The History of the Indian Revolt

Anatiposi

Anonymous

The History of the Indian Revolt

Reprint of the original, first published in 1859.

1st Edition 2023 | ISBN: 978-3-38231-000-4

Anatiposi Verlag is an imprint of Outlook Verlagsgesellschaft mbH.

Verlag (Publisher): Outlook Verlag GmbH, Zeilweg 44, 60439 Frankfurt, Deutschland
Vertretungsberechtigt (Authorized to represent): E. Roepke, Zeilweg 44, 60439 Frankfurt, Deutschland
Druck (Print): Books on Demand GmbH, In de Tarpen 42, 22848 Norderstedt, Deutschland

THE

HISTORY

OF THE

INDIAN REVOLT

AND OF THE EXPEDITIONS TO

PERSIA, CHINA, AND JAPAN

1856-7-8

WITH

Maps, Plans, and Wood Engravings

LONDON:
W. AND R. CHAMBERS 47 PATERNOSTER ROW
AND HIGH STREET EDINBURGH
1859

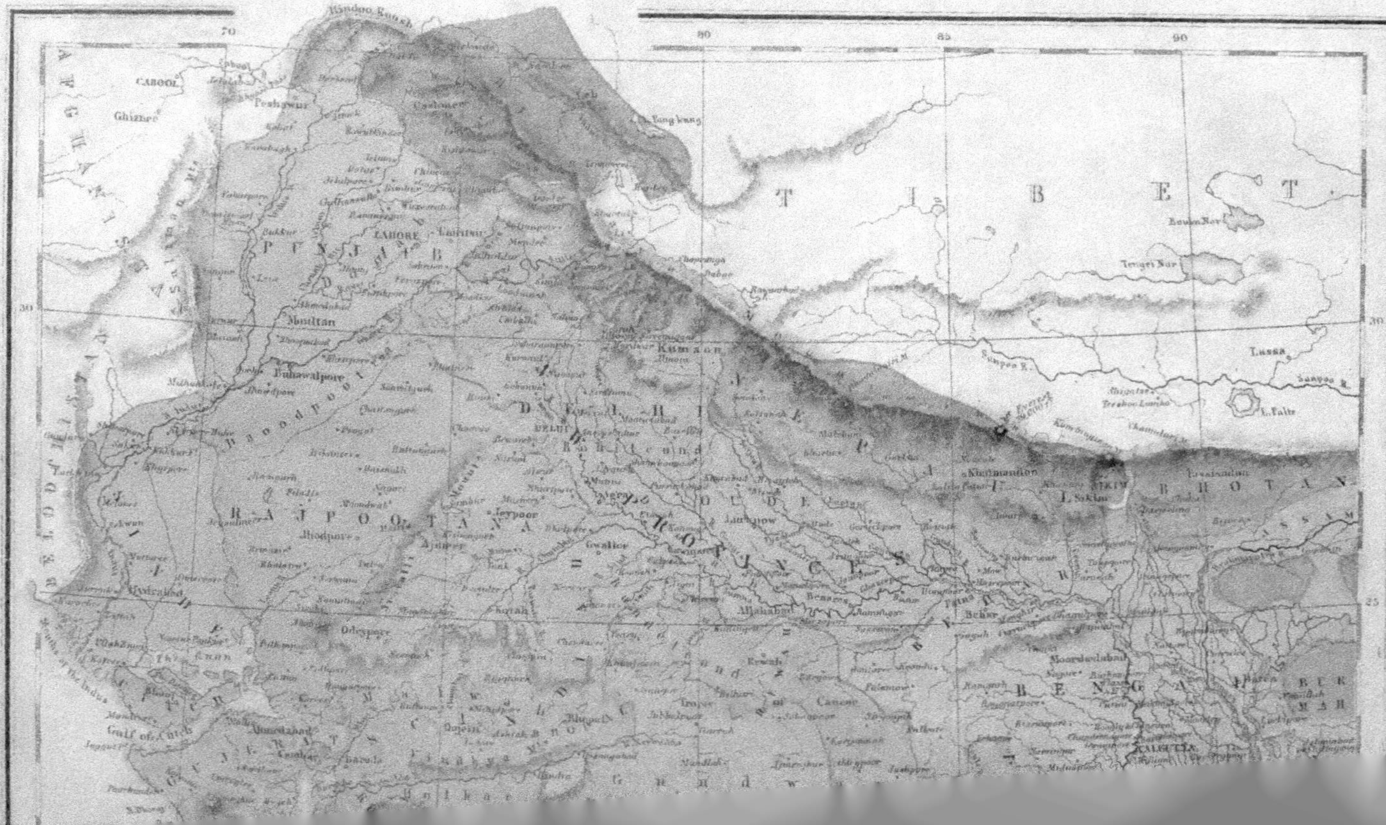

TIBET
PUNJAB
RAJPOOTANA
OUDE
BHOTAN
BENGAL
CABOOL
Peshawur
LAHORE
Moultan
Bahawalpore
DELHI
Lucknow
Allahabad
Benares
Lassa
Hindoo Kush
Gulf of Cutch
CALCUTTA

Printed in Colours by Schenck & Macfarlane, Edinburgh

W. & R. CHAMBERS LONDON & EDINBURGH.

PREFACE

IN the present volume is given a narrative of the chief events connected with one of the most formidable military Revolts on record. These events—from the first display of insubordination in the beginning of 1857, to the issue of the Royal Proclamation in the later weeks of 1858—form a series full of the romance as well as the wretchedness of war: irrespective of the causes that may have led to them, or the reforms which they suggested. The sudden rising of trained native soldiers in mutiny; the slaughter of officers who to the last moment had trusted them; the sufferings of gently-nurtured women and children, while hurrying wildly over burning sands and through thick jungles; and the heroism displayed amid unspeakable miseries—all tended to give an extraordinary character to this outbreak. Nor is it less interesting to trace the operations by which the difficulties were met. The task was nothing less than that of suppressing insurgency among a native population of nearly two hundred million souls by a small number of British soldiers and civilians, most of whom were at vast distances from the chief region of disaffection, and were grievously deficient in means of transport.

A chronicle of these events reveals also the striking differences between various parts of India. While Behar, Oude, Rohilcund, the Doab, Bundelcund, Malwah, and Rajpootana were rent with anarchy and plunged in misery, the rest of India was comparatively untouched. Most important, too, is it to trace the influence of nation, caste, and creed. Why the Hindoos of the Brahmin and Rajpoot castes rebelled, while those of the lower castes remained faithful; why the Sikhs and Mussulmans of the Punjaub shewed so little sympathy with the insurgents; why the Hindoos of Bengal were so timidly quiet, and those of Hindostan so boldly violent; why the native armies of Madras and Bombay were so tranquil, when that of Bengal was so turbulent?—were questions which it behoved the government to solve, as clues to the character of the governed, and to the changes of discipline needed. It was a time that brought into strong relief the peculiarities of the five chief classes of Europeans in India—Queen's soldiers, Company's soldiers, Company's 'covenanted' servants, 'uncovenanted' servants, and residents independent of the Company; and it shewed how nobly these classes forgot their differences when the honour of the British name and the safety of India were imperiled.

The history of home affairs during, and in relation to, that period of struggle, has its own points of interest—shewing in what manner, amid the stormy conflicts of party, the nation responded to the call for military aid to India, for pecuniary aid to individual sufferers, and for a great change in the government of that country.

Although the minor results of the Revolt may be visible to a much later date, it is considered that the month of November 1858 would furnish a convenient limit to the present narrative. The government of India had by that time been changed; the change had been publicly proclaimed throughout the length and breadth of that empire; the British army in the east had been so largely augmented as to render the prospects of the insurgents hopeless; the rebel leaders were gradually tendering their submission, under the terms of the Royal Proclamation; the skilled mutinous sepoys had in great proportion been stricken down by battle and privation; the military operations had become little more than a chasing of lawless marauders; and the armed men still at large were mostly dupes of designing leaders, or ruffians whose watchwords were pay and plunder rather than nationality or patriotism.

The remarkable Expeditions to Persia, China, and Japan are briefly noticed towards the close of the volume—on account of the links which connected them with the affairs of India, and of the aspect which they gave to the influence of England in the east.

Every endeavour has been made, by a careful examination of available authorities, to render the narrative a truthful one. It is hoped that the errors are few in number, and that hasty expressions of opinion on disputed points have in general been avoided. The Work is quite distinct from the HISTORY OF THE RUSSIAN WAR, issued by the same Publishers; yet may the two be regarded as companion volumes, relating to the affairs of England in the east—seeing that a few short months only elapsed between the close of the events of 1854–5–6 in Turkey, Russia, and Asia Minor, and the commencement of those of 1856–7–8 in India, Persia, and China.

G. D.

December 1858.

Contents

APPENDIX.

LIST OF ILLUSTRATIONS.

INTRODUCTION.

INDIA IN 1856: A RETROSPECT.

SCARCELY had England recovered from the excitement attendant on the war with Russia; scarcely had she counted the cost, provided for the expenditure, reprobated the blunderings, mourned over the sufferings; scarcely had she struck a balance between the mortifying incapacity of some of her children, and the Christian heroism of others—when she was called upon anew to unsheath the sword, and to wage war, not against an autocrat on this side of the Caspian, but against some of the most ancient nations in the world. Within a few months, almost within a few weeks, China, Persia, and India appeared in battle-array against her—they being the injurers or the injured, according to the bias of men's judgments on the matter. It may almost be said that five hundred millions of human beings became her enemies at once; there are at the very least this number of inhabitants in the three great Asiatic empires; and against all, proclamations were issued and armaments fitted out. Whether the people, the millions, sided more with her or with their own rulers, is a question that must be settled in relation to each of those empires separately; but true it is that the small army of England was called upon suddenly to render services in Asia, so many and varied, in regions so widely separated, and so far distant from home, that a power of mobility scarcely less than ubiquity, aided by a strength of endurance almost more than mortal—could have brought that small force up to a level with the duties required of it. Considering how small a space a month is in the life of a nation, we may indeed say that this great Oriental outbreak was nearly simultaneous in the three regions of Asia. It was in October 1856 that the long-continued bickerings between the British and the Chinese at Canton broke out into a flame, and led to the despatch of military and naval forces from England. It was while the British admiral was actually engaged in bombarding Canton that the governor-general of India, acting as viceroy of the Queen of England, declared war against the Shah of Persia for an infringement of treaty relating to the city of Herat. And lastly, it was while two British armaments were engaged in those two regions of warfare, that disobedience and disbanding began in India, the initial steps to the most formidable military Revolt, perhaps, the world has ever seen.

The theologian sees, or thinks he sees, the finger of God, the avenging rod of an All-ruling Providence, in these scenes of blood-shedding: a punishment on England for not having Christianised the natives of the East to the full extent of her power. The soldier insists that, as we gained our influence in the East mainly by the sword, by the sword we must keep it: permitting no disobedience to our military rule, but at the same time offending as little as possible against the prejudices of faith and caste among the natives. The politician smitten with Russo-phobia, deeply imbued with the notion, whether well or ill founded, that the Muscovite aims at universal dominion in Europe and Asia, seeks for evidences of the czar's intrigues at Pekin, Teheran, and Delhi. The partisan, thinking more of the ins and outs of official life, than of Asia, points triumphantly to the dogma that if *his* party had been in power, no one of these three Oriental wars would have come upon England. The merchant, believing that individual interest lies at the bottom of all national welfare, tells us that railways and cotton plantations would be better for India than military stations; and that diplomatic piques at Canton and at Teheran ought not to be allowed to drive us into hostility with nations who might be advantageous customers for our wares. But while the theologian, the soldier, the politician, the partisan, and the merchant are thus rushing to a demonstration, each of his favourite theory, without waiting for the evidence which can only by degrees be collected, England, as a nation, has had to bear up against the storm as best she could. Not even one short twelvemonth of peace was vouchsafed to her. The same year, 1856, that marked the closing scenes of one war, witnessed the commencement of two others; while the materials for a fourth war were at the same time fermenting, unknown to those whose duty it was to watch symptoms.

Few things in the history of our empire are more astonishing than the social explosion in India, taken in connection with the positive declarations of official men. Historical parallels have often been pointed out, striking and instructive; but here we have a historical contradiction. At the time when the plenipotentiaries of seven European empires and kingdoms were discussing at Paris the bases for a European peace, the Marquis of Dalhousie was penning an account of India, in the state to which Britain had brought it. A statesman of high ability, and of unquestioned earnestness of purpose, he evidently felt a pride in the work he had achieved as governor-general of India; he thought he had laid the foundation for a great future; and he claimed credit for England, not only in respect to what she had done, but also for the motives that had dictated her Indian policy. It was in the early part of 1848 that this nobleman went out to the East; it was in 1856 that he yielded the reins of power to Viscount Canning; and shortly before his departure from Calcutta he wrote a minute or narrative, formally addressed to the East India Company, but intended for his fellow-countrymen at large, giving an account of his stewardship. Remembering that that minute was written in March 1856, and that the Revolt commenced in January 1857, it becomes very important to know, from the lips or the pen of the marquis himself, what he believed to be the actual condition of the Anglo-Indian Empire when he left it. The document in question is worth more, for our present purpose, than any formal history or description of India; for it shews not only the sum-total of power and prosperity in 1848, but the additions made to that sum year after year till 1856. A parliamentary paper of fifty folio pages need not and cannot be reproduced here; but its substance may be rendered intelligible in a few paragraphs. This we will attempt at once, as a peculiarly fitting introduction to the main object of the present work; for it shews how little the Revolt was expected by him who was regarded as the centre of knowledge and influence in India. The marquis said: 'The time has nearly come when my administration of the government of India, prolonged through more than eight years, will reach its final close. It would seem that some few hours may be profitably devoted to a short review of those eventful years; not for the purpose of justifying disputed measures, or of setting forth a retrospective defence of the policy which may, on every several occasion, have been adopted; but for the purpose of recalling the political events that have occurred, the measures that have been taken, and the progress that has been made, during the career of the administration which is about to close. I enter on that review with the single hope that the Honourable Court of Directors may derive from the retrospect some degree of satisfaction with the past, *and a still larger measure of encouragement for the future.*' The words we have italicised are very remarkable, read by the light so soon and so calamitously to be afforded.

The minute first passes in review the proceedings of the Indian government with the independent native states, both east and west of the Ganges. How little our public men are able to foretell the course of political events in the East, is shown by the very first paragraph of the governor-general's narrative: 'When I sailed from England in the winter of 1847, to assume the government of India, there prevailed a universal conviction among public men at home that permanent peace had at length been secured in the East. Before the summer came, we were already involved in the second Sikh war.' Be it observed that public men *at home* are here adverted to: of what were the opinions of public men in India, the English nation was not kept sufficiently informed. There had been British officers murdered at Moultan; there was a rebellion of the Dewan Moolraj against the recognised sovereign of Lahore; but the renewal of war is attributed mainly to the 'spirit of the whole Sikh people, which was inflamed by the bitterest animosity against us; when chief after chief deserted our cause, until nearly their whole army, led by sirdars who had signed the treaties, and by members of the Council of Regency itself, was openly arrayed against us;' and when the Sikhs even joined with the Afghans against us. It was not a mere hostile prince, it was a hostile nation that confronted us; and the Indian government, whether wisely or not, declared war, put forth its power, maintained a long campaign, defeated and subdued the Sikhs, drove back the insurgent Afghans, and ended by annexing the Punjaub to the British territories. Scarcely had the Anglo-Indian armies been relieved from these onerous duties, when war called them to the regions beyond the Ganges. Certain British traders in the port of Rangoon had been subjected to gross outrage by the officers of the King of Ava, in violation of a pre-existing treaty; and the Marquis of Dalhousie, acting on a high-sounding dictum of Lord Wellesley, that 'an insult offered to the British flag at the mouth of the Ganges should be resented as promptly and as fully as an insult offered at the mouth of the Thames,' resolved to punish the king for those insults. That monarch was 'arrogant and overbearing'—qualities much disapproved, where not shewn by the Company's servants themselves; he violated treaties, insulted our traders, worried our envoys, and drove away our commercial agent at Rangoon; and as the government of India 'could never, consistently with its own safety, permit itself to stand for a single day in an attitude of inferiority towards a native power, and least of all towards the court of Ava, war was declared. After some sharp fighting, the kingdom of Pegu was taken and annexed, 'in order that the government of India might hold from the Burman state both adequate compensation for past injury, and the best security against future danger. . . . . A sense of inferiority has penetrated at last to the convictions of the nation; the Burman court and the Burman people alike have shewn that they now dread our power; *and in that dread is the only real security we can ever have, or ever could have had, for stable peace with the Burman state.*' These words are at once boastful and saddening; but the notions conveyed, of 'sense of inferiority' and 'dread of power,' are thoroughly Asiatic, and as such we must accept them. Another independent state, Nepaul, on the northern frontier of India, remained faithful during the eight years of the Dalhousie administration; it carried on a war of its own against Tibet, but it was friendly to England, and sent a be-jewelled ambassador, Jung Bahadoor, to visit the island Queen. The mountain region of Cashmere, stolen as it were from the Himalaya, was under an independent chieftain, Maharajah Gholab Sing, who, when he visited the Marquis of Dalhousie at Wuzeerabad, caught the vice-regal robe in his hand and said: 'Thus I grasp the skirts of the British government, and I will never let go my hold.' The governor-general expresses a belief that Gholab Sing 'will never depart from his submissive policy as long as he lives;' while Gholab's son and anticipated successor, Meean Rumbeer Sing, is spoken of as one who will never give 'any cause of offence to a powerful neighbour, which he well knows can crush him at will.' The Khan of Khelat, near the western frontier, was brought into close relationship, insomuch that he became 'the friend of our friends, and the enemy of our enemies,' and engaged to give us temporary possession of such military stations within his territory as we might at any time require for purposes of defence. At the extreme north-west of our Indian Empire, the Afghans, with whom we had fought such terrible battles during the Auckland and Ellenborough administrations of Indian affairs, had again been brought into friendly relations; the chief prince among them, Dost Mohammed Khan of Cabool, had been made to see that England was likely to be his best friend, and 'had already shewn that he regards English friendship as a tower of strength.'

Thus the governor-general, in adverting to independent states, announced that he had conquered and annexed the Punjaub and Pegu; while he had strengthened the bonds of amity with Nepaul, Cashmere, Khelat, and Cabool—amity almost degraded to abject servility, if the protestations of some of the chieftains were to be believed.

Having disposed of the independent states, the marquis directed attention to the relations existing between the British government and the protected or semi-independent states, of which there are many more than those really independent. The kingdom of Nagpoor became British territory by simple lapse, 'in the absence of all legal heirs.' In bygone years the British put down one rajah and set up another; and when this latter died, without a son real or adopted, or any male descendant of the original royal stock, 'the British government refused to bestow the territory in free gift upon a stranger, and wisely incorporated it with its own dominions'—a mode of acquiring territory very prevalent in our Eastern Empire. The King of Oude, another protected sovereign, having broken his engagements with the Company in certain instances, his state was treated like Nagpoor, and added to British India. Satara lost its rajah in 1849, and as no male heir was then living, that small state shared the fate of the larger Oude: it was made British. Jhansi, a still smaller territory, changed owners in an exactly similar way. The Nizam of Hyderabad, owing to the Company a sum of money which he was unable or unwilling to pay, and being in other ways under the Company's wrath, agreed in 1853 to give up Berar and other provinces to the exclusive sovereignty of the British. Early in 1848 the Rajah of Ungool, a petty chieftain in the Jungle Neehals, resisted the authority of the government; his raj was taken from him, and he died in exile. The Rajah of Sikim, a hill-chieftain on the borders of Nepaul, 'had the audacity' to seize a Company's official at Darjeling; as a punishment, all the territories he possessed within the plains were confiscated and annexed. In Sinde, Meer Ali Morad of Khyrpore, having involved himself in an act of forgery concerning the ownership of territory, 'the lands were taken from him, and his power and influence were reduced to insignificance.' The Nawab Nazim of Bengal having committed a murder by bastinado, 'his highness's peculiar jurisdiction and legal exemption were taken away from him; and he was subjected to the disgrace of losing a large portion of the salute of honour which he had previously received.' The Nawab of the Carnatic died suddenly in 1855; and as he left no male heir, and his relations lived very disreputably, the title of nawab 'was placed in abeyance:' that is, the Carnatic was made British territory, and the several members of the nawab's family were pensioned off. About the same time, the Rajah of Tanjore died, in like manner without male issue bearing his name; and the same process was adopted there as in the Carnatic—sovereign power was assumed by the Company, and the ex-royal family was pensioned off.

Counting up his treasures, the governor-general was certainly enabled to announce a most extraordinary accession of territory during the years 1848 to 1855. The Punjaub, Pegu, Nagpoor, Oude, Satara, Jhansi, Berar, Ungool, Darjeling, Khyrpore, the Carnatic, and Tanjore, all became British for the first time, or else had the links which bound them to England brought closer. While, on the one hand, it must be admitted that the grounds or excuses for annexation would be deemed very slight in any country but India; so, on the other, there can be no doubt that the Marquis of Dalhousie, and the directors with whom he was acting, believed that these annexing processes were essential to the maintenance of British power in the East. He takes credit to his government for having settled certain family quarrels among the petty royalties of Gujerat, Buhawalpore, Jummoo, and Mumdote, without paying itself for its services: as if it were a virtue to abstain from annexation at such times. The mention made of Delhi must be given in the governor-general's own words, to shew how much the descendant of the once mighty Mogul was regarded as a mere puppet—yet maintaining a certain hold on the reverence of the people, as was destined to be shewn in a series of events little anticipated by the writer of the minute. 'Seven years ago the heir-apparent to the King of Delhi died. He was the last of the race who had been born in the purple. The Court of Directors was accordingly advised to decline to recognise any other heir-apparent, and to permit the kingly title to fall into abeyance upon the death of the present king, who even then was a very aged man. The Honourable Court accordingly conveyed to the government of India *authority to terminate the dynasty of Timour*, whenever the reigning king should die. But as it was found that, although the Honourable Court had consented to the measure, it had given its consent with great reluctance, I abstained from making use of the authority which had been given to me. The grandson of the king was recognised as heir-apparent; but only on condition that he should quit the palace in Delhi in order to reside in the palace at the Kootub; and that he should, as king, *receive the governor-general of India at all times on terms of perfect equality*.' How strange do these words sound! A board of London merchants sitting in a room in Leadenhall Street, giving 'authority to terminate the dynasty of Timour;' and then, as a gracious condescension, permitting the representative of that dynasty to be on terms of 'perfect equality' with whomsoever may be the chief representative of the Company in India.

The Marquis of Dalhousie pointed to the revenues derivable from the newly annexed territories as among the many justifications for his line of policy. He shewed that four millions sterling were added to the annual income of the Anglo-Indian Empire by the acquisition of the Punjaub, Pegu, Nagpoor, Oude, Satara, Jhansi, and Berar—increasing the total revenue from about twenty-six millions in 1848 to above thirty millions in 1855.

The extreme importance of this official document lying in the evidence it affords how little dread was felt in 1856 of any approaching outbreak, we proceed with the governor-general's narrative of the augmentation and stability of British power in the East, power of which he was evidently proud—presenting, of course, as a mere outline, that which his lordship fills up in more detail.

Credit is claimed in the minute for the improved administrative organisation both of the old and of the newly acquired territories. Able men were selected to administer government in the Punjaub; and so well did they fulfil their duties that internal peace was secured, violent crime repressed, the penal law duly enforced, prison-discipline maintained, civil justice administered, taxation fixed, collection of revenue rendered just, commerce set free, agriculture fostered, national resources developed, and future improvements planned. Not only did the marquis assert this; but there is a general concurrence of opinion that the Punjaub fell into fortunate hands when its administration came to be provided for. In Pegu the administration, less brilliant than in the Punjaub, is nevertheless represented as being sound in principle; tranquillity was restored; effective police had secured the safety of all; trade was increased and increasing; a fair revenue was derived from light taxation; 'the people, lightly taxed and prosperous, are highly contented with our rule;' and, when population has increased, 'Pegu will equal Bengal in fertility of production, and surpass it in every other respect.' At Nagpoor the assumption of supreme authority by Britain was 'hailed with lively satisfaction by the whole population of the province;' no additional soldier had been introduced thither; the civil administration was introduced everywhere; the native army was partly embodied and disciplined in British pay, and partly discharged either with pensions or gratuities. In short, 'perfect contentment and quiet prevail; beyond the palace walls not a murmur has been heard; and in no single instance throughout the districts has the public peace been disturbed.' In Berar, we are told, the same phenomena were observed; as soon as the cession was made, our numerous disputes with the nizam ended; the civil administration was brought into working order; crime, especially the violent crime of *dacoitee* (gang-robbery without murder) was diminished; the 'admirable little army,' formerly called the Nizam's Contingent, was made available as part of the British force; the revenue rapidly increased; and the public tranquillity had 'not been disturbed by a single popular tumult.' The kingdom of Oude had only been annexed a few weeks before the Marquis of Dalhousie wrote his minute; but he states that a complete civil administration, and a resident military force, had been fully organised before the annexation took place; that the troops of the deposed native king were contentedly taking service in British pay; that no zemindar or chief had refused submission to our authority; that the best men who could be found available were selected from the civil and military services for the new offices in Oude; and that no popular resistance or disturbance had occurred.

Nothing could be more clear and positive th these assertions. Not only did the govern general announce that the Punjaub, Pegu, Nagpo Berar, and Oude had been completely annex bringing a large accession to the British revenue but that in every case a scheme of administrati had been framed and established, conducive to t lasting benefit of the natives, the honour of t British name, and the development of the natur resources of the several districts. Not a whisper discontent, of spirits chafed by change of ruler did the marquis recognise: if they occurred, the reached not him; or if they *did* reach him, h passed them by as trifles.

Nor was it alone in the newly acquired territories that credit for these advantageous change was claimed. Improvements in the government of India were pointed out in every direction. The governor-general had been relieved from an overwhelming press of duties by the appointment of a lieutenant-governor for Bengal. A Legislative Council had been organised, distinct from the Supreme Council; the public having access to its deliberations, and its debates and papers being printed and issued to the world. The Indian civil service, by an act passed in 1853, had been thrown open to all who, being natural-born subjects of the British sovereign, should offer themselves as candidates for examination and admission. Young cadets, who previously had been allowed nearly two years to 'idle and loiter' at the presidencies while studying for examination as civilians, were by a new regulation required to complete their studies in a much shorter period, thereby lessening their idleness and rendering them sooner useful. Periodical examinations of the civil servants had been established, to insure efficiency before promotion was given. A board of examiners had been founded, to conduct examinations and superintend studies. All officers of the Indian government had been formally prohibited from engaging in banking or trading companies; and any bankruptcy among them entailed suspension from office. In many of the civil offices, promotion, before dependent on seniority alone, had been made dependent on merit alone. A pension or superannuation list had been established in many departments, to insure steady and faithful service. Three boards of administration for salt, opium, and customs had been replaced by one board of revenue, simpler in its constitution. The annual financial reports, transmitted to the home government, had gradually been made more clear, full, and instructive. All the salaries throughout India had been placed under the consideration of a special commissioner, for equitable revision; and the authorities had determined that, in future, no salaries, with a few special exceptions, shall exceed fifty thousand rupees (about five thousand pounds) per annum.

Nor had legislative reform been wholly forgotten. During the eight years under review, laws had been passed or rules laid down for the punishment of officials guilty of corruption, or accountants guilty of default; for allowing counsel to prisoners on their trial; for abolishing the semi-savage custom of branding convicts; for rendering public officers more amenable to public justice; for vesting a right of pardon in the supreme government; for improving the procedure in all the civil and criminal courts; for rendering the reception of evidence more fair and impartial; and, among many less important things, for 'securing liberty of conscience, and for the protection of converts, and especially of Christian converts, against injury in respect of property or inheritance by reason of a change in their religious belief.' For the amelioration of prison-discipline, inspectors of prisons had been appointed in all the three presidencies, as well as in Oude, the Punjaub, and the north-west provinces.

Equally in moral as in administrative matters did the Marquis of Dalhousie insist on the manifold improvement of India during the eight years preceding 1856. Schools for the education of natives had been established; the Hindoo College at Calcutta had been revived and improved; a Presidency College had been founded in the same city, to give a higher scale of education to the youth of Bengal; similar colleges had been sanctioned at Madras and Bombay; grants-in-aid to all educational establishments had been authorised, subject to government inspection of the schools aided; a committee had been appointed to consider the plans for establishing regular universities at Calcutta, Bombay, and Madras; a distinct educational department had been formed at the seat of government, with director-generals of public instruction in all the presidencies and governments; and the East India Company had, by a dispatch framed in 1854, sanctioned a most extensive educational scheme for the whole of India, to be rendered available to all the natives who might be willing and able to claim its advantages. The delicate subject of female education had not been forgotten. Instructions had been given to the officers of the educational department to afford all possible encouragement to the establishment of female schools, whenever any disposition was shewn by the natives in that direction. There is a peculiar difficulty in all that concerns female education in India, arising from the reluctance which has always been shewn by the higher classes of natives to permit the attendance of their daughters at schools. Mr Bethune commenced, and the Marquis of Dalhousie continued, a delicate and cautious attempt to overcome this unwillingness by establishing a Hindoo ladies' school at Calcutta; and the minute gives expression to an earnest hope and belief that the female character in India will gradually be brought under the elevating influence of moral and intellectual education. As the native mind was thus sought to be ameliorated and strengthened by education; so had the prevention or cure of bodily maladies been made an object of attention. Additional advantages had been granted to natives who applied themselves to the study of the medical sciences; the number of dispensaries had been greatly increased, to the immense benefit of the poorer classes of Hindoos and Mohammedans; plans had been commenced for introducing a check to the dreadful ravages of the small-pox; admission to the medical service of the Company had been thrown open to natives; and, as a first-fruit of this change, one Dr Chuckerbutty, a Hindoo educated in England, had won for himself a commission as assistant-surgeon in the Company's service.

In so far as concerns superstition and religion, the minute narrates a course of proceeding of which the following is the substance. Among the extraordinary social customs—atrocities they are unquestionably considered in Europe—of India, those of Suttee, Thuggee, Infanticide, and the Meriah Sacrifice, are mentioned as having undergone much amelioration during the eight years to which the minute relates. The *suttee*, or burning of widows, had been almost suppressed by previous governor-generals, and the marquis had carried out the plans of his predecessors: remonstrating where any suttees occurred in independent states; and punishing where they occurred in the British and protected territories. *Thuggee*, or systematic murder of travellers for the sake of booty, had been quite suppressed east of the Sutlej; but having unexpectedly made its appearance in the Punjaub in 1851, it was thoroughly put down there as elsewhere; those who turned approvers or king's evidence against their brother Thugs now form—or rather did form in 1856—a peaceful industrious colony at Jubbulpoor, where they spun and wove muslins of exquisite fineness, instead of cutting the throats of unsuspecting travellers. *Female infanticide*, the result of pride of birth and pride of purse—parents murdering their infant daughters either because they cannot afford the marriage expenditure which must one day be incurred on their account, or because they see difficulties in marrying them suitably—had been greatly checked and discouraged. In the Punjaub a most signal and singular conquest had been achieved; for the British representative, calling together the chiefs of tribes in 1854, unfolded to them a plan, 'the observance of which would effectually secure that no man should feel any real difficulty in providing for his daughter in marriage;' whereupon the chiefs, as well as those of the Cashmere tribes, promised that, as the motive for infanticide would thus in great measure be removed, they would cheerfully aid in suppressing the practice. Lastly, the *Meriah sacrifice*—a horrible rite, in which young human victims are sacrificed for the propitiation of the special divinity which presides over the fertility of the earth—had been nearly rooted out from the only district where it was practised, among the hill and jungle tribes of Orissa. In religious matters, the ecclesiastical strength of the established church had been largely increased; clergymen had been occasionally sanctioned, besides those acting as chaplains to the Company; places of worship had been provided for the servants and soldiers of the Company; Protestant churches had been built in places where the worshippers were willing to contribute something towards the expenditure; Roman Catholics serving the Company had been provided with places of worship; salaries had been granted to three Roman Catholic bishops, one in each presidency; the salaries of the priests had been revised and augmented; and a wish was manifested to observe justice towards the Catholic as well as the Protestant who served his country well in the East.

Thus—in the acquisition of territory, in the augmentation of revenue consequent on that acquisition, in the administrative organisation, in the spread of education, in the provision for religious services, and in the plans for improving the moral conduct of the natives—the Marquis of Dalhousie claimed to have done much that would redound to the honour of the British name and to the advancement of the millions under British rule in India. The problem still remains unsolved—Why should India, or the native military of that country, have revolted from British service? Let us see, therefore, whether the governor-general says aught that throws light upon the matter in connection with trade and commerce; and in order to understand this subject clearly, let us treat separately of Productive Industry and Means of Communication.

Cotton is destined, according to the ideas of some thinkers, to mark a great future for India; but meanwhile we are told in the minute that, by the acquisition of Nagpoor and Berar, many fertile cotton districts were brought under British rule; and that since the acquisition of Pegu, an examination of the cotton-growing capabilities of the northern part of that kingdom had been commenced. The tea-culture in Assam had prospered greatly during the eight years from 1848 to 1856; the plant had been largely introduced into the upper districts of the north-west provinces; plantations had been established at Deyrah Dhoon, Kumaon, and Gurhwal; Mr Fortune had brought large supplies of Chinese seeds and Chinese workmen to India; many of the native zemindars had begun the cultivation on their own account in districts at the foot of the Himalaya; and every year witnessed a large increase in the production of Indian tea, which was excellent in quality, and sold readily at a high price. In agriculture generally, improvements of all kinds had been made; an Agricultural and Horticultural Society had been established in the Punjaub; carefully selected seeds had been procured from Europe; the growth of flax had been encouraged; the growth of the mulberry and the rearing of silkworms had been fostered by the government; and a grant had been made in aid of periodical agricultural shows in the Madras presidency. In relation to live-stock, plans had been formed for improving the breed of horses; merino and Australian rams had been introduced to improve the breed of sheep; and sheep had been introduced into Pegu, to the great delight of the natives and the advantage of all; 'for the absence of sheep leads to a privation in respect of food, which is severely felt, not only by European soldiers in the province, but also by all of every class who are employed therein.' The forests had been brought under due regulation by the appointment of conservators of forests at Pegu, Tenasserim, and Martaban; by the careful examination of the whole of the forests in the Punjaub; by the planting of new districts, hitherto bare; and by the laying down of rules for the future preservation and thrifty management of these important sources of timber and fuel. The inestimable value of coal being duly appreciated, careful researches had been made, by order of the government, in the Punjaub, Pegu, Tenasserim, Bengal, Silhet, and the Nerbudda Valley, to lay the groundwork for careful mining whenever and wherever good coal may be found. Practical chemists and geological surveyors had been set to work in the Simla Hills, Kumaon, Gurhwal, the Nerbudda Valley, Beerboom, and Jubbulpoor, either to discover beds of ironstone, or to organise ironworks where such beds had already been discovered; and an experimental mining and smelting establishment had been founded by the government among the Kumaon Hills, to apply tests likely to be valuable in future.

Next, in connection with means of communication, the channels by and through which commerce permeates the empire, the governor-general had a very formidable list of works to notice. Surveys, irrigation and canals, rivers and harbours, roads, railways, electric telegraphs, and postal communications—had all been made the subjects of great engineering activity during the eight years of the Dalhousie administration. A few words must be said here on each of these topics; for it becomes absolutely necessary, in order to a due appreciation of the narrative of Revolt about to follow, that we should, as a preliminary, know whether India really had or had not been neglected in these elements of prosperity in the years immediately preceding the outbreak.

Measures, we learn from the minute, had been taken for executing exact surveys of all the newly annexed territory in the Punjaub, Pegu, Sinde, Nagpoor, and Berar in the same careful manner as the survey of the older territories had been before carried out; and in Central India 'the consent of all the native states has been obtained to the making of a topographical survey, and to a demarcation of all the boundaries between the several native states, and between the British territories and those of native states:' a proceeding expected to lessen the frequency of feuds concerning disputed boundaries.

The activity in irrigation-works and canal-cutting had unquestionably been very great. In 1854 the Ganges Canal was opened in its main line, for the double purpose of irrigation and navigation. A mighty work this, which no mutiny, no angry feelings, should induce the English public to forget. It is 525 miles in length, and in some parts 170 feet in width; and considered as a canal for irrigation, 'it stands unequalled in its class and character among the efforts of civilised nations. Its length is fivefold greater than that of all the main lines of Lombardy united, and more than twice the length of the aggregate irrigation lines of Lombardy and Egypt together—the only countries in the world whose works of irrigation rise above insignificance.' Nor is this all. 'As a single work of navigation for purposes of commerce, the Ganges Canal has no competitor throughout the world. No single canal in Europe has attained to half the magnitude of this Indian work. It nearly equals the aggregate length of the four greatest canals in France. It greatly exceeds all the first-class canals of Holland put together; and it is greater, by nearly one-third, than the greatest navigation canal in the United States of America.' Pausing for one moment just to observe that the writer of the words here quoted seems to have temporarily forgotten the great canal of China, we proceed to state, on the authority of the minute, that when all the branches are finished, this noble Ganges Canal will be 900 miles in length. It will then, by its periodical overflowings, irrigate *a million and a half of acres*, thus lessening the terrible apprehensions of famine or dearth among millions of human beings. We may doubt or not on other subjects, but it is impossible to doubt the sincerity of the Marquis of Dalhousie when he says: 'I trust I shall not be thought vain-glorious if I say that the successful execution and completion of such a work as the Ganges Canal would, even if it stood alone, suffice to signalise an Indian administration.' But this work did not absorb all the energies of the canal engineers; much of a similar though smaller kind had been effected elsewhere. An irrigation canal had been begun in the Punjaub, which, when finished, would be 465 miles in length, fed from the river Ravee. All the old canals formed in the Moultan district of the Punjaub, 600 miles in length, had been cleansed, enlarged, and improved, and the distribution of the waters for the purpose of irrigation placed under judicious regulation. Irrigation canals had been made or improved in the Derajat, in the provinces east of the Sutlej, in Behar, and in Sinde. A magnificent work had been executed for carrying an irrigation canal over the river Godavery; and canals of much importance had been commenced in the Madras and Bombay presidencies.

Rivers and harbours had shared in the attention bestowed on irrigation and canal navigation. The Ganges had been opened to river steamers before 1848, and it only remained to advance in the same line of improvement. The Indus, by the conquest of the Punjaub, had been made a British river almost from the Himalaya down to the ocean; steamers had been placed upon it; and it had become a direct route for troops and travellers to many parts of Northern India, before attainable only by the Calcutta route. All the rivers in the upper part of the Punjaub had been surveyed, with a view to the determination of their capabilities for steam-navigation. No sooner was Pegu acquired, than steamers were placed upon the Irrawaddy, the great river of that country; and short canals of junction between various rivers had been so planned as to give promise of a complete line of river-steaming from Bassein to Moulmein. Arrangements had been made for placing steamers upon the river Burhampooter or Brahmaputra, to connect Assam with the Bay of Bengal. Extensive works had been commenced to improve the navigation of the Godavery. The channels that lead from Calcutta through the Sundurbunds to the sea had been enlarged; and a great bridge over the Hoogly near the city had been planned. The port of Bombay had been greatly improved, and large works for water-supply commenced. At Kurachee, at Madras, at Singapore, at Rangoon, and at other places, engineering improvements had been made to increase the accommodation for shipping.

We follow the Marquis of Dalhousie from the river to the land, and trace with him the astonishing length of new road constructed or planned during his administration. A great trunk-road from Calcutta to Delhi had been extended nearly to the Sutlej; and when the Punjaub became a British possession, plans were immediately marked out for prolonging the same road to Loodianah, Umritsir, Lahore, Jelum, Attock, and Peshawur—thus forming, if all be completed, a magnificent road 1500 miles in length from Calcutta to the Afghan frontier, available both for commercial and military operations. The difficulties of crossing so many broad rivers in Northern India is immense, and the cost great; but the road, as the minute tells us, 'will repay a thousandfold the labour and the treasure it has cost.' Then, fine roads had been formed from Patna to Gya, from Cuttack to Ungool and Sumbhulpore, from Dacca to Akyab, and thence towards Aracan and Pegu; while vast systems of roads had been brought under consideration for Pegu, the Punjaub, Sinde, and other newly acquired regions. Engineers had been employed to plan a road from Simla up to the very Himalaya itself, to connect India with Tibet; as it would greatly improve the social position of all the native tribes near it. When Pegu was attacked, and when a military force was sent thither overland from Calcutta, hundreds of elephants were employed to force a way through the forests and roadless tracts between Aracan and Pegu; but by the spring of 1855 a road had been formed, along which a battalion could march briskly on foot.

The Marquis of Dalhousie was not in a position to say so much concerning railways in India as ordinary roads. Although railways were brought under the consideration of the Company in 1843, nothing was done regarding them till 1849, when a contract was entered into with a separate company to construct a certain length of railway which, if continued, would connect Calcutta with the north and north-west of India. In the spring of 1853 the marquis recommended a bold line of policy in these matters: the sanction and support, in every available way, of great lines of railway to connect Calcutta with Lahore, Bombay with Agra, Bombay with Madras, and Madras with the Malabar coast. A qualified approval of these schemes had been accorded by the East India Company, and engagements to the extent of ten millions sterling had been made for a railway from Delhi to Burdwan: a line from Burdwan to Calcutta having been opened in 1855. The governor-general, not dreaming of mutinies and rebellions, named the year 1859 as the probable time of finishing the iron route from Calcutta to Delhi. Besides these engagements with the East India Railway Company in the Bengal presidency, contracts had been made with the Great India Peninsula Company for a railway from Bombay to the Ghaut Mountains; and another with the Bombay and Central India Company for a railway from Bombay to Khandeish and Nagpoor, and for another from Surat to Ahmedabad. On the eastern coast, the government had arranged with the Madras Railway Company for lines from Madras to the Malabar coast, *viâ* Coimbatore, and from Variembaddy to Bangalore. The English nation has long blamed the East India Company for a dilatory policy in regard to railways; but all we have to do in this place is, on the authority of the governor-general, to specify in few words what had been done in the years immediately preceding the outbreak.

The electric telegraph—perhaps the grandest invention of our age—found in India a congenial place for its reception. Where the officials had no more rapid means of sending a message to a distance of a thousand miles than the fleetness of a corps of foot-runners, it is no marvel that the achievements of the lightning-messenger were regarded with an eager eye. An experimental line of electric telegraph was determined on, to be carried out by Dr (now Sir William) O'Shaughnessy; and when that energetic man made his report on the result in 1852, it was at once determined to commence arrangements for lines of immense length, to connect the widely separated cities of Calcutta, Madras, Bombay, and Peshawur, and the great towns between them. It was a grand idea, and was worthily realised; for by the month of March 1854 an electric wire of 800 miles was established between Calcutta and Agra; by the month of February 1855, the towns of Calcutta, Agra, Attock, Bombay, and Madras were placed in telegraphic communication by 3000 miles of wire, serving nearly forty towns on the way; and by the beginning of 1856 another length of 1000 miles was added, from Attock to Peshawur, fro[m] Bangalore to Ootacamund, and from Rangoon t[o] the Burmese frontier. Many works of great mag[-]nitude were required; there were few good road[s] for the workmen to avail themselves of; ther[e] were few bridges; there were deadly jungles to b[e] passed; there was every variety of foundation, from loose black soil to hard rocky wastes; there were seventy large rivers to be crossed, either by cables in the water, or by wires extended on the tops of masts; there was a cable of two miles required to cross the Toongabudra, and one of three miles to cross the Sone—and yet the entire work was comprised within a cost of 500 rupees or £50 per mile; perhaps the wisest expenditure ever incurred in India. Repeatedly has a message, relating to news from England, been transmitted 1600 miles, from Bombay to Calcutta, in less than three-quarters of an hour; and it has become a regular routine that the government at Calcutta shall be in possession of a considerable body of telegraphic news from England within twelve hours after the anchoring of the mail-steamer at Bombay. Who can conceive the bewilderment of the Hindoo mind at such achievements! It is certainly permissible to the governor-general to refer with pride to two or three among many instances of the remarkable service rendered by these telegraphs. 'When her Majesty's 10th Hussars were ordered with all speed from Poonah to the Crimea, a message requesting instructions regarding their despatch was one day received by me at Calcutta from the government of Bombay, about nine o'clock in the morning. Instructions were forthwith sent off by the telegraph in reply; and an answer to that reply was again received at Calcutta from Bombay in the evening of the same day. A year before, the same communications for the despatch of speedy reinforcements to the seat of war, which occupied by the telegraph no more than *twelve hours*, could not have been made in less than *thirty days*.' Again: 'When it was resolved to send her Majesty's 12th Lancers from Bangalore to the Crimea, instead of her Majesty's 14th Dragoons from Meerut, orders were forthwith despatched by telegraph direct to the regiment at Bangalore. The corps was immediately got ready for service; it marched two hundred miles, and was there before the transports were ready to receive it.' Again: 'On the 7th of February 1856, as soon as the administration of Oude was assuredly under British government, a branch-electric telegraph from Cawnpore to Lucknow was forthwith commenced; in eighteen working-days it was completed, including the laying of a cable, six thousand feet in length, across the river Ganges. On the morning on which I resigned the government in India, General Outram was asked by telegraph: "Is all well in Oude?" The answer: "All is well in Oude," was received soon after noon, and greeted Lord Canning on his first arrival.' Little did the new governor-general then foresee in how few months he would receive painful proof that all was *not* well in Oude. However, the Marquis of Dalhousie was justified in adverting with satisfaction to the establishment of telegraphic communication during his reign of power; and he insists on full credit being due to the East India Company for what was done in that direction. 'I make bold to say, that whether regard be had to promptitude of executive action, to speed and solidity of construction, to rapidity of organisation, to liberality of charge, or to the early realisation and vast magnitude of increased political influence in the East, the achievement of the Honourable Company in the establishment of the electric telegraph in India may challenge comparison with any public enterprise which has been carried into execution in recent times, among the nations of Europe, or in America itself.'

The postal system had not been allowed to stagnate during the eight years under consideration. A commission had been appointed in 1850, to inquire into the best means of increasing the efficiency of the system; and under the recommendations of this commission, great improvements had been made. A director-general of the post-office for the whole of India had been appointed; a uniformity of rate irrespective of distance had been established (three farthings for a letter, and three half-pence for a newspaper); prepayment by postage-stamps had been substituted for cash payment; the privileges of official franking had been almost abolished; and a uniform sixpenny rate was fixed for letters between India and England. Here again the governor-general insists, not only that the Indian government had worked zealously, but that England herself had been outstripped in liberal policy. 'In England, a single letter is conveyed to any part of the British isles for one penny; in India, a single letter is conveyed over distances immeasurably greater—from Peshawur, on the borders of Afghanistan, to the southernmost village of Cape Comorin, or from Dehooghur, in Upper Assam, to Kurachee at the mouth of the Indus—for no more than three farthings. The postage chargeable on the same letter three years ago in India would not have been less than one shilling, or sixteen times the present charge. Again, since uniform rates of postage between England and India have been established, the Scotch recruit who joins his regiment on our furthest frontier at Peshawur, may write to his mother at John o' Groat's House, and may send his letter to her free for sixpence: three years ago, the same sum would not have carried his letter beyond Lahore.'

So great had been the activity of the Company and the governor-general, in the course of eight years, in developing the productive resources of our Oriental empire, that a department of Public Works had become essentially necessary. The Company expended from two to three millions sterling annually in this direction, and a new organisation had been made to conduct the various works on which this amount of expenditure was to be bestowed. When the great roads and canals were being planned and executed, numerous civil engineers were of course needed; and the minute tells us that 'it was the far-seeing sagacity of Mr Thomason which first anticipated the necessity of training engineers in the country itself in which they were to be employed, and which first suggested an effectual method of doing so. On his recommendation, the civil engineering college at Roorkee, which now rightly bears his honoured name, was founded with the consent of the Honourable Court. It has already been enlarged and extended greatly beyond its original limits. Instruction in it is given to soldiers preparing for subordinate employment in the Public Works department, to young gentlemen not in the service of government, and to natives upon certain conditions. A higher class for commissioned officers of the army was created some years ago, at the suggestion of the late Sir Charles Napier; and the government has been most ready to consent to officers obtaining leave to study there, as in the senior department at Sandhurst. Excellent fruit has already been borne by this institution; many good servants have already been sent forth into [from?] the department; and applications for the services of students of the Thomason College were, before long, received from other local governments.' But this was not all: civil engineering colleges and classes were formed at Calcutta, Madras, Bombay, Lahore, and Poonah.

So greatly had the various public works on rivers and harbours, roads and canals, telegraphic and postal communications, increased the trade of India, that the shipping entries increased regularly year by year. There were about six hundred vessels, exclusive of trading craft, that ascended the Hoogly to Calcutta in 1847; by 1856, the number had augmented to twelve hundred; and the tonnage had risen in a still greater ratio.

What is the English nation to think of all this, and how reconcile it with the tragedies destined so soon to afflict that magnificent country? Here we find the highest representative of the British crown narrating and describing, in words too clear to be misunderstood, political and commercial advancements of a really stupendous kind, effected within the short period of eight years. We read of vast territories conquered, tributary states annexed, amicable relations with other states strengthened, territorial revenues increased, improved administration organised, the civil service purified, legislative reforms effected, prison-discipline improved, native colleges and schools established, medical aid disseminated, thuggee and dacoitee put down, suttee and infanticide discouraged, churches and chapels built, ministers of religion salaried. We are told of the cultivation of raw produce being fostered, the improvement of live-stock insured, the availability of mineral treasures tested, exact territorial surveys completed, stupendous irrigation and navigation canals constructed, flotillas of river-steamers established, ports and harbours enlarged and deepened, magnificent roads formed, long lines of railway commenced, thousands of miles of electric telegraph set to work, vast postal improvements insured. We read all this, and we cannot marvel if the ruler of India felt some pride in his share of the work. But still the problem remains unsolved—was the great Revolt foreshadowed in any of these achievements? As the mutiny began among the military, it may be well to see what information is afforded by the minute concerning military reforms between the years 1848 and 1856.

It is truly remarkable, knowing what the English nation now so painfully knows, that the Marquis of Dalhousie, in narrating the various improvements introduced by him in the military system, passes at once to the *British* soldiers: distinctly asserting that 'the position of the *native* soldier in India has long been such as to leave hardly any circumstance of his condition in need of improvement.' The British troops, we are told, had been benefited in many ways. The terms of service in India had been limited to twelve years as a maximum; the rations had been greatly improved; malt liquor had been substituted for destructive ardent spirits; the barracks had been mostly rebuilt, with modifications depending on the climate of each station; separate barracks had been set apart for the married men of each regiment; lavatories and reading-rooms had become recognised portions of every barrack; punkhas or cooling fans had been adopted for barracks in hot stations, and additional bed-coverings in cold; swimming-baths had been formed at most of the stations; soldiers' gardens had been formed at many of the cantonments; workshops and tools for handicraftsmen had been attached to the barracks; sanitaria had been built among the hills for sick soldiers; and arrangements had been framed for acclimatising all recruits from England before sending them into hot districts on service. Then, as to the officers. Encouragement had been offered for the officers to make themselves proficient in the native languages. A principle had been declared and established, that promotion by seniority should no longer govern the service; but that the test should be 'the selection of no man, whatever his standing, unless he was confessedly capable and efficient.' With the consent of the Queen, the Company's officers had had granted to them the recognition, until then rather humiliatingly withheld, of their military rank, not only in India but throughout the world. A military orphan school had been established in the hill districts. All the military departments had been revised and amended, the commissariat placed on a wholly new basis, and the military clothing supplied on a more efficient system than before.

Again is the search baffled. We find in the minute proofs only that India had become great and grand; if the seeds of rebellion existed, they were buried under the language which described material and social advancement. Is it
England, in 1856, had yet to learn to underst
the native character? Such may be; for *thu*
came to the knowledge of our government w
astounding suddenness; and there may be so
other kind of thuggee, religious or social, stil
be learned by us. Let us bear in mind w
this thuggee or thugism was, and who were
Thugs. Many years ago, uneasy whispers pas
among the British residents in India. Rumo
went abroad of the fate of unsuspecting travell
ensnared while walking or riding upon the ro
lassoed or strangled by means of a silken co
and robbed of their personal property; t
rumours were believed to be true; but it was lo
ere the Indian government succeeded in bringi
to light the stupendous conspiracy or system o
which these atrocities were based. It was the
found that there exists a kind of religious body i
India, called Thugs, among whom murder an
robbery are portions of a religious rite, establishe
more than a thousand years ago. They worshi
Kali, one of the deities of the Hindoo faith. I
gangs varying from ten to two hundred, they
distribute themselves—or rather *did* distribute
themselves, before the energetic measures of the government had nearly suppressed their system—about various parts of India, sacrificing to their tutelary goddess every victim they can seize, and sharing the plunder among themselves. They shed no blood, except under special circumstances; murder being their religion, the performance of its duties requires secrecy, better observed by a noose or a cord than by a knife or firearm. Every gang has its leader, teacher, entrappers, stranglers, and gravediggers; each with his prescribed duties. When a traveller, supposed or known to have treasure about him, has been inveigled to a selected spot by the *Sothas* or entrappers, he is speedily put to death quietly by the *Bhuttotes* or stranglers, and then so dexterously placed underground by the *Lughahees* or gravediggers that no vestige of disturbed earth is visible.* This done, they offer a sacrifice to their goddess Kali, and finally share the booty taken from the murdered man. Although the ceremonial is wholly Hindoo, the Thugs themselves comprise Mohammedans as well as Hindoos; and it is supposed by some inquirers that the Mohammedans have ingrafted a system of robbery on that which was originally a religious murder—murder as part of a sacrifice to a deity.

We repeat: there *may* be some moral or social thuggee yet to be discovered in India; but all we have now to assert is, that the condition of India in 1856 did not suggest to the retiring governor-general the slightest suspicion that the British in that country were on the edge of a volcano. He

* The visitor to the British Museum, in one of the saloons of the Ethnological department, will find a very remarkable series of figures, modelled by a native Hindoo, of the individuals forming a gang of Thugs; all in their proper costumes, and all as they are (or were) usually engaged in the successive processes of entrapping, strangling, and burying a traveller, and then dividing the booty.

said, in closing his remarkable minute: 'My parting hope and prayer for India is, that, in all time to come, these reports from the presidencies and provinces under our rule may form, in each successive year, a happy record of peace, prosperity, and progress.' No forebodings here, it is evident. Nevertheless, there are isolated passages which, read as England can *now* read them, are worthy of notice. One runs thus: 'No prudent man, who has any knowledge of Eastern affairs, would ever venture to predict the maintenance of continued peace within our Eastern possessions. Experience, frequent hard and recent experience, has taught us that war from without, or rebellion from within, may at any time be raised against us, in quarters where they were the least to be expected, and by the most feeble and unlikely instruments. No man, therefore, can ever prudently hold forth assurance of continued peace in India.' Again: 'In territories and among a population so vast, occasional disturbance must needs prevail. Raids and forays are, and will still be, reported from the western frontier. From time to time marauding expeditions will descend into the plains; and again expeditions to punish the marauders will penetrate the hills. Nor can it be expected but that, among tribes so various and multitudes so innumerable, local outbreaks will from time to time occur.' But in another place he seeks to lessen the force and value of any such disturbances as these. 'With respect to the frontier raids, they are and must for the present be viewed as events inseparable from the state of society which for centuries past has existed among the mountain tribes. They are no more to be regarded as interruptions of the general peace in India, than the street-brawls which appear among the every-day proceedings of a police-court in London are regarded as indications of the existence of civil war in England. I trust, therefore, that I am guilty of no presumption in saying, that I shall leave the Indian Empire in peace, without and within.'

Such, then, is a governor-general's picture of the condition of the British Empire in India in the spring of 1856: a picture in which there are scarcely any dark colours, or such as the painter believed to be dark. We may learn many things from it: among others, a consciousness how little we even now know of the millions of Hindostan—their motives, their secrets, their animosities, their aspirations. The bright picture of 1856, the revolting tragedies of 1857—how little relation does there appear between them! That there *is* a relation all must admit, who are accustomed to study the links of the chain that connect one event with another; but at what point the relation occurs, is precisely the question on which men's opinions will differ until long and dispassionate attention has been bestowed on the whole subject.

Notes.

[This may be a convenient place in which to introduce a few observations on three subjects likely to come with much frequency under the notice of the reader in the following chapters; namely, the distances between the chief towns in India and the three great presidential cities—the discrepancies in the current modes of spelling the names of Indian persons and places—and the meanings of some of the native words frequently used in connection with Indian affairs.]

Distances.—For convenience of occasional reference, a table of some of the distances in India is here given. It has been compiled from the larger tables of Taylor, Garden, Hamilton, and Parbury. Many of the distances are estimated in some publications at smaller amount, owing, it may be, to the opening of new and shorter routes:

	To Calcutta.	To Madras.	To Bombay.
	Miles.	Miles.	Miles.
From Agra . .	796	1238	754
" Allahabad .	498	1151	831
" Arcot . .	1085	71	715
" Aracan .	598	1661	1795
" Benares . .	428	1151	927
" Bhopal .	849	944	492
" Bombay . .	1185	763	...
" Calcutta .	...	1063	1185
" Cawnpore .	628	1260	854
" Delhi . .	950	1372	868
" Dinapore .	376	1337	1072
" Furrukhabad .	722	1257	892
" Gwalior . .	782	1164	680
" Hyderabad* .	962	398	434
" Indore . .	965	979	378
" Jaunpore .	473	1196	972
From Jeypoor . .	921	1352	757
" Kolapoor .	1245	584	228
" Kurachee .	1610	1567	873
" Lahore .	1241	1712	1208
" Lucknow .	619	1253	907
" Madras .	1063	...	763
" Masulipatam .	797	322	654
" Meerut .	906	1405	912
" Moorshedabad .	123	1166	1308
" Mysore .	1245	290	635
" Nagpoor .	677	713	508
" Oodypoor .	1139	1209	606
" Patna . .	369	1299	1065
" Peshawur .	1543	2014	1510
" Pondicherry .	1157	98	803
" Poonah .	1107	667	94
" Rungpoor .	271	1334	1156
" Satara .	1160	609	163
" Seringapatam .	1236	281	626
" Shahjehanpoor	735	1320	936
" Simla . .	1112	1611	1086
" Surat . .	1232	867	191
" Tanjore . .	1257	212	871
" Trichinopoly .	1254	209	835
" Umballa . .	1033	1532	1007
" Umritsir .	1193	1664	1160
" Vellore . .	1100	86	709
" Vizagapatam .	557	501	834

* There are two Hyderabads—one in the Nizam's dominions in the Deccan, and the other in Sinde (spelt Hydrabad): it is the former here intended.

Orthography.—It is perfectly hopeless to attempt here any settlement of the vexed question of Oriental orthography, the spelling of the names of Indian persons and places. If we rely on one governor-general, the next contradicts him; the commander-in-chief very likely differs from both; authors and travellers have each a theory of his own; while newspaper correspondents dash recklessly at any form of word that first comes to hand. Readers must therefore hold themselves ready for these complexities, and for detecting the same name under two or three different forms. The following will suffice to shew our meaning:—Rajah, raja—nabob, nawab, nawaub—Punjab, Punjaub, Penjab, Panjab—Vizierabad, Wuzeerabad—Ghengis Khan, Gengis Khan, Jengis Khan—Cabul, Caboul, Cabool, Kabul—Deccan, Dekkan, Dukhun—Peshawur, Peshawar—Mahomet, Mehemet, Mohammed, Mahommed, Muhummud—Sutlej, Sutledge—Sinde, Scinde, Sindh—Himalaya, Himmaleh—Cawnpore, Cawnpoor—Sikhs, Seiks—Gujerat, Guzerat—Ali, Alee, Ally—Ghauts, Gauts—Sepoys, Sipahis—Faquir, Fakeer—Oude, Oudh—Bengali, Bengalee—Burhampooter, Brahmapootra—Asam, Assam—Nepal, Nepaul—Sikkim, Sikim—Thibet, Tibet—Goorkas, Ghoorkas—Cashmere, Cashmeer, Kashmir—Doab, Dooab—Sudra, Soodra—Vishnu, Vishnoo—Buddist, Buddhist, &c. Mr Thornton, in his excellent Gazetteer of India, gives a curious instance of this complexity, in *eleven* modes of spelling the name of one town, each resting on some good authority—Bikaner, Bhicaner, Bikaneer, Bicknneer, Bickanere, Bikkaneer, Bhikanere, Beekaneer, Beekaner, Beykaneer, Bicanere. One more instance will suffice. Viscount Canning, writing to the directors of the East India Company concerning the conduct of a sepoy, spelled the man's name *Shik Pultoo*. A fortnight afterwards, the same governor-general, writing to the same directors about the same sepoy, presented the name under the form *Shaik Phultoo*. We have endeavoured as far as possible to make the spelling in the narrative and the map harmonise.

Vocabulary.—We here present a vocabulary of about fifty words much used in India, both in conversation and in writing, connected with the military and social life of the natives; with the initials or syllables P., Port., H., M., A., T., Tam., S., to denote whether the words have been derived from the Persian, Portuguese, Hindustani, Mahratta, Arabic, Tatar, Tamil, or Sanscrit languages. Tamil or Tamul is spoken in some of the districts of Southern India. In most instances, two forms of spelling are given, to prepare the reader for the discrepancies above adverted to:

Ab, aub (P.), water; used in composition thus: *Punjaub*, five waters, or watered by five rivers; *Doab*, a district between two rivers, equivalent in meaning to the Greek *Mesopotamia*.
Abad (P.), inhabited; a town or city; such as *Allahabad*, city of God; *Hyderabad*, city of Hyder.
Ayah (Port.), a nurse; a female attendant on a lady.
Baba (T.), a term of endearment in the domestic circle, nearly equivalent to the English *dear*, and applied both to a father and his child.
Baboo, a Hindoo title, equivalent to our *Esquire*.
Bag, bâgh, a garden; *Kudsiya bâgh* is a celebrated garden outside Delhi.
Behadoor (P.), brave; a title of respect added to the names of military officers and others.
Bang (P.), an intoxicating potion made from hemp.
Bazar, bazaar, an exchange or market-place.
Begum (T.), a princess, a lady of high rank.
Bheestee, bihishti, a water-carrier.
Bobachee, bâwarchi (T.), an Indian officer's cook.
Budgerow, bajrâ (S.), a Ganges boat of large size.
Bungalow, banglâ (H.), a house or dwelling.
Cherry, cheri (Tam.), village or town; termination to the name of many places in Southern India; such as *Pondicherry*.
Chit, chitti (H.), a note or letter.
Chupatty, châpâti (P.), a thin cake of unleavened Indian-corn bread.
Coolie, kuli (T.), a porter or carrier.
Cutcherry, kacharî (H.), an official room; a court of justice.
Dacoit, dâkâit (H.), a gang-robber.
Dâk, dahk, dawk (H.), the Indian post, and the arrangements connected with it.
Dewan, a native minister or agent.
Dost (P.), a friend.
Feringhee, a Frank or European.
Fakeer, fakir (A.), a mendicant devotee.
Ghazee, ghazi (A.), a true believer who fights against infidels: hence *Ghazeepoor*, city of the faithful.
Golundauze, golandâz (P.), a native artilleryman.
Havildar (P.), a native sergeant.
Jehad (A.), a holy war.
Jemadar (P.), a native lieutenant.
Jhageerdar, jaghiredar, jâgirdâr (P.), the holder of land granted for services.
Mohurrum (A.), a fast held sacred by Mohammedans on the tenth day of the first month in their year, equivalent to the 25th of July.
Musjid (A.), a mosque; thence *jumma musjid* or *jum'aah masjid*, a cathedral or chief mosque.
Naik, naig (S.), a native corporal.
Nânâ, nena (M.), grandfather, a term of respect or precedence among the Mahrattas; *Nânâ Sahib*, so far from being a family or personal name, is simply a combination of two terms of respect (see *Sahib*) for a person whose real name was Dhundu Punt.
Nawab, nabob, nâwâb (A.), derived from *nâîb*, a viceroy or vicegerent.
Nuddee, nadi (S.), a river.
Nullah, nâlâ (H.), a brook, water-course, the channel of a torrent.
Puttum, pattanam (S.), a town; the termination of the names of many places in Southern India; such as *Seringapatam*, the city of Shri Ranga, a Hindoo divinity.
Peon (P.), a messenger or foot-attendant.
Pore, poor, a town; the final syllable in many significant names, such as *Bhurtpore* or *Bhurutpoor*, the town of Bharata.
Rajpoot, a Hindoo of the military caste or order; there is one particular province in Upper India named from them *Rajpootana*.
Ryot, a peasant cultivator.
Sahib, saheb, sâaib (A.), lord; a gentleman.
Sepoy, sipahi, in the Bengal presidency, a native soldier in the Company's service; in that of Bombay, it often has the meaning of a peon or foot-messenger.
Shahzadah (P.), prince; king's son.
Sowar (P.), a native horseman or trooper.
Subadar, soobahdar (A.), a native captain.
Tuppal, tappâl (H.), a packet of letters; the post.
Zemindar, zamindâr (P.), a landowner.

CHAPTER I.

THE ANGLO-INDIAN ARMY AT THE TIME OF THE OUTBREAK.

THE magnificent India which began to revolt from England in the early months of 1857; which continued that Revolt until it spread to many thousands of square miles; which conducted the Revolt in a manner that appalled all the civilised world by its unutterable horrors—this India was, after all, not really unsound at its core. It was not so much the *people* who rebelled, as the *soldiers.* Whatever grievances the hundred and seventy millions of human beings in that wonderful country may have had to bear; whatever complaints may have been justifiable on their parts against their native princes or the British government; and whatever may have been the feelings of those native princes towards the British—all of which matters will have to be considered in later chapters of this work—still it remains incontestable that the outbreak was a military revolt rather than a national rebellion. The Hindoo foot-soldier, fed and paid by the British, ran off with his arms and his uniform, and fought against those who had supported him; the Mohammedan trooper, with his glittering equipments and his fine horse, escaped with both in like manner, and became suddenly an enemy instead of a friend and servant. What effect this treachery may have had on the populace of the towns, is another question: we have at present only to do with the military origin of the struggle.

Here, therefore, it becomes at once necessary that the reader should be supplied with an intelligible clue to the series of events, a groundwork on which his appreciation of them may rest. As this work aims at something more than a mere record of disasters and victories, all the parts will be made to bear some definite relation one to another; and the first of these relations is—between the mutinous movements themselves, and the soldiers who made those movements. Before we can well understand what the sepoys *did,* we must know who the sepoys *are;* before we can picture to ourselves an Indian regiment in revolt, we must know of what elements it consists, and what are its usages when in cantonments or when on the march; and before we can appreciate the importance of two presidential armies remaining faithful while that of Bengal revolted, we must know what is meant by a presidency, and in what way the Anglo-Indian army bears relation to the territorial divisions of India. We shall not need for these purposes to give here a formal history of Hindostan, nor a history of the rise and constitution of the East India Company, nor an account of the manners and customs of the Hindoos, nor a narrative of the British wars in India in past ages, nor a topographical description of India—many of these subjects will demand attention in later pages; but at present only so much will be touched upon as is necessary for the bare understanding of the *facts* of the Revolt, leaving the *causes* for the present in abeyance.

What are the authoritative or official divisions of the country in reference to the governors who control and the soldiers who fight (or ought to fight) for it? What are the modes in which a vast region, extending more than a thousand miles in many different directions, is or may be traversed by rebel soldiers who fight against their employers, and by true soldiers who punish the rebels? What and who are the soldiers thus adverted to; how many, of what races, how levied, how paid and supported, where cantoned, how officered? These are the three subjects that will occupy a brief chapter; after which the narrative of the Revolt may with profit be at once entered upon.

And first, for India as an immense country governed by a people living eight or ten thousand miles distant. Talk as we may, there are few among us who can realise the true magnitude of this idea—the true bearing of the relation borne by two small islands in a remote corner of Europe to a region which has been famed since the time of Alexander the Great. The British Empire in India—what does it denote? Even before the acquisition of Oude, Pegu, and Nagpoor, the British possessions in India covered nearly 800,000 square miles; but as the influence of England is gradually extending over the protected and the hitherto independent states, we shall best conceive the whole (without Pegu, which is altogether eastward of what is considered India) as a compact territory of 1,400,000 square miles—twelve times as large as the United Kingdom, sixteen times as large as Great Britain, twenty-five times as large as

England and Wales: double the size, in fact, of Great Britain, France, Spain, Portugal, Italy, Belgium, Holland, Prussia, and Switzerland, all combined. Nor is this, like the Russian Empire, a vast but thinly populated region. It contains at least a hundred and eighty millions of human beings, more than a hundred and thirty millions of whom are the direct subjects of Queen Victoria—that is, if anything *can* be direct, connected with the anomalous relations between the Crown and the East India Company.

It comes within the knowledge of most intelligent English readers at the present day, that this Indian Empire, governed by a curiously complicated bargain between a sovereign and a company, has been growing for a hundred years, and still continues growing. In fits of national anger or international generosity, we inveigh against the Czar of Russia for processes of aggression and plans of annexation in regions around and between the Caspian and Black Seas, and we compassionate and assist his weak neighbours under the pressure of his ambition; but it is only in times of excitement or peril that we consider the extraordinary way in which our own Indian Empire has been built up—by conquest, by purchase, by forfeiture—and in some cases by means which, called robbery by our enemies, do at any rate demand a little compunction from us as a Christian people. Exactly a century ago, England scarcely occupied a foot of ground in India; her power was almost crushed out by the native nawab who rendered himself infamous by the episode of the Black Hole at Calcutta; and it was in the year after that atrocity—namely, in 1757, that Clive began those wonderful victories which established a permanent basis for a British Empire in Hindostan. And what a continuous growth by increment has since been displayed! The Pergunnahs, Masulipatam, Burdwan, Midnapore, Chittagong, Bengal, Bahar, the Northern Circars, Benares, all passed into British hands by the year 1775; the next twenty-five years brought to us the ownership of Salsette, Nagore, Pulo Penang, Malabar, Dindigul, Salem, Barramahal, Coimbatore, Canara, Tanjore, and portions of the Deccan and Mysore; in the first quarter of the present century the list was increased by the Carnatic, Gorukhpore, the Doab, Bareilly, portions of Bundelcund, Cuttack, Balasore, Delhi, Gujerat, Kumaon, Saugor, Khandeish, Ajmeer, Poonah, the Concan, portions of Mahratta country, districts in Bejapore and Ahmednuggur, Singapore, and Malacca; in the next period of equal length the acquisitions included Assam, Aracan, Tenasserim, the Nerbudda districts, Patna, Sumbhulpore, Koorg, Loodianah, Kurnaul, Sinde, and the Jullundur Doab; while during the eight years of the Marquis of Dalhousie's administration, as we learn on his own authority, there were added Pegu, the Punjaub, Nagpoor, Oude, Satara, Jhansi, and Berar—all these in exactly a century.

The whole of British India is placed under a governor-general, whose official residence is at Calcutta, and who is assisted by a kind of cabin or council of ministers. Formerly there were thre presidencies, under whom the whole territory wa placed; two being under the governors of Bombay and Madras, and the remainder, called the Benga presidency, being under the governor-general himself, who was to this extent vested with a special as well as a general government. But in process of time it was found impossible for this official to fulfil all the duties imposed upon him; and the great Bengal presidency became subdivided. There are now five local governors of great districts—the governor-general himself, who directly rules many of the newly acquired regions; the lieutenant-governor of the Northwest Provinces, who rules some of the country formerly included in the presidency of Bengal; the lieutenant-governor of the Lower Provinces, who rules the rest of that country; and the governors of Madras and Bombay, whose range of territory has not undergone much increase in recent years. Let us learn a little concerning each of these five.

Madras, as a presidency or government, includes the whole of the south of India, where its narrowed, peninsular form is most apparent, up to about latitude 16° north, together with a strip still further north on the east or Coromandel coast. Its greatest inland extent is about 950 miles in one direction, and 450 in another; while its shores are washed by the Indian Ocean and the Bay of Bengal along a coast-line of no less than 1700 miles—unfortunately, however, very ill provided with ports and anchorages. There are about thirty districts and states under the governor's rule—some as 'regulation districts,' others as 'non-regulation districts,' and others as 'native states.' The difference between these three kinds may be thus briefly indicated: the 'regulation' districts are thoroughly British, and are governed directly by the chief of the presidency; the 'non-regulation' districts are now equally British, though of more recent acquisition, but are governed by agents or commissioners; while the 'native states' have still their native princes, 'protected,' or rather controlled by the British. Without any formal enumeration, it may be well to remember that the following names of some of these districts, all more or less familiar to English readers as the names of towns or provinces, are included among those belonging to the presidency or government of Madras—Masulipatam, Nellore, Chingleput, Madras, Arcot, Cuddalore, Cuddapah, Salem, Coimbatore, Trichinopoly, Tanjore, Madura, Tinnevelly, Malabar, Canara, Vizagapatam, Kurnaul, Koorg,* Cochin, Mysore, Travancore. Some of these are not absolutely British; but their independence is little more than a name. There are various important towns, or places worth knowing in connection with Indian affairs, which are included in some or other of

* A young native princess was sent to England from this district to be educated as a *Christian* lady; and Queen Victoria became a sponsor for her at a baptismal ceremony.

these districts, but not giving their names to them—such as Seringapatam, Golcandah, Rajamaudry, Juggernaut, Vellore, Pulicat, Pondicherry (French), Tranquebar, Negapatam, Bangalore, Ootacamund, Mangalore, Calicut.

Bombay, as a presidency, is a curiously shaped strip. Exclusive of the subordinate territories of native princes (over which, however, the Company exercises paramount political sway) and of Sinde, which, though recently placed under the government of Bombay, may properly be regarded as a distinct territory—exclusive of these, the presidency occupies a narrow strip, of irregular outline, stretching for a considerable distance north and south. It occupies the western coast of the peninsula, from Gujerat on the north, to the small Portuguese settlement of Goa on the south; and has a length of 650 miles, with a maximum breadth of 240. The Bombay provinces included in the strip just noticed, the neighbouring territories administered by or on behalf of native princes, and Sinde, form three sections about equal in size, the whole collectively being thrice as large as England and Wales. To assist the memory, as in the last paragraph, we give the names of the chief districts likely to be known to English readers—all of which either belong absolutely to the presidency of Bombay, or are more or less under the control of the governor—Surat, Baroche, Ahmedabad, Khandeish, Poonah, Ahmednuggur, Bombay, Concan, Satara, Baroda, Kattywar, Kolapore, Cutch, the Mahratta districts, Kurachee, Hyderabad, Shikarpore, Khyrpore. The last four are districts of Sinde, conquered by the late Sir Charles James Napier, and placed under the Bombay presidency as being nearer at hand than any of the others. Besides the towns similarly named to most of these districts, the following may be usefully mentioned—Goa (Portuguese), Bejapore, Bassein, Aurungabad, Assaye, Nuseerabad, Cambay.

Lower Bengal, or the Lower Provinces of Bengal, considered as a sub-presidency or lieutenant-government, comprises all the eastern portion of British India, bounded on the east by the Burmese and Chinese Empires, and on the north by Nepaul, Sikim, and Bhotan; southward, it is washed by the Bay of Bengal; while inland or westward, it reaches to a point on the Ganges a little beyond Patna, but not so far as Benares. Fancy might compare it in shape to a dumb-bell, surmounting the upper part of the Bay of Bengal, which washes its shores throughout a distance of 900 miles. Without reckoning native states under the control of the Company, this lieutenant-governorship is considerably more than three times as large as England and Wales; and nearly the whole of it is in the basins of, or drained by, the two magnificent rivers Ganges and Brahmaputra. On the principle before adopted, we give the names of districts most likely to become familiarised to the reader—Jessore, Burdwan, Bancorah, Bhaugulpore, Monghir, Cuttack, Balasore, Midnapore, Moorshedabad, Rungpoor, Dacca, Silhet, Patna, Bahar, Chittagong, the Sunderbunds, Assam, Aracan. Most of these are also the names of towns, each the chief in its district; but there are other important towns and places not here named—including Calcutta, Cossimbazar, Barrackpore, Chandernagore, Serampore, Culpee, Purneah, Boglipore, Rajmahal, Nagore, Raneegunge, Jellasore, Dinapore, Bahar, Ramghur, Burhampore.

Northwest Bengal, or the Northwestern Provinces of the Bengal presidency, regarded as a sub-presidency or lieutenant-governorship, comprises some of the most important and densely populated districts of Northern India. It covers seven degrees of latitude and nine of longitude; or, if the portion of the 'non-regulation' districts under the control of this lieutenant-governor be included, the range extends to ten degrees of latitude and twelve of longitude. Its boundary is roughly marked by the neighbouring provinces or states of Sirhind, Kumaon, Nepaul, Oude, Lower Bengal, Rewah, Bundelcund, and Scindiah's Mahratta territory; but many of these are included among its 'non-regulation' territories. In its limited, strictly British territory, it is a little larger than England and Wales; but including the 'non-regulation' provinces, such as Kumaon, Ajmeer, Saugor, &c., it is vastly larger. As the chief city is Agra, the lieutenant-governorship is often called by that name: more convenient, perhaps, than the one officially adopted—indeed it was at one time determined, though the plan has been postponed *sine die*, to form an entirely new and distinct presidency, called the Presidency of Agra. The Ganges and the Jumna are the great rivers that permeate it. As before, we give the names of the most familiarly known divisions or districts—Delhi, Meerut, Allygurh, Rohilcund, Bareilly, Shahjehanpoor, Bijnour, Agra, Furruckabad, Allahabad, Cawnpore, Futtehpore, Benares, Gorukhpore, Azimghur, Jounpore, Mirzapore, Ghazeepore; and if to these we add the names of towns not indicated by the names of their districts—such as Simla, Sirhind, Umballa, Loodianah, Shahabad, Buxar—it will be seen how many places noted more or less in Indian affairs lie within this province or lieutenant-governorship.

For the sake of brevity, it may here be remarked, we shall frequently, in future chapters, use the names 'Northwest Bengal' and 'Lower Bengal,' instead of the tedious designations 'Northwestern Provinces' and 'Lieutenant Government of Bengal.'

As to the fifth or remaining sphere of government—that which is under the governor-general himself—it is with difficulty described; so many are the detached scraps and patches. The overworked representative of the crown, whether his name be Auckland or Ellenborough, Dalhousie or Canning, finding the governorship of Bengal too onerous when added to the governor-generalship of the whole of India, gives up his special care of Bengal, divides it into two sub-provinces, and hands it over to the two lieutenant-governors. But the increase of territory in British India has been so vast within the last few years, and the difficulty so great of deciding to which presidency they ought to belong, that they have been made into a fifth dominion or government, under the governor-general himself. The great and important country of the Punjaub, acquired a few years ago, is one of the list; it is under the governor-general, and is administered for him by a board of commissioners. The kingdom of Oude is another, annexed in 1856, and similarly represented by residents or commissioners acting for and under the orders of the governor-general. The province of Nagpoor is a third: a large country in the very centre of India, annexed in 1853, and nearly touching all the four governorships already described. Pegu is a fourth, wrested from the sultan of Burmah, in 1852, and placed under the governor-general's administration. A fifth is Tenasserim, a strip of country stretching five hundred miles along the eastern shore of the Bay of Bengal. There are other fragments; but the above will suffice to shew that the governor-general has no inconsiderable amount of territory under his immediate control, represented by his commissioners. If we look at the names of places included within these limits, we shall be struck with their number and importance in connection with stirring events in India. In the Punjaub we find Peshawur, Attock, Rawul Pindee, Jelum, Ramnugur, Chillianwalla, Wuzeerabad, Umritsir, Lahore, Jullundur, Ghoorka, Ferozpore, Ferozshah, Moodkee; in the once independent but now British province or kingdom of Oude will be found the names of Lucknow, Oude, Fyzabad, Sultanpore, Khyrabad; in the territory of Nagpoor is the town of the same name, but other towns of any note are scarce. In Pegu and Tenasserim, both ultra-Gangetic or eastward of the Ganges, we find Rangoon, Bassein, Prome, Moulmein, and Martaban.

The reader has here before him about a hundred and forty names of places in this rapid sketch of the great divisional governments of India, mostly the names of important towns; and—without any present details concerning modes of government, or numbers governed, natural wealth or social condition—we believe he will find his comprehension of the events of the great Revolt much aided by a little attention to this account of the five governments into which British India is at present divided. As for the *original* names of kingdoms and provinces, nawabships and rajahships, it scarcely repays the trouble to learn them: when the native chiefs were made pensioned puppets, the former names of their possessions became of lessened value, and many of them are gradually disappearing from the maps. We have 'political residents,' 'government agents,' or 'commissioners,' at the capital city of almost every prince in India; to denote that, though the prince may hold the trappings of royalty, there is a watchful master scrutinising his proceedings, and claiming something to do with his military forces. Such is the case at Hyderabad in the Nizam's territory, at Khatmandoo in Nepaul, at Gwalior in Scindiah's dominions, at Indore in Holkar's dominions, at Bhopal, in the country of the same name, at Bhurtpore and elsewhere in the Rajpoot princes' dominions, at Darjeeling in Sikim, at Baroda in the Guicowar's dominions, &c.

The semi-independent princes of India—mostly rajahs if Hindoos, nawabs if Mohammedans—are certainly placed in a most anomalous position. There are nearly two hundred of these vassal-kings, if we may so term them—some owning territories as large as European kingdoms, while others claim dominion over bits of country not larger than petty German principalities. The whole of them have treaties and engagements with the British government, involving the reciprocal obligations of protection and allegiance. Some of them pay tribute, others do not; but almost all have formally relinquished the right of self-defence, and also that of maintaining diplomatic relations with each other. The princes are regarded as children, expected to look up for protection only to their great mother, the Company. The Company undertakes not only to guarantee external safety but also internal tranquillity in these states, and is the umpire in all quarrels between native rulers. Though not called upon, and indeed not allowed, to defend themselves from an external attack, the princes mostly have armies, more for show than use under ordinary circumstances; but then they must obtain permission to do this, and they must limit the numbers; and in some cases there is a stipulation that if the British be at war in India, the prince must lend his troops. It is in this sense that the independent princes of India are said to possess, collectively, an armed force of little less than four hundred thousand men: many of them available, according to treaty, for British service.

Next, we may usefully pay a little attention to this question—How, in so immense a country, do the soldiers and subjects of these several states, British and native, travel from place to place: how do they cross mountains where passes are few, or marshes and sandy plains where roads are few and bad, or broad rivers where bridges are scarce? The distances traversed by the armies are sometimes enormous. Let us open a map of India, and see, for example, the relative positions of Calcutta, Madras, Bombay, Delhi, Peshawur, and Kurachee at the western mouth of the Indus. Delhi is nearly nine hundred miles from Bombay, more than nine hundred from Calcutta by land, fifteen or sixteen hundred miles from the same city by water-route up the Ganges and Jumna, and nearly fourteen hundred from Madras. Kurachee, the most westerly spot in India, and destined one day, perhaps, to be an important depôt for steamers from the Red Sea or the Persian Gulf, is more than sixteen hundred miles from Calcutta, nearly across the broadest part of India from east to west; while Peshawur, at the extreme north-west or Afghan frontier, acquired by England when the Punjaub was annexed, is no less than *two thousand* miles from Madras. All opinions and judgments, concerning the slowness of operations in India, must be tempered by a consideration of these vast distances.

The rivers were the great highways of that country before roads existed, as in other regions; and they have never ceased to be the most frequented routes. At least such is the case in relation to the larger rivers—such as the Ganges, Indus, Nerbudda, Kishna, Jumna, Sutlej, and Jelum. Hindoos and Mohammedans, too poor to hire horses or palkees for land-travel, may yet be able to avail themselves of their river-boats.

The native boats which work on the Ganges are numerous and curious in kind. The *patella* or baggage-boat is of saul-wood, clinker-built, and flat-bottomed, with rather slanting outsides, and not so manageable as a punt or a London barge; its great breadth gives it a very light draught of water, and renders it fittest for the cotton and other up-country products, which require little more than a dry and secure raft to float them down the stream. The *oolak* or common baggage-boat of the Hoogly and Central Bengal, has a sharp bow and smooth rounded sides; it is fitted for tracking and sailing before the wind, and is tolerably manageable with the oar in smooth water. The Dacca *pulwar* is more weatherly, although, like the rest, without keel, and the fastest and most handy boat in use for general traffic. The *budgerow*, the *baulcah*, and the ketch-rigged pinnace, are employed by Europeans for their personal conveyance. Besides these, there are numerous others—such as the wood-boats of the Sunderbunds, of various forms and dimensions—from one hundred to six thousand maunds burden (a maund being about equal to 100 pounds troy); the salt-boats of Tumlook; the light boats which carry betel-leaf; the Calcutta *bhur*, or cargo-boat of the port; the Chittagong boats; the light *mug*-boats, with floors of a single hollowed piece of timber, and raised sides, neatly attached by sewing, with strips of bamboo over the seams; the *dinghee*; and the *panswee*—all found within the limits of the Bengal presidency. 'A native traveller, according to his degree and substance, engages a dinghee or a panswee, a pulwar or an oolak; the man of wealth puts his baggage and attendants in these, and provides a budgerow or a pinnace for his personal accommodation. Officers of high standing in the civil or military service, travelling with a large retinue of servants and a quantity of baggage, seldom have less than five or six boats (one of them a cooking-boat, and another fitted with an oven for baking bread): sometimes as many as fifteen when they carry their horses and equipages, and the materials of housekeeping for their comfortable establishment on arrival.'

Before Indian steamers were introduced, or Indian railways thought of, the Ganges was the great highway from Calcutta to Benares, Allahabad, and the northwestern provinces generally, in all cases where speed was not required. The Indian government used to allow their military servants two months and a half for proceeding to Benares, three to Allahabad, five to Meerut, and nine to Loodianah—periods that seem to us, in the old country, outrageous in their length. The boats were chiefly of two of the kinds mentioned in the preceding paragraph—namely, the pinnace, very European in its appearance, and the lofty sterned budgerow, peculiarly Indian. Even after steamers were placed upon the Ganges, the slow-going budgerow continued to be much used by the Company's officers, and by other persons going northwest—chiefly in cases where a family and a large quantity of luggage or personal effects had to be conveyed; for every other mode than the budgerow then becomes very costly—and will probably so continue until the great trunk-railway is completed. Budgerow boating is, it must be confessed, enough to stagnate the blood of an active man who wishes to speed onward to a scene of usefulness. As the tide ends at a few miles above Calcutta, there is a constant downward current throughout all the rest of the Ganges; and this current has to be struggled against during the up-passage. If the wind be favourable, sails are hoisted; but if otherwise, progress is made by *gooning* or tracking, an operation performed by the greater part of the crew proceeding on shore, and with ropes attached to the mast-head, dragging the vessel bodily along: wading for hours, it may be, through nullahs or creeks more than breast high. The travellers spend much of their time on shore in the cooler hours of the morning and evening, walking, fishing, or shooting, or otherwise whiling away their time; for they can easily keep up with a boat that only makes ten miles per average day. The Company have been accustomed to make a certain allowance to each officer for boat-accommodation up the country; and it is not unusual for two or three to join in the hire of one budgerow, to their mutual comfort, and with a small saving out of their allowance. They engage an attendant dinghee as a cook-boat, to keep the culinary operations at a respectful distance; and they fit up their budgerow with camp-tables, camp-stools, charpoys or light bedsteads, copper chillumchees or wash-basins, rugs, hanging lamps, canteens, bullock or camel trunks, and a few other articles of furniture; with wine, spirits, ale, preserves, cheeses, pickles, salt meats, hams, tongues, and other provisions, which are cheaper at Calcutta than if purchased on the way; and with their wardrobes, articles for the toilet, books, chess and backgammon boards, guns, musical instruments, and other aids to lessen the tedium of a long voyage.

Hitherto, commerce has had so much more to do with this Ganges traffic than passenger travel, that the slowness of the progress was not felt: as in the instance of the canals of England, which, made for goods and not for passengers, are not blameable on the score of tardiness. The Ganges is now, as it has been for ages, the main channel for the commerce of Northern India. The produce of Europe, of Southern India, of the Eastern Archipelago, of China, brought to Calcutta by ocean-going steamers or sailing-ships, is distributed upwards to Patna, Benares, Allahabad, Lucknow, Cawnpore, Agra, Delhi, and other great towns, almost exclusively by the Ganges route; and the same boats which convey these cargoes, bring down the raw cotton, indigo, opium, rice, sugar, grain, rich stuffs, piece-goods, and other grown or manufactured commodities from the interior, either for consumption at Calcutta and other towns on the route, or for shipment to England and elsewhere. It is probable that the cargo-boats and the budgerows will continue to convey a large proportion of the traffic of India, let steamers and railways make

Boats on the Ganges.

what progress they may; for there is much local trading that can be better managed by this slow, stopping, free-and-easy Ganges route of boating.

The Ganges steamers are peculiar. Each consists of two vessels, a *tug* and a *flat*, neither of which is of much use without the other. The tug contains the engine; the flat contains the passengers and cargo; and this double arrangement seems to have been adopted as a means of insuring light draught. Each flat contains fifteen or twenty cabins, divided into three classes according to the accommodation, and obtainable at a fare of twenty to thirty pounds for each cabin for a voyage from Calcutta up to Allahabad—less in the reverse direction, because the aid of the stream shortens the voyage. Besides this, the passenger pays for all his provisions, and most of the furniture of his cabin. Every passenger is allowed to take one servant free of passage fare. The steamer proceeds only during the day, anchoring every night; and it stops every three or four days, to take coals into the tug, and to deliver and receive passengers. The chief of these stopping-places are at the towns of Berhampore, Monghir, Patna, Dinapoor, Chupra, Buxar, Ghazeepore, Benares, Chunar, and Mirzapore, all situated on the banks of the Ganges between Calcutta and Allahabad; and it is only during the two or three hours of these stoppages that the passengers have an opportunity of rambling on the shore by daylight. The tug is of iron, and drags the flat by means of hawsers and a long beam, which latter serves both as a gangway and to prevent collision between the two vessels. The East India Company first established these steamers, but others have followed their example, and help to keep up a healthy competition. The river distance to Allahabad being eight hundred miles (three hundred in excess of the land route), and the time of transit being about twenty days, this gives forty miles per day as the average rate of progress of the tug and its attendant flat or accommodation-boat. Of proposed plans for improving this Ganges steaming, we do not speak in this place.

The Indus is less traversed by boats and steamers; but, being nearer to England than the Ganges, it is becoming more and more important every year, especially since the annexation of the Punjaub by the British. The boats on the Indus take up the produce of the Persian and Arabian gulfs, Cutch, the western districts of India, and so much of the produce of Europe as is available for Sinde, the Punjaub, and the northwest of India generally: taking back the produce of Afghanistan, Cashmere, the Punjaub, Sinde, and the neighbouring countries. The boats on this river, having fewer European travellers, do not possess so many accommodations as those on the Ganges; the scantiness of the population, too, and the semi-barbarous condition of the natives, tend towards the same result. The Sutlej boats, mostly employed, are long and clumsy; when going downwards, the stream gives them a velocity of about two miles an hour, while the oars and sail give them barely another extra mile. They correspond, indeed, rather with our idea of a Thames coal-barge, than with that of a boat. The steersman and two oarsmen are at the stern, working with a broad paddle and two oars. The passengers occupy the rest of the vessel, in a rude bamboo cabin twelve or fourteen feet long. When the wind and the stream are unfavourable, the sail is hauled down, and tracking is resorted to. As the up-river return-voyage is exceedingly slow, a passenger travelling down towards the sea is obliged to pay for the return-voyage as well. As there are hardly any important towns on the banks below the Punjaub, except Hyderabad, a traveller is obliged to take almost the whole of his provisions and necessaries with him. The journey up the stream is so insupportably tedious by these boats, that small steamers are generally preferred; but these require very light draught and careful handling, to prevent them from grounding on the shoals and sandbanks, which are more numerous in the Indus than in the Ganges.

River-travelling, it hence appears, is a very slow affair, ruinously inadequate to the wants of any but a population in a low scale of commercial advancement. Let us inquire, therefore, whether land-travelling is in a condition to remedy these evils.

There are so few good roads in India, that wheel-carriages can scarcely be trusted for any long distances. The prevailing modes of travel are on horseback or in a palanquin. Technically, the one mode is called *marching;* the other, *dâk*, *dakh*, or *dawk*. The former is sometimes adopted for economy; sometimes from necessity while accompanying troops; and sometimes, on short trips, through inclination; but as it is almost impossible to travel on horseback during the heat of the day, the more expensive but more regular dâk is in greater request. The horseman, when he adopts the equestrian system, accomplishes from twelve to twenty miles a day: sending on his servants one march or day in advance, with tent, bedding, tent-furniture, canteen, &c., in order that they may have a meal ready for the traveller by the time he arrives. They daily buy fodder, fowls, eggs, milk, rice, fruit, or vegetables at the villages as they pass through; the traveller, if a sportsman, aids the supply of his larder with snipe, wild-fowl, quail, partridges, hares, jungle-cocks, or bustard; but a week's provision at a time must be made of all such supplies as tea, coffee, dried or preserved meats, sauces, spices, beer, or wine, at the principal towns—as these commodities are either unattainable or very costly at the smaller stations and villages. Thus the traveller proceeds, accomplishing eighty to a hundred and fifty miles per week, according to his supply of horse-relays. We may get rid of the European notions of inns and hotels on the road: the India officer must carry his hotel with him.

We come next to the *dâk* system, much more prevalent than travelling by horseback. The dâk is a sort of government post, available for private individuals as for officials. A traveller having planned his journey, he applies to the postmaster of the district, who requires from one to three days' notice, according to the extent of accommodation needed. The usual complement for one traveller consists of eight *palkee-burdars* or palanquin-bearers, two *mussanjees* or torch-bearers, and two *bangey-burdars* or luggage-porters: if less than this number be needed, the fact must be notified. The time and place of starting, and the duration and localities of the halts, must also be stated; for everything is to be paid beforehand, on the basis of a regular tariff. The charge is about one shilling per mile for the entire set of twelve men—shewing at how humble a rate personal services are purchasable in India. There is also an extra charge for demurrage or delays on the road, attributable to the traveller himself. For these charges, the postmaster undertakes that there shall be relays of dâk servants throughout the whole distance, even if it be the nine hundred miles from Calcutta to Delhi; and to insure this, he writes to the different villages and post stations, ordering relays to be ready at the appointed hours. The stages average about ten miles each, accomplished in three hours; at the end of which time the twelve men retrace their steps, and are succeeded by another twelve; for each set of men belong to a particular station, in the same way as each team of horses for an English stage-coach belongs to a particular town. The rivers and streams on the route are mostly crossed by ferry-boats, for bridges are scarce in India; and this ferrying is included in the fare charged by the postmaster; although the traveller is generally expected to give a small fee, the counterpart to the 'drink-money' of Europe, to ferrymen as well as bearers. The *palanquin*, *palankeen*, or *palkee*, is a kind of wooden box opening at the sides by sliding shutters; it is about six feet in length by four in height, and is suspended by two poles, borne on the shoulders of four men. The eight bearers relieve one another in two gangs of four each. The postmaster has nought to do with the palanquin; this is provided by the traveller; and on its judicious selection depends much of his comfort during the journey, for a break-down entails a multitude of petty miseries. The average value of a palanquin may be about ten pounds; and the traveller can generally dispose of it again at the end of his journey. On account of the weight, nothing is carried that can be easily dispensed with; but the traveller manages to fit up his palanquin with a few books, his shaving and washing apparatus, his writing materials, and a few articles in frequent use. The regular fittings of the palanquin are a cushion or bed, a bolster, and a few light coverings. The traveller's luggage is mostly carried in *petarrahs*, tin boxes or wicker-baskets about half a yard square: a porter can carry two of these; and one or two porters will suffice for the demands of any ordinary traveller, running before or by the side of the palanquin. The petarrahs are hung, each from one end of a

Palanquin.

bangey or bamboo pole, the middle of which rests on the bearer's shoulder. The torch-bearers run by the side of the palanquin to give light during night-travelling; the torch is simply a short stick bound round at one end with a piece of rag or a tuft of hemp, on which oil is occasionally dropped from a flask or a hollow bamboo; the odour of the oil-smoke is disagreeable, and most travellers are glad to dispense with the services of a second torch-bearer.

Bishop Heber's journey from Delhi to Benares was a good example of dâk-travelling in his day; and the system has altered very little since. He had twelve bearers, on account of his route lying partly through a broken country. His clothes and writing-desk were placed in the two petarrahs, carried by the two bangey-burdars. 'The men set out across the meadows at a good round trot of about four miles an hour, grunting all the way like paviers in England: a custom which, like paviers, they imagine eases them under their burden.' Only four men can usually put their shoulders to a palanquin at the same time; but the bishop observed that whenever they approached a deep nullah or steep bank, the bearers who were not at that time bearing the palanquin, but were having their interval of rest, thrust stout bamboos under the bottom of the palanquin, and took hold of the ends on each side; so that the strength of several additional men was brought into requisition. In crossing a stream, 'the boat (the spot being a regular ferry), a broad and substantial one, had a platform of wood covered with clay across its middle. The palanquin, with me in it, was placed on this with its length athwart the middle; the mangee steered, and some of the dâk-bearers took up oars, so that we were across in a very short time.'

Private dâks are occasionally employed, a speculator undertaking to supply the bearers. Having no large establishments to keep up, these men can afford to undersell the government—that is, establish a lower tariff; and they provide a little additional accommodation in other ways. Some travellers, however, think these speculators or *chowdries* not sufficiently to be trusted, and prefer the government dâk at higher rates. Experienced men will sometimes dispense with the preliminary of 'laying a dâk,' or arranging for the whole journey: depending on their own sagacity for hunting up bearers at the successive stations. There have also been introduced horse-dâks, wheeled palanquins drawn by horses; but these are only available on the great trunk-roads recently executed by the government.

It was observed, in relation to 'marching' or horse-travelling, that there are no hotels or inns on the road; there is a partial substitute, however, that may here be noticed. The Company have established dâk-bungalows at certain stations, varying from fifteen to fifty miles apart, according as the road is much or little frequented. These places are under the control of government officers: a *khitmutgar* or servant, and a porter, attend at each; the traveller pays a fixed sum for the use of the room, and makes a separate bargain for any few articles of provisions that may be obtainable. The building is little more than a thatched house of one story, divided into two small rooms, to each of which a bathing-room is attached. The servant cooks and serves a meal, while the porter assists in subsidiary offices. If a traveller does not choose to avail himself of these bungalows, he can travel continuously in his palanquin, sleeping and waking by turns. This, however, is a great trial for most persons; because the bearers make an unpleasant grunting noise as an accompaniment to their movements; and moreover,

Indian Domestics.

1. Dirgee—tailor. 2. Khitmutgar writing the accounts of the previous day. 3. Sepoy after parade. 4. Maitre, or house-cleaner. 5. Dobee—washerman. 6. Chuprassee going out with gun before a shooting-party. 7. Chuprassee—letter-carrier. 8. Bengalee Pundit, or scholar.

unless well drilled, they do not balance the palanquin well, but subject its inmate to distressing joltings.

It has been placed upon record, as an instructive commentary on the immense distances to be traversed in India, the imperfection of most of the roads, and the primitive detail of travelling arrangements—that when Viscount Hardinge was engaged in the Punjaub campaign in 1846, one hundred European officers were sent off from Calcutta to aid him. Although the distance was nearly fifteen hundred miles, nothing more rapid than palanquin travelling was available; and, as a consequence, the journey became so tediously prolonged that only thirty out of the hundred officers arrived at the Sutlej before the campaign was over. Palanquin-bearers were posted at different stations to carry three persons daily; and it was calculated that, assuming twelve bearers to be posted at every station, and the stations eight miles apart on an average, the duty must have required the services of *seven thousand* of these men—all to carry one hundred officers: a waste of muscular energy singular to contemplate by the light of an Englishman's home experience.

The Indian post is still more simple than the dâk. It is conducted by runners, each of whom slings his mail-bag on the end of a stick over his shoulder. He runs five miles in an hour, and then gives his bag to another man, who runs five miles in an hour; and so on. Strictly speaking, dâk is an appellation properly belonging to this letter-carrying system. It is equivalent to the English *post;* and as the English have adopted the custom of applying the term post to quick travelling as well as to letter-carrying, in like manner have the Anglo-Indians adopted a double application of the word dâk. It is only the express or quick dâk which maintains a speed of five miles an hour; the ordinary speed, when the letter-bag is heavy, is four miles. In order that the runners may not be required to go far from their homes, each man carries his bag one stage, exchanges bags with another runner who has come in the opposite direction, and then returns. A letter may thus be conveyed a hundred miles in a day—a distance which, considering the nature of the system, is quite as great as can reasonably be expected. Horse and camel dâks are occasionally employed; but they are not easily available, except on good roads. Besides the letter-dâk, there is a parcel-dâk or *bangey*, the runner carrying a packet or box, in which small parcels or newspapers are placed.

It will become a duty, in a later portion of this work, to notice somewhat fully the railway schemes of India, in relation to the plans for developing the industrial resources of that great region; but at present this would be out of place, since the Revolt has been dependent on the actual, not the prospective. This actuality, so far as concerns means and modes of travelling, is summed up in a few words. An Indian officer, we have seen, must travel to his station by horse or by palanquin if on land, by drag-boat or by steam-boat if on the rivers. In any case his rate of progress is slow; his movements are encumbered by a train of servants, by a whole bazarful of furniture and culinary apparatus, and by an anxiously selected provision for his larder. To move quickly is well-nigh impossible: all the conditions for it are wanting. Improvements, it is true, are in progress: steamers of light draught and rapid movement are being planned for the rivers; the great trunk-road from Calcutta to the Afghan frontier is beginning to offer facilities for wheel-carriage transport; and the railways are beginning to shew their iron tracks in various regions; nevertheless, these are rather indications of the future than appliances for the present; and the Indian officers are not yet in a position to say much about them from personal experience. The humbler soldiers, whether Europeans or sepoys, are of course less favourably served than the officers. There is no Weedon in India, connected by rail with a Chatham, a Portsmouth, a Liverpool, a Leeds, along which a whole regiment can be conveyed in a few hours; and as saddle-horses and palanquins are out of the question for infantry privates, it becomes necessary to trudge on foot along such roads as may be available, or to linger on the tardy river route. Once now and then, it is true, a daring man, a Napier or an Edwardes, will swiftly send a small body of troops over a sandy desert or a marshy plain on camels, horses, elephants, or some exceptional modes of conveyance; but the prevale characteristics of travel are such as have here be described, and such will doubtless be the case f many years to come.

Such, then, being the territorial arrangemen by which Anglo-Indian troops are considered belong to different presidencies and states; an such the modes in which military as well civilians must move from place to place in thos territories; we shall be prepared next to under stand something about the soldiers themselves— the Anglo-Indian army.

In no country in Europe is there an army so anomalous in its construction as that which until lately, belonged to the East India Company. Different kinds of troops, and troops from different provinces, we can well understand. For instance, the French avail themselves of a few Algerine Arabs, and a small foreign legion, as components in the regular army. The English have a few colonial corps in addition to the Queen's army. The Prussians have a *landwehr* or militia equal in magnitude to the regular army itself. The Russians have military colonists as well as military tributaries, in addition to the great *corps d'armée*. The Austrians have their peculiar Military Frontier regiments, besides the regular troops furnished by the dozen or score of distinct provinces and kingdoms which form their empire. The German States provide their several contingents to form (if the States can ever bring themselves to a unity of opinion) an Army of the Confederation. The Neapolitans employ Swiss mercenaries as a portion of their army. The Romans, the subjects of the pope as a temporal prince, have the 'protection' of French and Austrian bayonets, in addition to a small native force. The Turks have their regular army, aided (or sometimes obstructed) by the contingents of vassal-pachas and the irregulars from mountain districts. But none of these resemble the East India Company's army. Under an ordinary state of affairs, and without reference to the mutiny of 1857, the Indian army is in theory a strange conglomerate. The Queen *lends* some of her English troops, for which the Company pay; the Company enlist other English troops on their own account; they maintain three complete armies among the natives of India who are their subjects; they raise irregular corps or regiments in the states not so fully belonging to them; they claim the services of the troops belonging to certain tributary princes, whenever exigency arises; and the whole of these troops are placed under the generalship of a commander-in-chief, who is appointed—not by the Company, who have to pay for all—but by the Queen or the British government.

The Company's army rose by degrees, as the territorial possessions increased. At first the troops were little better than adventurers who sold their swords to the highest bidders, and fought for pay and rations without regard to the justice of the cause in which they were engaged; many were liberated convicts, many were deserters from various European armies, some were Africans, while a few were Topasses, a mixed race of Indo-Portuguese. The first regular English troops seen in Bengal were an ensign and thirty privates, sent from Madras to quell a petty disturbance at the Company's factory in the Hoogly. Gradually, as the numbers increased and the organisation improved, the weapons underwent changes. The troops originally were armed with muskets, swords, and pikes twelve or fourteen feet long: the pikemen in the centre of the battalion or company, and the musketeers on the flank. In the beginning of the last century the pikes were abandoned, and the soldiers armed with bayonets in addition to the muskets and swords. When the custom was adopted, from European example, of forming the companies into a regular battalion, the swords were abolished, and the common soldiers left only with muskets and bayonets. Various changes were made during the century, assimilating the troops more and more to those of the English crown, in weapons and accoutrements.

The regiments became, by successive ameliorations, composed almost wholly of native Hindoos and Mohammedans, officered to some extent by Europeans. An English sergeant was given to each company, and a drill-sergeant and sergeant-major to each battalion. Afterwards, when the battalions were formed into regiments, natives were appointed as sergeants of companies; and then the only European non-commissioned officers were a sergeant-major and a quartermaster-sergeant. By the time of Lord Clive's achievements, just about a century ago, three armies were owned by the Company—one in Bengal or the Calcutta presidency, one in the Coromandel or Madras presidency, and one on the Malabar coast, south of the present station of Bombay. These three armies were totally separate and distinct, each under its own commander, and each presenting some peculiarities of organisation; but they occasionally joined as one army for large military operations. There were many native corps, and a few European corps; but all alike were officered by Europeans. The cadet, the young man sent out from England to 'make his fortune' in India, was appointed to a native corps or a European corps at the choice of the commander. The pay being good and regular, and the customs and prejudices respected, the sepoys, sipahis, or native soldiers became in most cases faithful servants to the Company, obeying their native officers, who, in their turn, were accountable to the European officers. The European and the native corps were alike formed by enlistment: the Company compelling no one to serve but those who deemed the pay and other arrangements sufficient. An endeavour was made at that time (afterwards abandoned) to equalise the Hindoos and Mohammedans in numbers as nearly as possible.

From an early period in the Company's history, a certain number of regiments from the British royal army were lent for Indian service; the number being specified by charter or statute; and the whole expense, of every kind, being defrayed by the Company—including, by a more modern arrangement, retiring pay and pensions. There were thus, in effect, at all times two English armies in India; the one enlisted by the Company, the other lent by the Crown; and it was a matter of some difficulty to obviate jealousies and piques between the two corps. For, on the one hand, the officers of the Company's troops had better pay and more profitable stations assigned to them; while, on the other hand, the royal officers had precedence and greater honour. A Company's captain, however so many years he might have served, was subordinate even to the youngest royal captain, who assumed command over him by right. At length, in 1796, the commissions received by the Company's officers were recognised by the crown; and the two corps became placed on a level in pay and privileges.

The year just named witnessed a new organisation also of the native army. A regiment was ordered to be of two thousand men, in two corps or battalions of one thousand each; and each battalion was divided into ten companies, with two native officers to each company. Thus there were forty native officers in each of these large regiments. Besides these, there were half as many European officers as were allowed to a European regiment of the same magnitude. There had before been a native commandant to each battalion; but he was now superseded by a European field-officer, somewhat to the dissatisfaction of the men. The service occasionally suffered from this change; for a regiment was transferred at once from a native who had risen to command by experience and good conduct, to a person sent out from England who had to learn his duties as a leader of native troops after he went out. The youngest English ensign, perhaps a beardless boy, received promotion before any native, however old and tried in the service. And hence arose the custom, observed down to recent times, of paying no attention to the merits of the natives as a spur to promotion, allowing seniority to determine the rise from one grade to another.

While on the one hand the natives volunteered as soldiers in the Company's service, and were eligible to rise to a certain rank as regimental officers; the English officers, on the other, had their own particular routine and hopes of preferment. The cadets or youths went out partially educated by the Company in England, especially those intended for the artillery and engineer departments; and when settled with their regiments in India as officers, all rose by seniority; the engineers and artillery in their own corps, the cavalry and infantry in their own regiments. It often happened, however, that when few deaths occurred by war, officers reached middle life without much advancement, and retired after twenty years or more of service with the pay of the rank they then held. In 1836, however, a law was made to insure that the retiring allowance should not be below a certain minimum: if an officer served twenty-three years, he retired with captain's pay; if twenty-seven years, with major's pay; if thirty-one years, with lieutenant-colonel's pay; if thirty-five years, with colonel's pay—whatever might have been his actual rank at the date of his retirement. There was also permission for them to sell their commissions, although those commissions were not bought by them in the first instance.

Unquestionably the sepoy was well paid, considering the small value of labour and personal services in his country; and thus it arose that the Company had seldom any difficulty in obtaining troops. The sepoys were volunteers in the full sense of the word. Their pay, though small in our estimation, was high in proportion to the station they formerly held. The Bengal Infantry sepoy received seven rupees (fourteen shillings) per month, with an additional rupee after sixteen years' service, and two after twenty years. A havildar or sergeant received fourteen rupees; a jemadar or lieutenant twenty-four rupees; and a subadar or captain sixty-seven rupees. This pay was relatively so good, that each man was usually able to send two-thirds of it to his relations. And he was not a stranger to them at the end of his term, like a Russian soldier; for it was a part of the system to allow him periodical furlough or leave of absence, to visit his friends. If unfit for military service after fifteen months' duty, he retired on a life-pension sufficient to support him in his own simple way of life. Whether he *ought*, in moral fairness, to be grateful towards the rulers who fed and clothed him, is just one of those questions on which Indian officers have differed and still differ. Viewed by the aid of the experience furnished by recent events, many of the former encomiums on the sepoys, as men grateful for blessings conferred, read strangely. The Marquis of Dalhousie's statement, that 'The position of the native soldier in India has long been such as to leave hardly any circumstance of his condition in need of improvement,' has already been adverted to. To this we may add the words of Captain Rafter: 'We assert, on personal knowledge and reliable testimony, that the attachment of the sepoy to his English officer, and through him to the English government, is of an enduring as well as an endearing nature, that will long bid defiance to the machinations of every enemy to British supremacy, either foreign or domestic.'* In another authority we find that the sepoy, when his term of military service has expired, 'goes back to live in ease and dignity, to teach his children to love and venerate that mighty abstraction the Company, and to extend the influence of England still further throughout the ramifications of native society. Under such a system, although temporary insubordination may and sometimes does occur in particular regiments, it is invariably caused by temporary grievances. General disaffection cannot exist—desertion is unknown.' But the validity or groundlessness of such opinions we do not touch upon here: they must be reserved to a later chapter, when the *causes* of the mutiny will come under review. We pass on at once, therefore, from this brief notice of the origin of the Company's army, to its actual condition at and shortly before the period of the outbreak.

* *Our Anglo-Indian Army.*

Should it be asked what, during recent years, has been the number of troops in India, the answer must depend upon the scope given to the question. If we mention Queen's troops only, the number has been usually about 24,000; if Queen's troops and the Company's European troops, about 42,000; if the Company's native regulars be added to these, the number rises to 220,000; if the Company's irregular corps of horse be included, there are 280,000; if it include the contingents supplied by native princes, the number amounts to 320,000; and lastly, if to these be added the armies of the independent and semi-independent princes, more or less available by treaty to the Company, the total swells to 700,000 men.

As exhibiting in detail the component elements of the Company's Anglo-Indian army at a definite period, the following enumeration by Captain Rafter may be adopted, as applicable to the early part of 1855. Certain minor changes were made in the two years from that date to the commencement of the outbreak; but these will be noticed in later pages when necessary, and do not affect the general accuracy of the list. The three presidencies are kept separate, and the three kinds of troops—regiments of the royal army, the Company's native regular regiments, and native irregular regiments—are also kept separate.

First we take the Bengal presidency in all its completeness, stretching almost entirely across Northern India from the Burmese frontier on the east, to the Afghan frontier on the west:

BENGAL PRESIDENCY.

Queen's Troops.

Two regiments of light cavalry.
Fifteen regiments of infantry.
One battalion of 60th Rifles.

Company's Regular Troops.

Three brigades of horse-artillery, European and native.
Six battalions of European foot-artillery.
Three battalions of native foot-artillery.
Corps of Royal Engineers.
Ten regiments of native light cavalry.
Two regiments of European fusiliers.
Seventy-four regiments of native infantry.
One regiment of Sappers and Miners.

Irregular and Contingent Troops.

Twenty-three regiments of irregular native cavalry.
Twelve regiments of irregular native infantry.
One corps of Guides.
One regiment of camel corps.
Sixteen regiments of local militia.
Shekhawuttie brigade.
Contingents of Gwalior, Jhodpore, Malwah, Bhopal, and Kotah.

The European troops here mentioned, in the Company's regular army, are those who have been enlisted in England or elsewhere by the Company's agents, quite irrespective of the royal or Queen's army. The above forces, altogether, amounted to somewhat over 150,000 men. Let us now glance at another presidency:

MADRAS PRESIDENCY.

Queen's Troops.

One regiment of light cavalry.
Five regiments of infantry.

Company's Regular Troops.

One brigade of horse-artillery, European and native.
Four battalions of European foot-artillery.
One battalion of native foot-artillery.
Corps of Royal Engineers.
Eight regiments of native light cavalry.
Two regiments of European infantry.
Fifty-two regiments of native infantry.

No irregular or contingent troops appear in this entry.

BOMBAY PRESIDENCY.

Queen's Troops.

One regiment of light cavalry.
Five regiments of infantry.

Company's Regular Troops.

One brigade of horse-artillery, European and native.
Two battalions of European foot-artillery.
Two battalions of native foot-artillery.
Corps of Royal Engineers.
Three regiments of native light cavalry.
Two regiments of European infantry.
Twenty-nine regiments of native infantry.

Irregular and Contingent Troops.

Fifteen regiments of irregular native troops.

The European and the native troops of the Company are not here separated, although in effect they form distinct regiments. So costly are all the operations connected with the Anglo-Indian army, that it has been calculated that every English soldier employed in the East, whether belonging to the Queen's or to the Company's forces, costs, on an average, one hundred pounds before he becomes available for service, including his outfit, his voyage, his marching and barracking in India. This of course relates to the privates; an officer's cost is based upon wholly distinct grounds, and can with difficulty be estimated. The greatly increased expenditure of the Company on military matters has partly depended on the fact that the European element in the armies has been regularly augmenting: in 1837 there were 28,000 European troops in India; in 1850 the number was 44,000, comprising 28,000 Queen's troops, and 16,000 belonging to the Company; while the new charter of 1854 allowed the Company to raise 24,000, of whom 4000 were to be in training in England, and the rest on service in India. What was the number in 1857, becomes part of the history of the mutiny. In the whole Indian army, a year or two before this catastrophe, there were about 5000 European officers, governing the native as well as the European regiments; but of this number, so many were absent on furlough or leave, so many more on staff appointments, and so many of the remainder in local corps and on civil duties, that there was an insufficiency of regimental control—leading, as some authorities think, in great part to the scenes of insubordination; for the native officers, as we shall presently see, were regarded in a very subordinate light. There was a commander-in-chief for each of the three presidencies, controlling the three armies respectively; while one of the three, the commander-in-chief of the Bengal army, held at the same time the office of commander-in-chief of the whole of the armies of India, in order that there might be a unity of plan and purpose in any large combined operations. Thus, when Sir Colin Campbell went out to India in the summer of 1857, his power was to be exerted over the armies of the whole of India generally, as well as over that of Bengal in particular.

Continuing to speak of the Indian army as it was before the year 1857, and thereby keeping clear of the changes effected or commenced in that year, we proceed to mention a few more circumstances connected with the Company's European element in that army. The formation of an Indian officer commenced in England. As a youth, from fourteen to eighteen years of age, he was admitted to the Company's school at Addiscombe, after an ordeal of recommendations and testimonials, and after an examination of his proficiency in an ordinary English education, in which a modicum of Latin was also expected. A probation of six months was gone through, to shew whether he possessed the requisite abilities and inclination; and if this probation were satisfactory, his studies were continued for two years. His friends paid the larger portion of the cost of his maintenance and education at the school. If his abilities and progress were of a high class, he was set apart for an appointment in the engineers; if next in degree, in the artillery; and if the lowest in degree, for the infantry. At the end of his term the pupil must have attained to a certain amount of knowledge, of which, however, very little was professional. Supposing all to be satisfactory, he became a military *cadet* in the service of the Company, to be available for Indian service as occasion arose. Having joined one of the regiments as the lowest commissioned officer, his subsequent advancement depended in part on his qualifications and in part on seniority. He could not, by the more recent regulations of the Company, become a captain until he had acquired, besides his professional efficiency, a knowledge of the spoken and written Hindustani language, and of the Persian written character, much used in India. When placed on the general staff, his services might be required in any one of a number of ways quite unknown in the Queen's service in England: he might have a civil duty, or be placed at the head of the police in a tract of country recently evacuated by the military, or be made an adjutant, auditor, quarter-master, surveyor, pay-master, judge-advocate, commissary-general, brigade-major, aid-de-camp, barrack-master, or clothing agent. Many of these offices being lucrative, the military liked them; but such a bestowal created some jealousy among the civil servants of the Company, whose prizes in the Indian lottery were thereby diminished; and, what was worse, it shook the connection between an officer and his regiment, rendering him neither able nor willing to throw his sympathies into his work. No officer could hold any of these staff appointments, as they were called, until he had been two years in the army.

The officers noticed in the last paragraph were appointed to the command both of European and of native regiments. As to privates and non-commissioned officers in the European regiments, they were much the same class of men, and enlisted much in the same way, as those in the Queen's army. The privates or sepoys of the native regiments were of course different, not only from Europeans, but different among themselves. Four-fifths of the Bengal native infantry were Hindoos, mainly of the Brahmin and Rajpoot castes; and the remainder Mohammedans. On the other hand, three-fourths of the Bengal native cavalry were Mohammedans, the Hindoos being generally not equal to them as troopers. In the Madras native army, the Mohammedans predominated in the cavalry, while the infantry comprised the two religions in nearly equal proportions. In Bombay, nearer the nations of Western Asia, the troops comprised volunteers of many countries and many religions—more easily managed, our officers found, on that account.

Without at present going into the question how far the religious feelings and caste prejudices of the natives induced a revolt, it may be useful to shew how a regiment was constituted, of what materials, and in what gradations. An infantry regiment in the Bengal presidency will serve as a type.

The organisation of a Bengal native regiment, before the mutiny, was nearly as follows: An infantry regiment consisted of about 1000 privates, 120 non-commissioned officers, and 20 native commissioned officers. It was divided into ten companies, each containing one-tenth of the above numbers. When stationary, the regiment seldom had barracks, but was quartered in ten lines of thatched huts, one row for each company. In front of each row was a small circular building for containing the arms and accoutrements of that particular company, under the charge of a *havildar* or native sergeant. All these natives rose by a strict rule of seniority: the sepoy or private soldier becoming a *naik* or corporal, the naik being promoted to be *havildar* or sergeant, the havildar in time assuming the rank of *jemadar* or lieutenant, and the jemadar becoming a *subadar* or captain. All these promotions were necessarily slow; for the English colonel of the regiment had very little power to promote a worthy native officer or non-commissioned officer to a higher rank. The jemadar often became a gray-headed man of sixty before he rose to the rank of subadar, the highest attainable by a native. As a rule, there were four or five Hindoos to one Mohammedan in a Bengal infantry regiment; and of these eight hundred Hindoos, it was not unfrequent to find four hundred Brahmins or hereditary priests, and two hundred Rajpoots, a military caste only a little lower in rank than the former; while the remaining two hundred were low-caste Hindoos. The European officers, as will be explained more fully further on, lived in bungalows or detached houses near the lines of their regiment; but as the weather is too hot to admit of much open-air duty in the daytime, these officers saw less of their men than is customary in European armies, or than is necessary for the due preservation of discipline. The head of a regiment was the commander, generally a lieutenant-colonel; below him was an adjutant, who attended to the drill and the daily reports; below him was a quarter-master and interpreter, whose double duties were to look after the clothes and huts of the men, and to interpret or translate orders. Besides these three, there were ten subordinate officers for the ten companies, each expected to make a morning scrutiny into the condition and conduct of his men. The Europeans in a native regiment were thus fourteen or fifteen. It is true that the *theory* of a regiment involved a complement of about five-and-twenty European officers; but the causes of absenteeism, lately adverted to, generally brought down the effective number to about twelve or fifteen. The arrangements of the infantry in the other presidencies, and of the native cavalry all over India, each had their peculiarities.

Leaving for future chapters a further elucidation of the relations between the European officers and the native troops—so important in connection with the Revolt—and a description of the sepoys in their dresses, usages, and personal characteristics—we shall now proceed to view the native army under two different aspects—first, when barracked and cantoned in time of peace; and, secondly, when on the march towards a scene of war.

And first, for the army when stationary. At Calcutta, Bombay, and Madras, there are solidly built barracks for the whole of the soldiery, men as well as officers; but in almost all other parts of India the arrangements are of a slighter and less permanent character. At the cantonments, it is true, the officers have houses; but the sepoys are lodged in huts of their own construction. Around the cantonments at the stations, and generally skirting the parade-grounds, are the houses or bungalows of the officers. Within the lines of the cantonment, too, the officers' mess-rooms are situated; and at the larger stations may be seen ball-rooms, theatres, and racket-courts; while outside is a race-stand for witnessing the sports which Englishmen love in India as well as at home.

The Indian bungalows, the houses inhabited by European officers at the different towns and stations in India, have a certain general resemblance, although differing of course much in details. A bungalow of good size has usually a central room

5 4 3 2 1 6

Group of Sepoys.

1. Subadar—major. 2. Jemadar—Lieutenant. 3. Subadar—Captain. 4. Naik—Corporal. 5. Havildar—Sergeant. 6. Sepoy—Private.

called the hall, a smaller room opening on the front verandah, a similar one opening on the back verandah, three narrower rooms on each side of these three, and bathing-rooms at the four corners. A verandah runs entirely round the exterior. The central hall has only the borrowed light derived from eight or a dozen doors leading out of the surrounding apartments: these doors are always open; but the doorways are covered, when privacy is desired, with the *chick*, a sort of gauze-work of green-painted strips of fine bamboo, admitting air and light, but keeping out flies and mosquitoes. The floors are usually of *chunam*, finely tempered clay, covered with matting, and then with a sort of blue-striped carpet or with printed calico. The exterior is usually barn-like and ugly, with its huge roof, tiled or thatched, sloping down to the pillars of the verandah. Air and shade are the two desiderata in every bungalow, and adornment is wisely sacrificed to these. The finest part of the whole is the surrounding space or garden, called the *compound*, from a Portuguese word. The larger the space allowed for this compound, the more pleasant is the residence in its centre, and the more agreeable to the eye is a cantonment of such bungalows. The trees and fruits in these enclosures are delicious to the sight, and most welcome to the heat-wearied occupants of the dwellings. Officers in the Company's service, whether military or civil, live much under canvas during the hot seasons, at some of the stations; and the tents they use are much larger and more like regular habitations than those known in Europe. The tents are double, having a space of half a yard or so between the two canvas walls, to temper the heat of the sun. The double-poled tents are large enough to contain several apartments, and are furnished with glass-doors to fit into the openings. A wall of canvas separates the outer offices and bathing-rooms. Gay chintz for wall-linings, and printed cotton carpets, give a degree of smartness to the interior. Movable stoves, or else fire-dishes for wood-fuel called *chillumchees*, are provided as a resource against the chill that often pervades the air in the evening of a hot day. The tents for the common soldiers hold ten men each

Bungalow.

with great ease, and have a double canvas wall like the others.

An important part of every cantonment is the bazaar, situated in convenient proximity to the huts or tents of the troops. It comprises an enormous number of sutlers, who sell to the soldiers those commodities which cannot well be dispensed with, but which cannot conveniently be provided and carried about by them. Curry stuffs, tobacco, rice, arrack (in addition to the Company's allowance), cotton cloth, and a multiplicity of other articles, are sold at these bazaars; and the market-people who supply these things, with their families, the coolies or porters, and their hackeries or carts—add enormously to the mass that constitutes an Indian cantonment. The sepoy has little to spend with his sixpence a day; but then his wants are few; and his copper *pice*, somewhat larger than the English farthing, will buy an amount of necessaries little dreamed of in England. The Hindoos have such peculiar notions connected with food and cooking, that the government leave them as much to themselves as possible in those matters; and the bazaar and sutlers' arrangements assume a particular importance from this circumstance.

An Anglo-Indian army we have seen at rest, in cantonments. Now let us trace it when on a march to a scene of war; but while describing this in the *present* tense, we must make allowance for the changes which the Revolt has inevitably produced.

The non-fighting men who accompany the troops greatly exceed in number the troops themselves. Captain Munro says: 'It would be absurd for a captain to think of taking the field without being attended by the following enormous retinue—namely, a *dubash* (agent or commissionaire), a cook, and a *maty* boy (servant-of-all-work); if he cannot get bullocks, he must assemble fifteen or twen *coolies* to carry his baggage, together with a hor keeper and grass-cutter, and sometimes a dulcin and her train, having occasionally the assistance a barber, a washer, and an ironer, in comm with the other officers of his regiment. H tent is furnished with a good large bed, mattres pillows, &c., a few camp stools or chairs, a foldin table, a pair of glass shades for his candles, six seven trunks, with table equipage, his stock linens (at least twenty-four suits), some dozens wine, porter, brandy, and gin; with tea, sugar and biscuit, a hamper of live poultry, and hi milch-goat. A private's tent for holding hi servants and the overplus of his baggage is als requisite; but this is not at the Company' expense.' Of course it must be inferred tha all this luxury belongs to the best of times only, and is not available in the exigency of sudden military movements. The sepoys or common soldiers, too, have their satellites. Each man is accompanied by his whole family, who live upon his pay and allowances of rice from the Company. Every trooper or horse-soldier, too, has his grass-cutter; for it is a day's work for one person to dig, cut, and prepare a day's grass for one horse.

When on the march, the tents are generally struck soon after midnight. At the first tap of the drum, the servants knock up the tent-pins, and down fall the tents; horses begin to neigh and the camels to cry, the elephants and camels receive their loads of camp-equipage, the bullocks are laden with the officers' tents and boxes, the coolies take up their burdens, and all prepare for the road. During the noise and bustle of these preliminaries, the officers and men make their few personal arrangements, aided by their servants or families; while the officers' cooks and agents are sent on in advance, to prepare breakfast at the next halting-place. Between one and two o'clock the regiments start off, in columns of sections: the camp-followers, baggage, bullocks, elephants, and camels, bringing up the rear. The European soldiers do not carry their own knapsacks on the march; they have the luxury of cook-boys or attendants, who render this service for them. The natives, it is found, are able to carry heavier loads than the Europeans; or—what is perhaps more nearly the case—they bear the burdens more patiently, as the Europeans love soldiering better than portering. The tedium of the journey is sometimes relieved by a hunt after antelopes, hares, partridges, wild ducks, or wild boars, which the officers may happen to espy, according to the nature of the country through which they are passing. Arrived at the halting-place, everything is quickly prepared for a rest and a breakfast; the quarter-masters push forward to occupy the ground; the elephants and camels are disburdened of the tents; the natives and the cattle plunge into some neighbouring pool or tank to refresh themselves; the cooks have been already some time at work; and the officers sit down to a breakfast of tea, coffee, curry, rice, pillau, ham, and other obtainable dishes. The fakeers often recognise their friends or admirers among the natives of the cavalcade, and give loud blessings, and tom-tom drummings, in exchange for donations of the smallest Indian coins. The quartermasters' arrangements are so quickly and so neatly made, that in a short time the general's *durbar* appears in the centre of a street of tents for staff-officers, dining-tents on the one side and sleeping-tents on the other; while the bazaar-dealers open their temporary shops in the rear. The horses are picketed in long lines; while the elephants and camels browse or rest at leisure. Under ordinary circumstances, the day's marching is over by nine o'clock in the morning, at which hour the sun's heat becomes too fierce to be willingly borne. Repose, amusements, and light camp-duties fill up the remainder of the day, to be followed by a like routine on the morrow.

While one of these extraordinary marches is in progress, 'when the moving masses are touched here and there by the reddening light of the dawn, it seems to be a true migration, with flocks and herds, cattle loaded with baggage, men, women, and children, all in a chaos of disorder but the troops whose wants and wishes have attracted this assemblage. At length the country appears to awake from its sleep, and with the yell of the jackal, or the distant baying of the village dogs, are heard to mingle the voices of human beings. Ruddier grows the dawn, warmer the breeze, and the light-hearted sepoy, no longer shivering with cold, gives vent to the joyous feelings of morning in songs and laughter. The scenes become more striking, and the long array of tall camels, led by natives in picturesque costume, with here and there a taller elephant mingling with droves of loaded bullocks, give it a new and extraordinary character to a European imagination. The line of swarthy sepoys of Upper India, with their moustached lips and tall handsome figures, contrasts favourably with the shorter and plainer soldiers of Britain; the grave mechanical movements of the regular cavalry in their light-blue uniforms are relieved by the erratic evolutions and gay and glittering dresses of the irregulars, who with loud cries and quivering spears, and their long black locks streaming behind them, spur backwards and forwards like the wind from mere exuberance of spirits. . . . . . The camp-followers in the meantime present every possible variety of costume; and among them, and not the least interesting figures in the various groups, may frequently be seen the pet lambs of which the sepoys are so fond,

Troops on the March.

dressed in necklaces of ribbons and white shells, and the tip of their tails, ears, and feet dyed orange colour. The womenkind of the troops of the Peninsula (Southern India) usually follow the drum; but the Bengalees have left their families at home; and the Europeans bidden adieu to their temporary wives with the air the band strikes up on quitting the station, "The girl I left behind me."' *

* Leitch Ritchie. *British World in the East.*

Such, before the great Revolt, were the usual characteristics of an Anglo-Indian army when on the march; and, considering the *impedimenta*, it is not surprising that the daily progress seldom exceeded ten or twelve miles. The system was very costly, even at the cheap rate of Indian service; for the camp-followers, one with another, were ten times as numerous as the troops; and all, in one way or other, lived upon or by the Company.

Note.

A parliamentary paper, issued in 1857 on the motion of Colonel Sykes, affords valuable information on some of the matters treated in this chapter. It is 'A Return of the Area and Population of each Division of each Presidency of India, from the Latest Inquiries; comprising, also, the Area and Estimated Population of Native States.' It separates the British states from the native; and it further separates the former into five groups, according to the government under which each is placed. These five, as indicated in the present chapter, are under the administration of 'the governor-general of India in council'—the 'lieutenant-governor of Bengal'—the 'lieutenant-governor of the Northwest Provinces'—the 'government of Madras'—and the 'government of Bombay.' In each case the 'regulation districts' are treated distinct from the 'non-regulation provinces,' the former having been longer under British power, and brought into a more regular system than the latter. Without going again over the long list of names of places, it will suffice to quote those belonging to the group placed immediately under the governor-general's control. This group comprises the Punjaub, in the six divisions of Lahore, Jelum, Moultan, Leia, Peshawur, and Jullundur; the Cis-Sutlej states, four in number; the lately annexed kingdom of Oude; the central district of Nagpoor or Berar; the recently acquired region of Pegu; the strip of country on the east of the Bay of Bengal, known as the Tenasserim Provinces; and the 'Eastern Straits Settlements' of Singapore, Penang, and Malacca. The whole of British India is divided into nearly a hundred and eighty districts, each, on an average, about the size of Inverness-shire, the largest county, except Yorkshire, in the United Kingdom. The population, however, is eight times as dense, per average square mile, as in this Scottish shire. Keeping clear of details concerning divisions and districts, the following are the areas and population in the five great governments:

		Area. Square Miles.	Population.
Governor-general's Provinces.	. . .	246,050	23,255,972
Lower Bengal Provinces.	Regulation, .	125,133	37,962,163
	Non-regulation,	95,836	3,506,224
Northwest Provinces.	Regulation, .	72,052	30,271,885
	Non-regulation,	33,767	3,783,302
Madras Presidency.	Regulation, .	119,596	20,139,495
	Non-regulation,	13,284	2,316,802
Bombay Presidency.	Regulation, .	57,723	9,015,534
	Non-regulation,	73,821	9,774,509
	Total,	857,412	131,990,901

In some of the five governments, the population is classified more minutely than in others. Thus, in the Punjaub member of the governor-general's group, Hindoos are separated from non-Hindoos; then, each of these classes is divided into agricultural and non-agricultural; and, lastly, each of these is further separated into male and female. The most instructive feature here is the scarcity of females compared with males, contrary to the experience of Europe; in the Punjaub and Sirhind, among thirteen million souls, there are a million and a half more males than females—shewing, among other things, one of the effects of female infanticide in past years. The ratio appears to be about the same in the Northwest Provinces, around Delhi, Meerut, Rohilcund, Agra, Benares, and Allahabad. Not one place is named, throughout India, in which the females equal the males in number. In the Bombay presidency, besides the difference of sex, the population is tabulated into nine groups—Hindoos, Wild Tribes, Low Castes, Shrawniks or Jains, Lingayets, Mussulmans, Parsees, Jews, Christians. Of the last named there are less than fifty thousand, including military, in a population of twelve millions.

The area and population of the native states are given in connection with the presidencies to which those states are geographically and politically related, and present the following numbers:

	Area. Square Miles.	Population.
In Bengal Presidency, . .	515,533	38,702,206
In Madras Presidency, . .	51,802	5,213,671
In Bombay Presidency, . .	60,575	4,460,370
	627,910	48,376,247

The enumeration of these native states is minute and intricate; and it may suffice to shew the complexity arising out of the existence of so many baby-princedoms, that one of the native states of Bundelcund, Kampta by name, figures in the table as occupying an area of *one* square mile, and as having *three hundred* inhabitants!

Including the British states, the native states, the few settlements held by the French and Portuguese, and the recent acquisitions on the eastern side of the Bay of Bengal, the grand totals come out in the following numbers:

1,466,576 Square miles,
180,884,297 Inhabitants,

or 124 dwellers per square mile. Of these inhabitants, it is believed—though the returns are not complete in this particular—that there are fifteen Hindoos to one Mohammedan; if so, then India must contain more than a *hundred and sixty million* worshippers of Hindoo deities—even after allowance is made for Buddhists, Parsees, and a few savage tribes almost without religion.

CHAPTER II.

SYMPTOMS:—CHUPATTIES AND CARTRIDGES.

LITTLE did the British authorities in India suspect, in the early weeks of 1857, that a mighty CENTENARY was about to be observed—a movement intended to mark the completion of one hundred years of British rule in the East; and to mark it, not by festivities and congratulations, but by rebellion and slaughter.

The officers in India remembered and noted the date well; but they did not know how well the Mohammedans and Hindoos, the former especially, had stored it up in their traditions. The name of Robert Clive, the 'Daring in War,' was so intimately associated with the date 1757, that the year 1857 naturally brought it into thought, as a time when Christian rule began to overawe Moslem rule in that vast country. True, the East India Company had been connected with India during a period exceeding two hundred years; but it was only at the commencement of the second half of the last century that this connection became politically important. It was remembered that —1756 having been marked by the atrocities of the Black Hole at Calcutta, and by the utter extinction for a time of the East India Company's power in Bengal—the year 1757 became a year of retribution. It was remembered, as a matter of history among the British, and of tradition among the natives, how wonderful a part the young officer Clive performed in that exciting drama. It was remembered that he arrived at Calcutta, at that time wholly denuded of Englishmen, on the 2d of January in the last-named year, bringing with him a small body of troops from Madras; that on the 4th of February, with two thousand men, he defeated an army ten times as large, belonging to Suraj-u-Dowlah, Nawab of Bengal—the same who had caused the atrocities at the Black Hole, when a hundred and thirty persons died from suffocation in a room only fitted to contain a fourth of the number. It was further remembered how that, on the 9th of February, Clive obtained great concessions from the nawab by treaty; that Suraj broke the treaty, and commenced a course of treachery, in which Clive was not slow to imitate him; that on the 13th of June, Clive, having matured a plan equally bold and crafty, declared renewed hostilities against the nawab; that on the 23d he gained the brilliant battle of PLASSEY, conquering sixty thousand men with a force of only three thousand; that within a week, Suraj-u-Dowlah, a miserable fugitive, ended his existence; and that from that day British power had ever been supreme in Bengal. This was a series of achievements not likely to be forgotten by Englishmen. Ere yet the news of mutiny and murder reached Europe, steps had been taken to render homage to Clive on the hundredth anniversary of the battle of Plassey; the East India Company had subscribed largely towards a statue of the hero; and a meeting in London had decided that the chief town in Clive's native county of Shropshire should be selected as the spot wherein the statue should be set up.

Judging from the experience afforded by recent events, it is now clear that the Mohammedans in India had thought much of these things, and that the year 1857 had been marked out by them as a centenary to be observed in a special way—by no less an achievement, indeed, than the expulsion of the British, and the revival of Moslem power. In the spring of the year it was ascertained that a paper was in circulation among the natives, purporting to be a prophecy made by a Punjaub fakeer seven hundred years ago—to the effect that, after various dynasties of Mohammedans had ruled for some centuries, the *Nazarenes* or Christians should hold power in India for one hundred years; that the Christians would then be expelled; and that various events foretold in the Koran would then come to pass, connected with the triumph of Islamism. That this mysterious prediction was widely credited, is probable — notwithstanding that the paper itself, if really circulated, must manifestly have been an imposture of recent date; for the English nation was not known even by name to the natives of India seven hundred years ago. Setting aside, at present, all inquiries concerning the first authors of the plot, the degree to which the Company's annexations had provoked it, the existence of any grievances justifiably to be resisted, the reasons which induced Hindoos to join the Mohammedans against the British, or the extent to which the general population shared the views of the native military

—laying aside these inquiries for the present, there is evidence that a great movement was planned for the middle of the year 1857. Of this plan the British government knew nothing, and suspected little.

But although no vast plot was suspected, several trifling symptoms had given cause for uneasiness; and the English public learned, when too late, that many Indian officers had long predicted the imminency of some outbreak. Insubordination and mutiny, it was found, are not faults of recent growth among the native troops of India. Now that the startling events of 1857 are vividly presented to the public mind, men begin to read again the old story of the outbreak at Vellore, and seek to draw instruction therefrom. A little more than half a century ago—namely, on the 10th of July 1806—the European barracks at Vellore were thrown into a state of great excitement. This town is in the Carnatic, a few miles west of Madras, and in the presidency of the same name. At two o'clock in the morning, the barracks, containing four companies of the 69th regiment, were surrounded by two battalions of sepoys in the Company's service, who poured in a heavy fire of musketry, at every door and window, upon the soldiers. At the same time the European sentries, the soldiers at the main-guard, and the sick in the hospital, were put to death. The officers' houses were ransacked, and everybody found in them murdered. Upon the arrival of the 19th Light Dragoons, under Colonel Gillespie, the sepoys were immediately attacked; six hundred were cut down upon the spot, and two hundred taken from their hiding-places to be shot. There perished of the four European companies, a hundred and sixty-four, besides officers; and many British officers of the native troops were also murdered. Nothing ever came to light concerning the probable cause of the outrage, but this—that an attempt had been made by the military men at Madras to *change the shape of the sepoy turban* into something resembling the helmet of the light infantry of Europe, which would prevent the native troops from wearing on their foreheads the marks characteristic of their several castes. The sons of Tippoo Saib, the deposed ruler of Mysore, together with many distinguished Mohammedans deprived of office, were at that time in Vellore; and the supposition is, that these men contributed very materially to excite or inflame the suspicions of the Hindoos, concerning an endeavour to tamper with their religious usages. There was another mutiny some time afterwards at Nundeydroog, in the same presidency; and it was found indispensable to disarm four hundred and fifty Mohammedan sepoys, who had planned a massacre. At Bangalore and other places a similar spirit was exhibited. The governor of Madras deemed it necessary, in very earnest terms, to disclaim any intention of tampering with the native religion. In a proclamation issued on the 3d of December, he said: 'The right honourable the governor in council having observed that, in some late instances, an extraordinary degree of agitation has prevailed among several corps of the native army of this coast, it has been his lordship's particular endeavour to ascertain the motives which may have led to conduct so different from that which formerly distinguished the native army. From this inquiry, it has appeared that many persons of evil intention have endeavoured, for malicious purposes, to impress upon the native troops a belief that it is the wish of the British government to convert them by forcible means to Christianity; and his lordship in council has observed with concern that such malicious reports have been believed by many of the native troops. The right honourable the governor in council, therefore, deems it proper, in this public manner, to repeat to the native troops his assurance, that the same respect which has been invariably shewn by the British government for their religion and their customs, will be always continued; and that no interruption will be given to any native, whether Hindoo or Mussulman, in the practice of his religious ceremonies.' Notwithstanding the distinctness of this assurance, and notwithstanding the extensive promulgation of the proclamation in the Tamul, Telinga, and Hindustani languages—the ferment continued a considerable time. Even in March 1807, when some months had elapsed, so universal was the dread of a general revolt among the native troops, that the British officers attached to the Madras army constantly slept with loaded pistols under their pillows.

In the interval between 1806 and 1857, nothing so murderous occurred; but, among the Bengal troops, many proofs of insubordination were afforded; for it repeatedly occurred that grievances, real or pretended, led to combinations among the men of different regiments. In 1835, Lord William Bentinck, acting on a principle which had often been advocated in England, abolished flogging in the Indian army; this appears to have raised the self-pride rather than conciliated the good-will of the troops: insubordination ensued, and several regiments had to be disbanded. Again, in 1844, when several Bengal regiments were ordered to march to Sinde, the 34th native infantry refused; whereupon Lord Ellenborough, at that time governor-general, ignominiously disbanded the regiment in presence of the rest of the army. Again, in 1849, Sir Colin Campbell, serving under Sir Charles Napier, reported that the 22d Bengal regiment had mutinied on a question of pay, in which they were clearly in the wrong; but as the Punjaub was at that time in a critical state, Sir Charles did that which was very opposite to his general character—he yielded to an unjust demand, as a measure of prudence. It may have been that the sepoys counted on this probability when they mutinied. No less than forty-two regiments were ascertained to be in secret correspondence on this matter, under Brahminical influence—one of whom went so far as to threaten the commanding officer that they could stop enlistment if they chose. In 1850, Napier was compelled to disband the 66th regiment, for mutiny at Peshawur. In 1852, the 38th regiment was ordered to proceed to Burmah; the men objected to the sea-voyage, and refused to depart; and the authorities in this case gave way.

Like as, in the ordinary affairs of life, men compare notes after a disaster, to ascertain whether any misgiving had silently occupied their minds concerning causes and symptoms; so did many military officers, observing that the troubles were all or mostly in Bengal, or where Bengal troops operated, come forward to state that they had long been cognizant of a marked difference between the Bengal army on the one hand, and the Bombay and Madras armies on the other. Lord Melville, who, as General Dundas, had held a command during the Punjaub campaign, expressed himself very strongly in the House of Lords shortly after news of the mutiny arrived. He stated that, in the Bengal army, the native officers were in nearly all cases selected by seniority, and not from merit; that they could not rise from the ranks till old age was creeping on them; and that a sort of hopelessness of advancement cankered in the minds of many sepoys in the middle time of life. In the Bombay and Madras armies, on the contrary, the havildars or sergeants were selected for their intelligence and activity, and were recommended for promotion by the commanding officers of the regiments. It might possibly be a theory unsusceptible of proof, that this difference made the one army mutinous and the other two loyal; but Lord Melville proceeded to assert that the Bengal troops were notoriously less fully organised and disciplined, more prone to insubordination, than the troops of the other two presidencies. He stated as an instance, that when he commanded the Bombay army in the Punjaub frontier in 1849, the Bengal regiments were mutinous; while the Bombay troops remained in soldierly subordination. Indeed these latter, which he commanded in person, were credited by his lordship with having exhibited the highest qualities of brave and faithful troops. He detailed an incident which had occurred at the siege of Moultan. A covering-party having been ordered into the trenches, some disturbance soon afterwards arose; and an English officer found that many soldiers of the Bengal army had been endeavouring to prevent the men belonging to one of the Bombay regiments from digging in the trenches in discharge of their duty, on the ground that the sepoys' duty *was to fight and not to work.* Again: after the assault of Moultan, an officer in command of one of the pickets was requested to post a sergeant and twelve men at one of the gates of the town; this was done; but not long afterwards, three native officers of the Bengal engineers were detected in an endeavour to pass the gate with stores which they were about to plunder or appropriate. Although the views of Lord Melville were combated by a few other officers, there was a pretty general concurrence of opinion that the Bengal native army, through some circumstances known or unknown, had long been less obedient and orderly than those of the other two presidencies.

As it is the purpose of the present chapter to treat rather of the facts that preceded the horrors of Meerut and Cawnpore, than of the numerous theories for explaining them, we shall not dwell long in this place on the affairs of Oude, in connection with the Revolt; but so general is the opinion that the annexation of that kingdom was one of the predisposing causes of the late calamities, that it may be right to glance slightly at the subject.

Oude—once a nawabship under the great Mogul, then a kingdom, and the last remaining independent Mohammedan state in Northern India—was annexed in the early part of 1856; and although the governor-general sought to give a favourable account, both in its reasons and its results, of that momentous measure, there are not wanting grounds for believing that it made a deep impression on the minds of the natives, unfavourable to the English—among the military, if not among the people at large. The deposed king, with his family and his prime-minister, came to live at Calcutta in April 1856; and in the following month his mother, his brother, and one of his sons, proceeded in great state to England, to protest before Queen Victoria against the conduct of the governor-general and of the East India Company, in having deprived them of their regal position: prepared to prove, as they everywhere announced, that no justifiable grounds had existed for so harsh a step. Whether they sincerely believed this, or whether it was a blind to hide ulterior objects, could not at that time be determined. It is one among many opinions on the subject, that the courtiers around the deposed king gradually organised a plot against the British power; that the Queen of Oude's visit to England was merely intended to mask the proceedings arising out of this plot; that the conspirators brought over to their views the Mogul of Delhi, the shadowy representative of a once mighty despot; that they then sought to win over the Hindoos to side with them; and that, in this proceeding, they adduced any and all facts that had come to their knowledge, in which the British had unwittingly insulted the religious prejudices of the worshippers of Brahma—craftily insinuating that the insult was premeditated. The wisdom or justice of the annexation policy we do not discuss in this place; there is a multiplicity of interpretations concerning it—from that of absolute necessity to that of glaring spoliation; but the point to be borne in mind is, that a new grievance was thereby added to others, real or pretended, already existing. It is especially worthy of note, that any distrust of England, arising out of annexation policy, was likely to be more intense in Oude than anywhere else; for three-fourths of the infantry in the Bengal army had been recruited from the inhabitants of that state; they were energetic men, strongly attached to their native country; and when the change of masters took place, they lost certain of the privileges they had before enjoyed. The Bengalees proper, the natives of the thickly populated region around the lower course of the Ganges, have little to do with the Bengal army; they are feeble, indolent, and cowardly, glad by any excuses to escape from fighting.

Let us now—having said a few words concerning the centenary of British rule, and the state of feeling in Oude—attend to the strange episode of the *chupatties*, as a premonitory symptom of something wrong in the state of public feeling in India.

The chupatties—small cakes of unleavened bread, about two inches in diameter, made of Indian corn-meal, and forming part of the sepoys' regular diet—were regarded in England, as soon as the circumstances of the Revolt became known, as signs or symptoms which the various officers of the Company in India ought sedulously to have searched into. Ever since the middle of 1856—ever since, indeed, the final arrangements for the annexation of Oude—these chupatties were known to have been passing from hand to hand. A messenger would come to a village, seek out the headman or village elder, give him six chupatties, and say: 'These six cakes are sent to you; you will make six others, and send them on to the next village.' The headman accepted the six cakes, and punctually sent forward other six as he had been directed. It was a mystery of which the early stages were beyond our ken; for no one could say, or no one would say, which was the *first* village whence the cakes were sent. During many months this process continued: village after village being brought into the chain as successive links, and relays of chupatties being forwarded from place to place. Mr Disraeli, attacking on one occasion in the House of Commons the policy of the Indian government, adverted sarcastically to this chupatty mystery: 'Suppose the Emperor of Russia, whose territory, in extent and character, has more resemblance to our Eastern possessions than the territory of any other power—suppose the Emperor of Russia were told—"Sire, there is a very remarkable circumstance going on in your territory; from village to village, men are passing who leave the tail of an ermine or a pot of caviare, with a message to some one to perform the same ceremony. Strange to say, this has been going on in some ten thousand villages, and we cannot make head or tail of it." I think the Emperor of Russia would say: "I do not know whether you can make head or tail of it, but I am quite certain there is something wrong, and that we must take some precautions; because, where the people are not usually indiscreet and troublesome, they do not make a secret communication unless it is opposed to the government. This is a secret communication, and therefore a communication dangerous to the government."' The opposition leader did not assert that the government could have penetrated the mystery but that the mystery ought to have been regarded as significant of something dangerous, worthy of close scrutiny and grave consideration.

The chupatties first appeared in the Northwest Provinces, around Delhi; and subsequent events offered a temptation for rebuking the governor-general and the commander-in-chief, in having failed to strengthen the posts with English troops after the indications of some secret conspiracy had thus been made. In some places it was ascertained that the cakes were to be kept *till called for* by the messengers, other cakes being sent on instead of them; but what was the meaning of this arrangement, the English officials could not, or at least did not find out. In Scotland, in the clannish days, war-signals were sent from hut to hut and from clan to clan with extraordinary rapidity; and, however little an unleavened cake might appear like a war-signal, military men and politicians ought certainly to have been alive to such strange manifestations as this chupatty movement. From the Sutlej to Patna, throughout a vast range of thickly populated country, was the secret correspondence carried on. One thing at any rate may safely be asserted, that the military stations required close watching at such a time; something was fermenting in the minds of the natives which the English could not understand; but that very fact would have justified—nay, rendered almost imperative—the guarding of the chief posts from sudden surprise. Little or nothing of this precautionary action seems to have been attempted. Throughout nearly the whole of the great trunk-road from Calcutta to the Punjaub, the military stations were left as before, almost wholly in the hands of the sepoys. At Benares there was only a single company of European foot-artillery; the rest of the troops consisting of two regiments of native infantry, and one of the Cis-Sutlej Sikh regiments. At Allahabad, the great supply magazine of the province was left almost wholly to the guard of the sepoys. Lucknow had only one European regiment and one company of artillery; notwithstanding that, as the capital of Oude, it was in the midst of a warlike and excited population; while the native army of the province, capable of soon assembling at the city, comprised no less than fourteen regiments of infantry, six of cavalry, and six companies of artillery. Cawnpore, a very important station with a large medical depôt, contained three regiments of native infantry, one of native cavalry, and two companies of native artillery with twelve guns; while the English force was only a company of infantry, and about sixty artillerymen with six guns. The large magazine of Delhi, the great storehouse of ammunition for the military stations all around it, was left to be guarded entirely by sepoys. The late General Anson, at that time commander-in-chief, was among the hills at Simla, relaxing from his duties; and neither at Simla nor at Calcutta did it seem to be felt that, with existing symptoms, more European troops were necessary in the Bengal and Northwest Provinces.

The chupatty was not the only symbol of some mystery: the *lotus* was another. It was a common occurrence for a man to come to a cantonment with a lotus-flower, and give it to the chief native officer of a regiment; the flower was circulated from hand to hand in the regiment; each man took it, looked at it, and passed it on, saying nothing. When the lotus came to the last man in the regiment, he disappeared for a time, and took it to the next military station. This strange process occurred throughout nearly all the military stations where regiments of the Bengal native army were cantoned.

Chupatties and lotus-flowers, together with the incendiarism and the cartridge grievances presently to be noticed, unquestionably indicated some widely spread discontent among the natives—military if not general. 'It is clear,' in the words of an observant officer, writing from one of the Cis-Sutlej stations, 'that a certain ferment had been allowed gradually to arise throughout the mass of the Bengal army. In some it was panic, in some excitement, in some a mere general apprehension or expectation, and in some it was no doubt disaffection, or even conspiracy. Governing an alien people and a vast army, we had divested ourselves of all the instruments of foreign domination so familiar to Austria and all other continental powers. We had no political police, no European strongholds, no system of intelligence or espionage, comparatively little real military discipline; and even our own post-office was the channel of free, constant, and unchecked intercourse between all the different regiments. Not a letter even was opened; that would have been too abhorrent to English principles. The sepoy mind had probably become prepared to distrust us, as we had begun to distrust them. There were strange new legislative acts, and new post-office rules, and new foreign service enlistments, and new employment of armed races in our army, and other things disagreeable and alarming to the true old sepoy caste. And then it came about that from a small and trifling beginning, one of those ferments to which the native mind is somewhat prone, took possession of the sepoy army.'

One of the strange facts connected with the chupatty movement was, that the cakes were transmitted to the heads of villages who have *not* been concerned in the mutiny, while many sepoys who broke out in revolt had received no cakes. They appear to have been distributed mostly to the villagers; whereas the lotus passed from hand to hand among the military.

The chupatties and the lotus-flowers, however indicative they may have been of the existence of intrigue and conspiracy, were quiet indications; but there were not wanting other proofs of a mutinous spirit, in acts of violence and insubordination—apart from the incendiarisms and the cartridge difficulties. On one evening, early in the year, information was given by a sepoy of the intention of the men to rise against their officers and seize on Fort William, at Calcutta. On another occasion, a fanatic moulvie, a high Mohammedan priest at Oude, was detected preaching war against the infidels; and on his person was found a proclamation exciting the people to rebellion. On a third day, two sepoys were detected in an attempt to sap the fidelity of the guard at the Calcutta mint. An English surgeon in an hospital at Lucknow, by the bedside of a sepoy, put his lips to a bottle of medicine before giving it to his patient; this being regarded as a pollution, a pundit was sent for to break the bottle and exorcise the evil: on that night the doctor's bungalow was burned down by incendiaries who could not be discovered. A refusal to accept a furlough or leave of absence might not usually be regarded as a symptom of a mutinous spirit; yet in India it conveyed a meaning that could not safely be disregarded. On the 6th of March, the commander-in-chief, with the sanction of the governor-general, notified that the native army would receive, as usual, the annual indulgence of furlough from the 1st of April to a certain subsequent date. When this order was read or issued, about fourteen men of the 63d native infantry, stationed at Soorie, and under orders to proceed to Berhampore, evinced a disinclination to avail themselves of the indulgence, on the plea that none of the regiments at Barrackpore intended to take theirs. It certainly appears to have been a circumstance worthy of a searching inquiry by the military authorities, *why* the troops should have declined to take their furlough at that particular time.

We must now pass on to that series of events which, so far as outward manifestations are concerned, was more especially the immediate forerunner of the Revolt—namely, the disturbances connected with the *greased cartridges*. Let not the reader for a moment regard this as a trivial matter, merely because it would be trivial in England: the sepoys may have been duped, and indeed were unquestionably duped, by designing men; but the subject of suspicion was a serious one to them. The fat of cows and of pigs is regarded in a peculiar light in the East. The pig is as much held in abhorrence by the Mohammedans as the cow is venerated by the Hindoos; to touch the former with the lips, is a defilement to the one religion; to touch the latter, is a sacrilege to the other. The religious feelings are different, but the results in this case are the same. So sacred, indeed, are cattle regarded by the Hindoos, that the Company's officers have been accustomed to observe much caution in relation to any supply of beef for their own tables; the slaughter of a cow in a Hindoo village would in itself have been a sufficient cause for revolt; in large towns where Europeans are stationed, a high-walled paddock or compound is set apart for the reception of bullocks intended for food; and scrupulous care is taken that the natives shall know as little as possible of the proceedings connected with the slaughtering. The use of cow's fat in ammunition would therefore be repulsive to the Hindoo sepoy. Many experienced men trace the mutiny to a false report concerning the cartridges, acting on the minds of natives who had already become distrustful by the machinations of agitators and emissaries. 'It is a marvel and a mystery that so many years should have passed away without an explosion. At last a firebrand was applied to what a single spark might have ignited; and in the course of a few weeks there was a general conflagration; but a conflagration which still bears more marks of accident than of deliberate conspiracy and incendiarism. In a most unhappy hour—in an hour laden with a concurrence of adverse circumstances—the incident of the greased cartridges occurred. It found the Bengal army in a season of profound peace, and in a state of relaxed discipline. It found the sepoys pondering over the predictions and the fables which had been so assiduously circulated in their lines and their bazaars; it found them with imaginations inflamed and fears excited by strange stories of the designs of their English masters; it found them, as they fancied, with their purity of caste threatened, and their religious distinctions invaded, by the proselytising and annexing Englishmen. Still, there was no palpable evidence of this. Everything was vague, intangible, obscure. Credulous and simple-minded as they were, many might have retained a lingering confidence in the good faith and the good intentions of the British government, had it not been suddenly announced to them, just as they were halting between two opinions, that, in prosecution of his long-cherished design to break down the religion both of Mohammedan and Hindoo, the Feringhee had determined to render their military service the means of their degradation, by compelling them to apply their lips to a cartridge saturated with animal grease—the fat of the swine being used for the pollution of the one, and the fat of the cow for the degradation of the other. If the most astute emissaries of evil who could be employed for the corruption of the Bengal sepoy had addressed themselves to the task of inventing a lie for the confirmation and support of all his fears and superstitions, they could have found nothing more cunningly devised for their purpose.'*

It was on the 7th of February 1857 that the governor-general communicated to the home government the first account of anything mysterious or unpleasant in relation to the greased cartridges. He had to announce that a dissatisfaction had exhibited itself among the native troops attached to the musketry-depôt at Dumdum. There are two Dumdums, two Dumdumas, one Dumdumma, and one Dumdumineah in India; but the place indicated is in Bengal, a few miles out of Calcutta, and about half-way between that city and Barrackpore. It was formerly the head-quarters of artillery for the presidency of Bengal; and near it is an excellent cannon-foundry, with casting-rooms, boring-rooms, and all the appliances for making brass guns. It is a sort of Woolwich on a humble scale, connected with ordnance and firearms.

The sepoys at Dumdum had heard rumours which induced them to believe that the grease used for preparing the cartridges for the recently introduced Enfield rifles was composed of the fat of pigs and cows—substances which their religion teaches them to regard in a light altogether strange to Europeans. It was not the first time by three or four years that the cartridge-question had excited attention in India, although in England the public knew absolutely nothing concerning it. From documents brought to light during the earlier months of the mutiny, it appears that in 1853 the commander-in-chief of the forces in India directed the adjutant-general of the Bengal army to call the attention of the governor-general to the subject of cartridges as connected with the prejudices of the natives. For what reason grease of any kind is employed on or with cartridges, may be soon explained. A cartridge, as most persons are aware, is a contrivance for quickly loading firearms. Instead of inserting the powder and bullet separately into the musket, rifle, or pistol, as was the earlier wont, the soldier is provided with a supply of small cartridge-paper tubes, each containing a bullet and the proper proportion of powder; and by the employment of these cartridges much time and attention are saved under circumstances where both are especially valuable. The missiles are called *ball* or *blank* cartridges, according as they do or do not each contain a bullet. Now the Enfield rifle, an English improvement on the celebrated Minié rifle invented and used by the French, was largely manufactured by machinery in a government establishment at Enfield, for use in the British and Indian armies; and in firing from this or other rifles it was necessary that the ball-end of the cartridge should have an external application of some greasy substance, to facilitate its movement through the barrel. In the year above named, the East India Company informed the Calcutta government, that a supply of new-greased cartridges had been sent, which the Board of Ordnance wished should be subjected to the test of climate. It was concerning these cartridges that the commander-in-chief recommended caution; on the ground that 'unless it be known that the grease employed in these cartridges is not of a nature to offend or interfere with the prejudices of caste, it will be expedient not to issue them for test to native corps, but to Europeans only, to be carried in pouch.' It was not until June

* *Edinburgh Review*, No. 216.

1854 that the cartridges were received in India; and during the next twelve months they were subjected to various tests, at Calcutta, at Cawnpore, and at Rangoon. The cartridges had been greased in four ways—with common grease, with laboratory grease, with Belgian grease, and with Hoffman's grease, in each case with an admixture of creosote and tobacco; one set was tested by being placed in the ordnance magazines, a second by being kept in wagons, and a third by being tied up in pouch-bundles. The result of these tests was communicated to the directors in the autumn of 1855; and as a consequence, a modification was effected in the cartridges afterwards sent from England for service with the Enfield rifles in India.

To return now to the affair at Dumdum. When the complaints and suspicions of the sepoys were made known, inquiries were sent to England for exact particulars relating to the obnoxious missiles. It was ascertained that the new cartridges were made at the Royal Laboratory at Woolwich; and that Captain Boxer, the superintendent of that department, was accustomed to use for lubrication a composition formed of five parts tallow, five parts stearine, and one part wax—containing, therefore, ox or cow's fat, but none from pigs. He had no prejudices in the matter to contend against in England, and used therefore just such a composition as appeared to him most suitable for the purpose. The cartridges were not sent out to India ready greased for use; as, in a hot country, the grease would soon be absorbed by the paper: there was, therefore, a part of the process left to be accomplished when the cartridges reached their destination.

It appears to have been in the latter part of January that the first open manifestation was made at Dumdum of a disinclination to use the cartridges; and immediately a correspondence among the authorities commenced concerning it. When the complaint had been made, the men were seemingly appeased on being assured that the matter would be duly represented; and as a means of conciliation, cartridges without grease were issued, the men being allowed to apply any lubricating substance they chose. It was further determined that no more ready-made cartridges should be obtained from England, but that bullets and paper should be sent separately, to be put together in India; that experiments should be made at Woolwich, to produce some lubricating substance free from any of the obnoxious ingredients; and that other experiments should meanwhile be made by the 60th Rifles—at that time stationed at Meerut—having the same object in view.

During the inquiry into the manifestation and alleged motives of this insubordination, one fact was elicited, which, if correct, seems to point to a date when the conspirators—whoever they may have been—began to act upon the dupes. On the 22d of January, a low-caste Hindoo asked a sepoy of the 2d Bengal Grenadiers to give him a little water from his lota or bottle; the other, being a Brahmin, refused, on the ground that the applicant would defile the vessel by his touch—a magnificence of class-superiority to which only the Hindoo theory could afford place. This refusal was met by a retort, that the Brahmin need not pride himself on his caste, for he would soon lose it, as he would ere long be required to bite off the ends of cartridges covered with the fat of pigs and cows. The Brahmin, alarmed, spread the report; and the native troops, as is alleged, were afraid that when they went home their friends would refuse to eat with them. When this became known to the English officers, the native troops were drawn up on parade, and encouraged to state the grounds of their dissatisfaction. All the native sergeants and corporals, and two-thirds of all the privates, at once stepped forward, expressed their abhorrence of having to touch anything containing the fat of cows or pigs, and suggested the employment of wax or oil for lubricating the cartridges. It was then that the conciliatory measures, noticed above, were adopted.

Still were there troubles and suspicious circumstances; but the scene is now transferred from Dumdum to Barrackpore. This town, sixteen miles from Calcutta, is worthy of note chiefly for its connection with the supreme government of India. The governor-general has a sort of suburban residence there, handsome, commodious, and situated in the midst of a very beautiful park. There are numerous bungalows or villas inhabited by European families, drawn to the spot by the salubrity of the air, by the beauty of the Hoogly branch of the Ganges, at this place three-quarters of a mile in width, and by the garden and promenade attached to the governor-general's villa. In military matters, before the Revolt, there was a 'presidency division of the army,' of which some of the troops were in Calcutta, some at Barrackpore, and a small force of artillery at Dumdum, nearly midway between the two places; the whole commanded by a general officer at Barrackpore, under whom was a brigadier to command that station only. The station is convenient for military operations in the eastern part of Bengal, and for any sudden emergencies at Calcutta. Six regiments of native infantry were usually cantoned at Barrackpore, with a full complement of officers: the men hutted in commodious lines, and the officers accommodated in bungalows or lodges.

It was at this place that the discontent next showed itself, much to the vexation of the government, who had hoped that the Dumdum affair had been satisfactorily settled, and who had explained to the native regiments at Barrackpore what had been done to remove the alleged cause of complaint. The sepoys at this place, however, made an objection to bite off the ends of the cartridges—a necessary preliminary to the loading of a rifle—on account of the animal fat contained, or supposed to be contained, in the grease with which the paper was lubricated: such fat not being permitted to touch the lips or tongues of the men, under peril of defilement. Some of the authorities strongly suspected that this renewed discontent was the work of secret agitators rather than a spontaneous expression of the men's real feeling. There was at the time a religious Hindoo society or party at Calcutta, called the Dhurma Sobha, suspected of having spread rumours that the British government intended to compel the Hindoos to become Christians. Contemporaneously, too, with this movement, three incendiary fires took place at Barrackpore within four days; and a native sergeant's bungalow was burnt down at Raneegunge, another military station in Lower Bengal. It was natural, therefore, that General Hearsey, the responsible officer at Barrackpore, should wish to ascertain what connection, if any, existed between these incendiarisms, intrigues, complainings, and greased cartridges. This was the more imperative, on account of the relative paucity of English troops in that part of India. There were four native regiments quartered at that time at Barrackpore—namely, the 2d Grenadiers, the 34th and 70th Native Infantry, and the 43d Native Light Infantry; whereas, in the four hundred miles between Calcutta and Dinapoor there was only one European regiment, the Queen's 53d foot, of which one half was at Calcutta and the other half at Dumdum. The general held a special court of inquiry at Barrackpore on the 6th of February, and selected a portion of the 2d native Grenadier regiment to come forward and explain the cause of their continued objection to the paper of which the new rifle-cartridges were composed. One of the sepoys, Byjonath Pandy, stated that he felt a suspicion that the paper might affect his caste. On being asked his reason for this suspicion, he answered that the paper was a new kind which he had not seen before; and there was a 'bazaar report' that the paper contained animal fat. On being requested to examine the paper carefully in the light, and to explain to the court what he saw objectionable in it, he replied that his suspicion proceeded from the paper being stiff and cloth-like, and from its tearing differently from the paper formerly in use. Another sepoy, Chaud Khan, was then examined. He objected to the paper because it was tough, and burned as if it contained grease. He stated that much dismay had been occasioned in the regiment by the fact that 'on the 4th of February a piece of the cartridge-paper was dipped in water, and then burned; when burning, it made a fizzing noise, and smelt as if there were grease in it.' Thereupon a piece of the paper was burned in open court; Chaud Khan confessed that he could not smell or see grease in it; but he repeated his objection to the use of the paper, on the plea that 'everybody is dissatisfied with it on account of its being glazed, shining like waxed cloth.' Another witness, Khadu Buksh, filling the rank of subadar or native captain, on being examined, frankly stated that he had no objection to the cartridge itself, but that there was a general report in the cantonment that the paper was made up with fat. A jemadar or lieutenant, named Golal Khan, said very positively: 'There is grease in it, I feel assured; as it differs from the paper which has heretofore been always used for cartridges.' As shewing the well-known power of what in England would be called 'public opinion,' the answer of one of the sepoys is worthy of notice; he candidly confessed that he himself had no objection to use the cartridges, but he could not do so, as his companions would object to it. While these occurrences were under scrutiny, a jemadar of the 34th regiment came forward to narrate what he knew on the matter, as affording proof of conspiracy. On the 5th, when the fear of detection had begun to work among them, two or three of the sepoys came to him, and asked him to accompany them to the parade-ground. He did so, and there found a great crowd assembled, composed of men of the different regiments at the station; they had their heads tied up in handkerchiefs or cloths, so that only a small part of the face was exposed. They told him they were determined to die for their religion; and that if they could concert a plan that evening, they would on the next night plunder the station and kill all the Europeans, and then depart whither they pleased. The number he stated to be about three hundred. It was not at the time known to the authorities, but was rendered probable by circumstances afterwards brought to light, that letters and emissaries were being despatched, at the beginning of February, from the native troops at Barrackpore to those at other stations, inviting them to rise in revolt against the British.

Under any other circumstances, a discussion concerning such petty matters as bits of cartridge-paper and items of grease would be simply ridiculous; but at that time and place the ruling authorities, although ignorant of the real extent of the danger, saw clearly that they could not afford to regard such matters as otherwise than serious. There was either a sincere prejudice to be conciliated, or a wide-spread conspiracy to be met; and it was at once determined to test again the sincerity of the sepoys, by yielding to their (apparently) religious feelings on a matter which did not affect the efficiency of the service. A trial was made, therefore, of a mode of loading the rifle without biting the cartridge, by tearing off the end with the left hand. The commander-in-chief, finding on inquiry that this method was sufficiently efficacious, and willing to get rid of mere formalism in the matter, consented that the plan should be adopted both for percussion-muskets and for rifles. This done, the governor-general, by virtue of his supreme command, ordered the adoption of the same system throughout India.

The scene now again changes: we have to attend to certain proceedings at Berhampore, following on those at Barrackpore. Of Berhampore as a town, little need be said here; and that little is called for principally to determine *which* Berhampore is meant. Under the forms Berhampore, Berhampoor, or Burhampore, there are no less than four towns in India—one in the native state of Nepaul, sixty miles from Khatmandoo; another in the Nagpoor territory, sixty miles from the city of the same name; another in the Madras presidency, near Orissa; and a fourth in the district of Moorshedabad, Lower Bengal. It is this last-named Berhampore to which attention is here directed. The town is on the left bank of the river Bhagruttee, a great offset of the Ganges, and on the high road from Calcutta to Moorshedabad—distant about a hundred and twenty miles from the first-named city by land, and a hundred and sixty by water. It is in a moist, unhealthy spot, very fatal to Europeans, and in consequence disliked by them as a station in past times; but sanitary measures, draining, and planting have greatly improved it within the last few years. As a town, it is cheerful and attractive in appearance, adorned by stately houses in the neighbourhood, to accommodate permanent British residents. The military cantonments are large and striking; the grand square, the excellent parade-ground, the quarters of the European officers—all are handsome. Before the Revolt, Berhampore was included within the presidency division in military matters, and was usually occupied by a body of infantry and another of artillery. There is painful evidence of the former insalubrity of the station met with in a large open space filled with tombstones, contrasting mournfully with the majestic cantonments of the military. Berhampore has, or had a few years ago, a manufactory of the silk bandana handkerchiefs once so popular in England.

The troubles in this town were first made manifest in the following way. On or about the 24th of February, a portion of the 34th regiment of Bengal infantry changed its station from Barrackpore to Berhampore, where it was greeted and feasted by the men of the 19th native infantry, stationed there at that time. During their feasting, the new-comers narrated all the news from Dumdum and Barrackpore concerning the greased cartridges; and the effects of this gossip were very soon made visible. To understand what occurred, the mode of piling or storing arms in India must be attended to; in the Bombay army, and in the Queen's regiments, the men were wont to keep their arms with them in their huts; but in the Bengal army, it was a custom to deposit them in circular brick buildings called bells, which were kept locked under native guard, each in front of a particular company's lines. The men of the 19th regiment, then, excited by the rumours and stories, the fears and suspicions of their companions in arms elsewhere, but not knowing or not believing—or perhaps not caring for—the promises of change made by the military authorities, broke out into insubordination. On the 26th of February, being ordered to parade for exercise with blank cartridges, they refused to receive the percussion-caps, as a means of rendering their firing impossible—alleging that the cartridge-paper supplied for the charge was of two kinds; that they doubted the qualities of one or both; and that they believed in the presence of the fat of cows or pigs in the grease employed. That the men were either dupes or intriguers is evident; for it so happened that the cartridges offered to them were the very same in kind as they had used during many years, and had been made up before a single Enfield rifle had reached India. This resistance was a serious affair; it was something more than a complaint or petition, and needed to be encountered with a strong hand. It is a matter of opinion, judged differently even by military men accustomed to India and its natives, whether the proper course was on that occasion taken. The commanding officer, Lieutenant-colonel Mitchell, ordered a detachment of native cavalry and a battery of native artillery—the only troops at Barrackpore besides those already named—to be on parade on the following morning. Between ten and eleven o'clock at night, however, the men of the 19th regiment broke open the armouries or bells, took possession of their muskets and ammunition, and carried them to their lines. The next day, the guns were got ready, and the officers proceeded to the parade-ground, where they found the men in undress, but armed, formed in line, and shouting. The officers were threatened if they came on. Mitchell then expostulated with them; he pointed out the absurdity of their suspicions, and the unworthiness of their present conduct, and commanded them to give up their arms and return peaceably to their lines; whereupon the native officers said the men would refuse so to do unless the cavalry and artillery were withdrawn. The lieutenant-colonel withdrew them, and then the infantry yielded. It was a difficult position for an officer to be placed in; if he had struggled, it would have been with natives against natives; and, doubtful of the result of such a contest, he assented to the men's conditional surrender.

The affair could not be allowed to end here. The Calcutta authorities, receiving news on the 4th of March of this serious disaffection, but deeming it unsafe to punish while so few European troops were at hand, sent quietly to Rangoon in Pegu, with orders that Her Majesty's 84th foot should steam up to Calcutta as quickly as possible. On the 20th, this regiment arrived; and then the governor-general, acting in harmony with Major-general Hearsey, resolved on the disbandment of the native regiment which had disregarded the orders of its superiors. Accordingly, on the 31st of March, the 19th regiment was marched from Berhampore to Barrackpore, the head-quarters of the military division; the men were disarmed, paid off, marched out of the cantonments as far as Palta Ghaut, and conveyed across the river in steamers placed for the purpose. In short, the regiment, in a military sense, was destroyed, without personal punishment to any of the men composing it. But though not punished, in the ordinary sense, the infliction was a great one; for the men at once became penniless, unoccupied, objectless. The governor-general, in describing these proceedings for the information of the home government, added: 'We trust that the severe measures which we have been forced to adopt will have the effect of convincing the native troops that they will only bring ruin c themselves by failing in their duty to the state an in obedience to their officers.'

On the occasion just adverted to, Gener Hearsey addressed the men very energetically while an official paper from the governor-general read to the troops, asserted in distinct terms tha the rumour was wholly groundless which impute to the government an intention to interfere with

Viscount Canning.

the religion of the people. It was a charge soon afterwards brought in England against the governor-general, that, having subscribed to certain missionary societies in India, he did not like to abjure all attempts at the conversion of the natives; and that, being thus balanced between his public duty and his private religious feeling, he had issued the general order to the whole army, but had not shewn any solicitude to convey that positive declaration to all the natives in all the cantonments or military stations. This, however, was said when Viscount Canning was not present to defend himself; reasonable men soon saw that the truth was not to be obtained by such charges, unless supported by good evidence. It is, however, certain, that much delay and routine formality occurred throughout all these proceedings. As early as the 11th of February, General Hearsey wrote from Barrackpore the expressive words: 'We are on a mine ready to explode'—in allusion to the uneasy state of feeling or opinion among the sepoys that their religious usages were about to be tampered with; and yet it was not until the 27th of March that the Supreme Council at Calcutta agreed to the issue of a general order declaring it to be the invariable rule of the government to treat the religious tendencies of all its servants with respect; nor until the 31st that this general order was read to the troops at Barrackpore. Considering the mournful effects of dilatoriness and rigid formalism during the Crimean war, the English public had indulged a hope that a healthy reform would be introduced into the epistolary mechanism of the government departments; and this was certainly to some extent realised in England; but unfortunately the reform had not yet reached India. During these early months of the mutiny, an absurd waste of time occurred in the writing and despatching of an enormous number of letters, where a personal interview, or a verbal message by a trusty servant, might have sufficed. Eight letters were written, and four days consumed, before the Calcutta authorities knew what was passing at Dumdum, eight miles distant. A certain order given by the colonel of a regiment at Calcutta being considered injudicious by the general, an inquiry was made as to the grounds for the order; eight days and nine letters were required for this inquiry and the response to it, and yet the two officers were within an hour's distance of each other during the whole time. Although the affair at Barrackpore on the 6th of February was assuredly of serious import, it was not known to the government at Calcutta until the evening of the 10th, notwithstanding that a horseman might easily have ridden the sixteen miles in two hours. General Hearsey's reply to a question as to the cause of the delay is truly instructive, as exemplifying the slowness of official progress in India: 'I have no means of communicating anything to the government; I have no mounted orderly, no express camels; I must always write by the post; and that leaves Barrackpore at the most inconvenient hour of three o'clock in the afternoon.' These facts, trivial in themselves, are worthy of being borne in mind, as indicative of defects in the mechanism of government likely to be disastrous in times of excitement and insubordination.

Barrackpore was destined to be a further source of vexation and embarrassment to the government. It will be remembered that a part of the 34th native infantry went from that town to Berhampore in the last week in February; but the bulk of the regiment remained at Barrackpore. Inquiries, afterwards instituted, brought to light the fact that the European commander of that regiment had been accustomed to distribute religious tracts among his men; and it was surmised that the scruples and prejudices of the natives, especially the Brahmins, had been unfavourably affected by this proceeding. But whether the cause had or had not been rightly guessed, it is certain that the 34th displayed more mutinous symptoms at that time than any other regiment. When the news of the disturbance at Berhampore reached them, they became greatly excited: they attended to their duties, but with sullen doggedness; and they held nightly meetings, at which speeches were made sympathetic with the Berhampore mutineers. The authorities, not wholly ignorant of these meetings, nevertheless remained quiet until a European regiment could arrive to aid them. When the Queen's 84th arrived at Calcutta, the 34th were more excited than ever, believing that something hostile was intended against them; their whispers became murmurs, and they openly expressed their sympathy. When, in accordance with the plan noticed in the last paragraph, the 19th were marched off from Berhampore to be disbanded at Barrackpore, the 34th displayed still greater audacity. The 19th having rested for a time at Barraset, eight miles from Barrackpore, a deputation from the 34th met them, and made a proposal that they should that very night kill all their officers, march to Barrackpore, join the 2d and 34th, fire the bungalows, surprise and overwhelm the Europeans, seize the guns, and then march to threaten Calcutta. Had the 19th been as wild and daring, as irritated and vengeful, as the 34th, there is no knowing what calamities might have followed; but they exhibited rather a repentant and regretful tone, and submitted obediently to all the details of their disbandment at Barrackpore.

It will therefore be seen that the seeds of further disaffection had been already sown. As the 34th native infantry had been instrumental in inciting the 19th to mutiny, ending in disbandment, so did it now bring a similar punishment on itself. On the 29th of March, one Mungal Pandy, a sepoy in the 34th, roused to a state of excitement by the use of intoxicating drugs, armed himself with a sword and a loaded musket, traversed the lines, called upon his comrades to rise, and declared he would shoot the first European he met. Lieutenant Baugh, adjutant of the corps, hearing of this man's conduct, and of the excited state of the regiment generally, rode hastily to the lines. Mungal Pandy fired, missed the officer, but struck his horse. The lieutenant, in self-defence, fired his pistol, but missed aim; whereupon the sepoy attacked him with his sword, wounded him in the hand, brought him to the ground, and tried to entice the other soldiers to join in the attack. The sergeant-major of the corps, who went to the lieutenant's assistance, was also wounded by Mungal Pandy. The dark feature in this transaction was that many hundred men in the regiment looked on quietly without offering to protect the lieutenant from his assailant; one of them, a jemadar, refused to take Mungal into custody, and forbade his men to render any assistance to the lieutenant, who narrowly escaped with his life. Major-general Hearsey, on being informed of the occurrence, proceeded to the parade-ground, where, to his astonishment, he saw the man walking to and fro, with a blood-smeared sword in one hand, and a loaded musket in the other. He advanced with some officers and men to secure the sepoy, which was accomplished with much difficulty; and it was only by the most resolute bearing of the major-general that the rest of the men could be induced to return quietly to their lines. A court-martial was held on Mungal Pandy, and on the rebellious jemadar, both of whom were forthwith found guilty, and executed on the 8th of April. No assignable cause appeared for the conduct of this man: it may have been a mere drunken frenzy; yet there is more probability that a mutinous spirit, concealed within his breast during sober moments, made its appearance unchecked when under the influence of drugs. There was another sepoy, however, who acted faithfully on the occasion; this man, Shick Paltoo, was accompanying Lieutenant Baugh as orderly officer at the time of the attack; and by his prompt assistance the lieutenant was saved from further injury than a slight wound. Shick Paltoo was raised to the rank of supernumerary havildar for his brave and loyal conduct.

The outrage, however, could not be allowed to terminate without further punishment. For a time, the government at Calcutta believed that the execution of the two principal offenders would suffice, and that the sepoys would quietly return to

Calcutta.

their obedience; but certain ominous occurrences at Lucknow and elsewhere, about the end of April, shewed the necessity for a stern line of conduct, especially as the 34th still displayed a kind of sullen doggedness, as if determined on further insubordination. After mature consideration the whole of the disposable troops in and around Calcutta were, on the 5th of May, marched off to Barrackpore, to effect the disarming and disbanding of such sepoys among the 34th as were present in the lines when Lieutenant Baugh was wounded. The force comprised the Queen's 84th regiment, a wing of the 53d, the 2d, 43d, and 70th native infantry, two squadrons of cavalry, and a light field-battery with six guns. When these troops had been drawn up in two sides of a square, on the morning of the 6th, about four hundred sepoys of the 34th were halted in front of the guns. The order for disbandment was read out by the interpreter, Lieutenant Chamier; and after a few energetic remarks upon the enormity of their offence, General Hearsey commanded them to pile their arms, and strip off the uniform which they had disgraced. When this was done, the work of paying up their arrears was commenced. They were then dismissed with their families and baggage, to Chinsura, a town a few miles higher up the Hoogly. The grenadiers of the 84th, and a portion of the cavalry, accompanied them to see that they went to and settled at Chinsura, and did not cross the river to Chittagong, where three other companies of the same regiment were stationed. Four of the disbanded sepoys were officers; one of whom, a subadar, sobbed bitterly at his loss and degradation, although it was strongly suspected that he had been one of the leaders in the insubordination. In the general order which the governor-general ordered to be read to every regiment in the service, concerning this disbandment, words occur which shew that the old delusion was still working in the breasts of the natives. 'The sepoy who was the chief actor in the disgraceful scene of the 29th of March called upon his comrades to come to his support, for the reason that their religion was in danger, and that they were about to be compelled to employ cartridges, the use of which would do injury to their caste; and from the words in which he addressed the sepoys, it is to be inferred that many of them shared this opinion with him. The governor-general in council has recently had occasion to remind the army of Bengal that the government of India has never interfered to constrain its soldiers in matters affecting their religious faith. He has declared that the government of India never will do so; and he has a right to expect that this declaration shall give confidence to all who have been deceived and led astray. But, whatever may be the deceptions or evil counsels to which others have been exposed, the native officers and men of the 34th regiment native infantry have no excuse for misapprehension on this subject. Not many weeks previously to the 29th of March, it had been explained to that regiment—first by their own commanding officer, and subsequently by the major-general commanding the division—that their fears for religion were groundless. It was carefully and clearly shewn to them that the cartridges which they would be called upon to use contained nothing which could do violence to their religious scruples. If, after receiving these assurances, the sepoys of the 34th regiment, or of any other regiment, still refuse to place trust in their officers and in the government, and still allow suspicions to take root in their minds, and to grow into disaffection, insubordination, and mutiny, the fault is their own, and their punishment will be upon their own heads.'

Five weeks elapsed between the offence of the 19th native infantry and its punishment by disbandment; five weeks similarly elapsed between the offence and the disbandment of the 34th; and many observant officers were of opinion that these delays worked mischief, by instilling into the minds of the sepoys a belief that the authorities were afraid to punish them. Whether the punishment of disbanding was, after all, sufficiently severe, is a question on which military men are by no means agreed.

At a later date than the events narrated in this chapter, but closely connected with them in subject, was the circulation of a report manifestly intended to rouse the religious prejudices of the Hindoos by a false assertion concerning the designs of the ruling powers. In some of the towns of Southern India, far away from Bengal, unknown emissaries circulated a paper, or at least a story, of which the following was the substance: That the padres, probably Christian missionaries, had sent a petition to the Queen of England, complaining of the slowness with which Hindoos were made to become Christians; they adduced the conduct of some of the Mohammedan potentates of India in past times, such as Tippoo Saib, who had compelled the Hindoos to embrace Islamism; and they suggested a similar authoritative policy. The story made the padres give this advice: to mix up bullocks' fat and pigs' fat with the grease employed on the cartridges; in order that, by touching these substances with their teeth or lips, the sepoys might lose caste, and thus induce them to embrace Christianity as their only resource. The climax of the story was reached by making the Queen express her joy at the plan, and her resolve that it should be put in operation. The success of such a lying rumour must, of course, have mainly depended on the ignorance and credulity of the natives.

A far-distant region now calls for notice. At a time when the Upper and Lower Bengal provinces were, as the authorities hoped and believed, recovering from the wild excitement of the cartridge question, the commissioner of the Cis-Sutlej territory had ample means for knowing that the minds of the natives in that region were mischievously agitated by some cause or other. It is necessary here to understand what is meant by this geographical designation. If we consult a map in which an attempt is made, by distinct colouring, to define British territory from semi-independent states, we shall find the region between Delhi and Lahore cut up in a most extraordinary way. The red British patches are seen to meander among the scraps of native territory with great intricacy: so much so, indeed, that a map on a very large scale could alone mark the multitudinous lines of boundary; and even such a map would soon become obsolete, for the red, like a devouring element, has been year by year absorbing bits of territory formerly painted green or yellow. The peculiar tribe of the Sikhs, besides occupying the Punjaub, inhabit a wide region on the east or left bank of the river Sutlej, generally included under the name of Sirhind. For fifty years the British in India have had to deal, or have made a pretext for dealing, with the petty Sikh chieftains of this Sirhind region: at one time 'protecting' those on the east of the Sutlej from the aggression of the great Sikh leader, Runjeet Singh, on the west of that river; then 'annexing' the small territories of some of these chieftains on failure of male heirs; then seizing others as a punishment for non-neutrality or non-assistance during war-time. Thus it arose that—before the annexation of the Punjaub itself in 1849—much of the Sikh country in Sirhind had become British, and was divided into four districts marked by the towns of Ferozpore, Umballa or Umballah, Loodianah, and Kythul; leaving Putialah, Jeend, and Furreedkote as the three principal protected or semi-independent Sikh states of that country. Meanwhile a region somewhat to the east or north-east of Sirhind was subject to just the same process. Being hilly, it is called the Hill Country; and being ruled by a number of petty chieftains, the separate bits of territory are called the Hill States. During about forty years the process of absorption has been going on—arising primarily out of the fact that the British aided the Hill chieftains against the Nepaulese, and then paid themselves in their wonted manner. Part of Gurhwal was annexed; then Sandock, Malowa, and a number of other places not easily found in the maps; and afterwards Ramgurh was given back in exchange for Simla, to form a healthy holiday-place among the hills, a sort of Balmoral for sick governors and commanders. As a final result, much of the Hill Country became British, and the rest was left in the hands of about twenty petty chieftains.

Now, when the Cis-Sutlej territory is mentioned, it must be interpreted as including all the region taken by the British from the minor Sikh chieftains in Sirhind; together with such of the Hill States of Gurhwal and its vicinity as have become British. The whole together have been made a sub-government, under a commissioner responsible to the governor-general; or, more strictly, the commissioner rules the Sirhind region, while the Hills are included among the non-regulation districts of the Agra government. The four towns and districts of Ferozpore, Loodianah, Umballa, and Kythul, east of the Sutlej, will suffice for our purpose to indicate the Cis-Sutlej territory—so named in a Calcutta point of view, as being on the *cis* or *hither* side of the Sutlej, in reference to that city.

It was at Umballa, one of the towns in the Cis-Sutlej territory, that the commissioner, Mr Barnes, reported acts of incendiarism that much perplexed him. On the 26th of March, Hurbunsee Singh, a subadar or native captain in the 36th regiment native infantry, attached to the musketry depôt at that place, became an object of attack to the other men of the regiment; they endeavoured to burn his hut and his property. It was just at the time when reports reached Umballa relative to the cartridges, the using of which was said by the sepoys to be an innovation derogatory to their caste and religion. Hurbunsee Singh had at once come forward, and publicly stated his willingness to fire with such cartridges, as being, in his opinion, free from objection. The incendiarism took place on the day named; and the commissioner directly inferred that there must be something wrong in the thoughts of men who would thus seek to injure one of their own native officers on such grounds. Nothing further occurred, however, until the 13th of April, when another fire broke out. This was followed by a third on the 15th, in some outhouses belonging to the 60th native infantry; by two fires on the 16th, when government property was burned to the value of thirty thousand rupees; by the burning on the 17th of an empty bungalow in the 5th regiment native infantry lines, of a stable belonging to an English officer of the 60th, and of another building. On the 20th, attempts were made on the houses of the jemadar and havildar of the 5th regiment, two native officers favourable to the new cartridges; and under the bed of the jemadar were found gunpowder and brimstone, as if to destroy the man as well as his property. Some of the buildings are believed to have been set on fire by dropping burning brimstone through holes in the roof; and on one occasion, when the attempt at incendiarism had failed, a paper containing powder and brimstone was found. On the 21st and two following days, similar fires occurred. On the 25th, the house of the band-master of Her Majesty's 9th Lancers was fired and burned; and two or three similar attempts were shortly afterwards made, but frustrated. At all these fires, the engines of the cantonment were set to work; but it was observed that many of the sepoys worked listlessly and indifferently, as if their thoughts were bent rather upon fire-raising than fire-quenching.

That such occurrences produced uneasiness among the English authorities at Umballa may well be supposed. Captain Howard, magistrate of the cantonment, wrote thus to the Calcutta government: 'The emanating cause of the arson at this cantonment, I conceive, originated with regard to the newly introduced cartridges, to which the native sepoy shews his decided objection: it being obnoxious to him from a false idea—which, now that it has entered the mind of the sepoy, is difficult to eradicate—that the innovation of this cartridge is derogatory both to his caste and his religion . . . . That this has led to the fires at this cantonment, in my own private mind I am perfectly convinced. Were it the act of only one or two, or even a few persons, the well-disposed sepoys would at once have come forward and forthwith informed; but that there is an organised leagued conspiracy existing, I feel confident. Though all and every individual composing a regiment may not form part of the combination, still I am of opinion that such a league in each corps is known to exist; and such being upheld by the majority, or rather connived at, therefore it is that no single man dared to come forward and expose it.' Although proof could not be obtained of the culpability of any one sepoy, the incendiarism was at once attributed to them rather than to the peasantry. The existence of some oath or bond of secrecy was further supposed from the fact that a reward of one thousand rupees failed to bring forward a single witness or accuser. After about twenty attempts at burning buildings, more or less successful, the system was checked—by the establishment of mounted and foot patrols and pickets; by the expulsion of all fakeers and idle persons not belonging to the cantonment; by the refusal of a passage through it to sepoys on furlough or discharged; and by the arrest of such sepoys in the Umballa regiments as, having furloughs, still remained in the cantonment—influenced, apparently, by some mischievous designs.

Every one coincided in opinion with Captain Howard that there had been an organised plan among the sepoys; but some of the officers in the Company's service, civil as well as military, differed from him in attributing it solely to the cartridge affair—they thought this a blind or pretence to hide some deeper scheme. The commissioner of the Cis-Sutlej states, however, agreed with the magistrate, and expressed an opinion that nothing would restore quiet but a concession to the natives in the matter of greased cartridges; and he recommended to the government at Calcutta the adoption of that line of policy. Writing on the 7th of May, he said: 'Fires, for the present, have ceased; but I do not think that this is any indication that the uneasy feeling among the sepoys is on the wane.' Considering the position of Umballa, it is no wonder that those in authority at that spot should feel anxiety concerning the safety of their position. Umballa is more than a thousand miles from Calcutta, separated from it by the whole of the important states in which the cities of Delhi, Meerut, Agra, Cawnpore, Lucknow, Allahabad, and Benares are situated, and deprived of assistance from thence in the event of the intermediate regions being disturbed. Umballa is a somewhat important town, too, in itself, with more than twenty thousand inhabitants; it is large, and surrounded with a wall, well supplied with water, bounded by a highly fertile district, and capable of furnishing abundant supplies to rebels, if held by them.

The authorities, awakened by these events in so many parts of India, sought to inquire whether the native newspaper press of India had fermented the anarchy. It seemed at first ridiculous to suppose that those miserable little sheets, badly written and worse printed, and having a small circulation, could have contributed much to the creation of the evil. Yet many facts tended to the support of this view. It was a frequent custom in those papers to disguise the writer's real sentiments under the flimsy mask of a dialogue, in which one side was uniformly made victor. When the government was not actually abused and vilified, it was treated with ridicule, and its motives distorted. There were not many copies of these papers printed and sold; but a kind of ubiquity was afforded to them by the practice of news-mongers or tale-bearers, who went from hut to hut, retailing the various items of news or of comment that had been picked up.

Indeed, the tendency of the people to listen to attacks against the government is now known to have been very marked among the Hindoos. Predictions of the downfall of rulers were a favourite subject with them. Of course, such predictions would not be openly hazarded in newspapers; but they not less surely reached the ears of the natives. Thirty years ago, Sir John Malcolm spoke on this subject in the following way: 'My attention has been, during the last twenty-five years, particularly directed to this dangerous species of secret war against our authority, which is always carrying on by numerous though unseen hands. The spirit is kept up by letters, by exaggerated reports, and by pretended prophecies. When the time appears favourable, from the occurrence of misfortune to our arms, from rebellion in our provinces, or from mutiny in our troops, circular-letters and proclamations are dispersed over the country with a celerity almost incredible. Such documents are read with avidity. The contents in most cases are the same. The English are depicted as usurpers of low caste, and as tyrants who have sought India with no other view but that of degrading the inhabitants and of robbing them of their wealth, while they seek to subvert their usages and their religion. The native soldiery are always appealed to, and the advice to them is, in all instances I have met with, the same—"*Your European tyrants are few in number: kill them!*"' This testimony of Malcolm is especially valuable, as illustrating, and illustrated by, recent events.

The native press of India will come again under notice in a future chapter, connected with the precautionary measures adopted by the governor-general to lessen the power of those news-writers, whether English or native, who shewed a disposition to encourage rebellion by their writings. News and rumours always work most actively among credulous people—an important fact, knowing what we now know of India and its Hindoo inhabitants.

When General Anson, commander-in-chief of the forces in India, found that the small events at Dumdum, Berhampore, and Barrackpore had grown into great importance, and that the cartridge grievance still appeared to press on the consciences or influence the conduct of the sepoys, he deemed it right to make an effort that should pacify the whole of the native troops. Being at Umballa on the 19th of May, to which place he had hastened from his sojourn at Simla, he issued a general order to the native army, informing the troops that it had never been the intention of the government to force them to use any cartridges which could be objected to, and that they never would be required to do so. He announced his object in publishing the order to be to allay the excitement which had been raised in their minds, at the same time expressing his conviction that there was no cause for this excitement. He had been informed, he said, that some of the sepoys who entertained the strongest attachment and loyalty to the government, and who were ready at any moment to obey its orders, were nevertheless under an impression that their families would believe them to be in some way contaminated by the use of the cartridges used with the Enfield rifles recently introduced in India. He expressed regret that the positive assertions of the government officers, as to the non-existence of the objectionable substances in the grease of the cartridges, had not been credited by the sepoys. He solemnly assured the army, that no interference with their caste-principles or their religion was ever contemplated; and as solemnly pledged his word and honour that no such interference should ever be attempted. He announced, therefore, that whatever might be the opinions of the government concerning the cartridges, new or old, he had determined that the new rifle-cartridge, and every other of new form, should be discontinued; balled ammunition being made up by each regiment for its own use, by a proper establishment maintained for the purpose. Finally, he declared his full confidence, 'that all in the native army will now perform their duty, free from anxiety or care, and be prepared to stand and shed the last drop of their blood, as they had formerly done, by the side of the British troops, and in defence of their country.' The central government at Calcutta, on receipt of the news of this order having been promulgated, hastily sent to state that, in implying that new cartridges *had* been issued, the commander-in-chief had overstepped the actual facts of the case; nothing new in that way had been introduced throughout the year except to the troops at the Depôt of Musketry Instruction at Dumdum. From this fact it appears certain that the credulity of the sepoys at the more distant stations had been imposed upon, either by their fellow-Hindoos engaged in a conspiracy, or by Mohammedans.

In this chapter have been discussed several subjects which, though strange, exhibit nothing terrible or cruel. The suspicions connected with the Oude princes, the mystery of the chupatties, the prophecies of British downfall, the objections to the greased cartridges, the insubordination arising out of those objections, the incendiarism, the inflammatory tendency of the native newspaper press—all were important rather as symptoms, than for their immediate effects. But the month of May, and the towns of Meerut and Delhi, will now introduce us to fearful proceedings—the beginning of a series of tragedies.

Council-house at Calcutta.

King's Palace, Delhi.

CHAPTER III.

MEERUT, AND THE REBEL-FLIGHT TO DELHI.

THE first week in May marked a crisis in the affairs of British India. It will ever remain an insoluble problem, whether the hideous atrocities that followed might have been prevented by any different policy at that date. The complainings and the disobedience had already presented themselves: the murders and mutilations had not yet commenced; and there are those who believe that if a Lawrence instead of a Hewett had been at Meerut, the last spark that ignited the inflammable materials might have been arrested. But this is a kind of cheap wisdom, a prophecy after the event, an easy mode of judgment, on which little reliance can be placed. Taking the British officers in India as a body, it is certain that they had not yet learned to distrust the sepoys, whom they regarded with much professional admiration for their external qualifications. The Brahmins of the Northwest Provinces—a most important constituent, as we have seen, of the Bengal army—are among the finest men in the world; their average height is at least two inches greater than that of the English soldiers of the line regiments; and in symmetry they also take the lead. They are unaddicted to drunkenness; they are courteous in demeanour, in a degree quite beyond the English soldier; and it is now known that the commanding officers, proud of the appearance of these men on parade, too often ignored those moral qualities without which a good soldier is an impossible production. Whether, when the disturbances became known, the interpretation was favourable to the sepoys, depended much on the peculiar bias in the judgment of each officer. Some believed that the native soldier was docile, obedient, and loyal as long as his religious prejudices were respected; that he was driven to absolute frenzy by the slightest suspicion, whether well or ill grounded, of any interference with his creed or his observances; that he had been

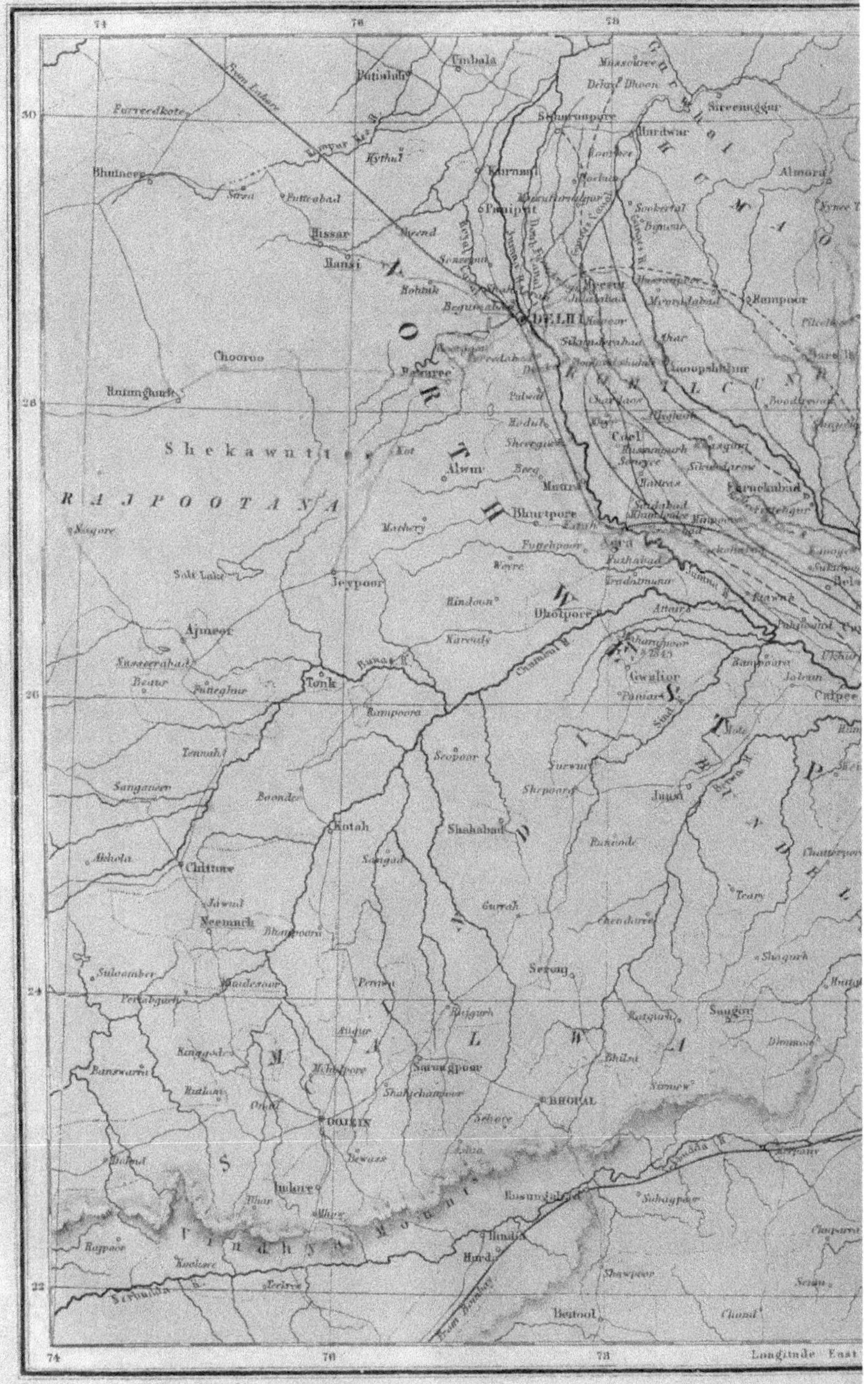

Printed in Colours by Schenck & McFarlane Edinburgh.

W. & R. CHAMBERS, L

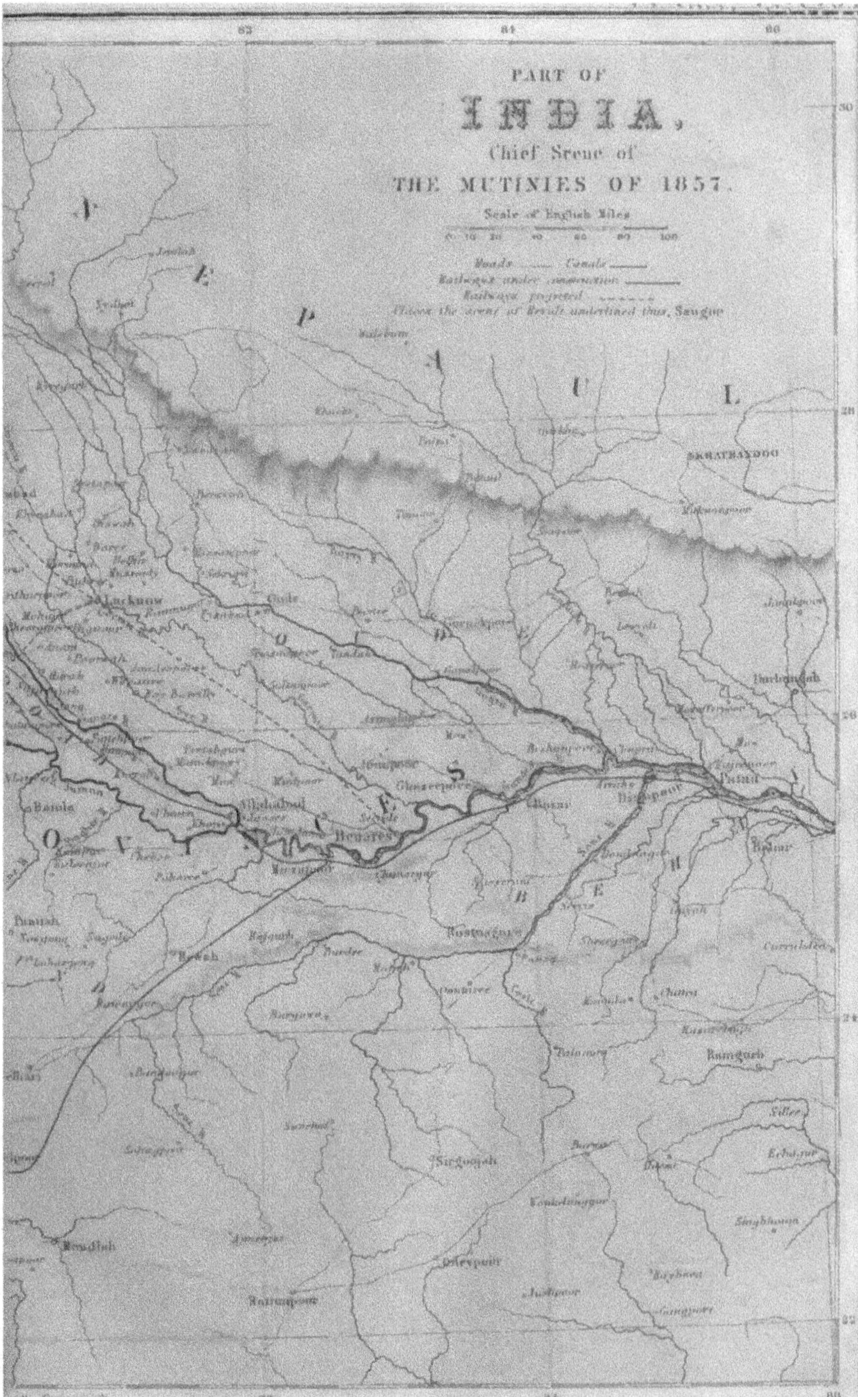

Constructed & Engraved by W. & A.K. Johnston, Edinburgh

ally rendered distrustful by the government y of forbidding suttee and infanticide, by withholding of government contributions to oo temples and idol-ceremonies, by the orities at Calcutta subscribing to missionary ties, and lastly by the affair of the greased idges; and that the sensibilities of Brahmin- thus vitally outraged, prepared the native l for the belief that we designed to proceed ome stratagem or other to the utter and final ition of caste. This interpretation is wholly the Hindoo side, and is respectful rather otherwise to the earnestness and honesty of Brahmins. Other officers, however, directed r attention at once to the Mohammedan nent in the army, and authoritatively pro- nced that the Hindoo sepoys were simply es and tools in the hands of the Moslem. se interpreters said—We have superseded the hammedan power in India; we have dethroned descendants of the great Aurungzebe and the ater Akbar; we have subjected the mogul's utenants or nawabs to our authority; we have ly extinguished the last remaining monarchy Northern India held by a son of the Faithful; have reduced a conquering and dominant race a position of inferiority and subserviency; and nce their undying resentment, their implacable tred, their resolute determination to try one ore struggle for supremacy, and their crafty nployment of simple bigoted Hindoos as worthy struments when sufficiently excited by dark hints d bold lies.

But there was one fact which all these officers dmitted, when it was too late to apply a remedy. Whether the Hindoo or the Mohammedan element as most disturbed, all agreed that the British orces were ill placed to cope with any difficulties rising out of a revolt. Doubt might be enter- ained how far the disloyalty among the native roops would extend; but there could be no doubt hat European troops were scanty, just at the laces where most likely to be needed. There were omewhat over twenty thousand Queen's troops at he time in India, with a few others on the way hither. Of these, as has been shewn in a former page, the larger proportion was with the Bengal troops; but instead of being distributed in the various Bengal and Oude provinces, they were rather largely posted at two extreme points, certainly not less than two thousand miles apart —on the Afghan frontier of the Punjaub, and on the Burmese frontier of Pegu. Four regiments of the Queen's army were guarding the newly annexed country of the Punjaub, while three others were similarly holding the recent conquests in Pegu. What was the consequence, in relation to the twelve hundred miles between Calcutta and the Sutlej? An almost complete denudation of European troops; a surrendering of most of the strongholds to the mercy of the sepoys. Only one European regiment at Lucknow, and none other in the whole of Oude; two at Meerut, one at Agra, one at Dinapoor, and one at Calcutta—none at Cawnpore or Allahabad. The two great native capitals of India—Delhi, of the Mohammedans: Benares, of the Hindoos—had not one European regiment in them. Indeed, earlier in the year, Calcutta itself had none; but the authorities, as narrated in the last chapter, became so uneasy at the thought of being without European supporters at the seat of government, that they sent to Rangoon in Pegu for one of the Queen's regiments, and did not venture upon the Barrackpore disbandments until this regiment had arrived. The lieutenant-governor of the Northwest Provinces, comprising Delhi and the surrounding regions, had in his whole government only three European regiments, and a sepoy army, soon found to be faithless. Oude had a considerable native force; but Bengal proper had very few troops of any kind. In short, the Company's forces were almost as unfavourably distributed as they could possibly be, to stem the Revolt at its beginning; and there may not be much hazard in assuming that the natives were as well acquainted with this fact as the British.

The reader will find it useful to bear in mind, that the unfavourable symptoms during the first four months of the year did not present themselves in those districts which were afterwards associated with such terrible deeds. Meerut and Delhi, Dinapoor and Ghazeepore, Benares and Allahabad, Cawnpore and Lucknow, Mirzapore and Agra—these were not in open disaffection during the period under notice, however much the elements for a storm may have been gathering. It was at Dumdum, Barrackpore, and Berhampore, on the Hoogly branch of the Lower Ganges—and at Umballa near the Sutlej, separated from them by more than a thousand miles—that the insubordination was chiefly shewn. Now, however, the scene shifts to the Jumna and the Upper Ganges—with which it will be well to become familiar by means of maps. Especially must the positions of Meerut and Delhi be attended to, in relation to the events detailed in this and the next following chapters.

Meerut, as a district, is a part of the Doab or delta enclosed between the rivers Ganges and Jumna; but it is Meerut the town with which this narrative is concerned. It came into the possession of the British in 1836, and is now included in the territories of Northwest Bengal. The town, standing on the small river Kalee Nuddee, is about equidistant from the Ganges and the Jumna, twenty-five or thirty miles from each, and nearly nine hundred miles from Calcutta. Meerut is interesting to the Indian antiquary in possessing some good architectural remains of mosques and pagodas; and to the European residents, in possessing one of the largest and finest Christian churches in India, capable of accommodating three thousand persons, and provided with a good organ; but the houses of the natives are wretchedly built, and the streets narrow and dirty, as in most oriental towns. It is as a military station, however, that Meerut is most important. The cantonment is two miles north of the town, and is divided into two portions by a small branch of the river, over which two bridges have been thrown. The northern half of the cantonment contains lines for the accommodation of a brigade of horse-artillery, a European cavalry corps, and a regiment of European infantry—separated respectively by intervals of several hundred yards. In front of these is a fine parade-ground, a mile in width and four miles in length, having ample space for field-battery practice and the manœuvres of horse-artillery; with a heavy battery on the extreme right. Overlooking the parade are the barracks, with stables, hospitals, riding-schools, canteens, and other military offices. The barracks consist of a series of separate brick-built low-roofed structures, each comprising one large and lofty room, surrounded by a spacious enclosed verandah, divided into apartments for the non-commissioned officers and the families of married men. Behind the barracks, in a continued line three deep, are the bungalows or lodges of the officers, each surrounded by a garden about a hundred yards square. The opposite or southern half of the cantonment is mainly occupied by the huts (not barracks) for native troops, and by the detached bungalows for the officers who command them. This description, applicable in some degree to many parts of India, may assist in conveying an idea of the manner in which the European officers have usually been lodged at the cantonments—in detached bungalows at no great distance from the huts of the native troops: it may render a little more intelligible some of the details of the fearful tragedies about to be narrated. Before the Revolt, it was customary to keep at Meerut a regiment of European cavalry, a regiment of European infantry, one of native cavalry, and three of native infantry, besides horse and foot artillery. The station is a particularly healthy one; and, both politically and geographically, is an important place to the British rulers of India.

Meerut, in some respects, was one of the last towns in which the mutiny might have been expected to commence; for there was no other place in the Northwest Provinces containing at the time so many English troops. There were the 60th (Rifle) regiment, 1000 strong; the 6th Dragoon Guards or Carabineers, 600 strong (but not fully mounted); a troop of horse-artillery; and 500 artillery recruits—altogether about 2200 men, with a full complement of officers. The native troops were but little more numerous: comprising the 3d Bengal cavalry, and the 11th and 20th Bengal infantry. In such a relative state of the European and native forces, no one for an instant would have admitted the probability of a revolt being successful at such a time and place.

Although it was not until the second week in May that those events took place which carried grief and mourning into so many families, M began its troubles in the latter part of the ceding month. The troops at this station not been inattentive to the events transpirin Lower Bengal; they knew all the rumours cerning the greased cartridges; they had b duped into a belief in the truth of those rumo and, moreover, emissaries had been at w among them, instilling into their minds anot preposterous notion—that the government plotted to take away their caste and insult t religion, by causing the pulverised bones bullocks to be mixed up with the flour sold in public markets or bazaars. Major-general Hew commanding the military division of wh Meerut was the chief station, sought by eve means to eradicate from the minds of the m these absurd and pernicious ideas; he pointed o how little the government had to gain by such course, how contrary it would be to the poli adopted during a hundred years, and how impro able was the whole rumour. He failed, howeve in his appeal to the good sense of the men; an equally did the European officers of the nati regiments fail: the sepoys or infantry, the sowa or cavalry, alike continued in a distrustful an suspicious state. Many British officers accus tomed to Indian troops aver that these men ha been rendered more insubordinate than ever b the leniency of the proceedings at Barrackpor and Berhampore; that disbandment was not sufficiently severe punishment for the offence committed at those places; that the delay in the disbanding was injurious, as denoting irresolution on the part of the authorities at Calcutta; and that the native troops in other places had begun to imbibe an opinion that the government were afraid of them. But whatever be the amount of truth in this mode of interpretation, certain it is that the troops at Meerut evinced a mutinous spirit that caused great uneasiness to their commanders. Bungalows and houses were set on fire, no one knew by whom; officers were not saluted as had been their wont; and whispers went about that the men intended to adopt a bold course in reference to the greased cartridges.

The military authorities on the spot resolved to put this matter to the test. On the 23d of April, Colonel Smyth, the English commander of the 3d regiment of native Bengal cavalry, ordered a parade of the skirmishers of his regiment with carabines on the following morning, to shew them the newly introduced mode of adjusting their cartridges without biting, hoping and believing that they would be gratified by this indication of the willingness of the government to consult their feelings in the matter. He caused the havildar-major and the havildar-major's orderly to come to his house, to shew them how it was to be done; and the orderly fired off a carabine under the new system. At night, however, uneasiness was occasioned by the burning down of the orderly's tent, and of a orse-hospital close to the magazine. Although this t of incendiarism looked ominous, the colonel evertheless determined to carry out his object on e morrow. Accordingly, on the morning of the th, the troops assembled on parade; and the avildar-major fired off one cartridge to shew em how it was to be done. The men demurred, owever, to the reception of the cartridges, though he same in kind as had been used by them during long period, and *not* the new cartridges. An nvestigation ensued, which was conducted on the 5th by Major Harrison, deputy-judge advocate. On being examined, the men admitted that they ould discern nothing impure in the composition or glazing of the paper; but added that they had *heard* it was unclean, and believed it to be so. The inquiry, after a few conciliatory observations on the part of the judge, ended in the men expressing contrition for their obstinacy, and promising a ready obedience in the use of the cartridges whenever called upon.

A hope was now entertained that the difficulties had been smoothed away; but this hope proved to be fallacious. Major-general Hewett, wishing to put an end to the stupid prejudice, and to settle at once all doubts as to the obedience of the men, ordered a parade of the 3d cavalry for the morning of the 6th of May. On the evening of the 5th, preparatory to the parade, cartridges were given out to the men, the same in quality as those which had been freely in use during many years. Eighty-five of the sowars or troopers—either still incredulous on the grease-question, or resolved to mutiny whether with just cause or not—positively refused to receive the cartridges. This conduct, of course, could not be overlooked; the men were taken into custody, and tried by a court-martial; they were found guilty of a grave military offence, and were committed to imprisonment with hard labour, for periods varying from six to ten years. The governor-general, seeing the necessity of promptitude at this crisis, had just sent orders to the military stations that the judgments of all court-martials should be put in force instantly, as a means of impressing the troops with the seriousness of their position; and Major-general Hewett, acting on these instructions, proceeded on the 9th to enforce the sentence of the court-martial. A European guard of 60th Rifles and Carabiniers was placed over the convicted men; and at daybreak the whole military force at the station was assembled on the rifle parade-ground. All were there—the European 60th, Carabiniers, and artillery—the native 3d, 11th, and 20th. The European cannon, carbines, and rifles were loaded, to prepare for any emergency. The eighty-five mutineers of the 3d native cavalry were marched upon the ground; they were stripped of their uniforms and accoutrements; they were shackled with irons riveted on by the armourers. While this was being done, very meaning looks were exchanged between the culprits and the other sowars of the same regiment—the former looking reproachfully at the latter, while the latter appeared gloomy and crestfallen: it was evident that the unconvicted men had promised to resist and prevent the infliction of the degrading punishment on their convicted associates; but it was equally evident that the presence of so many armed European troops would have rendered any attempt at rescue worse than useless. The manacles having been adjusted, the men were marched off to jail. And herein a grave mistake appears to have been committed. Instead of keeping a watchful eye over these men at such a perilous time, and retaining them under a guard of European troops until the excitement had blown over, they were sent to the common jail of Meerut, two miles distant from the cantonment, and there handed over to the police or ordinary civil power of the town. How disastrous was the result of this course of proceeding, we shall presently see. The native troops, when the culprits had been removed from the parade-ground, returned to their lines furious with indignation—at least the 3d cavalry were so, and they gradually brought over the infantry to share in their indignant feelings. It was a degrading punishment, unquestionably: whether the remainder of the native troops at the station would be terrified or exasperated by it, was just the problem which remained to be solved. All the afternoon and evening of that day were the men brooding and whispering, plotting and planning. Unfortunately, the European officers of native regiments were accustomed to mix so seldom with their men, that they knew little of what occurred except on parade-ground; this plotting was only known by its fruits. Judged by subsequent events, it appears probable that the native troops sent emissaries to Delhi, forty miles distant, to announce what had occurred, and to plan an open revolt. The prime plotters were the 3d; the 20th were nearly as eager; but the 11th, newly arrived at Meerut, held back for some time, although they did not betray the rest.

Little did the European inhabitants, their wives and their children, at Meerut, dream what was in store for them on Sunday the 10th of May—a day of peace in the eyes of Christians. It was on the 9th that the sentence of the court-martial on the eighty-five mutineers was enforced; it was on the 10th that the Revolt, in its larger sense, began. Whether these two events stood to each other in the relation of cause and effect, is a question not easily to be answered; but it may safely be asserted that the Revolt would not have resulted from the punishment unless the men had been generally in a state of disaffection. The Sunday opened as most Sundays open in India, quiet and uneventful, and remained so till evening. Ladies and families were then going to evening-service at the church. Some of them passed the mess-room of the 3d cavalry, and there saw servants looking towards the road leading to the native infantry lines. Something was evidently wrong. On inquiry it appeared that a mutiny had broken out, and that fighting was going on in the bazaar. Crowds of armed men soon hurried that way; and families who had been on the route to church, drove or walked back in haste to escape danger. So it was on all sides; whoever on that evening ventured forth, found that blood-shedding instead of church-service would fill their thoughts. The Rev. Mr Smyth, chaplain of Meerut, while driving to church for the seven o'clock service, met two of the 60th Rifles covered with blood; and on reaching the church, he saw buggies and carriages driving away in great confusion, and a body of people pointing to a column of fire and smoke in the direction of the city: frequent shots were heard, amid the cries of a large mob. In another direction the wife of an officer in the 3d cavalry, going like other Europeans to church, and startled like them by sounds of violence, saw a private of the Carabiniers unarmed, and running for very life from several men armed with *latthies* or long sticks; she stopped her carriage and took in the English soldier; but the men continued to strike at him until the vehicle rolled away. This lady, on reaching her bungalow in haste and dismay, was the first to give notice to her husband that something was wrong among the native troops: he instantly started off on foot to the lines, without waiting for his horse. In another part of the scene, an English officer of the 11th native infantry, at about six o'clock on that evening, while in his bungalow preparing for a ride with Colonel Finnis of the same regiment, had his attention attracted to his servants, and those in the bungalows of other officers, going down towards the front of the several compounds or gardens, and looking steadily into the lines or cantonment of the regiment. He heard a buzzing, murmuring noise, which at first he deemed of no consequence; but as it continued and increased, he hastily finished dressing and went out. Scarcely had he reached his gate, when he heard the sound of firearms, which his practised ear at once told him were loaded with ball-cartridge. An European non-commissioned officer came running towards him, with others, and exclaimed: 'For God's sake, sir, leave! Return to your bungalow, change that dress, and fly!' Shortly afterwards shots came into his own compound; and the havildar-major of the 11th, rushing terrified and breathless into the bungalow, exclaimed: 'Fly, sahib—fly at once! the regiments are in open mutiny, and firing on their officers; and Colonel Finnis has just been shot in my arms!' The officer mounted and started off—at first leisurely—because 'a Briton does not like actually running away under any circumstances;' but when the havildar-major (native sergeant-major) advised him to gallop off to the European cavalry lines, he saw that the suggestion was good; and he immediately started—over a rugged and barren plain, cut up by nullahs and ravines—towards the lines of the Queen's Carabiniers.

When these, and a dozen similar mysteries came to receive their solution, it was found that a mutiny had indeed broken out. Shortly before five o'clock on that Sunday afternoon, the men of the 3d native cavalry, and of the 20th native infantry rushed out of their lines on a given signal, and proceeded to the lines of the 11th native infantry, all fully armed. After a little hesitation, their comrades joined them; and then all three regiments proceeded to open acts of violence. Colonel Finnis of the 11th, the moment he heard of this startling proceeding, rode to the parade-ground, harangued the men, and endeavoured to induce them to return to their duty. Instead of listening to him, the men of the 20th fired a volley, and he fell, riddled with bullets—the first victim of the Indian Revolt. The other officers present, feeling that their remaining longer on the ground would effect no good, escaped. Whether a daring man might have stemmed the torrent, cannot now be told: no one attempted it after Finnis's death; his brother-officers were allowed to escape to the lines of the artillery and the Carabiniers, on the other side of the encampment. So far as the accounts are intelligible, the first shots appear to have been fired by the 20th, the 11th joining afterwards in the violence.

While the infantry were thus engaged, the ominous but natural step was taken by the 3d cavalry of releasing their eighty-five imprisoned companions—ominous, because those men, enraged at their incarceration, would join in the disorder with heated blood and excited passions. The troopers proceeded to the jail, set their companions free, armed them, and invited them to share in the mutiny. All this was evidently preconcerted; for native smiths were at hand to strike off the manacles. Yelling and threatening, the whole returned to the lines; and then commenced the direful mischief. Within a very short time, all three regiments became busily engaged in burning and murdering. But this was not all; when the eighty-five troopers were liberated, the other prisoners in the jail, *twelve hundred* in number, were set at liberty at the same time; and then the scum of Indian society entered into the scenes of violence with demoniac relish, adding tenfold to the horrors perpetrated by the sepoys and sowars. The mutineers and the ruffians set fire to nearly all the bungalows of the native lines, and to the government establishments near at hand, murdering, as they went, the Europeans who fell in their way. The bungalows being mostly thatched with straw, the destruction was very rapid; the cowardly assailants, setting fire to the thatch, waited till the flames had driven out the inmates of the bungalow, and then fell upon them as assassins. The conflagrations were accompanied by the yells of the rioters and the shrieks of the sufferers, rendered more terrible by the approach of darkness. The rabble of the bazaar, and the lowest portion of the population generally, as if intoxicated by release from the dread of Europeans, now joined the mutineers and the released felons, and the horrors thickened. On all sides shot up columns of flame and smoke; on all sides were heard the shouts and curses of some, the cries and lamentations of others. One redeeming feature—there may have been others—marked these proceedings; the sepoys of the 11th, in most instances, connived at the escape of their officers—nay, strove earnestly to save them: it was not by men of his own regiment that poor Colonel Finnis had been shot down.

A few individual examples, drawn from the simple but painful narratives of eye-witnesses, will shew in what way misery and death were brought into homes where the peace of a Christian Sabbath had reigned only a few hours before.

The Rev. Mr Smyth, after returning hurriedly from the church where he had intended to perform divine service, took shelter in the house of an officer of the artillery in the English lines. Shots had just before been aimed at that officer and his wife by eight or ten sepoys of the artillery depôt or school, while standing at the very gate of their compound; and yet Mr Smyth himself was saluted respectfully by several sepoys during his hurried retreat—shewing the strange mixture of deference and ferocity exhibited by these misguided men. Presently afterwards another shot was heard, a horse was seen galloping past with a buggy; and it was soon found that the surgeon and the veterinary surgeon of the 3d cavalry had been wounded and mutilated. The clergyman escaped unhurt, to learn and to mourn over the events transpiring in other parts of the town and cantonment.

A captain of horse, the husband of the lady mentioned in a former paragraph, hastened on the first news from his bungalow to the lines of the 3d cavalry, in which he commanded a troop. He was respected by his men, who offered him no hurt, and who seemed to hesitate for a time whether to join the rest in mutiny or not. Soon, however, the mania infected them; and the captain, seeing the jail opened and the prisoners liberated, hastened back. The road from the town to the cantonment was in an uproar; the infantry and the bazaar-people were in crowds, armed and firing; and he saw one of the miscreant troopers stab to death an Englishwoman, the wife of the Meerut hotel-keeper, as she passed. Soon a ball whizzed past his own ear, and he saw one of his own troopers aiming at him; he shouted: 'Was that meant for me?' 'Yes,' was the reply; 'I will have your blood!' The captain detected this man as one whom he had been obliged to punish for carelessness and disobedience. The man fired again, but again missed his aim; and although the other troopers did not join in this, they made no attempt to check or seize the assailant. The captain, abandoned gradually by all but a very few troopers, at length reached the European lines, where he took part in the proceedings afterwards adopted. Meanwhile the poor wife had passed two hours of terrible suspense. Believing at first that the carabinier whom she had saved might have been the main object of attack, she hid his uniform, dressed him in a coat of her husband's, and bade him sit with herself and family, for mutual safety. Out of doors she heard shots and shouts, and saw houses burning. In the next bungalow, speedily fired, was the wife of an adjutant lately arrived from England; she was entreated to come over for shelter, but not arriving, servants were sent in to seek her. A horrid sight met them: the hapless lady lay on the floor in a pool of blood, dead, and mutilated in a way that the pen refuses to describe. The noises and flames increased; eight or ten flaming bungalows were in sight at once; and many a struggle took place between the captain's servants and the mutineers, during which it was quite uncertain whether one more burning, one more massacre, would ensue. Troopers rushed into the bungalow, endeavouring to fire it; while others, with a lingering affection towards the family of their officer, prevented them. The husband arrived, in speechless agony concerning the safety of those dear to him. Wrapped in black stable-blankets, to hide their light dresses, all left the house amid a glare of flame from neighbouring buildings, and hid under trees in the garden; whence they sped to a small ruin near at hand, where, throughout the remainder of the night, they crouched listening to the noises without. Bands of armed men passed in and out of the bungalow compound during the night, and were only prevented from prosecuting a search, by an assurance from the domestics that the officer's family had effected their escape. When morning came, the (now) houseless Europeans, with about twenty troopers who remained faithful to the last—though agitated by strange waverings and irresolution—left the place, taking with them such few clothes and trinkets as could be hastily collected, and started off for the Carabiniers' lines, passing on their way the smouldering ruins of many bungalows and public buildings.

Howsoever the narratives might vary in details, in substance they were all alike; they spoke of a night of burning, slaughter, and dismay. Wherever there was a bungalow, the European inhabitants of which did not succeed in escaping to the English lines, there was murder perpetrated. The escape of Mr Greathed, civil commissioner for Meerut, was a narrow one. His house—flat-roofed, as it fortunately happened—was one of the first attacked by the mutineers: at the first alarm, Mr and Mrs Greathed fled to the roof; thither, on the least intimation from any of the servants, the miscreants would have followed them; but the servants persisted that the family had departed; and the assailants, after searching every room in the house, took their departure. One officer after another, as he rushed from his bungalow to call his men back to their allegiance, was shot down; and wherever the mutineers and their ruffian companions brought murder into a house, they mingled with the murder a degree of barbarity quite appalling and unexpected. There were a few Europeans in the town and vicinity not connected with the military department; and these, unless they effected their escape, were treated like the rest; rank, age, and sex were equally disregarded—or, if sex made any difference, women, gentle English women, were treated more ruthlessly than men. An officer of the 20th, living in his bungalow with his wife and two children, was sought out by the ruffians: the father and mother were killed; but a faithful ayah snatched up the two children and carried them off to a place of safety—the poor innocents never again saw their parents alive. An English sergeant was living with his wife and six children beyond the limits of the cantonment; he and three of his little ones were massacred in a way that must for very shame be left untold: the mother, with the other three, all bleeding and mutilated, managed to crawl to the European lines about midnight.

With what inexpressible astonishment were the narratives of these deeds heard and perused! Men who had been in India, or were familiar with Indian affairs, knew that the sepoys had before risen in mutiny, and had shot their officers; but it was something strange to them, a terrible novelty, that tender women and little children—injuring none, and throwing a halo of refinement around all—should be so vilely treated as to render death a relief. The contrast to all that was considered characteristic of the Hindoo was so great, that to this day it remains to many an Indian veteran a horrid enigma—a mystery insoluble even if his heart-sickness would lead him to the attempt. Be it remembered that for a whole century the natives had been largely trusted in the relations of social life; and had well justified that trust. Many an English lady (it has been observed by an eloquent reviewer, whose words we have before quoted) has travelled from one end of the country to the other—along desert roads, through thick jungles, or on vast solitary rivers—miles and miles away from the companionship of white men, without the slightest anxiety. Her native servants, Mohammedans and Hindoos, were her protectors; and she was as safe in such custody as in an English home. Her slightest caprice was as a law to her attendants. These swarthy bearded men, ready at her beck, ever treated her with the most delicate respect, ever appeared to bear about with them a chivalrous sense of the sacredness of their charge. Not a word or a gesture ever alarmed her modesty or excited her fear; and her husband, father, brother never hesitated to confide her to such guardianship. It was in the year 1857 that the charm of this delicate fidelity was first broken; and broken so appallingly, that men were long incredulous that such things could be.

But the children, the sabred and mangled little ones—that these could be so treated by the same natives, was more astounding to the Anglo-Indians than even the treatment of the women. 'Few of our countrymen have ever returned from India without deploring the loss of their native servants. In the nursery they are, perhaps, more missed than in any other part of the establishment. There are, doubtless, hundreds of English parents in this country who remember with feelings of kindliness and gratitude the *nusery* bearers, or male nurses, who attended their children. The patience, the gentleness, the tenderness with which these white-robed swarthy Indians attend the little children of their European masters, surpass even the love of women. You may see them sitting for hour after hour, with their little infantine charges, amusing them with toys, fanning them when they slumber, brushing away the flies, or pacing the verandah with the little ones in their arms, droning the low monotonous lullaby which charms them to sleep; and all this without a shadow on the brow, without a gesture of impatience, without a single petulant word. No matter how peevish, how wayward, how unreasonable, how exacting the child may be, the native bearer only smiles, shews his white teeth, or shakes his black locks, giving back a word of endearment in reply to young master's imperious discontent. In the sick-room, doubly gentle and doubly patient, his noiseless ministrations are continued through long days, often through long nights, as though hunger and weariness were human frailties to be cast off at such a time. It is little to say that these poor hirelings often love their master's children with greater tenderness than their own. Parted from their little charges, they may often be seen weeping like children themselves; and have been known, in after-years, to travel hundreds of miles to see the brave young ensign or the blooming maiden whom they once dandled in their arms.' These men, it is true, were domestic servants, not sepoys or soldiers fighting in the army of the Company; but it is equally true that the British officers, almost without exception, trusted implicitly to the sepoys who acted as orderlies or servants to them; and that those orderlies shewed themselves worthy of the trust, by their scrupulous respect to the ladies of each household, and their tender affection for the little ones born under the roof of the bungalow. Hence the mingled wonderment and grief when fiend-like cruelties suddenly destroyed the charm of this reliance.

Allowing the veil to remain, at present, drawn over still greater horrors in other places, it must be admitted that the principal atrocities at Meerut were perpetrated by the twelve hundred miscreants liberated from the jail, aided by the general rabble of the town. The native troops had something in their thoughts besides firing bungalows and murdering a few Europeans; they had arranged some sort of plot with the native troops of Delhi; and they set out in a body for that city long before the deplorable transactions at Meerut had ceased. Those scenes continued more or throughout the night; officers and their wives, ...nts and their children, were not relieved from agony of suspense before morning broke.

...he number massacred at Meerut on this even... and night was not so large as the excited ...ings of the survivors led them to imply; but it ...s large to *them;* for it told of a whole cluster ...happy homes suddenly broken up, of bungalows ...uced to ashes, of bleeding corpses brought in ... by one, of children rendered fatherless, of property consumed, of hopes blasted, of confidence destroyed. The European soldiers, as will presently be seen, soon obtained the mastery so far as Meerut was concerned; but the surviving women and children had still many hours, many days, of discomfort and misery to bear. The School of Instruction near the artillery laboratory became the place of shelter for most of them; and this place was much crowded. How mournfully does it tell of large families rendered homeless to read thus:

Laboratory at Meerut.

'We are in a small house at one end of the place, which consists of one large room and verandah rooms all round; and in this miserable shed—for we can scarcely call it anything else—there are no less than forty-one souls'—then are named thirteen members of one family, ten of another, three other families of four each, and two others of three each—'besides having in our verandah room the post-office, and arranging at present a small room adjoining the post-office as the telegraph-office.' Some of the houseless officers and their families found temporary homes in the sergeants' rooms of the European lines; space was found for all, although amid much confusion; and one of the refugees writes of 'a crowd of helpless babies' that added to the misery of the scene. Adverting to others like herself, she remarks: 'Ladies who were mere formal acquaintances now wring each other's hands with intense sympathy; what a look there was when we first assembled here!—all of us had stared death in the face.'

Let us turn now to a question which has probably presented itself more than once to the mind of the reader during the perusal of these sad details—What were the twenty-two hundred European troops doing while the three native regiments were imbuing their hands in the blood of innocent women and children? Could not they have intervened to prevent the atrocities? It must be borne in mind that these fine English troops, the Carabiniers and 60th Rifles, with artillery, were nearly equal in number to the rebels; and that, if quickly moved, they would have been a match for five or ten times their number. Whether or not they *were* quickly moved, is just the question at issue. Major-general Hewett's dispatch to the adjutant-general thus describes the course adopted as soon as the outbreak became known to him: 'The artillery, Carabiniers, and 60th Rifles were got under arms; but by the time we reached the native infantry parade-ground, it was too dark to act with efficiency in that direction; consequently, the troops retired to the north of the nullah, so as to cover the barracks and officers' lines of the artillery, Carabiniers, and 60th Rifles; which were, with the exception of one house, preserved; though the insurgents—for I believe the mutineers had by that time retired by the Allygurh and Delhi roads —burned the vacant Sapper and Miner lines.'

One thing is quite certain—the mutineers were not pursued: they were allowed to go to Delhi, there to raise the standard of rebellion in a still more alarming way. The Carabiniers, it is true, were deficient in horses to join in pursuit; but this might assuredly have been obviated by precautionary arrangements during the many days on which the 3d native cavalry had shewn symptoms of insubordination. An officer of the 11th native infantry, who narrowly escaped death in his gallop to the European cantonment, accompanied the Queen's regiments to the scene of anarchy; but there is evidence that he considered the movements somewhat tardy. 'It took us a long time, in my opinion,' he says, 'to get ready, and it was dark before the Carabiniers were prepared to start in a body.' In the latitude of Meerut, we may remark, in the second week in May, darkness can hardly come on until near seven o'clock, whereas the outbreak occurred two hours earlier. He continues: 'When the Carabiniers were mounted, we rode off at a brisk trot, through clouds of suffocating dust, and darkness, in an easterly direction, and along a narrow road —*not advancing in the direction of the conflagration*, but, on the contrary, leaving it behind on our right rear. In this way we proceeded for some two or three miles, to my no small surprise, when suddenly the "halt" was sounded, and we faced about, retracing our steps, and verging off to our left. Approaching the conflagration, we debouched on the left rear of the native infantry lines, which of course were all in a blaze. Skirting along behind these lines, we turned them at the western end, and wheeling up to the left, came upon the 11th parade-ground, where, at a little distance, we found the horse-artillery and her Majesty's 60th Rifles. It appears that the three regiments of mutineers had by this time commenced dropping off to the westward to the Delhi road, for here some firing took place between them and the Rifles; and presently the horse-artillery, coming to the front and unlimbering, opened upon a copse or wood in which they had apparently found cover, with heavy discharges of grape and canister, which rattled among the trees; and all was silent again. The horse-artillery now limbered up again, and wheeled round; and here I joined them, having lost the Carabiniers in the darkness. By this time, however, the moon arose. The horse-artillery column, with Rifles at its head, moving across the parade-ground, we entered the long street turn from the southward behind the light cavalry li There it was that the extent and particulars of conflagration first became visible; and, passing burning bungalow of the adjutant of the 11 native infantry, we proceeded along the straig road or street, flanked on both sides with flami and crashing houses in all stages of combusti and ruin; the Rifles occasionally firing volleys we proceeded. It was by this time past ten o'cloc and having made the entire circuit of the lines, passed up to the east of them, and, joined by th Carabiniers and Rifles, bivouacked for the night.'

Collating various accounts of this evening events, it becomes evident that the military move ments of the Europeans were anything but promp Even if the two regiments and the artillery coul not have reached the scene of tumult before dar —a supposition not at all borne out—still it seem strange that all should have 'bivouacked for th night' at the very time when three mutinous nativ regiments were on the way to Delhi. Hasty critics, as is usual in such circumstances, at once condemned the military commander at Meerut; and an ex-governor-general, dwelling, in his place in the House of Lords, on the occurrences in India, spoke in a contemptuous tone of 'an unknown man named Hewett' as one whose misconduct had allowed the rebel troops to escape from Meerut to Delhi. It was hard for a soldier who had served for forty years in India, without once returning to his native country, to find contumely thus hurled at him; it is one of the bitter things to which public men are subjected, not only from anonymous writers, but from other public men whose names carry authority with them. A near relation of the major-general afterwards took up his defence, urging that it might have been unwise policy to send the only European troops in pursuit to Delhi, at a time when the magazines and stores at Meerut required so much attention. The defence may possibly be insufficient; but the history of the Crimean war had shewn how hastily Lord Raglan had been accused of offences, things committed and things omitted, for which he was afterwards known not to have been responsible; and this experience ought to have suggested caution to assailants, especially remembering how long a time must often elapse between an accusation and a refutation, during which time the wound is festering. Declining years certainly did not prevent the officer whose name is now under notice from taking a part in the operations, such as they were, of the English troops at Meerut; although in his sixty-eighth year, he slept on the ground among the guns, like his men, on the 10th of May, and for fourteen consecutive nights he did the same; while for many following weeks he never doffed his regimentals, except for change of apparel, night or day. Whether such details are trivial or not, depends on the nature of the accusations. It is only the hasty judgments of those at a distance that are here commented on;

[th]e dissatisfaction of the Calcutta authorities will [b]e adverted to in a future page.

The sympathies of the Europeans at Meerut [w]ere drawn in a forcible way towards the inmates [o]f a convent and school at Sirdhana—an estab[li]shment remarkable as existing in that part of [I]ndia. We must go back sixty years to understand [t]his. Towards the close of the last century, there [w]as a Cashmerian bayadère or dancing-girl, who [b]ecame associated with a German adventurer, [a]nd then, by a course of unscrupulous intrigue and fearless sanguinary measures, obtained pos[s]ession of three considerable jaghires or princi[p]alities in the region around and between Meerut and Delhi. These cities, as well as Agra and others in the Doab, were at that time in the hands of the great Mahratta chief, Dowlut Rao Scindia. After a series of brilliant victories, the British obtained possession of the Doab in 1803, but awarded a petty sovereignty to the female adventurer, who became thenceforth known as the Begum Sumroo. She retained her queendom until her death in 1836, after which the three jaghires passed into the hands of the British. This remarkable woman, during the later years of her life, professed the Roman Catholic faith; she had a spacious and handsome palace at Sirdhana, about twelve miles from Meerut; and near it she built a Catholic church, imitative on a small scale of St Peter's at Rome, with a beautiful altar inlaid with mosaics and precious stones. Out of twelve thousand inhabitants in Sirdhana, about one-tenth now profess themselves Christians, having imitated the begum in her change of religion; and there is a Christian convent there, containing a number of priests, nuns, and pupils. When, therefore, the outrages occurred at Meerut, apprehensions naturally arose concerning the fate of the European women and girls at this convent. About five days after the Revolt commenced, rumours came in that the inmates of the convent at Sirdhana were in peril; and it was only by great exertions that the postmaster at Meerut was enabled to bring some of them away. A letter written in reference to this proceeding said: 'The poor nuns begged of him, when he was coming away, to try and send them some help; he tried all he could to get a guard to escort them to this station, but did not succeed; and yesterday morning (16th of May), having given up the idea of procuring a guard from the military authorities, he went round, and by speaking to some gentlemen, got about fifteen persons to volunteer their services, to go and rescue the poor nuns and children from Sirdhana; and I am happy to say they succeeded in their charitable errand without any one having been injured.'

It will be remembered that, during the burnings and murderings at Meerut on the evening of the 10th, most of the mutineers of the three regiments started off to Delhi. They took, as was afterwards found, the high road from Meerut, and passing the villages of Begumabad, Moradnuggur, Furrucknuggur, and Shahderuh, reached Delhi early on Monday; the infantry making forced marches, and the cavalry riding near them for support. Proof was soon afforded that the native troops in that city, or some of them, had been waiting for the mutineers, prepared to join them in an organised attack on the Europeans. What aspect that attack put on, and what were the calamities to which it gave rise, will be narrated in the next two chapters.

Many days elapsed before Meerut recovered its tranquillity. Such men of the 3d, 11th, and 20th regiments as remained faithful—especially the 11th, of whom there were more than a hundred—were received at the cantonment, and their previous insubordination pardoned on account of their subsequent fidelity; but still there were many causes for anxiety. In the major-general's first report on the disasters, he said: 'Nearly the whole of the cantonment and Zillah police have deserted.' These police or watchmen are referred to by an officer familiar with the district, who says: 'Round about Meerut and Delhi there are two or three peculiar castes or tribes, something similar to our gipsies, only holding human life at less value, and which in former days gave constant trouble. Of late years, they have lived in more peace and quietness, contenting themselves with picking up stray cattle and things that did not belong to them. They have now, however, on the earliest occasion broken out again, and have been guilty of all kinds of depredations. Skinner's Horse was originally raised to keep these people in order, about the time of Lord Lake; such men have hitherto been necessary at Meerut, Delhi, and those parts, as watchmen; every one was obliged to keep one, to avoid being robbed to a certainty.' The Meerut inhabitants had thus, in addition to their other troubles, the knowledge that gangs of desperadoes would be likely to acquire renewed audacity through the defection of the native police.

It was soon ascertained that the dâk communications on many of the roads were cut off, and the military commandant found much difficulty in transmitting intelligence to the seat of government. Five days after the great outbreak, another cause of uneasiness ensued. Six companies of native Sappers and Miners arrived at Meerut from Roorkee, under their commander, Major Fraser. The place here named is interesting in a twofold point of view. Being situated in one of the most elevated sites in the Doab between the Jumna and the Ganges, about eighty miles north of Meerut, it was selected as the head-quarters for operations on the great Ganges Canal, the noblest British work in India; and here has been made a magnificent aqueduct nine hundred feet in length, with arches of fifty feet span. This aqueduct, and the necessary workshops and model-rooms of the engineers, have converted the place from a small village to a considerable station. Roorkee also contains an establishment called the 'Thomason College,' for affording instruction in civil engineering to

Europeans and natives. When the native Sappers and Miners, about eight hundred strong, arrived at Meerut from this place, on the 16th of May—either excited by the news of the late occurrences, or moved by some other impulse—they suddenly shot their commanding officer, and made off for the open country. A force of the Carabiniers and horse-artillery went in pursuit of them, and shot down many; but a greater number escaped, probably to Delhi. Such of the companies as did not attempt flight were disarmed and carefully watched.

Too soon, alas! did the Europeans at Meerut know that atrocities were being committed at Delhi. By twos and threes did fugitives come in, glad to sacrifice all else for the sake of very life. Now several officers of the 38th native regiment; now a merchant and his family; now officers of the 74th and their families; now civil servants of the Company; now officers of the 54th—all toil-worn, dirty, ragged, hungered, weighed down by the miseries of their forty miles' flight from brutal assailants: women, as is usual with English women, bearing their share of these miseries with the truest heroism. All was doubt as to the occurrences in other quarters; dâks were cut off, telegraphic wires were severed; the wishes and orders of the governor-general at one place, and the commander-in-chief at another, could not yet be known. On the night of the outbreak, two Europeans had endeavoured to travel by dâk from Meerut to Delhi; they encountered the rebels, and were murdered; and this was the commencement of indications, afterwards abundant enough, that the roads were no longer safe. All that was certain was, that a sudden social earthquake had overturned the homes of families distant nine hundred miles from Calcutta, bringing death to many, mourning and loss to others, distrust and anxiety to all.

Dak Runner.

CHAPTER IV.

DELHI, THE CENTRE OF INDIAN NATIONALITY.

THE course of this narrative now requires that attention—more particular than will be required in relation to other cities in India—should be bestowed on the world-renowned Delhi, the great focus of all that can be called truly national in that vast country. Three regiments fled from Meerut to Delhi, and there found other regiments ready to join them in scenes of revolt and violence, of spoliation and murder; but it is necessary, in order to appreciate what followed, to know why Delhi is regarded in a peculiar light by the natives: why a successful resistance to British rule was, and must long continue to be, more serious in that locality than in any other part of the East. Not only ought the position of the city, considered as the residence of a hundred and sixty thousand Mohammedans and Hindoos, to be rendered familiar; but the reader should know how it has happened that the sovereign of that city has, for eight or nine hundred years, been regarded in a peculiar sense as the autocrat of Hindostan, the one man before whom millions of natives have been wont to bend the knee, or rather to lie prostrate in abject submission.

What India was before the arrival of the Mussulmans, need not be told here at any length. We know, in truth, very little on that matter. It was from the days of the first Moslem conqueror that the greatness of Delhi began. Long before the Christian era, Arab merchants brought rich spiceries from Sinde and Malabar, and sold them to Phœnician merchants, who conveyed them on laden camels by way of Petra to the shores of the Mediterranean. Other portions of Indian merchandise were carried up the Persian Gulf and the Euphrates to a point whence they were transported westward to Aleppo or Antioch—a route almost identical with that advocated in the present day for a Euphrates railway and a Euphrates telegraph. The Greeks derived all their knowledge of Indian commodities through the Phœnicians; while their information concerning the country itself was obtained from the Persians, who at one time held sway as far as the Indus. The expedition of Alexander the Great into India, about 326 B.C., first gave the Greeks a personal knowledge of this wonderful land; and many successors of the great Macedonian added to the then existing amount of information concerning the tribes, the productions, the customs of the region beyond the Indus. Consequent on those discoveries, the merchants of the newly founded city of Alexandria gradually obtained a command of the trade with India: bringing the rich produce of the East by ship to Berenice on the Red Sea, and then transporting it overland to Alexandria. The commodities thus imported were chiefly precious stones, spices, perfumes, and silks; and during some centuries the Roman Empire was drained of much specie to pay for these imports. Alexandrians were the principal merchants who furnished the nations of Europe with Indian articles till the discovery of the passage round the Cape of Good Hope by Vasco de Gama in 1498. The western nations of Asia, however, continued to be supplied principally by the merchants of Basra or Bussorah, a very flourishing commercial city near the point where the Euphrates empties itself into the Persian Gulf; and there was also an extensive caravan-trade from Northern India through Northern Persia to the Caspian and the Black Sea. The discovery of the Cape of Good Hope route naturally attracted the attention of the maritime nations of Europe towards India, followed by the settlement of Portuguese and Dutch traders on the coast, and ultimately by the wonderful rise of British power in those regions through the instrumentality of the East India Company.

But although trading instincts thus laid India open to the commercial dealings of merchants, and to the cupidity of European princes, it was not until modern erudition had been applied to the subject that the true history of the land of the Hindoos became at all known. Scholars found, when they had mastered the Sanscrit or sacred language of that people, that a wonderful mine of information was thrown open to them. They ascertained that the nation, whatever it may have been called, from which the genuine Hindoos are descended, must at some period have inhabited the central plains of Asia, whence they migrated into the northern parts of India; that for at least a thousand years before the Christian era, great and powerful empires existed in Hindostan, which made considerable progress in knowledge, civilisation, and literature; that Southern India, or the Deccan, was conquered and peopled by the Hindoos at a much later date than the rest; that Buddhism, the religion of the earlier inhabitants, was overruled and driven out by Brahminism or Hindooism in the fifth century of our era; and that for five centuries longer, the Hindoos were the true rulers of this much-coveted land.

It was, however, as has been already implied, only with the arrival of the Mohammedans that the course of Indian history took that turn which is now interesting to us, especially in connection with the city of Delhi.

The year 1000 was marked by the invasion of India by Mahmoud of Ghiznee, a Tatar sovereign who held sway among the chieftains of Afghanistan. He defeated the rajah of Lahore at Peshawur; then penetrated beyond the Sutlej; and returned laden with spoil. In a second expedition he conquered Moultan; in a third, he reconquered the same city after a revolt. A fourth expedition found Mahmoud opposed by a confederacy of all the sovereigns of Northern India, who, seeing a common danger, resolved to unite for a common cause; they were rapidly gaining an advantage over him, when the sudden fright of an elephant induced a panic in the Hindoo army, and left the victory to Mahmoud, who returned to Ghiznee still more richly laden with booty than ever. For a time, the Hindoo king who reigned over the region of which Delhi was the chief city, managed to ward off the hostility of the great invader; but taking offence at a departure from neutrality during one of the later expeditions, Mahmoud captured that city, and returned to Ghiznee with forty thousand prisoners. For thirty years did these raids and spoliations continue. The most celebrated next to that which resulted in the sack of Delhi, was the expedition intended for the destruction of the Hindoo temple of Somnauth in Gujerat; a temple which, if native annals are to be believed, had fifty thousand worshippers, and was endowed with a revenue of two thousand villages; which had two thousand Brahmins officiating as priests, five hundred daughters of noble Hindoos as dancing-girls, three hundred musicians; and the sandal-wood gates of which were the theme of magniloquence from the pen of an English governor-general eight centuries afterwards.* Mahmoud broke all the idols, and carried off countless treasures to Ghiznee.

From that time to the period of the rise of British power, the Mohammedans never lost the hold upon India, however much it may have been shaken by occasional success on the part of the Hindoos; nor did they ever cease to regard Delhi as the chief Indian city. Although Mahmoud made twelve expeditions across the Indus, the object was mainly booty, rather than permanent settlement. His successors, however, established a regular government in the Punjaub, and in the region thence eastward to Delhi. The Ghiznee dynasty was put an end to in the year 1184, when it was overcome by the Seljuks; and in 1193 Delhi was formally appointed capital of the Moslem sovereigns of India. After a succession of rebellions and murders, exhibiting all the hideous features of Oriental politics, the Seljuk dynasty fell to pieces in the year 1289. Then arose a third Mohammedan dynasty, that of the Afghans or Patans, who came like all the other conquerors of India from the north-west, and who like them coveted Delhi as their capital. For about a century did these Patan emperors reign, continually struggling against Hindoo rajahs on the one hand, and Mussulman adventurers on the other.

It was in the year 1398 that Tamerlane—familiar to all school-boys in England by the famous name of Timour the Tatar—first set foot in India, and laid the foundation of the Mogul dynasty. Properly speaking, he was not a true Mogul, but belonged to the rival Tatar nation of Turcomans; nevertheless the line of emperors to which he gave origin has always been known as the Mogul dynasty. He was a ruthless conqueror, who, having ravaged all Central Asia from the Black Sea to the Chinese frontier, turned his attention towards India. He crossed the Indus at Attock, went to Moultan, and extended his march to Delhi, wading through Hindoo blood, which he shed without resistance and almost without cause. The native annalists record how he put a hundred thousand beings to death in the great city; how he caused himself to be proclaimed Emperor or Great Mogul of India; how he departed suddenly to end his days on the other side of the Indus; and how Delhi mourned for many a year over its miseries. No pen can describe what India suffered during the next century and a quarter, with a Mogul emperor at Delhi, constantly fighting with the Mohammedan chieftains who resisted his authority.

The long but often broken line of wretched despots need not be enumerated here; a few landmarks of great names—Baber, Akbar, Jehanghire,

* When General Nott returned to India after his victorious campaign in Afghanistan in 1842, he brought away with him the gates of Somnauth, which, according to the tradition, had remained at Ghiznee since the days of Mahmoud. This and other trophies gave occasion to an address from Lord Ellenborough to the native princes of India, conceived in somewhat bombastic language, in which the recapture of the gates was characterised as an achievement 'avenging the insult of eight hundred years.' The chiefs and princes of Sirhind, Rajwarra, Malwah, and Gujerat, were enjoined to transmit, 'with all honour,' the gates to Somnauth. The address was much ridiculed in England; but those on the spot believed it to be calculated to make an impression on the natives. The home government, however, would not permit the gates—even if the genuine sandal-wood originals, which is not free from doubt—to be sent to the still-existing temple of Somnauth; they considered such an act would identify the Company injuriously with one of the two great parties of religionists in India, and deeply offend the other.

…hjehan, Aurungzebe, Nadir Shah—will furnish … that is needful for our present purpose.

Baber—or, in more majestic form, Zahireddin …hammed Baber—a descendant of Tamerlane, …s the first really great Mohammedan emperor … Delhi, the first Mogul who regarded his subjects … any other light than as a prey to be spoliated. …ntering his power at Delhi, he extended it …stward to the mouth of the Ganges; and …hough, in his short reign of four years, from …26 to 1530, constantly engaged in military …peditions, he nevertheless found time to culti…te the arts of peace, and to attend to whatever …peared calculated to promote the prosperity of …s empire. In blood-shedding, he was scarcely …rpassed by his predecessor Tamerlane: indeed …is was a propensity among all the Tatar chief…ains of those times. When his warlike and angry …assions were not excited, Baber could, however, …ome forth in a very different light, as a kind and …rgiving man, one fond of friends and friendship, …nd not without a tinge of poetry in his tastes. He …as a man of business, who attended personally …o the affairs of government, and passed fewer …ours in sensual idleness than is customary with …riental princes. With the Hindoos he had little …rouble; their national character was by this time much broken; the rapid succession of reigning families had inured them to change; and they had imbibed a feeling of horror and dismay from the atrocities to which the various Moslem conquerors had subjected them. When opposition to his progress had once ceased in India, he became an altered man. He made or improved roads; established serais or resting-places for travellers at suitable distances; caused the land to be measured, in order to fix taxation by equitable adjustment; planted gardens, and introduced many trees and plants until then unknown in India; established a regular post from Agra, through Delhi, Lahore, and Peshawur, to Cabool; and wrought many improvements in the city of Delhi.

Akbar, unquestionably the wisest and greatest prince who ever ruled India—a prince who was really a benefactor to his people—was the grandson of Baber. Becoming emperor of Delhi in 1556, he established the Mogul dynasty on a firmer basis than it had before occupied. The native Hindoos enjoyed, under him, greater prosperity than they had ever experienced since the first invasion of the Mohammedans. He was distinguished by a spirit of toleration and a love of justice; and the memory of his virtues is to this day treasured up by the Hindoos as well as the Mussulmans of India. As the worshippers of Islam had, by the time of Akbar, fallen out much among themselves, in various parts of Asia, the Mogul Moslems of India gradually became weaned from sympathy with the rest, and prepared for more thorough amalgamation with the Hindoos than had ever before been possible. If not an amalgamation by family ties, it was at least an incorporation by civil and social usages; and thus it is that from the time of Akbar may be dated the remarkable mixture of Mohammedans and Hindoos in so many towns of India. Ambitious chieftains might continue to struggle for supremacy; but the populace of the two religions began to wish rather to trade together than to exterminate each other. Akbar had the genius to see the full force of this tendency, and the honesty to encourage it. He never crushed those whom he conquered; but invited all alike, Hindoos as well as Mohammedans, to settle down as peaceful citizens, assured that they would receive equal justice from him regardless of their religious differences. He placed natives of both races in offices of trust; he abolished the capitation-tax on infidels; he forbade the degradation of war-prisoners to the position of slaves; he abrogated such of the Hindoo laws as were most repulsive to reason or humanity, without being vital parts of their religion; he discouraged fanaticism among those of his own faith; he encouraged trade and commerce; he reduced taxation; and he kept a strict watch over the conduct of the officers of his government. The mildness of his character, his strict impartiality to the different classes of his subjects, the magnanimity which he shewed to his enemies, and his great personal courage are mentioned with praise even by the Jesuits, who visited India during his reign. Well did this eminent man, during his long reign of forty-nine years, deserve the title of Akbar the Great; and natural was it that his subjects should look up with reverence to Delhi, the centre and seat of his empire. His reign, both in its beginning and its end, was almost exactly contemporaneous with that of Queen Elizabeth in England.

Jehanghire, a far inferior prince to Akbar, succeeded him in 1605, and soon became involved in troubles. The Uzbeks obtained possession of his dominions in Cabool; the King of Persia took Candahar from him; the Afghans revolted from his rule; the Hindoo Rajpoots commenced their struggles for independence; and, at a later date, his son Shahjehan rebelled against him. Nevertheless, Jehanghire, judged by an oriental standard, was not a bad ruler of Hindostan. The country enjoyed considerable prosperity under him; literature was extensively cultivated; many new cities were built; the Hindoo religion experienced even greater toleration than in the reign of Akbar; and he gave a courteous reception to Sir Thomas Roe, sent on an embassy from England to the Great Mogul. He was, however, a strange being. In a fit of anger against certain rebels, he caused several hundreds of them to be impaled, and placed in a row leading out of the Lahore gate at Delhi; and he himself rode past them on an elephant, 'to receive the obeisance of his friends.' His native ferocity also shone out, in his causing one of his principal councillors to be sewed up in the hide of a newly flayed ox, and thrown into the street; the hide, shrinking in the heat of the sun, compressed him to death; but as the compression came too soon to satisfy the savage feelings of the monarch, he caused the next victim, when similarly incased, to be sprinkled with water occasionally, to prolong the torture. One of the most remarkable circumstances in the career of Jehanghire was the influence gradually acquired over him by his Sultaness Nurmahal, the 'light of the palace,' whose name became changed to Nurjehan, the 'light of the world;' her exquisite beauty, wit, and accomplishments, won the love of the monarch; and as she was in mind and heart far his superior, her power over him was often exerted for good purposes.

Shahjehan, an ungrateful son to Jehanghire, was destined to be, in turn, the victim of his own son Aurungzebe. He was an emperor from 1627 to 1659, and then a miserable uncrowned captive for seven years longer. He attacked all the neighbouring princes whose dominions or wealth he coveted; and blinded or murdered all his relations whose ambition he dreaded. And yet, amid his atrocities, he was a man of much ability. Delhi, Agra, and other cities, benefited by his rule. The internal government of his kingdom was very complete. The great mosque at Delhi, and the Taj Mahal at Agra, which rose at his command, are, to this day, objects of admiration to the natives of India. Though it may, to English minds, have been a waste of public money to spend six millions sterling on the far-famed peacock's throne; yet, as all his establishments were formed on a scale of great magnificence, and as numerous other cities and towns throughout the Empire vied with the splendour of Delhi and Agra—there is evidence that the Mogul and his dominions must have owned vast wealth. He possessed both taste and financial tact; and thus, with all his atrocities, Shahjehan left behind him a full treasury and a splendid and prosperous empire.

Aurungzebe, the last Mogul who maintained the real greatness of the native court of Delhi, became emperor in 1659, by an act of violence against his royal parent. He captured the cities of Hyderabad, Bejapore, and Golconda, and extended his dominions nearly to the limits of the Carnatic. There were, however, the germs of mischief perceptible in his reign: the warlike Hindoo tribe of Mahrattas rose into note; and though they were frequently defeated in the plains by the troops of Aurungzebe, he was unable to subdue the country inhabited by these mountaineers. Sevajee, the founder of the Mahratta empire, gradually conquered the greater part of the Deccan; he died in 1682, and his son, Sambajee, was put to a cruel death by Aurungzebe in 1689; but the Mogul emperors of the north could never afterwards wholly subdue the Mahratta rajah of the south. Aurungzebe was illiberal towards his Hindoo subjects; and this circumstance threw them into closer sympathy than would otherwise have been produced with the rude Mahratta mountaineers. He was not without ability; but he had neither the wisdom nor the justice to maintain his wide-spreading empire in a state of greatness; and when he died in 1707, he the Mogul power at Delhi much weaker than found it at the period of his seizure of crown.

Nadir Shah, although never emperor of Del must be named here as one who contributed the crumbling of the Mogul dynasty. This m one of the grand barbarians whom Central A has so often sent forth, was the son of a sheep-sk cap-maker. He became a soldier of fortune; th the leader of a band of robbers; then governor Khorassan; then Shah of Persia; then a formi able opponent of the Turks and the Afghan and then a scourge to India. While devastati Afghanistan in 1738, he required of the Emperor Delhi that none of the Afghans should find shelt in his (the Mogul's) dominions; but as no attentic was paid to his demands, he marched into Hi dostan in the following year, and entered Del with an enormous army on the 8th of March. H seized the whole of the vast treasures which ha been amassed in the course of nearly two centuri by the Mogul monarchs. The citizens not bein so submissive as he wished, he ordered a genera massacre. His commands were only too we obeyed; for, from sunrise till noon, the inhabitant were slaughtered by his soldiers without distinctio of sex or age. At the earnest intercession of th emperor, Nadir ordered the butchery to be stopped Where the estimates of human beings murdered varies from 8000 to 150,000, it is clear that no trustworthy data are obtainable; but it is unquestionable that Delhi suffered immensely, both in its population and its wealth. The ruthless despoiler not only refrained from claiming the crown of Hindostan, but he did not make any conquests whatever: he came simply as a Shah of Persia on an errand of vengeance; he remained two months at Delhi; and then departed westward, carrying with him treasures that have been variously estimated at from thirty to seventy millions sterling.

The Delhi monarchs no longer need or deserve our attention; they had fallen from their high estate, and were forced to struggle constantly for the maintenance of their authority. A number of obscure names meet our view after the time of Aurungzebe—Shah Alum, Moez-Eddin, Furrucksir, Mohammed Shah, Ahmed Shah, Alumghir, and Shah Alum II.: each more powerless than the preceding. Now they were attacked by the warlike Mahrattas; now by the Rajpoots, a military Hindoo tribe which had never been wholly subdued by the Moslems; now by the Sikhs, a kind of Hindoo dissenters, brave and independent in their bearing; now by the Rohillas, an Afghan race, who effected a settlement in the very neighbourhood of Delhi; now by many of the Mohammedan nawabs or viceroys, who, like other Asiatic viceroys in parallel circumstances, were willing to rise on the fall of their masters; now by the competing sons and nephews who surrounded every emperor; and now—more striking in its onsequences than all the rest—by the ever-ncroaching British.

Nevertheless, amid all this decadence of Mogul power, the natives of Hindostan never ceased to ook up to the emperor as the centre of power, to Delhi as the centre of nationality. Their traditions old them of Mahmoud, of Tamerlane, of Baber, of he great Akbar, of Jehanghire, of Shahjehan, of Aurungzebe; and although ruthless barbarities were connected with the names of many of these rulers, there was still a grandeur that impressed the imagination. The Hindoos, it is true, had their sacred associations connected with Benares rather than with Delhi; but their distinct nationality had been almost stamped out of them during eight centuries of Mohammedan supremacy; and they, like the rest, held in reverence the city where the peacock's throne had glittered on the world.

By what strange steps the descendants of the Great Mogul became pensioners of the East India Company, will be explained presently; but it will be well first to describe Delhi itself.

This far-famed city is situated on the river Jumna, about five hundred miles by road above Allahabad, where the Jumna flows into the Ganges, and nine hundred by road from Calcutta. In the opposite direction, Delhi is nearly four hundred miles from Lahore, and six or seven hundred from Peshawur—so great are the distances between the chief towns in India: distances that terribly hamper the operations of a British army during any sudden emergency. Striking as Delhi may be, it presents but a faint approach in splendour to the city of past days, the home of the grand old Moguls. Of the original Delhi, the natives give the most extravagant account; they even run back to a period three thousand years before the Christian era for its foundation. All that is certain, however, is, that Inderput or Indraprestha, the name of the old city, was the capital of a Hindoo kingdom under a rajah, long before its conquest by the Mohammedans. When or how the original city went to ruin, is not exactly known; but modern Delhi owes its chief adornments to Shahjehan. A traveller from the south or Agra direction is struck with the evidences of ruined Inderput before he sees anything of modern Delhi. 'Everywhere throughout the plain rise shapeless half-ruined obelisks, the relics of massive Patan architecture, their bases buried under heaps of ruins bearing a dismal growth of thorny shrubs. Everywhere we tread on overthrown walls. Brick mosaics mark the ground-plan of the humbler dwellings of the poorer classes. Among the relics of a remote age, are occasionally to be seen monuments of light and elegant style of architecture, embellished with brilliant colours, gilt domes, and minarets incased in enamelled tiles.' Some travellers have asserted that they have traced these ruins thirty miles along the Jumna; but these cannot all have been the ruins of one city. Approaching the present Delhi, it is seen that the ruins are spread over a plain, in the midst of which the city is situated; and they give place, after a time, to the tasteful villas of the Europeans who exercise civil or military control within Delhi. Most of these villas are on the site of the once famous garden of Shalimar. On the northern side of the city, close under a ridge of sandstone rocks called the Mijnoon Pahar, are the cantonments—an alternation of bungalows, huts, and groups of trees.

So much for the environs. Although not entitled to take rank among the great cities of the earth, Delhi is nevertheless a considerable place, for it is seven miles in circumference. The Jumna bounds it on the east, while a lofty crenellated wall, of horseshoe shape, completes the boundary on the other sides. This wall has been an object of much attention at different times. As built by Shahjehan, it possessed little strength. When the British obtained ascendency over the city in 1803, the wall was found to be in a ruinous state, without other flanking defences than small circular bastions placed at intervals; the ditch was imperfect; there was scarcely any vestige of a glacis or exterior slope; and the crumbling ruins of dilapidated buildings had been allowed to accumulate all round the wall. Captains Hutchinson and Smith, of the Bengal engineers, were thereupon deputed to restore and strengthen the fortifications. It was determined to establish a series of bastions, with faces and flanks to defend the curtain or plain wall, and to mount them with heavy artillery. The walls were repaired; and to shield them from escalade, they were protected, especially on the river-front, with beams of timber, the sharpened ends of which were pointed at an acute angle downward into the ditch. The ditch was cleared out and deepened; the glacis was made to cover, in some degree, the scarp of the wall; the ground outside was cleared to some distance of ruins and houses; and the ravines were filled up to check the approach of marauding horsemen. To prepare for a rising within the city as well as an attack from without, detached martello towers were constructed, entirely separate from the walls, and accessible from them only by drawbridges; each tower had a gun mounted on a pivot, so that in the event of a tumult in the city, the towers might be occupied by artillerymen, the drawbridges drawn up, and the guns swiveled round to pour a fire upon the insurgents. The gateways of the city were strengthened; outworks were provided in front of some of them, while others were provided with guard-houses and *places-d'armes*. At a much later date—in 1838—Lord Auckland caused the walls and towers to be strengthened, and one of the new defences, called the Wellesley Bastion, to be reconstructed.

In what relation these defences stood to a British besieging force in 1857, will remain to be told in a future chapter: we proceed here with the description of the city.

Delhi has seven gates on the land-side, named, respectively, the Lahore, Ajmeer, Turcoman,

BIRD'S-EYE VIEW OF DELHI.—From a Coloured Lithograph by A. Maclure: taken from original native Drawings.

Cabool, Mohur or Moree, Cashmere, and Agra Gates; while along the river-front are four others, the Rajghat, Negumbod, Lall, and Kaila Gates. Some little diversity is shown by travellers in giving these names; and some make the number of gates twelve instead of eleven. The Cashmere Gate is provided with casemated or shot-proof chambers, for the accommodation of a city-guard. A bridge of boats over the Jumna connects Delhi with the road leading north-eastward to Meerut, and the chief magazine is, or was, between the centre of the city and this bridge. Eight of the defences on the walls are called the Shah Bastion, Burn Bastion, Garstin Bastion, College Bastion, Ochterlony Bastion, Lake Bastion, Wellesley Bastion, and Nawab Bastion—names obviously derived, in most instances, from military officers engaged in the Company's service. Strictly speaking, the wall does not quite surround the city; for on one side it abuts on a small branch of the river, where there is a short bridge across to the old fort of Selimgurh, built in a very heavy style by one of the early emperors. Entirely outside the wall, north of the city, is a custom-house, which affords a curious commentary on the relations existing between the civil and military officers of the Company. It was first built by a medical officer, then sold to the Company for a treasury, and then adapted as a custom-house. The engineers wanted to get rid of this building, as an obstruction to their plan of defences, in the same way as they had swept away numerous outhouses, bazaars, and ruins; but the civilians prevented this; and so the custom-house remained till 1857, when the building and its garden became a ready prey to the rebels.

The city, considered without relation to its defences, presents many of those features so familiar in oriental towns. As seen by the approaching traveller, few of the dwelling-houses peep above the ramparts; but the Jumna Musjid or principal mosque, the turreted and battlemented palace, the minarets, and other public buildings, combine to form a majestic picture; while the graceful acacias and lofty date-trees bending over the ramparts, and the grouping of tombs with sombre foliage on the glacis, add new features to the scene. Arrived within the city, it is seen that the streets are mostly narrow. The chief exception is that of a handsome street running south from the palace to the Agra Gate: three quarters of a mile long by a hundred and fifty feet wide. This street has, therefore, length and breadth enough to afford space for much splendour; but the Delhians have not fully availed themselves of this opportunity, for they have built blocks of small houses in the midst of this street, analogous in some degree to the 'Middle Rows' known to the inhabitants of London. Another large street, similarly shorn of its due dignity, runs from the palace westward to the Lahore Gate. Both streets are, however, enlivened by raised water-courses flowing in channels of red stone—part of a great work begun and finished by the Company, for supplying Delhi with water.

The glories of Delhi are the great mosque and the still greater palace. The Jumma Musjid, situated in the centre of the city, is one of those buildings to which Mohammedans point with pride: famous not only in Hindostan, but all over Southern and Central Asia. It presents to the eye an open court on an elevated platform, nearly five hundred feet square; in the middle of which is a marble fountain for the ablutions necessary in the ceremonials of Islamism. On three sides of this court are open arcades and octagonal pavilions; while on the fourth side is the mosque, a structure of great splendour approached by a magnificent flight of marble steps. White marble cornices inlaid in black marble with inscriptions from the Koran; walls, ceilings, and pavements of the same delicate materials; beautiful domes and lofty minarets—all combine to render the Jumma Musjid a truly gorgeous structure. The Emperor Shahjehan built it more than two centuries ago; and the British government gave orders in 1851 that it should be kept in repair.

But, splendid as is the Jumma Musjid, the imperial palace is still more striking—partly for what it is, but principally for what it has been. The palace stands between the two principal streets and the bridge. Some travellers have compared it with Windsor Castle, some with the Kremlin at Moscow, in size and majesty; while others insist that it has no compeer. Bishop Heber was quite enthusiastic in its praise. In the first place, the palatial buildings are surrounded by a wall to which there is certainly no parallel either at Windsor or at Moscow; it is of red granite, three quarters of a mile in circuit, nearly forty feet high, flanked with turrets and domes, and entered by two noble gates with barbicans. This wall is a grand work in itself, irrespective of the structures it encloses. Strictly speaking, the wall is only on three sides, the fourth abutting on a small branch of the Jumna, where occurs the short bridge crossing to the old fort of Selimgurh. The palace itself is entered by a series of beautiful gateways, all of red granite, and all sculptured with flowers and inscriptions from the Koran. The vaulted aisles and the open octagonal courts are spoken of by Heber with great admiration. The Dewani Khas, or private council-chamber, although allowed to become filthy by the visits of crows and kites, is an exquisite structure; it is a pavilion of white marble, supporting four cupolas of the same delicate material, with pillars and arches elaborately inlaid with gilt arabesques, flowers, and inscriptions. The garden around it has numerous white marble fountains of elegant form, and a small octagonal pavilion with bath-rooms, but all dirty and neglected. The Moti Musjid or private mosque for the court, and the Dewani-aum or public hall of audience, are, like the rest of the palace, ornate in marble and in carving, in sculpture and in inscriptions, in gilding and in inlaying; and, also like the rest, disfigured with filth—a combination truly oriental. In the hall of audience is, or was before the Revolt, the dais on which once stood the world-renowned peacock's throne, formed entirely of gold and jewels; and it was in this same chamber that the victorious Nadir Shah, by exchanging turbans with the defeated Mogul Mohammed Shah, obtained possession of a treasure almost as renowned as the peacock's throne itself—the *koh-i-noor*, the 'mountain of light,' the glorious diamond which, after various vicissitudes, now occupies a place in the regalia of Queen Victoria.

Passing from a scene of decayed splendour to one of living interest, we find Delhi to be inhabited by almost an exactly equal number of Hindoos and Mohammedans, eighty thousand of each; but it is essentially a Mohammedan city, the centre of their prestige and influence in India; and all the dwellings and public buildings of the Hindoos are indicative of a race locally less powerful. Besides the imperial palace just described, there is, about nine miles from Delhi, near an extraordinary pillar called the Kootub Minar, the country residence of the emperor, or, as it has been more customary in recent years to call him, the King. It is a large but paltry building, in an inferior style of Italian architecture, with a public road running through the very court-yard. Within the city a palace was built for the British resident a few years ago; and around this building a number of elegant houses have since been erected, by the natives as well as by the Europeans. Since the once great Mogul has been a king without a kingdom, a pensioned puppet of the Company, a potentate having nothing to employ his thoughts and his pension but political intrigue and sensual indulgence—the representative of England has been a sort of envoy or resident, ostensibly rendering honour to the Mogul, but really watching that he does no mischief, really insuring that he shall be a king only in name. But more on this point presently. The British civil staff in the city comprises—or did comprise before the Revolt—a resident or commissioner, a revenue collector, a magistrate, and other officials. There have usually been three regiments barracked or stationed in the cantonment; but the military importance of the place has been rather due to the fact that Delhi has been made a depôt for a large park of artillery—valuable enough when in the hands of the British, but a source of dismay and disaster when seized by mutineers.

Although this narrative has little to do with the merits or demerits of Delhi as a place of residence; yet, knowing something of what Englishmen and Englishwomen have had to bear when cooped up within a town or fort menaced by ruthless natives, every compatriot at home would like further to know in what way those trials are likely to have been aggravated by the incidents of climate. A lady-traveller furnishes a vivid picture of Delhi in a *hot-wind*, such as frequently visits towns in India during certain seasons of the year. 'Every article of furniture is burning to the touch; the hardest wood, if not well covered with blankets, will split with a report like that of a pistol; and linen taken from the drawers appears as if just removed from a kitchen-fire. The nights are terrible, every apartment being heated to excess. Gentlemen usually have their beds placed in the verandahs, or on the chubootiar or terrace on the top of the house: as they incur little risk in sleeping in the open air, at a season in which no dew falls, and when there is scarcely any variation in the thermometer. Tornadoes are frequent during these hot winds; while they last, the skies, though cloudless, are darkened with dust, the sun is obscured, and a London fog cannot more effectually exclude the prospect. The birds are dreadful sufferers at this season; their wings droop, and their bills are open as if gasping for breath; all animals are more or less affected.' Then, when this frightful heat is about to depart, ensues a storm, more terrible to look at, though easier to bear. 'The approaching strife is made known by a cloud, or rather a wall of dust, which appears at the extremity of the horizon, becoming more lofty as it advances. The air is sultry and still; for the wind, which is tearing up the sand as it rushes along, is not felt in front of the billowy masses, whose mighty ramparts gather strength as they spread. At length the plain is surrounded, and the sky becomes as murky as midnight. Then the thunder breaks forth, but its most awful peals are scarcely heard in the deep roar of the tempest; burst succeeds to burst, each more wild and furious than the former; the forked lightnings flash in vain, for the dust, which is as thick as snow, flings an impenetrable veil around them. The wind having spent itself in a final effort, suddenly subsides, and the dust is as speedily dispersed by torrents of rain, which in a very short time flood the whole country.' This is the last agony of the storm; after which the temperature lowers and nature becomes more tranquil.

Such is Delhi—such the city which, amid all its changes of fortune, has for so many centuries been an object of reverential affection to the natives of Hindostan. When the disorganised regiments from Meerut entered the imperial gates, they found an aged mogul or king, with sons and grandsons, courtiers and retainers, willing to make him a stepping-stone to their own advancement. Who this king was, and how he had come into that position, may soon be told.

Precisely a century ago, when Clive was preparing to revenge the atrocities connected with the Black Hole at Calcutta, the Delhi empire was rapidly losing all its power; the northern and northwestern provinces were seized upon by the Afghans and the Sikhs; the Rajpoots extended their dominions as far as Ajmeer; and the Emperor Alumghir was too weak to protect his capital from the monstrous barbarities of the fghan insurgents. The next emperor, Shah lum II., unable either to repel invaders or to ontrol his rebellious nawabs, virtually yielded the rapidly rising power of the East India ompany. He signed a treaty with Clive in 765, involving mutual obligations; he was to ield to the British certain provinces, and to ward to a resident appointed from Calcutta considerable power at the court of Delhi; while the ritish were to protect him from his numerous ssailants, and to secure him a pension of £260,000 er annum, which, with other sources of wealth, rought the degenerate descendant of the Moguls early half a million annually. Troubled by the Mahrattas on one side, by the Rohillas on a econd, and by the Nawab of Oude on a third, he paralysed emperor became so bewildered that he knew not which way to turn. About 1788 a Rohilla chieftain suddenly entered Delhi, and put out the eyes of the unfortunate emperor with a poniard; then the Mahrattas defeated this chieftain, seized the capital, and reduced Shah Alum himself to a mere puppet. During this anarchy the British in India were so fully occupied in other quarters, that they could not make a resolute demonstration in the centre of the once great Mogul empire; but in the year 1803 all was prepared by Lord Lake for a resolute attempt to break down the Mahratta and Rohilla power in the north, and to insure that the emperor should have no other master than the Company—a kindness, the motives for which will not bear very close scrutiny. The battle of Delhi, fought on the 11th of September 1803, opened the gates of the city to the British, and relieved the emperor from his thraldom. A reverse had very nearly occurred, however. While Lake was reposing after his victory, Holkar, the great Mahratta chief, leaving his cavalry to attract the notice of the British at Muttra, suddenly appeared before Delhi with a force of 20,000 infantry and 100 guns. The garrison comprised only two battalions and four companies of native troops, with a few irregular horse; and as some of these deserted at the first affright, there were left only 800 men and 11 guns to defend a city seven miles in circuit. By unwearied patience and daring intrepidity, however, Colonel Burn, who was military commandant in the city at the time, and who was ably assisted by Colonel Ochterlony and Lieutenant Rose, succeeded in repelling all the attacks of the Mahrattas; and Holkar retired discomfited.

From that day—from the 16th of October 1803, until the 11th of May 1857—an enemy was never seen before the gates of Delhi; a day had never passed during which the city had been other than the capital of a state governed nominally by a Mogul king, but really by a British resident. Shah Alum, after thirty years of a troubled life, was vouchsafed three years of peace, and died in 1806—a pensioner of that great abstraction, that inscrutable mystery to the millions of Hindostan, the 'Coompanee Bahadoor,' the Most Honourable Company.

The behaviour of the Company's servants towards the feeble descendant of the Great Moguls was, until about thirty years ago, the most absurd mockery. They took away all his real power, and then offered him a privilege, the least exercise of which, if he had ventured on such a thing, they would at once have resented. Shah Akbar, who succeeded his old, blind, feeble father, Shah Alum, in 1806, became at once a pensioner. He was really king, not over a kingdom, but only over the twelve thousand inmates of the imperial palace at Delhi, his relations and retainers—the whole of whom he supported on a pension of about a hundred thousand pounds per annum, paid by the Company. Hindoo and Mussulman, notwithstanding his fallen state, alike looked up to him as the only representative of the ancient glories of India; numerous princes received their solemn and legal investiture from him; and until 1827, the Company acquired no new province *without applying for his nominal sanction and official firman.* He was permitted to bestow dresses of honour on native princes at their accession to the musnud, as a token of suzerainty; and the same ceremony was attempted by him occasionally towards the governor-general. At length, under the rule of Earl Amherst in 1827, it was determined to put an end to a system which was either a mockery, or an incentive to disaffection on the part of the Delhians. The pension to the king was increased to a hundred and fifty thousand pounds, but the supposed or implied vassalage of the East India Company to the nominal Padishah or Mohammedan ruler of India was brought to an end; Shah Akbar being, from that date, powerless beyond the walls of his palace—except as the representative, the symbol, of something great, still venerated by the natives.

Palace intrigues have not been wanting at Delhi during the twenty years that preceded the Revolt; and these intrigues have borne some relation to the state of disaffection that accompanied that outbreak. Shah Akbar reigned, if reigning it can be called, from 1806 until 1837. He wished to be succeeded by his second son, Shah-zadah Jehanghire; but the British authorities insisted that the succession should go, as before, to the eldest son; and consequently Meerza Abu Zuffur became emperor on Shah Akbar's death in 1837, under the title of Mahomed Suraj-u-deen Shah Ghazee. This monarch, again, exhibited the same distrust of the next heir that is so often displayed in Oriental countries; the British authorities were solicited to set aside the proper heir to the peacock's throne, in favour of a younger prince who possessed much influence in the zenana. Again was the request refused; and the palace at Delhi was known to have been a focus of discontent and intrigue for some time previous to the Revolt. The mode in which the Marquis of Dalhousie treated these matters, in his minute of 1856, has already been adverted to; but it may be well to repeat his words here, to shew the exact state of Delhi palace-politics at that time. 'Seven years ago [that is, in 1849], the heir-apparent to the King of Delhi died. He was the last of the race who had been born in the purple. The Court of Directors was accordingly advised to decline to recognise any other heir-apparent, and to permit the kingly title to fall into abeyance upon the death of the present king, who even then was a very aged man. The Honourable Court accordingly conveyed to the government of India authority to terminate the dynasty of Timour, whenever the reigning king should die. But as it was found that, although the Honourable Court had consented to the measure, it had given its consent with great reluctance, I abstained from making use of the authority which had been given to me. The grandson of the king was recognised as heir-apparent; but only on condition that he should quit the palace in Delhi, in order to reside in the palace at the Kootub; and that he should, as king, receive the governor-general of India at all times on terms of perfect equality.' It was therefore simply a suspension of the absolute extinction of the kingly title at Delhi: a suspension dictated, apparently, by the existence of a little more hesitation in the court of directors, than in the bold governor-general.

The king who occupied the nominal throne of Delhi at the time of the Revolt was neither better nor worse than the average of his predecessors. pensioned prince with no responsibilities, he a true Oriental sensualist, and had become almost imbecile old man between eighty ninety years of age. Nevertheless, for the reas already more than once stated, he was inves with a certain greatness in the eyes of the nati of Hindostan; and Delhi was still their gr city. Hindoos, Afghans, Patans, Seljuks, Rajpo Tatars, Moguls, Persians, Rohillas, Mahratt Sikhs—all had left their impress upon the capit and with one or other of these, the millions India had sympathies either of race or of cre Even to the hour of the outbreak, the king w approached with the reverence due to royalty. the ruined paradise of Oriental sensualism, t great palace of Delhi, 'the house of Tamerlane st revelled in unchecked vileness. The royal famil consisting of many hundreds—idle, dissolute, sham less, too proud or too effeminate for military servi —lived in entire dependence on the king's allow ance. For their amusement were congregated fro all India the most marvellous jugglers, the mo cunning bird-tamers and snake-charmers, the mo fascinating dancing-girls, the most skilled Persia musicians. Though the population was exactl balanced between Mohammedans and Hindoos, i was the Moslem who here reigned supreme.*

* *Quarterly Review*, No. 204.

Howdah of an Indian Prince.

King of Delhi.

CHAPTER V.

THE EVENTFUL ESCAPES FROM DELHI.

REMEMBERING that in the month of May 1857 there was a very aged king living in the great palace at Delhi; that the heir-apparent, his grandson, resided in the palace of Kootub Minar, eight or nine miles from the city; that the Moslem natives still looked up to the king with a sort of reverence; and that his enormous family had become dissatisfied with the prospective extinction of the kingly power and name—remembering these facts, the reader will be prepared to follow the fortunes of the Meerut mutineers, and to understand on what grounds the support of the royal family was counted upon.

The distance to be passed over being forty miles, it was not till the day after the outbreak at Meerut—namely, the 11th of May—that the three mutinous regiments reached Delhi. The telegraphic wires were so soon cut, and the dáks so effectually interrupted, that it is doubtful at what hour, and to what extent, the transactions at Meerut became known to Brigadier Graves, who commanded at Delhi. The position of that officer was well calculated to produce uneasiness in his mind at a time of insubordination and distrust; for he had no European regiments with him. The garrison consisted of the 38th, 54th, and 74th native regiments, and a battery of native artillery; the English comprised only a few officers and sergeants of those regiments, the various servants of the Company, and private traders within the city. The 54th and 74th had not up to that time shewn any strong symptoms of disaffection; but the 38th, which had achieved a kind of triumph over the Marquis of Dalhousie in 1852, in reference to the proposed expedition to Pegu, had ever since displayed somewhat of a boastful demeanour, a pride of position and influence. The three regiments and the artillery had their regular quarters in the cantonment, about two miles north of the city: sending into Delhi such companies or drafts as were necessary to man the bastions, towers, magazine, &c. As the river Hindoun, a tributary to the Jumna, crosses the Meerut and Delhi road near Furrucknuggur, about ten miles from Delhi, it might be a fair problem whether the mutineers could have been met and frustrated at the crossing of that river: the solution of this problem, however, would necessarily depend partly on the time available, and partly on the prudence of marching the Delhi force across the Jumna at such a period, placing a broad river between the brigadier and a city likely to be readily affected by notions of disaffection. Whether influenced by want of time, want of due information, or by strategical reasons, no such movement was made by him. The mutineers would obviously cross the Jumna by the bridge of boats, and would then pass southwestward into the city, or northwestward towards the cantonment, or possibly both. A necessity arose, therefore, for adopting defensive measures in two different quarters; and as the non-military portion of the European inhabitants, especially women and children, would be a source of much anxiety at such a time, the brigadier made arrangements to accommodate them, or some of them, in the Flagstaff Tower, a strong circular brick building on the heights near the cantonment, a mile and a half north of the nearest or Cashmere Gate of the city. The military commandant ordered out his regiments, drew forth his guns, and delivered a pithy address, in which he exhorted the sepoys to stand true to their colours, and repel the mutineers as soon as they should appear. His address was received with cheers, the insincerity of which was soon to be made manifest.

So many Europeans were cut and shot down at Delhi on this day of misery, and so precipitate was the escape of others, that not one single person was in a position to give a connected narrative of the dismal work. Startling, indeed, were the sights and the sounds which riveted the attention of the European inhabitants on this morning. A peaceful Sunday had passed over in its ordinary way; for none knew what were the deeds being perpetrated at Meerut. The native troops, it is true, were to some extent cognizant of that movement, for the insurgents had unquestionably arranged the outlines of a plan; and some of the European officers at Delhi had observed, not without uneasiness, a change in the behaviour of the sepoys at that station; nevertheless, to the Europeans generally, this social avalanche was a wholly unexpected visitation. Resistance was needed from those too powerless to resist effectually; and flight was the only resource for many too weak, too young, too sick, to bear up under such a necessity. All the letters, since made public, relating to the sad events of that day, tend to shew how little the European inhabitants of Delhi looked forward to such scenes. One lady, after a hurried retreat, said: 'We can hardly ourselves believe how we escaped. The way in which poor helpless men, women, and children were slaughtered without a moment's warning was most dreadful. We were surprised on the morning of the 11th of May (baby's birthday) by a party of mutineers from Meerut.' It is evident that 'baby's birthday' had dawned with much happier thoughts in the poor mother's mind, than were destined to remain there. Another lady, with her husband and child, were just about to leave Delhi for Calcutta; their dâk-passage was paid, and their travelling arrangements nearly completed. Suddenly a messenger hastened to their home to announce that the Meerut mutineers had crossed the bridge, and were within the city walls; and very soon afterwards, fearful sights told them that immediate escape was the only mode of saving their lives. So it was all over the city; terror and blood began the week, instead of peace and commerce.

The train of circumstances, as we have just said, having involved either the death or the hasty flight of nearly all the English within the city and the cantonment, it follows that the narrative of the day's ruthless work must be constructed from materials derived from various quarters, each supplying some of the links. When Major Abbott of the 74th found himself, on the next day, the senior officer among those who escaped to Meerut, he deemed it his duty to write an account to Major-general Hewett of the proceedings, so far as his sad tale could tell them. With this we begin.

The city, according to Major Abbott's narrative, was entered first by a small number of the mutinous 3d native cavalry, who crossed by the bridge of boats. While proceeding westward, they were met by a wing of the 54th native infantry, under the command of Colonel Ripley. But here a serious symptom at once presented itself; the 54th excused themselves from firing on the mutineers, on the plea of their muskets not being loaded; the guard of the 38th native infantry likewise refused, on some pretence, to fire; and thus the insurgents were enabled to enter the city by the Cashmere Gate. Captain Wallis, the field-officer of the week, on ordering the men of the mainguard at the gate to wheel up and fire, was met by insulting jeers; and he only desisted from importuning them when he found the work of death going on in other quarters. Six British officers of the 54th speedily fell, either killed or wounded—namely, Colonel Ripley, Captains Smith and Burrowes, Lieutenants Edwardes, Waterfield, and Butler. Major Abbott, willing to hope that his own regiment, the 74th, was still faithful, hastened to the cantonment, got as many of his men together as he could, and explained to them that the time was come to shew their fidelity as true soldiers; he announced his intention to go down to the Cashmere Gate, and called for volunteers to follow him. All for a while went favourably; the men stepped up to the front, loaded promptly, and marched off briskly after the major. On arriving at the Cashmere Gate, the 74th took possession of the mainguard, drawn up in readiness to receive any attack that might be made. Affairs remained quiet near that gate until towards three o'clock, when a heavy firing of guns, followed by a terrific explosion, announced that fighting had been going on near the magazine, and that a vast store of ammunition had been blown into the air. Whether this explosion had been caused by friends or enemies was not at first known; but the news soon spread abroad that a gallant artillery-officer, Lieutenant Willoughby, had adopted this terrible mode of preventing an enormous supply of warlike material from falling into the hands of the insurgents.

Before proceeding with the narrative of events in the city, it will be necessary to describe more particularly the occurrence last adverted to. There were two magazines, one near the cantonment, and a much larger and more important one in the city. It was the last named that became the scene of such desperate work. This magazine was an enclosure of considerable size, about midway between the Selimgurh Fort and the Cashmere Gate, almost close to the British residency. As a storehouse filled with a greater quantity of guns, gunpowder, and ammunition, than any other place in India, a struggle for its possession between the British and the insurgents became inevitable: hence it arose that the destruction of the magazine was an achievement worthy of record, no less for its vast importance in relation to the ultimate fate of the city, than for the cool heroism that marked its planning and execution. The magazine contained no less than three hundred guns and mortars, twenty thousand stand of arms, two hundred thousand shot and shell, and other warlike stores. Lieutenant Willoughby was himself too severely wounded by the explosion to write; but the details of this gallant affair have been very exactly given by Lieutenant G. Forrest, who was assistant-commissary of ordnance in Delhi at the time. Between seven and eight o'clock in the morning of this eventful day, Sir Theophilus Metcalfe, one of the civil servants of the Company, residing between the city and the cantonment, came to the lieutenant, and requested him to go to the magazine for the purpose of planting two guns on the bridge, as a means of barring the passage of the mutineers. Arrived at the magazine, they met Lieutenants Willoughby and Raynor, and several officers and privates of the ordnance establishment. The three principals went to the small bastion on the river-face, commanding a full view of the bridge; there they could distinctly see the mutineers marching in open columns, headed by their cavalry; and they also saw that the Delhi side of the bridge was already in the possession of a smaller body of horse. Any attempt to close or guard the city-gates was found to be too late; for the mutineers were admitted, with great cheering, into the gate of the palace. Lieutenant Willoughby, seeing the critical state of affairs, returned quickly to the magazine, closed and barricaded the gates, and prepared for defence. Conductor Crow and Sergeant Stewart were placed near one of the gates, with lighted matches in their hands, in command of two six-pounders double-charged with grape, which they were ordered to fire if any attempt were made to force the gate from without. The principal gate of the magazine was similarly defended by two guns, with *chevaux-de-frise* laid down on the inside. There were five other six-pounders, and a twenty-four pounder howitzer, quickly placed at such spots as might render them more readily available for defence—all double-loaded with grape-shot. A more doubtful task was that of arming the native artillerymen or ordnance servants within the magazine; for they were in a state, not only of excitement, but of insubordination, much more inclined to aid the assailants without than the defenders within. This arming being effected so far as was practicable, a train of gunpowder was laid down from the magazine to a distant spot; and it was agreed that, on Lieutenant Willoughby giving the order, Conductor Buckley should raise his hat as a signal to Conductor Scully to fire the train and blow up the magazine with all its contents. Having done all that a cool and circumspect leader could do to prepare for the worst, Lieutenant Willoughby awaited the issue. Very soon, mutinous sepoys—or rather the palace guards, who had not until that hour been mutinous—came and demanded possession of the magazine, *in the name of the King of Delhi!* No answer being vouchsafed to this demand, scaling-ladders were sent from the palace, and placed against the wall of the magazine. This decided the wavering of the native artillerymen; they all as with one accord deserted, climbed up to the sloping roofs on the inside of the magazine, and descended the ladders to the outside. The insurgents now appearing in great numbers on the top of the walls, the little band of Europeans commenced a brisk fire of grape-shot, which worked much mischief among the enemy; although only nine in number, they kept several hundred men at bay. At last, the stock of grape at hand was exhausted, and the beleaguered garrison was shot at instead of shooting: seeing that none could run to the storehouses for more grape-shot without leaving to the mutineers freedom of entry by leaping from the walls. Two of the small number being wounded, and the impossibility of longer holding out being apparent, Lieutenant Willoughby gave the signal; whereupon Conductor Scully instantly fired the train. An awful explosion followed, amid the din and confusion of which, all who were not too much injured made their way out of the sally-port, to escape in the best manner they could. What was the number of insurgents killed and wounded by the grape-shot discharges and by the explosion, no one knew; some of the English officers estimated it at more than a thousand. It was at the time hoped by the authorities that the whole of the vast store of ammunition had been blown into the air, beyond the reach of the mutineers; but subsequent events shewed that the destruction was not so complete.*

To return to the agitating scenes within the city. Major Abbott, immediately on hearing of the explosion at the magazine, found himself placed in a painful position: urged to different courses by different persons, and doubtful how long his own regiment would remain faithful. He was requested by the commandant to send back two guns to the cantonment, as a means of defence; while, on the other hand, he was entreated by Major Paterson, and by the civil collector who had charge of the treasury, to retain his small force for guarding the various government establishments within the city. Major Abbott listened to this latter suggestion for a time, but then made arrangements for sending off the two guns to the cantonment. By this time, however, he found it was of little consequence what orders he gave: the native troops were fast getting beyond his control. The two guns, and some men of the 38th regiment, returned; the gunners had deserted on the road, and the guns had therefore been brought back again. A few of the native officers who were still faithful now importuned him to leave the city as soon as possible; he at first interpreted their request as an advice to hasten to defend the cantonment; but soon found that it bore relation to his own safety. Presently he heard shots whizzing in the main-guard. He asked what they meant, and was told: 'The 38th are shooting the European officers.' He then ordered about a hundred of his men to hasten with him to the rescue; but they replied: 'Sir, it is useless. They are all killed by this time, and we shall not save any one. We have saved you, and we are happy; we will not allow you to go back and be murdered.' The history of the Revolt presented many such incidents as this; in every native regiment there were some men who wished to remain faithful, and some officers who were favourites among them. The sepoys formed a ring round the major, and hurried him on foot along the road leading to the cantonment. He stopped some time at the quarter-guard, and sent a messenger to the saluting tower to obtain information of the proceedings in other parts of the city.

The sun was now setting, and evening approaching, giving omen of a night of danger and difficulty. Major Abbott espied two or three carriages belonging to officers of his own regiment, going northward on the road to Kurnaul; and on inquiry, he was told by the men at the quarter-guard: 'Sir, they are leaving the cantonment; pray follow their example. We have protected you so far; but it will be impossible for us to do so much longer. Pray fly for your life!' Willing as he was to remain at his post to the last, the major felt that the men around him were so far faithful as to deserve credence for what they had just uttered; and that his own life, if now taken, would be sacrificed without in any way contributing towards the retention of Delhi in British hands. He therefore replied: 'Very well; I am off to Meerut. Bring the colours; and let me see as many of you at Meerut as are not inclined to become traitors.' Major Abbott and Captain Hawkey now mounted one horse and started off after the carriages. They overtook some guns going the same road; but after a progress of four miles, the drivers refused to go any further, and insisted on driving the guns back again to Delhi. The officers, thus entirely deserted by the native troops, having no European troops with or near them, and being powerless to effect any good, rode or drove off to seek safety in other directions.

Major Abbott afterwards learned at what point in the day's proceedings his own regiment, the 74th, first broke out in mutiny. As soon as the explosion of the magazine was heard, he ordered Captain Gordon to take a company with him, to see whether he could render any aid in that quarter; the captain found, however, not only that his aid would be useless, but that his men exhibited great unwillingness to move. Somewhat later, several officers of the 74th were about to march out with a detachment, when a ball whistled among them: Captain Gordon fell dead. Another ball was heard, and Lieutenant Revely was laid low. It now became a matter of life and death: each officer, without any imputation of selfishness, looking after his own safety. Among others, Ensign Elton made for the bastion of the fort, jumped over the parapet, descended into the ditch, clambered up the counterscarp on the other side, ran across the country to the cantonment, and then followed the road which many of the other officers had taken. Captain Tytler, Captain Nicoll, and some others, went towards Kurnaul; Major Abbott, Captains Hawkey and Wallace, Lieutenant Aislabie, Ensign Elton, and Farrier-sergeant Law, took the Kurnaul road for some distance, and then struck off on the right to Meerut, where

* Rightly did the governor-general, when officially informed of this achievement, speak of 'the noble and cool soldiership of the gallant defenders' of the magazine: 'The governor-general in council desires to offer his cordial thanks to Lieutenants Raynor and Forrest, and the other survivors among the brave men mentioned in this report, and to express the admiration with which he regards the daring and heroic conduct of Lieutenant G. D. Willoughby and the warrant and non-commissioned officers by whom he was supported on that occasion. Their names are Lieutenants Raynor and Forrest, Conductors Shaw, Buckley, Scully, Sub-conductor Crow, Sergeants Edwards and Stewart. The family of the late Conductor Scully, who so devotedly sacrificed himself in the explosion of the magazine, will be liberally provided for, should it be ascertained that they have survived him.'

ey arrived at eight o'clock in the evening of uesday the 12th—thirty-six hours after the utineers from Meerut had reached Delhi.

After stating that almost all the European inhabitants of Delhi had been murdered, except those ho had at once been able to effect their escape, ajor Abbott thus expressed the opinion which e formed during these two days of terrible xcitement, concerning the successive steps of the utiny at Delhi: 'From all I could glean, there is ot the slightest doubt that this insurrection has een originated and matured in the palace of the King of Delhi, with his full knowledge and sanction, in the mad attempt to establish himself in the sovereignty of this country. It is well known that he has called on the neighbouring states to co-operate with him in thus trying to subvert the existing government. The method he adopted appears to have been to gain the sympathy of the 38th light infantry, by spreading the lying reports now going through the country, of the government having it in contemplation to upset their religion, and have them all forcibly inducted to Christianity. The 38th, by insidious and false arguments, quietly gained over the 54th and 74th native infantry, each being unacquainted with the other's real sentiments. I am perfectly persuaded that the 54th and 74th were forced to join the combination

Escape from Delhi.

by threats that the 38th and 54th would annihilate the 74th if they refused; or, *vice versâ*, that the 38th and 74th would annihilate the 54th. I am almost convinced that had the 38th not been on guard at the Cashmere Gate, the results would have been very different; the men of the 74th would have shot down every man who had the temerity to assail the post.' It may be that this officer, anxious to lessen the dishonour of his own regiment, viewed somewhat too partially the relative merits of the native troops; but it is unquestionable that the 74th remained faithful much longer than the 38th. To what extent the King of Delhi was really implicated, neither Major Abbott nor any other Englishman could at that time correctly tell.

It was not during the dire confusion of this terrible day that the course of events in the streets and buildings of Delhi could be fully known. The facts came to light one by one afterwards. When the 3d Bengal troopers, who preceded the mutinous infantry in the march from Meerut, arrived at the Jumna about seven in the morning, they killed the toll-keeper of the bridge of boats, took the money found in his office, and crossed the bridge. Arrived in Delhi, they hastened to the royal palace, where they made some sort of announcement of their arrival and its purport. Mr Simon Fraser, the commissioner for Delhi, Captain Douglas, his assistant, and one or two other officials, hearing of this movement, and seeing the approach of insurgent infantry on the other side of the river, hastened to the palace to watch the conduct of the royal personages at such a suspicious time. No sooner did they enter the palace precincts, however, than they were shot down. Shortly afterwards, the Rev. Mr Jennings, chaplain of the residency, was killed; as were likewise his daughter and another lady near him—after, it is to be feared, atrocities worse than death. It was seen that the insurgent troopers were in a state of the greatest excitement and fury, as if they had worked themselves up, by indulgence in the intoxicating *bang*, to a level with their terrible plans. While the military operations, already noticed, were going on at the Cashmere Gate, the magazine, and the cantonment, all the ruffians of Delhi and the neighbouring villages, eager for *loot* or plunder, joined the insurgents. Every European residence was searched: the troopers and sepoys seeking the lives of the inmates; while the rabble followed, and swept off every shred of property. Bungalows were fired one by one, until glaring sheets of flame were visible in every direction. Bands of Goojurs—a kind of Hindoo gipsy tribe—were lying in wait after nightfall all along the line of road twenty miles out of Delhi, on the watch for refugees. It was a day of jubilee for all the miscreants; they did not stay their hands when the Europeans had been pillaged, but attacked the houses of all the Hindoo bankers, carrying off great treasure. Some of the Europeans concealed themselves for a time within the palace gardens—a vain refuge, for they were all detected, tied to trees in a row, and shot or sabred by the mutineers. Many of the troopers, during the savage scenes of these days, pointed to the marks of manacles on their ankles; they were of the eighty-five who had been put in irons at Meerut on the preceding Saturday; and they now shewed how deep was the revenge which they intended to take for that degrading punishment. The military officers and their families were, from various causes, those whose fate became more publicly known; but the number of civil servants, Christians of humble grade, and half-castes, put to death, was very great. The bank-clerks, with their wives and children, were murdered; and similar scenes occurred at most of the public offices.

Mr Farrington, deputy-commissioner, when at Jullundur two or three weeks afterwards, received a written account from a native of the occurrences at Delhi during the days immediately following the Revolt—an account considered worthy of credence. A part of this narrative comprised the following sad tale: 'On the third day they [the mutineers] went to a house near the mosque where some Europeans had taken refuge. As they were without water, &c., they called for a subadar and five others, and asked them to take their oaths that they would give them water, and take them alive to the king: he might kill them, if he liked. On this oath, the Europeans came out: the mutineers placed water before them, and said: "Lay down your arms, and then you get water." They gave over two guns, all they had. The mutineers gave no water. They seized eleven children—among them infants—eight ladies, eight gentlemen. They took them to the ca sheds. One lady, who seemed more self-posse than the rest, observed that they were not tak them to the palace; they replied they were tak them by the way of Duryagunge (one of the g on the river-side of the city). Deponent says t he saw all this, and saw them placed in a r and shot. One woman entreated to give her ch water, though they might kill her. A sepoy t her child, and dashed it on the ground. T people looked on in dismay, and feared Delhi.' The imagination can, too truly, alas! up the deficient incidents in this tale of treache Mr Farrington deemed his informant worthy reliance. He said: 'The man has been with m He speaks frankly, and without fear. He is ab evidently, to narrate many a harrowing tale; b I did not wish to hear any. He seemed really recall with dismay what he had witnessed.'

The aged but wretched king of Delhi—wretche in having the hopes of earlier years revived, on to be crushed again—for a time distrusted th mutineers; he entertained misgivings that a might not end well. The shops and bazaars wer being plundered; the king was in the palace; an some of those around him urged that order coul be restored only by his assumption of the imperia purple. After three or four days, he went i a kind of state through the city, advising o commanding the people to re-open their shops and resume their former commercial dealings—advice more easily given than acted upon; for the devastation had been terrible, striking grief into the more peaceful portion of the native inhabitants. The king assumed command in the city; he named Mirza Mogul commander-in-chief, and gave the title of general of cavalry to Mirza Abu Bukur; he collected around him eight or nine thousand mutineers and volunteers, who were posted at the several gates of the city, or cantoned in the Duryagunge Bazaar. Additional guns were placed on the ramparts; and the native sappers and miners were placed in command of the cannon in the old fort of Selimgurh. The Company's treasury, one of the largest in India, is said to have been respected by the mutineers to this extent—that they did not appropriate it among themselves as spoil, but guarded it as belonging to their newly chosen leader, the King of Delhi. To shew how perplexed the Calcutta government must have been at the first news of these events, it may be mentioned that the king's name was adverted to as that of a friend rather than an enemy. On the 14th of May, three days after the arrival of the Meerut mutineers at Delhi, Mr Colvin, lieutenant-governor of the North-west Provinces, telegraphed from Agra to the governor-general as follows: 'We have authentic intelligence in a letter from the king that the town and fort of Delhi, *and his own person*, are in the hands of the insurgent regiments of the place, which joined about one hundred of the troops from Meerut and opened the gates.' Judged by the ordinary rules of probability, it would appear that the mutineers first secured the person of the king, and then compelled him to head them: the old man being further urged by the entreaties and threats of his intriguing sons and grandsons. It is difficult, under any other supposition, to account for his transmission of a message of information and warning to the chief British authority in those regions. On the 15th Mr Colvin sent a further telegraphic communication to Calcutta, containing this information: 'The rebels have declared the heir-apparent king. They are apparently organising the plan of a regular government; they still remain in the place. Their policy is supposed to be to annex the adjoining districts to their newly formed kingdom. They are not likely, therefore, to abandon the country or leave Delhi; they have probably strengthened themselves there. They may have secured fifty lacs of rupees [half a million sterling].' No further mention was here made of the old man; it was a younger relation who had been set up as king; and this younger prince may possibly have been the one whom the Marquis of Dalhousie had insisted should be the heir-apparent, with such prospective limitations of authority as the Company might hereafter declare to be expedient. The ordinary motives which influence men's conduct would be quite strong enough to induce this prince to avail himself of any accidental or unexpected means of insuring the crown without the limitations here adverted to. Ambition was almost the only sentiment not absolutely degrading left to the pensioned, sensual, intriguing dwellers in the palace.

The details of this chapter have hitherto been confined chiefly to the course of events within the city—as collected from the dispatches of military officers, the letters from commissioners and other civil servants of the Company, and the published statements of Europeans who survived the dangers of the day. But we now come to adventures which, politically of less importance, touch more nearly the hearts and sympathies of those who would know how Englishmen, and more particularly Englishwomen, bore up against the accumulated miseries that pressed upon them. We have to accompany the fugitives to the fields and jungles, the ditches and rivers, the swampy marshes and scorching sandy roads; we have to see how they contended against privation and trial—on their way forty miles in one direction towards Meerut, or eighty miles in another towards Kurnaul. Many of the narratives of the fugitives, afterwards made public, supply details not furnished in any official dispatches; while they illustrate many points worth knowing—among others, the greater hostility of the Mohammedan than the Hindoo natives near Delhi, and the indications of individual kindness in the midst of general brutality. A selection from these narratives will suffice for the present purpose, shortened and thrown into a different form so as to throw light on each other, and on the general events of the day. In most cases, the names of the fugitives, especially of ladies, will be withheld, from a motive which a considerate reader will easily appreciate. This scruple must not, however, be interpreted as affecting the authenticity of the narratives, which was verified only too abundantly by collateral evidence.

We select first a family of three fugitives to Kurnaul. The wife of an officer of the 54th native regiment, in the forenoon of this eventful Monday, hastened with her child to the Flagstaff Tower; where, in accordance with the advice of the brigadier-commandant, many other families had assembled. The gentlemen remained outside on guard; the ladies assisted in loading the guns, and in other services towards the common defence of all. Here they remained many hours, in all the horrors of suspense; for the husbands and fathers of many were away, and their fate unknown. At length came the news that the 38th had openly revolted; that none of the native regiments at Delhi could now be depended upon; and that the inmates of the tower ought to effect their escape as speedily as possible. There had been one company of the 38th at the Flagstaff Tower all day; and as the building was very strong, and armed with two guns, the brigadier long deemed himself able to protect the numerous persons there assembled; but as soon as the defection of the main body of this regiment became known, all reliance on the smaller corps was at an end. Such carriages and horses as could be obtained were immediately put in requisition, and various parties hastened off, mostly northward on the Kurnaul road. The small group whom we have here under notice—namely, the officer with his wife and child, reached Kurnaul the next day; but danger was all around, and the fugitives were forced to continue their flight, as soon as they could obtain means of conveyance. It is touching to read how 'baby' occupied the mother's thoughts through all this agitating escape. During a sojourn at a place called Thwanessur, on the road between Kurnaul and Umballa, they stopped at the assistant-commissioner's house. 'Before we had rested two hours we were alarmed by being told that a regiment of sepoys was come to attack us; we had to fly from the house and hide as best we could, under the bushes, &c., in the garden; and I kept dear baby in my own arms the whole time until morning.' The alarm proved to be false, and the fugitives proceeded. They arrived safely at Umballa on the morning of Thursday the 14th, having left Delhi on Monday evening. That the brave wife was 'quite fatigued and worn out' may well be conceived when she adds, 'for dear baby had never left me since we left Delhi.'

This adventure, however, was far exceeded in length, in privation, in strange situations, in hair-breadth escapes, by one which befell a party of four persons—an officer of the 38th regiment, an army

Delhi from Flagstaff Tower.

surgeon, and their two wives: all of whom, in the wilderness of confusion, sought the Kurnaul route rather than that to Meerut. These ladies were among the many who sought refuge in the Flagstaff Tower. There they had the pain of witnessing the sufferings of poor Colonel Ripley, who, as already narrated, had been bayoneted by men of his own regiment, and had been brought thither for succour; they tended him as women only can tend the sick; but their ministrations were of brief avail. After hours of suspense, in which small hope was mingled with large despair, the necessity for escape became obvious. A little bitterness is expressed, in the narratives of some of the fugitives, concerning the delay in making any preparations for the escape of the women and children; and a few of the head officers are blamed for supineness; but those who suffer are not always, at the time, the best judges of the cause of their sufferings. When evening approached, many of the native coachmen drove away the vehicles belonging to the Europeans, and appropriated them, thus leaving the women and children in dreadful perplexity how to reach Kurnaul or Meerut. The two Englishwomen whose narrative we now follow were among the last of those who left the city, when evening was approaching. They were in a buggy, but had been parted from their husbands during the confusion of the arrangements for departure, and one of them had lost her little child. They drove on, with no male protector, across rugged fields, fearful of the high road: treated sometimes respectfully by the natives, but at other times robbed and vilely addressed. Even the velvet head-dress of one of them was torn off, for the value of the bugles that adorned it. A jewel-box had been brought away in haste, as the only treasure preserved; and it became every hour more uncertain whether this would be a prey to the spoilers. Returning to the high road, the ladies met some gunners with two guns; and as the men told them certain death would be the result if they took the road to Kurnaul, they drove in another direction to the Company's garden outside Delhi. Here, marauding was everywhere going on; the poor ladies soon had the misery of seeing their carriage, horse, jewel-box, and most of their outer clothing reft from them. In the dead of the night they ventured to a neighbouring village. The surgeon, husband to one of the ladies, here managed to join them; but being enfeebled by previous sickness, and wounded in the jaw during the day's exciting troubles, he was powerless as a defender, and —far from being able to succour others—needed succour himself. During the next fifteen hours were these three persons hiding in fields and huts, befriended by a few natives, and conscious that roving sepoys were near, ready for murder or pillage. Sallying forth again on the evening of Tuesday, they were speedily stopped by six men, who robbed them of a further portion of their scanty apparel, and only stopped short of murder when the officer's wife pleaded for mercy, on the ground that she was searching for her husband and her child, both of whom had gone she knew not whither. The three fugitives walked all that night, the wounded surgeon dragging himself along. In the morning they were again accosted, and only escaped death by the ladies yielding up a further part of their attire, the only property they had left to give. During the remainder of that day they crept on, obtaining a little food and water from some villagers, who were, however, too much afraid of the sepoys to afford the fugitives the shelter of a roof; and it was terrible work indeed to roam along the roads with a burning sun overhead and burning sand under foot. They sat down by a well-side, and drank some water; but rude fellows accosted them, and after insulting the hapless women, compelled them to withdraw. They next encountered a party of irregular horse, who had not yet joined the mutineers; the men were at first inclined to befriend them; but fears of the consequences supervening, they soon deserted the fugitives. Here were these two Englishwomen, gently nurtured, and accustomed to all the amenities of good society, again compelled to wander like miserable outcasts, helping along a male companion whose under-jaw had been shattered, and who was otherwise in a weak state. They crawled on during another night, and then reached a village, which, as they saw it was Hindoo, they did not scruple to enter. Kindness was accorded to them for one whole day; after which the humane natives, timid lest the sepoys should burn their village if they heard of Feringhees having been harboured, declared they could no longer afford shelter. Once more, therefore, were the fugitives driven forth: having seen renewed symptoms that the sepoys, or rather the marauding ruffians, would not scruple to murder them, if opportunity offered. They had now been five days wandering about, and yet were only ten miles distant from Delhi: so completely had each day's plans been frustrated by the events of the next day. Again they entered a friendly village, and again were they compelled soon to depart, after receiving simple but kind assistance. No villagers, it was found, were free from dread at having assisted a Feringhee. Once they hid for shelter under a bridge; but an armed ruffian detected them, and behaved so unbearably towards the women that the surgeon, who was a Roman Catholic, took a gold cross from his bosom, and gave it as the price of their freedom from further molestation; a wounded, shattered, sinking man, he could not offer them a strong arm as a shield from insult. On the night of the 17th, at a little more than twenty miles from Delhi, they were glad to obtain the shelter of an outhouse containing twenty cows, the only roof that the owner dared to offer them. They made an attempt to have a letter forwarded to Kurnaul, praying for assistance; but none in those parts could be depended upon for faithfulness beyond an hour or two: so much was there of treachery on the one hand, and timidity on the other. On the 18th they heard that Major Paterson, of the 54th regiment, was in the same village as themselves; and he, powerless to succour, contrived to send a short message to them, written with a burnt stick on a piece of an old broken pan. Shortly afterwards they were greatly astonished, and not a little delighted, to see an officer, the husband of one of the ladies, enter the village; but more like a naked savage, blistered from head to foot, than like an English gentleman.

An eventful tale had this officer to narrate. When the scenes of violence on the 11th at Delhi had reached such a point that to remain longer was to meet certain slaughter, he sent off his little boy with friends towards Meerut, and saw his wife and her lady-companion start for Kurnaul. After being robbed of his horse, and having three bullets sent through his hat, and one through the skirt of his coat, he ran past the blazing houses of the cantonment, and, being ill at the time, sank down under a tree exhausted. A gang of ruffians found him, stripped him, robbed him of everything, and endeavoured, Thug-like, to strangle him—using, however, the sleeve of his own shirt instead of a silken cord. Happily the choking was only partial; he recovered, staggered on a mile or two, rested briefly in a hut, and then walked twelve miles to Alipore in a broiling sun. He obtained a little water, a little bread, and a few fragments of clothing, but was refused shelter. He wended his painful way barefoot, keeping to ploughed fields as safer than the high road, and reached a village where the headman gave him an asylum for five days. During these days, however, he twice narrowly escaped death from sepoys prowling about the village. On the sixth he received information which led him to believe that his wife and her travelling companions were within six or seven miles of him. He hastened on, with swollen and blistered feet, wretched substitutes for raiment, and a frame nearly worn out by sickness and anxiety; but a gleam of joy burst upon him when at length he overtook the surgeon and the two wives, though dismayed to see the plight to which they had been reduced. The poor ladies he found to be, like himself, reft of everything they had in the world except a few torn and toil-worn fragments of garments. The surgeon had been less rudely stripped, simply because the clothes of a wounded man were less acceptable to the spoliators. The fugitives, now four in number, continued their journey, their feet pierced with thorns and sharp stones, and the difficulty of carrying or dragging a wounded man becoming greater and greater. The officer's wife, having had no head-covering for many days, felt the sun's heat to be gradually affecting her brain; she was thankful when a villager gave her a wet cloth to bind round her temples. Matters now began to mend; the villagers were less afraid of the Delhi sepoys; the vicinity of Kurnaul exhibited less violence and marauding; horses and mules were obtained on one day to take them to Lursowlie; and on the next a carriage was provided for their conveyance to Kurnaul. How they got on from Kurnaul to Umballa, and from Umballa to Simla, need not be told—the romance of the incident was over when the three fugitives, two women and a wounded man, were joined by a fourth; although much physical and mental suffering had still to be endured. The little son of this lady, it was afterwards found, had been carried by some friends safely to Meerut on the 12th. The four fugitives, when they reached friendly quarters, were poor indeed: no beggars could be more completely dependent on the sympathy of those whom they now happily met.

Next we will follow the steps of some of those who chose Meerut rather than Kurnaul as their place of refuge. Their adventures partake of a new interest, because there was a broad and swift river to be crossed. A young ensign of the 54th regiment, a stripling who had just commenced military service under the Company, had a sad tale to tell, how the European officers of his regiment had fallen almost to a man. He was in the cantonment when the news arrived of the approach of the Meerut mutineers; his regiment was ordered to hasten to the city; and he, like other officers, was fain to hope that the men would remain true to their colours. Leaving two companies to follow with two guns, the other eight marched off to the city, distant, as has already been stated, about two miles. Arriving at the mainguard of the Cashmere Gate, the regiment encountered the mutinous 3d Bengal cavalry, who immediately shot down nearly all the officers of the eight companies: the men of those companies shewing, by a refusal to defend their officers, that they were quite ready for revolt. The colonel, indeed, was bayoneted by one of his own men after a trooper had shot him. In about half an hour the other two companies arrived with the two guns; but as the few remaining officers of the regiment knew not which of their men, if any, could be depended on, they formed a kind of small fort or citadel of the mainguard, into which they brought their few remaining companions one by one. The poor youth, who had just commenced soldiering, and who had never seen a dead body, was nearly overwhelmed with grief at the sight of his brother-officers, with whom he had laughed and chatted a few hours before, lying side by side dead and mutilated. The main body of the regiment remained sullen, though not mutinous, until about five o'clock in the evening; but then the spirit of evil seemed to seize them, and they turned upon the Europeans near them, shooting indiscriminately. The scene became agonising. Many women and children had gone to the mainguard for security; and now they as well as the officers found it necessary to flee for very life. Some ran, leaped, clomb, until they got beyond the wall of the city; others waited to help those who were weaker or of more tender years. Some of the ladies, though wounded, lowered themselves by handkerchiefs into the ditch, from embrasures in the parapet, and were caught by officers below; and then ensued the terrible labour of dragging or carrying them up the counterscarp on the other side of the ditch. (A ditch, in military matters, be it remembered, is a dry, broad, very deep trench outside a fortified wall, with nearly vertical sides, called the scarp and counterscarp.) The young officer tells how that he and his male companions would have made a dash towards Meerut, sword in hand, or have sold their lives at once; but that their chief thoughts were now for the women and children. What were the privations of such a company as this, in fords and jungles, in hunger and nakedness, we shall presently see by means of a narrative from another quarter.

It is an officer of the 38th who shall now tell his tale—how that his own personal troubles, when alone, were slight compared with those which he had afterwards to bear in company with other fugitive Europeans. This officer states that, while the refugees were anxiously watching the course of events at the Flagstaff Tower, they were momentarily expecting aid from Meerut. They could not believe that Major-general Hewett would have allowed the mutineers to march from Meerut to Delhi without either making an attempt to intercept them, or following on their heels; and their disappointment in this particular led to some of the unfavourable comments made on that general's

..e of conduct. The officer of the 38th, whose ..rrative is now under notice, shared the difficulty .. all the others in endeavouring to keep the men .. their duty; and he speaks of the terrible sight, ..ore than once adverted to, which met his eye .. the mainguard inside the Cashmere Gate: 'By ..e gate, side by side, and covered by pretty ladies' ..esses taken from some house, as if in mockery, ..y the bodies of poor Captain Smith, Burrowes, ..dwardes, and Waterfield, and the quarter-master-..rgeant; some lying calm as shot dead, and ..thers with an expression of pain, mutilated by ..ayonets and swords.' When all became hopeless ..ithin the city, and the brigadier had given orders ..o retire, the officers made a show of bringing off ..heir regiments as well as their families; but it ..vas only a show; for such of the men as had ..emained faithful up to this time now fell away, ..nd the Europeans found themselves compelled to ..scape as best they could. The officer hastened ..o the cantonment, disconsolate and helpless, but having no immediate idea of escape. With the colonel of the same regiment, however, he was urged to adopt that course, as the cantonment itself was now in a blaze. The two ran off in the dead of the night towards the river, crouching beneath trees when enemies seemed near; they forded the Jumna Canal, slaking their parched lips as they waded or swam; and they tore off the brighter parts of their glittering accoutrements, to prevent betrayal. In the morning, faint and hungered, they took refuge in a hut while a body of sepoys was searching around, as if for victims. A few Hindoo peasants discovering them, told them where they could hide in a tope of trees, and brought them chupatties and milk. Being able to ford across a narrow branch of the Jumna soon afterwards, they concealed themselves in the wild jungle; and there, to their joy and surprise, they found others of their friends in the same kind of concealment—joy damped, it is true, at the thought of educated English men and women crouching among long jungle-grass like savages or wild beasts. On counting numbers, they found they were thirteen, eight gentlemen and five ladies and children; and as they had several guns and swords among them, they took heart, and prepared to struggle against further difficulties.

To bring up the two parallel threads of the story, the escapes of the larger party, comprising the women and little ones, must now be told. In the afternoon of the preceding day, after arrangements had been made for conveying the ladies on gun-carriages from the city to the cantonment, the natives who had been trusted with this duty turned faithless, and the Europeans within the Cashmere Gate, finding themselves shot at, sought to escape beyond the walls in any way they could. One after another, women and children as well as men, leaped over into the ditch, scrambled up the other side, and ran off towards the house of Sir T. Metcalfe. One lady, the mother of three daughters who had to share in the flight, was shot through the shoulder, yet still kept on. The native servants—in the absence of their master, who afterwards had his own tale to tell of jungle-life and narrow escapes—gave them a little food; but just before the house was about being fired by the insurgents, the fugitives left it, and succeeded in fording the narrow stream to the spot mentioned above. When the thirteen had told their adventures, and formed a plan, they started anew, and sought a spot where they could ford the majestic Jumna. The officer must here tell the story of this perilous fording: 'Our hearts failed, and no wonder, where ladies were concerned, as we looked at the broad swift river. It was getting dark, too. Two natives went across. We watched them anxiously wade a considerable portion of the river; then their heads alone appeared above water. It was our only chance of life, and our brave ladies never flinched. The water was so deep, that where a tall man would wade, a short man would be drowned. I thought it was all over when, on reaching the deep water with Mrs —— on my left arm, a native supporting her on the other side, we were shot [drifted] down the river; however, by desperate efforts and the assistance of another native, we reached the bank in safety. I swam back once more for another of our party; and so ultimately we all got safe over. It was a brave feat for our ladies to do.' But so it was throughout these terrific scenes: the heroism, the patience, the long-suffering endurance of these gentlewomen, bore up to the last; feebleness of frame was vanquished by nobility of spirit; and the men were often kept in heart, though deeply pained, by the uncomplaining perseverance of their gentle companions in misery. Our fugitives passed a wretched night after this fording of the Jumna, crouching in the jungle, with no sound 'but the chattering of their teeth.' The next day threw them into the hands of a large band of ruffians; and as the guns of the officers had been rendered useless by wet, the consequence was direful: the whole party were stripped and robbed, and then left without food, without clothing, without resource, to wander whither they could. With naked feet, and skins blistering in the sun, they toiled on. 'How the ladies stood it,' says the officer whose narrative we are following, 'is marvellous; they never murmured or flinched, or distressed us by a show of terror.' Fortunately, a fakeer, in a Hindoo village, ventured to give them shelter; they remained three days, obtaining a little food, but nothing more. A German zemindar or landowner, who had been so long in India as to be hardly distinguishable from a Hindoo, hearing of their plight, sent for them, gave them some rough cloth to huddle on as substitutes for garments, and caused a message to be sent to Meerut, which brought relief to them; and they reached that town in seven days after leaving Delhi—worn out in mind and body, haggard, lame, penniless, but thankful that their lives had been spared.

Strange as these escapes and perils were, they

were eclipsed in individual daring and fertility of resource by one which remains to be told, and which may form the last of this little group of painful narratives. Mr Batson, surgeon of the 74th regiment, was unheard of during so long a time after the events at Delhi on the fatal Monday that he was given up for lost; but in a letter which he wrote to announce his safety, he detailed such a series of adventures as appear to belong rather to romance than to real life—Defoe-like, but entirely true instead of fictitious. And here it may be again remarked that these narratives must not be suspected of boastful exaggeration; there were links which connected all the eventful stories into one chain—each receiving corroborative strength from the others. Mr Batson states that when it was found that the three regiments at Delhi refused to act against the mutineers from Meerut, and that when such of the women and children as could be collected were placed in the mainguard and the Flagstaff Tower, he went to Brigadier Graves, volunteering to convey a letter to Meerut, in hope of obtaining the aid of European troops. His offer being accepted, he took leave of his wife and three daughters in the Flagstaff Tower, went to his house, dressed himself like a native fakeer or mendicant devotee, and coloured his face, hands, and feet. Off he set on his perilous errand. He first tried to cross the Jumna by the bridge of boats, but found it broken. Then he ran to the cantonment, and endeavoured to cross by a ferry near that spot, but found the insurgent cavalry and the neighbouring villagers plundering and marauding. Next he hastened across the parade-ground, and, after escaping two or three shots, was seized by some of the villagers and stripped of every bit of his fakeer clothing. On he ran again, in his now truly forlorn state, towards the Kurnaul road, hoping to overtake some of the officers who were escaping by that route; but before he could do so, two of the insurgent troopers intercepted him. Just as they were about to cut him down with their drawn swords, his tact and knowledge saved him. Being familiar both with the Hindostani language and with the Mohammedan customs, he threw himself into a supplicating position, and uttered the most exalted praises of the great Prophet of Islam: begging them to spare his life for the sake of the Moslem. Had his assailants been infantry sepoys, he would probably not have attempted this manœuvre, for most of them were Hindoos; but knowing that the cavalry sowars were chiefly Mohammedans, he made the venture. It succeeded. Whether they knew him as a fugitive Englishman, is not certain; but they let him go, saying: 'Had you not asked for mercy in the name of the Prophet, you should have died like the rest of the Kaffirs [infidels].' After running another mile—at once shivering with nakedness and burning with excitement—he encountered some Mussulman villagers, who rushed upon him, crying: 'Here is a Feringhee; kill the Kaffir! You Feringhees want to make us all Christians!' They dragged him to a village, tied his hands behind him, and sent one of their number to a house hard by to get a sword, with which to despatch him. At this critical moment some excitement—the nature of which Mr Batson could not understand—caused them all to leave him, and he ran off again. He fortunately fell in with some smiths who had been employed in the Delhi magazine, and who were willing to save him; they urged him not to go forward, or the villagers would certainly murder him. They took him to a hut, gave him an article or two of apparel, and fed him with milk and bread. He tried to sleep, but could not; he lay awake all night, restless and excited. In the morning he bethought him of informing his protectors that he was a physician, a doctor, a 'medicine-man;' and this proved to be an aid to him; for the villagers, finding that he could answer questions relating to maladies, and was familiar with their religion, language, and customs, began to take much interest in the Feringhee doctor. He found that two officers were in hiding at no great distance, but he could reach neither of them. To get to Meerut in time to deliver his message was of course now out of the question: all that Mr Batson could do was to secure his own safety. More perils were in store for him. The villagers of Badree were informed that if they harboured any Feringhees, the now triumphant King of Delhi would direfully punish them; they became alarmed, and hid him in a small mango tope. 'Here,' the surgeon says, 'I was left night and day alone. I was visited at night by some one or other of the villagers, who brought me bread and water in a ghurrah. I am unable to describe my feelings during this trying time. I was all day in the sun, in the extreme heat, and alone at night, when the jackals came prowling about and crying. It is only God and myself know what I have endured. After five nights and days in this tope of trees, I was again taken back to the village and concealed in a bhoosa house. I was here shut in for twenty-four hours; the heat and suffocation I cannot find language to describe. I do not know which was the greatest misery, the tope of trees in solitude or the bhoosa kotree.' At length the villagers, afraid to keep him any longer, dismissed him—enabling him to dress himself up again as a fakeer. Tramping on from village to village, he acted his part so well as to escape detection. He gave himself out as a Cashmerian; and although one of the villagers suspected his European origin by his blue eyes, he did not betray him. He observed from village to village—and the fact is worthy of note in relation to the causes and details of the Revolt—that the Mohammedans were much more savage than the Hindoos in their expressions and threats against the Feringhees. The further he proceeded from Delhi, the less did Mr Batson find himself involved in danger; and he was fortunately picked up by Captain M'Andrews and Lieutenant Mew of his own regiment. He had been out no less than twenty-five days, wandering from village to village, from tope to tope; suffering privations which none but himself could know, and not even he adequately describe. One great anxiety gnawed him the while—the fate of his family: one great joy awaited him—his family escaped.

Here this chapter may close. We have seen that on the morning of Monday the 11th of May, the European inhabitants of Delhi arose from their beds in peace; and that by the close of the same day there was not a single individual of the number whose portion was not death, flight, or terrified concealment. So far as the British rule or influence was concerned, it was at an end. The natives remained masters of the situation; their white rulers were driven out; and a reconquest, complete in all its details, could alone restore British rule in Delhi. At what time, in what way, and by whom, that reconquest was effected, will remain to be told in a later portion of this work. Much remains to be narrated before Delhi will again come under notice.

Elephant and State Howdah.

LUCKNOW.

CHAPTER VI.

LUCKNOW AND THE COURT OF OUDE.

ANOTHER regal or once-regal family, another remnant of Moslem power in India, now comes upon the scene—one which has added to the embarrassment of the English authorities, by arraying against them the machinations of deposed princes as well as the discontent of native troops; and by shewing, as the King of Delhi had shewn in a neighbouring region, that a pension to a sovereign deprived of his dominions is not always a sufficient medicament to allay the irritation arising from the deprivation. What and where is the kingdom of Oude; of what rank as an Indian city is its capital, Lucknow; who were its rulers; why and when the ruling authority was changed—these matters must be clearly understood, as a preliminary to the narrative of Sir Henry Lawrence's proceedings about the time of the outbreak.

Oude, considered as a province of British India, and no longer as a kingdom, is bounded on the north and northeast by the territory of Nepaul; on the east by the district of Goruckpore; on the southeast by those of Azimghur and Jounpoor; on the south by that of Allahabad; on the southwest by the districts of the Doab; and on the northwest by Shahjehanpoor. It is now about thrice the size of Wales; but before the annexation, Oude as a kingdom included a larger area. On the Nepaul side, a strip of jungle-country called the Terai, carries it to the base of the sub-Himalaya range. This Terai is in part a wooded marsh, so affected by a deadly malaria as to be scarcely habitable; while the other part is an almost impassable forest of trees, underwood, and reeds, infested by the elephant, the rhinoceros, the bear, the wild hog, and other animals. Considered generally, however, Oude surpasses in natural advantages almost every other part of India—having the Ganges running along the whole of its southwest frontier, a varied and fertile soil, a genial though hot climate, and numerous facilities for irrigation and water-carriage. It cannot, however, be said that man has duly aided nature in the development of these advantages; for the only regularly made road in the whole province is that from Lucknow to Cawnpore: the others being mostly wretched tracks, scarcely passable for wheel-carriages. The railway schemes of the Company include a line through Oude, which would be of incalculable benefit; but no definite contract had been made at the time when the Revolt commenced; nor would such a railway be profitable until the trunk-line is finished from Calcutta to Benares and Allahabad. Although the Mohammedans have, through many ages, held the ruling power in Oude, the Hindoos are greatly more numerous; and nearly the whole of the inhabitants, five millions in number, speak the Hindostani language; whereas those nearer Calcutta speak Bengali. As shewing the kind of houses in which Europeans occasionally sought concealment during the disturbances, the following description of the ordinary dwelling-places of Oude may be useful. They are generally built either of unburnt brick, or of layers of mud, each about three feet in breadth and one foot high. The roofs are made of square beams, placed a foot apart, and covered with planks laid transversely; over these are mats, and a roofing of well-rammed wet clay half a yard in thickness. The walls are carried to a height six or seven feet above the upper surface of the roof, to afford a concealed place of recreation for the females of the family; and during the rainy season this small elevated court is covered with a slight awning of bamboos and grass. Though so simply and cheaply constructed, these houses are very durable. Around the house there is usually a verandah, covered with a sloping tiled roof. Inside, the beams overhead are exposed to view, without any ceiling. The floors are of earth, well beaten down and smoothed, and partially covered with mats or cotton carpets. In the front of the house is a chabootra or raised platform of earth, open to the air at the sides, and provided with a roof of tiles or grass supported on pillars. This platform is a pleasant spot on which neighbours meet and chat in the cool of the evening. The dwellings of the wealthy natives of course present an aspect of greater splendour; while those of the Europeans, in the chief towns, partake of the bungalow fashion, already described.

There are few towns of any distinction in Oude compared with the area of the province; and of these few, only two will need to be mentioned in the present chapter. As for the city whence the province originally obtained its name—Oude, Oudh, or Ayodha—it has fallen from its greatness. Prinsep, Buchanan, and other authorities, regard it as the most ancient, or at any rate one of the most ancient, among the cities of Hindostan. Some of the coins found in Oude are of such extreme antiquity, that the characters in which their legends are graven are totally unknown. Buchanan thinks that the city was built by the first Brahmins who entered India, and he goes back to a date fourteen hundred years before the Christian era for its foundation; while Tod and Wilford claim for Oude an origin even six centuries earlier than that insisted on by Buchanan. The value of such estimates may not be great; they chiefly corroborate the belief that Oude is a *very* ancient city. With its eight thousand inhabitants, and its mud and thatch houses, the grandeur of Oude lives in the past; and even this grandeur is in antiquity rather than in splendour; for the ruins and fragments give a somewhat mean idea of the very early Hindoo architecture to which they belong. On the eastern side of the town are extensive ruins, said to be those of the fort of Rama, king of Oude, celebrated in the mythological and romantic legends of India. According to Buchanan: 'The heaps of bricks, although much seems to have been carried away by the river, extend a great way—that is, more than a mile in length, and half a mile in width—and, although vast quantities of materials have been removed to build the Mohammedan Ayodha or Fyzabad, yet the ruins in many parts retain a very considerable elevation; nor is there any reason to doubt that the structure to which they belonged was very large, when we consider that it has been ruined for above two thousand years.' A spot among the ruins is still pointed out by the reverential Hindoos from which Rama took his flight to heaven, carrying all the people of the city with him: a hypothetical emigration which had the effect of leaving Oude desolate until a neighbouring king repopulated it, and embellished it with three hundred and sixty temples. The existing buildings connected with the Hindoo faith are four establishments kept up in honour of the fabled monkey-god, the auxiliary of Rama; they have annual revenues, settled on them by one of the rulers of Oude; they are managed by *maliks* or spiritual superiors; and the revenues are dispensed to several hundreds of *bairagis* or religious ascetics, and other lazy Hindoo mendicants—no Mussulman being ever admitted within the walls.

Lucknow, however, is the city to which our attention will naturally be most directed—Lucknow, as the modern capital of the kingdom or province; as a city of considerable importance, political, military, commercial, and architectural; and as a scene of some of the most memorable events in the Revolt.

The city of Lucknow stands on the right bank of the river Goomtee, which is navigable thence downwards to its confluence with the Ganges between Benares and Ghazeepore. It is rather more than fifty miles distant from Cawnpore, and about a hundred and thirty from Allahabad. As Cawnpore is on the right bank of the Ganges, that majestic river intervenes between the two towns. The Goomtee is crossed at Lucknow by a bridge of boats, a bridge of substantial masonry, and an iron bridge—an unusual fulness of transit-channels in an Indian city. Lucknow displays a varied, lively, and even brilliant prospect, when viewed from a position elevated above the level of the buildings; but, once in the streets, the traveller has his dream of beauty speedily dissipated; for oriental filth and abomination meet his eye on all sides. The central portion of the city, the most ancient, is meanly built with mud-houses roofed with straw; many of them are no better than booths of mats and bamboos, thatched with leaves or palm-branches. The streets, besides being dirty, are narrow and crooked, and are dismally sunk many feet below the level of the shops. The narrow avenues are rendered still less passable by the custom of employing elephants as beasts of burden: unwieldy animals which almost entirely block up the way. In the part of the city occupied by Europeans, however, and containing the best public buildings, many of the streets are broad and lively. Until 1856, when Oude was annexed to British India, Lucknow was, to a stranger, one of the most remarkable cities of the east, in regard to its armed population. Almost every man went armed through the streets. One had a matchlock, another a gun, another a pistol; others their bent swords or *tulwars;* others their brass-knobbed buffalo-hide shields. Men of business and idlers—among all alike it was a custom to carry arms. The black beards of the Mussulmans, and the fierce moustaches of the Rajpoots, added to the warlike effect thus produced. Oude was the great storehouse for recruits for the Company's native army; and this naturally gave a martial bent to the people. The Company, however, deemed it a wise precaution to disarm the peaceful citizens at the time of the annexation.

Three or four structures in and near Lucknow require separate description. One is the Shah Nujeef, or Emanbarra of Azof-u-Dowlah, a model of fantastic but elegant Mohammedan architecture. English travellers have poured out high praise upon it. Lord Valentia said: 'From the brilliant white of the composition, and the minute delicacy of the workmanship, an enthusiast might suppose that genii had been the artificers;' while Bishop Heber declared: 'I have never seen an architectural view which pleased me more, from its richness and variety, as well as the proportions and general good taste of its principal features.' The structure consists of many large buildings surrounding two open courts. There are three archways to connect the courts; and in the centre of these is the tomb of the founder, watched by soldiers, and attended by moullahs perpetually reading the Koran. This structure is often called the king's Emanbarra or Imaumbarah, a name given to the buildings raised by that sect of Moslems called Sheahs, for the celebration of the religious festival of the Mohurrum. Every family of distinction has its own emanbarra, large or small, gorgeous or simple, according to the wealth of its owner, who generally selects it as his own burial-place. The central hall of the Shah Nujeef, the king's emanbarra, is of vast size and very magnificent; and the combination of Moslem minarets with Hindoo-pointed domes renders the exterior remarkably striking; nevertheless the splendour is diminished by the poverty of the materials, which are chiefly brick coated with chunam or clay cement. Near or connected with this building is the Roumee Durwaza or Gate of the Sultan, having an arch in the Saracenic style. Another public building is the mosque of Saadut Ali, one of the former nawabs of Oude; its lofty dome presents a remarkable object as seen from various parts of the city; and, being provided with terraces without and galleries within, it is especially attractive to a sight-seer. Southeast of the city, and near the river, is a fantastic mansion constructed by Claude Martine, a French adventurer who rose to great wealth and power at the late court of Lucknow. He called it Constantia, and adorned it with various kinds of architectural eccentricities—minute stucco fretwork, enormous lions with lamps instead of eyes, mandarins and ladies with shaking heads, gods and goddesses of heathen mythology, and other incongruities. The house is large, and solidly built of stone; and on the topmost story is the tomb of Martine; but his body is deposited in a sarcophagus in one of the lower apartments. The favourite residence of the former nawabs and kings of Oude was the Dil Koosha or 'Heart's Delight,' a richly adorned palace two miles out of the city, and placed in the middle of an extensive deer-park. When Colonel (afterwards General Sir James) Outram was appointed British resident at the court of Lucknow, about a year before the annexation, the Dil Koosha was set apart for his reception; and the whole ceremonial illustrated at once the show and glitter of oriental processions, and the honour paid to the Englishman. As soon as the colonel arrived at Cawnpore from Calcutta, the great officers of state were sent from Lucknow to prepare for his reception. After crossing the Ganges, and thereby setting foot in the Oude dominions, he entered a royal carriage replete with gold and velvet; a procession was formed of carriages, cavalry, and artillery, which followed the fifty miles of road to the capital. On the next day, the king was to have met the colonel half-way between the city palace and the Dil Koosha; but being ill, his place was taken by the heir-apparent. The one procession met the other, and then both entered Lucknow in state. A Lucknow correspondent of a Bombay journal said: 'Let the reader imagine a procession of more than three hundred elephants and camels, caparisoned and decorated with all that barbaric pomp could lavish, and Asiatic splendour shower down; with all the princes and nobles of the kingdom blazing with jewels, gorgeous in apparel, with footmen and horsemen in splendid liveries, swarming on all sides; pennons and banners dancing in the sun's rays, and a perfect forest of gold and silver sticks, spears, and other insignia of imperial and royal state.'

A work of remarkable character has appeared, ating to Lucknow and the court of Oude. It is lled the *Private Life of an Eastern King*, and has en edited from the notes of an Englishman who ld a position in the household of the king of ude, Nussir-u-Deen, in 1834 and following years.* iough the name of the author does not appear, e work is generally accepted as being trustworthy, many corroborations of its statements having peared in other quarters. Speaking of the ng's palace within the city, this writer says: The great extent of the buildings, generally called e king's palace, surprised me in the first instance. t is not properly a palace, but a continuation f palaces, stretching all along the banks of the oomtee, the river on which Lucknow is built. n this, however, the royal residence in Oude ut resembles what one reads of the Seraglio at onstantinople, the khan's residence at Teheran, nd the imperial buildings of Pekin. In all riental states, the palaces are not so much the bode of the sovereign only, as the centre of the overnment; little towns, in fact, containing extenive lines of buildings occupied by the harem and its vast number of attendants; containing courts, gardens, tanks, fountains, and squares, as well as the offices of the chief ministers of state. Such is the case in Lucknow. One side of the narrow Goomtee—a river not much broader than a middle-sized London street—is lined by the royal palace; the other is occupied by the *rumna* or park, in which the menagerie is (or was) maintained. . . . There is nothing grand or striking about the exterior of the palace, the Fureed Buksh, as it is called. Its extent is the only imposing feature about it; and this struck me more forcibly than any magnificence or loftiness of structure would have done.'

These few topographical and descriptive details concerning Oude and its two capitals, the former and the present, will prepare us to enter upon a subject touching immediately the present narrative: namely, the relations existing between the East India Company and the Oudians, and the causes which have generated disaffection in the late royal family of that country. It will be needful to shew by what steps Oude, once a Hindoo *kingdom*, became under the Mogul dynasty a Mohammedan *nawabship*, then a *nawab-viziership*, then under British protection a Mohammedan *kingdom*, and lastly an Anglo-Indian *province*.

Whether or not historians are correct in asserting that Oude was an independent Hindoo sovereignty fourteen hundred years before the Christian era, and that then, for an indefinite number of centuries, it was a Hindoo dependency of a prince whose chief seat of authority was at Oojein—it seems to be admitted that Bakhtiar Khilzi, towards the close of the twelfth century, was sent to conquer the country for the Mohammedan sovereign at that time paramount in the north of India; and that Oude became at once an integral part of the realm of the emperor of Delhi. Under the powerful Baber, Oude was a lieutenancy or nawabship: the ruler having sovereign power within his dominions, but being at the same time a vassal of the Great Mogul. This state of things continued until about a century ago, when the weakening of the central power at Delhi tempted an ambitious nawab of Oude to throw off the trammels of dependency, and exercise royalty on his own account. At that time the Mohammedan rulers of many states in Northern India were troubled by the inroads of the fierce warlike Mahrattas; and although the nawabs cared little for their liege lord the emperor, they deemed it expedient to join their forces against the common enemy. One result of this struggle was, that the nawab of Oude was named 'perpetual' nawab—the first loosening of the imperial chain. The nawab-vizier, as he was now called, never afterwards paid much allegiance to the sovereign of Delhi: nay, the effete Mogul, in 1764, asked the British to defend him from his ambitious and disobedient neighbour. This assistance was so effectively given, that in the next year the nawab-vizier was forced to sue humbly for peace, and to give up some of his possessions as the price of it. One among many stipulations of the East India Company, in reference to the military forces allowed to be maintained by native princes, was made in 1768, when the nawab-vizier was limited to an army of 35,000 troops; namely, 10,000 cavalry, 10,000 sepoys or infantry, 5000 matchlock-men, 500 artillery, and 9500 irregulars. In 1773, Warren Hastings had become so completely involved in the perplexities of Indian politics, and made treaties so unscrupulously if he could thereby advance the interests of the Company—that Company which he served with a zeal worthy of a better cause—that he plotted with the nawab-vizier against the poor decrepit Mogul: the nawab to obtain much additional power and territory, and the British to obtain large sums of money for assisting him. When the next nawab-vizier, Azof-u-Dowlah, assumed power in Oude in 1775, he hastened to strengthen himself by an alliance with the now powerful British; he gave up to them some territory; they agreed to protect him, and to provide a certain contingent of troops, for which he was to pay an annual sum. This was the complicated way in which the Company gained a footing in so many Indian provinces and kingdoms. It was in 1782 that that shameful proceeding took place, which—though Warren Hastings obtained an acquittal concerning it at his celebrated trial in the House of Lords—has indubitably left a stain upon his name; namely, the spoliation of two begums or princesses of Oude, and the cruel punishment, almost amounting to torture, of some of their dependents. The alleged cause was an arrear in the payment of the annual sum due from the nawab. Even if the debt were really due, the mode of extorting the money, and the selection of the persons from whom it was

* By Mr Knighton, author of *Forest Life in Ceylon*.

extorted, can never be reconciled to the principles of even-handed justice. The truth may be compressed into a short sentence—the Company being terribly in want of money to carry on a war against Hyder Ali, the governor-general determined to obtain a supply from some or other of the native princes in Northern India; and those natives being often faithless, he did not hesitate to become faithless to them. During the remainder of the century, the Company increased more and more its 'protection' of the nawab-vizier, and received larger and larger sums in payment for that protection. Azof-u-Dowlah was succeeded in 1797 by Vizier Ali, and he in 1798 by Saadut Ali.

We come now to the present century. In 1801, the Marquis Wellesley placed the relations with Oude on a new footing: he relinquished a claim to any further subsidy from the nawab-vizier, but obtained instead the rich districts of Allahabad, Azimghur, Goruckpore, and the Southern Doab, estimated to yield an annual revenue of nearly a million and a half sterling. Oude was larger than England before this date; but the marquis took nearly half of it by this transaction. Matters remained without much change till 1814, when Saadut Ali was succeeded by Ghazee-u-Deen Hyder. During the war between the British and the Nepaulese, soon afterwards, the nawab-vizier of Oude lent the Company two millions sterling, and received in return the Terai or jungle-country between Oude and Nepaul. A curious system of exchanges, this; for after receiving rich districts instead of money, the Company received money in return for a poor district inhabited chiefly by wild beasts. In 1819, the Company allowed Ghazee-u-Deen Hyder to renounce the vassal-title of nawab-vizier, which was a mockery as connected with the suzerainty of the now powerless Emperor of Delhi, and to become *King* of Oude—a king, however, with a greater king at his elbow in the person of the British resident at the court of Lucknow. The Company again became a borrower from Ghazee, during the Mahratta and Burmese wars. In 1827, the throne of Oude was ascended by Nussir-u-Deen Hyder—an aspirant to the throne who was favoured in his pretensions by the Company, and who was, as a consequence, in bitter animosity with most of his relations during the ten years of his reign. Complicated monetary arrangements were frequently made with the Company, the nature and purport of which are not always clearly traceable; but they generally had the effect of increasing the power of the Company in Oude. On the death of Nussir, in 1837, a violent struggle took place for the throne. He, like other eastern princes, had a large number of sons; but the Company would not acknowledge the legitimacy of any one of them; and the succession therefore fell upon Mahomed Ali Shah, uncle to the deceased sovereign. The begum or chief wife of Nussir fomented a rebellion to overturn this arrangement; and it cost Colonel (afterwards General) Low, resident at Lucknow, much trouble to preserve peace among the wrangling members of the royal family.

Now approaches the arrangement which led to the change of rulers. Oude had been most miserably governed during many years. The king and his relations, his courtiers and his dependents grasped for money as a substitute for the political power which they once possessed; and in the obtainment of this money they scrupled at no atrocities against the natives. The court, too, was steeped in debaucheries of the most licentious kind, outraging the decencies of life, and squandering wealth on the minions who ministered to its pleasures. The more thoughtful and large-hearted among the Company's superior servants saw here what they had so often seen elsewhere: that when the Company virtually took possession of a native state, and pensioned off the chief and his family, a moral deterioration followed; he was not allowed to exercise real sovereignty; he became more intensely selfish, because he had nothing to be proud of, even if he wished to govern well; and he took refuge in the only oriental substitute—sensual enjoyment. When Mahomed Ali Shah died in 1842, and his son, Umjud Ali Shah, was sanctioned by the Company as king, a pledge was exacted and a threat foreshadowed: the pledge was, that such reforms should be made by the king as would contribute to the tranquillity and just government of the country; the threat was, that if he did *not* do this, the sovereignty would be put an end to, and the Company would take the government into its own hands. In 1847, Umjud Ali Shah was succeeded by his son, Wajid Ali Shah: a king who equalled or surpassed his predecessors in weakness and profligacy, and under whom the state of matters went from bad to worse. The Marquis of Dalhousie was governor-general when matters arrived at a crisis. There can be no question that the Company, whatever may be said about aggressive views, wished to see the millions of Oude well and happily governed; and it is equally unquestionable that this wish had not been gratified. The engagement with Umjud Ali Shah had assumed this form: 'It is hereby provided that the King of Oude will take into his immediate and earnest consideration, in concert with the British resident, the best means of remedying the existing defects in the police, and in the judicial and revenue administration of his dominions; and that if his majesty should neglect to attend to the advice and counsel of the British government or its local representative, and if (which God forbid!) gross and systematic oppression, anarchy, and misrule, should hereafter at any time prevail within the Oude dominions, such as seriously to endanger the public tranquillity, the British government reserves to itself the right of appointing its own officers to the management of whatsoever portion of the Oude territory, either to a small or great extent, in which such misrule as that above alluded to may have occurred, for so long a period as it may deem necessary.' The marquis, finding that thirteen years had presented no improvement in the internal government of Oude, resolved to adopt decisive measures. He drew up a treaty, whereby the administration of the territory of Oude was to be transferred to the British government; ample provision being made for the dignity, affluence, and honour of the king and his family. The king refused to sign the treaty, not admitting the allegations or suppositions on which it was based; whereupon the marquis, acting with the sanction of the Company and of the imperial government in London, announced all existing treaties to be null and void, and issued a proclamation declaring that the government of the territories of Oude was henceforth vested exclusively and for ever in the East India Company. The governor-general in his minute, it will be remembered, spoke of this transfer of power in the following brief terms: 'The kingdom of Oude has been assumed in perpetual government by the Honourable East India Company; in pursuance of a policy which has so recently been under the consideration of the Honourable Court, that I deem it unnecessary to refer to it more particularly here.'

Everything tends to shew that the king violently opposed this loss of his regal title and power. When the governor-general and the resident at Lucknow waited on him with the draft of the proposed treaty, towards the close of 1855, he not only refused to sign it, but announced his intention to proceed to England, with a view of obtaining justice from Queen Victoria against the Company. This the marquis would not prevent; but he intimated that the king must travel, and be treated by the Company's servants, as a *private individual*, if he adopted this step. The stipend for the royal family was fixed by the Company—of course without the consent of the king and his relations—at £120,000 per annum. The reasons for putting an end to the title of King of Oude were thus stated, in a document addressed by the directors of the East India Company to the governor-general of India in council, many months after the transfer of power had been effected, and only a short time before the commencement of the Revolt: 'Half a century ago, our new and critical position among the Mohammedans of Northwestern India compelled us to respect the titular dignity of the Kings of Delhi. But the experiences of that half-century have abundantly demonstrated the inconveniences of suffering an empty nominal sovereignty to descend from generation to generation; and the continuance of such a phantom of power must be productive of inconvenience to our government, and we believe of more mortification than gratification to the royal pensioners themselves. It fosters humiliating recollections; it engenders delusive hopes; it is the fruitful source of intrigues that end in disappointment and disgrace. The evil is not limited to the effect produced upon the members of the royal house; prone to intrigue themselves, they become also a centre for the intrigues of others. It is natural, also, that the younger members of such a family should feel a greater repugnance than they otherwise would to mix with the community and become industrious and useful subjects. Strongly impressed with these convictions, we therefore observe with satisfaction that no pledge or promise of any kind with regard to the recognition by our government of the kingly title after the death of the present titular sovereign, Wajid Ali Shah, has been made to him or to his heirs.' The reasoning in this declaration is probably sound; but it does not apply, and was not intended to apply, to the original aggressive movements of the Company. Because the shadow of sovereignty is not worth retaining without the substance, it does not necessarily follow that the Company was right in taking the substance fifty-five years earlier: that proceeding must be attacked or defended on its own special ground, by any one who wishes to enter the arena of Indian politics.

It appears from this document, that four of the British authorities at Calcutta—the Marquis of Dalhousie, General Anson, Mr Dorin, and Mr Grant—had concurred in opinion that, as the king refused to sign the treaty, he should, as a punishment, be denied many of the privileges promised by that treaty. They proposed that the annual stipend of twelve lacs of rupees (£120,000) should be 'reserved for consideration' after the demise of the king—that is, that it should not necessarily be a perpetual hereditary stipend. To this, however, Colonel Low, who had been British resident at Lucknow, very earnestly objected. He urged that the king's sons were so young, that they could not, in any degree, be blamed for his conduct in not signing the proposed treaty; that they ought not to be made to lose their inheritance through the father's fault; that the father, the king, would in any case be pretty severely punished for his obstinacy; and that it would not be worthy of a great paramount state, coming into possession of a rich territory, to refuse a liberal stipend to the descendants of the king. These representations were listened to, and a pension to the amount already named was granted to the king and his heirs—'not heirs according to Mohammedan usages, but only those persons who may be direct male descendants of the present king, born in lawful wedlock.' A difficult duty was left to the Calcutta government, to decide how many existing persons had a claim to be supported out of the pension, seeing that an eastern king's family is generally one of great magnitude; and that, although he has many wives and many children, they fill various ranks in relation to legitimacy. The Company proposed, if the king liked the plan, that one-third of the pension should be commuted into a capital sum, with which jaghires or estates might be bought, and vested in the family for the use of the various members—making them, in fact, zemindars or landed proprietors, having something to do instead of leading lives of utter idleness. In what light the directors viewed the large and important army of Oude, will be noticed presently; but in reference to the transfer of mastership itself, they said: 'An expanse of territory embracing an area of nearly twenty-five thousand square miles, and containing five million of inhabitants, has passed from its native prince to the Queen of England without the expenditure of a drop of blood, and almost without a murmur. The peaceable manner in which this great change has been accomplished, and the tranquillity which has since prevailed in all parts of the country, are circumstances which could not fail to excite in us the liveliest emotions of thankfulness and pleasure.' This was written, be it remembered—and the fact is full of instruction touching the miscalculations of the Company—less than two months before the cartridge troubles began, and while the mysterious chupatties were actually in circulation from hand to hand.

The deposed King of Oude did not go to England, as he had threatened; he went to Calcutta, and took up his abode, in April 1856, at Garden Reach, in the outskirts of that city, attended by his late prime minister, Ali Nuckee Khan, and by several followers. The queen, however, achieved the adventurous journey to the British capital, taking with her a numerous retinue. This princess was not, in accordance with European usages, the real Queen of Oude; she was rather a sort of queen-dowager, the king's mother, and was accompanied by the king's brother and the king's son—the one claiming to be heir-presumptive, the other heir-apparent. All felt a very lively interest in the maintenance of the regal power and revenues among the members of the family, and came to England in the hope of obtaining a reversal of the governor-general's decree. They left Lucknow in the spring of 1856, and arrived in England in August. An attempt was made by an injudicious agent to enlist public sympathy for them by an open-air harangue at Southampton. He bade his hearers picture to themselves the suppliant for justice, 'an aged queen, brought up in all the pomp and luxury of the East, the soles of whose feet were scarcely allowed to tread the ground, laying aside the prejudices of travel, and undertaking a journey of some ten thousand miles, to appeal to the people of England for justice;' and the 'fellow-countrymen' were then exhorted to give 'three cheers' for the royal family of Oude —which they undoubtedly did, in accordance with the usual custom of an English assemblage when so exhorted; but this momentary excitement soon ceased, and the oriental visitors settled in London for a lengthened residence. What official interviews or correspondence took place concerning the affairs of Oude, was not publicly known; but there was an evident disinclination on the part both of the government and the two Houses of parliament to hold out any hopes of a reversal of the policy adopted by the East India Company; and the ex-royal family of Oude maintained no hold on the public mind, except so far as the turbaned and robed domestics attracted the attention of metropolitan sight-seers. In what fashion these suppliants disowned and ignored the Revolt in India, a future chapter will shew.

The reader will, then, picture to himself the state of Oude at the period when the Revolt commenced. The deposed king was at Calcutta; his mother and other relations were in London; while the whole governing power was in the hands of the Company's servants. Sir Henry Lawrence, a man in whom sagacity, energy, and nobleness of heart were remarkably combined, had succeeded Sir James Outram as resident, or rather chief-commissioner, and now held supreme sway at Lucknow.

It is important here to know in what light the East India Company regarded the native army of Oude, at and soon after the annexation. In the directors' minute, of December 1856, just on the eve of disturbances which were quite unexpected by them, the subject was thus touched upon: 'The probable temper of the army, a force computed on paper at some 60,000 men of all arms, on the announcement of a measure which threw a large proportion of them out of employment, and transferred the remainder to a new master, was naturally a source of some anxiety to us. In your scheme for the future government and administration of the Oude provinces, drawn up on the 4th of February, you proposed the organisation of an Oude irregular force, into which you suggested the absorption of as large a number of the disbanded soldiers of the king as could be employed in such a corps, whilst others were to be provided for in the military and district police; but you observed at the same time that these arrangements would not absorb one-half of the disbanded troops. To the remainder you determined to grant pensions and gratuities, graduated according to length of service. There were no better means than these of palliating a difficulty which could not be avoided. But only partial success was to be expected from so partial a measure. As a further precaution, the chief-commissioner deemed it expedient to promise pensions of one hundred rupees per month to the commandants of the regiments of the late king, some sixty in number, conditional on their lending their cordial co-operation to the government in this crisis, and provided that their regiments remained quiet and loyal. We recognise the force of the chief-commissioner's argument in support of these grants; and are willing to adopt his suggestion that, in the event of any of these men accepting office as tuhseeldars or other functionaries under our government, the amount of their pensions should still be paid to them.' It was found that the King of Oude had allowed the pay of his soldiers to run into arrear. On this point the directors said: 'The army, a large number of whom are necessarily thrown out of employment, and who cannot immediately find, even if the habits of their past lives fitted them for, industrial occupations, are peculiarly entitled to liberal consideration. It is doubtless true that, as stated by the chief-commissioner, the soldiery of Oude have "fattened on rapine and plunder;" and it is certain that the servants of the Oude government enriched themselves at the expense of the people. But this was only part of the system under which they lived; nothing better, indeed, was to be expected from men whose pay, after it had been tardily extracted from the treasury, was liable to be withheld from them by a fraudulent minister. Whatever may have been the past excesses and the illicit gains of the soldiers, it was the duty of the British government in this conjuncture to investigate their claims to the arrears of regular pay alleged to be due to them by the Oude government, and, having satisfied ourselves of the justice of these claims, to discharge the liabilities in full. We observe with satisfaction that this has been done. . . . . We concur, moreover, in the very judicious remark made by Viscount Canning, in his minute of the 5th of March, "that a few lacs* spent in closing the account, without injustice, and even liberality, will be well repaid if we can thereby smooth down discontent and escape disturbance."'

The plan adopted, therefore, was to disband the army of the deposed king, pay up the arrears due by him to the soldiers, re-enlist some of the discharged men to form a new Oude force in the Company's service, and give pensions or gratuities to the remainder.

We are now in a condition to follow the course of events at Lucknow during the months of April and May 1857: events less mutinous and tragical than those at Meerut and Delhi, but important for their consequences in later months.

It was in the early part of April that the incident occurred at Lucknow concerning a medicine-bottle, briefly adverted to in a former chapter: shewing the existence of an unusually morbid feeling on the subjects of religion and caste. Dr Wells having been seen to taste some medicine which he was about to administer to a sick soldier, to test its quality, the Hindoos near at hand refused to partake of it, lest the taint of a Christian mouth should degrade their caste. They complained to Colonel Palmer, of the 48th native regiment, who, as he believed and hoped, adopted a conciliatory course that removed all objection. This hope was not realised, however; for on that same night the doctor's bungalow was fired and destroyed by some of the sepoys, whom no efforts could identify. Very soon afterwards, nearly all the huts of the 13th regiment were burned down, under similarly mysterious circumstances.

Sir Henry Lawrence's difficulties began with the vexatious cartridge-question, as was the case in so many other parts of India. Towards the close of April, Captain Watson found that many of the recruits or younger men in his regiment, the 7th Oude infantry, evinced a reluctance to bite the cartridges. Through some oversight, the new method of tearing instead of biting had not been shewn to the sepoys at Lucknow; and there was therefore sufficient reason for adopting a conciliatory course in explaining the matter to them. The morbid feeling still, however, remained. On the 1st of May, recusancy was again exhibited, followed by an imprisonment of some of the recruits in the quarter-guard. The native officers of the regiment came forward to assure Captain Watson that this disobedience was confined to the 'youngsters,' and that the older sepoys discountenanced it. He believed them, or seemed to do so. On the 2d he addressed the men, pointing out the folly of the conduct attributed to the young recruits, and exhorting them to behave more like true soldiers. Though listened to respectfully, he observed so much sullenness and doggedness among the troops, that he brought the matter under the notice of his superior officer, Brigadier Grey. The native officers, when put to the test, declined taking any steps to enforce obedience; they declared their lives to be in danger from the men under them, should they do so. The brigadier, accompanied by Captains Watson and Barlow, at once went to the lines, had the men drawn up in regular order, and put the question to each company singly, whether it was willing to use the same cartridges *which had all along been employed*. They refused. The brigadier left them to arrange plans for the morrow; placing them, however, under safe guard for the night. On the morning of the 3d, the grenadier company (picked or most skilful company) of the regiment went through the lines, threatening to kill some of the European officers; and soon afterwards the tumult became so serious, that the fulfilment of the threat seemed imminent. By much entreaty, the officers, European and native, allayed in some degree the excitement of the men. While this was going on, however, at the post or station of Moosa Bagh, a messenger was sent by the intriguers of the 7th regiment to the cantonment at Murreeaun, with a letter inciting the 48th native infantry to join them in mutiny. This letter was fortunately brought, by a subadar true to his duty, to Colonel Palmer, the commandant. Prompt measures were at once resolved upon. A considerable force—consisting of the 7th Oude cavalry, the 4th Oude infantry, portions of the 48th and 71st Bengal infantry, a portion of the 7th Bengal cavalry, a wing of her Majesty's 32d, and a field-battery of guns—was sent from the cantonment to the place where the recusants were posted. The mutineers stood firm for some time; but when they saw cannon pointed at them, some turned and fled with great rapidity, while others quietly gave up their arms. The cavalry pursued and brought back some of the fugitives. The 7th Oude irregular infantry regiment, about a thousand strong, was thus suddenly broken into three fragments

* Lacs or lakhs of rupees: a lac being 100,000, value about £10,000.

—one escaped, one captured, and one disarmed. A letter from the Rev. Mr Polehampton, chaplain to the English residents at Lucknow, affords one among many proofs that Sunday was a favourite day for such outbreaks in India—perhaps purposely so selected by the rebellious sepoys. The 3d of May was Sunday: the chaplain was performing evening-service at the church. 'Towards the end of the prayers, a servant came into church, and spoke first to Major Reid, of the 48th; and then to Mr Dashwood, of the same regiment. They both went out, and afterwards others were called away. The ladies began to look very uncomfortable; one or two went out of church; one or two others crossed over the aisle to friends who were sitting on the other side; so that altogether I had not a very attentive congregation.' When it was found that the officers had been called out to join the force against the mutineers, the chaplain 'felt very much inclined to ride down to see what was going on; but as the Moosa Bagh is seven miles from our house, and as I should have left my wife all alone, I stayed where I was. I thought of what William III. said when he was told that the Bishop of Derry had been shot at the ford at the Battle of the Boyne, "What took him there?"'

The course of proceeding adopted by Sir Henry Lawrence on this occasion was quite of an oriental character, as if suggested by one who well knew the Indian mind. He held a grand military durbar, to reward the faithful as well as to awe the mutinous. In the first instance he had said that the government would be advised to disband the regiment, with a provision for re-enlisting those who had not joined the rebels; but pending the receipt of instructions from Calcutta, he held his durbar (court; levee; hall of audience). Four native soldiers—a havildar-major, a subadar, and a sepoy of the 48th regiment, and a sepoy of the 13th—who had proved themselves faithful in an hour of danger, were to be rewarded. The lawn in front of the residency was carpeted, and chairs were arranged on three sides of a square for some of the native officers and sepoys; while a large verandah was filled with European officials, civil and military, upwards of twenty in number. Sir Henry opened the proceedings with an address in the Hindostani language, full of point and vigour. After a gorgeous description of the power and wealth of the British nation—overwrought, perhaps, for an English ear, but well suited to the occasion—he adverted to the freedom of conscience in British India on matters of religion: 'Those amongst you who have perused the records of the past must well know that Alumghir in former times, and Hyder Ali in later days, forcibly converted thousands and thousands of Hindoos, desecrated their fanes, demolished their temples, and carried ruthless devastation amongst the household gods. Come to our times; many here present well know that Runjeet Singh never permitted his Mohammedan subjects to call the pious to prayer—never allowed the Afghan to sound from the lofty minarets which adorn Lahore, and which remain to this day a monument to their munificent founders. The year before last a Hindoo could not have dared to build a temple in Lucknow. All this is changed. Who is there that would dare *now* to interfere with our Hindoo or Mohammedan subjects?' He contrasted this intolerance of Mohammedan and Hindoo rulers in matters of religion with the known scruples of the British government; and told his hearers that the future would be like the present, in so far as concerns the freedom of all religions over the whole of India. He rebuked and spurned the reports which had been circulated among the natives, touching meditated insult to their faith or their castes. He adverted to the gallant achievements of the Company's native troops during a hundred years of British rule; and told how it pained him to think that disbandment of such troops had been found necessary at Barrackpore and Berhampore. And then he presented the bright side of his picture: 'Now turn to these good and faithful soldiers—Subadar Sewak Tewaree, Havildar Heera Lall Doobey, and Sipahi Ranura Doobey, of the 48th native infantry, and to Hossein Buksh, of the 13th regiment—who have set to you all a good example. The first three at once arrested the bearer of a seditious letter, and brought the whole circumstance to the notice of superior authority. You know well what the consequences were, and what has befallen the 7th Oude irregular infantry, more than fifty of whose sirdars and soldiers are now in confinement, and the whole regiment awaits the decision of government as to its fate. Look at Hossein Buksh of the 13th, fine fellow as he is! Is he not a good and faithful soldier? Did he not seize three villains who are now in confinement and awaiting their doom. It is to reward such fidelity, such acts and deeds as I have mentioned, and of which you are all well aware, that I have called you all together this day—to assure you that those who are faithful and true to their salt will always be amply rewarded and well cared for; that the great government which we all serve is prompt to reward, swift to punish, vigilant and eager to protect its faithful subjects; but firm, determined, resolute to crush all who may have the temerity to rouse its vengeance.' After a further exhortation to fidelity, a further declaration of the power and determination of the government to deal severely with all disobedient troops, Sir Henry arrived at the climax of his impassioned and vigorous address: 'Advance, Subadar Sewak Tewaree—come forward, havildar and sepoys—and receive these splendid gifts from the government which is proud to number you amongst its soldiers. Accept these honorary sabres; you have won them well: long may you live to wear them in honour! Take these sums of money for your families and relatives; wear these robes of honour at your homes and your festivals; and may the bright example which you have so conspicuously t, find, as it doubtless will, followers in every giment and company in the army.' To the subar and the havildar-major were presented each, handsomely decorated sword, a pair of elegant awls, a choogah or cloak, and four pieces of nbroidered cloth; to the other two men, each, decorated sword, a turban, pieces of cloth, and ree hundred rupees in cash. Hossein Buksh as also made a naik or corporal.

Let not the reader judge this address and these roceedings by an English standard. Sir Henry awrence knew well what he was doing; for w of the Company's servants ever had a deeper nsight into the native character than that eminent nan. There had been, in the Company's general ystem, too little punishment for misconduct, too ittle reward for faithfulness, among the native roops: knowing this, he adopted a different olicy, so far as he was empowered to do.

When the news of the Lucknow disturbance reached Calcutta, a course was adopted reminding us of the large amount of written correspondence involved in the mode of managing public affairs. The governor-general, it may here be explained, was assisted by a supreme council, consisting of four persons, himself making a fifth; and the council was aided by four secretaries, for the home, the foreign, the military, and the financial affairs of India. All these officials were expected to make their inquiries, communicate their answers, state their opinions, and notify their acts in writing, for the information of the Court of Directors and the Board of Control in London; and this is one reason why parliamentary papers touching Indian affairs are often so voluminous. At the period in question, Viscount Canning, Mr Dorin, General Low, Mr Grant, and Mr Peacock, were the five members of council, each and all of whom prepared 'minutes' declaratory of their opinions whether Sir Henry Lawrence had done right or wrong in threatening to disband the mutinous 7th regiment. The viscount wished to support the chief-commissioner at once, in a bold method of dealing with the disaffected. Mr Dorin went further. He said: 'My theory is that no corps mutinies that is well commanded;' he wished that some censure should be passed on the English officers of the 7th, and that the men of that regiment should receive more severe treatment than mere disbanding. General Low advocated a course midway between the other two; but at the same time deemed it right to inquire how it happened that the men had been required to bite the cartridges; seeing that instructions had already been issued from head-quarters that the platoon exercises should be conducted without this necessity. Mr Grant's minute was very long; he wanted more time, more reports, more examinations, and was startled at the promptness with which Lawrence had proposed to act. Mr Peacock also wanted further information before deciding on the plan proposed by the ruling authority at Oude. The governor-general's minute was written on the 9th; the other four commented on it on the 10th; the governor-general replied to their comments on the 11th; and they commented on his reply on the 12th. Thus it arose that the tedious system of written minutes greatly retarded the progress of business at Calcutta.

There cannot be a better opportunity than the present for adverting to the extraordinary services rendered by the electric telegraph in India during the early stages of the Revolt, when the mutineers had not yet carried to any great extent their plan of cutting the wires. We have just had occasion to describe the routine formalities in the mode of conducting business at Calcutta; but it would be quite indefensible to withhold admiration from the electro-telegraphic system established by the East India Company. This matter was touched upon in the Introduction; and the middle of May furnished wonderful illustrations of the value of the lightning-messenger. Let us fix our attention on two days only—the 16th and 17th of May—less than one week after the commencement of violent scenes at Meerut and Delhi. Let us picture to ourselves Viscount Canning at Calcutta, examining every possible scheme for sending up reinforcements to the disturbed districts; Sir John Lawrence at Lahore, keeping the warlike population of the Punjaub in order by his mingled energy and tact; Sir Henry Lawrence at Lucknow, surrounded by Oudians, whom it required all his skill to baffle; Mr Colvin at Agra, watching with an anxious eye the state of affairs in the Northwest Provinces; General Anson at Simla, preparing, as commander-in-chief, to hasten down to the Delhi district; Lord Elphinstone at Bombay, as governor of that presidency; and Lord Harris, filling an analogous office at Madras. Bearing in mind these persons and places, let us see what was done by the electric telegraph on those two busy days—deriving our information from the voluminous but ill-arranged parliamentary papers on the affairs of India: papers almost useless without repeated perusals and collations.

First, then, the 16th of May. Sir Henry Lawrence sent one of his pithy, terse telegrams* from Lucknow to Calcutta, to this effect: 'All is quiet here, but affairs are critical; get every European you can from China, Ceylon, and elsewhere; also all the Goorkhas from the hills. Time is precious.' On the same day he sent another: 'Give me plenary military power in Oude; I will not use it unnecessarily. I am sending two troops of cavalry to Allahabad. Send a company of Europeans into the fort there. It will be good to raise regiments of irregular horse, under good officers.' In the reverse direction—from Calcutta to Lucknow—

* The word *telegram*, denoting a message sent, as distinguished from the *telegraph* which sends it, has been a subject of much discussion among Greek scholars, concerning the validity of the grammatical basis on which it is formed; but as the new form is convenient for its brevity and expressiveness, and as it has been much used by the governor-general and the various officers connected with India, it will occasionally be employed in this work.

this message was sent: 'It appears that the regiment of Ferozpore [Sikhs] has already marched to Allahabad, and that, under present circumstances, no part of that regiment can be spared.' And another, in like manner answering a telegram of the same day: 'You have full military powers. The governor-general will support you in everything you think necessary. It is impossible to send a European company to Allahabad; Dinapoor must not be weakened by a single man. If you can raise any irregulars that you can tru do so at once. Have you any good officers spare for the duty?' All this, be it remember was telegraphed to and from two cities six seven hundred miles apart. On the same da questions were asked, instructions requested, an information given, between Calcutta, on the on hand, and Agra, Gwalior, Meerut, Cawnpore, an Benares on the other. Passing thence to Bomba —twelve hundred miles from Calcutta by roa

Sir Henry Lawrence.

and very much more by telegraph-route—we find the two governors conversing through the wires concerning the English troops which had just been fighting in Persia, and those about being sent to China; all of whom were regarded with a longing eye by the governor-general at that critical time. Viscount Canning telegraphed to Lord Elphinstone on the 16th: 'Two of the three European regiments which are returning from Persia are urgently wanted in Bengal. If they are sent from Bombay to Kurachee, will they find conveyance up the Indus? Are they coming from Bushire in steam or sailing transports? Let me know immediately whether General Ashburnham is going to Madras.' The general here named was to have commanded the troops destined for China. The replies and counter-replies to this on the 17th, we will mention presently. Lord Harris, on this same day of activity, sent the brief telegram: 'The Madras Fusiliers will be sent immediately by *Zenobia*; but she is hardly fit to take a whole regiment.' This was in reply to a request transmitted shortly before.

Next, the 17th of May. Sir Henry Lawrence telegraphed from Lucknow: 'You are quite right to keep Allahabad safe. We shall do without Sikhs or Goorkhas. We have concentrated the troops as much as possible, so as to protect the treasury and magazine, and keep up a communication. A false alarm last night.' He sent another, detailing what he had done in managing the turbulent 7th regiment. In the reverse direction, a message was sent to him, that 'The artillery invalids at Chunar, about 109 in number, have been ordered to proceed to Allahabad immediately.' The telegrams were still more numerous than on the 16th, between the various towns mentioned in the last paragraph, in Northern India. From Bombay, Lord Elphinstone telegraphed to ask whether an extra mail-steamer should be sent off to Suez with news for England; and added: 'The 64th will arrive in a few days from Bushire; their destination is Bengal; but we can keep them here available, or send them round to Calcutta if you wish it.' To which the governor-general replied from Calcutta, still on the same day, expressing his wishes about the mail, and adding: 'If you can send the 64th to Calcutta by steam, do so without any delay. If steam is not available, I will wait for an answer to my last message before deciding that they shall come round in sailing-vessels. Let me know when

Residency at Lucknow.

you expect the other European regiments and the artillery, and what steam-vessels will be available for their conveyance. Have you at present a steam-vessel that could go to Galle to bring troops from there to Calcutta? This must not interfere with the despatch of the 64th.' Another, from Lord Elphinstone, on the very same day, announced that the best of the Indus boats were in Persia; that it would be impossible to send up three European regiments from Kurachee to the Punjaub, within any reasonable time, by the Indus boats then available; that he nevertheless intended to send one regiment, the 1st Europeans, by that route; and that the 2d Europeans were daily expected from Persia. He further said: 'Shall I send them round to Calcutta; and shall I send the 78th also? General Ashburnham leaves this to-day by the steamer for Galle, where he expects to meet Lord Elgin; he is not going to Madras.' While this was going on between Calcutta and Bombay, Madras was not idle. The governor-general telegraphed to Lord Harris, to inform him of the mutiny, on the previous day, of the Sappers and Miners who went from Roorkee to Meerut; and another on the same day, replying to a previous telegram, said: 'If the *Zenobia* cannot bring all the Fusiliers, the remainder might be sent in the *Bentinck*, which will be at Madras on the 26th; but send as many in the *Zenobia* as she will safely hold. Let me know when the *Zenobia* sails, and what force she brings.' If we had selected three days instead of two, as illustrating the wonders of the electric telegraph, we should have had to narrate that on the third day, the 18th of May, Lord Harris announced that the Fusiliers would leave Madras that evening; that Viscount Canning thanked him for his great promptness; that Lord Elphinstone received instructions to send one of the three regiments up the Indus, and the other two round to Calcutta; that he asked and received suggestions about managing a Beloochee regiment at Kurachee; and that messages in great number were transmitted to and from Calcutta, Benares, Allahabad, Cawnpore, Lucknow, Agra, and other large towns.

The imagination becomes almost bewildered at contemplating such things. Between the morning of the 16th of May and the evening of the 17th, the great officers of the Company, situated almost at the extreme points of the Indian empire—east, west, north, and south—were conversing through four thousand miles of wire, making requests, soliciting advice, offering services, discussing difficulties, weighing probabilities, concerting plans; and all with a precision much greater than if they had been writing letters to one another, in ordinary official form, in adjoining rooms of the same building. It was, perhaps, the greatest triumph ever achieved up to that time by the greatest of modern inventions—the electric telegraph.

We shall find the present part of the chapter an equally convenient place in which to notice a series of operations strikingly opposed to those just described—slow travelling as compared with quick telegraphy. It is full of instruction to see how earnestly anxious Viscount Canning was to send troops up to the northern provinces; and how he was baffled by the tardiness of all travelling appliances in India. The railway was opened only from Calcutta to Raneegunge, a very small portion of the distance to the disturbed districts. The history of the peregrinations of a few English troops in May will illustrate, and will receive illustration from, the matters treated in Chapter I.

The European 84th regiment, it will be remembered, had been hastily brought from Rangoon in the month of March, to assist in disbanding the sepoys who had shewn disaffection at Barrackpore and Berhampore. When the troubles began at Meerut and Delhi, in May, it was resolved to send on this regiment; and the governor-general found no part of his onerous duties more difficult than that of obtaining *quick* transmission for those troops. On the 21st of May he telegraphed to Benares: 'Pray instruct the commissariat officer to prepare cooking-pots and other arrangements for the 84th regiment, now on its way to Benares; and the barrack department to have cots ready for them.' On the 23d, Sir Henry Lawrence asked: 'When may her Majesty's 84th be expected at Cawnpore?' to which an answer was sent on the following day: 'It is impossible to convey a wing of Europeans to Cawnpore (about six hundred and thirty miles) in less time than twenty-five days. The government dâk and the dâk companies are fully engaged in carrying a company of the 84th to Benares, at the rate of 18 men a day. A wing of the Madras Fusiliers arrived yesterday, and starts to-day; part by bullock-train, part by steamer. The bullock-train can take 100 men per day, at the rate of thirty miles a day. The entire regiment of the Fusiliers, about 900 strong, cannot be collected at Benares in less than 19 or 20 days. About 150 men who go by steam will scarcely be there so soon. I expect, that from this time forward troops will be pushed upwards at the rate of 100 men a day from Calcutta; each batch taking ten days to reach Benares; from Benares they will be distributed as most required. The regiments from Pegu, Bombay, and Ceylon will be sent up in this way. Every bullock and horse that is to be had, except just enough to carry the post, is retained; and no troops will be sent by steam which can be sent more quickly by other means.' These details shew that Cawnpore and Benares were both asking for troops at the same time; and that the governor-general, even if he possessed the soldiers, had not the means of sending them expeditiously. On the 24th, a message was sent to Raneegunge, ordering that a company of Madras troops might be well attended to, when they arrived by railway from Calcutta; and on the next day, Benares received notice to prepare for four companies proceeding thither by bullock-train, one company per day. The Benares commissioner announced the arrival of *fifteen* English soldiers, as if that were a number to be proud of, and stated that he would send them on to Cawnpore. (It will be seen, on reference to a map, that Benares lies in the route to almost all the upper and western provinces, whether by road or by river.) The Raneegunge agent telegraphed on the 26th: 'If the men reach Sheergotty, there is no difficulty in conveying them to Benares; the only difficulty is between Raneegunge and Sheergotty. *Ekahs* are not, I think, adapted for Europeans; nor do I think that time would be gained.' An ekah or ecka, we may here remark, is a light pony-gig on two wheels, provided with a cloth cushion on which the rider (usually a native) sits cross-legged. It shews the nature of Indian travelling, to find the officials discussing whether English soldiers should be thus conveyed—one cushioned vehicle to convey each cross-legged soldier. At Benares, the commissioner borrowed from the rajah the use of a house in which to lodge the English troops as fast as they came; and he sent them on by dâk to Allahabad and Cawnpore. Nevertheless Sir Henry Lawrence, disturbed by ominous symptoms, wished for ekahs, dâks—anything that would give him English soldiers. He telegraphed on this day: 'I strongly advise that as many ekah-dâks be laid as possible, from Raneegunge to Cawnpore, to bring up European troops. *Spare no expense;*' and on the next day he received the reply: 'Every horse and carriage, bullock and cart, which could be brought upon the road, has been collected, and no means of increasing the number will be neglected.' On the 27th it was announced from Benares that 'the steamer had stuck,' and that all the land-dâks were being used that could possibly be procured. On the same day the Allahabad commissioner spoke hopefully of his plan that—by the aid of 1600 siege-train bullocks from that place, 600 from Cawnpore, the government bullocks, the private wagon-trains, and magazine carts—he might be able to send 160 Europeans per day up to Cawnpore. On the 28th, the Calcutta authorities sent a telegram to Benares, to announce that 'Up to the 1st of June seven dâk-carriages will be despatched daily, with one officer and 18 soldiers. On the 1st of June, and daily afterwards, there will be despatched nine dâk-carriages, with one officer and 24 Europeans; and 28 bullock-carts, with one officer, 90 Europeans, a few followers, and provisions to fill one cart. The Calcutta steamer and flat, with four officers, 134 Europeans, and proportion of followers; and the coal-steamer, with about the same numbers, will reach Benares on the 10th or 11th of June.' From this it will be seen that a 'dâk-carriage' conveyed three soldiers, and a 'bullock-cart' also three, the 'followers' probably accompanying them on foot. The Benares commissioner on the same day said: 'Happily we have good metalled roads all over this division'—thereby implying what would have been the result if the roads were not good. The use of bullocks was more particularly adverted to in a telegram of the 30th of May: 'Gun-bullocks would be most useful between Raneegunge and the Sone, if they could be sent from Calcutta in time; if there are carts, the daily dispatches can be increased; not otherwise. Gun-bullocks would save a day, as they travel quicker than our little animals.' Immediately afterwards, forty-six elephants were sent from Patna, and one hundred from Dacca and Barrackpore, to Sheergotty, to assist in the transport of troops. On a later occasion, when more troops had arrived from England, Viscount Canning sent two steamers from Calcutta to Pegu, to bring over cargoes of elephants, to be used as draught-animals!

Thus it continued, day after day—all the servants of the Company, civil and military, calculating how long it would take to send driblets of soldiers up the country; and all harassed by this dilemma—that what the Ganges steamers gained in roominess, they lost by the sinuosities of the river; and that what the dâks and bullock-trains gained by a direct route, they lost by the inevitable slowness of such modes of conveyance, and the smallness of the number of soldiers that could be carried at a time. Thankful that they possessed telegraphs, the authorities had little to be thankful for as concerned railways or roads, vehicles or horses.

We now return to the proceedings of Sir Henry Lawrence at Lucknow.

Before the collective minutes of the five members of the Supreme Council were fully settled, he had acted on the emergency which gave rise to them. He held a court of inquiry; the result of which was that two subadars, a jemadar, and forty-four sepoys of the mutinous 7th were committed to prison; but he resolved not at present to disband the regiment. His grand durbar has been already described. In the middle of the month, as just shewn, he sent many brief telegrams indicating that, though no mutinies had occurred at Lucknow, there was nevertheless need for watchfulness. He had asked for the aid of some Sikhs, but said, on the 18th: 'As there is difficulty, do not send the Sikhs to Lucknow.' On the next day, his message was: 'All very well in city, cantonment, and country;' but after this, the elements of mischief seemed to be gathering, although Lawrence prepared to meet all contingencies resolutely. 'All quiet,' he said on the 21st, 'but several reports of intended attacks on us.' He was, however, more solicitous about the fate of Cawnpore, Allahabad, and Benares, than of Lucknow.

The military position of Sir Henry towards the last week in May was this. He had armed four posts for his defence at Lucknow. In one were four hundred men and twenty guns; in another, a hundred Europeans and as many sepoys; in another was the chief store of powder, well under command. A hundred and thirty Europeans, two hundred sepoys, and six guns, guarded the treasury; the guns near the residency being under European control. The old magazine was denuded of its former contents, as a precautionary measure. Six guns, and two squadrons of the 2d Oude irregular cavalry, were at the Dâk bungalow, half-way between the residency and the cantonment. In the cantonment were three hundred and forty men of her Majesty's 32d, with six European guns, and six more of the Oude light field-battery. By the 23d of the month, nearly all the stores were moved from the old magazine to one of the strongholds, where thirty guns and one hundred Europeans were in position, and where ten days' supplies for five hundred men were stored. On the 29th, Lawrence's telegram told of 'great uneasiness at Lucknow. Disturbances threatened outside. Tranquillity cannot be much longer maintained unless Delhi be speedily captured.' The residency, a place rendered so memorable by subsequent events, must be here noticed. The cantonment was six miles from the city, and the residency was itself isolated from the rest of Lucknow. The Rev. Mr Polehampton, describing in his letter the occurrences about the middle of May, said: 'The sick have been brought to the residency; so have the women; and the residency is garrisoned by 130 men of the 32d, and by the battery of native artillery. All the ladies, wives of civilians, who live in different parts of the city, have come into the residency. By the residency, I mean a piece of ground a good deal elevated above the rest of the city, allotted by the King of Oude, when he first put himself under British "protection" some fifty years ago, to the British civil residents. It is walled round almost entirely; on one side native houses abut upon it, but on the other three sides it is tolerably clear. Roads without gates in some places connect it with the city; but it is not at all a bad place to make a stand—certainly the best in Lucknow, to which it is a sort of acropolis. The residency contains the chief-commissioner's house, Mr Gubbins's, Mr Ommaney's, Foyne's, the post-office, city hospital, electric-telegraph office, church, &c.' The ever-memorable defence made by a little band of English heroes in this 'acropolis' of Lucknow, will call for our attention in due time. Mr Polehampton spoke of the gravity with which Sir Henry Lawrence regarded the state of public affairs; and of the caution which led him to post *one* English soldier at every gun, to watch the native artillerymen. The chaplain had means of knowing with what assiduity crafty lying men tried to gain over the still faithful sepoys to mutiny. 'Another most absurd story they have got hold of, which came out in the examination of some of the mutineers before Sir Henry Lawrence. They say that in consequence of the Crimean war there are a great many widows in England, and that these are to be brought out and married to the Rajahs in Oude; and that their children, brought up as Christians, are to inherit all the estates! The natives are like babies—they will believe anything.'—Babies in belief, perhaps; but fiends in cruelty when excited.

The last two days of May were days of agitation at Lucknow. Many of the native troops broke out in open mutiny. They consisted of half of the 48th regiment, about half of the 71st, some few of the 13th, and two troops of the 7th cavalry—all of whom fled towards Seetapoor, a town nearly due north of Lucknow. Lawrence, with two companies of her Majesty's 32d, three hundred horse, and four guns, went in pursuit; but the horse, Oude native cavalry, evinced no zeal; and he was vexed to find that he could only get within round-shot of the mutineers. He took thirty prisoners—a very inadequate result of the pursuit. Many disaffected still remained in Lucknow; for bungalows were burned, and a few English officers shot. The city was quiet, but the cantonment was in a disturbed state. In his last telegrams for the month, the chief-commissioner, who was also chief military authority, used these words: 'It is difficult to say who are loyal; but it is believed the majority are so; only twenty-five of the 7th cavalry proved false;' and he further said: 'The faithful remnants of three infantry regiments and 7th cavalry, about seven hundred men, are encamped close to the detachment of two hundred of her Majesty's 32d and four European guns.' Even then he did not feel much uneasiness concerning the city and cantonment of Lucknow: it was towards other places, Cawnpore especially, that his apprehensive glance was directed.

What were the occurrences at Lucknow, and in other towns of the territory of Oude, in June, will be better understood when the progress of the Revolt in other places during May has been narrated.

Ekah, or Officer's Travelling Wagon.

General View of CALCUTTA from Fort William.

CHAPTER VII.

SPREAD OF DISAFFECTION IN MAY.

THE narrative has now arrived at a stage when some kind of classification of times and places becomes necessary. There were special reasons why Delhi and Lucknow should receive separate attention, connected as those two cities are with deposed native sovereigns chafed by their deposition; but other cities and towns now await notice, spread over many thousand square miles of territory, placed in various relations to the British government, involved in various degrees in mutinous proceedings, and differing much in the periods at which the hostile demonstrations were made. Two modes of treatment naturally suggest themselves. The towns might be treated topographically, beginning at Calcutta, and working westward towards the Indus; this would be convenient for reference to maps, but would separate contemporaneous events too far asunder. Or the occurrences might be treated chronologically, beginning from the Meerut outbreak, and advancing, as in a diary, day by day throughout the whole series; this would facilitate reference to dates, but would ignore local connection and mutual action. It may be possible, however, to combine so much of the two methods as will retain their advantages and avoid their defects; there may be groups of days and groups of places; and these groups may be so treated as to mark the relations both of sequence and of simultaneity, of causes and of co-operation. In the present chapter, a rapid glance will be taken over a wide-spread region, to shew in what way and to what degree disaffection spread during the month of May. This will prepare us for the terrible episode at one particular spot—Cawnpore.

To begin, then, with Bengal—the fertile and populous region between the Anglo-Indian city of Calcutta and the sacred Hindoo city of Benares; the region watered by the lower course of the majestic Ganges; the region inhabited by the patient, plodding, timid Bengalee, the type from which Europeans have generally derived their idea of the Hindoo: forgetting, or not knowing, that Delhi and Agra, Cawnpore and Lucknow, exhibit the Hindoo character under a more warlike aspect, and are marked also by a difference of language.

A fact already mentioned must be constantly borne in mind—that few Bengalees are (or were) in the Bengal army; a population of forty millions furnished a very small ratio of fighting men.

Although not a scene of murder and atrocity during the Revolt, Calcutta requires a few words of notice here: to shew the relation existing between the native and the European population, and the importance of the city as the head-quarters of British India, the supreme seat of legislation and justice, the residence of the governor-general, the last great city on the course down the Ganges, and the port where more trade is conducted than in all others in India combined.

Calcutta stands on the left bank of the Hoogly, one of the numerous streams by which the Ganges finds an outlet into the sea. There are no less than fourteen of these streams deep enough for the largest craft used in inland navigation, but so narrow and crooked that the rigging of vessels often becomes entangled in the branches of the trees growing on the banks. The delta formed by these mouths of the Ganges, called the Sunderbunds, is nearly as large as Wales; it is little else than a cluster of low, marshy, irreclaimable islands, very unhealthy to the few natives living there, and left almost wholly to tigers, wild buffaloes, wild boars, and other animals which swarm there in great numbers. The Hoogly is one of the few really navigable mouths of the Ganges; and by this channel Calcutta has free access by shipping to the sea, which is about a hundred miles distant. The city, extending along the river four or five miles, covers an area of about eight square miles. A curved line nearly bounds it on the land-side, formed by the Mahratta ditch, a defence-work about a century old. Beyond the ditch, and a fine avenue called the Circular Road, the environs are studded with numerous suburbs or villages which may be considered as belonging to the city: among these are Nundenbagh, Bahar-Simla, Sealdah, Entally, Ballygunge, Bhowaneepore, Allipore, Kidderpore, Seebpore, Howrah, and Sulkea. The three last are on the opposite or west bank of the river, and contain the dock-yards, the ship-building establishments, the railway station, the government salt-warehouses, and numerous extensive manufactories. The approach to the city from the sea presents a succession of attractive features. First, a series of elegant mansions at a bend in the river called Garden Reach, with lawns descending to the water's edge; then the anchorage for the Calcutta and Suez mail-steamers; then the dock-yards; next the canal junction, the arsenal and Fort William. Above these is the Chowringhee, once a suburb, but now almost as closely built as Calcutta itself, containing the Esplanade, the Town Hall, the Government House, and many European residences. 'Viewed from Garden Reach,' says Mr Stocqueler, 'the *coup d'œil* is one of various and enchanting beauty. Houses like palaces are studding the bank on the proper left of the river, and a verdure like that of an eternal summer renovates the eye, so long accustomed to the glitter of the ocean. Anon, on *your* left, appears the semi-Gothic Bishop's College and in front of you, every moment growing more distinct, are beheld a forest of stately masts, a noble and beautiful fortress, a thousand small boats, of shapes new and undreamed of by the visitant, skimming over the stream; the large vessels of the country, pleasant to look upon ever for their strange dis-symmetry and consequent unwieldiness; the green barge or budgerow, lying idly for hire; and the airy little bauleahs, with their light venetianed rooms.' All this relates to the portion of the city lying south or seaward of the Chandpaul Ghat, the principal landing-place. Northward of this stretches a noble strand, on which are situated the Custom-house, the New Mint, and other government offices.

It must be noted that, although the chief British city in India, Calcutta in ordinary times contains no less than *seventy times* as many natives as English—only six thousand English out of more than four hundred thousand inhabitants. Even if Eurasians (progeny of white fathers and native mothers) be included, the disparity is still enormous; and is rendered yet more so by the many thousands of natives who, not being inhabitants, attend Calcutta at times for purposes of trade or of worship. Many wild estimates were made a few years ago concerning the population of Calcutta, which was sometimes driven up hypothetically to nearly a million souls; but a census in 1850 determined the number to be four hundred and seventeen thousand persons, living in sixty-two thousand houses and huts. The Hindoos alone exceed two hundred and seventy thousand. Circumstances of site, as well as the wishes and convenience of individuals, have led the Europeans to form a community among themselves, distinct from the native Calcutta. Many natives, it is true, live in the southern or British town; but very few British live in the northern or native town. The latter differs little from Indian towns generally, except in the large size of the dwellings belonging to the wealthy inhabitants. The southern town is European in appearance as in population; it has its noble streets, sumptuous government offices, elegant private residences surrounded with verandahs. On the esplanade is situated Fort William (the official name given to Calcutta in state documents), one of the strongest in India; it is octagonal, with three sides towards the river, and the other five inland; and it mounts more than six hundred guns. Whatever force holds Fort William may easily reduce Calcutta to ashes. The public buildings, which are very numerous, comprise the following among others—the Government House, that cost £130,000; the Town Hall, in the Doric style; the Supreme Court of Judicature; the Madrissa and Hindoo Colleges; the Martinière, an educational establishment founded by Martine the Frenchman, who has been mentioned in connection with Lucknow; the

Metcalfe Hall; the Ochterlony Monument; the Prinsep Testimonial; the Calcutta Asiatic Society's Rooms; St Paul's Cathedral, the finest Christian church in India; the Bishop's Palace and College; the European Female Orphan Asylum; the Botanic Gardens. The Episcopalians, the National and the Free Churches of Scotland, the Independents, the Baptists, the Roman Catholics, the Armenians, the Jews, the Greeks—all have places of worship in Calcutta. The native temples and mosques are of course much more numerous, amounting to two hundred and fifty in number.

Concerning the inhabitants, the English comprise the Company's civil and military servants, a few members of the learned professions, merchants, retail-dealers, and artisans. Of the native Hindoos and Mohammedans, exclusive of the degraded castes of the former, it is supposed that one-third are in the service of the English, either as domestic servants, or as under-clerks, messengers, &c. A majority of the remainder pick up a living on the street or the river—carrying palanquins as bearers, carrying parcels as coolies, rowing boats, attending ships, &c. The native artisans, shopkeepers, and market-people, fill up the number.

It will be remembered, from the details given in Chapter II., that the authorities at Calcutta, during the first four months of the year, were frequently engaged in considering the transactions at Dumdum, Barrackpore, and Berhampore, connected with the cartridge grievances. These did not affect the great city itself, the inhabitants of which looked on as upon events that concerned them only remotely. When the middle of May arrived, however, and when the startling news from Meerut and Delhi became known, an uneasy feeling resulted. There was in Calcutta a kind of undefined alarm, a vague apprehension of some hidden danger. At that time there were six companies of the 25th Bengal infantry, and a wing of the 47th Madras infantry, barracked on the esplanade between the Coolie Bazaar and the fort. They were without ammunition. There were, however, detachments of two other regiments acting as guards in the fort, provided with ten rounds of ammunition per man. It came to light that, on the 17th of May, the men of the 25th asked the guards privately to be allowed to share this ammunition, promising to aid them in capturing the fort during the following night. This treason was betrayed by the guards to the town-major, who at once ordered bugles to sound, and preparations to be made for defending the fort; the drawbridges were raised, the ladders withdrawn from the ditches, additional guards placed upon the arsenal, European sentries placed at various points on the ramparts, and armed patrols made to perambulate the fort during the night. The refractory sepoys, thus checked, made no attempt to carry out their nefarious project. An express was at once sent off to Dumdum for the remaining portion of her Majesty's 53d regiment, to join their comrades already at Calcutta. Although the immense value of these English troops was at once felt, the inhabitants of Calcutta were thrown into great excitement by the rumoured outbreak; they talked of militia corps and volunteer corps, and they purchased muskets and powder, rifles and revolvers, so rapidly, that the stores of the dealers were speedily emptied.

Two demonstrations of loyalty—or rather two sets of demonstrations—were made on this occasion, one from the Christian inhabitants, and one from the natives. The mutineers found head-quarters not quite suited for their operations; order was soon restored; and then all parties came forward to state how faithful, contented, and trustworthy they were. It is not without interest to glance at some of these demonstrations. One was from the Calcutta Trade Association, which held a meeting on the 20th of May. The resolution agreed to was to the effect that 'This body do send up to government a statement that they are prepared to afford the government every assistance in their power towards the promotion of order and the protection of the Christian community of Calcutta, either by serving as special constables or otherwise, in such manner as may appear most desirable to government; and at the same time suggesting to government that their services should be availed of in some manner, as they deem the present crisis a most serious one, and one in which every available means should be brought into action for the suppression of possible riot and insurrection.' The answer given by the governor-general in council to the address sent up in virtue of this resolution is worthy of note; shewing, as it does, how anxious he was to believe, and to make others believe, that the mutiny was very partial, and that the sepoy army generally was sound at heart. He thanked the Trade Association for the address; he announced that he had no apprehension whatever of riot or insurrection amongst any class of the population at Calcutta; he asserted his possession of sufficient means to crush any such manifestation if it should be made; but at the same time he admitted the prudence of civilians enrolling themselves as special constables, ready for any emergency. In reference, however, to an opinion in the address that the sepoys generally exhibited a mutinous spirit, he expressed uneasiness at such an opinion being publicly announced. 'There are in the army of this presidency many soldiers and many regiments who have stood firm against evil example and wicked counsels, and who at this moment are giving unquestionable proof of their attachment to the government, and of their abhorrence of the atrocious crimes which have lately been perpetrated in the Northwestern Provinces. It is the earnest desire of the governor-general in council that honourable and true-hearted soldiers, whose good name he is bound to protect, and of whose fidelity he is confident, should not be included in a condemnation of rebels and murderers.' Alas, for the 'honourable and true-hearted soldiers!'

Another movement of the same kind was made by the Freemasons of Calcutta—a body, the numbers of which are not stated. They passed a resolution on the same day, 'That at the present crisis it is expedient that the masonic fraternity should come forward and offer their services to government, to be employed in such manner as the governor-general may deem most expedient.'

The Armenians resident in the city met on the following day, and agreed to a series of resolutions which were signed by Apcar, Avdall, Agabeb, and others of the body—declaratory of their apprehension for the safety of Calcutta and its inhabitants; their sincere loyalty to the British government; their grateful appreciation of its mild and paternal rule; and their fervent hope that the energetic measures adopted would suffice to quell the insurrectionary spirit: concluding, 'We beg most respectfully to convey to your lordship in council the expression of our willingness and readiness to tender our united services to our rulers, and to co-operate with our fellow-citizens for maintaining tranquillity and order in the city.' The Armenians, wherever settled, are a peaceful people, loving trade better than fighting: their adhesion to the government was certain.

The French inhabitants in like manner held a meeting, and sent up an address to the governor-general by the hands of Consul Angelucci. They said: 'Viewing the dangers that, from one moment to another, may menace life and property at Calcutta, all the French resident in the city unite with one accord, and place themselves at the disposal of your excellency in case of need; beseeching that their services may be accepted for the common good, and as a proof of their loyalty and attachment towards her Majesty, the Queen of England.'

It is more interesting, however, in reference to such a time and such a place, to know in what way the influential native inhabitants comported themselves on the occasion. The meetings held, resolutions passed, and addresses presented, were remarkable for their earnestness, real or apparent. Although Viscount Canning gladly and promptly acknowledged them as valuable testimonials; yet the subsequent lying and treachery in many quarters were such that it is impossible to decide how much or how little sincerity was involved in declarations of loyalty. There was a body of Hindoo gentlemen at Calcutta, called the British Indian Association. The committee of the Association held a meeting on the 22d of May, and the secretary, Issur Chunder Singh, forwarded an address from the committee to the government. The address asseverated that the atrocities at Meerut and Delhi had been heard of with great concern; that the committee viewed with disgust and horror the excesses of the soldiery at those stations; and that such excesses would not meet with countenance or support from the bulk of the civil population, or from any reputable or influential classes among them. The committee recorded 'their conviction of the utter groundlessness of the reports which have led a hitherto faithful body of the soldiers of the state to the commission of the gravest crimes of which military men or civil subjects can be guilty; and the committee deem it incumbent on them on the present occasion to express their deep abhorrence of the practices and purposes of those who have spread those false and mischievous reports.' Finally, they expressed their belief that the loyalty of the Hindoos, and their confidence in the power and good intentions of the government, would be unimpaired by 'the detestable efforts which have been made to alienate the minds of the sepoys and the people of the country from their duty and allegiance to the beneficent rule under which they are placed.'

Three days later, a meeting was held of Hindoo persons of influence generally, at Calcutta, without reference to the British Indian Association; and the chairman of this meeting, Bahadoor Radhakant Rajah, was commissioned to forward a copy of resolutions to the governor-general. These resolutions were similar in character to those passed by the Association; but two others were added of very decided character: 'That this meeting is of opinion that, should occasion require, it would be the duty of the native portion of her Majesty's subjects to render the government every aid in their power for the preservation of civil order and tranquillity; and that, with a view to give an extensive circulation to the proceedings of this meeting, translations of the same into the vernacular dialects of the country shall be printed and distributed amongst the native population.'

Another Hindoo manifestation was remarkable for the mode in which the intentions of the persons concerned were proposed to be carried out. A meeting was held on the 23d, of 'some young men, at the premises of Baboo Gooroo Churn Dey, Bhowanipore, Chuckerbaria, in the suburbs of Calcutta: to consider the best means of keeping the peace in the said suburban town at this crisis of panic caused by some mutinous regiments.' These 'young men,' who appointed Baboo Gooroo Churn Dey and Essan Chunder Mullick as secretary and assistant-secretary, threw into their deliberations an abundance of youthful enthusiasm not to be found in the resolutions of their seniors. Their plan—not expressed in, or translated into, very good English—was: 'That some of the members will alternately take round at every night, with the view of catching or detecting any wrong-doer that may be found in the work of abetting some such malicious tales or rumours, as the town will be looted and plundered by the sepoys on some certain day, and its inhabitants be cut to pieces; and will, by every means in their power, impress on the minds of timid and credulous people the idea of the mightiness of the power of the British government to repel aggression of any foreign enemy, however powerful and indomitable, or put down any internal disturbance and disorder.' They announced their success in obtaining many 'strong and brave men' to aid them in this work.

The Mohammedans of Calcutta were a little behind the rest of the inhabitants in time, but not in expressed sentiment, concerning the position of public affairs. On the 27th, many of the leading men of that religion held a meeting; one was a deputy-magistrate; two were pleaders in the sudder or native courts of law; others were moulvies, moonshees, hadjis, agas, &c.; and all signed their names in full—such as Hadji Mahomed Hashim Ishphahanee, and Aga Mahomed Hassan Kooza Kenanee. Nothing could be more positive than some of the assertions contained in the resolutions passed by this meeting: 'We subjects are well aware that the members of the British government, from the commencement of their dominion in Hindostan, have repeatedly declared and made known their determination not to interfere with the religion or religious observances of any of their subjects; and we repose entire faith in this declaration, and assert, that up to the present time, a space of nearly one hundred years, our religion has never been interfered with. A number of us having left our homes, have found a dwelling and asylum under this government, where we live in peace and safety, protected by the equity and fostering care of the British government, and suffering no kind of injury or loss. As we have ever lived in safety and comfort under the British rule, and have never been molested or interfered with in religious matters; we therefore, with the utmost eagerness and sincerity, hereby determine, that in case of necessity we will serve the government to the utmost of our abilities and means.' In true oriental form the resolutions ended, in allusion to the governor-general, 'May his prosperity increase!'

What *could* Viscount Canning say to all this? How could he, in that early stage of the commotions, but believe in the sincerity of these men: and, believing, to thank them for their expression of loyalty and support? His official reply, in each case, conveyed in pointed terms his conviction that the disaffection among the sepoys was only local and temporary. He could not at that time foresee how severely this conviction would be put to the test.

The hostility to the governor-general, manifested at a later date by some of the English inhabitants of Calcutta, will be noticed in its due place.

Leaving Calcutta, the reader is invited to direct his attention to towns and districts north and northwest, following the course of the Hoogly and the Ganges, up to the busy scenes of mutiny and warfare. The whole district from Calcutta to Benares *by land* is singularly devoid of interest. The railway is open through Burdwan to Raneegunge; but thence to the great Hindoo capital there is scarcely a town or village worthy of note, scarcely one in which the mutineers disturbed the peaceful occupations of the inhabitants.

Three military stations on the Hoogly—Dumdum, Barrackpore, and Berhampore—all concerned, as we have seen, in the cartridge disturbances—remained quiet during the month of May, after the disbandments. One inquiry connected with those occurrences, not yet adverted to, must here be noticed. The conduct of Colonel S. G. Wheler, commanding the 34th regiment B. N. I.,* occupied much attention on the part of the Calcutta government, during and after the proceedings relating to the disbanding of the seven companies of that regiment at Barrackpore. Rumours reached the government that the colonel had used language towards his men, indicating his expectation that they would be converted to Christianity, and that he had addressed them on religious subjects generally. In the usual epistolary formalism of routine, the secretary to the government was requested to request Major-general Hearsey to request Brigadier Grant to request Colonel Wheler to furnish some reply to those rumours. The substance of the colonel's reply was contained in these words: 'During the last twenty years and upwards, I have been in the habit of speaking to the natives of all classes, sepoys and others, making no distinction, since there is no respect of persons with God, on the subject of our religion, in the highways, cities, bazaars, and villages—not in the lines and regimental bazaars. I have done this from a conviction that every converted Christian is expected, or rather commanded, by the Scriptures to make known the glad tidings of salvation to his lost fellow-creatures: our Saviour having offered himself as a sacrifice for the sins of the whole world, by which alone salvation can be secured.' He quoted from the Epistle to the Romans to prove that a Christian must necessarily be a better subject to any state than a non-Christian. He declared, however, that he had not given the sepoys cause for believing that any proselyting violence would be used against their own religion. Viscount Canning, passing over in silence the Scriptural phraseology used by Colonel Wheler, wished to ascertain whether the colonel's religious conversations had been held with the men of the 34th regiment as well as with other natives: seeing that the critical subject at that particular time was the dogged suspicion of the sepoys of that regiment on matters affecting their faith. In a second letter, Colonel Wheler adopted a still more decidedly evangelical tone. He stated that it was his custom to address *all* natives, whether sepoys or not, on religious matters. 'I have told them plainly that they are all lost and ruined sinners both by nature and by practice, like myself; that we can do nothing to save ourselves in the way of justifying ourselves in the sight of God. Our hearts being sinful, all our works must consequently be sinful in His sight; and therefore there can be no salvation by works, on which

* The initials N. I., B. N. I., M. N. I., &c., are frequently used in official documents as abbreviations of 'Native Infantry,' 'Bengal Native Infantry,' 'Madras Native Infantry,' &c.

they are all resting and depending.' This homily, singular as forming part of a military reply to a military question, was carried to a considerable length. On matters of plain fact, Colonel Wheler stated that it was most certain that he had endeavoured by argument and exhortation to convert sepoys as well as others to Christianity; that he was in the habit of enforcing by the only standard which he could admit to be valid, objections concerning 'the efficacy of their own works of washing in the Ganges, proceeding on pilgrimage, worshipping all kinds of creatures instead of the Creator, and other methods of man's invention.' Finally, he announced his determination to adhere to the same policy, even if his worldly position were injured thereby; taking shame to himself for his past lukewarmness as a soldier of Christ.

The whole of the members of the Supreme Court at Calcutta at once decided that an officer, holding Colonel Wheler's views of duty, ought not to remain in command of a native regiment, especially at such a critical period. The question was not, whether that officer was a good Christian, anxious to communicate to others what he himself fervently believed; but whether the black gown was not more suitable to him than the red coat, in such a country and at such a time.

The native troops at Barrackpore and Chittagong, after the disbandment of the mutinous corps, made professions of loyalty and fidelity to the government, concerning the sincerity of which it is now exceedingly difficult to judge. One theory is, that the men were designing hypocrites from the first; but the frequent examples of wavering and irresolution, afforded during the progress of the mutiny, seem to shew rather that the sepoys were affected by the strength of the temptation and example at each particular time and place. Be this as it may, some of the petitions and addresses deserve notice. Towards the close of May a petition, written in the Persian character (much used in India), was prepared by the native officers of the 70th regiment B. N. I., stationed at Barrackpore, and presented to their commander, Colonel Kennedy. In the names of themselves and the sepoys they said: 'It is reported that European troops are going up to Delhi and other places, to coerce the mutinous and rebellious there; and we wish to be sent with them also. In consequence of the misconduct of these traitors and scoundrels, confidence in us is weakened, although we are devoted to government; and we therefore trust that we may be sent wherever the European troops go; when, having joined them, we will, by bravery even greater than theirs, regain our good name and trustworthiness. You will then know what really good sepoys are.' Colonel Kennedy, in a letter to Major-general Hearsey, expressed his full belief that the men were sincere in their protestations; and added, that hitherto he had always been satisfied with the regiment. So important did this manifestation appear to Viscount Canning, that he went to Barrackpore in order to thank the men in person. He appeared before them on parade, on the 27th, and said, among other things: 'Men of the 70th, I will answer your petition. You have asked to be sent to confront the mutineers of Delhi. You shall go. In a few days, as soon as the arrangements can be made for your progress, you shall proceed to the northwest.' He expressed his conviction that they would keep their promise to vie with the Europeans in fidelity and bravery; and added: 'You have another duty to perform. You are going where you will find men, your brothers in arms, who have been deluded into the suspicion against which *you* have kept firm, that the government has designs against their religion or their caste. Say to them that you at least do not credit this; that you know it to be untrue; that for a hundred years the British government has carefully respected the feelings of its Indian subjects in matters of caste and religion.'

Arrangements were immediately made for sending this faithful, or apparently faithful, regiment to districts where it might render useful service. As there was an insufficient supply of steamers available, the government resolved to send the regiment the whole distance from Barrackpore to Allahabad by country boats on the Ganges —an excessively protracted voyage of eight hundred miles, as the reader is already aware. When the men were about to start, they expressed to Colonel Kennedy a wish that the new Enfield rifle should be served out to them. They declared themselves entirely satisfied with the explanations concerning the cartridges; and they added, in a written petition to which the names of twelve subadars and jemadars were appended: 'We have thought over the subject; and as we are now going up the country, we beg that the new rifles, about which there has been so much said in the army and all over the country, may be served out to us. By using them in its service, we hope to prove beyond a doubt our fidelity to government; and we will explain to all we meet that there is nothing objectionable in them; otherwise, why should we have taken them? Are we not as careful of our caste and religion as any of them?' All the native officers of this regiment, so far as can be judged from the names appended to the petition, were Hindoos. When the 70th started to the northwest, every effort was made by the government to set the unhappy cartridge troubles wholly at rest, and to enlist the services of the sepoys of that regiment in diffusing among their compatriots a knowledge of the real facts. Orders, instructions, memoranda, circulars were brought into requisition to explain—that the new rifle fired nine hundred yards, against the two hundred yards' range of the old musket; that it was lighter than the musket; that its great range and its lightness caused it to be introduced into the Anglo-Indian army; that the new rifle-bullets, requiring machinery for heir manufacture, were sent out from England in a finished state; that a few cartridges for those bullets were in the first instance sent out ready prepared with a lubricant, but that the Indian government resolved not to issue them to the native troops, in deference to their religious scruples; that the cartridge-paper had long been, and would continue to be, made at Serampore, without any admixture of grease; that every native regiment would be allowed to lubricate its cartridges with any suitable substance preferred by the men; and that the practice of biting off the ends of the cartridges might be wholly dispensed with. In short, everything that could be done, was done, to remove a suspicion unsound in its origin, and pernicious in its continuance.

Another regiment, the 34th B. N. I., adopted nearly the same course as the 70th. The larger portion of this regiment, it will be remembered, was at Barrackpore at the time of the cartridge troubles; but the rest was at Chittagong. The sepoys in this last-named detachment came forward with a very pointed declaration of their loyalty. Captain Dewaal, in command of that detachment, assembled his men one day towards the end of April, and told them how shamefully their companions had acted at Barrackpore, and how much disgrace had thereby been brought upon the regiment. Two days afterwards, an address or petition was presented to him, signed by the subadars and havildars in the names of all; in which regret was expressed for the conduct of the mutineers at Barrackpore. 'By a careful performance,' the petitioners said, 'of our duties, we have gained a reputation for fidelity to government. These men have deprived us of it. We well know that the government will not interfere with our religion. We hope that the government will consider us as faithful as ever; and we pray that this petition may be sent to the governor-general, in order that his lordship may know the state of our feelings.' Three or four weeks later, when this remnant of the regiment had been removed to Barrackpore, the men made another profession of their loyalty. In a petition to their commander, they said: 'Some evil-disposed men of the regiment have deprived us of the reputation for loyalty which we have ever held. They have received the fruits of their misconduct by being disbanded. We that remain are willing to serve against the mutineers at Delhi, and are anxious to recover our lost name. We pray that the government will ever regard us as faithful soldiers.'

Two further examples of a similar kind were presented, one by the 43d and another by the 63d regiments B. N. I. About the end of May, the commandant of the first of these two regiments at Barrackpore, received a petition signed by the native commissioned officers, praying that the regiment might be allowed to proceed against the mutineers at Delhi—a wish that had been previously expressed to him on parade. Nearly at the same time Captain Poster, commanding the 63d at Berhampore, received a petition signed by the whole of the native officers on parade, intended to be forwarded to the governor-general; and, this petition being afterwards read in the native language to the whole regiment, the sepoys unanimously expressed their concurrence in the sentiments it conveyed. The petitioners said: 'We have this day heard on parade the order issued by your lordship consequent on the petition forwarded by the native officers and sepoys of the 70th regiment of native infantry. On hearing the same, we were greatly rejoiced; for, in truth, all the men of that regiment have behaved as becomes loyal and faithful soldiers, and your lordship has in every way been pleased with them. Now do we also all petition that we may be numbered among the good and trustworthy soldiers of the state, as we have always been; and we are prepared and ready, with heart and hand, to go wherever, and against whomsoever you may please to send us, should it even be against our own kinsmen.'

The governor-general could do no other than receive these demonstrations. Whether he acceded to the request for permission to 'march against the mutineers,' depended necessarily on the military arrangements of the time; whether he fully believed the protestations, may perhaps be doubted, although no disbelief was expressed.

Happily for Bengal, it was affected by few of the disturbances that agitated the more western provinces. Consulting a map, we shall see that the banks of the Hoogly and the Lower Ganges are thickly studded with towns; and it may here at once be stated, that the peaceful industry of these towns was very little interrupted during the month of May. Tracing upwards from Calcutta, we meet with Dumdum, Barrackpore, and Serampore, the first two of which experienced a lull after the storm. Serampore was once the *Alsatia* of Calcutta, a place of refuge for schemers, insolvent debtors, and reckless adventurers; but the Company bought it from the Danish government, to which it had belonged, and the Baptist missionaries helped to civilise it; it is now a clean cheerful town, with a large paper manufactory. Higher up is the once flourishing but now decayed town of Chandernagore, one of the few places in India still belonging to the French. Near this is Chinsura, held by the Dutch until 1825, but now a flourishing settlement belonging to the Company, provided with an extensive military depôt for Europeans, with a magnificent hospital and barracks. Then we come to Hoogly, a town bearing the same name as the river on whose banks it stands; a busy place, with many civil and educational establishments. Further north is Plassy, the place near which Clive fought the great battle that virtually gave India to the British. Beyond this is Berhampore, which, very refractory in March and April, had become tractable and obedient in May. Next we meet with Moorshedabad and its suburb Cossimbazar. Once the capital of

Bengal when a Mohammedan dominion, Moorshedabad contained a splendid palace belonging to the nawab; but though no longer possessed of this kind of greatness, the city is commercially very important, as standing on the great highway, or rather water-way, from Calcutta to the northwest. All the places above named are situated either on the Hoogly or on the Bhagruttee, those two rivers combining to form the most convenient outlet from the Ganges to the sea.

The Ganges itself, too—the majestic, far-famed, sacred Ganges—was little disturbed by commotions in May throughout the lower part of its course. Rajmahal, Bhagulpore, Curruckpore, Monghir, Behar, Futwah, Patna, Hajeepoor, Dinapoor, Chupra, Arrah, Bishunpore, Buxar, Ghazeepore—all lie on or near the Ganges between the Hoogly and Benares. Some of these places are centres of commerce for the opium-trade; some are busy with the trading in rice grown in neighbouring districts; others are shipping-places for corn and other agricultural produce; while all regard the Ganges as an invaluable channel, affording intercourse with the rich districts of the west, and with the great focus of authority and trade at Calcutta. Such of these towns as were involved in trouble in later months of the year, will be noticed in the proper chapters; of the others, this narrative is not called upon to treat. One fact, however, may be mentioned in connection with Dinapoor. So early in the year as the middle of February, the Calcutta authorities wrote to the commander at that town, apprising him that a messenger was known to have been sent to the native regiment at Dinapoor, from some men of the 2d Bengal grenadiers, inciting them to mutiny. Major-general Lloyd promised to look out sharply for the messenger, but candidly expressed a doubt whether the astute native would suffer himself to be caught.

Benares may conveniently be described at once; for, whether disturbed or not by mutineers, it is so remarkably situated as to lie in the line of route of all commerce, all aggression, all military movement, between Calcutta and the upper provinces, whether by road, by rail, or by water. Regarded in this light, its possession and security are, and were in an especial degree during the mutiny, objects of the highest importance. This renowned city stands on the left bank of the Ganges, about four hundred and twenty miles by road from Calcutta, and seventy-four from Allahabad. The magnificent river, half a mile wide in the rainy season, forms a kind of semicircular bay in front of the city, which has thus three miles of river-frontage. Among the chief characteristics of Benares are the ghats or flights of fine broad freestone steps, giving access to the river; mostly very solid in construction, and in some cases highly decorated. So numerous are they, that they extend almost in a continuous line along the river's banks, interrupted here and there by temples. 'Upon these ghats,' says a lively traveller, 'are passed the busiest and happiest hours of every Hindoo's day: bathing, dressing, praying, preaching, lounging, gossiping, or sleeping, there will be found. Escaping from the dirty, unwholesome, and confined streets, it is a luxury for him to sit upon the open steps and taste the fresh air of the river; so that on the ghats are concentrated the pastimes of the idler, the duties of the devout, and much of the necessary intercourse of business.' Artists in India have delighted to portray the beauty and animation of this scene; but they cannot, if they would, reveal the hideous accompaniments—the fakeers and ascetics of revolting appearance, 'offering every conceivable deformity which chalk, cow-dung, disease, matted locks, distorted limbs, and repulsive attitudes of penance, can shew.'

Benares, beyond any other place in India, perhaps, is studded with religious structures. Thirty years ago the Moslem mosques were more than three hundred in number, while the Hindoo temples exceeded a thousand. The pinnacles of the Hindoo pagodas combine to give a very picturesque appearance to the city, viewed from a distance. Large as the number is, the Benares temples, as has been sarcastically observed, are not too many, for religion is 'the staple article of commerce, through which the holy city flourishes and is enriched.' The Mohammedan mosques, mostly situated in the northeast quarter of the city, are generally elegant little edifices crowned by small slender minarets, each standing in a garden planted with tamarinds. Most of them have been constructed on the sites, and with the materials, of demolished Hindoo temples. By far the grandest is the great mosque of Aurungzebe, built by that emperor on the site of a temple of Vishnu, which he destroyed to signalise the triumph of Islamism over Brahminism. It rises from the platform above the Madhoray Ghat. The minars or minarets, admired for their simplicity and boldness, taper from eight feet in diameter at the bottom to seven at the top; and though so slender, they are carried up to a height of a hundred and fifty feet, and have each an interior staircase from bottom to top. The streets of Benares have the usual oriental character of narrowness, crookedness, and dirtiness; they are mere alleys, indeed, that will admit no wheel-carriages; nor can beasts of burden pass without sorely disturbing pedestrians. The houses are more lofty than in most Indian cities, generally from three to six stories high; and as the upper stories usually project beyond the lower, the narrow street is almost closed in above: nay, in some cases, the inmates of one house can walk over to the opposite tenement through the upper windows. The houses are, in the better streets, built of stone, small-windowed and gaily painted. During the hot season the citizens are much accustomed to sleep in screened enclosures on the roof, open to the sky above, and to the night-breezes around. There are somewhat under two hundred thousand inhabitants, who live in about thirty thousand houses.

Benares is a religious, not a military city. The district around was at a very remote period the seat of an independent Hindoo state, founded, according to native tradition, twelve hundred years before the Christian era. It subsequently formed part of the dominions of the Rajpoot sovereigns. Then began the Mussulman rule, and Benares became a dependent province under the Moguls. The nawab-viziers of Oude, when the Mogul power was declining, seized Benares; and during some of the political jugglery of the year 1775, the territory was transferred to the East India Company, by whom it has ever since been held. But under whatever dynasty it has been placed, Benares has from remote ages been known as the sacred city of the Hindoos, where all that is remarkable, all that is abominable, in Brahminism, flourishes. It has been described

Ghat on the Ganges.

as the Jerusalem of Hindostan—swarming with religious teachers, devotees, mendicants, and sacred bulls. To wash in the Ganges in front of Benares, to die in that city, are precious privileges to the Hindoo. Some writers have given the inhabitants a bad character in what concerns loyalty to their present British rulers. 'Benares is one of the most unsafe and rebellious cities in Hindostan. It once successfully opposed a house-tax imposed on the people by the British government. There was also recently a strong commotion when the magistrate attempted to equalise the weights and measures. To show the hostility of the Hindoos of Benares to the English, it may be mentioned that when we lay before Bhurtpore in 1826, no less than thirty thousand sabres were sharpened at the cutlers' in expectation of our repulse.' If this statement be well founded, it does indeed denote a perilous state of feeling at the time in question.

Benares, we have said, is not a military city; but so important a place could not safely be left unguarded. Accordingly a British cantonment has been built at Secrole, two or three miles to the northwest. Secrole contains not only the barracks and huts for soldiers, but various civil establishments, and the residences of most of the British population of Benares. The cantonment consists of the usual buildings belonging to the head-quarters of a military division of the Company's army, and capable of accommodating three or four regiments; it lies on both sides of a small stream called the Burnah Nuddee, crossed by the great road from Benares to Allahabad. On the side of the cantonment furthest from the city are the bungalows of the various officials and European residents: substantially built, well fitted and appointed, and surrounded by pleasant gardens. There are, among the public buildings, a Christian church and chapel, a court of justice, the treasury, the jail, and a mint—the last named never yet appropriated to its destined purpose. Secrole is thus, in effect, the British portion of Benares.

Another military station, subordinate to Benares, Chunar or Chunargur, is about sixteen miles distant; indeed, being nearly midway between Benares and Mirzapore, it may be an auxiliary to either in time of need. Chunar is a town of about twelve thousand inhabitants, standing on a plateau or elevated cliff close to the Ganges. It was regarded as a stronghold more than three centuries ago; and, like many other places in the neighbourhood, belonged to the great Mogul; from whom, in lapse of time, it was wrested by the ambitious nawab-viziers of Oude; until at length it fell into the hands of the British. It was for some years the Company's principal artillery depôt for the Northwestern Provinces. The fortified portion of the town, on the heights, is surrounded by a rampart a little over a mile in circuit, and from ten to twenty feet high, guarded by towers, and in its turn completely commanding the river and its banks. The space enclosed by this wall or rampart, however, has very little of a military aspect; part is open grass-land; part occupied by bungalows and gardens of Europeans; part by the governor's house, the hospital, and the state prison; and part by the ancient Hindoo palace, a massy vaulted edifice presenting little of its original splendour. An article of Hindoo faith is recorded in connection with a slab of black marble in a small square court of this palace; to the effect that 'the Almighty is seated personally, though invisibly, on this stone, for nine hours each day, removing during the other three hours to Benares;' so that the fort, in sepoy belief, can only be taken between the hours of six and nine in the morning. Considered in a military sense, the fort is by no means strong; nevertheless the steepness of the ascent would render storming difficult; and to increase this difficulty, the garrison was wont in former times to keep a number of large rudely made stone-cylinders at hand, to roll down upon a besieging force. The citadel or stronghold is in the northeastern part of the enclosure; it is mounted with several cannon, and has a bomb-proof magazine. The native town, consisting principally of two-storied stone houses, is spread over a slope lying eastward of the fortifications. The English dwellings, and the station for invalid soldiers, are lower down the slope.

As soon as the Revolt began, the safety of Benares became an object of much solicitude to the governor-general at Calcutta, to Sir Henry Lawrence at Lucknow, and indeed to all the Company's servants; seeing that the maintenance of free communication would greatly depend on the peaceful condition of that city. We have seen that telegrams passed almost daily between Benares and the other chief cities in May; intended partly to facilitate the transport of reinforcements to the northwest, and in part also to insure the tranquillity of Benares itself. About the middle of the month the military commandant had to announce that there had been some excitement in the 37th native infantry; that a Sikh regiment had been sent on to Mirzapore and Allahabad; that the 13th irregular cavalry were at Sultanpore; and that his position was rather weak. On the 18th he telegraphed for aid: stating that 'if one hundred European infantry could be spared for duty here, it would restore confidence, and make Benares more secure, so as to maintain communication with the northwest.' General Lloyd was asked whether he could spare that much-coveted reinforcement—a hundred Europeans—from Dinapoor. About the same time the commandant was directed to defend Chunar fort with European invalids and veterans, and to keep the native infantry regiment at hand in Benares. Mr Tucker, civil commissioner, writing to the government on the same day, spoke of the 'bold policy' which had been adopted when the 37th shewed disaffection; the Europeans remaining in their houses, and acting so as neither to exhibit nor inspire distrust—instead of attempting to escape. On the 19th, arrangements were completed for sending a company of her Majesty's 84th from Dumdum to Benares, in five separate parties of twenty-one each, in transit-carriages. By the 19th, the irregular cavalry had been brought in from Sultanpore, and every precaution taken to guard against a surprise—insomuch that the Europeans at neighbouring stations were looking to Benares as a sort of stay and support. More than once allusion was made, by the civil commissioner at that city, to the tactics of serenity, as a medium between severity and fright. One of the telegrams told that 'Brigadier Ponsonby carries out Colonel Gordon's quiet policy of shewing no fear or distrust; not a muscle is moved.' Until towards the close of the month, Benares was included in the military command of which Dinapoor was the centre; but as the distance between the two towns is a hundred and fifty miles, Brigadier Ponsonby received permission to act for himself, irrespective of control from General Lloyd.

The 31st of May found Benares and its neighbourhood at peace. How close at hand were days of violence and bloodshed—a future chapter will shew.

We have now left Bengal, both in its original and in the Company's acceptation of that term, and have arrived within the territories grouped together as the Northwest Provinces. From Benares and Chunargur, as a glance at the map will shew, the course of the Ganges, of the great trunk-road, and of the railway in process of construction, brings us to Mirzapore—a town not actually thrown into rebellion during the month of May, but placed between two foci of inflammable materials, Benares and Allahabad, and liable at any time to be inflamed by them. Mirzapore is on the right bank of the Ganges, which is half a mile wide at this spot, and is crossed by a ferry in the absence of a bridge. It is a great commercial city, with about eighty thousand inhabitants; the emporium of the cotton trade of Bundelcund and the adjacent provinces; not rich in Mohammedan or Hindoo antiquities or splendour, associated with few military events, but wealthy on account of its industry. The Company's military cantonment, as in so many other parts of India, is two or three miles out of the town; indeed, this is a fact that must be borne in mind throughout, as a necessary condition to the understanding of events connected with the Revolt.

Approaching now the Jumna regions, the plot thickens and the characters increase in number. We come to that rich country, the Doab, watered on the one side by the Ganges and on the other by the Jumna, with Oude and Rohilcund on the north, Bundelcund and Scindiah's territory on the south. We find a considerable number of large and important towns—Lucknow, Fyzabad, Bareilly, Allahabad, Futtehpoor, Cawnpore, Furruckabad, Gwalior, Bhurtpore, Agra, Delhi, Meerut—in the immediate vicinity of one or other of these two rivers. The Company's military stations are far more thickly posted in that region than in any other part of India—a source of weakness in the midst of apparent strength; for as the native troops were predominant in all these places, their numbers became a manifest evil as soon as a mutinous spirit appeared among the men.

This chapter being mainly intended, as already explained, to shew how remarkably the materials for explosion were accumulating during the month of May, to burst forth with frightful violence in June, we shall glance rapidly and touch lightly here on many of the towns situated westward of Mirzapore, in order to place the reader in a position to understand what will follow—treating of sudden outrages and strange escapes in some few cases, and in others of a deceitful calm before a storm.

Allahabad, in a military sense, is a more important post than any between it and Calcutta: indeed, there are few to equal it throughout India. This is due principally to the fact that it lies at the junction of the two great rivers Ganges and Jumna, the northern side being washed by the one, the southern by the other. It occupies the most eastern, or rather southeastern point of the rich and fertile Doab; it lies in the direct water-route from Calcutta to both of the upper rivers; it is a main station on the great trunk-road from Calcutta to the Punjaub, and on the East India Railway now in course of construction; and a bridge will carry that railway across the Jumna close to it. No wonder, therefore, if the eyes of all were directed anxiously towards Allahabad during the mutinies and consequent struggles. The fort and arsenal are among the largest and finest in India. The fort rises direct from the point of confluence of the two rivers, and is on that side nearly impregnable. It is a mile and a half in circuit, five-sided, stone built, and bastioned. Two of the sides, near the water, are old, and weak as against a European force; the other three are modern, and, with their bastions and ravelins, command the city and the country beyond. Bishop Heber remarked that Allahabad fort had lost in grandeur what it had gained in strength; the lofty towers having been pruned down into bastions and cavaliers, and its high stone ramparts obscured by turf parapets and a sloping external glacis. The principal gate of the fort, surmounted by a dome with a wide hall beneath, and surrounded by arcades and galleries, forms a very majestic ornament. The arsenal, situated within the fort, is one of great magnitude, containing (before the Revolt) arms for thirty thousand men, an immense park of artillery, and the largest powder-magazine in Upper India. Altogether, it is a place of great strength, probably impregnable to natives, and fitted to bear a prolonged and formidable siege. In a part of the fort overlooking the Jumna is an ancient and spacious palace, formerly fitted up as residences for the superior European officers, but latterly used for state prisoners. From a balcony perched near the summit of a tower on which the windows of one of the chambers open, a scene is presented, of which European travellers in India speak with much admiration. The spectator looks down upon a grove of mango-trees, flanking a fine esplanade, and peopled with innumerable ring-necked paroquets. Above, on pediment, pinnacle, and turret, others of the feathered tribe build their nests and plume their wings. Along the thickly wooded shores on the north or Allahabad side of the Jumna, buildings of various degrees of interest are seen interspersed with the small islands which speckle the river; while the opposite or Bundelcund shore forms a noble background to the picture. In the days before the Revolt, the European troops of the garrison were accommodated in well-constructed barracks within the fort; while the military cantonment for the native troops lay northwest of it.

The city of Allahabad, westward of the fort, and on the Jumna shore, is scarcely worthy of its magnificent situation. It contains seventy thousand inhabitants; but its streets and houses are poor; nor do the mosques and temples equal those in many other parts of Hindostan, though the gardens and tomb of Sultan Khosroo and his serai are almost unequalled in India. There is a particular spot, outside the fort, where the actual confluence of the two great rivers is considered to take place; and this presents the liveliest scene in the whole city. One traveller tells of the great numbers of pilgrims of both sexes, anxious to bathe in the purifying waters; and of devotees who, causing earthen vessels to be fastened round their waists or to their feet, proceed in a boat to the middle of the stream, and precipitate themselves into the water—supposing that by this self-immolation they secure eternal bliss. Another states that when a pilgrim arrives here—Benares, Gyayah, and Allahabad being frequently included in the same pilgrimage—he sits down on the brink of the river, and causes his head and body to be so shaved that each hair may fall into the water—for the sacred writings promise the pilgrim a million years' residence in heaven for every hair thus deposited—and that, after shaving and bathing, he performs the obsequies of his deceased ancestors. The Brahmins are the money-makers at these spots; each has his little platform, standing in the water, where he assists in the operations by which the pilgrim is supposed to become holy. Skinner describes the whole scene as a kind of religious fair.

When the events at Meerut and Delhi became

City and Fort of ALLAHABAD.

known at Allahabad, the native troops shewed much excitement. One of them, the 6th Bengal infantry, drew down encomiums for fidelity, in offering to march and fight against the insurgents; whether all the officers believed the men, may be doubted; but the chief authorities did not deem themselves justified in shewing distrust. Thanks came from Calcutta for the manifestation of loyalty made by the regiment—a loyalty destined to be of brief duration. A detachment of her Majesty's 84th reached Allahabad on the 23d of May, sent up from Calcutta by the laboriously tedious methods lately described. There being some disturbance expected at the jail, the detachment was sent into the fort, and held in readiness to proceed to the cantonment with two guns; but as the alarm ceased for a time, the troops were sent on to Cawnpore, where much more anxiety was felt. Lieutenant Brasyer commanded four hundred Sikhs of the Ferozpore regiment in the fort; while Captain Hazelwood took charge of the European artillerymen. About two hundred Englishwomen and children were in the fort; and all hoped that the native troops in the cantonment could and would be kept in subjection. How far this hope was well founded, will be shewn in a future chapter.

Lucknow and the important territory of Oude, so far as concerns the events in May, have already been treated. The relations of the British government to the court of Oude, the assiduous exertions of Sir Henry Lawrence to maintain subordination and tranquillity, and the vigorous measures adopted by him against the mutineers at Lucknow towards the close of the month of May, were followed by occurrences in June which will come for notice in their proper place.

Of Cawnpore—a name never to be uttered by

English tongue without a thrill of horror, an ony of exasperated feeling—all notice will be stponed until the next chapter; not because the pless beings there residing were free from peril the month of May, but because the tragedy ust be treated continuously as a whole, each ene leading forward to the hideous climax. ffice it at present to know that Cawnpore coned so many English men and women, and so any mutinous native troops, that all eyes were anxiously directed towards the progress of events at that city.

Let us turn to towns and districts further westward.

Agra, once the capital of the Patan emperors, is the chief city of the Northwestern Provinces. Delhi is historically, and in population, more important; but was still at that time nominally under another sovereign; whereas Agra has been British territory since 1803, and is very well suited for a seat

Agra Fort.

of government. The city, like Delhi, is situated on the right bank of the Jumna, and will, like it, be at some future time accommodated by the East India railway. In round numbers, its distance from Delhi is a hundred and fifty miles; from Calcutta, a little under eight hundred; and from Lahore, five hundred. The boundary of the old city encloses a space of twelve square miles; but not more than half of this is at present occupied by houses. There is one fine street, with houses built of red sandstone; the remaining streets are mostly narrow, with very small, insignificant-looking shops. The public buildings are numerous, and some of them very magnificent, telling of the past days of imperial glory and splendour. One is the palace of Shahjehan; small, but rendered very beautiful by its white marble surfaces, arabesques and mosaics, carvings of flowers, inlayings of black and yellow marble, enrichments of gilding, screen-works of marble and metal, fountains in the mosaic pavements. Near this is Shahjehan's audience-chamber, as large as the palace itself, originally enclosed by arcades hung with tapestries. And also close at hand is the Moti Musjid or Pearl Mosque; with an exterior of red sandstone and an interior of white marble; a court with arcades and a fountain; a vestibule raised on steps; three terraces surmounted by beautiful domes; and nine elegant kiosks equidistant along the front. But the crowning beauty of Agra in its Mohammedan aspect is the celebrated Taj Mahal, a little way outside the city. This was the mausoleum of Shahjehan and his favourite sultaness Nurjehan, the 'Light of the World,' and occupied in its construction twenty thousand men during a period of more than twenty years. Page after page of travellers' descriptions are occupied with this glorious structure—its façade of a thousand feet in length; its dazzling whiteness of marble; its mosques at either end, with their domes; its stupendous marble terraced platform, with steps and pillars, minarets and kiosks; its great dome surmounted by gilded globes and crescents; its octagonal shrine or sepulchral apartment, with enclosures of extraordinary marble lattice-work; and its sarcophagi, literally covered with arabesques, fanciful mouldings, sculptured flowers, and inscriptions from the Koran.

What a mockery of past grandeur is all this now! Shahjehan, two centuries ago, was kept closely a prisoner in his splendour at Agra, while his ambitious son, Aurungzebe, was seizing the throne at Delhi; and now another race is dominant in both of those cities. Shahjehan's audience-chamber has had its arcades walled up, and is converted into an arsenal for and by the British; and near it are now an armoury, a medical depôt, and a district collectorate treasury. Nearly all the once-imperial buildings are within the fort, a large place nearly a mile in circuit; it contained a hundred and sixty guns when Lord Lake captured it in 1803. Adjacent to the city, on the west, is the government-house, the official residence of the lieutenant-governor of the Northwestern Provinces; and in various places are numerous buildings belonging to the Company, for revenue, magisterial, and judicial establishments. The military lines are outside the city-wall. Before the Revolt, this station was within the Meerut military division, and was usually occupied by a considerable body of European and native troops. It was a fact of small importance in peaceful times, but of some moment when rebellion arose, that the civilians and writers in the public offices were accustomed to live three or four miles from the cantonment containing the military, quite on the opposite suburb of Agra. None would live in the city itself, unless compelled, owing to the intense heat. It will be well to bear in mind that the fort at Agra was, as just noticed, not merely a post or stronghold, indicated by its name, but a vast enclosure containing most of the palatial as well as the defensive buildings, and ample enough to contain all the Europeans usually residing in the city and its vicinity—large enough in dimensions, strong enough in defences, provided a sufficient supply of food were stored within its walls. Here, as at Delhi, Lucknow, Allahabad, and other places, the due understanding of the mutinous proceedings requires an appreciation of this fact—that the *city*, the *fort*, and the *cantonment* were all distinct.

Agra, being the seat of government for the Northwest Provinces, was naturally the city to which the Calcutta authorities looked for information touching the Revolt; and Mr Colvin, the lieutenant-governor, was assiduously engaged in collecting details, so far as telegraphs and dâks permitted. On the night of the 10th of May he received sinister news from the postmaster at Meerut, telling of deeds of violence being at that moment committed. Next he heard th a young sepoy, mounted on a travelling troo horse, was stopped at Bolundshuhur, on suspicic of being *en route* to excite other sepoy reg ments to rebellion. On the 13th, it was ascertaine that a few sepoys were on their way from Meer through Allygurh to Agra, bent on mischief; an that others were supposed to be advancing fror Delhi. So little, however, did Mr Colvin appre hend serious results, that when Scindiah, th maharajah of Gwalior, came forward to offer hi body-guard of three hundred men, and a battery o artillery, as an aid to the Company, the governo accepted the offer as 'a personal compliment fo a short time;' but in the same message saying, 'though we really do not require more troops.' This was obviously said on the supposition that the native troops in and near Agra would not be affected by the rebellious epidemic prevailing further northward; a supposition destined to be sadly overturned. Nevertheless the government made arrangements for placing at the disposal of Mr Colvin two regiments of irregular horse from regions further west. Day after day did evidence arrive shewing that the various districts around were gradually becoming disturbed. On the 15th, the governor reviewed the native regiments in Agra, and, finding them deeply impressed with a conviction that the government intended in some way to degrade their caste, gave them the most positive assurance that they had been grossly deceived by such reports. He believed his explanation to have given satisfaction.

Towards the close of the month a step was taken by Mr Colvin which brought him into collision with his superiors in power. As lieutenant-governor of the Northwest Provinces, surrounded on every side by a teeming population, he wished to believe that the native troops as a body would still remain faithful, and that an indulgent tone towards them would effect more than severity to bring the erring back to a sense of their duty. It was not a thoughtless proceeding: if wrong, the mistake arose from the estimate formed of the native character, and of the effect which indulgence would produce. 'Hope,' he said, in a letter to the governor-general, 'I am firmly convinced, should be held out to all those who were not ringleaders or actually concerned in murder and violence. Many are in the rebels' ranks because they could not get away; many certainly thought we were tricking them out of their caste; and this opinion is held, however unwisely, by the mass of the population, and even by some of the more intelligent classes.' When he found some of the troopers of the Gwalior Contingent, on whose fidelity much reliance had been placed, become mutinous on the 24th of May, he resolved on issuing a proclamation, based on the supposition that 'this mutiny was not one to be put down by indiscriminating high-horsed authority.' The pith of his proclamation was contained in these words: Soldiers, engaged in the late disturbances, who are desirous of going to their own homes, and who give up their arms at the nearest government civil or military post, and retire quietly, shall be permitted to do so unmolested.' To this another sentence was added, in a less prominent form: 'Every evil-minded instigator in the disturbances, and those guilty of heinous crimes against private persons, shall be punished.' Mr Colvin earnestly solicited the assent of the Calcutta government to this proclamation; but the assent was as earnestly withheld. Viscount Canning telegraphed orders back to Agra to recall the proclamation as quickly as possible, and to substitute another sent for that purpose. 'Use every possible means to stop the circulation of the proclamation . . . do everything to stop its operation.' Mr Colvin was obliged to announce the abrogation of his own proclamation by a second which contained these words: 'Every soldier of a regiment which, although it has deserted its post, has not committed outrages, will receive free pardon if he immediately deliver up his arms to the civil or military authority, and if no heinous crimes be shewn to have been perpetrated by himself personally. This offer of free and unconditional pardon *cannot be extended to those regiments which have killed or wounded their officers or other persons, or which have been concerned in the commission of cruel outrages.*' Mr Colvin wished to pardon *all* who would give up their arms, except a few ringleaders, and persons individually engaged in outrage; while Viscount Canning wished to exempt from this pardon such regiments as had been engaged in the murderous atrocities at Meerut, Delhi, and elsewhere. General Anson, the commander-in-chief, died before his opinion could be sought; but the Calcutta government, and (at a later date) the British government and the British public, agreed with the governor-general. Mr Colvin was placed in a most perplexing position; for he was called upon to overturn his own proceedings, thereby departing from a plan which he believed adequate for the purpose in view, and weakening his authority in the eyes of the natives. Canning telegraphed to Colvin: 'The embarrassment in which your proclamation will place the government and the commander-in-chief is very great;' while Colvin telegraphed to Canning: 'Openly to undo my public act, where really no substantial change is made, would fatally shake my power for good.' Brigadier Sibbald, commanding the Rohilcund division, with Bareilly for his head-quarters, joined Mr Colvin in opinion on this matter; he said: 'Were the men under my command fully convinced that *the past should be forgotten*, I feel assured their loyalty and good conduct may be relied upon.' The general tendency of opinion has been that stern measures were necessary at that crisis; but it was unquestionably infelicitous that these contradictory views should have been held at such a time in high quarters.

Mr Colvin, perpetually harassed with the accounts daily received from the various important towns included in his government, was nevertheless secure at Agra itself until towards the close of the month of May. Then, however, he found stern measures necessary. Having two regiments of native infantry with him, the 44th and the 67th, he sent two companies, one of each regiment, to Muttra (on the Delhi road), to bring down treasure to Agra. On the road, they mutinied, murdered some of their officers, and hastened to join the insurgents at Delhi. Mr Colvin at once resolved to disarm the remaining companies of those regiments; this he was enabled to do by the presence of the 3d Europeans and Captain D'Oyley's European field-battery; and the disarming was quietly effected on the 1st of June. Shortly afterwards, a corps of volunteer horse was raised among the Europeans at Agra, and placed under the command of Lieutenant Greathed—one of three brothers at that time actively engaged in the Company's service. This corps rendered good service by putting down rebellious petty chieftains in the neighbourhood. Mr Colvin felt the full weight of his position; the governor-general was far from him in one direction, Sir John Lawrence far in another; while Sir Henry Lawrence had no troops to spare, and the commander-in-chief could scarcely be heard of.

The great Mahratta stronghold, Gwalior, did not become a scene of mutiny until June; we therefore need not notice the city or its chief, Scindiah, in this place; but by following the fortunes of a portion of the Gwalior Contingent, a regiment of irregular horse, we shall learn much concerning the state of the country round Agra, and of the active services required from the English officers. Mr Colvin having accepted the proffered services of the contingent from the maharajah, Lieutenant Cockburn received orders to head half the regiment, together with a battery of guns. He started on the 13th of May from Gwalior, and accomplished the distance of ninety miles to Agra by the 15th, without knocking up man or horse. On the 18th, news arrived that troubles had broken out at Allygurh, fifty-five miles north of Agra, and that the services of the contingent were necessary for the protection of the ladies and the civilians. Cockburn with his troopers marched thirty-four miles to Hattrass on that day, and the remaining twenty-one miles on the 19th—seeking shelter from the tremendous mid-day heat in any dilapidated building that might offer; and each officer keeping in store his only clean shirt 'to meet the fugitive ladies from Allygurh.' What he saw, and what he had yet to see, at Allygurh, was serious enough. This town was destined to affect the operations of the British, not so much by its intrinsic importance, as by its position on one of the great lines of route between the eastern and western provinces of India. Allygurh commands the road from Agra to Meerut; and thus, in hostile hands, it would necessarily add to the difficulties attending the temporary loss of Delhi; seeing that the road both to Simla and to Lahore would thus be interrupted. The town is so surrounded by marshes and shallow pools, as to be almost unassailable in the rainy season. The fort consists of a regular polygon, with a broad and very deep ditch outside; it was of simple construction at the time of its capture by the British in 1803, but has since been much strengthened and improved. The military cantonment, the civil establishments, and the bazaar, are situated towards Coel, a little southward of the fort. At the beginning of the troubles in May, Allygurh was under the care of Mr Watson, as magistrate and collector. There were in the place, at the time, the head-quarters and three or four companies of the 9th regiment B. N. I.: the remainder of the regiment being in detachments at Minpooree, Etawah, and Bolundshuhur, towns further to the southeast. The troops at Allygurh behaved well and steadily during the first half of the month; but gradually a change supervened. A spy was one day caught endeavouring to excite the men. Lieutenant Cockburn, in a private letter, thus narrates the manner—quite melodramatic in its way—in which this villain was foiled: 'An influential Brahmin of this neighbourhood having been seen lurking about the lines for the past day or two, a native non-commissioned officer concealed a number of sepoys, and induced the Brahmin to accompany him to where the men lay hidden; under pretence of its being a secluded spot where they might safely concert matters. The Brahmin then made overtures to the soldier, and told him that if he would persuade the men of the regiment to mutiny, he would furnish two thousand men to assist in murdering the Europeans and plundering the treasury. At a preconcerted signal, the sepoys jumped up and secured the ruffian.' He was hanged the same day. The troops at Bolundshuhur, really or affectedly expressing horror at the hanging of a Brahmin, marched to Allygurh, and, on the 20th, succeeded in inducing their companions to mutiny. This result was so wholly unforeseen, the 9th had hitherto behaved so well, and had displayed such alacrity in capturing the treacherous Brahmin, that neither the civilians nor the English officers were prepared to resist it. Cockburn at first intended to dash at them with his troopers; but the approaching darkness, and other considerations—possibly a doubt concerning the troopers themselves—led to a change of plan. 'One holy duty remained to be performed—to save the ladies and children. This we accomplished; and whilst they were being put into carriages, we shewed a front to the mutineers, and hindered their advance. An occasional bullet whistled by our heads, but it was too dark for taking aim. One man was shot through the wrist, and five are missing. We then heard that the inhabitants were rising, so we determined on retreating. The ladies were sent on direct to Agra, and we went on to Hattrass. We had not gone far, when the bright light behind us told too plainly that the cantonment was in flames.' The civilians and the officers of the 9th lost all except their horses and the clothes on their backs. Allygurh remained for a considerable time in the hands of the insurgents: almost cutting off communication between the southeast and the northwest.

While the refugees remained in safety at Hattrass, the troopers scoured the country to put down marauders and murderers—for it was a saturnalia of lawlessness. On the 21st, many of the ruffians were captured, and speedily hanged. On the 22d, two headmen of neighbouring villages joined the marauders in an attack on some English refugees, but were frustrated. On the 23d, Cockburn and his troop galloped off from Hattrass to Sarsnee, and rescued eighteen refugees from Allygurh. 'Poor people! They have sad tales to tell. One indigo planter, Mr ——, has had one son murdered; another son, his wife, and himself, are wounded. His house and all he possessed have been destroyed. The very clothes were torn from their backs; and even the poor women, naked and bleeding, insulted and abused, had to walk many miles. At length they received shelter from a kind-hearted native banker in the village where I found them; but even there the house in which they were sheltered was twice attacked.' The good Samaritan—for there were some good and kind amid all the villainies that surrounded them—gave two or three sheets to the poor sufferers, to cover their nakedness, and to enable them to proceed to Hattrass.

The 24th of May shewed how little the Gwalior troopers could be depended upon. Of two hundred and thirty that had been intrusted to Lieutenant Cockburn, a hundred and twenty suddenly mutinied, and galloped off to join the insurgents at Delhi. As the villagers began to shew symptoms of attacking him in his weakness, and as a hundred and ten troopers still stuck by their colours, he marched off that night nineteen miles from Hattrass to Kundowlie. On the road, the troopers told the lieutenant of many little grievances that had affected them at Gwalior, and that had partly led to the mutiny of the rest of their body; and he felt grateful that some at least of the number had remained true. During the remainder of the month, and in the early part of June, this diminished body of troopers was incessantly engaged in skirmishing, attacking, or resisting attacks; the country around being in such a frightful state, that a dozen villages were sometimes seen in flames at once—the work of desperadoes, who took advantage of a time of anarchy. On one occasion, Cockburn baffled a horde of scoundrels by a capital stratagem. They had collected to the number of about five hundred, and were plundering every one on the road in a shameful manner. The lieutenant went after them with fifty troopers. He sent four of his men in a bullock-cart, a curtained vehicle such as women usually ride in.

When the marauders saw this, they made a rush for plunder, and perhaps something worse, believing the cart to contain defenceless women; they approached, but the four men jumped up, fired their muskets, and by that signal brought Cockburn and his party forward. An exciting chase ensued, which ended in the death of fifty of the marauders, and the capture of many others.

The 9th native regiment, it will be remembered, was quartered in four detachments at Allygurh, Minpooree, Etawah, and Bolundshuhur. At all four places the troops mutinied. At Etawah and Bolundshuhur, the course of events was not so exciting as at Allygurh, although amply sufficient to try the tact and courage of the few officers and civilians stationed at those places. Minpooree, on the road from Agra to Furruckabad, was, however, the scene of so smart an affair, that the governor-general, amid all his harassing employments, made it a matter of special comment. The officer chiefly concerned was Lieutenant de Kantzow; the date was May the 23d, when three companies of the 9th broke out into revolt. On the night of the 22d, news arrived that the chief portion of the regiment had mutinied at Allygurh, and it thence became at once doubtful whether the three companies at Minpooree could be depended upon. The magistrate and the collector of the district, acting with Lieutenant Crawford, resolved on removing all the English women and children for safety to Agra: this was done, promptly and successfully. A plan was agreed on, relating to the three companies of native troops on the morrow; but the sepoys anticipated this plan by mutinying at four in the morning, and endeavouring to shoot down their officers. They loaded themselves with a great store of ammunition, and tried—first to bring down their officers, and then to plunder the treasury and the bungalows. Lieutenant de Kantzow, second in command under Crawford, confronted them undauntedly, reasoned with them, and endeavoured to stop them in their mad career. Some of the men, attached to the chivalrous officer, dashed down several muskets levelled at him, and saved his life. But a terrible scene occurred at the treasury. De Kantzow, with a mere handful of ill-armed jail-guards and jail-officials, maintained a three hours' struggle against three companies of fully armed troops. The commandant had gone off; the collector also had made a hasty escape, deeming the magistrate's conduct 'romantic' in remaining behind; and thus De Kantzow was left to do the best he could at the treasury, the magistrate elsewhere. De Kantzow sent a hasty message, requesting the magistrate *not* to come to the treasury, as it would make one European the more for the sepoys to yell at and attack. How long the unequal struggle would have been maintained, cannot be said; but the magistrate found an influential native, Ras Bhowanee Singh, willing and able to visit the excited sepoys, and induce them to desist from further violence. They did so: they decamped with a good deal of property, but *without* three lacs of rupees deposited in the treasury, and without taking one English life. Right indeed was it that De Kantzow should receive the thanks of the government;* for if he had flinched, Minpooree with its twenty thousand inhabitants would have been at the mercy of three hundred brutal armed men, ready to plunder natives as well as Feringhees.

It was about one week after this event that Captain Carey, of the 17th B. N. I., rode into Minpooree, the only remaining one of four English officers who had been endeavouring to render useful service in the neighbourhood. They were at the head of a small body of native cavalry. The sowars suddenly turned upon them in an open road. Major Hayes, military secretary to Sir Henry Lawrence—a great oriental scholar and most able officer, whom General Wheeler had just before solicited Sir Henry to send him, to open the communications with Agra—was instantly cut down with a sword, his head frightfully hacked, his right hand cut off, his left mutilated. Another, Lieutenant Fayers, had his head nearly severed from his body by a dastardly villain, while the unfortunate young officer was drinking at a well. An old Sikh rushed forward to prevent the atrocity, but was repelled with the words: 'What! are you with these Kaffirs? Look to yourself!' Lieutenant Barber, adjutant of the 2d irregular cavalry, made an attempt to escape, but was shot down, cut to pieces, robbed, and left dead. The fourth, Captain Carey, trusted to the heels of his good horse; on he galloped over fields and roads, followed by a troop of blood-thirsty miscreants, yelling and firing as they rode. Happily, just as his steed was about to sink through exhaustion, his pursuers gave up the chase. He reached Minpooree in safety; and on the 1st of June, followed the mangled remains of his three poor companions to the grave.

Another exploit connected with Minpooree shall be given in the words of Lieutenant de Kantzow, affording as it does one among many examples of the extraordinary risks to which the officers were exposed at that turbulent period, and of the rattling, quick-witted, fearless, persevering way in which such dangers were met, and afterwards described in the letters written to friends at home—letters that admit the reader behind the scenes in a way not possible in official dispatches: 'I was returning from reconnoitring, when information was brought me that five troopers of the 7th light cavalry (native) were coming along the road. An

* Viscount Canning, in a letter written on the 7th of June to Lieutenant de Kantzow, said: 'I have read the account of your conduct with an admiration and respect I cannot adequately describe. Young in years, and at the outset of your career, you have given to your brother-soldiers a noble example of courage, patience, good judgment, and temper, from which many may profit. I beg you to believe that it will never be forgotten by me. I write this at once, that there may be no delay in making known to you that your conduct has not been overlooked. You will, of course, receive a more formal acknowledgment, through the military department of the government, of your admirable service.'

immediate pursuit was of course ordered by me, and my thirty-nine troopers tore away at full speed after them. I was just coming up to them, and had already let drive among the murdering villains; when, lo! I came upon two hundred of their comrades, all armed with swords, and some with carbines. A smart fire was kept up at a distance of not more than twenty-five yards. What could thirty-nine do against two hundred regular troopers, well horsed and armed—particularly when walked into by the bullets of a hundred of the infantry! I ordered a retreat, but my cavalry could not get away from troopers mounted upon good stud-bred horses; so we were soon overtaken, and then commenced the shindy in earnest. Twelve troopers surrounded me: the first, a Mohammedan priest, I shot through the breast just as he was cutting me down. This was my only pistol, so I was helpless as regards weapons, save my sword; this guarded off a swingeing cut given me by number two, as also another by number three; but the fun could not last. I bitterly mourned not having a couple of revolvers, for I could have shot every man. My sword was cut down, and I got a slash on the head that blinded me; another on the arm that glanced and only took a slice off; the third caught me on the side, but also glanced and hit me sideways. I know not how I escaped: God only knows, as twelve against one were fearful odds, especially as I was mounted on a pony bare back. Escape, however, I did.' Twenty-four out of his thirty-nine troopers were killed, wounded, or missing.

The region lately noticed, including the towns of Allygurh, Hattrass, Etawah, Minpooree, &c., was formerly included in Rohilcund, or the land of the Rohillas; but according to the territorial or political division adopted by the Company, it is now partly in the Meerut division, and partly in that of Agra; while the present Rohilcund division is wholly on the left bank of the Ganges. These technical distinctions are, however, a matter of very little importance in connection with the progress of the Revolt; for the insubordinate sepoys tempted and imitated each other wholly in disregard of mere conventional boundaries. We must now follow the stream of insurrection across the Ganges, and shew how deplorable was the anarchy, how sad the sufferings, that began there towards the close of May.

The districts of Rohilcund in its modern or limited sense are Bareilly, Boodayoum or Budaon, Shahjehanpoor, Mooradabad, and Bijnour, each named after a chief town; and not only were the whole of these towns more or less disturbed, but throughout the intervening country the military cantonments were set into a flame—figuratively and often literally. In some instances the civil servants of the Company, chiefly magistrates and revenue collectors, made their escape with their wives and children, leaving the mutineers to occupy the stations and pillage the treasuries; in others the civil servants, led by one of their number possessing tact and resolution, held the marauders at bay until assistance could be procured; while in many cases the English officers of native regiments, as well as the civilians, yielded—by flight or by death—only after a determined resistance.

Two of the towns above named, Bareilly and Boodayoun, will suffice at present to illustrate the state of affairs in Rohilcund. Sunday, as we have often had occasion to observe, was a favourite day for the native outbreaks; and it was on Sunday the 31st of May that the miseries at Bareilly began. The 18th and 68th regiments N. I. were cantoned there. The bungalow of Colonel Troup was suddenly surrounded by two companies of his own regiment, the 68th: and it was only by a hasty exit through a side-door that he escaped death. During many previous days and nights the troops had been in a rebellious state; the English, civilians and military, had slept in their clothes, with pistols ready loaded, and horses kept ready saddled. The ladies had all been sent up for safety to Nynee Tal; and thus, when the struggle arose, the officers had only themselves to protect. This word 'ladies,' however, is to be interpreted in its conventional sense; for many women in a humbler grade of life, together with their children, remained in the town; and among these some deplorable scenes occurred. The members of one family were brought before a ruthless fellow who assumed some kind of authority; and in a very few minutes their heads were severed from their bodies. At the same time, Mr Robertson the judge, two medical men, the professors of the college, and others, were subjected to a mock trial and publicly hanged. The mutinous sepoys took aim in the most deliberate way at their officers, while the latter were fleeing; Mr Alexander, commissioner of Bareilly, though ill at the time, was forced to mount his horse and gallop off as the only means of saving his life, amid a shower of bullets and grape-shot—for the treacherous villains not only used muskets and rifles, but fired grape from the cannon. Many of the gentlemen rode off in haste without any head-coverings, the rays of an Indian sun pouring down upon them in full force. When the English were driven out, the Mohammedans and Hindoos began to fight fiercely against each other for possession of the treasure—one among many indications that plunder was at least as strong a desire as revenge in impelling the natives to deeds of violence.

The name of Nynee Tal is mentioned in the above paragraph; and it may be well to understand on what ground that town was so often named with earnest solicitude by officers engaged in arduous struggles in various parts of the north of India. Nynee Tal is a healthy spot on the banks of a beautiful lake, a few miles from Almora in Kumaon, and not far from the Nepaulese border: indeed it belonged to the Goorkhas of Nepaul until recent times, when it was conquered om them by the British; since which occurnces the late owners have been friendly neighours within their own territory of Nepaul. ynee Tal became a second Simla during the sturbances. Women and children, if their lives ere spared at the scenes of tumult, were hurried f to the places just named, and to one or two ther towns among the hills—there to remain till ays of peace returned, or till means of safe coneyance to Calcutta or Bombay could be procured. When the troubles in Rohilcund commenced; when Bareilly and Boodayoun, Mooradabad and hahjehanpoor, fell into the hands of the rebels—ll fled to Nynee Tal who could. Captain Ramsey, commanding at that town, at once made arrangements for protecting the poor fugitives; he formed he gentlemen of the station into a militia, who ook it in turn to fulfil the duties of an armed patrol, to keep in order the dacoits and other ruffians in the neighbourhood; he laid in a store of three months' provisions for all the mouths in the place; and he armed the station and the roads with companies of a Goorkha regiment. These Goorkhas, it may be well here to explain, are of Mongol origin, but smaller and darker than the real Chinese. They belong to Nepaul, and first became familiar to the British by their resolute soldierly qualities during the Nepaulese war. Although Hindoos by religion, they have little or nothing of caste prejudice, and sympathise but slightly with the Hindoos of the plains. Being natives of a somewhat poor country, they have shewn a readiness in recent years to accept Company's pay as auxiliary troops; and it was a very important fact to those concerned in quelling the revolt, that the Goorkhas manifested a disposition rather to remain faithful to their British paymasters, than to join the standard of rapine and murder.

Bareilly, we have just seen, was one of the towns from which fugitive ladies were sent for safety to Nynee Tal; and now the town of Boodayoun, on the road from Agra to Bareilly, comes for notice under similar conditions. Considering that the course of public events often receives illustration of a remarkable kind from the experience of single individuals, we shall treat the affairs of Boodayoun in connection with the strange adventures of one of the Company's civil servants—adventures not so deeply distressing as those of the fugitives from Delhi, but continued during a much longer period, and bringing to light a much larger number of facts connected with the feelings and position of the natives in the disturbed districts. The wanderer, Mr Edwards, collector of the Boodayoun district, was more than *three months* in reaching Cawnpore from Boodayoun—a distance scarcely over a hundred miles by road. About the middle of May, the districts on both sides of the Ganges becoming very disturbed, Mr Edwards sent his wife and child for refuge to Nynee Tal. He was the sole European officer in charge of the Boodayoun district, and felt his anxieties deepen as rumours reached him of disturbances in other quarters. At the end of the month, news of the revolt at Bareilly added to his difficulties; for the mutineers and a band of liberated prisoners were on their way from that place to Boodayoun. Mr Edwards expresses his opinion that the mutiny was aggravated by the laws, or the course adopted by the civil courts, concerning landed property. Landed rights and interests were sold by order of the courts for petty debts; they were bought by strangers, who had no particular sympathy with the people; and the old landowners, regarded with something like affection by the peasantry, were thrown into a discontented state. Evidence was soon afforded that these dispossessed landowners joined the mutineers, not from a political motive, but to seize hold of their old estates during a time of turmoil and violence. 'The danger now is, that they can never wish to see the same government restored to power; fearing, as they naturally must, that they will have again to give up possession of their estates.' This subject, of landed tenure in India, will call for further illustration in future pages, in relation to the condition of the people.

Narrowly escaping peril himself, Mr Edwards, on the 1st of June, saw that flight was his only chance. There were two English indigo-planters in the neighbourhood, together with another European, who determined to accompany him wherever he went, thinking their safety would be thereby increased. This embarrassed him, for friendly natives who might shelter one person, would probably hesitate to receive four; and so it proved, on several occasions. He started off on horseback, accompanied by the other three, and by a faithful Sikh servant, Wuzeer Singh, who never deserted him through all his trials. The worldly wealth of Mr Edwards at this moment consisted of the clothes on his back, a revolver, a watch, a purse, and a New Testament. During the first few days they galloped from village to village, just as they found the natives favourable or hostile; often forced to flee when most in need of food and rest. They crossed the Ganges two or three times, tracing out a strange zigzag in the hope of avoiding dangers. The wanderers then made an attempt to reach Futteghur. They suffered much, and one life was lost, in this attempt; the rest, after many days, reached Futteghur, where Mr Probyn was the Company's collector. Native troops were mutinying, or consulting whether to mutiny; Europeans were departing; and it soon became evident that Futteghur would no longer be a place of safety either for Probyn or for Edwards. Flight again became necessary, and under more anxious circumstances, for a lady and four children were to be protected; but how to flee, and whither, became anxious questions. Day after day passed, before a friendly native could safely plan an escape for them by boat; enemies and marauders were on every side; and at last the danger became so imminent that it was resolved to cross the Ganges, and seek an asylum in a very desolate spot, out of the way of the mutineers. Here was presented a curious exemplification of 'lucky' and 'unlucky' days as viewed by the natives. 'A lucky day having been found for our start,' says Mr Edwards, 'we were to go when the moon rose; but this moon-rise was not till three o'clock on the morning after that fixed for the start. This the Thakoors were not at first aware of. I was wakened about eleven o'clock by one them, who said that the fact had just come to h knowledge, and that it was necessary that som thing belonging to us should start at once, as th would equally secure the lucky influence of th day, even though we ourselves should not start ti next morning. A *table-fork* was accordingly give him, with which he went off quite satisfied, an which was sent by a bearer towards the villag we were to proceed to.' Under the happy influenc of this table-fork, the wanderers set forth by nigh

Nynee Tal—a refuge for European fugitives.

Mrs Probyn and her children riding on an elephant, and the men walking on roads almost impassable with mud. They reached the stream; they crossed in a boat; they walked some distance amid torrents of rain, Mr Edwards 'carrying poor baby;' and then they reached the village, Runjpoonah, destined for their temporary home. What a home it was! 'The place intended for the Probyns was a wretched hovel occupied by buffaloes, and filthy beyond expression, the smell stifling, and the mud and dirt over our ankles. My heart sank within me as I laid down my little charge on a charpoy.' By the exercise of ingenuity, an extemporaneous chamber was fitted up in the roof. During a long sojourn here in the rainy season, Mr Edwards wrote a letter to his wife at Nynee Tal, under the following odd circumstances: 'I had but a small scrap of paper on which to write my two notes, and just the stump of a lead-pencil: we had neither pens nor ink. In the middle of my writing, the pencil-point broke; and when I commenced repointing it, the whole fell out, there being just a speck of lead left. I was in despair; but was fortunately able to refix the atom, and to finish two short notes—about an inch square each: it was all the man could conceal about him. I then steeped the notes in a little milk, and put them out to dry in the sun. At once a crow pounced on one and carried it off, and I of course thought it was lost for ever. Wuzeer Singh, however, saw and followed the creature, and recovered the note after a long chase.' Several weeks passed; 'poor baby' died; then an elder child—both sinking under the privations they had had to endure: their anxious mother, with all her tender solicitude, being unable further to preserve them. Mr Edwards, who was one of those that thought the annexation of Oude an unwise measure, said, in relation to a rumour that Oude had been restored to its king: 'I would rejoice at such an equitable measure at another time; but now it would be, if true, a sign of a falling cause and of great weakness, which is I fear our real case.' On another occasion, he heard 'more rumours that the governor-general and the King of Oude had arrived at Cawnpore; and that Oude is then formally to be made over to the king.' Whether Oudians or not, everywhere he found the Mohammedans more hostile to the British than the Hindoos; and in some places the two bodies of religionists fought with each other. After many more weeks of delays and disappointments, the fugitives were started off down the Ganges to Cawnpore. In effecting this start, the 'lucky-day' principle was again acted on. 'The astrologer had fixed an hour for starting. As it was not possible for us to go at the fortunate moment and secure the advantage, a shirt of mine and some garments of those who were to accompany me, were forwarded to a village some way on the road, which is considered equivalent to ourselves starting.' Half-a-dozen times on their voyage were they in danger of being shot by hostile natives on shore; but the fidelity and tact of the natives who had befriended them carried them through all their perils. At length they reached Cawnpore on the 1st of September, just three calendar months after Mr Edwards took his hasty departure from Boodayoun.

This interesting train of adventures we have followed to its close, as illustrating so many points connected with the state of India at the time; but now attention must be brought back to the month of May.

West of the Rohilcund district, and north-west of Allygurh and its neighbouring cluster of towns, lie Meerut and Delhi, the two places at which the atrocities were first manifested. Meerut, after the departure of the three mutinous regiments on the night of the 10th of May, and the revolt of the Sappers and Miners a few days afterwards, remained unmolested. Major-general Hewett was too strong in European troops to be attacked, although his force took part in many operations against the rebels elsewhere. Several prisoners, proved to have been engaged in the murderous work of the 10th, were hanged. On the other hand, many sowars of the 3d native cavalry, instead of going to Delhi, spread terror among the villagers near Meerut. One of the last military dispatches of the commander-in-chief was to Hewett, announcing his intention to send most of his available troops from Kurnaul by Bhagput and Paniput, to Delhi, and requesting Hewett to despatch from Meerut an auxiliary force. This force he directed should consist of two squadrons of carabiniers, a wing of the 60th Rifles, a light field-battery, a troop of horse-artillery, a corps of artillerymen to work the siege-train, and as many sappers as he could depend upon. General Anson calculated that if he left Umballa on the 1st of June, and if Hewett sent his force from Meerut on the 2d, they might meet at Bhagput on the 5th, when a united advance might be made upon Delhi; but, as we shall presently see, the hand of death struck down the commander-in-chief ere this plan could be carried out; and the force from Meerut was placed at the disposal of another commander, under circumstances that will come under notice in their proper place.

Delhi, like Cawnpore, must be treated apart from other towns. The military proceedings connected with its recapture were so interesting, and carried on over so long a period; it developed resources so startlingly large among the mutineers, besieging forces so lamentably small on the part of the British—that the whole will conveniently form a subject complete in itself, to be treated when collateral events have been brought up to the proper level. Suffice it at present to say, that the mutineers over the whole of the north of India looked to the retention of Delhi as their great stronghold, their rock of defence; while the British saw with equal clearness that the recapture of that celebrated city was an indispensable preliminary to the restoration of their prestige and power in India. All the mutineers from other towns either hastened to Delhi, or calculated on its support to their cause, whatever that cause may have been; all the available British regiments, on the other hand, few indeed as they were, either hastened to Delhi, or bore it in memory during their other plans and proceedings.

Just at the time when the services of a military commander were most needed in the regions of which Agra is the centre, and when it was necessary to be in constant communication with the governor-general and authorities, General Anson could not be heard of; he was supposed at Calcutta to be somewhere between Simla and Delhi; but dâks and telegraphs had been interfered with, and all remained in mystery as to his movements. Lawrence at Lucknow, Ponsonby at Benares, Wheeler at Cawnpore, Colvin at Agra, Hewett at Meerut, other commanders at Allahabad, Dinapoor, and elsewhere—all said in effect: 'We can hold our own for a time, but not unless Delhi be speedily recaptured. Where is the commander-in-chief?' Viscount Canning sent messages in rapid succession, during the second half of the month of May, entreating General Anson to bring all his power to bear on Delhi as quickly as possible. Duplicate telegrams were sent by different routes, in hopes that one at least might reach its destination safely; and every telegram told the same story—that British India was in peril so long as Delhi was not in British hands, safe from murderers and marauders. Major-general Sir Henry Barnard, military commander of the Umballa district, received telegraphic news on the 11th of May of the outrages at Meerut and Delhi; and immediately sent an aid-de-camp to gallop off with the information to General Anson at Simla, seventy or eighty miles distant. The commander-in-chief at once hastened from his retirement among the hills. Simla, as was noticed in a former page, is one of the sanataria for the English in India, spots where pure air and moderate temperature restore to the jaded body some of the strength, and to the equally jaded spirits some of the elasticity, which are so readily lost in the burning plains further south. The poorer class among the Europeans cannot afford the indulgence, for the cost is too great; but the principal servants of the Company often take advantage of this health-restoring and invigorating climate—where the average temperature of the year is not above 55° F. The question has been frequently discussed, and is not without cogency, whether the commander-in-chief acted rightly in remaining at that remote spot during the first twenty weeks in the year, when so many suspicious symptoms were observable among the native troops at Calcutta, Dumdum, Barrackpore, Berhampore, Lucknow, Meerut, and Umballa. He could know nothing of the occurrences at those places but what the telegraphic wires and the postal dâks told him; nevertheless, if they told him the truth, and *all* the truth, it seems difficult to understand, unless illness paralysed his efforts, why he, the chief of the army, remained quiescent at a spot more than a thousand miles from Calcutta.

Startled by the news, the commander-in-chief quitted Simla, and hastened to Umballa, the nearest military station on the great Indian highway. It then became sensibly felt, both by Anson and Barnard, how insufficient were the appliances at their disposal. The magazines at Umballa were nearly empty of stores and ammunition; the reserve artillery-wagons were at Phillour, eighty miles away; the native infantry were in a very disaffected state; the European troops were at various distances from Umballa; the commissariat officers declared it to be almost impossible to move any body of troops, in the absence of necessary supplies for a column in the field; and the medical officers dwelt on the danger of marching troops in the hot season, and on the want of conveyance for sick and wounded. In short, almost everything was wanting, necessary for the operations of an army. The generals set to work, however; they ordered the 2d European Fusiliers to hasten from Subathoo to Umballa; the Nusseree Battalion to escort a siege-train and ammunition from Phillour to Umballa; six companies of the Sappers and Miners to proceed from Roorkee to Meerut; and the 4th Irregular Cavalry to hold themselves in readiness at Hansi. Anson at the same time issued the general order, already adverted to, inviting the native regiments to remain true to their allegiance, explaining the real facts concerning the cartridges, and reiterating the assurances of non-intervention with the religious and caste scruples of the men. On the 17th there were more than seven regiments of troops at Umballa—namely, the Queen's 9th Lancers, the 4th Light Cavalry Lancers, the Queen's 75th foot, the 1st and 2d European Fusiliers, the 5th and 60th native infantry, and two troops of European horse-artillery; but the European regiments were all far short of their full strength. Symptoms soon appeared that the 5th and 60th native infantry were not to be relied upon for fidelity; and General Anson thereupon strengthened his force at Umballa with such European regiments as were obtainable. He was nevertheless in great perplexity how to shape his course; for so many wires had been cut and so many dâks stopped, that he knew little of the progress of events around Delhi and Agra. Being new to India and Indian warfare, also, and having received his appointment to that high command rather through political connections than in reference to any experience derived from Asiatic campaigning, he was dependent on those around him for suggestions concerning the best mode of grappling with the difficulties that were presented. These suggestions, in all probability, were not quite harmonious; for it has long been known that, in circumstances of emergency, the civil and military officers of the Company, viewing occurrences under different aspects or from different points of view, often arrived at different estimates as to the malady to be remedied, and at different suggestions as to the remedy to be applied. At the critical time in question, however, all the officers, civil as well as military, assented to the conclusion that Delhi must be taken at any cost; and on the 21st of May, the first division of a small but well-composed force set out from Umballa on the road to Delhi. General Anson left on the 25th, and arrived on the 26th at Kurnaul, to be nearer the scene of active operations; but there death carried him off. He died of cholera on the next day, the 27th of May.

With a governor-general a thousand miles away, the chief officers at and near Kurnaul settled among themselves as best they could, according to the rules of the service, the distribution of duties, until official appointments could be made from Calcutta. Major-general Sir Henry Barnard became temporary commander, and Major-general Reid second under him. When the governor-general received this news, he sent for Sir Patrick Grant, a former experienced adjutant-general of the Bengal army, from Madras, to assume the office of commander-in-chief; but the officers at that time westward of Delhi—Barnard, Reid, Wilson, and others—had still the responsibility of battling with the rebels. Sir Henry Barnard, as temporary chief, took charge of the expedition to Delhi—with what results will be shewn in the proper place.

The regions lying west, northwest, and southwest of Delhi have this peculiarity, that they are of easier access from Bombay or from Kurachee than from Calcutta. Out of this rose an important circumstance in connection with the Revolt—namely, the practicability of the employment of the Bombay native army to confront the mutinous regiments belonging to that of Bengal. It is difficult to overrate the value of the difference between the two armies. Had they been formed of like materials, organised on a like system, and officered in a like ratio, the probability is that the mutiny would have been greatly increased in extent—the same motives, be they reasonable or unreasonable, being alike applicable to both armies. Of the degree to which the Bombay regiments shewed fidelity, while those of Bengal unfurled the banner of rebellion, there will be frequent occasions to speak in future pages. The subject is only mentioned here to explain why the western parts of India are not treated in the present chapter. There were, it is true, disturbances at Neemuch and Nuseerabad, and at various places in Rajpootana, the Punjaub, and Sinde; but these will better be treated in later pages, in connection rather with Bombay than with Calcutta as head-quarters. Enough has been said to shew over how wide an area the taint of disaffection spread during the month of May—to break out into something much more terrible in the next following month.

Notes.

Indian Railways.—An interesting question presents itself, in connection with the subject of the present chapter—Whether the Revolt would have been *possible* had the railways been completed? The rebels, it is true, might have forced up or dislocated the rails, or might have tampered with the locomotives. They might, on the other hand, if powerfully concentrated, have used the railways for their own purposes, and thus made them an auxiliary to rebellion. Nevertheless, the balance of probability is in favour of the government—that is, the government would have derived more advantage than the insurgents from the existence of railways between the great towns of India. The difficulties, so great as to be almost insuperable, in transporting troops from one place to another, have been amply illustrated in this and the preceding chapters; we have seen how dâk and palanquin bearers, bullocks and elephants, ekahs and wagons, Ganges steamers and native boats, were brought into requisition, and how painfully slow was the progress made. The 121 miles of railway from Calcutta to Raneegunge were found so useful, in enabling the English soldiers to pass swiftly over the first part of their journey, that there can hardly be a doubt of the important results which would have followed an extension of the system. Even if a less favourable view be taken in relation to Bengal and the Northwest Provinces, the advantages would unquestionably have been on the side of the government in the Bombay and Madras presidencies, where disaffection was shewn only in a very slight degree; a few days would have sufficed to send troops from the south of India by rail, *viâ* Bombay and Jubbulpoor to Mirzapore, in the immediate vicinity of the regions where their services were most needed.

Although the Raneegunge branch of the East Indian Railway was the only portion open in the north of India, there was a section of the main line between Allahabad and Cawnpore nearly finished at the time of the outbreak. This main line will nearly follow the course of the Ganges, from Calcutta up to Allahabad; it will then pass through the Doab, between the Ganges and the Jumna, to Agra; it will follow the Jumna from Agra up to Delhi; and will then strike off northwestward to Lahore—to be continued at some future time through the Punjaub to Peshawur. During the summer of 1857, the East India Company prepared, at the request of parliament, an exact enumeration of the various railways for which engineering plans had been adopted, and for the share-capital of which a minimum rate of interest had been guaranteed by the government. The document gives the particulars of about 3790 miles of railway in India; estimated to cost £30,231,000; and for which a dividend is guaranteed to the extent of £20,314,000, at a rate varying from 4½ to 5 per cent. The government also gives the land, estimated to be worth about a million sterling. All the works of construction are planned on a principle of solidity, not cheapness; for it is expected they will all be remunerative. Arrangements are everywhere made for a double line of rails—a single line being alone laid down until the traffic is developed. The gauge is nine inches wider than the 'narrow gauge' of English railways. The estimated average cost is under £9000 per mile, about one-fourth of the English average.

Leaving out of view, as an element impossible to be correctly calculated, the amount of delay arising from the Revolt, the government named the periods at which the several sections of railway would probably be finished. Instead of shewing the particular portions belonging respectively to the five railway companies—the East Indian, the Great Indian Peninsula, the Bombay and Central India, the Sinde, and the Madras—we shall simply arrange the railways into two groups, north and south, and throw a few of the particulars into a tabulated form.

NORTHERN INDIA.

Railways.	*Lengths.*	*Probable Time of Opening.*
	Miles.	
Calcutta to Raneegunge, .	121	Opened in 1855.
Burdwan to Rajmahal, . .	130	December 1859.
Rajmahal to Allahabad,	440	1860.
Allahabad to Cawnpore, .	126	December 1857.
Cawnpore to Delhi, . . .	260	October 1858 (excepting bridge at Agra over the Jumna).
Mirzapore to Jubbulpoor, .	300	No date specified.
Jubbulpoor to Bhosawal, .	314	End of 1861.
Bhosawal to Oomrawuttee,	125	December 1860.
Oomrawuttee to Nagpoor, .	138	March 1861.
Bhosawal to Callian, . .	241	October 1859.
Callian to Bombay, . . .	33	Opened in 1854.
Surat to Ahmedabad, . .	160	1858 and 1859.
Kurachee to Hydrabad, .	120	October 1859.

SOUTHERN INDIA.

Bombay to Poonah, . .	124	February 1858.
Poonah to Sholapore, . .	165	1860.
Sholapore to Kistnah, . .	101	End of 1861.
Kistnah to Madras, . . .	310	1861 and 1862.
Madras to Arcot, . . .	65	Opened in 1856.
Arcot to Vaniembaddy, . .	60	January 1859.
Madras to Beypore, . . .	430	March 1859.

The plans for an Oude railway were drawn up, comprising three or four lines radiating from Lucknow; but the projeet had not, at that time, assumed a definite form.

'Headman' of a Village.—It frequently happened, in connection with the events recorded in the present chapter, that the *headman* of a village either joined the mutineers against the British, or assisted the latter in quelling the disturbances; according to the bias of his inclination, or the view he took of his own interests. The general nature of the village-system in India requires to be understood before the significancy of the headman's position can be

appreciated. Before the British entered India, private property in land was unknown; the whole was considered to belong to the sovereign. The country was divided, by the Mohammedan rulers, into small holdings, cultivated each by a village community under a headman; for which a rent was paid. For convenience of collecting this rent or revenue, *zemindars* were appointed, who either farmed the revenues, or acted simply as agents for the ruling power. When the Marquis of Cornwallis, as governor-general, made great changes in the government of British India half a century ago, he modified, among other matters, the zemindary; but the collection of revenue remained.

Whether, as some think, villages were thus formed by the early conquerors; or whether they were natural combinations of men for mutual advantage—certain it is that the village-system in the plains of Northern India was made dependent in a large degree on the peculiar institution of caste. 'To each man in a Hindoo village were appointed particular duties which were exclusively his, and which were in general transmitted to his descendants. The whole community became one family, which lived together and prospered on their public lands; whilst the private advantage of each particular member was scarcely determinable. It became, then, the fairest as well as the least troublesome method of collecting the revenue to assess the whole village at a certain sum, agreed upon by the *tehsildar* (native revenue collector) and the headman. This was exacted from the latter, who, seated on the chabootra, in conjunction with the chief men of the village, managed its affairs, and decided upon the quota of each individual member. By this means, the exclusive character of each village was further increased, until they have become throughout nearly the whole of the Indian peninsula, little republics; supplied, owing to the regulations of caste, with artisans of nearly every craft, and almost independent of any foreign relations.' *

Not only is the headman's position and duties defined; but the whole village may be said to be socially organised and parcelled out by the singular operation of the caste principle. Each village manages its internal affairs; taxes itself to provide funds for internal expenses, as well as the revenue due to the state; decides disputes in the first instance; and punishes minor offences. Officers are selected for all these duties; and there is thus a local government within the greater government of the paramount state. One man is the scribe of the village; another, the constable or policeman; a third, the schoolmaster; a fourth, the doctor; a fifth, the astrologer and exorciser; and so of the musician, the carpenter, the smith, the worker in gold or jewels, the tailor, the worker in leather, the potter, the washerman—each considers that he has a prescriptive right to the work in his branch done within the village, and to the payment for that work; and each member of his family participates in this prescriptive right. This village-system is so interwoven with the habits and customs of the Hindoos, that it outlives all changes going on around. Sir T. Metcalfe, who knew India well, said: 'Dynasty after dynasty tumbles down; revolution succeeds to revolution; Hindoo, Patan, Mogul, Mahratta, Sikh, English, are all masters in turn; but the village community remains the same. In times of trouble they arm and fortify themselves. If a hostile army passes through the country, the village communities collect their cattle within their walls, and let the enemy pass unprovoked. If plunder and devastation be directed against themselves, and the force employed be irresistible, they flee to friendly villages at a distance; but when the storm has passed over, they return and resume their occupations. If a country remain for a series of years the scene of continued pillage and massacre, so that the village cannot be inhabited, the scattered villages nevertheless return whenever the power of peaceable possession revives. A generation may pass away, but the succeeding generation will return. The sons will take the places of their fathers; the same site for their village, the same positions for the houses, the same lands will be reoccupied by the descendants of those who were driven out when the village was depopulated; and it is not a trifling matter that will drive them out, for they will often maintain their post through times of disturbance and convulsion, and acquire strength sufficient to resist pillage and oppression with success. This union of the village communities, each one forming a separate little state in itself, has, I conceive, contributed more than any other cause to the preservation of the people of India through all the revolutions and changes which they have suffered.' *

It is easily comprehensible how, in village communities thus compactly organised, the course of proceeding adopted by the headman in any public exigency becomes of much importance; since it may be a sort of official manifestation of the tendencies of the villagers generally.

* Irving: *Theory and Practice of Caste.*

* Report of Select Committee of House of Commons, 1832.

Palanquin.

Parade-ground, Cawnpore.

CHAPTER VIII.

TREACHERY AND ATROCITIES AT CAWNPORE.

NO other events connected with the Revolt in India made so deep an impression on the public mind, or produced so utter an astonishment and dismay, as those relating to Cawnpore—the treachery of an arch-villain, and the sufferings that resulted therefrom. The mystery that for so many weeks veiled the fate of the victims heightened the painful interest; for none in England knew how the troubles in May gave rise to the miseries in June, and these to the horrors of July, until nearly all were dead who could faithfully have recorded the progress of events. Now that the main incidents are known, they come upon the reader almost with the force of a tragic drama; associating themselves in succession with five scenes—the intrenchment, the boats, the ghat, the house of slaughter, the well—the intensity deepening as the plot advances towards its end.

So unutterably revolting were the indignities to which some of the unfortunates were subjected, at Cawnpore as at other places, that no one dared to speak or write fully of them; even men, hardy and world-worn men, almost shrank from whispering the details to each other. Vague generalities of language were employed, in sheer dismay lest the use of precise words should lift too high the veil that hid the hideous scene. So much was this felt, so much were the facts understated, that persons of unblemished moral character almost regretted the reticence of the press. A nobleman held in very high estimation, the Earl of Shaftesbury, on one occasion expressed at a public meeting a wish that the daily journals would proceed one stage further in making the mournful tale known; on the ground that Englishmen, by learning more of the real truth, would appreciate more fully the sufferings of our countrymen and countrywomen, the heroism and Christian patience with which those sufferings were borne, and the necessity for (not vengeance, but) retributive justice on those who had ordered and executed the devilish barbarities. It is not a trifling compliment to the delicacy of the English press, that a Christian nobleman should thus have suggested less scruple, less reserve, in the treatment of a most trying subject. In every narrative of these mournful events, the reader feels, and must continue to feel, that the *worst* is left unsaid.

The first matters to treat are—the locality in which, and the native chieftain by whom, these wrongs were inflicted. Cawnpore, a terrible word to English readers, is the name both of a district and of its chief town. The district, a part of the Doab or delta between the Ganges and the Jumna, is included within the government of the North-western Provinces. The city of Cawnpore is on the right bank of the Ganges, about two hundred and seventy miles below Delhi; and the river flows down nearly a thousand miles below this point to Calcutta; the land-distance, however, from Cawnpore to Calcutta is between six and seven hundred miles. The Ganges here is sometimes more than a mile in width at and soon after the rainy season, and is at such time very difficult to be crossed by bodies of troops. Cawnpore is an important city to the British in India, both commercially and in a military sense. The ghat or landing-place, in peaceful times, is a scene of great liveliness and bustle. When Skinner was there, 'Every description of vessel that can be imagined was collected along the bank. The pinnace, which with its three masts and neat rigging might have passed for a ship; budgerows, the clumsiest of all clumsy things, with their sterns several times higher than their bows; the bauleahs, ugly enough, but lightly skimming along like gondolas compared with the heavy craft around them; the drifting haystacks, which the country-boats appear to be when at a distance, with their native crews straining every nerve upon their summits, and cheering themselves with a wild and not unfrequently a sweet song; panswees shooting swiftly down the stream, with one person only on board, who sits at the head, steering with his right hand, rowing with his foot, and in the left hand holding his pipe. A ferry-boat constantly plying across the stream adds to the variety of the scene, by its motley collection of passengers—travellers, merchants, fakeers, camels, bullocks, and horses—all crowded together. The vessels fastened to the shore are so closely packed, that they appear to be one mass, and, from their thatched roofs and low entrances, might easily pass for a floating village.' Cawnpore is (or rather was) remarkable in its military arrangements. The cantonment, six miles long by half a mile broad, often contained, before the Revolt, a native population of fifty thousand persons, besides sixty thousand in the city itself, irrespective of military and Europeans. The native infantry of the station encamped here in the cool part of the year, when there were regular streets and squares of canvas stretching over an immense space; each regiment was provided with its bazaar; in the rear and far beyond the lines, were the bivouacs of every kind of camp-followers, in immense numbers. All these with many hundred bungalows or lodges of officers and European residents, gave great animation to the cantonment. The bungalows, though tiled or thatched, were here, as in other parts of India, large and commodious; each standing pleasantly in the midst of its compound or enclosure, richly planted with grapes, peaches, mangoes, shaddocks, plantains, melons, oranges, limes, guavas, and other fruits especially acceptable in a hot climate. There was accommodation for seven thousand troops, but the number actually stationed there was generally much less. In accordance with the Company's regulations, the English military officers, whether of European or native regiments, always resided within the cantonment where their services were required; while the civilians, although residing chiefly in the suburbs, had their offices and places of business within the city itself. There were thus, to some extent, two sets of English residents.

The next point to render clear is, the position of the man who so fatally influenced the affairs at Cawnpore in the summer months of 1857. Nena Sahib was his name to an English eye and tongue, and as Nena Sahib he will ever be execrated; but that was his titular or honorary, not his real name, which appears to have been Dhundu Punt or Dhoondhoopunt. When called the Nena or Nana, the Nena Sahib, the Peishwa, the Maharajah, the Nena Bahadoor, he was recognised by one of his oriental titles of honour. Let him to us be the Nena Sahib. There was a motive, however inadequate in the estimate of persons possessing a spark of human feeling, for the black treachery and monstrous cruelty of this man. He had a quarrel with the East India Company: a quarrel which the Company had nearly forgotten, but not he. The disagreement arose out of the prevalent Eastern custom of adoption, in default of legitimate male heirs. Bithoor, a town six or eight miles from Cawnpore, and within the same district, had long been the residence of the chief of the Mahrattas or Peishwa, with whom, as with other native princes, the Company had had many negotiations and treaties. Bithoor itself, a town of about fourteen thousand inhabitants, possesses numerous Hindoo temples, and several ghats or flights of steps giving access to the Ganges, to which the Brahmins and their followers frequently resort for the purpose of ritual ablution. The place is not without fortification, but it does not take rank among the strongholds of India. The last chief, Maharajah Bajee Rao Peishwa, died in 1851; and in consequence of that event, a jaghire or estate, near the town, which had been bestowed upon him during pleasure by the Company, lapsed to the government, and was subjected to the general regulations in force in Cawnpore. Being sonless, he had adopted a son, or indeed two sons—not merely to inherit the vast wealth which belonged to him independently of the arrangements with the Company, but also to perform certain filial duties which high-caste Hindoos deem it necessary to their religion that a son should perform. This adoption was legal so far as concerned the Peishwa's personal property; but the Company would not admit its validity in relation to a pension of £50,000 per annum which he had been in the habit of receiving. A slight obscurity in the wording of an official document led to some doubt on this matter. On the 1st of June 1818, Sir John Malcolm, on the part of the Company, signed a treaty with Bajee Rao, granting a pension to the rajah *and his family*. This has since been interpreted, by the Bithoor intriguers, as a perpetual grant *to the heirs*; but there is abundant evidence that Sir John and the Company meant the pension to be for Bajee Rao's life only, to be shared by his family then living. Nine years afterwards, namely, in 1827, Bajee Rao adopted two children, Suddehoo Rao and Dhundu Punt, the one four years and the other two years and a half old; they were the sons of two Brahmins, natives of the Deccan, who had come to reside at Bithoor about a year before. There is no evidence that Bajee Rao ever considered these two adopted sons, or either of them, entitled to a continuance of the Company's pension; although Dhundu Punt may very possibly have thrown out frequent hints, to sound the Company on this subject. It has been supposed that when the old King of Delhi was reproclaimed after the Meerut outbreak, he offered to acknowledge the Nena Sahib, Dhundu Punt, as the proper successor of the Peishwa of Bithoor, on condition of receiving his aid and allegiance. This was probably true, but would not suffice, without the incentive of private animosity, to account for his subsequent actions. So little was known of him in England when the Revolt began, that doubt prevailed whether he was really the adopted son of Bajee Rao; some writers asserting that that honour had been conferred upon another Dhundu Punt, and that the Nena himself was the eldest son of the rajah's subadar, Ramchunder Punt.

If hatred ruled his heart during the six years from 1851 to 1857, he must indeed have been a consummate hypocrite; for the English were always courteously received by him at his petty court, and generally came away impressed in his favour—impressed, however, at the same time, with a conviction that he entertained a sort of hope that the Queen of England would graciously befriend him in his contest with the Calcutta government, the Court of Directors, and the Board of Control, all of whom disputed his adoptive claims. He had a curious taste for mingling the English with the oriental in his palace at Bithoor. An English traveller, who visited him a few years before the Revolt, and was received with an amount of flattery that appeared to have a good deal of shrewd calculation in it, found the rooms set apart for him decked with English furniture arranged in the most incongruous manner—a chest of drawers and a toilet-table in the sitting-room; a piano and a card-table in the bedroom; tent-tables and camp-stools in the same room with elegant drawing-room tables and chairs; a costly clock by the side of cheap japan candlesticks; good prints from Landseer's pictures, in juxtaposition with sixpenny coloured plates of Wellington and Napoleon; sacred prints, and prints of ballet-girls and Epsom winners—all kinds were mingled indiscriminately, as if simply to make a show. The guest was most struck by the oriental compliments he received from the Nena, and by the odd attempt to provide English furniture where English habits and customs were so little known; yet there were not wanting dark tints to the picture. He heard rumours 'that two women of rank were kept in a den not far from my apartments, and treated like wild beasts; and that a third, a beautiful young creature, had recently been *bricked up in a wall*, for no other fault than attempting to escape.' An agent of the Nena, one Azimullah, resided some time in London, about the year 1855; he came to England to advocate the Nena's claims, and managed to ingratiate himself with many persons moving in the upper circles of society, by his manifest abilities, his winning grace, his courtesy to all with whom he came into relation. Yet there were strange fits of moody silence observable in him; and when the failure of his mission became evident, he was heard to throw out dark mysterious threats, which were disregarded at the time, but were brought vividly to recollection afterwards, when the deeds of his master forced themselves into notice.

It will presently be seen that Nena Sahib, whatever were his thoughts at the time, did not depart, when the Revolt commenced, from his usual demeanour towards the English; he was courteous to them, and was always courteously saluted by them when he rode past.

How interesting it is—nay, how affecting—to trace the mode in which the unfortunate Europeans at Cawnpore became gradually shut out from communication with the external world; neither knowing what was occurring east and west of them, nor able to communicate news of their own sufferings! In May, messages and letters passed to and from them; in June, authentic intelligence was superseded by painful rumours; in July, a deadly silence was followed by a horrible revelation.

When the Meerut and Delhi outbreaks occurred, the attention of the civil and military authorities was turned to the importance of securing Cawnpore: because of its native troops, its store of ammunition, its large treasury, its considerable English population, and its position on the Ganges and the great road. Sir Henry Lawrence, knowing that Sir Hugh Wheeler's force in European troops was weak, sent him fifty English infantry in the third week in May, and also sent the aid (aid as it was hoped to be) of two squadrons of Oude irregular horse. But Lucknow could ill spare these armed men, and hence the telegrams already briefly adverted to. First, Lawrence to Canning: 'Cawnpore to be reinforced with all speed. When may her Majesty's 84th be expected?' Then Canning to Lawrence: 'It is impossible to place a wing of Europeans at Cawnpore in less time than twenty-five days.' Then Wheeler to Canning: 'All is quiet here, but impossible to say how long it will continue so.' Next a telegram from Benares, announcing that every possible exertion would be made to send on troops to Cawnpore as fast as they came from Calcutta. Then, on the 25th, Wheeler telegraphed to Canning: 'Passed anxious night and day, in consequence of a report on very good authority that there would be an outbreak during one or the other. All possible preparations to meet it, but I rejoice to say that none occurred.' On this, Lawrence sent his earnest message recommending the establishment of ekah dâks—

NENA SAHIB. From a picture painted at Bithoor in 1850, by Mr Beechy, portrait-painter to King of Oude.

anything at any expense—to carry troops on to Cawnpore. Towards the close of the month, about seventy men of the Queen's 84th reached the city; and Sir Hugh telegraphed 'All quiet:' at the same time making very evident the existence of anxiety on his mind concerning his prospects. The governor-general telegraphed to him: 'Your anxious position is well understood; and no means have been neglected to give you aid.' On another day Sir Hugh telegraphed: 'All quiet still, but I feel by no means certain it will continue so. The civil and military are depending entirely upon me for advice and assistance.' He announced to Lawrence that he had been obliged to send irregular cavalry to clear the roads of insurgent ruffians; and added, 'Europeans are arriving but very slowly here.' The dilemma and doubt were painful to all; for Viscount Canning had few troops to send up from Calcutta, and no facilities for sending them rapidly; while, on the other hand, he did not know that death had cut off General Anson ere an advance could be made to Delhi and Cawnpore from the northwest. Hence such telegrams as the following from Canning to Anson: 'Cawnpore and Lucknow are severely pressed, and the country between Delhi and

Cawnpore is passing into the hands of the rebels. It is of the utmost importance to prevent this, and to relieve Cawnpore; but nothing but rapid action will do this. . . . It is impossible to overrate the importance of shewing European troops between Delhi and Cawnpore.' Sir Hugh Wheeler's anxieties did not relate wholly to Cawnpore; he knew that a wide region depended on that city for its continuance in loyalty. By the 2d of June only ninety European troops had reached him. On the next day he telegraphed that the population was much excited, and that unfavourable reports were coming in from the districts between Cawnpore and Lucknow. To make matters worse, Lawrence was becoming weak at the last-named place, and Wheeler sent him fifty-two of his highly cherished English troops—a number that shews how precious, from its scarcity, this military element was regarded by the two commanders. 'This leaves me weak,' said Wheeler; and well might he say so. Then occurred the cutting of the telegraph wires on all sides of Cawnpore, and the stoppage of the dâk-runners. After this, all was doubt and mystery, for it was only by stealthy means that letters and messages could leave or enter that city. By degrees there reached the Company's officers at Lucknow, Allahabad, and Benares, indirect news telling of disaster—of a rebellious rising of the native troops at Cawnpore; of the mutineers being aided and abetted by the Nena Sahib of Bithoor; of all the Europeans taking refuge in an intrenched barrack; of the forlorn band being regularly besieged in that spot; of terrible sufferings being endured; and of the soldiers and civilians, the women and children, being brought to death by numerous privations. The commissioner at Benares, when these rumours of disaster reached him, telegraphed to Calcutta: 'May God Almighty defend Cawnpore; for no help can we afford.' And so it was throughout June—Benares, Allahabad, Lucknow, Agra, all were equally unable to send aid to the beleaguered garrison. Gradually the messages became fewer, and the rumours darker; escaped fugitives and native messengers came in stealthily to one or other of the neighbouring towns; and men talked of a massacre at Cawnpore of English fugitives from Futtehgur, of another massacre of English in boats bound for Calcutta, of women and children placed in confinement, and of Nena Sahib's cruelty.

Such was the condition of Cawnpore as viewed from without, by those who could necessarily know but little of the truth. Let us now enter and trace the course of events as experienced by the sufferers themselves.

There is abundant evidence that, previous to the actual outbreak at Cawnpore, the native troops —consisting of the 1st, 53d, and 56th B. N. I., and the 2d native cavalry—were much agitated by the rumours of mutiny elsewhere; and that the European inhabitants felt sensibly the paucity of English soldiers at that place. A lady, the wife of the magistrate and collector of Cawnpore—one of those who, with all her family, were barbarously slaughtered in cold blood a few weeks afterwards —writing to her friends on the 15th of May, said: 'Cawnpore is quiet, and the regiments here are stanch; but there is no saying that they would remain long so if they came in contact with some of their mutinous brethren. We have only about a hundred European soldiers here altogether, and six guns. . . . Down-country, from Meerut to Dinapore, there is but one regiment of Europeans, of which we have a hundred.' Nevertheless, although the sepoys at Cawnpore were restless, an impression prevailed that, even if they joined in the mutiny, and marched off to Delhi, they would not inflict any injury on the military commander, Sir Hugh Wheeler, or the other English officers, who were much respected by them. The general thought it right to obtain correct though secret information from spies who mixed among the men in the cantonment; and these spies reported that the three infantry regiments, except a few refractory sepoys, appeared well disposed towards the government; whereas the 2d native cavalry, discontented and surly, had sent their families to their homes, to be out of danger, and were in the habit of holding nightly meetings or *punchayets* (a kind of jury of five persons, one of the Hindoo institutions of very ancient formation), in their lines, to concert measures of insubordination. These troopers endeavoured to bring over the foot regiments to a scheme for rising in revolt, seizing the government treasure, marching off to Delhi, and presenting that treasure to the newly restored Mogul as a token of their allegiance. The European inhabitants were numerous; for they comprised not only the officers and civilians with their families, but European merchants, missionaries, engineers, pensioners, &c., and also many non-residents, who had either come to Cawnpore from parts of the country supposed to be less protected, or had been stopped there on their way up-country by the mutineers in the Doab. These, relying on the report concerning the apparently favourable feeling among the native infantry, made no immediate attempt to quit the place. Sir Hugh Wheeler, however, did not deem it consistent with his duty to remain unprepared. Cawnpore is built on a dead level, without stronghold or place of refuge, and could not long be held against a rebel besieging force; the cantonment was at a considerable distance; and the general resolved on making some sort of defensive arrangement irrespective both of the city and the cantonment. He secured sufficient boats to convey the whole of the Europeans down the Ganges if danger should appear; and he formed a plan for protection at night in an intrenched position. This stronghold, if so it may be called, afterwards rendered memorable as 'the Intrenchment,' was a square plot of ground on the grand military parade, measuring about two hundred yards in each direction; within it were two barrack hospitals, a few other buildings, and a well; while the boundary was formed by a trench and parapet or breast-work of earth, intended to be armed and defended in case of attack. The intrenchment was entirely distinct both from the city and from the cantonment, and was further from the Ganges than either of them, about a quarter of a mile out of the Allahabad and Cawnpore high road. On the side of it furthest from the river were several barracks in course of construction. It was not intended that the European civilians should at once enter the intrenchment, but that they should regard that spot as a place of shelter in time of need. Sir Hugh brought into this place a supply of grain, rice, salt, sugar, tea, coffee, rum, beer, &c., calculated at thirty days' consumption for one thousand persons. He gave orders to the assistant-commissary to blow up the magazine if a mutiny should take place; while the collector was instructed to convey all the Company's cash, estimated at ten or twelve lacs of rupees, from the treasury in the city to the cantonment—an instruction which, as we shall see, he was able only to obey in part. As another precaution, the executive commissariat and pay-officers, with all their records and chests, were removed into bungalows adjacent to the intrenchment. There is reason to believe that the ringleaders among the native troops sought to terrify the rest into mutiny by representing that the digging, which had been seen actively in progress at the intrenchment, was the beginning of the construction of a series of mines, intended to blow them all up.

One of the most painful considerations associated with these events in May was, that the heartless man who afterwards wrought such misery was trustingly relied upon as a friend. The magistrate's wife, in a series of letters before adverted to, wrote under date May 16th: 'Should the native troops here mutiny, we should either go into cantonments, or to a place called Bithoor, where the Peishwa's successor resides. He is a great friend of C——'s [the magistrate's], and is a man of enormous wealth and influence; and he has assured C—— that we should all be quite safe there. I myself would much prefer going to the cantonment, to be with the other ladies; but C—— thinks it would be better for me and our precious children to be at Bithoor.' Again, on the 18th: 'If there should be an outbreak here, dearest C—— has made all the necessary arrangements for me and the children to go to Bithoor. He will go there himself, and, with the aid of the rajah, to whose house we are going, he will collect and head a force of fifteen hundred fighting-men, and bring them into Cawnpore to take the insurgents by surprise. This is a plan of their own, and is quite a secret; for the object of it is to come on the mutineers unawares.' Here, then, in the month of May, was Nena Sahib plotting with the English against the mutineers. It was on the 20th that Sir Hugh, rendered uneasy by the symptoms around, sent to Lucknow for three hundred European soldiers; but as Sir Henry Lawrence could hardly spare one-sixth of that number, arrangements were made for accommodating as many English families as possible in the cantonment, and for fitting up the intrenchment as a place of refuge. On the 21st, the magistrate, with Wheeler's consent, wrote to the Nena, begging him to send the aid of a few of his Mahratta troops. The native soldiers being hutted in the cantonment, and the few English soldiers barracked in the intrenchment, it was speedily determined that—while the English officers should sleep at the cantonment, to avoid shewing distrust of the native troops—their wives and families, and most of the civilians, should remain at night in the intrenchment, under protection of English soldiers. On the first night of this arrangement, 'there were an immense number of ladies and gentlemen assembled in the intrenchment; and oh! what an anxious night it was! The children added much to our distress and anxiety,' said the lady whose letters were lately quoted; 'it was some hours before I could get them to sleep. I did not lie down the whole night. Extraordinary it was, and most providential too, that we had a thunder-storm that night, with a good deal of rain, which cooled the air a little; had it not been for this, we should have suffered much more.' An English officer, in relation to this same night, said: 'Nearly all the ladies in the station were roused out of their houses, and hurried off to the barracks. The scene in the morning you can imagine. They were all huddled together in a small building, just as they had left their houses. On each side were the guns drawn up; the men had been kept standing by them all night through the rain, expecting an instant attack. There are few people now in the station but believe this attack had been intended, and had merely been delayed on finding us so well prepared.' On the last day of the month—a day that seems to have ended all communication from this hapless lady to her friends in England—she wrote: 'We are now almost in a state of siege. We sleep every night in a tent pitched by the barracks, with guns behind and before. We are intrenched, and are busy getting in a month's provisions in case of scarcity. For the first four or five nights, we scarcely closed our eyes. . . . . Last night, the sepoys of the 1st regiment threatened to mutiny, and poor Mrs Ewart was in dreadful distress when Colonel Ewart went to sleep in the lines, according to orders; and he himself fully expected to be killed before morning; but, thank God, all passed off quietly. The general remains in the barracks day and night, to be at hand if anything should happen. We still pass the day at the Ewarts' house; but at night every one returns to the barracks, which is a wretched place. . . . . Poor Mrs —— has quite lost her reason from terror and excitement. Oh! it is a hard trial to bear, and almost too much; but the sight of the children gives us strength and courage.'

Colonel Ewart, mentioned in the above

paragraph, and Major Hillersdon, were the commandants of the 1st and 53d native regiments, respectively; they lived in pleasant bungalows outside Cawnpore; but at this perilous time they slept near their men in the cantonment, while their families took refuge within the intrenchment. Mrs Ewart—destined, like the magistrate's wife, to be in a few weeks numbered among the outraged and slaughtered—wrote like her of the miseries of their position, even at that early period of their privation. Speaking of the interior of the intrenchment, she said: 'We have a tent, which is, of course, more private and comfortable for the night; and at present there is no occasion to spend days as well as nights there, though many people do so. This is fortunate, since the weather is fearfully hot. God grant that we may not be exposed to such suffering as a confinement within that intrenchment must entail; even should we be able to bear it, I know not how our poor little ones could go through the trial.' The general feelings of the English in the place towards the close of May cannot be better conveyed than in the following words: 'We are living face to face with great and awful realities—life and property most insecure, enemies within our camp, treachery and distrust everywhere. We can scarcely believe in the change which has so suddenly overcast all the pleasant repose and enjoyment of life. We are almost in a state of siege, with dangers all around us—some seen, some hidden . . . . Major Hillersdon joins us daily at our four o'clock dinner, and we stay together till half-past seven, when we go to our melancholy night-quarters, behind guns and intrenchments. My husband betakes himself to his couch in the midst of his sepoys; and you can fancy the sort of nights we have to pass. These are real trials, but we have not experienced much actual physical suffering yet.' In another letter she further described the intrenchment and barracks as they were at night: 'We returned to those melancholy night-quarters. Oh, such a scene! Men, officers, women and children, beds and chairs, all mingled together inside and outside the barracks; some talking or even laughing, some very frightened, some defiant, others despairing. Such sickening sights these for peaceful women; and the miserable reflection that all is caused not by open foes, but by the treachery of those we had fed and pampered, honoured and trusted, for so many years.' Colonel Ewart, in probably the last letter received from him by his friends in England, wrote on the 31st: 'The treasury, containing some ten or twelve lacs of rupees, is situated five miles from the cantonment. It has hitherto been thought inexpedient to bring the treasure into the cantonment; but the general has now resolved on making the attempt to-morrow. Please God, he will succeed. He is an excellent officer, very determined, self-possessed in the midst of danger, fearless of responsibility—that terrible bugbear that paralyses so many men in command.' This was the character generally given to Sir Hugh Wheeler, who was much liked and trusted. The state of suspense in which the officers themselves were placed, not knowing whether revolt and outrage would speedily mark the conduct of regiments that had up to that moment remained faithful, was well expressed in a letter written by one of the infantry officers: 'I only wish that I might get orders to go out with my regiment, or alone with my company, against some of the mutineers; so that we could put the men to the test, and see whether they really mean to stick to us or not, and end this state of suspense.'

Numerous scraps of local information, portions of letters, diaries, conversations, and scarcely intelligible messages, in English, Hindustani, and Persian, help to make up the materials out of which alone a connected narrative of the events at Cawnpore can be prepared. These would all have been very insufficient, had it not fortunately happened that an officer of the Company, an educated man, lived to record upon paper his experience of four weeks spent in the intrenchment, and three subsequent weeks of imprisonment in the city. This was Mr Shepherd, belonging to the commissariat department. How his life was saved, and how those dear to him were savagely butchered, will be seen further on; at present, it will suffice to remark that he lived to prepare, for the information of the government, a record of all he knew on this dreadful subject; and that the record thus prepared contains more information than any other brought to light amid that dismal wreck of human hopes and human existence.

When the month of June opened, symptoms became so unfavourable that the non-military Christian residents thought it expedient to move from the city, and obtain shelter in the English church and other buildings near the intrenchment. Day after day small portions of cash, and Company's papers of various kinds, were brought by the commissariat officers to head-quarters. The collector, acting on Sir Hugh's instructions, had endeavoured to bring the Company's treasure from the city to the intrenchment; but he met too much opposition to enable him to effect this, save in part; and the aid of three or four hundred men was obtained from Nena Sahib, to guard the treasury and its contents. What was passing through the heart of that treacherous man at the time, none but himself could know; but the English officers, whether forgetful or not of his grudge against the Company, seem to have acted as though they placed reliance on him. On the 2d, it being thought improper to keep any public money under the sepoy guard at the office, the commissariat treasure-chest, containing about thirty-four thousand rupees in cash, together with numerous papers and account-books, was brought into the intrenchment, and placed in the quarter-guard there. In short, nothing was deemed safe by Wheeler and the other officials, unless it was under their own immediate care.

On the 5th of June arrived the crisis which

was to tax to the utmost the firmness and courage, the tact and discrimination, the kindness and thoughtfulness, of the general on whom so many lives now depended. He had appealed, and appealed in vain, for reinforcements from other quarters: no one possessed troops that could readily be sent to him; and he had therefore to meet his troubles manfully, with such resources as were at hand. At two o'clock in the morning, after a vain attempt to draw the native infantry from their allegiance, the 2d cavalry rose in a body, gave a great shout, mounted their horses, set fire to the bungalow of their quarter-master-sergeant, and took possession of thirty-six elephants in the commissariat cattle-yard. The main body then marched off towards Nawabgunge; while the ringleaders remained behind to assail once more the honesty of the infantry. The 1st regiment N. I. yielded to the temptation, and marched out of the lines about three o'clock; but before doing

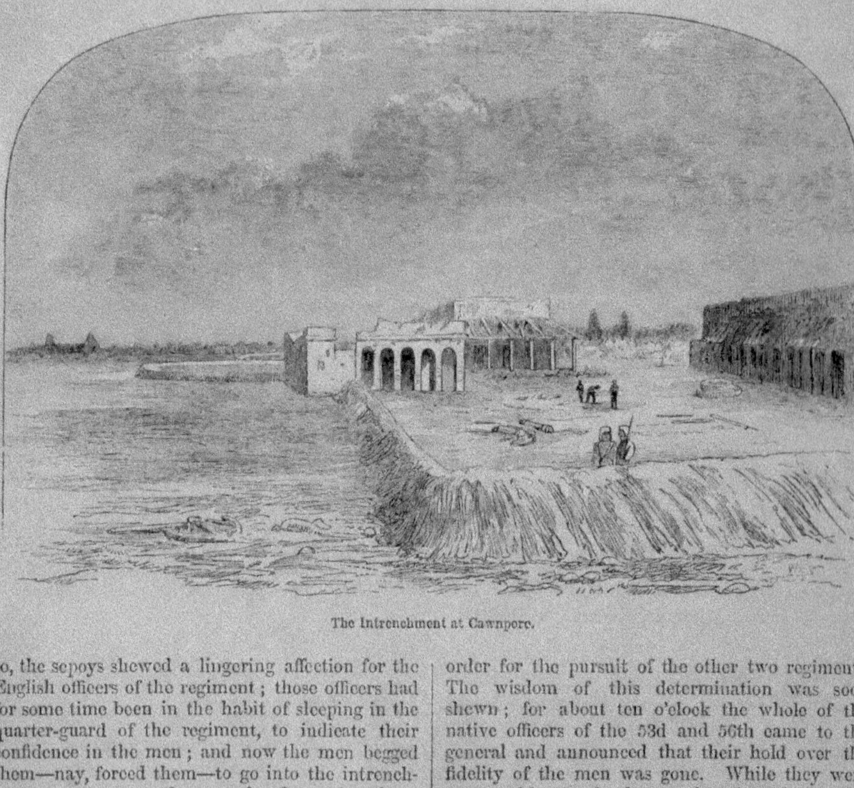

The Intrenchment at Cawnpore.

so, the sepoys shewed a lingering affection for the English officers of the regiment; those officers had for some time been in the habit of sleeping in the quarter-guard of the regiment, to indicate their confidence in the men; and now the men begged them—nay, forced them—to go into the intrenchment, as a means of personal safety. An alarm gun was fired, and all the non-combatants were brought from the church-compound into the intrenchment—a necessary precaution, for burning bungalows were seen in various directions. A few days previously, a battery of Oude horse-artillery had been sent from Lucknow by Lawrence to aid Wheeler at Cawnpore; and this battery was, about seven o'clock on the eventful morning of the 5th, ordered with a company of English troops to pursue the two mutinous regiments. But here a dilemma at once presented itself. Could the 53d and 56th regiments be relied upon? Sir Hugh thought not; and therefore he countermanded the order for the pursuit of the other two regiments. The wisdom of this determination was soon shewn; for about ten o'clock the whole of the native officers of the 53d and 56th came to the general and announced that their hold over the fidelity of the men was gone. While they were yet speaking, a bugle was heard, and the two regiments were seen to march off to join their companions at Nawabgunge; any attempt on the English being checked by the pointing of a gun at them. The apparently faithful native officers were directed to organise a few stragglers who had not joined the mutineers; they left the intrenchment for this purpose, but did not return: whether they joined in the revolt, or went quietly to their own homes to avoid the resentment of the sepoys, was not fully known. As soon as possible, carts were sent to the cantonment to bring away the sick from the hospital, and such muskets and other property as might be useful. In consequence of this, the two hospitals or barracks in the intrenchment became very much crowded, many of the people being compelled to sleep in the open air through want of room. All the civilians were then armed, and directed what they should do for the common good. The Oude artillery, shewing signs of being smitten by the prevailing mania for revolt, were disarmed and dismissed that same evening.

The scene must now be shifted, to shew Nena Sahib's share in the work. Rumours came to the intrenchment that when the rebels reached Nawabgunge, he quitted Bithoor and came out to meet them; that he placed himself at their head; that they all went together to the treasury; that he carried off a large amount of government treasure on the government elephants; and that he gave up the rest to the sepoys as a prize. Thereupon the papers were burnt, and the treasury and the collector's office destroyed. The sepoys guarding the magazine would not allow that building to be blown up by the government

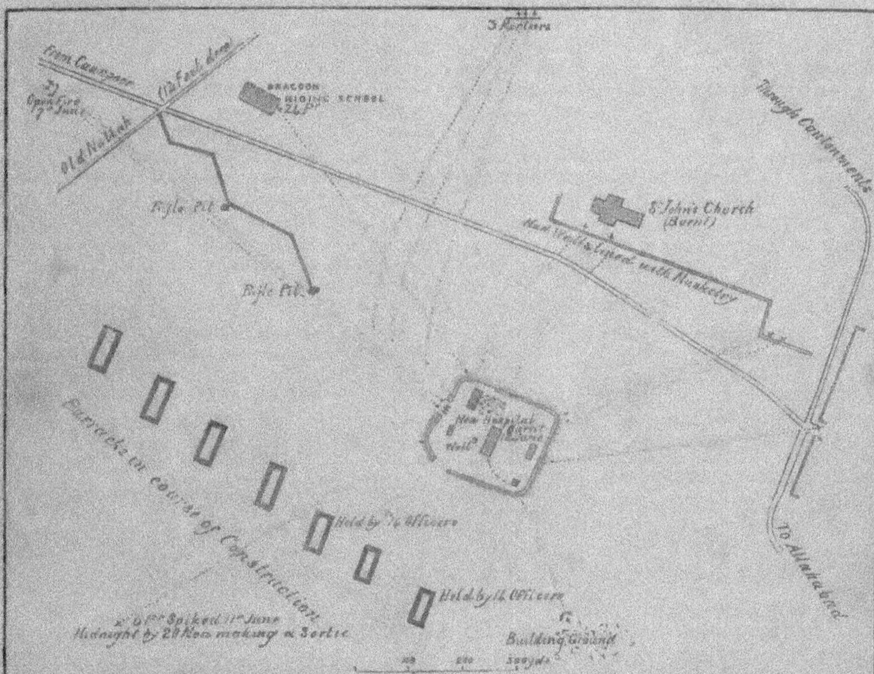

Plan of Sir H. Wheeler's Intrenchment at Cawnpore. From an official survey.

officer; the mutineers brought as many country carts as they could procure, and carried off a considerable quantity of baggage and ammunition. All then marched off to Kullianpore, being one stage on the road to Delhi, except a few troopers who remained to finish the work of destruction among the bungalows. The Oude artillery, lately disarmed and dismissed by Wheeler, now went to Nena Sahib, and laid before him a plan for attacking the intrenchment, concerning which they were able to give much information. They reported that the cantonment contained many guns, and much powder and ammunition, with which the intrenchment might safely be attacked. There was another fact favourable to the rebels. One end of the great Ganges Canal enters the river near Cawnpore; and it had been contemplated by the government to send a large store of shot and shell by that canal up to Roorkee, through Allygurh and Meerut; but as the Doab and Rohilcund were in too disturbed a state to permit this, thirty-five boats laden with shot and shell were this day lying in the canal near the cantonment. This large store of ammunition the rebel artillerymen suggested should be at once seized; and the advice was acted on. A native inhabitant, who afterwards gave information to the English, said that when the Nena openly took part with the rebels, he released four hundred prisoners in the town, whose fetters he ordered to be knocked off; 'and having opened the door of the armoury, he gave the order that whatever prisoner was willing to follow him should arm himself with gun, pistol, or sword, as he liked best'—a story highly probable, though not within the power of Mr Shepherd to confirm. Before the Nena finally committed himself to a course of rebellion and war, the 1st native infantry made their head subadar a general; and the general then promoted all the havildars and naiks to be subadars and jemadars.

Two officers of the 56th regiment were fortunate enough to be away from Cawnpore and the cantonment altogether, on the day of the mutiny. They had been sent with two hundred men to Ooral, a village or town at some distance, on the 2d of June. When that regiment mutinied at the cantonment, and when the news of the mutiny reached Ooral, the two hundred did not long delay in following their example. The officers, seeing their danger, at once galloped off, taking nothing with them but the clothes on their backs, and their swords and revolvers. Their tale was as full of adventure as many that have already occupied these pages. They found their way to Calpee, to Humeerpoor, to various places; they met with two brother-officers escaping from mutineers at Humeerpoor; the four rowed boats, swam rivers, entered villages where they were plundered of their weapons and clothes, roamed through jungles, fed on chupatties and water when they could obtain such fare, picked up bits of native clothing, encountered friendly Hindoos at one time and marauding enemies at another. Of the two officers from Cawnpore, one died mad in the jungle, from heat, thirst, and suffering; but the other, Ensign Browne, joined the body of English troops at Futtehpoor, after thirty-seven days of wandering. All the other English officers of the four native regiments appear to have been at or near Cawnpore at the time of the outbreak; and all were called upon to bear their bitter share in the woes that followed—woes rendered more distressing by falling equally on innocent women and children as on themselves—nay, much more heavily.

The sun rose upon an anxious scene on the 6th of June. Sir Hugh Wheeler and nearly all the Europeans—men, women, and children—military, civilians, and servants—were crowded within the intrenchment; while the rebel troops, four regiments and an artillery battery, had not only abandoned their allegiance, but were about to besiege those who were lately their masters. The rebels brought into requisition all the government work-people and the bullocks, in the town and cantonment, to drag guns into position near the intrenchment, and to convey thither a store of powder and ammunition. They brought six guns (two of them 18-pounders) to bear in a line, and opened fire about ten o'clock in the forenoon. Instantly a bugle sounded within the intrenchment; and every man, from the highest officers down to the clerks and the drummers, flew to arms, and took up the position assigned to him. There was only a breast-high earthen parapet, bounded by a small trench, between the besiegers and the besieged: hence there was nothing but indomitable courage and unceasing watchfulness that could enable the English to hold their own against the treacherous native troops. Here, then, were nine hundred persons* hemmed into a small space, forming their citadel, while the surrounding country was wholly in the hands of the rebels. Out of the nine hundred, barely one-third were fighting-men; while considerably more than one-third were women and children, to be fed and protected at all hazards. The few guns within the intrenchment answered those from without; but all the men not employed with those guns crouched down behind the breast-work, under the hot wind and scorching sun of a June day, ready to defend the spot with musketry if a nearer attack were made. The rebels did not attempt this; they adopted the safer course of bringing up their guns nearer to the beleaguered place. Sir Hugh Wheeler had eight pieces of ordnance—two brass guns of the Oude battery, two long 9-pounders, and four smaller; he had also a good store of ammunition, buried underground, and had thus a defensive power of some importance. On the other hand, his anxieties were great; for one of the two buildings (they had been used as hospitals for European troops) was thatched, liable to be fired by a chance shot; the commissariat officers were unable to bring in more supplies; the shelter was direfully insufficient for nine hundred persons in a fierce Indian climate; and the women and children could do little or nothing to assist in the defence of all.

The native informant, above adverted to, states that when Nena Sahib found the mutineers about to depart to Delhi, 'he represented to the native officers that it would not be correct to proceed towards Delhi until they had entirely destroyed the officers and European soldiers, and women and children of the Christian religion; and that they should, if possible, by deceiving the officers, accomplish this grand object, or they would be good for nothing.' Such words were certainly consistent with the machinations of a villain who sought a terrible revenge for some injury, real or pretended; but they do not the less illustrate the remarkable subtlety and secretiveness of the Hindoo character, so long concealing a deadly hatred under a friendly exterior. This same native, who was in Cawnpore at the time, further said: 'In the city it was as if the day of judgment had come, when the sepoys of

* The number of persons in the intrenchment on that day will probably never be accurately known; but Mr Shepherd, from the best materials available to him, made the following estimate:

First company, 6th battalion, artillery,	61
Her Majesty's 32d foot,	84
Her Majesty's 84th foot,	50
1st European Fusiliers,	15
English officers, mostly of mutinied regiments,	100
Merchants, writers, clerks, &c.,	100
English drummers of mutinied regiments,	40
Wives and children of English officers,	50
Wives and children of English soldiers,	160
Wives and children of civilians,	120
Sick, native officers, and sepoys,	100
Native servants, cooks, &c.,	100

the infantry and the troopers of the cavalry, the jingling of whose sword-scabbards and the tread of whose horses' feet resounded on all sides, proceeded with guns of various sizes, and ammunition, from the magazine through the suburbs of Cawnpore towards the intrenchment.' In relation to the conduct of native servants of the Company on that day, Mr Shepherd said: 'None of the native writers, Bengalees and others in government offices or merchants' employ, went into the intrenchment; they remained in the city, where they appear to have received much annoyance from the mutineers; and some had to hide themselves to save their lives. The (native) commissariat contractors' [those who supplied provisions and stores for the troops, ordered and paid for by the head commissary] 'all discontinued their supplies from the 6th; or rather, were unable to bring them in, from the way the mutineers surrounded the intrenchment on all sides, permitting no ingress or egress at any time except under cover of night.' Those natives must, in truth, have been placed in a perplexing position, between employers whom they wished to serve but could not, and rebels who sought to tamper with their honesty.

Another day broke, revealing a further strengthening of the rebels' attack. They increased their number of guns, four of which were 24-pounders; and with the shot from these guns not only were many valuable men struck down, but the walls and verandahs of the hospitals pierced, spreading terror among the helpless inmates. There was but one well within the intrenchment; and so hot was the fire from without, that, to use the words of Mr Shepherd, 'it was as much as giving a man's life-blood to go and draw a bucket of water; and while there was any water remaining in the large jars, usually kept in the verandah for the soldiers' use, nobody ventured to the well; but after the second day, the demand became so great that a bheestee bag of water was with difficulty got for five rupees, and a bucket for a rupee. Most of the servants deserted, and it therefore became a matter of necessity for every person to fetch his own water, which was usually done during the night, when the enemy could not well direct their shots.' What was the degree of thirst borne under these circumstances, none but the forlorn garrison could ever know. As there was no place under which to shelter live cattle, some of the animals were let loose, and others slaughtered; entailing a necessary exhaustion of meat-rations after three or four days. The commissariat servants, however, now and then managed to get hold of a stray bullock or cow near the intrenchment at night, which served for a change. Not only was it difficult to obtain suitable food to eat, but the native servants took every opportunity to escape, and the cooking was in consequence conducted under very sorry conditions.

The tale of accumulated suffering need not, and indeed cannot, be followed day by day: several days must be grouped together, and the general character of the incidents noted—so far as authentic recitals furnish the materials. Meat, as has just been intimated, soon became scarce; hogsheads of rum and malt liquor were frequently burst by cannon-balls, but the supply still remained considerable; chupatties and rice were the chief articles of food for all. The English found their troubles increase in every way: the rebels at first fired only cannon on them; but by degrees, after burning the English church and all other buildings around and near the intrenchment, the sepoys masked themselves behind the ruined walls, and kept up an almost incessant fire of musketry, shooting down many who might have escaped the cannon-balls. There were seven unfinished barracks outside the intrenchment, three of them at about a furlong distance. These were scenes of many an exciting encounter. Captain Moore of the 32d foot, a gallant and intrepid officer, often encountered the rebels near those places. He would send some of his men, with field-telescopes, to watch the position of the enemy's guns, from the roof of one of the barracks, as a guidance for the besieged; and as soon as these men were attacked, a handful of gallant companions would rush out of the intrenchment, and drive off the assailants with a fire of musketry. The enemy having no cannon on this side, a sort of drawn battle ensued: the besiegers holding three or four of the barracks, and the besieged maintaining a hold of the three nearest to the intrenchment. After a while, the enemy brought one gun round to this quarter; but twenty English made a sortie at midnight on the 11th, spiked the gun, and returned safely. Whenever fighting on anything like terms of equality took place, the European troops proved themselves a match for many times their number of natives; but any daring achievements for effectual liberation were rendered nugatory by the presence of so many helpless women and children, whose safety was the first thought in the minds of the men, whether civilians or military. Numbers of the poor creatures died within the first week, from illness, heat, fright, want of room, want of proper food and care. In the obituary of many an English newspaper, when news of the terrible calamity had crossed the ocean, might be read that such a one, probably an officer's wife, had 'died in the intrenchment at Cawnpore;' what that intrenchment meant, few readers knew, and fewer knew what sufferings had preceded the death. The dead bodies were thrown into a well outside the intrenchment, lest they should engender disease by any mode of burial within the crowded and stifling enclosure; and even this sad office could only be rendered under a shower of shot and shell. 'The distress was so great,' says Mr Shepherd, 'that none could offer a word of consolation to his friend, or attempt to administer to the wants of each other. I have seen the dead bodies of officers, and tenderly brought-up young ladies of rank (colonels' and captains' daughters), put outside the verandah amongst the rest, to await the time when the fatigue-party usually went round to carry the dead to the well; for there was scarcely room to shelter the living.'

During all these days, Cawnpore itself, and the country between it and the intrenchment, became prey to a marauding host of sepoys, liberated prisoners, and ruffians of every kind. The native before adverted to, one Nujeer Jewarree, referring to this period, said: 'In whatever shop the sepoys entered to ask for sugar or rice, they plundered everything belonging to the citizen that they could find; so much so, that plunder and oppression were the order of the day. Every violent man did what came into his mind; and the troopers got possession of a note, the value of which amounted to twenty-five thousand rupees, belonging to Eman-u-Dowlah and Bakir Ali. One troop, or thereabouts, left the cantonment and proceeded to the buildings in which the civil and revenue and judicial courts were held, and commenced firing them. In the city and gardens there was so much villainy committed that travelling became dangerous, and to kill a man was quite easy. They (the marauders) committed deeds of oppression and plundered each other; some forcibly cut the grain out of the fields, and others were occupied in picking up plundered property. He then spoke of the houses and offices of certain English merchants and traders—Greenway, Crump, Mackintosh, Reid, Marshall, Kirk, &c.—and of the 'lacs' of treasure that were plundered from each; too vaguely estimated to be relied on in detail, but evidently denoting a scene of unscrupulous pillage. Another native, Nerput, presently to be noticed more particularly, said: 'Zemindars of the neighbourhood are fighting among themselves in payment of old quarrels; sepoys, making for their homes with plundered treasure, have been deprived of their plunder, and, if any opposition is made, immediately murdered. Such few Europeans as had remained beyond the intrenchment, were caught and put to death.'

The native authority just referred to states (although the statement is not confirmed by Mr Shepherd), that on the 9th of June Sir Hugh Wheeler sent a message to Nena Sahib, demanding why he had thus turned against the English, who had hitherto been treated by him in a friendly spirit; and why he was causing the death of innocent women and children—to which the Nena gave no other reply than from the cannon's mouth.

One day was so much like another, after the actual commencement of the siege, that the various narrators make little attempt to record the particular events of each. Every day brought its miseries, until the cup nearly overflowed. The food was lessening; the water was difficult to obtain; strength was sinking; lives were being rapidly lost; the miscreant rebels were accumulating in greater and greater number outside the intrenchment; the two buildings were becoming every day more and more riddled with shot; the wounded had their wretchedness increased by the absence of almost everything needful to the comfort of the sick; the hearts of the men were wrung with anguish at seeing the sufferings borne by the women; and the women found their resolution and patience terribly shaken when they saw their innocent little ones dying from disease and want.

A scene was presented on the 13th that filled every one with horror. The officers and their families had hitherto lived chiefly in tents, within the intrenchment; but the rebels now began to fire *red-hot* shot, which not only necessitated the removal of the tents, but ignited the thatch-roof of one of the two hospitals. This building contained the wives and children of the common soldiers, and the sick and wounded. The flames spread so rapidly, and the dire confusion among the wretched creatures was such, that forty of the helpless invalids were burned to death before aid could reach them. The rebels appeared to have calculated on all the men within the intrenchment rushing to save the victims from the flames, leaving the besiegers to enter with musket and sword; and so threatening was the attack, so close the approach of the enemy, that the Europeans were forced to remain watchful at their frail earthen defence-work, despite their wish to rescue the shrieking sufferers in the hospital. Nearly all the medicines and the surgical instruments were at the same time destroyed by the fire, affording a hopeless prospect to those who might afterwards fall ill or be wounded. The rebels by this time amounted to four thousand in number, and their attacks increased in frequency and closeness; but the besieged had not yielded an inch; every man within the intrenchment, a few only excepted, was intrusted with five or six muskets, all of which were kept ready loaded, to pour a fire into any insurgents who advanced within musket-shot. Bayonets and swords were also ready at hand, for those who could use them. The condition of every one was rendered more deplorable than before by this day's calamity; the fire had wrought such mischief that many of the men, who had until then occasionally sheltered themselves under a roof for a few hours at a time, were now forced to remain permanently in the open air, exposed to a fierce Indian sun at a date only one week before the summer solstice. That many were struck down by *coup de soleil* at such a time may well be conceived. The poor ladies, too, and the wives of the soldiers, were rendered more desolate and comfortless than ever, by the destruction of much of their clothing during the fire, as well as of many little domestic comforts which they had contrived to bring with them in their hurried flight from their homes in the city or the cantonment.

What transpired outside the intrenchment, none of the captives knew; and even at later times it was difficult to ascertain the real truth. The native chronicler already referred to speaks of many deeds of cruelty, but without affording means of verification. On one day, he says, a family was seen approaching from the west in a carriage; the husband was at once killed; the others, 'one lady and one grown-up young lady and three children,' were brought before the Nena, who ordered them to be instantly put to death. 'The lady begged the Nena to spare her life; but this disgraceful man would not in any way hearken to her, and took them all into the plain. At that time the sun was very hot, and the lady said: "The sun is very hot, take me into the shade;" but no one listened. On four sides the children were catching hold of their mother's gown and saying: "Mamma, come to the bungalow and give me some bread and water." At length, having been tied hand to hand, and made to stand up on the plain, they were shot down by pistol-bullets.' This story, touching amid all its quaintness of recital, was probably quite true in its main features. Another lady, whom he calls the wife of Mukan Sahib, merchant, and who had been hiding for four or five days in the garden of her bungalow, 'came out one evening, and was discovered. She had through fear changed her appearance by putting on an Hindustani bodice, and folding a towel around her head. She was taken before the Nena, who ordered her to be killed. The writer of this journal having gone in person, saw the head of that lady cut off, and presented as a nazir (gift of royalty).' There can be no question that the vicinity of Cawnpore was at that time in a frightful state. Not only were mutinous sepoys and sowars engaged in hostilities against the 'Feringhees,' whom they had so lately served, and whose 'salt' they had eaten; but many of the ambitious petty rajahs and chieftains took advantage of the anarchy to become leaders on their own special account; plunderers and released prisoners were displaying all their ferocious recklessness; while timid, sneaking villagers, too cowardly to be openly aggressive, were in many instances quite willing to look complacently at deeds of savage brutality, if those deeds might leave a little *loot*, or plunder, as their share. Consequently, when any English refugees from other towns passed that way, their chance of safety was small indeed.

Before tracing the course of events in the intrenchment during the third week in June, we must advert to another calamity. The griefs and sufferings endured by the English soldiers and residents at Cawnpore did not fill up the measure of Nena Sahib's iniquity. Another stain rests on his name in connection with the fate of an unfortunate body of fugitives from Futteghur. It is an episode in the great Cawnpore tragedy; and must be narrated in this place, in connection with the events of the month.

Futteghur, as will be seen by reference to a map, is situated higher up the Ganges than Cawnpore, near Furruckabad. Practically, it is not so much a distinct town, as the military station or cantonment for the place last named. Furruckabad itself is a city of sixty thousand inhabitants; handsome, cleaner, and more healthy than most Indian cities, carrying on a considerable trading and banking business, and standing in the centre of a fertile and cultivated region. It has no other fortifications than a sort of mud-fort connected with the native nawab's residence. When this nawab became, like many others, a stipendiary of the modern rulers of India, the British built a military cantonment at Futteghur, about three miles distant, on the right bank of the river. Towards the close of May, Futteghur contained the 10th regiment Bengal native infantry, together with a few other native troops. Among the chief English officers stationed there, were General Goldie, Colonels Smith and Tucker; Majors Robertson, Phillot, and Munro; Captains Phillimore and Vibert; Lieutenants Simpson, Swettenham, and Fitzgerald; and Ensigns Henderson and Eckford. The troops displayed much insubordination as the month closed; and on the 3d of June the symptoms were so threatening, that it was deemed prudent to arrange for sending off the women and children for safety to Cawnpore—in ignorance that the Europeans in that city were in a still more perilous state. Boats had already been procured, and held in readiness for any such exigency. On the next day the 10th infantry exhibited such ominous signs of mutiny, that a large party of the English at once took to their boats. After a short voyage, finding the natives on the banks of the Ganges likely to be troublesome, the fugitives resolved on separating themselves into two parties; one, headed by Mr Probyn, the Company's collector, and consisting of about forty persons, sought refuge with a friendly zemindar named Herden Buksh, living about twelve miles from Futteghur, on the Oude side of the river; while the other party proceeded on the voyage down the Ganges to Cawnpore. This last-named party amounted to more than a hundred and twenty persons, nearly all non-combatants; missionaries, merchants, indigo planters, estate stewards, agents, collectors, clerks, shopkeepers, schoolmasters, post and dâk agents—such were the male members of this hapless band of fugitives; most of them had wives; and the children far exceeded the adults in number. It is pitiable, knowing as we now know the fate that was in store for them, to read such entries as the following, in a list of the occupants of the boats—'Mr and Mrs Elliott and five children;' 'Mr and Mrs Macklin and eight children;' 'Mr and Mrs Palmer and nine children.'

So few persons survived from Futteghur, that it is not certain at what places and on what days they separated into parties; nor how many lives were lost on the way; but there is evidence that while some pursued their way down the Ganges without much interruption until they reached Bithoor, others went back to Futteghur. This retrograde movement was due to two causes; for while, on the one hand, the officers trusted to a report that the sepoys had returned to a sense of their duty; Herden Buksh, on the other, was threatened by the Oude mutineers if he harboured any of the English. We will follow the fortunes of this second party.' From about the 12th to the 18th of June there was a lull in the station; but on the last-named day the 10th infantry broke out in earnest, and being joined by the mutinous 41st from the other side of the Ganges, seized the treasure and threatened the officers. There were about a hundred Europeans now in the place; and as the river was at the time too low to render a boat-voyage to Cawnpore safe, it was resolved to defend a post or fort at Futteghur, and there remain till succour arrived. Out of the hundred there were scarcely more than thirty fighting-men, so numerous were the women and children; nevertheless, Colonel Smith, of the 10th, organised the whole, and prepared for the worst. He had a fair store both of ammunition and of food within the fort. Until the 4th of July they maintained a manly struggle against the mutineers, holding their fort until they could hold it no longer. Colonel Tucker and one of the civil officers were shot in the head while acting as artillerymen; General Goldie was slightly wounded, as was likewise one of his daughters; and many other casualties occurred. The besieged had great difficulty in making a covered-way to protect their servants, to enable them to pass to and fro with the meals for the ladies and children, who were collected in a room or godown overlooked by a two-storied house held by the insurgents. Then commenced a voyage full of miseries, in boats that contained all the Europeans still remaining at that spot. First the rebels fired on the boats as they rowed along; then one of the boats ran aground; then a boatful of rebels approached, and the ladies in the stranded boat jumped overboard to avoid capture. Death by bullets, death by drowning, took place every hour; and the fugitives were thrown into such dire confusion that none could help the rest. Some crept on shore, and wandered about the fields to escape detection; others found shelter under friendly roofs; one boat-load succeeded in prosecuting their voyage down to Cawnpore, or rather Bithoor.

There were thus two sets of Futteghur fugitives; one that reached the clutches of the Nena towards the middle of June; the other, much smaller, that was spared that fate until the middle of July. So complete was the destruction of both, however; so sweeping the death-stroke hurled against them by Nena Sahib, that the details of their fate have been but imperfectly recorded. Towards the close of June, Mr Court and Colonel Neill, at Allahabad, received information touching the events at Cawnpore from a native named Nerput, an opium *gomashta* or agent at the last-named city; he gave them or sent them a narrative written in Persian, portions of which were afterwards translated and published among the official papers. Nerput was one of the few who wrote concerning the arrival of the first party of Futteghur fugitives at Cawnpore. Under the date of June the 12th he said: 'Report that Europeans were coming in boats to relieve Cawnpore; and two companies sent westward to make inquiries. They found that a hundred and twenty-six men, women, and children, were in boats, sick.' Another narrative of the Futteghur calamity simply states, that when the unhappy fugitives arrived at the part of the Ganges opposite Bithoor, Nena Sahib 'stopped their boats, brought the fugitives on shore, and shot every one. He then tied their bodies together, and threw them into the river.' A native resident at Cawnpore, who was examined a few weeks afterwards by Colonel Neill concerning his knowledge of the atrocities committed by the rajah, and of the sufferings borne by the English, gave an account of the Futteghur catastrophe corresponding nearly with those derived from other quarters. He states that on the 12th of June, just as the customary daily cannonading of the intrenchment was about to recommence, a report came in that Europeans were approaching from the west. Immediately a troop of cavalry and two companies of infantry were sent to reconnoitre (probably to the vicinity of Bithoor). There were found three boats, containing about a hundred and thirty men, women, and children. 'The troopers seized them all and took them to the Nena, who ordered that they should all be killed; and sundry Rampoorie troopers of the Mussulmans of the 2d Cavalry, whom the Nena kept with him for the express purpose, killed them all. Among them was a young lady, the daughter of some general. She addressed herself much to the Nena, and said: "No king ever committed such oppression as you have, and in no religion is there any order to kill women and children. I do not know what has happened to you. Be well assured that by this slaughter the English will not become less; whoever may remain will have an eye upon you." But the Nena paid no attention, and shewed her no mercy; he ordered that she should be killed, and that they should fill her hands with powder and kill her by the explosion.'

The fate of the second party of fugitives from Futteghur will be noticed presently. We must return now to the unfortunate occupants of the intrenchment at Cawnpore.

When three weeks of the month of June had transpired, the rebels, joined by a number of ruffians who had crossed over the Ganges from Oude, made a more determined effort than ever to capture the intrenchment; they had made the subadar-major of the 1st N. I. a sort of general over them; and he swore to vanquish the weakened garrison, or die in the attempt. They brought large bales of cotton, which they rolled along the ground, and approached in a crouching position under cover of these bales, firing their muskets at intervals. About a hundred sepoys thus advanced within a hundred and fifty yards of the intrenchment, backed up by a strong body, who seemed bent on storming the position. In this, as in every former attempt, they failed; their leader was struck down, nearly two hundred were killed or wounded by a fire of grape-shot, and the rest driven back to their former distance. At the very same time, contests were maintained on all sides of the enclosure; for what with musketeers in the unfinished barracks, guns and mortars in four different directions, and rifle-pits approached under cover of zigzags, the rebels maintained a tremendous fire upon the besieged. Wheeler's guns, under a gallant young officer, St George Ashe, were manned at all hours, loaded and fired with great quickness and precision, and pointed in such directions as might produce most mischief among the enemy. But the contest was unequal in this as in most other particulars; one gun after another was disabled by the more powerful artillery of the insurgents—until the eight were reduced to six, then to four, three, and at last two. As the forlorn garrison became weaker and weaker, so did the heroic men redouble their exertions in defence. One day a shot from the enemy blew up an ammunition-wagon within the intrenchment; and then it became a question of terrible import how to prevent the other wagons from being ignited. Lieutenant Delafosse, a young officer of the once trusted but now disloyal 53d, ran forward, laid himself down under the wagons, picked up and threw aside the burning fragments, and covered the flaming portions with handfuls of earth—all the while subject to a fearful cannonading from a battery of six guns, aimed purposely by the enemy at that spot! Two soldiers ran to him, with two buckets of water; and all three succeeded in rescuing the other ammunition-wagons from peril, and in returning from the dangerous spot in safety.

Unspeakable must have been the misery of those nine hundred persons—or rather, nine hundred wofully diminished by deaths—after twenty days of this besieging. The hospitals were so thoroughly riddled with shot, and so much injured by the fire, as to afford little or no shelter; and yet the greater portion of the non-combatants remained in them rather than be exposed to the scorching glare of the sun outside. Some made holes for themselves behind the earthen parapet that bounded the intrenchment; these holes were covered with boxes, cots, &c., and whole families of wretched beings resided in them—more after the fashion of the Bushmen of Africa, than of Christian civilised people. Apoplexy struck down many in these fearfully heated abodes. At night, all the men had to mount guard and keep watch in turn; and the women and children, to be near their male protectors in the hour of trouble, slept near them behind the parapet—or rather they tried to sleep; but the bomb-shells vomited forth from three mortars employed by the enemy, kept the terrified people in an agony that 'murdered sleep;' and thus the existence of the women and children was spent in perpetual fear. The soldiers had their food prepared by the few remaining cooks; but all the rest shifted for themselves in the best way they could; and it was often difficult, for those who received their scanty rations of rice and grain, to provide a mouthful of cooked victuals for themselves and their children. Money would hardly, one would suppose, be thought of at such a time and place; yet it appears that the richer bought with money the services of the poorer, at a rupee or two per meal, for cooking. The innumerable troubles and distresses felt by all were deepened at the sight of the sick and wounded, to whom it was now utterly impossible to render proper assistance. The stench, too, from the dead bodies of horses and other animals that had been shot in the enclosure and could not be removed, added to the loathsomeness of the place. Oppressed as they were with heat, the English nevertheless dreaded the setting in of the rains; for one single day of Indian rain would have converted the earthen abodes of the poor people into pools of water, deluged the shot-riddled buildings, and rendered the muskets useless. Nothing can better denote the extraordinary scene of ruin and devastation which the interior of the intrenchment must have presented, than the descriptions given a few weeks afterwards by English officers concerned in the recovery of Cawnpore. Or rather, it would be more correct to say, that those descriptions, by relating only to the intrenchment when deserted, necessarily fell far short of the reality as presented when many hundreds of suffering persons were residing there day after day. One officer wrote: 'We are encamped close to poor old Wheeler's miserable intrenchment. Of all the wonders which have passed before us since this outbreak commenced, the most wonderful is that this ruinous intrenchment should have held that horde of blood-thirsty ruffians off so long. This is a strong statement; but none who have visited it can call it too strong.' Another said: 'I have had a look at the barracks in which the unfortunate people were intrenched. They consist of a couple of oblong buildings; in one of them, the roof is completely fallen in; and both are battered with round shot. The verandahs as well as the walls have been torn up by the shot; and round the buildings are some pits dug in the ground, and breast-works. The ground inside and out is strewed with broken bottles, old shoes, and quantities of books and other documents and letters. It was a melancholy sight; and the suffering must have been more than humanity could bear.' A third officer corroborated this general description, but mentioned one or two additional particulars: 'These buildings formed what was called the European Cavalry Hospital. Right well and heroically must it have been defended. The walls are riddled with cannon-shot like the cells of a honey-comb. The doors, which seem to have been the principal points against which the Nena's fire was directed, are breached and knocked into large shapeless openings. Of the verandahs, which surrounded both buildings, only a few splintered rafters remain, and at some of the angles the walls are knocked entirely away, and large chasms gape blackly at you. Many of the enemy's cannon-shot have gone through and through the buildings; portions of the interior walls and roof have fallen; and here and there are blood-stains on wall and floor. Never did I yet see a place so terribly battered.'

As a sad story is often most touchingly told in the fewest words, we may here advert to the contents of two scraps of paper, shewing how the members of a family were cut off one by one during these days of misery. When Cawnpore fell again into the hands of the British, by a train of operations hereafter to be described, there were found among other wrecks two small pieces of paper, covered with blood, and containing a few words in pencil; they appeared to have been written by two persons, both females. One gave a brief and confused narrative of some of the events in the intrenchment; while the other consisted simply of a record of the dates on which members of the writer's family were struck down by the hand of death.* The dates were irregular, and extended into July; but every line told, in its simplicity, how agonising must have been the position of one who had to record such things of those who were dear to her. The contents of the two pieces of paper were printed in a Calcutta journal; and when the mournful tale reached Scotland, it was at once concluded, almost as a certainty, from the Christian names mentioned, that the sufferers were all members of a family of Lindsays, who had been stationed at Cawnpore. The writers of the two notes were themselves numbered with the dead before the gloomy tragedy was ended.

All these evidences render only too plain to us the deplorable position of the Europeans, after eighteen days of siege, and thirty-three of enforced residence in the intrenchment. When duly considered, who can wonder that the beleaguered garrison pondered on two possible contingencies—a defeat of the rebels by a daring sally, or a release by parley? If the officers could have known the treachery which was about to be practised on them, they would probably have attempted the former; but they could receive no intelligence or warning, and they did not like to quit their wives and children at such a perilous time, in uncertainty of their chances of success.

Their first knowledge of the state of affairs at Cawnpore was obtained in an unexpected way. Among the commercial firms in the city was that of Greenway Brothers, of which the members and the family had hastily left Cawnpore at the beginning of the troubles, and taken refuge at Nujjubgurh, a village about sixteen miles distant. They were discovered by Nena Sahib, however, and only saved from death by promising a ransom of a lac of rupees. Mrs Greenway, a very aged lady, the mother and grandmother of a number of the sufferers, was sent by this treacherous villain with a message to Sir Hugh Wheeler at the intrenchment, intended to mask a nefarious and bloody scheme. The message was to this effect—that the general and all his people should be allowed to proceed to Allahabad unmolested, on condition that he abandoned Cawnpore, the intrenchment, the public treasure, the guns, and the ammunition. This message was delivered on the 24th of June; but whether in consequence of Mr Shepherd's adventure on that same day, presently to be mentioned, does not clearly appear. On the next day an interview took place, outside the intrenchment, between Sir Hugh and an agent of Nena named Azimoollah (probably the same who had visited London two years before), who was accompanied by a few of the leading mutineers. The terms were agreed to, with a few modifications; and Nena Sahib gave his signature, his seal, and his oath to a contract binding him to provide the Europeans with boats and a safe escort to Allahabad.

Such was the account given by Mr Shepherd of a transaction narrated somewhat differently by other persons; but before noticing certain anomalies in this matter, it will be well to treat of an occurrence in which that gentleman was unquestionably the best judge of the facts. When the 24th of June arrived, Mr Shepherd adopted a course which led to his own preservation, and enabled him to write his brief but mournful narrative. The besieged civilians, not being under the command of Sir Hugh Wheeler further than might be consistent with their own safety, naturally thought with yearning hearts of their former abodes in the city, and compared those abodes with the present deep misery and privation. Wheeler would gladly have allowed them to return to Cawnpore; but could they cross the intervening ground in safety, or would they find safety in the city itself? To ascertain these points, was a project adopted on the suggestion of Mr Shepherd, who—as a commissariat officer in a place where scarcely any commissariat services could be rendered—occupied a position somewhat midway between the military and the civil. He had a large family within the intrenchment, comprising his wife, daughter, brother, sister, three nieces, and two other relatives; an infant daughter had been killed by a musket-shot a few days earlier. Mr Shepherd's mission was—to make his way to the city; to ascertain the state of public affairs there; to enter into negotiations with influential persons who were not friendly to the mutineers; and to spend

* 'Mamma died, July 12.' 'Alice died, July 9.' 'George died, June 27.' 'Entered the barracks, May 21.' 'Cavalry left, June 5.' 'First shot fired, June 6.' 'Uncle Willy died, June 18.' 'Aunt Lilly, June 17.'

or promise a lac of rupees in any way that might bring about a cessation of the siege. The arrangement made with Sir Hugh was, that if Mr Shepherd succeeded in returning to the intrenchment with any useful information, he should be allowed to go with his family to Cawnpore. He started; but he never returned, and never again saw those hapless beings whose welfare had occupied so much of his solicitude. He disguised himself as a native cook, left the intrenchment, passed near the new barracks, and ran on towards Cawnpore; but he was speedily descried and captured, and carried before Nena Sahib. Two native women-servants had shortly before escaped from the intrenchment to the city, and had reported that the garrison was starving; the new captive, designedly, gave a very different account; and as the Nena did not know which to believe, he imprisoned all three. Mr Shepherd remained in prison, suffering great hardships, from the 24th of June to the 17th of July, as we shall presently see.

It is not easy to reconcile the various accounts of the convention between the besiegers and the besieged, the Nena and the general. According to Mr Shepherd, as we have just seen, the Nena sent a message by Mrs Greenway on the 24th; and Sir Hugh had an interview with one of Nena's agents on the 25th. An ayah, or native nurse, however, who had been in the service of Mrs Greenway, and who afterwards gave a narrative in evidence before some English officers at Cawnpore, said that the message was taken, not by Mrs Greenway, but by a Mrs Jacobi. She proceeded to aver that Nena Sahib himself went to the intrenchment; and then she gave a curious account of the interview, which, to say the least of it, is quite consistent with the relative characters and positions of the two leaders. According to her narrative: 'The Nena said: "Take away all the women and children to Allahabad; and if your men want to fight, come back and do so: we will keep faith with you." General Wheeler said: "You take your solemn oath, according to your custom; and I will take an oath on my Bible, and will leave the intrenchment." The Nena said: "Our oath is, that whoever we take by the hand, and he relies on us, we never deceive; if we do, God will judge and punish us." The general said: "If you intend to deceive me, kill me at once: I have no arms." The Nena replied: "I will not deceive you; rely on us. I will supply you with food, and convey you to Allahabad." On this the general went inside the intrenchment, and consulted with the soldiers. They said: "There's no reliance to be placed on natives; they will deceive you." A few said: "Trust them; it is better to do so." On this the general returned, and said: "I agree to your terms; see us away as far as Futtehpoor, thence we can get easily to Allahabad." The reply was: "No; I will see you all safe to Allahabad."'

That Sir Hugh Wheeler was mortally wounded before his unfortunate companions left the intrenchment under a solemn pledge of safety, seems to be generally admitted, but the date of his death is not clearly known; nor do the narrators agree as to the names of the persons by whom the convention was signed. But on the main point all evidence coincides—that a safe retirement to Allahabad was guaranteed. How villainously that guarantee was disregarded, we shall now see.

It was on the 27th of June that those who remained of the nine hundred took their departure from the intrenchment where they had borne so many miseries. Collateral facts lead to a conjecture that the sepoys, belonging to the native regiments that had mutinied, had become wearied with their three-weeks' detention outside the intrenchment, and wished to start off to a scene of more stirring incidents at Delhi. This would not have suited the Nena's views; he wanted their aid to grasp the remainder of the Company's treasure and ammunition at Cawnpore; and hence he formed the plan for getting rid of the Europeans and obtaining their wealth without any more fighting. Cannonading ceased on both sides from the evening of the 24th; and from thence to the 27th all was done that could be done to fit out the boat-expedition. But under what miserable circumstances was this done! The unburied bodies of relations and friends lay at the bottom of a well; the sick and wounded were more fit to die than to be removed; the women and children had become haggard and weak by almost every kind of suffering; the clothes of all had become rent and blood-stained by many a terrible exigency; and misgivings occupied the thoughts of those who remembered that the same Nena Sahib, at whose mercy they were now placed, was the man who had proved a traitor three weeks before. Twenty boats were provided, each with an awning. The English were forced to give up the three or four lacs of rupees which had been brought to the intrenchment. Early on the morning of the 27th, the Nena sent a number of elephants, carts, and doolies, to convey the women, children, sick, and wounded, to the river-side, a distance of about a mile and a half: the hale men proceeding on foot—if hale they can be called, who were worn down with hunger, thirst, fatigue, heat, grief for the dear ones who had fallen, anxiety for those who still lived to be succoured and protected. If Mr Shepherd is right in his statement that the number who took their departure in this mournful procession from the intrenchment was four hundred and fifty, then one half of the original number of nine hundred must have fallen victims to three weeks of privation and suffering. Those who first reached the river took boat, and proceeded down-stream; but the later comers were long detained; and while they were still embarking, or preparing to embark, they were startled by the report of a masked battery of three guns.

The dreadful truth now became evident; the execrable rebel-chief, in disregard of all oaths and treaties, had given orders for the slaughter of the hapless Europeans. Some of the boats were set on fire, and volley upon volley of musketry fired at the unfortunates—scores of whom were shot dead, others picked off while endeavouring to swim away. A few boats were hastily rowed across the river; but there a body of the 17th N. I., just arrived from Azimghur, intercepted all escape. The ruffians on both banks waded into the water, seized the boats within reach, and sabred all the men yet remaining alive in them. The women were spared for a worse fate; though many of them wounded, some with two or three bullets each, these poor creatures, with the children, were taken ashore, and placed in a building called the Subadar Kothee, in Nena Sahib's camp.

The fortunes of two separate boat-parties must be traced. Lieutenant Delafosse, whose name has already been mentioned in connection with a gallant achievement in the intrenchment, has placed upon record the story of one boat's adventure, shewing how it happened that he was among the very few who escaped the Cawnpore tragedy. After stating that nearly all the boats which attempted to descend the Ganges were either stopped one by one, or the persons in them shot down where they sat, he proceeds thus: 'We had now one boat, crowded with wounded, and having on board more than she could carry. Two guns followed us the whole of that day, the infantry firing on us the whole of that night. On the second day, 28th June, a gun was seen on the Cawnpore side, which opened on us at Nujjubgurh, the infantry still following us on both sides. On the morning of the third day, the boat was no longer serviceable; we were aground on a sandbank, and had not strength sufficient to move her. Directly any of us got into the water, we were fired upon by thirty or forty men at a time. There was nothing left for us but to charge and drive them away; and fourteen of us were told off to do what we could. Directly we got on shore the insurgents retired; but, having followed them up too far, we were cut off from the river, and had to retire ourselves, as we were being surrounded. We could not make for the river; we had to go down parallel, and came to the river again a mile lower down, where we saw a large force of men right in front waiting for us, and another lot on the opposite bank, should we attempt to cross the river. On the bank of the river, just by the force in front, was a temple. We fired a volley, and made for the temple, in which we took shelter, having one man killed and one wounded. From the door of the temple we fired on every insurgent that happened to shew himself. Finding that they could do nothing against us whilst we remained inside, they heaped wood all round and set it on fire. When we could no longer remain inside on account of the smoke and heat, we threw off what clothes we had, and, each taking a musket, charged through the fire. Seven of us out of the twelve got into the water; but before we had gone far, two poor fellows were shot. There were only five of us left now; and we had to swim whilst the insurgents followed us along both banks, wading and firing as fast as they could. After we had gone three miles down the stream [probably swimming and wading by turns], one of our party, an artilleryman, to rest himself, began swimming on his back, and not knowing in what direction he was swimming, got on shore, and was killed. When we had got down about six miles, firing from both sides [of the river] ceased; and soon after we were hailed by some natives, on the Oude side, who asked us to come on shore, and said they would take us to their rajah, who was friendly to the English.' This proved to be the case; for Lieutenant Delafosse, Lieutenant Mowbray Thomson, and one or two companions, remained in security and comparative comfort throughout the month of July, until an opportunity occurred for joining an English force.

Although the boat-adventure just narrated was full of painful excitement, ending in the death of nearly all the persons by shooting or drowning—yet there is one still to be noticed more saddening in its character, for the sufferers were reserved for a worse death. The name of Sir Hugh Wheeler is connected with this adventure in a way not easily to be accounted for; Mr Shepherd and Lieutenant Delafosse were not witnesses of it, and no reliable personal narrative is obtainable from any one who was actually present when it occurred. The probability is, that Sir Hugh, although wounded in the intrenchment, did not die until the boat-expedition had commenced, and that the same boat contained his daughter and his (living or dead) body. At anyrate, this was the last the world could hear of a brave old soldier, who went to India fifty-four years before; who fought with Lord Lake before Delhi in 1804; who took an active part in the Punjaub war; and who had been military commander of the Cawnpore district from 1850 to 1857. It was also the last to be heard of Brigadier Jack, who commanded the Cawnpore cantonment; and of many brave English officers, from colonels down to ensigns, of both the English and the native regiments.

Whether the general was alive or dead, and by whomsoever accompanied, it appears certain that a large party rowed many miles down the Ganges. One account states that Baboo Rambaksh, a zemindar of Dowreea Kheyra near Futtehpoor, stopped the boats, captured the persons who were in them, and sent them in carts as prisoners back to Cawnpore. The names of Mr Reid, Mr Thomas Greenway, Mr Kirkpatrick, Mr Mackenzie, Captain Mackenzie, and Dr Harris, were mentioned in connection with this band of unfortunates; but accuracy in this particular is not to be insured. The narrative given by Nujoor Jewarree, the native afterwards examined by English officers at Cawnpore, was different in many points, and much more detailed. He stated that the boat in question, after proceeding some distance, got upon a sand-bank, where there was a severe encounter; the sepoys not only ran along the shore, but followed in boats shooting at the victims as soon as they got within musket-range, and receiving many fatal shots in return. A freshet in the river released the boat, and the voyage recommenced. Meanwhile, the probable escape of this party being reported to Nena Sahib, he ordered three companies of the 3d Oude infantry to pursue the boat, and effect a complete capture. The boat was soon after taken, and all the occupants seized as prisoners. 'There came out of that boat,' said Nujoor Jewarree, 'sixty sahibs (gentlemen), twenty-five memsahibs (ladies), and four children—one boy and three half-grown girls.' His story then proceeded to details which, if correct, shew that Sir Hugh Wheeler was in the boat, and still alive; for a contest ensued between Nena and some of the soldiers whether or not the old general should be put to death: many of the sepoys wishing to preserve his life.

It will become apparent to the reader, from the nature of the above details, that the true story of the boat-catastrophe at Cawnpore will probably never be fully told. All that we positively know is, that one portion of the wretched victims met their death in the river, by muskets, swords, and drowning; and that two other portions were carried back to a captivity worse even than that of the intrenchment.

The proceedings of Nena Sahib, after the iniquitous treachery of the 27th of June, bore evident relation to his own advancement as an independent chieftain. At sunset on that day he held a review of all the rebel troops around Cawnpore on a plain between the now deserted intrenchment and the Ganges. They appear to have consisted of five regiments of Bengal native infantry, two of Oude native infantry, one of Bengal cavalry, two of Oude cavalry, two of irregular cavalry, a battery of field-guns, besides sundry detachments of regiments, and marauders who became temporary soldiers in the hope of sharing pillage. Guns were fired in honour of the Nena as sovereign, of his brother as governor-general, and of an ambitious Brahmin as commander-in-chief, of the newly restored Mahratta kingdom. From day to day more troops joined his standard, after mutinying at various stations on all sides of Cawnpore. Twenty thousand armed men are said to have been in that city by the 10th of July; and as the Nena was very slow in awarding to them any of his ill-gotten wealth, they recompensed themselves by plundering the inhabitants, under pretext of searching for concealed Europeans. Cawnpore was thus plunged into great misery, and speedily had cause to lament the absence of its former masters. Nena created new offices, for bestowal upon those who had served him; and he ordered the neighbouring zemindars to pay to him the revenue that had wont to be paid to the Company. He caused to be proclaimed by beat of tom-tom, throughout Cawnpore and the surrounding district, that he had entirely conquered the British; and that, their period of reign in India having been completed, he was preparing to drive them out foot by foot. During this heyday of self-assumed power, he issued many remarkable proclamations, worthy of note as indications of his ambitious views, of his hopes as dependent on the mass of the native people, and of the stigma which he sought to throw on the British government. Some of these proclamations are given in full at the end of the present chapter. There are many facts which lend support to the supposition that this grasp at power and wealth was suggested to him by the gradual development of events. He probably entertained crafty designs and suppressed vindictiveness from the outset; but these did not shew themselves openly until the native troops at the cantonment had rebelled. Seeing a door opened by others, which might possibly lead him to power and to vengeance, he seized the occasion and entered.

The last acts of the Cawnpore tragedy now await our attention.

What horrors the poor women suffered during their eighteen days of captivity under this detestable miscreant, none will ever fully know; partial glimpses only of the truth will ever come to light. According to the ayah's narrative, already noticed, the women and children who were conveyed from the boats into captivity were a hundred and fifteen in number. The poor creatures (the women and elder girls) were sought to be tempted by an emissary of the Nena to enter quietly into his harem; but they one and all expressed a determination to die where they were, and with each other, rather than yield to dishonour. They were then destined to be given up to the sensual licence of the sepoys and sowars who had aided in their capture; but the heroic conduct of Sir Hugh Wheeler's daughter is said to have deterred the ruffians. What this 'Judith of Cawnpore' really did, is differently reported. Her heroism was manifested, in one version of the story, by an undaunted and indignant reproach against the native troops for their treachery to the English who had fed and clothed them, and for their cowardice in molesting defenceless women; in another version, she shot down five sepoys in succession with a revolver, and then threw herself into a well to escape outrage; in a third, given by Mr Shepherd, this English lady, being taken away by a trooper of the 2d native cavalry to his own hut, rose in the night, secured the trooper's sword, killed him and three other men, and then threw herself into a well; while a fourth version, on the authority of the ayah, represents the general's daughter as cutting off the heads of no less than five men in the trooper's hut. These accounts, incompatible one with another, nevertheless reveal to us a true soldier's daughter, an English gentlewoman, resolved to proceed to any extremity in defence of her own purity.

The victims were detained three days at Nena's camp, with only a little parched grain to eat, dirty water to drink, and the hard ground to lie upon, without matting or beds of any kind. The ayah states that the Nena, after the events of the 27th of June, sent to ask the temporarily successful King of Delhi what he should do with the women and children; to which a reply was received, that they were not to be killed. Whether this statement be right or wrong, the captives were taken from the camp to Cawnpore, and there incarcerated in a house near the Assembly Rooms, consisting of outbuildings of the medical depôt, shortly before occupied by Sir George Parker. Here they were joined by more than thirty other European women and children, the unhappy relics of the boat-expedition that had been recaptured near Futtehpoor in the vain attempt to escape. Without venturing to decide whether the ayah, Nujoor Jewarree, Mr Shepherd, or Lieutenant Delafosse was most nearly correct in regard of numbers; or whether Sir Hugh Wheeler was at that time alive or dead—it appears tolerably certain that many unhappy prisoners were brought back into Cawnpore on the 1st of July. All the men were butchered in cold blood on the evening of the same day. One officer's wife, with her child, clung to her husband with such desperate tenacity that they could not be separated; and all three were killed at once. The other women were spared for the time. This new influx, together with five members of the Greenway family, swelled the roll of prisoners in the small building to a number that has been variously estimated from a hundred and fifty to two hundred, nearly all women and children. Their diet was miserably insufficient; and their sufferings were such that many died through want of the necessaries of life. 'It is not easy to describe,' says Mr Shepherd, 'but it may be imagined, the misery of so many helpless persons: some wounded, others sick, and all labouring under the greatest agony of heart for the loss of those, so dear to them, who had so recently been killed (perhaps before their own eyes); cooped up night and day in a small low pukha-roofed house, in the hottest season of the year, without beds or punkahs, for a whole fortnight—and constantly reviled and insulted by a set of brutish ruffians keeping watch over them.'

Added to all these suffering women and children, were those belonging to the second boat-expedition from Futteghur. It will be remembered, from the details given in a former page, that one party from this fort reached Bithoor about the middle of June, and were at once murdered by orders of Nena Sahib; while another body, after a manly struggle against the rebels for two or three weeks, did not prosecute their voyage downwards until July. It will throw light on the perils and terrors of these several boat-adventures to transcribe a few sentences from an official account by Mr G. J. Jones, a civil servant of the Company, who left Futteghur with the rest on the 4th of July, but happily kept clear of the particular boat-load which went down to Cawnpore. 'We had not proceeded far, when it was found that Colonel Goldie's boat was much too large and heavy for us to manage; it was accordingly determined to be abandoned; so all the ladies and children were taken into Colonel Smith's boat. A little delay was thus caused, which the sepoys took advantage of to bring a gun to bear on the boats; the distance, however, was too great; every ball fell short. As soon as the ladies and children were all safely on board, we started, and got down as far as Singheerampore without accident, although fired upon by the villagers. Here we stopped a few minutes to repair the rudder of Colonel Smith's boat; and one out of the two boatmen we had was killed by a matchlock ball. The rudder repaired, we started again, Colonel Smith's boat taking the lead; we had not gone beyond a few yards, when our boat grounded on a soft muddy sand-bank; the other boat passed on; all hands got into the water to push her; but, notwithstanding all our efforts, we could not manage to move her. We had not been in this unhappy position half an hour, when two boats, apparently empty, were seen coming down the stream. They came within twenty yards of us, when we discovered they carried sepoys, who opened a heavy fire, killing and wounding several. Mr Churcher, senior, was shot through the chest; Mr Fisher, who was just behind me, was wounded in the thigh. Hearing him call out, I had scarcely time to turn round, when I felt a smart blow on my right shoulder; a bullet had grazed the skin and taken off a little of the flesh. Major Robertson was wounded in the face. The boats were now alongside of us. Some of the sepoys had already got into our boat. Major Robertson, seeing no hope, begged the ladies to come into the water rather than fall into their hands. While the ladies were throwing themselves into the water, I jumped into the boat, took up a loaded musket, and, going astern, shot a sepoy. . . . Mr and Mrs Fisher were about twenty yards from the boat; he had his child in his arms, apparently lifeless. Mrs Fisher could not stand against the current; her dress, which acted like a sail, knocked her down, when she was helped up by Mr Fisher. . . . Early the next morning a voice hailed us from the shore, which we recognised as Mr Fisher's. He came on board, and informed us that his poor wife and child had been drowned in his arms.'

The occupants of the boat that prosecuted the voyage down to Cawnpore, or rather Bithoor, suffered greatly: the hands of the gentlemen who were on board, and who pulled the boat, were terribly blistered; the women and children suffered sad hardships; and all were worn down by fatigue and anxiety. At Bithoor, so far as the accounts are intelligible, Nena Sahib's son seized the boat, and sent all the unfortunate Europeans in her into confinement at Cawnpore. As in other parts of this mournful tragedy, it will be vain to attempt accuracy in the statement of the numbers of those that suffered; but there is a subsidiary source of information, possessing a good deal of interest in connection with the July occurrences. When, at a later date, the reconquerors of Cawnpore were in a position to attempt a solution of the terrible mystery; when the buildings of Cawnpore were searched, and the inhabitants examined, for any documents relating to the suffering Europeans—a paper was found, written in the Mahratta language, in the house of a native doctor who had been in charge of the prisoners, or some of them. It was, or professed to be, a list of those who were placed under his care on Tuesday the 7th of July; but whether invalids only, does not clearly appear. All the names were given, with some inaccuracy in spelling; which, however, cannot be considered as rendering the document untrustworthy. In it were to be found large families of Greenways, Reids, Jacobis, Fitzgeralds, Dempsters, and others known to have been in Cawnpore about that time. They were a hundred and sixty-three in number. To this hapless group was added another list, containing

House at Cawnpore in which the women and children were massacred.

the names of forty-seven fugitives belonging to the *second* boat-party from Futteghur, who are reported as having arrived on the 11th of July, and who included many members of the families of the Goldies, Smiths, Tuckers, Heathcotes, &c., already named in connection with the Futteghur calamities. The Mahratta document gave altogether the names of two hundred and ten persons; but it was silent on the question how many other Europeans were on those days in the clutches of the ruthless chieftain of Bithoor. A further list contained the names of about twenty-six persons, apparently all women and children, who died under this native doctor's hands between the 7th and the 15th, diminishing to that extent the number of those left for massacre. To most of the names 'cholera,' or 'diarrhœa,' or 'dysentery' was appended, as the cause of death; to two names, 'wounds;' while one of the patients was 'a baby two days old.' In what a place, and under what circumstances, for an infant to be born, and to bear its two wretched days of life!

Let us follow Mr Shepherd's two narratives—one public, for government information; one in a letter, relating more especially to his own personal troubles and sufferings—concerning the crowning iniquity of Nena Sahib at Cawnpore.

After his capture, on attempting to hasten from the intrenchment to the city, the commissary was subjected to a sort of mock-trial, and condemned to three years' imprisonment with hard labour; on what plea or evidence, is not stated. He implies that if he had been known as an Englishman, he would certainly have been put to death. On the third day after his capture he heard a rumour of certain movements among his unfortunate compatriots in the intrenchment. 'Oh! how I felt,' he exclaims, 'when, in confinement, I heard that the English were going in safety! I could not keep my secret, but told the subadar of the prison-guard that I was a Christian;

I nearly lost my life by this exposure.' Mr Shepherd was confined for twenty-four days in a miserable prison, with heavy fetters on his legs, and only so much parched grain for food as would prevent actual starvation. As days wore on, he obtained dismal evidence that the departure from the intrenchment had not been safely effected; that coward treachery had been displayed by the Nena; that innocent lives had been taken; and that the survivors were held in horrible thraldom by that cruel man. The commissary was a prisoner within the city during all the later days of the tragedy; whether he was within earshot of the sufferers, is not stated; but the following contains portions of his narrative relating to that period: 'Certain spies, whether real or imaginary is not known, were brought to the Nena as being the bearers of letters supposed to have been written to the British [at Allahabad] by the helpless females in their captivity; and with these letters some of the inhabitants of the city were believed to be implicated. It was therefore decreed by Nena Sahib that the spies, together with all the women and children, as also the few gentlemen whose lives had been spared, should be put to death.' Mr Shepherd connected these gentlemen with the Futteghur fugitives, concerning whom, however, he possessed very little information. It was a further portion of Nena's decree, that all the baboos (Bengalees employed as clerks) of the city, and every individual who could read or write English, should have their right hands and noses cut off. At length, on the 15th, just before quitting Cawnpore in the vain hope of checking the advance of a British column, this savage put his decrees into execution. 'The native spies were first put to the sword; after them the gentlemen, who were brought from the outbuildings in which they had been confined, and shot with bullets. Then the poor females were ordered to come out; but neither threats nor persuasions could induce them to do so. They laid hold of each other by dozens, and clung so closely that it was impossible to separate or drag them out of the building. The troopers therefore brought muskets, and after firing a great many shots through the doors, windows, &c., rushed in with swords and bayonets. Some of the helpless creatures in their agony fell down at the feet of their murderers, and begged them in the most pitiful manner to spare their lives; but to no purpose. The fearful deed was done deliberately and determinedly, in the midst of the most dreadful shrieks and cries of the victims. From a little before sunset till dark was occupied in completing the dreadful deed. The doors of the buildings were then locked for the night, and the murderers went to their homes. Next morning it was found, on opening the doors, that some ten or fifteen females, with a few of the children, had managed to escape from death by hiding under the murdered bodies of their fellow-prisoners. A fresh command was thereupon sent to murder these also; but the survivors not being able to bear the idea of being cut down, rushed out into the compound, and seeing a well there, threw themselves into it. The dead bodies of those murdered on the previous evening were then ordered to be thrown into the same well; and julluds were appointed to drag them away like dogs.'

Mr Shepherd himself did not witness this slaughter; no looker-on, so far as is known, has placed upon record his or her account of the scene. Nor does there appear any trustworthy evidence to shew what the poor women endured in the period, varying from four to eighteen days, during which they were in the Nena's power; but the probability is fearfully great that they passed through an ordeal which the mind almost shrinks from contemplating. Mr Shepherd was evidently of this opinion. While telling his tale of misery relating to those poor ill-used creatures, he hinted at 'sufferings and distresses such as have never before been experienced or heard of on the face of the earth.' It was in his agony of grief that he wrote this; when, on the 17th of July, a victorious English column entered Cawnpore; and when, immediately on his liberation, he hastened like others to the house of slaughter. Only when the manacles had been struck from his limbs, and he had become once more a free man, did he learn the full bitterness of his lot. 'God Almighty has been graciously pleased to spare my poor life,' was the beginning of a letter written by him on that day to a brother stationed at Agra. 'I am the only individual saved among all the European and Christian community that inhabited this station.' [Nearly but not exactly true.] 'My poor dear wife, my darling sweet child Polly, poor dear Rebecca and her children, and poor innocent children Emmeline and Martha, as also Mrs Frost and poor Mrs Osborne' [these being the members of his family whom he had left in the intrenchment on the 24th of June, when he set out disguised on his fruitless mission], 'were all most inhumanly butchered by the cruel insurgents on the day before yesterday;' and his letter then conveyed the outpourings of a heart almost riven by such irreparable losses.

While reserving for a future chapter all notice of the brilliant military movements by which a small band of heroes forced a way inch by inch from Allahabad to Cawnpore; and of the struggle made by the Nena, passionately but ineffectually, to maintain his ill-gotten honours as a self-elected Mahratta sovereign—it may nevertheless be well in this place to follow the story of the massacre to its close—to know how much was left, and of what kind, calculated to render still more vividly evident the fate of the victims.

Never, while life endures, will the English officers and soldiers forget the sight which met their gaze when they entered Cawnpore on the 17th of July. It was frequently observed that all were alike deeply moved by the atrocities that came to light in many parts of Northern India. Calcutta, weeks and even months afterwards, contained ladies who had escaped from various towns and stations, and who entered the Anglo-Indian capital in most deplorable condition: ears, noses, lips, tongues, hands, cut off; while others had suffered such monstrous and incredibly degrading barbarities, that they resolutely refused all identification, preferring to remain in nameless obscurity, rather than their humiliation should be known to their friends in England. Their children, in many instances, had their eyes gouged out, and their feet cut off. Many were taken to Calcutta in such hurry and confusion, that it remained long in doubt from what places they had escaped; and an instance is recorded of a little child, who belonged no one knew to whom, and whose only account of herself was that she was 'Mamma's pet:' mournfully touching words, telling of a gentle rearing and a once happy home. An officer in command of one of the English regiments, speaking of the effect produced on his men by the sights and rumours of fiend-like cruelty, observed: 'Very little is said among the men or officers, the subject being too maddening; but there is a curious expression discernible in every face when it is mentioned—a stern compression of the lips, and a fierce glance of the eye, which shew that when the time comes, no mercy will be shewn to those who have shewn none.' He told of fearful deeds; of two little children tortured to death, and portions of their quivering flesh forced down the throats of their parents, who were tied up naked, and had been compelled to witness the slaughter of their innocent ones. The feelings of those who were not actually present at the scenes of horror are well expressed in a letter written by a Scottish officer, who was hemmed in at Agra during many weeks, when he longed to be engaged in active service chastising the rebels. He had, some months before, been an officer in one of the native regiments that mutinied at Cawnpore; and, in relation to the events at that place, he said: 'I am truly thankful that most of the officers of my late corps died of fever in the intrenchment, previous to the awful massacre. Would that it had been the will of Heaven that all had met the same fate, fearful as that was. For weeks exposed to a scorching sun, without shelter of any kind, and surrounded by the dying and the dead, their ears ringing with the groans of the wounded, the shouts of sun-struck madmen, the plaintive cries of children, the bitter sobs and sighs of bereaved mothers, widows, and orphans. Even such a death was far better than what fell to the lot of many. Not even allowed to die without being made witnesses of the bloody deaths of all they loved on earth, they were insulted, abused, and finally, after weeks of such treatment, cruelly and foully murdered. One sickens, and shudders at the bare mention of it. . . . . Oh! how thankful I am that I have no wife, no sisters out here.' It was a terrible crisis that could lead officers, eight or ten thousand miles away from those near and dear to them, to say this.

It is necessary, as a matter of historical truth, to describe briefly the condition of the house of slaughter on the 17th of July; and this cannot be better done than in the words employed by the officers and soldiers in various letters written by them, afterwards made public. The first that we shall select runs thus: 'I have seen the fearful slaughter-house; and I also saw one of the 1st native infantry men, according to order, wash up part of the blood which stains the floor, before being hanged.' [This order will presently be noticed in the words of Brigadier Neill.] 'There were quantities of dresses, clogged thickly with blood; children's frocks, frills, and ladies' underclothing of all kinds; boys' trousers; leaves of Bibles, and of one book in particular, which seems to be strewed over the whole place, called *Preparation for Death;* broken daguerreotypes; hair, some nearly a yard long; bonnets, all bloody; and one or two shoes. I picked up a bit of paper with the words on it, "Ned's hair, with love;" and opened and found a little bit tied up with ribbon. The first [troops] that went in, I believe, saw the bodies with their arms and legs sticking out through the ground. They had all been thrown in a heap in the well.' A second letter: 'The house was alongside the Cawnpore hotel, where the Nena lived. I never was more horrified. I am not exaggerating when I tell you that the soles of my boots were more than covered with the blood of these poor wretched creatures. Portions of their dresses, collars, children's socks, and ladies' round hats, lay about, saturated with their blood; and in the sword-cuts on the wooden pillars of the room, long dark hair was sticking, carried by the edge of the weapon, and there hung their tresses—a most painful sight. I picked up a mutilated Prayer-book; it appeared to have been open at page 30 of the Litany, where I have little doubt those poor creatures sought and found consolation in that beautiful supplication; it is there sprinkled with blood.' A third: 'We found that the Nena had murdered all the women and children that he had taken prisoners, and thrown them naked down a well. The women and children had been kept in a sort of zenana, and no attention whatever paid to cleanliness. In that place they had been butchered, as the ground was covered with clotted blood. One poor woman had evidently been working, as a small work-box was open, and the things scattered about. There were several children's small round hats, evidently shewing that that was their prison. The well close by was one of the most awful sights imaginable.' A fourth: 'It is an actual and literal fact, that the floor of the inner room was several inches deep in blood all over; it came over men's shoes as they stepped. Tresses of women's hair, children's shoes, and articles of female wear, broad hats and bonnets, books, and such like things, lay scattered all about the rooms. There were the marks of bullets and sword-cuts on the walls—not high up, as if men had fought—but low down, and about the corners where the poor crouching creatures had been cut to pieces. The bodies of the victims had been thrown indiscriminately into a well—a mangled heap, with arms and legs protruding.' Some of the officers, by carefully examining the walls, found scraps of writing in pencil, or scratched in the plaster, such as, 'Think of us'—'Avenge us'—'Your wives and families are here in misery and at the disposal of savages'—'Oh, oh! my child, my child.' One letter told of a row of women's shoes, *with bleeding amputated feet in them*, ranged in cruel mockery on one side of a room; while the other side exhibited a row of children's shoes, filled in a similarly terrible way; but it is not certain whether the place referred to was Cawnpore. Another writer mentioned an incident which, unless supported by collateral testimony, seems wanting in probability. It was to the effect that when the 78th Highlanders entered Cawnpore, they found the remains of Sir Hugh Wheeler's daughter. They removed the hair carefully from the head; sent some of it to the relations of the unfortunate lady; divided the rest amongst themselves; counted every single hair in each parcel; and swore to take a terrible revenge by putting to death as many mutineers as there were hairs. The storm of indignant feeling that might suggest such a vow can be understood easily enough; but the alleged mode of manifestation savours somewhat of the melodramatic and improbable.

A slight allusion has been made above to Brigadier Neill's proceedings at Cawnpore, after the fatal 17th of July. In what relation he stood to the reconquering force will be noticed in its due place; but it may be well here to quote a passage from a private letter, written independently of his public dispatches: 'I am collecting all the property of the deceased, and trying to trace if any have survived; but as yet have not succeeded in finding one.' [Captain Bruce's research, presently to be mentioned, had not then been made.] 'Man, woman, and child, seem all to have been murdered. As soon as that monster Nena Sahib heard of the success of our troops, and of their having forced the bridge about twenty miles from Cawnpore, he ordered the wholesale butchery of the poor women and children. I find the officers' servants behaved shamefully, and were in the plot, all but the lowest-caste ones. They deserted their masters and plundered them. Whenever a rebel is caught, he is immediately tried, and unless he can prove a defence, he is sentenced to be hanged at once; but the chief rebels or ringleaders I make first clean up a certain portion of the pool of blood, still two inches deep, in the shed where the fearful murder and mutilation of women and children took place. To touch blood is most abhorrent to the high-caste natives; they think by doing so they doom their souls to perdition. Let them think so. My object is to inflict a fearful punishment for a revolting, cowardly, barbarous deed, and to strike terror into these rebels. . . . The well of mutilated bodies—alas! containing upwards of two hundred women and children—I have had decently covered in and built up as one grave.'

With one additional testimony, we will close this scene of gloomy horror. The Earl of Shaftesbury, as was noticed in a former page, took occasion soon after the news of the Cawnpore atrocities reached London, to advert at a public meeting to the shrinking abhorrence with which those deeds were regarded, and to the failure of the journalists to present the full and fearful truth. He himself mentioned an incident, not as an example of the worst that had been done by the incarnate fiends at Cawnpore, but to indicate how much remains to be told if pen dare write or tongue utter it: 'I have seen a copy of a letter written and sent to England by an officer of rank who was one of the first that entered Cawnpore a few hours after the perpetration of the frightful massacre. . . . To his unutterable dismay, he saw a number of European women stripped stark naked, lying on their backs, fastened by the arms and legs; and there many of them had been lying four or five days exposed to a burning sun; others had been more recently laid down; others again had been actually hacked to pieces, and so recently, that the blood which streamed from their mangled bodies was still warm. He found children of ten, twelve, thirteen, and fourteen years of age treated in the same horrible manner at the corners of the streets and in all parts of the town: attended by every circumstance of insult, the most awful and the most degrading, the most horrible and frightful to the conception, and the most revolting to the dignity and feelings of civilised men. Cawnpore was only a sample of what was perpetrated in various parts of that vast region, and that with a refinement of cruelty never before heard of. Women and children have been massacred before; but I don't believe there is any instance on record where children have been reserved in cold blood to be most cruelly and anatomically tortured in the presence of their horrified parents before being finally put to death.'

Something must be said here concerning the devastated property at Cawnpore, in relation to the miserable beings to whom it had once belonged. When the city was again in British hands, and the Rajah of Bithoor driven out with the curses of all English hearts resting on him, it was found to be in such a devastated state, so far as regarded Europeans, that Brigadier Neill was at a loss what to do with the wrecks of spoliated property. He requested Captain Bruce, of the 5th Punjaub cavalry, whom he had appointed temporarily superintendent of police, to write to the Calcutta newspapers, inviting the aid of any one able to identify the property. The letter said: 'The property of the unfortunate people who lost their lives here has been collected in one spot; and any which can be recognised will be handed over to the owners, or put up to auction for the benefit of the estates of the deceased. There is a good deal of property belonging to the different mercantile firms here, as well as to the heirs of deceased officers, &c.; but when I mention that every house was gutted, and the property scattered over sixty or seventy square miles of country, it will be apparent how impossible it was to take care of individual interests. . . . . Almost all the former European residents here having been murdered by the miscreant Nena Sahib, there is no one forthcoming to recognise or give any information concerning the property that has been saved.' At a later date Captain Bruce captured one of the boatmen who had come down from Futteghur with the first party of unhappy fugitives from that place; the man had a large amount of English jewellery in his possession, comprising brooches, earrings, bracelets, clasps, studs, shawl-pins, hair-lockets, gold chains, and similar articles. The boatman had probably secreted the jewel-caskets of the unfortunate ladies, at or shortly before the forcible landing of the boat-party at Bithoor.

A much more painful inquiry, than any relating to property, was that relating to the loss of life. When Captain Bruce, after many days of sedulous inquiry, had collected all the available information bearing on the fate of the hapless sufferers, he arrived at these conclusions—that the only Europeans who escaped from the boat-massacre, and really obtained their liberty, were two officers and two soldiers—probably Lieutenant Delafosse and three of his companions; that the only one who remained in Cawnpore and yet preserved his life, was a pensioner of the 3d light dragoons, who was concealed in the city by a trooper of the 4th light cavalry; and that there were, on the 31st of July, six Englishmen, three Englishwomen, and three children, concealed and protected by the Rajah of Calpee, across the Jumna; but it was not stated, and perhaps not known, whether they had gone thither from Cawnpore. Mr Shepherd himself was not included in this list. When Lieutenant Delafosse, about a fortnight after the recapture of Cawnpore, was requested by Brigadier Neill to furnish the best list he could of the English sufferers at that place, he endeavoured to separate the victims into three groups, according as they had died in the intrenchment, in the boats, or in the house of slaughter. But this was necessarily a very imperfect list; for, on the one hand, he knew nothing of the two parties of fugitives from Futteghur; while, on the other, he speaks of many persons who came into the station with their families on account of disturbance, and whose names he did not know. Taking the matter in a military estimate, however, he gave the names of one general (Wheeler), one brigadier (Jack), three colonels, five majors, thirteen captains, thirty-nine lieutenants, five ensigns, and nine doctors or army-surgeons; Lady and Miss Wheeler, Sir George Parker, and two clergymen or missionaries, were among the other members in his melancholy list. No guess can be made of the total numbers from this document, for the persons included under the word 'family' are seldom specified by name or number. The mournful truth was indeed only too evident that many complete families—families consisting of very numerous members—were among the slaughtered. When the lists began to be made out, of those who had been known as Cawnpore residents or Futteghur fugitives, and who were found dead when the English recaptured the place, there were such entries as these—'Greenway: Mr, two Mrs, Martha, Jane, John, Henry'—'Fitzgerald: John, Margaret, Mary, Tom, Ellen'—'Gilpin: Mrs, William, Harriet, Sarah, Jane, F.'—'Reid: Mr, Susan, James, Julia, C., Charles'—'Reeve: Mrs, Mary, Catherine, Ellen, Nelly, Jane, Cornelia, Deon.'

Religious men, thoughtful men—and, on the other hand, men wrought up to a pitch of exasperated feeling—afterwards spoke of the fatal well as a spot that should be marked in some way for the observance of posterity. Two church missionaries were among the murdered at Cawnpore; and it was urged in many quarters that a Christian church, built with the splendour and resources of a great nation, would be a suitable erection at that spot—as an appropriate memorial to the dead, a striking lesson to the living, and the commencement of a grand effort to Christianise the heathen millions of India. Whether a church be the right covering for a hideous pit containing nearly two hundred mangled bodies of gentle English women and children; and whether rival creeds would struggle for precedency in the management of its construction, its details, and the form of its service—may fairly admit of doubt; but with or without a church, the English in no parts of the world are ever likely to forget THE WELL AT CAWNPORE!

Note.

Nena Sahib's Proclamations.—When Generals Neill and Havelock were at Cawnpore, during a period subsequent to that comprised within the range of the present chapter, they found many proclamations which had been printed in the Mahratta language by order of Nena Sahib, as if for distribution among the natives under his influence. These proclamations were afterwards translated into English, and included among the parliamentary papers relating to India. A few of them may fittingly be reproduced here, to shew by what means that consummate villain sought to attain his ends.

The following appears to have been issued on or about

the 1st of July:—'As, by the kindness of God and the ikbal or good-fortune of the Emperor, all the Christians who were at Delhi, Poonah, Satara, and other places, and even those 5000 European soldiers who went in disguise into the former city and were discovered, are destroyed and sent to hell by the pious and sagacious troops, who are firm to their religion; and as they have all been conquered by the present government, and as no trace of them is left in these places, it is the duty of all the subjects and servants of the government to rejoice at the delightful intelligence, and to carry on their respective work with comfort and ease.'

This was accompanied by another: 'As, by the bounty of the glorious Almighty God and the enemy-destroying fortune of the Emperor, the yellow-faced and narrow-minded people have been sent to hell, and Cawnpore has been conquered, it is necessary that all the subjects and landowners should be as obedient to the present government as they had been to the former one; that all the government servants should promptly and cheerfully engage their whole mind in executing the orders of government; that it is the incumbent duty of all the ryots and landed proprietors of every district to rejoice at the thought that the Christians have been sent to hell, and both the Hindoo and Mohammedan religions have been confirmed; and that they should as usual be obedient to the authorities of the government, and never to suffer any complaint against themselves to reach the ears of the higher authority.'

On the 5th of the same month the Nena issued the following to the kotwal or Mayor of Cawnpore: 'It has come to our notice that some of the city people, having heard the rumours of the arrival of the European soldiers at Allahabad, are deserting their houses and going out into the districts; you are, therefore, directed to proclaim in each lane and street of the city that regiments of cavalry and infantry and batteries have been despatched to check the Europeans either at Allahabad or Futtehpoor; that the people should therefore remain in their houses without any apprehension, and engage their minds in carrying on their work.'

Another proclamation displayed in an extraordinary way the Rajah's mode of practising on the credulity of the natives, by the most enormous and barefaced fictions: 'A traveller just arrived in Cawnpore from Calcutta states that in the first instance a council was held to take into consideration the means to be adopted to do away with the religion of the Mohammedans and Hindoos by the distribution of cartridges. The council came to this resolution, that, as this matter was one of religion, the services of seven or eight thousand European soldiers would be necessary, as 50,000 Hindustanis would have to be destroyed, and then the whole of the people of Hindostan would become Christians. A petition with the substance of this resolution was sent to the Queen Victoria, and it was approved. A council was then held a second time, in which English merchants took a part, and it was decided that, in order that no evil should arise from mutiny, large reinforcements should be sent for. When the dispatch was received and read in England, thousands of European soldiers were embarked on ships as speedily as possible, and sent off to Hindostan. The news of their being despatched reached Calcutta. The English authorities there ordered the issue of the cartridges, for the real intention was to Christianise the army first, and this being effected, the conversion of the people would speedily follow. Pigs' and cows' fat was mixed up with the cartridges; this became known through one of the Bengalese who was employed in the cartridge-making establishment. Of those through whose means this was divulged, one was killed and the rest imprisoned. While in this country these counsels were being adopted, in England the vakeel (ambassador) of the Sultan of Roum (Turkey) sent news to the sultan that thousands of European soldiers were being sent for the purpose of making Christians of all the people of Hindostan. Upon this the sultan issued a firman to the King of Egypt to this effect: "You must deceive the Queen Victoria, for this is not a time for friendship, for my vakeel writes that thousands of European soldiers have been despatched for the purpose of making Christians the army and people of Hindostan. In this manner, then, this must be checked. If I should be remiss, then how can I shew my face to God; and one day this may come upon me also, for if the English make Christians of all in Hindostan, they will then fix their designs upon my country." When the firman reached the King of Egypt, he prepared and arranged his troops before the arrival of the English army at Alexandria, for this is the route to India. The instant the English army arrived, the King of Egypt opened guns upon them from all sides, and destroyed and sunk their ships, and not a single soldier escaped. The English in Calcutta, after the issue of the order for the cartridges, and when the mutiny had become great, were in expectation of the arrival of the army from London; but the Great God, in his omnipotence, had beforehand put an end to this. When the news of the destruction of the army of London became known, then the governor-general was plunged in grief and sorrow, and beat his head.

'Done by order of the Peishwa Bahadoor, 13 Zekaida, 1273 Hegira.'

The Well at Cawnpore.

House of the Rajah at ALLAHABAD.

CHAPTER IX.

BENGAL AND THE LOWER GANGES: JUNE.

WHEN, through the media of telegrams, dispatches, and letters, the tragical events at Cawnpore became known in England, and were invested with an additional horror on account of a vague suspicion that worse remained untold, a painful and widely spread sensation was produced. Nay, more; in almost every part of the civilised world, whether or not in harmony with the British government on political and international questions, astonishment was excited by these recitals of unapproachable barbarity among a people who had acquired a sort of traditional character for mildness and gentleness. It was about the end of June when news of the Meerut outbreak reached London; and from that time each fortnightly mail revealed the truth that a larger and larger area of India was becoming involved in the troubles of insurrection—that a gradually increasing number of military officers and civil servants of the Company, with their wives and children, were placed in circumstances of imminent peril. Residents in the United Kingdom, any of whose relations and friends were stationed at Cawnpore, sought eagerly and anxiously, as each mail arrived, for indications that escape had been effected, or a rescuing force obtained. No such news came, no such hopes were realised; darker and more silent was everything relating to that much-dreaded city, until at length the frightful climax became known.

There has been a designed avoidance, in the preceding chapters of this work, of any account of the measures adopted by the British government in military matters, or by the British nation in active benevolence, to remedy the disasters and allay the sufferings to which the Anglo-Indians had so suddenly been exposed; for, in truth, India knew little of such measures until August was far advanced. Whether all was done that might have been done to expedite the passage of British troops to India, is a question that will have to be considered in its proper place; the significant truth now to be borne in mind is that the Calcutta government had to meet the difficulties as best it could, with the scanty supply of troops at that time in India—sending to the Mauritius and the

Cape of Good Hope for such reinforcements as might be available, but knowing that aid from England could not arrive for many months. The mode of treatment adopted here is naturally suggested by the course of events themselves. When the ramifications of the Revolt have been traced throughout the month of June, a chapter will then be devoted to the subjects above indicated; for, although Cawnpore carried us into July, we have yet to watch what was concurrently passing at other places.

We begin with the region extending from the Burmese frontier to the Doab, and forming the eastern portion of Northern India; it may for convenience be called Bengal, without any rigid adherence to territorial subdivision.

The Indian government was not as yet troubled with any serious outbreaks at Chittagong or Dacca, or in any of the districts bounding the Bay of Bengal on the north and east. There were a few native troops at the first named of these two towns, belonging to one of the mutinous regiments at Barrackpore; but tranquillity was not disturbed by them. It is true that, when the disloyalty of the 34th became known, the inhabitants of Chittagong and Tipperah experienced some alarm lest the detachment of this regiment stationed at the first-named town might follow the pernicious example; but the Company's collector, having three lacs of rupees in hand, quietly removed his treasure on board a steamer; and all uneasiness was soon allayed. Along the extreme eastern border of the Bengal presidency, from Assam down through Dacca to Chittagong, the month of June similarly passed over without any disturbances calling for notice, although a temporary panic was excited in more than one spot. At Dacca, for instance, the approach of disbanded native mutineers was apprehended; and a mischievous set of Mohammedans, under one Keramut Ali, were detected in the endeavour to sow the seeds of disaffection; but by the firmness of the civil authorities, and the arrival of a hundred seamen in two pinnaces from the Company's steamers *Zenobia* and *Punjaub*, tranquillity was soon restored.

In the Calcutta and Barrackpore district, although no actual mutiny occurred, symptoms were presented that gave much anxiety to the Europeans residing at the capital, and prompted energetic preventive measures. We have seen, in Chapter II., that much discontent was exhibited at Dumdum, Barrackpore, and Berhampore, between the months of January and May, by the native troops; that this discontent was (professedly) associated with the affair of the greased cartridges; that insubordination led to disarming and disbandment; that the news of the Meerut and Delhi atrocities in May greatly alarmed the Calcutta inhabitants; and that many addresses of loyalty and sympathy with the government were thenceforth presented. During the first half of June, the European residents looked with a sort of suspicious watchfulness at everything that was occurring around them, prepared to find the native troops treacherous, yet hoping for better things. The reliable forces in Calcutta at that time comprised H.M. 53d foot, nine hundred strong, and five hundred of H.M. 37th. A company of the 3d battalion Madras artillery; No. 2 horse field-battery; forty men of the royal artillery, recently arrived from Ceylon; and a wing of H.M. 35th foot, were at Barrackpore. The 78th Highlanders were at Chinsura. On the 13th of June, Calcutta was thrown into great agitation. A messenger was captured by the authorities, and confessed that the sepoys at Barrackpore and Calcutta had agreed to mutiny on that very night. Arrangements were immediately made for defending the city by the aid chiefly of volunteers, who had before then begun to organise themselves. The civilians took arms, marshalled themselves into companies and corps, and paraded the streets in the English part of the city. During the two following nights, this patrolling was conducted very vigilantly; and every native met in the streets was required to give an account of his movements. On one occasion, Lady Canning, accompanied by the governor-general, the commander-in-chief, Generals Windham and Beatson, and a glittering staff, went to the parade-ground; where, the volunteers being all drawn up in full array, her ladyship presented them with colours, and made a complimentary address; to which Major Turnbull replied, as commandant of the 'Calcutta Volunteer Guards.'

The military proceedings on this occasion were as follow. Before light on Sunday morning the 14th, in consequence of a message received from head-quarters, a body of the 78th Highlanders was sent off hastily from Chinsura to Barrackpore, to disarm the native troops there; while five hundred of her Majesty's 37th foot, landed from Ceylon only the day before, were marched off to a point about midway between Calcutta and Barrackpore, to command the road during the disarming. About midnight an order arrived that some of the 37th should return instantly to the capital. It had been discovered that the deposed King of Oude, residing in a handsome house at Garden Reach, was engaged in some machinations with a prince of the Delhi family, inimical to the interests of the Europeans. A military force marched to his house at four o'clock on the morning of the 15th, surrounded the grounds, entered, and seized the king and his prime minister, together with a large quantity of papers. Arrangements were immediately made for the safe custody of the two Oudians, until the papers could be fully examined. A document came to light, containing a Mohammedan sketch-map of Calcutta, dividing the city into sections; together with the plan for a general rising of natives on the centenary day of the battle of Plassy, the murder of all the Feringhees, and the establishment of a native 'raj' or dynasty on the ruins of that of the Company. It was deemed proper to adopt prompt measures on this occasion; all the native troops in Calcutta were disarmed as a precautionary measure, including the Calcutta militia, but excluding the governor-general's body-guard. The sepoys, who made no demur whatever, were disarmed in parties wherever they happened to be—at the Government House guard, the treasury, the mint, the bank, and the fort. Each party was confronted by a party of Europeans, and gave up arms on being so commanded; the arms and ammunition were then taken away by the European soldiers, nothing being left with the sepoys but their ramrods, with which to 'shoulder arms.' It was explained to them that the disarming was only a temporary precautionary measure; that they would receive pay and perform sentinel-duty as before; and that the arms would be restored to them as soon as public tranquillity was insured.

The inhabitants of Calcutta long continued to bear well in remembrance the 14th of June. For nearly a month the civilians had been in the habit of taking revolvers with them to church, balls, and parties; but on this day, such were the vague terrors of slaughter whispered from mouth to mouth, that the excitement rose to a height of panic. One who was there at the time said: 'The infection of terror raged through all classes. Chowringhee and Garden Reach were abandoned for the fort and the vessels in the river. The shipping was crowded with fugitives; and in houses which were selected as being least likely to be attacked, hundreds of people gladly huddled together, to share the peculiar comfort which the presence of crowds imparts on such occasions. The hotels were fortified; bands of sailors marched through the thoroughfares, happy in the expectation of possible fighting and the certainty of grog. Every group of natives was scanned with suspicion. The churches and the course were abandoned for that evening. A rising, either of Hindoos or of Mussulmans, or perhaps of both, was looked upon as certain to happen in the course of the night. From Chandernagore the whole body of European and East Indian inhabitants emigrated to Calcutta; the *personnel* of government, the staff of the army, all in short who had anything to lose, preferred to come away and run the risk of losing it, rather than encounter the unknown danger.' A somewhat unworthy timidity seems, at first sight, to mark all this; but the civilians and private families of Calcutta, utterly unused to war, had been so horror-stricken by the accounts of murders of officers, violations of women, mutilations of little children, burnings of sick and wounded, and other atrocities perpetrated in Upper India, as to become in a certain sense paralysed. After the decisive measures adopted by the government on the 14th and next following day, the inhabitants of the capital gradually recovered their equanimity; and the month closed peacefully.

Early in June, the sepoys cantoned at Barrackpore made the same kind of demonstration as at an earlier date—that is, they professed fidelity, and asked to be furnished with the new Enfield rifle. In the 43d regiment B.N.I., there was a general application made to Major Matthews, by native officers as well as sepoys, to this effect; accompanied by the expression of a desire to be sent to fight against the rebels at Delhi. The 70th B.N.I., almost to a man, came forward on the 5th of the month, and presented a petition to Colonel Kennedy, with a similar prayer. The petition began somewhat boastfully: 'From the day on which his lordship the governor-general condescended to come in person to answer our petition, on which occasion General Hearsey translated to us his address, and which was fully explained to us by our colonel, interpreter, adjutant, and all the other officers of the regiment, our honour and name have been raised amongst our countrymen;' and it ended with an abundant profession of loyalty towards the government. The 34th regiment B.N.I., or such of the men as were at Barrackpore, imitated the example of their fellow-soldiers; they sent a petition to Lieutenant-colonel Wheler on the 9th of June, expressive of their loyalty, and requesting that the new rifle might be served out to them. The government, in reply to all these petitions and demonstrations, stated that the supply of Enfield rifles received from England was too small to permit the granting of the request; but that the request itself was received with much gratification by the governor-general, 'proving as it does that the men of these regiments consider there is nothing objectionable either in the rifles or in the cartridges to their caste or religion.'

Little was it suspected in how short a time all these complimentary exchanges of good words would be brought to nought. On the evening of the 13th came to light those plottings or suspicions of plottings which led to an imperative order for the disarming of the sepoys. In a private letter on this subject, the major-general said: 'Some villains in the corps were trying to incite the good men and true to mutiny; these good men ought to have given the villains up to justice;' but as they did not, he thought it a safe plan to disarm them all. When this determination was made known by the authorities, many of the English officers of the native regiments felt much vexed and hurt; they still relied on their men, and deemed it a humiliation to themselves that such a course should be deemed necessary. Captain Greene, of the 70th N.I., wrote to Major-general Hearsey, on the Sunday morning: 'Is it of any use my interceding with you on behalf of my old corps, which, for nigh twenty-five years, has been my pride and my home? I cannot express to you the pain with which I have just heard that they are this evening to be subjected to the indignity of being disarmed. Had the men misbehaved, I should have felt no sympathy for them; but they have not committed themselves in any way; and surely after the governor-general's laudatory order and expression of confidence, it would not be too much to expect that a fair trial of their sincerity should be afforded.' Captain Greene proceeded to say that he knew the men thoroughly, and had the most firm and undoubted reliance on their fidelity. The authorities were not affected by this appeal. At four o'clock in the afternoon, the 35th and 78th British regiments were marched to the parade-ground at Barrackpore, with loaded muskets, and supported by six 12-pounders loaded with grape-shot. The native troops were then summoned to the parade, and ordered at once to surrender their arms; this they did quietly and promptly, for even if disposed to resist, the force against them was too formidable. In little more than an hour, the muskets of the disarmed regiments were on the way to Calcutta. The sepoys bore the trial quietly, but with many expressions of mortification.

Captain Greene, in the postscript to a letter written on the following day to the major-general, mentioned certain facts which ought to have opened his eyes to the possibility of deceit and danger. A Mussulman sepoy of the 70th regiment came to him on the 9th of the month, and after conversation on some contemplated movements of the captain, said: 'Whatever you do, do not take your lady with you.' He gave as a reason: 'Because the minds of the native soldiers are now in a state of inquietude; and it would be better to let the lady remain here till everything is settled in the country, as there is no knowing what might happen.' On being asked whether he had reason to doubt the regiment, he exclaimed: 'Who can tell the hearts of a thousand men!' He implied that a few evil men were endeavouring to corrupt the rest. This communicative sepoy went on to observe, that the cartridge grievance, although founded on a misconception in the first instance, was afterwards used as a means of imposing on the ignorant. There were men who went about saying that the English endeavoured to destroy the caste and religion of the people; that the government ought to be uprooted; and that as the Company had been driven out of Cabool, so might it be driven out of the whole of India, if the people acted resolutely and with one accord. Another sepoy, a Hindoo, in the same regiment, told Captain Greene that the Mussulmans generally in all regiments were in the habit of talking to the effect that their 'raj' or supremacy was coming round again. Many others spoke indistinctly to him about dangers, and promised to protect him if peril arose. It may not be improbable that most of the men in that regiment were really disposed to be faithful, and that the danger arose from a smaller number of malcontents. Captain Greene went to see his men in the lines after the disarming; it was a painful interview to them all. 'I have been for upwards of an hour,' he wrote, 'endeavouring to allay the excited feelings of our men, who were in such a state of depression, that many were crying bitterly, and none could cook their food. Some, too, had sold their cooking utensils for a mere trifle in the bazaar.' The regiment had not been disbanded as if in disgrace, only disarmed as if for precaution; but the men nevertheless regarded it as a degradation. Some budmashes (scoundrels) had been amongst them in the night, and had urged them to desert, telling them that handcuffs and manacles had been sent for. The captain earnestly implored that their arms should be given back to them: 'Unless something be speedily done to reassure them, the influence of their European officers will cease to exist, and a good regiment will crumble away before hopelessness and desertion. All of us, black and white, would be so thankful to you if you would get us back our arms, and sent away from here at once.' This request was not acceded to.

Within ten days after the disarming, a hundred and thirty-three men of the disarmed regiments (2d, 34th, 43d, and 70th) deserted from Barrackpore and Calcutta, nearly all belonging to the 43d. The magistrates and military authorities in many parts of Bengal were troubled with the arrival of these deserters, who came two or three at a time, and endeavoured to excite disaffection against a government which, as they alleged, had disgraced them without a cause. A reward of fifty rupees was offered for the apprehension of every deserter.

Departing from Calcutta and Barrackpore as centres, it may be well now to sketch the state of the surrounding districts during the month of June. Towards the northeast, many towns, especially Jessore, were thrown occasionally into excitement by occurrences which would have been regarded as trivial if happening at any other time, but which required watchful attention on the part of the authorities in the peculiarly sensitive state of the native mind. In the Dinagepore district, near the Bhotan frontier, several moulvies spread reports of the intention of the government forcibly to convert native children to Christianity: these reports caused many of the children in the vernacular school at Muthoorapore to be withdrawn by their parents; and on an examination of the moulvies being ordered by the authorities, it was found that the fakeers and other religious mendicants were accustomed to carry treasonable letters and concealed correspondence within the bamboo sticks with which most of them were provided. North and west of the Anglo-Indian capital, a similar state of public affairs was presented; a succession of troublous symptoms that required attention, but without entailing serious consequences. In some instances disarmed sepoys were detected exciting disaffection; in others, seditious placards were posted up in the towns. In the country around Ramgurh a few circumstances transpired to produce temporary disquietude. The Ramgurh battalion was believed to be stanch; but as some discontent had spread among the troops in relation to the cartridge grievance, and as two or three petty chieftains exhibited symptoms of disloyalty, judicious and early precautions were taken against disaster—especially at Hazarebagh, where the treasury contained a lac of rupees, and where the jail, containing nine hundred prisoners, was guarded solely by two companies of a native regiment: a kind of guard which had proved very perilous at Meerut a few weeks earlier. At Midnapore, a sepoy of the jail-guard, detected in an attempt to excite mutiny among the men of the Shekhawuttie battalion, was tried, found guilty, and hanged.

The most serious event in the districts around Calcutta, perhaps, was one that occurred in the Sonthal Pergunnahs; in which the 5th irregular cavalry displayed a tendency, fatal on a small scale, and likely to have become much more disastrous if not speedily checked. Lieutenant Sir N. R. Leslie was adjutant of that regiment at Rohnee. On the 12th of June, this officer, Major Macdonald, and Assistant-surgeon Grant, while sitting in Sir Norman Leslie's compound, in the dusk of the evening, were suddenly attacked by three men armed with swords. Major Macdonald received a blow which laid his head open, and rendered him insensible for many hours; Mr Grant received sword-wounds on the arm and the leg; while Sir Norman was so severely wounded that he expired within half an hour. The miscreants escaped after this ferocious attack, without immediate detection.* At first it was hoped and believed that the regiment had not been dishonoured by the presence of these murderers on the muster-roll; Mr Grant was of this opinion; but Major Macdonald, commandant of the regiment, took a less favourable view. The offenders, it soon appeared, belonged to the regiment; a chase was ordered; two of the men were found after a time, with their clothes smeared with blood; while the third, when taken, candidly owned that it was his sword that had given the death-stroke to Leslie. The murderers were speedily executed, but without giving any information touching the motives that led to their crime. Three sowars of the regiment, Ennus Khan, Kurreem Shere Khan, and Gamda Khan, received encomiums and rewards for the alacrity with which they had pursued the reckless men who had thus brought discredit on their corps. The official dispatches relating to this affair comprised two letters written by Major Macdonald to Captain Watson, an officer commanding a squadron of the same regiment at Bhagulpore; they afford curious illustration of the cheerful, daring, care-for-naught spirit in which the British officers were often accustomed to meet their difficulties during those exciting scenes: 'I am as fairly cut and neatly scalped as any Red Indian could do it. I got three cracks in succession on the head before I knew I was attacked. I then seized my chair by the arms, and defended myself successfully from two of them on me at once; I guarded and struck the best way I could; and at last Grant and self drove the cowards off the field. This is against my poor head, writing; but you will be anxious to know how matters really were; I expect to be in high fever to-morrow, as I have got a bad gash into the skull besides being scalped.' This was written on the day after the murderous attack; and three days later the major wrote: 'My dear fellow, I have had a sad time of it, and am but little able to go through such scenes, for I am very badly wounded; but, thank God, my spirits and pluck never left me for a moment. When you see my poor old head, you will wonder I could hold it up at all. I have preserved my scalp in spirits of wine—such a jolly specimen!'

In Cuttack, bounding the northwest corner of the Bay of Bengal, many Mohammedans were detected in the attempt to sap the loyalty of the Shekhawuttie battalion. Lieutenant-colonel Forster, with the head-quarters of that corps at Midnapore, succeeded by his personal influence in keeping the men from anything beyond slight acts of insubordination; but he had many proofs, in that town and in the Cuttack district, that the Company's 'raj' or rule was being preached against by many emissaries of rebellion.

This rapid sketch will have shewn that the eastern divisions of Bengal were not disturbed by any very serious tumults during the month of June. Incipient proofs of disaffection were, it is true, manifested in many places; but they were either unimportant in extent, or were checked before they could rise to perilous magnitude. In the western divisions, however, the troubles were more serious; the towns were further from Calcutta, nearer to the turbulent region of Oude; and these conditions of locality greatly affected the steadiness and honesty of the native troops.

During the earlier days of the month, considerable excitement prevailed in the districts of which Patna and Dinapoor are the chief towns; in consequence of the general spread of a belief, inculcated by the deserters from Barrackpore, that the government contemplated an active

* The following is an extract of a letter written by Major Macdonald, after the attack upon him and his brother-officers: 'Two days after, my native officer said he had found out the murderers, and that they were three men of my own regiment. I had them in irons in a crack, held a drumhead court-martial, convicted, and sentenced them to be hanged the next morning. I took on my own shoulders the responsibility of hanging them first, and asking leave to do so afterwards. That day was an awful one of suspense and anxiety. One of the prisoners was of very high caste and influence, and this man I determined to treat with the greatest ignominy, by getting the lowest caste man to hang him. To tell you the truth, I never for a moment expected to leave the hanging scene alive; but I was determined to do my duty, and well knew the effect that pluck and decision had on the natives. The regiment was drawn out; wounded cruelly as I was, I had to see everything done myself, even to the adjusting of the ropes, and saw them looped to run easy. Two of the culprits were paralysed with fear and astonishment, never dreaming that I should dare to hang them without an order from government. The third said he would not be hanged, and called on the Prophet and on his comrades to rescue him. This was an awful moment; an instant's hesitation on my part, and probably I should have had a dozen of balls through me; so I seized a pistol, clapped it to the man's ear, and said, with a look there was no mistake about: "Another word out of your mouth, and your brains shall be scattered on the ground." He trembled, and held his tongue. The elephant came up, he was put on his back, the rope adjusted, the elephant moved, and he was left dangling. I then had the others up, and off in the same way. And after some time, when I had dismissed the men of the regiment to their lines, and still found my head on my shoulders, I really could scarcely believe it.'

interference with the religion of the people. A similar delusion, it was speedily remembered, had existed in the same parts about two years earlier; the government had adopted such measures as, it was hoped, would remove the prejudice; but the events of 1857 shewed that the healing policy of 1855 had not been effective for the purpose in view. Until the 13th of June, the disaffection was manifested only by sullen complainings and indistinct threats; but on that day matters presented a more serious aspect. The various magistrates throughout the Patna division reported to the lieutenant-governor of Bengal, that although no acts of violence had been committed, the continuance of tranquillity would mainly depend on the fidelity of the native troops at Dinapoor, the most important military station in that part of India. Dinapoor may, in fact, be regarded as the military post belonging to the great city of Patna, which is about ten miles distant.* The magistrates also reported, as one result of their inquiries, that the Mohammedans in that division were thoroughly disaffected; and that if any disturbance occurred at head-quarters (Dinapoor), a rapid extension of the revolt would be almost inevitable. When these facts and feelings became known, such precautionary measures were adopted as seemed best calculated to avert the impending evils. An increase was made in the police force at Behar; the ghats or landing-places were carefully watched and regulated; the frontiers of the neighbouring disaffected districts were watched; a portion of the Company's treasure at Arrah and Chupra was sent off to Calcutta, and the rest removed to Patna for safe custody under a guard of Sikhs; a volunteer guard was formed in that city; measures were taken to defend the collectorate and the opium factories; six companies of the Sikh police battalion were marched from Soorie to Patna; and places of rendezvous for European residents were appointed at many of the stations, to facilitate a combined plan of action in the event of mutinous symptoms appearing among the native troops. The Rajahs of Bettiah and Hutwah addressed letters expressive of loyalty and affection towards the government, and placed men and elephants at the disposal of the local authorities, to assist in the maintenance of tranquillity.

Towards the middle of the month, an alarm prevailed at Chupra and Arrah, consequent on the mutinous proceedings in certain towns further to the west, presently to be noticed. Large works were under construction near those places in connection with the East India Railway; and the Europeans engaged in those operations, as well as others resident in the two towns, made a hasty retreat, and sought for refuge at Dinapoor. The magistrates and most of the civil officers remained at their posts, and by their firmness prevented the alarm from degenerating into a panic. At Gayah or Gya, a town between Patna and the great trunk-road—celebrated for its Bhuddist and Hindoo temples, and the great resort of pilgrims of both religions—considerable apprehension prevailed, on account of the unprotected state of a large amount of Company's treasure in the collectorate; an apprehension increased by the presence of many desperate characters at that time in the jail, and by the guard of the jail being wholly composed of natives who would remain steady only so long as those at Dinapoor were 'faithful to their salt.' Fortunately, the authorities were enabled to obtain a guard of European soldiers, chiefly from her majesty's 64th regiment; and thus the ruffians, more to be dreaded than even the rebellious sepoys, were overawed.

It is impossible to avoid seeing, in the course of events throughout India, how much importance ought to be attached to the matter just adverted to—the instrumentality of robbers and released prisoners in producing the dreadful scenes presented. India swarms with depredators who war on the peaceful and industrious inhabitants—not merely individual thieves, but robber-tribes who infest certain provinces, directing their movements by the chances of war or of plunder. Instead of extirpating these ill-doers, as Asiatic sovereigns have sometimes attempted to do, the East India Company has been accustomed to capture and imprison them. Hence the jails are always full. At every important station we have several hundred, sometimes two or three thousand, such prisoners. The mutiny set loose these mischievous elements. The release of crowds of murderers and robbers from prison, the flocking of others from the villages, and the stimulus given to latent rogues by the prospect of plunder, would account for a large amount of the outrage committed in India—outrage which popular speech in England attaches to the sepoys alone.

On the 13th of June, the first indications of a conspiracy at Patna were detected. A nujeeb of the Behar station guards was discovered in an attempt to tamper with the Sikhs of the police corps, and to excite them to mutiny: he was tried, convicted, sentenced to death, and hanged; while three Sikhs, who had been instrumental in his apprehension, were publicly rewarded with fifty rupees each. In singular contrast to this, three other nujeebs of the same force, on the same day, placed in the commissioner's hands a letter received from sepoys at Dinapoor, urging the Behar guards to mutiny, and to seize the treasure at Patna before the Sikhs could arrive to the rescue: this, as a valuable service rendered at a critical period, was rewarded by donations of two hundred rupees to each of the three men. The next symptoms were exhibited by certain members of the Wahabee sect of Mohammedans at Patna. The fanatical devotion of these Mussulmans to their spiritual

* Dinapoor is remarkable for the fine barracks built by the Company for the accommodation of troops—for the officers, the European troops, and the native troops; most of the officers have commodious bungalows in the vicinity; and the markets or bazaars, for the supply of Europeans as well as natives, are unusually large and well supplied.

leaders, their abnegation of self, and their mode of confidential communication with each other without written documents, render it at all times difficult to produce legal proof of any machinations among them; while their mutual fidelity enables them to resist all temptation to betrayal. The commissioner of Patna, having suspicions of the proceedings of the Wahabees in that city, deemed it politic to detain four of their number as hostages for the sect generally—a sect formidable for its organisation, and peculiarly hostile to Christians. They were placed in a sort of honourable confinement, while a general disarming of the inhabitants took place. On another occasion a police jemadar, Waris Ali, was ascertained to be in possession of a large amount of treasonable correspondence; he was known to be in some way related to the royal family of Delhi; and the letters found in his house threw suspicion on more than one native official in the service of the Company.

The most serious affair at Patna, however, occurred about the close of the period to which this chapter more particularly relates. At about eight o'clock in the evening of the 3d of July, a body of Mohammedans, variously estimated from eighty to two hundred, assembled at the house of one of their number, one Peer Ali Khan, a bookseller, and proceeded thence to the Roman Catholic church and mission-house in Patna, with two large green flags, a drum beating, and cries of 'Ali! Ali!' The priest, whom they probably intended to murder, fortunately escaped. They emerged into the street, reiterated their cries, and called on the populace to join them. Dr Lyell, principal assistant to the opium agent, immediately went to the spot, accompanied by nine Sikhs. He rode ahead of his support, was shot down by the rioters, and his body mangled and mutilated before the Sikhs could come up. A force of Sikhs and nujeebs speedily recovered the unfortunate gentleman's body, killed some of the insurgents, and put the rest to flight. This appeared at first to be a religious demonstration; a Mohammedan fanatic war-cry was shouted, and the property of the Catholic mission was destroyed, but without any plunder or removal. Thirty-six of the insurgents were afterwards captured and tried; sixteen of the number, including Peer Ali Khan, who was believed to be the murderer of Dr Lyell, were condemned to death; eighteen, including a jemadar, were sentenced to various terms of imprisonment; and two were acquitted. All the facts of this temporary outbreak were full of significance; for it soon became evident that something more than mere religious hostility had been intended. Peer Ali Khan was offered a reprieve if he would divulge the nature of the conspiracy; but, like a bold, consistent fanatic, he remained defiant to the last, and nothing could be got out of him. It was afterwards ascertained that he had been in secret communication with an influential native at Cawnpore ever since the annexation of Oude, and that the details of some widely-spread plot had been concerted between them. The capture of the thirty-six rioters had been effected by the disclosures of one of the band, who was wounded in the struggle; he declared that a plot had been in existence for many months, and that men were regularly paid to excite the people to fight for the Padishah of Delhi. Letters found in Peer Ali's house disclosed an organised Mussulman conspiracy to re-establish Mohammedan supremacy on the ruins of British power; and besides the correspondence with Cawnpore and Delhi, a clue was obtained to the complicity of an influential Mohammedan at Lucknow.

Patna was sufficiently well watched and guarded to prevent the occurrence of anything of more serious import. Nevertheless, the European inhabitants were kept in great anxiety, knowing how much their safety depended on the conduct of the sepoys at Dinapoor. The commissioner at the one place, and the military commandant at the other, were naturally rejoiced to receive any demonstrations of fidelity on the part of the native troops, even if the sincerity of those demonstrations were not quite free from doubt. On the 3d of June, Colonel Templer assembled the 7th regiment B. N. I. on the military parade at Dinapoor, to read to them the flattering address which Viscount Canning had made to the 70th regiment at Barrackpore, on the manifestation of loyalty by that corps. On the conclusion of this ceremony, the native commissioned officers came up to the colonel, and presented to him a petition, signed by two subadars and five jemadars on the part of the whole regiment. The petition is worth transcribing,* to shew in what glowing language the native troops could express their grateful allegiance—but whether sincere or insincere, no European could at that time truly tell. Colonel Templer desired that all the men who acknowledged the petition to contain an expression of their real sentiments and wishes, would shoulder their arms in token thereof; on which every one present

* 'At present the men of bad character in some regiments, and other people in the direction of Meerut and Delhi, have turned from their allegiance to the bountiful government, and created a seditious disturbance, and have made choice of the ways of ingratitude, and thrown away the character of sepoys true to their salt.

'At present it is well known that some European regiments have started to punish and coerce these rebels; we trust that by the favour of the bountiful government, we also may be sent to punish the enemies of government, wherever they are; for if we cannot be of use to government at this time, how will it be manifest and known to the state that we are true to our salt? Have we not been entertained in the army for days like the present? In addition to this, government shall see what their faithful sepoys are like, and we will work with heart and soul to do our duty to the state that gives us our salt.

'Let the enemies of government be who they may, we are ready to fight them, and to sacrifice our lives in the cause.

'We have said as much as is proper; may the sun of your wealth and prosperity ever shine.

'The petition of your servants:

HEERA SING, Subadar,
ELLAHEE KHAN, Subadar,
BHOWANY SING, Jemadar,
MUNROOP SING, Jemadar,
HEERA SING, Jemadar,
ISSERAEE PANDY, Jemadar,
MURDAN SING, Jemadar,

of the Burra Crawford's, or 7th regiment, native infantry, and of every non-commissioned officer and sepoy in the lines. Presented on the 3d June 1857.'

shouldered arms. The native officers afterwards assured the colonel, with apparent earnestness, that it was the eager wish of the whole regiment to be afforded an opportunity of removing even a suspicion of their disaffection. When Colonel Templer repeated this to Major-general Lloyd, the military commander of the Dinapoor division, and when Lloyd forwarded the communication to Calcutta, the regiment of course received thanks for the demonstration, and were assured that 'their good conduct will be kept in remembrance by the governor-general in council.' It was not until a later month that the small value of these protestations was clearly shewn; nevertheless the Europeans at Dinapoor continued throughout June to be very uneasy. Almost every one lived in the square; the guns were kept ready loaded with grape; the few European troops were on the alert; and pickets were posted all round the station. A motley assemblage—planters, soldiers, civilians, railway men, and others—was added to the ordinary residents, driven in from the surrounding districts for protection. The officers gave up their mess-house to the ladies, who completely filled it.

In Tirhoot, a district north of Patna, on the other side of the Ganges, the planters and others were thrown into great excitement during the month of June, by the events occurring around them. About the middle of the month, planters left their estates and civilians their homes, to go for refuge to the Company's station at Mozufferpoor. Eighty gentlemen, thirty ladies, and forty children, were all crowded into two houses; the ladies and children shut up at night, while the men slept in verandahs, or in tents, or took turns in patrolling. The nujeebs, stationed at that place, were suspected of being in sympathy with the mutineers; one of the Company's servants, disguised as a native, went to their quarters one night, and overheard them conversing about murdering the Europeans, looting the treasury (which contained seven lacs of rupees), and liberating the prisoners. This was the alarm that led to the assembling of the Europeans at the station for mutual protection; and there can be little doubt that the protection would have been needed had Dinapoor fallen. One of the Mohammedan inhabitants was seized at Mozufferpoor, with a quantity of treasonable correspondence in his possession; and the commandant at Segowlie condemned to the gallows with very little scruple several suspicious characters in various parts of the district.

Advancing up the Ganges, we come to Ghazeepore, on its northern or left bank. This town, containing forty thousand inhabitants, is rendered somewhat famous by a palace once belonging to the Nawab of Oude, but now in a very ruinous state; also by the beautiful Grecian tomb erected to the Marquis of Cornwallis; and by the rose-gardens in its vicinity, where rose-leaves are gathered for making the celebrated otto or attar. The bungalows of the Company's civil servants are situated west of the town; and beyond them is the military cantonment. During the early part of the month of June, the 65th native infantry, stationed at Ghazeepore, was sorely tempted by the mutinying of so many other regiments at stations within forty or fifty miles; but they remained stanch for some time longer.

Not so the sepoys at Azimghur, a town north-west of Ghazeepore, containing twelve or fourteen thousand inhabitants, and a military station. At this place the 17th regiment Bengal native infantry was posted at the beginning of June. On the 3d of the month an escort of thirty troopers of the 13th irregular cavalry brought in seven lacs of rupees from Goruckpore, *en route* to Benares. At six o'clock in the evening the treasure was started again on its journey; and in three hours afterwards the 17th mutinied, influenced apparently rather by the hope of *loot* than by any political or religious motives. During several days previously the authorities had been employed in throwing up a breastwork around the cutchery or government offices; but this was not finished. The sepoys killed their quartermaster, and wounded the quartermaster-sergeant and two or three others. The officer on guard at the fort of the cutchery sent out a picket to the lines, and ordered the native artillerymen to load their guns: this they refused to do; and hence the infantry were left to follow out their plan of spoliation. The officers were at mess when the mutiny began; seeing the danger, they placed the ladies on the roof of the cutchery. When the sepoys came up, they formed a square round the officers, and swore to protect them; but stated that, as some men of the regiment were very hostile, it would be better for all the officers to depart. The men brought carriages for them, and escorted them ten miles on the road to Ghazeepore. Many of the civilians hurried away to the same town, reaching that place in terrible plight. The marauders from the neighbouring villages did not fail in their usual course; they plundered the bungalows of the Europeans at Azimghur, or such of them as were left unprotected.

Far more serious were the events at Benares, than at any city or station eastward of it, during the month of June. It would in all probability have been still more deplorable, had not European troops arrived just at that time. Lieutenant-colonel Neill reached Benares on the 3d of June, with sixty men and three officers of the 1st Madras Fusiliers (Europeans), of which regiment five more companies were in the rear, expecting to reach that city in a few days. The regiment had been despatched in great haste by Viscount Canning, in the hope that it would appear before Cawnpore in time to relieve Sir Hugh Wheeler and his unfortunate companions. Neill intended, after a day's repose, to have started from Benares for Cawnpore on the 4th; but he received timely notice from Lieutenant Palliser that the 17th B. N. I. had mutinied at Azimghur; and that the treasure, passing through Azimghur in its way from Goruckpore to Benares (mentioned in the last paragraph), had been plundered by the mutinous sepoys. Brigadier Ponsonby, the commandant at Benares, at once consulted with Colonel Neill concerning the propriety of disarming the 37th regiment Bengal infantry, stationed at that city. Neill recommended this to be done, and done at once. It was then arranged that Neill should make his appearance on parade at five o'clock that same afternoon, accompanied by a hundred and fifty of H.M. 10th foot, sixty of the Madras Fusiliers, and three guns of No. 12 field-battery, with thirty artillerymen. They were to be joined on parade by the Sikh regiment, in which Lieutenant-colonel Gordon placed full confidence, and about seventy of the 13th irregular cavalry. The 37th, suspecting what was intended, ran to the bells of arms, seized and loaded their muskets, and fired upon the Europeans; several men fell wounded, and the brigadier was rendered powerless by a sun-stroke. Thereupon Colonel Neill, assuming the command, made a dash on the native lines. What was now the perplexity of the colonel, and the mortification of Gordon, at seeing the Sikhs halt, waver, turn round, wound several of their officers, fire at the Europeans, and disperse! It was one of those inexplicable movements so frequently exhibited by the native troops. Neill, now distrusting all save the Europeans, opened an effective fire with his three guns, expelled the 37th from their lines, burnt the huts, and then secured his own men and guns in the barrack for the night. Early on the morning of the 5th he sent out parties, and brought in such of the arms and accoutrements of the 37th as had been left behind; he also told off a strong body to bring the Company's treasure from the civil offices to the barracks. Colonel Neill fully believed that if he had delayed his bold proceeding twelve hours, the ill-protected treasury would have been seized by the 37th, and that the numerous European families in the cantonment would have been placed in great peril before he could reach them. The barracks were between the cantonment and the city; and near them was a building called the mint. Into this mint, before going on parade on the 4th, he had arranged that all the families should go for refuge in the event of any disturbance taking place. A few of the Sikhs and of the irregular cavalry remained faithful; and Colonel Neill, with his two hundred and forty Europeans* and these fragments of native regiments, contrived to protect the city, the barracks, the mint, and the cantonment—a trying task, to defend so large an area from mutinous sepoys and troopers, and predatory budmashes. He had to record the deaths of Captain Guise, an army-surgeon, and two privates; and the wounding of about double this number—casualties surprising for their lightness, considering that there were nearly two thousand enemies to contend against altogether. Of the insurgents, not less than two hundred were killed or wounded. It was at once determined to strengthen the neighbouring fort of Chunar or Chunargur; for which duty a small detachment of Europeans was drafted off.

Such were the military operations of the 4th and 5th of June, as told in the brief professional language of Colonel Neill. Various officers and civilians afterwards dwelt more fully on the detailed incidents of those two days. The 13th irregular cavalry and the Sikhs (Loodianah regiment) had been relied on as faithful; and the 37th had greatly distinguished itself in former years in the Punjaub and Afghanistan. This infantry regiment, however, exhibited signs of insubordination on the 1st of the month; and on the 3d, Lieutenant-colonel Gordon, second in command under Ponsonby, told the brigadier that the men of the 37th were plotting with the ruffians of the city. The brigadier, Mr Tucker the commissioner, and Mr Gubbins the judge, thereupon conferred; and it was almost fully determined, even before Colonel Neill's arrival, and before the receipt of disastrous news from Azimghur, that the disbandment of the regiment would be a necessary measure of precaution. The irregular cavalry were stationed at Sultanpore and Benares, and were called in to aid the Europeans and Sikhs in the disarming. A few of the officers, unlike their brethren, distrusted these troopers; and the distrust proved to be well founded. The Sikhs, at the hour of need, fell away as soon as the 37th had seized their arms; and the irregulars were not slow to follow their example; so that, in effect, the insurgents were to the Europeans in the ratio of eight or ten to one. One of the English officers of the 37th has placed upon record a few facts shewing how strangely unexpected was this among many of the Indian outbreaks, by the very men whose position and experience would naturally lead them (one might suppose) to have watched for symptoms. In the first instance, Major Barrett, indignant at the slight which he believed to have been put upon the good and faithful sepoys of the 37th, by the order for disarming, went openly towards the regiment during the struggle at the bells of arms, to shew his confidence in them; but when he saw some of his men firing at him, and others approach him with fixed bayonets, he felt painfully that he must both change his opinions and effect a retreat. Some of the 37th did, however, remain 'true to their salt;' and these, under the major, who had escaped the shots aimed at him, were among the troops sent to guard Chunar Fort. As a second instance: after Captain Guise, of the 13th irregulars, had been shot down by men of the 37th, the brigadier appointed Captain Dodgson

* The exact components of this gallant little band appear to have been as follow:

	Guns.	Officers.	Men.
Artillery,	3	1	30
Queen's troops,	0	3	150
Madras Fusiliers,	0	3	60
	3	7	240

Irrespective of the officers belonging to the mutinous regiments.

to supply his place; but the irregulars, instead of obeying him, flashed their swords, muttered some indistinct observations, fired at him, and at once joined the rebels whom they had been employed and expected to oppose. A third instance, in relation to the Sikhs, shall be given in the words of the officer above adverted to: 'Just as the irregulars were flashing their swords in reply to Captain Dodgson's short address, I was horrified by noticing about a dozen of the Sikhs fire straight forward upon the European soldiers, who were still kneeling and firing into the 37th. The next moment some half-dozen of their muskets were staring me in the face, and a whole tempest of bullets came whizzing towards me. Two passed through my forage-cap, and set my hair on fire; three passed through my trousers, one just grazing my right thigh. I rushed headlong at one of the fellows whom I had noticed more especially aiming at me, but had scarcely advanced three paces when a second volley of bullets saluted me.' This volley brought the officer low; he lay among the wounded, unrecognised for many hours, but was fortunate enough to obtain surgical aid in time to avert a fatal result. Many circumstances afterwards came to light, tending to shew that, had not Neill and Ponsonby taken the initiative when they did, the native troops would probably have risen that same night, and perhaps imitated the Meerut outrages. One of the missionaries at Benares, who escaped to Chunar as soon as the outbreak occurred, said in a letter: 'Some of the 37th have confessed to their officers that they had been told out in bands for our several bungalows, to murder all the Europeans at ten o'clock that night; and that, too, at the time they were volunteering to go to Delhi, and Colonel Spottiswoode was walking about among them in plain clothes with the most implicit confidence.'

The fighting, during this exciting day at Benares, was practically over as soon as the rebels began to retreat; but then the perils of the civilians commenced. More correctly, however, it might be said that the wild confusion began earlier; for while the brief but fierce military struggle was still in progress on the parade-ground, the native guards of the 37th at the treasury, the hospital, the mess-house, the bazaar, and other buildings, broke from their duty, and proceeded to molest the Europeans, with evident hopes of plunder. A Sikh, one Soorut Singh, has been credited with an act which saved many lives and much treasure. He was among the Sikhs of the treasury-guard; and when the rising began, talked to his comrades, and prevented them from rising in mutiny; many civilians, with their families, who had taken refuge in the collector's cutcherry, were saved through this friendly agency; while the treasure was held intact till the following morning, when European troops convoyed it to a place of safety. The Rev. Mr Kennedy, a resident in Benares at that time, states that the faithfulness of these Sikhs, about seventy in number, was deemed so remarkable under the circumstances, that £1000 was given to them as a reward for their safe guardianship of the £60,000 in the treasury. After the discomfiture on the parade-ground, the rebels, maddened by defeat and thirsting for blood, streamed through many of the compounds in the cantonment as they retreated, and fired as they passed, but happily so much at random that little danger was done. Several of the Europeans took refuge in stables and outhouses. Others climbed to the roofs of their houses, and hid behind the parapets. At the house of the commissioner, Mr Tucker, many ladies and children found concealment under straw on the flat roof; while the gentlemen stood by to defend them if danger should approach. Three or four families took boat, and rowed out into the middle of the Ganges, there to remain until news of returning tranquillity should reach them; much booming of cannon and rattling of musketry, much appearance of fire and smoke hovering over city and cantonment, kept the occupants of the boats in constant anxiety; but when victory had declared for the British, and these boat-parties had returned to land, escorts arrived to convey the non-combatants and some of the officers to the mint, in accordance with the arrangement already made. They arrived at that building about midnight. Mr Kennedy described in a letter the scene presented at the mint when he and his family reached it: 'What a scene of confusion and tumult was there. All in front, bands of English soldiers, ready to act at a moment's notice; men, women, and children, high and low, huddled together, wondering at meeting at such a time and in such a place, not knowing where they were to throw themselves down for the night, and altogether looking quite bewildered.' A young officer, throwing into his narrative that light-heartedness which so often bore up men of his class during the troubles of the period, gave a little more detail of the first night and day at the place of refuge: 'I found everybody at the mint, which several had only reached after many adventures. We bivouacked in the large rooms, and slept on the roof—ladies, children, ayahs, and punkah-coolies; officers lying down dressed, and their wives sitting up fanning them. In the compound or enclosure below, there was a little handful of Europeans, perhaps a hundred and fifty in all; others were at the barracks half a mile off. There was a picknicking, gipsifying look about the whole affair, which prevented one from realising that the small congregation were there making a stand for a huge empire, and that their lives were upon the toss-up of the next events.'

During a considerable portion of the month of June, the Europeans made the mint their chief place of residence, the men going out in the daytime to their respective duties, and the ladies and children remaining in their place of refuge. On the 5th, few ventured out of the building, unless heavily armed or strongly escorted. The mint ad a most warlike appearance, bristling with rms, and soon became almost insupportably hot o the numerous persons congregated within it. The hot winds of Benares at that time, nearly midsummer, were terrible for Europeans to bear.

On the 7th, which was Sunday, Mr Kennedy performed divine service at the mint, and a church-missionary at the barracks. Gradually, on subsequent days, whole families would venture out for a few hours at a time, to take a hasty glance at homes which they had so suddenly been called upon to quit; but the mint continued for two or three weeks to be the refuge to which they all looked. As European troops, however, were arriving at Benares every day, on the way to the upper provinces, it soon became practicable, under the energetic Neill, to insure tranquillity in and near that city with a very small number of these so much-valued Queen's troops. The capture and execution of insurgents, under the combined orders of Neill, Tucker, and Gubbins, respectively the commandant, commissioner, and judge, were conducted with such stern promptness as struck terror into the hearts of evildoers. It may be instructive to see in what light Mr Kennedy, as a clergyman, regarded these terrible

Mess-house of the Officers of the 6th Native Infantry at ALLAHABAD.

executions, which are admitted to have been very numerous: 'The gibbet is, I must acknowledge, a standing institution among us at present. There it stands, immediately in front of the flagstaff, with three ropes always attached to it, so that three may be executed at one time. Scarcely a day passes without some poor wretches being hurled into eternity. It is horrible, very horrible! To think of it is enough to make one's blood run cold; but such is the state of things here, that even fine delicate ladies may be heard expressing their joy at the rigour with which the miscreants are treated. The swiftness with which crime is followed by the severest punishment strikes the people with astonishment; it is so utterly foreign to all our modes of procedure, as known to them. Hitherto the process has been very slow, encumbered with forms, and such cases have always been carried to the Supreme Court for final decision; but now, the commissioner of Benares may give commissions to any he chooses (the city being under martial law), to try, decide, and execute on the spot, without any delay and without any reference.'

Jounpoor or Juanpoor, a town about thirty miles northwest of Benares, was one of those which shared with that city the troubles of the month of June. A detachment of the Loodianah Sikh regiment, under Lieutenant Mara, stationed at that place, mutinied most suddenly and unexpectedly on the 5th, within less than an hour after they had shaken hands with some of the European residents as a token of friendly feeling. The men revolted through some impulse that the English in vain endeavoured to understand at the time; but it was afterwards ascertained that some of the mutinous 37th from Benares had been tampering with them. In the first whirl of the tumult, the lieutenant and a civilian were shot down, and the rest of the Europeans sought safety by flight. Information reached Benares, after some days, that the fugitives were in hiding; and a small detachment was at once despatched for their relief. It was now found, as in many other instances, that amid all the brutality and recklessness of the mutineers and budmashes, there were not wanting humane natives in the country villages, ready to succour the distressed; one such, named Hingun Lall, had sheltered and fed the whole of the fugitives from Jounpoor for five days.

There were many stations at which the number of insurgent troops was greater; there were many occasions on which the Europeans suffered more general and prolonged miseries; there were many struggles of more exciting character between the dark-skinned soldiers and the light—but there was not perhaps, throughout the whole history of the Indian mutinies, an outbreak which excited more astonishment than that at Allahabad in the early part of June. It was totally unexpected by the authorities, who had been blinded by protestations of loyalty on the part of the troops. This place (see p. 107) occupies a very important position in relation to Upper India generally; being at the point where the Jumna and Ganges join, where the Benares region ends and the Oude region begins, where the Doab and Bundelcund commence, where the river-traffic and the road-traffic branch out in various directions, and where the great railway will one day have a central station. As stated in a former page, the 6th Bengal Native Infantry, stationed at Allahabad, voluntarily came forward and offered their services to march against the Delhi mutineers. For this demonstration they were thanked by their officers, who felt gratified that, amid so much desertion, fidelity should make itself apparent in this quarter. Rather from a vague undefined uneasiness, than from any suspicion of this particular regiment, the Europeans at Allahabad had for some time been in uneasiness; there had been panics in the city; there had been much patrolling and watching; and the ladies had been looking anxiously to the fort as a place of refuge, whither most of them had taken up their abode at night, returning to their homes in the cantonment or the city in the daytime. From Benares, Lucknow, or other places, they apprehended danger—but not from within.

It was on the 5th of June that Colonel Simpson, of the 6th regiment, received Viscount Canning's instructions to thank his men for their loyal offer to march and fight against the rebels at Delhi; and it was on the same day that news reached Allahabad, probably by telegraph, of the occurrences at Benares on the previous day, and of the possible arrival of some of the insurgents from that place. The officers still continued to trust the 6th regiment, not only in virtue of the recent protestation of fidelity by the men but on account of their general good conduct indeed, this was one of the most trusted regiments in the whole native army. Nevertheless instructions were given to arm the civilians as well as the military, and to prepare for making a good stand at the fort. Many civilians, formed into a militia, under the commandant of the garrison, slept in the fort that night, or relieved each other as sentinels at the ramparts. There were at that time in the fort, besides the women and children, about thirty invalid artillerymen, under Captain Hazelwood; a few commissariat and magazine sergeants; about a hundred volunteer civilians; four hundred Sikhs, of the Ferozpore regiment, under Lieutenant Brasyer; and eighty men of the 6th regiment, guarding the main gate. Several Europeans with their families, thinking no danger nigh, slept outside the fort that night. Two companies of the native regiment under three English officers, and two guns under Captain Harward, were sent to guard the bridge of boats across the Ganges in the direction of Benares. Captain Alexander, with two squadrons of the 3d regiment Oude irregular cavalry, was posted in the Alopee Bagh, a camping-ground commanding the roads to the station. The main body of the 6th remained in their lines, three miles from the fort. All proceeded quietly until about nine o'clock on the evening of the 6th of June; when, to the inexpressible astonishment and dismay of the officers, the native regiment rose in revolt. The two guns were seized by them at the bridge-head, and Harward had to run for his life. In the cantonment the officers were at mess, full of confidence in their trusted troops, when the sepoys sounded the alarm bugle, as if to bring them on parade; those who rushed out were at once aimed at, and nearly all shot dead; while no fewer than nine young ensigns, mere boys who had just entered on the career of soldiering, were bayoneted in the mess-room itself. It was a cruel and bloody deed, for the poor youths had but recently arrived, and were in hostility with none. Captain Alexander, when he heard of the rising, hastened off to the lines with a few of his troopers; but he was caught in an ambush by a body of the sepoys, and at once shot down. The sepoys, joined by released prisoners and habitual plunderers, then commenced a scene of murder and devastation in all directions; Europeans were shot wherever they could be seen; the few English women who had not been so fortunate as to seek refuge in the fort, were grossly outraged before being put to death; the telegraph wires were cut; the boats on the river were seized; the treasury was plundered; the houses of native bankers, as well as those of European residents, were pillaged; and wild licence reigned everywhere. Terrible were the deeds recorded—a whole family roasted alive; persons killed by the slow process of cutting off in succession ears, nose, fingers, feet, &c.; others chopped to pieces; children tossed on bayonets before their mother's eyes.

An affecting incident is related of one of the unfortunate young officers so ruthlessly attacked at the mess-house. An ensign, only sixteen years of age, who was left for dead among the rest, escaped in the darkness to a neighbouring ravine. Here he found a stream, the waters of which sustained his life for four days and nights. Although desperately wounded, he contrived to raise himself into a tree at night-time, for protection from wild beasts. On the fifth day he was discovered, and dragged by the brutal insurgents before one of their leaders. There he found another prisoner, a Christian catechist, formerly a Mohammedan, whom the sepoys were endeavouring to terrify and torment into a renunciation of Christianity. The firmness of the native was giving way as he knelt before his persecutors; but the boy-officer, after anxiously watching him for a short time said: 'Oh, my friend, come what may, do not deny the Lord Jesus!' Just at this moment the arrival of Colonel Neill and the Madras Fusiliers (presently to be noticed) at Allahabad was announced; the ruffians made off; the poor catechist's life was saved; but the gentle-spirited young ensign sank under the wounds and privations he had endured. When this incident became known through the medium of the public journals, the father of the young officer, town-clerk of Evesham, told how brief had been the career thus cut short. Arthur Marcus Hill Cheek had left England so recently as the 20th of March preceding, to commence the life of a soldier; he arrived at Calcutta in May, was appointed to the 6th native regiment, reached Allahabad on the 19th of the same month, and was shot down by his own men eighteen days afterwards.

The inmates of the fort naturally suffered an agony of suspense on the night of the 6th. When they heard the bugle, and the subsequent firing, they believed the mutineers had arrived from Benares; and as the intensity of the sound varied from time to time, so did they picture in imagination the varying fortunes of the two hypothetical opposing forces—the supposed insurgents from the east, and the supposed loyal 6th regiment. Soon were they startled by a revelation of the real truth—that the firing came from their own trusted sepoys. The Europeans in the fort, recovering from their wonder and dismay, were fortunately enabled to disarm the eighty sepoys at the gate through the energy of Lieutenant Brasyer; and it was then found that these fellows had loaded and capped their muskets, ready to turn out. Five officers succeeded in entering during the night, three of them naked, having had to swim the Ganges. For twelve days did the Europeans remain within the fort, not daring to emerge for many hours at a time, lest the four hundred Sikhs should prove faithless in the hour of greatest need. The chief streets of the city are about half a mile from the fort; and during several days and nights troops of rioters were to be seen rushing from place to place, plundering and burning. Day and night the civilians manned the ramparts, succeeding each other in regular watches—now nearly struck down by the hot blazing sun; now pouring forth shot and shell upon such of the insurgents as were within reach. The civilians or volunteers formed themselves into three corps; one of which, called the Flagstaff Division, was joined by about twenty railway men—sturdy fellows who had suffered like the rest, and were not slow to avenge themselves on the mutineers whenever opportunity offered. After a time, the volunteers sallied forth into the city with the Sikhs, and had several skirmishes in the streets with the insurgents—delighted at the privilege of quitting for a few hours the hot crowded fort, even to fight. It was by degrees ascertained that conspiracy had been going on in the city before the actual outbreak occurred. The standard of insurrection was unfurled by a native unknown to the Europeans; some supposed him to be a moulvie, or Mohammedan religious teacher; but whatever may have been his former position, he now announced himself as viceroy of the King of Delhi. He quickly collected about him three or four thousand rebels, sepoys and others, and displayed the green flag that constitutes the Moslem symbol. The head-quarters of this self-appointed chieftain were in the higher part of the city, at the old Mohammedan gardens of Sultan Khoosroo; there the prisoners taken by the mutineers were confined—among whom were the native Christian teachers belonging to the Rev. Mr Hay's mission.

The movements of Colonel Neill must now be traced. No sooner did this gallant and energetic officer hear of the occurrences at Allahabad, than he proceeded to effect at that place what he had already done at Benares—re-establish English authority by a prompt, firm, and stern course of action. The distance between the two cities being about seventy-five miles, he quickly made the necessary travelling arrangements. He left Benares on the evening of the 9th, accompanied by one officer and forty-three men of the Madras Fusiliers. The horses being nearly all taken off the road, he found much difficulty in bringing in the dâk-carriages containing the men; but this and all other obstacles he surmounted. He found the country between Mirzapore and Allahabad infested with bands of plunderers, the villages deserted, and none of the authorities remaining. Major Stephenson, with a hundred more men, set out from Benares on the same evening as Neill; but his bullock-vans were still more slow in progress; and his men suffered much from exposure to heat during the journey. Neill reached Allahabad on the afternoon of the 11th. He found the fort almost completely invested; the bridge of boats over the Ganges in the hands of a mob, and partly broken; and the neighbouring villages swarming with insurgents. By cautious manœuvring at the end of the Benares road, he succeeded in obtaining boats which conveyed him and his handful of men over to the fort. He at once assumed command, and arranged that on the following morning the enemy should be driven out of the villages, and the bridge of boats recaptured. Accordingly, on the morning of the 12th he opened fire with several round-shot, and then attacked the rebels in the village of Deeragunge with a detachment of Fusiliers and Sikhs: this was effectively accomplished, and a safe road opened for the approach of Major Stephenson's detachment on the evening of that day. On the 13th the insurgents were driven out of the village of Kydgunge. Neill had now a strange enemy to combat within the fort itself—drunkenness and relaxed discipline. The Sikhs, during their sallies into the city before his arrival, had gained entrance into some of the deserted warehouses of wine-merchants and others in the town, had brought away large quantities of beverage, and had sold these to the European soldiers within the fort—at four *annas* (sixpence) per bottle for wine, spirits, or beer indiscriminately; drunkenness and disorganisation followed, requiring determined measures on the part of the commandant. He bought all the remaining liquors obtainable, for commissariat use; and kept a watchful eye on the stores still remaining in the warehouses in the town. Neill saw reason for distrusting the Sikhs; they had remained faithful up to that time, but nevertheless exhibited symptoms which required attention. As soon as possible, he got them out of the fort altogether, and placed them at various posts in the city where they might still render service if they chose to remain faithful. His opinion of the native troops was sufficiently expressed in this passage in one of his dispatches: 'I felt that Allahabad was really safe when every native soldier and sentry was out of the fort; and as long as I command I shall not allow one to be on duty in it.' Nothing can be more striking than the difference of views held by Indian officers on this point; some distrusted the natives from the first, while others maintained faith in them to a very disastrous extent.

From the time when Neill obtained the upper-hand in Allahabad, he was incessantly engaged in chastising the insurgents in the neighbourhood. He sent a steamer up the Jumna on the 15th, with a howitzer under Captain Harward, and twenty fusiliers under Lieutenant Arnold; and these worked much execution among the rebels on the banks. A combined body of fusiliers, Sikhs, and irregular cavalry made an attack on the villages of Kydgunge and Mootingunge, on the banks of the Jumna, driving out the insurgents harboured there, and mowing them down in considerable numbers. On subsequent days, wherever Neill heard of the presence of insurgents in any of the surrounding villages, he at once attacked them; and great terror seized the hearts of the malcontents in the city at the celerity with which guns and gibbets were set to work. On the 18th he sent eighty fusiliers and a hundred Sikhs up the river in a steamer, to destroy the Patan village of Durriabad, and the Meewattie villages of Sydabad and Russelpore. It was not merely in the villages that these active operations were necessary; a large number of the mutinous sepoys went off towards Delhi on the day after the outbreak, leaving the self-elected chief to manage his rabble-army as he liked; and it was against this rabble that many of the expeditions were planned. The city suffered terribly from this double infliction; for after the spoliation and burning effected by the marauders, the English employed cannon-balls and musketry to drive those marauders out of the streets and houses; and Allahabad thus became little other than a mass of blackened ruins. Colonel Neill organised a body of irregular cavalry by joining Captain Palliser's detachment of the 13th irregulars with the few men of Captain Alexander's corps still remaining true to their salt. A force of about a hundred and sixty Madras Fusiliers started from Benares on the 13th, under Captain Fraser; he was joined on the road by Captain Palliser's detachment of troopers, just adverted to, of about eighty men, and the two officers then proceeded towards Allahabad. They found the road almost wholly in the hands of rebels and plunderers; but by fighting, hanging, and burning, they cleared a path for themselves, struck terror into the evildoers, and recovered much of the Company's treasure that had fallen into hostile hands. It is sad to read of six villages being reduced to ashes during this one march; but stringent measures were absolutely necessary to a restoration of order and obedience. Fraser and Palliser reached Allahabad on the 18th, and their arrival enabled Neill to prosecute two objects which he had at heart—the securing of Allahabad, and the gradual collection of a force that might march to the relief of poor Sir Hugh Wheeler and the other beleaguered Europeans at Cawnpore. During these varied operations, the officers and men were often exposed during the daytime to a heat so tremendous that nothing but an intense interest in their work could have kept them up. 'If I can keep from fever,' wrote one of them, 'I sha'nt care; for excitement enables one to stand the sun and fatigue wonderfully. At any other time the sun would have knocked us down like dogs; but all this month we have been out in the middle of the day, toiling like coolies, yet I have never been better in my life—such an appetite!' To meet temporary exigencies, the church, the government offices, the barracks, the bungalows—all were placed at the disposal of the English troops, as fast as they arrived up from Calcutta. These reinforcements, during the second half of the month, consisted chiefly of detachments of her Majesty's 64th, 78th, and 84th foot. The peaceful inhabitants began to return to the half-ruined city, shattered houses were hastily rebuilt or repaired, trade gradually revived, bullocks and carriages arrived in considerable number, supplies were laid in, the weather became cooler, the cholera abated, and Colonel Neill found himself enabled to look forward with much confidence to the future. The fort, during almost the whole of the month, had been very much crowded, insomuch that the inmates suffered greatly from heat and cholera. Two steam-boat loads of women and children were therefore sent down the river towards Calcutta; and all the non-combatants left the fort, to reoccupy such of their residences as had escaped demolition. Some of the European soldiers were tented on the glacis; others took up quarters in a tope of trees near the dâk-bungalow; lastly, a hospital was fitted up for the cholera patients.

With the end of June came tranquillity both to Benares and to Allahabad, chiefly through the determined measures adopted by Colonel Neill; and then he planned an expedition, the best in his power, for Cawnpore—the fortunes of which will come under our notice in due time.

Notes.

The Oude Royal Family.—When the news reached England that the deposed King of Oude had been arrested at Calcutta, in the way described in the present chapter, on suspicion of complicity with the mutineers, his relations, who had proceeded to London to appeal against the annexation of Oude by the Company, prepared a petition filled with protestations of innocence, on his part and on their own. The petition was presented to the House of Lords by Lord Campbell, though not formally received owing to some defect in phraseology. A memorial to Queen Victoria was couched in similar form. The petition and memorial ran as follows:

'The petition of the undersigned Jenabi Auliah Tajara Begum, the Queen-mother of Oude; Mirza Mohammud Hamid Allie, eldest son and heir-apparent of his Majesty the King of Oude; and Mirza Mohammud Jowaad Allie Sekunder Hushmut Bahadoor, next brother of his Majesty the King of Oude, sheweth:

'That your petitioners have heard with sincere regret the tidings which have reached the British Kingdom of disaffection prevailing among the native troops in India; and that they desire, at the earliest opportunity, to give public expression to that solemn assurance which they some time since conveyed to her Majesty's government, that the fidelity and attachment to Great Britain which has ever characterised the royal family of Oude continues unchanged and unaffected by these deplorable events, and that they remain, as Lord Dalhousie, the late governor-general of India, emphatically declared them, "a royal race, ever faithful and true to their friendship with the British nation."

'That in the midst of this great public calamity, your petitioners have sustained their own peculiar cause of pain and sorrow in the intelligence which has reached them, through the public papers, that his Majesty the King of Oude has been subjected to restraint at Calcutta, and deprived of the means of communicating even with your petitioners, his mother, son, and brother.

'That your petitioners desire unequivocally and solemnly to assure her Majesty and your lordships, that if his Majesty the King of Oude has been suspected of any complicity in the recent disastrous occurrences, such suspicion is not only wholly and absolutely unfounded, but is directed against one, the whole tenor of whose life, character, and conduct directly negatives all such imputations. Your petitioners recall to the recollection of your lordships the facts relating to the dethronement of the King of Oude, as set forth in the petition presented to the House of Commons by Sir Fitzroy Kelly on the 25th of May last, that when resistance might have been made, and was even anticipated by the British general, the King of Oude directed his guards and troops to lay aside their arms, and that when it was announced to him that the territories of Oude were to be vested for ever in the Honourable East India Company, the king, instead of offering resistance to the British government, after giving vent to his feelings in a burst of grief, descended from his throne, declaring his determination to seek for justice at her Majesty's throne, and from the parliament of England.

'That since their resort to this country, in obedience to his Majesty's commands, your petitioners have received communications from his Majesty which set forth the hopes and aspirations of his heart; that those communications not only negative all supposition of his Majesty's personal complicity in any intrigues, but fill the minds of your petitioners with the profound conviction that his Majesty would feel, with your petitioners, the greatest grief and pain at the events which have occurred. And your petitioners desire to declare to your lordships, and to assure the British nation, that although suffering, in common with his heart-broken family, from the wrongs inflicted on them, from the humiliations of a state of exile, and their loss of home, authority, and country, the King of Oude relies only on the justice of his cause, appeals only to her Majesty's throne and to the parliament of Great Britain, and disdains to use the arm of the rebel and the traitor to maintain the right he seeks to vindicate.

'Your petitioners therefore pray of your lordships that, in the exercise of your authority, you will cause justice to be done to his Majesty the King of Oude, and that it may be forthwith explicitly made known to his Majesty and to your petitioners wherewith he is charged, and by whom, and on what authority, so that the King of Oude may have full opportunity of refuting and disproving the unjust suspicions and calumnies of which he is now the helpless victim. And your petitioners further pray that the King of Oude may be permitted freely to correspond with your petitioners in this country, so that they may also have opportunity of vindicating here the character and conduct of their sovereign and relative, of establishing his innocence of any offence against the crown of England, or the British government or people, and of shewing that, under every varying phase of circumstance, the royal family of Oude have continued steadfast and true to their friendship with the British nation.

'And your petitioners will ever pray, &c.'

Some time after the presentation of this petition and memorial, a curious proof was afforded of the complexity and intrigue connected with the family affairs of the princes of India. A statement having gone abroad to the effect that a son of the King of Oude had escaped from Lucknow during the troubles of the Revolt, a native representative of the family in London sought to set the public mind right on the matter. He stated that the king had had only three legitimate sons; that one of these, being an idiot, was confined to the zenana or harem at Lucknow; that the second died of small-pox when twelve years of age; that the third was the prince who had come to London with the queen-mother; and that if any son of the king had really escaped from Lucknow, he must have been illegitimate, a boy about ten years old. This communication was signed by Mahmoud Museehooddeen, residing at Paddington, and designating himself 'Accredited Agent to his Majesty the King of Oude.' Two days afterwards the same journal contained a letter from Colonel R. Ouseley, also residing in the metropolis, asserting that *he* was 'Agent in Chief to the King of Oude,' and that Museehooddeen had assumed a title to which he had no right.

Castes and Creeds in the Indian Army.—The Indian officers being much divided in opinion concerning the relative insubordination of Mohammedans and Hindoos in the native regiments, it may be useful to record here the actual components of one Bengal infantry regiment, so far as concerns creed and caste. The information is obtained from an official document relating to the cartridge grievance, before the actual Revolt began.

The 34th regiment Bengal native infantry, just before its disbandment at Barrackpore in April, comprised 1089 men, distributed as follows:

	Subadar-major.	Subadars.	Jemadars.	Havildars.	Naiks.	Drummers.	Sepoys.	Total.
Brahmin Caste,	1	2	4	24	10	..	294	335
Lower Castes, .	..	5	5	25	26	1	406	468
Christians, .	..	..	..	..	..	10	2	12
Mussulmans, .	..	2	1	12	24	8	153	200
Sikhs, . .	..	..	..	..	..	..	74	74
	1	9	10	61	60	19	929	1089

The portion of this regiment present at Barrackpore—the rest being at Chittagong—when the mutinous proceedings took place, numbered 584, thus classified under four headings:

	Subadar-major.	Subadars.	Jemadars.	Havildars.	Naiks.	Drummers.	Sepoys.	Total.
Brahmin Caste,	1	2	1	12	5	..	175	196
Lower Castes, .	..	1	4	13	14	1	193	226
Mussulmans,	..	1	..	7	14	4	85	111
Sikhs, . .	..	..	..	..	..	..	51	51
	1	4	5	32	33	5	504	584

When 414 of these men were dismissed from the Company's service, their religions appeared as follows:

	Commissioned Officers.	Non-commissioned Officers.	Sepoys.	Total.
Brahmin Caste,	2	12	135	149
Lower Castes,	4	19	150	173
Mussulmans, .	..	14	49	63
Sikhs, .	..	..	29	29
	6	45	363	414

It is not clearly stated how many Rajpoots, or men of the military caste, were included in the Hindoos who were not Brahmins.

If the regiment thus tabulated had been cavalry, instead of infantry, the preponderance, as implied in Chapter I., would have been wholly on the side of the Mussulmans.

Sikh Cavalry.

CHAPTER X.

OUDE, ROHILCUND, AND THE DOAB: JUNE.

THE course of events now brings us again to that turbulent country, Oude, which proved itself to be hostile to the British in a degree not expected by the authorities at Calcutta. They were aware, it is true, that Oude had long furnished the chief materials for the Bengal native army; but they could not have anticipated, or at least did not, how close would be the sympathy between those troops and the Oude irregulars in the hour of tumult. Only seven months before the beginning of the Revolt, and about the same space of time after the formal annexation, a remarkable article on Indian Army Reform appeared in the *Calcutta Review*, attributed to Sir Henry Lawrence; in which he commented freely on the government proceedings connected with the army of Oude. He pointed out how great was the number of daring reckless men in that country; how large had been the army of the king before his deposition; how numerous were the small forts held by zemindars and petty chieftains, and guarded by nearly sixty thousand men; how perilous it was to raise a new British-Oudian army, even though a small one, solely from the men of the king's disbanded regiments; how serious was the fact that nearly a hundred thousand disbanded warlike natives were left without employment; how prudent it would have been to send Oudians into the Punjaub, and Punjaubees into Oude; and how necessary was an increase in the number of British troops. The truth of these comments was not appreciated until Sir Henry himself was ranked among those who felt the full consequence of the state of things to which the comments referred. Oude was full of zemindars, possessing considerable resources of various kinds, having their retainers, their mud-forts, their arsenals, their treasures. These zemindars, aggrieved not so much by the annexation of their country, as by the manner in which territorial law-proceedings were made to affect the tenure of their estates, shewed sympathy with the mutineers almost from the first. The remarks of Mr Edwards, collector at Boodayoun, on this point, have already been adverted to (p. 115). The zemindars did not, as a class, display the sanguinary and vindictive passions so terribly evident in the reckless soldiery; still they held to a belief that a successful revolt might restore to them their former position and influence as landowners; and hence the formidable difficulties opposed by them to the military movements of the British.

Sir Henry Lawrence, as chief authority both military and civil in Oude, found himself very awkwardly imperiled at Lucknow in the early days of June. Just as the previous month closed, nearly all the native troops raised the standard of rebellion (see p. 96); the 13th, 48th, and 71st infantry, and the 7th cavalry, all betrayed the infection, though in different degrees; and of the seven hundred men of these four regiments who still remained faithful, he did not know how many he could trust even for a single day. The treasury received his anxious attention, and misgivings arose in his mind concerning the various districts around the capital, with their five millions of inhabitants. Soon he had the bitterness of learning that his rebellious troops, who had fled towards Seetapoor, had excited their brethren at that place to revolt. The Calcutta authorities were from that day very ill informed of the proceedings at Lucknow; for the telegraph wires were cut, and the insurgents stopped all dâks and messengers on the road. About the middle of the month, Colonel Neill, at Allahabad, received a private letter from Lawrence, sent by some secret agency, announcing that Seetapoor and Shahjehanpoor were in the hands of the rebels; that Seerora, Beraytch, and Fyzabad, were in like condition; and that mutinous regiments from all these places, as well as from Benares and Jounpoor, appeared to be approaching Lucknow on some combined plan of operations. He was strengthening his position at the Residency, but looked most anxiously for aid, which Neill was quite unable to afford him. Again, it became known to the authorities at Benares that Lawrence, on the 19th, still held his position at Lucknow; that he had had eight deaths by cholera; and that he was considering whether, aid from Cawnpore or Allahabad being unattainable, he could obtain a few reinforcements by steamer up the Gogra from Dinapoor. Another letter, but without date, reached the chief-magistrate of Benares, to the effect that Lawrence had got rid of most of the remaining native troops, by paying them their due, and giving them leave of absence for three months; he evidently felt disquietude at the presence even of the apparently faithful sepoys in his place of refuge, so bitterly had he experienced the hollowness of all protestations on their part. He had been very ill, and a provisional council had been appointed in case his health should further give way. Although the Residency was the stronghold, the city and cantonment also were still under British control: a fort called the Muchee Bhowan, about three-quarters of a mile from the Residency, and consisting of a strong, turreted, castellated building, was held by two hundred and twenty-five Europeans with three guns. The cantonment was northeast of the Residency, on the opposite side of the river, over which were two bridges of approach. Sir Henry had already lessened from eight to four the number of buildings or posts where the troops were stationed—namely, the Residency, the Muchee Bhowan, a strong post between these two, and the dâk-bungalow between the Residency and the cantonment; but after the mutiny, he depended chiefly on the Residency and the Muchee Bhowan. News, somewhat more definite in character, was conveyed in a letter written by Sir Henry on the 20th of June. So completely were the roads watched, that he had not received a word of information from Cawnpore, Allahabad, Benares, or any other important place throughout the whole month down to that date; he knew not what progress was being made by the rebels, beyond the region of which Lucknow was more immediately the centre; he still held the fort, city, Residency, and cantonment, but was terribly threatened on all sides by large bodies of mutineers. On the 27th he wrote another letter to the authorities at Allahabad, one of the very few (out of a large number despatched) that succeeded in reaching their destination. This letter was still full of heart, for he told of the Residency and the Muchee Bhowan being still held by him in force; of cholera being on the decrease; of his supplies being adequate for two months and a half; and of his power to 'hold his own.' On the other hand, he felt assured that at that moment Lucknow was the only place throughout the whole of Oude where British influence was paramount; and that he dared not leave the city for twenty-four hours without danger of losing all his advantages. His sanguine, hopeful spirit shone out in the midst of all his trials; he declared that with one additional European regiment, and a hundred artillerymen, he could re-establish British supremacy in Oude; and he added, in a sportive tone, which shewed what estimate he formed of some, at least, of the contingent corps, 'a thousand Europeans, a thousand Goorkhas, and a thousand Sikhs, with eight or ten guns, will thrash anything.' The Sikhs were irregulars raised in the Punjaub; and throughout the contests arising out of the Revolt, their fidelity towards the government was seldom placed in doubt.

The last day of June was a day of sad omen to the English in Lucknow. On the evening of the 29th, information arrived that a rebel force of six or seven thousand men was encamped eight miles distant on the Fyzabad road, near the Kookra Canal. Lawrence thereupon determined to attack them on the following day. He started at six o'clock on the morning of the 30th, with about seven hundred men and eleven guns.* Misled, either by accident or design, by informants on the road, he suddenly fell into an ambush of the enemy, assembled in considerable force near Chinhut. Manfully struggling against superior numbers, Lawrence looked forward confidently to victory; but just at the most critical moment, the Oude artillerymen proved traitors—overturning their six guns into ditches, cutting the traces of the horses, and then going over to the enemy. Completely outflanked, exposed to a terrible fire on all sides, weakened by the defection, having now few guns to use, and being almost without ammunition, Sir Henry saw that retreat was imperative. A disastrous retreat it was, or rather a complete rout; the heat was fearful, the confusion was dire; and the officers and men fell rapidly, to rise no more. Colonel Case, of H.M. 32d, receiving a mortal wound, was immediately succeeded by Captain Steevens; he in like manner soon fell, and was succeeded by Captain Mansfield, who escaped the day's perils, but afterwards died of cholera.

Sir Henry Lawrence now found himself in a grave difficulty. The English position at Lucknow needed all the strengthening he could impart to it. He had held, as already explained, not only the Residency, but the fort of Muchee Bhowan and other posts. The calamity of the 30th, however, having weakened him too much to garrison all, or even more than one, he removed the troops, and then blew up the Muchee Bhowan, at midnight on the 1st of July, sending 240 barrels of gunpowder and 3,000,000 ball-cartridges into the air. From that hour the whole of the English made the Residency their stronghold. Later facts rendered it almost certain that, if this abandonment and explosion had not taken place, scarcely a European would have lived to tell the tale of the subsequent miseries at Lucknow. By incessant exertions, he collected in the Residency six months' food for a thousand persons. The last hour of the gallant man was, however, approaching. A shell, sent by the insurgents, penetrated into his room on this

* *Artillery:* 4 guns, horse light field-battery; 6 guns, Oude field-battery; and 1 8-inch howitzer. *Cavalry:* 120 troopers of 1st, 2d, and 3d Oude irregular cavalry; and 40 volunteer cavalry, under Captain Radcliffe. *Infantry:* 300 of H.M. 32d foot; 150 of 13th native infantry; 60 of the 48th native infantry; and 20 of the 71st.

day; his officers advised him to remove to another spot, but he declined the advice; and on the next day, the 2d of July, another shell, entering and bursting within the same room, gave him a mortal wound. Knowing his last hour was approaching, Sir Henry appointed Brigadier Inglis his successor in military matters, and Major Banks his successor as chief-commissioner of Oude.

Grief, deep and earnest, took possession of every breast in the Residency, when, on the 4th of July, it was announced that the good and great Sir Henry Lawrence had breathed his last. He was a man of whom no one doubted; like his gifted brother, Sir John, he had the rare power of drawing to himself the respect and love of those by whom he was surrounded, almost without exception. 'Few men,' said Brigadier Inglis, at a later date, 'have ever possessed to the same extent the power which he enjoyed of winning the hearts of all those with whom he came in contact, and thus insuring the warmest and most zealous devotion for himself and the government which he served. All ranks possessed such confidence in his judgment and his fertility of resource, that the news of his fall was received throughout the garrison with feelings of consternation only second to the grief which was inspired in the hearts of all by the loss of a public benefactor and a warm personal friend. . . . . I trust the government of India will pardon me for having attempted, however imperfectly, to portray this great and good man. In him every good and deserving soldier lost a friend and a chief capable of discriminating, and ever on the alert to reward merit, no matter how humble the sphere in which it was exhibited.' Such was the soldier whom all men delighted to honour,* and to whom the graceful compliment was once paid, that 'Sir Henry Lawrence enjoyed the rare felicity of transcending all rivalry except that of his illustrious brother.'

How the overcrowded Residency at Lucknow bore all the attacks directed against it; how the inmates, under the brave and energetic Inglis, held on against heat, disease, cannon-balls, thirst, hunger, and fatigue; how and by whom they were liberated—will come for notice in proper course.

The other districts of Oude fell one by one into the hands of the insurgents. The narratives subsequently given by such English officers as were fortunate enough to escape the perils of those evil days, bore a general resemblance one to another; inasmuch as they told of faith in native troops being rudely broken, irresolute loyalty dissolving into confirmed hostility, treasuries of Company's rupees tempting those who might otherwise possibly have been true to their salt, military officers and their wives obliged to flee for succour to Nynee Tal or some other peaceful station, the families of civilians suddenly thrown homeless upon the world, and blood and plunder marking the footsteps of the marauders who followed the example set by the rebellious sepoys and troopers. A few examples will suffice to illustrate the general character of these outbreaks.

The mutiny at Fyzabad, besides being attended with a sad loss of life, was note-worthy for certain peculiarities in the tactics of the insurgents—a kind of cool audacity not always exhibited in other instances. A brief description will show the position and character of this city. In a former chapter (p. 83) it was explained that Oude or Ayodha, the city that gave name to the province, is very ancient as a Hindoo capital, but has become poor and ruinous in recent times; and that the fragments of many of its old structures were employed in building Fyzabad, the Mohammedan Ayodha, nearly adjoining it on the southwest. It was scarcely more than a hundred and thirty years ago that the foundation of Fyzabad was established, by Saadut Ali Khan, the first nawab-vizier of Oude; its advance in prosperity was rapid; but since the selection of Lucknow as the capital in 1775, Fyzabad has fallen in dignity; the chief merchants and bankers have migrated to Lucknow, and the remaining inhabitants are mostly poor.

On the 3d of June, rumours circulated in Fyzabad that the mutinous 17th regiment B. N. I. was approaching from Azimghur. Colonel Lennox, the military commandant, at once conferred with the other officers, and formed a plan for defending the place. The immediate alarm died away. On the 7th, however, renewed information led the colonel to propose an advance to Surooj-khoond, a place about five miles away, to repel the mutineers before they could reach Fyzabad. The native troops objected to go out, on the plea of disinclination to leave their families and property behind; but they promised to fight valiantly in the cantonment if necessary, and many of them shook hands with him in token of fidelity. The evening of the 8th revealed the hypocrisy of this display. The native troops, cavalry, infantry, and artillery, joined in a demonstration which rendered all

* 'Every boy has read, and many living men still remember, how the death of Nelson was felt by all as a deep personal affliction. Sir Henry Lawrence was less widely known, and his deeds were in truth of less magnitude than those of the great sea-captain; but never probably was a public man within the sphere of his reputation more ardently beloved. Sir Henry Lawrence had that rare and happy faculty (which a man in almost every other respect unlike him, Sir Charles Napier, is said also to have possessed) of attaching to himself every one with whom he came in contact. He had that gift which is never acquired, a gracious, winning, noble manner; rough and ready as he was in the field, his manner in private life had an indescribable charm of frankness, grace, and even courtly dignity. He had that virtue which Englishmen instinctively and characteristically love—a lion-like courage. He had that fault which Englishmen so readily forgive, and when mixed with what are felt to be its naturally concomitant good qualities, they almost admire—a hot and impetuous temper; he had in overflowing measure that Godlike grace which even the base revere and the good acknowledge as the crown of virtue—the grace of charity. No young officer ever sat at Sir Henry's table without learning to think more kindly of the natives; no one, young or old, man or woman, ever heard Sir Henry speak of the European soldier, or ever visited the Lawrence Asylum, without being excited to a nobler and truer appreciation of the real extent of his duty towards his neighbour. He was one of the few distinguished Anglo-Indians who had attained to something like an English reputation in his lifetime. In a few years, his name will be familiar to every reader of Indian history; but for the present it is in India that his memory will be most deeply cherished; it is by Anglo-Indians that any eulogy on him will be best appreciated, it is by them that the institutions which he founded and maintained will be fostered as a monument to his memory.'—*Fraser's Magazine*, No. 336.

the officers powerless; every officer was, in effect, made a prisoner, and placed under armed guard for the night; two tried to escape, but were fired at and brought back. The leader of the mutiny, Dhuleep Singh, subadar-major of the 22d regiment, came to Colonel Lennox in the morning, and told him plainly that he and the other officers must yield to the course of circumstances; that boats would be provided to take them down the river Gogra towards Dinapoor, but that he would not guarantee their safety after once they had embarked. There was a cool impudence about the proceeding, unlike the wild confusion exhibited at many of the scenes of outbreak. A moulvie, who had been imprisoned in the quarter-guard for a disturbance created in the city, and who had just been liberated by the mutineers, sent the sub-assistant surgeon to Colonel Lennox with a message; thanking him for kindnesses received during the imprisonment, and requesting that the colonel's full-dress regimentals might be sent to the moulvie. The native surgeon begged pardon for his change of allegiance; urging that times were altered, and that he must now obey the mutineers. There was something more than mere effrontery, however, in the proceedings of these insurgents;* there was a subordination amid insubordination. 'The men,' said one of the narrators, 'guarded their officers and their bungalows after mutinying, placed sentries over the magazines and all public property, and sent out pickets to prevent the towns-people and servants from looting. They held a council of war, in which the cavalry proposed to kill the officers; but the 22d, objecting to this, informed their officers that they would be allowed to leave, and might take with them their private arms and property, but no public property—as that all belonged to the King of Oude.'

Let us briefly trace the course of some of the European fugitives. Colonel Lennox, powerless to resist, gave up his regimentals, and prepared for a melancholy boat-departure with his wife and daughter. They were escorted to the banks of the Gogra, and pushed off on their voyage. From two in the afternoon on the 8th of June, until nearly midnight, their boat descended the stream—often in peril from sentries and scouts on shore, but befriended by two sepoys who had been sent to protect them for a short distance. Much care and manœuvring were required to effect a safe passage near the spot where the mutinous 17th regiment was encamped; for it now became manifest that the 22d had in effect sold the fugitives to the other corps. Early on the following morning, information received on shore rendering evident the danger of a further boat-voyage, the houseless wanderers, leaving in the boat the few fragments of property they had brought away from Fyzabad, set out on foot towards Goruckpore. With nothing but the clothes on their backs, the family began their weary flight. After stopping under trees and by the side of wells to rest occasionally, they walked until the heat of day rendered necessary a longer pause. By a narrow chance they avoided being dragged to the camp of the 17th regiment, by a trooper who professed to have been offered two hundred rupees for the head of each member of the family. A friendly chieftain, one Meer Mohammed Hossein Khan, came to their rescue just at the moment of greatest peril. One of the retainers of this man, however, more disposed for enmity than amity, spoke to the colonel with great bitterness and fierceness of manner, shewing that the prevalent rumours had made a deep impression in Oude; he expressed a longing to shoot the English, 'who had come to take away their caste, and make them Christians.' Meer Mohammed rebuked this man for saying that a stable would do to shelter the refugees, for that he was prepared 'to kill them like dogs.' The fugitives were taken to a small fort, one of the numerous class lately adverted to, where the zemindars and petty chieftains maintained a kind of feudal or clannish independence. On the second day, the danger to sheltered Europeans becoming apparent, Colonel Lennox, his wife, and daughter, put on native dresses, and remained nine days concealed in a reed-hut behind the zenana, treated very kindly and considerately by their protector. Meer Mohammed went once or twice to Fyzabad, to learn if possible the plans of the mutineers; he was told that they meant to attack Lucknow, and then depart for Delhi. On the 10th day of the hiding, when news arrived that the fort was likely to be attacked, the ladies went for shelter into the zenana, while the colonel was hid in a dark wood-shed. Happily, however, it turned out that the suspected strangers were a party sent by the collector of Goruckpore for the rescue of the family. Danger was now nearly over. The fugitives reached Amorah, Bustee, Goruckpore, Azimghur, and Ghazeepore, at which place they took steamer down to Calcutta. This fortunate escape from great peril was almost wholly due to 'the noble and considerate' Meer Mohammed, as Colonel Lennox very properly characterises him.

Far more calamitous were the boat-adventures of the main body of Fyzabad officers, of which an account was afterwards written, for the information of government, by Farrier-sergeant Busher, of the light field-battery. On the morning of the 8th, the wives and families of many civilians, and of five non-commissioned European officers, had been sent by Captain Orr to a place called Sheergunge, under the protection of a friendly native, Rajah Maun Singh, to be free from peril if tumult should arise. Early on the 9th, while Colonel Lennox was still at the station, all or nearly all the other English were sent off by the mutineers in four

* The troops stationed at that time at Fyzabad comprised the 22d regiment native infantry; the 6th regiment irregular Oude infantry; the 5th troop of the 15th regiment irregular cavalry; No. 5 company of the 7th battalion of artillery; and No. 13 horse-battery. The chief officers were Colonels Lennox and O'Brien; Major Mill; Captain Morgan; Lieutenants Fowle, English, Bright, Lindesay, Thomas, Ouseley, Cautley, Gordon, Parsons, Percival, and Currie; and Ensigns Anderson and Ritchie. Colonel Goldney held a civil appointment as commissioner.

boats. One of these boats (mere dinghees, in which little more than a bundle for each person could be put) contained eight persons, one six, one five, and the remaining boat three. Only one female was of the party, Mrs Hollum, wife of Sergeant-major Hollum of the 22d native regiment. The first and second boats got ahead of the other two, and proceeded about twenty miles down the river without molestation; but then were seen troopers and sepoys approaching the banks, with an evidently hostile intent. The firing soon became so severe that the occupants of the first boat struck in for the off-shore, and seven of them took to their heels—the eighth being unequal to that physical exertion. They ran on till checked by a broad stream; and while deliberating how to cross, persons approached who were thought to be sepoys; the alarm proved false, but not before Lieutenants Currie and Parsons had been drowned in an attempt to escape by swimming. The other five, running on till quite exhausted, were fortunate enough to meet with a friendly native, who sheltered them for several hours, and supplied them with food. At midnight they started again, taking the road to Amorah, which they were enabled to reach safely through the influence of their kind protector—although once in great peril from a gang of freebooters. They were glad to meet at Amorah the three occupants of the fourth boat, who, like themselves, had escaped the dangers of the voyage by running across fields and fording streams. At seven in the morning of the 10th, the fugitives, now eight in company, recommenced their anxious flight—aided occasionally by friendly natives, but at length betrayed by one whose friendship was only a mask. They had to cross a nullah or stream knee-deep, under pursuit by a body of armed men; here Lieutenant Lindesay fell, literally cut to pieces; and when the other seven had passed to the opposite bank, five were speedily hewn to the ground and butchered—Lieutenants Ritchie, Thomas, and English, and two English sergeants. The two survivors ran at their topmost speed, pursued by a gang of ruffians; Lieutenant Cautley was speedily overtaken, and killed; and then only Sergeant Busher remained alive. He, outrunning his pursuers, reached a Brahmin village, where a bowl of sherbet was given to him. After a little rest, he ran on again, until one Baboo Bully Singh was found to be on the scent after him; he endeavoured to hide under some straw in a hut; but was discovered and dragged out by the hair of the head. From village to village he was then carried as an exhibition to be jeered and scoffed at by the rabble; the Baboo evidently intended the cruel sport to be followed by murder; but this intention underwent a change, probably from dread of some future retribution. He kept his prisoner near him for ten days, but did not further ill treat him. On the eleventh day, Busher was liberated; he overtook Colonel Lennox and his family; and safely reached Ghazeepore seventeen days after his departure from Fyzabad. The boat containing Colonel O'Brien, Lieutenants Percival and Gordon, Ensign Anderson, and Assistant-surgeon Collinson, pursued its voyage the whole way down to Dinapoor; but it was a voyage full of vicissitudes to the fugitives. At many places they were obliged to lie flat in the boat to prevent recognition from the shore; at others they had to compel the native boatmen, on peril of sabring, to continue their tugging at the oars; on one occasion they narrowly escaped shooting by a herd of villagers who followed the boat. For three days they had nothing to eat but a little flour and water; but happening to meet with a friendly rajah at Gola, they obtained aid which enabled them to reach Dinapoor on the 17th.

The occupants of the remaining boat, the civilians, and the ladies and children who had not been able to effect a safe retreat to Nynee Tal, suffered terribly; many lives were lost; and those who escaped to Goruckpore or Dinapoor arrived in distressing plight—especially a party of women and children who had been robbed of everything while on the way, and who had been almost starved to death during a week's imprisonment in a fort by the river-side. When it is stated that, among a group of women and children who reached a place of safety after infinite hardships, *an infant was born on the road*, the reader will easily comprehend how far the sufferings must have exceeded anything likely to appear in print. Many persons were shot, many drowned, while the fate of others remained doubtful for weeks or even months. Colonel Goldney and Major Mill were among the slain. The wanderings of Mrs Mill and her three children were perhaps among the most affecting incidents of this mutiny. Amid the dire haste of departure, she became separated from her husband, and was the last Englishwoman left in Fyzabad. How she escaped and how she fared, was more than she herself could clearly narrate; for the whole appeared afterwards as a dreadful dream, in which every kind of misery was confusedly mixed. During two or three weeks, she was wandering up and down the country, living in the jungle when man refused her shelter, and searching the fields for food when none was obtainable elsewhere. Her poor infant, eight months old, died for want of its proper nourishment; but the other two children, seven and three years old, survived all the privations to which they were exposed. On one occasion, seeing some troopers approaching, and being utterly hopeless, she passionately besought them, if their intentions were hostile, to kill her children without torturing them, and then to kill her. The appeal touched the hearts of the rude men; they took her to a village and gave her a little succour; and this facilitated their conveyance by a friendly native to Goruckpore, where danger was over.

Sultanpore was another station at which mutiny and murder occurred. On the 8th of June, a wing of the 15th irregular cavalry entered that place from Seetapoor, in a state of evident excitement. Lieutenant Tucker, who was a favourite with them, endeavoured to allay their mutinous spirit, and succeeded for a few hours; but on the following morning they rose in tumult, murdered Colonel Fisher, Captain Gubbings, and two other Europeans, and urged the lieutenant to escape, which he did. After much jungle-wanderings, and concealment in a friendly native's house, he safely arrived at Benares, as did likewise four or five other officers, and all the European women and children at the station. In this as in other instances, the revolt of the troops was followed by marauding and incendiarism on the part of the rabble of Sultanpore; in this, too, as in other instances, the mutineers had a little affection for some one or more among their officers, whom they endeavoured to save.

The station of Pershadeepore experienced its day of trouble on the 10th of June. The 1st regiment Oude irregular infantry was there stationed, under Captain Thompson. He prided himself on the fidelity of his men; inasmuch as they seemed to turn a deaf ear to the rumours and suspicions circulating elsewhere; and he had detected the falsity of a mischief-maker, who had secretly caused ground bones to be mixed with the attah (coarse flour with which chupatties are made) sold in the bazaar, as the foundation for a report that the government intended to take away the caste of the people. This pleasant delusion lasted until the 9th; when a troop of the 3d Oude irregular cavalry arrived from Pertabghur, followed soon afterwards by news of the rising at Sultanpore. The fidelity of the infantry now gave way, under the temptations and representations made to them by other troops. When Captain Thompson rose on the morning of the 10th, he found his regiment all dressed, and in orderly mutiny (if such an expression may be used). He tried with an aching heart to separate the good men from the bad, and to induce the former to retire with him to Allahabad; but the temptation of the treasure was more than they could resist; they all joined in the spoliation, and then felt that allegiance was at an end. At four in the afternoon all the Europeans left the station, without a shot or an angry word from the men; they were escorted to the fort of Dharoopoor, belonging to a chieftain named Rajah Hunnewaut Singh, who treated them courteously, and after some days forwarded them safely to Allahabad. There was not throughout India a mutiny conducted with more quietness on both sides than this at Pershadeepore; the sepoys had evidently no angry feeling towards their officers. Captain Thompson remained of opinion that his men had been led away by rumours and insinuations brought by stragglers from other stations, to the effect that any Oude regiment which did *not* mutiny would be in peril from those that had; and that, even under this fear, they would have remained faithful had there been no treasure to tempt their cupidity. It is curious to note Colonel Neill's comment on this incident, in his official dispatch; his reliance on the native troops was of the smallest possible amount; and in reference to the captain's honest faith, he said: 'This is absurd; they were as deeply in the plot as the rest of the army; the only credit due to them is that they did not murder their officers.'

Seetapoor, about fifty miles north of Lucknow, was the place towards which the insurgent troops from that city bent their steps at the close of May. Whether those regiments kept together, and how far they proceeded on the next few days, are points not clearly made out; but it is certain that the native troops stationed at Seetapoor—comprising the 41st Bengal infantry, the 9th and 10th Oude irregular infantry, and the 2d Oude military police, in all about three thousand men—rose in mutiny on the 3d of June. The 41st began the movement. A sepoy came to one of the officers in the morning, announced that the rising was about to take place, declared that neither he nor his companions wished to draw blood, and suggested that all the officers should retreat from the station. The regiment was in two wings, one in the town and one in the cantonment; the plundering of the treasury was begun by the first-named party; the other wing, obedient at first, broke forth when they suspected they might be deprived of a share in the plunder. After the 41st had thus set the example, the 9th revolted; then the military police; and then the 10th. Lieutenant Burnes, of the last-named regiment, entreated his men earnestly to remain faithful, but to no effect. Seeing that many officers had been struck down, the remainder hastily retired to the house of Mr Christian the commissioner; and when all were assembled, with the civilians, the ladies, and the children, it was at once resolved to quit the burning bungalows and ruthless soldiers and seek refuge at Lucknow. Some made their exit without any preparation; among whom was Lieutenant Burnes—roaming through jungles for days, and aiding women and children as best they could, suffering all those miseries which have so often been depicted. The great body of Europeans, however, left the station in buggies and other vehicles; and as the high roads were perilous, the fugitives drove over hills, hollows, and ploughed fields, where perhaps vehicles had never been driven before. Fortunately, twenty troopers remained faithful to them, and escorted them all the way to Lucknow, which place they reached on the night of the third day—reft of everything they possessed, like many other fugitives in those days. Many of the Europeans did not succeed in quitting Seetapoor in time; and among these the work of death was ruthlessly carried on—the sepoys being either unwilling or unable to check these scenes of barbarity.

As at Lucknow, Fyzabad, Sultanpore, Pershadeepore, Seetapoor; so at Secrora, Durriabad, Beraytch, Gonda, and other places in Oude—wherever there was a native regiment stationed, or a treasury of the Company established, there, in almost every instance, were exhibited scenes of violence attended by murder and plunder. The lamented Lawrence, in the five weeks preceding his death, was, as has been lately pointed out, placed in an extraordinary position. Responsible to the supreme government both for the political and the military management of Oude, and knowing that almost every station in the province was a focus of treachery and mutiny, he was notwithstanding powerless to restore tranquillity. So far from Cawnpore assisting him, he yearned to assist Cawnpore; Rohilcund was in a blaze, and could send him only mutineers who had thrown off all allegiance; Meerut, after sending troops to Delhi, was doing little but defending itself; Agra, with a mere handful of European troops, was too doubtful of its Gwalior neighbours to do anything for Lucknow and Oude; Allahabad and Benares were too recently rescued, by the gallant Neill, from imminent peril, to be in a position to send present assistance to Sir Henry; and the Nepaul sovereign, Jung Bahadoor, had not yet been made an ally of the English in such a way as might possibly have saved Oude, and as was advocated by many well-wishers of India.

The position of the sovereignty just named may usefully be adverted to here. Nepaul, about equal in area to England, is one of the few independent states of Northern India; it reaches to the Himalaya on the north; and is bounded on the other sides by the British territories of Behar, Oude, and Kumaon. The region is distinguished by the magnificent giant mountain-chain which separates it from Tibet; by the dense forest-jungle of the Terai on the Oude frontier; by the beautiful valley in which the capital, Khatmandoo, lies, and which is dotted with flourishing villages, luxuriant fields, and picturesque streams; and by its healthy and temperate climate. It is with the people, however, that this narrative is more particularly concerned. The Nepaulese, about two millions in number, comprise Goorkhas, Newars, Bhotias, Dhanwars, and Mhanjees. The Goorkhas are the dominant race; they are Hindoos in religion, but very unlike Hindoos in appearance, manners, and customs. The Newars are the aborigines of Nepaul, decidedly Mongolian both in faith and in features; they are the clever artisans of the kingdom, while the Goorkhas are the hardy soldiers. The other three tribes are chiefly cultivators of the soil. In the latter half of the last century, Nepaul was for a short time a dependency of the Chinese Empire; but a treaty of commerce with the British in 1782 initiated a state of affairs which soon enabled Nepaul to throw off Chinese supremacy. Conventions, subsidies, border encroachments, and family intrigues, checkered Nepaulese affairs until 1812; when the Company made formal war on the ground of a long catalogue of injuries and insults—such a catalogue as can easily be concocted by a stronger state against a weaker. The war was so badly conducted, that nothing but the military tact of Sir David Ochterlony, who held one-fourth of a command which seems to have had no head or general commander, saved the British from ignominious defeat. Broken engagements led to another war in 1816, which terminated in a treaty never since ruptured; the Nepaulese court has been a focus of intrigue, but the intrigues have not been of such a character as to disturb the relations of amity with the British. Jung Bahadoor—a name well known in England a few years ago, as that of a Nepaulese ambassador who made a sensation by his jewelled splendour—was the nephew of a man who became by successive steps prime minister to the king. Instigated by the queen, and by his own unscrupulous ambition, Jung Bahadoor caused his uncle to be put to death, and became commander-in-chief under a new ministry. Many scenes of truly oriental slaughter followed—that is, slaughter to clear the pathway to power. Jung Bahadoor treated kings and queens somewhat as the Company was accustomed to do in the last century; setting up a son against a father, and treating all alike as puppets. At a period subsequent to his return from England, he caused a marriage to be concluded between his daughter, six years old, and the heir-apparent to the Nepaulese throne, then in his ninth year. Whether king or not, he was virtually chief of Nepaul at the time when the Revolt broke out; and had managed, by astuteness in his diplomacy, to remain on friendly terms with the authorities at Calcutta: indeed he took every opportunity, after his English visit, to display his leaning towards his neighbours. Like Nena Sahib, he had English pianos and English carpets in his house, and prided himself in understanding English manners and the English language; and it is unquestionable that both those men were favourites among such of the English as visited the one at Bithoor or the other at Khatmandoo.

It has been mentioned in a former chapter (p. 115) that Goorkha troops assisted to defend Nynee Tal when that place became filled with refugees; and Goorkha regiments have been adverted to in many other parts of the narrative. Jung Bahadoor permitted the Nepaulese of this tribe to enlist thus in the Company's service; and he also offered the aid of a contingent, the non-employment of which brought many strictures upon the policy of the Calcutta government. At a later date, as we shall see, this contingent was accepted; and it rendered us good service at Juanpore and Azimghur by protecting Benares from the advance of Oude mutineers. About the middle of June, fifteen Europeans (seven gentlemen, three ladies, and five children) escaped from the Oude mutineers into the jungle region of Nepaul, and sought refuge in a post-station or serai about ten days' journey from Goruckpore and eighteen from Khatmandoo. The officer at that place wrote to Jung Bahadoor for instruction in the matter; to which he received a speedy reply —'Treat them with every kindness, give them elephants, &c., and escort them to Goruckpore.' Major Ramsey, the Company's representative at Khatmandoo, sent them numerous supplies in tin cases; and all the English were naturally disposed to bless the Nepaulese chieftain as a friend in the hour of greatest need, without inquiring very closely by what means he had gained his power.

The course of the narrative now takes us from Oude northwestward into the province of Rohilcund; the districts of which, named after the towns of Bareilly, Mooradabad, Shahjehanpoor, Boodayoun, and Bijnour, felt the full force of the mutinous proceedings among the native troops. The Rohillas were originally Mussulman Afghans, who conquered this part of India, gradually settled down among the Hindoo natives, and imparted to them a daring reckless character, which rendered Rohilcund a nursery for irregular cavalry—and afterwards for mutineers.

Brigadier Sibbald was commandant of Bareilly, one of the towns of Rohilcund in which troops were stationed. These troops were entirely native, comprising the 18th and 68th Bengal native infantry, the 8th irregular cavalry, and a battery of native artillery—not an English soldier among them except the officers. The brigadier, although these troops appeared towards the close of the month of May to be in an agitated state, nevertheless heard that all was well at Mooradabad, Shahjehanpoor, Almora, and other stations in Rohilcund, and looked forward with some confidence to the continuance of tranquillity—aided by his second in command, Colonel Troup, and the commissioner, Mr Alexander. As a precaution, however, the ladies and children were sent for safety to Nynee Tal; and the gentlemen kept their horses saddled, ready for any emergency. Bareilly being a city of a hundred thousand inhabitants, the temper of the natives was very anxiously watched. Scarcely had the month closed, before the hopes of Brigadier Sibbald received a dismal check, and his life a violent end. We have already briefly mentioned (p. 114) that on Sunday the 31st, Bareilly became a scene of violence and rapine; the brigadier himself being shot by a trooper, the treasure seized, the bungalows plundered and burned, and the Europeans either murdered or impelled to escape for their lives. When Colonel Troup, who commanded the 68th native infantry, and who became chief military authority after the death of Sibbald, found himself safe at Nynee Tal, he wrote an official account of the whole proceeding, corroborating the chief facts noted by the brigadier, and adding others known more especially to himself. From this dispatch it appears that the colonel commanded at Bareilly from the 6th to the 19th of May, while the brigadier was making a tour of inspection through his district; that from the 19th to the 29th, Sibbald himself resumed the command; and that during those twenty-three days nothing occurred to shew disaffection among the troops, further than a certain troubled and agitated state. On that day, however, the Europeans received information, from two native officers, that the men of the 18th and 68th native regiments had, *while bathing in the river*, concerted a plan of mutiny for that same afternoon. Most of the officers were quickly on the alert; and, whether or not through this evidence of preparedness, no émeute took place on that day. On the 30th, Colonel Troup, who had relied on the fidelity of the 8th irregular cavalry, received information that those sowars had sworn not to act against the native infantry and artillery if the latter should rise, although they would refrain from molesting their own officers. After a day and night of violent excitement throughout the whole station, the morning of Sunday the 31st (again Sunday!) ushered in a day of bloodshed and rapine. Messages were despatched to all the officers, warning them of some intended outbreak; but the bearers, sent by Troup, failed in their duty, insomuch that many of the officers remained ignorant of the danger until too late to avert it. Major Pearson, of the 18th, believed his men to be stanch; Captain Kirby, of the artillery (6th company, 6th battalion), in like manner trusted his corps; and Captain Brownlow, the brigade major, disbelieved the approach of mutiny—at the very time that Colonel Troup was impressing on all his conviction that the sinister rumours were well founded. At eleven o'clock, the truth appeared in fatal colours; the roar of cannon, the rattle of musketry, and the yells of men, told plainly that the revolt had begun, and that the artillery had joined in it. The 8th irregular cavalry, under Captain Mackenzie, were ordered or invited by him to proceed against the lines of the insurgent infantry and artillery; but the result was so disastrous, that all the Europeans, military as well as civilians, found their only safety would be in flight. Ruktawar Khan, subadar of artillery, assumed the rank of general, and paraded about in the carriage of the brigadier, attended by a numerous string of followers as a 'staff.' Colonel Troup, writing on the 10th of June, had to report the deaths of Brigadier Sibbald and three or four other officers, together with that of many of the civil servants. About twenty-five military officers escaped; but the list of 'missing' was large, and many of those included in it were afterwards known to have been brutally murdered. Captain Mackenzie, who clung to his troopers in the earnest hope that they would remain faithful, found only nineteen men who did so, and who escorted their officers all the way to Nynee Tal.

A despicable hoary traitor, Khan Bahadoor Khan, appears to have headed this movement. He had for many years been in receipt of a double pension from the Indian government—as the living representative of one of the early Rohilla chieftains, and as a retired judge of one of the native courts. He was an old, venerable-looking, insinuating man; he was thoroughly relied on by the civil authorities at Bareilly; he had loudly proclaimed his indignation against the Delhi mutineers; and yet he became ringleader of those at Bareilly—deepening his damning atrocities by the massacre of such of the unfortunate Europeans as did not succeed in making their escape. It was by his orders, as self-elected chief of Rohilcund, that a rigorous search was made for all Europeans who remained in Bareilly; and that Judge Robertson, and four or five other European gentlemen, were hung in the Kotwal square, after a mock-trial. During the month of June, Bareilly remained entirely in the hands of the rebels; not an Englishman, probably, was alive in the place; and the Mussulmans and Hindoos were left to contend for supremacy over the spoil.

Of Boodayoun it will be unnecessary to say more here; Mr Edwards's narrative of an eventful escape (pp. 115, 116), pointed to the 1st of June as the day when the Europeans deemed it necessary to flee from that station—not because there were any native troops at Boodayoun, but because the mutineers from Bareilly were approaching, and joyfully expected by all the scoundrels in the place, who looked forward to a harvest of plunder as a natural result.

Mooradabad, which began its season of anarchy and violence on the 3d of June, stands on the right bank of the Ramgunga, an affluent of the Ganges, at a point about midway between Meerut and Bareilly. It is a town of nearly 60,000 inhabitants—having a civil station, with its cutcherry and bungalows; a cantonment west of the town; a spacious serai for the accommodation of travellers; and an enormous jail sufficiently large to contain nearly two thousand prisoners. In this, as in many other towns of India, the Company's troops were wont to be regarded rather as guardians of the jail and its inmates, than for any active military duties. So early as the 19th of May, nine days after the mutineers of Meerut had set the example, the 29th regiment native infantry proceeded to the jail at Mooradabad, and released all the prisoners. Although Mr Saunders, collector and magistrate, wrote full accounts to Agra of the proceedings of that and the following days, the dâks were so completely stopped on the road that Mr Colvin remained almost in ignorance of the state of affairs; and on that account Saunders could obtain no assistance from any quarter. The released prisoners, joined by predatory bands of Goojurs, Meewatties, and Jâts, commenced a system of plunder and rapine, which the European authorities were ill able to check. The 29th, however, had not openly mutinied; and it still remained possible to hold control within the town and the surrounding district; several native sappers and miners were stopped and captured on their way from Meerut, and several of the mutinous 20th regiment on the way from Mozuffernugger. When, however, news of the Bareilly outbreak on the 31st reached Mooradabad, the effect on the men of the 29th regiment, and of a native artillery detachment, became very evident. On the 3d of June, the sepoys in guard of the treasury displayed so evident an intention of appropriating the money, that Mr Saunders felt compelled to leave it (about seventy thousand rupees) together with much plate and opium in their hands—being powerless to prevent the spoliation. The troops manifested much irritation at the smallness of the treasure, and were only prevented from wreaking their vengeance on the officials by an oath they had previously taken. To remain longer in the town was deemed a useless risk, as bad passions were rising on every side. The civil officers of the Company, with their wives and families, succeeded in making a safe retreat to Meerut; while Captain Whish, Captain Faddy, and other officers of the 29th, with the few remaining Europeans, laid their plans for a journey to Nynee Tal. All shared an opinion that if the Bareilly regiments had not mutinied, the 29th would have remained faithful—a poor solace, such as had been sought for by many other officials similarly placed. Mr Colvin afterwards accepted Mr Saunders's motives and conduct in leaving the station, as justifiable under the trying circumstances.

Rohilcund contained three military stations, Bareilly, Mooradabad, and Shahjehanpoor—Boodayoun and the other places named being merely civil stations. As at Bareilly and Mooradabad, so at Shahjehanpoor; the native troops at the station rose in mutiny. On Sunday the 31st of May—a day marked by so many atrocities in India—the 28th native infantry rose, surrounded the Christian residents as they were engaged in divine worship in church, and murdered nearly the whole of them, including the Rev. Mr M'Callum in the sacred edifice itself. The few who escaped were exposed to an accumulation of miseries; first they sought shelter at Mohammerah in Oude; then they met the 41st regiment, after the mutiny at Seetapoor, who shot and cut them down without mercy; and scarcely any lived to tell the dismal tale to English ears.

Thus then it appears that, in Rohilcund, the 18th, 68th, 28th, and 29th regiments native infantry, together with the 8th irregular cavalry and a battery of native artillery, rose in revolt at the three military stations, and murdered or drove out nearly the whole of the Europeans from the entire province—European troops there were none; only officers and civilians. They plundered all the treasuries, containing more than a quarter of a million sterling, and marched off towards Delhi, five thousand strong—unmolested by the general who commanded at Meerut.

Nynee Tal became more crowded than ever with refugees from Oude and Rohilcund. Under the energetic command of Captain Ramsey, this hill-station remained in quiet during the month of May (p. 115); but it was not so easily defended in June. Some of the native artillery at Almora, not far distant, gave rise to uneasiness towards the close of the month; yet as the ill-doers were promptly put into prison, and as the Goorkhas remained stanch, confidence was partially restored. The sepoys from the rebel regiments dreaded a march in this direction, on account of the deadly character of the Terai, a strip of swampy forest, thirty miles broad, which interposes between the plains and the hills; but that jungle-land itself contained many marauders, who were only prevented by fear of the Goorkhas from going up to Nynee Tal. At the end of June, there were five times as many women and children as men among the Europeans at that place; hence the anxious eye with which the proceedings in surrounding districts were regarded.

The third region to which this chapter is appropriated—the Doab—now calls for attention. Like Oude and Rohilcund, it was the scene of terrible anarchy and bloodshed in the month of June. In its two parts—the Lower Doab, from Allahabad to a little above Furruckabad; and the Upper Doab, from the last-named city up to the hill-country—it was nearly surrounded by mutineers, who apparently acted in concert with those in the Doab itself.

Of Allahabad and Cawnpore, the two chief places in the Lower Doab, sufficient has been said in Chapters VIII. and IX. to trace the course of events during the month of June. About midway between the two is Futtehpoor, a small civil station in the centre of a group of Mohammedan villages; it contained, at the beginning of June, about a dozen civil servants of the Company, and a small detachment of the 6th native regiment from Allahabad. The residents, as a precautionary measure, had sent their wives and children to that stronghold, and had also arranged a plan for assembling at the house of the magistrate, if danger should appear. On the 5th of the month, disastrous news arriving from Lucknow and Cawnpore, the residents took up their abode for the night on the flat roof of the magistrate's house, with their weapons by their sides; and on the following day they hauled up a supply of tents, provisions, water, and ammunition—a singular citadel being thus extemporised in the absence of better. On the 7th, their small detachment aided in repelling a body of troopers who had just arrived from Cawnpore on a plundering expedition; and the residents congratulated themselves on the fidelity of this small band. Their reliance was, however, of short duration; for, on the receipt of news of the Allahabad outbreak, the native officials in the collector's office gave way, like the natives all around them, and Futtehpoor soon became a perilous spot for Europeans. On the 9th, the residents held a council on their roof, and resolved to quit the station. A few troopers befriended them; and they succeeded, after many perils and sufferings, in reaching Banda, a town southward of the Jumna. Not all of them, however. Mr Robert Tucker, the judge, resisting entreaty, determined to remain at his post to the last. He rode all over the town, promising rewards to those natives who would be faithful; he endeavoured to shame others by his heroic bearing; he appealed to the gratitude and good feeling of many of the poorer natives, who had been benefited by him in more peaceful times. But all in vain. The jail was broken open, the prisoners liberated, and the treasury plundered; and Mr Tucker, flying to the roof of the cutcherry, there bravely defended himself until a storm of bullets laid him low. Robert Tucker was one of those civilians of whom the Company had reason to be proud.

Advancing to the northwest, we come to a string of towns and stations—Etawah, Minpooree, Allygurh, Futteghur, Muttra, Bolundshuhur, Mozuffernugger, &c.—which shared with Oude and Rohilcund the wild disorders of the month of June. The mutiny at Futteghur has already engaged our notice (p. 133), in connection with the miserable fugitives who swelled the numbers put to death by Nena Sahib at Bithoor and Cawnpore. It needs little further mention here. The 10th native infantry, and a small body of artillery, long resisted the temptation held out by mutineers elsewhere; but, on the appearance of the insurgent regiments from Seetapoor, their fidelity gave way. Four companies went off with the treasure; the remainder joined the other mutinous regiments in besieging the fort to which so many Europeans had fled for refuge, and from which so disastrous a boat-voyage was made down the Ganges. Mr Colvin, at Agra, knew of the perilous state of things at Futteghur; he knew that a native nawab had been chosen by the mutineers as a sort of sovereign; but, as we shall presently see, he was too weak in reliable troops to afford any assistance whatever. Thus it happened that the two boat-expeditions, of June and July, ended so deplorably to the Europeans, and left Futteghur so wholly in the hands of the rebels. It was a great loss to the British in many ways; for most of the Company's gun-carriages were made, or at least stored, at Futteghur; and the agency-yard was surrounded by warehouses containing a large supply of material belonging to the artillery service. Indeed it was this court-yard of the gun-carriage agency that constituted the fort, as soon as a few defensive arrangements had been made. Many circumstances had drawn rather a large English population to Futteghur; and hence the terrible severity of the tragedy. There were officers of the 10th regiment; other military officers on leave; gun-carriage agents; civil servants; merchants and dealers; a few tent-makers and other artisans; indigo-planters from the neighbouring estates; and many native Christians under the care of the American Presbyterian mission.

We have already seen (pp. 112, 113) by how small a number of native troops several stations were set in commotion in May. The 9th regiment Bengal native infantry was separated into four portions, which were stationed at Allygurh, Bolundshuhur, Etawah, and Minpooree, respectively; and all mutinied nearly at the same time. The fortune of war, if war it can be called, at these stations during the month of June, may be traced in a very few words. It was on the 20th of May that the four companies at Allygurh mutinied; and on the 24th that one-half of Lieutenant Cockburn's Gwalior troopers, instead of assisting him to retain or regain the station, rose in mutiny and galloped off to join the insurgents elsewhere. There were, however, about a hundred who remained faithful to him; and these, with fifty volunteers, made an advance to Allygurh, retook it, drove out the detachment of the 9th native regiment, released a few Europeans who had been in hiding there, captured one Rao Bhopal Singh, and hanged him as a petty chieftain who had continued the rapine begun by the sepoys. Throughout the month of June this station was maintained in British hands—not so much for its value in a military sense, as for its utility in keeping open the roads to Agra and Meerut; but, in the direction

SIMLA, the summer residence of the Governor-general of India.

of Delhi, the volunteers could obtain very little news, the dâks being all cut off by the Goojurs and other predatory bands. At Minpooree the three companies of the 9th checked, it will be remembered, by the undaunted courage and tact of Lieutenant de Kantzow, departed to join the insurgents elsewhere; but Minpooree remained in British hands. The remaining companies mutinied at Etawah and Bolundshuhur without much violence.

Agra, when the narrative last left it (p. 111), had passed through the month of May without any serious disturbances. The troops consisted of the 44th and 67th regiments Bengal native infantry, the 3d Europeans, and a few artillery. After two companies of these native troops had mutinied while engaged in bringing treasure from Muttra to Agra, Mr Colvin deemed it necessary to disarm all the other companies; and this was quietly and successfully effected on the 1st of June, by the 3d Europeans and Captain D'Oyley's field-battery. Many facts afterward came to light, tending to show that if this disarming had not taken place, the 44th and 67th would have stained their hands with the same bloody deeds as the sepoys were doing elsewhere. The native lines had been more than once set on fire during the later days of May—in the hope, as afterwards appears, that the handful of Europeans, by rushing out unarmed to extinguish the flames, would afford the native troops a favourable opportunity to master the defences of the city, and the six guns of the field-battery. A curious proof was supplied of the little knowledge possessed by the Europeans of the native character, and the secret springs that worked unseen as moving powers for their actions. There had long seemed to be an angry feeling between the 44th and the 67th; and Mr Colvin, or the brigadier acting with him, selected one company from each regiment for the mission to Muttra, in the belief that each would act as a jealous check upon the other; instead of which, the two companies joined in revolt, murdered many of their officers, and carried off their treasure towards Delhi. After the very necessary disarming of the two regiments, the defence of this important city was left to the 3d European Fusiliers, Captain D'Oyley's field-battery of six guns, and a corps of volunteer European cavalry under Lieutenant Greathed. Most of the disarmed men deserted, and swelled the ranks of the desperadoes that wrought so much ruin in the surrounding districts—a result that led many military officers to doubt whether disarming without imprisonment was a judicious course under such circumstances; for the men naturally felt exasperated at their humbled position, whether deserved or not; and their loyalty, as soldiers out of work, was not likely to be in any way increased. Whether or not this opinion be correct, the Europeans in Agra felt their only reliance to be in each other. During the early days of June, most of the ladies resorted at night to certain places of refuge allotted by the governor, such as the fort, the post-office, the office of the *Mofussilite* newspaper, and behind the artillery lines; while the gentlemen patrolled the streets, or maintained a defensive attitude at appointed places. Trade was continued, British supremacy was asserted, bloodshed was kept away from the city, and the Europeans maintained a steady if not cheerful demeanour. Nevertheless Mr Colvin was full of anxieties; he was responsible to the Calcutta government, not only for Agra, but for the whole of the Northwest Provinces; yet he found himself equally unable to send aid to other stations, and receive aid from them. Agra was troubled on the night of the 23d of June by the desertion of the jail-guard, to whom had been intrusted the custody of the large central prison. A guard from the 3d Europeans was thereupon placed on the outside; while the inside was guarded by another force under Dr Walker the superintendent. So far as concerned military disturbances within the city, Mr Colvin was not at that time under much apprehension; but he knew that certain regiments from Neemuch—the mutiny of which will be described in the next chapter—had approached by the end of the month to a point on the high road between Agra and Jeypoor, very near the first-named city; and he heard that they contemplated an attack. He estimated their strength at two regiments of infantry, four or five hundred cavalry, and eight guns; but as the whole of the civil and military authorities at Agra were on the alert, he did not regard this approaching force with much alarm. To strengthen his position, and maintain public confidence, he organised a European militia of horse and foot, among the clerks, railway men, &c., to which it was expected and desired that nearly all civilians should belong. This militia, placed under the management of Captains Prendergast and Lamb, Lieutenants Rawlins and Oldfield, and Ensign Noble, who had belonged to the disarmed native regiments, was divided into two corps, to which the defence of the different parts of the station was intrusted. How the Europeans, both military and civilians, became cooped up in the fort during July, we shall see in a future chapter.

Meerut, during June, remained in the hands of the British; but there was much inactivity on the part of the general commanding there, in relation to the districts around that town. On the 10th of May, when the mutiny began (p. 50), there were a thousand men of the 60th Rifles, six hundred of the Carabiniers, a troop of horse-artillery, and five hundred artillery recruits—constituting a force unusually large, in relation to the general distribution of English troops in India. Yet these fine soldiers were not so handled as to draw from them the greatest amount of service. They were not sent after the three mutinous regiments who escaped to Delhi; and during the urgent and critical need of Lawrence, Colvin, and Wheeler, Major-general Hewett kept his Europeans almost constantly in or near Meerut. It is true that he, and others who have defended him, asserted that the maintenance of the position at Meerut, a very important consideration, could not have been insured if he had marched out to intercept rebels going from various quarters towards Delhi; but this argument was not deemed satisfactory at Calcutta; Major-general Hewett was superseded, and another commander appointed in his place. It was not until June that dâks were re-established between Meerut and Agra on the one hand, and Meerut and Kurnaul on the other. Some of the Europeans were sent off to join the besieging army before Delhi; while a portion of the remainder were occasionally occupied in putting down bands of Goojurs and other predatory robbers around Meerut. The town of Sirdhana, where the Catholic nuns and children had been placed in such peril (p. 57), was too near Meerut to be held by the rebels. Early in June, one Wallee Dad Khan set himself up as subadar or captain-general of Meerut, under the King of Delhi; raised a rabble force of Goojurs; held the fort of Malagurh with six guns; and seized the district of Bolundshuhur. News arriving that he was advancing with his force towards Meerut, about a hundred European troops, Rifles and Carabiniers, with a few civilians and two guns, started off to intercept him. They had little work to do, however, except to burn villages held by the insurgents; for the robber Goojurs having quarrelled with the robber Jâts about plunder, the latter compelled Wallee Dad Khan and his general, Ismail Khan, to effect a retreat before the English came up. In the last week of the month the force at Meerut, chiefly in consequence of the number sent off to Delhi, was reduced to about eight hundred; these were kept so well on the alert, and the whole town and cantonment so well guarded, that the Europeans felt little alarm; although vexed that they could afford no further assistance to the besiegers of Delhi, nor even chastise a portion of the 4th irregular cavalry, who mutinied at Mezuffernugger. All the English, civilians and their families as well as military officers, lived at Meerut either in barracks or tents—none venturing to sleep beyond the immediate spot where the military were placed.

Simla, during these varied operations, continued to be a place where, as at Nynee Tal, ladies and children, as well as some of the officers and civilians, took refuge after being despoiled by mutineers. A militia was formed after the hasty departure of General Anson; Simla was divided into four districts under separate officers; and the gentlemen aided by a few English troops, defended those districts, throughout June. The people at the bazaar, and all the native servants of the place, were disarmed, and the arms taken for safe custody to Kussowlie.

Delhi—a place repeatedly mentioned in every chapter of this narrative—continued to be the centre towards which the attention of all India was anxiously directed. Fast as the native regiments mutinied in Bengal, Oude, Rohilcund, the Doab, Bundelcund, and elsewhere, so did they either flee to Delhi, or shape their course in dependence on the military operations going on there; and fast as the British troops could be despatched to that spot, so did they take rank among the besiegers. But in truth this latter augmentation came almost wholly from the Punjaub and other western districts. Lloyd, Neill, Wheeler, Lawrence, Hewett, Sibbald, were so closely engaged in attending to the districts around Dinapoor, Benares, Allahabad, Cawnpore, Lucknow, Meerut, and Bareilly, that they could not send aid to the besiegers of Delhi, during several weeks of siege operations. These operations will be noticed in systematic order, when the other threads of the narrative have been traced to the proper points. Meanwhile the reader will bear in mind that the siege of Delhi was in progress from the middle of June to an advanced period in the summer.

Tomb at Futtehpore Sikri.

CHAPTER XI.

CENTRAL REGIONS OF INDIA: JUNE.

IN the political and territorial arrangements of the East India Company, the name of Central India is somewhat vaguely employed to designate a portion of the region lying between the Jumna and Bundelcund on the northeast, and the Nizam's territory and Gujerat on the southwest; a designation convenient for general reading, without possessing any very precise acceptation. In the present chapter, we shall change the expression and enlarge the meaning so as to designate a belt of country that really forms Central India in a geographical sense, extending from Lower Bengal to Rajpootana, and separating Northern India from the southern or peninsular portion of the empire. This will carry the narrative into regions very little mentioned in former chapters—such as Nagpoor, the Saugor and Nerbudda territories, Bundelcund and Rewah, the Mahratta states and the Rajpoot states—regions that will be briefly described, so far as to render the proceedings of the native troops intelligible.

We begin with Nagpoor, a country now belonging to the British government, and considerably larger than England and Wales.

This province was acquired, not so much by conquest, as by one of those intricate arrangements concerning dynasty which have brought so many native states under British rule. It is in general an elevated country, containing many offshoots from the Vindhya range of mountains. Some parts of it, towards the southeast, have never been explored by Europeans, but are believed to be hilly, wooded, and full of jungles, inhabited by the semi-barbarous tribe of Ghonds. The remainder is better known and better cultivated; and being on the high road from Calcutta to Bombay, possesses much political importance. The population exceeds four millions and a half. Early in the last century, one of the Mahratta chieftains conquered Nagpoor from the rajahs who had before governed it; and he and his descendants, or other ambitious members of the Mahratta family, continued to hold it as Rajahs of Nagpoor or Berar. Although constantly fighting one with another, these Mahrattas were on fair terms with the East India Company until 1803, when, unluckily for the continuance of his rule, the native rajah joined Scindia in the war against the British. As a consequence, when peace was restored in 1804, he was forced to yield Cuttack and other provinces to the conquerors. In 1817, another Rajah of Nagpoor joined the Peishwa of the Mahrattas in hostilities against the British—a course which led to his expulsion from the raj, and to a further increase of British influence. Then followed a period during which one rajah was imbecile, another under age, and many unscrupulous chieftains sought to gain an ascendency one over another. This was precisely the state of things which rendered the British resident more and more powerful, setting up and putting down rajahs, and allowing the competitors to weaken the whole native rule by weakening each other. The history of British India may be almost told in such words as these. At length, in 1853, the last rajah, Ragojee, died—not only without heirs, but without any male relations who could support a legitimate claim to the raj. Thereupon, the governor-general quietly annexed this large country to the Company's dominions. It will be remembered (p. 4) that the Marquis of Dalhousie, in his minute, despatched this subject in a very few lines; not asserting that the British had actually any right to the country; but 'wisely incorporated it,' as no one else could put in a legitimate claim for it, and as it would have been imprudent 'to bestow the territory in free gift upon a stranger.' The Nagpoor territory was placed under the management of a commissioner, who was immediately subordinate to the governor-general in council; seeing that the Bengal Presidency was already too large to have this considerable country attached to it for governmental purposes.

At and soon after the time of the outbreak, there were the 1st regiment irregular infantry, the Kamptee irregulars, an irregular horse-battery, and a body of European gunners, stationed in the city of Nagpoor, or in Kamptee, eleven miles distant; the 2d infantry and a detachment of the 1st were at Chandah; a detachment of the 1st at Bhandara;

the chief portion of the 3d at Rajpoor; and the remainder of the same regiment at Bilaspoor. The arsenal, containing guns, arms, ammunition, and military stores of every description; and the treasury of the province, with a large amount of Company's funds—were close to the city. Mr Plowden filled the office of commissioner at that period. With a mere handful of Europeans in the midst of a very extensive territory, he often trembled in thought for the safety of his position, and of British interests generally, in the region placed under his keeping. He had numerous native troops with him, and a large city under his control; if anything sinister should arise, he was far away from any extraneous aid—being nearly six hundred miles distant from Madras, and still further from Calcutta. But, whatever were his anxieties (and they were many), he put on a calm bearing towards the natives of Nagpoor. This city, the capital of the territory bearing the same name, is a dirty, irregular, straggling place, nearly seven miles in circumference. Most of the houses are mud-built; and even the palace of the late rajah is little more than a clumsy pile of unfinished masonry. The city has become rather famous for its banking business, and for its manufactures of cottons, chintzes, turbans, silks, brocades, woollens, blankets, tent-cloths, and other textile goods. The population exceeds a hundred thousand. There is nothing of a military appearance about the city; but whoever commands the Seetabuldee, commands Nagpoor itself. This Seetabuldee is a hilly ridge close to the city on the west, having two summits, the northern the higher, the southern the larger, but every part overlooking the city, and fortified. Such being the topographical position of his seat of government, Mr Plowden proceeded to disarm such of his troops as excited disquietude in his mind, and to strengthen the Seetabuldee. A corps of irregular cavalry shewed symptoms of disloyalty; and indeed rumours were afloat that on a particular day the ascent of a balloon was to be a signal for the revolt of the troops. Under these circumstances, Mr Plowden arranged with Colonel Cumberlege, the commandant, to disarm them on the morning of the 23d of June—the colonel having the 4th regiment of Madras cavalry, on whom he fully relied, to enforce the order for disbanding. The irregulars were paraded, mounted and fully armed, to shew that the authorities were not afraid of them. Mr Plowden having addressed them, they quietly gave up their arms and their saddles, which were taken in carts to the arsenal; and thus six hundred and fifty troopers were left with nothing but their bare horses, and ropes to picket them. Some of the men and of the native officers were arrested, and put on their trial for an attempt to excite mutiny. The roll was called over every four hours, and every native soldier absent, or found outside the lines without a pass, was treated as a deserter. The 1st regiment irregular infantry assisted in the disarming of the troopers. Following up the measures thus promptly taken, the commissioner strengthened the defences on the Seetabuldee hill, as a last refuge for the Europeans at Nagpoor in the event of any actual mutiny at that place. The Residency became a barrack at night for all the civil and military officers; and a watchful eye was kept on the natives generally. At present, all was safe in Nagpoor.

Another province, and another commissioner in charge of it, now come for notice. This province, bearing the rather lengthened name of the Saugor and Nerbudda Territories, is about half the size of England, and is bounded by the various provinces or regions of Nagpoor, Mirzapore, Allahabad, Banda, Bundelcund, Gwalior, Bhopal, and the Nizam's state of Hyderabad. It corresponds more nearly with the exact centre of India than any other portion of territory. One half of its name is derived from the town of Saugor, the other half from the river Nerbudda. To describe the scraps and patches of which it consists, and the means by which they were acquired, would be neither easy nor necessary. Within its limits is the small independent state of Rewah, the rajah of which was bound to the British government by a treaty of alliance. Four other petty states—Kotee, Myhir, Oocheyra, and Sohawul—were in the hands of native chieftains, mere feudatories of the Company, under whose grants they held their possessions; allowed to govern their small sovereignties, but subject at any moment to the supervision and interference of the paramount power. The larger portion, now entirely British, is marked by the towns and districts of Saugor, Jubbulpoor, Hosungabad, Seuni, Nursingpore, Baitool, Sohagpoor, and others of less importance. There are still many aboriginal Ghonds in the province, as in Nagpoor, lurking in the gloomiest recesses of dense forests, and subsisting for the most part on wild roots and fruits. There are other half-savage tribes of Koles, Palis, and Panwars; while the more civilised population comprises a singular mixture of Brahmins, Bundelas, Rajpoots, Mahrattas, and Patans. The Mahrattas at one time claimed this region, on the same plea as those east and west of it—the right of conquest; and the British obtained it from the Mahrattas, about forty years ago, by cession after a course of hostilities.

Major Erskine was commissioner of the Saugor and Nerbudda territories during the early weeks of the mutiny; responsible, not immediately to the governor-general at Calcutta, but to the lieutenant-governor of the Northwest Provinces at Agra. Like Mr Plowden at Nagpoor, he felt how imperiled he and his fellow-Europeans would be if the native troops were to rebel. At Jhansi and at Nuseerabad, as we shall presently see, revolt and massacre marked the first week in June; and Major Erskine sought earnestly for means to prevent his own Saugor troops from being tempted to a similar course. He was with the 52d native infantry at Jubbulpoor. He wrote on the 9th of

June to Brigadier Prior at Kamptee, praying him —while keeping that station and Seuni intact— to prevent, if possible, all news of the mutineers from passing to Jubbulpoor by that route; he feared lest his 52d should yield to the influence of pernicious example. Seuni was a small civil station, nearly midway between Jubbulpoor and Nagpoor, and about eighty miles distant from each; while Kamptee was a cantonment of Madras regulars, eleven miles north of Nagpoor. The four places named, in fact, stand nearly in a line north and south, and interpose between the Mahratta states and Lower Bengal. Mr Plowden at Nagpoor, Major Erskine at Jubbulpoor, and Brigadier Prior at Kamptee, thereupon concerted measures for preserving, so far as they could, that region of India from disturbance; they all three agreed that 'tranquillity will be most effectually secured by crushing disaffection before it approaches too near to agitate men's minds dangerously.' One consequence of this arrangement was, that a force was sent on the 13th to Seuni, under Major Baker; consisting of the 32d native infantry, a squadron of the 4th light cavalry, a squadron of irregular cavalry, and three field-guns.

The Europeans at Jubbulpoor were not allowed to pass through the month of June without many doubts and anxieties. The native troops, though not actually in mutiny, were seized with a mingled feeling of fear and exasperation when European troops were mentioned; they were in perpetual apprehension, from the countless rumours at that time circulating throughout India, that Europeans were about to approach and disarm them, as degraded and distrusted men. Jubbulpoor is a large thriving town, which at the time of the mutiny contained a small cantonment for native troops, and a political agency subsidiary to that at Saugor. On one occasion, this report of the approach of European troops seized so forcibly on the minds of the sepoys, that the subadar-major, a trusted and influential man, lost all control over them; and they were not satisfied until their English colonel allowed two or three from each company to go out and scour the country, to satisfy themselves and the rest whether the rumour were true or false. On another occasion, one of the sepoys rose with a shout of 'Death to the Feringhees,' and endeavoured to bayonet the adjutant; but his companions did not aid him; and the authorities deemed it prudent to treat him as a madman, to be confined and not shot. When troops were marched from Kamptee to Seuni, in accordance with the arrangements mentioned in the last paragraph, the sepoys at Jubbulpoor were at once told of it, lest their excited minds should be again aroused on the subject of Europeans. Some of the English officers felt the humiliation involved in this kind of petting and pampering; but danger was around them, and they were obliged to temporise. A few ladies had been sent to Kamptee; all else remained with their husbands, seldom taking off their clothes at night, and holding themselves ready to flee at an hour's warning. Such a state of affairs, though less perilous, was almost as mentally distressing as actual mutiny. As the month drew to a close, and the perpetual anxiety and expectation were becoming wearisome to all, the Europeans resolved to fortify the Residency. This they did, and moreover stored it with six months' provision for about sixty persons, including thirty ladies and children; and for several civilians, who had also to be provided for.

Saugor was placed in some such predicament as Jubbulpoor; its European officers had much to plan, much to execute, to enable them to pass safely through the perils of the month of June. This town, the capital of the province in political matters, possessed a military cantonment on the borders of a lake on which the town stands; a large fort, which had been converted into an ordnance depôt; and a population of fifty thousand souls, chiefly Mahrattas. At the time of the outbreak, Brigadier Sage commanded the Saugor district force, and had under him the 31st and 42d native infantry regiments, a regiment of native cavalry, and about seventy European gunners. The fort, the magazine, and the battering-train were at one end of the cantonment; an eminence, called the Artillery Hill, was at the other end, three miles off; and the brigadier felt that if mutiny should occur, he would hardly be able to hold both positions. During many minor transactions in the district, requiring the presence of small detachments from Saugor, the temper of the troops was made sufficiently manifest; sometimes the 31st shewed bad symptoms, sometimes the 42d; two or three men were detected in plans for murdering their officers; and petty rajahs in the district offered the sepoys higher pay if they would change their allegiance. The European inhabitants of Saugor becoming very uneasy, the brigadier cleared out the fort, converted it into a place of refuge for women and children, supplied it with useful furniture and other articles, and succeeded in supplanting sepoys by Europeans in guard of the fort, the magazine, and the treasury. The fort being provisioned for six months, and the guns secured, Brigadier Sage felt himself in a position to adopt a resolute tone towards the native troops, without compromising the safety of the numerous persons congregated within it—comprising a hundred and thirty officers and civilians, and a hundred and sixty women and children, all the Europeans of the place. Thus ended June. It may simply be added here, that during the early part of the following month, the 31st and 42d regiments had a desperate fight, the former willing to be faithful, and the latter to mutiny. The brigadier, not feeling quite sure even of the 31st, would not place either his officers or his guns at their mercy, but he sent out of the fort a few men to aid them. The irregular cavalry joined the 42d; but both corps were ultimately beaten off by the 31st—to carry wild disorder into other towns and districts.*

Without dwelling on minor mutinies at Dumoh and other places in the Saugor province, we will transfer our attention northward to Bundelcund; where Jhansi was the scene of a terrible catastrophe, and where riot and plunder were in the ascendant throughout the month of June. Bundelcund, the country of the Bundelas, affords a curious example of the mode in which a region became in past times cut up into a number of petty states, and then fell in great part into British hands. It is a strip of country, about half the size of Scotland, lying south or southwest of the Jumna, and separated by that river from the Doab. The country was in the hands of the Rajpoots until the close of the fourteenth century; when another tribe, the Bundelas, began a system of predatory incursions which led to their ultimate possession of the whole tract. Early in the last century there was a chief of Western Bundelcund tributary to the Great Mogul, and another in Eastern Bundelcund supported by the Mahrattas against that sovereign. How one chief rose against another, and how each obtained a patch of territory for himself, need not be told; it was only an exemplification of a process to which Asiatics have been accustomed from the earliest ages. About the close of the century, the East India Company began to obtain possession here, by conquest or by treaty; and in 1817, after a war with the Mahrattas, a large increase was made in this ownership. These are matters needful to be borne in mind here; for, though the country is but small, it now contains five or six districts belonging to the British, and nine native princedoms or rajahships; besides numerous petty jaghires or domains that may in some sense be compared to the smallest states of the Germanic confederation. At the time of the mutiny, the British districts were managed under the lieutenant-governor of the Northwest Provinces; while the 'political superintendence,' as it was called, of the native states was in the hands of an agent appointed by, and directly responsible to, the governor-general. With the principal native states, of which Jhansi was one, the British government had engagements, varying on minor points according to circumstances, but all recognising its supremacy, and binding the dependent state to the relinquishment of all political relations except with the superior power. Some were tributary; some exempt from that obligation. The chief towns in the portion of Bundelcund belonging to the British are Jhansi, Banda, and Jaloun.

Bundelcund, we have said, was the scene of much outrage, especially at Jhansi. This town, lying on the main route from Agra to Saugor, was much frequented in the last century by caravans of merchants who traded between the Doab and the Deccan; and it is still a prosperous commercial place, rendered conspicuous by the castellated residence of the former rajahs. The Jhansi mutiny was not followed by so many adventures and wanderings as that at other places—for a very mournful reason; nearly all the Europeans were at once put to death. A fort in the town had been previously supplied with food and ammunition, and had been agreed on as a place of refuge in time of danger. Major Skene and Captain Gordon, civil officers of the Company, received information which tended to shew that a petty chieftain near Jhansi was tampering with the troops; and Captain Dunlop, in command there, made what defensive preparations he could. Besides the fort in the town, there was one called the Star Fort in the cantonment, containing the guns and the treasure. The native troops—portions of the 12th infantry and of the 14th irregular cavalry, and a few artillery—rose on the afternoon of the 4th of June, seized the Star Fort, and shot at all the officers in the cantonment; many were killed, and the rest ran to the Town Fort, which they barricaded as well as they were able. The little garrison of Europeans then prepared for a siege; but it could be only of short duration, as the place was too weak to contend against the rebel besiegers. Musketry and sword-cuts (for the garrison often met their assailants hand to hand at the gates) brought down many; and some of the civilians, who tried to escape disguised as natives, were caught by the insurgents and killed. At last, when Captains Dunlop and Gordon, and many other officers had fallen, and when the remaining Europeans had become disheartened, by the scarcity of ammunition and of food, Major Skene accepted terms offered to him, on oath—that the whole of the garrison should be spared if he opened the gate and surrendered. The blood-thirsty villains soon shewed the value of the oath they had taken. They seized all—men, women, and children—and bound them in two rows to ropes, the men in one row and the women and children in the other. The whole were then deliberately put to death; the poor ladies stood with their infants in their arms, and their elder children clinging to their gowns; and when the husbands and fathers had been slaughtered, then came the other half of the tragedy. It is even said that the innocent children were cut in halves before their mothers' eyes. One relief, and one only, marked the scene; there was not, so far as is known, torture and violation of women as

* A curious example was afforded, in relation to the affairs of Saugor, of the circuitous manner in which public affairs were conducted in India, when different officials were residing in different parts of that vast empire. The brigadier commanding the Saugor district adopted a certain course, in a time of peril, concerning the management of the troops under his command. He sent information of these proceedings to Neill at Allahabad (300 miles). Neill forwarded the information to Calcutta (500 miles). The military secretary to the government at Calcutta sent a dispatch to the adjutant-general of the army outside Delhi (900 miles), requesting him to 'move' the commander-in-chief to send a military message to Saugor (400 miles), calling upon the officer of that station to explain the motives for his conduct in the matter at issue. The explanation, so given, was to be sent 400 miles to Delhi, and then 900 miles to Calcutta; and lastly, if the conduct were not approved, a message to that effect would be sent, by any route that happened to be open for dâk, from Calcutta to Saugor.

precursors of death. The death-list was a sad one. Skene, Dunlop, Gordon, Ryves, Taylor, Campbell, Burgess, Turnbull—all were military officers in the Company's service, employed either on military or civil duties; and all were killed. Twenty-four civil servants and non-commissioned officers likewise met with their death; and most painful of all, nineteen ladies and twenty-three children were butchered by the treacherous miscreants. Mr Thornton, the collector for a district between Jhansi and Cawnpore, was afterwards in a position to inform the government that the mutinous troops intended to have left Jhansi after they had captured the treasure; that a Bundelcund chieftainess, the Ranee of Jhansi, wishing to regain power in the district, bribed them with large presents to take the fort and put all the Europeans to death before they finally departed for Delhi; and that it was thus to a *woman* that was due the inhuman slaughtering of more than forty European ladies and children. One account, that reached the ears of officers at other stations, was to the effect that when Major Skene became aware of the miscreant treachery, he kissed his wife, shot her, and then shot himself, to avert apprehended atrocities worse than death; while another narrative or rumour represented the murderers as having chopped off the heads of the victims, instead of merely shooting them; but, in truth, the destruction was so complete that scarcely one was left to tell the tale except natives, who contradicted each other in some of the particulars.

Jhansi of course soon became a prey to lawless marauders; while the mutineers marched off to Delhi or elsewhere. Lieutenant Osborne, at Rewah, was placed in a difficult position at that time. Rewah is a small Rajpoot state, ruled by a native rajah, who is bound by treaties with the British government, and who has a British agent as resident at his court. Rewah was nearly surrounded by mutinous districts, such as Benares, Allahabad, Futtehpoor, Jhansi, Saugor, and Jubbulpoor; and it became a difficult problem for Lieutenant Osborne, the British agent, how to keep wild disorder away from that place. On the 8th of June, by an energetic use of his influence, he was able to announce that the Maharajah of Rewah had placed his troops at the disposal of the government; that the offer had been accepted; and that eight hundred of those troops, with two guns, had been sent off to Ummapatan, a place which commanded the roads to Jubbulpoor, Nagode, and Saugor—ready to oppose insurgents from any of those towns, and to intercept communication with other mutinous towns on the Jumna. He also sent eleven hundred of the Maharajah's troops, with five guns, to Kuttra Pass: a spot whence a rapid advance could be made to Benares, Chunar, or Mirzapore, according as military exigencies might render desirable. A week later, he obtained permission from the Maharajah to send seven hundred troops to Banda; and at the same time to issue a proclamation, promising rewards to any of his soldiers who should distinguish themselves by their gallantry and fidelity. With no higher military rank than that of lieutenant did this active officer thus lay plans, not only for the peace of the Rewah territory itself, but also in aid of the Company's officers all around him. His position at a later date was very perilous.

If the destruction of life was less at Nowgong than at Jhansi, the proceedings of mutinous troops were followed by much more adventure and varied interest. Nowgong or Nowgaon is situated about a hundred miles southeast of the last-named town, but, like it, in the Bundelcund territory. At the beginning of June there were stationed at that place about four hundred men of the 12th native infantry, and rather over two hundred of the 14th irregular cavalry—wings of the same two regiments as at Jhansi; together with a company of the 9th battalion of artillery, and a light field bullock-battery. Major Kirke, commanding the station, had in earlier weeks often discussed the cartridge question with his men, and believed he had removed from their minds all misgivings on that unfortunate subject. Nevertheless, as June approached, the major deemed the appearance of affairs so suspicious, that he made such precautionary arrangements as were practicable to resist an outbreak. Bungalows were now and then discovered to be in flames, without any means of detecting the incendiaries. When the atrocities at Meerut and elsewhere became known, the troops stationed at Nowgong made ardent demonstrations of loyalty—so ardent, that Kirke almost upbraided himself for his momentary distrust of them; the infantry embraced their colours, the artillery embraced their guns, and all asserted their burning desire to chastise the rebels who had proved faithless to the Company Bahadoor. So late as the 6th of June, even while whisperings and ominous signs were passing between them, these unreliable men sent in a grandiloquent petition, in which they said: 'As it is necessary to avenge the government on those cowardly rascals who now, in Delhi and other places, are exciting rebellion, and for which purpose many European regiments are being despatched; we, hearing of this, are exceedingly desirous that we be sent as volunteers to chastise these scoundrels. And that we may shew from our hearts our faithfulness, we are ready to go wherever sent'—and more to the same purpose. This petition or address was presented to Major Kirke by the wing of the 12th regiment. On that same day news arrived that the other wing of the same regiment had mutinied at Jhansi; and the Neemuch men, either with childish indecision or with profound duplicity, sent off a letter to them, reproving them for their insubordination! On the 10th, a petition was presented by the commandant of the artillery (4th company, 9th battalion), couched in similar language; demanding that the artillery might be sent against the rebels; 'in order,' as the petition averred, 'that we may fulfil the wish of our hearts by shewing our bravery and loyalty.'

Never were words uttered more hollow and treacherous. By nightfall on that same 10th of June, the native troops at Nowgong were nearly all rebels, and the Europeans nearly all fugitives. A few hours sufficed to shew the English officers that they were powerless to contend against their opponents. Flight commenced. The officers and civilians, with their families, and Europeans of humbler station, all took their departure from Nowgong—some in buggies, some on horseback, and some on foot; but all equally reft of their worldly property. Were it not that this Chronicle has already contained examples, mournfully numerous, of similar wanderings over the scorching roads and through the thick jungle of India, the fate of the Nowgong party might afford materials for a very exciting narrative; but with the reader's experience on this matter, a few lines of description will suffice. The party was a large one. It comprised Major Kirke, Captain Scot, Lieutenants Townshend, Jackson, Remington, Ewart, Franks, and Barber, about forty other Europeans of both sexes and all ages, and about ninety sepoys of the mutinous infantry, who had not joined their brethren. The fugitives lessened in number every day; some or other of them sank under the heat and fatigue; while the sepoys deserted when they approached towns where insurgents were in the ascendant. Either collectively or separately the wanderers found themselves on different days at Chutterpore, at Logassee, at Churkaree, at Maheba, at Callingurh, at Kabrai, at Banda—places mostly belonging to petty rajahs of Bundelcund. The principal survivors of the party were about ten or twelve days on the roads and fields, before they reached friendly quarters at Banda. On one occasion they were attacked by a band of marauders, and had to buy security with rupees; on another, their sepoys were seized with a panic, and ran off in large numbers; on a third, a body of matchlock-men suddenly confronted them, and shot down Lieutenant Townshend. On one part of the journey, Captain Scot found himself in the midst of a distressing group of women and children: having poor Townshend's horse with him, he loaded both horses with as many as he could carry; but it made him heart-sick to see the others fall away one by one, utterly broken down by fatigue, and with insufficient men to help them along—for the flight appears to have been wanting in every semblance of organisation. A bandsman's wife dropped dead through a sunstroke; then an artillery sergeant, worn out, went into a hut to die. Captain Scot came up with a lady and her child, reeling along the road as if delirious; he readjusted his horse-load, took up the fugitives, and the lady very speedily died in his arms. Shortly after this a fine hale sergeant-major sank, to rise no more; Major Kirke died through a sunstroke; and others dropped off in a similar way. Dr Mawe died from illness and fatigue; and then his wife, while laving her blistered feet in a pool, was set upon by ruffians and robbed of the little she had about her. Captain Scot, after many changes in his horse-load, took up Dr Mawe's child; and 'little Lotty,' of two years' old, seemed to him a blessing rather than a burden; for on the few occasions when he met friendly natives, their friendship was generally gained for him by the sight of the little girl, whose head he endeavoured to shield from the burning sun by a portion of his shirt—the only resource for one who had lost both hat and coat, and whose own head was nearly driven wild by the intense solar heat. It is pleasant to know that the captain and 'little Lotty' were among the few who reached a place of safety.

Banda was another of the stations affected; but the details of its troubles need not be traced here. Suffice it to say that, on the 14th of June, there was a mutiny of a detachment of native infantry, and a few troops belonging to the Nawab of Banda—a titular prince, possessing no political power, but enjoying a pension from the Company, and having a sort of honorary body-guard of native troops. The officers and their families were at first in great peril; but the nawab aided them in making a safe retreat to Nagode. On the 16th of June, Major Ellis had to announce to the government that his station at Nagode was beginning to be filled with anxious fugitives from Banda, Futtehpoor, Humeerpoor, and Ameerpoor; comprising military officers, magistrates, salt-agents, revenue servants, railway officials, and private persons. Twenty-eight of these fugitives arrived on one day. He sent to many petty chieftains of Bundelcund, who were pensioners under the Company or had treaties with it, to exert themselves to the utmost in recovering all property seized during the events of the preceding two or three days in the Banda district. Major Ellis at Nagode, and Mr Mayne at Banda, applied earnestly to Calcutta for military assistance; but they were told plainly that none could be sent to them, every European soldier being needed in the Ganges and Jumna regions.

It now becomes necessary, on removing the scene further to the west, to know something concerning the Mahrattas, their relations to the two great families of Scindia and Holkar, the conventions existing between those two families and the British government, and the military arrangements of the Mahratta territories at the time of the outbreak. These matters can be rendered intelligible without any very lengthened historical narrative.

After the death of the Emperor Aurungzebe, a century and a half ago, India was distracted and impoverished by the contentions of his sons and descendants; each of whom, in claiming the throne, secured the partisanship of powerful nobles, and the military aid of fighting-men in the pay of those nobles. A civil war of terrible kind was the natural result; and equally natural was it that other chieftains, in nowise related to the imperial family, should take advantage of the anarchy to found dynasties for themselves. One such chieftain was Sevajee, a Mahratta in the service of the King of Bejapore, in the southern part of India. The Mahrattas were (and are) a peculiar tribe of Hindoos, more fierce and predatory than most of their fellow-countrymen. Long before Europeans settled in India, the Mahrattas were the chief tribe in the region north, south, and east of the present city of Bombay. After many struggles against the competitors for the throne of Delhi, the Mahrattas were left in possession of a sovereign state, of which Satara and Poonah were the chief cities. From 1707 till 1818, the nominal sovereign or rajah of the Mahrattas had no real power; he was a sort of state or honorary prisoner, confined in the hill-fortress of Satara; while the government was administered by the Peishwa or prime minister, whose office became hereditary in a particular family, and whose seat of government was at Poonah. After many Peishwas had held this singular kind of sovereignty at the one city—the nominal rajah being all the time powerless at the other—circumstances occurred which led to an intermeddling of the East India Company with Mahratta politics, followed by the usual results. Narrain Rao Peishwa was murdered in 1773; many relations of the murdered man competed for the succession; and as the Company greatly desired to possess the island of Salsette and the town of Bassein, at that time belonging to the Mahrattas, it was soon seen that this wish might be gratified by aiding one competitor against another. Battles and intrigues followed, ending in the possession of the two coveted places by the British, and in the appointment of a British resident at the Peishwa's court at Poonah. Thus matters remained until 1817, when the Peishwa engaged in intrigues with other Mahratta chiefs against the British; a course that led to his total overthrow after a few fierce contests in the field. The Mahratta sovereignty at Poonah was entirely put an end to, except a small principality assigned to the Rajah of Satara, the almost forgotten representative of the founder of the Mahratta rule. The British took all the remaining territory, pensioning off the Peishwa; and as to Satara, after several rajahs had reigned, under the close control of the British resident at that city, the principality 'lapsed' in 1848, in default of legitimate male heirs—a lapse that led to the preparation of many ponderous blue books concerning the grievances and complaints of a certain adopted son of the last rajah.

Thus much for the south Mahratta country, having Poonah and Satara for its chief cities; but the British have had fully as much to do with the northern portion of the Mahratta region, represented by the two cities of Gwalior and Indore, and held by the two great Mahratta families of Scindia and Holkar. As the Peishwas in past years cared little for the nominal head of the Mahrattas at Satara, so did the Scindias and Holkars care little for the Peishwas. Each chieftain endeavoured to become an independent sovereign. The Scindia family is traceable up to the year 1720, when Ranojee Scindia was one of the dependents of the Peishwa. From that year, by predatory expeditions and by intrigues, the successive heads of the Scindia family became more and more powerful—contending in turn against the Mogul, the Rajpoots, the Peishwa, and the British; until at length, in 1784, Madhajee Scindia was recognised as an independent sovereign prince, with the hill-fortress of Gwalior as his stronghold and seat of government. In 1794, when Madhajee died, the Scindia dominions extended from beyond Delhi on the north to near Bombay on the south, and from the Ganges to Gujerat—a vast region, held and acquired by means as atrocious as any recorded in the history of India. Early in the present century, the power of the Scindia family received a severe check. Hostilities having broken out with the British, Sir Arthur Wellesley (afterwards Duke of Wellington) defeated Dowlut Rao Scindia at Assaye in 1803, while Lord Lake drove the Mahrattas from the whole of the Doab. Many desperate wars occurred in later years, ending, in 1844, by a treaty which left Bajerut Rao Scindia king or rajah of a state barely equalling England in area, with Gwalior as his capital. A contingent or body of troops was to be supplied by him for the service of the British, beyond which he was permitted to have an independent army of nine thousand men; and there were numerous minor details which gave much influence to the British resident at Gwalior.

Of the family of Holkar, almost the same account may be given as of that of Scindia; inasmuch as it has sprung from a Mahratta leader who acquired power a century and a half ago. The city of Indore has always been the centre of dominion belonging to this family—a dominion extending over a very wide region at some periods, but greatly contracted in recent times. The ruler of the Indore territory at the time of the mutiny was one Mulkerjee Holkar, who had been appointed by the Calcutta government at a time of disputed succession, in such a way as to imply that the territory might pass into British hands whenever the Company chose. Holkar's territory is now much smaller than Scindia's, scarcely exceeding Wales in area.

It will suffice, then, to bear in mind that the southern Mahratta power, that of the courts of Poonah and Satara, had wholly fallen into British hands before the time of the mutiny; and that the northern power, held by the courts of Gwalior and Indore, extended over a country no larger than England and Wales united. Nevertheless, considering that that portion of central India is bounded by Bundelcund, the Doab, Rajpootana, Gujerat, the Nizam's dominions, and the Saugor and Nerbudda territories, it was of much importance to the British that Scindia and Holkar should remain faithful to their alliances at a critical period.

Although Nuseerabad is properly in Rajpootana, of which a few words of description will be given shortly, the mutiny at that place may conveniently be treated here; because it was a link in a chain which successively affected Neemuch, Indore, Mhow, and Gwalior.

Nuseerabad is near Ajmeer, the chief town of a British district surrounded by the dominions of independent or semi-independent rajahs. Ajmeer, though far smaller than most of the principal cities in India, is an ancient and important place, about two hundred and sixty miles southwest of Delhi; at the time of the mutiny, it was the seat of a British political agency; and in a ruined palace of the Emperor Akbar, converted into an arsenal, was a powder-magazine. Nuseerabad, fifteen miles from Ajmeer, may be regarded as the military station for that city, and for the neighbouring British districts; it had an extensive and well-laid-out cantonment, and was the head-quarters of the corps known as the Rajpootana Field-force. Nuseerabad had been nearly drained of troops early in the year, on account of the Persian expedition; but this gap was afterwards partially filled up. In the month of May there were at the station the 1st regiment Bombay lancers, the 15th and 30th Bengal native infantry, and the 2d company of the 7th battalion of Bengal native artillery. An instructive fact was made manifest; the Bombay troops remained faithful, while those of the Bengal army became first restless, then mutinous, then murderous. Unfortunately, the good were not strong enough to coerce the bad; the Bombay lancers numbered only two hundred and fifty sabres. The month of May had not closed when the disturbances at Nuseerabad began. The officers had been nightly in the habit of sleeping with revolvers and swords near at hand; while the Bombay lancers patrolled the cantonment—so suspicious were the symptoms observed. On the evening of the 28th a servant rushed into the bungalow of one of the lieutenants of the 15th infantry, announcing that the regiment had risen. The officers hastened to the lines, and there found the regiment drawn up in companies—the martial array being maintained in mutiny as it had been in regular drill. The men looked sternly at their officers; and soon worse news arrived. The native artillerymen who worked the six guns joined the revolters—not actually firing on the officers, but ready to do so. The Englishmen connected with the two regiments were a mere handful; they were powerless, for none of the sepoys would aid them against the rest. Colonel Penny, in command of the Bombay lancers, instantly hastened down, armed and mounted his troopers, and drew them up into position. Galloping to the artillery lines, and finding the guns pointed against him, he immediately ordered a charge for capturing them, each troop charging in succession. Captain Spottiswoode began, and soon fell mortally wounded; other officers led subsequent charges, but the guns could not be taken. Penny then felt obliged to relinquish this attempt, and to hold himself in readiness to check the mutineers in other ways; but as the two regiments of native infantry refused to listen to their officers, nothing was left but flight. Cornet Newberry, as well as Captain Spottiswoode, fell while charging; Colonel Penny became suddenly ill and died in a few hours; while two or three other officers were wounded. How perilous were those cavalry-charges against the six guns may be judged from a letter written by one of the officers: 'I galloped towards the guns, and must have been eighty or a hundred yards from them when I began to experience the unpleasant sensation of bullets whizzing past my head, and saw a lot of sepoys taking shots at me as I came along. I immediately turned my pony's head, and endeavoured to retreat under cover of a wall which ran in front of the artillery lines. Here I saw more men running up with the kind intention of having a crack at me; so I had to keep along the parade-ground right in the line of fire, and had one or two men popping at me from over the wall on my right. My tât (pony) went as fast as ever he could go, and, thanks be to God, carried me back in perfect safety..... Off we started towards the cavalry lines amid showers of bullets. I dodged round the first bell of arms; and as I passed the bells, saw three or four men behind each, who deliberately shot at us as we passed.' The ladies had been sent off from the station just in time. The surviving officers joined them beyond the cantonment about nightfall, and then all hastened away. They rode forty miles during the night, on roads and fields and rocky hills, and reached a place of safety, Beaur or Beawur, towards noon—hungry, tired, and reft of everything but the clothes on their backs.

As this small body of Bombay native cavalry remained stanch when the Bengal troops were faithless all around them, it was deemed right to make some public acknowledgment of the fact. Lord Elphinstone, as president or governor of Bombay, issued a general order on the subject, thanking the troopers, and passing lightly over the fact that a few of them afterwards disgraced themselves.* The commander-in-chief afterwards ordered the report of the transaction by Captain

* 'To mark the approbation with which he has received this report, the Right Honourable the Governor in Council will direct the immediate promotion to higher grades of such of the native officers and men as his Excellency the Commander-in-chief may be pleased to name as having most distinguished themselves on this occasion, and thereby earned this special reward; and the Governor will take care that liberal compensation is awarded for the loss of property abandoned in the cantonment and subsequently destroyed, when the Lancers, in obedience to orders, marched out to protect the families of the European officers, leaving their own unguarded in cantonment.

'By a later report the Governor in Council has learned with regret that eleven men of the Lancers basely deserted their comrades and their standards, and joined the mutineers; but the Governor in Council will not suffer the disgrace of these unworthy members of the corps to sully the display of loyalty, discipline, and gallantry which the conduct of this fine regiment has eminently exhibited.'

Hardy, who took the control of the lancers when Colonel Penny died, to be translated into the Hindustani and Mahratta languages, and read to all the regiments of the Bombay native army, as an encouragement to them in the path of duty. After the English officers and their families had escaped to Beaur, the mutinous troops made off towards Delhi. Nuseerabad being considered an important station in regard to the control of the surrounding districts, a force was sent to reoccupy it towards the end of June; comprising a detachment of H.M. 83d foot, another of the 20th Bombay native infantry, another of the Jhodpore legion, and a squadron of the 2d Bombay cavalry—Nuseerabad being sufficiently near Bombay to derive advantages not possessed by stations further east.

The usual consequences of the revolt of native regiments followed. Nuseerabad furnished a bad example to Neemuch. As a village, Neemuch is of small consequence; as a military station, its importance is considerable. During some of the negotiations with Scindia in past years, it was agreed that the British should have a cantonment at this spot, which is on the confines of Malwah and Mewar, about three hundred miles south-west of Agra; a force in British pay was to be stationed there, by virtue of certain terms in a treaty, and a small district, with the village in the centre, was made over to the Company for this purpose. The cantonment thereupon built was two or three miles long by a mile in width, and comprised the usual native infantry lines, cavalry lines, artillery lines, head-quarters, offices, bungalows, bazaar, parade-ground, &c. There was also a small fort or fortified square built, as a place of refuge for the families of the military when called to a distance on duty.

In the early part of June, the troops stationed at Neemuch comprised the 72d Bengal N. I., the 7th regiment of Gwalior infantry, two troops of the 1st Bengal light cavalry, and a troop of horse-artillery. Every effort had been made in the early weeks of the mutiny to insure the confidence of these troops, and prevent them from joining the standard of rebellion. Colonel Abbott, and most of the officers of the 72d, as well even as some of their families, slept within the sepoy lines, to win the good-will of the men by a generous confidence. One wing (three companies) of the Gwalior troops held the fortified square and treasury; while the other wing (five companies), now quartered in a vacant hospital, about a quarter of a mile distant, was encamped just outside the walls; Captain Macdonald, the chief officer, residing with the first-named wing. Colonel Abbott, who commanded the station generally, as well as the 72d regiment in particular, became convinced, on the morning of the 2d of June, that all the hopeful expectations of himself and brother-officers were likely to be dashed; for the troops at Neemuch had heard of the mutiny at Nuseerabad, and could be restrained no longer. While the superintendent, Captain Lloyd, hastened to secure some of the Company's records and accounts, and to open a line of retreat for fugitives along the Odeypore road, Colonel Abbott made such military arrangements as were practicable on the spur of the moment. The colonel brought his native officers together, and talked to them so earnestly, that he induced them to swear, 'on the Koran and on Ganges water,' that they would be true to their salt; while he, at their request, swore to his confidence in their faithful intentions. This singular compact, in which Mohammedans, Hindoos, and a Christian swore according to the things most solemn to them respectively, remained unbroken for twenty-four hours; who broke it, after that interval, will at once be guessed. During many preceding days, a panic had prevailed in the Sudder Bazaar; incendiary fires occurred at night; great numbers of persons had removed with their property; the wildest reports were set afloat by designing knaves to increase the distrust; and the commonest occurrences were distorted into phantoms of evil intended against the troops. At last, on the night of the 3d, the troops threw off their oath and their allegiance at once. The artillery, disregarding Lieutenant Walker's entreaties and expostulations, fired off two guns; the cavalry, on hearing this signal, rushed out to join them; and the 72d broke from their lines immediately afterwards. Captain Macdonald instantly ordered into the fort the one wing of the Gwalior regiment which had been encamped outside, under Lieutenants Rose and Gurdon; and then prepared for defence. A bold and singular expedient had just before been adopted by the civil superintendent; he authorised Macdonald to promise to the Gwalior troops, if they faithfully defended the fort during any mutiny outside, a reward of a hundred rupees to each sepoy or private, three hundred to each naik or corporal, five hundred to each havildar or sergeant, higher sums to the jemadars and subadars, and five thousand rupees to the senior native officer, or to the one who should most distinguish himself in preserving the loyalty of the regiment. These are large sums to the natives of India; and the superintendent must have considered long and fully before he promised the Company's money in such a manner. All was, however, in vain. The Gwalior troops remained faithful under the temptation of this promise for a short time; but at length, headed by a subadar named Heera Singh, they demanded that the gates of the fort should be opened, and requested that the officers would make arrangements for their own safety. Macdonald, Rose, Gurdon, and other officers of the Gwalior regiment, expostulated with their men; but entreaty was now of no avail; the troops forcibly opened the gates, and the officers took their departure when the last vestige of hope had been destroyed.

Of the flight, little need be said; it was such a flight as almost every province in Northern India exhibited in those sad days. Some of the ladies and children had been sent off a few hours earlier, hurried away with no preparations for their comfort or even their sustenance; while others waited to accompany their husbands or fathers. Very few had either horses or vehicles; they laboured on footsore to Baree, to Chota Sadree, to Burra Sadree, to Doogla—straggling parties meeting and separating according as their strength remained or failed, and all dependent on the villagers for food. At Doogla, where they arrived on the third night, the officers strengthened a sort of mud-fort about forty yards square, within which forty persons were huddled. After being much straitened, they were relieved by Brigadier Showers on the 9th. The fugitive party now broke up; some returned to Neemuch, which the mutineers had abandoned; but the greater number went to Odeypore, the rana of which place gave them a hospitable reception; some of them afterwards went further west to Mount Aboo or Aboo Gurh—a celebrated place of Hindoo pilgrimage to a sacred temple, and a sanatarium for the Europeans stationed at the

Fort of Mhow.

cantonment of Deesa, about forty miles distant. Those of the party who returned to Neemuch, found everything devastated, the bungalows and offices burnt, and the villagers stripped of their stores by the mutineers, who had afterwards started off for Agra. The officers and their families were literally beggars; they had lost their all. No Europeans were killed save the wife and three children of a sergeant, who could not leave Neemuch in time.

Thus were lost to the British about fourteen hundred men and six guns at Nuseerabad, and sixteen hundred men and six guns at Neemuch, all of which went to swell the insurgent forces inside Delhi or outside Agra.

The stations of Indore and Mhow must now engage a little of our attention—situated nearly south of Neemuch, and about four hundred miles from Agra. Indore, as has already been stated, is the capital of Holkar's Mahratta dominions. It is an ill-built place, standing on the small river Kutki, and is less than a century old: the original Indore, or Jemnah, being on the opposite side of the river. Holkar's palace is a building possessing few attractions; and the like may be said of the other native structures. The relation existing at that time between Indore and Mhow was this—that Indore was the residence of the British political agent at the court of Holkar; whereas Mhow, thirteen miles distant, was the military station or cantonment. The house of the British agent, and those of the other Europeans, were on the eastern side of the town. The agent, at the time of the mutiny, had an escort of cavalry and infantry at his disposal; but it was simply an escort, not a regular military force. The agent, in addition to his duties connected with Holkar's court, was the immediate representative of the British government in relation to various petty states under its protection, but in other points differing greatly in their circumstances.

The Indore agent in May and June was Colonel

Durand. All was peaceful at that place, although much agitation was visible, until the 1st of July; on which day mutiny occurred. Holkar's troops rose against the English, without, as it afterwards appeared, the privity or the wish of the Maharajah himself. Two companies, set apart for the protection of the Residency in the bazaar square, brought two guns to bear upon the building; and the Europeans were horror-stricken at finding themselves suddenly exposed to cannon and musketry. Fortunately a few men of the Bhopal Contingent under Colonel Travers, were on duty at the Residency; and a few of these remained faithful long enough to allow the colonel and the other European officers, with their families, to escape. Not so the civilians, however; many of the civil servants, and of the clerks in the telegraph department, with their wives and children, were butchered in cold blood. As soon as Holkar heard of the outbreak, he ordered some of his own Mahratta troops to hasten to the Residency and aid Colonel Durand; but they told him it was a matter of *deen* (religion), and that they could not act against their brethren. During the next three days Holkar was almost a prisoner in his own palace; his troops rose in revolt, and were speedily joined by those from Mhow, presently to be mentioned; they plundered the treasury, the Residency, and many parts of the town; but as he would not countenance their proceedings, they at length marched off towards Gwalior. This affair at Indore led to the flight of many European families, amid great misery. They collected hastily a few ammunition-wagons, two or three bullock-carts, an elephant, and some horses, and started off towards Sehore and Hosungabad; escorted by a portion of the Bhopal Contingent from several small stations in that part of India.

An important question arose—how was Mhow affected by the mutinous proceedings? As the news of the Nuseerabad mutiny had thrown the troops at Neemuch into agitation, so did the subsequent events at Neemuch immediately affect the sowars and sepoys at Mhow.* Mhow contained a squadron of the same cavalry regiment, the 1st B. N. C., two troops of which had mutinied at Neemuch; and in addition to these was the 23d regiment native infantry, and a company of European artillery. Mhow presented much the appearance of an English town; having a steepled church on an eminence, a spacious lecture-room, a well-furnished library, and a theatre; the cantonment was large and well appointed; and a force was maintained there in virtue of one of the treaties made with Holkar. This relates to the station or British part of the town; the small native town of Mhow is a mile and a half distant. The excitement caused at this station by the news from Neemuch was visible in the conduct of the troops throughout the whole of the month of June. Colonel Platt and the other officers, however, kept a vigilant watch on them, and by combined firmness and kindness hoped to surmount the difficulty. Captain Hungerford afterwards stated that such had been the excessive confidence of some of the officers in their respective regiments, that he could not induce them to strengthen the fort or fortified square, by occupying it with their artillery, until almost the last hour before the Revolt. The fortified square had for some time, however, been a rendezvous for all the ladies and children, who slept within it; the officers remaining in the lines. Thus matters passed until the 1st of July, when Colonel Platt received a pencil-note from Colonel Durand, announcing that the Residency at Indore had been attacked by Holkar's soldiers, and that aid was urgently needed. A troop of cavalry and a few guns were immediately despatched from Mhow; but when they had reached within four miles of Indore, news arrived that the Europeans yet living at that station were about to effect a retreat; upon which the small force returned to Mhow. This duty the troops performed, but it was the last they rendered. The colonel, fearing the arrival of mutinous sepoys from Indore, but not suspecting his own men, made such arrangements as seemed to him befitting, bringing a European battery of artillery into the fort. Soon did the crisis arrive. At eleven o'clock on that same night the plans and hopes were cruelly disappointed; that terrible yell was heard which so often struck dismay into the hearts of the Europeans at the various military stations: the yell of native troops rising in mutiny. Lieutenant Martin, adjutant of the cavalry, while quietly conversing with one of the troopers, became the victim of that dastardly fellow; the war-cry arose, and the trooper turned round and shot the unfortunate officer without a moment's warning. The other officers, hearing the report, but not suspecting the real truth, thought that Holkar's Mahrattas had arrived; they rushed forward to head their respective companies and troops, but sepoys and sowars alike opened fire on them. The officers, now rendered painfully aware of their critical position, ran swiftly across the parade towards the fort, having no time to mount their horses; and it is a marvel that only one of the number, Major Harris, commandant of the cavalry, was shot by the heavy fire poured on them during this run. Colonel Platt, who was in the fort, was almost incredulous when the breathless officers rushed in; he could with difficulty believe the truth now presented to his notice—so fully had he relied on the fidelity of the men. Colonel Platt and Captain Fagan rode down to the lines of the 23d, to which regiment they both belonged, to ascertain the real facts and to exhort the men; but they were never seen alive again by their brethren in arms; they fell, riddled with bullets and gashed with sword-cuts. Captain Hungerford, of the artillery, brought two guns to bear on

* It is well to observe, for the aid of those consulting maps, that there are five or six towns and villages of this name in India. The Mhow here indicated is nearly in lat. 22½°, long. 76°.

the mutineers, which gradually drove them from the lines, but not before they had fired the regimental mess-house and several bungalows; and during the darkness of night, plunderers carried off everything that was valuable. Hungerford would have followed the mutineers with his guns; but the roads were too dark for the pursuit, and the Europeans too unprotected to be left. The remaining English officers, having now no troops to command, acted as a cavalry guard in support of the European battery in the fortified square, under Captain Hungerford. As all the civilians, women, and children were in this place; as the square itself was quite unfitted for a long defence; and as only five native soldiers out of the whole number remained with the officers—the prospect was precarious enough: nevertheless all did their best; Hungerford collected in a few days a large store of provisions, and routed many of the insurgents in neighbouring villages. The impulses that guided the actions of the sepoys were strangely inconsistent; for two of the men saved the life of Lieutenant Simpson, who had been on outpost-duty on the fatal night, and brought him safely into the fort; and yet, though offered promotion for their fidelity, they absconded on the following morning to join their mutinous companions. The Europeans, about eighty in number, maintained their position at Mhow, until a force from Bombay arrived to reoccupy all that region. The ladies, there as everywhere, strove to lessen rather than increase the anxieties of their male companions. One of the officers thus shut up in the extemporised stronghold said in a letter: 'Throughout all this I cannot express the admiration I feel at the way the ladies have behaved—cheerful, and assisting in every way in their power. Poor things, without servants or quarters, huddled together; they have had to do everything for themselves, and employ all their time in sewing bags for powder for the guns, well knowing the awful fate that awaits them if the place is taken. There has not been a sign of fear; they bring us tea or any little thing they can, and would even like to keep watch on the bastions if we would let them. . . . You should see the state we are in—men making up canister, ladies sewing powder-bags, people bringing plunder recovered, artillery mounting guns; all of us dirty and tired with night-watching; we mount sentry-duty to take the weight of it off the artillerymen, and snatch sleep and food as we can.'

Many other stations in that part of India were disturbed in June and July by the mutinies of wings and detachments of regiments too small in amount to need notice here. At one place, Asseerghur, Colonel Le Mesurier warded off mutiny by a prompt and dexterous manœuvre, for which he received the marked thanks of the government.

Gwalior now comes under notice, in relation to a mutiny of troops at that place, and to the conduct of Scindia, the most important of the Mahratta chieftains. Considered as a city or town (about sixty-five miles south of Agra), Gwalior is not very important or interesting, being irregularly built and deplorably dirty, and possessing few public buildings of any note. It is for its hill-fortress that Gwalior is so famed. The rock on which the fortress stands is an elongated mass, a mile and a half long by a quarter of a mile in width, and reaching in some places to a height of about three hundred and fifty feet. It is entirely isolated from other hills; and—partly from the natural stratification of the sandstone, partly from artificial construction—is in many parts quite perpendicular. A rampart runs round the upper edge, conforming to the outline of the summit. The entrance to the enclosure within the rampart is near the north end of the east side; in the lower part by a steep road, and in the upper part by steps cut in the rock, wide enough to permit elephants to make the ascent. A high and massive stone-wall protects the outer side of this huge staircase; seven gateways are placed at intervals along its ascent; and guns at the top command the whole of it. Within the enclosure of the rampart is a citadel of striking appearance, an antique palace surmounted by kiosks, six lofty round towers or bastions, curtains or walls of great thickness to connect those towers, and several spacious tanks. It is considered that fifteen thousand men would be required to garrison this fortress completely. So striking is this rock, so tempting to a chieftain who desires a stronghold, that Gwalior is believed to have been a fortress during more than a thousand years. It has been captured and recaptured nearly a dozen times, by contending Hindoos and Mohammedans, in the course of centuries. The last celebrated contest there was in 1779, when the Company's forces captured it through a clever and unexpected use of ladders and ropes during a dark night. In the next sixty-five years it was possessed successively by the British, the Jâts, the Mahrattas, the British again, the Mahrattas again, and finally by the British, according to the intricacies of treaties and exchanges. Since 1844, Gwalior has been the head-quarters of a corps called the Gwalior Contingent, commanded by British officers; and thus the hill-fortress has virtually been placed within the power of the British government. Besides this famous stronghold, there is at Gwalior a place called the Lashkar. This, in former times, was the stationary camp of the Maharajah Scindia—a dirty collection of rude buildings, extending to a great distance from the southwest foot of the rock; but the great reduction in the number of troops allowed to be held independently by Scindia has materially lessened the importance of the Lashkar.

The loyalty of Scindia became a question of very anxious importance at the time of the mutinies. Holkar was possessor of a much smaller territory than Scindia; and yet, when a rumour spread that the rising at Indore on the 1st of July had the sanction of the first-named sovereign, numerous petty chieftains in that part of India rose against the British, and prepared to cut off all retreat for Europeans. It was not until Holkar had given undoubted evidence of his hostility to the mutineers, that these movements were checked. Much more was this rendered manifest in Scindia's dominions. If Scindia had failed us, the mutineers from Neemuch, Nuseerabad, and Jhansi, by concentrating at Gwalior, might have rendered that hill-fortress a second Delhi to the British. Scindia and Holkar both remained steady; it was the Contingents that failed. These contingents were bodies of native troops, paid by the native princes of the states or countries whose name they bore, but organised and officered by the British, in the same way as the ordinary battalions of the sepoy army. If the native princes, for whose defence ostensibly, and at whose expense really, these contingents were maintained, wished and were permitted to have any independent military force of their own, that could only be done additionally to the contingent which they were bound to furnish. As a consequence of this curious system, a distinction must be drawn between the contingent troops and the prince's troops. At Indore, Holkar's little army as well as Holkar's contingent proved hostile to the British. Scindia was in like manner paymaster for a double force; and the British often anxiously pondered whether one or both of these might prove faithless at Gwalior, with or without the consent of Scindia himself. The Gwalior Contingent, though connected with a Mahratta state, consisted chiefly of Hindustanis, like the sepoys of the Bengal army; the Mahrattas formed quite a minority of the number. The contingent consisted of all three arms of the service—infantry, cavalry, and artillery—and formed a compact army.

The disasters at Gwalior began on Sunday the 14th of June—as usual, on Sunday. It will be remembered (p. 112) that Scindia, three or four weeks earlier, had offered the aid of his own body-guard, which had been accepted by Mr Colvin at Agra; that a portion of the Gwalior Contingent (cavalry) was also sent; that this contingent, under Lieutenant Cockburn, was actively engaged against the insurgents in the region between Agra and Allygurh; and that about one-half of the troopers composing it revolted on the 28th of May, placing that gallant officer in a very embarrassing position. They were portions of the same contingent that mutinied at Neemuch and one or two other places; and on this account the European inhabitants at Gwalior were subject to much anxiety—knowing that that station was the head-quarters; and that, although the contingent was paid for by the Maharajah, the troops had been raised mostly in Oude, and, being disciplined and officered by the British, were likely to share the same sentiments as the Oudians and other Hindustanis of the Bengal army elsewhere. The Maharajah had little or no influence over them; for neither were they his countrymen, nor had he any control over their discipline or movements. During fourteen years, as boy, youth, and man, he had been in great measure a pupil under the British resident at Gwalior; and if he remained an obedient pupil, this was nearly all that could be expected from him—shorn, as the Mahratta court was, of so much of its former influence. Dr Winlow Kirk, superintending surgeon of the contingent, placed upon record, ten days before the bloody deed which deprived him of life, a few facts relating to the position of the Europeans at Gwalior in the latter part of May and the beginning of June. The resident received information which led him to believe that the contingent—seven regiments of infantry, two of cavalry, and four batteries of artillery—was thoroughly disaffected, both the main body at Gwalior and the detachments elsewhere. The brigadier commandant shared this opinion with the resident; and, as a precautionary measure, all the ladies were sent from the station to the Residency, a distance of six miles, on the 28th of May. Dr Kirk, and most of the military officers, dissented from this opinion; they thought the troops were behaving in a respectful manner, and they offered to sleep among the men's lines to shew their confidence in them. On the 29th and 30th, the ladies returned to cantonment, much to the apparent delight of the sepoys at the generous reliance thus placed in them. Bitter was the disappointment and grief in store for those who had trusted these miscreants.

It was on the 14th of June, we have said, that the uprising at Gwalior began. The Europeans had long wished for the presence of a few English troops; but as none were to be had, they watched each day's proceedings rather anxiously. At nine o'clock in the evening of the disastrous Sunday, the alarm was given at the cantonment; all rushed out of their respective bungalows, and each family found others in a similar state of alarm. Shots were heard; officers were galloping or running past; horses were wildly rushing with empty saddles; and no one could give a precise account of the details of the outbreak. Then occurred the sudden and mournful disruption of family ties; husbands became separated from their wives; ladies and children sought to hide in gardens and grass, on house-tops and in huts. Then arose flames from the burning bungalows; and then came bands of reckless sepoys, hunting out the poor homeless English who were in hiding. On the morning of that day, Dr Kirk, although he had not shared the resident's alarm seventeen days before, nevertheless thought with some anxiety of the ladies and children, and asked what arrangements had been made for their safety in the event of an outbreak; but the officers of the regiments, most of whom relied fully on their men, would not admit that there was any serious need for precautionary measures. Two of these unfortunate officers, Major Blake and Major Hawkins, were especially trustful; and these were two among the number who fell by the hands of their own men that very night. Captain Stewart, with his wife and child, were killed, as also Major Sheriff. Brigadier Ramsey, and several others, whose bungalows were on the banks of a small river, escaped by fording. Dr Kirk was one of those who, less fortunate, were furthest from the river. With Mrs Kirk and his child, he hid in the garden all night; in the morning they were discovered; Mrs Kirk was robbed without being otherwise ill treated; but her husband was shot dead before her eyes. Thus fell an amiable and skilful man, who for nearly twenty years had been a medical officer of the Company—first with the Bundelcund legion in Sinde; then as a medical adviser to Sir Charles Napier on matters connected with the health of troops in that sandy region; then with the Bengal troops at Bareilly; then with the European artillery at Ferozpore; and lastly, as superintending surgeon to the troops of the Gwalior Contingent, who shewed their gratitude for his medical aid by putting him to death. After this miserable sight, Mrs Kirk begged the murderers to put an end to her also; but they replied: 'No, we have killed you already'—pointing to the dead body of her husband.

The rest of this story need not be told in detail. Agra was the place of refuge sought by those who had now to flee; and it is some small alleviation of the crimes of the mutineers that they allowed the ladies and children to depart—with their lives, but with little else. How the poor things suffered during five days of weary journeying, they could themselves hardly have told; hunger, thirst, heat, illness, fatigue, and anxiety of mind accumulated on them. Many arrived at Agra without shoes or stockings; and all were beggared of their worldly possessions when they reached that city. When, shortly afterwards, Lieutenant Cockburn wrote to private friends of this event, he had to tell, not only of his own mortification as the officer of a disloyal corps, but of the wreck suffered by the British station at Gwalior. 'I fear there is no chance of my ever recovering any of your portraits; for the ruffians invariably destroy all they cannot convert into silver or gold. All our beautiful garden at Gwalior, on which I spent a good deal of money and care, has been dug up; our houses have been turned into cattle-sheds; there is not a pane of glass in the station; our beautiful church has been gutted, the monuments destroyed, the organ broken up, the stained-glass windows smashed, and the lovely floor of encaustic tiles torn up. The desecration of the tombs is still more horrible; in many places the remains of our countrymen have been torn from the earth, and consigned to the flames!'

The position of Scindia was sufficiently embarrassing at that time. As soon as the troops of the contingent had murdered or driven away their officers, they went to him, placed their services at his disposal, and demanded that he would lead them against the British at Agra. There were eight or ten thousand men in the contingent altogether, and his own Mahratta army was little less numerous; it was therefore a matter of critical importance to the English that he remained steady and faithful. He not only refused to sanction the proceedings of the mutineers, but endeavoured to prevent them from marching towards Agra. In this he succeeded until an advanced period of the autumn; for the troops that troubled Agra at the end of June and the beginning of July were those from Mhow and Neemuch, not the larger body from Gwalior. These mutineers proceeded towards Agra by way of Futtehpore or Futhepore Sikri—a town famed for the vast expanse of ruined buildings, erected by Akbar and destroyed by the Mahrattas; for the great mosque, with its noble gateway and flight of steps; and for the sumptuous white marble tomb, constructed by Akbar in memory of a renowned Mussulman ascetic, Sheik Selim Cheestee.* The battle that ensued, and the considerations that induced Mr Colvin to shut up himself and all the British in the fort at Agra, will be better treated in a later page.

Many of the events treated in this chapter occurred in, or on the frontiers of, the region known as Rajpootana or Rajasthan—concerning which a few words may be desirable. The name denotes the land of the Rajpoots. These Hindoos are a widely spread sept of the Kshetrigas or military caste; but when or where they obtained a separate name and character is not now known. Some of the legends point to Mount Aboo as the original home of the Rajpoots. They were in their greatest power seven hundred years ago, when Rajpoot princes ruled in Delhi, in Ajmeer, in Gujerat, and in other provinces; but the Mohammedan conquerors drove them out of those places; and during many centuries the region mainly belonging to the Rajpoots has been nearly identical with that exhibited at the present time. This region, situated between Central India and Sinde, is about twice as large as England and Wales. Warlike as the Rajpoots have ever been, and possessing many strongholds and numerous forces, they were no match for the Mahrattas in the last century; indeed it was this inequality that led to the interference of the British, who began to be the 'protector' of the Rajpoot princes early in the present century. This protection, insured by various treaties, seems to have been beneficial to the Rajpoots, whose country has advanced in industry and prosperity during a long continuance of peace. The chief Rajpoot states at present are Odeypore or Mewar, Jeypoor, Jhodpore or Joudpore, Jhallawar, Kotah, Boondee, Alwur, Bikaneer, Jeysulmeer, Kishengurh, Banswarra, Pertabghur, Dongurpore, Kerowlee, and Sirohi. The treaties with these several states, at the time of the mutiny, were curiously complicated and diverse: Odeypore paid tribute, and shared with the Company the expense of maintaining a Bheel corps; Jeypoor,

* See page 175.

though under a rajah, was virtually governed by a British resident; Jhodpore, under a sort of feudal rule, paid tribute, and maintained a Jhodpore legion besides a force belonging to the feudatories; Kotah bore the expense of a corps called the Kotah Contingent, organised and officered by the British; Jeysulmeer gave allegiance in return for protection, and so did Kishengurh and many other of the states included in the above list. Most of the Rajpoot states had a feudal organisation for internal affairs; and most of them maintained small native corps, in addition to the contingents furnished by three or four under arrangements with the British. For the whole of the Rajpoot states collectively an agent was appointed by the governor-general to represent British interests, under whom were the civil officers at various towns and stations; while the military formed a Rajpootana Field-force, with head-quarters at Nusserabad.

At the extreme north of Rajpootana is a small British district named Hurrianah, of which the chief towns are Hansi and Hissar. A military corps, called the Hurrianah Light Infantry Battalion, mutinied a few weeks after the Meerut outbreak, killing Lieutenant Barwell and other Europeans; the men acted in conjunction with a part of the 4th regiment irregular cavalry, and, after a scene of murder and pillage, marched off towards Delhi. At Bhurtpore, on the northeast frontier of Rajpootana, a similar scene was exhibited on a smaller scale; a corps called the Bhurtpore Levies revolted against Captain Nixon and other officers, compelling them to flee for their lives: the mutineers, as in so many other instances, marching off at once towards Delhi. There were other mutinies of small detachments of native troops, at minor stations in the Mahratta and Rajpoot countries, which need not be traced in detail.

The vast region in the centre of India has thus passed rapidly under review. We have seen Hindustanis, Bundelas, Jâts, Mahrattas, Bheels, Rajpoots, and other tribes of India revolting against English authority; we have seen native princes and chiefs perplexed how to act between the suzerain power on the one hand, and the turbulent soldiery on the other; we have seen that soldiery, and the attendant rabble of marauders, influenced quite as much by love of plunder as by hate of the Company's raj; we have seen British officers sorely wounded at heart by finding those men to be traitors whom they had trusted almost to the last hour; we have seen ladies and children driven from their bungalows, and hunted like wild beasts from road to river, from jungle to forest; and lastly, in this vast region, we have tracked over considerably more than a thousand miles of country in length without meeting with a single regiment of British troops. The centre of India was defended from natives by natives; and the result shewed itself in deplorable colours.

Girls at the Ganges.

Akali of the Sikhs.

CHAPTER XII.

EVENTS IN THE PUNJAUB AND SINDE.

A VERY important and interesting region in Northern India has scarcely yet been mentioned in this narrative; that, namely, which comprises the Punjaub and Sinde—the Punjaub with its offshoot Cashmere, and Sinde with the delta of the Indus. It will now be necessary, however, to obtain a few general notions on the following points—the geographical position of the Punjaub; the national character of the Sikhs as the chief inhabitants; the transactions which rendered the British masters of that country; and the circumstances that enabled Sir John Lawrence at once to hold the Punjaub intact and to aid the besiegers of Delhi. Of Sinde, a still shorter account will suffice.

The name Punjaub is Persian; it signifies 'five waters;' and was given in early days to the region between the five rivers Indus, Jelum, Chenab, Ravee, and Sutlej. The Punjaub is somewhat triangular in shape, extending from the Himalaya and Cashmere as a northern base to an apex where the five rivers have all coalesced into one. It is about equal in area to England and Scotland without Wales. The northern part is rugged and mountainous; the southern almost without a hill, comprising the several 'Doabs' between the rivers. The natural facilities for inland navigation and for irrigation are great; and these, aided by artificial channels, render the Punjaub one of the most promising regions in India. If the Beas, an affluent of the Sutlej, be added to the five rivers above named, then there are five Doabs or tongues of land between the six rivers, named severally the Doabs of Jullundur, Baree, Rechna, Jetch, and Sinde Sagur, in their order from east to west. The Baree Doab, between the rivers Beas and Ravee, is the most populous and important, containing as it does the three cities of Lahore, Umritsir, and Moultan.

The population of this country is a very mixed one; the Punjaub having been a battle-ground whereon Hindoos from the east and Mohammedans from the west have often met; and as the conquerors all partially settled on their conquests, many races are found in juxtaposition, though each prevailing in one or other of the Doabs. For instance, the Afghans are mostly west of the Indus; the Sikhs, in the Baree Doab; and so on. The inhabitants exceed ten millions in number; nearly two-thirds of them are Mohammedans—a very unusual ratio in India. The Sikhs, however, are the most interesting constituent in this population. They are a kind of Hindoo dissenters, differing from other Hindoos chiefly in these three points—the renunciation of caste, the admission of proselytes, and the practice of the military art by nearly all the males. They trace their origin to one Nanac, who was born in 1469 in a village about sixty miles from Lahore; he founded a new religion, or a new modification of Brahminism; and his followers gave him the designation of *Guru* or 'spiritual pastor,' while they took to themselves that of *Sikhs* or 'disciples.' After many contests with the Mohammedans of the Punjaub, the Sikhs ceased to have a spiritual leader, but acquired temporal power—some assuming the general surname or tribe-name of *Singh* or 'lion,' to denote their military prowess; while the rest became *Khalasas*, adherents to the more peaceful and religious doctrines of Nanac. Some of the Singhs are Akalis, a sort of warlike priests. The Sikhs are more robust than the generality of Hindoos, and more enterprising; but they are more illiterate, and speak a jargon composed of scraps from a multitude of languages.

Such being the country, and such the inhabitants, we have next to see how the British gained influence in that quarter. From the eleventh century until the year 1768 the Mohammedans—Afghans, Gorians, Moguls, and other tribes—ruled in the Punjaub; but in that year the Sikhs, who had gradually been growing in power, gained the ascendency in the region eastward of the Jelum. At the close of the last century an adventurer, named Runjeet Singh, a Sikh of the Jât tribe, became ruler of the district around the city of Lahore; and from that time the Sikh power was in the ascendant. The Sikhs constituted a turbulent and irregular republic; holding, in cases of emergency, a parliament called the Guru-mata at Umritsir; but at other times engaged in petty warfare against each other. Runjeet Singh was ambitious of putting down these competitors for power. He built at Umritsir the great fort of Govindgurh, ostensibly to protect, but actually to overawe and control some of the chieftains. In 1809 he crossed the Sutlej, and waged war against some of the Sikh chieftains of Sirhind who had obtained British protection. This led, not to a war, but to a treaty; by which Runjeet agreed to keep to the west of the Sutlej, and the British not to molest him there. This treaty, with a constancy rare in Asia, the chief of Lahore respected throughout the whole of his long career: maintaining a friendly intercourse with the British. In other directions, however, he waged ruthless war. He conquered Moultan, then Peshawur, then the Derajat, then Cashmere, then Middle Tibet, then Little Tibet, and finally became Maharajah of the Sikhs. In 1831 an interview, conducted with gorgeous splendour, took place between Runjeet Singh and Lord Auckland, in which the governor-general strengthened the ties of amity with the great Sikh. Runjeet died in 1839, and his son and grandson in 1840. From that year a total change of affairs ensued; competitors for the throne appeared; then followed warlike contests; and then a period of such excessive anarchy and lawlessness that British as well as Sikh territory became spoliated by various chieftains. War was declared in 1845, during which it required all the daring and skill of the victors at Moodkee, Ferozshah, Aliwal, and Sobraon, to subdue the fierce and warlike Sikhs. This was ended by a treaty, signed in March 1846; but the treaty was so frequently broken by the chieftains, that another war broke out in 1848, marked by the battles of Moultan, Chillianwalla, and Gujerat. Then ended the Sikh power. The British took the Punjaub in full sovereignty, dated from the 29th of March 1849. Commissioners were appointed, to organise a thoroughly new system of government; and it was herein that Sir Henry Lawrence so greatly distinguished himself. In less than three years from that date, the progress made towards peaceful government was so great, that the court of directors enumerated them in a eulogistic dispatch to the governor in council. The progress was one of uninterrupted improvement from 1849 to 1857; and it will ever remain a bright page in the East India Company's records that, finding the Punjaub a prey to wild licence and devastating intrigues, the Company converted it into a peaceful and prosperous country. The reward for this was received when the rest of Northern India was in a mutinous state. It may here be stated that, when the Punjaub was annexed, a distinct arrangement was made with Cashmere. This interesting country, almost buried among the Himalaya and its offshoots, is one of the few regions in India which have suffered more from natural calamities than from the ravages of man; its population has been diminished from eight hundred thousand to two hundred thousand in the course of thirty years, by a distressing succession of pestilences, earthquakes, and famines. It was governed by Mohammedans during about five centuries; and was then held by the Sikhs from 1819 till the end of their power. Circumstances connected with the annexation of the Punjaub led to the assignment of Cashmere as a rajahship to Gholab Singh, one of the Sikh chieftains; he was to be an independent prince, subsidiary to the British so far as concerned a contingent of troops. The two Tibets were abandoned by the Sikhs before the date when British sovereignty crossed the Sutlej.

For administrative purposes, the Punjaub has been separated into eight divisions—Lahore, Jelum, Moultan, Leia, Peshawur, Jullundur, Hoshyapoor, and Kangra; of which the Lahore

SIR JOHN LAWRENCE.

division alone contains three millions and a half of souls. Each division comprises several revenue and judicial districts. For military purposes, the divisions are only two, those of Lahore and Peshawur, each under a general commandant.

In the middle of May 1857, when the mutinies began, Sir John Lawrence, who had been knighted for his eminent services while with his brother Sir Henry, and had succeeded him as chief-commissioner in the Punjaub, was absent from the capital of that country. He was at Rawul Pindee, a station between Lahore and Peshawur; but happily he had left behind him men who had learned and worked with his brother and himself, and who acted with a promptness and vigour worthy of all praise. To understand what was done, we must attend to the city and cantonment of Lahore. This famous capital of the Punjaub is situated about a mile east of the river Ravee. It contains many large and handsome buildings—such as the Padshah Mosque, said to have been built by Aurungzebe, but converted into a barrack by Runjeet Singh, who cared little about mosques; the Vizier Khan Mosque, once celebrated for its lofty minarets, but afterwards desecrated by the Sikhs in being used as stables for horses and shambles for swine; the Sonara Mosque; and many other Mohammedan mosques and Hindoo temples. Beyond the limits of the city are the large and once-magnificent tomb of the Emperor Jehanghire; the tomb of Anarkalli; and the exquisite garden of Shahjehan, the Shalimar or 'House of Joy'—at one time the pride of the Mussulmans of Lahore, with its three marble terraces and its four hundred marble fountains, but afterwards ruthlessly despoiled of its marble by Runjeet Singh, to adorn Umritsir. Lahore presents every trace of having been a much larger city before the time of the Sikh domination; for the ruins of palaces, serais, and mosques spread over a great area. The city now contains about a hundred thousand inhabitants, a great declension from its population in former days. Considered in a military sense, Lahore is surrounded by a brick wall, formerly twenty-five feet high, but recently lowered. Runjeet Singh ran a trench round the wall, constructed a line of works, mounted the works with many cannon, and cleared away many ruins. This line of fortification exceeds seven miles in circuit; and within the northwest angle is a fort or citadel, containing extensive magazines and manufactories of warlike stores.

From evidence educed at different times, it appears certain that many of the native troops in the Punjaub were cognizant of a conspiracy among the 'Poorbeahs,' by which name the sepoys of the eastern regions are known to the inhabitants of the Punjaub; and that they held themselves ready to join in any mutiny arising out of such conspiracy. How the authorities checked this conspiracy, was strikingly shown by the proceedings at different stations immediately after news arrived of disaster in the eastern provinces. We will rapidly glance in succession at Lahore, Umritsir, Ferozpore, Jullundur, and Phillour; and will then proceed to the Peshawur region. The British military cantonment for the city of Lahore was six miles distant, at a place called Meean Meer; where were stationed three native infantry regiments, and one of cavalry, the Queen's 81st foot, two troops of horse-artillery, and four reserve companies of foot-artillery. In the fort, within the city-walls, were half a native infantry regiment, a company of Europeans, and a company of foot-artillery. The plot, so far as concerned the Punjaub, is believed to have been this.* On a particular day, when one wing of a native regiment at the fort was to be exchanged for another, there would, at a particular moment, be about eleven hundred sepoys present; they were to rise suddenly, murder their officers, and seize the gates; take possession of the citadel, the magazine, and the treasury; overpower the Europeans and artillery, only a hundred and fifty men in all; and kindle a huge bonfire as a signal to Meean Meer. All the native troops in cantonment were then to rise, seize the guns, force the central jail, liberate two thousand prisoners, and then commence an indiscriminate massacre of European military and civilians. The other great stations in that part of the Punjaub—Umritsir, Ferozpore, Jullundur, Phillour—were all in the plot, and the native troops at these places were to rise in mutiny about the 15th of May. There were many proofs, in the Punjaub and elsewhere, that the plotters at Meerut began a little too early for their own object; the scheme was not quite ripe at other places, else the English might have been almost entirely annihilated throughout the northern half of India.

The authorities at Lahore knew nothing of this plot as a whole, though they possibly observed symptoms of restlessness among the native troops. When the crisis arrived, however, they proved themselves equal to the difficulties of their position. On the 10th of May, the outbreak at Meerut occurred; on the 11th an obscure telegram reached Lahore, telling of some disaster; on the 12th the real nature of the affair became known. Sir John Lawrence being at Rawul Pindee, the other authorities—Mr Montgomery, Mr M'Leod, Mr Roberts, Colonel Macpherson, Colonel Lawrence (another member of this distinguished family), Major Ommaney, and Captain Hutchinson—instantly formed a sort of council of war; at which they agreed on a plan, which was assented to by Brigadier Corbett, commandant of the station at Meean Meer. This plan was to consist in depriving the native troops of their ammunition and percussion-caps, and placing more Europeans within the fort. A native officer in the Sikh police corps, however, revealed to the authorities the outlines of a conspiracy which had come to his knowledge; and the brigadier then resolved on the complete disarming of the native regiments—a bold step where he had so few Europeans to assist him, but carried out with admirable promptitude and success. It so happened that a ball was to be given that night (the 12th) by the military officers at Meean Meer; the ball *was* given, but preparations of a kind very different from festive were at the same time quietly made, wholly unknown to the sepoys. Early on the morning of the 13th, the whole of the troops, native and European, were ordered on parade, avowedly to hear the governor-general's order relating to the affairs at Barrackpore, but really that the Europeans might disarm the natives. After this reading, a little manœuvring was ordered, whereby the whole of the native regiments—the 16th, 26th, and 49th Bengal infantry, and the 8th Bengal cavalry—were confronted by

* The events of the mutiny relating to the Punjaub have been ably set forth in a series of papers in *Blackwood's Magazine*, written by an officer on the spot.

the guns and by five companies of the Queen's 81st. At a given signal, the sepoys were ordered to pile arms, and the sowars to unbuckle sabres; they hesitated; but grape-shot and port-fires were ready—they knew it, and they yielded. Thus were disarmed two thousand five hundred native troops, by only six hundred British soldiers. Meanwhile the fort was not forgotten. Major Spencer, who commanded the wing of the 26th stationed there, had the men drawn up on parade on the morning of that same day; three companies of the 81st entered the fort under Captain Smith; and these three hundred British, or thereabouts, found it no difficult task to disarm the five or six hundred sepoys. This done, the 81st and the artillery were quickly placed at such posts as they might most usefully strengthen—in the lines of the 81st, on the artillery parade-ground, and in an open space in the centre of the cantonment, where the brigadier and his staff slept every night. The ladies and children were accommodated in the barracks; while the regimental officers were ordered to sleep in certain selected houses in the lines of their own regiments—regiments disarmed but not disbanded; and professedly disarmed only as a matter of temporary expediency. Thus was Lahore saved.

Umritsir is the next station to which attention must be directed relatively to the Punjaub. It was an important place to hold in due subordination, not only on account of its size and population, but for a certain religious character that it possesses in the eyes of the Sikhs. Umritsir or Amritsir has had a career of less than three centuries. In 1581, Ram Das, the fourth *Guru* or spiritual pastor of the Sikhs, ordered a reservoir or fountain to be formed at a particular spot, and named it *Amrita Saras*, or 'Fount of Immortality.' This Amrita Saras or Umritsir at once became a place of pilgrimage, and around it gradually grew up a considerable city. One of the Mohammedan sovereigns, Ahmed Shah, uneasy at the increasing power of the Sikhs, sought to terrify and suppress them by an act of sacrilege at Umritsir; he blew up a sacred shrine, filled up the sacred pool, and caused the site to be desecrated by slaughtering kine upon it. But he miscalculated. It was this very act which led to the supremacy of the Sikhs over the Mohammedans in the Punjaub; they purified and refilled the pool, rebuilt the shrine, and vowed unceasing hostility to the Mussulmans. At present, the holy place at Umritsir is a very large square basin, in which Sikhs bathe as other Hindoos would do in the Ganges; and in the centre, on a small island, is a richly adorned temple, attended by five hundred Akalis or armed priests. Considered as a city, Umritsir is large, populous, industrial, and commercial. The most striking object in it is the Govindgurh, the fortress which Runjeet Singh constructed in 1809, professedly to protect the pilgrims at the sacred pool, but really to increase his power over the Sikhs generally. Its great height and heavy batteries, rising one above another, give it a very imposing appearance; and it has been still further strengthened since British occupation began.

Directly the unfavourable news from Meerut was received at Lahore, or rather immediately after the disarming at the last-named place had been effected—a company of H.M. 81st foot, under Lieutenant Chichester, was sent off in eckas to Umritsir, to strengthen the garrison at Govindgurh. It was known that this fort was regarded almost in a religious light in the Punjaub; and that if the Poorbeahs or rebellious sepoys should seize it, the British would be lowered in the eyes of the Sikhs generally. In the fort, and in the cantonment near the town, were two companies of artillery, one European and one native; together with the 59th B. N. I., and a light field-battery. The wing of the Queen's 81st, despatched from Lahore on the evening of the 13th of May, reached Umritsir on the following morning; and a company of foot-artillery, under Lieutenant Hildebrand, intended for Phillour, was detained at Umritsir until the authorities should feel sure of their position. The officers of the 59th had, some time previously, discussed frankly with their men the subject of the greased cartridges, and had encouraged them to hold a committee of inquiry among themselves; the result of which was a distinct avowal of their disbelief in the rumours on that unfortunate subject. It is only just towards the regimental officers to say that the highest authorities were as unable as themselves to account for the pertinacious belief of the sepoys in the greased-cartridge theory; Sir John Lawrence spoke of it as a 'mania,' which was to him inexplicable. With the miscellaneous forces now at hand, the authorities made no attempt to disarm the native regiment, but kept a watchful eye on the course of events. On the night of the 14th, an alarm spread that the native troops at Lahore had mutinied, and were advancing on Umritsir; the ladies and children were at once sent into the fort, and a small force was sent out on the Lahore road, to check the expected insurgents; but the alarm proved to be false, and the troops returned to their quarters. Peace was secured at Umritsir by the exercise of great sagacity. The Mohammedans were strong in the city, but the Sikhs were stronger; and Mr Cooper, the deputy-commissioner, succeeded in preventing either religious body from joining the other against the British—a task requiring much knowledge of the springs of action among the natives in general. It was not the first time in the history of India that the British authorities had deemed it expedient to play off the two religions against each other.

Ferozpore was not so happily managed as Lahore and Umritsir in this exciting and perilous week; either because the materials were less suitable to work upon, or because the mode of treatment was not so well adapted to the circumstances.

Ferozpore is not actually in the Punjaub; it is one of the towns in Sirhind, or the Cis-Sutlej states—small in size and somewhat mean in appearance, but important through its position near the west bank of the Sutlej, and the large fort it comprises. In the middle of May, this station contained H.M. 61st foot, the 45th and 57th Bengal native infantry, the 10th Bengal native cavalry, about 150 European artillery, and one light-horse field-battery, with six field-guns—a large force, not required for Ferozpore itself, but to control the district of which it was the centre. Ferozpore had been the frontier British station before the annexation of the Punjaub, and had continued to be supplied with an extensive magazine of military stores. When Brigadier Innes heard on the 12th of May of the mutiny at Meerut, he ordered all the native troops on parade, that he and his officers might, if possible, judge of their loyalty by their demeanour. The examination was in great part, though not wholly, satisfactory. At noon on the 13th the disastrous news from Delhi arrived. The intrenched magazine within the fort was at that time guarded by a company of the 57th; and the brigadier, rendered somewhat uneasy on this matter, planned a new disposition of the troops. There had been many 'cartridge' meetings held among the men, and symptoms appeared that a revolt was intended. The relative positions of all the military were as follows: In the middle of the fort was the intrenched magazine, guarded as just stated; outside the fort, on the west, were the officers' bungalows and the official buildings; still further to the west were the sepoy lines of the 45th and 57th; northward of these lines were the artillery barracks; still further north were the lines of the cavalry; south of the fort were the barracks of the European regiment; on the north of the fort was the Sudder Bazaar; while eastward of it was an open place or *maidan*. The brigadier sought to avert danger by separating the two native regiments; but the Queen's 61st, by the general arrangements of the cantonment, were too far distant to render the proper service at the proper moment. The 45th were to be removed to an open spot northeast of the cantonment, and the 57th to another open space on the south, two miles distant; the native cavalry were to take up a position near their own lines; the 61st were to encamp near the south wall of the fort; while one company, with artillery and guns, was to be placed within the fort. After a parade of the whole force, on the afternoon of the 13th, each corps was ordered to the camping-ground allotted for it. The 57th obeyed at once, but some companies of the 45th, while marching through the bazaar, refused to go any further, stopped, loaded their muskets, and prepared for resistance; they ran towards the fort, clambered over a dilapidated part of the ramparts, and advanced towards the magazine, where scaling-ladders were thrown over to them by a company of the 57th who had been on guard inside. This clearly shewed complicity to exist. A short but severe conflict ensued. Captain Lewis and Major Redmond had only a few Europeans with them, but they promptly attacked the mutineers, drove out the 45th, and made prisoners the treacherous guard of the 57th. All was now right in the fort and magazine, but not in the cantonment. About two hundred men of the 45th commenced a system of burning and looting; officers' bungalows, mess-houses, hospitals, the church—all were fired. Many isolated acts of heroism were performed by individual Europeans, but no corps was sent against the ruffians. Fortunately, a powder-magazine beyond the cavalry lines, containing the enormous quantity of three hundred thousand pounds of gunpowder, did not fall into the hands of the rebels; it might have done so, for no preparations had been made to defend it. All this time the Queen's troops chafed at their enforced inaction; their camping-ground had been so badly chosen that they dared not in a body attack the 45th lest the 57th should in the meantime surprise them in the rear; and there is no evidence that they were ordered to do what any English regiment would cheerfully have undertaken—divide into two wings, each to confront a whole regiment of sepoys. During the night and the following morning nearly all the sepoys decamped, some with arms and some without. Ferozpore was saved for the present; but mutinous proceedings were encouraged at Jullundur, Jelum, and Sealkote, by the escape of the 45th and 57th; and the brigadier fell into disgrace for his mismanagement of this affair. He had only just arrived to take command of that station, and it may be that he was on this account less able to judge correctly the merits or demerits of the forces placed at his disposal.

Jullundur, which gives name to the Jullundur Doab between the Sutlej and the Beas, is another of this group of stations. It is situated on the high road from Umballa and Umritsir to Lahore; and was formerly the capital of an Afghan dynasty in the Punjaub. Although shorn of much of its former greatness, it is still an important and flourishing town, with forty thousand inhabitants. Jullundur received the news from Meerut on the 11th of May, and immediately precautionary measures were taken. Brigadier-general Johnstone, the commandant, being absent at the time, a plan was at once formed by Colonel Hartley of H.M. 8th foot, and Captain Farrington, the deputy-commissioner, and agreed to by all the other officers. The station at that time contained H.M. 8th foot, the 6th light cavalry, the 36th and 61st native infantry, and one troop of horse-artillery. The chief officers in command were Colonels Longfield and Hartley, Majors Barton, Innes, and Olpherts, and Captain Faddy. When the telegraph of the 12th of May confirmed the Meerut news of the 11th, it was resolved at once to control the native troops at Jullundur, and to disarm them if mutinous symptoms should appear.

Part of the Queen's troops were marched into the artillery lines; the guns were pointed at the lines of the native regiments in such a way as to render the sepoys and sowars somewhat uneasy; two field-guns were kept with horses ready harnessed for movement; careful patrolling was maintained during the night; and the ladies and children were safely if not comfortably placed in barracks and rooms guarded by their own countrymen. Captain Farrington was placed in charge of the civil lines, the public buildings, and the town generally; and most fortunate was it for him, and the English generally, that the native Rajah of Jullundur, Rundheer Singh Alloowalla, remained friendly. This prince had been deprived of part of his territory at the period of the annexation of the Punjaub, but the deprivation had not rendered him hostile to his powerful superiors; he promptly aided Farrington with guns and men, instead of throwing in his lot with the mutineers. Jullundur, like Lahore, Umritsir, and Ferozpore, was saved for the present.

Phillour, the fifth station in this remarkable group, was in one sense more perilously placed than any of the others, owing to its nearer proximity to the mutineers of Meerut and Delhi. It stands on the right bank of the Sutlej, on the great high road from Umballa and Loodianah to Umritsir and Lahore. Phillour is of no account as a town, but of great importance as a military station on the frontier of the Punjaub, and as commanding the passage of the grand trunk-road across the Sutlej. At the time of the mutiny it had a magazine containing a vast supply of warlike material, without any European troops whatever. The adjoining cantonment contained one native regiment, of which one company guarded the fort and magazine. The military authorities all over the Punjaub and Sirhind well knew that Phillour contained munitions of war that would be most perilous in the hands of mutineers. Lieutenant Hildebrand, as was lately stated, was sent from Lahore with a company of artillery to Phillour; but he stopped on the way to aid the operations at Umritsir. When the news from Meerut arrived, Colonel Butler made such precautionary arrangements as he could at the lines, while Lieutenant Griffith looked watchfully after the fort and arsenal. Securing the telegraph, in order that the sepoys of the 3d native infantry might not tamper with it, they communicated with Jullundur, and were rejoiced to find that a small force was about to be despatched from that place for their relief. As soon as the authorities at the last named station became aware of the insurgent proceedings, they determined, besides attending to the safety of their own station, to aid Phillour; they sent a telegraphic officer to make such arrangements as would keep the wire in working order; they sent a message to Loodianah, to warn the deputy-commissioner to guard the bridge of boats across the Sutlej; and they sent a small but compact force to Phillour. This force consisted of a detachment of the Queen's 8th foot, two horse-artillery guns, spare men and horses for the artillery, and a small detachment of the 2d Punjaub cavalry. Knowing that this welcome force was on the road, Colonel Butler and Lieutenant Griffith sought to maintain tranquillity in Phillour during the night; they closed the fort-gate at sunset; they placed a loaded light field-piece just within the gate, with port-fires kept burning; and the little band of Europeans remained on watch all night. At daybreak their succour arrived; the force from Jullundur, commanded by Major Baines and Lieutenants Sankey, Dobbin, and Probyn, marched the twenty-four miles of distance without a single halt. The guns and cavalry, being intended only as an escort on the road, and to aid in recovering the fort in the event of its having been captured by the sepoys during the night, returned to Jullundur, together with fifty of the infantry. The actual reinforcement, therefore, was about a hundred of H.M. 8th foot, and a few gunners to work the fort-guns if necessary. The little garrison opened the fort-gates to admit this reinforcement—much to the dismay of the sepoys in the cantonment; for, as was afterwards ascertained, a plot had been formed whereby the fort was to be quietly taken possession of on the 15th of the month, and used as a rendezvous for the sepoy regiments in the Punjaub, when they had risen in mutiny, and formed a system of tactics in reference to the great focus of rebellion at Delhi.

Thus were the days from the 11th to the 14th of May days of critical importance in the eastern part of the Punjaub. Evidence almost conclusive was obtained that the 15th was intended to have been a day of grand mutiny among the Bengal sepoys stationed in that region: the regimental officers knew nothing of this; some of them would not believe it, even at the time of the disarming; but the current of belief tended in that direction afterwards. There is very little doubt, as already implied, that the Meerut outbreak occurred before the plans were ready elsewhere; that event seemed to the British, and rightly so, a dreadful one; but, if delayed five days, it would probably have been followed by the shedding of an amount of European blood frightful to contemplate.

Having noticed the prompt measures taken at Lahore, Umritsir, Ferozpore, Jullundur, and Phillour, shortly before the middle of May; it will be useful, before tracing the course of subsequent revolt in some of the eastern Punjaub stations, to attend to the state of affairs in the western division, of which Peshawur was the chief city.

Peshawur was beyond the limits of British India until the annexation of the Punjaub. Situated as it is on the main road from the Indus at Attock to the Indian Caucasus range at the Khyber Pass, it has for ages been regarded as an important military position, commanding one of the gates of India. The Afghans and other Mohammedan tribes generally made their irruptions into India by this route. During the complexities of

Indian politics and warfare, Peshawur passed from the hands of the Afghans to those of the Sikhs, and then to the British, who proceeded to make it the head-quarters of a military division. Peshawur had been so ruthlessly treated by Runjeet Singh, after his capture of that place in 1818, that its fine Moslem buildings were mostly destroyed, its commerce damaged, and its population diminished. At present, its inhabitants are believed to be about sixty thousand in number. The fort is very strong; it consists of lofty walls, round towers at the angles, semicircular ravelins in front, faussebraies of substantial towers and walls, a wet ditch, and one only gateway guarded by towers; within the enclosure are capacious magazines and storehouses.

When the mutiny began, the Peshawur division contained about fourteen thousand troops of all arms. A peculiar military system was found necessary in this division, owing to the large proportion of semi-civilised marauders among the inhabitants. The western frontier is hilly throughout, being formed of the Indian Caucasus and the Suliman Range, and being pierced by only a few roads, of which the Khyber Pass and the Bolan Pass are the most famous. These passes and roads are for the most part under the control of hardy mountaineers, who care very little for any regular governments, whether Afghan, Sikh, or British, and who require constant watching. Many of these men had been induced to accept British pay as irregular horsemen; and Colonel (formerly Major) Edwardes acquired great distinction for his admirable management of these rough materials. The fourteen thousand troops in the Peshawur division of the Punjaub comprised about three thousand European infantry and artillery, eight thousand Bengal native infantry, three thousand Bengal native cavalry and artillery, and a few Punjaubees and hill-men. These were stationed at Peshawur, Nowsherah, Hoti Murdan, and the frontier forts at the foot of the hills. Major-general Reid was chief military authority at Peshawur. On the 13th of May he received telegraphic news of the mutiny at Meerut and of the disarming at Lahore, and immediately held a council of war, attended by himself, Brigadiers Cotton and Neville Chamberlain, Colonels Edwardes and Nicholson. Edwardes was chief-commissioner and superintendent of the Peshawur division, besides being a military officer. It was resolved that, as senior military officer in the Punjaub, General Reid should assume chief command, and that his head-quarters should be with those of the Punjaub civil government, at Lahore or elsewhere; while Cotton should command in the Peshawur division. The council also agreed that, besides providing as far as was possible for the safety of each station individually, a 'movable column' should be formed at Jelum, a station on the great road about midway between Lahore and Peshawur—ready to move on any point in the Punjaub where mutinous symptoms might appear. This force, it will be seen,* was made up of a singular variety of troops, comprising all arms of the service, irregulars as well as regulars, Europeans as well as natives; but the Oudian or 'Poorbeah' element was almost wholly absent, and by this absence was the efficiency of the column really estimated. Various arrangements were at the same time made for so distributing the European troops as to afford them the best control over the sepoy regiments. At Peshawur itself, the Company's treasure was sent into the fort for safety, and the Residency was made the head-quarters of the military authorities.

On the 21st of May, news reached Peshawur that the 55th Bengal native infantry—encouraged probably by the withdrawal of the 27th foot from Nowsherah to aid in forming the movable column—had mutinied at Murdan on the preceding day, keeping their officers under strict surveillance, but not molesting them; and that Colonel Spottiswoode, their commander, had put an end to his existence through grief and mortification at this act. The crisis being perilous, it was at once resolved to disarm the native troops at Peshawur, or so much of them as excited most suspicion. This was successfully accomplished on the morning of the 22d—much to the chagrin of the officers of the disbanded regiments, who, here as elsewhere, were among the last to admit the probability of insubordination among their own troops. The 24th, 27th, and 51st regiments of Bengal native infantry, and the 5th of light cavalry, were on this occasion deprived of their arms; and a subadar-major of the 51st was hanged in presence of all his companions in arms. The disarming was effected by a clever distribution of the reliable forces; small parties of European artillery and cavalry being confronted with each regiment, in such way as to prevent aid being furnished by one to another. The men were disarmed, but not allowed to desert, on pain of instant death if caught making the attempt; and they were kept constantly watched by a small force of Europeans, and by a body of irregular troopers who had no sympathy whatever with Hindustanis. This done, a relieving force was at once sent off to Murdan; a step which would have been dangerous while sepoy troops still remained so strong at Peshawur. The small force of Europeans and irregulars was found to be sufficient for this duty; it arrived at Murdan, attacked the mutinous 55th, killed or captured two hundred, and drove the rest away. These misguided insurgents ill calculated the fate in store for them. Knowing that Mohammedan hill-tribes were near

* This column was made up as follows:

1. H.M. 27th foot, from Nowsherah.
2. H.M. 24th foot, from Rawul Pindee.
3. One troop European horse-artillery, from Peshawur.
4. One light field-battery, from Jelum.
5. The Guide Corps, from Murdan.
6. The 16th irregular cavalry, from Rawul Pindee.
7. The 1st Punjaub infantry, from Bunnoo.
8. The Kumaon battalion, from Rawul Pindee.
9. A wing of the 2d Punjaub cavalry, from Kohat.
10. A half company of Sappers, from Attock.

at hand, and that those tribes had often been hostile to the English, they counted on sympathy and support, but met with defeat and death. The chivalrous Edwardes, who had so distinguished himself in the Punjaub war, had gained a powerful influence among the half-trained mountaineers on the Afghan border. While the detachment from Peshawur was pursuing and cutting down many of the mutineers, the hill-men were at that very time coming to Edwardes to ask for military employment. These hill-men hated the Brahmins, and had something like contempt for traitors; when, therefore, Edwardes sent them against the mutineers, the latter soon found out their fatal error. 'The petted sepoy,' says one who was in the Punjaub at the time, 'whose every whim had been too much consulted for forty years—who had been ready to murder his officer, to dishonour his officer's wife, and rip in pieces his officer's child, sooner than bite the end of a cartridge which he well knew had *not* been defiled—was now made to eat the bread and drink the water of affliction: to submit at the hazard of his wretched life, which he still tenaciously clung to, to ceremonies the least of which was more damning to his caste than the mastication of a million of fat cartridges.' Even this was not the end; for the sepoys were brought back to the British cantonment, in fives and tens, and there instantly put to death; no quarter was given to men who shewed neither justice nor mercy to others. There were other forts in the Peshawur Valley similar to that at Murdan, places held by native regiments, in which little or no reliance could be placed. There were four native regiments altogether in these minor forts; and it became necessary to disarm these before the safety of the British could be insured. Peshawur contained its full Asiatic proportion of desperate scoundrels, who would have begun to *loot* at any symptom of discomfiture of the paramount power.

When this disarming of the native troops at the surrounding forts had been effected, the authorities at Peshawur continued to look sharply after the native troops at this important station. The disarmed 5th irregular cavalry, having refused to go against the 55th at Murdan, were at once and successfully disbanded. By a dexterous manœuvre, the troopers were deprived of horses, weapons, coats, and boots, while the mouths of cannon were gaping at them; they were then sent off in boats down the Indus, with a hint to depart as far as possible from any military stations. The authorities in the Punjaub, like Neill at Benares and Allahabad, believed that mercy to the sepoys would be cruelty to all besides at such a time; they shot, hanged, or blew away from guns with terrible promptness, all who were found to be concerned in mutinous proceedings. On one occasion a letter was intercepted, revealing the fact that three natives of high rank (giving names) were to sit in council on the morrow to decide what to do against the British; a telegraphic message was sent off to Sir John Lawrence, for advice how to act; a message was returned: 'Let a spy attend and report;' this was done, and a plot discovered; another question brought back another telegram: 'Hang them all three;' and in a quarter of an hour the hanging was completed. The importance of retaining artillery in European hands was strongly felt at Peshawur; to effect this, after many guns had been sent away to strengthen the moving column, a hundred and sixty European volunteers from the infantry were quickly trained to the work, and placed in charge of a horse-battery of six guns, half the number on horseback, and the other half sitting on the guns and wagons—all actively put in training day after day to learn their new duties. Fearful work the European gunners had sometimes to perform. Forty men of the 55th regiment were 'blown from guns' in three days. An officer present on the occasion says: 'Three sides of a square were formed, ten guns pointed outwards, the sentence of the court read, a prisoner bound to each gun, the signal given, and the salvo fired. Such a scene I hope never again to witness—human trunks, heads, arms, legs flying about in all directions. All met their fate with firmness but two; so to save time they were dropped to the ground, and their brains blown out by musketry.' It sounds strangely to English ears that such a terrible death should occasionally be mentioned as a *concession* or matter of favour; yet such was the case. Mr Montgomery, judicial commissioner of the Punjaub, issued an address to one of the native regiments, two sepoys of which had been blown away from guns for mutinous conduct. He exhorted them to fidelity, threatened them with the consequences of insubordination, and added: 'You have just seen two men of your regiment blown from guns. This is the punishment I will inflict on all traitors and mutineers; and your consciences will tell you what punishment they may expect hereafter. These men have been blown from guns, and not hanged, because they were Brahmins, and *because I wished to save them from the pollution of the hangman's touch*; and thus prove to you that the British government does not wish to injure your caste and religion.' The treachery and cruelty of the mutinous sepoys soon dried up all this tenderness as to the mode in which they would prefer to be put to death. We have seen Neill at Cawnpore, after the revelation of the horrors in the slaughter-room, compelling the Brahmin rebels to pollute themselves by wiping up the gore they had assisted to shed, as a means of striking horror into the hearts of miscreant Brahmins elsewhere.

In addition to the severe measures for preserving obedience, other precautions were taken involving no shedding of blood. A new levy of Punjaubee troopers was obtained by Edwardes from the Moultan region; the disarmed sepoys were removed from their lines, and made to encamp in a spot where they could be constantly watched; a land-transport train was organised, for the conveyance of European troops from place to place; the fort was strengthened, provisioned, and guarded against all surprises; the artillery park was defended by an earthwork; and trusty officers were sent out in various directions to obtain recruits for local irregular corps—enlisting men rough in bearing and unscrupulous in morals, but who knew when they were well commanded, and who had no kind of affection for Hindustanis. Thus did Cotton, Edwardes, Nicholson, and the other officers, energetically carry out plans that kept Peshawur at peace, and enabled Sir John Lawrence to send off troops in aid of the force besieging Delhi. Colonel Edwardes, it may here be stated, had been in Calcutta in the month of March; and had there heard that Sikhs in some of the Bengal regiments were taking their discharge, as if foreseeing some plot then in preparation; this confirmed his predilection for Punjaub troops over 'Poorbeahs.' The activity in raising troops in the remotest north-west corner of India appears to have been a double benefit to the British; for it provided a serviceable body of hardy troops, and it gratified the natives of the Peshawur Valley. This matter was adverted to in a letter written by Edwardes. 'This post (Peshawur), so far from being more arduous in future, will be more secure. Events here have taken a wonderful turn. During peace, Peshawur was an incessant anxiety; now it is the strongest point in India. We have struck two great blows—we have disarmed our own troops, and have raised levies of all the people of the country. The troops (sepoys) are confounded; they calculated on being backed by the people. The people are delighted, and a better feeling has sprung up between them and us in this enlistment than has ever been obtained before. I have also called on my old country, the Derajat, and it is quite delightful to see how the call is answered. Two thousand horsemen, formerly in my army at Moultan, are now moving on different points, according to order, to help us in this difficulty; and every post brings me remonstrances from chiefs as to why they have been forgotten. This is really gratifying.' It may be here stated that Sir John Lawrence, about the end of May, suggested to Viscount Canning by telegraph the expediency of allowing Bengal sepoys to retire from the army and receive their pay, if they preferred so doing, and if they had not been engaged in mutinous proceedings—as a means of sifting the good from the bad; but Canning thought this would be dangerous east of the Sutlej; and it does not appear to have been acted on anywhere.

These exertions were materially aided by the existence of a remarkable police system in the Punjaub—one of the benefits which the Lawrences and their associates introduced. The Punjaub police was of three kinds. First was the *military* police, consisting of two corps of irregular infantry, seven battalions of foot, one regiment cavalry, and twenty-seven troops of horse—amounting altogether to about thirteen thousand men. These men were thoroughly disciplined, and were ready at all times to encounter the marauding tribes from the mountains. Then came the *civil* police, comprising about nine thousand men, and distributed over nearly three hundred thannahs or subordinate jurisdictions, to protect thirty thousand villages and small places: the men were armed with swords and carbines. Lastly were the *constabulary*, thirteen hundred men in the cities, and thirty thousand in the rural districts; these were a sort of watchmen, dressed in a plain drab uniform, and carrying only a staff and a spear. This large police army of more than fifty thousand men was not only efficient, when well officered, in maintaining tranquillity, but furnished excellent recruits for regiments of Sikh and Punjaubee soldiers.

Sir John Lawrence issued a vigorous proclamation, encouraging the native troops to remain faithful, and threatening them with dire consequences if they revolted; but from the first he relied very little on such appeals to the Bengal troops. Leaving this subject, however, and directing attention to those events only which bore with any weight on the progress of the mutiny, we shall now rapidly glance at Punjaub affairs in the summer months. Many struggles took place, too slight to require much notice. One was the disarming of a native regiment at Noorpore. Another, on June 13th, was the execution of twelve men at Ferozpore, belonging to the 45th N. I., for mutiny after being disarmed.

It was early in June that the station at Jullundur became a prey to insurgent violence. On the 3d of the month, a fire broke out in the lines of the 61st native infantry—a bad symptom wherever it occurred in those days. On the following night a hospital was burned. On the 6th, the 4th regiment Sikh infantry marched into the station, as well as a native troop of horse-artillery; but, owing to some uneasiness displayed by the Bengal troops, the Sikh regiment was removed to another station—as if the brigadier in command were desirous not to offend or irritate the petted regiments from the east. At eleven o'clock at night on the 7th, the close of a quiet Sunday—again Sunday!—a sudden alarm of fire was given, and a lurid glare was seen over the lines of the 36th native infantry. The officers rushed to their respective places; and then it was found that the 6th native cavalry, wavering for a time, had at last given way to the mutinous impulse that guided the 36th and 61st infantry, and that all three regiments were threatening the officers. The old sad story might again be told; the story of some of the officers being shot as they spoke and appealed to the fidelity of their men; of others being shot at or sabred as they ran or rode across the parade-ground; of ladies and children being affrighted at the artillery barracks, where they had been wont to sleep for greater security. The mutineers had evidently expected the native artillery to join them; but fortunately these latter were so dove-tailed with the European artillery, and were so well looked after by a company of the 8th foot, that they could not mutiny if they would. All the Europeans who fled to the artillery barracks and lines were safe; the guns protected them. The mutineers, after an hour or two of the usual mischief, made off. About one half the cavalry regiment mutinied, but as all confidence was lost in them, the rest were deprived of horses and arms, and the regiment virtually ceased to exist. The officers were overwhelmed with astonishment and mortification; some of them had gone to rest on that evening in perfect reliance on their men. One of the cavalry officers afterwards said: 'Some of our best men have proved the most active in this miserable business. A rough rider in my troop, who had been riding my charger in the morning, and had played with my little child, was one of the men who charged the guns.' This officer, like many others, had no other theory to offer than that his troopers mutinied in a 'panic,' arising from the sinister rumours that ran like wildfire through the lines and bazaars of the native troops, shaking the fidelity of those who had not previously taken part in any conspiracy. It was the only theory which their bitterness of heart allowed them to contemplate with any calmness; for few military men could admit without deep mortification that they had been ignorant of, and deceived by, their own soldiers down to the very last moment.

While a portion of the 6th cavalry remained, disarmed and unhorsed but not actually disbanded, at Jullundur, the two regiments and a half of mutineers marched off towards Phillour, as if bound for Delhi. At the instant the mutiny began, a telegraphic message had been sent from Jullundur to Phillour, to break the bridge of boats over the Sutlej, and thereby prevent the rebels from crossing from the Punjaub into Sirhind.

Unfortunately, the telegraphic message failed to reach the officer to whom it was sent. The 3d regiment Bengal native cavalry, at Phillour, might, as the commanding officer at that time thought, have been maintained in discipline if the Jullundur mutineers had not disturbed them; but when the 36th and 61st native infantry, and the 6th cavalry were approaching, all control was found to be lost. The telegraphic wires being cut, no news could reach Phillour, and thus the insurgents from Jullundur made their appearance wholly unexpected—by the Europeans, if not by the troopers. The ladies and families were at once hastened off from the cantonment to the fort, which had just before been garrisoned by a hundred men of H.M. 8th foot. The officers then went on parade, where they found themselves unable to bring the 3d regiment to a sense of their duty; the men promised to keep their hands clear of murder, but they would not fight against the approaching rebels from Jullundur. The officers then returned to the fort powerless; for the handful of Europeans there, though sufficient to defend the fort, were unable to encounter four mutinous regiments in the cantonment. In a day or two, all the ladies and children were sent off safely to the hills; and the cavalry officers were left without immediate duties. The tactics of the brigadier at Jullundur were at that crisis somewhat severely criticised. It was considered that he ought to have made such arrangements as would have prevented the mutineers from crossing the Sutlej. He followed them, with such a force as he could spare or collect; but while he was planning to cut off the bridge of boats that spanned the Sutlej between Phillour and Loodianah, they avoided that spot altogether; they crossed the river six miles further up, and proceeded on their march towards Delhi—attacked at certain places by Europeans and by Sikhs, but not in sufficient force to frustrate their purpose.

Although belonging to a region east of the Punjaub, it may be well here to notice another of the June mutinies nearer the focus of disaffection. One of the regiments that took its officers by surprise in mutinying was the 60th B. N. I.; of which the head-quarters had been at Umballa, but which was at Bhotuck, only three marches from Delhi, when the fidelity of the men gave way. One of the English officers, expressing his utter astonishment at this result, said: 'All gone! The men that we so trusted; my own men, with whom I have shot, played cricket, jumped, entered into all their sports, and treated so kindly!' He thought it almost cruel to subject that regiment to such temptation as would be afforded by close neighbourhood with the mutineers at Delhi. But, right or wrong, the temptation was afforded, and proved too strong to be resisted. It afterwards became known that the 60th received numerous letters and messages from within Delhi, entreating them to join the national cause against the Kaffir Feringhees. On the 11th of June, the sepoys suddenly rose, and fired a volley at a tent within which many of the officers were at mess, but fortunately without fatal results. Many of the officers at once galloped off to the camp outside Delhi, feeling they might be more useful there than with a mutinous regiment; while others stayed a while, in the vain hope of bringing the men back to a sense of their duty. After plundering the mess of the silver-plate and the wine, and securing the treasure-chest, the mutineers made off for Delhi. Here, however, a warm reception was in store for them; their officers had given the alarm; and H.M. 9th Lancers cut the mutineers up terribly on the road leading to the Lahore Gate. Of those who entered the city, most fell in a sortie shortly afterwards. At the place where this regiment had been stationed, Umballa, another death-fiend—cholera—was at work. 'We have had that terrible scourge the cholera. It has been raging here with frightful violence for two months (May to July); but, thank God, has now left us without harming the Sahibs. It seemed a judgment on the natives. They were reeling about and falling dead in the streets, and no one to remove them. It is the only time we have looked on it as an ally; though it has carried off many soldiers, two native officers, and six policemen, who were guarding prisoners; all fell dead at the same place; as one dropped, another stepped forward and took his place; and so on the whole lot.' It was one of the grievous results of the Indian mutiny that English officers, in very bitterness of heart, often expressed satisfaction at the calamities which fell on the natives, even townsmen unconnected with the soldiery.

Jelum, which was the scene of a brief but very fierce contest in July, is a considerable town on the right bank of the river of the same name; it is situated on the great line of road from Lahore to Peshawur; and plans have for some time been under consideration for the establishment of river-steamers thence down through Moultan to Kurachee. Like many other places on the great high road, it was a station for troops; and like many other stations, it was thrown into uneasiness by doubts of the fidelity of the sepoys. The 14th regiment Bengal native infantry, about three-fourths of which were stationed at Jelum, having excited suspicions towards the end of June, it was resolved to disarm them; but as no force was at hand to effect this, three companies of H.M. 24th foot, under Colonel Ellice, with a few horse-artillery, were ordered down from Rawul Pindee. On the 7th of July the English troops arrived, and found the native regiment drawn up on parade. Whether exasperated at the frustration of a proposed plan of mutiny, or encouraged by their strength being thrice that of the English, is not well known; but the 14th attacked the English with musketry directly they approached. This of course brought on an immediate battle. The sepoys had fortified their huts, loopholed their walls, and secured a defensive position in a neighbouring village. The English officers of the native regiment, deserted and fired at by their men, hastened to join the 24th; and a very severe exchange of musketry soon took place. The sepoys fought so boldly, and disputed every inch so resolutely, that it was found necessary to bring the three guns into requisition to drive them out of their covered positions. At last they were expelled, and escaped into the country; where the British, having no cavalry, were unable to follow them. It was an affair altogether out of the usual order in India at that time; instead of being a massacre or a chasing of treacherously betrayed individuals, it was a fight in which the native troops met the British with more than their usual resolution. The loss in this brief conflict was severe. Colonel Ellice was terribly wounded in the chest and the thigh; Captain Spring was killed; Lieutenants Streathfield and Chichester were wounded, one in both legs, and the other in the arm; two sergeants and twenty-three men were killed; four corporals and forty-three men wounded. Thus, out of this small force, seventy-six were either killed or wounded. The government authorities at Jelum immediately offered a reward of thirty rupees a head for every fugitive sepoy captured. This led to the capture of about seventy in the next two days, and to a fearful scene of shooting and blowing away from guns.

On the same day, July 7th, when three companies of H.M. 24th were thus engaged at Jelum, the other companies of the same regiment were engaged at Rawul Pindee in disarming the 58th native infantry and two companies of the 14th. The sepoys hesitated for a time, but seeing a small force of horse-artillery confronted to them, yielded; some fled, but the rest gave up their arms. Two hundred of their muskets were found to be loaded, a significant indication of some murderous intent.

The mutiny at Sealkote, less fatal than that at Jelum in reference to the conflict of troops in fair fight, was more adventurous, more marked by 'hair-breadth 'scapes' among the officers and their families. Sealkote is a town of about twenty thousand inhabitants, in the Doab between the Chenab and the Ravee, on the left bank of the first-named river, and about sixty miles distant from Lahore. At the time of the mutiny there was a rifle-practice depôt at this place. The sepoys stationed at Sealkote had often been in conversation with their European officers concerning the cartridge-question, and had expressed themselves satisfied with the explanations offered. During the active operations for forming movable columns in the Punjaub, either to protect the various stations or to form a Delhi siege-army, all the European troops at Sealkote were taken away, as well as some of the native regiments; leaving at that place only the 46th Bengal native infantry, and a wing of the 9th native cavalry, in cantonment, while within the fort were about a hundred and fifty men of the new Sikh levies. The brigadier commandant was rendered very uneasy by this removal of his best troops; some of his officers had already recommended the disarming of the sepoys before the last of the Queen's troops were gone; but he was scrupulous of shewing any distrust of the native army; he felt and acted in this matter more like a Bengal officer than a Punjaub officer—relying on the honour and fidelity of the 'Poorbeah' troops. His anxieties greatly increased when he heard that the 14th native infantry, after revolting at Jelum, were approaching Sealkote. Many of them, it is true, had been cut up by a few companies of the Queen's 24th; but still the remainder might very easily tempt his own sepoys and troopers. Nevertheless, to the last day, almost to the last hour, many of the regimental officers fully trusted the men; and even their ladies slept near the lines, for safety.

The troops appear to have laid a plan on the evening of the 8th of July, for a mutiny on the following morning. At four o'clock on the 9th, sounds of musketry and cries of distress were heard, rousing all the Europeans from their slumbers. An officer on night-picket duty near the cavalry lines observed a few troopers going towards the infantry lines. It was afterwards discovered that these troopers went to the sepoys, told them 'the letters' had come, and urged them to revolt at once—implying complicity with mutineers elsewhere; but the officer could not know this at the time; he simply thought the movement suspicious, and endeavoured to keep his own sepoy guards from contact with the troopers. In this, however, he failed; the sepoys soon left him, and went over to the troopers. He hurried to his bungalow, told his wife to hasten in a buggy to the fort, and then went himself towards the lines of his regiment. This was a type of what occurred generally. The officers sought to send their wives and families from their various bungalows into the fort, and then hastened to their duties. These duties brought them into the presence of murderous troops at the regimental lines; troops who fired on the very officers that to the last had trusted them. Especially was the mortification great among the Europeans connected with the 46th; for when they begged their sepoys to fire upon the mutinous troopers, the sepoys fired at them instead. A captain, two surgeons, a clergyman, and his wife and child, were killed almost at the very beginning of the outbreak; while Brigadier Brind and other officers were wounded.

There were no wanderings over burning roads and through thick jungles to record in this case; but a few isolated adventures may be briefly noticed. Two or three roads from the lines and bungalows to the fort became speedily marked by fleeing Europeans—officers, ladies, and children—in vehicles, on horseback, and on foot—all trying to reach the fort, and all attacked or pursued by the treacherous villains. Dr Graham, the superintending surgeon, on the alarm being raised, drove quickly with his daughter towards the fort; a trooper rode up and shot him dead; his bereaved daughter seized the reins, and, with the corpse of her parent on her lap, drove into the nearest compound, screaming for help. A young lieutenant of the 9th cavalry, when it came to his turn to flee, had to dash past several troopers, who fired many shots, one only of which hit him. He galloped thirty miles to Wuzeerabad, wounded as he was; and, all his property being left behind him only to be ruthlessly destroyed, he had, to use his own words, to look forward to begin the world again, 'with a sword, and a jacket cut up the back.' Three officers galloped forty miles to Gujeranwalla, swimming or wading the rivers that crossed their path. One of the captains of the 46th, who was personally much liked by the sepoys of his own company, was startled by receiving from them an offer of a thousand rupees per month if he would become a rebel like them, and still remain their captain! What answer he gave to this strange offer may easily be conceived; but his company remained kind to him, for they saw him safely escorted to the fort. In one of the bungalows fourteen persons, of whom only three were men, sought refuge from the murderous sepoys and troopers. The women and children all congregated in a small lumber-room; the three gentlemen remained in the drawing-room, pistols in hand. Then ensued a brisk scene of firing and counter-firing; during which, however, only one life appears to have been lost: the love of plunder in this case overpowered the love of murder; for the insurgents, compelling the gentlemen to retreat to their poor companions in the lumber-room, and there besieging them for a time, turned their attention to loot or plunder. After ten hours sojourn of fourteen persons in a small room in a sultry July day, the Europeans, finding that the mutineers were wandering in other directions, contrived to make a safe and hasty run to the fort, a distance of upwards of a mile. Some of the Europeans at the station, as we have said, were killed; some escaped by a brisk gallop; while the rest were shut up for a fortnight in the fort, in great discomfort, until the mutineers went away. There being no European soldiers at Sealkote, the sepoys and sowars acted as they pleased; they pillaged the bungalows, exploded the magazine, let loose the prisoners in the jail, and then started off, like other mutineers, in the direction of Delhi.

One of the most touching incidents at Sealkote bore relation to a nunnery, a convent of nuns belonging to the order of Jesus Marie of Lyon, a Roman Catholic establishment analogous to that at Sirdhana near Meerut, already brought under notice (p. 57). The superior at Lyon, many weeks afterwards, received a letter from one of the sisters,* giving an affecting account of the way in which the quiet religieuses were hunted about by the mutineers.

* 'Very Dear and Good Mother—On the 8th of the present month the native soldiers heard they were to be disarmed the following day. They became furious, and secretly planned a revolt. They carried their plans into execution at an early hour on the following morning. We were immediately apprised of it, and I hastened to awake our poor children, and all of us, half-clad, prayed for shelter at a Hindoo habitation. Some vehicles had been prepared for us to escape, when the servants desired us to conceal ourselves, as the sepoys were coming into the garden. We returned to our hiding-place; the soldiers arrived; they took away our carriages, and a shot was fired into the house where we were concealed. The ball passed close to where our chaplain was sitting, and slightly wounded a child in the leg. At the same moment three soldiers, well armed, presented themselves at the door. The good father, holding the holy sacrament, which he never quitted, advanced to meet them. Several of us accompanied him. "We have orders to kill you," said the sepoys; "but we will spare you if you give us money. Go out, all, that we may see there are no men concealed here." Having searched and found nothing, one of the soldiers raised his sabre over the chaplain, and cried out: "You shall die." "Mercy, in the name of God!" exclaimed I. "I will open every press to shew you that there is no money concealed here." He followed me, and having satisfied himself that there was no money, the soldiers went away. We then broke a hole in the wall of our garden, and fled into the jungle. We had scarcely escaped when thirty more sepoys entered the house; but the Almighty preserved us from this danger. We were crossing the country, when a faithful servant brought us to a house where several Europeans had taken refuge. We breathed freely there for a moment, but the government treasure was deposited there, and the house was soon attacked by the mutinous sepoys. We believed that our last hour was at hand; but the savages were too much occupied with pillage to notice us, and the

When the Sealkote mutineers had taken their departure towards Delhi, a force was organised at Jelum as quickly as possible to pursue them. This force, under Colonel Brown, comprised three companies of H.M. 24th foot, two hundred Sikhs, a hundred irregular horse, and three horse-artillery guns. The energetic Brigadier Nicholson, in command of a flying column destined for Delhi, comprising the 52d light infantry, the 6th Punjaub cavalry, and other troops, made arrangements at the same time for intercepting the mutineers. It thus happened that on the 12th of July, the insurgent 46th and 9th regiments when they reached the Ravee from Sealkote, found themselves hemmed in; and after an exciting contest on an island in the river, they were almost entirely cut up.

About the close of July, the disarmed 26th native infantry mutinied at Lahore, killed Major Spencer and two native officers, and fled up the left bank of the Ravee; but the police, the new levies, and the villagers pursued them so closely and harassed them so continuously, that hardly a man remained alive. In August, something of the same kind occurred at other places in the Punjaub; native Bengal regiments still were there, disarmed but not disbanded; and it could not be otherwise than that the men felt chafed and discontented with such a state of things. If faithful, they felt the degradation of being disarmed; if hollow in their professed fidelity, they felt the irksomeness of being closely watched in cantonment. At Ferozpore, on the 19th of August, a portion of the 10th native cavalry, that had before been disarmed, mutinied, and endeavoured to capture the guns of Captain Woodcock's battery; they rushed at the guns while the artillerymen were at dinner, and killed the veterinary surgeon and one or two other persons; but a corps of Bombay Fusiliers, in the station at that time, repulsed and dispersed them. At Peshawur, where it was found frequently necessary to search the huts and tents of the disarmed sepoys, for concealed weapons, the 51st native infantry resisted this search on the 28th of the month; they beat their officers with cudgels, and endeavoured to seize the arms of a Sikh corps while those men were at dinner. They were foiled, and fled towards the hills; but a disastrous flight was it for them; more than a hundred were shot before they could get out of the lines, a hundred and fifty more were cut down during an immediate pursuit, nearly four hundred were brought in prisoners, to be quickly tried and shot, and some of the rest were made slaves by the mountaineers of the Khyber Pass, who would by no means 'fraternise' with them. Thus the regiment was in effect annihilated. There were then three disarmed native regiments left in Peshawur, which were kept so encamped that loaded guns in trusty hands might always point towards them.

The course of events in the Punjaub need not be traced further in any connected form. From first to last the plan adopted was pretty uniform in character. When the troubles began, there were about twenty regiments of the Bengal native army in the Punjaub; and these regiments were at once and everywhere distrusted by Sir John Lawrence and his chief officers. If hope and confidence were felt, it was rather by the regimental officers, to whom disloyalty in their respective corps was naturally mortifying and humiliating. All the sepoys were disarmed and the sowars dismounted, as soon as suspicious symptoms appeared; some regiments remained at the stations, disarmed, throughout the whole of the summer and autumn; some mutinied, before or after disarming; but very few indeed lived to reach the scene of rebel supremacy at Delhi; for they were cut up by the Europeans, Sikhs, Punjaubees, or hill-men which the Punjaub afforded. Gladly as every one, whether civilian or military, acknowledged the eminent services of Sir John Lawrence; there were, it must be admitted, certain advantages available to him which were utterly denied to Mr Colvin, the responsible chief of the Northwest Provinces, in which the mutiny raged more fiercely than anywhere else. When the troubles began, the Punjaub was better furnished with regiments of the Queen's army than any other part of India; while the native Sikhs, Punjaubee Mohammedans, and hill-men, were either indifferent or hostile to the sepoys of Hindostan proper. The consequences of this state of things were two: the native troops were more easily disarmed; and those who mutinied were more in danger of annihilation before they could get east of the Sutlej. In the Northwest Provinces the circumstances were far more disastrous; the British troops were relatively fewer; and the people were more nearly in accord with the sepoys, in so far as concerned national and religious sympathies. In the Meerut military division, when the mutiny had fairly commenced, besides those at Meerut station, there was only one European regiment (at Agra), against ten native regiments, irrespective of those which mutinied at Meerut and Delhi. In the Cawnpore military division, comprising the great stations of Lucknow, Allahabad, Cawnpore, and the whole of Oude, there was scarcely more than one complete European regiment, against thirty native Bengal and Oude regiments, regular and irregular. In the Dinapoor military division, comprising Benares, Patna, Ghazeepore, and other large cities, together with much government wealth in the form of treasure and opium, there was in like manner only one British regiment, against sixteen native corps. There was at the same time this additional difficulty; that no such materials were at hand as

Europeans escaped. At this moment a Catholic soldier offered to guide us to the fort, where we arrived at twelve o'clock. We do not know how long we shall remain in the fort. The English officers have treated us with the greatest kindness and attention, and have supplied us with provisions both for ourselves and our pupils. We trust we shall one day make our way to Bombay; but that will depend on the orders we receive from the government.'

in the Punjaub, for raising regiments of horse and foot among tribes who would sympathise but little with the mutineers.

Sir John Lawrence was at first in some doubt what course to follow in relation to the liberty of the press. The Calcutta authorities, as we shall see in the next chapter, thought it proper to curtail that liberty in Bengal and the Northwest Provinces. Sir John, unwilling on the one hand to place the Europeans in the Punjaub in the tormenting condition of seclusion from all sources of news, and unwilling on the other to leave the news-readers at the mercy of inaccurate or unscrupulous news-writers at such a critical time, adopted a medium course. He caused the *Lahore Chronicle* to be made the medium of conveying official news of all that was occurring in India, so far as rapid outlines were concerned. The government secretary at that place sent every day to the editor of the newspaper an epitome of the most important public news. This epitome was printed on small quarter-sheets of paper, and despatched by each day's post to all the stations in the Punjaub. The effect was—that false rumours and sinister reports were much less prevalent in the Punjaub than in Bengal; men were not thrown into mystery by a suppression of journalism; but were candidly told how events proceeded, so far as information had reached that remote part of India. The high character of the chief-commissioner was universally held as a guarantee that the news given in the epitome, whether little or much in quantity, would be honestly rendered; the scheme would have been a failure under a chief who did not command respect and win confidence. As the summer advanced, and dâks and wires were interrupted, the news obtainable became very scanty. The

Camel and Rider.

English in the Punjaub were placed in a most tantalising position. Aware that matters were going wrong at Delhi and Agra, at Lucknow and Cawnpore, they did not know *how* wrong; for communication was well-nigh cut off. As the cities just named lie between the Punjaub and Calcutta, all direct communication with the seat of government was still more completely cut off. The results of this were singularly trying. 'Gradually,' says an officer writing from the Punjaub, 'papers and letters reached us from Calcutta *vid* Bombay. It is not the least striking illustration of the complete revolution that has occurred in India, that the news from the Gangetic valley—say from Allahabad and Cawnpore—was known in London sooner than at Lahore. We had been accustomed to receive our daily letters and newspapers from every part of the empire with the same unfailing regularity as in England. Suddenly we found ourselves separated from Calcutta for two months of time. Painfully must a letter travel from the eastern capital to the western port—from Calcutta to Bombay; painfully must it toil up the unsettled provinces of the western coast; slowly must it jog along on mule-back across the sands of Sinde; many queer twists and unwonted turns must that letter take, many enemies must it baffle and elude, before, much bestamped, much stained with travel—for Indian letter-bags are not water-proof—it is delivered to its owner at Lahore. . . . Slowly, very slowly, the real truth dragged its way up the country. It is only this very 29th of September that this writer in the Punjaub has read anything like a connected account of the fearful tragedy at Cawnpore, which, once read or heard, no Englishman can ever forget.'

Attention must now for a brief space be directed to the country of Sinde or Scinde; not so much for the purpose of narrating the progress of mutiny there, as to shew how it happened that there were few materials out of which mutiny could arise.

Sinde is the region which bounds the lower course of the river Indus, also called Sinde. The name is supposed to have had the same origin as Sindhi or Hindi, connected with the great Hindoo race. When the Indus has passed out of the

Punjaub at its lower apex, it enters Sinde, through which it flows to the ocean, which bounds Sinde on the south; east is Rajpootana, and west Beloochistan. The area of Sinde is about equal to that of England without Wales. The coast is washed by the Indian Ocean for a distance of about a hundred and fifty miles; being, with very few exceptions, little other than a series of mud-banks deposited by the Indus, or low sand-hills blown in from the sea-beach. So low is most of the shore, that a wide expanse of country is overflowed at each high tide; it is a dreary swamp, scarcely observable from shipboard three or four miles out at sea. The mouths of the Indus are numerous, but so shallow that only one of them admits ships of any considerable burden; and even that one is subject to so many fluctuations in depth and in weather, that sea-going vessels scarcely enter it at all. Kurachee, the only port in Sinde, is a considerable distance west of all these mouths; and the mercantile world looks forward with much solicitude to the time when a railway will be formed from this port to Hydrabad, a city placed at the head of the delta of the Indus. This delta, in natural features, resembles that of the Nile rather than that of the Ganges, being nearly destitute of timber. On each side of the Indus, for a breadth varying from two to twelve miles, is a flat alluvial tract, in most places extremely fertile. Many parts of Sinde are little better than desert; such as the *Pât*, between Shikarpore and the Bolan Pass, and the *Thur*, nearer to the river. In general, it may be said that no part of Sinde is fertile except where the Indus irrigates it; for there is little either of rain or dew, and the climate is intensely hot. Camels are largely reared in Sinde; and the Sindians have abundant reason to value this animal. It is to him a beast of burden; its milk is a favourite article of diet; its hair is woven into coarse cloth; and it renders him service in many other ways.

The Sindians are an interesting race, both in themselves and in their political relations. They are a mixture of Jâts and Beloochees, among whom the distinction between Hindoo and Mussulman has a good deal broken down. The Beloochees are daring, warlike Mohammedans; the Jâts are Hindoos less rigorous in matters of faith and caste than those of Hindostan; while the Jâts who have become Mohammedans are a peaceful agricultural race, somewhat despised by both the others. The Sindians collectively are a dark, handsome, well-limbed race; and it was a favourite opinion of Sir William Jones, that they were the original of the gipsies. The languages spoken are a mixture of Hindi, Beloochee, and Persian.

The chain of events which brought Sinde under British rule may be traced in a few sentences. About thirteen centuries ago the country was invaded by the Persians, who ravaged it without making a permanent settlement. The califs at a later date conquered Sinde; from them it was taken by the Afghans of Ghiznee; and in the time of Baber it fell into the hands of the chief of Candahar. It was then, for a century and a half, a dependency of the Mogul Empire. For a few years Nadir Shah held it; next the Moguls retook it; and in 1756 Sinde fell under the rule of the Cabool khans, which was maintained nearly to the time when the British seized the sovereign power. Although subject to Cabool, Sinde was really governed by eight or ten native princes, called Ameers, who had among them three distinct territories marked by the cities of Hydrabad, Khyrpore, and Meerpoor. Under these ameers the government was a sort of military despotism, each ameer having a power of life and death; but in warlike affairs they were dependent on feudal chieftains, each of whom held an estate on condition of supplying a certain number of soldiers. The British had various trading treaties with the ameers; one of which, in 1832, opened the roads and rivers of Sinde to the commerce of the Company. When, in 1838, the eyes of the governor-general were directed anxiously towards Afghanistan, Sinde became involved in diplomatic conferences, in which the British, the Afghans, the Sindians, and Runjeet Singh were all concerned. These conferences led to quarrels, to treaties, to accusations of breach of faith, which we need not trace: suffice it to say that Sir Charles James Napier, with powers of the pen and of the sword intrusted to him, settled the Sinde difficulty once for all, in 1848, by fighting battles which led to the annexation of that country to the Company's dominions. The former government was entirely put an end to; and the ameers were pensioned off with sums amounting in the aggregate to about fifty thousand pounds per annum. Some of these Ameers, like other princes of India, afterwards came to England in the hope of obtaining better terms from Queen Victoria than had been obtainable from the Company Bahadoor.

When Sinde became a British province, it was separated into three collectorates or districts—Shikarpore, Hydrabad, and Kurachee; a new system of revenue administration was introduced; annual fairs were established at Kurachee and Sukur; and peaceful commerce was everywhere so successfully established, that the country improved rapidly, greatly to the content of the mass of the people, who had formerly been ground down by the ameers' government. For military purposes, Sinde was made a division, under the Bombay presidency.

Sinde, at the commencement of the mutiny, contained about seven thousand troops of all arms, native and European. The military arrangements had brought much distinction to Colonel (afterwards Brigadier-general) John Jacob, whose 'Sinde Irregular Horse' formed a corps much talked of in India. It consisted of about sixteen hundred men, in two regiments of eight hundred each, carefully drilled, and armed and equipped in the European manner, yet having only five

European officers; the squadron and troop commanders were native officers. The brigadier uniformly contended that it was the best cavalry corps in India; and that the efficiency of such a regiment did *not* depend so much on the number of European officers, as on the manner in which they fulfilled their duties, and the kind of discipline which they maintained among the men. On these points he was frequently at issue with the Bengal officers; for he never failed to point out the superiority of the system in the Bombay army, where men were enlisted irrespective of caste, and where there were better means of rewarding individual merit.* Nationally speaking, they were not Sindians at all; being drawn from other parts of India, in the ratio of three-fourths Mohammedans to one-fourth Hindoos.

When the mutiny began in the regions further east, ten or twelve permanent outposts on the Sinde frontier were held by detachments of the Sinde Irregular Horse, of forty to a hundred and twenty men each, wholly commanded by native officers. These men, and the head-quarters at Jacobabad (a camp named after the gallant brigadier), remained faithful, though sometimes tempted by sepoys and troopers of the Bengal army. A curious correspondence took place later in the year, through the medium of the newspapers, between Brigadier Jacob and Major Pelly on the one side, and Colonel Sykes on the other. The colonel had heard that Jacob ridiculed the greased cartridge affair, as a matter that would never be allowed to trouble *his* corps; and he sought to show that it was no subject for laughter: 'Brigadier John Jacob knows full well that if he were to order his Mohammedan soldiers (though they may venerate him) to bite a cartridge greased with pigs' fat, or his high-caste troopers to bite a cartridge greased with cows' fat, both the one and the other would promptly refuse obedience, and in case he endeavoured to enforce it, they would shoot him down.' Jacob and Pelly at once disputed this; they both asserted that the Mohammedans and Hindoos in the Sinde Horse would never be mutinous on such a point, unless other sources of dissatisfaction existed, and unless they believed it was *purposely* done to insult their faith. 'If it were really necessary,' said the brigadier, 'in the performance of our ordinary military duty, to use swine's fat or cows' fat, or anything else whatever, not a word or a thought would pass about the matter among any members of the Horse, and the nature of the substances made use of would not be thought of or discussed at all, except with reference to the fitness for the purpose to which they were to be applied.' The controversialists did not succeed in convincing each other; they continued to hold diametrically opposite opinions on a question intimately connected with the early stages of the mutiny—thereby adding to the perplexities of those wishing to solve the important problem: 'What was the cause of the mutiny?'

Owing partly to the great distance from the disturbed provinces of Hindostan, partly to the vicinity of the well-disposed Bombay army, and partly to the activity and good organisation of Jacob's Irregular Horse, Sinde was affected with few insurgent proceedings during the year. At one time a body of fanatical Mohammedans would unfurl the green flag, and call upon each other to fight for the Prophet. At another time, gangs of robbers and hill-men, of which India has in all ages had an abundant supply, would take advantage of the troubled state of public feeling to rush forth on marauding expeditions, caring much for plunder and little for faith of any kind. At another, alarms would be given which induced European ladies and families to take refuge in the forts or other defensive positions at Kurachee, Hydrabad, Shikarpore, Jacobabad, &c., where English officers were stationed. At another, regiments of the Bengal army would try to tamper with the fidelity of other troops in Sinde. But of these varied incidents, few were so serious in results as to need record here. One, interesting in many particulars, arose out of the following circumstance: When some of the Sinde forces were sent to Persia, the 6th Bengal irregular cavalry arrived to supply their place. These troopers, when the mutiny was at least four months old, endeavoured to form a plan with some Beloochee Mohammedans for the murder of the British officers at the camp of Jacobabad. A particular hour on the 21st of August was named for this outrage, in which various bands of Beloochees were invited to assist. The plot was revealed to Captain Merewether, who immediately confided in the two senior native officers of the Sinde Irregular Horse. Orders were issued that the day's proceedings should be as usual, but that the men should hold themselves in readiness. Many of the border chiefs afterwards sent notice to Merewether of what had been planned, announcing their own disapproval of the conspiracy. At a given hour, the leading conspirator was seized, and correspondence found upon him tending to shew that the Bengal regiment having failed in other attempts to seduce the Sinde troops from their allegiance, had determined to murder the European officers as the chief obstacles to their scheme. The authorities at Jacobabad wished Sir John Lawrence to take this

* The brigadier's confidence in his men was conditional on their implicit obedience; and he was wont to affirm that his 'Irregulars' were as 'regular' in conduct and discipline as the Queen's Life-guards themselves. He would allow no religious scruples to interfere with their military efficiency. On one occasion, during the *Mohurrum* or Mohammedan religious festival in 1854, there was great uproar and noise among ten thousand Mussulmans assembled in and near his camp of Jacobabad to celebrate their religious festival. He issued a general order: 'The commanding officer has nothing to do with religious ceremonies. All men may worship God as they please, and may act and believe as they choose, in matters of religion; but no men have a right to annoy their neighbours, or to neglect their duty, on pretence of serving God. The officers and men of the Sinde Horse have the name of, and are supposed to be, excellent soldiers, and not mad fakeers. . . . . He therefore now informs the Sinde Irregular Horse, that in future no noisy processions, nor any disorderly display whatever, under pretence of religion or anything else, shall ever be allowed in, or in neighbourhood of, any camp of the Sinde Irregular Horse.'

Bengal regiment off their hands; but the experienced chief in the Punjaub would not have the dangerous present; he thought it less likely to mutiny where it was than in a region nearer to Delhi.

The troops in the province of Sinde about the middle of August were nearly as follows: At Kurachee—the 14th and 21st Bombay native infantry; the 2d European infantry; the depôt of the 1st Bombay Fusiliers; and the 3d troop of horse-artillery. At Hydrabad—the 13th Bombay native infantry; and a company of the 4th battalion of artillery. At Jacobabad—the 2d Sinde irregular horse; and the 6th Bengal irregular cavalry. At Shikarpore and Sukur, the 16th Bombay native infantry; and a company of the 4th battalion of artillery. The whole comprised about five thousand native troops, and twelve hundred Europeans.

At a later period, when thanks were awarded by parliament to those who had rendered good service in India, the name of Mr Frere, commissioner for Sinde, was mentioned, as one who 'has reconciled the people of that province to British rule, and by his prudence and wisdom confirmed the conquest which had been achieved by the gallant Napier. He was thereby enabled to furnish aid wherever it was needed, at the same time constantly maintaining the peace and order of the province.'

Notes.

This will be a suitable place in which to introduce two tabular statements concerning the military condition of India at the commencement of the mutiny. All the occurrences narrated hitherto are those in which the authorities at Calcutta were compelled to encounter difficulties without any reinforcements from England, the time elapsed having been too short for the arrival of such reinforcements.

Military Divisions of India.—At the period of the outbreak, and for some time afterwards, India was marked out for military purposes into divisions, each under the command of a general, brigadier, or other officer, responsible for all the troops, European and native, within his division. The names and localities of these divisions are here given; on the authority of a military map of India, engraved at the Topographical Depôt under the direction of Captain Elphinstone of the Royal Engineers, and published by the War Department. Each division was regarded as belonging to, or under the control of, one of the three presidencies. We shall therefore group them under the names of the three presidential cities, and shall append a few words to denote locality:

UNDER CALCUTTA GOVERNMENT.

Name.	Limits.
Presidency Division,	Calcutta and its vicinity, and the east and northeast of Bengal.
Dinapoor Division,	From the Nepaul frontier, southwest towards Nagpoor.
Cawnpore Division,	Including Oude, the Lower Doab, and part of Bundelcund.
Saugor Division,	On both sides of the Nerbudda river, south of Bundelcund.
Gwalior Division,	Scindia's Dominions, bordering on Rajpootana.
Meerut Division,	Rohilcund, from the Himalaya down to Agra and the Jumna.
Sirhind Division,	The Cis-Sutlej and Hill states, northwest of Delhi.
Lahore Division,	Eastern part of Punjaub, from Cashmere down to Sinde.
Peshawur Division,	Western part of Punjaub, on the Afghan frontier.

UNDER BOMBAY GOVERNMENT.

Name.	Limits.
Sinde Division,	On the Beloochee frontier, both sides of the Lower Indus.
Rajpootana Field-force,	East of Sinde, and west of Scindia's Gwalior dominions.
Northern Division,	From Cutch nearly to Bombay, including Gujerat.
Poonah Division,	Around Bombay, and the South Mahratta country near it.
Southern Division,	Southernmost part of the Bombay Presidency.

UNDER MADRAS GOVERNMENT.

Name.	Limits.
Nagpoor Subsidiary Force,	The recently acquired Nagpoor territory, near Nizam's states.
North Division,	Northern part of Madras Presidency, on sea-coast.
Centre Division,	Madras city, and the coast-region north and south of it.
Ceded Districts,	Northwest of Madras city, towards Bombay.
Mysore Division,	Seringapatam, and the country once belonging to Tippoo Saib.
Southern Division,	Southernmost part of the Indian peninsula, towards Ceylon.

UNDER MADRAS GOVERNMENT.—*Continued.*

It may be useful to remark that these military divisions are not necessarily identical in area or boundaries with the political provinces or collectorates, the two kinds of territorial limits being based on different considerations.

Armies of India, at the Commencement of the Mutiny.—During the progress of the military operations, it was frequently wished in England that materials were afforded for shewing the exact number of troops in India when the troubles began. The Company, to respond to this wish, caused an elaborate return to be prepared, from which a few entries are here selected. The names and limits of the military divisions correspond nearly, but not exactly, to those in the above list.

BENGAL ARMY, MAY 10, 1857.

Military Divisions.	Europeans.	Natives.	Total.
Presidency,	1,214	13,976	15,190
Dinapoor,	1,597	15,063	16,660
Cawnpore,	277	5,725	6,002
Oude,	993	11,319	12,312
Saugor,	327	10,627	10,954
Meerut,	3,096	18,357	21,453
Sirhind,	4,790	11,049	15,839
Lahore,	4,018	15,939	19,957
Peshawur,	4,613	15,916	20,529
Pegu,	1,763	692	2,455
	22,698	118,663	141,361

The Europeans in this list include all grades of officers as well as rank and file; and among the officers are included those connected with the native regiments. The natives, in like manner, include all grades, from subadars down to sepoys and sowars. The Punjaub, it will be seen, alone contained 40,000 troops. The troops were stationed at 160 cantonments, garrisons, or other places. As shewing gradations of rank, the Europeans comprised 2271 commissioned officers, 1602 non-commissioned officers, and 18,815 rank and file; the natives comprised 2325 commissioned officers, 5821 non-commissioned officers, and 110,517 rank and file. The stations which contained the largest numbers were the following:

Peshawur,	9500	Sealkote,	3500
Lahore,	5500	Benares,	3200
Meerut,	5000	Rawul Pindee,	3200
Lucknow,	5000	Bareilly,	3000
Jullundur,	4000	Moultan,	3000
Dinapoor,	4000	Saugor,	2800
Umballa,	3800	Agra,	2700
Cawnpore,	3700	Nowsherah,	2600
Delhi,	3600	Jelum,	2400
Barrackpore,	3500	Allahabad,	2300

These 20 principal stations thus averaged 3800 troops each, or nearly 80,000 altogether.

MADRAS ARMY, MAY 10, 1857.

Military Divisions.	Europeans.	Natives.	Total.
Centre,	1,580	6,430	8,010
Mysore,	1,088	4,504	5,592
Malabar,	604	2,513	3,117
Northern,	215	6,169	6,384
Southern,	726	5,718	6,444
Ceded Districts,	135	2,519	2,654
South Mahratta,	16	375	391
Nagpoor,	289	3,585	3,874
Nizam's,	1,322	5,027	6,349
Penang and Malacca,	49	2,113	2,162
Pegu,	2,880	10,154	13,034
	10,194	49,737	59,931

This list was more fully made out than that for the Bengal army; since it gave the numbers separately of the dragoons, light cavalry, horse-artillery, foot-artillery, sappers and miners, European infantry, native infantry, and veterans. The ratio of Europeans to native troops was rather higher in the Madras army (about 20 per cent.) than in that of Bengal (19 per cent.) More fully made out in some particulars, it was less instructive in others; the Madras list pointed out the location of all the detachments of each regiment, whereas the Bengal list gave the actual numbers at each station, without mentioning the particular regiments of which they were composed. Hence the materials for comparison are not such as they might have been had the lists been prepared on one uniform plan. There were about 36 stations for these troops, but the places which they occupied in small detachments raised the total to a much higher number. Although Pegu is considered to belong to the Bengal presidency, it was mostly served by Madras troops. Besides the forces above enumerated, there were nearly 2000 Madras troops out of India altogether, on service in Persia and China.

BOMBAY ARMY, MAY 10, 1857.

Military Divisions.	Europeans.	Natives.	Total.
Bombay Garrison,	695	3,394	4,089
Southern,	283	5,108	5,391
Poonah,	1,838	6,817	8,655
Northern,	1,154	6,452	7,606
Asseerghur Fortress,	2	446	448
Sinde,	1,087	6,072	7,159
Rajpootana,	50	3,312	3,362
	5,109	31,601	36,710

The Bombay army was so dislocated at that period, by the departure of nearly 14,000 troops to Persia and Aden, that the value of this table for purposes of comparison becomes much lessened. Nevertheless, it affords means of knowing how many troops were actually in India at the time when their services were most needed. On the other hand, about 5000 of the troops in the Bombay presidency belonged to the Bengal and Madras armies. The different kinds of troops were classified as in the Madras army. The regular military stations where troops took up their head-quarters, were about 20 in number; but the small stations where mere detachments were placed nearly trebled this number. The Europeans were to the native troops only as 16 to 100.

As a summary, then, we find that India contained, on the day when the mutinies began, troops to the number of 238,002 in the service of the Company, of whom 38,001 were Europeans, and 200,001 natives—19 Europeans to 100 natives. An opportunity will occur in a future page for enumerating the regiments of which these three armies were composed.

Catholic Church, Sirdhana.—Built by Begum Sumroo (See p. 57).

Sir Colin Campbell.

CHAPTER XIII.

PREPARATIONS: CALCUTTA AND LONDON.

BEFORE entering on a narrative of the great military operations connected with the siege of Delhi, and with Havelock's brilliant advance from Allahabad to Cawnpore and Lucknow, it will be necessary to glance rapidly at the means adopted by the authorities to meet the difficulties arising out of the mutiny—by the Indian government at Calcutta, and by the imperial government in London. For, it must be remembered that—however meritorious and indispensable may have been the services of those who arrived in later months—the crisis had passed before a single additional regiment from England reached the scene of action. There was, as we have seen in the note appended to the preceding chapter, a certain definite amount of European military force in India when the mutiny began; there were also certain regiments of the Queen's army known to be at different spots in the region lying between the Cape of Good Hope on the west and Singapore on the east; and it depended on the mode of managing those materials whether India should or should not be lost to the English. There will therefore be an advantage in tracing the manner in which the Calcutta government brought into use the resources immediately or proximately available; and the plans adopted by the home government to increase those resources.

It is not intended in this place to discuss the numerous questions which have arisen in connection with the moral and political condition of the natives of India, or the relative fitness of different forms of government for the development of their welfare. Certain matters only will be treated, which immediately affected the proceedings of those intrusted with this grave responsibility at so perilous a time. Three such at once present themselves for notice, in relation to the Calcutta government—namely, the military measures taken to confront the mutineers; the judicial treatment meted out to them when conquered or captured; and the precautions taken in reference to freedom of public discussion on subjects likely to foster discontent.

First, in relation to military matters. England, by a singular coincidence, was engaged in two Asiatic wars at the time when the Meerut outbreak marked the commencement of a formidable mutiny. Or, more strictly, one army was returning after the close of a war with Persia; while another was going out to begin a war with China. It will ever remain a problem of deep significance what would have become of our Indian empire had not those warlike armaments, small as they were, been on the Indian seas at the time. The responsible servants of the Company in India did not fail to recognise the importance of this problem—as will be seen from a brief notice of the plans laid during the earlier weeks of the mutiny.

On the 13th of May, three days after the troubles began at Meerut, Mr Colvin, lieutenant-governor of the Northwest Provinces, telegraphed to Calcutta, suggesting that the returning force from Persia should be ordered round to Calcutta, in order to be sent inland to strengthen the few English regiments by which alone the Revolt could be put down. On the next day, Viscount Canning, knowing that the Queen's 43d foot and the 1st Madras Fusiliers were at Madras, telegraphed orders for those two regiments to be forwarded to Calcutta—seeing that the Bengal presidency was more likely than that of Madras to be troubled by mutinous sepoys. On the same day orders were sent to Pegu to bring the depôt of the Queen's 84th foot to Calcutta, the bulk of the regiment being already in or near that city. On the 16th, a message was sent to Lord Elphinstone at Bombay, requesting him to send round to Calcutta two of the English regiments about to return from Persia; another message was sent to Pegu, summoning every available soldier of the Queen's 35th foot from Rangoon and Moulmein; and orders were issued that all government river-steamers and flats in India should be held ready for army use. On the 17th, Lord Harris at Madras telegraphed to Canning, recommending him to stop the army going to China under Lord Elgin and General Ashburnham, and to render it immediately available for Indian wants. It was on this day, too, that Sir John Lawrence announced his intention of disarming the Bengal sepoys in the Punjaub, and of raising new Punjaub regiments in their stead; and that Mr Frere, commissioner of Sinde, was ordered by Lord Elphinstone to send the 1st Bombay Europeans from Kurachee up the Indus to Moultan, and thence to Ferozpore. On the 18th, Canning telegraphed to Elphinstone, naming the two regiments—the Queen's 78th foot and the 2d Europeans—which were to be sent round to Calcutta, together with artillery; on the same day Elphinstone telegraphed to Canning that he would be able to send the Queen's 64th as well as 78th foot; and on the same day the authorities at Sinde arranged for sending a Beloochee regiment up from Hydrabad to Ferozpore. On the 19th, the Madras Fusiliers started for Calcutta; and on the same day Sir Henry Lawrence, to strengthen his military command in Oude, was raised from the rank of colonel to that of brigadier-general. Without dwelling, day by day, on the proceedings adopted, it will suffice to say that, during the remaining period of May, the Madras Fusiliers, which were destined to render such good service under the gallant Neill, arrived at Calcutta; that the Queen's 64th and 78th made their voyage from Bombay to Calcutta; and that steamers were sent to Ceylon to bring as many royal troops as could be spared from that island.

When June arrived, the same earnest endeavours were made to bring troops to bear upon the plague-spots of mutiny. Orders were sent to transfer a wing of the Queen's 29th foot from Pegu, the 12th Lancers from Bombay, and cavalry horses from Bushire and elsewhere, to Calcutta. Later in the month, messages were transmitted to Madras, commanding the sending to Calcutta of everything that had been prepared there for the service of the expedition to China; such as tents, clothing, harness, and necessaries; but it was at the same time known that the regiments on that service available for India could be very few for a considerable time to come—the only certain news being of the 5th Fusiliers, which left Mauritius on the 23d of May, and the 90th foot, which left England on the 18th of April. Towards the close of the month, an arrangement was made for accepting the aid of an army of Nepaulese from Jung Bahadoor, to advance from Khatmandoo through Goruckpore towards Oude—a matter on which Lord Canning was much criticised, by those who thought the arrangement ought to have been made earlier. As soon as news reached Calcutta of the death of General Anson, Sir Patrick Grant, commander-in-chief of the Madras army, was summoned from Madras to hold the office of commander-in-chief of the army of Bengal, subject to sanction from the home authorities. When he had accepted this provisional appointment, and had arrived at Calcutta, Sir Patrick wrote a 'memorandum,' expressing his views of his own position towards the supreme government. It was to the effect that—seeing that there was in fact no native army to rely upon; that the European army was very small; and that this army had to operate on many different points, in portions each under its own commandant—it would be better for the commander-in-chief to remain for a while at Calcutta, than to move about from station to station. If near the seat of government, he would be in daily personal communication with the members of the supreme council; he would learn their views in relation to the innumerable questions likely to arise; and he would be in early receipt of the mass of intelligence forwarded every day to Calcutta from all parts of India. On these grounds, Sir Patrick proposed to make Calcutta his head-quarters. All the members of the council—Canning, Dorin, Low, J. P. Grant, and Peacock—assented at once to these views; the governor-general added: 'I am of opinion, however, that as soon as the course of events shall tend to allay the general disquiet, and to shew to what points our force should be mainly directed, with the view of crushing the heart of the rebellion, it will be proper that his excellency should consider anew the question of his movements.'

As it was difficult in those days of interrupted dâks and severed wires to communicate intelligence between Calcutta and Lahore, the general officers in the Punjaub and Sirhind made the best readjustment of offices they could on hearing of Anson's death; but when orders could be given from Calcutta, Sir Henry Barnard, of the Sirhind division, was made commander of the force against Delhi; General Penny, from Simla, replaced General Hewett at Meerut; General Reid, of the Peshawur division, became temporary commander in the west until other arrangements could be made; and Brigadier Cotton was appointed to the command at Peshawur, with Colonel Edwardes as commissioner. Later in the month, when Henry Lawrence was hemmed in at Lucknow, Wheeler beleaguered at Cawnpore, and Lloyd absorbed with the affairs of Dinapoor brigade, commands were given to Neill and Havelock, the one from Madras and the other from the Persian expedition; while Outram, who had been commander of that expedition, also returned to assume an important post in India. Several colonels of individual regiments received the appointment of brigadier-general, in command of corps of two or more regiments; and in that capacity became better known to the public than as simple commandants of regiments.

When the month of July arrived, the British troops in India, though lamentably few for the stern work to be done, were nevertheless increasing in number; but it is doubtful whether, at the end of the month, the number was as large as at the beginning; for many desperate conflicts had taken place, which terribly thinned the European ranks. The actual reinforcements which arrived at Calcutta during eight months, irrespective of any plans laid in England arising out of news of the mutiny, consisted of about twenty regiments, besides artillery. Some of these had been on the way from England before the mutiny began; the 84th foot arrived in March from Rangoon; none arrived in April; in May arrived the 1st Madras Fusiliers; in June, the 35th, 37th, 64th, and 78th Queen's regiments, together with artillery belonging to all the three presidential armies; in July, the 5th Fusiliers, the 90th foot, and a wing of the 29th; in August, the 59th foot, a military train, a naval brigade from Hong Kong, and royal marines from the same place; in September, the 23d Welsh Fusiliers, 93d Highlanders, four regiments of Madras native infantry (5th, 17th, 27th, and 36th), and detachments of artillery and engineers; in October, the 82d foot, the 48th Madras native infantry, and recruits for the East India Company's service—all these, be it again remarked, were troops which reached Calcutta without any reference to the plans laid by the home government to quell the mutiny; those which came from England started before the news was known; the rest came from Rangoon, Moulmein, Madras, Bombay, Ceylon, Mauritius, Hong Kong, Cape of Good Hope, &c. A few observations may be made in connection with the above list—that some of these regiments were native Madras troops, on whom reliance was placed to fight manfully against the Bengal sepoys; that some of the Madras companies advanced inland to Bengal, without taking the sea-voyage to Calcutta; that no cavalry whatever were included in the list; and that the list does not include the regiments which advanced from Bombay or Kurachee towards the disturbed districts.

Cavalry, just adverted to, was the arm of the service in which the Indian government was throughout the year most deficient. During a long period of peace the stud-establishments had been somewhat neglected; and as a consequence, there were more soldiers able and willing to ride, than horses ready to receive them. In the artillery and baggage departments, also, the supply of horses was very deficient. When news of this fact reached Australia, the colonists bestirred themselves to ascertain how far they could assist in remedying the deficiency. The whole of New South Wales was divided into eight districts, and committees voluntarily undertook the duty of ascertaining how many available horses fit for cavalry were obtainable in each district. Colonel Robbins was sent from Calcutta to make purchases; and he was enabled to obtain several hundred good strong horses at prices satisfactory both to the stock-farmers and to the government. The good effected by the committees consisted in bringing together the possible sellers and the willing buyer.

By what means the troops, as they arrived at Calcutta from various quarters, were despatched to the scene of action in the upper provinces, and by what difficulties of every kind this duty was hampered—need not be treated here; sufficient has been said on this subject in former pages.

We pass to the second of the three subjects marked out, in reference to the proceedings at Calcutta for notice—the arrangements for preventing the mutiny of native troops, or for punishing those who had already mutinied: a very important and anxious part of the governor-general's duty.

Unfortunately for all classes in India, there was a hostile feeling towards the governor-general, entertained by many of the European inhabitants unconnected with the Company; they accused him of favouring the natives at the expense of the English. There was also a sentiment of deep hatred excited against the natives, owing to the barbarous atrocities perpetrated by the mutinous sepoys and the rabble budmashes on the unfortunate persons at the various military and civil stations of the Company during the course of the Revolt. There was at the same time a certain jealousy existing between the military and civil officers in India. These various feelings conspired to render the supreme government at Calcutta, and especially Viscount Canning as its head, the butt for incessant ridicule and the object of incessant vituperation. When the mutiny was many months old, the Calcutta government gave a full reply to insinuations which it would have been undignified to rebut at the time when made, and which, indeed, would have fallen with little force on the public mind while convulsed with passion at the unparalleled news from India.

It was repeatedly urged upon the governor-general to proclaim martial law wherever the Europeans found or fancied themselves in peril; to encounter the natives with muskets and cannon instead of courts of justice; and to adopt these summary proceedings all over India. In reply, Viscount Canning states that this was actually done wherever it was necessary, and as soon as it could answer any good purpose. Martial law was proclaimed in the Delhi province in May; in the Meerut province about the same time; in Rohilcund on the 28th of the same month; in the Agra province in May and the early part of June; in the Ajmeer district on the 12th of June; in Allahabad and Benares about the same date; in Neemuch also at the same time; in the Patna district on the 30th of June; and afterwards in Nagpoor. In the Punjaub and Oude, governed by special regulations, it was not necessary that martial law should be proclaimed, but the two Lawrences acted as if it was. Martial law, where adopted, was made even more stringent than in European countries; for there only military men take part in courts-martial; whereas in India, the military officers at the disposal of the government being too few for the performance of such duties at such a time, an act of the Calcutta legislature was passed directly after the news from Meerut arrived, authorising military officers to establish courts-martial for the trial of mutineers and others, and empowering them to obtain the aid at such courts, not only of the Company's civil servants, but of indigo-planters and other Europeans of intelligence and of independent position. On the 30th of May, to meet the case of a rebellious populace as well as a mutinous soldiery, another act was passed authorising all the local executive governments to issue special commissions for the summary trial of delinquents, with power of life and death in addition to that of forfeiture of property—without any tedious reference to the ordinary procedures of the law-courts. On the 6th of June a third act was passed, intended to reach those who, without actually mutinying or rebelling, should attempt to excite disaffection in the native army, or should harbour persons guilty of that offence; general officers were empowered to appoint courts-martial, and executive bodies to appoint special commissions, to try all such offenders at once and on the spot, and to inflict varying degrees of punishment according to the offence. Some time afterwards a fourth act gave an extended application of these stringent measures to India generally. In all these instances Europeans were specially exempted from the operation of the statutes. The enormous powers thus given were largely executed; and they were rendered still more formidable by another statute, enabling police-officers to arrest without warrant persons suspected of being mutineers or deserters, and rendering zemindars punishable if they failed to give early information of the presence of suspicious persons on their respective estates. 'Not only therefore,' says the governor-general in council, 'is it not the case that martial law was not proclaimed in districts in which there was a necessity for it; but the measures taken for the arrest, summary trial, and punishment of heinous offenders of every class, civil as well as military, were far more widely spread and certainly not less stringent than any that could have resulted from martial law.'

The outcry against Viscount Canning became so excessively violent in connection with two subjects, that the Court of Directors sought for explanations from him thereon, superadded to the dispatches forwarded in the regular course. The one referred to the state of Calcutta; the other to the proceedings of special commissioners in the Allahabad district. A petition was presented from about two hundred and fifty inhabitants of Calcutta, praying that martial law should at once be proclaimed throughout the whole of the Bengal presidency; on the ground that the whole native population was in a disaffected state, that the native police were as untrustworthy as the native soldiery, and that the Company's civil authorities were wholly unable to cope with an evil of so great magnitude. The governor-general in council declined to accede to this request. He urged in reply—that there was no evidence of the native population of Bengal being in so disaffected a state as to render martial law necessary; that such law had already been enforced in the north-west provinces, where the mutineers were chiefly congregated; that in Bengal the native police, aided by the European civilians, would probably be strong enough to quell ordinary disturbances; that, as all his European troops were wanted to confront the mutinous sepoys, he had none to spare for ordinary police duties; and that in Calcutta especially, where a zealous volunteer guard had been organised, the peace might easily be preserved by ordinary watchfulness on the part of the European inhabitants. This reply was in many quarters interpreted into a declaration that the natives would be petted and favoured more than the Europeans.

The second charge, as stated above, related to the proceedings in the Allahabad district. When the power of appointing special commissions for trying the natives was given, the civilians in that region entered on the duty in a more stern manner than anywhere else. In about forty days a hundred and seventy natives were tried, of whom a hundred were put to death. When a detailed report of the proceedings reached Calcutta, grave doubts were entertained whether the offences generally were proportionate to the punishment. Many persons had been put to death for having plundered property in their possession, without being accused of having actually been engaged in mutiny; some were put to death for obtaining by threats salary that was not due to them from the revenue establishments; several others for 'robbing their masters,' and some for 'plundering salt;' six were condemned to death in one day for having in their possession more rupees than they could or would account for. The question forced itself on Lord Canning's attention, whether such offences and such punishments as these were intended to be met by the extraordinary tribunals established in time of danger. The culprits might have been and probably were rogues; but it did not follow that they deserved death at the hands of civilians, irrespective of military proceedings. The Calcutta authorities considered, from all the information that reached them, that these large powers 'had been in some cases unjustly and recklessly used; that the indiscriminate hanging, not only of persons of all shades of guilt, but of those whose guilt was at the least very doubtful, and the general burning and plunder of villages, whereby the innocent as well as the guilty, without regard to age or sex, were indiscriminately punished, and in some instances sacrificed,' were unjustifiable. It further became manifest that 'the proceedings of the officers of government had given colour to the rumour, which was industriously spread and credulously received in all parts of the country, that the government meditated a general bloody prosecution of Mohammedans and Hindoos in revenge for the crimes of the sepoys, and only awaited the arrival of European troops to put this design into execution.' This led the governor-general to issue a resolution on the 31st of July, containing detailed instructions for the guidance of civil officers in the apprehension, trial, and punishment of natives charged with or suspected of offences. This resolution was interpreted by the opponents of Viscount Canning as a check upon all the heroes who were fighting the battles of the British against the mutinous natives; but it was afterwards clearly shewn that the resolution applied, and was intended to apply, only to the civil servants, among whom such vast powers were novel and often susceptible of abuse; it did not cramp the energies of generals or military commanders who might feel that martial law was necessary to the successful performance of their duties. So obstructive, however, was the bitter hostility felt in many quarters against the supreme government at Calcutta, that it led to a ready belief in charges which were afterwards shewn to be wholly untrue. When the Northwest Provinces had fallen into such utter anarchy by the mutiny, that the rule of the lieutenant-governor was little better than a name, a new government was formed called the Central Provinces, comprising the regions of Goruckpore, Benares, Allahabad, the Lower Doab, Bundelcund, and Saugor, and placed under the lieutenant-governorship of Mr Grant, who had until that time been one of the members of the supreme council. A rumour reached London, and was there credited three months before Viscount Canning knew aught concerning it, that 'Mr Grant had liberated a hundred and fifty mutineers or rebels placed in confinement by Brigadier-general Neill.' As a consequence of this rumour, it was often asserted in London that Mr Grant was more friendly to the native mutineers than to the British soldiery. Knowing the gross improbability of such a story, Viscount Canning at once appealed to the best authority on the subject—Mr Grant himself. It then appeared that the lieutenant-governor had never pardoned or released a single person seized by Neill or any other military authority; that he had never commuted or altered a single sentence passed by such authorities; that he had never written to or even seen Neill; that he had neither found fault with, nor commented upon, any of that general's proceedings—in short, the charge was an unmitigated, unrelieved falsehood from beginning to end. As a mere *canard*, the governor-general would not have noticed it; but the calumny assumed historical importance when it affected public opinion in England during a period of several months.

We now arrive at the third subject marked out—the attitude of the Indian government towards the European population. It has been shewn in former chapters that, when the mutinies began, addresses were presented from various classes of persons at Calcutta, some expressing alarm, but all declaratory of loyalty. Similar declarations were made at Madras and Bombay—two cities of which we have said little, because they were happily exempt from insurgent difficulties. A few lines will suffice to shew the relation between these two cities and Calcutta, as seats of presidential government. Madras is situated on the east coast, far down towards Ceylon—perhaps the worst port in the world for the arrival and departure of shipping, on account of the peculiar surf that rages near the shore. Fort St George, the original settlement, is the nucleus around which have collected the houses and buildings which now constitute Madras. As Calcutta is called 'Fort William' in official documents, so is Madras designated 'Fort St George.' The principal streets out of the fort constitute 'Black Town.' Bombay, on the opposite coast, boasts of a splendid harbour that often excites the envy of the Madras inhabitants. The city is built on two or three islands, which are so connected by causeways and other constructions as to enclose a magnificent harbour. Nevertheless Madras has the larger population, the numbers being seven hundred and twenty thousand against five hundred and sixty thousand. So far as this

Chronicle is concerned, both cities may pass without further description. Each was a metropolis, in all that concerned military, judicial, and civil proceedings; and each remained in peace during the mutiny, chiefly owing to the native armies of Madras and Bombay being formed of more manageable materials than that of Bengal. Lord Harris at the one city, and Lord Elphinstone at the other, received numerous declarations of loyalty from the natives; and were enabled to render military service to the governor-general, rather than seek aid from him.

In Calcutta, there was more difficulty than in Madras and Bombay. The government had to defend itself against Europeans as well as natives. It has already been stated that great hostility was shewn towards this government by resident Europeans not belonging to the Company's service. On the one side, the Company was accused of regarding India as a golden egg belonging to its own servants; on the other, the Company sometimes complained that missionaries and newspapers encouraged disaffection among the natives. This had been a standing quarrel long before the mutiny broke out. As ministers of religion, missionaries of various Christian denominations were allowed to pursue their labours, but without direct encouragement. They naturally sympathised with the natives; but, however pure may have been their motive, it must be admitted that the missionaries often employed language that tended to place the Company and the natives in the antagonistic position of the injurers and the injured. In September 1856 certain missionaries in the Bengal presidency presented a memorial, setting forth in strong terms the deplorable social condition of the natives—enumerating a series of abuses and defects in the Indian government; and recommending the appointment of a commission of inquiry, to comprise men of independent minds, unbiassed by official or local prejudices. The alleged abuses bore relation to the police and judicial systems, gang-robberies, disputes about unsettled boundaries, the use of torture to extort confession, the zemindary system, and many others. The memorialists asserted that if remedies were not speedily applied to those abuses, the result would be disastrous, as 'the discontent of the rural population is daily increasing, and a bitter feeling of hatred towards their rulers is being engendered in their minds.' Mr Halliday, lieutenant-governor of Bengal, in reply to the memorial, pointed out the singular omission of the missionaries to make any even the most brief mention of the numerous measures undertaken by the government to remove the very evils complained of; thereby exhibiting a one-sided tendency inimical to the ends of justice. He declined to accede to the appointment of a commission on these grounds: That without denying the existence of great social evils, 'the government is in possession of full information regarding them; that measures are under consideration, or in actual progress, for applying remedies to such of them as are remediable by the direct executive or legislative action of the government; while the cure of others must of necessity be left to the more tardy progress of national advancement in the scale of civilisation and social improvement.' He expressed his 'absolute dissent from the statement made, doubtless in perfect good faith, that the people exhibit a spirit of sullen discontent, on account of the miseries ascribed to them; and that there exists amongst them that bitter hatred to the government which has filled the memorialists, as they declare, with alarm as well as sorrow.' The British Indian Association, consisting of planters, landed proprietors, and others, supported the petition for the appointment of a commission, evidently with the view of fighting the missionaries with their own weapons, by shewing that the missionaries were exciting the natives to disaffection. Mr Halliday declined to rouse up these elements of discord; Viscount Canning and the supreme council supported him; and the Court of Directors approved of the course pursued.

In the earlier weeks of the mutiny, or rather before the mutiny had actually begun, the colonel of a regiment at Barrackpore, as has already been shewn, brought censure upon himself by taking the duties of a missionary or Christian religious teacher among his own troops. Whatever judgment may be passed on this officer, or on those who condemned him, it is at least important to bear in mind that, throughout the whole duration of the mutiny and the battles consequent on it, one class of theorists persisted in asserting that the well-meant exertions of pious Christians had alarmed the prejudices of the native soldiers, and had led to the Revolt. Right or wrong, this theory, and the line of conduct that had led to it, greatly increased the embarrassments of the governor-general, and rendered it impossible for him to pursue a line of conduct that would please all parties.

Much more hostile, however, was the feeling raised against him in relation to an important measure concerning newspapers—turning against him the bitter pens of ready writers who resented any check placed upon their licence of expression. On the 13th of June, the legislative council of Calcutta, on the motion of the governor-general, passed an act whereby the liberty of the press in India was restricted for one year. The effect of this law was to replace the Indian press, for a time, very much in the position it occupied before Sir Charles Metcalfe's government gave it liberty in 1835. Sir Thomas Munro and other experienced persons had, long before this last-named date, protested against any analogy between England and India, in reference to the freedom of the press. Sir Thomas was connected with the Madras government; but his observations were intended to apply to the whole of British India. In 1822 he said: 'I cannot view the question of a free press in this country without feeling that the tenure by which we hold our power never has been and never can be the liberties of the people. Were the people all our own countrymen, I would prefer the utmost freedom of the press; but as they are, nothing could be more dangerous than such freedom. In place of spreading useful knowledge among the people and tending to their better government, it would generate insubordination, insurrection, and anarchy. . . . . A free press and the dominion of strangers are things which are incompatible, and which cannot long exist together. For what is the first duty of a free press? It is to deliver the country from a foreign yoke, and to sacrifice to this one great object every meaner consideration; and if we make the press really free to the natives as well as to Europeans, it must inevitably lead to this result.' Munro boldly, whether wisely or not, adopted the theory of India being a conquered country, and of the natives being more likely to write against than for their English rulers, if allowed unfettered freedom of the press. He pointed out that the restrictions on this freedom were really very few; extending only to attacks on the character of government and its officers, and on the religion of the natives. In reply

General View of MADRAS.—From a Drawing by Thomas Daniell.

to a suggestion that the native press might be placed under restriction, without affecting the Indo-British newspapers read by Europeans, he said: 'We cannot have a monopoly of the freedom of the press; we cannot confine it to Europeans only. There is no device or contrivance by which this can be done.' In fine, he declared his opinion that if the native press were made free, 'it must in time produce nearly the same consequences here which it does everywhere else; it must spread among the people the principles of liberty, and stimulate them to expel the strangers who rule over them, and to establish a national government.' When the liberty of the press was made free and full in 1835, the Court of Directors severely censured Sir Charles Metcalfe's government for having taken that step without permission from London, and directed that the subject should be reconsidered; but Lord Auckland, who succeeded Sir Charles as governor-general, pointed out what appeared to him the difficulty of rescinding the liberty when once granted; and the directors yielded, though very unwillingly. The minute, in which the alteration of the law was made in 1835, was from the pen of Mr (afterwards Lord) Macaulay; but this eminent person at the same time admitted that the governor-general had, and ought to have, a power suddenly to check this liberty of the press in perilous times. The members of the supreme council at Calcutta, in their minutes on this subject, asserted the power and right of the government to use the check in periods of exigency.

Viscount Canning, conceiving that all his predecessors had recognised the possible necessity of curbing the liberty of the press, considered whether the exigency for so doing had arrived. He found that it would be of little use to control the native press unless that of the English were controlled also; because he wished to avoid invidious distinctions; and because some of the newspapers, though printed in the English language, were written, owned, and published by natives, almost exclusively for circulation among native readers. The natives, it was found, were in the habit of procuring English newspapers, not only those published in India, but others published in England, and of causing the political news relating to their own country to be translated and read to them. This might not be amiss if the government were made responsible for such articles only as emanated from it; but the natives were often greatly alarmed at articles and speeches directed against them, or against their usages and religion, in the Calcutta, Madras, and Bombay newspapers—not by the government, but by individual writers. The newspaper press in India, whether English or native, has generally been distinguished by great violence in the mode of opposing the government; this violence, in times of peace, was disregarded by those against whom it was directed; but at a time when a hundred thousand native troops were more or less in mutiny, and when Mohammedan leaders were endeavouring to enlarge this military revolt into a national rebellion, Viscount Canning and his colleagues deemed it right to place a restriction on the liberty of the press, during the disturbed state of India.

Very little has hitherto been known in England concerning the native newspapers of India; for few except the Company's servants have come in

BOMBAY.—From a View in the Library of the East India Company.

contact with them. Their number is considerable, but the copies printed of each are exceedingly limited. In the Agra government alone, a few years ago, there were thirty-four native papers, of which the aggregate circulation did not reach *two thousand*, or less than sixty each on an average. Some appeared weekly, some twice a week. Some were printed in Persian, others in Oordoo, others in Hindee. About twenty more were published in various towns in the northwest regions of India. A few were sensible, many more trivial, but nearly all abusive of the government. As estimated by an English standard, the extremely small circulation would have rendered them wholly innocuous; but such was not the case in the actual state of affairs. The miserably written and badly lithographed little sheets of news had, each, its group of men seated round a fluent reader, and listening to the contents; one single copy sufficed for a whole regiment of sepoys; and it was observed, during a year or two before the Revolt, that the sepoys listened with unwonted eagerness to the reading of articles grossly vituperative of the government. The postal reform, effected by the Marquis of Dalhousie, exceeding in liberality even that of England itself, is believed to have led to an unexpected evil connected with the dissemination of seditious intelligence in India. To save expense, he placed natives instead of Europeans in most of the offices connected with this service; and it appears probable, from facts elicited during the mutiny, that Hindoo and Mohammedan postmasters were far too well acquainted with the substance of many of the letters which passed through their hands.

It may be well here to state that Lord Harris, governor of the presidency of Madras, dwelt on the unfair tone of the British press in India, before the actual commencement of the mutiny at Meerut. On the 2d of May he made a minute commencing thus: 'I have now been three years in India, and during that period have made a point of keeping myself acquainted with the tenor of the larger portion of the British press, throughout the country; and I have no hesitation in asserting my impression to be that it is, more particularly in this presidency, disloyal in tone, un-English in spirit, and wanting in principle—seeking every opportunity, whether rightly or wrongly, of holding up the government to opprobrium.' He denied that any analogy could be furnished from the harmlessness of such attacks in the home country; because, in England, 'every man is certain of having an opportunity of bringing his case before the public, either by means of rival newspapers or in parliament.' This facility is not afforded in India; and thus the newspaper articles are left to work their effects uncompensated. 'I do not see how it is possible for the natives, in the towns more especially, with the accusations, misrepresentations, and calumnies which are constantly brought before them, to come to any other conclusion than that the government of their country is carried on by imbecile and dishonest men.'

The legislative statute of the 13th of June may be described in a few words. All printing-presses, types, and printing-machinery throughout British India were, by virtue of this act, to be registered, and not used without licence from the government. Magistrates were empowered to order a search of suspected buildings, and a seizure of all unregistered printing-apparatus and printed paper found therein. All applications for a printing-licence were to be made on oath of the proprietor, with full particulars on certain specified matters. The licence might be refused or granted; and, if granted, might be at any time revoked. A copy of every paper, sheet, or book was required to be sent to the authorities, immediately on being printed. The government, by notice in the government gazette, might prohibit the publication of the whole or any part of any book or paper, either in the whole or any part of India; and this was equally applicable whether the book or paper were printed in India or any other country. The penalty—for using unlicensed printing-machinery, or for publishing in defiance of a gazette order—was a fine of 5000 rupees (£500), or two years' imprisonment, or both. This punishment was so rigorous, that the instances were very few in which the press disobeyed the new law; it produced great exasperation in some quarters; but the proprietors of newspapers generally placed such a check upon editors and writers as to prevent the insertion of such articles as would induce the government to withdraw the printing-licence.

So alien are such restrictions to the genius of the English people, that nothing but dire necessity could have driven the Calcutta government to make them. They must be judged by an Indian, not an English standard. It is well to remark, however, as shewing the connection of events, that this statute was one cause of the violent attacks made against Lord Canning in London; the freedom, checked in India, appeared in stronger form than ever when several of the writers came over to England, or sent for printing in England books or pamphlets written in India. When one of these editors arrived in London, he brought with him a petition or memorial, signed by some of the Europeans at Calcutta not connected with the government, praying for the removal of Viscount Canning from the office held by him.

Having thus passed in review three courses of proceeding adopted by the Indian government consequent on the outbreak—in reference to military operations, to judicial punishments, and to public opinion—we will now notice in a similarly rapid way the line of policy adopted by the home government to stem the mutiny, and by the British nation to succour those who had suffered or were suffering by it.

It was on the 27th of June that the government, the parliament, and the people of England were startled with the news that five or six native regiments had revolted at Meerut and Delhi, and that the ancient seat of the Mogul Empire was in the hands of mutineers and rebels. During some weeks previously, observations had occasionally been made in parliament, relating to the cartridge troubles at Barrackpore and Berhampore; but the ministers always averred that those troubles were slight in character. The Earl of Ellenborough, who had been governor-general from 1842 to 1844, and who possessed extensive knowledge of Indian affairs generally, had also drawn attention occasionally to the state of the Indian armies. While India was in commotion, but six or seven weeks before England was aware of that fact, the earl asked the ministers (on May 19th) what arrangements had been made for reinforcing the British army in India. Lord Panmure, as war-minister, replied that certain regiments intended for India had been diverted from that service and sent to China; but that four other regiments would be ready to depart from England about the middle of June, to relieve regiments long stationed in the East Indies; irrespective of four thousand recruits for the Company's service. On the 9th of June Lord Ellenborough expressed suspicions that a mutinous feeling was being engendered among the sepoys, by a fear on their part that their religion was about to be tampered with; this expression of opinion led to various counter-views in both Houses of parliament.

Two or three paragraphs may here be usefully given, to shew to how great an extent the number and distribution of European troops in India had been a subject of consideration among the governing authorities, both at Calcutta and in London. Towards the close of 1848 the Marquis of Dalhousie drew attention to the propriety, or even necessity, of increasing the European element in the Indian armies; and, to this end, he suggested that an application should be made to the crown for three additional regiments of the royal army. This was attended to; three regiments being promptly sent. In March 1849, consequent on the operations in the Punjaub, application was made for two more Queen's regiments; which was in like manner quickly responded to. All these additions, be it observed, were to be fully paid for by the Company. These five regiments, despatched during the early months of 1849, comprised 220 commissioned officers, and 5335 non-commissioned, rank and file. In 1853, after the annexation of Pegu, the marquis wrote home to announce that that newly-acquired province could not be securely held with a less force than three European regiments, eight native regiments, and a proportionate park of artillery; and he asked: 'Whence is this force to be derived?' The British empire in India was growing; the European military element, he urged, must grow with it; and he demanded three new regiments from England to occupy Pegu, seeing that those already in India were required in the older provinces and presidencies. There were at that time five regiments of European cavalry in India, all belonging to the Queen's army; and thirty regiments of European infantry, of which twenty-four were Queen's, and the remaining six belonging to the Company. As the crown retained the power of drawing away the royal regiments from India at any time of emergency, the marquis deemed it prudent that the three additional regiments required should belong to the Company, one to each presidential army, and not to the royal forces. The Company, by virtue of the act passed that year (1853), obtained permission to increase the number of European troops belonging absolutely to it in India; and, that permission being obtained, three additional regiments were planned in the year, to comprise about 2760 officers and men. Only two out of the three, however, were really organised. When the war with Russia broke out in 1854, a sudden demand was made for the services of several of the Queen's regiments in India—namely, the 22d, 25th, 96th, and 98th foot, and the 10th Hussars; at the same time, as only the 27th and 35th foot were ordered out to India, the royal troops at the disposal of the governor-general were lessened by three regiments. This step the Marquis of Dalhousie, and his colleagues at Calcutta, most earnestly deprecated. A promise was made that two more regiments, the 82d and 90th foot, should be sent out early in 1855; but the marquis objected to the weakening of the Indian army even by a single English soldier. In a long dispatch, he dwelt upon the insufficiency of this army for the constantly increasing area of the British army in India. The European army in India, the Queen's and the Company's together, was in effect only two battalions stronger in September 1854 than it had been in January 1847; although in that interval of nearly eight years the Punjaub, Pegu, and Nagpoor, had been added to British India. The army was so scattered over this immense area, that there was only one European battalion between Calcutta and Agra, a distance of nearly eight hundred miles. The marquis earnestly entreated the imperial government not to lessen his number, already too small, of European troops—not only because the area to be defended had greatly increased; but because many of the princes of India were at that time looking with a strange interest at the war with Russia, as if ready to side with the stronger power, whichever that might be. There were symptoms of this kind in Pegu, in Nepaul, and elsewhere, which he thought ought not to be disregarded. No document penned by the marquis throughout his eight years' career in India was more energetic, distinct, or positive than this; he protested respectfully but earnestly against any further weakening of the European element in his forces. The home government, however, had engaged in a war with a great power which needed all its resources; the withdrawal of the regiments was insisted on; and the governor-general was forced to yield.

The year 1855 presented nothing worthy of comment in relation to the Indian armies; but in February 1856, just on surrendering the reins of government to Viscount Canning, the Marquis of Dalhousie drew up a minute bearing on this subject. At that time, fifteen months before the commencement of the mutiny at Meerut, there were thirty-three regiments of European infantry in India.* The marquis sketched a plan for so redistributing the forces as to provide for the principal stations during peace, and also for a field-army in case of outbreak in Cabool, Cashmere, Nepaul, Ava, or other adjacent states; he required two additional regiments to effect this, and shewed how the whole thirty-five might most usefully be apportioned between the three presidencies.† He suggested that this number of 24 Queen's regiments of foot should be a *minimum*, not at any time reducible by the imperial government without consent of the Indian authorities; he remembered the Crimean war, and dreaded the consequence of any possible future war in depriving India of royal troops. These were suggestions, made by the Marquis of Dalhousie when about to leave India; they possessed no other authority than as suggestions, and do not appear to have been taken officially into consideration

* Presidency.	Queen's Regiments.	Company's Regiments.	Total.
Bengal, . .	16	3	19
Madras, . .	4	3	7
Bombay, . .	4	3	7
	24	9	33

† Presidency.	Queen's Regiments.	Company's Regiments.	Total.
Bengal, . .	15	4	19
Madras, . .	5	4	9
Bombay, . .	4	3	7
	24	11	35

until the mutiny threw everything into confusion. During the later months of 1856, Viscount Canning, the new governor-general, drew the attention of the Court of Directors to the fact that the English officers in the native regiments had become far too few in number; some were appointed to irregular corps, others to civil duties, until at length the regiments were left very much under-officered. As a means of partially meeting this want, the directors authorised in September that every regular native infantry or cavalry regiment should have two additional officers, one captain and one lieutenant; and that each European regiment in the Company's service should have double this amount of addition. In the same month it was announced by the military authorities in London that the two royal regiments, 25th and 89th, *borrowed* from India for the Russian war in 1854, should be replaced by two others early in 1857; and that at the same time two additional regiments of Queen's foot should be sent out, to relieve the 10th and 29th, which had been in India ever since 1842.

The year of the mutiny, 1857, witnessed the completion of the military arrangement planned in 1856, and the organisation of others arising out of the complicated state of affairs in Persia, China, and India. About the middle of February, the second division of the army intended for the Persian expedition left Bombay, making, with the first division, a force of about 12,000 men under the command of Sir James Outram. About 4000 of that number were European troops.* Viscount Canning, speculating on the probability that a third division would be needed, pointed out that India could not possibly supply it; and that it would be necessary that the home government should send out, not only the four regiments already agreed on, but three others in addition, and that the 10th and 29th regiments should not return to Europe so early as had been planned. There was another complication, arising out of the Chinese war; the 82d and 90th foot, intended to replace the two regiments withdrawn from India during the Crimean war, were now despatched to the Chinese seas instead of to India; and the directors had to make application for two others. Early in May, before any troubles in India were known to the authorities in London, it was arranged that the plan of 1856 should be renewed—two Queen's regiments to be sent out to replace those withdrawn for the Crimean war; and two others to relieve the 10th and 29th—bringing the royal infantry in India to the usual number of twenty-four regiments. Of these four regiments, two were to proceed to Calcutta, one to Madras, and one to Kurachee. They were to consist of the 7th Fusiliers, the 88th and 90th foot, and the 3d battalion of the Rifle Brigade. It was also planned that the 2d and 3d Dragoons should go out to India to relieve the 9th Lancers and 14th Dragoons. Furthermore, it was arranged that these six regiments should take their departure from England in June and July, so as to arrive in India at a favourable season of the year; and that with them should go out drafts from Chatham, in number sufficient to complete the regiments already in India up to their regular established strength. So far as concerned Persia, the proposed third division was not necessary; the Shah assented to terms which—fortunately for British India—not only rendered this increased force unnecessary, but set free the two divisions already sent.

Such was the state of the European element in the Indian army at, and some time before, the commencement of the mutiny. It was on the 27th of June, we have said, that the bad news from Meerut reached London. Two days afterwards, the Court of Directors ordered officers at home on furlough or sick-leave to return to their regiments forthwith, so far as health would permit. They also made a requisition to the government for four full regiments of infantry, in addition to those already decided on; to be returned, or replaced by other four, when the mutiny should be ended. On the 1st of July—shewing thereby the importance attached to the subject—the government announced, not only its acquiescence in the demand, but the numbers or designations of the regiments marked out—namely, the 19th, 38th, and 79th foot, and the 1st battalion of the 1st foot. It was also agreed to that the four regiments intended to have been relieved—namely, the 10th and 29th foot, and the 9th and 14th Dragoons—should *not* be relieved at present, but that, on the contrary, drafts should go out to reinforce them. Another mail arrived, making known further disasters; whereupon the directors on the 14th of July made another application to government for *six* more regiments of infantry, and eight companies of royal artillery—the artillerymen to be sent out from England, the horses from the Cape of Good Hope, and the guns and ammunition to be provided in India itself. Two days afterwards—so urgent did the necessity appear—the government named the six regiments which should be sent out in compliance with this requisition—namely, the 20th, 34th, 42d, 54th, and 97th foot, and the 2d battalion of the Rifle Brigade; together with two troops of horse-artillery, and six companies of royal (foot) artillery.

Summing up all these arrangements, therefore, we find the following result: Two regiments of royal infantry—7th Fusiliers and 88th foot—were to go to India, to replace two borrowed or withdrawn from the Company in 1854; two others—the 90th foot and the 3d battalion of the Rifle

* *First Division*, under Major-general Stalker—

Natives,	3550
Europeans,	2270
	5820

Second Division, under Brigadier-general Havelock—

Natives,	4370
Europeans,	1770
	6140

Brigade—to relieve the 10th and 29th foot, and two regiments of cavalry—the 2d and 3d Dragoons—to relieve the 9th Lancers and 14th Dragoons, but the four relieved regiments not to return till the mutiny should be quelled; four regiments of infantry—the 19th, 38th, and 79th foot, and the 1st battalion of the 1st foot—to go out in consequence of the bad news received from India at the end of June; six regiments of infantry—the 20th, 34th, 42d, 54th, 97th, and 2d battalion of the Rifle Brigade—together with several troops and companies of artillery, were to go out in consequence of the still more disastrous news received in the middle of July; drafts were to go out to bring up to the full strength the whole of the Queen's regiments in India; and, lastly, recruits were to go out, to bring up to the full complement the whole of the European regiments belonging to the Company. These various augmentations to the strength of armed Europeans in India amounted to little less than twenty-four thousand men, all placed under orders by the middle of July.

Various discussions bearing on the military arrangements for India, took place in the two houses of parliament. Lord Ellenborough frequently recommended the embodiment of the militia and the calling out of the yeomanry, in order that England might not be left defenceless by sending a very strong royal army to India. The Earl of Hardwicke suggested that all the troops at Aldershott camp, about sixteen thousand in number, should at once be sent off to India. These, and other members of both Houses, insisted on the perilous position of India; whereas the ministers, in their speeches if not in their proceedings, treated the mutiny as of no very serious importance. Differences of opinion existed to a most remarkable extent; but the president of the Board of Control, Mr Vernon Smith, subjected himself at a later period to very severe criticism, on account of the boldness of the assertions made, or the extent of the ignorance displayed, in the earlier stages of the mutiny. When the news from Meerut and Delhi arrived, he said in the House of Commons: 'I hope that the House will not be carried away by any notion that we exaggerate the danger because we have determined upon sending out these troops. It is a measure of security alone with respect to the danger to be apprehended. I cannot agree with the right honourable gentlemen (Mr Disraeli) that our Indian empire is imperiled by the present disaster. I say that our Indian empire is *not* imperiled; and I hope that in a short time the disaster, dismal as it is, will be effectually suppressed *by the force already in that country*. . . . . Luckily the outrage has taken place at Delhi; because it is notorious that that place *may be easily surrounded;* so that if we could not reduce it by force, we could by famine. . . . . Unfortunately, the mail left on the 28th of May; and I cannot, therefore, apprise the House that the fort of Delhi has been razed to the ground; but I hope that ample retribution has by this time been inflicted on the mutineers.' That other persons, military as well as civil, felt the mutiny to be a wholly unexpected phenomenon, is true; but this minister obviously erred by his positive assertions; his idea of 'easily surrounding' a walled city seven miles in circuit was preposterous; and there was displayed an unpardonable ignorance of the state of the armies in that country in the further assertion that 'there are troops in India equal to *any* emergency.'

A question of singular interest and of great importance arose—how should the reinforcements of troops be sent to India? But before entering on this, it will be well to notice the arrangements made for providing a commander for them when they should reach their destination. As soon as it was known in London, early in July, that General Anson was dead, the government appointed Sir Colin Campbell as his successor. The provisional appointment of Sir Patrick Grant as commander of the forces in India was approved as a judicious step on the part of the Calcutta government; but, rightly or wrongly, the permanent appointment to that high office had come to be considered a ministerial privilege in London; and thus Sir Colin was sent out to supersede Sir Patrick. Fortunately, the general selected carried with him the trust and admiration of all parties. For a time, it is true, there was a disposition to foster a Campbell party and a Grant party among newspaper writers. One would contend that Sir Colin, though a brave and good soldier, and without a superior in command of a brigade, had nevertheless been without opportunity of shewing those powers of combination necessary for the suppression of a wide-spread mutiny, perhaps the reconquest of an immense empire; whereas Sir Patrick was just the man for the occasion, possessing the very experience, temper, and other qualities for dealing with the native soldiers. On the other hand, it was contended that Campbell was something more than a mere general of brigade, having successfully commanded masses of troops equal in extent to armies during the Punjaub war; whereas Grant, being by professional education and military sympathies a Bengal officer—although afterwards commander at Madras—had imbibed that general leaning towards the sepoys which rendered such officers unfit to deal sternly with them in time of disaffection. Happily, this controversy soon came to an end; Sir Colin was pronounced by the public verdict to be the right man, without any disparagement to Sir Patrick; and it was judiciously suggested by the Earl of Ellenborough that the last-named general might, with great advantage to the state, be made a military member of the supreme council at Calcutta, to advise the governor-general on army and military subjects. The nation recognised in Sir Colin the soldierly promptness which had distinguished Wellington and Napier, and which he illustrated in the following way: On the morning of Saturday the 11th of July, the news of General Anson's death reached London; at two o'clock on the same day a cabinet council was held; immediately after the council an interview took place between the minister of war and the commander of the forces; consequent on this interview, Sir Colin Campbell was offered the post of commander-in-chief in India; he accepted it; he was asked how soon he could take his departure; his reply was 'To-morrow;' and, true to his word, he left England on the Sunday evening—taking very little with him but the clothes on his back. Men felt that there would be no unnecessary amount of 'circumlocution' in the proceedings of such a general—a veteran who had been an officer in the army forty-nine years; and who, during that long period, had served in the Walcheren expedition; then in the Peninsular battles and sieges of Vimieira, Corunna, Barossa, Vitoria, San Sebastian, and Bidassoa; then in North America; then in the West Indies; then in the first Chinese war; then in the second Sikh war; and lastly in the Crimea.

Sir Colin Campbell, as a passenger remarkably free from luggage and baggage of every kind, was able to take advantage of the quickest route to India—by rail to Folkestone, steam to Boulogne, rail to Marseille, steam to Alexandria, rail and other means to Suez, and thence steam to Calcutta. Whether the troops could take advantage of this or any other kind of *swift* conveyance, was a question whereon public authorities and public advisers soon found themselves at variance. There were four projects—to proceed through France to Alexandria and Suez; to reach Alexandria by sea from Southampton; to steam from England to Calcutta round the Cape of Good Hope; and to take this last-named route by sailing-ships instead of steamers. A few words may usefully be said on each of these four plans.

As the overland route through France is the quickest, some advisers urged that it would therefore be the best; but this was by no means a necessary inference. It would require an immense amount of changing and shifting. Thrice would the men of the various regiments have to enter railway-trains—at London or some other English station, at Boulogne, and at Alexandria—perhaps also a fourth time at Paris; thrice would they have to leave railway-trains—at Folkestone, at Marseille, and at Cairo or some other place in Egypt; thrice would they have to embark in steamers—at Folkestone, at Marseille, and at Suez; and thrice would they have to disembark—at Boulogne, at Alexandria, and at Calcutta. The difficulties incidental to these many changes would be very great, although of course not insuperable. There would, in addition, be involved a delicate international question touching the passage of large bodies of troops through the territories of another sovereign. The Emperor of France, at a time of friendly alliance, would possibly have given the requisite permission; but other considerations would also have weight; and it is, on the whole, not surprising that the route through France was left unattempted.

It does not follow, however, from difficulties in the French route, that the sea-route to Alexandria would be unavailable; on the contrary, that mode of transit found many advocates. The distance from Southampton to Alexandria is about three thousand miles; and this distance could obviously be traversed, in a number of days easy of estimate, by a steamer requiring no transhipment of cargo. Another steamer would make the voyage from Suez to Calcutta; and an overland passage through Egypt would complete the route. This is a much shorter route to Calcutta than that *viâ* the Cape of Good Hope, in the ratio of about eight thousand miles to twelve thousand; it is adopted for the heavy portion of the India mail; and many persons thought it might well be adopted also for the transmission of troops. The ministers in parliament, however, explained their reasons for objecting to this route. These objections referred principally to steamers and coal, of which there were no more in the Indian seas than were necessary for the mail service. The matter was argued thus: The first mail from England, after the news of the mutiny, left on the 10th of July; it would reach Bombay about the 10th of August; a return mail would start from Bombay on the 16th of August, describing the arrangements made for receiving at Suez any troops sent by the Egyptian route; that letter would reach London about the 16th of September; and if troops were sent off immediately, with everything prepared, they could not have reached India till towards the end of October—four months after the receipt of the first disastrous news from Meerut. A vessel by the Cape route, if sent off *at once*, would reach as soon. This argument depended wholly on the assumption that it would be necessary to spend three months in sending and receiving messages, before the troops could safely be started off from Southampton to Alexandria. Some of those who differed from the government on this point admitted that only a small number of troops could be conveyed by this route, owing to the unfinished state of the land-conveyance from Alexandria to Suez.* The thirty miles of sandy desert to be traversed, either by marching or in vehicles, would necessarily entail much difficulty and confusion if the number of troops were large, especially as neither the isthmus nor its railway belonged to England. Then, again, there are questions concerning calms, storms, monsoons, trade-winds, shoals, and coral reefs, which were warmly discussed by the advocates of different systems; some of whom contended that the Red Sea cannot safely be depended on by ship-loads

* In August 1857, of the whole railway distance marked out from Alexandria through Cairo to Suez, 205 miles in length, about 175 miles were finished—namely, from Alexandria to the crossing of the Nile, 65 miles; from the crossing of the Nile to Cairo, 65 miles; from Cairo towards Suez, 45 miles. The remainder of the journey consisted of 30 miles of sandy desert, not at that time provided with a railway, but traversed by omnibuses or vans.

of troops during the second half of the year; while others argued that the dangers of the route are very slight. On the one side, it was represented that, by adopting the Suez route, there would be many changes in the modes of travel, many sources of confusion wherever those changes were made, many uncertainties whether there would be steamers ready at Suez, many doubts about the supply of coal at Aden and elsewhere, many perils of wreck in and near the Red Sea, much deterioration of health to the troops during the hot weather in that region, and much embarrassment felt by Viscount Canning if the troops came to him faster than he could transfer them up the country. Certain of these government doubts were afterwards admitted to be well founded; others were shewn to be erroneous; and though a few regiments were sent by the Suez route later in the year, it became pretty generally admitted, that if only one or two regiments had taken that route *early in July*, the benefit to India would have been very great, and the difficulties not more than might have been easily conquered.

Next for consideration was the Cape route. Those who admitted that the overland journey was suited only for a *small* body of troops, and not for an army of thirty thousand men, had yet to settle whether sailing-ships or steamers were best fitted for this service. In some quarters it was urged: 'Employ our screw war-steamers; we are at peace in Europe, and can send our soldiers quickly by this means to India, without the expense of chartering steamers belonging to companies or private persons. If sufficient bounties are offered, in one week we could obtain seamen enough to man twenty war-steamers. Take the main and lower-deck guns out of the ships; place fifteen hundred troops in each of the large screw line-of-battle ships; and man each ship with half the war complement, the soldiers themselves serving as marines.' To this it was replied that line-of-battle ships would be dearer rather than cheaper than chartered vessels, because they could not lessen the charge by back-cargoes. Sir Charles Napier contended, moreover, that screw war-steamers could not be fitted out as troop-ships in less than three months after the order was given; and that great difficulty would be found in raising men for them. The government was influenced by these or similar considerations; for no troops were sent out in war-vessels—possibly owing to a prudential wish to keep all war-ships ready for warlike exigencies.

There remained, lastly, the question whether, the Cape route being adopted, it would be better to hire steam-ships or sailing-ships for conveying troops to India. Eager inquiries on this question were made in parliament soon after the news of the outbreak arrived. The ministers, in reference to the superiority of steamers over sailing-ships, stated that, from the difficulty in procuring steamers of the requisite kind, and the delay caused by the number of intermediate points at which they would have to touch for coal, steamers would probably not reach the Indian ports more quickly than sailing-ships. Lord Ellenborough admitted that, when he was in India, sailing-vessels were found better than steamers for India voyages in the autumnal half of the year; but this left untouched the important improvements effected in steam-navigation during the intervening period of fourteen years. The battle was much contested. Sir Charles Wood, First Lord of the Admiralty, pointed out that fast sailing-ships often went from England to Calcutta in 90 to 100 days; that auxiliary screws had been known to take from 90 to 120 days; and therefore that we were not certain of quicker voyages by steam than by sail, even (which was doubtful) if coal enough were procurable at the Cape. This roused the advocates of steaming, who complained that the minister had compared quick sailing-ships with slow steamers. Mr Lindsey asserted that the average duration of twenty-two sail-voyages was 132 days; and that the steam-average would not exceed 94 days. Another authority averred that the average of ninety-eight sail-voyages was 130 days; and that of seven screw-steam voyages, 93 days.

Such were a few of the points brought under consideration, in connection with the schemes for sending troops to India. We mention them here, because they bore intimately on the mutiny and its history. A compromise between the various schemes was effected by the government, in this way:—The ten thousand troops intended to be sent out, as reinforcements, reliefs, and recruits, *before* the news of the disasters reached England, were despatched as originally intended, in ordinary sailing-vessels; the four thousand additional troops, immediately applied for by the Company, were despatched, half in screw-steamers, and half in fast-sailing clippers; while the six thousand supplied on a still later requisition were sent almost wholly in steamers. It was not until late in the year, when the slowness of most of the voyages had been made manifest, that the superiority of steaming became unquestionable—provided the various coal-depôts could be kept well supplied. Setting aside all further controversy as to the best mode of transit, the activity of the movements was unquestionable. In May and June few of the regiments and ships were ready, and therefore few only were despatched; but after that the rapidity was something remarkable. In July more than thirty troop-laden ships departed from our shores, carrying numbers varying from 131 to 438 soldiers each. August was a still more busy month, in relation both to the number of ships and the average freight of each; there being forty troop-laden ships, carrying from 208 to 1057 soldiers each. In July not a single steam-ship was included in the number; but in August nearly half were steamers. The most remarkable shipments were those in the *James Baines* clipper sailing-ship (1037 men of the 42d and 92d foot), the *Champion of the Seas* clipper (1032 men of the 42d and 20th foot) and the *Great Britain* screw-steamer (1057 men of the 8th Hussars and 17th Lancers. In these three splendid ships the troops were conveyed with a degree of comfort rarely if ever before attained in such service. While the necessary arrangements were in progress for shipping off the twenty-four thousand men chosen by the middle of July, other plans were being organised for despatching further regiments; insomuch that, by the end of the year, very nearly forty thousand men had been sent off to the scene of mutiny. In what order and at what times these troops reached their destination, may usefully be noted in a later page. Towards the close of the year the Suez route was adopted for a few regiments; and the rapidity of passage was such as to lead to much expression of regret that that route had not been adopted earlier—although an opinion continued to prevail on the part of the government and the Company that it would not have been practicable to send the bulk of the army by that means.

Another important question arose during the year, how these troops ought to be clothed, and their health secured. English soldiers complain of their tightly buttoned and buckled garments in hot weather, even in an English climate; but in an Indian summer the oppression of such clothing is very grievous; and much anxiety was manifested, when it became known that thirty or forty thousand troops were to set out for the East, as to the dress to be adopted. The War-office issued a memorandum on the subject, chiefly with the view of allaying public anxiety;* but it became afterwards known that, owing to blunders and accidents similar to those which so disastrously affected the Crimean army, the light clothing, even if sufficient in quantity, was not in the right place at the right time; and our gallant men were only kept from complaining by their excitement at the work to be done. It must at the same time be admitted that, owing to the slowness of the voyages, the majority of the reinforcements did not land in India till the intense heat of summer had passed. In reference to the important question of the health of the troops, Dr James Harrison, of the Company's service, drew up a series of rules or suggestions, for the use of officers in the management of their troops. These rules, which received the approval of Sir Colin Campbell, bore relation to the hours of marching; the length of each march; the kind of beverage best for the soldier before starting; the marching-dress in hot weather; the precautions against sitting or lying in wet clothes; the necessity for bathing; the best choice of food and the best mode of cooking; the stimulants and beverages, &c.

It would be difficult to enumerate all the modes in which the government, the legislature, and the press, sought to meet the difficulties and remedy the evils arising out of the Indian mutiny; nor would such an enumeration be necessary, further than concerned the really practicable and adopted measures. At a time when each mail from India increased the sum-total of disastrous news, each grievance found its own peculiar expositor, who insisted that *that* particular grievance had been the main cause of the mutiny, and that a remedy must be found in that particular direction. Nevertheless, in a series of short paragraphs to close the present chapter, it may be possible to sketch the general character of the plans and thoughts that occupied the public mind.

Railways were not forgotten. It was strongly urged that if Indian railways had been begun earlier, and carried to a further stage towards completion, the mutiny either could not have happened at all, or might have been crushed easily by a small force having great powers of locomotion. The disorders in India did not prevent the forwarding of schemes for new lines of railway—such as the Sinde Railway, from Kurachee to Hydrabad, there to be connected with steamers up the Indus to Moultan; the Punjaub Railway, from Moultan to Lahore, there to join the grand trunk railway; the Oude Railway, to supply Lucknow with a series of lines radiating in various directions; and the East Bengal Railway, to accommodate the region eastward of Calcutta. But besides these, the mutiny gave a new impetus to schemes for carrying railways across Western Asia towards India; either from Scutari (opposite Constantinople) to Bagdad, or from Antioch to the Euphrates, with a railway or a steam-route thence through Mesopotamia to the Persian Gulf. Some parts of these schemes were very wild; the projectors, in every case, required guaranteed interest from government, on the ground that the particular railway advocated would form a new and quick route from England to India available for government purposes; but as no guarantee was forthcoming, the schemes remained in abeyance.

Electric telegraphs did not fail to occupy a portion of public favour; and there is no question that their benefit was immense. Every lessening of the time for transmitting a message from India to London, or *vice versâ*, was so much gained to those responsible for quelling the mutiny. In the middle of 1857, small portions of submarine cable were

* 'According to existing regulations of some years' standing, every soldier on his arrival in India is provided with the following articles of clothing, in addition to those which compose his kit in this country:

'Mounted Men.—4 white jackets, 6 pair of white overalls, 2 pair of Settringee overalls, 6 shirts, 4 pair of cotton socks, 1 pair of white braces.

'Foot-soldiers.—4 white jackets, 1 pair of English summer trousers, 5 pair of white trousers, 5 white shirts, 2 check shirts, 1 pair of white braces.

'These articles are not supplied in this country, but form a part of the soldier's necessaries on his arrival in India, and are composed of materials made on the spot, and best suited to the climate.

'During his stay in India, China, Ceylon, and at other hot stations, he is provided with a tunic and shell-jacket in alternate years; and in the year in which the tunic is not issued, the difference in the value of the two articles is paid to the soldier, to be expended (by the officer commanding) for his benefit in any articles suited to the climate of the station.

'The force recently sent out to China and India has been provided with white cotton helmet and forage-cap covers.

'Any quantity of light clothing for troops can be procured on the spot in India at the shortest notice.'

immersed in the Mediterranean; but by the end of the year the islands of Corsica, Sardinia, Malta, and Corfu were all connected, greatly shortening the time for transmitting a telegram from Alexandria to Marseille. Superadded to this, the usefulness of the telegraph encouraged the projectors of new lines—from Corfu to Alexandria; from Antioch to the Euphrates and the Persian Gulf; from Suez down the Red Sea to Aden and Kurachee. Rival companies occupied much of the public attention; and, had the British government been favourably disposed towards a guarantee or subsidy, engineers were not wanting who would have undertaken to connect London with Calcutta by an unbroken wire.

River-steaming was advocated as one of the great things needed for India. One scheme was for an Indus flotilla. Supposing a hundred miles of railway to be constructed from Kurachee to Hydrabad, then the Indus would be reached at a point whence it is navigable to Moultan for five hundred and seventy miles; and it was proposed for this service to establish a flotilla of fifteen steamers, fitted up for passengers and a little cargo, and each towing two flat-bottom barges for the conveyance of troops and heavy cargo. Irrespective of the success or failure of any particular project, the establishment of steamers on the Indus was unquestionably a practical good to which India had a right to look forward; for, as a glance at a map will shew, the Indus instead of the Ganges seems the natural route of communication from Europe to the upper provinces of India. The Ganges provinces also would undergo an immense development of resources by the increase of steam-navigation on that noble river.

Gun-boats for India did not fail to find advocates. It was deemed almost a certainty that if light-draught vessels of this description had been on two or three of the Indian rivers, especially the Ganges and the Jumna, the mutineers would have met with formidable opponents; and even if the mutiny were quelled, a few gun-boats might act as a cheap substitute for a certain number of troops, in protecting places near the banks of the great rivers. Impressed with this conviction, the East India Company commissioned Messrs Rennie to build a small fleet of high-pressure iron gun-boats; each to have one boiler, two engines, two screw-propellers, and to carry a twelve-pounder gun amidships. The boats were seventy-five feet long by twelve wide, and were so constructed as to be stowed away in the hold of a ship for conveyance from England to India.

The means of locomotion or communication—railways, electric telegraphs, river-steamers, river gun-boats—formed only one portion of the schemes which occupied public thought during the first six months of the mutiny. Still more attention was paid to men—men for fighting in India and for defending our home-coasts. Shortly before the bad news began to arrive from India, a council order announced that the militia would *not* be called out in 1857; two months afterwards, in reply to a question in the House of Commons, Viscount Palmerston would not admit that circumstances were so serious as to necessitate a change in this arrangement; he thought that recruiting would be cheaper than the militia, as a means of keeping up the strength of the army. In August, however, the ministers obtained an act of parliament empowering them to embody some of the militia during the recess, if the state of public affairs should render such a step necessary. A system of active recruiting commenced, and was continued steadily during several months. These recruits were intended, not to increase the number of regiments, but to add a second battalion to many regiments, and to increase the number of men in each battalion; some of the regiments were, by this twofold process, raised from 800 or 1000 to 2000 or 2400 men each. Volunteers, also, came forward from France, Belgium, Germany, Italy, and other foreign countries; but these were mostly adventurers who sought officers' commissions in India, and their services were not needed. The government made an attempt to encourage enlisting by offering commissions in the army to any private gentlemen who could bring forward a certain number of men each—a project not attended with much success. At certain crises, when the news from India was more than usually disastrous, appeals to patriotism shewed themselves in the newspapers—'A Young Englishman;' 'Another Young Englishman;' 'A True Briton;' 'One of the Middle Class;' or 'A Young Scotsman'—would write to the journals, pour out his patriotism or his indignation, and shew what he would do if he only had the power. One proposed that clerks and shopmen out of situations should be embodied into a distinct volunteer corps; another said that, as he was a gentleman, and wished to avenge the foul murder of innocent women and children, he thought that he and such as he ought to be encouraged by commissions in the Indian army; another suggested that, if government would use them well, many young men would volunteer to serve in India, to return to their former mode of life when the mutiny was over. Some, rather in sarcasm than in earnest, suggested that drapers' shopmen should drop the yard-measure, and go to India to fight; leaving to women the duty of serving muslins, and laces, and tapes. There was a certain meaning in all the suggestions, as expressive of honest indignation at the atrocities in India, especially those at Cawnpore; but, in its practical result, volunteering fell to the ground; and even the militia was not much appealed to. Various improvements were made in the condition of the common soldier; and recruits for the regular army came forward with much readiness.

We must now mention those who offered their monetary instead of their personal services in alleviation of the difficulties experienced in our Indian empire. Long before the mutinies in

India had arrived at their greatest height, the question was anxiously debated both in that country and in England, what would be the worldly condition of the numerous families driven from their homes and robbed of all they possessed by the sepoys and marauders at the various stations? Every mail brought home fresh confirmation of the fact that the number of families thus impoverished was rapidly increasing; while on the other hand it was known that the East India Company could not reimburse the sufferers without much previous consideration. For, in the first place, it would have to be considered whether any distinction ought to be made between the two classes of Europeans in India—the civil and military servants of the Company, and those who, independent of the Company, had embarked capital in enterprises connected with indigo factories, opium farms, banks, printing-presses, &c.; and then would come a second inquiry whether the personal property only, or the commercial stock in trade also, should be considered as under the protection of the government. It was felt that immediate suffering ought not to wait for the solution of these questions; that when families had been burnt out or driven out of their homes, penniless and almost unclothed, immediate aid was needed from some quarter or other. This was admitted in the Punjaub, where Sir John Lawrence organised a fund for the relief of the necessitous; and it was admitted at Calcutta, where Lord and Lady Canning headed a subscription for providing shelter, raiment, and food to the hundreds of terrified fugitives who were constantly flocking to that capital. By the time the principal revolts of June were known in England, the last week of August had arrived; and then commenced one of those wonderful efforts in which London takes the lead of all the world—the collection of a large sum of money in a short time to ameliorate the sufferings arising out of some great calamity.

It was on the 25th of August that the lord-mayor presided at a meeting at the Mansion House to establish a fund for the relief of the sufferers by the Indian mutiny. The sum subscribed at the meeting did not much exceed a thousand pounds; but the whole merits of the case being set forth in newspapers, contributions poured in from all quarters, in the same noble spirit as had been manifested during the Crimean disasters. The high-born and the wealthy contributed large sums; the middle classes rendered their aid; country committees and town committees organised local subscriptions; large sums, made up of many small elements, were raised as collections after sermons in the churches and chapels; and when the Queen's subjects in foreign and colonial regions heard of this movement, they sought to shew that they too shared in the common English feeling. Thousands swelled to tens of thousands, these to a hundred thousand, until in the course of a few months the fund rose to three or four hundred thousand pounds. In order to give system to the operations, thirty-five thousand circulars were issued, by the central committee in London, to all the authorities in church and state, to the ambassadors and ministers at foreign courts, to the governors of British colonies, and to the consuls at foreign ports.

This Mutiny Relief Fund was administered by four committees—General, Financial, Relief, and Ladies' Committees. The General Committee settled the principles on which the fund was to be administered, determined the amount and destinations of the remittances to India, and controlled the proceedings of the subordinate committees. The Financial Committee supervised the accounts, the investments of the money, and the arrangement of remittances. The Relief Committee decided on applications for relief, on the administration of relief by donation or by loan, and on the application of means for the maintenance and education of children. The Ladies' Committee took charge of such details as pertained more particularly to their own sex. Each of these committees met once a week. The first remittance was a sum of £2000 to Calcutta, to relieve some of the families who had been driven by the mutineers to seek shelter in that city. This was followed by frequent large remittances to the same place, and to Agra, Delhi, Lucknow, Bombay, and Lahore. Committees, formed in Calcutta and Bombay, corresponded with the head committee in London, and joined in carrying out plans for the expenditure of the fund. The donations and loans to persons who had arrived in England were small in amount; most of the aid being afforded to those who had not been able to leave India. The money was put out at interest as fast as the amount in hand exceeded the immediate requirements. At one time the government made an offer to appoint a royal commission for the administration of the fund; but this was declined; and there has been no reason for thinking that the transference of authority would have been beneficial. It was soon found that there were five classes of sufferers who would greatly need assistance from this fund—families of civil and military officers whose bungalows and furniture had been destroyed at the stations; the families of assistants, clerks, and other subordinate *employés* at the stations; European private traders and settlers, many of whom had been utterly impoverished; many missionary families and educational establishments; and the families of a large number of pensioners, overseers, artificers, indigo-workers, school-masters, shop-keepers, hotel-keepers, newspaper printers, &c. To apportion the amount of misery among these five classes would be impossible; but the past chapters of this work have afforded examples, sufficiently sad and numerous, of the mode in which all ranks of Europeans in India were suddenly plunged into want and desolation. At Agra, when the fort had been relieved from a long investment or siege by the rebels, almost the entire Christian population was not only houseless, but the majority were without the most essential articles of furniture or clothing; nearly all were living in cellars and vaults. At many other stations it was nearly as bad; at Lucknow it was still worse.

India speedily raised thirty thousand pounds on its own account, irrespective of aid from England; and most of this was expended at Calcutta in providing as follows: Board and lodging on arrival at Calcutta for refugees without homes or friends to receive them; clothing for refugees; monthly allowances for the support of families who were not boarded and lodged out of the fund; loans for purchasing furniture, clothing, &c.; free grants for similar purposes; passage and diet money on board Ganges steamers; loans to officers and others to pay for the passage of their families to England; free passage to England for the widows and families of officers; and education of the children of sufferers. These were nearly the same purposes as those to which the larger English fund was applied. The East India Company adopted a wholly distinct system in recognising the just claims of the officers more immediately in its service, and of the widows and children of those who fell during the mutiny—a system based on the established emoluments and pensions of all in the Company's service.

It will thus be seen that the news of the Indian Revolt, when it reached London by successive mails, led to a remarkable and important series of suggestions and plans—intended either to strengthen the hands of the executive in dealing with the mutineers, or to succour those who had been plunged into want by the crimes of which those mutineers were the chief perpetrators.

Note.

At the end of the last chapter a table was given of the number of troops, European and native, in all the military divisions of India, on the day when the mutiny commenced at Meerut. It will be convenient to present here a second tabulation on a wholly different basis—giving the *designations* of the regiments instead of the *numbers* of men, and naming the *stations* instead of the *divisions* in which they were cantoned or barracked. This will be useful for purposes of reference, in relation to the gradual annihilation of the Bengal Hindustani army. The former table applied to the 10th of May 1857; the present will apply to a date as near this as the *East India Register* will permit—namely, the 6th of May; while the royal troops in India will be named according to the *Army List* for the 1st of May—a sufficiently near approximation for the present purpose. A few possible sources of error may usefully be pointed out. 1. Some or other of the India regiments were at all times moving from station to station; and these movements may in a few cases render it doubtful whether a particular corps had or had not left a particular station on the day named. 2. The station named is that of the head-quarters and the bulk of the regiment: detachments may have been at other places. 3. The Persian and Chinese wars disturbed the distribution of troops belonging to the respective presidencies. 4. The disarming and disbanding at Barrackpore and Berhampore are not taken into account; for they were not known in London at the time of compiling the official list. 5. The *Army List*, giving an enumeration of royal regiments in India, did not always note correctly the actual stations at a particular time. These sources of error, however, will not be considerable in amount.

REGIMENTS AND STATIONS OF BENGAL ARMY—MAY 1857.

GENERAL ANSON, Commander-in-chief.

European Cavalry.

Regiment	Station
6th Carabiniers (Queen's),	Meerut.
9th Lancers "	Umballa.

Native Regular Cavalry.

Regiment	Station	Regiment	Station
1st Regiment,	Mhow.	6th Regiment,	Nowgong.
2d "	Cawnpore.	7th "	Lucknow.
3d "	Meerut.	8th "	Lahore.
4th "	Umballa.	9th "	Sealkote.
5th "	Peshawur.	10th "	Ferozpore.

Irregular and Local Cavalry.

Regiment	Station	Regiment	Station
1st Bengal Ir. C.,	Jelum.	3d Bengal Ir. C.,	Jhansi.
2d " "	Goordaspore.	4th " "	Hansi.

Irregular and Local Cavalry.—Continued.

Regiment	Station	Regiment	Station
5th Bengal Ir. C.,	Sonthal.	12th Bengal Ir. C.,	Segowlie.
6th " "	Moultan.	13th " "	Bareilly.
7th " "	Peshawur.	14th " "	Jhansi.
8th " "	Sultanpore.	15th " "	Oude.
9th " "	Hosheapore.	16th " "	Rawul Pindee.
10th " "	Goordaspore.	17th " "	Shumshabad.
11th " "	Berhampore.	18th " "	Peshawur.

Regiment	Station
1st Gwalior Contingent Cavalry,	Gwalior.
2d " " "	Augur.
1st Punjaub Cavalry,	Dera Ismael.
2d " "	" "
3d " "	Bunnoo.
4th " "	Kohat.
5th " "	Asnee.
1st Oude Irregular Cavalry,	Seerora.
2d " " "	Lucknow.
3d " " "	Pertabghur.
Nagpoor Irregular Cavalry,	Taklee.

European Infantry.

Regiment	Station	Regiment	Station
8th Ft. (Qun.'s),	Cawnpore.	53d Ft. (Qun.'s),	Dugshai.
10th "	Wuzeerabad.	60th "	Jullundur.
24th "	Sealkote.	61st "	Wuzeerabad.
27th "	"	70th "	Ferozpore.
29th "	Thayet Mhow.	75th "	Rawul Pindee.
32d "	Kussowlie.	81st "	Lahore.
35th "	Calcutta.	87th "	Peshawur.
52d "	Lucknow.		

Regiment	Station
1st Europeans (East India Company's),	Dugshai.
2d " " "	Umballa.
3d " " "	Agra.

Native Regular Infantry.

Regiment	Station	Regiment	Station
1st Regiment,	Cawnpore.	19th Regiment,	Berhampore.
2d* "	Barrackpore.	20th "	Meerut.
3d "	Phillour.	21st "	Peshawur.
4th "	Noorpore.	22d "	Fyzabad.
5th "	Umballa.	23d "	Mhow.
6th "	Allahabad.	24th "	Peshawur.
7th "	Dinapoor.	25th "	Thayet Mhow.
8th "	"	26th "	Meean Meer.
9th "	Allygurh.	27th "	Peshawur.
10th "	Futteghur.	28th "	Shahjehanpoor.
11th "	Allahabad.	29th "	Jullundur.
12th "	Nowgong and Jhansi.	30th "	Agra.
		31st "	Barrackpore.
13th "	Lucknow.	32d "	Sonthal.
14th "	Moultan.	33d "	Hosheapore.
15th "	Meerut.	34th "	Barrackpore.
16th* "	Meean Meer.	35th "	Sealkote.
17th "	Goruckpore.	36th† "	Jullundur.
18th "	Bareilly.	37th† "	Benares.

* Grenadiers. † Volunteers.

Native Regular Infantry.—Continued.

Regiment	Station	Regiment	Station
38th* Regiment,	Delhi.	57th Regiment,	Ferozpore.
39th* 〃	Jelum.	58th 〃	Rawul Pindee.
40th* 〃	Dinapoor.	59th 〃	Umritsir.
41st 〃	Seetapoor.	60th 〃	Umballa.
42d 〃	Saugor.	61st 〃	Jullundur.
43d 〃	Barrackpore.	62d 〃	Moultan.
44th 〃	Agra.	63d 〃	Barrackpore.
45th 〃	Ferozpore.	64th 〃	Peshawur.
46th 〃	Sealkote.	65th* 〃	Dinapoor.
47th* 〃	Prome.	66th† 〃	Almora.
48th 〃	Lucknow.	67th* 〃	Etawah.
49th 〃	Meean Meer.		Minpooree.
50th 〃	Nagode.	68th 〃	Bareilly.
51st 〃	Peshawur.	69th 〃	Moultan.
52d 〃	Jubbulpoor.	70th 〃	Barrackpore.
53d 〃	Cawnpore.	71st 〃	Lucknow.
54th 〃	Delhi.	72d 〃	Agra.
55th 〃	Nowsherah.	73d 〃	Jumalpore.
56th 〃	Cawnpore.	74th 〃	Cawnpore.

Irregular and Local Infantry.

1st Oude Irregular Infantry, ... Persadpore.
2d 〃 〃 〃 . . . . . Seerora.
3d 〃 〃 〃 . . . . . Gonda.
4th 〃 〃 〃 . . . . . Lucknow.
5th 〃 〃 〃 . . . . . Durriabad.
6th 〃 〃 〃 . . . . . Fyzabad.
7th 〃 〃 〃 . . . . . Lucknow.
8th 〃 〃 〃 . . . . . Sultanpore.
9th 〃 〃 〃 . . . . . Seetapoor.
10th 〃 〃 〃 . . . . . Mullaong.

1st Gwalior Contingent Infantry, . . . Gwalior.
2d 〃 〃 〃 . . . 〃
3d 〃 〃 〃 . . . 〃
4th 〃 〃 〃 . . . 〃
5th 〃 〃 〃 . . . Seepree.
6th 〃 〃 〃 . . . Lullutpore.
7th 〃 〃 〃 . . . Augur.

1st Punjaub Infantry, ... Kohat.
2d 〃 〃 . . . . . 〃
3d 〃 〃 . . . . . 〃
4th 〃 〃 . . . . . Dera Ghazi.
5th 〃 〃 . . . . . Bunnoo.
6th 〃 〃 . . . . . Dera Ismael.

1st Sikh Infantry, ... Hazara.
2d 〃 〃 . . . . . Kangra.
3d 〃 〃 . . . . . Khan.
4th 〃 〃 . . . . . Umballa.

1st Nagpoor Irregular Infantry, ... Seetabuldee.
2d 〃 〃 〃 . . . . Chandah.
3d 〃 〃 〃 . . . . Raypoor.

Regiment of Guides (foot and horse), . . . Peshawur.
〃 of Kelat-i-Ghilzi, ... Shubkuddur.
〃 of Loodianah (Sikhs), ... Benares.
〃 of Ferozpore (Sikhs), ... Mirzapore.
Ramgurh Light Infantry, ... Dorunda.
Hill Rangers, ... Bhagulpore.
Nusserree Rifles, ... Simla.
Pegu Light Infantry, ... Myan Owng.
Sirmoor Rifles, ... Almora.
Kumaon Battalion, ... Deyra.
Assam Light Infantry, 1st, ... Debroogurh.
〃 〃 〃 , 2d, ... Gowhatti.
Mhairwarra Battalion, ... Bewar.
Aracan Battalion, ... Akyab.
Hurrianah Light Infantry, ... Hansi.
Silhet Light Infantry, ... Cherrah.
Malwah Bheel Corps, ... Sirdarpore.
Mewar Bheel Corps, ... Khairwarah.
Sebundee Corps, ... Darjeeling.

Artillery, Engineers, Sappers and Miners.

Horse-artillery, 1st Brigade:
3 European Troops.
2 Native Troops.
〃 〃 2d Brigade:
3 European Troops.
1 Native Troop.
〃 〃 3d Brigade:
3 European Troops.
1 Native Troop.
Foot-artillery, . . 6 European Battalions.
(4 Companies each.)
〃 〃 3 Native Battalions.
(6 Companies each.)

Head-quarters: Meerut. Jullundur. Peshawur. Umballa. Cawnpore. Sealkote. Dumdum.

Engineers, ... } Head-quarters:
Sappers and Miners, . . . 8 Companies, } Roorkee.

* Volunteers. † Goorkhas.

Mixed Corps—Cavalry, Infantry, and Artillery.

Shekhawuttie Battalion, ... Midnapore.
Jhodpore Legion, ... Erinpoora.
Malwah Contingent, ... Mehidpore.
Bhopal 〃 . . . . Sehore.
Kotah 〃 . . . . Kurrowlee.

REGIMENTS AND STATIONS OF MADRAS ARMY—MAY 1857.

SIR PATRICK GRANT, Commander-in-chief.

European Cavalry.

12th Lancers (Queen's), ... Madras.

Native Cavalry.

1st Madras Light Cavalry, ... Trichinopoly.
2d 〃 〃 〃 . . . . . . Sholapore.
3d 〃 〃 〃 . . . . . . Bangalore.
4th 〃 〃 〃 . . . . . . Kamptee.
5th 〃 〃 〃 . . . . . . Bellary.
6th 〃 〃 〃 . . . . . . Jaulnah.
7th 〃 〃 〃 . . . . . . Secunderabad.
8th 〃 〃 〃 . . . . . . Bangalore.

European Infantry.

74th Foot (Queen's), ... Madras.
84th 〃 〃 . . . . Burmah.*

1st Europeans (East India Company's), . . . [Persia].
2d 〃 〃 〃 〃 . . . . Burmah.
3d 〃 〃 〃 〃 . . . Secunderabad.

Native Infantry.

Regiment	Station	Regiment	Station
1st Regiment,†	Secunderabad.	27th Regiment,	Vellore.
2d 〃	Quilon.	28th 〃	Hosungabad.
3d 〃	Cananore.	29th 〃	Penang.
4th 〃	Burmah.	30th 〃	Cuddapah.
5th† 〃	Berhampore.	31st 〃	Vizianagram.
6th 〃	Burmah.	32d 〃	Kamptee.
7th 〃	Moulmein.	33d 〃	〃
8th 〃	Rangoon.	34th 〃	Trichinopoly.
9th 〃	Samulcottah.	35th 〃	Hurryhur.
10th 〃	Rangoon.	36th† 〃	Madras.
11th 〃	Cananore.	37th‡ 〃	Burmah.
12th 〃	Madras.	38th† 〃	Singapore.
13th 〃	Moulmein.	39th 〃	Madras.
14th 〃	Singapore.	40th 〃	Cuttack.
15th 〃	Burmah.	41st 〃	Secunderabad.
16th† 〃	Mangalore.	42d 〃	〃
17th 〃	Madras.	43d 〃	Vizagapatam.
18th 〃	〃	44th 〃	Burmah.
19th 〃	Bangalore.	45th 〃	Rangoon.
20th 〃	French Rocks.	46th 〃	Henzana.
21st 〃	Paulghaut.	47th 〃	Bellary.
22d 〃	Secunderabad.	48th 〃	Moulmein.
23d 〃	Russelcondah.	49th† 〃	Secunderabad.
24th† 〃	Secunderabad.	50th 〃	Bangalore.
25th 〃	Trichinopoly.	51st 〃	Pallamcottah.
26th† 〃	Kamptee.	52d 〃	Mercara.

Artillery, Engineers, Sappers and Miners.

Horse-artillery, 4 European Troops.
〃 〃 2 Native Troops.
Foot-artillery, 4 European Battalions.
(4 Companies each.)
〃 〃 1 Native Battalion.
(6 Companies.)

Head-quarters: St Thomas's Mount, Bangalore, Kamptee, Saugor, Secunderabad.

Engineers, ... Head-quarters: Fort St George.
Sappers and Miners, . . Head-quarters: Dowlaishweram.

REGIMENTS AND STATIONS OF BOMBAY ARMY—MAY 1857.

SIR HENRY SOMERSET, Commander-in-chief.

European Cavalry.

14th Light Dragoons (Queen's), ... Kirkee.

Native Regular Cavalry.

1st Lancers, ... Nuseerabad.
2d Light Cavalry, ... Rajcote.
3d 〃 〃 . . . . [Persia.]

Native Irregular Cavalry.

1st Sinde Irregular Horse, ... Jacobabad.
2d 〃 〃 〃 . . . . . . Jacobabad.
Poonah Irregular Horse, ... [Persia.]
Gujerat Irregular Horse, ... Ahmedabad.
South Mahratta Irregular Horse, ... [Persia.]
Cutch Irregular Horse, ... Bhooj.

* Removed to Calcutta. † Rifles. ‡ Grenadiers.

European Infantry.

Regiment	Station
64th Foot (Queen's),	[Persia.]
78th " "	Poonah.
86th " "	Kurachee.
1st Fusiliers (East India Company's),	Kurachee.
2d Light Infantry (East India Company's),	[Persia.]
3d " " " "	Poonah.

Native Regular Infantry.

Regiment	Station	Regiment	Station
1st Regiment,*	Baroda.	16th Regiment,	Shikarpore.
2d* "	Ahmedabad.	17th "	Bhooj.
3d "	Sholapore.	18th "	[Aden.]
4th† "	[Persia.]	19th "	Mulligaum.
5th "	Bombay.	20th "	[Persia.]
6th "	Poonah.	21st "	Neemuch.
7th "	"	22d "	Satara.
8th "	Baroda.	23d "	[Persia.]
9th "	Surat.	24th "	Ahmednuggur.
10th "	Nuseerabad.	25th "	Ahmedabad.
11th "	Bombay.	26th "	[Persia.]
12th "	Deesa.	27th "	Kolapore.
13th "	Hydrabad.	28th "	Dharwar.
14th "	Kurachee.	29th "	Belgaum.
15th "	Bombay.		

* Grenadiers. † Rifles.

Native Irregular Infantry.

Corps	Station
1st Belooch Battalion,	Kurachee.
2d " "	[Persia.]
Khandeish Bheel Corps,	Dhurrungaum.
Rutnagherry Rangers,	Rutnagherry.
Sawunt Waree Corps,	Sawunt Waree.
Satara Local Corps,	Satara.
Kolapore Infantry Corps,	Kolapore.

Artillery, Engineers, Sappers and Miners.

Horse-artillery, 1 European Brigade, (4 Troops.)* Foot-artillery, 2 European Battalions, (4 Companies each.) " " 2 Native Battalions, (6 Companies each.)	Head-quarters: Bombay. Ahmedabad. Ahmednuggur.
Engineers,	Head-quarters: Bombay,
Sappers and Miners,	Head-quarters: Poonah and Aden

* The first troop of horse-artillery was called Leslie's Troop.

Jumma Musjid, Agra.—Mosque built by Shah Jehan in 1656.

CHAPTER XIV.

THE SIEGE OF DELHI: JUNE AND JULY.

WHILE these varied scenes were being presented; while sepoy regiments were revolting throughout the whole breadth of Northern India, and a handful of British troops was painfully toiling to control them; while Henry Lawrence was struggling, and struggling even to death, to maintain his position in Oude; while John Lawrence was sagaciously managing the half-wild Punjaub at a troublous time; while Wheeler at Cawnpore, and Colvin at Agra, were beset in the very thick of the mutineers; while Neill and Havelock were advancing up the Jumna; while Canning was doing his best at Calcutta, Harris and Elphinstone at Madras and Bombay, and the imperial government at home, to meet the trying difficulties with a determined front—while all this was doing, Delhi was the scene of a continuous series of operations. Every eye was turned towards that place. The British felt that there was no security for their power in India till Delhi was retaken; the insurgents knew that they had a rallying-point for all their disaffected countrymen, so long as the Mogul city was theirs; and hence bands of armed men were attracted thither by antagonistic motives. Although the real siege did not commence till many weary weeks had passed, the plan and preparations for it must be dated from the very day when the startling news spread over India that Delhi had been seized by rebellious sepoys, under the auspices of the decrepit, dethroned, debauched representative of the Moguls.

It was, as we have already seen (p. 70), on the morning of Monday the 11th of May, that the 11th and 20th regiments Bengal native infantry, and the 3d Bengal cavalry, arrived at Delhi after a night-march from Meerut, where they had mutinied on the preceding evening. At Delhi, we have also seen, those mutineers were joined by the 38th, 54th, and 74th native infantry. It was on that same 11th of May that evening saw the six mutinous regiments masters of the imperial city; and the English officers and residents, their wives and children, wanderers through jungles and over streams and rivers. What occurred within Delhi on the subsequent days is imperfectly known; the few Europeans who could not or did not escape were in hiding; and scanty notices only have ever come to light from those or other sources. A Lahore newspaper, three or four months afterwards, gave a narrative prepared by a native, who was within Delhi from the 21st of May to the 23d of June. Arriving ten days after the mutiny, he found the six regiments occupying the Selimgurh and Mohtabagh, but free to roam over the city; where the sepoys and sowars, aided by the rabble of the place, plundered the better houses and shops, stole horses from those who possessed them, 'looted' the passengers who crossed the Jumna by the bridge of boats, and fought with each other for the property which the fleeing British families had left behind them. After a few days, something like order was restored, by leaders who assumed command in the name of the King of Delhi. This was all the more necessary when new arrivals of insurgent troops took place, from Allygurh, Minpooree, Agra, Muttra, Hansi, Hissar, Umballa, Jullundur, Nuseerabad, and other places. The mutineers did not, at any time, afford proof that they were really well commanded; but still there *was* command, and the defence of the city was arranged on a definite plan. As at Sebastopol, so at Delhi; the longer the besiegers delayed their operations, the greater became the number of defenders within the place, and the stronger the defence-works.

It must be remembered, in tracing the history of the siege of Delhi, that every soldier necessary for forming the siege-army had to be brought from distant spots. The cantonment outside the city was wholly in the hands of the rebels; and not a British soldier remained in arms in or near the place. Mr Colvin at Agra speedily heard the news, but he had no troops to send for the recapture. General Hewett had a British force at Meerut—unskilfully handled, as many persons thought and still think; and it remained to be seen what arrangements the commander-in-chief could make to render this and other forces available for the reconquest of the important city.

Major-general Sir Henry Barnard was the medium of communication on this occasion. Being stationed at Umballa, in command of the Sirhind military division, he received telegraphic messages on the 11th of May from Meerut and Delhi, announcing the disasters at those places. He immediately despatched his aid-de-camp to Simla, to point out the urgent need for General Anson's presence on the plains instead of among the hills. Anson, hearing this news on the 12th, first thought about his troops, and then about his own movements. Knowing well the extreme paucity of European regiments in the Delhi and Agra districts, and in all the region thence eastward to Calcutta, he saw that any available force to recover possession of Delhi must come chiefly from Sirhind and the Punjaub. Many regiments were at the time at the hill-stations of Simla, Dugshai, Kussowlie, Deyrah Dhoon, Subathoo, &c., where they were posted during a time of peace in a healthy temperate region; but now they had to descend from their sanitaria to take part in stern operations in the plains. The commander-in-chief sent instant orders to transfer the Queen's 75th foot from Kussowlie to Umballa, the 1st and 2d Bengal Europeans from Dugshai to Umballa, the Sirmoor battalion from Deyrah Dhoon to Meerut, two companies of the Queen's 8th foot from Jullundur to Phillour, and two companies of the Queen's 81st foot, together with one company of European artillery, from Lahore to Umritsir. These orders given, General Anson himself left Simla on the evening of the 14th, and arrived at Umballa early on the 15th. Before he started, he issued the proclamation already adverted to, announcing to the troops of the native army generally that no cartridges would be brought into use against the conscientious wishes of the soldiery; and after he arrived at Umballa, fearing that his proclamation had not been strong enough, he issued another, to the effect that no new cartridges whatever should be served out—thereby, as he hoped, putting an end to all fear concerning objectionable lubricating substances being used; for he was not aware how largely hypocrisy was mixed up with sincerity in the native scruples on this point.

Anson and Barnard, when together at Umballa, had to measure well the forces available to them. The Umballa magazines were nearly empty of stores and ammunition; the artillery wagons were in the depôt at Phillour; the medical officers dreaded the heat for troops to move in such a season; and the commissariat was ill supplied with vehicles and beasts of burden and draught. The only effectual course was found to be, that of bringing small detachments from many different stations; and this system was in active progress during the week following Anson's arrival at Umballa. On the 16th, troops came into that place from Phillour and Subathoo. On the 17th arrived three European regiments from the Hills,* which were shortly to be strengthened by artillery from Phillour. The prospect was not altogether a cheering one, for two of the regiments at the station were Bengal native troops (the 5th and 60th), on whose fidelity only slight reliance could be placed at such a critical period. In order that no time might be lost in forming the nucleus of a force for Delhi, some of the troops were despatched that same night; comprising one wing of a European regiment, a few horse, and two guns. On successive days, other troops took their departure as rapidly as the necessary arrangements could be made; but Anson was greatly embarrassed by the distance between Umballa and the station where the siege-guns were parked; he knew that a besieging army would be of no use without those essential adjuncts; and it was on that account that he was unable to respond to Viscount Canning's urgent request that he would push on rapidly towards Delhi.

On the 23d of May, Anson sketched a plan of operations, which he communicated to the brigadiers whose services were more immediately at his disposal. Leaving Sir Henry Barnard in command at Umballa, he proposed to head the siege-army himself. It was to consist† of three brigades—one from Umballa, under Brigadier Halifax; a second from the same place, under Brigadier Jones; and a third from Meerut, under Brigadier Wilson. He proposed to send off the two brigades from Umballa on various days, so that all the corps should reach Kurnaul, fifty miles nearer to Delhi, by the 30th. Then, by starting on the 1st of June, he expected to reach Bhagput on the 5th, with all his Umballa force except the siege-train, which might possibly arrive on the 6th. Meanwhile Major-general Hewett was to organise a brigade at Meerut, and send it to Bhagput, where it would form a junction with the other two brigades. Ghazeeoodeen Nuggur being a somewhat important post, as a key to the Upper Doab, it was proposed that Brigadier Wilson should leave a small force there—consisting of a part of the Sirmoor battalion, a part of the

* The troops at Umballa on the 17th comprised:
Queen's 75th foot.
1st Bengal European Fusiliers. } Weak: only 1800 bayonets in all.
2d " " "
5th Bengal native infantry.
60th " " "
Queen's 9th Lancers.
4th Bengal cavalry.
Two troops European horse-artillery.

† 1st Umballa Brigade. Brigadier Halifax. { Queen's 75th foot. 1st Bengal Europeans. Two squadrons 9th Lancers. One troop horse-artillery.

2d Umballa Brigade. Brigadier Jones. { 2d Bengal Europeans. 60th native infantry. Two squadrons 9th Lancers. One squadron 4th Bengal Lancers. One troop horse-artillery.

Meerut Brigade. Brigadier Wilson. { One wing Queen's 60th Rifles. Two squadrons Carabiniers. One light field-battery. One troop horse-artillery. Native Sappers (if reliable). 120 artillerymen.

Rampore horse, and a few guns—while he advanced with the rest of his brigade to Bhagput. Lastly, it was supposed that the Meerut brigade, by starting on the 1st or 2d of June, could reach the rendezvous on the 5th, and that then all could advance together towards Delhi. Such was General Anson's plan—a plan that he was not destined to put in execution himself.

It will be convenient to trace the course of proceeding in the following mode—to describe the advance of the Meerut brigade to Bhagput, with its adventures on the way; then to notice in a similar way the march of the main body from Umballa to Bhagput; next the progress of the collected siege-army from the last-named town to the crest or ridge bounding Delhi on the north; and, lastly, the commencement of the siege-operations themselves—operations lamentably retarded by the want of a sufficient force of siege-guns.

Major-general Hewett, at Meerut, proceeded to organise a brigade in accordance with the plan

SIR HENRY BARNARD.

laid down by General Anson; retaining at his head-quarters a force sufficient to protect Meerut and its neighbourhood. It was on the 27th of May that this brigade was ready, and that Colonel Archdall Wilson was placed in command of it—a gallant officer afterwards better known as Brigadier or General Wilson. The brigade was very small; comprising less than 500 of the 60th Rifles, 200 of the Carabiniers, one battery and a troop of artillery. They started on the evening of the 27th; and after marching during the cooler hours of the 28th and 29th, encamped on the morning of the 30th at Ghazeeoodeen Nuggur (Ghazee-u-deen Nuggur, Guznee de Nuggur). This was a small town or village on the left bank of the river Hindoun, eighteen miles east of Delhi, important as commanding one of the passages over that river from Meerut, the passage being by a suspension-bridge.

On that same day, the 30th of May, Brigadier Wilson was attacked by the insurgents, who had sallied forth from Delhi for this purpose, and who were doubtless anxious to prevent a junction of the Meerut force with that from Kurnaul. The enemy appeared in force on the opposite side of the river, with five guns in position. Wilson at once sent a body of Rifles to command the suspension-bridge; while a few Carabiniers were despatched along the river-bank to a place where they were able to ford. The insurgents opened fire with their five heavy guns; whereupon the brigadier sent off to the attacked points all his force except sufficient to guard his camp; and then the contest became very brisk. The Rifles, under Colonel Jones, were ordered to charge the enemy's guns; they rushed forward, disregarding grape and canister shot, and advanced towards the guns. When they saw a shell about to burst, they threw themselves down on their faces to avoid the danger, then jumped up, and off again. They reached the guns, drove away the gunners, and effected a capture. The enemy, beaten away from the defences of the bridge, retreated to a large walled village, where they had the courage to stand a hand-to-hand contest for a time—a struggle which no native troops could long continue against the British Rifles. As evening came on, the enemy fled with speed to Delhi, leaving behind them five guns, ammunition, and stores. Colonel Constance followed them some distance with the Carabiniers; but it was not deemed prudent to continue the pursuit after nightfall. In this smart affair 11 were killed, 21 wounded or missing. Captain Andrews, with four of his riflemen, while taking possession of two heavy pieces of ordnance on the causeway, close to the toll-house of the bridge, were blown up by the explosion of an ammunition-wagon, fired by one of the sepoy gunners.

The mutineers did not allow Brigadier Wilson to remain many hours quiet. He saw parties of their horse reconnoitring his position all the morning of the 31st; and he kept, therefore, well on the alert. At one o'clock the enemy, supposed to be five thousand in number, took up a position a mile in length, on a ridge on the opposite side of the Hindoun, and about a mile distant from Wilson's advanced picket. Horse-artillery and two 18-pounders were at once sent forward to reply to this fire, with a party of Carabiniers to support; while another party, of Rifles, Carabiniers, and guns, went to support the picket at the bridge. For nearly two hours the contest was one of artillery alone, the British guns being repeatedly and vainly charged by the enemy's cavalry; the enemy's fire then slackening, and the Rifles having cleared a village on the left of the toll-bar, the brigadier ordered a general advance. The result was as on the preceding day; the mutineers were driven back. The British all regretted they could not follow, and cut up the enemy in the retreat; but the brigadier, seeing that many of his poor fellows fell sun-stricken, was forced to call them back into camp when the action was over. This victory was not so complete as that on the preceding day; for the mutineers were able to carry off all their guns, two heavy and five light. The killed and wounded on the side of the English were 24 in number, of whom 10 were stricken down by the heat of the sun—a cause of death that shews how terrible must have been the ordeal passed through by all on such a day. Among the officers, Lieutenant Perkins was killed, and Captain Johnson and Ensign Napier wounded.

After the struggle of the 31st of May, the enemy did not molest Wilson in his temporary camp at Ghazeeoodeen Nuggur. He provided for his wounded, refitted his brigade, and waited for reinforcements. On the morning of the 3d of June he was joined by another hundred of the 60th Rifles from Meerut, and by a Goorkha regiment, the Sirmoor battalion, from Deyrah Dhoon; and then lost no time in marching to the rendezvous. The route taken was very circuitous, hilly, and rugged; and the brigade did not reach the rendezvous head-quarters at Bhagput till the morning of the 6th.

We have now to trace the fortunes of the Umballa force. It was on the 23d of May, as has been shewn, that General Anson put forth the scheme for an advance towards Delhi, in which the brigade from Meerut was to take part. He left Umballa on the 24th, and reached Kurnaul on the 25th. All the proposed regiments and detachments from Umballa had by that time come in to Kurnaul except two troops of horse-artillery; but as the siege-train was far in arrear, Anson telegraphed to Calcutta that he would not be in a position to advance from Kurnaul towards Delhi until the 31st of the month. On the 26th, the commander-in-chief's plans were ended by the ending of his life; an attack of cholera carried him off in a few hours. He hastily summoned Sir Henry Barnard from Umballa; and his last words were to place the Delhi force under the command of that officer. At that time news and orders travelled slowly between Calcutta and the northwest; for dâks were interrupted and telegraph wires cut; and it was therefore necessary that the command should at once be given to some one, without waiting for sanction from the governor-general. Viscount Canning heard the news on the 3d of June, and immediately confirmed the appointment of Sir Henry to the command of the siege-army; but that confirmation was not known to the besiegers till long afterwards. Major-general Reed, by the death of Anson, became provisional commander-in-chief; and he left Rawul Pindee on the 28th of May to join the head-quarters of the siege-army, but without superseding Barnard. It was a terrible time for all these generals: Anson and Halifax had both succumbed to cholera; Reed was so thoroughly broken down by illness that he could not command in person; and Barnard was summoned from a sick-bed by the dying commander-in-chief.

Sir Henry Barnard did not feel justified in advancing from Kurnaul until heavier guns than those he possessed could arrive from the Punjaub. On the 31st, a 9-pounder battery—those already at hand being only 6-pounders—came into camp; and the march from Kurnaul to Paniput commenced on that evening. Sir Henry expected to have met Brigadier Wilson at Racc, where there was a bridge of boats over the Jumna; but through some misconstruction or countermanding of orders, Wilson had taken a much more circuitous route by Ghazeeoodeen Nuggur, and could not join the Umballa brigade at the place or on the day expected. Barnard, after a brief sojourn and a slight change of plan, sent out elephants to aid in bringing forward the Meerut brigade, and advanced with the greater portion of his own force to Alipore (or Aleepore), where he arrived on the morning of the 5th of June. The chief artillery force being with the Meerut brigade, Sir Henry waited for Wilson, who effected a junction with him on the 6th; and on the 7th, the united forces were reorganised, at a point so near Delhi that the troops looked forward eagerly to a speedy encounter with the enemy.

Many of the soldiers who thus assembled at a place distant only a few miles from the famous city, which they all hoped soon to retake from the hands of the enemy, had marched great distances. Among the number was the corps of Guides, whose march was one of those determined exploits of which soldiers always feel proud, and to which they point as proof that they shrink not from fatigue and heat when a post of duty is assigned to them. This remarkable corps was raised on the conclusion of the Sutlej campaign, to act either as regular troops or as guides and spies, according as the exigencies of the service might require. The men were chosen for their sagacity and intelligence, as well as for their courage and hardihood. They were inhabitants of the Punjaub, but belonged to no one selected race or creed; for among them were to be found mountaineers, borderers, men of the plains, and half-wild warriors. Among them nearly all the dialects of Northern India were more or less known; and they were as familiar with hill-fighting as with service on the plains. They were often employed as intelligencers, and in reconnoitring an enemy's position. They were the best of all troops to act against the robber hill-tribes, with whom India is so greatly infested. Among the many useful pieces of Indian service effected by Sir Henry Lawrence, was the suggestion of this corps; and Lord Hardinge, when commander-in-chief, acted on it in 1846. The corps was at first limited to one troop of cavalry and two companies of artillery, less than three hundred men in all; but the Marquis of Dalhousie afterwards raised it to three troops and six companies, about eight hundred and fifty men, commanded by four European officers and a surgeon. The men were dressed in a plain serviceable drab uniform. Their pay was eight rupees per month for a foot-soldier, and twenty-four for a trooper. These, then, were the Guides of whom English newspaper-readers heard so much but knew so little. They were stationed at a remote post in the Punjaub, not far from the Afghan frontier, when orders reached them to march to Delhi, a distance of no less than 750 miles. They set off, horse and foot together, and accomplished the distance in twenty-eight days—a really great achievement in the heat of an Indian summer; they suffered much, of course; but all took pride in their work, and obtained high praise from the commander-in-chief. One of the English officers afterwards declared that he had never before experienced the necessity of 'roughing' it as on this occasion. Captain Daly commanded the whole corps, while Captain Quintin Battye had special control of that portion of it which consisted of troopers.

The Guides, as has just been shewn, were an exceptional corps, raised among the natives for a peculiar service. But the siege-army contained gallant regiments of ordinary troops, whose marching was little less severe. One of these was the 1st Bengal European Fusiliers; a British regiment wholly belonging to the Company, and one which in old times was known as Lord Lake's 'dear old dirty shirts.' On the 13th of May it was at Dugshai, a sanatarium and hill-station not far from Simla. Major Jacob rode in hastily from Simla, announced that Meerut and Delhi were in revolt, and brought an order for the regiment to march down to Umballa forthwith, to await further orders. At five o'clock that same day the men marched forth, with sixty rounds in pouch, and food in haversack. After a twenty-four miles' walk they refreshed on the ground, supping and sleeping as best they could. At an hour after midnight they renewed their march, taking advantage—as troops in India are wont to do—of the cool hours of the night; they marched till six or seven, and then rested during the heat of the day at Chundeegurh. From five till ten in the evening they again advanced, and then had supper and three hours' rest at Mobarrackpore. Then, after a seven hours' march during the night of the 14th–15th, they reached Umballa—having accomplished sixty miles in thirty-eight hours. Here they were compelled to remain some days until the arrangements of the general in other directions were completed; and during this detention many of their number were carried off by cholera. At length four companies were sent on towards Kurnaul on the 17th, under Captain Dennis; while the other companies did not start till the 21st. The two wings of the regiments afterwards effected a junction, and marched by Paniput, Soomalka, and Sursowlie, to Raee, where they arrived on the 31st of May. Under a scorching sun every day, the troops were well-nigh beaten down; but the hope of 'thrashing the rebels at Delhi' cheered them on. One officer speaks of the glee with which he and his companions came in sight of a field of onions, 'all green above and white below,' and of the delightful relish they enjoyed during a temporary rest. The regiment, after remaining at Raee till the morning of the 5th of June, was then joined by its commandant, Colonel Welchman. Forming now part of Brigadier Showers' brigade, the 1st Europeans marched to Alipore, where its fortunes were mixed up with those of the other troops in the besieging army.

Many at Calcutta wondered why Barnard did not make a more rapid advance from Paniput and Race to Alipore; and many at Race wondered why Wilson did not come in more quickly from Ghazeeoodeen Nuggur. The brigadier was said to have had his plans somewhat changed by suggestions from one of the Greatheds (Mr H. H. Greathed was agent, and Lieutenant W. H. Greathed, aid-de-camp, for the lieutenant-governor of the Northwest Provinces in the camp of the siege-army); while Sir Henry was anxious both to secure Wilson's co-operation as soon as he started, and to preserve the health of his men during the trying season of heat. It is greatly to the credit of him and all the officers, that the various regiments, notwithstanding their long marches and fierce exposure to heat, reached Delhi in admirable health—leaving cholera many miles behind them. Having been joined by a siege-train on the 6th of June, and by Brigadier Wilson's forces on the 7th, Barnard began at once to organise his plans for an advance. The reinforcements brought by Wilson were very miscellaneous;* but they had fought well on the banks of the Hindoun, and were an indispensable aid to the general. Major-general Reed arrived from Rawul Pindee at midnight, not to take the command from Barnard, but to sanction the line of proceedings as temporary commander-in-chief.

It was at one o'clock on the morning of the 8th of June that the siege-army set out from Alipore, to march the ten miles which separate that village from Delhi. Some of the reinforcements, such as the Guides, had not yet arrived; but the troops which formed the army of march on this morning, according to Sir Henry's official dispatch, were as noted below.† They advanced to a village, the name of which is variously spelt in the dispatches, letters, and maps as Badulla Serai, Bardul-ki-Serai, Badulee-ke-Serai, Bardeleeke Serai, Budlee-ka Surnee, &c., about four miles from Delhi. Here the fighting began; here the besiegers came in contact with the enemy who had been so long sought. When within a short distance of the village, the sepoy watch-fires were seen (for day had scarcely yet broken). Suddenly a report was heard, and a shot and shell came roaring down the road to the advancing British force; and then it became necessary to plan a mode of dealing with the enemy, who were several thousands in number, in a strongly intrenched position, with artillery well served. Sir Henry Barnard intrusted Brigadiers Showers, Graves, and Grant with distinct duties—the first to advance with his brigade on the right of the main trunk-road; the second to take the left of the same road; and the third to cross the canal, advance quietly, and recross in the rear of the enemy's position at such a time as a signal should direct them to effect a surprise. The guns were placed in and on both sides of the road. When the hostile forces met, the enemy opened a severe fire—a fire so severe, indeed, that the general resolved to stop it by capturing the battery itself. This was effected in a gallant manner by the 75th foot and the 1st Europeans; it was perilous work, for the troops had to pass over open ground, with very little shelter or cover. Several officers were struck down at this point; but the most serious loss was produced by a cannon-shot which killed Colonel Chester, adjutant-general of the army. The battery was charged so determinedly that the artillerymen were forced to flee, leaving their guns behind them; while the advance of the other two brigades compelled them to a general flight. Colonel Welchman, of the 1st Fusiliers, in his eagerness galloped after three of the mutineers and cut one of them down; but the act would have cost him his own life, had not a private of his regiment come opportunely to his aid.

A question now arose, whether to halt for a while, or push on towards Delhi. It was between five and six o'clock on a summer morning; and Barnard decided that it would be advisable not to allow the enemy time to reassemble in or near the village. The men were much exhausted; but after a hasty taste of rum and biscuit, they resumed their march. Advancing in two columns, Brigadiers Wilson and Showers fought their way along the main trunk-road; while Barnard and Graves turned off at Azadpore by the road which led through the cantonment of Delhi—a cantonment lately in the hands of the British authorities, but now deserted. This advance was a continuous fight the whole way: the rebels disputing the passage inch by inch. It then became perceptible that a rocky ridge which bounds Delhi on the north was bristling with bayonets and cannon, and that the conquest of this ridge would be a necessary preliminary to an approach to Delhi. Barnard determined on a rapid flank-movement to turn the right of the enemy's position. With a force consisting of the 60th Rifles under Colonel Jones, the 2d Europeans under Captain Boyd, and a troop of horse-artillery under Captain Money, Sir Henry rapidly advanced, ascended the ridge, took the enemy in flank, compelled them to flee, and swept the whole length of the ridge—the enemy

* Four guns of Major Tombs' horse-artillery.
Major Scott's horse field-battery.
Two 18-pounders, under Lieutenant Light.
Two squadrons of Carabiniers.
Six companies of 60th Rifles.
400 Sirmoor Goorkhas.

† Head-quarters and six companies of H.M. 60th Rifles.
" " and nine companies of H.M. 75th foot.
1st Bengal European Fusiliers.
2d " " " head-qurs. and six companies.
Sirmoor battalion (Goorkhas), a wing.
Head-quarters detachment Sappers and Miners.
H.M. 9th Lancers.
" 6th Dragoon-guards (Carabiniers), two squadrons.
Horse-artillery, one troop of 1st brigade.
" " , two troops of 3d brigade.
Foot-artillery, two companies,
and No. 14 horse-battery.
Artillery recruits, detachment.

abandoning twenty-six guns, with ammunition and camp-equipage. The Rifles rendered signal service in this movement; taking advantage of every slight cover, advancing closer to the enemy's guns than other infantry could safely do, and picking off the gunners. Brigadier Wilson and his companions were enabled to advance by the main road; and he and Barnard met on the ridge. From that hour the besieging army took up its position before Delhi—never to leave it till months of hard fighting had made them masters of the place. During the struggle on the ridge, two incidents greatly exasperated the troops: one was the discovery that a captured cart, which they supposed to contain ammunition, was full of the mangled limbs and trunks of their murdered fellow-Christians; the other was that two or three Europeans were found fighting for and with the rebels—probably soldiers of fortune, ready to sell their services to the highest bidders. Every European—and it was supposed that Delhi contained others of the kind—so caught was sure to be cut to pieces by the enraged soldiery, with a far more deadly hatred than sepoys themselves could have inspired. This day's work was not effected without serious loss. Colonel Chester, we have said, was killed; as were Captains Delamain and Russell, and Lieutenant Harrison. The wounded comprised Colonel Herbert; Captains Dawson and Greville; Lieutenants Light, Hunter, Davidson, Hare, Fitzgerald, Barter, Rivers, and Ellis; and Ensign Pym. In all, officers and privates, there were 51 killed and 133 wounded. Nearly 50 horses were either killed or wounded.

Here, then, in the afternoon of the 8th of June, were the British posted before Delhi. It will be necessary to have a clear notion of the relative positions of the besiegers and the besieged, to understand the narrative which is to follow. Of Delhi itself an account is given elsewhere, with a brief notice of the defence-works; * but the gates and bastions must here be enumerated somewhat more minutely, as the plan of the siege mainly depended on them. A small branch or nullah of the Jumna is separated from the main stream by a sand-bank which forms an island; the junction or rejoining of the two takes place where the Jumna is crossed by a bridge of boats, and where the old fort called the Selimgurh was built. Beginning at this point, we trace the circuit of the wall and its fortifications. From the Selimgurh the wall borders—or rather bordered (for it will be well to speak in the past tense)—the nullah for about three-quarters of a mile, in a northwest direction, marked by the Calcutta Gate, a martello tower, the Kaila Gate, the Nuseergunje Bastion, and the Moree or Moira Bastion. The wall then turned sharply to the west, or slightly southwest; and during a length of about three-quarters of a mile presented the Moree Bastion just named, the Cashmere Gate, the Moree Gate, and the Shah Bastion. To this succeeded a portion about a mile in length, running nearly north and south, and marked by the Cabool Gate, a martello tower, Burn Bastion, the Lahore Gate, and the Gurstin Bastion. Then, an irregular polygonal line of two miles in length carried the wall round to the bank of the Jumna, by a course bending more and more to the east; here were presented the Turushkana Gate, a martello tower, the Ajmeer Gate, the Akbar Bastion, another martello tower, the Ochterlony Bastion, the Turcoman Gate, a third and a fourth martello towers, and the Delhi Gate. Lastly, along the bank of the river for a mile and a half, and separated from the water at most times by a narrow sandy strip, was a continuation of the wall, broken by the Wellesley and Nawab Bastions, the Duryagunje Gate, a martello tower, the Rajghat Gate, the wall of the imperial palace, and the defence-wall entirely surrounding the Selimgurh. Such were the numerous gates, bastions, and towers at that period; many parts of the wall and bastions were formed of masonry twelve feet thick, and the whole had been further strengthened by the rebels during four weeks of occupation. Outside the defences was a broad ditch twenty feet deep from the ground, or thirty-five from the top of the wall.

The position taken up by the besiegers may be thus briefly described. The camp was pitched on the former parade-ground of the deserted encampment, at a spot about a mile and a half from the northern wall of the city, with a rocky ridge acting as a screen between it and the city. This ridge was commanded by the rebels until the afternoon of the 8th; but from that time it was in the hands of the besiegers. The British line on this ridge rested on the left on an old tower used as a signal-post, often called the Flagstaff Tower; at its centre, upon an old mosque; and at its right, upon a house with enclosures strongly placed at the point where the ridge begins to slope down towards the plain. This house, formerly occupied by a Mahratta chief named Hindoo Rao, was generally known as Hindoo Rao's house. Owing to the ridge being very oblique in reference to the position of the city, the right of the line was of necessity thrown much forward, and hence Hindoo Rao's house became the most important post in the line. Near this house, owing to its commanding position, the British planted three batteries; and to protect these batteries, Rifles, Guides, and Sirmoor Goorkhas were posted within convenient distance. Luckily for the British, Hindoo Rao's house was 'pucka-built,' that is, a substantial brick structure, and bore up well against the storm of shot aimed at it by the rebels.

When the British had effected a permanent lodgment on the ridge, with the camp pitched in the old cantonment behind the ridge as a screen, the time had arrived when the detailed plan for the siege was to be determined, if it had not been determined already. Some military critics averred that Sir Henry Barnard, only acquainted in a

* Chapter iv., pp. 63-65.

slight degree with that part of India, displayed indecision, giving and countermanding orders repeatedly, and leaving his subordinates in doubt concerning the real plan of the siege. Others contended that the sudden assumption of command on the death of General Anson, the small number of troops, and the want of large siege-guns, were enough to render necessary great caution in the mode of procedure. The truth appears to be, that the rebels were found stronger in Delhi, than was suspected before the siege-army approached close to the place; moreover, they had contested the advance from Alipore more obstinately than had been expected—shewing that, though not equal to British soldiers, it would not be safe to despise their prowess. The plan of attack would obviously depend upon the real or supposed defensive measures of the besieged. If the rebels risked a battle outside the walls, they might very likely be defeated and followed into the city and palace; but then would come a disastrous street-fighting against enemies screened behind loopholed walls,

Hindoo Rao's House—Battery in front.

and firing upon besiegers much less numerous than themselves. Or the half-crumbled walls might easily be scaled by active troops; but as these troops would be a mere handful against large numbers, their success would be very doubtful. A third plan, suggested by some among the many advisers of that period, was to make an attack by water, or on the river-side. The Jumna is at certain times so shallow at Delhi as to be almost fordable, and leaving a strip of sand on which batteries might be planted; these batteries might breach the river-wall of the palace, and so disturb the garrison as to permit a large body of the besiegers to enter under cover of the firing; but a rise in the river would fatally affect this enterprise. A fourth plan suggested was to attack near the Cashmere Gate, on the north side of the city; the siege-army would in this case be protected on its left flank by the river, and might employ all its force in breaching the wall between the gate and the river; the guns would render the mainguard untenable; when the assault was made, it would be on a part where there is much vacant ground in the interior; and the besieging troops would have a better chance than if at once entangled among the intricacies of loopholed houses. Any project for starving out the garrison, if it ever entered the mind of any soldier, was soon abandoned; the boundary was too extensive, the gates too many, and the besiegers too few, to effect this.

During the early days after the arrival of the British, indications appeared of an intention to blow open the Cashmere Gate, and effect a forcible entry into the city at once; but these indications soon ceased; and the besiegers found themselves compelled rather to resist attacks than to make them; for the enemy, strong in numbers, made repeated sorties from the various gates of the city, and endeavoured to dislodge the British. One such sortie was made about noon on the 9th, within twenty-four hours after the arrival of the besiegers; the enemy were, however, easily repulsed, and driven in again. The corps of Guides met with a loss on this day which occasioned much regret. Among those who accompanied the hardy men all the way from the Afghan frontier was Captain Quintin Battye, a young officer much beloved as commandant of the cavalry portion of the corps. They arrived on the 8th; and on the next day poor Battye was shot through the body; he lived twenty-four hours in great agony, and then sank. The Guides had a large share in this day's work; many of them fell, in dislodging the enemy from a rocky position which they temporarily occupied. On the 10th a little skirmishing took place, but not so serious as on the preceding day; it was found, however, that the white shirts of the men were a little too conspicuous; and they underwent an extemporaneous process of dyeing to deepen the colour. On the 12th, early in the morning, the enemy made a sudden attack on both flanks; but all points were speedily defended. They were first driven back on the left; then, after a repulse on the right, they advanced a second time under the cover of thickly wooded gardens near the Subzee Mundee—a suburb of Delhi about a mile and a quarter northwest of the Cabool Gate. Major Jacob was then sent against them with some of the Bengal Europeans; he beat them back till they got beyond the suburb, and then returned to the camp. This morning's affair was supposed to have cost the enemy 250 men; the British loss was very small. On this day, the British had the mortification of seeing two regiments of Rohilcund mutineers, the 60th native infantry and the 4th native cavalry, enter Delhi with bands playing and colours flying; the defiant manner was quite as serious an affair as the augmentation of the strength of the garrison. On the 13th a large enclosure in advance of the British left, known as Metcalfe House, was occupied by them, and the erection of a battery of heavy guns and mortars commenced.

Not a day passed without some such struggles as have just been adverted to. The besieging of the city had not really commenced, for the British had not yet a force of artillery sufficient for that purpose; indeed, they were now the besieged rather than the besiegers; for the enemy came out of the city—horse, foot, and guns—and attempted to effect a surprise on one part or other of the position on the ridge. Against the battery at Metcalfe House a sortie was made on the 15th, and another was made on the same day at the right of the line. On the 17th an exciting encounter took place. A shot from the city struck the corner of Hindoo Rao's house, and glancing off, killed Lieutenant Wheatley of the Goorkhas. It was then suspected that the enemy, besides their attacks on this house in front, were throwing up a battery outside the western gates of the town, at a large building known as the Eedghah, formerly used as a serai. Thereupon a force was immediately organised, consisting of horse-artillery, cavalry, Goorkhas, and Rifles, to drive them away from that position. They passed through the Subzee Mundee to the Eedghah, drove out the enemy, and captured the only gun which had yet been placed there. One of the officers on this duty had a finger shot off, a bullet through the wrist, another through the cheek, and another which broke the collar-bone; yet he recovered, to fight again.

On the 19th of June it came to the knowledge of Brigadier Grant that the enemy intended to attack the camp in the rear; and as the safety of the camp had been placed under his keeping, he made instant preparations to frustrate the insurgents. These troops are believed to have been augmentations of the insurgent forces, consisting of the 15th and 30th native regiments from Nusseerabad. The brigadier advanced with six guns and a squadron of lancers to reconnoitre, and found the enemy in position half a mile in rear of the Ochterlony Gardens, northwest of the camp. Troops quickly arrived, and a rapid exchange of fire began, the enemy being strong in artillery as well as in infantry. Just as the dusk of the evening came on, the enemy, by a series of skilful and vigorous attacks, aided by well-served artillery, very nearly succeeded in turning the flank of the British, and in capturing two guns; but both these disasters were frustrated. The dusk deepened into darkness; but the brigadier felt that it would not do to allow the enemy to occupy that position during the night. A charge was made with great impetuosity by horse and foot, with so much success, that the enemy were driven back quite into the town. The brigadier had to regret the loss of Colonel Yule of the 9th Lancers, who was knocked off his horse, and not found again by his men till next morning; when they were shocked to see him dead and mangled, with both thighs broken, a ball through the head just over the eyes, his throat cut, and his hands much gashed. He had been on leave of absence in Cashmere, but directly he heard of the work to be done, travelled night and day till he reached his regiment just before its arrival at Delhi. Lieutenant Alexander was also among the killed. Captain Daly of the Guides, and six other officers, were wounded. All the officers of the Guides, but one, received wounds. Altogether, the day's fighting resulted to the British in the loss of 19 killed and 77 wounded; and it was a source of much regret that a few of these fell by the hands of their own comrades, while fighting in some confusion as darkness approached. No less than sixty horses fell. The brigadier did not fail to mention the names of three private soldiers—Thomas Hancock, John Purcell, and Roopur Khan—who behaved with great gallantry at a critical moment.

Sir Henry Barnard, for very cogent reasons, watched every movement on the part of the mutineers who sallied forth from Delhi. On the

22d, he saw a body of them come out of the city; and as they were not seen to return at night, he suspected a masked attack. At six in the evening, he sent out a party of infantry, Guides, and Sappers, to demolish two bridges which carried the great road across a canal westward of the camp, and over which the enemy were in the habit of taking their artillery and columns when they wished to attack the camp in the rear; this was a work of six hours, warmly contested but successfully accomplished. On the 23d, Sir Henry, expecting a valuable convoy from the Punjaub, adopted prompt measures for its protection. He sent out a strong escort, which safely brought the convoy into camp. Scarcely had this been effected, when his attention was drawn to the right of his position, near Hindoo Rao's house. It was afterwards ascertained that the enemy, remembering the 23d of June as the centenary of the battle of Plassy, had resolved to attempt a great victory over the British on that day; incited, moreover, by the circumstance that two festivals, one Mussulman and the other Hindoo, happened to occur on that day; and they emerged from the city in vast force to effect this. They commenced their attack on the Subzee Mundee side, having a strong position in a village and among garden-walls. Here a combat was maintained during the whole of the day, for the rebels continued their attacks with much pertinacity; they lodged themselves in loopholed houses, a serai, and a mosque, whence they could not be dislodged till they had wrought much mischief by musketry. At length, however, they were driven back into the city. The value of the precaution taken on the preceding evening, in destroying the bridges, was made fully evident; for the rebels were unable to cross the canal to get to the rear of the camp. The 1st Europeans had a desperate contest in the Subzee Mundee, where street-fighting, and firing from windows and house-tops, continued for many hours. The British troops suffered terribly from the heat of the midsummer sun, to which they were exposed from sunrise to sunset. Many officers were brought away sun-struck and powerless. The Guides fought for fifteen hours uninterruptedly, with no food, and only a little water. At one o'clock, when the enemy were strengthened by large reinforcements from the city, the Guides found themselves without ammunition, and had to send back to the camp for more; but as great delay occurred, they were in imminent peril of annihilation. Fortunately a corps of Sikhs, who had arrived at camp that morning, rushed forward at a critical moment, and aided the Guides in driving back the enemy. One of the incidents of the day has been thus narrated, shewing how little scruple a Goorkha felt when he met a sepoy: 'In the intense heat, a soldier of the 2d Europeans and a Goorkha sought the shade and protection of a house near the Subzee Mundee, a window of which looked into a lane where they were seated. Not long had they rested when, from the open window, was seen to project the head of a sepoy. Now all Hindoos have what ladies at home call "back-hair," and this is usually turned up into a knot; by this the unlucky wretch was at once seized, and before he could even think of resistance, his head was at a stroke severed from his body by the sharp curved knife of the Goorkha!' This day's work was in every way very severe, and shewed the besiegers that the rebels were in great strength. Lieutenant Jackson was killed; Colonel Welchman, Captain Jones, and Lieutenant Murray, wounded. The total loss of the day was 39 killed and 121 wounded. The enemy's loss was very much larger; indeed, one of the estimates raised the number up to a thousand. The loss appears to have somewhat dispirited the mutineers, for they made very few attacks on the following three days.

But although there was a temporary cessation, Sir Henry Barnard, in his official dispatches, shewed that he was much embarrassed by this condition of affairs. His forces were few; those of the enemy were very large; and the attacks were rendered more harassing by the uncertainty of the point on which they would be made, and the impossibility of judging whether they were about to be made on more points than one. The onslaughts could only be successfully repulsed by the untiring and unflinching gallantry of a small body of men. The enemy, instead of being beleaguered within Delhi, were free to emerge from the city and attack the besiegers' position. The British did not complain; it was not their wont; but they suffered greatly from this harassing kind of warfare. Reinforcements were slowly coming in; in the last week of June the Europeans numbered about three thousand; and they were well satisfied with the native corps who fought by their side—the Guides, the Goorkhas, and the Sikhs—all of whom joined very heartily in opposing the rebel sepoys. The siege-material at this time consisted of five batteries, mounting about fifteen guns and mortars, placed on various points of the ridge; the bombardment of the city by these guns was not very effective, for the distance averaged nearly a mile, and the guns were not of large calibre.

The interval from the 23d to the 30th of June passed much in the same way as the two preceding weeks; the British siege-guns wrought very little mischief to the city; while the enemy occasionally sallied forth to attack either the camp or the works on the ridge. It was often asserted, and facts seemed to corroborate the statement, that when mutinous regiments from other places appeared before Delhi, they were not afforded reception and shelter until they had earned it by making an attack on the British position; and thus it happened that the besiegers were opposed by a constantly increasing number of the enemy. The defenders of the garrison fitted up a large battery on the left of the Cashmere Gate, one at the gate itself, one at the Moree Gate, one at the Ajmeer Gate, and one directly opposite Hindoo Rao's house; against these five batteries, for a long time, the British had only three; so that the besieged were stronger than the besiegers in every way. The gunners, too, within Delhi, were fully equal to those of the siege-army in accuracy of aim; their balls and shells fell near Hindoo Rao's house so thickly as to render that post a very perilous one to hold. One shell entered the gateway, and killed eight or nine officers and men who were seeking shelter from the mid-day heat.

It was pretty well ascertained, before June was half over, that Delhi was not to be taken by a *coup de main;* and when Sir John Lawrence became aware of that fact, he sent reinforcements down from the Punjaub as rapidly as they could be collected. Every sepoy regiment that was either disbanded or disarmed lessened his own danger, for he trusted well in his Sikhs, Punjaubees, and Guides; and on that account he was able to send Europeans and artillery. The reserve and depôt companies of the regiments already serving before Delhi were sent down from the hills to join their companions. A wing of H.M. 61st foot, a portion of the 8th, artillery from Jullundur, and artillery-men from Lahore, followed the Guides and Sikhs, and gradually increased the besieging force. Then

The General and his Staff at the Mosque Picket before Delhi.

came Punjaub rifles and Punjaub light horse; and there were still a few Hindustani cavalry and horse-artillery in whom their officers placed such unabated confidence that they were permitted to take part in the siege-operations, on the ground that there were Europeans enough to overawe them if they became unruly. These reinforcements of course came in by degrees: we mention them all in one paragraph, but many weeks elapsed before they could reach the Delhi camp. Fortunately, supplies were plentiful; the country between Delhi and the Sutlej was kept pretty free from the enemy; and the villagers were glad to find good customers for the commodities they had to sell. It hence arose that, during the later days of June, the British were well able to render nugatory all sallies made by the enemy; they had food and beverages in good store; and they were free from pestilential diseases. On the other hand, they suffered intensely from the heat; and were much dissatisfied at the small progress made towards the conquest of the city. Some expressed their dissatisfaction by adverse criticisms on the general's tactics; while others admitted that a storming of Delhi would not be prudent without further reinforcements. As to the heat, the troops wrote of it in all their letters, spoke of it in all their narrations. One officer, who had seventy-two hours of outpost-duty on a plain without the slightest shelter, described his sensation in the daytime as if 'a hot iron had been going into his head.' On a certain day, when some additional troops arrived at camp after a twenty-two miles' march, they had scarcely lain down to rest when they were ordered out to repel an attack by the enemy: they went, and gallantly did the work cut out for them; but some of them 'were so exhausted that they sank down on the road, *even under fire*, and went off to sleep.'

July arrived. Brigadier Chamberlain had recently joined the camp, and reinforcements were coming in; but on the other hand the rebels were increasing their strength more rapidly than the British. The enemy began the month by an attack which tried the prowess of the Guides and Punjaubees, in a manner that brought great praise to those corps. In the afternoon of the 1st, Major Reid, who was established with the headquarters of the Sirmoor battalion at Hindoo Rao's house, observed the mutineers turning out in great force from the Ajmeer and Turcoman Gates, and assembling on the open plain outside. Then, looking round on his rear right, he saw a large force, which was supposed to have come out of Delhi on the previous day; comprising thirteen guns and mortars, besides cavalry and infantry. The two forces joined about a mile from the Eedghah Serai. At sunset 5000 or 6000 infantry advanced, passed through the Pahareepore and Kissengunje suburbs, and approached towards the British lines, taking cover of the buildings as they passed. The extreme right of the line was attacked at the Pagoda picket, which was held only by 150 Punjaubees and Guides, under Captain Travers. Major Reid sent him a message to reserve his fire till the enemy approached near, in order to husband his resources; while 150 British were being collected to send to his aid. Throughout the whole night did this little band of 300 men resist a large force of infantry and artillery, never yielding an inch, but defending the few works which had been constructed in that quarter. At daybreak, the enemy renewed the attacks with further troops; but Reid brought a few more of his gallant fellows to repel them. Evening, night, morning, noon, all passed in this way; and it was not until the contest had continued twenty-two hours that the enemy finally retired into the city. There may have been sufficient military reasons why larger reinforcements were not sent to Major Reid from the camp behind the ridge; but let the reasons have been what they may, the handful of troops fought in the ratio of hundreds against thousands, and never for an instant flinched during this hard day's work. Major Reid had the command of all the pickets and defence-works from Hindoo Rao's house to the Subzee Mundee. During the first twenty-eight days of the siege, his positions were attacked no fewer than twenty-four times; yet his singular medley of troops—Rifles, Guides, Sikhs, Punjaubees, Goorkhas, &c.—fought as if for one common cause, without reference to differences of religion or of nation. The officers, in these and similar encounters, often passed through an ordeal which renders their survival almost inconceivable. An artillery officer, in command of two horse-artillery guns, on one occasion was surprised by 120 of the enemy's cavalry; he had no support, and could not apply his artillery because his guns were limbered up. He fired four barrels of his revolver and killed two men; and then knocked a third off his horse by throwing his empty pistol at him. Two horsemen thereupon charged full tilt, and rolled him and his horse over. He got up, and seeing a man on foot coming at him to cut him down, rushed at him, got inside his sword, and hit him full in the face with his fist. At that moment he was cut down from behind; and was only saved from slaughter by a brother-officer, who rode up, shot one sowar and sabred another, and then carried him off, bleeding but safe.

On the 2d, the Bareilly mutineers—or rather Rohilcund mutineers from Bareilly, Moradabad, and Shahjehanpoor, consisting of five regiments and a battery of artillery—crossed the Jumna and marched into Delhi, with bands playing and colours flying—a sight sufficiently mortifying to the besiegers, who were powerless to prevent it; for any advance in that direction would have left the rear of their camp exposed. It afterwards became known that the Bareilly leader was appointed general within Delhi. The emergence of a large body of the enemy from the city on the night of the 3d of July, induced Sir Henry Barnard to send Major Coke to oppose them; with a force made up of portions of the Carabiniers, 9th Lancers, 61st foot, Guides, Punjaubees, horse and foot artillery. Coke started at two in the morning of the 4th. He went to Azadpore, the spot where the great road and the road from the cantonment met. He found that the enemy had planned an expedition to seize the British depôt of stores at Alipore, and to cut off a convoy expected to arrive from the Punjaub. When the major came up with them near the Rohtuk road, he at once attacked them. During many hours, his troops were confronted with numbers greatly exceeding their own; and what with the sun above and swamps below, the major's men became thoroughly exhausted by the time they returned to camp. The rebels, it was true, were driven back; but they got safely with their guns into Delhi; and thus was one more added to the list of contests in which the besiegers suffered without effecting anything towards the real object of the siege. The enemy's infantry on this occasion seem to have comprised the Bareilly men. An officer of the Engineers, writing concerning this day's work, said: 'The Bareilly rascals had the impudence to come round to our rear, and our only regret is that one of them ever got back. I was out with the force sent against them, and cannot say that I felt much pity for the red-coated villains with "18," "28," and "68" on their buttons.' This officer gives expression to the bitter feeling that prevailed generally in the British camp against the 'Pandies'* or mutinous sepoys, for their treachery, black ingratitude, and cruelty. 'This is a war in its very worst phase, for generosity enters into no one's mind.

* After the execution of Mungul Pandy at Barrackpore on the 8th of April, for mutiny, the rebel sepoys acquired the sobriquet of 'Pandies'—especially those belonging to the Brahmin caste.

Mercy seems to have fled from us; and if ever there was such a thing as war to the knife, we certainly have it here. If any one owes these sepoys a grudge, I think I have some claim to one; but I must say that I cannot bring myself to put my sword through a wounded man. I cannot say that I grieve much when I see it done, as it invariably is; but grieve or not as you please—he is a clever man who can now keep back a European from driving his bayonet through a sepoy, even in the agonies of death.' These were the motives and feelings that rendered the Indian mutiny much more terrible than an ordinary war. In allusion to sentiments at home, that the British soldiers were becoming cruel and bloodthirsty, the same officer wrote to a friend: 'If you hear any such sentiments, by all means ship off their propounder to this country at once. Let him see one half of what *we* have seen, and compare our brutality with that of the rebels; then send him home again, and I think you will find him pretty quiet on the subject for the rest of his life.'

A new engineer officer, Colonel Baird Smith, arrived to supersede another whose operations had not met with approval. The colonel took into consideration, with his commander, a plan for blowing in the Moree and Cashmere Gates, and escalading the Moree and Cashmere Bastions; but the plan was abandoned on account of the weakness of the siege-army.

The 5th of July was marked by the death of Major-general Sir Henry Barnard, who had held practical command of the Delhi field-force during about five weeks, and had during that time borne much anxiety and suffering. He knew that his countrymen at Calcutta as well as in England would be continually propounding the question, 'Why is Delhi not yet taken?' and the varied responsibilities connected with his position necessarily gave him much disquietude. During the fierce heat of the 4th he was on horseback nearly all day, directing the operations against the Bareilly mutineers. Early on the following morning he sent for Colonel Baird Smith, and explained his views concerning the mode in which he thought the siege-operations should be carried on; immediately afterwards he sent for medical aid; and before many hours had passed, he was a corpse. Many of his friends afterwards complained that scant justice was done to the memory of Sir Henry Barnard; in the halo that was destined to surround the name of Wilson, men forgot that it was his predecessor who had borne all the burden of collecting the siege-force, of conducting it to the ridge outside Delhi, and of maintaining a continued series of conflicts almost every day for five or six weeks.

Major-general Reed, invalid as he was, immediately took the command of the force after Barnard's death; leaving, however, the active direction mainly to Brigadier Chamberlain. It became every day more and more apparent that, notwithstanding reinforcements, the British artillery was too weak to cope with that of the enemy—whose artillerymen, taught by those whom they now opposed, had become very skilful; and whose guns were of heavier metal. The besiegers' batteries were still nearly a mile from the walls, for any nearer position could not be taken up without terrible loss. To effect a breach with a few 18-pounders at this distance was out of the question; and although the field-guns were twenty or thirty in number, they were nearly useless for battering down defences.

The attacks from the enemy continued much as before, but resistance to them became complicated by a new difficulty. There were two regiments of Bengal irregular cavalry among the troops in the siege-army, and there were a few 'Poorbeahs' or Hindustanis in the Punjaub regiments. These men were carefully watched from the first; and it became by degrees apparent that they were a danger instead of an aid to the British. Early in the month a Brahmin subadar in a Punjaubee regiment was detected inciting his companions-in-arms to murder their officers, and go over to Delhi, saying it was God's will the Feringhee 'raj' should cease. One of the Punjaubees immediately revealed this plot to the officers, and the incendiary was put to death that same evening. The other Poorbeahs in the regiment were at once paid up, and discharged from the camp—doubtless swelling the number of insurgents who entered Delhi. Again, on the 9th, a party of the enemy's cavalry, while attempting an attack on the camp, was joined by some of the 9th irregulars belonging to the siege-army, and with them tried to tempt the men of the native horse-artillery. They were beaten back; and the afternoon of the same day, the 9th of July, was marked by one of the many struggles in the Subzee Mundee, all of which ended by the enemy being driven into Delhi. If the rebel infantry had fought as well as the artillery, it might have gone hard with the besiegers, for the sallies were generally made in very great force. The rebels counted much on the value of the Subzee Mundee; as a suburb, it had been rendered a mass of ruins by repeated conflicts, and these ruins precisely suited the sepoy mode of fighting. The sepoys found shelter in narrow streets and old houses, and behind garden-walls, besides being protected by heavy guns from the city. In this kind of skirmishing they were not far inferior to their opponents; but in the open field, and especially under a charge with the bayonet, they were invariably beaten, let the disparity of numbers be what it might. All the officers, in their letters, spoke of the terrible efficacy of the British bayonet; the sepoys became paralysed with terror when this mode of attack was resorted to. On one occasion they were constructing a defensive post at the Eedghah; the British attacked it and drove in the entrance; there was no exit on the other side, and the defenders were all bayoneted in the prison-house which they had thus unwittingly constructed for themselves.

On the morning of the 14th, the mutineers poured out in great numbers, and attacked the batteries at Hindoo Rao's house, and the picket in the Subzee Mundee. The troops stationed at those places remained on the defensive till three o'clock in the afternoon, struggling against a force consisting of many regiments of insurgent infantry, a large body of cavalry, and several field-pieces. It was indeed a most determined attack, supported, moreover, by a fire of heavy artillery from the walls. Why it was that so many hours elapsed before succour was sent forth, is not very clear; but the troops who had to bear the brunt of this onslaught comprised only detachments of the 60th and 75th foot, with the Goorkhas of the Sirmoor battalion and the infantry of the Guides. A column was formed, however, at the house above named, under Brigadier Showers, consisting of the 1st Punjaub infantry, the 1st Europeans, and six horse-artillery guns. Then commenced a double contest; Showers attacking the enemy at the picket-house, and Major Reid at Hindoo Rao's house. After a fierce struggle the enemy were driven back into the city, and narrowly escaped losing some of their guns. It was a day's work that could not be accomplished without a serious loss. None of the officers, it is true, were killed in the field; but the list of wounded was very large, comprising Brigadier Chamberlain (at that time adjutant-general of the army), and Lieutenants Roberts, Thompson, Walker, Geneste, Carnegie, Rivers, Faithful, Daniell, Ross, Tulloch, Chester, Shebbeare, Hawes, Debrett, and Pollock. The wounding of so many subalterns shews how actively different companies of troops must have been engaged. Altogether, the operations of this day brought down 15 men killed and 193 officers and men wounded.

The heat was by this time somewhat alleviated by rains, which, however, brought sickness and other discomforts with them. Men fell ill after remaining many hours in damp clothes; and it was found that the fierce heat was, after all, not so detrimental to health. Many young officers, it is true, lately arrived from England, and not yet acclimatised, were smitten down by sun-stroke, and a few died of apoplexy; but it is nevertheless true that the army was surprisingly healthy during the hot weather. One of the Carabiniers, writing in the rainy season, said: 'The last three days have been exceedingly wet; notwithstanding which we are constantly in the saddle; no sooner has one alarm subsided than we are turned out to meet the mutineers in another quarter.' An officer of Sappers, employed in blowing up a bridge, said: 'We started about two P.M., and returned about twelve at night drenched through and thoroughly miserable, it having rained the whole time.'

The state of affairs in the middle of July was peculiar. It seemed to the nation at home that the army of Delhi ought to be strong enough to retake the city, especially when a goodly proportion of the number were Europeans. Yet that this was not the case, was the opinion both of Reed and of Wilson; although many daring spirits in the army longed to breach the walls and take the place by storm. Twelve hundred wounded and sick men had to be tended; all the others were kept fully employed in repelling the sallies of the enemy. Major-general Reed, who ought never to have assumed the command at all—so broken-down was he in health—gave in altogether on the 17th, after the wounding of Chamberlain; he named Brigadier Wilson, who had brought forward the Meerut brigade, as his successor. The new commander immediately wrote to Sir John Lawrence a letter (in French, as if distrusting spies), in which he candidly announced that it would be dangerous and disastrous to attempt a storm of the city; that the enemy were in great force, well armed, strong in position, and constantly reinforced by accessions of insurgent regiments; that they daily attacked the British, who could do little more than repel the attacks; that his army was gradually diminishing by these daily losses; that it would be impossible to take Delhi without at least one more European regiment and two more Sikh regiments from the Punjaub; and that if those additions did not speedily reach him, he would be obliged to raise the siege, retreat to Kurnaul, and leave the country all around Delhi to be ravaged by the mutineers. This letter shewed the gravity with which Brigadier Wilson regarded the state of matters at that critical time. Lawrence fully recognised the importance of the issue, for he redoubled his exertions to send 900 European Fusiliers and 1600 Punjaubees to the camp.

General Reed's resignation was twofold. He resigned the provisional command-in-chief of the Bengal army as soon as he was officially informed of the assumption of that office by Sir Patrick Grant; and he resigned the command of the Delhi field-force to Brigadier Wilson, because his health was too far broken to permit him to take part in active duties. It was the virtual ending of his part in the wars of the mutiny; he went to the hills, in search of that health which he could never have recovered in the plains.

Among the many contests in the second half of the month was one near Ludlow Castle, a name given to the residence of Mr Fraser, the commissioner of Delhi, one of those foully murdered on the 11th of May. This house was within half a mile of the Cashmere Gate, near the river; the enemy were found to be occupying it; but their works were attacked and destroyed by a force under Brigadier Showers; while Sir T. Metcalfe's house, further northward, was taken and strengthened as a defensive post by the British.

Mr Colvin, writing from Agra to Havelock on the 22d of July, giving an account of such proceedings at Delhi as had come to his knowledge, made the following observations on the character which the struggle had assumed: 'The spirit by which both Hindoos and Mohammedans act together at Delhi is very remarkable. You would well understand a gathering of Mohammedan fanatical feeling at that place; but what is locally, I find, known by the name of "Pandyism," is just as strong. Pandies are, among the Hindoos, all Brahmins. What absurd, distorted suspicions of our intentions (which have been so perfectly innocent towards them) may have been first worked upon, it is scarcely possible to say; but the thing has now got beyond this, and it is a struggle for mastery, not a question of mistrust or discontent. Mohammedans seem to be actively misleading Hindoos for their own purposes. Sir Patrick Grant will not know the Bengal army again. The Goorkhas, Sikhs, and Punjaubee Mohammedans have remained quite faithful, and done their duty nobly at Delhi; the bad spirit is wholly with the Poorbeahs.' Mr Greathed, Colvin's commissioner with the siege-army, made every attempt to ascertain, by means of spies and deserters, what were the alleged and what the real motives for the stubborn resistance of the mutineers to British rule. He wrote on this

General Wilson.

subject: 'The result of all questionings of sepoys who have fallen into our hands, regarding the cause of the mutiny, is the same. They invariably cite the "cartouche" (cartridge) as the origin; no other cause of complaint has been alluded to. His majesty of Delhi has composed a couplet, to the effect that the English, who boast of having vanquished rods of iron, have been overthrown in Hindostan by a single cartridge. A consciousness of power had grown up in the army, which could only be exercised by mutiny. The cry of the cartridges brought the latent spirit of revolt into action.' Mr Muir of Agra, commenting on these remarks, said: 'I fully believe this to be the case with the main body of the sepoys. There were ringleaders, no doubt, who had selfish views, and possibly held correspondence with the Delhi family, &c.; but they made use of the cartridge as their argument to gain over the mass of the army to the belief that their caste was threatened.'

It will be unnecessary to trace day by day the struggles outside Delhi. They continued as before; but the frequency was somewhat lessened, and the danger also, for the defence-works on the ridge had been much strengthened. Every bridge over the canal was blown up, except that on the main road to Kurnaul and Umballa; and thus the enemy could not easily attack the camp in the rear. It was not yet really a siege, for the British poured very few shot or shell into the city or against the walls. It was not an investment; for the British could not send a single regiment to the southwest, south, or east of the city. It was little more than a process of *waiting* till further reinforcements could arrive.

At the close of July, Brigadier Wilson forwarded to the government a very exact account of the state of his army, shewing what were his resources for maintaining the siege on the one hand, and repelling attacks by the enemy on the other. We present the chief particulars in a footnote, in an altered and more condensed form.* It appears that out of this army of something more than 8000 men, above 1100 were rendered non-effective by sickness or wounds; that of the whole number of effectives, just about one-half were Europeans, belonging either to the Queen's or to the Company's army; and that no European corps, except perhaps the Lancers, comprised more than a fractional percentage of a full regiment. A return sent in about the middle of the month had comprised 300 men of the 4th and 17th Bengal irregular cavalry; but the omission of this element at the end of the month shewed that those dangerous companions had been got rid of. The corps of Guides and Goorkhas

Engineer Officers in Battery before Delhi.

had in a fortnight diminished from an aggregate number of 923 to 571—so rapidly had those gallant men been brought down by balls, bullets, and cholera. Ranked among the artillery and engineers were many hundred syces and bildars, natives who merely aided in certain labouring operations; and among the Sappers and Miners the Punjaubees were only just learning their trade.

The casualty list of officers was a very serious one. From the time when Brigadier Wilson encountered the enemy at Ghazeeoodeen Nuggur at the end of May, till he made up his report at the end of July, the officers who were killed or wounded were 101 in number. Anson, Barnard, Reed, Chamberlain, Halifax, Graves—nearly all the general officers except Wilson and Showers, were either dead or in some way disabled; and these frequent changes in command doubtless affected the organisation and movements of the army.

Brigadier Wilson made every attempt, while doing the best he could with his own forces, to ascertain the number and components of those possessed by the enemy. Military commanders always aim at the acquisition of such knowledge, effected by a species of espionage which, however opposed to general feeling at other times, is deemed quite fair in war. From the 11th of May, when

* *Infantry*—	Officers and Men.	
H.M. 8th foot, head-quarters,	198	
H.M. 61st foot, "	296	
H.M. 75th foot, "	513	
H.M. 60th Rifles, "	299	
1st European Bengal Fusiliers,	520	
2d " " "	556	
Guide Infantry,	275	
Sirmoor battalion, Goorkhas,	298	
1st Punjaub Infantry,	723	
4th Sikh Infantry,	345	
		= 4023
Cavalry—		
H.M. Carabiniers,	153	
H.M. 9th Lancers,	428	
Guide Cavalry,	338	
1st Punjaub Cavalry,	148	
2d " "	110	
5th " " (at Alipore),	116	
		= 1293
Artillery and Engineers—		
Artillery, European and Native,	1129	
Bengal Sappers and Miners,	209	
Punjaub " "	264	
		= 1602
		6918

Besides these effectives, there were as non-effectives, 765 sick + 351 wounded = 1116.

the troubles began in Delhi, to the end of July, there arrived in the city mutinous regiments from Meerut, Hansi, Muttra, Lucknow, Nuseerabad, Jullundur, Ferozpore, Bareilly, Jhansi, Gwalior, Neemuch, Allygurh, Agra, Rohtuk, Jhuggur, and Allahabad. The list given in a note * is taken from the official dispatch, which was itself a record of information obtained from various native sources; but after making allowance for the fact that portions only of many of the regiments had entered Delhi, and that the numbers had been considerably lessened by the thirty or more encounters which had taken place outside the walls, the military authorities brought down the supposed number to a much lower limit than had before been named—namely, 4000 disciplined cavalry, and 12,000 infantry, besides 3000 undisciplined levies. The rebels retained the formidable defensive artillery which they found in Delhi, and brought thirty field-guns also with them; but these guns were lessened in number one-half by successive seizures made by the British.

The condition and proceedings of the rebels within the city could, of course, be known only imperfectly. The old king was looked up to by all as the centre of authority, but it is probable that his real power was small. Where regiments had arrived from so many different quarters, we may suppose that the apportionment of military command was no easy matter; and indeed there was, throughout, little evidence that the rebel force had one head, one leader whose plans were obeyed by all. The *Lahore Chronicle* some time afterwards printed a narrative by a native, of a residence in Delhi from the 13th to the 30th of July. Such narratives can seldom be relied on; but so far as it went, this revelation spoke of great discord among the leaders; great discontent among the troops because their pay was in arrear; great perplexity on the part of the old king because he had not funds enough to pay so large an army; and great plundering of the citizens by the rude soldiery, who deemed themselves masters of the situation. 'When the sepoys,' said this native, 'find out a rich house in the city, they accuse the owner after the following manner, in order to plunder his property. They take a loaf of bread and a bottle of grog with them, and make a noise at the door and break it in pieces, get into the house, take possession of the cash and valuables, and beat the poor householder, saying: "Where is the Englishman you have been keeping in your house?" When he denies having done so, they just shew him the bread and the bottle, and say: "How is it that we happened to find these in your house? We are quite sure there was an Englishman accommodated here, whom you quietly sent elsewhere before our arrival." Soon after, the talk is over, and the poor man is disgracefully put into custody, where there is no inquiry made to prove whether he is innocent or guilty; he cannot get his release unless he bribes the general.' The known attributes of oriental cunning give a strong probability to this curious story.

Here, for the present, we take leave of the siege of Delhi, and of the stage at which it had arrived by the end of July. Much has to be narrated, in reference to other places, other generals, other operations, before the final capture of the imperial city will call for description.

* Bengal native infantry: 3d, 9th, 11th, 12th, 15th, 20th, 28th, 29th, 30th, 36th, 38th, 44th, 45th, 54th, 57th, 60th, 61st, 67th, 68th, 72d, 74th, 78th.
Other native infantry: 5th and 7th Gwalior Contingent, Kotah Contingent, Hurrianah battalion; together with 2600 miscellaneous infantry.
Native cavalry: Portions of five or six regiments, besides others of the Gwalior and Malwah Contingents.

Bullock-wagon.

Sir Henry Havelock.

CHAPTER XV.

HAVELOCK'S CAMPAIGN: ALLAHABAD TO LUCKNOW.

IF there be one name that stands out in brighter colours than any other connected with the mutiny in India, perhaps it is that of Henry Havelock. There are peculiar reasons for this. He came like a brilliant meteor at a time when all else was gloomy and overshadowed. Anson had died on the way to Delhi; Barnard had died in the camp before that city; Reed had retired, broken down by age and sickness; Wilson had not yet shewn whether he could work out victory at the great Mogul capital; Wheeler was falling, or had fallen, a miserable victim to the treachery of Nena Sahib; Henry Lawrence was no more; Hewett and Lloyd were under a cloud, for mismanagement as military commanders—all this had rendered the British nation grieved and irritated; and men fiercely demanded 'Who's to blame?'—as if it were necessary to seek relief by wreaking vengeance on some persons or other. It was a crisis that pressed heavily on Viscount Canning; but it was at the same time a crisis that insured fervid gratitude to any general who could achieve victories with small means. Such a general was Havelock. The English public knew little of him, although he was well known in India. Commencing his career as a soldier in 1816, Henry Havelock had borne his full share in all a soldier's varied fortune. He went to India in 1823; engaged in the Burmese war in 1824; took part in a mission to the court of Siam in 1826; was promoted from lieutenant to captain in 1838; took an active share in the stirring scenes of the Afghan campaign, which brought him a brevet majority, and the order of C. B.; acted as Persian interpreter to generals Elphinstone, Pollock, and Gough; fought at Gwalior in 1843; became brevet lieutenant-colonel in 1844; fought with the bravest in 1845 at Moodkee, Ferozshah, and Sobraon; and in 1846 received the appointment of deputy adjutant-general of the Queen's troops at Bombay. An Indian climate during so many years having told—in its customary sad way—on his constitution, Henry Havelock returned for a sojourn in England. Returning to Bombay in 1851, he became brevet colonel; and in after years he was appointed quarter-master-general, and then adjutant-general, of the whole of the Queen's troops in India. When the war with Persia broke out, he took command of one of the divisions in 1857; and when that war was ended, he returned to Bombay. All this was known to official persons in India, but very few of the particulars were familiar to the general public in the home-country; hence, when Havelock's victories were announced, the public were surprised as if by the sudden appearance of a great genius. That he bore so heavy a responsibility, or suffered such intense mental anxiety, as Wheeler at Cawnpore, Inglis at Lucknow, or Colvin at Agra, is not probable; for he had not hundreds of helpless women and children under his charge; but the astonishing victories he achieved with a mere handful of men, and the moral influence he thereby acquired for the British name throughout the whole of the Doab, well entitled him to the outburst of grateful feeling which the nation was not slow to exhibit. The only danger was, lest this hero-worship should render the nation blind for a time to the merits of other generals.

Neill and Havelock, who worked so energetically together in planning the relief of Lucknow, were brought from other regions of India to take part in the operations on the Ganges. Neill, as colonel of the 1st Madras European Fusiliers, accompanied that regiment to Calcutta, and thence proceeded up the country to Benares, where his contest with the rebels first began. Havelock, landing at Bombay from Persia, set off by steam to go to Calcutta; he was wrecked on the way near Ceylon, and experienced much perilous adventure before he could proceed on his journey. At Calcutta—where he arrived, in the same steamer which brought Sir Patrick Grant, on the 17th of June—he received the appointment of brigadier-general,* to command such a force as could be hastily collected for the relief, first of the Europeans at Cawnpore, and then of those at Lucknow; and it was towards the close of June that he made his appearance at Allahabad.

Sufficient has been stated in former chapters to shew what was the state of affairs at that time. Lucknow, Cawnpore, Agra, and Delhi were either in the hands of the rebels, or were so beset by them that no British commander was able to assist his brother-officers. Oude, the Doab, and Rohilcund were in deplorable anarchy; and it depended either upon Viscount Canning at Calcutta, or Sir John Lawrence at Lahore, to send aid to the disturbed districts. Lawrence, as we have seen, and as we shall see again in a future chapter, with admirable energy and perseverance, sent such assistance as enabled Wilson to conquer Delhi; while Canning, under enormous difficulty, sent up troops to Allahabad by scores and fifties at a time, as rapidly as he could collect them at Calcutta.

Brigadier Neill preceded Havelock in the operations connected with the repression of the mutiny in the Doab and adjacent regions. His own regiment, the 1st Madras European Fusiliers, had been ordered to proceed to Persia in the spring, but had received counter-orders in consequence of the sudden termination of the war in that country. While at Bombay, uncertain whether commands might be received to proceed to China, the regiment heard the news of a revolt among the Bengal troops; and very speedily, both Persia and China were forgotten in matters of much greater exigency and importance. After making the voyage back from Bombay to Madras, the regiment proceeded to Calcutta, and the men were then sent up the country as rapidly as possible to Benares, some by road and the rest by steamers. Neill himself reached that city on the 3d of June, and was immediately engaged, as we have already seen (p. 154), in disarming a mutinous regiment, and in maintaining order in the vicinity. After six days of incessant work at Benares, the brigadier, hearing of the mutiny at Allahabad, started off on the 9th to render service in that region. With what a powerful hand he put down the rebels; with what stern and prompt firmness he retained possession of that important city, the 'key to Upper India'—has already been briefly shewn.† The various corps of the Madras Fusiliers reached

* It may be useful to note, for readers unfamiliar with military matters, the meaning of the words *brevet* and *brigadier*. A brevet is a commission, conferring on an officer a degree of rank *next above* that which he holds in his particular regiment; without, however, conveying the power of receiving the corresponding pay. Besides being honorary as a mark of distinction, it qualifies the officer to succeed to the full possession of the higher rank on a vacancy occurring, in preference to one not holding a brevet. In the British army brevet rank only applies to captains, majors, and lieutenant-colonels. A *brigadier* is a colonel or other officer of a regiment who is made temporarily a general officer for a special service, in command of a brigade, or more than one regiment. It is not a permanent rank, but is considered as a stepping-stone to the office of major-general. Many Indian officers who were colonels when the Indian mutiny began, such as Henry Lawrence and Neill, were appointed brigadier-generals for a special service, and rose to higher rank before the mutiny was ended.

† Chapter ix., pp. 159-161.

Benares and Allahabad by degrees; and fragments of other European regiments were sent up as fast as possible, as the nucleus of a little army forming at Allahabad.

The 1st of July may be taken as the day that marked the commencement of General Havelock's career in relation to the Indian Revolt. He and his staff arrived at Allahabad on that day, after a rapid journey from Calcutta. A few hours before his arrival, the first relieving column had been sent off by Neill towards Cawnpore: consisting of 200 Madras Fusiliers, 200 of the 84th foot, 300 Sikhs, and 120 irregular cavalry, under Major Renaud; and a second, of larger proportions, was to follow in a week or ten days' time. The immediate object held in view, in the march of both columns, was to liberate Sir Hugh Wheeler and his hapless companions at Cawnpore; and, if this were accomplished, the second work to be done was to advance and relieve Sir Henry Lawrence and the British at Lucknow. It was not at that time known that, before the second column could start from Allahabad, both Wheeler and Lawrence had been numbered with the dead. Neill superseded the officer previously in command at Allahabad; Havelock superseded Neill in command of the relieving force; we shall have to speak of Outram superseding Havelock; and we have already spoken of Patrick Grant superseding Reed, and of Colin Campbell superseding Grant. All these supersessions were in virtue of military routine, depending either on seniority, or on the exercise of a right to make appointments. If these various officers had been unsuccessful, the system of supersession would have been attacked by adverse judges as the cause of the failure; but there was so much nobility of mind displayed by four or five of the gallant men here named, that the vexation often caused by supersession was much alleviated; while the nation at large had ample reason to admire and be thankful for the deeds of arms that accompanied generosity of feeling.

On the 3d, an auxiliary force under Captain Spurgin, left Allahabad for Cawnpore, irrespective of the two columns. It consisted only of 100 Madras Europeans armed with rifles, 12 artillery-men, and two 6-pounder guns; it went by steamer up the Ganges, partly in order to control the mutineers on the banks, but in part also on account of the paucity of means for land-conveyance. No steamer had had much success in that part of the Ganges; and hence great interest was felt in the voyage of the *Brahmaputra*. As a first difficulty, the engineers, having no coals, were obliged to forage for wood every day on shore. On the second day of the trip, this foraging had to be protected by half the force, against a body of 500 insurgents on the Oude bank, provided with a large piece of ordnance; the wood was not obtained without a regular battle, in which 50 English 'thrashed'—to use a very favourite term among the soldiers—just ten times their number of rebels, and captured their gun. On they went, struggling against the rapid stream of the Ganges, and never making more than two miles an hour. The enemy hovered on the banks, and sent several round shot into the little iron steamer—a sort of irritation that kept the crew and soldiers well on the alert. Day after day passed in this way, Captain Spurgin timing his movements so as to accord with the march of the land-columns. The steamer reached Cawnpore on the 17th, just a fortnight after the departure from Allahabad—a degree of slowness not altogether dependent on the difficulty of the navigation, but partly due to the necessity of not advancing more rapidly than the columns could fight their way on shore.

The dismal news gradually reached Allahabad that some dreadful calamity had occurred at Cawnpore. This information led Havelock to modify his plans and quicken his movements; and, full of heart, he transmitted to Calcutta the telegram already quoted, to the effect that '1000 Europeans, 1000 Goorkhas, and 1000 Sikhs, with 8 or 10 guns, will thrash everything.' Among the troops he collected was a handful of volunteer cavalry, consisting chiefly of officers who had been left without command by the mutiny of their respective native regiments, or had narrowly escaped massacre; the number amounted only to a score; but it comprised just the sort of men who would be ready for any enterprise at such a time.

Major Renaud had every reason to be satisfied with the gallantry of the Madras Fusiliers—to which corps he belonged—and of the other troops who aided in forming his small column, in various minor operations during the first nine days of the march from Allahabad. He everywhere pacified the country by punishing the ringleaders in mutiny and rebellion wherever and whenever they fell into his hands. Suddenly, however, he found himself placed in an awkward position on the 10th. Cawnpore had fallen; the British at that station had either been killed or thrown into prison; and the rebel force thus freed from occupation had rapidly pushed down to the vicinity of Futtehpoor—a town which had been in the hands of the rebels since the 9th of June (see p. 172). That force was at least 3500 strong, with 12 guns; whereas Renaud had at that time only 820 men and 2 guns. General Havelock, becoming aware of this state of things, saw that his force ought to join that of Renaud as quickly as possible. He marched twenty miles on the 11th, under a frightful sun, to Synee; then, after resting a few hours, he and his troops resumed their march at eleven o'clock in the evening, overtook Renaud during the night, and marched with him by moonlight to Khaga, five miles short of Futtehpoor. His little army consisted of about 2000 men, made up of a curious collection of fragments from various regiments; and as it was destined to achieve great results with limited resources, it may be interesting to tabulate the component elements of this admirable little band.* Havelock's information proved to be better than that of the enemy, for when he sent forward Colonel Tytler with a reconnaissance, the enemy supposed they had only Renaud's small force to contend with; they fired on the colonel and his escort, and pushed forward two guns and a force of infantry and cavalry. When the enemy began to cannonade his front and threaten his right and left, Havelock saw that the time was come to undeceive them: he would have preferred to give his worn-out soldiers a few hours' rest; but this was not now to be thought of, as, to use his own words, 'it would have injured the *morale* of the troops to permit them thus to be bearded.' The work before him was sufficiently formidable; for there was only the main trunk-road by which to approach Futtehpoor easily; the fields on either side were covered with a depth of two or three feet of water; there were many enclosures of great strength, with high walls; and in front of the city were many villages, hillocks, and mango-groves which the enemy occupied in force. Havelock placed his eight guns on and near the main road, protected by 100 riflemen of the 64th; the infantry came up at deploying distance, covered by rifle-skirmishers; and the cavalry moved forward on the flanks. The struggle was literally decided in ten minutes. The enemy saw a few riflemen approach; but they knew little of the Enfield rifle; and were panic-stricken with the length and accuracy of its range; they shrank back in astonishment; and then Captain Maude, who had dashed over the swamps with his artillery, poured into them a fire so rapid and accurate as to complete their discomfiture. Three guns were abandoned at once, and Havelock steadily advanced, with the 64th commanding the centre, the 78th the right, the 84th and the Sikhs the left. He drove the enemy before him at every point, capturing their guns one by one; the garden enclosures, the barricades on the road, the city wall, the streets of Futtehpoor, all were gained in turn. The enemy retreated right through the city, till they reached a mile beyond it; but they then attempted to make a stand. This attempt gave Havelock some trouble, because his infantry were almost utterly exhausted by fatigue, and because the few irregular horse showed symptoms of a tendency to go over to the enemy unless narrowly watched. Again the guns and rifles came to the front, and again they attacked in a manner so irresistible as to put the enemy effectively to flight. Havelock thus became master of Futtehpoor, and parked 12 captured guns. It was with a justifiable pride that the general, in sending his list of 'casualties,' remarked that it was 'perhaps the lightest that ever accompanied the announcement of such success. Twelve British soldiers were struck down by the sun, and never rose again;' but not one was either killed or wounded in the action; his casualties, 6 killed and 3 wounded, were among his native troops. The truth seems to be, that the enemy were dismayed, first by finding that Havelock had joined Renaud, and then by the wonderful range of the Enfield rifles. 'Our fight was fought neither with musket, nor bayonet, nor sabre, but with Enfield rifles and cannon; so we took no prisoners. The enemy's fire scarcely reached us; ours, for four hours, allowed him no repose.' It was with good cause that he thanked and congratulated his troops on the following day, in a 'morning order,' short but pithy.*

While encamped at Kullenpore or Kullianpore, on the 14th, to which he had marched after a sojourn at Futtehpoor sufficient to afford his troops that rest which had become absolutely necessary, Havelock sent off a brief telegram, announcing that his capture of artillery at Futtehpoor would enable him to substitute nine excellent field-guns for six of lighter calibre, and also to bring into action two light 6-pounders.

This, then, was the brigadier-general's first victory over the rebels; it elated his own troops, and checked the audacity of those to whom he was opposed. Neill, meanwhile, was anxiously watching at Allahabad. He had worked hard to organise and send off the first portion of the force under Renaud, the second under Spurgin, and the third under Havelock. He had received from Renaud, on the 4th of the month, information which rendered only too probable the rumour that an act of black treachery on the part of Nena Sahib at Cawnpore had been followed by a wholesale destruction of hapless fugitives in boats on the Ganges. Neill was thus especially anxious that Renaud should advance at once with the first column, and Spurgin with the detachment up the river; but Havelock saw reason why those officers should somewhat delay their advance until he could come up to them, in order that all might if possible enter Cawnpore together.

Havelock, after marching and resting on the 13th and 14th, came up again with the enemy on the 15th. When approaching the small stream

* *British Troops:*

H.M. 64th foot (from Persia), . .	435 men;	Major Stirling.
H.M. 78th Highlanders (from Persia),	284 "	Col. Hamilton.
H.M. 84th foot (from Pegu), . .	190 "	Lieut. Ayrton.
1st Madras Fusiliers (from Madras), .	376 "	Major Renaud.
Voluntary cavalry (from Allahabad), .	20 "	Capt. Barrow.
Royal artillery (from Ceylon), .	98 "	Capt. Maude.
	1403	

Native Troops:

Regiment of Ferozpore (Sikhs), . .	448 men;	Capt. Brasyer.
13th Irr. Cav., and 3d Oude Cav.,	95 "	Lieut. Palliser.
Artillery, ...	18 "	
	561	

Colonel Tytler and Captain Beatson officiated as quarter-master-general and adjutant-general of the force, irrespective of particular regiments.

* 'Brigadier-general Havelock thanks his soldiers for their arduous exertion of yesterday, which produced, in four hours, the strange result of a whole army driven from a strong position, eleven guns captured, and their whole force scattered to the winds, without the loss of a single British soldier!

'To what is this astonishing effect to be attributed? To the fire of the British artillery, exceeding in rapidity and precision all that the brigadier-general has ever witnessed in his not short career; to the power of the Enfield rifle in British hands; to British pluck, that good quality that has survived the revolution of the hour; and to the blessing of Almighty God on a most righteous cause—the cause of justice, humanity, truth, and good government in India.'

called the Pandoo Nuddee, it became important to him to ascertain what was the state of the bridge which carried the high road over that river, at a spot about twenty miles from Cawnpore. The stream was too deep to be fordable at that season: hence the importance of obtaining command of the bridge. His intelligencers ascertained that the enemy intended to dispute his passage at the village of Aong, four miles short of the Nuddee; by means of two guns commanding the high road, skirmishers on the right and left of those guns, and cavalry to hover on the flanks of any advancing force. This information being obtained, Havelock sent forward his skirmishers on the right and left of the road; then his volunteer cavalry on the road itself; then the ten guns in line, mostly on the left of the road; and then the infantry in line—the 64th and 84th on the right flank; the 78th, Fusiliers, and Sikhs, on the left. The struggle ahead was not a severe one, for the enemy receded as the British under Colonel Tytler advanced; but Havelock was much harassed by the attempts of the hostile cavalry to get into his rear and plunder his baggage: attempts that required much exertion from his infantry to resist, seeing that the thickly wooded country interfered with the effect of cannon and musketry. The enemy after a time abandoned guns, tents, ammunition, and other materials of war, and made a hasty retreat through the village.

This difficulty over, Havelock prepared for another struggle at the Pandoo Nuddee, which it was necessary for him to cross as speedily as possible. He rested and refreshed his troops for a few hours, and advanced the same afternoon, on a fiercely hot July day. The enemy had not destroyed the bridge, but had placed two guns in épaulement to command it at the opposite side of the stream. Captain Maude disposed his artillery so as to bring a converging fire upon the two guns of the enemy; while the Madras Fusiliers commenced a fire with Enfield rifles to pick off the gunners. The two guns were fired directly down the road at the advancing British column; but after Maude had somewhat checked this fire, the Fusiliers gallantly closed, rushed upon the bridge, and captured both guns—an exploit in which Major Renaud was wounded. The mutineers precipitately retreated. Thus did the brigadier-general achieve two victories in one day—those of Aong and Pandoo Nuddee. True, the victories were not great in a military sense; but they were effected over a numerous force by a mere handful of troops, who fought after wearying marches under a solar heat such as residents in England can with difficulty imagine. Havelock had only 1 man killed during these two actions; 25 were wounded. The loss of the enemy was at least ten times greater; but the chief result of the battles was the dismay into which Nena Sahib was thrown.

General Havelock, like other commanders at that critical time, found the native Bengal troops in his force not to be trusted. Their conduct in presence of the enemy on the 12th excited his suspicion; it was, indeed, worse than doubtful; and on the 14th he found it necessary to disarm and dismount his sowars of the 13th Irregulars and 3d Oude Irregulars—at the same time threatening with instant death any one of their number who should attempt to escape. One of the officers at Allahabad who joined the volunteer cavalry, and had opportunity of observing the conduct of the irregulars at the battle of Futtehpoor, wrote thus concerning it: 'On seeing the enemy, Palliser called to the men to charge, and dashed on; but the scoundrels scarcely altered their speed, and met the enemy at the same pace that they came down towards us. Their design was evident; they came waving their swords to our men, and riding round our party, making signs to them to go over to their side. When our men thus hung back, a dash out would certainly have ended in our being cut up.' During a subsequent skirmish, 'our rear-men turned tail and left us, galloping back as hard as their horses could go; and we were forced to commence a regular race for our necks. . . . . I write this with shame and grief; but it was no fault of Palliser's or ours.' Havelock saw the necessity of disarming and dismounting such fellows.

The scene of operations now approaches Cawnpore, that city of unutterable horrors! It was a desperate struggle that Nena Sahib made to retain the supremacy he had obtained at Cawnpore. He probably cared little for kings of Delhi or for greased cartridges, provided he could maintain a hold of sovereign power. When he had broken faith with Sir Hugh Wheeler, and had carried his treachery to the extent of indiscriminate slaughter in the Ganges boats, he naturally hoped to become leader of the rebellious sepoys. In this object, however, he did not wholly succeed; he and his immediate followers were Mahrattas; the mutineers were mostly Hindustanis; and the latter made little account of the Nena's claim to sovereignty. Had the issue depended upon the infantry sepoys, who were in chief part Hindoos, and who chiefly looked for plunder, his projects might speedily have come to an end; but the cavalry sepoys, being mostly Mohammedans, and exhibiting a more deadly hatred towards the British, more readily joined him in a combined plan of operations, and drew the sepoys to act with them. Leaving Delhi to be held by the large body of mutineers, Nena Sahib took upon himself the office of crushing any British force that might make its appearance from Allahabad. When he heard that Renaud had started with his little band, he got together a force of sowars, sepoys, Mahrattas, artillery, and rabble; having motives of fear as well as of self-interest to induce him to prevent the advance of his opponent. Not knowing that Renaud had been joined by Havelock, the Mahratta chieftain sent bodies of troops sufficient, as he believed, to check the advance; but when the gallant general swept everything before him, the arch-fiend of Bithoor saw that the matter was becoming serious. He had had experience of the indomitable resistance, under accumulated suffering, of the hapless Sir Hugh Wheeler and his companions; but now a British general had to be encountered in the open field. So far as is known, it appears that as soon as he heard of the passage of the Pandoo Nuddee by Havelock, Nena Sahib ordered the slaughter of all the captives yet remaining alive at Cawnpore—in order either that the dead might tell no tales, or that he might wreak vengeance on the innocent for the frustration of his plans. Having committed this bloody deed, he went out with an army, and took up a position at Aherwa, the point at which the road to the cantonment branches out from the main trunk-road to Cawnpore city. Nena Sahib commanded five villages, with numerous intrenchments, armed with seven guns; and in the rear was his infantry. Havelock, after advancing

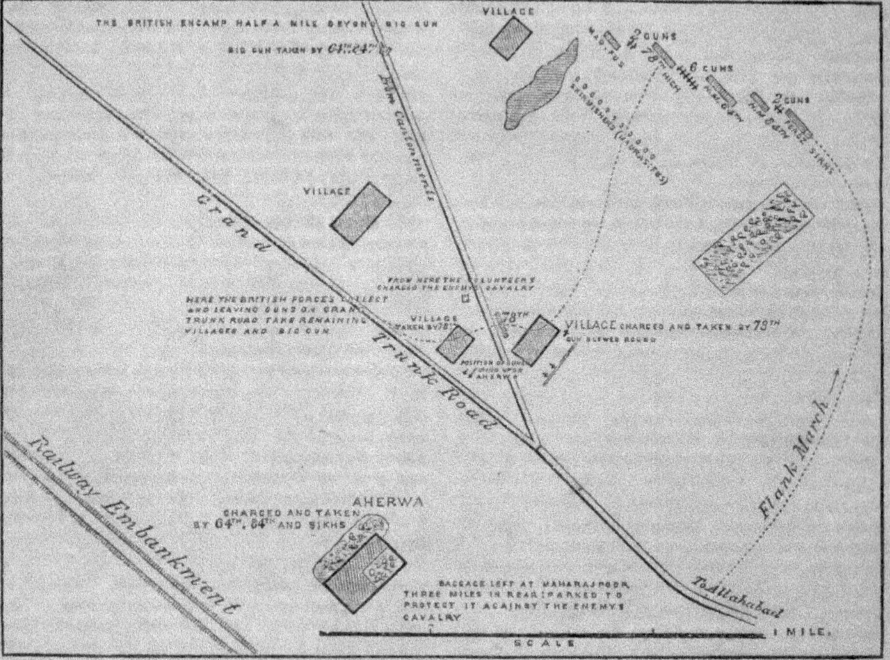

Plan of action near Cawnpore, July 16, 1857.

sixteen miles from the Pandoo Nuddee to Aherwa during the night of the 15th, and after measuring the strength of this force, saw that his troops would be shot down in alarming numbers before the guns could be silenced and the intrenchments carried; he resolved, therefore, on a flank-movement on the enemy's left. As a preliminary, he left his camp and baggage under proper escort at Maharajpoor, a few miles in the rear; and gave his sunburnt and exhausted troops two or three hours' rest in a mango-grove during mid-day of the 16th, until the fierce heat should have somewhat abated. The hour of struggle having arrived, Havelock quietly wheeled his force round to the left flank of the enemy's position, behind a screen of clumps of mango. When the enemy detected this manœuvre, great sensation was displayed; a body of horse was soon sent to the left, and cannon opened fire in that direction. Then came a series of operations in which the superb qualities of British infantry were strikingly displayed. Villages were attacked and captured one after another, by fragments of regiments so small that one marvels how the enemy could have yielded before them. One such exploit is thus narrated in Havelock's own language: 'The opportunity had arrived, for which I have long anxiously waited, of developing the prowess of the 78th Highlanders. Three guns of the enemy were strongly posted behind a lofty hamlet, well intrenched. I directed this regiment to advance; and never have I witnessed conduct more admirable. They were led by Colonel Hamilton, and followed him with surpassing steadiness and gallantry under a heavy fire. As they approached the village, they cheered and charged with the bayonet, the pipes sounding the pibroch. Need I add that the enemy fled, the village was taken, and the guns captured?' After three or four villages had thus changed hands, the enemy planted a 24-pounder gun on the cantonment road in such a position as to work much mischief upon Havelock, whose artillery cattle were so worn out with heat and fatigue that they could not drag the guns onward to a desired position. The Nena appearing to have in project a renewed attack, Havelock resolved to anticipate him; he cheered on his infantry to a capture of the 24-pounder; they rushed along the road amid a storm of grape-shot from the enemy, and never slackened till they had reached the gun and captured it. Especially was the 64th, led by Major Stirling, conspicuous in this bold enterprise. The enemy lost all heart; they retreated, blew up the magazine of Cawnpore on their way, and then went on to Bithoor.

Thus was fought the battle of Cawnpore, the conquest of which place had for so many weeks been anxiously looked forward to by the British. True, they had heard, and under too great a variety of detail to warrant disbelief, that Sir Hugh Wheeler and his gallant companions had been most treacherously murdered by the ruthless chieftain of Bithoor; but yet a hope clung to them that some of their compatriots at least might be alive at Cawnpore. On this 16th of July, Havelock's small force was lessened by the loss of 6 killed and 98 wounded or missing—a loss wonderfully slight under the circumstances, but serious to him. Captain Currie of the 84th received a wound so desperate that he sank under it in a few hours; Major Stirling was slightly wounded; Captain Beatson, attacked with cholera on the morning of the fight, held up with heroic bearing during the whole day, but died soon afterwards. The enemy lost seven guns on this day, of which three were 24-pounders.

Some of the Europeans bore an almost incredible amount of hard labour on this day of fierce July heat. One, a youth of eighteen who had joined the volunteer cavalry, had been on picket all the preceding night, with no refreshment save biscuit and water; he then marched with the rest sixteen miles during the forenoon; then stood sentry for an hour with the enemy hovering around him; then fought during the whole afternoon; then lay down supperless to rest at nightfall, holding his horse's bridle the while; then mounted night-guard from nine till eleven o'clock; and then had his midnight sleep broken by an alarm from the enemy. It was on this occasion, too, that Lieutenant Marshman Havelock, son of the general, to whom he acted as aid-de-camp, performed a perilous duty in such a way as to earn for himself the Victoria Cross—a badge of honour established in 1856 for acts of personal heroism. The general thus narrated the incident, in one of his dispatches: 'The 64th regiment had been much under artillery-fire, from which it had severely suffered. The whole of the infantry were lying down in line, when, perceiving that the enemy had brought out the last reserved gun, a 24-pounder, and were rallying round it, I called up the regiment to rise and advance. Without any other word from me, Lieutenant Havelock placed himself on his horse, in front of the centre of the 64th, opposite the muzzle of the gun. Major Stirling, commanding the regiment, was in front, dismounted; but the lieutenant continued to move steadily on in front of the regiment at a foot-pace, on his horse. The gun discharged shot until the troops were within a short distance, when it fired grape. In went the corps, led by the lieutenant, who still steered steadily on the gun's muzzle until it was mastered by a rush of the 64th.' It is difficult for civilians adequately to comprehend the cool courage required in an act like this; where a soldier walks his horse directly up in front of a large piece of cannon which is loaded and fired at him and his comrades as rapidly as possible.

What the British troops saw when they entered Cawnpore, has already engaged our attention (pp. 142–145). None could ever forget it to their dying day. It was on the 17th of July that Havelock, after a night's rest for his exhausted troops, entered the city, and learned the hideous revelations of the slaughter-room and the well. What steps were immediately taken in Cawnpore, has been noticed in the chapter just cited; and the dismal story need not be repeated. The general could not wait to attend to those matters at that time; he had still to learn what were the movements of Nena Sahib after the battle of the preceding day—whether the Mahratta intended or not to make a stand in his palace at Bithoor. Sending forward part of his troops therefore on the afternoon of the 17th, he found the enemy in a very strong position. Their force consisted of the insurgent 31st and 42d Bengal infantry from Saugor, the 17th from Fyzabad, sepoys from various other regiments, troops of the cavalry regiments, and a portion of Nena Sahib's Mahrattas—about 4000 men in all. The plain in front of Bithoor, diversified by thickets and villages, had two streams flowing through it, not fordable, and only to be crossed by two narrow bridges. The enemy held both bridges, and defended them well. The streams prevented Havelock from turning the enemy's flanks; and when his infantry assaulted the position, they were received with heavy rifle and musketry fire. After an hour of very severe struggle, he effected a crossing, drove them back, captured their guns, and chased them towards Sorajpore. He had no cavalry to maintain a pursuit—indeed the want of cavalry was felt sadly by him in every one of his battles. This contest cost the enemy about 250 men, the British about one-fifth of the number; in this last-named list was included only one officer, Captain Mackenzie of the 78th Highlanders, who was slightly wounded.

Here, then, was one part of the enterprise accomplished. Cawnpore had been recaptured, and the road cleared of rebels between that place and Allahabad. It was on the 30th of June that Renaud had left the last-named place with the first division, and on the 3d of July that Spurgin had set off with the detachment by steamer. It was on the 7th that Havelock had placed himself at the head of the second division, and marched forth to overtake the two others—carrying with him the recollection of a scowl from many of the Mussulman inhabitants of the city. He had seen, as he went along, evidences of Renaud's stern energy, in the number of rebellious sepoys hanging from gibbets and trees by the roadside. He and his troops had made ordinary Indian marches the first three or four days, in alternate rain and fierce heat, and within sight of destroyed bungalows and devastated homesteads; but when the news from Renaud arrived, forced marches were made. Then came the battle of Futtehpoor on the 12th, that of Aong on the morning of the 14th, that of Pundoo Nuddee on the afternoon of the same day, that of Cawnpore on the 16th, and that of Bithoor on the 17th—five victories in six days, spreading the fame of Havelock far and wide throughout the surrounding districts. The future tactics had then to be resolved upon. Cawnpore had been recovered, although the garrison could not be saved; but there was another British garrison, another group of suffering British women and children, to be thought of—at Lucknow. The general well knew how desperate was the work before him, with the reduced and sickened force at his command; but he was not the man to shrink from making an attempt, at least, to relieve Brigadier Inglis and his companions. Feeling the urgent need of more troops, and the imperative necessity of holding Cawnpore safely while he himself advanced into Oude, Havelock had already sent to Allahabad, requesting Neill to come if possible in person to Cawnpore, and to bring reinforcements with him. It was easier for Neill to respond to the first of these two appeals than to the second; he would have gone anywhere, borne any amount of fatigue, to share in the good work; but he found himself already reduced to so few troops at Allahabad as to be barely able to maintain that place. Nevertheless, after counting heads and measuring strength, he ventured to draft off 227 men of the 84th foot from his little force; he started them forth on the 15th, partly by bullock-trains, to reach Cawnpore on the 20th. He himself set out on the 16th—the day of the battle of Cawnpore—leaving Allahabad under the command of Captain Drummond Hay of the 78th Highlanders, until Colonel O'Brien could arrive. After a rapid journey, Neill reached Cawnpore, took military command of that place and its neighbourhood, and assisted Havelock in the preparations necessary for crossing the Ganges into Oude. One great necessity was perceived on the instant by both generals; English soldiers, with all their good qualities, are prone to drink; and Havelock soon found, to use his own words, that 'half his men would be needed to keep the other half from getting drunk' if they had easy access to liquor; he therefore bought up all spare beverages in Cawnpore, and placed them in the hands of the commissariat. A calamity much grieved the little army at this time. Major Renaud, who had so successfully brought forward the first column from Allahabad, sank under the effects of a wound he had received. A bullet had hit him above the knee, forcing part of the scabbard of his sword into the wound, and causing much suffering; amputation seemed to afford some relief, but only for a time; he died soon after the arrival of Neill, who had highly valued him as a trusty officer in his own Madras Fusiliers.

Glancing at a map, we see that the high road from Cawnpore to Lucknow is broken at its very commencement by the river Ganges, which, at this point, varies from five hundred to two thousand yards in width. There is, of course, no bridge here; and as the stream is usually very rapid, the transport of troops necessarily becomes slow, difficult, and dangerous work. Havelock began to cross on the 20th of July, but many days elapsed before the task was completed. The *Brahmaputra* steamer, which brought Spurgin's detachment to Cawnpore on the 17th, was, with a few open boats, the only available resource for this work. By the 23d, about 1100 of his troops had crossed over into Oude—every boat-load having to battle against a broad and swift current. All possible baggage was left behind, each man taking with him a very small supply of clothing and food.

On the 20th, Havelock sent a short telegram to the commander-in-chief—announcing that Nena Sahib's followers appeared to be deserting him; that he had fled from Bithoor; that the British had re-entered that place on the 19th; and that the palace had been reduced to ashes, and 13 guns captured. On the next day a further communication was sent to the effect that three more guns, and a number of animals, had been brought along from Bithoor, and that the magazine had been blown up. Subsequent events proved that the Nena, though forced to flee, still retained a body of troops under his command.

When the brigadier-general, on the 23d of July, had so far succeeded in transporting his gallant little army over the majestic Ganges; and when his sanguine hopes had led him to believe that he could conquer Lucknow in two or three days, then arose in his mind the important strategic question—What next? Should he remain in Oude after the capture of Lucknow, and effect the thorough reconquest of that province; or should he hastily recross the Ganges, march to Agra, liberate Colvin and the other Europeans in the fort, pick up any available force there, and advance to aid in the siege of Delhi? Sir Patrick Grant, who was commander-in-chief at that time, was solicited by telegram for an answer to this query. He strenuously recommended that Havelock, once in Oude, should remain there if possible. 'If he merely relieves the beleaguered garrison of Lucknow, and, after accomplishing that object, instantly recrosses the Ganges into our own provinces, it will be thought and believed throughout India that he had signally failed to reconquer Oude, and that he was driven out of the province by force of arms. The insurgents, though beaten before Lucknow, would assuredly collect again, and follow up the retiring army, prevent supplies from coming into camp, and reduce our troops to great straits and hazards when recrossing the Ganges—the passage of which, even when wholly unopposed, the brigadier-general describes as having been a very difficult and tedious operation.' This exactly coincided with Havelock's own view; and he therefore turned a deaf ear to all applications for aid made to him by the commanders at Agra and Delhi.

It was not until the 25th that Havelock, after seeing his army safely across the river, made the passage himself from the Doab into Oude. Neill, with a very small number of troops, prepared to hold Cawnpore safely during Havelock's absence. He re-established British power throughout the place; offered government rewards for bringing in captured rebels and public property; appointed Captain Bruce to the post of superintendent of the police and intelligence departments; purchased troop-horses in the neighbouring districts; and made arrangements for keeping the road open and unmolested between Cawnpore and Allahabad. All this he did, besides taking care of Havelock's sick and wounded, with a force of only 300 men—such was the result of the bravery of a soldier and the skill of a commander, when combined in the same person.

When Havelock had advanced six miles from the Ganges, at a place called Mungulwar, he was met by a messenger who had succeeded in eluding the vigilance of the insurgents at Lucknow, and had brought a plan of that city prepared by Major Anderson, together with some brief but valuable information from Brigadier Inglis. The details were partly written in Greek character, as a measure of precaution. Havelock now saw the full importance and difficulty of the work before him. His own little band was reduced to 1500 men, supported by 10 badly equipped and manned guns. On the other hand, he learned that the enemy had intrenched and covered with guns the long bridge across the Sye (Saee) at Bunnee, and had made preparations for destroying it if the passage were forced. Nor was his rear less imperiled than his front; for Nena Sahib had collected 3000 men and several guns, with which he intended to get between Havelock and the Ganges, to cut off his retreat. Nothing but the anxious dangers and difficulties of the Europeans at Lucknow would have induced the gallant man to advance under such perilous odds. He said in one of his despatches to the government on the 28th: 'The communications convince me of the extreme delicacy and difficulty of any operation to relieve Inglis; it shall be attempted, however, at every risk.' Could he have known how anxiously the beleaguered British in the Residency at Lucknow was looking for him, his heart would have bled for them; Major Anderson had sent him a military plan, but the messenger was too much imperiled to bring any lengthened narrative.

The battle of Onao or Oonao was one of the most surprising of the series in which Havelock was engaged. His passage towards Lucknow was disputed on the 29th by the enemy, who had taken up a strong position. Their right was protected by a swamp which could neither be forced nor turned; their advanced corps was in a garden enclosure which assumed the form of a bastion; and the rest of their force was posted in and behind a village, the houses of which were loopholed and defended by 15 guns. The passage between the village and the town of Onao was very narrow; but along this passage the attack had to be made—because the swamp precluded an advance on the one flank, while the flooded state of the country equally rendered the other impassable. The attack was commenced by the 78th Highlanders and the 1st Fusiliers, who, with two guns, soon drove the enemy out of the bastioned enclosure; but when they approached the village, they were exposed to a hot fire from the loopholed houses. A party of the 84th foot advanced in aid; and then a determined struggle ensued; the village was set on fire, but still the enemy resisted with a bravery worthy of a better cause. At length the passage between the town and the village was forced; and then the enemy were seen drawn up in great strength in an open plain—infantry, cavalry, and artillery. Nevertheless Havelock attacked them, captured their guns, and put the horse and foot to flight. During all this time a large detachment of Nena Sahib's troops, under Jupah Singh, threatened the left flank of the British, in the not unreasonable hope of being able to annihilate such a handful of men. No sooner had Havelock given his troops two or three hours' rest, than he advanced from Onao to Busherutgunje. This was a walled town, with wet ditches, a gate defended by a round tower, four pieces of cannon on and near the tower, loopholed and strengthened buildings within the walls, and a broad and deep pond or lake beyond the town. Havelock sent the Highlanders and Fusiliers, under cover of the guns, to capture the earthworks and enter the town; while the 64th made a flank movement on the left, and cut off the communication from the town by a chaussée and bridge over the lake. His few horse could do nothing for want of open ground on which to manœuvre; but his guns and his infantry soon captured the place and drove the enemy before them. In these two battles on one day, he had 12 killed and 76 wounded; while the enemy is supposed to have lost half as many men as Havelock's whole force. He also captured 19 guns, but as he had no gunners to work them, or horses to draw them, they were destroyed—two by spiking, and seventeen by shot. In a dispatch relating to this day's hard work, the general, after describing the brief but desperate contest among the loopholed houses, said: 'Here some daring feats of bravery were performed. Private Patrick Cavanagh, of the 64th, was cut literally in pieces by the enemy, while setting an example of distinguished gallantry. Had he lived I should have deemed him worthy of the Victoria Cross; it could never have glittered on a more gallant breast.' This mode of noticing the merit of private soldiers endeared Havelock to his troops. Cavanagh had been the first to leap over a wall from behind which it was necessary to drive the enemy; he found himself confronted by at least a dozen troopers, two or three of whom he killed; but he was cut to pieces by the rest before his comrades could come to his aid.

It must have been with a pang of deep regret that the general, hitherto successful in every encounter, found it necessary, on the 31st of July, to make his first retrograde movement. He never scrupled to attack thousands of the enemy with hundreds of his own troops, in open battle; the odds, whether five to one or ten to one, did not deter him; but when his whole force, his miniature army of operations, became reduced to little more than the number for one full regiment, the question arose whether any men would be left at all, after fighting the whole distance to Lucknow. He had no means for crossing the Sye river or the great canal, as the enemy had taken care either to destroy or to guard all the bridges; and in every military requirement—except courage—his force was becoming daily weaker. Besides officers and men who had been killed or wounded in fair fight, numbers had been struck down by the sun; while others, through exposure to swamps and marshes, had been seized with cholera, diarrhœa, and dysentery; insomuch that Havelock was losing at the rate of fifty men a day. In addition to all this, as he could leave no men behind him to keep open the communication with Cawnpore, he was obliged to take all his sick and wounded with him. His little band being now reduced by battle and disease to 1364 men, he determined on receding two short marches, to wait until reinforcements of some kind could reach him. Colonel Tytler, his quartermaster-general, strongly confirmed the necessity of this retreat. He saw no possibility of more than 600 men reaching Lucknow alive and in fighting condition; and they would then have had two miles of street-fighting before reaching the Residency. He recommended a retreat from Busherutgunje to Mungulwar; and this retreat was made under the earnest hope that aid would arrive soon enough to permit an advance to Lucknow within a week—aid most urgently needed, seeing that the garrison at that place was becoming very short of provisions. The troops, of course, were a little disheartened by this retrograde movement. They rested in Busherutgunje from the early morning of the 30th to the afternoon, when they received the order to retreat. It was not till after the reasons were explained to them, that his gallant companions in arms could at all reconcile themselves to this order from the general. They marched back that evening to Onao, and the following morning to Mungulwar.

The month of August began under dispiriting circumstances to Havelock. His chance of reaching Lucknow was smaller than ever; although greater than ever was the need of the garrison at that place for his assistance. He sent back his sick and wounded from Mungulwar to Cawnpore, across the Ganges, and committed them to Neill's keeping. He explained to that general the reasons for his retreat, and asked for further reinforcements if such were by any means obtainable. Neill was able simply to send a few dozens of men, bringing Havelock's effective number up to about 1400. With these he set about reorganising his little band during the first three days of the month—counting each man as if he had been a gem above price. Every native had been got rid of; all his troops were British; and therefore, few as they were, he felt entire reliance on them. On the 4th he sent out his handful of volunteer cavalry to reconnoitre the Lucknow road, to see what had become of the enemy. The troopers dashed through Onao without interruption; but on approaching Busherutgunje they saw ample evidence that the enemy were endeavouring to block up the line of communication, by occupying in force a series of hamlets between the town and the lake beyond it. The cavalry, having thus obtained news critically important to the general, galloped back the same evening to Onao, where they were joined by Havelock and his force from Mungulwar. After a night's bivouac at Onao, the British marched forth in early morn, and met their old enemy for a second time at Busherutgunje. Havelock, after a reconnaissance, resolved to deceive the enemy by a show of cavalry in front, while he sent round guns and infantry to turn their flanks. This manœuvre completely succeeded; the enemy were surprised, shelled out of the town, and pursued by the bayonet and the rifle through the whole of the hamlets to an open plain beyond. They suffered much, but safely drew off all their guns except two. Though a victory for Havelock, shewing the high qualities of his men, it was not one that cheered him much. The enemy were still between him and Lucknow, and he would have to encounter them again and again, with probably great reinforcements on their side, ere he could succeed in the object he had at heart. The morning of the 6th of August rose gloomily to him; for he was forced to a conclusion that an attack on Lucknow was wholly beyond his force. He returned from Busherutgunje through Onao to his old quarters at Mungulwar;

and when encamped there, wrote or telegraphed to the commander-in-chief that he must abandon his long-cherished enterprise until strengthened. All his staff-officers joined in the opinion that to advance now to Lucknow would be 'to court annihilation,' and would, moreover, seal the doom of the heroic Inglis in that city—seeing that that officer could not possibly hold out without the hopeful expectation, sooner or later, of relief from Cawnpore. 'I will remain,' added Havelock in his notification, 'till the last moment in this position (Mungulwar), strengthening it, and hourly improving my bridge-communication with Cawnpore, in the hope that some error of the enemy may enable me to strike a blow against them, and give the garrison an opportunity of

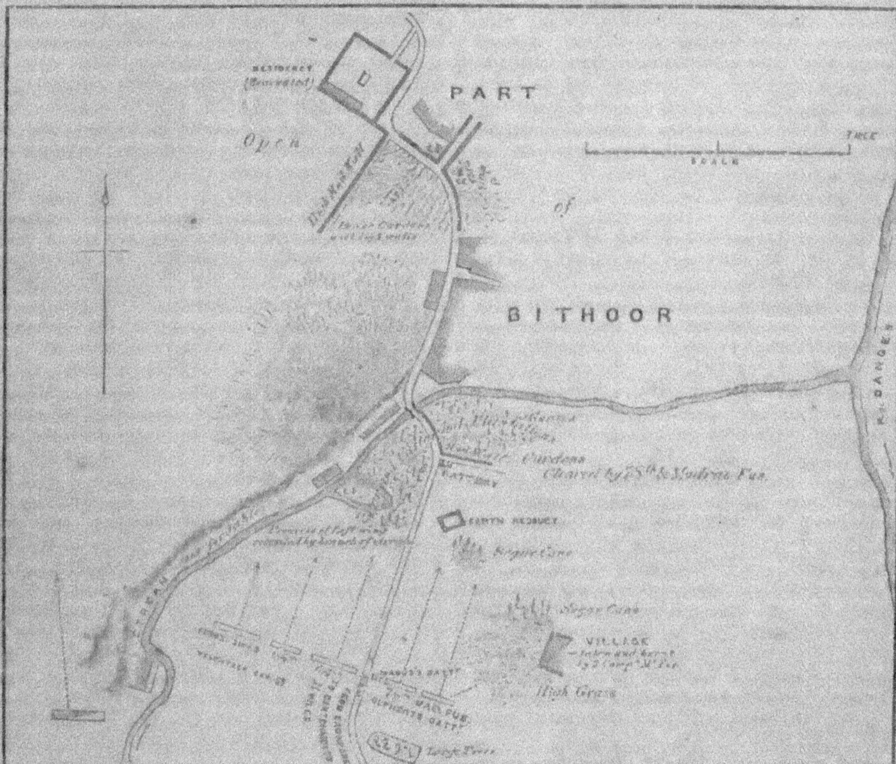

Plan of action near Bithoor, August 16, 1857.

blowing up their works and cutting their way out.' Havelock's army now only just exceeded 1000 effective men—a number absurd to designate as an army, were it not for its brilliant achievements. Between Mungulwar and Lucknow it was known that there were three strong posts, defended by 50 guns and 30,000 men. Every village on the road, too (this being, in the turbulent province of Oude), was found to be occupied by zemindars deadly hostile to the British. Neill had only 500 reliable troops at Cawnpore, of whom one-half were on the sick-list. Who can wonder, then, that even a Havelock shrank from an advance to Lucknow at such a time?

From the evening of the 6th to the morning of the 11th was the small overworked column encamped at Mungulwar—fighting against cholera as a more dreaded opponent than rebellious sepoys, and keeping a guarded watch on the distrusted Oudians around. On the 11th, however, this sojourn was disturbed; and the British found themselves called upon to meet the enemy for the third time at the town of Busherutgunje. Early in the morning Havelock received information that 4000 rebels, with some guns, had advanced from Nawabgunge to that place. It did not suit his views to have such a hostile force in position within a few hours' march of him; he therefore put his column in motion. His advanced guard drove the enemy's parties out of Onao; but when he marched onward to the vicinity of Busherutgunje, he found the enemy far more numerous than he had expected—spread out to a great distance right and left, and strongly intrenched in the centre. Havelock saw reasons for postponing his attack till the following day. He returned to Onao, where his troops bivouacked on the wet ground amid much discomfort, and after a very scanty supper. Such men, however, were not likely to make the worst of their troubles; they rose on the 12th, ready to vanquish the enemy in their usual style. In the two former battles of Busherutgunje, the enemy had depended chiefly on defences in and behind the town; but in this instance they had adopted the plan of intrenching the village of Boursekee Chowkee, in advance of the town. Havelock was much retarded in bringing his battery and supporting troops across the deep and wide morasses which protected the enemy's front, during which operation the enemy's shot and shell caused him some loss; but when these obstacles were surmounted, and his artillery brought into play, the 78th Highlanders, without firing a shot, rushed with a cheer upon the principal redoubt, and captured two out of the three horse-battery guns with which it was armed. The enemy's extreme left being also turned, they were soon in full retreat. But here, as before, the victory was little more than a manifestation of British superiority in the field of battle; the enemy lost six to one of the British, but still they remained on or near the Lucknow road. The brigadier, just alike to his humble soldiers and to his brother-officers, did not fail to mention the names of those who particularly distinguished themselves. On one occasion it was his own son Lieutenant Havelock; on another it was Patrick Cavanagh the private; and now it was Lieutenant Crowe of the 78th Highlanders, who, on this 12th of August, had been the first man to climb into the enemy's redoubt at Boursekee Chowkee—an achievement which afterwards brought him the Victoria cross.

The conqueror for the third time retreated from Busherutgunje to Mungulwar, of course a little weaker in men than in the morning. Havelock's object, in this third retreat, was not merely to reach Mungulwar, but to recross the Ganges to Cawnpore, there to wait for reinforcements before making another attempt to relieve Lucknow. The advance of the 4000 rebels on the 11th had been mainly with the view of cutting off the little band of heroes during this embarkation; but the battle of the 12th frustrated this; and by evening of the 13th the whole of the British had crossed the Ganges from the Oude bank to the Cawnpore bank, by a bridge of boats and a boat-equipage which Colonel Tytler and Captain Crommelin had used indefatigable exertions to prepare.

There can be no question that this retreat was regarded by the insurgents as a concession to their superior strength, as an admission that even a Havelock could not penetrate to Lucknow at that time; it elated them, and for the same reason it depressed the little band who had achieved so much and suffered so severely. The general himself was deeply grieved, for the prestige of the British name, but more immediately for the safety of Brigadier Inglis and his companions. But though grieved, he was too good a soldier to despond: he looked at his difficulties manfully. Those difficulties were indeed great. While he was fighting in Oude, bravely but vainly striving to advance to Lucknow, Nena Sahib had been collecting a motley assemblage of troops near Bithoor, for the purpose of re-establishing his power in that region. A whole month had been available to him for this purpose, from the middle of July to the middle of August; and during this time there had been assembled the 31st and 42d native infantry from Saugor, the 17th from Fyzabad, portions of the 34th disbanded at Barrackpore, troops of three mutinied cavalry regiments, and odds and ends of Mahrattas. The Nena had imitated Havelock in crossing into Oude, but had afterwards recrossed into the Doab, with the evident intention of attacking Neill's weak force at Cawnpore. Bithoor he re-occupied without difficulty, for Neill had no troops to station at that place, but now he planned an advance to Cawnpore itself. As soon as Havelock had brought his column across the Ganges on the 13th, the two generals concerted a plan; they resolved to rest the troops on the 14th, attack Nena Sahib's left wing on the 15th, and march to Bithoor on the 16th. Neill, with a mere handful of men, went out of his intrenchment, surprised the enemy's left, and drove them with precipitation from the vicinity of Cawnpore. This done, Havelock laid his plan for a third visit to Bithoor on the 16th. He marched out with about 1300 men—nearly all that he and Neill possessed between them—and came up to the enemy about mid-day. They had established a position in front of Bithoor, which Havelock characterised as one of the strongest he had ever seen. They had two guns and an earthen redoubt in and near a plantation of sugar and castor-oil plants, intrenched quadrangles filled with troops, and two villages with loopholed houses and walls. Havelock, after surveying the position, sent his artillery along the main road; consisting of Maude's battery, which had already rendered such good service, and Olphert's battery, recently forwarded from Allahabad under Lieutenant Smithett. While the guns proceeded along the main road, the infantry advanced in two wings on the right and left. After a brief exchange of artillery-fire, the 78th Highlanders and the Madras Fusiliers advanced in that fearless way which struck such astonishment and panic into the mutineers; they captured and burned a village, then forced their way through a sugar-plantation, then took the redoubt, then captured two guns placed in a battery, and drove the rebels before them at every point. The battery, redoubt, quadrangles, villages, and plantations having been thus conquered, the British crossed a bridge over a narrow but unfordable stream, and pursued the enemy into and right through the town of Bithoor. Beyond this it was impossible to pursue them, for Havelock had now scarcely a dozen troopers, and his infantry were utterly exhausted by marching and fighting during a fiercely hot day. The 64th and 84th foot, with the Ferozpore Sikhs, were disabled from taking a full share in the day's operations, by a bend or branch of the unfordable stream which intercepted their intended line of march; the chief glory of the day rested with the 78th Highlanders and the Madras Fusiliers. Havelock, in his dispatch relating to this battle, said: 'I must do the mutineers the justice to pronounce that they fought obstinately; otherwise they could not for a whole hour have held their own, even with such advantages of ground, against my powerful artillery-fire.' Worn out with fatigue, the British troops bivouacked that night near Bithoor; and on the 17th they returned to Cawnpore. They had been fighting for six or seven weeks under an Indian sun, almost from the day of their leaving Allahabad. 'Rest they must have,' said Neill, in one of his pithy telegrams. Captain Mackenzie, of the Highlanders, was among those who received wounds on this day.

This may be regarded as terminating the Havelock campaign in the strict sense of the term; that is, the campaign in which he was undisputed chief. He was destined, before the hand of death struck him down, to fight again against the rebellious sepoys, but under curious relations towards a brother-officer—relations strikingly honourable to both, as will presently be explained. A wonderful campaign it must indeed be called. Between the 12th of July and the 17th of August, Havelock had fought and won three battles in the Doab east of Cawnpore, three in the vicinity of Cawnpore and Bithoor, and four in Oude—ten battles in thirty-seven days; and this against an enemy manifold superior in numbers, and with an army which naturally became weaker by each battle, until at length its fighting power was almost extinguished.

Precarious, indeed, was the state to which Havelock's little force was reduced. Shells, balls, bullets, sabres, heat, fatigue, and disease, laid his poor fellows low; while his constant cry for reinforcements was—not unheeded, certainly—but left unsatisfied. The cry was everywhere the same—'Send us troops;' and the reply varied but little: 'We have none to send.' On the 19th of August, he had 17 officers and 466 men sick at Cawnpore; while those who were not sick were so exhausted as to be scarcely fit for active service. Havelock and Neill thirsted to encourage their handful of men by some brilliant achievement; but the one essential would be the relief of Lucknow, and for this they were not strong enough. The rebels, encouraged by this state of affairs, assembled in great force on the Oude side of the Ganges; they threatened to cross at Cawnpore, at a spot twelve miles lower down, and at Futtehpoor; while, on the other side, the Gwalior Contingent threatened the small British force from Calpee. Havelock telegraphed to the commander-in-chief: 'I could bring into the field 8 good guns, but the enemy are reported to have 29 or 30; these are great odds, and my 900 soldiers may be opposed to 5000 organised troops. The loss of a battle would ruin everything in this part of India.' After deducting his sick and wounded, and two detachments to guard the cantonment and the road to it, he had only 700 men ready for the field—perhaps the smallest 'army' that modern warfare has exhibited. Every day the general became more earnest and urgent in the language of his telegrams; he was quite willing to 'fight anything, and at any odds;' but his failure of victory would be ruinous at such a critical time. There were 5000 Gwalior troops threatening his rear on the Jumna; there were 20,000 Oudians watching him from the other side of the Ganges; there were 12,000 of the enemy on his left at Furruckabad; and to oppose these 37,000 armed and disciplined soldiers, he had only 700 effective men! The contrast would have been ridiculous, but for the moral grandeur which gave almost a sublimity to the devotedness of this little band. On the 21st, he announced that unless reinforcements arrived soon, he would be compelled to abandon all his hopes and plans, and return to Allahabad, whence he had started on his career of conquest seven weeks before. He endeavoured, meanwhile, to strengthen his position at Cawnpore, and to send off sick and wounded to Allahabad, as a temporary relief.

It would not be easy to decide who was beset by most anxiety towards the close of August—Havelock or Inglis. The former, after his vain attempt to reach Lucknow, wrote a note on the 4th which happily reached Inglis; telling him of what had occurred, and adding, 'You must aid us in every way, even to cutting your way out, if we can't force our way in. We have only a small force.' This note reached Inglis on the 15th; he wrote a reply on the 16th, which—after the messenger had been exposed to seven days of great peril—Havelock received on the 23d. This reply told how terrible was the position of the Lucknow garrison—120 sick and wounded; 220 women, and 230 children; food and all necessaries scanty; disease and filth all about them; officers toiling like common labourers from morning till night; soldiers and civilians nearly worn out with fatigue; enemy attacking every day, and forming mines to blow up the feeble intrenchments; and no means of carriage even if the garrison succeeded in quitting the place. The remaining days of the month were spent by Havelock inactively but hopefully. True, he was becoming almost invested by the rebels at Cawnpore, who saw that his handful of men could do little against them; but, on the other hand, telegraphic communication was well kept up with Allahabad, Benares, and Calcutta. He learned that Canning, Campbell, and Outram were busily engaged in sending up every possible reinforcement to him; and he wrote again and again to Inglis, urging him to remain firm to the last, in the cheerful trust that aid would come before the last act of despair—a surrender to the insurgents at Lucknow. There was mention of nearly 2000 men being either on their way or about to start from Calcutta, belonging to the 5th, 64th, 78th, 84th, and 90th regiments, the Madras Fusiliers, and the artillery; and there were confident hopes expressed of great service being rendered by the Naval Brigade, 500 'blue jackets,' under Captain Peel, who left Calcutta by steamer on the 20th. The governor-general knew that Brigadier Inglis had a quarter of a million sterling of government money under his charge in the Residency of Lucknow; and he sent telegrams to Havelock and Neill, urging them, if possible, to convey instructions to Inglis not to care about the money, but rather to use it in any way that might best contribute to the liberation of his heroic and suffering companions.

New names now appear upon the scene—those of Outram and Campbell. Major-general Sir James Outram, after successfully bringing the Persian war to an end, had been appointed by the governor-general to the military command of the Dinapoor and Cawnpore divisions; succeeding Wheeler, who was killed at Cawnpore, and Lloyd, who had fallen into disgrace at Dinapoor. This was a very important trust, seeing that it placed under his control all the British officers engaged in the various struggles at Lucknow, Cawnpore, Allahabad, Benares, Dinapoor, &c. He arrived at Dinapoor to assume this command on the 18th of August, two days after the date when Havelock had ended his series of ten battles. It happened, too, that Sir Colin Campbell arrived in India about the same time, to fill the office of commander-in-chief of all the armies of the crown and the Company in India. For a period of two months, Sir Patrick Grant had superintended military matters, remaining in consultation with Viscount Canning at Calcutta, and corresponding with the generals in the various provinces and divisions. Now, however, Sir Patrick returned to his former post at Madras, and Sir Colin assumed military command in his stead—remaining, like him, many weeks at Calcutta, where he could better organise an army than in the upper provinces. Campbell and Outram, the one at Calcutta and the other at Dinapoor, speedily settled by telegram that every possible exertion should be made to send up reinforcements to Havelock and Neill at Cawnpore; and that those gallant men should be encouraged to hold on, and not retreat from their important position. Outram had formed a plan entirely distinct from that in which Havelock was concerned—namely, to advance from Benares direct to Lucknow *viâ* Jounpoor, a route altogether northeast of the Ganges and the Doab; and to relieve Brigadier Inglis and the devoted garrison of that city. When, however, it became known that Inglis could not cut his way out of Lucknow without powerful assistance, and that Havelock himself was in danger at Cawnpore, Sir Colin Campbell suggested to Sir James Outram a reconsideration of his plan; pointing out that an advance of a hundred and fifty miles from Benares to Lucknow, through a country mostly in the hands of the enemy, would under any circumstances be very perilous; and submitting that a march by Allahabad to Cawnpore might probably be better. The great problem in effect was—how could Outram best assist Havelock and Neill, and how could all three best liberate Inglis from his difficulties? To solve this problem, the few remaining days of August, and the month of September, were looked forward to with anxiety.

The plan of operations once agreed upon, Sir James Outram engaged in it as quickly as possible. On the 1st of September, having made the necessary military arrangements for the safety of the Dinapoor region, he arrived at Allahabad, making a brief sojourn at Benares on his way. He took with him 90 men of H.M. 90th foot—a small instalment of the forces with which he hoped to strengthen Havelock's little band. Three days afterwards, 600 men of the same regiment reached Allahabad by steamers—a slow and sure way which the government was forced to adopt owing to the miserable deficiency in means of land-transport. No time was lost in making these valuable troops available. Reckoning up the various fragments of regiments which had arrived at Allahabad since Havelock took his departure from that place two months before, Outram found them to amount to something over 1700 men; he set off himself on the 5th with a first column of 673 men; Major Simmonds started on the same day with a second column of 674; about 90 more followed on the 6th; and 300 remained to guard Allahabad, and to form the nucleus for further reinforcements. On the 7th, Outram was at Hissa, progressing at a rate that would probably carry him to Cawnpore by the 15th—all his men eagerly hoping to have a brush with the 'Pandies,' and to aid in augmenting the gallant little band under Havelock.

While Sir James was on his march, he received information that a party of insurgents from Oude were about to cross the Ganges into Doab, at a place called Koondun Puttee, between Allahabad and Futtehpoor, and about twenty miles from the last-named town. Seeing the importance of frustrating this movement, he made arrangements accordingly. Being at Thureedon on the 9th of September, he placed a small force under the charge of Major Vincent Eyre, who had lately much distinguished himself at Arrah; consisting of 100 of H.M. 5th, and 50 of the 64th regiments, mounted on elephants, with two guns, tents, two days' cooked provisions, and supplies for three days more. These troops, not sorry at being selected for such a novel enterprise, started off and reached Hutgong by dusk on the 10th, where they were joined by 40 troopers of the 12th Irregular Horse under Captain Johnson. Eyre, after resting his men, made a moonlight march to Koondun Puttee, where he arrived at daybreak. The enemy, in surprise, rushed hastily to their boats, with a view of recrossing the Ganges into Oude; but this escape was not allowed to them. The sword, musket, rifle, and cannon brought them down in such numbers that hardly any saw Oude again. The number of the enemy was about 300; a number not large, but likely to prove very disastrous if they had obtained command of the road between Allahabad and Cawnpore. Havelock evidently attached much importance to this service, for he said in his dispatch: 'I now consider my communications secure, which otherwise must have been entirely cut off during our operations in Oude; and a general insurrection, I am

Brigadier-general Neill.

assured, would have followed throughout the Doab had the enemy not been destroyed—they being but the advanced-guard of more formidable invaders.' This work achieved, the different columns continued their march, until at length they safely reached Cawnpore.

The three generals—Outram, Havelock, and Neill—met on the 15th of September at Cawnpore, delighted at being able to reinforce each other for the hard work yet to be done. And now came a manifestation of noble self-denial, a chivalrous sacrifice of mere personal inclination to a higher sense of justice. Outram was higher in rank as a military officer, and held a higher command in that part of India; he might have claimed, and officially was entitled to claim, the command of the forthcoming expedition; but he, like others, had gloried in the deeds of Havelock, and was determined not to rob him of the honour of relieving Lucknow. On the 16th, Sir James Outram issued an order,* in which, among other things, he announced that Havelock had been raised from brigadier-general to major-general; that that noble soldier should have the opportunity of finishing what he had so well begun; that Outram would accompany him as chief-commissioner of Oude, and would fight under him as a volunteer, without interfering with his command; and that Havelock should not be superseded in the command by Outram until the relief of Lucknow should have been achieved. It was a worthy deed, marking, as Havelock well expressed it, 'characteristic generosity of feeling;' he announced it to his troops by an order on the same day, and 'expressed his hope that they would, by their exemplary and gallant conduct in the field, strive to justify the confidence thus reposed in them.'

The two generals wished at once to ascertain from Calcutta what were the views of Viscount Canning and Sir Colin Campbell concerning any ulterior proceedings at Lucknow. Outram sent a telegram to Canning to inquire whether, if Lucknow were recaptured, it should be held at all hazards, as a matter of success and prestige. The governor-general at once sent back a reply: 'Save the garrison; never mind our prestige just now, provided you liberate Inglis; we will recover prestige afterwards. I cannot just now send you any more troops. Save the British in the Residency, and act afterwards as your strength will permit.' The two generals proceeded to act on these instructions. Just two months had elapsed since Havelock had made his appearance at Cawnpore as a victor; and it was with great pain and anxiety that he had been forced to allow those two months to pass away without sending one single soldier, one single ration of food, to the forlorn band who so wonderfully stood their ground in the Residency at Lucknow. Now, however, he looked forward with brighter hopes; Outram was with him, under relations most friendly and honourable; and both generals were fully determined to suffer any sacrifice rather than leave Inglis and his companions unrelieved.

Outram himself planned the organisation of the new force for operations in Oude; but he placed Havelock at the head of it, and took care that Neill should have a share in the glory.† It consisted of two brigades of infantry, one of cavalry, one of artillery, and an engineer department.

It was on the 19th of September that the two generals crossed with this army into Oude, making use for that purpose of a bridge of boats over the Ganges, most laboriously constructed by Captain Crommelin. The enemy, assembled near the banks, retired after a nominal resistance to Mungulwar. The heavy guns and the baggage were crossed over on the 20th. On the 21st the British again came up with the enemy, turned their right flank, drove them from their position, inflicted on them a severe loss, and captured four guns. With the heroism of a true soldier, Sir James Outram headed one of the charges that brought about this victory; serving as a volunteer under Havelock. The enemy were not permitted to destroy the Bunnee bridge over the Sye; and thus the victors were enabled to pursue their route towards Lucknow. On the 23d, Havelock again found himself in presence of the enemy, who had taken up a strong position; their left posted in the enclosure of the Alum Bagh—a place destined to world-wide notoriety—and their centre and right on low hills. Alum Bagh is so near Lucknow that firing in the city could be distinctly heard; and Havelock therefore gave a volley with his largest guns, to tell the beleaguered garrison that aid was near. The British, in order to encounter the enemy, had to pass straight along the high road between morasses, during which they suffered much from artillery; but when once enabled to deploy to the right and left, they gradually gained an advantage, and added another to the list of their victories—driving the enemy before them, but at the same time suffering severely from the large numbers and the heavy firing of those to whom they were opposed. They had been marching three days under a perfect deluge of rain, irregularly fed, and badly housed in villages. Havelock determined, therefore, to pitch camp, and to give his exhausted troops one whole day's rest on the 24th.

At last came the eventful day, the 25th of September, when the beleaguered garrison at Lucknow were to experience the joy of seeing those whose arrival had been yearned for during

* 'The important duty of first relieving the garrison of Lucknow has been intrusted to Major-general Havelock, C.B.; and Major-general Outram feels that it is due to this distinguished officer, and to the strenuous and noble exertions which he has already made to effect that object, that to him should accrue the honour of the achievement.

'Major-general Outram is confident that the great end for which General Havelock and his brave troops have so long and so gloriously fought will now, under the blessing of Providence, be accomplished.

'The major-general, therefore, in gratitude for and admiration of the brilliant deeds in arms achieved by General Havelock and his gallant troops, will cheerfully waive his rank on the occasion, and will accompany the force to Lucknow in his civil capacity as chief-commissioner of Oude, tendering his military services to General Havelock as a volunteer.

'On the relief of Lucknow, the major-general will resume his position at the head of the forces.'

† 'FIRST INFANTRY BRIGADE.

'The 5th Fusiliers; 84th regiment; detachments 64th foot and 1st Madras Fusiliers:—Brigadier-general Neill commanding, and nominating his own brigade staff.

'SECOND INFANTRY BRIGADE.

'Her Majesty's 78th Highlanders; her Majesty's 90th Light Infantry; and the Sikh regiment of Ferozpore:—Brigadier Hamilton commanding, and nominating his own brigade staff.

'THIRD (ARTILLERY) BRIGADE.

'Captain Maude's battery; Captain Olphert's battery; Brevet-Major Eyre's battery:—Major Cope to command, and to appoint his own staff.

'CAVALRY.

'Volunteer cavalry to the left; Irregular cavalry to the right:—Captain Barrow to command.

'ENGINEER DEPARTMENT.

'Chief-engineer, Captain Crommelin; assistant-engineers, Lieutenants Leonard and Judge.

'Major-general H. Havelock, C.B., to command the force.'

so long and anxious a period. Early on that morning, after depositing his baggage and tents under an escort in the Alum Bagh, Havelock pursued his march. The 1st brigade, with Outram attached to it as a volunteer, drove the enemy from a succession of gardens and walled enclosures; while the other brigades supported it. From the bridge of the Char Bagh over the canal, to the Residency at Lucknow, was a distance in a straight line of about two miles; and this interval was cut by trenches, crossed by palisades, and intersected by loopholed houses. Progress in this direction being so much obstructed, Havelock resolved to deploy along a narrow road that skirted the left bank of the canal. On they went, until they came opposite the palace of Kaiser or Kissurah Bagh, where two guns and a body of insurgents were placed; and here the fire poured out on them was so tremendous that, to use the words of the general, 'nothing could live under it;' his troops had to pass a bridge partly under the influence of this fire; but immediately afterwards they received the shelter of buildings adjacent to the palace of Fureed Buksh. Darkness now coming on, it was at one time proposed that the force should halt for the night in and near the court of this palace; but Havelock could not bear the idea of leaving the Residency for another night in the hands of the enemy; he therefore ordered his trusty Highlanders, and little less trusty Sikhs, to take the lead in the tremendous ordeal of a street-fight through the large city of Lucknow. It was a desperate struggle, but it was for a great purpose—and it succeeded. On that night, within the British Residency, Havelock and Outram clasped hands with Inglis, and listened to the outpourings of full hearts all around them. The sick and the wounded, the broken-down and the emaciated, the military and the civilians, the officers and the soldiers, the women and the children—all within the Residency had passed a day of agonised suspense, unable to help in their own deliverance; but when at length Havelock's advanced column could be seen in a street visible from the buildings of the Residency—then broke forth such a cheer as none can know but those placed in similar circumstances.

When General Havelock penned a hasty dispatch narrating the events of this day, he said: 'To form a notion of the obstacles overcome, a reference must be made to the events that are known to have occurred at Buenos Ayres and Saragossa. Our advance was through streets of flat-roofed and loopholed houses, each forming a separate fortress. I am filled with surprise at the success of operations which demanded the efforts of 10,000 good troops.' The advantage cost him dearly. Sir James Outram received a flesh-wound in the arm early in the day, but nothing could subdue his spirit; though faint from loss of blood, he continued till the end of the operations to sit on his horse, from which he only dismounted at the gate of the Residency. Greatest loss of all was that of the gallant and energetic Brigadier-general Neill, who from the 3d of June to the 25th of September had been almost incessantly engaged in conflicts with the enemy, in and between the cities of Benares, Allahabad, Cawnpore, and Lucknow. He fell, to fight no more. From the time when he left his native home in Ayrshire, a stripling sixteen years of age, he had passed thirty years of his life in service, and had been a trusty and trusted officer.* But although the loss of Neill was the most deplored, on account of the peculiar services which he had rendered, Havelock had to lament the melancholy list of gallant officers who had equally desired to shew themselves as true soldiers on this day.† No less than ten officers were either killed or wounded in the 78th Highlanders alone—shewing how terrible must have been the work in which that heroic regiment led. The whole list of casualties comprised 119 officers and men killed, 339 wounded, and 77 missing. Of these last Havelock said: 'I much fear that, some or all, they have fallen into the hands of a merciless foe.' Thus was the force reduced by more than five hundred men in one day.

On the evening of this day, the 25th of September, Major-general Havelock, within the Residency at Lucknow, gave back to Sir James Outram the charge which had so generously been intrusted to him. He became second in command to one who had all day fought chivalrously under him as a volunteer. Here, then, this chapter may end. It was the last day of Havelock's campaign as an independent commander. What else he did before disease ended his valuable life; what the Lucknow garrison had effected to maintain their perilous position during so many weary weeks; what were the circumstances that rendered necessary many more weeks of detention in the Residency; by whom and at what time they were really and finally relieved—are subjects that will engage our attention in future pages.

* The Queen afterwards gave to the brigadier-general's wife the title which she would have acquired in the regular way if her gallant husband had lived a few weeks longer—that of Lady Neill.

† *Officers Killed.*—Brigadier-general Neill; Brigade-major Cooper; Lieutenant-colonel Bazely; Captain Pakenham; Lieutenants Crump, Warren, Bateman, Webster, Kirby, Poole, and Moultrie.

Officers Wounded.—Major-general Sir J. Outram; Lieutenant-colonel Tytler; Captains Becher, Orr, Dodgson, Crommelin, Olphert, L'Estrange, Johnson, Lockhart, Hastings, and Willis; Lieutenants Sitwell, Havelock, Lynch, Palliser, Swanston, Birch, Crowe, Swanson, Grant, Jolly, Macpherson, Barry, Oakley, Woolhouse, Knight, Preston, Arnold, and Bailey. Some of the wounded officers afterwards died of their wounds.

CHAPTER XVI.

THE DINAPOOR MUTINY, AND ITS CONSEQUENCES.

AFTER the first startling outbreak at Meerut, there was no instance of mutiny that threw consternation over a more widely spreading range of country than that at Dinapoor. This military station is in the midst of the thickly populated province of Behar, between Bengal and Oude; a province rich in opium, rice, and indigo plantations, and inhabited chiefly by a class of Hindoos less warlike than those towards the west. The Dinapoor mutiny was the one great event in the eastern half of Northern India during July and August; and on this account it may conveniently be treated as the central nucleus around which all the minor events grouped themselves. In the regions surrounding the lower course of the Ganges, and its branch the Hoogly, the disturbances were of minor character; but along both sides of the great trunk-road there was much more agitation, especially after the mutiny at the station above named. Nevertheless, it will be desirable to take a bird's-eye glance at Bengal and Behar generally in this chapter, in relation to the events of July and August—keeping steadily in mind the 25th of July, as the day on which the occurrences at Dinapoor agitated all the natives, paralysed many of the Europeans, and led to a train of truly remarkable proceedings in and near the town of Arrah.

First, then, for Calcutta, the Anglo-Indian capital. This city was not afflicted by a mutiny, in the usual meaning of the term, at any time during the year. Many reasons might be assigned for this exemption. There were on all occasions more Europeans at Calcutta than in any other city in India, who could have presented a formidable defence-corps if they chose to combine for that purpose. There was the majesty of a vice-regal court at Calcutta, not without its effect on the impressionable minds of Asiatics. There were the head-quarters of all authority in the city, insuring the promptest measures if exigency should demand them. And lastly, Calcutta being the landing-place for most of the English troops, rebel sepoys could never hope for much chance of success in that capital. Mutiny there was not, but panic unquestionably appeared—panic among the Europeans who did not belong to the Company's service, and whose imaginations were excited by the terrible narratives brought in from the northwest, and highly coloured during their transmission. It was an unfortunate circumstance that many of these persons were hostile to the government of Viscount Canning; and this hostility was especially displayed by those connected with the press, on account of the restrictions already adverted to. Whatever may be the varieties of opinion on the matters at issue, it is unquestionable that difficulties were thrown in the way of the executive by this want of accord. India has for a long period been rich in coteries and parties. Among military men, the Queen's officers and the Company's officers have had a little emulative pique; among non-military men, there has been an envy by the non-officials of the civil servants of the Company; and the military and the civilians have had their own grounds for antagonism. Calcutta, above all other places, has been marked by these sources of discord.

Towards the close of July the government deemed it prudent to ascertain what was the state of affairs in Calcutta with reference to the possession, sale, or concealment of arms. The Europeans in the city, in a state of perpetual alarm, kept up by unauthenticated paragraphs in the newspapers, had indulged a belief that the natives had lately made large purchases of arms, as if plotting mischief. Especially was this suspicion entertained when news arrived from Havelock and Neill that all the Europeans at Cawnpore had been murdered; almost wild with excitement, rage, and terror, the Calcutta community set no bounds to their apprehensions; they would fain have shot all the natives around them, in vague dread of some diabolical plot. Mr Wauchope, commissioner of police, was ordered to make strict inquiry concerning the possession of arms. He found that the sale of weapons had been very large during three months, but that nearly all the purchases had been made by Europeans, and that hardly a house in Calcutta, inhabited by Christians, was without one or more muskets or pistols. Many arms also had been purchased in Calcutta, and taken into the provinces for the use of indigo-planters, zemindars, and others, who naturally wished to have near them a few weapons at such a turbulent period. Of any considerable purchases of arms by the native population of Calcutta there was no proof, and the superintendent disbelieved the rumour. This was the third time in two months that the Anglo-Indian capital had been thrown into a paroxysm of terror on this subject; and although the panic was shown to be groundless, the authorities nevertheless believed it to be expedient to cause all firearms in the city to be registered.

No small part of the agitation at Calcutta arose

MAJOR VINCENT EYRE.

from the shackles on the press, already adverted to. Men of extreme opinions, and men of excited feelings, longing to pour out their thoughts on paper, found themselves less able so to do than in times gone by; there was the seizure of their printing apparatus, the infliction of a heavy fine, confronting them, and checking the movement of their pens. Sufficient transpired, however, to render manifest these two facts—that the European community at Calcutta violently hated the natives generally, and violently opposed Viscount Canning personally. There was a very general acquiescence in some such code of rules as the following, for dealing with the natives—that every mutineer who had taken up arms or quitted his ranks should be put to death; that every native, not a soldier, who aided the mutineers, should in like manner be put to death; that in every village in which a European had been murdered, a telegraph wire cut, or a dâk stolen, a swift tribunal should exercise summary justice; that every village in which a European fugitive had been insulted or refused aid should be heavily fined; and that vengeance, burning vengeance, was the only adequate measure to deal out to all who had offended. The distressing tales brought by the fugitives had much effect in keeping up the feeling denoted by such suggestions as these. It was under the influence of the same disturbed state of the public mind, that an address or petition was got up, condemnatory alike of Viscount Canning and of the East India Company; it was intended to work a considerable effect in England; but the obviously one-sided line of argument vitiated its force and damaged its reception.

As the month of July advanced, and fugitives came in from the disturbed provinces, arrangements were made for accommodating them at

Calcutta, and—as we have seen—for alleviating their wants. It became also a point of much importance to provide barracks or temporary homes of some kind for the troops expected to arrive by sea from various regions. Among buildings set apart for this latter purpose were the Town Hall, the Free School, the Pleaders' Chambers in the Sudder Court, and the Lower Orphan School at Kidderpore. Many months would necessarily elapse before troops in large numbers could arrive; but even a single regiment would require considerable space to house it before it could be sent up the country. In what way, during July and August, the English troops were sent to the seats of disturbance, has already been sufficiently noticed; some were despatched by steamers up the Ganges to Patna, Benares, and Allahabad; while the rest mostly went from Calcutta to Raneegunge by railway, and thence pursued their land-journey by any vehicles obtainable.

It may here be remarked, that when Sir Colin Campbell arrived at Calcutta, an immense amount of labour presented itself to his notice. Before he could decide whether to advance northwest to the seat of war, or to remain at the capital, he had carefully to examine the military condition of India. The records of the war department were at Simla, while the centre of authority was at Calcutta. The principal officers were scattered throughout the disturbed districts; the desultory and isolated struggles had relaxed the bond of military obedience; the reinforcements as they arrived had to be fitted into their places; the detached forces had to be brought into subordination to some general plan; and the different branches of the service had to be brought into harmony one with another. Hence Calcutta was for several weeks the head-quarters of the veteran commander-in-chief, while these all-important details of military organisation were in progress.

In the wide belt of country forming the eastern margin of India, from the Himalaya in the north to Pegu in the south, there was no mutiny properly so called during July and August. All the disturbances were limited to threatening symptoms which, if not attended to, might have proved dangerous. The nature of these symptoms may be illustrated by a few examples. At Jelpigoree, early in July, two men were detected tampering with the sepoys of the 73d N.I.; and a trooper of the 11th irregular cavalry was found guilty of insubordination. At Dinagepore the moulvies or Mussulman religious teachers began to spread seditious rumours. At Jessore, similar Mussulman tendencies were manifested. In the third week of July tranquillity prevailed throughout the divisions of Aracan, Chittagong, Dacca, Assam, and Darjeeling, comprising the belt above adverted to; and if agitation were more observable towards the close of the month, it was traceable to news of the Dinapoor mutiny, presently to be noticed. Early in August the Jelpigoree native troops were found to be in a very unsettled state, ready to mutiny at any time; and on the 15th a plot was discovered for murdering the officers and decamping towards the west. In consequence of this, orders were sent to Assam and Darjeeling to aid the Jelpigoree officers in case of need. During the remainder of August, a close watch was kept on the 73d N. I., the chief native regiment in that part of India, sufficient to prevent actual outbreaks; and native servants were disarmed during the Mohurrum or Mohammedan festival, to guard against the effects of fanaticism. Perhaps, however, the tranquillity of this eastern belt was more efficiently secured by the near neighbourhood of half-civilised border tribes, who had but little sympathy with the real Hindustanis, and were willing to enter into the Company's service as irregular troops and armed police.

Passing westward, to the line of route along the Hoogly to the Ganges, and the country near it, we find traces of a little more turbulency, owing to the presence of a greater number of native troops. About the middle of July, the Barrackpore authorities asked for permission to disarm the villages near at hand, in order to render more effectual the previous disarming of native troops at Barrackpore itself—treated in a former chapter. Early in August the behaviour of the troops at Berhampore became suspicious; they had heard of the mutiny of the 8th N. I. at places further west, and were with difficulty kept from imitating the pernicious example. In the middle of the month, the commissioner of Bhagulpore deemed it necessary to detain two detachments of H.M. 5th Fusiliers, on their way up the Ganges, at Bhagulpore and Monghir; for the 32d native infantry, and the 5th irregular cavalry, exhibited symptoms not to be neglected. After the occurrences at Dinapoor, the region around Berhampore and Moorshedabad could no longer be kept in peace while the native troops retained their arms; it was determined therefore, by Mr Spencer the commissioner, and Colonel Macgregor the commandant, to adopt decisive measures while there was yet time. On the 1st of August, having the aid of H.M. 90th foot, they disarmed the 63d native infantry and the 11th irregular cavalry at Berhampore; and on the following day they similarly disarmed all the inhabitants of that place and of Moorshedabad. Colonel Campbell, of the 90th, who had brought that regiment from England in splendid condition in the *Himalaya* steamer, and who was on his way up the Ganges to the disturbed districts, was the officer who practically effected this disarming at Berhampore; he spoke of the 11th irregular cavalry as one of the most superb regiments he had ever seen, in men, horses, and equipments; they were rendered almost savage by the skill with which the colonel managed his delicate task; and they reproached the sepoys of the 63d for having submitted so quietly to the disarming. A little further up the country, at Bhagulpore, about 200 troopers of the 5th irregular cavalry mutinied on the 14th of August, taking the road towards Bowsee, but harming none of their officers; on the 15th they passed through Bowsee to Rownee; and on the 18th left Rownee for Gayah—bound for the disturbed regions in the west. At Monghir, still higher up the Ganges, a terrible commotion was produced by this occurrence; the civil commissioner shut himself up in a fort, with a few of H.M. 5th Fusiliers, and left the city to its fate; but fortunately Sir James Outram was at the time passing up the Ganges in a steamer; he rebuked this pusillanimity, and recommended the officials to shew a bolder front.

Arriving now at the Patna and Dinapoor district, we must trace the progress of affairs more in detail, to shew how the authorities were placed before, and how after, the mutiny which it is the chief object of this chapter to narrate. Patna is a large and important city, the centre of an industrious region; while Dinapoor, in the immediate vicinity, is the largest military station between Barrackpore and Allahabad. Mr Tayler, civil commissioner, was the chief authority at the one place; Major-general Lloyd was military commandant at the other; and it was essentially necessary, for the preservation of peace in all that region, that these two officials should act in harmony. We have already seen (pp. 151–154) that, about the middle of June, the Patna district became much agitated by the news of disturbances in other quarters; that the police force was thereupon strengthened, and the ghats or landing-places watched; that some of the Company's treasure was removed to other stations; that places of rendezvous were agreed upon in case of emergency; that conspiracies among the Moslem inhabitants were more than once discovered, in concert with other conspirators at Lucknow and Cawnpore; and that on the 3d of July some of the fanatics murdered Dr Lyell, principal assistant to the opium agent. We have also seen, in the same chapter, that Dinapoor reposed upon a sort of moral volcano throughout June; that although the native troops made loud professions of loyalty, the Europeans were nevertheless in a very anxious position—all living near together, all on the alert, and most of them believing that the fidelity of the sepoys was not worth many days' purchase. Being thus on their guard, a mutiny ought not to have occurred at their station; but it *did* occur, and brought disgrace to the general who was responsible for military affairs in that division.

An intelligent clue to this whole series of transactions will be obtained by tracing—first, the Dinapoor mutiny itself; then the mingled disasters and successes, blunders and heroism, at Arrah; then the effect of the mutiny on the districts of Behar north of the Ganges; and, lastly, the effects on the wide-spreading region south of that river.

The distance between the two cities is about ten miles. The barracks of the European troops at Dinapoor were situated in a large square westward of the native town; beyond this were the native lines; and most western of all, by a very injudicious arrangement, was the magazine in which the percussion-caps were stored—a matter apparently small in itself, but serious in its consequences, as we shall presently see. Major-general Lloyd, commander of the station, and of a vast military region called the Dinapoor Division, had for some weeks been an object of almost as much anxiety to the Europeans at the station as the sepoys themselves. He was advanced in years, infirm, and irresolute. Unable to mount his horse without assistance, and dreading to give orders that would have the effect of sending any European troops away from Dinapoor, he was singularly unfitted to cope with the difficulties of those times. It points to some great defect in military routine, when one who had been a gallant officer in his better days was thus left in possession of a command he was no longer fitted to wield. Towards the close of July there were three regiments of Bengal native infantry at that station, the 7th, 8th, and 40th. There was also the greater portion of H.M. 10th foot, together with two companies of the 37th, and two troops of artillery. Not a British officer, except the major-general, doubted that these Europeans could have disarmed and controlled the sepoys, had the attempt been made at the proper time. The Calcutta inhabitants had petitioned the governor-general to disarm the native regiments at Dinapoor, and the officers of the Queen's regiments at that station had all along advocated a similar measure; but General Lloyd, like many other Company's officers, was proud of the sepoys, and trusted them to the last; and Viscount Canning placed reliance on his experience, to determine whether and when to effect this disarming. This reliance ended in unfortunate results.

On the 25th of July, the appearance of affairs led the major-general to exhibit less than his former confidence in the native troops; he shrank, it is true, from disarming them; but he sought to render their arms less dangerous by quietly removing the percussion-caps from the magazine. Now these caps had to be brought in front of the whole length of the sepoy lines on the way from the magazine to the English barracks. Early in the morning he sent the 10th and the artillery to the grand square, ready to be moved towards the sepoy lines if disturbance should occur. Two hackeries went down to the magazine under charge of an officer; the caps were placed in them; and the vehicles were drawn some distance towards the English lines. There then arose a shout among the sepoys: 'Kill the sahibs; don't let the caps be taken away!' The caps were taken, however, and safely conveyed to the officers' mess-room. The 10th were kept idle in the square or in barracks all the forenoon; while the native officers were ordered to go to the native lines, and ask the sepoys to give up the caps already issued to them. Some of the sepoys obeyed this strange demand—strange, because backed by no display of power; while some fired their muskets and threatened to shoot the officers. At the sound of these shots the

10th were ordered hastily to advance; they did so, but only to see the rebel sepoys run off as fast as their legs could carry them. Inexpressible was the mortification of the officers at this sight; three entire regiments escaped across fields, with their arms and accoutrements, to swell the ranks of the mutineers elsewhere; and so stupid had been the orders given, that there was no force at hand to stop them. The 10th, two companies of the 37th, and the artillery, all were burning to castigate these men; yet was the escape so quickly and completely effected that very few of the sepoys fell. The English destroyed the sepoy lines, but did not pursue the mutineers, for their perplexed commander would not permit them to leave him in danger. A surgeon of the 10th, on seeing the officers threatened by the sepoys, brought his hospital-guards to confront them; and even some of his patients got upon the flat roof of the hospital, and fired at the rebels. He then galloped off, and brought all the ladies and children to the barracks for safety. Every man of the 10th regiment was vexed and irritated by this day's work; complaints against the general were loud, deep, and many; and all the officers' letters told plainly of the general feeling among them. The regiment numbered little more than four hundred bayonets; for many men were sick in hospital, and a detachment was at Benares; but the four hundred, highly disciplined men, would not have hesitated an instant to disarm, to fight, to pursue, the three thousand rebels, had they been properly instructed and permitted so to do. During eight or ten weeks the officers of that regiment had urged the disarming of the sepoys; but their recommendations had not been listened to, and now it was too late. The general himself, on the forenoon of the 25th, went on board a steamer in the Ganges: 'I had no horse in cantonment,' he said. 'My stable was two miles distant; and being unable at the time to walk far or much, I thought I should be most useful on board the steamer with guns and riflemen.' It is deeply to be regretted that an old soldier should have been so placed as to find such an explanation necessary. As a consequence of this retreat to a place of shelter, the officers remained without commands and without a commander. Some of the mutineers embarked in boats, with the intention of going down the Ganges to Patna, or of crossing the river; but the detachment of the 37th, on shore and in the steamer, killed most of them by rifle-shots. The steamer did its work, unquestionably; but it was not the place for a military commander at such a time.

The question at once presented itself to the minds of all—whither had the rebels gone? Evidence was soon afforded that the direction taken was that of Arrah, a town twenty-four miles from Dinapoor, and separated from it by the river Sone. Arrah, as a town, was not of great importance; but it was the chief place in the district of Shahabad, and was surrounded by a country whence much revenue was obtained by the East India Company. During the troubles arising out of the mutiny, the chief authority at Arrah was the magistrate, Mr Wake—a man who, by his energy and public spirit, proved to be eminently fitted to hold power in perilous times. During the whole of June and July he had watched the progress of events with an anxious eye. Very soon after the mutiny commenced, he wrote to the authorities at Calcutta, describing the contents of certain native newspapers published about that time, and suggesting the propriety of curbing the licence of those productions. On the 10th of June he announced—with something like contempt in his manner—that most of the Europeans employed on the railway-works near Arrah had hurried away frightened by reports of mutinous symptoms at Ghazeepore and Buxar; and he dwelt on the pernicious effects of the example afforded by this timidity. About a week afterwards he induced them all to return. From time to time he applied to Dinapoor, Patna, and Calcutta, for a small detachment of troops to protect Arrah; but none could be afforded. He suspected some of the chieftains and zemindars near at hand, and more than suspected numerous disbanded sepoys who were seen in the district; to detect plots, he detained and opened letters at the post-office; but this course met with disapproval, as commencing a system liable to great abuse. There were two influential men in the neighbourhood—Baboo Koer Singh, and the Rajah of Doomraon—whose conduct Mr Wake scrutinised very closely; they professed friendship and loyalty to the government, but he doubted them. On the 11th of July, Arrah had become surrounded by so many disbanded sepoys, and natives ready for any mischief, that he applied to Patna for a party of Captain Rattray's Sikh police, which was furnished to him.

Thus matters proceeded until the 25th of July, when rumours of something disastrous at Dinapoor arrived. Arrah was now about to become suddenly famous. The 'Defence of Arrah' was to be narrated in dispatches and letters, in pamphlets and books, and was to cheer up many who had been humiliated by blunders committed elsewhere. True, it was only a house defended, not a town; it was less than a score of Europeans saved, not a whole community; yet did it bring well-deserved praise to those concerned in it, and encouragement to a spirited line of conduct on the part of the Company's civil servants elsewhere.

On the evening of the day just named, Mr Wake received express news that the native troops at Dinapoor had actually mutinied, or shewed symptoms of so doing within a few hours. On the morning of the 26th, he heard that some of the mutineers were crossing the river Sone, at a point sixteen miles from Dinapoor, and advancing upon Arrah. His Hindustani local police speedily ran away; but he and a trusty band of civilians resolved to remain at their posts. They selected the bungalow of one of their number, Mr Boyle, an engineer of the main trunk railway, and made that their fortress. Or, more correctly, it was a building which Mr Boyle had selected for some such purpose as this many days or even weeks before, when the state of affairs began to look gloomy; it was a detached two-storied house, about fifty feet square, standing within the same compound as the bungalow inhabited by Mr Boyle; he fortified it with stones and timber, and always kept some provisions in it. When the other civilians learned this, some of them smiled; but the smile became one of gratitude on the 26th of July. The Europeans who now took up their abode in this fortified house were Messrs Wake, Boyle, Littledale, Combe, Colvin, Halls, Field, Anderson, Godfrey, Cock, Tait, Hoyle, Delpeiron, De Songa, and Dacosta; and a Mohammedan deputy-collector, Syud Azimoodeen—all employed in various civil duties in or near Arrah: not a military man among them. With them were 50 Sikhs of Captain Rattray's police battalion. The ladies and children had been sent

Mr Boyle's house at Arrah, defended for seven days against 3000 rebels.

away to a place of safety. All that the defenders could bring into the house was meat and grain for a few days' short allowance for the Europeans, with a very scanty supply of food for the Sikhs. As to weapons, most of the Europeans, besides revolvers and hog-spears, had two double-barrelled guns each, or a gun and a rifle; they had abundance of ammunition, and wherewithal to make cartridges by thousands. Early in the morning of the 27th, nearly the whole of the Dinapoor mutineers marched into Arrah, released the prisoners in the jail, about four hundred in number, rushed to the collectorate, and looted the treasury of eighty thousand rupees. They then advanced to Boyle's house, and kept up a galling fire against it during the whole day, finding shelter behind trees and adjacent buildings. And now did Baboo Koer Singh shew himself in his true colours; he threw off the mask of friendliness, and boldly headed the mutineers. It was afterwards ascertained that this man, supposed to be in league with Nena Sahib, had openly become a rebel instantly on hearing of the mutiny at Dinapoor: it was he who had procured the boats in which they crossed the Sone; and he formed a plan for joining the Oude insurgents after plundering the treasury of Arrah. When in front of Mr Boyle's house, Koer Singh and his myrmidons endeavoured to bribe the Sikhs to desert; but these stanch fellows remained true to their salt. On the 28th the insurgents having brought two small cannon, the hastily defended house had then to bear a torrent of cannon-balls as well as of musket-bullets. Thus the siege continued day after day. The rebels even dragged one of the cannon up to the roof of Mr Boyle's bungalow, about sixty yards off, whence they could fire into the defended house. 'Nothing,' said Mr Wake in his dispatch, 'but the cowardice, ignorance, and want of unanimity of our enemies, prevented our fortification from being brought down about our ears.' As fast as the strength of the attack was increased, so fast did the garrison increase their defences; to oppose a new battery, a new barricade was raised; to defeat a mine, a counter-mine was run out. The Sikhs worked untiringly, and seemed to glory in the gallant defence they were making. When provisions began to run low, they made a sally one night, and brought in four sheep—a precious treasure to them at such a time. Seven whole days and nights did this continue—three thousand men besieging seventy. On the last two days the cowards offered 'terms,' which were contemptuously rejected. On the 2d of August the mutineers marched off to the west of Arrah to fight Major Vincent Eyre; how they fared, we shall see presently; but the battle brought about the liberation of Mr Wake and his companions. Wonderful to relate, only one member of the garrison, a Sikh policeman, received a dangerous wound; all the rest escaped with mere bruises and scratches. The Sikhs were justly proud of their share in the work. During the siege, when water ran short, they dug a well underneath the house, and continued their labour till they came to a spring; when all was happily ended, they requested that the well might be built into a permanent one, as a memento of their services; and that the house itself should receive the inscription of 'Futtehgurh' or 'stronghold of victory'—requests with which Mr Boyle was not at all unwilling to comply.

We must now direct attention again to Patna and Dinapoor, and notice the measures taken to check if possible the triumph of the mutineers. Mr Tayler at the one place had civil control, and General Lloyd at the other had military control, over Arrah as well as all other towns in the neighbourhood; and both felt that that station was placed in peril as soon as the mutineers moved westward from Dinapoor. Some weeks earlier, when the railway officials had hurried away from Arrah to Dinapoor in affright, Mr Tayler rebuked them, saying that, 'this is a crisis when every Englishman should feel that his individual example is of an importance which it is difficult to calculate. It is of great consequence that Europeans should exhibit neither alarm nor panic; and that, whenever it is practicable, they should band together for mutual defence and protection.' This rebuke aided Mr Wake's advice in bringing the railway people back to Arrah. It may here be remarked that Mr Tayler himself was, during the early part of July, in a state of discord, not only with the natives, but with many of the Europeans at Patna. He had an unseemly wrangle with Mr Lowis the magistrate; and was himself frequently reprimanded by the lieutenant-governor of Bengal. This anarchy appears to have arisen from the fact that, at a time of much difficulty, different views were entertained concerning the best policy to be pursued—views, advocated in a way that much obstructed public business.

It was about one o'clock on the 25th that the authorities at Patna heard alarming intelligence from Dinapoor. Mr Tayler at once summoned all the Europeans resident in the city to his house, where measures of defence were planned in case of an attack. At three o'clock a distant firing announced that the mutiny had taken place; and within an hour or two came the news that the mutinous regiments had marched off towards the west. Mr Tayler made up an expeditionary force of about 100 persons—Sikhs, Nujeebs, recruits, and volunteers—and sent it off that same night towards Arrah, to watch the movements of the rebels. At dawn on the following morning, however, unfavourable news came in from many country stations; and the commissioner, uneasy about Patna and its neighbourhood, recalled the corps. Tayler and Lloyd did not work well together at that crisis. The commissioner wrote to the general on the day after the mutiny, urging him to send 50 European troops either to Chupra or to Mozufferpoor, or both, to protect those places from an attack threatened by insurgents. To this application Lloyd returned a somewhat querulous answer—that he had only 600 Europeans at Dinapoor; that he was afraid of treachery on the part of Koer Singh; that he had already been blamed by the Calcutta authorities for listening to applications for troops to defend Patna, instead of sending them on to Allahabad; and that he could render no aid for the purposes required. Mr Tayler renewed the subject by announcing that he would send 50 Sikhs to the two places named; and he strongly urged the general to send 200 men to rout the mutineers who had gone to Arrah—proposing, at the same time, the establishment of a corps of volunteer cavalry among the officers and gentlemen of Patna and Dinapoor. In most of these matters Mr Tayler appears to have judged more soundly than General Lloyd; but in one point he was fatally in error—he believed that Baboo Koer Singh of Jugdispore would remain faithful to the British government.

If the 'defence of Arrah' has acquired notoriety, so has the 'disaster' at that place—to which we must now direct attention. This disaster was peculiarly mortifying to the British, as giving a temporary triumph to the mutineers, and as involving a positive loss of many English soldiers at a critical period. The revolt at Dinapoor having occurred on Saturday the 25th of July, General Lloyd made no effort until Monday the 27th to look after the sepoys; but on that day he sent a party of the 37th foot from Dinapoor towards Arrah, for the purpose of dispersing the mutineers assembled at that place, and for rescuing the European community hemmed in there. The troops went in the *Horungotta* steamer; but this unfortunately went aground after three hours' steaming, and the plan was frustrated. On the evening of Tuesday the 28th, another expedition was organised; and it was to this that the disastrous loss occurred. The steamer *Bombay* happening to arrive at Dinapoor in her downward passage on the Ganges, Lloyd detained it, and arranged to send a detachment on board. The *Bombay* was to take a certain number of troops, steam up to the spot where the *Horungotta* had run aground, take in tow the detachment from that steamer, and proceed up the river Sone to a landing-place as near as possible to Arrah. This river enters the Ganges at a point a few miles west of Dinapoor. Early in the morning of Wednesday the 29th, the steamer started, and after picking up the other detachment, the whole disembarked in the afternoon at Beharee Ghat—over 400 men in all, under Captain Dunbar.* The landing having been safely effected on the left or west bank of the Sone, the troops marched to a nullah which it was necessary to cross by means of boats. When, after a considerable delay, this was accomplished, they resumed their march, with a bright moon above them, a rough road beneath them, and a very few of the enemy in sight; and the evening was far advanced when they reached a bridge about a mile and a half short of Arrah. Here Captain Harrison of the 37th suggested that they should halt until daylight, and not incur the danger of entering the town by night; but Captain Dunbar, of the 10th, who commanded the force, overruled this suggestion, under an unfortunate impression that there would be little or no opposition. This was the fatal mistake that wrecked the whole enterprise. The troops arrived at Arrah at eleven at night, in black darkness, for the moon had set; then passed through the outskirts of the town—the 10th leading, then the Sikhs, then the 37th. Suddenly, while passing by a large tope of mango-trees, a dreadful musketry-fire flashed out of the gloom; the enemy, it now appeared, had been lying in ambush awaiting the arrival of the unsuspecting force. Mr Wake and his companions were startled by the sound of this musketry, audible enough in their beleaguered but well-defended house; they at once inferred that something wrong had occurred to British troops, and in this inference they were only too correct. The suddenness of the attack, and the blackness of the night, seem to have overwhelmed the detachment; the men lost their officers, the officers their men: some ran off the road to fire into the tope, others to obtain shelter; Dunbar fell dead; and Harrison had to assume the command of men whom, at midnight and in utter darkness, he could not see. The main body succeeded in reassembling in a field about four hundred yards from the tope; and there they remained until daylight—being joined at various periods of the night by stragglers, some wounded and some unhurt, and being fired at almost continually by the mutineers. It was a wretched humiliating night to the British. At daybreak they counted heads, and then found how severe had been their loss. Captain Harrison at once collecting the survivors into a body, marched them back ten or eleven miles to the steamer. The men had fasted so long (twenty-four hours), through some mismanagement, that they were too weak to act as skirmishers; they defended themselves as long as their ammunition lasted, but kept in column, pursued the whole way by a large body of the enemy, who picked off the poor fellows with fatal certainty. Arrived at the banks of the nullah, all organisation ceased; the men rushed to the boats in disorder; some were run aground, some drowned, some swam over, some were shot by sepoys and villagers on shore. How the rest reached the steamer, they hardly knew; but this they did know—that they had left many of their wounded comrades on shore, with the certain fate of being butchered and mutilated by the enemy. It was a mournful boat-load that the *Bombay* carried back to Dinapoor on the evening of the 30th of July. Captain Dunbar, Lieutenants Bagnall and Ingilby, Ensigns Erskine, Sale, Birkett, and Anderson, and Messrs Cooper and Platt (gentlemen-volunteers) were killed; Lieutenant Sandwith, Ensign Venour, and Messrs Garstin and Macdonell (gentlemen-volunteers) were wounded. Out of fifteen officers, twelve were killed or wounded. The dismal list enumerated 170 officers and men killed, and 120 wounded—290 out of 415! Havelock won half-a-dozen of his victories with no greater loss than this.

Here, then, was one disaster on the heels of another. General Lloyd's vacillation had permitted the native troops at Dinapoor to mutiny; and now the unfortunate Captain Dunbar's mismanagement had led to the destruction of nearly two-thirds of the force sent to rout those mutineers. Happily, Messrs Wake and Boyle, and their companions, still held out; and happily there was a gallant officer near who had the skill to command as well as the courage to fight. This officer was Major Vincent Eyre, of the artillery. Being *en route* up the Ganges with some guns from Dinapoor to Allahabad, and having arrived at Ghazeepore on the 28th of July, he there learned the critical position of the handful of Europeans in the house at Arrah. He applied to the authorities at Ghazeepore for permission to make an attempt to relieve Mr Wake; they gave it; he steamed back to Buxar, and there met a detachment of the 5th Fusiliers going up the Ganges. Finding the officers and men heartily willing to aid him, he formed a plan for marching a field-force from Buxar to Arrah, and there attacking the Dinapoor mutineers and their accomplice Koer Singh. Although dignified with the name of a field-force, it consisted simply of about 160 men of H.M. 5th Fusiliers under Captain L'Estrange, 12 mounted volunteers of the railway department, and three guns; but under an able commander, it was destined to prove more than a match for nearly *twenty times* its number of native troops. On the 30th of July, the morning when the detachment

* H.M. 10th foot, ...	153	officers and men.
H.M. 37th foot, ...	197	" "
Sikhs of police battalion, . . .	50	" "
Sikhs of mutinied regiments, . .	15	" "
	415	

from Dinapoor retreated from Arrah under such deplorable circumstances, Eyre commenced a series of operations west of that town. He started from Buxar, and marched twenty-eight miles to Shawpoor, where he heard of the disaster that had overwhelmed Captain Dunbar's party. He at once stated to General Lloyd, in a dispatch: 'I venture to affirm confidently that no such disaster would have been likely to occur, had that detachment advanced less precipitately, so as to have given full time for my force to have approached direct from the opposite side; for the rebels would then have been hemmed in between the two opposing forces, and must have been utterly routed.' Regret, however, being useless, Eyre proceeded to carry out his own plan. Hearing that the enemy intended to destroy the bridges *en route*, he pushed on again towards Arrah. On the 1st of August, finding the bridge at Bullowtee just cut, he hastily constructed a substitute, and marched on to Gujeratgunje by nightfall. Here he bivouacked for the night. At daybreak on the 2d he started again, and soon came in sight of the enemy, drawn up in great force in plantations on either side of the road, with inundated rice-fields in front; they had sallied out of Arrah to meet him. Perceiving that the enemy intended to turn his flanks, he boldly pushed on against their centre, penetrated it, and advanced to the village of Beebeegunje. The enemy, baffled by his tactics, gave up their first plan, and hastily sought to prevent his passage over a bridge near the village. In this they succeeded for a time, by destroying the bridge. After resting his troops a while, Eyre—seeing that the enemy had formed extensive earthworks beyond the stream, and that they occupied the houses of the village in great force—determined to make a detour to the right, and try to cross about a mile higher up. The enemy, seeing his object, followed him quickly, and attacked him with great boldness, being flushed by their recent victory over the luckless river detachment. They were nearly 2500 strong in mutinous sepoys alone, besides Koer Singh and his followers. After an hour's hard fighting, Eyre ordered Captain L'Estrange to make a charge with infantry. Promptly and gallantly that officer obeyed the order; his skirmishers on the right turned the enemy's flank, the guns with grape and shrapnell shells drove in the centre; and then the infantry advanced—driving the enemy, panic-stricken, in all directions. Losing no time, the major crossed the stream, and advanced through an open country to within four miles of Arrah. Here he was suddenly brought up by an impassable river, which cost him many hours' hard labour to bridge over—obtaining, fortunately, for that purpose, the aid of labourers employed on the East Indian Railway, just close at hand. Koer Singh and the rebels were so dismayed at these proceedings, that they left Arrah altogether, and retreated in various directions. It seems almost incredible, although the detailed official list places the matter beyond all doubt, that Major Eyre, during nine hours' severe fighting on this day, lost only 2 killed and 14 wounded.

As a means of enabling this energetic officer to follow up his success, a reinforcement was sent to him from Dinapoor on the 7th of August, consisting of 200 of H.M. 10th foot. This reinforcement entered Arrah on the next day; and a party of 100 Sikhs having arrived a day or two afterwards, the major was enabled to lay his plans for an expedition to Jugdispore, twelve miles distant, to which place Koer Singh and a large number of the mutineers had retired. The enterprise was not to be commenced without some caution; for the roads were difficult for the passage of troops at that season of the year, and the rebel chief's fort at Jugdispore was represented as being very strong and well defended. All this, however, only whetted the desire of Eyre's troops to try their mettle against the enemy. The force consisted of just 500 men,* with three guns. On the afternoon of the 11th he took his departure from Arrah, marched eight miles, and encamped for the night on the bank of the Gagur Nuddee. Resuming his progress next morning, he passed over two miles of rice-fields nearly under water, which rendered the draught of his guns very difficult. At eleven o'clock he espied some of the enemy in the village of Tola Narainpore, evidently preparing to resist his passage of a river immediately beyond. After a fight of skirmishers, Eyre opened a fire of grape which roused up a large body of the enemy concealed behind bushes. The detachment of the 10th foot, eager to emulate the previous heroism of their comrades of the 5th Fusiliers, and exasperated by their previous loss under Captain Dunbar, asked to be permitted to charge the enemy at once; Eyre consented; Captain Patterson led them on; they rushed with a shout and a cheer, and the enemy gave way before a charge which they found irresistible. The other infantry came up and assisted in dispersing the enemy from another village, Dullaur, beyond the river. This accomplished, Eyre marched a mile and a half through thick jungle to Jugdispore, maintaining a running-fight the whole way. The treacherous Koer Singh's stronghold was but feebly defended; Eyre took possession of it early in the afternoon, and with it large stores of grain, ammunition, and warlike material. The villagers around Jugdispore immediately sent in tokens of submission to the conqueror. Here as in the former instance, Major Eyre suffered wonderfully small loss; not a man of his force was killed on this 12th of August, and only six were wounded. The enemy lost 300.

Eyre did not give Koer Singh much time to recover himself. The rebel chief fled with a few followers to the Jutowrah jungle, where he had

* H.M. 5th Fusiliers, 137 men, under Captain L'Estrange; H.M. 10th foot, 197 men, under Captain Patterson; Sikh battalion, 150 men, under Mr Wake, of Arrah celebrity; mounted volunteers, 16, under Lieutenant Jackson.

a residence. Thither the major followed him on the 14th, or rather sent Captain L'Estrange with a detachment; but all had dispersed, sepoys and rebels alike; and L'Estrange returned after destroying residences belonging to Koer Singh and his two brothers.

It may suffice here to mention, that, so far as concerned the region south and southwest of Arrah, the remaining days of August were spent in the marching of the Dinapoor mutineers from place to place, and the plundering or threatening of many towns as they passed. The authorities would gladly have checked the course of so many armed rebels; but it became a question whether Eyre or any other officer was strong enough in Europeans to do so, and whether their aid was not more urgently needed at Allahabad, Cawnpore, and Lucknow. The mutineers marched southward of Mirzapore into Bundelcund, with the treacherous Koer Singh at their head. The engineers and others connected with the works for the East Indian railway were among those most perplexed by this movement of the rebels; because the various places occupied temporarily by those persons were just in the way of the mutineers. A lady, wife to one of these officials, has recorded in a letter that she and her friends received early news on the 25th of July that something was wrong at Dinapoor; that on the 26th the rebels themselves made their appearance; that the family got into a boat on the Sone, with no property but the clothes on their backs; that they immediately rowed off towards Dinapoor as the only means of escape; and that scarcely had they embarked when they saw bungalows and property of every description—belonging to individuals, to the railway company, and to the East India Company—a prey to devastating flames. 'Everything we have in the world is gone,' said the disconsolate writer; 'what to do, or where to go, we know not.' It is no wonder that the letters of such sufferers contained bitter comments on the government and politics of India—bitter, but often unjust.

The effects of this mutiny of the Dinapoor sepoys were, as has already been remarked, deep and wide-spreading. It is scarcely too much to say that twenty or thirty millions of persons were thrown into agitation by it. Along the whole line of the Ganges it was felt, from Calcutta up to Allahabad; along the great trunk-road between these two cities, it was felt; in the belt of country north of the Ganges; in the belt between the Ganges and the great road; in the belt south of the great road—in all these extensive regions, the news from Dinapoor threw Christians and natives alike into a ferment. Some discontented natives had vague hopes of advantage by the threatened dissolution of the English 'raj;' some of the villagers dreaded the approach of marauders who made little scruple in pillaging friend as well as foe; while all the Europeans cried out as with one voice: 'Send us reliable British troops.' Viscount Canning had none to send; and when ship-loads of troops did at length arrive at Calcutta, they were so urgently wanted higher up the country that he could spare few or none for regions east of Allahabad.

The revenue-officers were placed in a position of trying difficulty in those days. Besides collecting the taxes on land, salt, &c., and keeping the money in the local treasuries until it could be sent safely to Calcutta, they stored up large quantities of opium at certain factories, which were in their special keeping. The Company were the purchasers of the opium from the poppy-growers, and the sellers of it (at a large profit) to British merchants at Calcutta or Bombay; and during the interval of time between the buying and selling, the opium was stored in godowns or warehouses at certain large towns. Patna was the chief of these towns; and thus the revenue-officers of that place were especially interested in the maintenance of tranquillity among the native troops in the neighbouring station at Dinapoor. Dr Lyell, as was stated in a former page, fell a victim to Mussulman fanaticism at Patna early in July, about three weeks before the mutiny at Dinapoor. On the very day before his murder, anxious for the responsibility thrown upon him, he wrote an official letter which is interesting as illustrating the matter now under consideration. He had just succeeded the chief opium-agent, lately deceased, and had under his charge opium to the enormous value of *two millions* sterling, together with other government property of a quarter of a million. He had endeavoured to strengthen the opium godowns by barricading the gates with timber, and raising a breastwork of chests filled with sand on the flat roofs—fearful lest an excited rabble should attack the place. He had less than twenty Europeans on whom he could rely. Major-general Lloyd at Dinapoor either could not or would not supply him with any troops; and he sent to Calcutta urgent requisitions for British troops, Sikh police, and guns. Matters became worse; Lyell himself was massacred, and the native troops at Dinapoor mutinied; then, at the end of July, the revenue-officers at Patna announced to the government that the property under their charge had accumulated to three millions sterling, and that they could not adequately protect it unless reinforcements were sent. This appeared so serious at Calcutta, that arrangements were made for throwing a few British troops, and a few reliable Sikhs, into Patna.

The region north of the Ganges and east of Oude was in a perpetual state of flutter and uneasiness during those troubled weeks. There were few troops, either native or British; but the rumours from other quarters, gaining strength as they passed from mouth to mouth, occasioned great uneasiness, especially among the Europeans engaged in indigo-planting and other industrial pursuits. There was a small military station at Segowlie, not far from the Nepaul frontier, under the charge of Major Holmes; and this officer thought proper, even before the month of June was ended, to proclaim martial law in the districts between Segowlie and Patna. Mr Tayler, commissioner at the last-named city, thought this a bold proceeding; but he sanctioned it on account of the disturbed state of the country. The Calcutta government, however, considered that the major had overstrained his authority, and rebuked him for so doing. Before he could be informed of this rebuke, Holmes had assumed absolute military control over all the region between Patna and Goruckpore—giving orders to magistrates to watch the ghats or landing-places, to arrest suspicious persons, to offer rewards for the apprehension of rebels, to keep an eye on the petty rajahs and chieftains, to strengthen the native police, and to act in all things subordinately to him as military commander throughout the districts of Sarun, Tirhoot, and Chumparun. Military men applauded this step, but the civilians took umbrage at an assumption of power not warranted by any instructions received from Calcutta. This energetic but hapless officer was not permitted to remain many weeks in the position which he had taken up; his chief troops were the 12th irregular cavalry; and these rose on the 24th of July at Segowlie, murdered him and Mrs Holmes, as well as other Europeans, and then bent their steps towards Azimghur. This atrocity caused great consternation; for the 12th had been much trusted among the native regiments, as one whose gallantry was a guarantee for its fidelity. Gallantry was exchanged for cowardice and villainy this day. While the major and his wife were riding out, four of the troopers came up to the vehicle and *beheaded them both* as they sat; this being the signal, the rest of the regiment rose in mutiny, murdered the surgeon, his wife, and children, plundered the treasury, and made off in the way just noticed. When this savage act became known, and when the mutiny at Dinapoor on the next following day was also known, nothing could exceed the agitation among the Europeans. At Chupra, a station nearly opposite Arrah, the Europeans at once abandoned their homes and occupations, and ran off to Dinapoor, to be behind the shelter of a few hundred English bayonets; this was, indeed, not to be wondered at, for Chupra itself was threatened by the Segowlie mutineers. On the 30th, when the events at Dinapoor became known at Calcutta, the government did all and more than all that Major Holmes had before done; they declared martial law—not only in the northern districts of Sarun, Tirhoot, and Chumparun, but also in those districts of the Patna division south of the Ganges—Patna, Behar, and Shahabad. All through the month of August, the districts north of the river were in the state just noticed; no further mutinies took place there, but the various stations were thrown into frequent panics by the threatened irruption of insurgents from other quarters. It was chiefly from Oude that these onslaughts were feared; for that province contained more rebels than any other—more natives who, without being actually soldiers, were quite ready to embark in any desperate enterprise, military or marauding, against the English.

We have said that the whole region right and left of the main trunk-road was thrown into commotion by the mutiny at Dinapoor; this was certainly the case, if we add to the disturbing causes the revolt of one or two minor corps within this region itself. To describe how the region is parcelled out into divisions, districts, and collectorates, is wholly unnecessary: few in England know, and still fewer care, much concerning these territorial details; but if the reader will roughly mark out with his eye a sweep of country four hundred miles long by a hundred and fifty in width, beginning at Moorshedabad or Midnapore, and ending at Benares, and lying on the right or south of the Ganges—he will there see that which, in July and August, was a region of perplexity. Small military stations, and much more numerous civil stations, dot this space. The dispatches relating to the events of those two months spoke of dangers and alarms at places not one half of which are known even by name to any but persons intimately connected with India—Hazarebagh, Sheergotty, Burhee, Ramgurh, Sasseram, Bhagulpore, Bagoda, Ranchee, Bowsee, Gayah, Pittorea, Raneegunge, Rownee, Dorunda, Chyebassa, Rotas, Purulia, Bancorah, Dehree, Rotasgurh—all were places either disturbed by the visits of mutineers, or thrown into commotion lest those visits should be made at a time when means of defence were scanty.

It not unfrequently happened, at that troubled period, that while the British officers were making arrangements to disarm suspected regiments, the men of those regiments anticipated that proceeding by marching off in mutiny, of course taking their arms with them. Such happened to Lieutenant Graham, commanding at Hazarebagh. Being at Dorunda on the 30th of July, and learning that the 8th B. N. I. were unreliable at Hazarebagh, he marched off with a view to disarm them; taking with him about 220 Ramgurh infantry, 30 Ramgurh cavalry, and two 6-pounder guns. On that very day, long before he could reach Hazarebagh, the sepoys rose in mutiny, plundered the treasury, and released all the prisoners. Graham soon found himself in difficulties; he could not pass his guns over the river Damoodah at Ramgurh, because his bullocks were too few and too weak; and his Ramgurh infantry shewed signs of a disposition to march back to Dorunda and take the guns with them. After an anxious night, he crossed the river on the morning of the 31st, with his few troopers; but his infantry broke their faith, and marched away with the two guns. So far, therefore, from being able to disarm a suspected regiment, the lieutenant had the mortification of hearing that the regiment had mutinied, and, in addition, of seeing his own infantry follow the pernicious example. One fact cheered

Lieutenant Graham in his anxious duty; his 30 sowars remained faithful to him.. When Captain Drew, who commanded the detachment at Hazarebagh, came to make his report, it appeared that the men of the 8th B. N. I. numbered just 200 bayonets, forming two companies of one of the regiments lately mutinied at Dinapoor. When news reached the captain, on the 28th, of this last-named mutiny, he made arrangements for removing the ladies and children from the station, as he had seen enough to make him distrust his own men; he also sent to Colonel Robbins at Dorunda, for the aid of Lieutenant Graham's Ramgurh force, and to Calcutta for any available aid in the shape of European troops. Four ladies and six children were forwarded to a place of safety, and Captain Drew passed the 29th in some anxiety. On the 30th he addressed his men, praising the sepoys who in certain regiments had remained faithful while their comrades revolted; his native officers seemed to listen to him respectfully, but the sepoys maintained an ominous silence. On that same afternoon the men ran to the bells of arms, broke them open, and seized their muskets. The die was cast. All the officers, military and civil, jumped on their horses, and rode for twelve hours through jungle, reaching Bagoda on the trunk-road on the morning of the 31st; after two hours' rest they galloped forty miles further, then took transit dâk to Raneegunge, whence they travelled to Calcutta by railway. Meanwhile the mutineers released 800 prisoners, burned the bungalows, and pillaged the treasury of seventy thousand rupees. Whether a bold front might have prevented all this, cannot now be known; Captain Drew asserted that if he and the other officers had remained, they must inevitably have been killed on the spot.

An instructive illustration was afforded towards the close of July, of the intimate connection between the rebel sepoys and the villages of Behar or Western Bengal. The government issued a proclamation, offering rewards for the apprehension of mutineers and deserters. Mr Money, magistrate at Gayah, found by inquiries that the inhabitants of the villages refused to aid in giving up such men; but he hit upon a mode of ascertaining at least the connection between the sepoys and the villages respectively. Every sepoy remitted to his village a portion of his pay, by means of remittance-bills and descriptive rolls; each bill went to the accountant; the receipt of the payee went back to the regiment; while the descriptive roll was kept and filed in the office of the magistrate, shewing the name and regiment of the remitter. Mr Money thought it useful to collect and tabulate all these descriptive rolls for two years; and thus was able to obtain a record of the name of every sepoy belonging to every village within his jurisdiction. He could thus track any rebel soldier who might return to his village in hope of escaping punishment; for the native police, if ordered to apprehend a particular man in a particular district would do so, although unwilling to initiate inquiries. The matter is noted here, as shewing how closely the ties of family were kept up by the sepoys in this regular transmission of money from the soldier in his camp to his relations in their village.

During the first half of the month of July, before the state of affairs at Dinapoor had assumed a serious import, the towns and districts recently named were troubled rather by vague apprehensions than by actual dangers. At Gayah, the chief town of a district south of Patna, the magistrate was in much anxiety; the native inhabitants, in part hopefully and in part fearfully, were looking out daily for news from the mutineers in the Jumna and Ganges regions; and he felt much doubt whether the Company's treasury at that place was safe. So it was in most of the towns and stations; from Raneegunge, where the finished portion of the railway ended (at about a hundred and twenty miles from Calcutta), to the districts approaching Benares and Patna, magistrates and revenue-collectors, feeling their responsibility as civil servants of the Company, cried aloud to Calcutta for a few, even a very few, English troops, to set at rest their apprehensions; but Calcutta, as these pages have over and over again shewn, had no troops to spare except for the great stations further to the northwest.

As the month advanced, these symptoms of uneasiness increased in number and intensity; and when the isolated mutineers at Rownee, Monghir, Hazarebagh, &c., became intensified by the more momentous outbreak at Dinapoor, fear grew in some instances up to panic, and the Company's officers hastened away from stations which they believed themselves unable to hold. But here, as elsewhere, difficulties raised different qualities in different minds; many of these gentlemen behaved with a heroism worthy of all praise, as Mr Wake and Mr Boyle had done at Arrah. At some of the places not a single English soldier could be seen, or was likely to be seen at that time; and under those circumstances it was a fact of high importance that Captain Rattray's battalion of Sikh police remained stanch and true—ready to march in small detachments to any threatened spot, and always rendering good service. When the two companies of the 8th B.N.I. mutinied at Hazarebagh, towards the close of the month, and when the Ramgurh force followed their example instead of opposing them, the civilians in this wide region were really placed in great peril; Hazarebagh wished to know what Ramgurh would do, Sheergotty looked anxiously towards Gayah, and Raneegunge feared for the safety of its railway station. The Raneegunge officials, after fleeing to Calcutta, returned to their station about the middle of August, under the protection of Sikh police. The wife of one of the civil servants of the Company, writing from Raneegunge on the 7th of August, told of the sad condition in which European fugitives reached that place, coming from various disturbed districts. 'We are overwhelmed with refugees from all places. Some of the poor creatures have come without a thing but what they have on, and I am obliged to give them all changes of clothes for a time. Many came after riding seventy miles on one horse, and one gentleman without a saddle—a doctor and two others in their night-clothes—as they started while the wretches were firing into their bungalows. My husband had to lend them clothes to go to Calcutta in.' The telegraphic messages or written letters that passed between Calcutta and the various stations in Western Bengal, in July and August, occupy a very large space in the blue-books relating to the mutiny; they everywhere tell of officials expressing apprehensions of being obliged to flee unless reinforcements could be sent to them; and of distinct replies from the governor-general that, as he had no troops to send them, they must bear up as long as their sagacity and resolution would permit. The Europeans at Sheergotty left that station in a body, not because they were attacked, but because they saw no hope of defence if enemies should approach. Many Europeans, however, similarly placed, afterwards regretted that they had fled; instances were not few of the moral power obtained over the native mind by men who resolutely clung to their duty in moments of peril; while in those cases where the abandonment took place, 'the thieves and rabble of the neighbourhood,' as an eye-witness remarked, 'plundered the cutcheries and private houses; and those who had grudges against their neighbours began to hope and to prepare for an opportunity of vengeance.'

August found matters in an equally unsettled state. Many of the magistrates and collectors now had a new difficulty. Mr Tayler, as commissioner for the whole of the Patna division, ordered such of them as were under his control to abandon their stations and come into Patna for shelter; many were quite willing to do so; but others, resolute and determined men, did not like this appearance of shrinking from their duty in time of trouble. Mr Money, the magistrate of Gayah, called a meeting of the Europeans at that station, and read Mr Tayler's order to them; it was decided by vote to abandon the place and its treasure, and retreat to Patna. 'We formed rather a picturesque cavalcade,' said one of the number, 'as we wound out from Gayah; the elephants and horses; the scarlet of the Europeans contrasting with the white dresses of the Sikh soldiery; the party of gentlemen, armed to the teeth, who rode in the midst; and the motley assemblage of writers, servants, and hangers-on that crowded in the rear.' While on the road towards Patna, two of the gentlemen, Mr Money and Mr Hollings, feeling some humiliation at the position they were in, resolved to march back to their posts even if none others accompanied them. It happened that a few men of the 64th foot had passed through Gayah a day or two before, and Mr Money was enabled to bring them back for a short period. These two officials, it is true, were afterwards driven away from Gayah by a band of released prisoners, and fled to Calcutta; but their firmness in an hour of difficulty won for them approval and promotion from the government. This transaction at Gayah was connected with a series of quarrels which led to much partisan spirit. Mr Tayler had long been in disfavour with Mr Halliday, lieutenant-governor of Bengal, as an official of a very intractable and insubordinate character; and after the issue of the order lately adverted to, Mr Tayler was removed from his office altogether—a step that led to a storm of letters, papers, pamphlets, charges, and counter-charges, very exciting to the Calcutta community at that time, but having little permanent interest in connection with the mutiny.

As the month advanced, the government were able to send a few English troops to some of the stations above named. When Mr Halliday had learned, by telegrams and letters, that not a single European remained in Sheergotty or Bagoda, and that the native troops of the Ramgurh battalion had mutinied at Ranchee, Purulia, and elsewhere, he earnestly begged Lord Canning to send a few troops thither, or the whole region would be left at the mercy of marauding bands. This the governor-general was fortunately enabled to do, owing to the arrival about that time of troops from the China expedition.

When August ended, the Dinapoor mutineers, under Koer Singh, were marching onwards to the Jumna regions, as if with the intention of joining the mutineers in Bundelcund; the 12th irregulars, after their atrocity at Segowlie, were bending their steps towards Oude; the Ramgurh mutineers were marching westward to the Sone, as if to join Koer Singh; while the petty chieftains, liberated prisoners, and ruffians of all kinds, were looking out for 'loot' wherever there was a chance of obtaining it. Bengal and Behar exhibited nothing that could be dignified with the name of battles or war; it was simply anarchy, with insufficient force on the part of the authorities to restore order.

One unfortunate result of the Dinapoor mutiny was, that the Europeans contracted a sentiment of hatred towards the natives, so deadly as to defeat all the purposes of justice and fairness. When Sir James Outram was at Dinapoor, on his way up the Ganges, he found that some of the English soldiers had murdered several sepoys against whom nothing could be charged—in revenge for the terrible loss suffered at Arrah. Sir James noticed in one of his dispatches, with strong expressions of regret, the distortion of feeling thus brought about by the mutiny; distortion, because those soldiers were not, at other times, less inclined to be just and manly than the other regiments of her Majesty's army. It was a sore trial for men, when scenes of brutal cruelty were everywhere before their eyes, coolly to draw the line between justice and vengeance, and to discriminate between the innocent and the guilty.

CHAPTER XVII.

MINOR MUTINIES: JULY AND AUGUST.

THE reader will easily appreciate the grounds on which it is deemed inexpedient to carry out uninterruptedly the history of the mutiny at any one spot. Unless contemporaneous events elsewhere be noticed, links in the chain of causes and effects will be wanting. We have traced the siege of Delhi down to a certain point in the line of operations; we have followed the footsteps of Havelock until he reached the ball-shattered home of the European residents at Lucknow; we have watched the more immediate effects of the Dinapoor mutiny in the regions of Bengal and Behar. It now, however, becomes necessary to inquire what was doing elsewhere during the months of July and August—how the Europeans at Agra fared, when the stations on all sides of them were in the hands of the insurgents; how far the affrighted women and tender children succeeded in finding refuge at the hill-stations of Nynee Tal and its neighbourhood; what the Mahratta followers of Scindia and Holkar were doing; to what extent Rohilcund and the Cis-Sutlej territory were thrown into anarchy; whether or not Bombay and Madras, Nagpoor and the Nizam's country, remained at peace; how, in short, India generally was affected during the two months above named. Fortunately, this duty will not demand so full a measure of treatment as the analogous narratives for earlier months. The isolated revolts in June occupied attention in three successive Chapters*—because of their great number, the wide-spreading area over which they occurred, the sufferings of many of the Europeans, the romantic adventures of others, the daring bravery of nearly all, and the necessity for describing the geographical and military peculiarities of the several provinces and stations. These matters having once been treated with moderate fulness, the narrative may now proceed at an accelerated pace; insomuch that we shall be enabled, in the present chapter, to take a bird's-eye glance at the isolated or miscellaneous events, whether mutinies or suppressions of mutiny, belonging to the months of July and August.

Let us begin by directing attention to that small but thickly populated country lying between Patna and Allahabad, and extending in the other direction from the Ganges to Nepaul. Goruckpore, Ghazeepore, Azimghur, Jounpoor, and Benares, all lie within this region; Dinapoor, Buxar, Mirzapore, Sultanpore, and Fyzabad, lie just beyond it; and towns and villages of smaller character bestrew it more thickly than any other part of India. When Henry Lawrence was dead, and Inglis powerless in Oude for anything beyond maintaining his position in Lucknow; when Wheeler had been killed at Cawnpore, and Lloyd superseded at Dinapoor; when Colvin was shut up in Agra, and could do very little as lieutenant-governor of the Northwest Provinces—there was scarcely any one who could exercise control within the region just marked out. If a magistrate, collector, or commandant, succeeded in maintaining British supremacy by mingled courage and sagacity, so far well; but he was in few instances able to exercise power beyond the limits of his own town or station. Under these circumstances, Viscount Canning created a new office, that of 'Lieutenant-governor of the Central Provinces,' and gave it to Mr J. P. Grant, one of the members of the Supreme Council at Calcutta. The object in view was to restore order to a large range of country that had been thrown into utter anarchy. The title was not, perhaps, happily chosen; for there was already a 'Central India,' comprising the Mahratta country around Indore or Malwah; and, moreover, a jurisdiction was hardly 'central' that ran up to the borders of Nepaul. Passing by this, however, the newly aggregated 'Central Provinces' comprised the Allahabad division, the Benares division, and the Saugor division; containing a large number of important cities and towns.

When Mr Grant assumed his new duties in August, he found that the Goruckpore district was entirely in the hands of rebels. The leader of the

* Chaps. ix., x., xi.; pp. 147-191.

rebels was one Mahomed Hussein, who was at the head of a poorly armed rabble, rather than of an organised military force, and who, with that rabble, had been perpetrating acts of great barbarity. One civilian, Mr Bird, had displayed that gallant spirit which so honourably marked many of the Company's servants: he remained behind, at his own request, when the rest of the civil officers fled from Goruckpore; he hoped to be able to maintain his position, but was forced after a time to yield to the pressure of adverse circumstances, and escape to Bettiah. The governor-general, during the month of June, accepted aid which had been offered some time previously, by Jung Bahadoor of Nepaul. In pursuance of this agreement, three thousand Goorkhas were sent down from Khatmandoo, and entered British territory northward of Goruckpore. They were ordered on shortly afterwards to Azimghur; and most of the Goruckpore officials, availing themselves of this escort, quitted the station with their movables and the government treasure. Some of the Goorkhas then remained for a time at Azimghur, while the rest went to escort the treasure to Jounpoor and Benares. While at Goruckpore, the Goorkhas assisted in disarming such native troops as were at the station. Much was expected from these hardy troops, and it is only just to observe that they generally warranted the expectation. It was late in June that the arrangement was entered into, the immediate object in view being the pacification of the very districts now under notice.

The Azimghur district had its full share in the troubles of the period. During the first half of July, mutinous sepoys from other stations were frequently threatening the town of Azimghur, and keeping the Europeans perpetually on the watch. The 65th native infantry were very turbulent in the vicinity. On a particular day the Company's servants at the station held a council of war; some voted that Azimghur was untenable, and that a retreat should be made to Ghazeepore; but bolder councils prevailed with the majority. At last a regular battle with the enemy took place; a battle which has been described in such a lively manner by Mr Venables, deputy-magistrate of Azimghur, that we cannot do better than quote a portion of a letter in which he narrated the events of the day.* The action was really worthy of note even in a military sense; for a small force, headed by a civilian, defeated an enemy ten times as numerous. Mr Venables received the thanks of the government for his skill and courage on this occasion. But afterwards came a time of mortification. Of the native troops which formed his little army on the 18th, more than half belonged to the very regiment which mutinied a few days afterwards at Segowlie, after murdering their commandant, Major Holmes. Mr Venables pondered on the question: 'Will the detachment of the 12th irregulars remain faithful at Azimghur, when another portion of the same regiment has mutinied at Segowlie?' He thought such a proof of fidelity improbable; and therefore, he and the other Europeans sought to avert danger by removing from Azimghur to Ghazeepore, which they did on the 30th of July. The district all around the station at Azimghur remained at the mercy of lawless marauders until the arrival of the Goorkhas from Goruckpore, mentioned in the last paragraph. Then began a struggle, which should act with the most effective energy—Oudian insurgents from the west, openly hostile to the British; or Nepaul Goorkhas from the north, serving in alliance with the British—a struggle in which, it hardly need be said, many villages were reduced to ashes, and much disturbance of peaceful industry produced.

The Jounpoor district was even more completely disorganised than those of Goruckpore and Azimghur; it had been almost entirely abandoned since the first mutiny of the troops at that station in June. Not until after a Goorkha force had marched into Jounpoor in August, could the civil officers feel any safety in returning to their duties at that station.

Benares, the most important place hereabouts, became a temporary home for many officers who, by the revolt of their several native regiments, had been suddenly and unwillingly deprived of active duties; there were eight or ten of them, mostly belonging to Oude regiments which had revolted. When Jung Bahadoor agreed to send a body of Goorkha troops from Nepaul to the disturbed districts, the Calcutta government transmitted orders for some of these unemployed officers to meet those troops at Goruckpore, and act with them. Among those officers were Captain Boileau and Lieutenants Miles, Hall, and Campbell. It was early in July when this order was sent to Benares, but some weeks elapsed ere the Goorkhas reached Goruckpore. Before this co-operation with the Goorkhas took place, Benares was enabled to render a little good service against the rebels by the aid of British troops, not stationed at that place, but while on transit to the upper provinces. The gallant 78th Highlanders, journeying from Calcutta to Alla-

* 'On the morning of the 18th they were not a mile off, so at noon we marched through the city to meet them. Our force consisted of 160 sepoys and 100 irregular cavalry or sowars, one six-pounder, and eight men to work it. This gun was an old one that had been put up to fire every day at noon. I rigged it out with a new carriage, made shot and grape, and got it all in order. With my gun I kept the fellows in front in check; but there were too many of them. There were from 2500 to 3000 fighting-men, armed with matchlocks and swords, and many thousands who had come to plunder. They outflanked us on both sides, and the balls came in pretty fast. Men and horses were killed by my side, but, thank God, I escaped unhurt! We retired through the city to our intrenchments, followed by the enemy. They made several attacks, coming up every time within a hundred yards; but they could not stand the grape. At five P.M. they made their last attempt; but a lucky shot I made with the gun sent them to the right-about. They lost heart, and were seen no more. We killed from 150 to 200 of them, our own loss being 18 killed and wounded, and eight horses. All their wounded and a lot of others were cut up during their retreat by the rascally villagers, who would have done the same to us had the day gone against us. Our victory was complete. Not a house in Azimghur was plundered, and the whole of the rebels have since dispersed. Please God, as soon as I hear of Lucknow being relieved, I'll be after them again. They have paid me the compliment of offering five hundred rupees for my head.'

habad, were divided into portions according as the means of transport were presented, and according to the necessities of the districts through which they passed. On the 5th of July, Lieutenant-colonel Gordon, commanding the Benares district, saw the necessity of checking some insurgents near that city; and he intrusted that duty to Major Haliburton of the 78th. The major started on the morning of the 6th, with a mixed detachment of Europeans and natives, and marched eight miles on the Azimghur road. His advanced cavalry reported a large body of the enemy half a mile ahead, with their centre posted across the road, and their flanks resting on villages, partially concealed behind trees and rising-ground. Their number was about 500, aided by an equal number of villagers apparently eager for mischief. The contest was soon over, and the enemy repelled. The chief point that rendered the incident worthy of note was that a few of the 12th irregular cavalry, employed by Haliburton, shewed bad symptoms during the day; they did not charge the enemy with alacrity; and they appeared inclined to listen to the appeals made to their religious feelings by the natives whom they were called upon to oppose. These troopers belonged to the same regiment as those who afterwards mutinied at Segowlie.

After the departure of the Highlanders, this great and important Hindoo city was frequently thrown into excitement by mutinies or reports of mutinies at other places. Rumours came in early in August, to the effect that the irregular cavalry from Segowlie, after murdering their officers, were on their way to Jounpoor, thirty-five miles from Benares, with the intention of visiting Benares itself. The city contained at that time only 300 English soldiers, none of whom could safely be spared to go out and confront the rebels. The civil lines at Benares comprised that portion of the British station which contained the jails, the courts of justice, and the residences of the commissioner, judge, surgeon, &c.; it lay on the north of the Burnah River, while the military lines were on the south, the two being connected by a bridge. The civil station was thus peculiarly open to attack; and all that the authorities could do for it was to post a party of soldiers and two guns on the bridge; the prisoners were removed to the other side of the river, the courts were abandoned, and all valuable property was taken from the civil station to that of the European military in the cantonment. The Rev. James Kennedy, chaplain of the station, has in a letter mentioned a fact which shews in how agitated a state the English community at Benares were at that time;* illustrating in a striking way—as was more than once shewn during those turmoils in India—that the panic arising from an apprehended danger was often worse than the reality, paralysing the exertions of those who would have rendered good service had actual fighting with an open enemy commenced. No sooner had the dread of the Segowlie mutineers passed away, than an approach of those from Dinapoor was threatened. Colonel Gordon, seeing the mischief that would accrue from such a step, resolved to prevent it: he sent out his handful of English soldiers, not merely to check the approach of the rebels, but to drive them from the district altogether. Koer Singh and his rabble army did not wait for this conflict; they gave Benares a 'wide offing,' and bent their steps towards Mirzapore. While the few English soldiers were engaged on this duty, the sentinels left behind were aided by the residents, headed by the judge—all keeping watch and ward in turn, for the common safety.

Mirzapore, from its large size and great importance as a commercial city, and its position on the banks of the Ganges between Benares and Allahabad, was often placed in considerable peril. No mutiny actually occurred there, but the city was repeatedly threatened by mutineers from other quarters, who, if successful, would certainly have been aided by all the budmashes of the place, and by many Mussulmans higher in station than mere rabble. The European residents were perpetually on the watch. When a battery of artillery came up the Ganges *en route* to Allahabad, they earnestly entreated to be allowed to retain it for their own protection; but Neill, the presiding genius at that time, would not listen to this; Allahabad and Cawnpore must be thought of, and Mirzapore must shift for itself. When the affairs at Segowlie and Dinapoor became known, measures were taken for making some kind of stronghold at Mirzapore. The Europeans intrenched the largest and strongest house belonging to them, barricaded the streets, buried much property, placed other property in guarded boats on the river, and prepared for service four small guns and five hundred rounds of ammunition. On numbering heads, they found 135 persons, all of whom had separate duties or posts assigned to them in the hour of need; they also secured provision for a month. This judicious line of policy answered the desired purpose: the Dinapoor mutineers did not enter or molest Mirzapore. Those marauders passed westward along a line of route further removed from the Ganges, plundering as they went, and committing great devastation. On the 19th of August, a small force set out from Mirzapore to check those acts of violence; but the Dinapoor men generally managed to keep beyond the reach of pursuers. A little later, when other regiments had mutinied in the Saugor division, it was deemed prudent by the Calcutta authorities to send a portion of a Madras regiment, with two guns, to aid in the protection of Mirzapore.

It may here be remarked, that along the line

* 'In the evening there was a fearful though causeless panic at Raj-ghat, where the intrenchment is being made. The cry arose: "The enemy are coming." The workmen, 3000 in number, rushed down the hill as for their lives. Prisoners who were at work tried to make their escape, and were with difficulty recovered. Gentlemen ran for their rifles; the soldiers got under arms; the gunners rushed to their guns; and altogether, there was indescribable confusion and terror. All this was the result of a succession of peals of thunder, which were mistaken for the firing of artillery!'

of country immediately adjacent to the eastern frontier of Oude, the influence of that turbulent province was made abundantly manifest during the period now under notice. There were many zemindars near the border who maintained bodies of armed men on foot. A rebel chief of Sultanpore, one Mehudee Hussein, appeared to direct the movements in that region; he was one among many who received direct commissions from the rebel authorities at Lucknow, as chieftains expected to bring all their forces to bear against the British. This fact alone suffices to shew how completely Oude was at that time in the hands of the enemy.

Mr Grant, as lieutenant-governor of the Central Provinces, was called upon to exercise authority in the districts of Allahabad, Futtehpoor, Cawnpore, Banda, and Humeerpoor, as well as in those of Goruckpore, Ghazeepore, Jounpoor, Benares, and Mirzapore. When he settled down at Benares as his head-quarters, towards the close of August, he found that no civil business of the Company was carried on throughout the Doab, from Allahabad to Cawnpore, except at Allahabad itself. Neill and Havelock, by the gallant operations already described, obtained military control of the great line of road; but their troops being lamentably small in number, they were nearly powerless beyond a few miles' distance on either side of that road; while the judges and magistrates, the commissioners and collectors, had in only a few instances been able to resume their duties as civil servants of the Company. A large portion of the population, driven from their villages either by the rebel sepoys or by the British, had not yet returned; and the fertile Doab had become, for a time, almost a desert. Banda and Humeerpoor, British districts immediately south of the Doab, were temporarily but completely given up; scarcely an Englishman remained within them, unless at hide-and-seek. Some of the petty chiefs, including the rajahs of Mundah and Churkarree, remained faithful. For a time, police in the service of the Company were able to retain command in that part of the Allahabad division which lay north of the Ganges; but the Oudians, as August advanced, crossed the frontier, and gradually drove them away, thus further narrowing the belt of country within which the Company's 'raj' was respected. Koer Singh, whose name has so often been mentioned, was ruler for a time south of the Jumna, with his Dinapoor mutineers; it was supposed that he had offered his services to Nena Sahib and to the King of Delhi, in hopes of some substantial authority or advantages as a reward for his co-operation. This unsettled state of the region south of the Jumna placed Lieutenant Osborne in an extraordinary position. He was, as we have already seen (p. 180), British representative at the court of the Rajah of Rewah, a place south-west of Allahabad—unimportant in itself, but surrounded by districts every one of which was in a state of anarchy. Although the young rajah was friendly to the English, and aided the lieutenant in his military plans for checking the mutineers, it was at all times uncertain how far the Rewah troops themselves could be depended on. At a somewhat later date than that to which this chapter relates, Osborne was living in a tent at Rewah, with no Englishman of any grade near him, and uncertain whether he could rely for an hour on the fidelity of the native troops belonging to the rajah—defended by little else than his own indomitable force of character. Koer Singh and the Dinapoor mutineers had asked the rajah either to join them, or to allow them to pass through his territory; he opposed it; his troops wished it; and thus the rajah and the lieutenant were thrown into antagonism with the Rewah troops.

Another region or division placed under Mr Grant's lieutenant-governorship, Saugor, had witnessed very great disturbance during the month of June, as has already been shewn;* and he found the effects of that disturbance manifested in various ways throughout July and August. Rewah, Nowgong, Jhansi, Saugor, Jubbulpoor, Hosungabad—all had suffered, either from the mutiny of troops at those towns, or by the arrival of mutineers from other stations. Nagpoor was under a different government or control; but it would not on that account have escaped the perils of those evil days, had it not been that the troops distributed over that province belonged to the Madras rather than to the Bengal army—a most important difference, as we have had many opportunities of seeing. Mr Plowden, commissioner of Nagpoor, found it comparatively easy to maintain his own territory in peace, for the reason just stated; and he used all possible exertion to bring up troops from Madras, and send them on to the Saugor province. His advice to Major Erskine was, to disarm his Bengal troops at all the stations as soon as he could obtain Madras troops; but the numbers of these latter were not sufficient to permit the carrying out of such a plan. The Saugor territory, in having the peaceful part of Bengal on the east, and Nagpoor territory on the south, was pretty safe from disturbance on those frontiers; but having the Jumna region on the north, and the Mahratta dominions on the west, it had many sources of disturbance in those directions.

In the town and military station of Saugor, the state of affairs was very remarkable. Brigadier Sage, in the month of June (p. 178), had converted a large fort into a place of refuge for the ladies and families of the officers, provisioned it for six months, placed the guns in position, and guarded the whole by a body of European gunners. This he did, not because the native regiments at the station (31st and 42d B. N. I., and 3d irregular cavalry) had mutinied, but because they appeared very unsettled, and received tempting offers from scheming chieftains in the vicinity. The Calcutta authorities called upon the brigadier for an

* Chapter xi., pp. 177-181.

explanation of the grounds on which he had shut up all the Europeans at Saugor, three hundred in number, in the fort, without any actual mutiny at that place; but on account of interrupted dâks and telegraphs, many weeks elapsed before the various official communications could take place, and during those weeks the brigadier was responsible for the safety of the residents. The remarkable feature in all this was, not that the native troops should mutiny, or that the Europeans should live in a fortified residence, but that one regiment should remain faithful when others at the same spot repudiated allegiance. Early in July the 42d and the cavalry endeavoured to incite the 31st to mutiny; but not only did the latter remain true to their salt—they attacked and beat off the rebels. On the 7th of the month a regular battle ensued; the 31st and some of the irregular cavalry attacking the 42d and the rest of the irregulars, and expelling them altogether from the station. 'Well done, 31st,' said Major Erskine, when news of this event reached Jubbulpoor. It was not merely that two infantry regiments were in antagonism; but two wings of one cavalry regiment were also at open war with each other. So delighted were the English officers of the 31st at the conduct of their men, that they were eager to join in the fray; but the brigadier would not allow this; he distrusted all these regiments alike, and would not allow the officers to place themselves in peril. Many at Saugor thought that an excess of caution was herein exhibited.

The other chief place in the province, Jubbulpoor, as shewn in a former chapter (p. 178), had been thrown into much perplexity in the month of June by the news of mutiny at Jhansi and Nuseerabad; and Major Erskine, commissioner of the province, sought how he might best prevent the pestilence from spreading southeastward. He was at Jubbulpoor with the 52d B. N. I. By a system of constant watchfulness he passed through that month without an outbreak. It was, however, a month of anxiety; for such of the ladies as did not retire to Kamptee for shelter, remained in continual dread near their husbands at Jubbulpoor, seldom taking off their clothes at night, and holding ready to flee at an hour's warning—a state of suspense entailing almost as much suffering as mutiny itself. Early in July the Europeans fortified the Residency, and stored it with half a year's provisions for thirty officers, thirty ladies and children, and several civilians; this was done on receipt of news that the 42d native infantry and the 3d irregular cavalry had mutinied at Saugor. The Residency was made very strong, being converted from a house into a fort; three officers were made garrison engineers, two acted as commissariat officers, and all the rest took specific duties. It became not only the stronghold, but the home, night and day, for nearly seventy persons. One of the officers who had the best means of knowing the temper of the troops, while praising the 52d for still remaining faithful under

Fort at Agra, from the river Jumna.

so many temptations from mutineers elsewhere, and while promising them extra pay for their fidelity, nevertheless acknowledged in a private letter that the regiment was a broken reed to rest upon. 'To tell the truth, I doubt the regiment being much better than any other. Circumstances alone keep the sepoys quiet. There is no treasure; we merely collect enough to pay ourselves and them. If they plundered the country, they could not take away the property; as the Bundelas would loot and murder them.' Speaking of the domestic economy of his brother-officers and their families in the fortified Residency, he said: 'The 52d mess manage everything in the *Khana peena* line (eating and drinking). Ladies and gentlemen all dine together—a strange scene, quite a barrack-life. In the evening a few of us drive out; others ride and walk. We cannot afford above six or eight to leave the garrison together.' July passed over in safety in Jubbulpoor. Early in August a relieving force arrived from the Nagpoor territory, which, nearly tranquil itself, was able to forward trusty Madras troops to regions troubled by the faithless sepoys of the Bengal army. This force consisted of the 33d Madras native infantry, a squadron of the 4th Madras cavalry, 75 European artillerymen, and six guns. Major Erskine, thus reinforced, set forth to restore order at Dumoh, and to proceed thence to Saugor; to which place a Bombay column was expected to come, *viâ* Indore and Bhopal. This was a part of the policy determined on by the government at that time. Calcutta could supply no troops except for the Cawnpore and Lucknow region; the Punjaub could furnish reinforcements only for the siege of Delhi; and therefore it was determined that columns should start from the Madras and Bombay presidencies, comprising *no* Bengal native troops, and should work their way inwards and upwards to the disturbed provinces, sweeping away mutineers wherever they encountered them. It was not until the latter part of August that the Madras movable column could safely leave the vicinity of Jubbulpoor for Dumoh and other disturbed stations, and even then Major Erskine found it necessary to retain a portion of the troops. How long the 52d remained faithful at Jubbulpoor we shall see in a future page; but it may here be remarked that the English officers of the native regiments were at that time placed in a position of difficulty hardly to be comprehended by others. They either trusted their sepoys, or felt a kind of shame in expressing distrust: if not in actual peril, they were at least mortified and vexed; for they felt their own honour touched when their regiments proved faithless.

The Bengal troops at Nagode appear to have remained untouched by mutiny until the 25th of August. On that day the 50th native infantry shewed symptoms which caused some anxiety to the officers; two days afterwards disturbances took place, and at a period somewhat beyond the limit to which this chapter is confined the bulk of the regiment mutinied, and marched off to join mutineers elsewhere. About 250 of the sepoys remained true to their colours; they escorted their officers, and all the ladies and children, safely from Nagode to Mirzapore. These divergences among the men of the same regiment greatly complicate any attempts to elucidate the causes of the Indian mutiny generally. That the sepoys were often excited by temporary and exceptional impulses, is quite certain; and such impulses were wholly beyond the power of the Europeans correctly to estimate. There was one station at which a portion of a native regiment mutinied and shot an officer; the sepoys of his company threw themselves upon his body and wept, and then—joined the mutineers!

We pass from the Saugor province to those which were nominally under the control of Mr Colvin as lieutenant-governor of the Northwest Provinces—nominally, for, being himself shut up in Agra, he exercised scarcely any control beyond the walls of the fort. Of the Doab, sufficient has already been narrated to shew in what condition that fertile region was placed during the months of July and August. Where Havelock and Neill pitched their tents, there was British supremacy maintained; but beyond the three cities of Allahabad, Futtehpoor, and Cawnpore, and the high road connecting them, British power was little more than a name. Higher up the Doab, at Etawah, Minpooree, Furruckabad, Futteghur, Allygurh, Bolundshuhur, &c., anarchy was paramount. Crossing the Ganges into Oude, the cessation of British rule was still more complete. Scarcely an Englishman remained alive throughout the whole of Oude, except in Lucknow; all who had not been killed had precipitately escaped. Almost every landowner had become a petty chieftain, with his fort, his guns, and his band of retainers. In no part of India, at no time during the mutiny, was the hostility of the villagers more strikingly shewn than in Oude: in other provinces the inhabitants of the villages often aided the British troops on the march; but when Havelock, Neill, and Outram were in Oude, every village on the road had to be conquered, as if held by an avowed enemy. It has been often said that the Indian outbreak was a revolt of soldiery, not a rebellion of a people; but in Oude the contest was unquestionably with something more than the military only. Whether their love for their deposed king was sincere or only professed, the Oudians exhibited much animosity against the British. What the beleaguered garrison of Lucknow were doing, we shall see in the proper place.

Of Agra city, and the fort or residency in which the Europeans were for safety assembled, it will be remembered (p. 173) that after peaceably but anxiously passing through the month of May, Mr Colvin, on the 1st of June, found it necessary or expedient to disarm the 44th and 67th Bengal native infantry—because two companies of those regiments had just mutinied near Muttra, and because the bulk of the regiments exhibited unmistakable signs of disaffection. This great and important city was then left under the charge of the 3d European Fusiliers, a corps of volunteer European cavalry under Lieutenant Greathed, and Captain D'Oyley's field-battery of six guns. Most of the disarmed native troops deserted, to swell the insurgent ranks elsewhere; and in the course of the month the jail-guard deserted also. Thus June came to its end—the European residents still remaining at large, but making certain precautions for their common safety at night.

When July arrived, however, the state of affairs became much more serious. The Europeans were forced into a battle, which ended in a necessity for their shutting themselves up in the fort. The force was very weak. The 3d Europeans only numbered about 600 men, the militia and volunteers 200, and a few artillerymen belonging to the guns. Among the officers present were several who had belonged to the Gwalior Contingent, the various regiments and detachments of which had mutinied at Hattrass, Neemuch, Augur, Lullutpore, and Gwalior, on various days between the 28th of May and the 3d of July; these officers, having now no commands, were glad to render aid in any available way towards the defence of Agra. Just at this critical time, when the approach of a hostile force was imminent, the Europeans were further troubled by the sudden mutiny of the Kotah Contingent. This force—consisting of infantry, cavalry, and artillery, about 700 men in all—having been deemed loyal and trustworthy, had been brought about a month previously to Agra from the southwest, and had during that time remained true—collecting revenue, burning disaffected villages, capturing and hanging rebels and mutineers. They were brought in from the vicinity towards the close of June, to aid if necessary against the Neemuch mutineers, and were encamped half-way between the barracks and government-house. Suddenly and unexpectedly, on the evening of the 4th, the cavalry portion of the Contingent rose in revolt, fired at their officers, killed their sergeant-major, and then marched off, followed by the infantry and the artillery—all but a few gunners, who enabled the British to retain the two guns belonging to the Contingent. This revolt startled the authorities, and necessitated a change of plan, for it had been intended to attack the Neemuch force that very evening; nay, matters were even still worse, for the Kotah villains at once joined those from Neemuch.

On the morning of Sunday the 5th of July (again Sunday!), an army of mutineers being known to be near at hand, a reconnoitring party was sent out to examine their position. The enemy were found to consist of about 4000 infantry and 1000 cavalry, with ten or twelve guns; they comprised the 72d B. N. I., the 7th Gwalior Contingent infantry, the 1st Bengal native cavalry, the Malwah Contingent cavalry—which had joined the Neemuch men at Mehidpore—and fragments of other mutinied regiments, together with a very efficient artillery corps. The arrival of the Neemuch mutineers had for some time been expected; and as soon as it was known, on the 3d, that the enemy had reached Futtehpore Sikri, about twenty miles from Agra, the ladies and children, as well as many of the civilians and traders, had as a measure of precaution abandoned their houses in the city, and gone into the fort, which had been cleaned out, made as habitable as possible, and largely supplied with provisions. The reconnoitring party returned to announce that the enemy were at Shahgunje, a village close to the lieutenant-governor's house, three miles from the cantonment and four from the fort. The authorities at Agra resolved at once to go out and fight the enemy in open field; seeing that the native citizens had begun to think slightingly of their British masters, and that it was necessary to remove any suspicion of fear or timidity. The brigadier made up a force equal to about one-eighth of the enemy's numbers; it consisted of seven very weak companies of the 3d European Fusiliers, the militia and volunteers, and a battery of artillery. The infantry were placed under Colonel Riddell, and the artillery under Captain D'Oyley. As to the volunteer cavalry, it was made up of a curious medley of unemployed military officers, civilians, merchants, and writers—all willing to share the common danger for the common good; but with untrained horses, and without regular cavalry drill, they laboured under many disadvantages. About 200 men of the 3d Europeans remained behind to guard the fort.

At noon, the opposing forces met. The enemy occupied a strong position behind Shahgunje, with their guns flanking the village, and the cavalry flanking the guns. The British advanced in line, with their guns on each flank, the infantry in the middle, and the mounted militia and volunteers in the rear. When about six hundred yards from the enemy, the infantry were ordered to lie down, to allow the guns to do their work against the village, from behind the houses and walls of which the enemy's riflemen opened a very destructive fire. It was a bad omen that women were seen in the village loading the rifles and muskets and handing them to the mutineers to fire. For two hours an exchange of artillery-fire was kept up—extremely fierce; shrapnel shells, round-shot, and grape-shot, filling the air. A tumbril belonging to D'Oyley's battery now blew up, disabling one of the guns; the enemy's cavalry took advantage of this to gallop forward and charge; but the 3d Europeans, jumping up, let fly a volley which effectually deterred them. Most of the officers and soldiers had wished during these two hours for a bolder course of action—a capture of the enemy's guns by a direct charge of infantry. Then followed a rapid musketry-fire, and a chasing of the enemy out of the village by most of the infantry—the rest guarding the guns. Unfortunately another tumbril blew up, disabling another gun; and, moreover, D'Oyley had used up all the ammunition which had been supplied to him. Upon this the order was given for retreat to the city; and the retreat was made—much to the mortification of the troops, for they had really won a victory. The rebels, it was afterwards known, were themselves out of ammunition, and were just about to retreat when they saw the retreat of the British; their infantry marched off towards Muttra, but their cavalry and one gun harassed the British during their return to the city. The artillery-fire of the mutineers during the battle was spoken of with admiration even by those who were every minute suffering from it; the native artillerymen had learned to use effectively against us those guns which they had been paid and fed to use in our defence. If the cavalry had been equally effective, the British would probably have been cut off to a man. This battle of Agra was a severe one to the British, for one-fourth of the small force were killed or wounded. The officers suffered much: Majors Prendergast and Thomas, Captains D'Oyley, Lamb, and Alexander, Lieutenants Pond, Fellowes, Cockburn, Williams, and Bramley, were wounded, as well as many gentlemen belonging to the volunteer horse. The loss of Captain D'Oyley was very much deplored, for he was a great favourite. While managing his guns, a shot struck him; he sat on the carriage, giving orders, in spite of his wound; but at last he fell, saying: 'Ah, they have done for me now! Put a stone over my grave, and say I died at my guns.' He sank the next day.

The British returned to Agra—not to the city, but to the fort; for three or four thousand prisoners had got loose during the day, and had begun to fire all the European buildings in the city. Officers and privates, civilians and ladies, all who wrote of the events at Agra at that time, told of the wild licence of that day and night. One eye-witness said: 'Hardly a house has escaped destruction; and such houses and their contents as were not consumed by fire have been completely gutted and destroyed by other means. In fact, even if we were to leave the fort to-morrow, there are not four houses in the place with roofs remaining under which we could obtain shelter; and as for household property and other things left outside, there is not a single article in existence in serviceable order. The very doors and windows are removed, and every bit of wood torn out, so that nothing remains but the bare brick walls. Things are strewed about the roads and streets in every direction; and wherever you move you see broken chairs and tables, carriages in fragments, crockery, books, and every kind of property wantonly destroyed.' An officer of the 3d Europeans, after describing the battle, and the return of the little force to the fort, said: 'Immediately afterwards the work of destruction commenced, the budmashes began to plunder, bungalows on every side were set on fire—one continued blaze the whole night. I went out the next morning. 'Twas a dreadful sight indeed; Agra was destroyed; churches, colleges, dwelling-houses, barracks, everything burned.'

But they had something more to think of than the devastation in Agra city; they had to contemplate their own situation in Agra Fort. Among the number of Europeans, some had already borne strange adversities. One officer had escaped, with his wife, in extraordinary guise, from Gwalior at the time of the mutiny of the Contingent at that place. He had been obliged to quit his wife at their bungalow in the midst of great danger, to hasten down to his regiment in the lines; and when he found his influence with his men had come to naught, and that shots were aimed at him, three sepoys resolved to save him. They took off his hat, boots, and trousers, wrapped him in a horse-cloth, huddled him between them, and passed him off as a woman. They left him on the bank of a stream, and went to fetch his wife from a position of great peril. She being too weak to walk, they made up a horse-cloth into a sort of bag, tied it to a musket, put her into it, shouldered the musket horizontally, and carried her seven miles—her husband walking by her side, barefoot over sharp stones. After meeting with further assistance, they reached Agra somewhat more in comfort. Another officer, who had likewise served in the Gwalior Contingent, and who had seen much hard service before the mutiny of his corps compelled him to flee to Agra, counted up the wreck of his property after the battle of the 5th of July, and found it to consist of 'a coat, a shirt, the greater portion of a pair of breeches, a pair of jack-boots, one sock, a right good sword'—and a cannon-ball through his leg; yet, recognising the useful truth that grumbling and complaining are but poor medicines in a time of trouble, he bore up cheerfully, and even cheered up Mr Colvin, who was at that time nearly worn to the grave by sickness and anxiety. An officer of the 3d Europeans said in a letter: 'I lost everything in the world. . . . . The enemy went quietly off; but here we are; we can't get out—no place to go to—nothing to do but to wait for assistance.' And a few days afterwards he added: 'Here we are like rats in a trap; there are from four to five thousand people in this fort, military and civil, Eurasians, half-castes, &c.; and when we shall get out, is a thing to be guessed at.' A surgeon of the recently mutinied Gwalior Contingent thus spoke of what he saw around him: 'The scene in the fort for the first few days was a trying one. All the native servants ran off. I had eleven in the morning, and at night not one. Ladies were seen cooking their own food, officers drawing and carrying water from the wells, &c. Many people were ruined, having escaped with only their clothes on their backs. We are now shut up here, five hundred fighting-men with ammunition, and about four or five thousand altogether, eagerly awaiting the arrival of European troops.' A commissariat officer said: 'Here we are all living in gun-sheds and casemates. The appearance of the interior is amusing, and the streets (of the fort) are named; we have Regent and Oxford Streets, the Quadrant, Burlington and Lowther Arcades, and Trafalgar Square.' The wife of one of the officers described her strange home: 'We are leading a very unsettled ship-like life. No one is allowed to leave the fort, except bodies of armed men. We are living in a place they call Palace Yard; it is a square, with a gallery round it, having open arches; every married couple are allowed two arches. . . . It is no easy matter to keep our arches clean and tidy.' As all the Europeans in Agra went to live in the fort, the number included the staff of the *Mofussilite* ('Provincial European') newspaper, one of the journals which had for some time been published in that city; the issue for the 3d of July had been printed at the usual office of the paper; but none other appeared for twelve days, when a *Mofussilite* was printed within the fort itself.

There was no exaggeration in the accounts of the number of persons thus strangely incarcerated. So completely were the Europeans and their native servants at Agra shut up within the fort, and so much was that place regarded as a refuge for those who had been forced to flee from other stations, that it gradually became crowded to an extraordinary degree. On the 26th of July Mr Colvin determined to take a census of all the persons who slept within the fort on that night; he did so, and found them to amount to no less a number than 5845 *—all of whom had to be supplied with their daily food under military or garrison arrangements. More than 2000 of the number were children, who could render little or no return for the services so anxiously demanded by and for them. Provided, however, the supply of food and other necessaries were sufficient, the danger of the position was not at all comparable to that of Sir Hugh Wheeler at Cawnpore or of Brigadier Inglis at Lucknow. The fort at Agra (see wood-cut, p. 109) was a very large structure, a sort of triangle whose sides extended from three to five eighths of a mile each; it contained numerous large buildings within the walls, of which the chief were the palace of Shahjehan, the Hall of Audience built by the same emperor, and the Moti Musjid or Pearl Mosque. All the buildings were at once appropriated, in various ways, to the wants of the enormous number of persons who sought shelter therein. The defences of the place, too, were greatly strengthened; sixty guns of heavy calibre were mounted on the bastions; thirteen large mortars were placed in position; the powder-magazines were secured from accidental explosion; the external defences were improved by the levelling of many houses in the city which approached too near the fort; and preparations were completed for blowing up the superb Jumma Musjid (p. 229) if any attempt were made by a hostile force to occupy it, seeing that its upper ranges commanded the interior of the fort. The only insurgent force at that time in possession of guns and mortars powerful enough to breach strong walls was the Gwalior Contingent; and even if Scindia lost all hold over that force, Agra was provisioned for ten months, and had ammunition enough to stand a whole year's siege. An officer of a mutinied Gwalior regiment, writing from Agra after some weeks' confinement, said: 'Almost all the roads are closed, and it is only by secret messengers and spies that we can get any intelligence of what is going on in the convulsed world around us. My letters from Scotland used to reach me in thirty days; now if I get one in eighty days I congratulate myself on my good-luck. . . . As for this fort, we can hold it against any number for months; our only fear being for the women and children, who would suffer much, and of whom we have some three thousand. The health of the troops, &c., is, thank God, excellent, and the wounded are doing well.' Nevertheless, with all their sense of security, the Europeans within the fort had enough to do to maintain their cheerfulness. On the day and night of the 5th of July, property had been burned and despoiled in the city to an enormous amount; and most of this had belonged to the present inmates of the fort. The merchants had been prosperous, their large shops had abounded with the most costly articles of necessity and luxury—and now nearly all was gone. The military officers had of course less to lose, but their deprivation was perhaps still more complete.

Throughout July and August the state of affairs thus continued at Agra. The danger was small, but the discomforts of course numerous. Mr Colvin sent repeated applications for a relieving force. There was, however, none to aid him. His health failed greatly, and he did not bear up against the anxieties of his position with the cheerful firmness exhibited by many other of the officials at that trying time. Brigadier Polwhele, former military commandant, was superseded by Colonel Cotton when the account of the battle of the 5th of July became known at Calcutta. Occasional sallies were made from the fort, to punish isolated bodies of rebels at Futtehpore Sikri, Hattrass, and Allygurh; but the European troops were too few to be very effective in this way. The most note-worthy exploit took place during the latter half of August, when Mr Colvin requested Colonel Cotton to organise a small force for driving some mutineers from Allygurh. Major

*	Men.	Women.	Boys.	Girls.	Total.
Europeans, . .	1065	289	341	294	1989
East Indians, .	413	531	423	339	1542
Native Christians,	287	177	295	299	858
Hindoos, . .	842	49	102	4	1157
Mohammedans, .	244	10	43	3	293
	2961	656	1192	840	5845

Montgomery set forth with this miniature army,* reached Hattrass on the 21st, and there learned that 6000 mutineers, under Ghose Mahomed Khan, naib or lieutenant of the King of Delhi, were prepared to resist him at Allygurh. Montgomery marched from Allygurh to Sarsnee on the 23d, rested for the night in an indigo factory and other buildings, and advanced on the following day to Allygurh. There ensued a sharp conflict of two hours' duration, in gardens and enclosures outside the town; it ended in the defeat and dispersion of the enemy, who left 300 dead on the field. The battle was a gallant affair, worthy of ranking with those of Havelock; for Montgomery contended against twenty times his own number; and, moreover, many of the troops among the enemy were Ghazees or fanatic Mussulmans who engaged fiercely in hand-to-hand contests with some of his troops. His detachment of men was too small to enable him to enter and re-occupy Allygurh: he was obliged to leave that place in the hands of the rebels, and to return to Hattrass; but having replenished his stock of ammunition and supplies, he advanced again to Allygurh, held it for several days, and left a detachment there when he took his departure.

Taking leave for the present of Agra, we may briefly state that almost every other city and station in that part of India was in the hands of the enemy during the months of July and August. Delhi was still under siege; but there was scarcely a British soldier in any part of the Delhi division except in the siege-camp before Delhi itself. In the Agra division, as we have just seen, British influence extended very little further than the walls of Agra Fort. In the Meerut division, the station at that town was still held; the military lines were strongly fortified, and supplied with provisions to an extent sufficient to remove immediate anxiety. The region between Delhi and the Sutlej, containing Hansi, Hissar, Sirsa, and other towns, was fortunately kept in some order by a column under General Van Cortlandt, which moved quickly from place to place, and put down a swarm of petty chieftains who were only too ready to take advantage of the mutinies of the native troops. In the Rohilcund division scarcely a town, except up in the hills, remained under British control.

Welcome as was the refuge which the wives and children of officers found at the hill-stations in the Rohilcund and Cis-Sutlej provinces, their tranquillity was frequently disturbed by the movements of rebels. Early in August the civil commissioner of Kumaon received intelligence that an attack was contemplated on Nynee Tal by Kalee Khan, one of the myrmidons of Khan Bahadoor Khan of Bareilly, who had 3000 rabble with him; the plunder and destruction of the station being the main objects in view. Captain Ramsey, commandant at Nynee Tal, and Colonel M'Causland, commanding the troops in the various stations of Kumaon, at once determined to remove the ladies and children, two hundred in number, from Nynee Tal to Almora, further away from Bareilly: this was done; and then the colonel prepared to meet the mutineers, and confront them with a detachment of the 66th Goorkhas. Kalee Khan set forth on his mission; but when he heard that M'Causland was calmly waiting for him, he changed his plan, returned to Bareilly, and avoided a conflict, the probable result of which presented itself very clearly to his mind. At Nynee Tal, at Almora, at Mussouree, at Simla, and at other places among the cool hilly regions, ladies and children were assembled in large numbers, some with their husbands and fathers, but many sent away from scenes of strife in which those dear to them were compelled to engage. It was not all idle hopelessness with them. Englishwomen can always find some useful service to render, and are always ready to render it. A lady, writing from Mussouree on the 9th of August, said: 'We are very busy working flannel clothes for our army before Delhi. They are very badly off for these things; and being so much exposed at such a season of the year, and in such a proverbially unhealthy locality, and fighting as they have done so nobly, they really deserve to be provided for by us.' After enumerating the sums subscribed towards this object from various quarters, the writer went on to say: 'Mrs —— and myself are constantly at work; for, with the exception of our tailors, and one or two others given up to us by ladies, we can get none. . . . Wonderful to say, though I never did such a thing in my life before, I have the management of our portion of the business, which keeps me employed from early morning till late at night. We meet, with several other ladies, at ——'s house every day, with as many tailors as we can collect, and stitch away.'

The great and important country of the Punjaub, though not free from disturbance, was kept pretty well under control during July and August, by the energy of Sir John Lawrence and the other officers of the Company. We have seen * that on the 13th of May the 16th, 26th, and 49th regiments of Bengal native infantry, and the 8th Bengal cavalry, were disarmed at Meean Meer, a cantonment six miles from the city of Lahore; that on the same day the 45th and 57th native infantry mutinied at Ferozpore, while the 10th cavalry was disarmed; that during the same week, Umritsir, Jullundur, and Phillour were only saved from mutiny by the promptness and spirit of some of the officers; that on the 20th, the 55th native infantry mutinied at Murdan in the Peshawur Valley; that consequent upon this, the 24th, 27th, and 51st native infantry, and the 5th native

* 3d Europeans,	154 officers and men.
Artillery,	61 " "
Militia,	22 " "
Jât matchlock-men,	70 " "

Two 9-pounders; one 24-pounder howitzer.

* Chapter xii., pp. 193-205.

cavalry, were on the 22d of the month disarmed in the station of Peshawur itself; that early in June, the 4th native regiment was disarmed at Noorpore; that on the 6th, the 36th and 61st native infantry, and the 6th native cavalry, mutinied at Jullundur, and marched off towards Phillour; that the 3d native cavalry, at the last-named station, mutinied on the following day, unable to resist the temptation thrown out to them by those from Jullundur; that the 14th native infantry mutinied at Jelum on the 7th of July, maintaining a fierce fight with a British detachment before their departure; that on the same day the 58th native infantry, and two companies of the 14th, were disarmed at Rawul Pindee; that on the 9th, the 46th native infantry, and a wing of the 9th native cavalry, mutinied at Sealkote, and decamped towards Delhi; that towards the close of July, the disarmed 26th mutinied at Meean Meer, murdered Major Spencer, and marched off with the intention of strengthening the insurgents at Delhi; that on the 19th of August, a portion of the disarmed 10th cavalry mutinied at Ferozpore; and that on the 28th of the same month, the disarmed 51st mutinied at Peshawur, fled to the hills, and were almost annihilated. It thus appears that about a dozen regiments mutinied in the Punjaub between the middle of May and the end of August; that some of these had been previously disarmed; and that others had been disarmed without having mutinied.

A few additional words may be given here relating to the partial mutiny at Meean Meer. The four native regiments at that station, disarmed on the 13th of May, remained in their lines until the 30th of July, peaceful and without arms. On the last-named day, however, it became known to the authorities that the men meditated flight. Major Spencer of the 26th, and two native officers, were killed by the sepoys of that regiment on that day—with what weapons does not clearly appear. The murder of the unfortunate English officer deranged the plans of the troops; all were to have decamped at a given signal; but now only the 26th made off, leaving the other three regiments in their lines. The authorities, not well knowing whither the fugitives had gone, sent off three strong parties of mounted police, to Umritsir, Hurrekee, and Kussoor, the three routes towards the Sutlej. The men, however, had gone northward; but within a few days they were almost entirely destroyed, for the villagers aided the police in capturing or shooting the miserable fugitives as they marched or ran in field and jungle.

Without going over in detail any proceedings already recorded, it may be convenient to condense in a small space a narrative of Brigadier-general Nicholson's operations in the later days of June and the first half of July with a movable column placed under his command by Sir John Lawrence. Having disarmed the 33d and 35th B. N. I., for reasons which appeared to him amply sufficient, he began on the 27th of June to retrace his steps from Phillour, and on the 5th of July he encamped at Umritsir, to overawe the 59th B. N. I., and to hold a central position whence he might march to any threatened point east or west. On the 7th, hearing of the mutiny of the 14th native infantry at Jelum, and receiving no satisfactory evidence that Colonel Ellice had been able to frustrate or defeat the mutineers, he at once resolved on a measure of precaution. He disarmed the 59th on the following morning—with very great regret; for he had nothing to censure in the conduct of the men; he took that step solely on account of the peril which, at such a time, threatened any station containing Bengal troops without British; and he added in his dispatch: 'I beg very strongly to recommend this corps, both as regards officers and men, to the favourable consideration of government.' On the 10th, receiving intelligence that the 46th native infantry, and a wing of the 9th native cavalry, had mutinied at Sealkote, Nicholson at once disarmed the other wing of the same cavalry regiment, which formed part of his column. In the course of the same day he learned that the Sealkote mutineers intended to march eastward, through Goordaspore, Noorpore, Hoshyapoor, and Jullundur, to Delhi—endeavouring to tempt to mutiny, on their way, the 2d irregular cavalry at Goordaspore, the 4th native infantry at Noorpore, and the 16th irregular cavalry at Hoshyapoor. The problem thence arose—could Nicholson intercept these mutineers before they reached Goordaspore? He found he would have to make a forced march of forty miles in a northeast direction to effect this. He did so, by energetic exertions, in twenty hours. He came up with them at the Trimmoo ford over the Ravee, nine miles from Goordaspore, on the 12th of July—his force now consisting of H.M. 52d foot, 184 men of the Punjaub infantry, a company of the police battalion, a few irregular horse, a troop of artillery, and three guns. Nicholson defeated them after a short but sharp conflict on the river's bank; but his horsemen were not trustworthy, and he could not pursue the enemy. About 300 mutineers, with one gun, took post on an island in the river; these, by a well-planned movement, were almost entirely annihilated on the 16th—and the 'Sealkote mutineers' disappeared from the scene. It was with justice that the active leader thanked his troops on the following day: 'By a forced march of unusual length, performed at a very trying season of the year, the column has been able to preserve many stations and districts from pillage and plunder, to save more than one regiment from the danger of too close a contact with the mutineers; while the mutineer force itself, 1100 strong, notwithstanding the very desperate character of the resistance offered by it, has been utterly destroyed or dispersed.'

Let us now, as in a former chapter, glance at the state of affairs in the vast region of India southward of the Ganges, the Jumna, and the Sutlej—passing over Sinde without special mention, as being nearly free from disturbing agencies. The reader will remember* that among the various states, provinces, and districts of Nagpoor, Hyderabad, Carnatic, Madras, Bombay, Holkar, Scindia, Rajpootana, &c., some became subject to anarchy in certain instances during the month of June—especially the three last-named states; and we have now to shew that this anarchy continued, and in some cases extended, during July and August; but it will also be made manifest that the amount of insurgency bore a very small ratio to that in the stormy districts further north.

Of Southwestern Bengal, Orissa, and Nagpoor, it is scarcely necessary here to speak. The native troops were not influenced by a hostility so fierce, a treachery so villainous, as those in Hindostan proper; there were not so many zemindars and petty chieftains who had been wrought up to irritation by the often questionable appropriations and annexations of the Company; and there was easier access for the troops of the Madras presidency, who, as has already been more than once observed, had small sympathy with the petted sepoys and sowars of the larger presidency. The mutinies or attempts at mutiny, in these provinces, were of slight character during July and August. Mr Plowden, commissioner of Nagpoor, was enabled, with troops sent by Lord Harris from Madras, not only to maintain British supremacy throughout that large country (nearly equal in size to England and Scotland combined), but also to assist Major Erskine in the much more severely threatened territory of Saugor and Nerbudda, lying between Nagpoor and the Jumna.

The Madras presidency remained almost entirely at peace. Not only did the native troops hold their faith with the government that fed and paid them, but they cheerfully volunteered to serve against the mutinous Bengal sepoys in the north. On the 3d of July the governor in council issued a proclamation, announcing that several regiments had expressed their desire to be employed in the North-west Provinces or wherever else their services might be required; that thanks would be publicly awarded to the native officers and men of all the regiments who had thus come forward; and that the favourable attention of the supreme government towards them would be solicited. The corps that thus proffered their services were the 3d, 11th, 16th, and 27th Madras native infantry, the 3d and 8th Madras native cavalry, a company of native foot-artillery, a troop of native horse-artillery, and a detachment of native sappers and miners. Many of these afterwards rendered good service in the battles which distinguished—and we may at the same time add devastated—Northern and Central India. Four days afterwards, Lord Harris was able to announce that other regiments—the 17th, 30th, 36th, and 47th native infantry, and the 5th native cavalry—had in a similar way come forward 'to express their abhorrence of the traitorous conduct of the mutineers of the Bengal army, and their desire to be employed wherever their services may be required.' Besides thus providing faithful soldiers, the governor of Madras was in a position, at various times during July and August, to send large supplies of arms, ammunition, and camp-equipage, from Madras to Calcutta. In the city of Madras itself, and in the various southern provinces and countries of Carnatic, Tanjore, Travancore, Canara, Malabar, and Mysore, the same exemption from mutiny was experienced. There were, it is true, discontents and occasional plottings, but no formidable resistance to the British power. Many persons there were who, without being rebels or open malcontents, thought that the Company had dealt harshly with the native princes, and were on that account deterred from such hearty sympathy with the British as they might otherwise possibly have manifested. An officer in the Madras army, writing when the mutiny was four months old, stated that in the previous February, when that terrible movement had not yet commenced, he went one day to take a sketch of a mosque, or rather a collection of mosques, in the suburbs of Madras—tombs that were the memorials of past Mussulman greatness. His conversation with an old man of that faith* left upon his mind the impression that there was a sentiment of injury borne, rights violated, nationality disregarded, conveyed in the words of his temporary companion.

There was, however, one occurrence in the Madras presidency which gave rise to much uneasiness. The 8th Madras native cavalry was ordered to march from Bangalore to Madras, and there embark for Calcutta. On arriving at a place about twenty-five miles from Madras, on the 17th of August, the men put forward a claim for the rates of pay, batta, and pension which existed before the year 1837, and which were more favourable than those of subsequent introduction. Such a claim, put forward at such a moment, was very perplexing to the officers; they hastened to Madras, and obtained the consent of the government to make conciliatory offers to the men. After a further march of thirteen miles to Poonamallee, the troopers again stopped, and

* Chapter xi., pp. 176-190.

* 'We were still looking at the scene and speculating upon the tenants of the tombs, when an old Mussulman came near us with a salam; he accosted us, and I asked him in whose honour the tomb had been erected. His reply struck me at the time as rather remarkable. "That," said he, pointing to the largest, "is the tomb of the Nawab Mustapha; he reigned about 100 years ago: and that," pointing to a smaller mausoleum near it, "is the tomb of his dewan, and it was he who counselled the nawab thus: 'Beware of the French, for they are soldiers, and will attack and dispossess you of your country; but cherish the Englishman, for he is a merchant, and will enrich it.' The nawab listened to that advice, and see here!" The old man was perfectly civil and respectful in his manner, but his tone was sad: it spoke the language of disappointment and hostility, if hostility were possible. In this case the man referred to our late assumption of the Carnatic, upon the death of the last nawab, who died without issue. As a general rule, never was a conquered country so mildly governed as India has been under our rule; but you can scarcely expect that the rulers we dispossessed, even though like ourselves they be foreigners, and only held the country by virtue of conquest, will cede us the precedence without a murmur.'

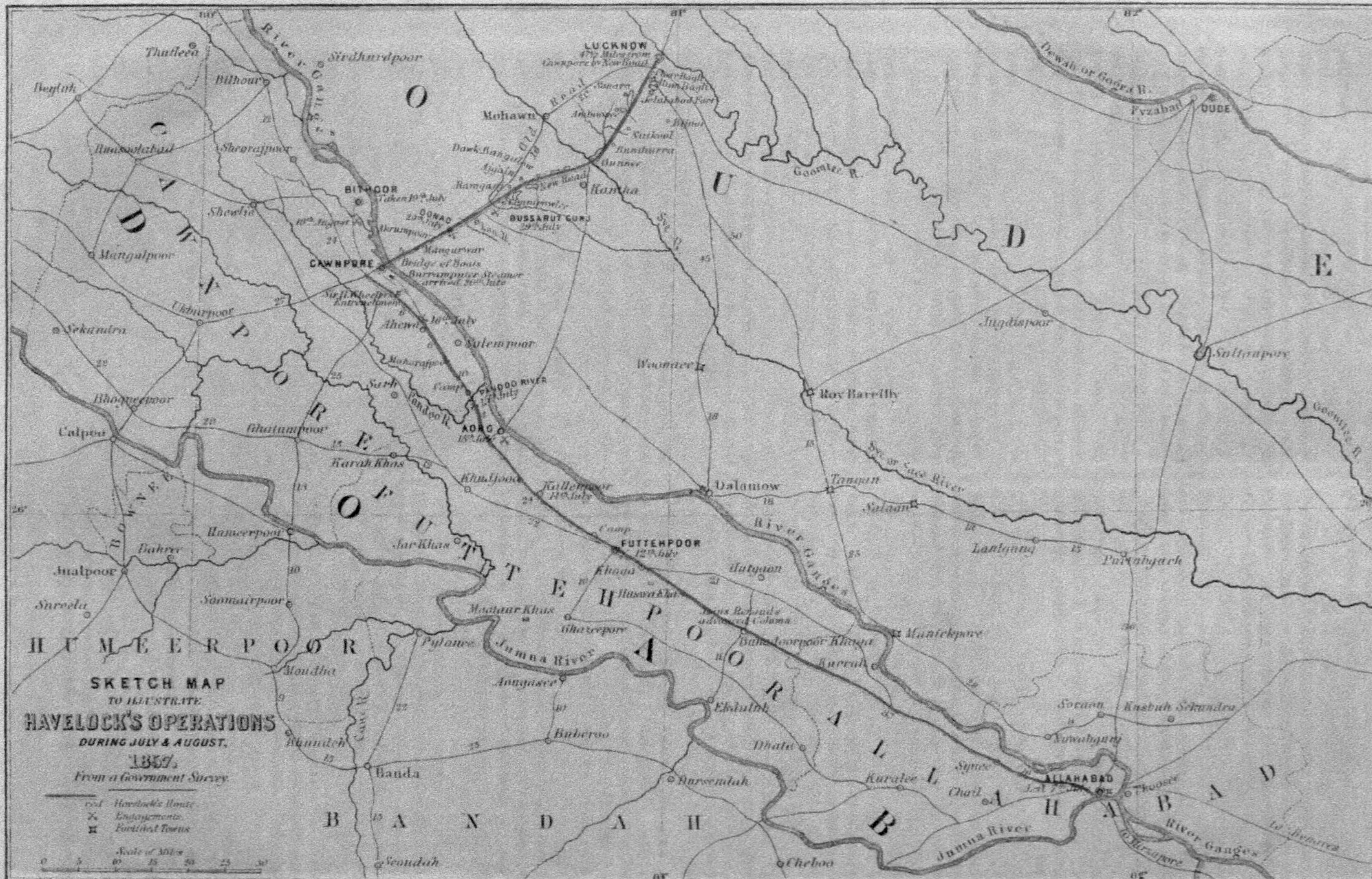
SKETCH MAP
TO ILLUSTRATE
HAVELOCK'S OPERATIONS
DURING JULY & AUGUST,
1857.
From a Government Survey.
Havelock's Route
Engagements
Fortified Towns
Scale of Miles
0 5 10 15 20 25 30
OUDE
CAWNPORE
FUTTEHPOOR
ALLAHABAD
HUMEERPOOR
BANDAH
LUCKNOW
Mohawn
Bithoor
Taken 16th July
CAWNPORE
Bridge of Boats
Kantha
Dalamow
Roy Barelly
Woonaee
Jugdispoor
Sultanpoor
Fyzabad
OUDE
Dewah or Gogra R.
Goomtee R.
River Ganges
Jumna River
FUTTEHPOOR
12th July
Khaga
Manickpore
Allahabad
Banda
Calpee
Jualpoor
Hameerpoor
Soomairpoor
Moudha
Pylanee
Aougasee
Baberoo
Durwendah
Cheboo
Seondah
Bhognepoor
Sekandra
Mangalpoor
Shewlie
Bilhour
Thatleea
Beylah
Sirdharpoor
Russoolabad
Shoorajpoor
Ukburpoor
Ghatampoor
Karah Khas
Jar Khas
Ghazeepore
Ekdulah
Dhata
Karalee
Chail
Syree
Sorann
Kusbah Sekundra
Lalgunj
Partabgarh
Tangan
Salaan
Hutgaon
Kurrah
Ahewa
Salempoor
Sarh
Pandoo R.
Pandoo River
Aong
Kalleanpoor
Khujooa
Camp
Dawk Bungalow
Mangurwar
Dussarut Gunj
Bunnee
Busheerutgunge
Sussaree
Ramgunge
Sunaree
Alumbagh
Charbagh
Jelalabad Fort
Bijnor
Sutkoul
Buntharra
Bahree
Sureela
Rhundeh
Cane R.
Sye R.
Sye or Saee River
to Benares
to Mirzapore
Jhoosee
81°
82°
26°

declared they would not go forth 'to war against their countrymen.' This being an act of insubordination which of course could not be overlooked, two guns and some artillerymen were promptly brought forward; the 8th cavalry were unhorsed and disarmed, and sent to do dismounted duty at Arcot; while their horses were forthwith shipped to Calcutta, where such accessions were specially valuable. The affair caused great excitement at Madras; the volunteers were warned that their services were to be available at a moment's notice; patrols were placed in the streets by day and night; and guns were planted in certain directions. Happily, the prompt disarming of this turbulent regiment prevented the poison from spreading further.

Bombay, like its sister presidency Madras, was affected only in a slight degree by the storms that troubled Bengal and the northwest. The Bombay troops, though, as the sequel shewed, not altogether equal in fidelity to those of Madras, did nevertheless pass through the perilous ordeal very creditably—rendering most valuable service in Rajpootana and other regions of the north. There was a wealthy and powerful native community at Bombay—that of the Parsees—which was nearly at all times ready to support the government, and which greatly strengthened the hands of Lord Elphinstone by so doing. It consisted of merchants, shipowners, and bankers, many of whom had made large fortunes in the ordinary way of trade. These Parsees may always be distinguished from the other natives of India by something peculiar in their names—Jamsetjee, Nowrojee, Cursetjee, Bomanjee, Rustomjee, Hormuzjee, Luxmonjee, Maneckjee, Sorabjee, Furdoonjee, Soonderjee, Ruttonjee, Wassewdewjee, Dhakjee, &c. The Parsees are the descendants of those Persians who, refusing to exchange the religion of Zoroaster for that of Mohammed, migrated to India more than a thousand years ago; those still remaining in Persia are few in number and degraded in position; but those at Bombay are wealthy and active, and bear a high character both morally and intellectually. The property in the island on which the city of Bombay stands is chiefly in the hands of the Parsees; and it is usual for the European commercial firms of Bombay to have a Parsee capitalist as one of the partners. Although wearing the Asiatic costume, and adhering very rigidly to their religious customs and observances, the Parsees assimilate more than other eastern people to the social customs of Europeans: they nearly all speak English, and have it carefully taught to their children. There is something remarkable in a Parsee holding the dignity of a baronet, in English fashion; such was the case a few years ago, when a Parsee of enormous wealth, and of liberality as great as his wealth, was made by Queen Victoria a baronet under the title of Sir Jamsetjee Jejeebhoy. It will at once be seen that such a body as the Parsees, having little or no sympathy with Hindustani sepoys, and having their worldly interests much bound up with the English, were likely to be sources of strength instead of weakness in troubled times. They headed an address to Lord Elphinstone, signed by about four hundred natives of various castes and creeds.* It was not more adulatory, not more filled with enthusiastic professions of loyalty, than many addresses presented to Viscount Canning in Bengal; but it more nearly corresponded with the conduct of those who signed it.

If Bombay city, however, remained nearly undisturbed during July and August, there were symptoms that required close watching in various districts to the north, south, and east. Kolapore, one of the places here adverted to, is distant about a hundred and eighty miles south from Bombay. It is the chief place of a raj or state of the same name, and was in the last century a scene of frequent contest between two Mahratta princes, the Peishwa of Satara and the Rajah of Kolapore, each of whom struggled against the claims to superiority put forth by the other. About half a century ago began those relations towards the Company's government, which, as in so many other parts of India, led to the gradual extinction of the rule of the native rajah; the British govern 'in the name of the rajah,' but the rajah's authority remains in abeyance. The military force belonging specially to the state, at the time of the mutiny, amounted to about ten thousand men of all arms. It was, however, among the Company's own troops that the disaffection above adverted to took place. The 27th Bombay native infantry, without any previous symptoms of disaffection, suddenly mutinied at Kolapore, on the day of a festival called the Buckree Eed (1st of August); or rather, a portion of the regiment mutinied. While the officers were assembled in the billiard-room of their mess-house on the evening of that day, a jemadar rushed in and informed them that some of the sepoys had risen in revolt; the officers hastened out; when three of them, ignorant of the place, or bewildered

* 'My Lord—We, the undersigned inhabitants of Bombay, have observed with sincere regret the late lamentable spread of mutiny and disaffection among the Bengal native soldiery, and we have read with feelings of horror and indignation the accounts of the cowardly and savage atrocities perpetrated by the ruthless mutineers on such unfortunate Europeans as fell into their hands.

'While those who have ever received at the hands of government such unvarying kindness and consideration have proved untrue to their salt and false to their colours, it has afforded us much pleasure to observe the unquestionable proof of attachment manifested by the native princes, zemindars, and people of Upper India in at once and unsolicited rallying around government and expressing their abhorrence of the dastardly and ungrateful conduct of the insurgent soldiery. Equally demanding admiration are the stanchness and fidelity displayed by the men of the Bombay and Madras armies.

'That we have not earlier hastened to assure your lordship of our unchangeable loyalty, and to place our services at the disposal of government, has arisen from the entire absence in our minds of any apprehension of disaffection or outbreak on this side of India.

'We still are without any fears for Bombay; but, lest our silence should be misunderstood, and with a view to allay the fears which false reports give rise to, we beg to place our services at the disposal of government, to be employed in any manner that your lordship may consider most conducive to the preservation of the public peace and safety.

'We beg to remain, my lord, your most obedient and faithful servants,

'Nowrojee Jamsetjee, &c., &c.'

in the darkness, went astray, and were taken and murdered by the mutineers. The mother of the jemadar went to the house of Major Rolland, the commanding officer, to warn the ladies of their danger, and to afford them means of escape. No sooner had the ladies hurried away, than the house was surrounded by mutineers, who, disappointed at finding it empty, revenged themselves by slaughtering the old woman. After plundering the treasury of forty thousand rupees, the mutineers retired to a religious edifice in the town, and marched off in early morning by the Phoonda Ghat towards Wagotun, on the coast. The native commissioned officers of the regiment remained faithful; none of them accompanied the mutineers. The outbreak ended most disastrously to those concerned in it. When they got some distance from Kolapore, they found themselves without food and without friends; and gradually nearly all were destroyed by detachments sent against them, headed by Major Rolland and Colonel Maughan, the latter of whom was British resident at Kolapore. There were circumstances which justify a belief that this was not so much a mutiny after the Bengal type, as an association of the bad men of the regiment for purposes of plunder.

This event at Kolapore threw the whole of the south Mahratta country into a ferment. At Poonah, Satara, Belgaum, Dharwar, Rutnagherry, Sawunt Waree, and other places, the threads of a Mohammedan conspiracy were detected; and fortunately the germs of insurrection were nipped in the bud. When Mr Rose, commissioner of Satara, found that the deposed royal family of that state were engaged in plots and intrigues, he took a small but reliable English force, entered Satara before daylight on the 6th of August, surrounded the palace, and ordered the rajah and the ranees to prepare for instant departure. Resistance being useless, the royal prisoners entered phaetons which had been brought for that purpose, and before eight o'clock they were on the way to Poonah—to be kept under the eye of the Bombay authorities until the political atmosphere should become clearer, in a navy depôt on an island near Bombay city. A plot was about the same time discovered at Poonah, concerted between the moulvies of that place and of Belgaum, for massacring the Europeans and native Christians of those stations; letters were intercepted at the Poonah post-office, which enabled the authorities to shun the coming evil. Many arrests of Mussulman conspirators were made; and it was then found that matters had gone so far as a preparation to blow up the arsenal at Poonah. The authorities at once disarmed the natives of the cantonment bazaar. From most of the out-stations, being troubled by these events, the English ladies were sent by military escort to Bombay or to Poonah. Among other measures of precaution, the remaining companies of the 27th native regiment were disarmed at Kolapore and Rutnagherry; and examples of the terrible 'blowing away from guns' were resorted to, to check this incipient revolution. The 28th Bombay native infantry, stationed at Dharwar, and the 29th, stationed at Belgaum, had been raised at the same time as the 27th; and a few symptoms of insubordination were manifested by sepoys of those regiments; but the timely arrival of a European regiment restored quiet. The English were greatly exasperated when the fact came to light that one of the conspirators detected at Belgaum was a moonshee who had been receiving a hundred and fifty rupees per month for instructing officers of regiments in Hindustani.

The three presidencies were all anxiously watching the state of feeling in the large and important country of Hyderabad, the dominions of the Nizam; for that country borders on Nagpoor on the northeast; while on the southeast and on the west it is conterminous with districts belonging to Madras and to Bombay respectively. Its two largest cities, Hyderabad in the southeast portion, and Aurungabad in the northwest, contained many English families belonging to military and civil servants of the Company; or at least the families were at stations not far from those cities. By the terms of various treaties between the Nizam and the Company, the latter had the right of maintaining a large military cantonment at Secunderabad, a few miles north of Hyderabad city. This cantonment was three miles in length, and was well provided with officers' bungalows and mess-houses, European barracks, sepoy lines, horse-artillery lines, foot-artillery barracks, native bazaars, parade-ground, hospitals, arsenal, and all the other requisites for a large military station. The cavalry lines were two miles north of the cantonment, at Bowenpilly. The military station for the troops belonging to the Nizam as an independent sovereign was at Bolarum, somewhat further away from Hyderabad, but still within easy reach of Secunderabad. At the time of the mutiny the British resident at Hyderabad was placed in a position of some difficulty. Although there was a large force at Secunderabad, it comprised scarcely any British troops; and therefore, if trouble arose, he could only look to defence from natives by natives. The capital of the Deccan, or the Nizam's territory, comprised within itself many elements of insecurity. The government and a large portion of the inhabitants were Mohammedan; the rabble of the city was numerous and ruthless; the Nizam's own army was formed on the same model as the contingents which had so generally mutinied in Hindostan; the Company's own forces, as just mentioned, were almost entirely native; and the city and province were at all times thronged with predatory bands of Rohillas, Afghans, Arabs, and other mercenaries, in the pay of the nobles and jaghiredars of the Hyderabad court. It is almost certain that if the Nizam had turned against us, Southern India would have been in a blaze of insurrection; but he was faithful; and his chief minister, Salar Jung, steadily supported him in all measures calculated to put down disturbance. The news of the rebel-triumph at Delhi set in tumultuous motion the turbulent Mussulmans of Hyderabad; and it has been well observed that 'a single moment of indecision, a single act of impolicy, a single false step, or a single admission of weakness, might have turned Hyderabad into a Lucknow and made a second Oude of the Deccan.' The Nizam, his prime minister, and the British resident, all brought sagacity and firmness to bear on the duties of their respective offices; and thus the Deccan and Southern India were saved. What might have been the case under other circumstances was foreshadowed by the events of the 17th of July. On the preceding day, intelligence was received at the Residency, which stands clear of the city, but at the distance of some few miles from the British cantonment at Secunderabad, that the mob in the city was much excited, and that a scheme was on foot to press the Nizam to attack the Residency. Notice was sent from the Residency to Salar Jung, and preparations were made. Early in the evening on the 17th, a Rohilla rabble stole forth from the city, and made for the Residency. An express was at once sent off to cantonments for aid; and in the meantime the guard, with three guns, went out to attack the insurgents. Captain Holmes plied his grape-shot effectively from the three guns; and when cavalry and horse-artillery arrived from Secunderabad, the Rohillas received a total discomfiture. This was almost the only approach to a mutiny that occurred in the portion of the Deccan near the Carnatic frontier.

Aurungabad, on the Bombay side of the Nizam's dominions, was, in regard to mutinies, less important than Hyderabad, because more easily accessible for European troops; but more important, in so far as the sepoy regiments of Malwah and Rajpootana were nearer at hand to be affected by evil temptation. The city is about seventy miles distant from Ahmednuggur, and a hundred and seventy from Bombay. Uneasiness prevailed here so early as June. The 1st cavalry and the 2d infantry, of the corps called the Hyderabad Contingent, were stationed at Aurungabad; and of these, the former showed signs of disaffection. Captain Abbott, commanding the regiment, found on the morning of the 13th that his men were murmuring and threatening, as if unwilling to act against mutineers elsewhere; indeed, they had sworn to murder their officers if any attempt were made to employ them in that way. Fortunately, the ressaldars—each being a native captain of a troop of cavalry, and there being therefore as many ressaldars in a regiment as there were troops or companies—remained faithful; and Captain Abbott, with Lieutenant Dowker, were enabled to discuss with these officers the state of the regiment. The ressaldars assured the captain that many of the troopers had begun to talk loudly about the King of Delhi as their rightful ruler. The resident at the court of the Nizam, through the military secretary, Major Briggs, advised Captain Abbott—seeing that no aid could be expected from any other quarter—to speak in as conciliatory a tone as possible to the men, and to promise them that they should not be required to act against the insurgents at Delhi, provided they would be obedient to other orders. Quiet was in this way restored; but it being a dangerous precedent thus to allow troops to decide where and against whom they would choose to fight, Major-general Woodburn, who had been placed in command of a movable column from Bombay, marched through Ahmednuggur to Aurungabad. This column consisted of the 28th Bombay native infantry, the 14th dragoons, Captain Woolcombe's battery, and a pontoon train. When Woodburn arrived, he found that the ladies had all left the Aurungabad station, that the officers were living barricaded in the mess-room, and that all the Nizam's troops exhibited unfavourable symptoms. The first native cavalry, when confronted with Woodburn's troops, behaved in a very daring way; and about a hundred of them made off, owing to the unwillingness of the general to open fire upon them, although Abbott and Woolcombe saw the importance of so doing.

In the country north of Bombay, and between it and Malwah, many slight events occurred, sufficient to shew that the native troops were in an agitated state, as if oscillating between the opposite principles of fidelity and treachery. It was worthy of note, however, that the troops thus affected were, in very few instances, those belonging to the Company's Bombay army; they were generally contingent corps, or Mahrattas, or Rajpoots, or men imbued with the same ideas as the Hindustanis and Oudians. Towards the close of July, a few troopers of the Gujerat Irregular Horse endeavoured to incite their companions to mutiny; they failed, and then decamped; but were pursued and captured, and then hung in presence of their own regiment.

Still further northward lies the country which, under the various names of Scindia's territory, Holkar's territory, Malwah, and Bhopal, has already been described as the chief seat of the Mahratta power, and which corresponds pretty nearly with the region marked out by the Company's officials as 'Central India.' We have seen in former pages * that Scindia, chief of the Mahratta state of which Gwalior is the capital, offered the aid of his Contingent army to Mr Colvin in May; that Lieutenant Cockburn, with half a cavalry regiment of this Contingent, rendered good service in the region around Agra, until the troopers deserted him; that the fidelity of Scindia to the British alone prevented his

* Chapter vii., p. 111; chapter xi., pp. 181-189.

troops generally from joining the rebels, for they belonged to the same Hindustani and Oudian families, though serving a Mahratta prince in a Mahratta state; that after certain detachments had mutinied at Neemuch and elsewhere, the main body rose in revolt at Gwalior on the 14th of June, murdered some of the English officers, drove away the rest with their families, and formally threw off all allegiance to the Company; and that Maharajah Scindia, under circumstances of great difficulty and peril, managed to keep peace at Gwalior—retaining and feeding the troops at that place, and yet discountenancing their mutinous tendencies against the British. If he had not acted with much tact and judgment, the Gwalior Contingent would have marched to Agra in a body, and greatly imperiled the British 'raj.' Not only did he keep those troublesome troops near him during the remaining half of June, but also during July and August. Scindia's

Mount Aboo—Military Sanitarium in Rajpootana.

special army, entirely under his own control, were chiefly Mahrattas, who had little sympathy with the soldiers of the Contingent; but they were too few in number to put down the latter, and therefore he was forced to temporise—partly by persuasions and promises, partly by threats. Major Macpherson, the British political agent, and Brigadier Ramsey, the military commandant, ceased to have influence at Gwalior; it was Scindia's good faith alone that stood the British in stead.

Holkar's Mahratta territory, with Indore for its chief city, we have, in like manner, seen to be troubled with a mutinous spirit in the Contingent troops, partly owing to temptation from other quarters. We have briefly shewn in the chapters lately cited, that on the 28th of May the 15th and 30th Bengal native infantry revolted at Nuseerabad; that on the 2d of June, influenced by this pernicious example, the 72d B. N. I., the 7th regiment of Gwalior Contingent infantry, and the main body of the 1st Bengal native cavalry, mutinied at Neemuch; that on the 1st of July, a portion of Holkar's Contingent rose against the British at Indore, without his wish or privity, and that he could not get even his own special troops to act against those of the Contingent; that, on the evening of the same day, the 23d Bengal native infantry, and one squadron of the 1st Bengal native cavalry, mutinied at Mhow; and that numerous British officers and their families were thrown into great misery by these several occurrences. It now remains to be stated that, during July and August, Holkar adopted nearly the same course as Scindia; he remained faithful to the British, and endeavoured to quell the mutinous spirit among his troops. Holkar possessed, however, less influence than his brother-chieftain; most of the mutineers from Indore and Mhow marched to Gwalior, and were only prevented by the shrewdness of Scindia from extending their march to Agra.

Among the troops in Rajpootana were the Deesa Field Brigade, commanded towards the close of August by Brigadier Creagh, who had under his control the troops at Deesa, those at the sanitarium on Mount Aboo, and those at Erinpoora and other places in the neighbourhood. These places were thrown into confusion during the last two weeks of the month, by the mutiny of the Jhodpore legion, consisting partly of cavalry and partly of infantry. Such of these men as were stationed at Erinpoora, about 550 in number, rose in mutiny on the 22d. They suddenly threw off their allegiance; seized the guns; made prisoners of Lieutenant Conolly and the European serjeants; plundered the bazaar and some of the native villages; burned all the officers' bungalows, and destroyed or appropriated all that they found therein; lived in tents on the parade-ground for three days; and then marched off in the direction of Nuseerabad. The cavalry, although forming part of the same legion, and sharing in the movement, protected the Europeans from the infantry. Among the latter, it was only the Hindustani portion which revolted; there were some Bheels in the legion who remained faithful. On the preceding day (21st), about 100 men of the legion had mutinied at Mount Aboo; but as there was a detachment of H.M. 83d there, the mutineers did nothing but hastily escape. A native chieftain, the Rao of Sihori, was prompt to render any aid he could to Captain Hall at Mount Aboo. Another portion of the Jhodpore legion was at Jhodpore itself, where the mutiny placed in great peril Captain Monck Mason, British resident at that native state; by his energy, he provided an asylum for many ladies and children who had been driven from other stations; but he himself fell by the swords of a body of mutinous troopers, under circumstances of mingled cowardice and brutality.

The state of this part of India during July and August may be summed up in a few words. By the revolt of the Contingents of Scindia, Holkar, and Bhopal, and of the Jhodpore legion, English residents were driven from station to station in much peril and suffering, and English influence became for a time almost a nullity; but the native chieftains for the most part remained faithful, even though their troops revolted; and there were hopes of ultimate success from the arrival of relieving columns belonging to the Bombay army. Of that army, a few fragments of regiments occasionally displayed mutinous symptoms, but not to such a degree as to leaven the whole mass. What the officers felt through the treachery of the troops, and what their families suffered during all these strange events, need not again be described; both phases of the Revolt have received many illustrations in former pages; but this chapter may fittingly close with two short extracts from letters relating to the mutinies at the stations of Mhow and Indore. An artillery officer, commenting on the ingratitude of the sepoys towards commanders who had always used them well, said: 'I must not forget to mention that Colonel Platt was like a father to the men; and that when he had an opportunity of leaving them and joining a European corps last summer, the men petitioned him to stay. He had been upwards of thirty years with them, and when the mutiny took place he had so much confidence in them that he rode up to their lines before we could get out. When we found him next morning, both cheeks were blown off, his back completely riddled with balls, one through each thigh, his chin smashed into his mouth, and three sabre-cuts between the cheek-bone and temple; also a cut across the shoulder and the back of the neck.' The following few words are from the letters of a lady who was among those that escaped death by flight from Indore: 'I have already given you an account of our three days and three nights of wandering, with little rest and not much food, no clothes to change, burning sun, and deluges of rain; but —— and I, perhaps, could bear these things better than others, and suffered less. When we heard the poor famishing children screaming for food, we could but thank God that ours were not with us, but safe in England. We found kind friends here, and I am in Mrs ——'s clothes; everything we had being gone. The destructive wretches, after we left Indore, commenced doing all the damage they could—cutting up carpets with their tulwars, smashing chandeliers, marble tables, slabs, chairs, &c.; they even cut out the cloth and lining of our carriages, hacking up the woodwork. The Residency is uninhabitable, and almost all have lost everything. I might have saved a few things in the hour and a half that elapsed between the outbreak and our retreat; but I had so relied on some of our defenders, and felt so secure of holding on, that flight never for a moment occurred to me.'

Note.

The British at the Military Stations.—The reader will have gathered, from the details given in various chapters, that the stations at which the military servants of the Company resided, in the *Mofussil* or country districts, bore a remarkable relation to the Indian towns and cities. They were in most cases separated from the towns by distances varying from one mile to ten, and formed small towns in themselves. Sometimes the civil officers had their bungalows and cutcheries near these military cantonments; while in other instances they were in or near the city to which the cantonment was a sort of appendage. Such, with more or less variety of detail, was the case at Patna (Dinapoor), Benares (Chunar), Cawnpore, Lucknow, Allahabad, Furruckabad (Futteghur), Agra, Delhi, Gwalior, Lahore (Meean Meer), Nagpoor (Kamptee), Indore (Mhow), Hyderabad (Secunderabad), Moorshedabad (Berhampore), Saugor, &c. The marked separation between the native and the British portions of the military stations has been described in a very animated way, by an able and distinguished correspondent of the *Times*, one of whose letters contains the following paragraph:

'For six miles along the banks of the Ganges extend the ruins of the English station of Cawnpore. You observe how distinct they are from the city. The palace of the Victoria Regia at Chatsworth is not more unlike the dirty ditch in which lives the humble duck-weed—Belgravia is not more dissimilar to Spitalfields—than is the English quarter of an Indian station to the city to which it is attached. The one is generally several miles away from the other. There is no common street, no link to connect the one with the others; and the one knows nothing of the other. Here are broad roads, lined on each side with trees and walls, or with park-like grounds, inside which you can catch glimpses of gaily-painted one-storied villas, of brick, covered with cement, decorated with Corinthian colonnades, porticoes, and broad verandahs—each in its own wide park, with gardens in front, orchards, and out-offices. There are narrow, tortuous, unpaved lanes, hemmed in by tottering, haggard, miserable houses, close and high, and packed as close as they can stand (and only for that they would fall), swarming with a hungry-eyed population. The mosque and the Hindoo temple are near each other, but they both shun the church, just as the station avoids the city. . . . In the station there are hotels, ball-rooms, magazines, shops, where all the habits and customs of Europe, sometimes improved and refined by the influence of the East, are to be found; and when the cool of the evening sets in, out stream the carriages and horses and buggies, for the fashionable drive past the long line of detached villas within their neat enclosures, surrounded by shadowing groves and rich gardens. They pass the lines or barracks of the native infantry—a race of whom they know almost less than they do of the people of the town; and they are satisfied with the respect of action, with the sudden uprising, the stiff attitude of attention, the cold salute, regardless of the insolence and dislike of the eye; they chat and laugh, marry and are given in marriage, have their horse-races, their balls, their card-parties, their dinners, their plate, their tradesmen's bills, their debts; in fact, their everything that English society has, and thus they lived till the deluge came upon them. We all know how nobly they stemmed its force, what heroic struggles they made against its fury. But what a surprise when it burst in upon them! What a blow to all their traditions! What a rebuke to their blind confidence! There is at the moment I write these lines a slight explosion close at hand, followed by the ascent of some dark columns of earth and bricks into the air. We are blowing up the Assembly-rooms of Cawnpore in order to clear the ground in front of the guns of our intrenchment, and billiard-rooms and ball-rooms are flying up in fragments to the skies. Is not that a strange end for all Cawnpore society to come to? Is it not a curious commentary on our rule, and on our position in India?'

Native Musicians at a Sepoy station.

BRIGADIER-GENERAL NICHOLSON.—Copied by permission from a Portrait published by Messrs Gambart.

CHAPTER XVIII.

THE SIEGE OF DELHI: FINAL OPERATIONS.

AFTER eleven weeks of hostile occupation, after seven weeks of besieging, the great city of Delhi still remained in the hands of a mingled body of mutineers and rebels—mutineers who had thrown off their soldierly allegiance to their British employers; and rebels who clustered around the shadowy representative of an extinct Mogul dynasty. Nay, more—not only was Delhi still unconquered at the end of July; it was relatively stronger than ever. The siege-army had been increased; but the besiegers had increased in number in a still larger ratio. General Anson* had had thirteen days of command, in reference to the preparations for the reconquest of the city, before his death; General Barnard, forty, before he likewise died; General Reed, twelve, before his retirement; General Wilson, thirteen, by the end of July; and now the last-named commander was called upon to measure the strength with which he could open the August series of siege-operations.

It may be convenient slightly to recapitulate a

* Chap. xiv., pp. 230-246.

few events, and to mention a few dates, connected with the earlier weeks of the siege, as a means of refreshing the memory of the reader concerning the train of operations which, in the present chapter, is to be traced to an end.

It will be remembered, then, that as soon as the startling mutinies at Delhi and Meerut became known to the military authorities at the hill-stations, the 75th foot were ordered down from Kussowlie, the 1st Europeans from Dugshai, and the 2d Europeans from Subathoo—all to proceed to Umballa, there to form portions of a siege-army for Delhi; that a siege-train was prepared at Phillour; that Generals Anson and Barnard, and other officers, held a council of war at Umballa on the 16th of May, and concerted such plans as were practicable on the spur of the moment; and that troops began at once to march southeastward towards Delhi. We have further seen that Anson was troubled by the presence of Bengal native troops whom he could not trust, and by the scarcity of good artillerymen to accompany his siege-train; and that his operations were suddenly cut off by a fatal attack of cholera, under which he sank on the 27th. Next we traced twelve days' operations of Sir Henry Barnard, during which he had advanced to Raneeput, Paniput, Rhye, Alipore, Badulla Serai, and Azadpore, to the ridge northward of Delhi, on which he established his siege-camp on the 8th of June; he had just been joined by General Wilson, who had beaten the enemy at Ghazeeoodeen Nuggur, and had crossed the Jumna from Meerut near Bhagput. Then came the diversified siege-operations of the month of June, with a force which began about 3000 strong, aided by 22 field-guns and 17 siege-guns and mortars—the arrival on the 9th of the Guide corps, after their surprising march in fiercely hot weather from Peshawur; the bold attack made by the rebels on the same day; the manifest proofs that the siege-guns were too light, too few, and too distant, to batter the defences of the city; the commencement on the 13th, but the speedy abandonment as impracticable, of a project for storming the place; the continual arrival of mutineers to swell the number of defenders within Delhi; the daily sallies of the enemy; the daily weakening of the small British force; and the necessity for employing one-half of the whole siege-army on picket-duty, to prevent surprises. We have seen how Hindoo Rao's house became a constant target for the enemy's guns, and Metcalfe House for attacks of less frequency; how Major Reid, with his Goorkhas and Guides, guarded the ridge with indomitable steadiness, and made successful attacks on the Eedghah and Kissengunje suburbs; and how sedulously Barnard was forced to watch the movements of the enemy in the rear of his camp. Passing from June to July, the details of the former chapter told us that the siege-army became raised to about 6000 men, by various reinforcements early in the last-named month; that an assault of the city was again proposed, and again abandoned; that insurgent troops poured into Delhi more rapidly than ever; that Sir Henry Barnard died on the 5th, worn down by anxiety and cholera; that numerous canal-bridges were destroyed, to prevent the enemy from gaining access to the rear of the camp; that the British were continually thrown on the defensive, instead of actively prosecuting the siege; that the few remaining Bengal native troops in the siege-army were either sent to the Punjaub, or disarmed and unhorsed, in distrust of their fidelity; that on the 17th, General Reed gave up the command which had devolved upon him after the death of Barnard, and was succeeded by Brigadier-general Wilson; and that towards the close of the month the enemy made many desperate attempts to turn the flanks and rear of the siege-camp, requiring all the skill of the British to frustrate them.*

August arrived. The besieged, in every way stronger than the besiegers, continued their attacks on various sides of the heights. They gave annoyance, but at the same time excited contempt by the manner in which they avoided open hand-to-hand conflicts. An officer of engineers, commenting on this matter in a private letter, said: 'At Delhi, they are five or six to one against us, and see the miserable attempts they make to turn us out of our position. They swarm up the heights in front of our batteries by thousands; the ground is so broken and full of ravines and rocks, that they can come up the whole way unseen, or you may depend upon it they would never venture. If they had the pluck of a goose, their numbers might terrify us. It is in the Subzee Mundee that most of the hard fighting goes on; they get into and on the tops of the houses, and fire into our pickets there; this goes on until we send a force from camp to turn them out, which we invariably do, but not without loss. We have now cleared the ground all around of the trees, walls, and houses; as a consequence, there is a large clear space around our pickets, and Pandy will not venture out of cover; so we generally let him pop away from a distance until he is tired.' Early in the month, an attempt was made to destroy the bridge of boats over the Jumna; the rains had set in, the river was high, the stream strong, and these were deemed favourable conditions. The engineers started three 'infernal machines,' each consisting of a tub containing fifty pounds of powder, a stick protruding from the tub, and a spring connected with an explosive compound; the theory was, that if the tubs floated down to the bridge, any contact with the stick would explode the contents

* By comparing two wood-cuts—'Bird's-eye View of Delhi' (p. 64), and 'Delhi from Flagstaff Tower' (p. 76)—the reader will be assisted in forming an idea of the relative positions of the mutineers within the city, and of the British on the ridge and in the camp behind it. The 'Bird's-eye View' will be the most useful for this purpose, as combining the characteristics of a *view* and a *plan*, and shewing very clearly the river, the bridge of boats, the camp, the ridge, the broken ground in front of it, the Flagstaff Tower, Metcalfe House, the Custom-house, Hindoo Rao's house, the Samee House, the Selimgurh fort, the city, the imperial palace, the Jumma Musjid, the walls and bastions, the western suburbs, &c.

of the tub, and destroy one or more of the boats of the bridge; but there is no record of success attending this adventure. The bridge of boats being a mile and a half distant from the batteries on the ridge, it could not be harmed by any guns at that time possessed by the British; and thus the enemy, throughout the siege, had free and unmolested passage over the Jumna. The supply of ammunition available to the mutineers seemed to be almost inexhaustible; the British collected 450 round shot that had been fired at them from the enemy's guns in one day; and as the British artillerymen were few in number, they were worked nearly to exhaustion in keeping up the necessary cannonade to repel the enemy's fire. Although the 'Pandies' avoided contests in the open field, many of their movements were made with much secrecy and skill—especially that of the 1st of August, when at least 5000 troops appeared in the vicinity of the British position, by a combined movement from two different quarters, and made an attack which nothing but the courage and skill of Major Reid and his handful of brave fellows could have withstood. In some of these numerous operations, when the rainy season commenced, the amount of fatigue borne by the troops was excessive. It was the special duty of the cavalry, not being immediately available for siege-services, to guard the rear of the camp from surprise; and to insure this result, they held themselves ready to 'boot and saddle' at a few minutes' notice—glad if they could insure only a few hours of sleep in the twenty-four. Many an officer, on picket or reconnoitring duty, would be in the saddle twelve hours together, in torrents of rain, without food or refreshment of any kind. Yet, with all their trials, they spoke and wrote cheerfully. An artillery-officer said: 'Our position here is certainly by nature a wonderfully secure one; and if the Pandies could not have found a better place than Delhi as the head-quarters of their mutiny, with an unlimited magazine at their disposal, I doubt if *we* could have been so well off anywhere else. Providence has assisted us in every way. From the beginning, the weather has been most propitious; and in cantonments I have never seen troops so healthy as they are here now. Cholera occasionally pays us a visit, but that must always be expected in a large standing camp. The river Jumna completely protects our left flank and front; while the large jheel (water-course) which runs away to the south-west is at this season quite impassable for miles, preventing any surprise on our right flank; so that a few cavalry are sufficient as a guard for three faces of our position'—that is, a few, if constantly on the alert, and never shirking a hard day's work in any weather.

The enemy gradually tired of attacks on the rear of the camp, which uniformly failed; but they did not cease to maintain an aggressive attitude. Early in the month, they commenced a series of efforts to drive the British from the Metcalfe post or picket. This Metcalfe House, the peaceful residence of a civil-service officer until the disastrous 11th of May, had become an important post to the besiegers. As early as four days after the arrival of the siege-army on the ridge, the enemy had emerged from the city, concealed themselves in some ravines around Sir T. Metcalfe's house, and thence made a formidable attack on the Flagstaff Tower. To prevent a recurrence of this danger, a large picket was sent to occupy the house, and to form it into a river-side or left flank to the siege-position. This picket was afterwards thrown in advance of the house, and divided into three portions—one on a mound near the road leading from the Cashmere Gate to the cantonment Sudder bazaar; a second in a house midway between this mound and the river; and a third in a range of stables close to the river. All the portions of this picket were gradually strengthened by the engineers, as reinforcements reached them. The Flagstaff Tower was also well guarded; and as the night-sentries paced the whole distance between the tower and the Metcalfe pickets, the belt of rugged ground between the ridge and the river was effectually rendered impassable for the enemy. These various accessions of strength, however, were made only at intervals, as opportunity offered; at the time now under notice, they were very imperfectly finished. The enemy plied the Metcalfe picket vigorously with shot and shell, from guns brought out of the Cashmere Gate and posted a few hundred yards in advance of the city wall; while a number of infantry skirmishers, many of whom were riflemen, kept up a nearly incessant fire from the jungle in front. Although the losses at the Metcalfe picket were not numerous, owing to the good cover, the approach to it for reliefs, &c., was rendered extremely perilous; and as this species of attack was in many ways annoying to the British, General Wilson resolved to frustrate it. He placed under the command of Brigadier Showers a force of about 1300 men,* by whom the insurgents were suddenly surprised on the morning of the 12th, and driven off with great loss. It was a sharp contest, for the brigadier had more than a hundred killed and wounded. Showers himself was in the list of wounded; as were also Major Coke, Captain Greville, Lieutenants Sherriff, James, Lindesay, Maunsell, and Owen. Four guns belonging to the enemy were captured and brought into camp; but the chief advantage derived from the skirmish was in securing the abandonment of a mode of attack likely to be very annoying to the besiegers. The insurgents, it is true, by placing guns on the opposite side of the Jumna, frequently

* H.M. 75th foot,	100 men.
1st Bengal Europeans,	350 "
Coke's Punjaub Rifles,	250 "
H.M. 8th foot,	100 "
2d Bengal Europeans,	100 "
Kumaon Goorkhas,	100 "
4th Sikh infantry,	100 "
H.M. 9th Lancers,	one squadron.
Horse artillery,	six guns.

sent a shot or shell across; but the danger here was lessened by shifting the camp of the 1st Punjaub infantry.

That the siege-army was weakened by these perpetual encounters, need hardly be said. Every day witnessed the carrying of many gallant fellows to the camp-hospital or to the grave. At about the middle of August, the force comprised 3571 European officers and men, and 2070 native officers and men, fit for duty; with 28 horse-artillery guns (6 and 9 pounders) and a small supply of siege-artillery. A detail of the component elements of the force, and of the ratio which the effectives bore to the sick and wounded, will be more usefully given presently in connection with the September operations. Knowing well from dearly-bought experience that he could not successfully assault and capture Delhi with his present force, General Wilson looked anxiously for reinforcements from the Punjaub, which were due about the middle of the month. Indeed, all in camp were prepared to welcome one who, from the daring and energy which characterised nearly all the operations with which he had been intrusted, had earned from some the title of the 'Lion,' from others that of the 'Bayard,' of the Punjaub. This was Brigadier-general Nicholson, a soldier who had attained to that rank at an unusually early age. About the end of June, Sir John Lawrence had intrusted to him a flying column which had been organised at Wuzeerabad,* but which had undergone many vicissitudes; for Nicholson had been compelled to disarm all the Bengal native troops who were in his column. As we have seen in former pages, the brigadier struck terror into the mutineers, and swept away bands of rebels in front and on either side of him in the region between the Chenab and the Sutlej. He nearly annihilated the Sealkote mutineers near Goordaspore,† and then cleared the country during a long march, in fearfully hot weather, to Delhi. He himself with a few companions reached the city on the 8th of August; but the bulk of his column did not arrive till the 14th. Its composition had undergone some change; and it now comprised H.M. 52d foot, the remaining wing of the 61st foot, the 2d Punjaub infantry, 200 Moultan horse, and a small force of artillery—in all, about 1100 Europeans and 1400 Punjaub troops. Valuable, however, as was this accession of strength, it could not immediately affect the siege-operations; seeing that it was necessary to await the arrival of another siege-train, which Sir John Lawrence had caused to be collected at Ferozpore, and which was on its way to Delhi, with great stores of ammunition.

As soon as General Wilson found himself aided by the energetic Nicholson, he gave additional efficiency to his army by grouping the infantry into four brigades, thus constituted: *First* brigade, under Brigadier Showers, H.M. 75th foot, 2d Bengal Europeans, and the Kumaon battalion of Goorkhas; *Second*, under Colonel Lenfield, H.M. 52d foot, H.M. 60th Rifles, and the Sirmoor battalion of Goorkhas; *Third*, under Colonel Jones, H.M. 8th foot, H.M. 61st foot, and Rothney's Sikhs; *Fourth*, under Brigadier Nicholson, 1st Bengal Europeans, 1st Punjaub infantry (Coke's rifles), and 2d Punjaub infantry (Green's Rifles). The Guides were not brigaded, but were left free for service in any quarter. The cavalry was placed under Brigadier Grant, and the artillery under Brigadier Garbett. Nicholson had brought with him a few guns; nevertheless it was necessary, as just remarked, to wait for a regular siege-train before a bombardment of the city could be attempted. The camp, organised as it now was, although it put on a somewhat more regular appearance than before, was a singular phenomenon, owing to the mode in which European and Asiatic elements were combined in it. An officer who was present through all the operations has given, in a letter which went the round of the newspapers, a graphic account of the camp, with its British and native troops, its varieties of costume, its dealers and servants, its tents and animals, and all the details of a scene picturesque to an observer who could for a moment forget the stern meaning which underlay it.* About the time of Nicholson's arrival, Lieutenant Hodson was intrusted by General Wilson with an enterprise small in character but useful in result. It was to watch a party of the enemy who had moved out from Delhi on the Rohtuk road, and to afford support, if necessary, either to Soneeput or to the Jheend rajah, who remained faithful to his alliance with the British. Hodson started on the night of the 14th of August with a detachment of about 350 cavalry, comprising 230 of the irregular horse named after himself, 100 Guide cavalry, and a few Jheend cavalry. The enemy were known

* H.M. 52d light infantry.
35th Bengal native infantry.
2d Punjaub infantry.
9th Bengal native cavalry, one wing.
Moultan horse.
Dawe's troop of horse-artillery.
Smyth's troop of native foot-artillery.
Bourchier's light-infantry battery.

† During that famous pursuit and defeat of the Sealkote mutineers, a wing of H.M. 52d foot marched sixty-two miles in forty-eight hours of an Indian summer, besides fighting with an enemy who resisted with more than their usual determination. It was work worthy of a regiment which had marched *three thousand miles in four years.*

* 'What a sight our camp would be even to those who visited Sebastopol! The long lines of tents, the thatched hovels of the native servants, the rows of horses, the parks of artillery, the English soldier in his gray linen coat and trousers (he has fought as bravely as ever without pipeclay), the Sikhs with their red and blue turbans, the Afghans with their red and blue turbans, their wild air, and their gay head-dresses and coloured saddle-cloths, and the little Goorkhas, dressed up to the ugliness of demons in black worsted Kilmarnock hats and woollen coats—the truest, bravest soldiers in our pay. There are scarcely any Poorbeahs (Hindustanis) left in our ranks, but of native servants many a score. In the rear are the booths of the native bazaars, and further out on the plain the thousands of camels, bullocks, and horses that carry our baggage. The soldiers are loitering through the lines or in the bazaars. Suddenly the alarm is sounded. Every one rushes to his tent. The infantry soldier seizes his musket and slings on his pouch, the artilleryman gets his guns harnessed, the Afghan rides out to explore; in a few minutes everybody is in his place.

'If we go to the summit of the ridge of hill which separates us from the city, we see the river winding along to the left, the bridge of boats, the towers of the palace, and the high roof and minarets of the great mosque, the roofs and gardens of the doomed city, and the elegant-looking walls, with batteries here and there, the white smoke of which rises slowly up among the green foliage that clusters round the ramparts.'

to have passed through Sampiah on the way to Rohtuk; and Hodson resolved to anticipate them by a flank-movement. On the 15th, at the village of Khurkowdeh, he captured a large number of mutineer cavalry, by a stratagem at once bold and ingenious. On the 16th the enemy marched to Rohtuk, and Hodson in pursuit of them. On the 17th skirmishes took place near Rohtuk itself; but on the 18th Hodson succeeded in drawing forth the main body of rebels, who suffered a speedy and complete defeat. They were not simply mutineers from Delhi; they comprised many depredatory bodies that greatly troubled such of the petty rajahs as wished to remain faithful to or in alliance with the British. Lieutenant Hodson, by dispersing them, aided in pacifying the district around the siege-camp—a matter of much consideration. A letter from one of the officers of the Guides will afford a good idea of the manner in which all fought in those stirring times, and of the language in which the deeds were narrated when the formality of official documents was not needed.*

For ten days after Nicholson's arrival, little was effected on either side save this skirmish of Hodson's at Rohtuk. Wilson did not want to begin; it was not his strategy; he steadily held his own until the formidable siege-train could arrive. On the other hand, the enemy were foiled in every movement; all their attacks had failed.

Nicholson was on the alert to render good service; and the opportunity was not long in presenting itself. His energy as a soldier and his skill as a general were rendered very conspicuous in his battle of Nujuffghur, resembling in its tactics some of those in which Havelock had been engaged. General Wilson obtained intelligence that a force of the enemy was advancing from Delhi towards Bahadoorghur, with the apparent intention of attacking the siege-camp in the rear; the distance between the city and the town being about twenty miles, and the latter being nearly due west of the former. Or, as seems more probable (seeing that all attacks on the rear of the camp had signally failed), the enemy may have intended to cross the Nujuffghur jheel or water-course, and intercept the siege-train which they as well as the British knew to be on the way from Ferozpore. One account of the matter is, that Bukhtar Singh, a rebel who had gained unenviable notoriety at Bareilly, had got into disfavour with the King of Delhi for his want of success as one of the military leaders within the city; that he had offered, if a good force were only placed at his disposal, to wipe off the discredit by a crowning victory over the Feringhees; and that, in pursuance of this object, he proposed to get in rear of the siege-camp, intercept the expected siege-train, capture it, and cut off all communication between the camp and Umballa. Whatever may have been the main purpose, the expeditionary force was of considerable strength, amounting to 7000 men, and comprising the whole or large portions of six mutinied infantry regiments, three of irregular cavalry, and numerous artillery. The general, on receipt of this information, at once placed a column* under the command of Brigadier Nicholson, with instructions to frustrate the operations of the enemy. The brigadier started at daybreak on the 25th of August, crossed two difficult swamps, and arrived at Nangiooe, a village about midway between Delhi and Bahadoorghur. During a halt and a reconnoitre, it was found that the enemy had crossed a bridge over the Nujuffghur jheel, and would probably encamp in the afternoon near the town of the same name. Nicholson determined to push on against them that same evening. After another ten-mile march, during which his troops had to wade through a sheet of water three feet deep, he came up with the enemy about five o'clock, and found them posted in a position two miles in length, extending from the bridge to the town: they had thirteen guns, of which four were in a strong position at an old serai on their left centre. The brigadier, after a brief reconnaissance, resolved first to attack the enemy's left centre, which was their strongest point, and then, 'changing front to the left,' sweep down their line of guns towards the bridge. His guns having fired a few rounds, the critical moment for a charge arrived; he addressed his men, told them what a bayonet charge had always been in the British army, and shouted—'Advance!' The infantry charged, and drove the enemy out of the

* 'The first day we marched to a place called Khurkowdeh, but such a march! We had to go through water for miles up to the horses' girths. We took Khurkowdeh by surprise, and Hodson immediately placed men over the gates, and we went in. Shot one scoundrel instanter, cut down another, and took a ressaldar (native officer) and some sowars (troopers) prisoners, and came to a house occupied by some more, who would not let us in at all; at last, we rushed in and found the rascals had taken to the upper story, and still kept us at bay. There was only one door and a kirkee (window). I shoved in my head through the door, with a pistol in my hand, and got a chip over my turban for my pains; my pistol missed fire at the man's breast (you must send me a revolver), so I got out of that as fast as I could, and then tried the kirkee with the other barrel, and very nearly got another cut. We tried every means to get in, but could not, so we fired the house, and out they rushed a muck among us. The first fellow went at ——, who wounded him, but somehow or other he slipped and fell on his back. I saw him fall, and, thinking he was hurt, rushed to the rescue. A Guide got a chop at the fellow, and I gave him such a swinging back-hander that he fell dead. I then went at another fellow rushing by my left, and sent my sword through him, like butter, and bagged him. I then looked round and saw a sword come crash on the shoulders of a poor youth; oh, such a cut; and up went the sword again, and the next moment the boy would have been in eternity, but I ran forward and covered him with my sword and saved him. During this it was over with seven men, —— had shot one with his revolver, and the other four were cut down at once. Having polished off these fellows, we held an impromptu court-martial on those we had taken, and shot them all—murderers every one, who were justly rewarded for their deeds.'

* H.M. 9th Lancers	(Captain Sarrell),	One squadron.
Guide cavalry	(Captain Sandford),	120 men.
2d Punjaub cavalry,		80 "
Moultan horse.		
H.M. 61st foot,	(Colonel Renny),	420 "
1st Bengal Europeans	(Major Jacob),	380 "
1st Punjaub infantry	(Coke's),	400 "
2d Punjaub infantry	(Green's),	400 "
Sappers and Miners,		30 "
Horse-artillery	(Tombs' and Olphert's),	Sixteen guns.

Captain (now Major) Olphert being ill, the command of his troop was taken by Captain Remington.

serai with great impetuosity. He then changed front to the left, and so completely outflanked the enemy that they fled at once from the field, leaving thirteen guns behind them. While this was being done, Lieutenant Lumsden advanced to Nujuffghur, and cleared it of insurgents. A small number of the enemy concealed themselves in the neighbouring village of Nuglee; and when attacked, in a way that left no loophole for escape, they fought so desperately as to bring down a considerable number of Lumsden's party, including the lieutenant himself. The enemy's cavalry effected little or nothing; while Nicholson's was employed chiefly in guarding baggage and escorting guns. Nicholson passed the night near the bridge, which had been the object of a fierce attack and defence during the evening, and which he succeeded in blowing up about two o'clock in the morning—thus cutting off one of the few approaches by which the mutineers from the city could get to the main line of road behind the camp. Nicholson returned to camp on the 26th, after a few hours' rest for his exhausted troops. They had indeed had a hard day's labour on the 25th; for they marched eighteen miles to the field of battle—starting at daybreak, and crossing two difficult swamps before they could arrive at Nanglooe; and, to use the words of their commander in his dispatch, 'as it would not have been prudent to take the baggage across the ford at Baprowla, they were obliged, after fourteen hours' marching and fighting, to bivouac on the field without food or covering of any kind.' There seems to have been something wrong here. One of the officers has said: 'Unfortunately, through some mistake, I suppose, the grog for the men had not arrived, nor commissariat rations; and it is wonderful how they bore up against the privations of a long march, some hard fighting, and no food. A little grumbling was occasionally heard, but good-humour and cheerfulness were the order of the day.' Such of them as had time to sleep at all during the night, slept on the damp ground; but all these exigencies of a soldier's life were soon forgotten, and the troops returned to camp in high spirits at their success. Nicholson had relied fully on the Punjaubees in the day of battle, and they justified his reliance, for they emulated the courage and soldierly qualities of the European troops who formed the *élite* of the force. He had to regret the loss of 25 killed, including Lieutenants Lumsden and Gabbett; and of 70 wounded, including Major Jacob and Lieutenant Elkington. The brigadier's official dispatch contained some curious particulars not always given in such documents. It appears that during the day his men fired off 17,000 musket and rifle charges, and 650 cannon-shot and shells—a murderous torrent, that may perhaps convey to the mind of a reader some faint idea of the terrible ordeal of a battle. He captured all the enemy's guns and ammunition; but a better result was, the frustration of an attack which might have been very annoying, if not dangerous, on the rear of the camp. Of the guns captured, nine were English field-pieces, formerly belonging to the regular Bengal army; while the other four were native brass guns belonging to the imperial palace at Delhi.

The Delhi insurgents, whether well or ill commanded, manifested no careless inattention to what was occurring outside the city walls. They were nearly always well informed of the proceedings of the besiegers. They knew that a large siege-train was expected, which they much longed to intercept; they knew that Brigadier Nicholson had gone out to Nujuffghur on the morning of the 25th; they knew that he had not returned to camp on the morning of the 26th; and they resolved on another attack on the camp in its then weakened state. All was in vain, however; in this as in every similar attempt they were beaten. As soon as they made their appearance, General Wilson strengthened his pickets. The enemy commenced by a fire with field-guns from Ludlow Castle against the Mosque picket; but the attack never became serious; it was steadily met, and the enemy, after suffering severely, retired into the city.

During the later days of August, the enemy attempted little more than a series of skirmishing attacks on the pickets. If, once now and then, they appeared in force outside the walls as though about to attack in a body, the intention was speedily abandoned, and they disappeared again within the city. No evidence was afforded that they were headed by any officer possessing unity of command and military ability. There was no Sevajee, no Hyder among them. 'Often,' as an eye-witness observed, 'like an undisciplined mob, at best merely an agglomeration of regiments, the rebels have attacked us again and again, and fiercely enough when under cover, but always with a poverty of conception and want of plan that betrayed the absence of a master-mind. And now that they know strong reinforcements have joined our army, and that the day of retribution is not far distant—although they may make an attempt to intercept the siege-train—yet by their vacillating and abortive gatherings outside the walls, and by the dissensions and desertions that are rife within, they shew that the huge body of the insurrection is still without a vigorous and life-giving spirit.'

True as this may have been in the particular instance, it is nevertheless impossible not to be struck with the fact that the mutineers maintained a remarkable degree of organisation after they had forsworn their allegiance; the men of all the corps rallied round the colours belonging to each particular regiment; and those regiments which had customarily been massed into brigades, long strove to maintain the brigade character. Although the insurrection possessed few elements of unity, although the rebels could not form an army, or operate comprehensively in the field, they sought to maintain the organisation which their late British masters had given to them. There had usually been a brigade of two, three, or four native regiments at each of the larger military stations; from the station the brigade took its name; and when the mutiny was many months old, the mutineers were still recognisable as belonging to the brigades which they had once loyally served—such as the Bareilly brigade, the Neemuch brigade, the Dinapoor brigade, the Nuseerabad brigade, &c. Although single regiments and fragments of regiments entered Delhi, to maintain the standard of rebellion against the English 'raj,' nevertheless the majority were distinguishable as brigaded forces. The Delhi brigade itself, consisting of the 38th, 54th, and 74th regiments native infantry, formed the material on which the Meerut brigade had worked on the 11th of May. This Meerut brigade comprised the 11th and 20th infantry, and the 3d cavalry. On the 16th of June arrived the Nuseerabad brigade, consisting of the 15th and 30th infantry, with horse and foot artillery; on the 22d, the Jullundur and Phillour brigades entered, comprising the 3d, 36th, and 61st infantry, and the 6th cavalry; on the 1st and 2d of June came the Bareilly or Rohilcund brigade, including the 18th, 28th, 29th, and 68th infantry, and the 8th irregular cavalry; and later in the same month came the Neemuch and Jhansi brigades. Even when combined within the walls of Delhi, each brigade constituted a sort of family or community, having to a great extent a way and a will of its own. The history of a hundred years has shown that the sepoys always fought well when well commanded; and their ineffective fighting as mutineers may hence be attributed in part to the fact that they were *not* well commanded.

It was about this period, the latter half of August, that an unfortunate English lady—unfortunate in being so long in the hands of brutal men—escaped from Delhi under circumstances which were narrated by the Bombay and Calcutta newspapers as below.* She was the wife of one of the civil officers of the Company engaged at Delhi before the mutiny; but as the newspaper narratives were not always correct in matters of identification, the name will not be given here.

September arrived, and with it many indications that the siege would soon present new and important features. Little is known of what passed within Delhi during those days; but General Wilson learned from various sources that the mutineers were in a very dissatisfied state at the failure of all their attempts to dislodge the besiegers, or even to disturb in any material degree the plan of the siege. They were without a responsible and efficient leader, and were split up into small sections; they had no united scheme of operations; nor were they adequately provided with money to meet their daily demands.

With the besiegers, on the other hand, prospects were brightening. The siege-train, when it arrived early in September, made a formidable increase in the ordnance before Delhi. As the name implies, the guns were larger, and carried shot and shell more weighty, than those used in battles and skirmishes; their main purpose being to make breaches in the defence-works of the city, through which infantry might enter and capture the place. Sir John Lawrence had been able to collect in the Punjaub, and send to Delhi from Ferozpore, a train of about thirty heavy pieces of artillery, consisting of guns, howitzers, and mortars of large calibre. The difficulty was not to obtain the guns, but to secure and to forward men to escort them, animals to draw them, ammunition to serve them, carriages to convey the auxiliary stores, food and camp-equipage for the men, fodder for the animals—whether horses, oxen, camels, or elephants. Such was the disturbed state of India at that time, that Lawrence had not been able to send this reinforcement until September; and even then, all his skill, influence, and energy, were required to surmount the numerous difficulties. About the same time there arrived in camp a Belooch battalion from Karachee, the 4th Punjaub infantry, the Patan Irregular Horse, and reinforcements to H.M. 8th, 24th, 52d, and 60th regiments. The siege-army now reached an aggregate of about 9000 men of all arms, effectives and non-effectives, including gun-lascars, syce-drivers, Punjaubee Sappers and Miners, native infantry recruits, and other men not comprised in regular regiments. There were also near the camp or on their march to it, numerous troops belonging to the Cashmere, Jheend, and Putialah Contingents. Out of the total number of troops of all kinds, Wilson hoped to be enabled to find 9000 effective infantry to make an assault on the city after a bombardment. To what extent this hope was realised, we shall see presently.

It is important to bear clearly in mind the relative positions of the besiegers and the besieged, the siege-camp and the fortified city, at that time. Let it not be forgotten that the British position before Delhi, from the early days of June to those of September, was purely a defensive one. The besiegers could neither invest the city nor

* 'Mrs ——, the wife of Mr ——, made her escape from Delhi on the morning of the 19th. Poor creature, she was almost reduced to a skeleton; as she had been kept in a sort of dungeon while in Delhi. Two chuprassees, who, it appears, have all along been faithful to her, aided her in making her attempt to escape. They passed through the Ajmeer Gate, but not wholly unobserved by the mutineers' sentries, as one of the chuprassees was shot by them. It being dark at the time, she lay hidden among the long web-grass until the dawn of day, when she sent the chuprassee to reconnoitre, and as luck would have it, he came across the European picket stationed at Subzee Mundee. So soon as he could discover who they were, he went and brought the lady into the picket-house amongst the soldiers, who did all they could to insure her safety. As soon as she arrived inside the square, she fell down upon her knees, and offered up a prayer to Heaven for her safe deliverance. All she had round her body was a dirty piece of cloth, and another piece folded round her head. She was in a terrible condition; but I feel assured that there was not a single European but felt greatly concerned in her behalf; and some even shed tears of pity when they heard the tale of woe that she related. After being interrogated by the officers for a short time, Captain Bailey provided a doolie for her, and sent her under escort safe to camp, where she has been provided with a staff-tent, and everything that she requires.'

batter down its walls; the troops being too few for the first of these enterprises, and the guns too weak for the second; while an assault, though twice intended, was not attempted, because there was no force sufficient to hold the city, even if it were captured. The position on the north of the city, from Metcalfe House to the Subzee Mundee, was the only one which they could successfully maintain. Nevertheless, though limited to that one side, it was invaluable, because it enabled the British to keep open a road of communication with the northwest, whence all supplies must necessarily be obtained. The English public, grieved and irritated by the astounding news from India, often reproached Barnard and Wilson for their delay in 'taking Delhi;' and many of the officers and soldiers on the spot longed for some dashing movement that would restore British prestige, and give them their hour of revenge against the mutineers. Subsequent experience, however, has gone far to prove that the generals were right. The grounds for so thinking have been thus set forth by an artillery-officer whose account of the siege has found a place among the Blue-books: 'Whether the city might or might not have been carried by a *coup de main*, as was contemplated first in June and afterwards in July, it is needless now to inquire; but judging from the resistance we afterwards experienced in the actual assault, when we had been greatly reinforced in men and guns, it appears to me fortunate the attempt was not made. The strength of the place was never supposed to consist in the strength of its actual defences, though these were much undervalued; but every city, even without fortifications, is, from its very nature, strongly defensible, unless it can be effectually surrounded or bombarded. Moreover, within Delhi, the enemy possessed a magazine containing upwards of two hundred guns, and an almost inexhaustible supply of ammunition; while their numbers were certainly never less than double those of the besiegers.' But, more than this, Delhi was not so weak a place as public opinion in England at that time represented it to be. The numerous bastions presented regular faces and flanks of masonry, with properly cut embrasures. The portions of wall or curtain between the bastions were twenty-four feet high, two-thirds of the height being twelve feet thick, and the remainder near the top being a parapet three feet in thickness. Outside the wall was a broad beam or ledge, screened by a parapet as a place for musketeers; below the beam was a ditch, sixteen feet deep by twenty feet wide at the bottom, with well-constructed escarp and counterscarp; and a good sloping glacis, descending from the outer edge of the ditch, covered nearly half the height of the wall from all assaults by distant batteries. Captain Norman, who was present during the whole of the siege as assistant adjutant-general, and who wrote a very lucid semi-official account of the siege-operations, fully corroborates this statement of the strength of the position.

As a memento of a remarkable event in the military history of India, it may be acceptable to present here a detailed list of all the troops constituting the siege-army of Delhi in the second week of September, when the assault was about to be made. The number, it will be seen, was 9866,* besides 'unarmed and undisciplined pioneers,' of whom no enumeration was given. These, it must be remembered, were all *effective* troops, and did not include those who were disabled by wounds or sickness. It should also be observed, that the Cashmere, Jheend, and Putialah Contingents find no place in this list; they were scarcely mentioned by General Wilson in his dispatches, although from other sources of information they seem to have reached nearly three thousand in number. Why the general and his staff should have had to make the entry 'strength unknown,' in reference to them, does not clearly appear. Concerning the other or more important elements of the army, many of the regiments were represented only by detachments or wings in the camp, the rest being at other places; but all that need be noted in the list is the exact number of men. Glancing over this list, it is impossible to avoid being struck with the fact how nearly the Oudian or Hindustani element is excluded from it. There are Europeans, Goorkhas, Sikhs, Punjaubees, Beloochees, and mountaineers from the Afghan frontier; but the only entry referring clearly to the Bengal native army is that of 78 men of the 4th irregular cavalry, and these appear in the unsoldierlike condition, 'disarmed and unhorsed.' The horse-artillery were frequently referred to in dispatches by the names of the officers in command—such as Tombs', Turner's, Renny's, and Remington's troops; while two light field-batteries were named after Scott and Bourchier. There were also several companies of

* *Artillery, Engineers, &c.*

European and Native.	Artillerymen of all kinds,	1350
	Engineers, Sappers, Miners, &c.,	722
	Pioneers, unarmed and undisciplined,	?
		2072

Cavalry.

European.	H.M. Carabiniers,	123
	H.M. 9th Lancers,	391
Native.	4th irregular cavalry (disarmed and unhorsed),	78
	1st Punjaub cavalry,	147
	2d " "	114
	5th " "	107
	Hodson's Irregular Horse,	462
	Guide corps, cavalry,	286
		1705

Infantry.

European.	H.M. 8th foot,	323
	" 52d "	302
	" 60th Rifles,	390
	" 61st foot,	403
	" 75th foot,	459
	1st Bengal European Fusiliers,	427
	2d " " "	370
Native.	Sirmoor battalion, Goorkhas,	212
	Kumaon " "	312
	Guide corps, infantry,	302
	4th Sikh infantry,	414
	1st Punjaub infantry,	664
	2d " "	650
	4th " "	541
	Belooch battalion,	322
		6089

foot-artillery serving with the siege-guns, which altogether numbered more than sixty heavy pieces of ordnance of various kinds. It has been said above that the list of 9866 excluded sick and wounded; these latter numbered at that time no less than 3074; therefore the total of all ranks and all degrees of efficiency nearly reached 13,000 men, even excluding the unenumerated pioneers and contingents. In five regiments alone there were 1300 men sick and wounded, almost equalling in number those in an effective state; the 52d royal regiment and the Sirmoor battalion exhibited a greater number on the sick-list than on that of the effectives.

Now commenced those operations of siege-warfare which depend more on engineers and artillerymen than on infantry and cavalry—the arrangements for bringing near the city guns numerous and powerful enough to batter the walls. All hands were busy. The engineers and their assistants had made 10,000 fascines, 10,000 gabions, and 100,000 sand-bags; field-magazines, scaling-ladders, and spare platforms had been made in great number. The north side of the city being that which was to be assaulted, it was resolved to maintain the right of the position strongly against the enemy, while the main attack was pushed on the left—first, because the river would protect the left flank of the advancing columns; and, secondly, because the troops would find themselves in comparatively open ground in that part after a successful assault, instead of being cooped up in narrow and fiercely defended streets. One of the subsidiary measures taken was to form a trench to the left of the Samee, and to construct at the end of it a battery for four guns and two large howitzers. This Samee, better known to the soldiers as the Sammy House, was an old temple, situated some way down the slope of the ridge towards the city, and about half a mile distant from the Moree Bastion; it had for some weeks been held by the British. The purpose of this newly constructed Samee Battery was to prevent sorties from the Lahore or Cabool Gates passing round the city wall to annoy the breaching-batteries, and also to assist in keeping down the fire of the Moree Bastion. The three main works on the north side of the city were the Moree, Cashmere, and Water Bastions—all of which had been strengthened by the British authorities some years before, when no one dreamed that those strengthenings would be a disaster to the power which ordered them to be effected.

It was on the 7th of September that the besiegers began to render visible those works which pertain especially to the storming of a fortified post. Until then, there had been few or no trenches, parallels, or zigzags, intended to enable the besiegers to approach near the beleaguered city, preparatory to a forcible entry. On that night, however, a working-party was sent out to establish two batteries about seven hundred yards distant from the Moree Bastion. The sappers, attacked by the enemy and defended by infantry, prosecuted their work amid the peril which always surrounds that species of military labour. One battery, on the left, of four 24-pounders, was intended to hold the Cashmere Bastion partially in check; while the other, of five 18-pounders and one 8-inch howitzer, was to silence the Moree Bastion, and prevent it interfering with the attack on the left. A trench was made to connect the two batteries, and extending beyond them a little to the right and left, so as to communicate with a wide and deep ravine which, extending very nearly up to the left attack, formed a sort of first parallel, affording good cover to the guard of the trenches. All this was completed during the night or by the forenoon of the 8th; and the two portions, with the trench connecting them, became known as Brind's Battery, named after the officer who worked it.

At dusk on the evening of the 8th, a second working-party set forth, to construct a battery to be called 'No. 2.' The enemy, influenced by an opinion that the attack would be made on the right, had neglected the ground at and near Ludlow Castle, a house situated barely seven hundred yards from the Cashmere Gate. The British engineers, taking advantage of this neglect, seized the position, occupied it with a strong detachment, and employed the nights of the 9th and 10th in constructing a battery upon it. The enemy, alarmed at this near approach, kept up a fierce cannonade from the Cashmere and Water Bastions and from the Selimgurh; but the besiegers had made their approach so carefully, that few of them suffered. This battery, like Brind's, was in two portions; one, immediately in front of Ludlow Castle, for nine 24-pounders, was intended to breach the wall between the Cashmere and Water Bastions, and to render the parapet untenable by musketeers; the other, two hundred yards further to the right, for seven 8-inch howitzers and two 18-pounders, was to aid in attaining the same objects. The 'No. 2' Battery, from its magnitude, and the important duty assigned to it, was placed under the control of two officers; Major Kaye commanded the right position; while the left was intrusted to Major Campbell, who, being wounded soon afterwards, was succeeded by Captain Johnson.

Still further was the powerful machinery for attack carried. On the night of the 10th, Battery No. 3 was commenced, within two hundred yards of the Water Bastion, behind a small ruined house in the custom-house compound; it was bold and hazardous work to construct a battery in such a spot, for the enemy kept up a destructive fire of musketry the whole time. The object of No. 3, when mounted with six 18-pounders, was to open a second breach in the Water Bastion. Battery No. 4 was in like manner constructed during the nights of the 10th and 11th, at the Koodseebagh near Ludlow Castle; it was mounted with ten

Jumma Musjid at Delhi.—From a Photograph.

heavy mortars, placed under the charge of Major Tombs. Later in the siege a battery of light mortars was worked by Captain Blunt from the rear of the custom-house. To enable the whole of the siege-batteries to be armed, most of the heavy guns were withdrawn from the ridge, leaving only a few that were necessary to defend it from any attacks made by the enemy from the Kissengunje and Subzee Mundee quarters. There being a deficiency of foot-artillerymen to man the heavy guns and mortars, nearly all the officers and men of the horse-artillery quitted the duties to which they more especially belonged, and worked in the batteries during the bombardment; as did likewise many volunteers from the British cavalry, who were eager to take part in the fray. Even the infantry regiments furnished volunteers from among the officers, who practised at the ridge-batteries for many days before the breaching-batteries opened their fire, when they transferred their services to the latter. The newly raised Sikh artillerymen, proud to share the dangers and emulate the courage of the British, were intrusted with the working of two of the great guns, a duty which they afterwards performed to admiration.

It thus appears that the works at the newly constructed breaching-batteries bristled with forty-four heavy pieces of ordnance, besides guns of lighter weight and smaller calibre at more distant points. The murderous conflict could not much longer be delayed. The besieged knew well the danger impending over them, and made arrangements for a desperate resistance. No sooner did Brind's Battery open fire on the 8th than the enemy made a sortie from the city, principally of cavalry; but they were soon driven in by the artillery. From the broken ground below the ridge, and from a trench in front of the battery, they kept up a constant fire of musketry; grape-shot had to be used against them, from a light gun-battery near the Samee House. In like manner, during the construction of the remaining breaching-batteries, the enemy kept up a fierce and continuous fire from every available point, causing great loss to the besiegers—not only among the fighting-men, but among the natives employed as porters, magazine lascars, ordnance-drivers, &c. The enemy went to work on the night of the 11th, and constructed an advanced trench parallel to the British left attack, three or four hundred yards distant from it; and from this they opened a very hot fire of musketry. They also got some light guns, and one of heavier calibre, into the open ground on the right of the siege-position, from which they maintained an annoying enfilade fire. At the Custom-house Battery, within two hundred yards of the city, the British were continually assailed with a storm of bullets, which rendered their passage to and from the spot extremely perilous. On more than one occasion, before Battery No. 2 was finished, the mutineers sallied out from the Cashmere Gate, and poured forth a volley of musketry at that spot; and it required a very strong guard of infantry to protect the battery from a closer attack. Some of the enemy's guns, planted to enfilade the batteries Nos. 1 and 2, were so sheltered that the ordnance on the ridge and at the Samee House were never able effectually to silence them. From another quarter, the Selimgurh or old fort, a constant fire of shells was kept up, so skilfully pointed as to drop with perilous accuracy upon three of the breaching-batteries. During the actual progress of the bombardment and assault, only one attempt was made by the enemy to annoy the besiegers in the rear; a body of horse crossed the canal at Azadpore (at the junction of the two roads leading from the city and the cantonment), drove in a picket of irregular horse, and created some confusion; but parties of Punjaub and Guide cavalry, quickly arriving at the spot, checked, pursued, and dispersed the intruders.

Now commenced the fearful thunder of a cannonading. The engineers having finished their work, handed it over to the artillerymen, who collected around them vast stores of shot and shell. It was on the 11th of September that the British siege-guns may be said to have opened their systematic fire, although some had been already tested, and others were not quite ready. The nine 24-pounders, in Major Campbell's No. 2 Battery, 'opened the ball,' to use the language of one of the engineers, and soon shewed their tremendous power in bringing down huge pieces of the wall near the Cashmere Bastion. The enemy's guns on that bastion attempted to reply, but were soon knocked over, and the bastion itself rendered untenable. The work was hot on the 11th, but much hotter on the 12th, when Battery No. 3 opened its fire, and upwards of forty ponderous pieces of ordnance belched forth ruin and slaughter on the devoted city. All that night, all the next day and night, until the morning of the 14th, did this cannonading continue, with scarcely an interval of silence. Soldiers like to be met in soldierly fashion, even if they suffer by it. The British did not fail to give a word of praise to the enemy; who, though unable to work a gun from any of the three bastions that were so fiercely assailed, stuck to their artillery in the open ground which enfiladed the right attack; they got a gun to bear through one of the holes breached in the wall; they sent rockets from one of their martello towers; and they poured forth a torrent of musketry from their advanced trench and from the city walls. Throughout the warlike operations here and elsewhere, the enemy were more effective in artillery than in infantry, and less in cavalry than in either of the other two.

When the great day arrived—the day with which hopes and fears, anxieties and responsibilities, had been so long associated—General Wilson made arrangements for the final assault. The plan of operations was dependent on the state to which the breaching-batteries had brought the defence-works of the city during two or three days' bombarding, by the engineers under Colonel Baird Smith, and the artillery under Major Gaitskell. It was known that the force of shot and shell poured against the place had made breaches near the Cashmere and Water Bastions, destroyed the defences of those bastions, and knocked down the parapets which had afforded shelter to the enemy's musketeers; but wishing to ascertain the exact state of matters, the general, on the night of the 13th, sent down Lieutenants Medley and Lang on the dangerous duty of examining the breach made in the city wall near the Cashmere Bastion; while Lieutenants Greathed and Home made a similar examination of the breach near the Water Bastion. These officers having announced that both breaches were practicable for the entrance of storming-parties, the general resolved that the next day, the 14th of September, should be signalised by a storming of the great Mogul stronghold. He marshalled his forces into columns,* the exact components of which it will be interesting to record here; and to each column he prescribed a particular line of duty. The 1st column, of 1000 men, was to assault the main breach, and escalade the face of the Cashmere Bastion, after the heavy siege-guns had finished their destructive work; it was to be covered by a detachment of H.M. 60th Rifles. The 2d column, of 850 men, similarly covered by a body of Rifles, was to advance on the Water Bastion and carry the breach. The 3d column, of 950 men, was to be directed against the Cashmere Gate, preceded by an explosion-party of engineers under Lieutenants Home and Salkeld, and covered by a party of Rifles. The 4th column (strength unrecorded) was to assail the enemy's strong position in the Kissengunje and Pahareepore suburbs, with a view both of driving in the rebels, and of supporting the main attack by forcing an entrance at the Cabool Gate; for this duty a miscellaneous body of troops, almost wholly native, was told off. In addition to the four columns, there was a reserve of 1300 men, covered by Rifles, which was to await the result of the main attack, and take possession of certain posts as soon as the columns entered the place. No more troops were left at camp than were absolutely necessary for its protection; a few convalescents of the infantry, and a few troopers and horse-artillery, were all that could be spared for this duty. Nearly all the pickets were handed over to the cavalry to guard. Arrangements were, however, made to send back a force as speedily as possible to the camp to guard the sick, wounded, stores, &c., which naturally became objects of much solicitude to the general at such a time. Brigadier Grant, with the bulk of the cavalry and some horse-artillery, moved down to the vicinity of No. 1 Battery, to check any attempt that might be made by the enemy, after a sortie from the Lahore or Ajmeer Gates, to attack the storming columns in flank.

The night which closed in the 13th and opened the 14th of September was not one to be soon forgotten by the soldiers of the siege-army. Few of them, officers or men, slept much; their thoughts were too intensely directed towards the stern realities of the morrow, which would end the career of so many among their number. At four o'clock on the morning of the 14th, the different columns set forth on their march from the camp to their respective places. The first three columns were, according to the programme just cited, to engage in the actual assault on the northern side of the city; the heads of those columns were to be kept concealed until the moment for assault had arrived; and the signal for that crisis was to be, the advance of the Rifles to the front, to act as skirmishers.

Brigadier Nicholson took the lead. He gave the signal; the Rifles rushed to the front with a cheer, and skirmished along through the low jungle which extended to within fifty yards of the ditch. The 1st and 2d columns, under himself and Brigadier Jones, emerged from behind the Koodseebagh, and advanced steadily towards the breached portions of the wall. Up to this time the enemy's guns had wrought little mischief on the columns; but as soon as the latter emerged into the open ground, a perfect storm of bullets met them from the front and both flanks; officers and men were falling fast on the glacis; and for several minutes it was impossible to get the ladders placed for a descent into the ditch and an ascent of the escarp. After a fierce struggle, the British bayonet, as usual, won the day; the troops dashed through and over all obstacles, and entered the city through the breaches which the guns had previously made in the walls. Now within the boundary of the imperial city, the two brigadiers at once turned to the right, proceeded along the ramparts, fought the sepoys inch by inch, overcame all opposition, and captured in succession a

---

* *1st Column*, under Brigadier-general Nicholson—

		Men.
H.M. 75th foot	(Lieutenant-colonel Herbert),	300
1st Bengal Europeans	(Major Jacob), ...	250
2d Punjaub infantry	(Captain Green), . . .	450

2d Column, under Brigadier Jones—

H.M. 8th foot	(Lieutenant-colonel Greathed),	250
2d Bengal Europeans	(Captain Boyd), . . .	250
4th Sikh infantry	(Captain Rothney), . .	350

3d Column, under Colonel Campbell—

H.M. 52d foot	(Major Vigors), . . .	200
Kumaon Goorkhas	(Captain Ramsay), ...	250
1st Punjaub infantry	(Lieutenant Nicholson), .	500

4th Column, under Major Reid—

Sirmoor Goorkhas, Guide infantry, European pickets, Native pickets,	Besides Cashmere Contingent, of which strength unknown.	850

Reserve, under Brigadier Longfield—

H.M. 61st foot	(Lieutenant-colonel Deacon), .	250
4th Punjaub infantry	(Captain Wilde), . . .	450
Belooch battalion	(Lieutenant-colonel Farquhar),	300
Jheend auxiliaries	(Lieutenant-colonel Dunsford),	300

The engineer officers were attached to the several columns as follows:

To the 1st column, Lieuts. Medley, Lang, and Bingham.
" " 2d " , " Greathed, Hovenden, and Pemberton.
" " 3d " , " Home, Salkeld, and Tandy.
" " 4th " , " Maunsell and Tennant.
" " Reserve, " Ward and Thackeray.

small battery, a tower between the Cashmere and Moree Bastions, the Moree itself, and the Cabool Gate; but the vigorous attempts they made to take the Burn Bastion and the Lahore Gate failed, so determined was the resistance opposed to them, and so terrible the loss they suffered in officers and men. It was in one of the many attacks on the Lahore Gate, when the troops had to advance along a narrow lane swept by the enemy's grapeshot and musketry, that the bullet was fired which laid low the gallant Nicholson—an officer in whom the whole army had reposed a full and deep reliance. As far as the Cabool Gate, the two columns were enabled to maintain their conquests; and they immediately made preparations for opening fire from the bastions inwards upon the yet unconquered buildings of the city—a sand-bag parapet being constructed across the gorge or open rear of each bastion.

We have now to see what was transpiring in another quarter, on this morning of heroism and slaughter. While the 1st column was engaged in forcing an entrance through the breach near the Cashmere Bastion, and the 2d column a similar entrance through that near the Water Bastion, the 3d directed its operations against the Cashmere Gate—through which, it will be remembered, the troops of that column were to rush after an explosion-party had blown in the gate itself. If there be any sublimity in bloody warfare, it is manifested in the self-devotion with which a soldier marches steadfastly to a position where he knows that death will be almost certain and immediate. Such self-devotion was shewn by the little band of heroes forming this explosion-party. They had to advance in broad daylight to the gate, amid a storm of bullets from above, from both flanks, and from a wicket in the gate itself; they had carefully to lay down and adjust the bags of gunpowder close to the gate, to arrange a train or fuse, to fire the bags, and to take their chance of being themselves blown up by the explosion. The gallant men intrusted with this dangerous duty were divided into two parties—an advanced and a firing party. The first consisted of an engineer officer, Lieutenant Home, two non-commissioned officers, Sergeants Smith and Carmichael, and a few native sappers, who carried the powder-bags. The firing-party consisted of Lieutenant Salkeld, Corporal Burgess, and a few native sappers. Owing to some delay, the two parties did not set out for their rendezvous at Ludlow Castle until broad daylight, and then they had to encounter a heavy fire of musketry all the way. When the advanced party reached the gate—a heavy wooden structure, flanked by massive walls—they found that a part of the drawbridge over the ditch had been destroyed; but, passing across the precarious footing afforded by the remaining beams, they proceeded to lodge their powder-bags against the gate. The wicket was open, and through it the enemy kept up a heavy fire. Sergeant Carmichael, and a native sapper named Madhoo, were killed while laying the bags; but Lieutenant Home only received a blow from a stone thrown up by a bullet. The perilous duty of laying the bags being completed, the advanced party slipped down into the ditch, to make room for the firing-party, which then advanced. 'Lieutenant Salkeld,' said Colonel Baird Smith, in his report of the engineering operations of the day, 'while endeavouring to fire the charge, was shot through the arm and leg, and handed over the slow match to Corporal Burgess, who fell mortally wounded just as he had successfully accomplished the onerous duty. Havildar Tilluh Singh, of the Sikhs, was wounded, and Ramloll Sepoy of the same corps, was killed during this part of the operation. The demolition being most successful, Lieutenant Home, happily not wounded, caused the bugler (Hawthorne) to sound the regimental call of the 52d, as the signal for the advancing columns. Fearing that amid the noise of the assault the sounds might not be heard, he had the call repeated three times, when the troops advanced and carried the gateway with complete success.' Sergeant Smith had a narrow escape from being blown up. Seeing Burgess fall, and not knowing the exact result of the gallant fellow's efforts to fire the train, he ran forward; but seeing the train alight, he had just time to throw himself into the ditch before the explosion took place. The perilous nature of this kind of duty gave rise to a correspondence in the public journals, from which a few lines may not unsuitably be given in a note.*

Colonel Campbell, with the 3d column, after the heroic explosion-party had forced an entry for him through the Cashmere Gate, marched boldly

* One of the writers remarked: 'The stout rope-mat which forms an efficient screen to the Russian artillerymen while serving their gun, impervious to the Minié ball, which lodges harmlessly in its rough and rugged surface, may surely suggest to our engineers the expediency of some effort to shield the valuable lives of our men when exposed to the enemy's fire. In ancient warfare, all nations appear to have defended themselves from the deadly arrow by shields, and why the principle of the testudo should be ignored in modern times is not obvious. Take the instance before us—Lieutenant Salkeld and a few others undertake the important, but most perilous duty of blowing in the Cashmere Gate, by bags of gunpowder, in broad daylight, and in the face of numerous foes, whose concentrated fire threatens the whole party with certain death. It is accomplished, but at what a loss! Marvellous indeed was it that one escaped. Now, as a plain man, without any scientific pretensions, I ask, could not, and might not, some kind of defensive screen have been furnished for the protection of these few devoted men? Suppose a light cart or truck on three wheels, having a semicircular framework in front, against which might be lashed a rope-matting, and inside a sufficient number of sacks of wool or hay, propelled by means of a central cross-bar pushed against by four men within the semicircle, the engineers could advance, and on reaching the gate, perform their work through a central orifice in the outer matting, made to open like a flap. The party would then retire in a similar manner, merely reversing the mode of propulsion, until the danger was past.' Another, Mr Rock of Hastings, said: 'In July 1848, I sent a plan for a movable shield for attacking barricades, to General Cavaignac, at Paris; and on the 13th or 14th of July your own columns (the *Times*) contained descriptions of my machine, and a statement by your Paris correspondent that it had been constructed at the Ecole Militaire in that city. Fortunately, it was never used there, but there seems to me no valid reason why such a contrivance should not be used on occasions like that which recently occurred at Delhi. The truck proposed, with a shield in front, would serve to carry the powder-bags, without incurring the chance of their being dropped owing to the fall of one or two of the men employed on the service, while the chances of premature ignition would be diminished. These, I think, are advantages tending to insure success which should induce military engineers to use movable cover for their men when possible, even if they despise it as a personal protection.'

through the city towards the Jumma Musjid—a perilous enterprise; for the distance was upwards of a mile even in a straight line, and many populous streets would need to be traversed. In this march he was aided by Sir Theophilus Metcalfe, a member of the Company's civil service, whose house outside Delhi has been so often mentioned, and who had been a valuable adviser to the siege-army during the whole period of its operations on the ridge. He knew Delhi well, and was thus enabled to render Campbell essential service. Conducting the column by a circuitous route, he kept it nearly free from opposition until the fine street, called the Chandnee Chowk, was reached, where they took possession of the Kotwallee. At this point, however, the troops began to fall rapidly under the muskets of the enemy, and it was found to be impracticable to achieve the object fondly hoped—the capture of the Jumma Musjid itself. After a gallant struggle, the column fell back to the neighbourhood of the English church near the Cashmere Gate, where it had the support

Corporal Burgess, blown up at Cashmere Gate.

of the reserve. The colonel at once placed the 52d regiment in the church, the Kumaon battalion in Skinner's house, and the Punjaub infantry in the houses at the junction of two streets that led from the centre of the city to the open space around the church. Guns, too, were posted at the last-named place, to check the advance of insurgents who had begun to treat Campbell as a fleeing and defeated officer. He was in one sense defeated; for he had to retreat nearly a mile, and saw his fine troops cut up terribly all around him; nevertheless, before nightfall he had placed himself in a position from which the enemy could not dislodge him, and which enabled him to take a prominent part in the subsequent operations.

Rather as a support to Colonel Campbell's 3d column, than as a leading corps, the reserve now comes for notice—its position being indeed denoted by its name. This reserve column, under Brigadier Longfield, had, it will be remembered, the duty of watching the result of the main attack, and of taking possession of certain posts as soon as the other columns had effected an entry into the city. The reserve followed the 3d column through the Cashmere Gate, having previously spared the Belooch battalion to render service near Hindoo Rao's house. Longfield at once cleared the college gardens of insurgents, and then told off his troops so as to obtain efficient hold of the Water Bastion, the Cashmere Gate, Skinner's house, and a large commanding building called Ahmed Ali Khan's house. Skinner's house, or in Indian form, Sikunder's, had at one time been the residence of Major Skinner, commander of a regiment of irregular horse, which had acquired much celebrity; the house was large, and presented many important advantages for a military force.

There is yet another portion of the siege-army, whose fortune on this 14th of September has to be noticed—namely, that which was placed under the command of Major Reid, for a series of operations in the western suburbs of the city. Everything here was under a cloud of disappointment; the operations were not attended with that degree of success which the officers and men had fondly hoped. Captain Dwyer, in command of the Cashmere field-force, was intrusted with the management of 400 men of that force, and four guns; and the object he was to endeavour to attain was the safe occupation of the Eedghah Serai, in dangerous proximity to the garrison within the city. Early in the morning he set out from the camp. Finding the road very difficult for artillery, he pulled down a portion of stone-wall to enable his guns to get upon the Rohtuk high road; the noise unfortunately attracted the enemy, who immediately sent down 2000 men to that point. Dwyer kept up a fire of artillery for three quarters of an hour; but finding that the enemy, instead of being discomfited, were about to outflank him, he resolved on a bold advance on the Eedghah. This resolve he could not carry out; his troops were widely spread in skirmishing order, and could not be collected in column; the guns could not be properly moved, for the grass-cutters had taken away the horses. In short, the attempt was a total failure, and the captain was compelled to retire without his guns. The force appears to have been too small, and the Cashmerian troops scarcely equal in soldierly discipline to the demands of the work intrusted to them. This attack on the Eedghah was to have been part of a larger enterprise intrusted to Major Reid, having in view the conquest of the whole western suburb of Delhi, and the command of all outlets by the western gates. The major advanced from the Subzee Mundee towards the Kissengunje suburb; but he found the enemy so numerous and strongly posted, and he met with such a strenuous opposition, that his progress was soon checked. The gallant Reid himself being struck down wounded, as well as many other officers, Captain Muter of the 60th Rifles, and Captain R. C. Lawrence, political agent with the Cashmere Contingent, felt it necessary promptly to decide on the course best to be pursued. They found the different detachments, of which the column consisted, so broken and disorganised by the heavy fire of the enemy, that it was impossible to re-form them on broken ground, and under a severe fire the attack on the Kissengunje could not be renewed; all they attempted was to keep the enemy in check for an hour, without losing ground. They waited for a reinforcement of artillery, which Reid had sent for before being wounded; but these guns, through some unexplained cause, failed to arrive. Seeing the enemy increase in force, and fearing for the safety of the batteries below Hindoo Rao's house, the officers gave up the attack and retired, strengthening the batteries and the Subzee Mundee picket. The failure of Captain Dwyer's attack greatly increased the difficulty of the position; for the enemy was thereby enabled to advance on the right flank of the main column, endanger its rear, and hotly press the Subzee Mundee picket. Reid, Lawrence, Dwyer, Muter—all were mortified at their failure in this suburban operation.

Thus ended the 14th of September, a day on which British authority was partially restored in the 'city of the Moguls,' after an interregnum of eighteen weeks. Partial, indeed, was the reconquest; for the portion of the city held bore so small a ratio to the whole, that the troops foresaw a terrible and sanguinary ordeal to be gone through before the British flag would again wave undisputed over the conquered city. The loss was very large, in relation to the strength of the army generally. There fell on this one day, 8 British officers, 162 British troops, and 103 native troops, killed; while the list of wounded comprised 52 British officers, 512 British troops, and 310 native troops—a total of 1135. When night closed around the survivors, the 1st and 2d columns held all the towers, bastions, and ramparts from the vicinity of the Cashmere Gate to the Cabool Gate; the 3d column and the reserve held the Cashmere Gate, the English church, Skinner's house, the Water Bastion, Ahmed Ali Khan's house, the college gardens, and many buildings and open spots in that part of Delhi; while the 4th column, defeated in the western suburbs, had retreated to the camp or the ridge.

Snatching a little occasional repose during the night, the besiegers found themselves at dawn on the 15th, as we have said, masters of a *part* only of Delhi; and they prepared for the stern work before them. They dragged several mortars into position, at various points between the Cashmere and Cabool Gates, to shell the heart of the city and the imperial palace. A battery, commanding the Selimgurh and a part of the palace, was also established in the college gardens; and several houses were taken and armed in advance or further to the south. The enemy, meanwhile, kept up a vigorous fire from the Selimgurh and the magazine upon the positions occupied by the British, and skirmishing went on at all the advanced posts. This, be it understood, was within the city itself; the British being in command of a strip of ground and buildings just within the northern wall; while all the rest was still in the hands of the rebels. It was in every way a strange position for an army to occupy; the city was filled with hostile soldiery, who had the command of an immense array of guns and a vast store of ammunition, and whose musketry told with fatal effect from loopholed walls and houses in all the streets within reach; while the besiegers themselves were separated by a lofty city wall from their own camp.

The 16th was marked by a greater progress than the 15th towards a conquest of the city, because the newly established batteries began to shew signs of work. The guns in the college garden having effected a breach in the magazine defences, that important building was stormed and taken, with a loss comparatively slight, by the 61st, the 4th Punjaub, and the Beloochees.* Outside the city, the Kissengunje suburb was this day evacuated by the enemy, leaving five guns, which were speedily captured by a detachment sent down from Hindoo Rao's house; it was then found that the enemy's position here had been one of immense strength, and the failure of Major Reid's attack received a ready explanation.

Another day dawned, and witnessed the commencement of operations which placed a further portion of the city in the hands of the conquerors. The magazine having been captured, it became important to secure the whole line of rampart and

* When the magazine was so heroically fired by Lieutenant Willoughby, four months earlier, the destruction caused was very much smaller than had been reported and believed. The stores in the magazine had been available to the rebels during the greater part of the siege.

forts from that point to the Cabool Gate, comprising the northeast as well as the north sides of the city. This was begun on the 17th, and completed on the 18th, giving to the British a firm hold of everything behind a straight line extending from the magazine to the Cabool Gate. A bold advance southward could now be made. Columns were sent forth, which captured the Delhi bank, Major Abbott's house, and the house of Khan Mohammed Khan, and made a near approach to the palace and the Chandnee Chowk. The pen can easily record this, but it must leave to the imagination of the reader to conceive how great must have been the peril of soldiers thus advancing inch by inch through a crowded city; field-artillery was brought to bear against them from almost every street, muskets from almost every house-top and window; and many a gallant fellow was laid low. One great advantage the besiegers now had, was in the command of mortars brought out from the magazine; these were placed in selected positions, and employed to shell the palace and the quarters of the town occupied by the enemy. It was now that the insurgents were seen to be gradually escaping from the palace into the southern parts of the city, and thence through the southern gates into open country not yet attacked by the British. Over the bridge of boats they could not go, for the guns of the conquerors commanded it. Or, it may more correctly be said, the command of the bridge of boats enabled the conquerors to check that passage if they chose; but General Wilson did not make war on women and children, or on such males as appeared to be peaceful citizens: he allowed them to depart from the city if they wished—which nearly all did, for they feared terrible retribution at the hands of the British soldiery.

After another night within the imperial city, the conquerors achieved further successes on the 19th. The post called the Burn Bastion, situated on the west side of the city, close to the Lahore Gate, was surprised and captured by a detachment sent from the already conquered Cabool Gate. This swept the enemy from another large extent of wall. On the following morning a detachment of cavalry, going from the ridge by way of the Kissengunje and the Eedghah, found that the enemy had evacuated a large and strong camp long occupied by them outside the Delhi Gate. Lieutenant Hodson at once took possession of it; and a mere glance shewed, by the quantities of clothing, plunder, and ammunition lying around, that the enemy must have made a very precipitate flight. The cavalry, entering the city by the Delhi Gate—which, together with the Gurstin Bastion, had just been attacked and taken by the infantry, galloped on to the sumptuous Jumma Musjid, of which they took possession, being speedily supported by infantry and guns. While all this was going on, the imperial palace was the object of a distinct attack. A column advanced along the Chandnee Chowk, placed powder-bags against the gate, blew it in, and entered the palace. The enormous building was found to be deserted by all but a few fanatics and numerous wounded sepoys.

Thus at length was the great city of Delhi reconquered by its former masters; thus again did the Feringhee become paramount over the Mogul. Captain Norman, whose semi-official account of the siege has already been adverted to, closed his narrative by saying: 'It is impossible to conclude without alluding to the trials and constancy of the troops employed in this arduous siege. Called on at the hottest season of the year to take the field, imperfectly equipped, and with the extent of difficulties to be faced very imperfectly known, all felt that a crisis had arrived, to meet which every man's cheerful, willing, and heartfelt energies must be put forth to the utmost; and how well this was done, those who were with the army know and can never forget. For the first five weeks every effort was required, not indeed to take Delhi, but even to hold our own position; and day after day, for hours together, every soldier was under arms under a burning sun, and constantly exposed to fire. Notwithstanding the daily casualties in action, the numerous deaths by cholera, the discouraging reports relative to the fidelity of some of the native portions of our own force, the distressing accounts from all parts of the country, the constant arrival of large reinforcements of mutineers, and the apparent impossibility of aid ever reaching in sufficient strength to enable us to take the place—the courage and confidence of the army never flagged. And, besides enduring a constant and often deadly cannonade, for more than three months, in thirty different combats, our troops invariably were successful, always against long odds, and often opposed to ten times their numbers, who had all the advantages of ground and superior artillery.'

Taking the 30th of May as the date when the first conflict between the besiegers and defenders of Delhi took place, at some distance from Delhi itself, the interval of 113 days between that date and the final capture on the 20th of September was marked by a very large death-list. It could not be otherwise. Where men were exposed during so many days and nights to shells, balls, bullets, swords, heat, swamps, fatigue, and disease, the hand of the destroyer must indeed have been heavy. And, as in all similar instances, the list of wounded was much larger than that of killed. The official list comprised the names of 46 European officers who had either been killed in battle, or died from wounds received; and of 140 others whose wounds had not proved fatal. But the adjutant-general is seldom accustomed to comprise in his lists those who fall with disease without being wounded; and thus the Delhi enumeration did not include the names of Generals Anson and Barnard, or of any of the numerous officers, who, though not wounded before Delhi, unquestionably met their death in connection with the preparations for, or conduct of, the siege.

Distributed under different headings, the killed and wounded amounted altogether to 3807,* to which were added 30 missing. Of the horses there were 186 killed and 378 wounded. Of the number of insurgents who fell during the struggle, no authentic knowledge could be obtained.

The official dispatches were nearly silent concerning the proceedings, except military, in the interval of six days between the first assault of the city and the final subjugation, and during the remaining ten days of September. General Wilson, shortly before the final attack was to be made, issued an address to his soldiers, from which a few sentences are here given in a note;† and in which, it will be seen, they were instructed to give no quarter to the mutineers—that is, make no prisoners, but put all armed rebels to death. This was attended to; but something more was done, something darker and less justifiable. It is not customary for soldiers to stab wounded and sick men in an enemy's army; but such was done at Delhi. The sense of hatred towards the mutinous sepoys was so intense, the recollection of the atrocities at Cawnpore was so vivid, that vengeance took place of every other feeling. The troops did that which they would have scorned to do against the Russians in the Crimean war—they bayoneted men no longer capable of resistance. They refused to consider the rules of honourable warfare applicable to black-hearted traitors; their officers joined them in this refusal; and their general's address justified them up to a certain point. If the rule laid down by Wilson had been strictly adhered to, there would have been military precedence to sanction it; but the common soldiers did not discriminate in their passion; and many a dark-skinned inhabitant of Delhi fell under the bayonet, against whom no charge of complicity with the mutineers could be proved. The letters written home to friends in England, soon after the battle, and made public, abundantly prove this; the soldiers were thirsting for vengeance, and they slaked their thirst. Many of the villagers of India, indeed, bore cruel injustice during that extraordinary period. Instances frequently came to light, such as the following: A revolted regiment or a predatory band would enter a village, demand and obtain money, food, and other supplies by threats of vengeance if the demand were not complied with, and then depart; an English corps, entering soon afterwards, would fine and punish the villagers for having aided the enemy. One thing, however, the British soldiers did *not* do; they did not murder women and children. This humanity, heroism, justice, or whatever it may best be called, was more than the natives generally expected: the leaders in the revolt had sedulously disseminated a rumour that the British would abuse all the women, and murder them and their children, in all towns and stations where mutinies had taken place; and under the influence of this belief, many of the natives put their wives to death rather than expose them to the apprehended indignities. While, at one part of Delhi, the conquerors (if the narrators are to be believed) found Christian women *crucified* against the walls in the streets; at another part, nearly twenty native women were found lying side by side with their throats cut, their husbands having put them to death to prevent them from falling into the hands of the conquerors.

What other scenes of wild licence took place within Delhi during those excited days, we may infer from collateral evidence. The mutineers, quite as much in love with plunder as with nationality, had been wont to carry about with them from place to place the *loot* which they had gathered during the sack of the stations and towns. As a consequence, Delhi contained temporarily an enormous amount of miscellaneous wealth; and such of this as the fugitives could not carry away with them, was regarded as spoil by the conquerors. There are certain rules in the English army concerning prizes and prize-money, which the soldiers more or less closely obey; but the Punjaubee and Goorkha allies, more accustomed to Asiatic notions of warfare, revelled in the unbridled freedom of their new position, and were with difficulty maintained in discipline. There was a large store of beverage, also, in the city, which the conquerors soon got at; and as intemperance is one of the weak points of English soldiers, many scenes of drunkenness ensued.

But all these are among the exigencies of war. The soldiers bore up manfully against their varied trials, fought heroically, and conquered; and it is not by the standards of conduct familiar to quiet persons at home that they should be judged. When General Wilson reported the result of his

*	Killed.	Wounded.
Europeans—		
Officers,	46	140
Non-commissioned officers,	59	113
Rank and file,	476	1313
Natives—		
Officers,	14	49
Non-commissioned officers,	37	104
Rank and file,	380	1076

† 'The force assembled before Delhi has had much hardship and fatigue to undergo since its arrival in this camp, all of which has been most cheerfully borne by officers and men. The time is now drawing near when the major-general commanding the force trusts that their labours will be over, and that they will be rewarded by the capture of a city for all their past exertions and for a cheerful endurance of still greater fatigue and exposure. . . . The artillery will have even harder work than they yet have had, and which they have so well and cheerfully performed hitherto; this, however, will be for a short period only, and when ordered to the assault, the major-general feels assured British pluck and determination will carry everything before them, and that the bloodthirsty and murderous mutineers against whom they are fighting will be driven headlong out of their stronghold or be exterminated.

'Major-general Wilson need hardly remind the troops of the cruel murders committed on their officers and comrades, as well as their wives and children, to move them in the deadly struggle. *No quarter should be given to the mutineers*; at the same time, for the sake of humanity, and the honour of the country they belong to, he calls upon them to spare all women and children that may come in their way . . . . It is to be explained to every regiment that indiscriminate plunder will not be allowed; that prize-agents have been appointed, by whom all captured property will be collected and sold, to be divided, according to the rules and regulations on this head fairly among all men engaged; and that any man found guilty of having concealed captured property will be made to restore it, and will forfeit all claims to the general prize; he will also be likely to be made over to the provost-marshal, to be summarily dealt with.'

hard labours, he said in his dispatch: 'Thus has the important duty committed to this force been accomplished, and its object attained. Delhi, the focus of rebellion and insurrection, and the scene of so much horrible cruelty, taken and made desolate; the king a prisoner in our hands; and the mutineers, notwithstanding their great numerical superiority and their vast resources in ordnance, and all the munitions and appliances of war, defeated on every occasion of engagement with our troops, are now driven with slaughter in confusion and dismay from their boasted stronghold. . . . . Little remains for me to say, but to again express my unqualified approbation of the conduct and spirit of the whole of the troops, not only on this occasion, but during the entire period they have been in the field. . . . . For four months of the most trying season of the year this force, originally very weak in number, has been exposed to the repeated and determined attacks of an enemy far outnumbering it, and supported by a numerous and powerful artillery. The duties imposed upon all have been laborious, harassing, and incessant, and notwithstanding heavy losses, both in action and from disease, have been at all times zealously and cheerfully performed.' And in similar language, when the news was known at Calcutta, did Viscount Canning acknowledge the heroism of those who had conquered Delhi.*

It will be seen above that the governor-general spoke of the 'king a prisoner.' This must now be explained. When all hope of retaining Delhi faded away, the aged king—who had in effect been more a puppet in the hands of ambitious leaders than a king, during four months—fled from the city, as did nearly all the members and retainers of the once imperial family. It fell to the lot of Captain (afterwards Major) Hodson to capture the king and other royal personages. This officer was assistant quartermaster-general, and intelligence-officer on General Wilson's staff. His long acquaintance as a cavalry officer with Sikhs, Punjaubees, and Afghans had given him much knowledge of the native character, and enabled him to obtain remarkably minute information concerning the movements and intentions of the enemy; to insure this, he was invested with power to reward or punish in proportion to the deserts of those who assisted him. It was known directly the Cashmere Gate was conquered that the exodus of the less warlike inhabitants of Delhi was beginning; but not then, nor until six days afterwards, could this be stopped, for the southern gates were wholly beyond reach of the conquerors. The imperial palace was captured, and was found nearly empty, on the 20th; and on the following day Captain Hodson learned that the king and his family had left the city with a large force by the Ajmeer Gate, and had gone to the Kootub, a suburban palace about nine miles from Delhi. Hodson urged that a detachment should be sent in pursuit, but Wilson did not think he could spare troops for this service. While this subject was under consideration, messengers were coming from the king, and among others Zeenat Mahal, a favourite begum, making ridiculous offers on his part, as if he were still the power paramount—all of which were of course rejected. As these offers could not be accepted; as Wilson could not or would not send a detachment at once to defeat or capture the mutinous troops who had departed with the king; and as it was, nevertheless, desirable to have the king's person in safe custody—Captain Hodson received permission to promise the aged sovereign his life, and exemption from immediate personal indignity, if he would surrender.

Thus armed, Hodson laid his plans. He started with fifty of his own native irregular troopers to Humayoon's Tomb, about three miles from the Kootub. Concealing himself and his men among some old buildings close by the gateway of the tomb, he sent his demand up to the palace. After two hours of anxious suspense, he received a message from the king that he would deliver himself up to Captain Hodson only, and on condition that he repeated with his own lips the pledge of the government for his safety. The captain then went

* 'The reports and returns which accompany this dispatch establish the arduous nature of a contest carried on against an enemy vastly superior in numbers, holding a strong position, furnished with unlimited appliances, and aided by the most exhausting and sickly season of the year.

'They set forth the indomitable courage and perseverance, the heroic self-devotion and fortitude, the steady discipline, and stern resolve of English soldiers.

'There is no mistaking the earnestness of purpose with which the struggle has been maintained by Major-general Wilson's army. Every heart was in the cause; and while their numbers were, according to all ordinary rule, fearfully unequal to the task, every man has given his aid, wherever and in whatever manner it could most avail, to hasten retribution upon a treacherous and murderous foe.

'In the name of outraged humanity, in memory of innocent blood ruthlessly shed, and in acknowledgment of the first signal vengeance inflicted upon the foulest treason, the governor-general in council records his gratitude to Major-general Wilson and the brave army of Delhi. He does so in the sure conviction that a like tribute awaits them, not in England only, but wherever within the limits of civilisation the news of their well-earned triumph shall reach.'

Some days afterwards, Lord Canning issued a more formal and complete proclamation, of which a few paragraphs may here be given: 'Delhi, the focus of the treason and revolt which for four months have harassed Hindostan, and the stronghold in which the mutinous army of Bengal has sought to concentrate its power, has been wrested from the rebels. The king is a prisoner in the palace. The head-quarters of Major-general Wilson are established in the Dewani Khas [the "Elysium" of the Mogul palace-builders, and of Moore's *Lalla Rookh*]. A strong column is in pursuit of the fugitives.

'Whatever may be the motives and passions by which the mutinous soldiery, and those who are leagued with them, have been instigated to faithlessness, rebellion, and crimes at which the heart sickens, it is certain that they have found encouragement in the delusive belief that India was weakly guarded by England, and that before the government could gather together its strength against them, their ends would be gained.

'They are now undeceived.

'Before a single soldier of the many thousands who are hastening from England to uphold the supremacy of the British power has set foot on these shores, the rebel force, where it was strongest and most united, and where it had the command of unbounded military appliances, has been destroyed or scattered by an army collected within the limits of the Northwestern Provinces and the Punjaub alone.

'The work has been done before the support of those battalions which have been collected in Bengal from the forces of the Queen in China and in her Majesty's eastern colonies could reach Major-general Wilson's army; and it is by the courage and endurance of that gallant army alone, by the skill, sound judgment, and steady resolution of its brave commander, and by the aid of some native chiefs true to their allegiance, that, under the blessing of God, the head of the rebellion has been crushed, and the cause of loyalty, humanity, and rightful authority vindicated.'

out into the middle of the road in front of the gateway, and said he was ready to receive his captives and renew the promise. 'You may picture to yourself,' said one familiar with the spot, 'the scene before that magnificent gateway, with the milk-white domes of the tomb towering up from within, one white man among a host of natives, yet determined to secure his prisoners or perish in the attempt.' After a time, a procession began to arrive from the palace. Threats and promises soon did their work; and the king, his begum Zeenat Mahal, and her son Jumma Bukht, were escorted to Delhi. It was a striking manifestation of moral power; for there were hundreds or even thousands of retainers in the procession, any one of whom could by a shot have put an end to Hodson's life; but he rode at the side of the imperial palanquins, cool and

Scene of Capture of the Princes of Delhi—Tomb of Emperor Humayoon.

undaunted, and they touched him not. As the city was approached, the followers and bystanders slunk away, being unwilling to confront the British troops. The captain rode on a few paces ahead, and ordered the Lahore Gate to be opened. 'Who have you there in the palanquin?' asked the officer on duty. 'Only the King of Delhi,' was the reply. The guard were all enraptured, and wanted to greet Hodson with a cheer; but he said the king would probably take the honour to himself, which was not desirable. On they went, through the once magnificent but now deserted Chaudnee Chowk; and the daring captor, at the gate of the palace, handed up his royal prisoners to the civil authorities.

Captain Hodson's work was not yet finished; there were other members of the royal family towards whom his attention was directed. Early on the following morning, he started to avail himself of information he obtained concerning three of the princes, who were known to have been guilty of monstrous deeds which rendered them worthy of instant death. He went with a hundred of his troopers to the Tomb of Humayoon, where the princes were concealed. After accepting 'king's evidence,' bribing, threatening, and manœuvring, Hodson secured his prisoners, and sent them off with a small escort to the city. Entering the tomb, he found it filled with an enormous number of palace scum and city rabble, mostly armed; but so thoroughly cowed were they by his fearless demeanour, that they quietly obeyed his order to lay down their arms and depart. The captain and his men then moved warily off to the city; and at a short distance from the gate, he found the vehicle containing the princes surrounded by a mob, who seemed disposed to resist him. What followed must be given in the words of an officer who was in a position to obtain accurate information. 'This was no time for hesitation or delay.

Hodson dashed at once into the midst—in few but energetic words explained "that these were the men who had not only rebelled against the government, but had ordered and witnessed the massacre and shameful exposure of innocent women and children; and that thus therefore the government punished such traitors, taken in open resistance"—shooting them down at the word. The effect was instantaneous and wonderful. Not another hand was raised, not another weapon levelled, and the Mohammedans of the troop and some influential moulvies among the bystanders exclaimed, as if by simultaneous impulse: "Well and rightly done! Their crime has met with its just penalty. These were they who gave the signal for the death of helpless women and children, and outraged decency by the exposure of their persons, and now a righteous judgment has fallen on them. God is great!" The remaining weapons were then laid down, and the crowd slowly and quietly dispersed. The bodies were then carried into the city, and thrown out on the very spot where the blood of their innocent victims still stained the earth. They remained there till the 24th, when, for sanitary reasons, they were removed from the Chibootra in front of the Kotwallee. The effect of this just retribution was as miraculous on the populace as it was deserved by the criminals.' Thus were put to death two of the old king's sons, Mirza Mogul Beg, and another whose name is doubtful, together with Mirza's son.

What was done to restore order in Delhi after its recapture; who was appointed to command it; what arrangements were made for bringing to justice the wretched king who was now a prisoner; and what military plan was formed for pursuing the mutinous regiments which had escaped from the city—will more conveniently be noticed in subsequent pages.

The country did not fail to do honour to those who had been concerned in the conquest of the imperial city. The commander of the siege-army was of course the first to be noticed. Although he had no European reputation, Archdale Wilson had served as an artillery officer nearly forty years in India. He was employed at the siege of Bhurtpore in 1824, and in many other active services; but his chief duties confined him to the artillery depôts. It is a curious fact that most of the guns employed by him at the siege of Delhi, as well as those used by the enemy against him, had been cast by him as superintendent of the gun-foundry at Calcutta many years before, and bore his name as part of the device. He held in succession the offices of adjutant-general of artillery and commandant of artillery. At the commencement of the mutiny, his regimental rank was that of lieutenant-colonel of the Bengal artillery; but he acted as brigadier at Meerut, and was afterwards promoted to the rank of major-general. The Queen, in November, raised him to the baronetcy, and made him a Knight Commander of the Order of the Bath; and thus the artillery officer had risen to the rank of 'Major-general Sir Archdale Wilson, K.C.B.' The East India Company, too, sought to bestow honour—or something more solid than honour—on the victorious commander; the court of proprietors, on the suggestion of the court of directors, voted a pension of £1000 per annum to Sir Archdale Wilson, to commence from the day when his troops entered Delhi.

What honours Brigadier Nicholson would have earned, had his valuable life been spared, it would be useless to surmise. He was an especial favourite among the soldiers in the Indian army—more so, perhaps, than some whose names are better known to English readers; and his death withinside the walls of Delhi was very generally deplored. He had not yet attained his 35th year—a very early age at which to obtain brigade command, either in the Company's or the Queen's armies. Nothing but the unbounded confidence of Sir John Lawrence in the military genius of Nicholson would have justified him in making so young a man, a simple regimental captain (brevet-major), brigadier of a column destined to fight the rebels all the way from the Punjaub to Delhi; yet even those seniors who were superseded by this arrangement felt that the duty was intrusted to one equal to its demands. He had seen hard service during the Afghan and Punjaub campaigns, as captain in the 27th Bengal native infantry; and had, instead of idling his time during a furlough visit to England, studied the armies and military organisation of continental Europe. An officer who served with him during the mutiny said: 'He had a constitution of iron. The day we marched to Murdan he was *twenty-six* hours in the saddle, following up the mutineers.' The Queen granted the posthumous dignity of Knight Commander of the Bath upon Brigadier-general John Nicholson; and as he was unmarried, the East India Company departed from their general rule, by bestowing a special grant of £500 per annum upon his widowed mother, who had in earlier years lost another son in the Company's service.

One among many civil servants of the Company who fell during the siege was Hervey Harris Greathed, a member of a family well known in India. After filling various official situations in the Punjaub, Rajpootana, and Meerut, he became chief-commissioner of Delhi, after the foul murder of Mr Simon Fraser on the 11th of May. Serve or remain in Delhi itself he could not, for obvious reasons; but he was with Wilson's army in the expedition from Meerut to Delhi, and then remained with the siege-army on the heights, where his intimate knowledge of India and the natives was of essential value. He died of cholera just before the conclusion of the siege. His brothers, Robert and George Herbert, had already died in the services of the Company or the crown; but two others, Edward Harris and William Wilberforce Harris, survived to achieve fame as gallant officers.

Another of those who fell on the day of the

assault was Lieutenant Philip Salkeld, of the Bengal engineers. He was the son of a Dorsetshire clergyman, and went to India in 1850, in his twentieth year, in the corps of Sappers and Miners. He was employed for four years as an engineer in connection with the new works of the grand trunk-road, in Upper India; and was then transferred to the executive engineers' department in the Delhi division. His first taste of war was in relation to the mutinies; he was engaged in all the operations of the siege of Delhi, and was struck down while gallantly exploding the Cashmere Gate. He lingered in great pain, and died about the 10th of October. The Rev. S. G. Osborne, in a letter written soon after the news of Salkeld's death reached England, said: 'This young officer has not more distinguished himself in his profession by his devotion to his country's service of his life, than he stands distinguished in the memory of those who knew him for his virtues as a son and brother. His father, a clergyman in Dorsetshire, by a reverse of fortune some years since, was with a large family reduced, I may say, to utter poverty. This, his soldier son, supported out of his own professional income one of his brothers at school, helping a sister, obliged to earn her own bread as a governess, to put another brother to school. Just before his death he had saved a sum of £1000, which was in the bank at Delhi, and was therefore lost to him, and, more than this, it was lost to the honourable purpose to which, as a son and brother, he had devoted it. In his native county it has been determined to erect a monument to his memory by subscription. Cadetships having been given to two of his young brothers, it is now wisely resolved that while the memorial which is to hand down his name to posterity in connection with his glorious death shall be all that is necessary for the purpose, every farthing collected beyond the sum necessary for this shall be expended as he would have desired, for the good of these his young brothers.'

Lieutenant Duncan Home, another hero of the Cashmere Gate, was not one of the wounded on that perilous occasion; he lived to receive the approval of his superior in the engineering department; but his death occurred even sooner than that of his companion in arms, for he was mortally wounded on the 1st of October while engaged with an expeditionary force in pursuit of the fleeing rebels. It was on that day, a few hours before he received the fatal bullet, that he wrote a letter to his mother in England; in which, after describing the operations at the Cashmere Gate, he said: 'I was then continually on duty until the king evacuated the palace. I had never more than four hours' sleep in the twenty-four, and then only by snatches. I had also the pleasure of blowing in the gate of the palace; luckily no one fired at me, there being so few men left in the palace.'

Salkeld and Home received the 'Victoria Cross,' a much-coveted honour among the British troops engaged in the Indian war. As did likewise Sergeant Smith, who so boldly risked, yet saved, his life; and also Bugler Hawthorne of the 52d, who blew his signal-blast in spite of the shots whistling around him. Poor Sergeant Carmichael and Corporal Burgess did not live to share in this honour; they fell bullet-pierced.

State Palanquin.

Sir J. E. W. Inglis, defender of Lucknow.

CHAPTER XIX.

THE STORY OF THE LUCKNOW RESIDENCY.

THERE were events that made a deeper impression on the minds of the English public; military exploits more grand and comprehensive; episodes more fatal, more harrowing; trains of operation in which well-known heroic names more frequently found place—but there was nothing in the whole history of the Indian mutiny more admirable or worthy of study than the defence of Lucknow by Brigadier Inglis and the British who were shut up with him in the Residency. Such a triumph over difficulties has not often been placed upon record. Nothing but the most resolute determination, the most complete soldierly obedience, the most untiring watchfulness, the most gentle care of those who from sex or age were unable to defend themselves, the most thorough reliance on himself and on those around him, could have enabled that gallant man to bear up against the overwhelming difficulties which pressed upon him throughout the months of July, August, and September. He occupied one corner of an enormous city, every other part of which was swarming with deadly enemies. No companion could leave him, without danger of instant death at the hands of the rebel sepoys and the Lucknow rabble; no friends could succour him, seeing that anything less than a considerable military force would have been cut off ere it reached the gates of the Residency; no food or drink, no medicines or comforts, no clothing, no ammunition, in addition to that which was actually within the place at the beginning of July, could be brought in. Great beyond expression were the responsibilities and anxieties of one placed in command during eighty-seven of such days—but there was also a moral grandeur in the situation, never to be forgotten.

In former chapters of this work,* much has been said concerning Lucknow, its relations towards the British government on the one hand, and the court of Oude on the other, and the operations which enabled Havelock and Neill to bring a small reinforcement to its British garrison towards the close of September; but what the garrison did and suffered during the three months before this succour could reach them, has yet to be told. The eventful story may be given conveniently in this place, as one among certain intermediate subjects between the military operations of Sir Henry Havelock and those of Sir Colin Campbell.

Let us endeavour, by recapitulating a few facts, to realise in some degree the position of the British at Lucknow when July commenced. The city is a little over fifty miles from Cawnpore—exactly fifty to the Alum Bagh, fifty-three to the Residency, and fifty-seven to the cantonment. Most of its principal buildings, including the Residency, were on the right or southwest bank of the river Goomtee. There was a cantonment Residency, and also a city Residency, at both of which, according to his daily duties, it was the custom of the lamented Sir Henry Lawrence to dwell, before the troubles of the mutiny began; but it is the city Residency which has acquired a notoriety that will never die. It is also necessary to bear in mind that the mere official mansion called the Residency bore but a small ratio to the area and the buildings now known to English readers by that name. This ambiguity is not without its inconveniences, for it denotes a Residency *within* a Residency. Understanding the Residency to mean English Lucknow, the part of the city containing the offices and dwellings of most of the official English residents, then it may be described as an irregular quadrangle a few hundred yards square, jutting out at the north corner, and indented or contracted at the west. Within that limit were numerous residences and other buildings, some military, some political or civil, some private. The word 'garrison' was applied after the defence began, to buildings which had previously been private or official residences; if, therefore, the reader meets in one map with 'Fayrer's House,' and in another with 'Fayrer's Garrison,' he must infer that a private residence was fortified as a stronghold when the troubles began. In this chapter we shall in most instances denominate the whole area as the *intrenchment* or *enclosure*, with the Residency itself as one of the buildings; and we shall furthermore retain the original designation of *house*, rather than *garrison*, for each of the minor residences. The northeast side of the whole enclosure was nearly parallel with the river; and the north corner was in near proximity to an iron bridge carrying a road over the river to the cantonment.

How the British became cooped up within that enclosure, the reader already knows; a few words will bring to recollection the facts fully treated in the chapters lately cited. We have there seen that there were burnings of bungalows, and cartridge troubles, as early as April, in the cantonment of Lucknow; that on the 3d of May some of the native troops became insubordinate at the Moosa Bagh, a military post three or four miles northwest of the Residency; that the 3d Oude infantry was broken into fragments by this mutiny and its consequences; that Sir Henry Lawrence sought to restore a healthy feeling by munificently rewarding certain native soldiers who had remained faithful under temptation; that towards the close of the month he attended very sedulously to various magazines and military posts in and near the city; that he fortified the English quarter by placing defence-works on and near the walls by which it was already three-fourths surrounded, and by setting up other defences on the remaining fourth side; that he brought all the women and children, and all the sick, of the English community, into the space thus enclosed and guarded; that on the last two days of the month he had the vexation of seeing most of the native troops in Lucknow and at the cantonment, belonging to the 13th, 48th, and 71st infantry, and the 7th cavalry, march off in mutiny towards Seetapoor; and that of the seven hundred who remained behind, he did not know how many he could trust even for a single hour. Next, under the month of June, we have seen that nearly all the districts of Oude fell one by one into the hands of the insurgents, increasing at every stage the difficulties which beset Sir Henry as civil and military chief of the province; that he knew the mutineers were approaching Lucknow as a hostile army, and that he looked around in vain for reinforcements; that he paid off most of the sepoys still remaining with him, glad to get rid of men whose continuance in fidelity could not be relied on; that he greatly strengthened the Residency, and also the Muchee Bhowan, a castellated structure northwest of it, formerly inhabited by the dependents of the King of Oude; that all his letters and messages to other places became gradually cut off, leaving him without news of the occurrences in other parts of India; that he stored the Residency with six months' provisions for a thousand persons as a means of preparing for the worst; and that on the last day of the month he fought a most disastrous battle with the mutineers at Chinhut, seven or eight miles out of Lucknow. Then, when July opened, we have seen the British in a critical and painful situation. Lawrence having lost many of his most valued troops, could no longer garrison the Muchee Bhowan, the cantonment, the dâk bungalow, or any place beyond

* Chap. vi., pp. 82-96. Chap. x., pp. 163-165. Chap. xv., pp. 247-263.

the Residency. No European was safe except within the Residency enclosure; and how little safety was found there was miserably shewn on the 2d of the month, when a shell from the insurgents wounded the great and good Sir Henry Lawrence, causing his death on the 4th, after he had made over the military command of Lucknow to Brigadier Inglis, and the civil command to Major Banks.

The Europeans, then, become prisoners within the walls of the Residency enclosure at Lucknow—officers, soldiers, revenue-collectors, judges, magistrates, chaplains, merchants, ladies, children. And with them were such native soldiers and native servants as still remained faithful to the British 'raj.' What was the exact number of persons thus thrown into involuntary companionship at the beginning of July appears somewhat uncertain; but an exact enumeration has been given of those who took up their quarters within the Residency on the 30th of May, when the symptoms of mutiny rendered it no longer safe that the women and children should remain in the city or at the cantonment. The number was 794.* The principal persons belonging to the European community at Lucknow were the following: Sir Henry Lawrence, chief-commissioner; Captain Hayes, military secretary; Major Anderson, chief-engineer; Brigadier Inglis, commandant of the garrison; Brigadier Handscomb, commandant of the Oude brigade; Captain Carnegie, provost-marshal; Captain Simons, chief artillery officer; Colonel Master, 7th native cavalry; Colonel Case and Major Low, H.M. 32d foot; Major Bruyère, 13th native infantry; Major Apthorp, 41st native infantry; Colonel Palmer and Major Bird, 48th native infantry; Colonel Halford, 71st native infantry; Brigadier Gray, Oude Irregulars; Mr Gubbins, finance commissioner; Mr Ommancy, judicial commissioner; Mr Cooper, chief-secretary. Some of these died between the 30th of May and the 4th of July, but a few only. When the whole of the Europeans, officers and privates, had been hastily driven by the mutiny from the cantonment to the Residency; when all the native troops who remained faithful had been in like manner removed to the same place; and when the Muchee Bhowan and all the other buildings in Lucknow had been abandoned by the British and their adherents—the intrenched position at and around the Residency became necessarily the home of a very much larger number of persons; comprising, in addition to the eight hundred or so just adverted to, many hundred British soldiers, and such of the sepoys as remained 'true to their salt.'

In one sense, the Europeans were not taken by surprise. They had watched the energetic exertions of Sir Henry during the month of June, in which he exhibited so sagacious a foresight of troubles about to come. They had seen him accumulate a vast store of provisions; procure tents and firewood for the Residency; arm it gradually with twenty-four guns and ten mortars; order in vast quantities of shot, shell, and gunpowder, from the Muchee Bhowan and the magazines; make arrangements for blowing up all the warlike *matériel* which he could not bring in; bury his barrels of powder beneath the earth in certain open spots in the enclosure; bury, in like manner, twenty-three lacs of the Company's money, until more peaceful days should arrive; destroy many outlying buildings which commanded or overtopped the Residency; organise all the males in the place as component elements in a defensive force; bring in everything useful from the cantonment; build up, in front of the chief structures in the enclosure, huge stacks of firewood, covered with earth and pierced for guns; bring the royal jewels and other valuables from the king's palace into the Residency for safety; and disarm—much to their chagrin—the servants and dependents of the late royal family. All this the Europeans had seen the gallant Lawrence effect during the five weeks which preceded his death. Of the non-military men suddenly converted into soldiers, Captain Anderson says: 'Sir Henry Lawrence deemed it expedient to enrol all the European and Eurasian writers in the public offices as volunteers, and he directed arms and ammunition to be served out to them. Some of these men were taken into the volunteer cavalry—which also comprised officers civil and military—and the remainder were drilled as infantry. At the commencement, when these men were first brought together, to be regularly drilled by sergeants from Her Majesty's 32d regiment, the chance of ever making them act in a body seemed almost hopeless. There were men of all ages, sizes, and figures. Here stood a tall athletic Englishman; there came a fat and heavy Eurasian, with more width about the waist than across the chest; next to the Eurasian came another of the same class, who looked like a porter-barrel, short and squat, and the belt round his waist very closely resembled a hoop; not far off you observed an old, bent-double man, who seemed too weak to support the weight of his musket and pouch. . . . We must not always judge by appearances. Amongst this

* General staff,	9
Brigade staff,	5
Artillery,	9
Engineers,	3
H.M. 32d foot,	22
〃 84th 〃	2
7th Bengal native cavalry,	13
13th 〃 〃 infantry,	10
41st 〃 〃 〃	11
48th 〃 〃 〃	14
71st 〃 〃 〃	11
Oude brigade,	26
Various officers,	9
Civil service,	9
Surgeons,	2
Chaplains,	2
Ladies,	69
〃 , children of,	68
Other women,	171
〃 〃 , children of,	196
Uncovenanted servants,	125
Martinière school,	8
	794

Another account gave the number 865, including about 50 native children in the Martinière school.

awkward-looking body there sprang up, during the siege, bold, intrepid, and daring men!'

Notwithstanding these preparations, however, the calamity fell upon the inmates too suddenly. The fatal result of the battle of Chinhut compelled every one to take refuge within the Residency enclosure; even those who had hitherto lived in the city, rushed in, without preparation, many leaving all their property behind them except a few trifling articles. No one was, or ever could be, bitter against Sir Henry Lawrence; yet were there many criticisms, many expressions of regret, at the policy which led to the battle; and it is unquestionable that much of the misery subsequently borne arose from the precipitate arrangements rendered inevitable on the 30th of June and the following day. When they saw the rebels march into Lucknow, invest the Residency, set up a howitzer-battery in front of it, and loophole the walls of houses for musketry, the Europeans could no longer wait to provide for domestic and personal comforts, or even conveniences: they hastened to their prison-house with such resources as could be hastily provided.

Here, then, was a British community thrown most unexpectedly into close companionship, under circumstances trying to all. It is no wonder that some among the number kept diaries of the strange scenes they witnessed, the sad distresses they bore; nor could there be other than a strong yearning on the part of the English public for a perusal of such diaries or narratives. Hence the publication of several small but deeply interesting volumes relating to the defence of Lucknow—one by Mr Rees, a Calcutta merchant, who happened, unluckily for himself, to be at Lucknow when the troubles began; another by the wife of one of the two English chaplains; a third by Captain Anderson; a fourth by a staff-officer.* Such diaries, when used in illustration and correction one of another, are and must ever be the best sources of information concerning the inner life of Lucknow during that extraordinary period.

Terrible was the confusion within the Residency enclosure for the first few days. Those who had hastened into the place from other spots were endeavouring to find or make something which they could call 'home;' those who had been wounded at Chinhut were suffering in agony within the walls of a building hastily fitted up for them; while the military men looked anxiously around at the defences of the place, to see what could be done to keep the enemy out. When the officers, civil or military, went on the roofs of the houses, they had the mortification of seeing the mutineers gradually concentrating their forces towards the Residency; they saw, also, that the prisoners had escaped from the jails, to join the ranks of those who hated or at any rate opposed the Feringhees.

Arrangements had for some time been in progress, and were now hastily completed, to fortify the principal buildings within the enclosure. If we imagine this English Lucknow to be an irregular diamond-shaped enclosure, with the acute angles very nearly north and south; then it may be said that the south angle was the nearest point to the Cawnpore road, and the north angle the nearest to the iron bridge over the Goomtee towards the cantonment. Near the south point was the house of Captain Anderson, standing in the middle of a garden or open court surrounded by a wall; the house was defended by barricades, and loopholed for musketry; while the garden was strengthened by a trench and rows of palisades. Next to this house, and communicating with it by a hole in the wall, was a newly constructed defence-work that received the name of the Cawnpore Battery, mounted with guns, and intended to command some of the houses and streets adjacent to the Cawnpore road. Mr Deprat's house had a verandah which, for defensive purposes, was blocked up with a mud-wall six feet high and two feet and a half thick; this wall was continued in a straight line to that of the next house, and carried up to a height of nine feet, with loopholes for musketry. Next to this was a house occupied as a school for boys of the Martinière College,* strengthened by a stockade of beams placed before it; and adjacent was a street or road defended by stockades, barricades, and a trench. Further towards the western angle of the enclosure was a building formerly known as the Daroo Shuffa or King's Hospital, but now called the Brigade Mess-house, having a well-protected and lofty terrace which commanded an exterior building called Johannes' house. In its rear was a parallelogram, divided by buildings into two squares or courts, occupied in various ways by officers and their families. Then came groups of low brick buildings around two quadrangles called the Sikh Squares, on the tops of which erections were thrown up to enable the troops to fire out upon the town. Separated from these by a narrow lane was the house of Mr Gubbins, the financial commissioner; the lane was barricaded by earth, beams, and brambles; the buildings were strengthened in every way; while the extreme western point was a battery formed by Mr

* *Personal Narrative of the Siege of Lucknow, from its Commencement to its Relief.* By L. E. Ruutz Rees, one of the Survivors.

A Lady's Diary of the Siege of Lucknow, written for the Perusal of Friends at Home.

A Personal Journal of the Siege of Lucknow. By Captain R. P. Anderson, 25th Regiment N. I., commanding an outpost.

The Defence of Lucknow: a Diary recording the Daily Events during the Siege of the European Residency. By a Staff-officer.

* In a former chapter (p. 84), a brief notice is given of Claude Martine, a French adventurer who rose to great wealth and influence at Lucknow, and who lived in a fantastic palace called Constantia, southeastward of the city. His name will, however, be more favourably held in remembrance as the founder of a college, named by him the Martinière, for Eurasian or half-caste children. This college was situated near the eastern extremity of the city; but when the troubles began, the principals and the children removed to a building hastily set apart for them within the Residency enclosure. The authoress of the *Lady's Diary*, whose husband was connected as a pastor with the Martinière, thus speaks of this transfer: 'The Martinière is abandoned, and I suppose we shall lose all our remaining property, which we have been obliged to leave to its fate, as nothing more can be brought in here. We got our small remnant of clothes; but furniture, harp, books, carriage-horses, &c., are left at the Martinière. The poor boys are all stowed away in a hot close native building, and it will be a wonder if they don't get ill.'

Gubbins himself. Then, passing along the northwest side were seen in turn the racket-court, the slaughter-house, the sheep-pen, and the butcher-yard, all near the boundary of the fortified position, and separated one from another by wide open spaces; there was a storehouse for *bhoosa* (cut chaff for cattle-food), and a guard-house for Europeans; and all the buildings were loopholed for musketry. In the rear of the Bhoosa Intrenchment, as this post was called, was Mr Ommaney's house, guarded by a deep ditch and a cactus-hedge, and provided with two pieces of ordnance. North of the slaughter-house a mortar-battery was formed. The English church was the next important building towards the north; it was speedily converted into a granary; and in the church-yard was formed a mortar-battery capable of shelling all the portion of the city between it and the iron bridge. This church-yard was destined afterwards to present melancholy proofs of the large number of deaths among the English defenders of the place. Beyond the church-yard was Lieutenant Innes's house, in dangerous proximity to many buildings held by the rebels, and bounded on two sides by a garden; it was a difficult but most important duty to strengthen this house as much as possible. The extreme northern part of the whole enclosure, not five hundred yards from the iron bridge, was scarcely susceptible of defence in itself; but it was fully protected by the Redan Battery, constructed by Captain Fulton: this was decidedly the best battery in the whole place, commanding a wide sweep of city and country on both banks of the river. Along the northeast side, connected at one end with the Redan, was a series of earthworks, fascines, and sand-bags, loopholed for musketry, and mounted with guns. A long range of sloping garden-ground was turned into a glacis in front of the line of intrenchment just named. In the centre of the northern half of the whole place was the Residency proper, the official home of the chief-commissioner; this was a large and beautiful brick building, which was speedily made to accommodate many hundred persons; and as it was on high ground, the terrace-roof commanded a view of the whole city—to whoever would incur the peril of standing there.* The hospital, a very large building near the eastern angle of the whole enclosure, had once been the banqueting-room for the British resident at the King of Oude's court; but it was now occupied as a hospital, a dispensary, officers' quarters, and a laboratory for making fuses and cartridges; it was defended by mortars and guns in various directions. The Ballee or Bailey guard was near the hospital, but on a lower level; various parts of it were occupied as a store-room, a treasury, and barracks; the portion really constituting the Bailey guard gate, the station of the sepoys formerly guarding the Residency, was unluckily beyond the limits of the enclosure, and was productive of more harm than good to the garrison; as a means of security, the gateway was blocked up with earth, and defended by guns. Dr Fayrer's house, south of the hospital, had a terrace-roof whence rifles were frequently brought to bear on the insurgents, and near it a gun or two were placed in position. Southward again was the civil dispensary; and near this the post-office, a building which, from its position and construction, was one of the most important in the whole place; soldiers were barracked in the interior, a shell and fuse room was set apart, the engineers made it their head-quarters, several families resided in it, and guns and mortars were planted in and around it. The financial-office, and the house of Mrs Sago (mistress of a charity-school), were on the southeast side of the enclosure, and were with great difficulty brought into a defensive state. The judicial office, near Sago's house, could only be protected from an open lane by a wall of fascines and earth. The jail, near the Cawnpore Gate, was converted into barracks; and the native hospital became a tolerably sheltered place. The Begum's Kothee, or 'lady's house' (formerly belonging to a native lady of rank), was in the centre of the whole enclosure; it comprised many buildings, which were afterwards parcelled off as commissariat store-rooms, cooking-rooms, and dwellings for officers' families.

It will thus be seen that the Residency at Lucknow, so often mentioned in connection with the history of the mutiny, was a small town rather than a single building. But it will also be seen that this small town was most dangerously placed, in juxtaposition to a large city full of hostile inhabitants and revolted sepoys. Before Sir Henry Lawrence took it in hand in June, it could be approached and entered from all sides; and at the beginning of July only a part of the defence-works above described were completed. The officers had to fight and build, to suffer and work, to watch and fortify, day after day, under privations difficult for others to appreciate. The various houses, more frequently designated *garrisons* by those engaged in the siege, did really deserve that title in a military sense; for they were gradually transformed into little forts or strongholds, each placed under one commander, and each defended indomitably against all attacks from the enemy. To give one as an example of many—Captain Anderson, who had resided at Lucknow, as assistant-commissioner, ever since the annexation of Oude, made his own house one of these fortified posts; he had under him eighteen men and one subaltern officer, with whose aid he withstood a *five months'* siege, notwithstanding the enemy had nine 9-pounder guns playing on his house. The wall of the compound around the house was levelled, and a stockade put in its place; within the stockade was a ditch, then an earthwork five feet high, and then another ditch

* The wood-cut at p. 93 represents a part of the Residency in this limited sense of the term; the view at p. 82 will convey some notion of the appearance of the city of Lucknow as seen from the terrace-roof of this building. The plan on next page will give an idea of the Residency before siege; and in the next Part will be given a plan of the Residency under siege, showing the relation which the enemies' guns bore to those of the besieged.

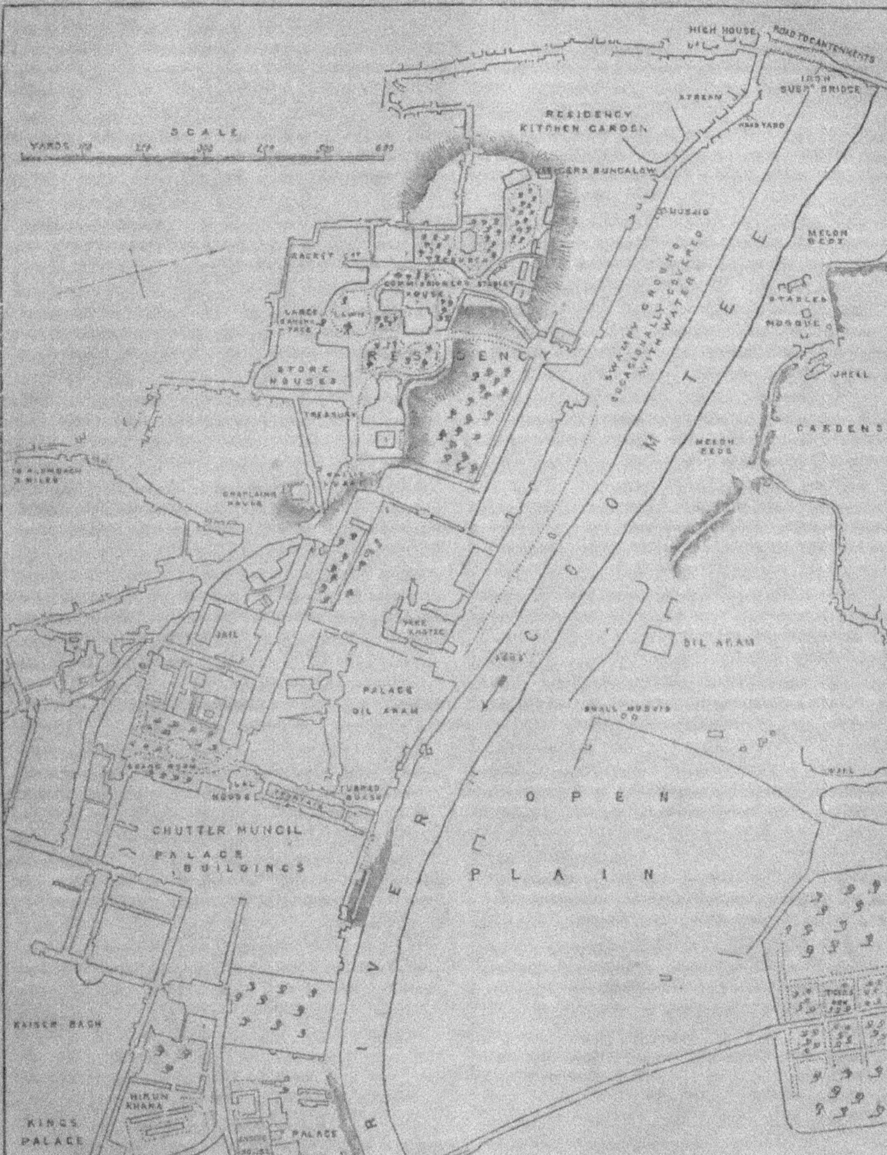

Plan of Residency and part of the City of Lucknow.

with pointed bamboos, forming a *chevaux-de-frise*. It was, in truth, a small citadel, and one very important for the safety of the whole place.

The siege began on the 1st of July, the day following the disastrous battle of Chinhut. It was indeed a siege, even more so than that to which Sir Hugh Wheeler had been exposed at Cawnpore; for there was not only constant firing of musketry, cannon, and mortars, by the mutineers against the Residency; but there were also subterranean mines or galleries dug from the outer streets under the enclosing wall, to blow up the defenders and their defence-works. At every hour of the day, at every corner of the Residency enclosure, was it necessary to keep strict watch. A telegraph, worked at the top of one of the buildings, gave signals to the officers at the Muchee Bhowan, directing them to blow up that fort, and retire to the Residency with the treasure and the guns. This was a most perilous enterprise, but under the skilful superintendence of Captain Francis and Lieutenant Huxhain it succeeded; 240 barrels of gunpowder, and 600,000 rounds of ammunition, were blown into the air, to prevent them from falling into the hands of the enemy; and then the few officers and soldiers marched from the Muchee Bhowan to the Residency, where they helped to strengthen the wofully small number of efficient fighting-men.* All this was done by midnight on the 1st. On the 2d, while resting on a couch after his exhausting and anxious labours, Sir Henry Lawrence was struck by the shell which took away his valuable life; for it was a day on which *ten thousand* rebels were firing shells, balls, and bullets into or at the Residency. Miss Palmer, daughter of Colonel Palmer of the 48th, had her thigh shattered by a ball which entered one of the buildings; and Mr Ommaney was among the wounded. On the 3d dire confusion was everywhere visible; for all felt that their great leader would die of his wound: none had yet fully realised the appalling difficulties of their position; yet were they distracted by family anxieties on the one hand, and public duty on the other. On the 4th, Lawrence descended to the grave; on that day his nephew, Mr G. H. Lawrence, was wounded; and on that day, also, all order or legitimate trade ceased in the city, for marauders and budmashes plundered the shops. No military honours marked the funeral of Sir Henry; there was neither time nor opportunity for any display; a hurried prayer was repeated amid the booming of the enemy's cannon, and a few spadefuls of earth speedily covered the mortal remains of one whose good name was not likely soon to die.* On or about the 5th, the enemy seized the building known as Johannes' house, from which they were able to keep up a deadly fire of musketry against Anderson's house, the jail barracks, the post-office, and the Begum's Kothee; it was afterwards much regretted that this house had not been included among those demolished by Sir Henry. On the 6th and 7th, the harassing fire continued from various points. Some of the bhoosa, or chopped straw for bullocks' fodder, had been left in an ill-defended place; it was fired by the enemy, and totally consumed, placing in imminent danger a powder-magazine at no great distance. Major Francis had both his legs cut off by a cannon-ball, while quietly sitting in the mess-room; Mr Marshall, an opium-merchant, was killed, and the Rev. Mr Polehampton was wounded, about this time. It was a cruel vexation to the garrison to see and feel how much they were suffering through the skilful gunnery which the British had taught to the miscreants now in the insurgent army. The enemy's artillerymen displayed great rapidity, ingenuity, and perseverance, in planting batteries in positions totally unlooked for; some even on house-tops, and others in spots where the garrison could not respond to their fire. It was more than suspected that Europeans were among them; indeed one reckless member of an otherwise worthy English family was recognised among the number, bringing discredit upon brothers and cousins who were at that very time gallantly serving the Company elsewhere. Many of the enemy's batteries were not more than fifty or a hundred yards distant from the marginal buildings of the Residency enclosure; the balls knocked down pillars and verandahs with fearful accuracy. Most of the deaths, however, from ten to twenty a day, were caused by musket-bullets; the enemy had many good marksmen—especially a rebel African, who used his musket with deadly effect from Johannes' house. If Sir Henry Lawrence had been a sterner soldier, if he had not been influenced by such considerate feelings for the opinions and prejudices of others, the British would have lost fewer lives than they did in Lucknow.

* Mr Rees relates a strange anecdote in connection with this retreat from the Muchee Bhowan to the Residency: 'We saved all but one man, who, having been intoxicated, and concealed in some corner, could not be found when the muster-roll was called. The French say, *Il y a un Dieu pour les ivrognes*; and the truth of the proverb was never better exemplified than in this man's case. He had been thrown into the air, had returned unhurt to mother-earth, continued his drunken sleep again, had awaked next morning, found the fort to his surprise a mass of deserted ruins, and quietly walked back to the Residency without being molested by a soul; and even bringing with him a pair of bullocks attached to a cart of ammunition. It is very probable that the débris of these extensive buildings must have seriously injured the adjacent houses and many of the rebel army—thus giving the fortunate man the means of escaping.

* The authoress of the *Lady's Diary* gives an affecting account of the hour that succeeded the wounding of Sir Henry Lawrence. She, with her husband, was at that time in the house of Dr Fayrer, a surgeon who had more than once urged upon Sir Henry the paramount duty of cherishing his own life as one valuable to others even if slighted by himself. 'He was brought over to this house immediately. ——— prayed with him, and administered the Holy Communion to him. He was quite sensible, though his agony was extreme. He spoke for nearly an hour, quite calmly, expressing his last wishes with regard to his children. He sent affectionate messages to them and to each of his brothers and sisters. He particularly mentioned the Lawrence Asylum, and entreated that government might be urged to give it support. He bade farewell to all the gentlemen who were standing round his bed, and said a few words of advice and kindness to each. . . . There was not a dry eye there; every one was so deeply affected and grieved at the loss of such a man.'

It may here be stated that the Queen afterwards bestowed a baronetcy on Sir Henry's eldest son, Alexander Lawrence; to whom also the East India Company voted a pension of £1000 per annum.

We have already said that many of the houses around the Residency were destroyed by orders of Sir Henry, to prevent the enemy from converting them into strongholds; but it was afterwards known that the military officers under him urged the necessity for a still greater demolition. Brigadier Inglis, when at a later date he made a military report of the siege and the defence, adverted to this point in very decisive language. 'When the blockade commenced,' he said, 'only two of our batteries were completed, part of the defences were yet in an unfinished condition, and the buildings in the immediate vicinity, which gave cover to the enemy, were only very partially cleared away. Indeed, our heaviest losses have been caused by the fire from the enemy's sharpshooters, stationed in the adjoining mosques and houses of the native nobility, to the necessity of destroying which the attention of Sir Henry had been repeatedly drawn by the staff of engineers; but his invariable reply was: "Spare the holy places, and private property too, as far as possible;" and we have consequently suffered severely from our very tenderness to the religious prejudices and respect to the rights of our rebellious citizens and soldiery. As soon as the enemy had thoroughly completed the investment of the Residency, they occupied these houses, some of which were within easy pistol-shot of our barricades, in immense force, and rapidly made loopholes on those sides which bore on our post, from which they kept up a terrific and incessant fire day and night.'

The second week of the siege began, bringing with it an augmentation of the troubles already bitterly tasted. One day the Bailey guard would be fiercely attacked, another day the Cawnpore Battery, demanding incessant watchfulness on the part of the officers and men posted at those outworks. Brigadier Inglis sent off letters and messages to Cawnpore and Allahabad; but none reached their destination, the messengers being all intercepted on the way. He did not know how his missives fared; he only knew that no aid, no intelligence, reached him, and he measured his resources with an anxious heart. Sometimes a few officers would retire to snatch a little rest just before midnight, and then would be roused at one or two o'clock in the morning by a message that Gubbins's house—or 'garrison,' as most of the houses within the enclosure were now called—or the Bailey guard, or some other important post, was closely attacked. Sleep, food, everything was forgotten at such moments, except the one paramount duty of repelling the enemy at the attacked point. One day a rebel musketeer pushed forward to such a spot as enabled him to shoot Lieutenant Charlton within side the very door of the church. The enemy sometimes fired logs of wood from their cannon and mortars, as if deficient in shot and shell; but they did not slacken from this or any other cause; they sent shots which set the commissioner's house on fire, causing much danger and difficulty in extinguishing the flames; and it became perilous for any one within the enclosure to be seen for an instant by the enemy—so deadly accurate were their marksmen. Once now and then the officers with a few men, longing for a dash that would inspirit them in the midst of their troubles, would astonish the enemy by making a sortie beyond the defences, spiking a gun or two, despatching a few of the rebels, and hastening back to the enclosure. Lives being, however, too valuable to be risked for advantages so small as these, the brigadier sought rather to discourage than encourage such acts of heroism. Mr Bryson and Lieutenant Baxter were among the many who fell at this time. The officers did men's duty, the civilians did military duty; for there were not hands enough to guard properly the numerous threatened points. One night all spare hands would be called upon to cover with tarpaulin the bhoosa stacks in the racket-court; on another, civilians who never before did labourers' work were called up to dig earth and to carry sand-bags for batteries or breast-works; or they would stand sentinels all night in drenching rains. And then, perhaps on returning to their houses or 'garrisons' in the morning, they would find them untenable by reason of the torrent of balls and bullets to which they had been exposed. The open spots between the several buildings became gradually more and more dangerous. 'A man could not shew his nose,' says Captain Anderson, 'without hearing the whiz of bullets close to his head. The shot, too, came from every direction; and when a poor fellow had nearly jerked his head off his shoulders in making humble salutations to passing bullets, he would have his penance disagreeably changed into a sudden and severe contortion of the whole body to avoid a round shot or shell. So soon as a man left his post he had no time for meditation; his only plan was to proceed rapidly. In fact, to walk slow was in some places very, very dangerous; and many a poor fellow was shot, who was too proud to run past places where bullets danced on the walls like a handful of pease in a frying-pan.'

The third week arrived. Now were the gallant defenders still more distressed and indignant than they had hitherto been; for the enemy commenced firing at the Brigade Mess, where large numbers of ladies and children had taken refuge; attacks were thus made on those who could not defend themselves, and the officers and soldiers found their attention distracted from necessary duties at other points. Anderson's house had by this time become so riddled with shot, that the stores were removed from it; and Deprat's house, similarly battered by the enemy, in like manner became uninhabitable. The buildings near the boundary naturally suffered most; and, as a consequence, those nearer the centre became more and more crowded with inmates. Day by day did officers and men work hard to strengthen the defences. Mortars were placed behind the earthwork at the post-office, to jet forth shells upon the troublesome Johannes' house; stockades and traverses were made, to screen the entrance to the Residency, within which so many persons were domiciled. Nevertheless the attack increased in vigour quite as rapidly as the defence; for the insurgents appear to have received large reinforcements. Their custom was to fire all night, so as to afford the garrison no rest, and thus tire them out; they so pointed a mortar as to send two shells directly into the Residency itself; they commenced a new battery, to bear upon Gubbins's house; their cannon-balls—of which there were indications of a new supply—fell upon and into Fayrer's and Gubbins's houses, the post-office and the Brigade Mess; a shot burst through a room in which many of the principal officers were breakfasting; a mine was sprung inside the Water Gate, intended to blow up the Redan Battery; and at the same time vigorous attacks were made with guns and musketry on almost every part of the enclosure, as if to bewilder the garrison with crushing onslaughts on every side. The pen cannot describe the state of incessant anxiety into which these daily proceedings threw the forlorn inmates of the place: no one could look forward to a night of sleep after a harassing day; for the booming of cannon, and the anticipated visit of a cannon-ball or a mortar-shell, drove away sleep from most eyelids. It was on the 20th that the specially vigorous attack, just adverted to, was made; so general and energetic, that it almost partook of the character of a storming or assault of a beleaguered city. Nothing but the most untiring assiduity could have saved the garrison from destruction. Every one who could handle a musket or load a cannon, did so; others helped to construct stockades and earthen barriers; and even many of the sick and wounded rose from their pallets, staggered along to the points most attacked, sought to aid in the general cause, and in some instances dropped dead while so doing. Almost every building was the object of a distinct attack. The Redan Battery was fortunately not blown up, the enemy having miscalculated the distance of their mine; but the explosion was followed by a desperate struggle on the glacis outside, in which the insurgents were mowed down by grape-shot before they would abandon their attempt to enter at that point. At Innes's house, Lieutenant Loughnan maintained a long and fierce contest against a body of insurgents twentyfold more numerous than the little band who aided him; before they desisted, no less than a hundred dead and wounded were carried off by the rebels. The financial office and Sago's house, entirely defended by non-military men, bore up bravely against the torrent brought against them. The judicial office, under Captain Germon, and Anderson's house, under Captain Anderson, were not only successfully defended, but the handful of troops aided other points where there were no military men. The Brigade Mess, Gubbins's house, the houses near the Cawnpore Battery—all were attacked with vigour, but every attack was repelled.

When the muster-roll was called after these exciting scenes, it was found that many valuable lives had been lost. Yet is it truly remarkable that less than thirty persons of all classes in the garrison were killed or wounded on the 20th. No officer was killed; among the wounded were Captains Lowe and Forbes, Lieutenants Edmonstone and M'Farlane, and Adjutant Smith. Mr Rees asserts that the loss of the enemy, during seven hours of incessant fighting, could hardly have been less than a thousand men. It was the grape-shot poured forth from the garrison that worked this terrible destruction. The week had been attended with its usual list of isolated losses within the enclosure. On one day Lieutenant Lester was killed; on another, Lieutenants Bryce and O'Brien were wounded; and on another, Lieutenant Harmer was laid low.

The arrival of the fourth week of the siege found Brigadier Inglis and his companions stout in heart, but yet depressed in spirits; proud of what they had achieved on the 20th, but fearful that many more such dangers would beset them. The detachment of the 32d foot was that on which Inglis most relied in a military point of view, and in that the casualties had been 150 in three weeks. He had sent out repeated messengers, but had hitherto obtained not a word of news from any quarter; shut out from the world of India, he knew of nothing but his own cares and responsibilities. On the 23d, however, a gleam of joy shot through the garrison; a messenger, amid imminent peril, had been to Cawnpore, and brought back news of Havelock's victories in the Doab. Inglis immediately sent him off again, with an urgent request to the gallant general to advance with his column to Lucknow as quickly as possible. The English residents began to count the days that must elapse before Havelock could arrive—a hopeful thing at the time, but bitterly disappointing afterwards; for they knew not how or why it was that succour did not arrive. Whatever might be the hopes or fears for the future, there was an ever-present danger which demanded daily and hourly attention. Although mortified by their late defeat, the enemy did not on that account give up their attacks. On narrowly watching, the engineers detected the enemy forming a mine beneath the ground from Johannes' house to the Sikh Square and the Brigade Mess; they could hear the miners at their subterraneous work, and they did what military engineers are accustomed to in such cases—run out a countermine, and destroy the enemy's handiwork by an explosion. Above ground the attack was maintained chiefly by artillery, the hurling of balls, shells, shrapnels, and those abominable compounds of pitchy and sulphureous substances which artillerymen call 'stinkpots.' The breakfast-table of the officers at the post-office was one morning visited by an eight-inch shell, which fell on it without exploding. On the 25th a letter arrived from Colonel Tytler at Cawnpore, the first received from any quarter throughout July; for the former messenger had brought rumours concerning Havelock, not a letter or a message. Great was the joy at learning that Havelock intended to advance to Lucknow; and Inglis at once sent off to him a plan of the city, to aid his proceedings—offering the messenger five thousand rupees if he safely brought back an answer. An anxious time indeed was it for all, and well might they look out for succour. Major Banks, the civil commissioner appointed by Sir Henry Lawrence, was shot dead while reconnoitring from the top of an outhouse; he was an officer who had served nearly thirty years in India, and who, both as a soldier and a linguist, had won a good name. Dr Brydon was wounded; the Rev. Mr Polehampton was killed, as were Lieutenants Lewin, Shepherd, and Archer, and many others whose lives were valuable, not only to their families, but to all in the garrison. The death of Major Banks increased the cares and responsibilities of Brigadier Inglis, who, now that there was no chief-commissioner, felt the necessity of placing the whole community under strict military-garrison rules.

In the official dispatch afterwards prepared by Inglis, full justice was done to the ingenuity and perseverance of the besiegers. Speaking of the large guns placed in batteries on every side of the enclosure, he said: 'These were planted all round our post at small distances, some being actually within fifty yards of our defences, but in places where our own heavy guns could not reply to them; while the perseverance and ingenuity of the enemy in erecting barricades in front of and around their guns, in a very short time rendered all attempts to silence them by musketry entirely unavailing. Neither could they be effectually silenced by shells, by reason of their extreme proximity to our position, and because, moreover, the enemy had recourse to digging very narrow trenches about eight feet in depth in rear of each gun, in which the men lay while our shells were flying, and which so effectually concealed them, even while working the gun, that our baffled sharpshooters could only see their hands while in the act of loading.'

And now, the reader may ask, what were the ladies and children doing during this terrible month of July; and how did the officers and men fare in their domestic and personal matters? It is a sad tale, full of trouble and misery; and yet it is a heroic tale. No one flinched, no one dreamed for an instant of succumbing to the enemy. It must be remembered, as a beginning of all the privations, that the Europeans went into the Residency very scantily supplied with personal necessaries. When the cantonment was burned during the mutiny of the 31st of May, much property belonging to the officers was destroyed; and when every one hurried in for shelter after the disastrous 30th of June, no time was allowed for making purchases in the city, or bringing in property from bungalows or storehouses outside the official stronghold. Hence every one was driven to make the best of such commodities as had been secured by the last day of June. Even during the greater part of that month the troubles were many; the enclosure Residency was full of officers and men, all hard at work; the heat was excessive; cholera, dysentery, and small-pox were at their deadly work; the church being full of grain, those who sought religious aid in time of need met for divine service in any available spot; most of the native servants ran away when the troubles began; and many of them ended their service by robbing their masters.

How July opened for the British, may faintly be imagined. The commissariat chief was ill; no one could promptly organise that office under the sudden emergency; the food and draught bullocks, unattended to, roamed about the place; and many of them were shot, or tumbled into wells. Terrible work was it for the officers to bury the killed bullocks, lest their decaying carcasses should taint the air in excessively hot weather. Some of the artillery horses were driven mad for want of food and water. Day after day, after working hard in the trenches, the officers had to employ themselves at night in burying dead bullocks and horses—officers, be it understood; for the men were all employed as sentries or in other duties. It was not until after many days that they could turn out of the enclosure all the spare horses, and secure the rest. As the heat continued, and as the dead bodies of animals increased in number, the stench became overpowering, and was one of the greatest grievances to which the garrison were exposed; the temperature at night was often less patiently borne than that by day, and the officers and men were troubled by painful boils. Even when wet days occurred, matters were not much improved; for the hot vapours from stagnant pools engendered fever, cholera, dysentery, and diarrhœa. The children died rapidly, and the hospital-rooms were always full; the sick and wounded could not be carried to upper apartments, because the enemy's shot and shell rendered all such places untenable. The officers were put on half-rations early in the month; and even those rations they in many cases had to cook for themselves, owing to the disappearance of the native servants. The English ladies suffered unnumbered privations and inconveniences. The clergyman's wife, in her *Diary*, told of the very first day of the siege in these words: 'No sooner was the first gun fired, than the ladies and children—congregated in large numbers in Dr Fayrer's house—were all hurried down stairs into an underground room called the Tye Khana, damp, dark, and gloomy as a vault, and excessively dirty. Here we sat all day, feeling too miserable, anxious, and terrified to speak, the gentlemen occasionally coming down to reassure us and tell us how things were going on. —— was nearly all the day in the hospital, where the scene was terrible; the place so crowded with wounded and dying men that there was no room to pass between them, and everything in a state of indescribable misery, discomfort, and confusion.' In the preceding month it had been a hardship for the ladies to be deprived of the luxuries of Anglo-Indian life; but they were now driven to measure comforts by a different standard. They were called upon to sweep their own rooms, draw water from the wells, wash their own clothes, and perform all the menial duties of a household; while their husbands or fathers were cramped up in little outhouses or stables, or anywhere that might afford temporary shelter at night. When food became scanty and disease prevalent, these troubles were of course augmented, and difference of rank became almost obliterated where all had to suffer alike. Many families were huddled together in one large room, and all privacy was destroyed. The sick and wounded were, as may be supposed, in sad plight; for, kind as the rest were, there were too many harassing duties to permit them to help adequately those who were too weak to help themselves. Officers and men were lying about in the hospital rooms, covered with blood and often with vermin; the *dhobees* or washermen were too weak-handed for the preservation of cleanliness, and few of the British had the luxury of a change of linen; the windows being kept closed and barricaded, to prevent the entrance of shot from without, the pestilential atmosphere carried off almost as many unfortunates as the enemy's missiles. The writer of the *Lady's Diary*, whose narrative is seldom relieved by one gleam of cheerfulness, departs from her habitual sadness when describing the mode in which eleven ladies and seven children slept on the floor in the Tye Khana or cellar, 'fitting into each other like bits into a puzzle.' Chairs being few in number, most of the ladies sat on the floor, and at meal-times placed their plates on their knees. The cellar being perfectly dark, candles were lighted at meal-times. The reason for keeping so many persons in this subterranean abode was to lessen the chance of their being shot in any upper apartment. Of one torment, the flies, every person complained bitterly who was shut up in the Residency enclosure on those fearfully hot days. Mr Rees says: 'They daily increased to such an extent that we at last began to feel life irksome, more on their account than from any other of our numerous troubles. In the day, flies; at night, mosquitoes. But the latter were bearable; the former intolerable. Lucknow had always been noted for its flies; but at no time had they been known to be so troublesome. The mass of putrid matter that was allowed to accumulate, the rains, the commissariat stores, the hospital, had attracted these insects in incredible numbers. The Egyptians could not possibly have been more molested than we were by this pest. They swarmed in millions, and though we blew daily some hundreds of thousands into the air, this seemed to make no diminution in their numbers; the ground was still black with them, and the tables were literally covered with these cursed flies. We could not sleep in the day on account of them. We could scarcely eat. Our beef, of which we got a tolerably small quantity every day, was usually studded with them; and when I ate my miserable boiled lentil-soup and unleavened bread, a number of scamps flew into my mouth, or tumbled into and floated about in my plate.'

Let us proceed, and watch the military operations of the month of August.

The fifth week of the siege opened with the same scenes as before, deepened in intensity. The enemy, it is true, did not attack with more vigour, but the defenders were gradually weakened in every one of their resources—except courage, and the resolution to bear all rather than yield to the enemy. Colonel Tytler's letter had afforded hope that the relieving column under Havelock would arrive at Lucknow before the end of July; but when the 30th and 31st had passed, and the 1st and 2d of August had passed also, then were their hopes cruelly dashed. It required all the energy of Brigadier Inglis to keep up the spirits of himself and his companions under the disappointment. He did not know, and was destined to remain for some time in ignorance, that Havelock had been forced to return to Cawnpore, owing to the losses suffered by his heroic little band. About the beginning of the month, great numbers of additional rebel sepoys entered Lucknow, increasing the phalanx opposed to the British. They began a new mine near Sago's house, and another near the Brigade Mess, in which many of the ladies and children were sheltered; and it required all the activity of the officers to frustrate these underground enemies. The rebels planted a 24-pounder near the iron bridge, to batter the church and the Residency. On one day a shell burst in a room of the Begum's Kothee, where Lieutenant James and Mr Lawrence were ill in bed, but without injuring them; and on another a soldier was shot dead by a cannon-ball in the very centre room of the hospital. Inglis tried, but tried in vain, to get any one to take a letter, even so small as to go into a quill, to Havelock; the enterprise was so perilous, that the offer of a great reward fell powerless. Thus reduced to his own resources, he began anxiously to count up his stores and supplies: he protected the powder-magazine with heavy beams, laden with a great thickness of earth; and he got the civilians to labour at the earthworks, and to watch the batteries, for nearly all his engineers were ill. One engineer-officer, Captain Fulton, was happily spared from illness longer than most of the others; and he laboured unremittingly and most skilfully to baffle the enemy's mining by countermining: he organised a body of sappers from among the humbler members of the garrison, and begged every one who did sentry-duty at night to listen for and give information concerning any underground sounds that denoted the driving of galleries or mines by the enemy. One of the ladies, Mrs Dorin, was among the number who this week fell from the shots of the enemy. An event of this kind was peculiarly distressing to all; an officer learns to brave death, but he is inexpressibly saddened when he sees tender women falling near him by bullets.

The sixth week arrived. The brigadier, by redoubling his offers, did at length succeed in obtaining the aid of a native, who started on the dangerous duty of conveying a small note to General Havelock at Cawnpore. This done, he renewed his anxious superintendence of matters within the enclosure. The enemy mounted on the top of Johannes' house, and thence kept up a very annoying fire on the Brigade Mess. They also recommenced mining near the Redan. On the 8th of August the garrison could hear and see much marching and countermarching of troops within the city, without being able to divine its cause; they fondly hoped, when the booming of guns was heard, that Havelock was approaching. This hope was, however, speedily and bitterly dashed; for on the following day a great force of rebels was seen to approach from the direction of the cantonment, cross the river, and join the main body of the insurgents within Lucknow. This was a bad omen, for it prefigured an increase in the number, frequency, and varieties of attack. On the 10th the enemy succeeded in exploding one of their mines opposite Johannes' house; it blew up sixty feet of palisades and earthen defences. Under cover of this surprise, and of a tremendous firing of guns, the enemy pushed forward into all the buildings near the Cawnpore Battery and Johannes' house; but they encountered so steady and determined a resistance that they were beaten at all points. Near Sago's house, too, they fired another mine, which blew up two soldiers; but here, in like manner, they were repulsed after a fierce contest. This explosion was accompanied or attended by an incident almost as strange as that connected with the soldier at Muchee Bhowan; the two men were blown into the air, but both escaped with their lives; one fell within the enclosure, slightly bruised, but not seriously injured; the other, falling into an open road between the enclosure and the enemy, jumped up when he found himself unhurt, and clambered over a wall or through the breach, untouched by the storm of bullets sent after him. On the same day there were other attacks on Innes's, Anderson's, and Gubbins's houses or garrisons. Of the attacks on the Brigade Mess, the Cawnpore Battery, and Anderson's house, Brigadier Inglis afterwards thus spoke in his dispatch: 'The enemy sprang a mine close to the Brigade Mess, which entirely destroyed our defences for the space of twenty feet, and blew in a great portion of the outside wall of the house occupied by Mr Schilling's garrison. On the dust clearing away, a breach appeared through which a regiment could have advanced in perfect order, and a few of the enemy came on with the utmost determination; but they were met with such a withering flank-fire of musketry from the officers and men holding the top of the Brigade Mess, that they beat a speedy retreat, leaving the more adventurous of their numbers lying on the crest of the breach. While this operation was going on, another large body advanced on the Cawnpore Battery, and succeeded in locating themselves for a few minutes in the ditch. They were, however, dislodged by hand-grenades. At Captain Anderson's post, they also came boldly forward with scaling-ladders, which they planted against the wall; but here, as elsewhere, they were met with the most indomitable resolution; and the leaders being slain, the rest fled, leaving the ladders, and retreated to their batteries and loopholed defences, whence they kept up for the rest of the day an unusually heavy cannonade and musketry fire.' All the attacks, it is true, were frustrated, but only by fearful labour on the part of the defenders; every man was worn down by exhaustion on this terrible day. A message or rather a rumour was received, obscure in its purport, but conveying the impression that Havelock had been baffled in his attempt to reach Lucknow: news that produced very great despondency in the garrison, among those who had become sick at heart as well as in body. When a cannon-ball rushed along and demolished the verandah of the Residency or chief-commissioner's house, it could not do less than add to the trepidation of the numerous families domiciled within the walls of that building, already brought into a state of nervous agitation by the incessant noises and dangers. Death and wounds were as rife as ever during this week. A shot broke the leg of Ensign Studdy while breakfasting in the Residency; Captain Waterman was wounded; Lieutenant Bryce died of a wound received some days earlier; Major Anderson, chief-engineer, died of dysentery and over-fatigue, bringing grief to the whole garrison for the loss of a most valuable and intrepid officer. These were the chief names: those of humbler rank who fell to rise no more were too many to be officially recorded; they were hastily buried in the churchyard, and soon driven from the memories of those who had no time to dwell on the past.

Up to the day when the seventh week of the siege opened, there had been twenty letters sent for succour, first by Sir Henry Lawrence, and then by Brigadier Inglis; and to only one of these had a direct reply been received. Only a few of them, indeed, had reached their destinations; and of these few, a reply from one alone safely passed through all the perils between Cawnpore and Lucknow. As has been already said, this reply was not such as to comfort the British residents; they had to rouse themselves to a continuance of the same kind of exertions as before. The enemy did not give them one day, scarcely one hour, of rest. On the 12th of August so fierce an attack was made on the Cawnpore Battery, that all the defenders were forced to shield themselves from the balls and bullets—still remaining at hand, however, in case a closer assault were attempted. It being found, too, that a mine was being run by the enemy in the direction of Sago's house, some of the officers made a daring sortie to examine this mine, much to their own peril. Then commenced, as before, a system of countermining, each party of miners being able to hear the other working in an adjoining gallery; it became a struggle which should blow the other up; the British succeeded, and shattered all the works of the enemy at that spot. Nothing in the whole progress of the siege was more extraordinary than this perpetual mining and countermining. While the infantry and artillery on both sides were at their usual deadly work in the open air, the Sappers and Miners were converting the ground beneath into a honeycomb of dark galleries and passages—the enemy attempting to blow up the defence-works, and the defenders attempting to anticipate this by blowing up the enemy. Whenever the firing by the mutineers slackened in any material degree, the defenders took advantage of the opportunity to make new sand-bags for batteries and earthworks, in place of the old ones which had been destroyed. The 15th of August was a white day within the enclosure; *no burial took place.* It was also rendered notable by the receipt of a letter from General Havelock—a letter telling of inability to afford present succour, and therefore a mournful letter; but still it was better than none, seeing that it pointed out to all the necessity for continued exertions in the common cause. Now came the time when a great increase of discomfort was in store for the numerous persons who had been accommodated in the Residency, the official house of the chief-commissioner. The building had been so shaken by shells and balls that it was no longer secure; and the inmates were removed to other quarters. On the 18th a terrible commotion took place; the enemy exploded a mine under the Sikh Square or barrack, and made a breach of thirty feet in the defence-boundary of the enclosure. Instantly all hands were set to work; boxes, planks, doors, beams, were brought from various quarters to stop up the gap; while muskets and pistols were brought to bear upon the assailants. Not only did the gallant fellows within the enclosure repel the enemy, but they made a sortie, and blew up some of the exterior buildings which were in inconvenient proximity. By the explosion on this day, Captain Orr, Lieutenant Meecham, and other officers and men, were hurled into the air, but with less serious results than might have been expected; several, however, were suffocated by the débris which fell upon them.

By the eighth week the garrison had become in a strange way accustomed to bullets and balls; that is, though always in misery of some kind or other, the report of firearms had been rendered so thoroughly familiar to them, through every day and night's experience, that it was a matter of course to hear missiles whiz past the ear. Mr Rees, speaking of his daily movements from building to building in the enclosure, says: 'At one time a bullet passed through my hat; at another I escaped being shot dead by one of the enemy's best riflemen, by an unfortunate soldier passing unexpectedly before me, and receiving the wound through the temples instead; at another I moved off from a place where in less than a twinkling of an eye afterwards a musket-bullet stuck in the wall; at another, again, I was covered with dust and pieces of brick by a round-shot that struck the wall not two inches away from me; at another, again, a shell burst a couple of yards away from me, killing an old woman, and wounding a native boy and a native cook.' Every day was marked by some vicissitudes. On the 20th, the enemy opened a tremendous cannonading, which knocked down a guard-room over the Mess-house, and lessened the number of places from which the garrison could obtain a look-out. The enemy were also on that day detected in the attempt to run new mines under the Cawnpore Battery and the Bailey guard. This led to a brilliant sortie, headed by Captain M'Cabe and Lieutenant Browne, which resulted not only in the spiking of two of the enemy's guns, but also in the blowing up of Johannes' house, which had been such a perpetual source of annoyance to the garrison. It was one of the best day's work yet accomplished, and cheered the poor, hard-worked fellows for a time. Yet they had enough to trouble them; the Cawnpore and Redan batteries were almost knocked to pieces, and needed constant repair; the judicial office became so riddled with shot that the women and children had to be removed from it; the enemy's sharpshooters were deadly accurate in their aim; their miners began new mines as fast as the old ones were destroyed or rendered innoxious; and Inglis's little band was rapidly thinning.

Another week arrived, the last in August, and the ninth of this perilous life in the fortified enclosure. The days exhibited variations in the degree of danger, but not one really bright gleam cheered the hearts of the garrison. An advantage had been gained by the successful mining and blowing up of Johannes' house, once the residence of a merchant of that name; it had been a post from which an African eunuch belonging to the late king's court had kept up a most fatal and accurate fire into the enclosure, bringing down more Europeans than any other person in the enemy's ranks. An advantage was thus gained, it is certain; but there were miseries in abundance in other quarters. Gubbins's house had become so shot-riddled, that the ladies and children domiciled there were too much imperiled to remain longer; they were removed to other buildings, adding to the number of inmates in rooms already sadly overcrowded. Among the natives in the enclosure, desertions frequently took place; a fact at which no one could reasonably be surprised, but which nevertheless greatly added to the labours of those on whom devolved the defence of the place. Distressingly severe as those labours had all along been, they were now doubly so; for the enemy erected a new battery opposite the Bailey guard, and commenced new mines in all directions. As the defenders could seldom venture on a sortie to examine the enemy's works of attack, they were driven to the construction of 'listening-galleries'—underground passages where the sound of the enemy's mining picks and shovels could be heard. And then would be renewed the digging of countermines,

English Church and Residency at Lucknow—from Officers' Quarters.

and a struggle to determine which party should be the first to blow up the other. The Mohurrum or Mohammedan festival commenced this week; a period in which fanatical Mussulmans are so fierce against all who dissent from their faith, that the garrison apprehended a new onslaught with more force than ever; this fear passed away, however, for though there was much 'tom-tom' processioning and buffalo-horn bugling in the city, the attacks on the enclosure did not differ much from their usual character. Another letter was received from Havelock, which gave joy to men who found that they were not wholly forgotten by friends in the outer world; but when they heard that a period of at least *three weeks* longer must elapse before he could possibly reach them, their overcharged hearts sank again, and deep despondency existed for a time among them.

During this month of August, the women and children, the sick and wounded, of course suffered much more terribly than in the previous month of July. Every kind of peril and discomfort had increased in severity; every means of succour and solace had diminished in quantity. Death struck down many; disease and wounds laid low a still greater number; and those who remained were a prey to carking cares, which wore down both mind and body. Those who, in a Christian country, are accustomed to pay the last token of respect to departed friends by decent funeral ceremonies, were often pained by their disability to do so in the Lucknow enclosure, under the straitened circumstances of their position. The Rev. Mr Polehampton, after working day and night in his kindly offices among the sick and wounded, was at length himself struck down by cholera; and then came the mournful question, whether he could have a coffin and a separate grave. The writer of the *Diary*, wife of the clergyman who succeeded Mr Polehampton in his duties as a pastor, says that her husband read the funeral-service over the dead body in presence of the mourning widow, on the day and in the room where the death took place, before removal for instant interment. 'She (the widow) was extremely anxious he should have a coffin, a wish it seemed impossible to gratify; but —— instituted a search, and found one stored away with some old boxes under the staircase in the hospital; and he also had a separate grave dug for him. Since the siege, the bodies have hitherto always been buried several in the same grave, and sewn up in their bedding, as there are no people and no time to make coffins.' In their troubled state of feeling, vexations affected the different members of the imprisoned community more acutely than would have been the case at other times. The plague of flies can be adverted to in a half-laughing manner by a man in health; but in the Lucknow enclosure it was a real plague, a source of exquisite misery, against which more complaints were uttered than almost anything else. There were also troublesome and painful boils on the person, brought on by high temperature and insufficient diet and medicines. Whatever might be the amount of care taken, bullocks were frequently killed by the shot of the enemy; and as animals so dying were not fit for human food, it became necessary to bury the carcasses at once. A frightful duty this was, mostly performed (as has already been stated) at night by officers, whose few hours of possible sleep were cut short by this revolting sort of labour. No one could leave the enclosure, except native servants determined on escape; not an inch of ground belonged to the British beyond the limits of the intrenched position; and therefore whatever had to be put out of sight—dead bodies of human beings, carcasses of bullocks and horses, garbage and refuse of every kind—could only so be treated by being buried underground in the few open spots between the buildings. And this, too, in the August of an Indian climate, when even the best sanitary arrangements fail to remove offensive odours. The officers, in all their letters and diaries, spoke of this portion of their labours as being most distressing; while the poor women, cabined by dozens together in single rooms, yearned, but yearned in vain, for the breathing of a little air free from impurities. They dared not move out, for the balls and bullets of the enemy were whizzing across and into every open spot. Sometimes an 18-pounder shot would burst into a room where two or three of them were dressing, or where a larger number were at meals. In some of the houses or 'garrisons,' where many ladies formed one community, they used to take it in turn to keep awake for hourly watches during the night; one of them said in a letter: 'I don't exactly know what is gained by these night-watchings—except that we are all very nervous, and are expecting some dreadful catastrophe to happen.' The little children died off rapidly, their maladies being more than could be met by the resources at hand; and those who bore up against the afflictions were much emaciated. The husbands and fathers, worn out with daily fatigue and nightly watching, had little solace to afford their families; and thus the women and children were left to pass the weary hours as best they could. A few little creatures, 'siege-babies,' as their poor mothers called them, came into the world during this stormy period; and with them each day was a struggle for life. When the native servants one by one escaped, the discomforts of the English women of course underwent much aggravation; and when the house or bungalow of Mr Gubbins became untenable through shot and bullet, the difficulty was immense of finding shelter elsewhere; every place was already overcrowded. Much additional misery befell the officers and men from this fact—that the commissariat quarter, offensive to every sense on account of the organic accumulations inseparable from the slaughtering and cutting up of animals—was one of the weakest parts in the whole enclosure, and required to be guarded at all hours by armed men, who loathed the spot for the reason just mentioned. The chaplain, too, found the church-yard getting into such a horrible state that he dared not go near the graves to read the funeral-service. Mr Rees mentions an instance to illustrate the anxieties of those who, willing to suffer themselves, were almost crushed by witnessing the privations of those dear to them. 'He' (mentioning one of the officers) 'had at first told me of his wife being feverish and quite overcome with the abominable life she had to lead. And then he talked to me of his boy Herbert; how he was attacked with cholera, and feared he was very ill; and how, instead of being able to watch by his bedside, he had been all night digging at Captain Fulton's mine; and then how his child next night was convulsed, and what little hope of his darling being spared to them—how heart-rending the boy's sufferings were to his parents' feelings—how even his (the father's) iron constitution was at last giving way—how he had neither medicine, nor attendance, nor proper food for the child—and how the blowing up of the mine so close to his sick child had frightened him. And then to-day he told me, with tears in his eyes, that yesterday—the anniversary of his birthday—his poor child was called away. "God's will be done," said he; "but it is terrible to think of. At night we dug a hole in the garden, and there, wrapped in a blanket, we laid him."' This case is not singular; many another poor parent's heart was thus torn.

The provisioning of the garrison was of course a perpetual source of anxiety to Brigadier Inglis and the other officers; or rather, the distribution of the food already possessed, and rapidly becoming exhausted, without any prospect of replenishing. Fresh meat was in store for the garrison as long as any healthy bullocks remained; but in other articles of food the deficiency became serious as the month advanced. An immense store of attah—the coarse meal from which chupatties or cakes were made—had been provided by Sir Henry

Lawrence; but this was now nearly exhausted, and the garrison had to grind corn daily, from the store kept in the impromptu granaries. The women and the older children were much employed in this corn-grinding, by means of hand-mills. To economise the meal thus laboriously ground, rice and unground wheat were served out to the natives. The animal food was likely to be limited, by the want not of bullocks, but of bhoosa or fodder to feed them; and the commissariat-officers saw clearly before them the approach of a time when the poor animals must die for want of food. The tea and sugar were exhausted, except a little store kept for invalids. The tobacco was all gone; and the soldiers, yearning for a pipe after a hard day's work, smoked dried leaves as the only obtainable substitute. A few casks of porter still remained, to be guarded as a precious treasure. Once now and then, when an officer was struck down to death, an auction would be held of the few trifling comforts which he had been able to bring with him into the enclosure; and then the prices given by those who possessed means plainly told how eager was the desire for some little change in the poor and insufficient daily food. A few effects left by Sir Henry Lawrence were sold; among them, £16 was given for a dozen bottles of brandy, £7 for a dozen of beer, the same amount for a dozen of sherry, £7 for a ham, £4 for a quart bottle of honey, £5 for two small tins of preserved soup, and £3 for a cake of chocolate. Sugar was the luxury for which most craving was exhibited.

We pass on now to another month, September, whose early days ushered in the tenth week of the captivity.

New mines were everywhere discovered. The British, officers and men, attended sedulously to the underground listening-galleries adverted to in a former paragraph, and there obtained unmistakable evidence that the enemy were running mines towards Sago's house, the Brigade Mess, the Bailey guard, and other buildings, with the customary intent of blowing them up, and making a forcible entry into the enclosure. Untiring exertions at countermining alone frustrated these terrible operations. On one day, the upper part of the Brigade Mess was smashed in by a shot; on another, a breach was made in the wall of the Martinière temporary school, requiring very speedy stockading and barricading to prevent the entrance of the enemy; on another, a few engineers made a gallant sortie from Innes's house, and succeeded in blowing up a building from which the enemy had maintained an annoying fire of musketry; and on another day, an officer had the curiosity to count the cannon-balls, varying from 3 to 24 pounds each, which had fallen on the roof of one building alone, the Brigade Mess—they were no less than 280 in number! On the 5th of the month, the enemy made a more than usually impetuous attack; there were 5000 of them in sight from the Residency; they had formed a battery on the other side of the river; they exploded two mines near the Bailey guard and the mess-house; they advanced to Gubbins's house and to the Sikh Square, bringing with them long ladders to effect an escalade—in short, they seemed determined to carry their point on this occasion. All was in vain, however; the garrison, though worked almost to death, gallantly rushed to every endangered spot and repelled the enemy, hastily reconstructing such defence-works as had been destroyed or damaged. Fortunately, the two exploded mines were short of their intended distance: they wrought but little damage. Much marching and countermarching were occasionally visible among the troops in the city: vague rumours reached the Residency that Havelock had a second time vanquished Nena Sahib's troops at Cawnpore or Bithoor; but to what extent these movements and rumours would influence the garrison was left painfully undecided. The nights were more terrible than the days; for the enemy, as if to destroy all chance of sleep, kept up a torrent of musketry, accompanied by much shouting and screaming. Many of the officers worked with almost superhuman energy at this time. Captains Fulton and Anderson, Lieutenants Aitken, Clery, Innes, Hutchinson, Tulloch, Birch, Hay, and others, were constantly on the watch for mines, and sedulously digging countermines to foil them.

The eleventh week found the garrison more than ever exposed to hourly peril. The officers, driven from place to place for their few hours of repast and repose, had latterly messed in one of the buildings of the Begum's Kothee; this fact seemed to be well known to the rebels, who were from the first better acquainted with what transpired inside the fort than the garrison were with external affairs; they directed their shells and balls so thickly on that spot, that ingress and egress were equally difficult. Two sides of Innes's house were blown in, and the whole structure made little else than a heap of ruins; the Residency, too, became so tottering, that renewed precautions had to be taken in that quarter; new mines were perpetually discovered, directed to points underneath the various buildings; and the enemy sought to increase their means of annoyance by booming forth shells filled with abominable and filthy compositions. Perhaps the most harassing troubles were owing to the uncertainty of the time and place when active services would be needed. The officers could not reckon upon a single minute of peace. 'In the midst of all these miseries,' says Captain Anderson, 'you would hear the cry of "Turn out;" and you had to seize your musket and rush to your port. Then there was a constant state of anxiety as to whether we were mined or not; and we were not quite sure, whilst we were at a loophole, that we might not suddenly see the ground open, or observe the whole materials of the house fly into the air by the explosion of a mine. Shells came smashing into our rooms, and dashed our property to pieces; then followed round-shot, and down tumbled huge pieces of masonry, while bits of wood and brick flew in all directions. I have seen beds literally blown to atoms, and trunks and boxes completely smashed into little bits.' Nevertheless, there was no flinching in the garrison; if a mine were discovered, a countermine was run out to frustrate it; if a wall or a verandah were knocked down by shot, the débris was instantly used to form a rampart, barricade, or stockade. On the 14th of the month, a loss was incurred which caused grief throughout the garrison. Captain Fulton, whose indomitable energy had won the admiration of all in his duties as engineer, and whose kindness of manner had rendered him a general favourite, was struck by a cannon-ball which took his head completely off. Brigadier Inglis felt this loss sensitively, for Fulton had been to him an invaluable aid in all his trials and difficulties. Fulton, who was especially marked by his skill and promptness in countermining, had succeeded Major Anderson as chief-engineer, and was himself now succeeded by Captain Anderson.

The twelfth week, the last which the beleaguered English were destined to suffer before the one which was to bring Havelock and Neill to Lucknow, found them in great despondency. They had lately lost a number of valuable officers. Lieutenant Birch fell; then M. Deprat, a merchant who worked and fought most valiantly at the defences; then Captain Cunliffe; and then Lieutenant Graham, whose mental firmness gave way under privation, grief, and wounds, leading him to commit suicide. As a natural consequence of these and similar losses, harder work than ever pressed on those who remained alive. Never for a moment was the look-out neglected. At all hours of the day and night, officers were posted on the roofs of the Residency and the post-office, finding such shelter as they could while watching intently the river, the bridges, the roads, and the buildings in and around the city; every fact they observed, serious in its apparent import, was at once reported to Brigadier Inglis, who made such defensive arrangements as the circumstances made desirable, and as his gradually lessened means rendered possible. What were the sleepless nights thus added to harassing days for the responsible guardian of the forlorn band, may to some extent be conceived. The enemy's batteries were now more numerous than ever. They were constructed near the iron bridge; in a piece of open ground that formerly comprised the Residency kitchen-garden; near a mosque by the swampy ground on the river's bank; in front of a range of buildings called the Captan Bazaar; in the Taree Kothee opposite the Bailey guard; near the clock-tower opposite the financial office; in a garden and buildings opposite the judicial office and Anderson's house; in numerous buildings that bore upon the Cawnpore Battery and the Brigade Mess; in fields and buildings that commanded Gubbins's house; and in positions on the northwest of the enclosure—in other words, the whole place was surrounded by batteries bristling with mortars and great guns, some or other of which were almost incessantly firing shot and shell into it.

And what, the reader may anxiously ask, was the domestic or personal life of the inmates of the enclosure during these three weeks of September? It was sad indeed—beyond the former sadness. If the men toiled and watched in sultry dry weather, they were nearly overcome by heat and noisome odours; if they slept in the trenches in damp nights after great heat, they suffered terribly in their limbs and bones, for they had neither tents nor change of clothing. Such was the state to which the whole of the ground was brought, by refuse of every kind, that a pool resulting from a shower of rain soon became an insupportable nuisance; sanitary cleansings were unattainable by a community who had neither surplus labour nor efficient drains at command. Half the officers were ill at one time, from disease, over-fatigue, and insufficient diet; and when they were thus laid prostrate, they had neither medicines nor surgeons sufficient for their need. There was not a sound roof in the whole place. On one day a cannon-ball entered at one end of the largest room in the hospital, traversed the whole length, and went out at the other—but, singular to relate, it did not hurt one human being in the whole crowded apartment. In the commissariat department, some of the bullocks yet remaining fell sick through privations, others were shot; thereby lessening the reserve store, and adding to the repulsive night-duties of the officers already adverted to. Of the few native servants still remaining, hardly one now could be retained; and the saving of their simple food was an inadequate counterbalance for the loss of their assistance in drudgery labours. There were not, however, wanting proofs of a fact abundantly illustrated in many walks of life—the moral healthiness of useful employment. One of the ladies, whose early weeks in the Residency had been weeks of misery, afterwards wrote thus: 'I now find every hour of the day fully occupied. It is a great comfort to have so much to do, and to feel one's self of some little use; it helps one to keep up one's spirits much better than would otherwise be possible under the circumstances.' The live-stock, the rum, the porter, were all getting low; tea, sugar, coffee, and chocolate had long disappeared from the rations. Such officers and civilians as had money in their pockets, were willing to give almost any prices for the few luxuries still remaining in private hands, in order that they might in some degree alleviate the sufferings of their wives and children. Forty shillings were eagerly given for a bottle of brandy; thirty-two for a bottle of curaçoa; forty for a small fowl; sixteen shillings per pound were offered, but offered in vain, for sugar; two shillings a pound for coarse flour; ten shillings a pound for a little half-rancid butter or ghee; tobacco, four shillings *a leaf;* a bottle of pickles, forty shillings. Mr

Rees sold a gold watch to a companion who had money to spare, and with it purchased the luxury of smoking cigars at two shillings each; but when those bits of rolled tobacco-leaf commanded three rupees or six shillings each, he bade adieu to his last remaining source of personal enjoyment. What any one *gave*, he gave out of kind sympathy to his suffering companions; but what he *sold*, he sold in the usual commercial spirit to the highest bidder. The attire was reduced to the most piteous condition. Many of the officers had found much of their clothing burned nearly four months earlier, during the mutiny at the cantonment; and the troubles of June had prevented them from making purchases in the city before the arrival of the day when they were all alike to be shut up in the enclosure. As a consequence, their remaining clothes wore away to rags, or something worse. There was scarcely a vestige of a military uniform visible throughout the place. Officers worked and fought, dined and slept, in shirt, trousers, and slippers; one made himself a coat out of a billiard table-cloth; and another contrived a sort of shirt out of a piece of floor-cloth. When the trifling effects of one of the deceased officers came to be examined and sold, a little under-clothing was sought for with an eagerness which sumptuous garments would not have excited; four pounds sterling were given for a new flannel-shirt, and twelve pounds for five others which had already rendered much service.

Joy, joy beyond expression rang through the enclosure when, on the 21st of September, the rumour ran round that a messenger had arrived with good news. Inglis had, a few days before, sent off a spy on the often-tried but generally unsuccessful attempt to carry a small note (enclosed in a quill); the peril had been great, but the man safely returned with a small written reply from Havelock, announcing that Outram and himself were on the road from Cawnpore, and expected to reach Lucknow in three or four days. Hearts were filled to overflowing with this announcement. Many wept for joy, some laughed and shouted, more sank on their knees in thanksgiving, while the sick and wounded rose from their pallets, as if wondrously strengthened by the glad tidings. All worked hard and vigorously, in their respective ways, to prepare for the struggle inevitable on any attempt of the two generals to penetrate through the streets of the city; the inmates of the garrison could not, it is true, leave their stronghold to join in the fight, but they might possibly aid when the forlorn-hope was approaching the Bailey guard, the probable place of entrance. The 22d passed over in hopes and fears, expectations and preparations. On the 23d, musketry was heard on the Cawnpore road, and much agitation was visible within the city. On the next day, cannonading and musketry were again heard; and then were the garrison rejoiced at seeing multitudes escaping out of the city, and over the bridge to the other side of the river—rejoiced, because this movement denoted success on the part of the advancing British.

The 25th arrived—the day of deliverance! Prodigious agitation and alarm had marked the city all night: movements of men and horses, and all the indications of a city in commotion. At noon, the increasing sounds told that street-fighting was going on; those who went on the top of the Residency for a look-out could see the smoke of musketry, but nothing else. As the afternoon advanced, the sounds came nearer and nearer;* then was heard the sharp crack of rifles; then was gradually perceived the flash of musketry; and then the well-known uniforms of a friendly band. Outram and Havelock, when they had fought their way over the canal by the Char Bagh Bridge (bridge of the 'four gardens'), intended to have taken the straight road to the Residency; but this road had been blocked up by the enemy with guns, palisades, stockades, barricades, concealed pits and trenches, and other obstacles. The two generals therefore diverged to the right, marched along a by-road to the eastern part of the city, and there fought their way through a continuous line of streets to the Bailey guard entrance of the Residency enclosure, suffering terribly as they went.† Great was the shout with which they were welcomed, and warm the grasp with which Inglis thanked his deliverers. 'The immense enthusiasm,' says Mr Rees, 'with which they were greeted defies description. As their hurrah and ours rang in my ears, I was nigh bursting with joy. . . . . We felt not only happy, happy beyond imagination, and grateful to that God of mercy who, by our noble deliverers, Havelock and Outram, and their gallant troops, had thus snatched us from imminent death; but we also felt proud of the defence we had made, and the success with which, with such fearful odds to contend against, we had preserved, not only our own lives, but the honour and lives of the women and children intrusted to our keeping. As our deliverers poured in, they continued to greet us with loud hurrahs. . . . . We ran up to them, officers

* The *Jersey Times* of December 10, 1857, contained what professed to be an extract of a letter from M. de Bannerol, a French physician in the service of Mussur Rajah, dated October 8, and published in *Le Pays* (Paris paper), giving an account of the feelings of the Christian women shut up within Lucknow just before their relief. It went on to state how Jessie Brown, a corporal's wife, cheered the party in the depth of their terrors and despair, by starting up and declaring that, amidst the roar of the artillery, she caught the faint sound of the *slogan* of the approaching Highlanders, particularly that of the Macgregor, 'the grandest of them a'!' The soldiers intermitted firing to listen, but could hear nothing of the kind, and despair once more settled down upon the party. After a little interval, Jessie broke out once more with words of hope, referring to the sound of the Highland bagpipes, which the party at length acknowledged they heard; and then by one impulse, all fell on their knees, 'and nothing was heard but the bursting sob and the voice of prayer.' The tale has made so great an impression on the public mind, that we feel much reluctance in expressing our belief that it is either wholly a fiction, or only based slightly in fact. What excited our distrust from the first was the allusion to the slogans or war-cries of the respective clans—things which have had no practical existence for centuries, and which would manifestly be inappropriate in regiments composed of a miscellany of clansmen, not to speak of the large admixture of Lowlanders. We are assured that the story is looked upon in the best-informed quarters as purely a tale of the imagination.

† See chap. xv., p. 263.

and men without distinction, and shook them by the hands—how cordially, who can describe? The shrill notes of the Highlanders' bagpipes now pierced our ears. Not the most beautiful music ever was more welcome, more joy-bringing. And these brave men themselves, many of them bloody and exhausted, forgot the loss of their comrades, the pain of their wounds, the fatigue of overcoming the fearful obstacles they had combated for our sakes, in the pleasure of having accomplished our relief.' What the women felt on this day, the *Lady's Diary* will tell us. 'Never shall I forget the moment to the latest day I live. It was most overpowering. We had no idea they were so near, and were breathing air in the portico as usual at that hour, speculating when they might be in—not expecting they could reach us for several days longer; when suddenly, just at dark, we heard a very sharp fire of musketry close by, and then a tremendous cheering. An instant after, the sound of bagpipes, then soldiers running up the road, our compound and verandah filled with our deliverers, and all of us shaking hands franticly, and exchanging fervent "God bless you's!" with the gallant men and officers of the 78th Highlanders. Sir James Outram and staff were the next to come in, and the state of joyful confusion and excitement was beyond all description. The big, rough-bearded soldiers were seizing the little children out of our arms, kissing them with tears rolling down their cheeks, and thanking God they had come in time to save them from the fate of those at Cawnpore. We were all rushing about to give the poor fellows drinks of water, for they were perfectly exhausted; and tea was made down in the Tye Khana, of which a large party of tired, thirsty officers partook, without milk or sugar; we had nothing to give them to eat. Every one's tongue seemed going at once with so much to ask and to tell; and the faces of utter strangers beamed upon each other like those of dearest friends and brothers.'

After a night, in which joy kept many awake whom fatigue would have else sent into a deep sleep, the dawn of the 26th ushered in a day in which there was again to be much severe fighting; for some of Havelock's heroic little band had been left in palatial buildings outside the Residency enclosure, which they managed to hold during the night. To succour these comrades, to bring in the guns which they had guarded, and to obtain firm possession of the buildings, were objects that required great exertion and daring courage. The attempt succeeded. The palaces of Fureed Buksh and Taree Kothee were conquered from the enemy, and formed into new intrenched positions, which greatly relieved the overcrowded Residency. When the further conquest of the Chuttur Munzil palace and other buildings near the riverside had been effected, the position held by the British was thrice as large in area as that which Brigadier Inglis had so long and so gallantly defended. It lay along the river-bank for a considerable distance; while on the other side it was bounded by a dense mass of the streets constituting the main portion of the city.

One of the results of Havelock and Outram's advance was the capture of an important outpost. At a spot three or four miles out of Lucknow, near the new road from Cawnpore, was the Alum Bagh, the 'garden of the Lady Alum or beauty of the world.' It comprised several buildings, including a palace, a mosque, and an emambarra or private temple, bounded by a beautiful garden, which was itself in the middle of a park, and the park enclosed in a wall with corner towers. There was abundant space within it for a large military force, and it was susceptible of being made a stronghold if the defences were well maintained. Havelock, on his advance from Cawnpore, found the enemy drawn up in considerable strength, within and without the wall of the Alum Bagh; and it was only after a hot and fierce contest that he could capture the place. He encamped there on the night of the 23d, and had to bear many attacks from the enemy near the same spot on the 24th. On the 25th he advanced to Lucknow, and maintained the sanguinary street-fight already noticed. The Alum Bagh was too important a place to be abandoned when once conquered. Havelock left there the baggage, ammunition, sick, and wounded, of his relieving force; with 300 men to protect them, and an immense array of elephants, camels, horses, camp-followers, and laden carts; and with four guns to aid in the defence. No one for an instant supposed that that detachment would be left there without further aid. Havelock and his men fully expected, that, Lucknow once conquered, the Alum Bagh would simply be one of the strongholds of his position with which he could communicate when he pleased. Little did he look forward to the state of things actually produced, when the occupants of the Alum Bagh were so completely isolated from the British in the city, that they could not send even a message, unless by good-fortune a *kossid* or native messenger succeeded in conveying, in a quill or in the sole of his shoe, a brief letter from the one place to the other.

This isolated position of the little garrison at Alum Bagh was, moreover, only one among many grave subjects that speedily presented themselves for consideration. After the first outburst of thankfulness at the arrival of the welcome deliverers, the residents in the Lucknow intrenchment had to ask themselves to what extent it was really a deliverance. Then did they find that, in effect, they were as close prisoners as ever. Havelock had lost nearly one-third of his small force during the desperate encounters of the past few days; and those who survived were far too weak for any considerable military operations. The one great, absorbing, sacred, deeply earnest object he had all along held in view, was to save his fellow-countrymen, their wives and children, from horrors such as had been perpetrated at Cawnpore. To his dying day he remained deeply grateful that he had been permitted to effect this; but what more could he do? Could he remain a conqueror in Lucknow, or could he bring away from that city all those who for four months had been exposed to such peril! He could do neither the one nor the other. The result of the fighting on the 25th and 26th of September had given to him the command of a larger portion of the city than the Residency enclosure, which had been so long and so gallantly maintained by Inglis; but he could neither gain another inch without struggling for it, nor retain the portion already acquired without incessant watchfulness and assiduity. Nor could he make the Residency and the Alum Bagh component parts of one great stronghold, seeing that the British were alike besieged in the one and the other, and could not hold intercommunication. Nor could he send the women and children to Allahabad or any other place of safety; they would all have been cut to pieces on the road, so small was the escort he could afford, and so overwhelming the force of the enemy. The whole of the immediate benefit consisted in an increase in the number of British for the defence-works; but as these hard-working and hard-fighting troops brought little or no supplies further than the Alum Bagh, there was an increase rather in the number of mouths to be fed than in the means of feeding them. The disappointment of Inglis's garrison, after the first joy had passed, was very severe. Captivity and short commons were still to be their lot. Many councils of war were held, to determine what should be done. A party of volunteer cavalry on one day set out with the intention of cutting their way to the Alum Bagh, and perhaps to Cawnpore, to seek for reinforcements and to give notice of the exact state of affairs; but they were driven back almost immediately, by a body of rebels too large to be resisted. Sir James Outram sought to ascertain whether any of the influential natives in the city were disposed, by tempting offers, to render him and his companions aid in their difficulties; but here in like manner failure resulted. The scene was very miserable until something like order could be restored. The poor fellows who had fallen on the 25th and 26th had been brought into the intrenchment, some to be buried, some to be healed if possible. The authoress of the *Lady's Diary* said: 'The hospital is so densely crowded, that many have to lie outside in the open air, without bed or shelter. —— says he never saw such a heart-sickening scene. It is far worse than that after Chinhut—amputated arms and legs lying about in heaps all over the hospital, and the crowd and confusion such that little can be done to alleviate the intense discomfort and pain of the poor sufferers.'

It might be interesting to surviving friends, but would be tedious to general readers, to present here a list of all the persons mentioned by name in Brigadier Inglis's dispatch as having distinguished themselves in this most gallant struggle. They amount to about ninety in number. Indeed, it may well be supposed that at such a time every soldier worthy of the name, every civilian with a drop of honest blood in him, would achieve things of which, at another time, he would scarcely deem himself capable. Not only British; for Captain Anderson mentions two gentlemen of foreign birth, a Frenchman and an Italian, who, shut up like the rest in the intrenchment, fought and worked as untiringly as their companions. In a foot-note we give the names of officers mentioned by Brigadier Inglis as having died during the siege;* and in another, of those who commanded eleven of the outposts or 'garrisons,' those fortified houses which were defended in so extraordinary a way.† Of all these he had a kindly word to say; as well as of the artillery and engineer officers, the infantry officers, the officers of the staff, the surgeons and the chaplains, the commissariat-officers, the gentlemen-volunteers, the humble rank and file, and the ladies who became the 'Florence Nightingales' of the garrison. Nothing, perhaps, in the whole course of the siege, was more remarkable than the conduct of the native troops. It will be remembered that when three native infantry regiments mutinied at the cantonment on the 30th of May, some of the sepoys in each remained faithful. This select band shared all the labours and sufferings of the British during the siege. With scanty food, little and broken sleep, harassing exertions, daily fightings, they remained steadfast to the last. Though sorely tempted by the mutineers, who would often converse with them over the palisades of the intrenchment, they never flinched from their duty. What they were on the 30th of May, they were on the 25th of September, soldiers 'true to their salt.' Few things are more embarrassing, in taking an estimate of the causes and progress of the Revolt, than to meet with such anomalies as this. Explain it how we may, it would be gross injustice to withhold from such men a tribute of admiration for their fidelity at so trying a time. May there not have been something of a moral grandeur, a sublimity of heroism, in the conduct of the devoted garrison, that touched the hearts of these sepoys, and appealed to their better nature?

Viscount Canning did not fail to give an official recognition of the merits of those who had made this glorious defence. In an 'Order in Council,' issued at Calcutta, after adverting to the receipt of a military account of the proceedings from Brigadier Inglis, his lordship said:

'The governor-general in council believes that

* Sir Henry Lawrence; Major Banks; Lieutenant-colonel Case, Captains Steevens, Mansfield, Radcliffe, and M'Cabe, 32d foot; Captain Francis, 13th N.I.; Lieutenants Shepherd and Archer, 7th native cavalry; Captain Hughes, 57th N.I.; Major Anderson and Captain Fulton, engineers; Captain Simons, artillery.

† Colonel Master and Captain Boileau, 7th N.C.; Major Apthorp and Captain Sanders, 41st N.I.; Captain Germon and Lieutenants Aitken and Loughnan, 13th N.I.; Captain Anderson, 25th N.I.; Lieutenant Graydon, 44th N.I.; Lieutenant Longmore, 71st N.I.; Mr Schilling, principal of the Martinière College.

never has a tale been told which will so stir the hearts of Englishmen and Englishwomen. . . . There does not stand recorded in the annals of war an achievement more truly heroic than the defence of the Residency at Lucknow. That defence has not only called forth all the energy and daring which belong to Englishmen in the hour of active conflict, but it has exhibited continuously, and in the highest degree, that noble and sustained courage which against enormous odds and fearful disadvantages, against hope deferred, and through increasing toil and wear of body and mind, still holds on day after day, and triumphs. The heavy guns of the assailants, posted almost in security within fifty yards of the intrenchments—so near, indeed, that the solicitations, threats, and taunts which the rebels addressed to the native defenders of the garrison were easily heard by those true-hearted men; the fire of the enemy's musketry, so searching that it penetrated the innermost retreat of the women and children and of the wounded; their desperate attempts, repeatedly made, to force an entry after blowing in the defences; the perpetual mining of the works; the weary night-watching for the expected signal of relief; and the steady waste of precious lives until the number of English gunners was reduced below that of the guns to be worked—all these constitute features in a history which the fellow-countrymen of the heroes of Lucknow will read with swelling hearts, and which will endure for ever as a lesson to those who shall hope, by treachery, numbers, or boldness in their treason, to overcome the indomitable spirit of Englishmen.'

The officer who so nobly held the command after Lawrence and Banks had been stricken down by death, well earned the honours which the Queen afterwards conferred upon him. He entered Lucknow as a lieutenant-colonel; he left it as Major-general Sir John Eardley Wilmot Inglis, K.C.B. Promotion in various ways awaited many of the other officers; but the immediate recognition by the governor-general of the services rendered by the garrison was embodied in the following general order: 'Every officer and soldier, European and native, who has formed part of the garrison of the Residency between the 29th of June and the 25th of September last shall receive six months' batta. Every civilian in the covenanted service of the East India Company who has taken part in the defence of the Residency within the above-named dates shall receive six months' batta, at a rate calculated according to the military rank with which his standing corresponds. Every uncovenanted civil officer or volunteer who has taken a like part shall receive six months' batta, at a rate to be fixed according to the functions and position which may have been assigned to him. Every native commissioned and non-commissioned officer and soldier who has formed part of the garrison shall receive the Order of Merit, with the increase of pay attached thereto, and shall be permitted to count three years of additional service. The soldiers of the 13th, 48th, and 71st regiments native infantry, who have been part of the garrison, shall be formed into a regiment of the line, to be called "the Regiment of Lucknow," the further constitution of which, as regards officers and men, will be notified hereafter.'

What was done at Lucknow during October and November must be recorded in a future chapter. While Outram, Havelock, and Inglis were maintaining themselves, by indomitable resolution, in the Residency and the Alum Bagh, Sir Colin Campbell was collecting a force adequate, if not to the actual reconquest of Lucknow, at least to the rescue of all the British of every class residing in that hateful city. Those two concurrent lines of proceeding will be treated in intimate connection, a few pages on.

Note.

Brigadier Inglis's Dispatch.—In order that the narrative contained in the foregoing chapter might not be interrupted by too many extracts from official documents, little has been said of the report which Brigadier Inglis drew up of the siege soon after the arrival of Outram and Havelock. So vividly, however, and in all respects so worthily, did that report or dispatch portray the trying difficulties of the position, and the heroic conduct of the garrison, that it may be well to give a portion of it in this place.

'The right honourable the governor-general in council will feel that it would be impossible to crowd within the limits of a dispatch even the principal events, much less the individual acts of gallantry, which have marked this protracted struggle. But I can conscientiously declare my conviction, that few troops have ever undergone greater hardships, exposed as they have been to a never-ceasing musketry-fire and cannonade. They have also experienced the alternate vicissitudes of extreme wet and of intense heat, and that, too, with very insufficient shelter from either, and in many places without any shelter at all. In addition to having had to repel real attacks, they have been exposed night and day to the hardly less harassing false alarms which the enemy have been constantly raising. The insurgents have frequently fired very heavily, sounded the advance, and shouted for several hours together, though not a man could be seen: with the view, of course, of harassing our small and exhausted force. In this object they succeeded, for no part has been strong enough to allow of a portion only of the garrison being prepared in the event of a false attack being turned into a real one; all, therefore, had to stand to their arms and to remain at their posts until the demonstration had ceased; and such attacks were of almost nightly occurrence. The whole of the officers and men have been on duty night and day during the 87 days which the siege had lasted up to the arrival of Sir J. Outram, G.C.B. In addition to this incessant military duty, the force has been nightly employed in repairing defences, in moving guns, in burying dead animals, in conveying ammunition and commissariat stores from one place to another, and in other fatigue-duties too numerous and too trivial to enumerate here. I feel, however, that any words of mine will fail to convey any adequate idea of what the fatigue and labours have been—labours in which all ranks and all classes, civilians, officers, and soldiers, have all borne an equally noble part. All have together descended into the mine, and have together handled the shovel for the interment of the putrid bullocks; and all, accoutred with musket and bayonet, have relieved each other on sentry without regard to the distinctions of rank, civil or military. Notwithstanding all these hardships, the garrison has made no less than five sorties, in which they spiked two of the enemy's heaviest guns, and blew up several of the houses from which they had kept up their most harassing fire. Owing to the extreme paucity of our numbers, each man was taught to feel that on his own individual efforts alone depended in no small measure the safety of the entire position. This consciousness incited every officer, soldier, and man, to defend the post assigned to him with such desperate tenacity, and to fight for the lives which Providence had intrusted to his care with such dauntless determination, that the enemy, despite their constant attacks, their heavy mines, their overwhelming numbers, and their incessant fire, could never succeed in gaining one single inch of ground within the bounds of this straggling position, which was so feebly fortified, that had they once obtained a footing in any of the outposts the whole place must inevitably have fallen.

'If further proof be wanting of the desperate nature of the struggle which we have, under God's blessing, so long and so successfully waged, I would point to the roofless and ruined houses, to the crumbled walls, to the exploded mines, to the open breaches, to the shattered and disabled guns and defences, and lastly, to the long and melancholy list of the brave and devoted officers and men who have fallen. These silent witnesses bear sad and solemn testimony to the way in which this feeble position has been defended.

'During the early part of these vicissitudes, we were left without any information whatever regarding the posture of affairs outside. An occasional spy did indeed come in with the object of inducing our sepoys and servants to desert; but the intelligence derived from such sources was, of course, entirely untrustworthy. We sent our messengers daily calling for aid, and asking for information, none of whom ever returned until the 26th day of the siege; when a pensioner named Ungud came back with a letter from General Havelock's camp, informing us that they were advancing with a force sufficient to bear down all opposition, and would be with us in five or six days. A messenger was immediately despatched, requesting that on the evening of their arrival on the outskirts of the city two rockets might be sent up, in order that we might take the necessary measures for assisting them while forcing their way in. The sixth day, however, expired, and they came not; but for many evenings after, officers and men watched for the ascension of the expected rockets, with hopes such as make the heart sick. We knew not then, nor did we learn until the 29th of August—or 35 days later—that the relieving force, after having fought most nobly to effect our deliverance, had been obliged to fall back for reinforcements; and this was the last communication we received until two days before the arrival of Sir James Outram, on the 25th of September.

'Besides heavy visitations of cholera and small-pox, we have also had to contend against a sickness which has almost universally pervaded the garrison. Commencing with a very painful eruption, it has merged into a low fever, combined with diarrhœa; and although few or no men have actually died from its effects, it leaves behind a weakness and lassitude which, in the absence of all material sustenance, save coarse beef, and still coarser flour, none have been able entirely to get over. The mortality among the women and children, and especially among the latter, from these diseases and from other causes, has been perhaps the most painful characteristic of the siege. The want of native servants has also been a source of much privation. Owing to the suddenness with which we were besieged, many of these people, who might perhaps have otherwise proved faithful to their employers, but who were outside the defences at the time, were altogether excluded. Very many more deserted, and several families were consequently left without the services of a single domestic. Several ladies have had to tend their children, and even to wash their own clothes, as well as to cook their scanty meals, entirely unaided. Combined with the absence of servants, the want of proper accommodation has probably been the cause of much of the disease with which we have been afflicted.

'I cannot refrain from bringing to the prominent notice of his lordship in council the patient endurance and the Christian resignation which have been evinced by the women of this garrison. They have animated us by their example. Many, alas! have been made widows and their children fatherless in this cruel struggle. But all such seem resigned to the will of Providence; and many—among whom may be mentioned the honoured names of Birch, of Polehampton, of Barbor, and of Gall—have, after the example of Miss Nightingale, constituted themselves the tender and solicitous nurses of the wounded and dying soldiers in the hospital.'

[After enumerating the officers and civilians who had wrought untiringly in the good cause, Brigadier Inglis did ample justice to the humbler combatants.]

'Lastly, I have the pleasure of bringing the splendid behaviour of the soldiers—namely, the men of her Majesty's 32d foot, the small detachment of her Majesty's 84th foot, the European and native artillery, the 13th, 48th, and 71st regiments of native infantry, and the Sikhs of the respective corps—to the notice of the government of India. The losses sustained by her Majesty's 32d, which is now barely 300 strong, by her Majesty's 84th, and by the European artillery, shew at least that they knew how to die in the cause of their countrymen. Their conduct under the fire, the exposure, and the privations which they have had to undergo, has been throughout most admirable and praiseworthy.

'As another instance of the desperate character of our defence, and the difficulties we have had to contend with, I may mention that the number of our artillerymen was so reduced, that on the occasion of an attack, the gunners, aided as they were by men of her Majesty's 32d foot, and by volunteers of all classes, had to run from one battery to another wherever the fire of the enemy was hottest, there not being nearly enough men to serve half the number of guns at the same time. In short, at last the number of European gunners was only 24, while we had, including mortars, no less than 30 guns in position.

'With respect to the native troops, I am of opinion that their loyalty has never been surpassed. They were indifferently fed and worse housed. They were exposed, especially the 13th regiment, under the gallant Lieutenant Aitken, to a most galling fire of round-shot and musketry, which materially decreased their numbers. They were so near the enemy that conversation could be carried on between them; and every effort, persuasion, promise, and threat, was alternately resorted to in vain to seduce them from their allegiance to the handful of Europeans, who, in all probability, would have been sacrificed by their desertion.'

MR COLVIN, Lieutenant-governor of Northwest Provinces.

CHAPTER XX.

MINOR CONFLICTS: SEPTEMBER AND OCTOBER.

LEAVING for a while the affairs of Lucknow—which by the progress of events had become far more important than those of Delhi or of any other city in India—we may conveniently devote the present chapter to a rapid glance at the general state of affairs during the months of September and October: noticing only such scenes of discord, and such military operations, as arose immediately out of the Revolt. The subject may be treated in the same style as in Chapter xvii., relating to the months of July and August, but more briefly; for, in truth, so few Bengal native regiments now remained 'true to their salt,' that the materials for further mutiny were almost exhausted.

Of Calcutta, and the region around it on all sides, little need be said. Mutiny in that neighbourhood would not have been easy during the autumn months; for British troops were gradually arriving, who would speedily have put down any rebellious risings. Sometimes alarms agitated the civilians and traders in the city; but nothing really serious called for notice. The ex-king of Oude continued to be watched carefully at Calcutta. Whatever honeyed phrases may have been used to render his detention more palatable, none of the government officers placed any reliance on his fidelity or peacefulness. In truth, if he *had* displayed those qualities, after being compelled to witness the annexation of his country to the British raj, he would have been something more (or less) than oriental. At various times during the summer and autumn months, scrutinising inquiries were made into the conduct of the king and his retainers. Thus, on the 16th of August, a person who had for some time resided at Calcutta, under the assumed title of Bishop of Bagdad, but whose real name was Syed Hossein Shubber, was with five others arrested, for complicity in plots affecting the British government; and, consequent on papers discovered, three retainers of the king were arrested about a week afterwards. The government kept secret the details of these affairs, pending further inquiry; but it was apparent enough that mischief was fermenting in the minds of the royal prisoner's retainers. Unquestionably many natives sincerely believed the king to have been an ill-used man—an opinion shared also by many Europeans—and they did not deem it treason to aid him in his misfortunes.

Much to the vexation of the government, the district of Assam, little known to Europeans except as a region where tea is experimentally grown, was drawn into the vortex of trouble early in September. Many of the sepoys of the 1st Assam native infantry came from the neighbourhood of Arrah, and were closely related to one regiment (the 40th) of the Dinapoor mutineers; while others were from the estates of Koer Singh. When, therefore, the news of the Dinapoor mutiny became known, the Assam regiment was thrown into much agitation. There was a rajah in Assam, one Saring Kunderpessawar Singh, who secretly engaged in treasonable correspondence, and who received offers of support from the Arrah men of the Assam regiment, if he would openly break with the British. There were also Hindustanis in the 2d Assam native regiment; while the artillery companies at Debrooghur were entirely Hindustanis. It was known likewise that many of the neighbouring tribes were in a disaffected state, and that a religious mendicant was rapidly moving about with some secret but apparently mischievous purpose. By degrees a plot was discovered. The conspirators planned on a given day to murder all the Christians in Assam, and then plunder the stations. Fortunately this project was known in time. The Calcutta government having no soldiers to spare, organised a force of English seamen, trained as gunners, and sent them by a steamer up the Brahmaputra to Debrooghur, to be employed as the local authorities might deem advisable. One of the circumstances connected with this movement illustrates the antagonism between governing authorities and newspaper writers on military matters—an antagonism frequently felt during the Indian Revolt as during the Russian war. A responsible leader wishes to keep his plans of strategy secret from the enemy; a newspaper writer wishes to give as much news as possible on all subjects; and these two modes of procedure do not always flow in harmonious concord. Mr Halliday, lieutenant-governor of Bengal, in reporting on this Assam affair, said: 'The utmost care was taken to despatch the force to Assam with the secrecy necessary to prevent its destination being known; but it is feared that this intention has been frustrated by the ill-judged publication of the departure of the steamer, and notification of its objects, by the Calcutta papers. It is hoped that this injudicious proceeding may not be attended with the serious results that would ensue from a revolt in the province in its present unprotected state. Such an untoward contingency was feared by the officers in Assam, who pointed out the urgent necessity of extreme care being observed in preventing the promulgation of the transmission, before its arrival, of any European force that might be sent; lest the knowledge of the approach of aid should cause a premature explosion of the expected revolt.' The force consisted of 100 armed sailors, with two 12-pounder guns; they set out on the 11th of September, under the charge of Lieutenant Davies, in the steamer *Horungotta;* and were to be at the disposal of Colonel Jenkins on arriving in Assam. As a curious example of the different light in which different tribes were at this time viewed, it may be stated that all the men of the 1st Assam infantry who were *not* Hindustanis were called in from the outposts to Debrooghur, as a protection in case the remainder of the regiment should mutiny. Captain Lowther, commanding a corps of Goorkhas, was sent from another station to capture the rajah; this he managed admirably, and in so doing, effectually crushed the incipient mutiny. The captain, in a private letter, told in excellent style the story of his expedition; from which we will extract so much as relates to the night-scene in the rajah's palace at Debrooghur.*

* 'I told off my men rapidly, and formed them into parties, so as completely to surround and cover every outlet and corner. The main party, consisting mostly of my own particular sharpshooters and bodyguard, watched the *front*; another moved towards the town, there to arrest an educated Bengalee, agent to the conspirators; another to the rear, to cut off escape towards the town; while my friend the Political crept quietly past some outhouses with his police, and under the palace walls awaited my signal for opening the ball.

'Before long the ominous barking of a disturbed cur in the direction of the party sent after the prime-minister proclaimed that no time was to be lost. Off I went towards the guard-shed in front of the palace, my personal sharpshooters following at the double. The noise, of course, awoke the sleeping guard, and as they started up from their slumbers I caught one firmly by the throat; the little Goorkha next me felled with a but-end blow another of them while they were getting to arms, I having strictly forbidden my men to fire until obliged; the remainder, as we rushed in, took to flight, and my eager party wished to fire on them, which I prevented, not considering such valiant game worth powder and shot. In the darkness and confusion, no means of entrance could at once be found. My police guide, however, having been often in the palace, knew every room in it, and, thrusting himself in at a door, acted ferret to perfection, and by dint of activity, soon brought me into the presence of the rajah, who, though young in years, is old in sin; he refused to surrender or admit any one—a resolution which cooled instanter on my

Some weeks afterwards, towards the close of October, Mr Halliday entertained much distrust of the 73d Bengal native infantry, of which two companies were at Dacca, and the main body at Jelpigoree, near the Bhotan frontier. By precautionary measures, however, he prevented for a time any actual outbreak of this particular regiment.

There were reasons why the towns on the banks of the Lower Ganges remained tolerably free from rebellion during the months now under notice. English regiments, in wings or detachments, were sent up the river in flats tugged by steamers, from Calcutta towards Upper India; and the turbulent rabble of the towns were awed into quietness by the vicinity of these red-coats. Berhampore, Moorshedabad, Rajmahal, Bhagulpore, Monghir, Patna, Dinapoor, Buxar, Ghazeepore, Benares, Mirzapore—all felt the benefit of this occasional passing of British troops along the Ganges, in the moral effect produced on the natives. True, the arrivals at Calcutta were few and far apart until October was well advanced; true, many of the troops were sent by land along the main trunk-road, for greater expedition; true, those who went by water were too urgently needed in the Doab and in Oude to be spared for intermediate service at the towns above named; but, nevertheless, the mere transit of a few English regiments effected much towards the tranquillising of Bengal. Early in the month of August, Lord Elgin had come to Calcutta, and placed at the disposal of Lord Canning two war-steamers, the *Shannon* and the *Pearl;* and from among the resources of these steamers was organised a splendid naval brigade, consisting of 400 able British seamen, and no less than ten of the enormous 68-pounder guns which such seamen know so well how to handle. They started from Calcutta up the Hoogly and the Ganges, under the command of Captain Peel, who had so gallantly managed a naval-battery in the Crimea during the siege of Sebastopol. If such a man could fret, he would have fretted at the slowness of his voyage. Week after week elapsed, without his reaching those districts where his services would be invaluable. Half of August and the whole of September thus passed wearily away in this most tedious voyage. The upward passage is always tardy, against the stream; and his ponderous artillery rendered slowness still more slow. It was not until the 30th of September that he, with 286 men of his brigade, arrived at Benares. Hastening on, he arrived with 94 men at Allahabad on the 3d of October; and four days afterwards the rest joined him, with their enormous guns and store of ammunition. A small naval brigade, under Captain Sotheby, was placed at the disposal of the Patna authorities, to be used against certain insurgents in the neighbourhood.

The portion of Bengal north of the Ganges was almost entirely free from disturbance during these two months; but the parallel portion of Behar was in a very different state. The actual mutinies there had been few in number, for in truth there had not been many native troops quartered in that region; but the rebellious chieftains and zemindars were many, each of whom could command the services of a body of retainers ready for any mischief. Patna, in September, as in earlier months, was disturbed rather by anarchy in other regions than by actual mutinies within the city itself. In what way the Dinapoor troubles affected it, we have seen in an earlier chapter. Its present difficulties lay rather with the districts north and northwest of the city, where the revenue collectors had been driven from place to place by mutinous sepoys, and by petty chieftains who wished to strengthen themselves at the expense of the English 'raj.' The abandonment of Goruckpore by the officials, in a moment of fright, had had the effect of exposing the Chupra, Chumparun, and Mozufferpoor districts to the attacks of rebels, especially such as had placed themselves under the banner of the Mussulman chieftain Mahomed Hussein Khan, the self-appointed 'ruler in the name and on behalf of the King of Oude.' This man had collected a considerable force, and had organised a species of government at Goruckpore. The military power in the hands of the Company's servants in the Chupra and Tirhoot districts consisted chiefly of a few Sikhs of the police battalion, quite unequal to the resistance of an incursion by Mahomed Hussein. The civilians of those districts sent urgent applications to Patna for military aid. But how could this be furnished? Troops and artillery were so imperatively demanded at Cawnpore, to aid the operations at Lucknow, that none could be detained on their passage up the river; the Dinapoor garrison, reduced by the mutiny and its consequences, could only spare a few troops for Patna itself; the troops going up the main trunk-road from Calcutta to Upper India could barely afford time and strength to encounter the Ramgurh insurgents, without attempting anything north of the Ganges. There happened, however, to be a Madras regiment passing up by steamer to Alla-

calling my men to set fire to the palace; he then with a bad grace delivered up to me his state-sword. A shout from the opposite doors proclaimed an entry there. The queen-mother and the rest of the female royalty and attendants were seized while trying to descend on that side. Then came a chorus of shouting and struggling, and bawling for lights and assistance; at last, a lamp being procured, we proceeded to examine the palace: we wandered in dark passages and cells, while I mounted a guard at every door. The air being confined and heated within the royal residence, I sat outside until after daybreak, and then proceeded to rummage for papers and letters; several boxes of these we appropriated, and counted out his treasure, all in gold vessels and ingots; we found a quantity of arms, spiked some guns, one of them of French make; all day we were hard at work, searching and translating papers. The prime-minister was found at his house, fast asleep. In the heat of the afternoon, we went to his residence in the town, and by dint of keeping fans going over us, carried out a thorough search. We did not get as many of his papers as we wanted, he having been told by his correspondents to destroy all letters after reading them.

'At sunset I carried off my prisoners over the same bad ground by which we had so stealthily arrived. We were followed by about 200 infuriated Mussulmans, crying, praying, and prostrating themselves to the object of their lingering hope of rebellion (the rajah), but we drove them off.'

habad; and permission was obtained to detain a portion of this regiment for service in the Goruckpore region; while the Rajahs of Bettiah and Hutwah were encouraged to maintain a friendly attitude in support of the British authorities. The rebel or rather rabble forces under Mahomed Hussein were ill armed and worse disciplined; and it was probable that a few men of the 17th M. N. I., with a few Sikhs, could have beaten them at any time; but it was felt necessary to reoccupy Goruckpore at once, to prevent the neighbouring zemindars and thalookdars from joining the malcontents.

That Lord Canning accepted an offer of several Goorkha regiments, from Jung Bahadoor of Nepaul, has been stated in a former chapter; but a very long time elapsed before those hardy little troops were enabled to render much service. The process of collecting them at Khatmandoo and elsewhere occupied several weeks, and it was not until the beginning of September that they reached Jounpoor, a station in the very heart of the disturbed districts. Even then, there was much tardiness in bringing them into active service; for the English officers appointed to command them did not at first understand the difference of management required by Hindustani sepoys and Nepaulese Goorkhas. Happily, an opportunity occurred for remedying this defect. A smart affair on the 20th of September afforded the Goorkhas an opportunity of shewing their gallantry. Colonel Wroughton, military commandant at Jounpoor, having heard that Azimghur was threatened with an attack by 8000 rebels under Madhoo Singh of Atrowlia, resolved to send a regiment of Goorkhas from Jounpoor to strengthen the force already at Azimghur. They started at once, marched the distance in a day and a half, and reached the threatened city on the evening of the 19th. This was the Shere regiment of Jung Bahadoor's force, under Colonel Shumshere Singh, a Nepaulese officer. At a very early hour on the morning of the 20th, it was ascertained that a large body of rebels had assembled in and near the neighbouring village of Mundoree. A force of 1200 men, mostly belonging to three Goorkha regiments, was immediately sent out to disperse them—Captain Boileau commanding, Colonel Shumshere Singh heading the Goorkhas, and Mr Venables (whose prowess had already been displayed in the same district) taking charge of a small body of local horse. Finding that the rebels were posted in a clump of trees and in a jheel behind the village, Captain Boileau directed Shumshere Singh to advance his Goorkhas at double pace. This was done, despite the fire from several guns; the little Goorkhas charged, drove the enemy away towards Captangunje, and captured three brass guns and all the camp-equipage. Mr Venables was seen wherever the fighting was thickest; he was up at the first gun taken, and killed three of the enemy with his own hand. About 200 of the enemy were laid low in this brief encounter, and one-sixth of this number on the part of the victors.

This little battle of Mundoree had a moral effect, superadded to the immediate dispersing of a body of rebels. It shewed the soldierly conduct of the Goorkhas, who had marched fifty miles in two days, and then won a battle in a kind of country to which they were unaccustomed. It proved the intrepidity of one of the civil servants of the Company, whose sterling qualities were brought forth at a critical time. Moreover, it dissipated a prejudice against the Goorkhas formed by some of the British officers. These troops had hitherto remained nearly inactive in the region between Nepaul and the Ganges. Jung Bahadoor had sent them, under a native officer, Colonel Puhlwan Singh, to be employed wherever the authorities deemed best. Colonel Wroughton, and other British officers, formed an opinion that the Nepaulese troops were incapable of rapid movement, and that their native officers dreaded the responsibility of independent action. Mr Grant, lieutenant-governor of the Central Provinces, in an official letter to Colonel Wroughton after the battle of Mundoree, pointed out that this opinion had been very detrimental to the public service, in discouraging any employment of the Goorkhas. He added: 'It was natural to expect that foreigners, and those foreigners mountaineers, unaccustomed either to the plains or to their inhabitants, should at first feel some awkwardness in the new position in which they were placed, with everything strange around them. The sagacity of Jung Bahadoor had already foreseen this difficulty; and it was at his earnest desire that British officers were attached to the Goorkha force, to encourage the officers and men, and to explain how operations should be carried on in such a country and such a climate as that in which they now for the first time marched, and against such an enemy as they now for the first time met. . . . The lieutenant-governor will now confidently look to you that the Goorkha force is henceforth actively employed in the service for which it was placed at the disposal of the British government by the Nepaulese.' It must be borne in mind, to prevent confusion, that this Goorkha force, lent by Jung Bahadoor, was distinct from the Goorkha battalions of Sirmoor and Kumaon, often mentioned in former chapters; those battalions were part of the Bengal native army, fortunately consisting of Goorkhas instead of 'Pandies;' whereas the new force was a Nepaulese army, lent for a special purpose.

Mr Grant, the temporarily appointed lieutenant-governor just mentioned, employed all his energies throughout September and October in promoting the transit of British troops from the lower to the upper provinces, to aid in the operations at Cawnpore and Lucknow. He could not, however, forget the fact that the eastern frontier of Oude adjoined the British districts of Goruckpore, Jounpoor, and Azimghur; and that the Oude rebels were continually making demonstrations on that side. He longed for British troops, to strengthen and encourage the Goorkhas in his service, and occasionally applied for a few; but he, as all others, was told that the relief of the residents at Lucknow must precede, and be paramount over, all other military operations whatever. Writing to Lord Canning from Benares on the 15th of October, he said: 'It is a point for consideration, how much longer it will be otherwise than imprudent to continue to send the whole of the daily arrivals of Europeans nearly half-way round the province of Oude, in order to create a pressure upon the rear of the mutineers and insurgents of that province from the direction of Cawnpore and Lucknow, whilst our home districts are left thus open to them in their front.' He expressed a hope that the Punjaub and Delhi regions would be able to supply nearly troops enough for immediate operations at Lucknow; and that a portion of the British regiments sent up from the lower provinces would be permitted to form the nucleus of a new army at Benares, for operations on the eastern frontier of Oude. Many weeks elapsed, however, before this suggestion could meet with practical attention.

Thus it was throughout the districts of Goruckpore, Jounpoor, Azimghur, and others eastward of Oude and north of the Ganges. If the British had had to contend only with mutinied sepoys and sowars, victory would more generally and completely have attended their exertions; but rebellious chieftains were numerous, and these, encouraged by the newly established rebel government at Lucknow, continually harassed the British officials placed in charge of those districts. The colonels, captains, judges, magistrates, collectors—all cried aloud for more European troops; their cries were heeded at Calcutta, but could not be satisfied, for reasons already sufficiently explained.

Let us cross the Ganges, and watch the state of affairs in the southwestern districts of Bengal and Behar during the months of September and October.

Throughout this wide region, the troubles arose rather from sepoys already rebellious, than from new instances of mutiny. Preceding chapters have shewn that the 8th Bengal native infantry mutinied at Hazarebagh on the 30th of July; that the infantry of the Ramgurh battalion followed the pernicious example on the next day; that the 5th irregular cavalry mutinied at Bhagulpore on the 14th of August; and that the 7th, 8th, and 40th regiments of native infantry which mutinied at Dinapoor on the 25th of July, kept the whole of Western Bengal in agitation throughout August, by rendering uncertain in which direction they would march, under the rebel chieftain, Koer Singh. The only additional mutiny, in this region, was that of the 32d native infantry, presently to be noticed. The elements of anarchy were, however, already numerous and violent enough to plunge the whole district into disorder. Some of the towns were the centres of opium-growing or indigo-producing regions; many were surrounded simply by rice or cornfields; others, again, were military stations, at which the Company were accustomed to keep troops; while several were dâk or post stations, for the maintenance of communication along the great trunk-road from Calcutta to Benares. But wherever and whatever they may have been, these towns were seldom at peace during the months now under notice. The towns-people and the surrounding villagers were perpetually affected by rumours that the mutinous 5th cavalry were coming, or the mutinous 8th infantry, or the Ramgurh mutineers, or those from Dinapoor. For, it must be borne in mind, we are now treating of a part of India inhabited chiefly by Bengalees, a race too timid to supply many fighting rebels—too fond of quiet industry willingly to belt on the sword or shoulder the matchlock. They may or may not have loved the British; if not, they would rather intrigue than fight against them. In the contest arising out of the mutiny, these Bengalees suffered greatly. The mutineers, joined by the released vagabonds from the jails, too frequently plundered all alike, Feringhee and native; and the quiet trader or cultivator had much reason to dread the approach of such workers of mischief. The Europeans, few in number, and oppressed with responsibility, knew not which way to turn for aid. Revenue collectors, with many lacs of the Company's rupees, feared for the safety of their treasure. Military officers, endeavouring with a handful of troops to check the passage of mutineers, were bewildered by the vague and conflicting intelligence which reached them. Officials at the dâk-stations, impressed daily by stringent orders from Calcutta to keep open the main line of road for the passage of English troops to Upper India, were in perpetual anxiety lest bands of mutineers should approach and cut off the dâks altogether. Every one begged and prayed the Calcutta government to send him a few trusty troops; every one assured the government that the salvation of that part of India depended on the request being acceded to.

Dorunda, sixty miles south of Hazarebagh, was a scene of violence on the 11th of September. The Ramgurh mutineers destroyed the public and private buildings at this place, plundered the town, committed great atrocities on the towns-people, beheaded a native surgeon belonging to the jail, and marched off in the direction of Tikhoo Ghat, taking with them four guns and a large amount of plunder and ammunition. Their apparent intention was to march through the Palamow district, and effect a junction with Koer Singh, with whom they had been in correspondence. Only four men of the Ramgurh irregular cavalry were of the party; all the rest were infantry. The cavalry, remaining faithful as a body, seized the first opportunity of joining their officers at Hazarebagh. This was another instance of divergence between the two parts of one corps, wholly inexplicable to the British officers, who could offer no reason why the infantry had lapsed, while the cavalry remained faithful. In this part of India the mutineers were not supported by the zemindars or landowners, as in other districts; and hence the few British troops were better enabled to lay plans for the frustration of these workers of mischief. Captain Fischer, Captain Dalton, Major English, Captain Oakes, Captain Davies, Captain Rattray, Lieutenant Graham, Lieutenant Birch, and other officers, were in command of small bodies of troops in this region during the greater part of the month; these troops consisted of Madras natives, Sikhs, and a very few British; and the numerous trifling but serviceable affairs in which they were engaged bore relation to the regiments which had mutinied at Ramgurh, Bhagulpore, and Dinapoor, and to the chieftains and marauders who joined those disloyal soldiers.

For the reasons already assigned, however, the British troops were very few in number; while the Madras troops were so urgently needed in the more turbulent Saugor provinces, that they could barely be spared for service in Bengal. Regiments had not at that time begun to arrive very rapidly from England; the few that did land at Calcutta, were eagerly caught up for service in the Doab and Oude. In most instances, the aid which was afforded by English troops to the region now under notice, depended on a temporary stoppage of a regiment or detachment on its passage to the upper provinces; in urgent cases, the government ordered or permitted a small British force to diverge from its direct line of march, and render aid to a Bengal town or station at a particular juncture. Such was the case with H.M. 53d foot. Major English, with a wing of this regiment, had a contest with the Ramgurh mutineers on the 29th of September. He marched from Hazarebagh to Sillis Chowk, where he heard news of these insurgents; and by further active movements he came up with them on the 2d of October, just as they had begun to plunder the town of Chuttra. The mutineers planted two guns so as to play upon the British; but the latter, in the way which had by this time become quite common with their comrades in India, determined to attack and take the guns by a fearless advance. On they went, through rice-fields, behind rocks and underwood, through lanes and round buildings, running and cheering, until they had captured four guns in succession, together with ammunition, ten elephants, and other warlike appliances, and sent the enemy fleeing. The officers dashed on at the head of their respective parties of men in a way that astonished the enemy; and the major, viewing these enterprises with the eye of a soldier, said in his dispatch: 'It was splendid to see them rush on the guns.' His loss was, however, considerable; 5 killed and 33 wounded out of three companies only. In addition to military trophies, Major English took fifty thousand rupees of the Company's treasure from the mutineers, who, like mutineers elsewhere, regarded the revenue collections as fair booty when once they had thrown off allegiance. During the operations of the 53d in this region—one, in many parts of which British soldiers had never been seen—an instance was afforded of the dismay into which the civilians were sometimes thrown by the withdrawal of trusty troops; it was narrated in a letter written by an officer of that regiment.*

The native regiments were often distributed in detachments at different stations; and it frequently happened—as just adverted to—for reasons wholly inexplicable to the authorities, that some of those component elements remained faithful long after others had mutinied. Such was the case in reference to the 32d B. N. I. Two companies of that regiment, stationed at Deoghur in the Sonthal district, rose in mutiny on the 9th of October, murdered Lieutenant Cooper and the assistant-commissary, looted the bazaar, and then marched off to Rohnee, taking with them Lieutenant Rennie as a prisoner. Two other companies of the regiment were at that time *en route* from Burhait to Soorie, while the head-quarter companies were at Bowsee. The authorities at Calcutta at once sought to ascertain what was the feeling among the men at the stations just named; but, pending these inquiries, orders were given to despatch a wing of H.M. 13th foot from Calcutta to the Sonthal district, to control the mutineers. Major English was at that time going to the upper provinces with a detachment of H.M. 53d foot; but he was now ordered to turn aside for a while, and aid in pacifying the district before pursuing his journey to Benares. Although the remaining companies of the native 32d did afterwards take rank among the mutineers, they were 'true to their salt' for some time after the treachery of their companions had become known.

This 32d mutinous regiment succeeded in crossing the Sone river, with the intention of joining Koer Singh and the Dinapoor mutineers—a feat managed in a way that greatly mortified Major English's 53d. On the 20th of October the wing of this latter regiment proceeded from Sheergotty to Gayah, to re-assure the uneasy officials at that station; and on the 22d they started again, to intercept the mutineers. After much hot and wearying marching, they returned to Gayah, without having encountered the mutineers, one portion of

* 'The ejected civilians from Dorunda had come on ahead and offered our small party breakfast, which we gladly accepted. While waiting until it was ready, the chief-commissioner got an electric-telegraph dispatch from the governor-general, ordering the whole of the 53d party under Major English back again to the main trunk-road. You never saw anything like the long faces they all had at this announcement; for the commissioner had just had intelligence on which he thought he could rely, that the mutineers were still kept at bay by the party at the pass, through which they must get through to effect their escape from us; and they did not think that 350 Madras sepoys with two guns would be sufficient to attack 830 desperate men caught in a trap. Moreover, the retirement of the Europeans would run like wildfire through the district; and I heard them all say they would not answer for what might happen.' The column *did* advance to Dorunda, and dispersed the miscreants; but it had to hasten to other regions, and then—'All the residents are very much disgusted at our going back, as the moral effect of our arrival must be great, the natives here having as much idea of a European soldier as they have of a whale, never having seen either; and the fact of their being put as prisoners under a European guard frightens them more than a thousand deaths.'

whom had crossed the Sone. Some days later, news arrived that the second portion of the 32d, that which had not at first mutinied, was, in like manner, marching towards the river. On the 1st of November the 53d started in pursuit, marched thirty miles during the night to Hurwa, rested a while, marched ten miles further to Nowada during the evening, and came up with the mutineers in the night. A skirmish by moonlight took place, greatly to the advantage of the rebels, who had a better knowledge of the country than their opponents. The sepoys did not want to fight, they wished to march towards the Sone; and this they did day after day until the 6th, followed closely all the way by the British. The pursued outstripped the pursuers, and safely crossed the river—much to the vexation of the major and his troops. One of the officers present has said: 'This was very provoking; for if we had but caught them, we should have got as much credit for it as for Chuttra. The country we went through was, for the most part, over swampy rice-fields; when we gave up the pursuit we had gone 130 miles in 108 hours; and, on our return to Gayah, we had been 170 miles in exactly one week. After the second day we sent our tents and bedding back; so that we marched as lightly as possible, and were by that means able to give the men an occasional lift on the elephants.'

Throughout these miscellaneous and often desultory operations in Bengal, if the Sikhs had proved faithless, all would have gone to ruin. It was more easy to obtain a thousand Sikhs than a hundred British, and thus they were made use of as a sort of military police, irrespective of the regular regiments raised in the Punjaub. Few circumstances are more observable throughout the Revolt, than the fidelity of these men. Insubordination there was, certainly, in some instances, but not in sufficient degree to affect the character of the whole. Captain Rattray's Sikhs have often been mentioned. These were a corps of military police, formed for rendering service in any part of Bengal; and in the rendering of this service they were most admirable. The lieutenant-governor of Bengal, in a paper drawn up early in September, said: 'The commandant of the Sikh Police Battalion has pleaded strongly on his own behalf, and on that of his men, for the assembling of the scattered fragments of his corps, to enable them to strike such a blow as to prove the high military spirit and discipline of the regiment. The urgent necessities which caused the separation of Captain Rattray's regiment renders it impossible, in existing circumstances, to call in all detachments to head-quarters; but its admirable discipline, daring, and devotion at Arrah and Jugdispore, and its good conduct everywhere, have fully established its character for soldierly qualities of the highest order. It would be difficult to exaggerate the value of the services which it has rendered to the state since the commencement of the present troubles; and the trust and confidence everywhere reposed in it, prove that these services are neither underrated nor disregarded. Of the men, all who have distinguished themselves for conspicuous deeds of valour and loyalty, have already been rewarded.' As individuals, too, the Sikhs were reliable in a remarkable degree, when Hindustanis were falling away on all sides. When the troubles broke out at Benares, early in the mutiny, a Sikh chieftain, by name Rajah Soorut Singh, rendered invaluable service to the British residents, which they did not fail gratefully to remember at a later period. A few of the Company's servants, civil and military, at Benares and other towns in that part of India, caused to be manufactured by Mr Westley Richards of Birmingham, for presentation to Soorut Singh, a splendid set of firearms, effective for use as well as superb in appearance.

We will now cross the Sone, and trace the progress of affairs in the Bundelcund and Saugor provinces.

It will be remembered, from the details given in former chapters, that the native inhabitants of Bundelcund, and other regions south of the Jumna and the Central Ganges, displayed a more turbulent tendency than those of Bengal. They had for ages been more addicted to war, and had among them a greater number of chieftains employing retainers in their pay, than the Bengalese; and they were within easier reach of the temptations thrown out by Nena Sahib, the King of Delhi, Koer Singh, and the agents of the deposed King of Oude. Lieutenant (now Captain) Osborne, the British resident at Rewah, was one who felt the full force of this state of circumstances. As he had been in August, so was he now in September, almost the only Englishman within a wide range of country south-west of Allahabad; the rajah of Rewah was faithful, but his native troops were prone to rebellion; and it was only by wonderful sagacity and firmness that he could protect both the rajah and himself from the vortex.

In a wide region eastward of Rewah, the question arose, every day throughout September, where is Koer Singh? This treacherous chieftain, who headed the Dinapoor mutineers from the day of their entering Arrah, was continually marching about with his rebel army of something like 3000 men, apparently uncertain of his plans—an uncertainty very perplexing to the British officials, who, having a mere handful of troops at their disposal, did not know where that handful might most profitably be employed. On one day Koer Singh, with his brother Ummer Singh, would be reported at Rotas, on another day at Sasseram; sometimes there was a rumour of the rebels being about to march to Rewah and Bundelcund; at others, that they were going to join the Goruckpore insurgents; and at others, again, that the Dinapoor and Ramgurh mutineers would act in concert. Wherever they went, however, plunder and rapine marked their footsteps. At one of the towns, the heirs of a zemindar, whose estates had been forfeited many years before, levied a thousand men to aid in seizing the property from the present proprietors. This was one among many proofs afforded during the mutiny, that chieftains and landowners sought to make the revolt of the native soldiery a means for insuring their own private ends, whether those ends were justifiable or not. The authorities at Patna and elsewhere endeavoured to meet these varied difficulties as best they could with their limited resources. They sent to Calcutta all the ladies and children from disturbed districts, so far as they possessed means of conveyance. They empowered the indigo-planters to raise small bodies of police force in their respective districts. They obtained the aid of two regiments of Goorkhas in the Chumparun district, by which the restoration of tranquillity might reasonably be expected. They seized the estates of Koer Singh and Ummer Singh at Arrah, as traitors. They imposed heavy fines on villages which had sent men to take active part in the disturbances. Lastly, they used all their energies to protect that part of the main trunk-road which passes near the river Sone; seeing that the march of European troops from Calcutta to the upper provinces would be materially affected by any interruption in that quarter. The newly arrived British regiments could not go up as an army, but as small detachments in bullock-wagons, and therefore were not prepared for sudden encounters with large numbers of the enemy.

The 5th irregular cavalry, who had mutinied in this part of India some weeks before, continued a system of plundering, levying contributions, and destroying public property. Every day that transpired, leaving these daring atrocities unchecked, weakened British prestige, and encouraged marauders on all sides to imitate the example so fatally set before them. The authorities felt and acknowledged this; yet, for the reasons already noticed, they could do little to check it. Captain Rattray, at the head of a portion of his Sikh police, encountered the 5th irregulars on the 8th of the month; but, as a cavalry force, they were too strong for him; they beat him in action, outgeneralled him in movement, released four hundred prisoners from one of the jails, and then marched west toward the river Sone. The mutinous sowars were subsequently heard of at Tikane, Daoodunggur, Baroon, and other places; everywhere committing great depredations. Thus was a large and important region, on either side of the main trunk-road, and extending two hundred miles along that road, kept in a state of daily agitation. The 5th irregular cavalry in one quarter, Koer Singh in another, and his brothers Ummer Singh and Nishan Singh in a third, were all busily employed in depredation; patriotism or nationality had little hold on their thoughts just then; for they plundered whomsoever had property to lose, without much regard to race or creed. The government offered large rewards for the capture of these leaders, but without effect: the rebels generally resisted this kind of temptation. Opium-crops to the value of half a million sterling were at that time ripening in the Behar and Arrah districts alone; and it was feared that all these would be devastated unless aid arrived from Calcutta.

Mr Wake, and the other civil servants who had so gallantly defended themselves at Arrah, against an enormous force of the enemy, returned to that station about the middle of September, to resume their duties; but as it was feared that Ummer Singh and the 5th irregulars would effect a junction, and attempt to reoccupy Jugdispore, those officers were authorised to fall back upon Dinapoor or Buxar, in the event of being attacked; although they themselves expressed a wish rather to remain at their posts and fortify themselves against the rebels as they had done before. The necessity of making this choice, however, did not arise. The 5th cavalry, after their victory over Rattray's Sikhs, and during their visits to the towns and villages near the Sone, committed, as we have just said, every kind of atrocity—plundering houses, levying contributions, breaking open the zenanas of Hindoo houses, abusing the women, and destroying property too bulky to be carried away—all this they did; but for some unexplained reason, they avoided the redoubtable little band at Arrah.

The Saugor and Nerbudda provinces, of which the chief towns and stations were Banda, Jaloun, Jhansi, Saugor, Jubbulpoor, Nagode, Dumoh, Nowgong, Mundlah, and Hosungabad, were, as we have seen, in a very precarious state in the month of August. At Saugor, so early as the month of June, Brigadier Sage had brought all the Europeans into a well-armed and amply provisioned fort, guarded by a body of European gunners, and by the still faithful 31st regiment of Bengal infantry; and there the Europeans remained at the close of August, almost cut off from communication with their fellow-countrymen elsewhere. Jubbulpoor had passed through the summer months without actual mutiny; but the revolt of the 42d infantry and the 3d irregular cavalry, at neighbouring stations, and certain suspicious symptoms afforded by the 52d at Jubbulpoor itself, led Major Erskine to fortify the Residency, and provision it for six months. Banda, Jhansi, and Jaloun, had long fallen into the hands of the rebels; Mundlah and Hosungabad were at the mercy of circumstances occurring at other places; Nagode would be reliable only so long as the 50th native infantry remained true; and Dumoh would be scarcely tenable if Jubbulpoor were in danger. Thus, at the end of August, British supremacy in the Saugor and Nerbudda territories hung by a thread. The Calcutta authorities, unable to supply British troops for Bengal or Behar, were equally debarred from rendering assistance to these territories. September opened very gloomily for the officers intrusted with duties in this quarter. The Punjaub and Calcutta could only furnish trustworthy troops for the Jumna and Doab regions, where the war raged with greatest fierceness; it was from Madras and Bombay alone that aid could be expected. Fortunately, the large regions of Nagpoor and Hyderabad were nearly at peace, and thus a passage could be afforded for troops from the south which would not have been practicable had those countries been plunged in anarchy.

Towards the middle of September, Lieutenant Clark, deputy-commissioner of Jubbulpoor, learned a few facts that put him on the track of a conspiracy. It came out, on inquiry, that Rajah Shunker Shah, and many other chieftains and zemindars in the neighbourhood of Jubbulpoor, acting in concert with some of the sepoys of the 52d B. N. I., intended to attack the cantonment on the last day of the Mohurrum, murder all the Europeans, burn the cantonments, and plunder the treasury and city. By a bold and prompt movement, the chief conspirators were seized on the 14th. The lieutenant, writing to the commissioner of Nagpoor, announced the result in brief but significant language. 'I have been fortunate enough to get conclusive evidence by means of spies, without the conspirators taking alarm; and this morning, with a party of sowars and police, bagged thirty, and two rajahs (ringleaders) among them. Of course they swing. Many of my principal zemindars, and some—I wish I knew how many—of the 52d, are in the plot.' In Rajah Shunker's house, among other treasonable papers, was found a sort of prayer, invoking his deity to aid him in the destruction of all Europeans, the overturning of the government, and the re-establishment of his own power. The paper was found in a silk bag in which he kept his fan, and was a scrap torn from a government proclamation issued after the massacre at Meerut. In this instance, therefore, the official expression of horror and wrath at the opening scene of the mutiny, instead of deterring, encouraged others to walk in the same bloody path. The prayer or invocation was afterwards translated from the Hindee into English, and published among the parliamentary papers.* The execution of the rajah and his son was something more terrible than was implied by the lieutenant's curt announcement, 'of course they swing.' It was one among many examples of that 'blowing away from guns' to which the records of the mutiny habituated English newspaper readers. An officer stationed at Jubbulpoor at the time, after noticing the complicity of these two guilty men, describes the execution in a brief but painfully vivid way. 'At the head of the conspiracy was Shunker Shah, the Ghond rajah, and his son. Their place of abode is about four miles from Jubbulpoor. In former days this family ruled over all this part of the country; they can trace their descent for sixty generations. The family had been deprived of everything by the Mahrattas, and were in great poverty when we took possession. Our government raised them up from this state, and gave them sufficient to support themselves comfortably; and now they shewed their gratitude by conspiring against us in our time of sore trial. The family have neither much property nor power, but the ancient name and prestige was a point on which to rally. . . . . On the 18th, at 11 o'clock A.M., our two guns were advanced a few hundred yards in front of the Residency, covered by a company of the 33d and a few troopers, and it became known that the Ghond rajah and his son were about to be blown away from the cannon's mouth. The old man walked up to the guns with a firm stride; the son appeared more dejected. The old man, with his snow-white hair and firm manner, almost excited compassion; and one had to remember, before such feelings could be checked, how atrociously he intended to deal with us had his conspiracy succeeded; the evidence of his guilt was overwhelming. All was over in a few minutes. The scattered remains were pounced upon by kites and vultures, but what could be collected was handed over to the ranee.'

Although Lieutenant Clark was thus enabled, by mingled caution and decision, to frustrate the atrocious plot of which Jubbulpoor was to have been the theatre, he could not prevent the mutiny of the 52d native regiment. That corps revolted, albeit without perpetrating the cruelties and rapine intended. It was on the 18th that this rising took place, the troops at once marching off quietly towards Dumoh. One old subadar they tied on a horse, because he did not wish to join, and because they did not choose to leave him behind. It was supposed that the 52d had gone towards Dumoh, to capture guns there, and then return to plunder Jubbulpoor. Two days before this, namely, on the 16th, the greater part of the 50th regiment Bengal infantry threw off allegiance. Being stationed at Nagode, they suddenly rose, released the prisoners from the jail, burned the bungalows, and rendered the place no longer safe for Europeans. Mr Ellis and the other civilians fled to Paunna, while Colonel Hampton and the other military officers made their escape towards Jokhie—leaving every vestige of their property behind, except the clothes on their backs. Two companies of the regiment, remaining faithful, accompanied their officers safely to Mirzapore, a journey which occupied them twelve days.

* Shut the mouth of slanderers, bite and
Eat up backbiters, trample down the sinners,
You, *Sutrsingharka*,
Kill the British, exterminate them,
Mat Chundee.
Let not the enemy escape, nor the offspring of such,
Oh, *Singharka*.
Shew favour to Shunker!
Support your slave!
Listen to the cry of religion,
Mathalka.
Eat up the unclean!
Make no delay!
Now devour them,
And that quickly,
Ghormatkalka.

The words in italics are various names of the goddess Devee or Deva, 'the destroyer.'

The Europeans at Dumoh, a civil station on the road from Saugor to Jubbulpoor, were thrown into much tribulation by news of these mutinies at other places. When both the 50th and 52d regiments had 'gone'—a term that acquired much significance in India at that time—Major Erskine, chief-commissioner of the Saugor and Nerbudda territories, who happened to be at Dumoh, summoned a council of war on the 20th of September, to consider what was best to be done. It was resolved that Dumoh could not long be held against any considerable body of mutineers; and that advantage should be taken of the temporary presence of a column of Madras native troops to employ that column as an escort for the civilians and the Company's treasure from Dumoh to Jubbulpoor. There was a detachment of the still faithful 31st at Dumoh; and this was sent to join the main body of the regiment at Saugor, to be out of the way of temptation from mutinous sepoys.

This convoy of men and money from Dumoh led to a smart military encounter. The Madras movable column which afforded the required protection numbered about 500 men of all arms, under Colonel Miller. Leaving Dumoh on the 21st, and being much obstructed in passing the river Nowtah, Colonel Miller reached Sigrampore on the 26th; where he heard that the main body of the mutineers were at Konee, on the banks of a river which the column would need to cross on its way to Jubbulpoor. The colonel at once despatched a force of about 100 men, under Lieutenant Watson, to secure the boats on the river; but the enemy baffled this officer, who had much difficulty in preserving his men. Miller then advanced with his whole column, met the enemy, and fought a brief but decisive battle, which ended in the utter rout of the rebel sepoys. If it had been a purely military affair, the colonel was strong enough to defeat a more numerous body of the enemy; but he was hampered by the presence of civilians, treasure, and 120 sepoys of the 52d, who had been disarmed at Dumoh on news of the revolt of the main body, and whom it was necessary to take with the column. It was, indeed, a strange state of things; for the disarmed men were of course eager enough to rush over and join their companions of the same regiment.

It is not matter for censure if men placed in authority at different stations, in time of peril, occasionally differed concerning the relative importance of those stations. Thus, when the 50th and 52d native regiments mutinied, a question arose which principal city, Saugor or Jubbulpoor, should be regarded as a last stronghold in the event of the British being nearly overpowered. Major Erskine, at Jubbulpoor, urged the claims of that city, as having certain facilities for the receipt of reinforcements, should such happily be afforded; and as having many European women and children within the fort, who could not be removed without danger. Brigadier Sage, on the other hand, urged—'Whatever you do, let me retain Saugor. It is the key to Central India. It has a good fort and magazine. It is provisioned for six or eight months for three hundred men, and has thirty thousand maunds of grain in addition. It has a siege-train, which will fall into the hands of the enemy if we leave the place. It contains 170 women and children, who could not be withdrawn without danger.' In such or similar words was the retention of Saugor advocated. The discussion happily ended by both towns being retained. Those officials of the Company, military or civil, who resolutely fortified, instead of abandoning their positions, were in most instances rewarded with success—unless the enemy were in unusually overwhelming force.

Nearly all parts of the Saugor and Nerbudda territories were in wild confusion at the close of September. The Kamptee column of Madras troops had, as we have just seen, broken up the 52d mutineers; but still those rebels lay concealed in jungles, ready for mischief whenever an opportunity might offer; while the Madrasses, distracted by many applications from different quarters, had been unable to prevent the mutinous 50th regiment, at Nagode, from marching off to join the Dinapoor mutineers near Banda. At Saugor, Brigadier Sage and the British were safe, because they were in a strong and well-provisioned fort, and because the 31st native infantry exhibited no signs of disaffection; nevertheless the whole country around was in the hands of rebellious chieftains. On one occasion he sent out the greater part of his force to attack the Rajah of Bankipore at Nurriowlee, ten miles from Saugor; but the attack was unskilfully made—it failed, and greatly lowered British prestige in the neighbourhood.

As in September, so in October; these provinces were held by a very slender tie. Nearly all the chiefs of Bundelcund, on the border, were ready to rise in rebellion at news of any discomfiture of the British. Numerous thakoors had risen, and, with their followers, were plundering the villages in every direction. At Jubbulpoor, Hosungabad, Nursingpore, Jaloun, Jhansi, Saugor, Mundlah, Dumoh, there was scarcely an English soldier; and the presence of a few hundred Madras troops alone stood between the authorities and frightful anarchy. Indeed, Jaloun, Jhansi, and Dumoh were out of British hands altogether. The commissioner of Nagpoor was unable to send up any more Madrasses from the south; Mr Grant was unable to send any from Benares; the independent and half-distrusted state of Rewah lay on one border; the thoroughly rebellious state of Banda on another—and thus Major Erskine looked with gloomy apprehensions on the fate of the provinces under his charge. As the month drew to a close, his accounts were still more dismal. In one letter he said: 'The mass of native chiefs disbelieve in the existence of a British army; and nothing but the presence of troops among them will convince them of their error.' Again and again were such messages and representations sent to Viscount Canning, as chief authority in India; again and again did he announce that he had no British troops to spare. To Major Erskine's letters he replied that he 'must say broadly and plainly that he would consider the sacrifice of the garrison in Lucknow as a far greater calamity and reproach to the government than an outbreak of the Rewah or Bundelcund states, even if followed by rebellion and temporary loss of our authority in our own territories on the Nerbudda.' At the close of the month, Koer Singh and the Dinapoor mutineers were somewhere between Banda and Calpee; while Captain Osborne—one of the most remarkable men whom the Indian Revolt brought into notice—still maintained his extraordinary position at Rewah.

We pass now further to the west—to the cities and towns on the Jumna river, and to the regions of Central India between that river and Bombay. Here, little need detain us until we come to Agra. Futtehpoor, Cawnpore, and Futteghur, though not in Oude, were on its frontier, and were involved in the fortunes of that province. Captain Peel's movements with his naval brigade, in the Doab, may be left for treatment in connection with the affairs of Lucknow.

Agra experienced a loss early in September, in the death of John Russell Colvin, the lieutenant-governor of the Northwest Provinces. He fell from sickness, brought on mainly by the intense anxieties arising out of his position. He was a remarkable man, a true specimen of those civilians developed into usefulness by the unique policy of the East India Company. In England a public man becomes a statesman through a multitude of minor and exceptional causes; in India, under the Company's 'raj,' statesmen were educated professedly and designedly for their work. In England, we have seen the same statesman transferred from the Exchequer to the India Board, and from thence to the Admiralty, as if the same kind of knowledge were required for all three situations; in India, the statesman's education bore more close relation to the duties of the offices he was likely to fill. No defects in the Company's government, no evils arising out of 'traditional policy,' no favouritism or nepotism—can blot out the fact that the system brought out the best qualities of the men in their service. Well will it be if the imperial government, in future ages, is served so faithfully, skilfully, and energetically in India as the Company's government, during the last half-century, has been served by the Malcolms, Metcalfes, Munros, Birds, Thomasons, Elphinstones, Montgomerys, Outrams, Lawrences, and Colvins—most of them civilians, whose apprenticeship to Indian statesmanship began almost from boyhood.

Mr Colvin, whose death has suggested the above few remarks, had seen as much political service as almost any man in India. He was born in Calcutta, the son of a merchant engaged in the Calcutta trade. After receiving his education in England, and carrying off high honours at Haileybury, he went to India in the Company's service in 1826; and for thirty-one years was seldom free from public duties, mostly special and local. The number of offices he served in succession was remarkably large. He was assistant to the registrar of the Sudder Court at Calcutta; assistant to the British resident at Hyderabad; assistant-secretary in the revenue and judicial department at Calcutta; secretary to the Board of Revenue in the Lower Provinces; private secretary to Governor-general Lord Auckland; British resident in Nepaul; commissioner of the Tenasserim provinces; judge of the Sudder Court; and lastly, lieutenant-governor of the Northwest Provinces—ruler over a territory containing as many inhabitants as the United Kingdom of Great Britain and Ireland. All these offices he filled in succession, and the first eight qualified him for the onerous duties of the ninth and last. Throughout the mutiny, the only point on which Mr Colvin differed from Viscount Canning was in the policy of the proclamation issued on the 25th of May. It was at the time, and will ever remain, a point fairly open to discussion, whether Colvin's proclamation* was or was not too lenient towards the rebellious sepoys. If Canning's decision partook more of that of John Lawrence, it is equally certain that Colvin's views were pretty nearly shared by Henry Lawrence, in the early stages of the mutiny. Irrespective of this question of the proclamation, Colvin's position at Agra was one of painful difficulty. He was not so successful as Sir John Lawrence in the Punjaub, and his name has not found a place among the great men whom the mutiny brought into notice; but it would be unfair to leave unnoticed the circumstances which paralysed the ruler of Agra. A distinguished civilian, who knew both Colvin and Lawrence, and who has written under the assumed name of 'Indophilus,' thus compares the position of the two men: 'Colvin, with a higher official position, had less real command over events than his neighbour in the Punjaub. John Lawrence ruled a people who had for generations cherished a religious and political feud with the people of Hindostan Proper; and Delhi was, in Sikh estimation, the accursed city drunk with the blood of saints and martyrs. John Colvin's government was itself the focus of the insurrection. Lawrence may be said to have been his own commander-in-chief; and after a European force had been detached to Delhi immediately on the outbreak, he still had at his disposal seven European regiments, including the one sent from Bombay to Moultan, besides European artillery and a local Sikh force of about 20,000 first-rate irregulars of all arms. Colvin was merely the civil governor of the Northwest Provinces; and as the posts (dâks) were stopped, he could not even communicate with the commander-in-chief, with whom the entire disposal of the military

* See p. 111.

Camp within the Fort, Agra.—From a Photograph.

force rested. Lawrence had three days' exclusive knowledge by telegraph of what had taken place at Meerut and Delhi, during which interval he made his arrangements for disarming the sepoy regiments stationed in the Punjaub. Colvin had no warning; and the military insurrection had actually broken out within his government, and the mutineers were in possession of Delhi, before he could begin to act; but he promptly and vigorously did what was in his power.' We have seen in former chapters what course Mr Colvin adopted between May and August.* He opened communications with the authorities all around him, as soon as he knew that the mutiny had begun; he disarmed the 44th and 67th native infantry on the 1st of June; he raised a corps of volunteer horse for service in the neighbourhood; he organised a foot-militia among the civilians and traders, for the protection of the city; and he kept a close watch on the proceedings of the Gwalior mutineers. In July occurred the mutiny of the troopers of the Kotah Contingent; then the ill-managed battle outside Agra on the 5th; then the shutting up of Mr Colvin and six thousand persons within the fort; and then the passing of two weary months, during which the lieutenant-governor was powerless through his inability to obtain trusty troops from any quarter whatever. His health and spirits failed, and he died on the 9th of September—still hemmed within the walls of the fort at Agra. Mr Reade, the leading civilian, assumed authority until orders could be received from Calcutta; Colonel Frazer afterwards received the appointment—not of lieutenant-governor of the Northwest Provinces, for that government had by this time disappeared under the force of the mutiny—but of chief-commissioner at Agra. Viscount Canning, in a government order, gracefully and properly acknowledged the merits of Mr Colvin.†

The Europeans resident in Agra, after Mr Colvin's decease, were still unable to liberate themselves; for Delhi had not yet fallen, nor had English prestige been yet restored by Havelock's success at Lucknow. The English officers felt their enforced idleness very irksome. They, like all the other Europeans, were confined within the fort; no daring military exploits could be looked forward to hopefully, because there were scarcely any troops to command. For three months the Gwalior mutineers had been their *bête noir*, their object of apprehension, as being powerful and not far distant. They occasionally heard news from Gwalior, but of too uncertain a nature to satisfy their doubts. Early in September one of the officers wrote: 'A portion of the rebel army of Gwalior has marched; but their intentions are not yet known. They still say they are coming to turn us out of the fort, and perform all sorts of gallant deeds. Had they come at first, they would have given us a good deal of trouble, as we were not prepared for a siege—guns not mounted, magazines not shell-proof, provisions not in sufficient quantity, and (worst of all) two thousand women and children without any protection from the enemy's fire. All this is now being rapidly remedied, and now we could stand a siege with comfort. One of the greatest wants is that of tobacco; the soldiers have none; and few men know so well as they do the comfort of a pipe after a hard day's work, whether under a broiling sun or in drenching rain.' The British officers at Agra were embittered by becoming acquainted with the fact, that many influential natives now in rebellion were among those who made the most fervent demonstrations of loyalty when the mutiny first began.

Of the affairs of Delhi we shall speak presently. Meanwhile, it may be well to describe the movements of a distinct corps, having its origin in the capture of that city. Although General Wilson seized all the gates and buildings of the imperial city one by one, he could not prevent the escape of the mutineers from the southern gate, the opposite to that where the siege-works had been carried on. By the 21st of September, when the conquest was completed, large bodies of the rebels were far away, on their march to other scenes of struggle. The chief body marched down the right bank of the Jumna on the Muttra road, with the intention of crossing over into the Doab. Brigadier Showers was sent with a force to pursue another body of rebels in another direction; but the operations now under notice were those of the column under Colonel E. H. Greathed (of H.M. 8th foot), organised at Delhi on the 23d of September—about 3000 strong.* Starting on the 24th, Greathed crossed the Jumna, and marched towards Bolundshuhur. Here a body of fugitive mutineers was encountered on the 28th. A sharp action ensued, which ended in the flight of the enemy,

* Chap. vii., pp. 109-111. Chap. x., pp. 173, 174. Chap. xvii., pp. 232-236.

† 'It is the melancholy duty of the Right Honourable the Governor-general in Council to announce the death of the Honourable John Russell Colvin, the lieutenant-governor of the North-west Provinces.

'Worn by the unceasing anxieties and labours of his charge, which placed him in the very front of the dangers by which of late India has been threatened, health and strength gave way; and the Governor-general in Council has to deplore with sincere grief the loss of one of the most distinguished among the servants of the East India Company.

'The death of Mr Colvin has occurred at a time when his ripe experience, his high ability, and his untiring energy would have been more than usually valuable to the state.

'But his career did not close before he had won for himself a high reputation in each of the various branches of administration to which he was at different times attached, nor until he had been worthily selected to fill the highest position in Northern India; and he leaves a name which not friends alone, but all who have been associated with him in the duties of government, and all who may follow in his path, will delight to honour.

'The Right Honourable the Governor-general in Council directs that the flag shall be lowered half-mast high, and that 17 minute-guns shall be fired at the seats of government in India upon the receipt of the present notification.'

* H.M. 8th foot.
H.M. 75th foot.
2d Punjaub infantry.
4th " "
H.M. 9th Lancers.
1st Punjaub cavalry.
2d " "
5th " "
Two troops horse-artillery.
Light field-battery.
Pearson's 9-pounder battery.

leaving behind them two guns and much ammunition. As a consequence of this defeat, a newly set-up rajah, one Waladad Khan, abandoned the fort of Malagurh, and fled. It was in the blowing-up of this fort, by order of the colonel, that Lieutenant Home, who had so distinguished himself at the storming of the Cashmere Gate, was killed. One of his brother-officers said in a letter: 'The loss of poor Home has thrown a cloud over all our successes. He was brave among brave men, and an honour to our service.' Greathed advanced day after day, burning villages which were known to have been nests of insurgents. In one of those places, Koorjah, he found the skeleton of a European woman, the head cut off, and the legs hacked and cut. On the 5th of October, the column reached Allygurh, scoured through the town, and cut up a large body of rebels, taking eleven guns from them. Greathed was at Akerabad the next day, where Mungal Singh and his brother had raised the standard of rebellion; but these chieftains were killed, as well as most of their retainers. On the 9th, he reached Hattrass. At this place his movements were suddenly disturbed; he had intended to march down the Doab to aid Havelock, Outram, and Inglis; but now news from Agra reached him that led to a change of plan. To understand this, attention must be turned to the state of affairs in the Mahratta dominions of Scindia, the northern boundary of which approached very near Agra.

From the day when Scindia's Gwalior Contingent rose in mutiny against British authority, on the 14th of June, nothing but the personal faithfulness of Scindia himself prevented the mutineers from joining their compatriots at Delhi or elsewhere. Every British officer being driven away from Gwalior, the powerful army forming the Contingent might easily have made itself master of all that part of the Mahratta dominions; but Scindia, by a remarkable exercise of steadiness and shrewdness, kept them near him. He would not make himself personally an enemy to them; neither, on the other hand, would he express approval of their act of mutiny. He still remained their paymaster, and held his power over them partly by keeping their pay in arrear. All through the months of July and August did this singular state of affairs continue. A few detachments of the Contingent had marched off from other stations, but the main body remained quiet. The Indore mutineers from Holkar's Contingent had for some time been encamped near them at Gwalior, much against Scindia's inclination. Early in September the two bodies disagreed concerning future plans—the Indore men wishing to speed to Delhi, the Gwalior men to Cawnpore. Some of the maharajah's own troops, distinct from the Contingent, were seduced from their allegiance by the Indore men, and marched off with them on the 5th, with seven guns and a good store of ammunition. Some of the budmashes or vagabonds of Gwalior joined them; but the Gwalior Contingent proper still remained quiet near that city. This quietness, however, did not promise to be of long continuance. On the 7th, the native officers went to Scindia, and demanded from him food and conveyance for a march either to Agra or to Cawnpore. The maharajah's response not being satisfactory to them, they began to seize oxen, buffaloes, mules, horses, camels, and carts from the neighbouring villagers, and a few elephants from the richer men. Some violence against Scindia himself appeared probable; but he found the main body of his own little army disposed to remain faithful, and hence the Contingent had little inducement to attack him. The landowners in the neighbourhood offered to aid him with their retainers, thus lessening the danger to which he might otherwise have been exposed. About the middle of the month a fierce struggle seemed imminent; but Scindia and his supporters continued firm, and the Contingent did not for some time attempt any manœuvre likely to be serious to the British. We can therefore follow the steps of the other army of mischief-workers.

When the miscellaneous body of Indore mutineers, Gwalior traitors, and budmashes left Gwalior, they proceeded towards the river Chumbul, which they crossed on the 7th of September, and then took possession of the fort of Dholpore, a place about thirty miles from Agra—at the point where the trunk-road from Delhi to Bombay crosses the Chumbul, and therefore a very important spot in relation to any arrival of reinforcements for the British. In that very week the final bombardment of Delhi began; and if the mutineers had marched thither, they might seriously have embarrassed General Wilson's operations. They appear, however, to have remained near Dholpore, supporting and strengthening themselves by plunder in the neighbouring region. When Delhi fell, and its defenders escaped, the Dholpore mutineers—as we may now conveniently call them—had no motive for marching towards the imperial city; but, near the close of the month, they began to lay plans for an attack on Agra.

When October arrived, Mr Reade, and Colonels Cotton and Frazer, had to direct their attention not only to these Dholpore mutineers, but to dangerous neighbours from other quarters. A glance at a map will shew that when mutineers and marauders escaped from Delhi towards the Lower Ganges, Agra would necessarily be not far from the line of route. When, therefore, the authorities at the last-named city heard of the fall of Delhi, they naturally looked with some anxiety to the course pursued by the fugitives. They speedily heard that a crowd of mutineers, fanatics, felons, and miscreants of every description, had found their way to Muttra, and were engaged in constructing a bridge of boats over the Jumna; in order, as appeared probable, to open a communication with the Indore or Dholpore mutineers. Hence the extreme anxiety of the Agra authorities that Greathed's column, in pursuit of the fugitive rebels, should march down the right instead of the left bank of the Jumna, in order to aid Agra, and cut off the communication with Dholpore; and hence great disappointment, when it was found that the active leader of that column was marching rapidly on towards Cawnpore without thinking of Agra. At such a time, each officer naturally thought first and principally of the safety of the city or station for which he was responsible; and the commanders of movable columns were often embarrassed by conflicting requisitions from different quarters.

Such was the state of feeling in Agra at the end of September. Early in October, matters became more serious. The authorities received news that an attack on Agra was meditated by the rebels—comprising the 23d B. N. I. and the 1st B. N. C. of the Indore Contingent, from Mhow; a part of the

LIEUTENANT HOME, Bengal Engineers

fugitive forces from Delhi; and malcontents from Dholpore and the neighbourhood. Means were immediately sought for frustrating this attack. The rebels were known to be on the advance on the 6th; it was also known that on that day Colonel Greathed had arrived with his column at Akrabad, one day's march from Allygurh, on his way towards Cawnpore. It was thereupon resolved to obtain the aid of Greathed at Agra, before he further prosecuted his march. This energetic officer, who was rapidly following up a fugitive brigade from Delhi, very unwillingly postponed an object on which he had set his heart; but the danger to Agra becoming very imminent, he turned aside to lend his aid at that point. After marching forty-four miles in twenty-eight hours—a tremendous achievement in an Indian climate—Greathed arrived at the parade-ground of Agra on the morning of the 10th of October. Before his tired troops could enjoy even three hours' rest, they found themselves engaged in battle with the enemy, who suddenly attacked their camp. The rebels made a spirited dash with their cavalry, and opened a brisk fire with artillery half hidden behind luxuriant standing corn. Not a moment did Greathed delay. He moved to the right with a view of outflanking the enemy and capturing their guns on that side; and his arrangements in other quarters soon enabled him to charge and capture the enemy's guns and standards. On they went, the mutineers retreating and Greathed following them up, until he reached a village three miles out on the Gwalior road. Here Colonel Cotton came up, and assumed the command; the infantry drove the rebels to the five-mile point, and the cavalry and artillery continued the pursuit; until at length the enemy were utterly routed. They lost twelve guns, and the whole of their tents, baggage, ammunition, and vehicles of every description. It was a complete discomfiture. Colonel Greathed obtained, and deservedly, high praise for the celerity and energy of his movements. By the time the battle and pursuit were over, his cavalry had marched sixty-four and his infantry fifty-four miles in thirty-six hours; while Captain Bourchier's 9-pounder battery had come in from Hattrass, thirty miles distant, during the night without a halt. Greathed's loss in the action was 11 killed and 56 wounded. It was a strange time for the mutineers to make an attack on Agra. During the siege of Delhi, Wilson could not have spared a single regiment from his siege-camp, nor could any other general have brought resources to bear on the relief of Agra; whereas now, in this second week of October, Greathed with a strong column was within two days' march of the city. If they were not aware of this fact, then was their information less complete than usual; if they hoped to check his advance down the Doab, then did they wofully underrate his strength and gallantry.

While tracing briefly the progress of the movable column after this battle of Agra, it may be well to advert to a source of vexation that sometimes presented itself during the wars of the mutiny, at Agra as elsewhere. Many of the gallant men concerned in struggling against the mutineers were occasionally much perplexed by questions of seniority, at times and places when they could refer for solution neither to the governor-general nor to the commander-in-chief. Such was the case in reference to Greathed's column. General Gowan in Sirhind, General Penny at Delhi, the chief-commissioner at Agra, all had some authority in military matters in the Northwest Provinces. Colonel Cotton, at Agra, finished the battle which Greathed began—not because it had been badly fought, but because Cotton was senior to Greathed. Again, while Greathed was marching quickly and fighting valiantly on the road to Cawnpore, after the battle of Agra, Colonel Hope Grant of the 9th Lancers, made brigadier in order that he might assume higher command, was sent out from Delhi *viâ* Agra to supersede him—not because he was a better officer than Greathed, but because he was senior in rank. Grant joined the column on the 19th of October, and became its leader. The change caused a busy paper-war between the generals and commissioners who had made the respective appointments, and who could not, at such a troubled time, rightly measure the relative strength of their own claims to authority. Whether under Hope Grant, however, or under Greathed, the column was in good hands. On the 19th, the column marched twenty-four miles, and entered Minpooree. A native rajah had long ruled that place during the anarchy of the provinces; but no sooner did he hear of the approach of the British than he fled—leaving behind him several guns, 14,000 pounds of powder, 230,000 rupees, and much other property, which had been taken from the Company's officers when the mutiny began. There was no fighting, only a reoccupation. After another severe punishment of the rebels at Kanouge on the 23d, the column marched towards Cawnpore, which was reached on the 26th.

Returning to the affairs of the various Mahratta states, it may now be mentioned that the Gwalior Contingent did at last, in the month of October, make a move. They marched slowly and heavily (six regiments, four batteries, and a siege-train), leaving Gwalior on the 15th, and advancing eastward towards Jaloun and Calpee, as if with the intention of crossing the Jumna at the last-named place into the Doab; but the month came to an end without any serious demonstration on their part. Had Nena Sahib been as bold and skilful as he was vicious, he might have wrought great mischief to the English at this time. If he had placed himself at the head of the Gwalior Contingent (which was fully expected), and had marched with them southward through Bundelcund to the Saugor and Nerbudda territories, he would have picked up rebellious Bundelas at every village, and have advanced towards the Nerbudda in such strength as to render it very doubtful whether the available Madras and Bombay troops could have confronted him. He had ambition enough to place himself at the head of all the Mahratta princes, but neither skill nor courage for such a position. So far as concerns Agra, the residents continued in the fort, in no great danger, but too weak in military to engage in any extensive operations. The only contest, indeed, during the rest of the month was on the 28th, when a party from the fort sallied out, and dispersed a body of rebels assembled at Futtehpore Sikri.

The wide region comprised within the political limits of the Mahratta and Rajpootana states was in a very disturbed condition during September and October. Besides the Gwalior Contingent in Scindia's dominions, there were Holkar's Contingent, the Bhopal and Kotah Contingents, the Jhodpore legion, and other bodies of native troops, the partial mutiny of which kept the country in perpetual agitation. All Bengal troops were sources of mischief, for they were the very elements among which the disaffection grew up; European troops could be sent neither from Calcutta nor the Punjaub; and therefore it depended either on Bombay or Madras (chiefly the former) to send troops by whom the insurgents could be put down. These troops, for reasons already sufficiently explained, were few in number; and it was a work of great difficulty to transfer them from place to place where anarchy most prevailed; indeed, the commanding officers were often distracted by appeals to them from various quarters for aid—appeals incompatible one with another.

Colonel Lawrence had a contest with the mutineers of the Jhodpore legion, about the middle of September, in Rajpootana. He marched to and through various places, the names of which have hardly been heard of in England, such as Beaur, Chiliamas, Barr, Peeplia, Bugree, Chaputtia, and Awah; these movements took place between the 14th and the 18th of the month; and on the last-named date he encountered the rebels at Awah. He had with him 200 of H.M. 83d foot, 250 Mhairwara battalion, two squadrons of Bombay native cavalry, and 5 guns. It was an artillery attack on both sides, lasting three hours. Lawrence seems to have distrusted his own strength; he would not bring his infantry and cavalry into action, fearful of losing any of his men just at that place and time. In short, his attack failed; the rebels retained hold of Awah, and Lawrence, finding his supplies running short, retired to Beaur. The rebels had the guns of the legion with them, and worked them well. It was an untoward affair; for the Rajah of Jhodpore, friendly to the English, had just before met with a defeat of his own troops by the same legion, in an action which involved the death of Captain Monck Mason, the British resident; and now prestige was still further damaged by the retreat of Lawrence after a desultory action. The colonel had come with a small Bombay column to Ajmeer, to watch the movements of rebels in and near Ajmeer, Nuseerabad, Awah, and other places in that part of Rajpootana; and any discomfiture at such a time was likely to afford a bad example. At Kotah, Neemuch, Mundisore, Mehidpore, Indore, Mhow, Bhopal, &c., an uneasy feeling similarly prevailed, arising out of disturbances too small to be separately noticed here, but important as indicating a wide belt of disaffected country between the Jumna and the Bombay presidency. The strange character of the whole of that region, in a political sense, was well expressed by an English officer, who, writing from Neemuch, said: 'This station is in the heart of Rajpootana, a country abounding in and surrounded by native states which compose anything but one family, and between any two of which it is very difficult to determine at any given time what relation exists. There are Holkar's troops, and Scindia's troops, and Salomba's troops, and the mercenary troops of Odeypore, the Kotah Contingent, the Jeypoor, Jhodpore, Meywar, and Malwar corps, and a host more; and when any little dispute arises in the country, a sort of jumble takes place between these bodies, during which two of them at least are pretty sure to come into collision.' These petty quarrels among the chieftains were sometimes advantageous to the British; but the soldiery were so strongly affected with mutinous tendencies, that a friendly rajah could seldom give practical value to his friendliness.

It is unnecessary to notice in detail the petty military operations of that region. No great success attended any of them. One was at Nimbhera, or Nimbhaira, between Neemuch and Nuseerabad. Here a contest took place on the 20th of September, in which a native rajah was worsted by Colonel Jackson and 350 miscellaneous troops. Another occurred some weeks later, when the Mundisore insurgents, on the 22d of October, made an attack on Jeerun, a town about ten miles from Neemuch. A force of about 400 men was at once sent out from this station, chiefly Bombay native troops, but headed by 50 of H.M. 83d foot, under Captains Simpson, Bannister, and Tucker. The enemy were found drawn up in force. Tucker brought two guns and a mortar to bear upon them, and sent his infantry to attack the town; but the enemy checked them by overpowering numbers, and captured the mortar. The cavalry now made an attack, followed by the infantry, and the mortar was speedily retaken. The enemy were driven into the fort, and their fire entirely silenced. The Neemuch force was not strong enough to take the fort at that time, but the insurgents evacuated it during the night, and marched off. The encounter was rather severe to the British officers engaged; for two of them (Captains Tucker and Read) were killed, and five wounded. The miscreants cut off Captain Tucker's head as soon as he had fallen.

One of the most pathetic stories of that period had relation, not to a battle or a wholesale slaughter, but to the assassination of a father and two sons under very cowardly and inexplicable circumstances. Major Burton was British political agent at Kotah, a Rajpootana state of which the chief town lies northeast of Neemuch—a situation he had filled for thirteen years, always on friendly terms with the native rajah and the people generally. He had been four months at Neemuch, but returned to Kotah on the 12th of October, accompanied by two sons scarcely arrived at manhood. On the 15th, two regiments of the rajah's native army revolted, and surrounded the Residency in which Major Burton and his sons had just taken up their abode. What followed may best be told in the words of a third son, Mr C. W. Burton, of Neemuch.*

* 'The political agent was himself the first to discover their approach; and, as he had only returned to Kotah three days previously from an absence of four months, he believed the number of people he saw advancing merely to be some of the chief subordinates coming to pay him the usual visit of ceremony and respect. In a second he was cruelly undeceived. The mutineers rushed into the house; the servants, both private and public, abandoned him with only one exception (a camel-driver); and the agent, his boys, and this one solitary servant fled to the top of the house for safety, snatching up such few arms as were within their reach. The fiends pursued; but the cowardly ruffians were driven back for the time by the youngest boy shooting one in the thigh. When there, they naturally hoped the agency-servants or their own would have returned with assistance from the chief; but no—all fled, and no help came. In the meantime, the mutineers proceeded to loot the house, and they (the major and his sons) saw from their position all their property carried away. A little while and two guns were brought to play upon the bungalow, the upper part of which caught fire from the lighted sticks which the miscreants from time to time threw up. Balls fell around them, the little room at the top fell in, and they were yet unhurt—and this for five long and weary hours. Major Burton wished to parley with the mutineers, in the hope they would be contented if he gave himself up, and allow his boys to escape; but his children would not allow of such a sacrifice for their sakes; and like brave men and good Christians, they all knelt down and uttered their last prayers to that God who will surely avenge their cause. All now seemed comparatively quiet, and they began to hope the danger over, and let down the one servant who was still with them on a mission to the Sikh soldiers and others, who were placed by the chief for the personal protection of the agent round his bungalow, and of whom at the time there were not less than 140, to beg of them to loosen the boat, that an escape might be attempted across the river. They said: "We have had no orders." At this moment a shot from a pistol was fired. Scaling-ladders had been obtained, the

Let us on to Delhi, and watch how the imperial city fared after the siege.

As soon as the conquest had been completely effected, on the 21st of September,* it became necessary to make arrangements for the internal government of the city, irrespective of any more permanent or important appointments. Colonel Burn was made military governor. This officer had been thirty years in the Company's service—first in the Bengal native infantry; then in raising three native regiments on the Afghan frontier; next in the operations of the Afghan war; then in those of the Sikh war; afterwards as secretary to the commissioners of the Punjaub; and, lastly, as an officer in Nicholson's movable column. Colonel Burn being made military governor of Delhi, Colonel Innes received the appointment of commandant of the palace. Mr Hervey Harris Greathed, who had been appointed civil commissioner for Delhi as soon as the murder of Mr Simon Fraser on the 11th of May became known, lived through all the vicissitudes of the siege, but sank through illness almost as soon as the victorious army entered the imperial city; he was succeeded in his office by Mr Saunders. Another change may here be mentioned. General Wilson, worn out by his anxieties and labours in the siege-camp, retired two or three weeks after the conquest, for the recovery of his health in the hill-country, and was succeeded in the supreme command at Delhi by General Penny—subject to any more authoritative change by order of the Calcutta government.

Within, the city of Delhi was a very desolation. Nearly all the native inhabitants left it, in dread lest the English soldiers should retaliate upon them the atrocities perpetrated by the insurgents upon defenceless Europeans. The authorities had no wish for the immediate return of these people, until it could be ascertained to what extent the traders and working population had connived at the rebellion of the sepoys. Even many weeks after all fighting had ceased in and near the city, one of the officers wrote of the state of Delhi in the following terms: 'Every wall or bastion that faced our camp is in almost shapeless ruin; but the white marble pavilions of the palace rise unharmed along the Jumna's bank. In one of these live the . . . . . There is no describing the beauty and quaintness of their rooms. I long for photographs to send home. They are all of inlaid marble, with semianahs pitched in the zenana courts between. But all around speaks of awful war—the rows on rows of captured guns—the groups of English soldiers at every post; and not English only, for our brave defenders the Goorkhas, Sikhs, and Punjaubees mingle among them. A strange army indeed, with not a trace of pipe-clay! It is a frightful drive from the palace to the Cashmere Gate—every house rent, riven, and tottering; the church battered, and piles of rubbish on every side. Alas! the burnt European houses and deserted shops! Desolate Delhi! and yet we are told it is clearing and much improved since the storming of the place. It has only as yet a handful of inhabitants in its great street, the Chandnee Chowk, who are all Hindoos, I believe. Many miserable wretches prowl through the camps outside the city begging for admission at the various gates; but none are admitted whose respectability cannot be vouched for. Cart-loads of ball are being daily dug out from the Moree Bastion, now a shapeless, battered mass.'

The conquerors of Delhi, wishing to prevent for ever the imperial city from becoming a stronghold for rebels, proposed to destroy at once all the fortifications. The Calcutta government, on receiving news of the final capture, telegraphed to General Wilson to the following effect: 'The governor-general in council desires that you will at once proceed to demolish the defences of Delhi. You will spare places of worship, tombs, and all ancient buildings of interest. You will blow up, or otherwise destroy all fortifications; and you will so far destroy the walls and gates of the city as to make them useless for defence. As you will not be able to do this completely with the force at present available at Delhi, you will select the points at which the work may be commenced with the best effect, and operate there.' After General Wilson had retired, and General Penny had assumed command at Delhi, information reached Sir John Lawrence at Lahore of the intended demolition. He evidently did not approve of the plan in its totality, and suggested delay even in commencing it, until further orders could be received from Calcutta. He thus telegraphed to Delhi on the 21st of October: 'I do not think any danger could arise from delay. If the fortifications be dismantled, I would suggest that it be done as was the case at Lahore; we filled in the ditches by cutting down the glacis, lowered the walls, and dismantled the covering-works in front of the gates and bastions. A wall of ten or twelve feet high could do no harm, and would be very useful for police purposes. Delhi, without any walls, would be exposed to constant depredations from the Meeras, Goojurs, and other predatory races. Even such a partial demolition will cost several lacs of rupees and take a long time; at Lahore it cost two lacs, and occupied upwards of two years.'

One subject connected with the capture of Delhi was curiously illustrative of the state of the public mind as exhibited during the autumn of 1857. Anything less than a sanguinary retaliation for the atrocities committed by the natives in India was in many quarters regarded almost as a treasonable shrinking from justice. Kill, kill, kill all—was the

murderers ascended the walls, and the father and his sons were at one fell stroke destroyed. . . . . The maharajah was enabled to recover the bodies of the agent and both his sons in the evening, and they were carefully buried by his order. Dr Saider's house was attacked at the same time with the agency-house. He was cut down outside, in sight of the agent, as was also Mr Savlell, the doctor of the dispensary in the city, and one or two others whose names are not certain.'

* Chap. xviii., pp. 295-315.

injunction implied, if not expressed. Among the British residents in India this desire for blood was so strong, that it distempered the judgment of persons otherwise amiable and generous. Instead of acting on the principle that it is better for a few guilty to escape than for one innocent man to be punished, the doctrine extensively taught at that time reversed this rule of conduct. It is of course not difficult to account for this. The feelings of those who, a few short months before, had been peacefully engaged in the usual Anglo-Indian mode of life, were suddenly rent by a terrible calamity. Husbands, brothers, sons—wives, sisters, daughters—were not only put to death unjustly, but the black deed was accompanied by brutalities that struck horror into the hearts of all survivors. It was not at such a time that men could judge calmly. The subject is mentioned here because it points to one of the difficulties, almost without parallel in intensity, that pressed upon the nobleman whose fate it

Colonel Burn, Military Governor of Delhi.

was to govern India at such a time. Every proclamation or dispatch, issued by Viscount Canning, which contained instructions to the Company's officers tending to leniency towards any of the dark skins, was misquoted, misrepresented, violently condemned, and attributed to what in bitter scorn was called the 'clemency of Canning.' It required great moral courage, at such a time, to form a definite plan of action, and to maintain it in spite of clamour. Differences of opinion on these difficult matters of state policy are of course reasonable enough; the point is mentioned here only in its historical relation to an almost frenzied state of public opinion at a particular time.

The treatment of the King of Delhi was one of the subjects connected with this state of feeling. When taken a prisoner, the dethroned monarch was not shot. 'Why is this?' it was asked. Because Captain Hodson promised the king his life if he would surrender quietly. For a long time this gallant officer was an object of violent abuse for this line of conduct. 'Why did Hodson dare to do this?' was the inquiry. It was not until evidence clear and decisive had been afforded, of General Wilson's sanction having been given to this proceeding, that the subject fell into its proper place as one open to fair and temperate discussion. Again, letters written anonymously at Delhi appeared in the Calcutta newspapers, announcing that the ex-royal family were treated with the most obsequious deference; and the 'clemency' was again contrasted with the 'righteous demand for blood.' So much of this as was untrue gradually fell out of repute; and then the simple fact became known that the king was to be tried as a traitor, but was not to be treated as a felon until found guilty. Mrs Hodson, wife to the officer who effected the capture, paid a visit to the royal captives, which she described in a highly interesting letter to an English relation, afterwards made public; whatever else it shewed, it afforded no indication that the aged profligate was treated with a degree of luxurious attention offensive to the European residents of the place.*

* 'There is a report, which has been mischievously set about, and may have mischievous consequences—namely, that the king has the whole of his retinue, and has returned to his own apartments in the palace.

'This is perfectly untrue. I went with Mr Saunders, the civil commissioner, and his wife, to see the unfortunate and guilty wretch. We mounted a flight of stone steps, at the bottom and top of which was a European sentry. A small low door opened into a room, half of which was partitioned off with a grass-matting called chitac, behind which was a woman cooking some atrocious compound, if I might judge from the smell. In the other half was a

For all else, Delhi furnished nothing calling for special notice during the six weeks following the siege.

Of two columns, despatched from Delhi to pursue and punish the rebels after the siege, that under Colonel Greathed has already been noticed. A second, under Brigadier Showers, was engaged throughout October, mostly west and northwest of Delhi. Some of the petty rajahs between the Jumna and the Sutlej were in an embarrassing position; they would have drawn down on their heads eventual defeat by the British if they joined the rebels; while they were in immediate danger from the enmity of marauders and mutineers if they remained faithful to the British. To their credit be it said, most of them remained true to their treaties; they assisted the British in a time of trouble to the extent of their means. Especially was this the case in relation to the Rajahs of Jheend and Putialah, without whose friendly aid it would have scarcely been possible for Sir John Lawrence to send reinforcements from the Punjaub to General Wilson at Delhi. An exception was afforded by the Rajah of Jhujjur, whose treacherous conduct earned for him a severe defeat by Brigadier Showers about the middle of October. That officer was, later in the month, actively engaged in defeating and punishing rebels at Sonah, Bullubgurh, and other places.

Of the country north and northeast of Delhi, little need be said. Rohilcund was almost wholly in the hands of the rebels during September and October. In the districts of Bareilly, Boodayoun, Mooradabad, Shahjehanpoor, and Bijnour, the English might be reckoned by tens—so fierce had been the tempest which had swept them away. Happily Nynee Tal still remained a refuge for many non-combatants, who could not yet be safely removed to Calcutta or Bombay. Khan Bahadoor Khan—a notorious offender whose name has more than once been mentioned in these pages, and who, after being a well-paid deputy-collector in the Company's service, shewed his gratitude by committing great atrocities as self-elected Nawab of Bareilly—planned an attack on Nynee Tal about the middle of September. He sent a force of 800 men, under his nephew, Nizam Ullie Khan. Major Ramsey, however, speedily mustered 300 Goorkhas, and about 50 miscellaneous volunteers and troopers; this force, sallying forth from Nynee Tal on the 18th, encountered the Bareilly rebels at Huldwanee, near the foot of the hills, and gave so effective a defeat to them as to prevent any repetition of the attack for a very long time.

All around the district of Meerut the movements of the rebels were sensibly checked by the fact that that important military station still remained in the hands of the British. After the first day of outbreak (10th of May), Meerut was provisioned and intrenched in such a way as to render it safe from all attacks, especially as the garrison had a good store of artillery; and as small bands of trusty troops could occasionally be spared for temporary expeditions, the mutineers were kept from any very near approach to Meerut itself. The chief annoyance was from the Goojurs and other predatory tribes, who sought to reap a golden harvest from the social anarchy around them.

Happily, the extreme northwest remained nearly at peace. The Punjaub, under the firm control of Sir John Lawrence, although occasionally disturbed by temporary acts of lawlessness, was in general tranquil. A few English troops ascended from Kurachee by way of the Indus and Moultan; and a few native regiments came from Bombay and Sinde; but the Sikhs and Mussulmans of the Punjaub itself were found to be for the most part reliable, under the able hands of Cotton and Edwardes. In Sinde a similar state of affairs was exhibited: a few isolated acts of rebellion, sufficient to set the authorities on the alert without seriously disquieting them. On one occasion a company of native artillery was disarmed at Hydrabad, on suspicion of being tainted with disloyalty. On another occasion the 21st native infantry was disarmed at Kurachee, because twenty or thirty of the men displayed bad symptoms. And on another, a few men of the 16th native infantry were detected in an attempt to excite their companions to mutiny. All these instances tended to show, that if Sinde had been nearer to Hindostan or Oude, the Bengal portion of the army there stationed would in all probability have revolted; but being in a remote region, and among a people who had few sympathies with Brahmin sepoys, the incendiarism died out for lack of fuel.

Happily, again, the southern or peninsular portion of India was left nearly free from the curse of rebellion during the two months now under notice

native bedstead—that is, a frame of bamboo on four legs, with grass-rope strung across it; on this was lying and smoking a hookah an old man with a long white beard; no other article of furniture whatever was in the room, and I am almost ashamed to say that a feeling of pity mingled with my disgust at seeing a man recently lord of an imperial city, almost unparalleled for riches and magnificence, confined in a low, close, dirty room, which the lowest slave of his household would scarcely have occupied, in the very palace where he had reigned supreme, with power of life and death, untrammelled by any law, within the precincts of a royal residence as large as a considerable-sized town; streets, galleries, towers, mosques, forts, and gardens, a private and a public hall of justice, and innumerable courts, passages, and staircases. Its magnificence can only be equalled by the atrocities which have been committed there. But to go back to the degraded king. The boy, Jumma Bukht, repeated my name after Mr Saunders. The old man raised his head and looked at me, then muttered something I could not hear, and at the moment the boy, who had been called from the opposite door, came and told me that his mother, the begum, wished to see me. Mrs Saunders then took possession of me, and we went on into a smaller, darker, dirtier room than the first, in which were some eight or ten women crowding round a common "charpoy" or couch, on which was a dark, fat, shrewd, but sensual-looking woman, to whom my attention was particularly drawn. She took hold of my hand—I shuddered a little—and told me that my husband was a great warrior; but that if the king's life and her son's had not been promised them by the government, the king was preparing a great army which would have annihilated us. The other women stood round in silence till her speech was finished, and then crowded round, asking how many children I had, and if they were all boys; examined my dress, and seemed particularly amused by my bonnet and parasol. They were, with one exception, coarse, low-caste women, as devoid of ornament as of beauty. Zeenat Mahal asked me—a great honour, I found, which I did not appreciate—to sit down on her bed; but I declined, as it looked so dirty. Mr Saunders was much amused at my refusal, and told me it would have been more than my life was worth six months before to have done so; and I have no doubt of it.'

In Nagpoor, in the Deccan or Nizam's dominions, in Mysore, in the various provinces of the Madras presidency, in the South Mahratta country, and in the provinces around Bombay, the disturbances were few. In the Deccan, the Nizam and his prime minister remained stanch throughout; and although the city of Hyderabad was kept in much commotion by fanatical moulvies and fakeers, and by turbulent Rohillas and Deccanees, there was no actual mutiny of entire regiments, or successful scheme of rebellion. At Ahmedabad, midway between Bombay and the disturbed region of Rajpootana, one of those terrible events occurred on the 26th of October—a blowing away of five men from guns. All the officers whose duty it was to attend on those fearful occasions united in hoping that such a sight might never again meet their eyes.

Ruins near Kootub Minar, Delhi.

Lucknow, from the Observatory.

CHAPTER XXI.

THE RESCUE AT LUCKNOW, BY SIR COLIN CAMPBELL.

A LITTLE care is needed to avoid confusion in the use of the words 'siege,' 'defence,' and 'relief,' relating to Lucknow—so peculiar and complicated were the military operations in and near that city during the mutiny. In the first place, there was the defence of the Residency by Brigadier Inglis, during July, August, and September: the mutineers and rebels in the city itself being the besiegers. Secondly, in the closing week of September, came the siege of Lucknow city by the British under Havelock, Outram, and Neill: the rebels being the besieged, and Inglis's little band, still shut up within the Residency enclosure, being unable to take an active part in the operations. Next, for a further period of seven or eight weeks, a renewed defence of the British position was maintained by Havelock, Outram, and Inglis—the mutineers and rebels being, as in the first instance, the besiegers. Then, in the third week of November, occurred a siege of the city by Sir Colin Campbell: the mutineers and rebels being the defenders, and the British inmates of the Residency being enabled to aid the operations of the commander-in-chief. After this, there was another defence of the Alum Bagh against the rebels by Outram, and another siege of Lucknow by Campbell. It follows, therefore, that the 'siege,' the 'defence,' or the 'relief' of Lucknow should not be mentioned without defining the period to which the expression refers.

With this explanatory remark, the scope of the present chapter may be easily shewn. In former pages* the eventful defence of the Residency at Lucknow from the beginning of July to near the close of September, by Brigadier Inglis, was described; together with the arrival of a small army under Havelock and Outram, and the terrible conflict in the streets of the city. In the present chapter the sequel of the story will be given—shewing how it arose that Havelock and Outram could not escort the suffering women and children, sick and wounded, from Lucknow to a place of safety; how they struggled on for eight weeks longer; what preparations Sir Colin Campbell made to collect an army of relief; how he

* 'Story of the Lucknow Residency,' chap. xix. pp. 316-337.

fought his way to Lucknow; and by what felicitous arrangements he safely brought away those who, from sex, age, sickness, or wounds, were unable to defend themselves against a fierce and relentless enemy.

On the 26th of September, when a few hours' sleep had closed the agitating proceedings of the previous day, it was found that the 'relief' of Lucknow was a relief rather in name than in substance. Sir Henry Havelock surrendered the command which had been generously left in his hands up to this time by a superior officer; Brigadier Inglis surrendered the military control of the intrenched position, or rather continued to hold it under the supervision of another; while Sir James Outram, in virtue of an arrangement previously made, assumed the leadership of all the British forces, and the exercise of all British power, throughout Oude. At present, this leadership and power were of humble dimensions, for he commanded very little more of the province than the few acres at the Residency and the Alum Bagh. Of the gallant troops, under 3000 in number, who, led by Havelock, Outram, and Neill, had left Cawnpore on the 19th of September, nearly one-third were stricken down by the time the Residency was reached. The survivors were too few in number to form a safe escort for the women and children from Lucknow to Cawnpore; the march would have been an awful one, marked by bloodshed at every step; the soldiers, distracted by the double duties of protectors and combatants, would have been too weak for either. They brought muscle and sinew to aid in constructing countermines and batteries; they enlarged the area of the intrenched or fortified position—but they could not rescue those who had so long borne the wonderful siege.

Some of the troops, in charge of guns, baggage, and baggage animals, had defended a position outside the Residency enclosure during the night; and arrangements were now made to secure the new or enlarged area—including the Clock Tower, the Jail, a mosque, the Taree Kothee, the Chuttur Munzil palace, the Fureed Buksh palace, the Pyne Bagh, and other buildings and gardens. It was not without severe fighting and much loss on the 26th that the wounded were placed in safety, the guns secured, and the new position fortified. When these palaces, which had until now been respected, were conquered from the enemy, they were regarded as fair military spoil. The buildings formed a labyrinth of courtyards, inner gardens, balconies, gateways, passages, verandahs, rotundas, outhouses, and pavilions; and all became a scene of plunder. 'Everywhere,' says Mr Rees, 'might be seen people helping themselves to whatever they pleased. Jewels, shawls, dresses, pieces of satin, silk, broadcloths, coverings, rich embroidered velvet saddles for horses and elephants, the most magnificent divan carpets studded with pearls, dresses of cloth of gold, turbans of the most costly brocade, the finest muslins, the most valuable swords and poniards, thousands of flint-guns, caps, muskets, ammunition, cash, books, pictures, European clocks, English clothes, full-dress officers' uniforms, epaulettes, aiguillettes, manuscripts, charms; vehicles of the most grotesque forms, shaped like fish, dragons, and sea-horses; imauns or representations of the Prophet's hands, cups, saucers, cooking-utensils, china-ware sufficient to set up fifty merchants in Lombard Street, scientific instruments, ivory telescopes, pistols; and (what was better than all) tobacco, tea, rice, grain, spices, and vegetables.' There is no proof that much order was observed in the partition or distribution; every one appears to have helped himself to what he pleased; and many collected large stores of useful and ornamental articles which they afterwards sold at high prices. There was a good deal of luxurious living for the first few days, on the savoury provisions found in the palaces; and we may in some degree imagine how this was enjoyed, after such sorry rations of chupatties, stewed peas, and morsels of tough gun-bullock beef. There was, perhaps, something undignified in all this scrambling spoliation that jars with one's notions of heroism and exalted courage; but military men are accustomed to overlook it in the moment of victory.

When Sir James Outram clearly ascertained that the rebels and mutineers, instead of escaping from the city, were closing in more and more resolutely, he saw that no departure would be practicable either for officers or men, military or civilians, women or children. He endeavoured to open negotiations with Maun Singh, a powerful thalookdar or landowner;* to win him over to the

* The *thalookdaree* system of Oude requires a little explanation, in relation to the participants in the Revolt. Most of the annexations effected by the East India Company were followed by changes either in the ownership of the soil, or in the assessment of land-tax—such land-tax being the chief item in the Company's revenue. When the several annexations occurred, it was found throughout a great part of India that superior holders—whether proprietors, hereditary farmers of revenue, or hereditary middlemen—held large tracts of land, in a middle position between the native governments and the cultivating communities, and were responsible for the revenue to the state. In Bengal, these influential men were generally recognised by the Company as proprietors, and the rights of the sub-holders almost wholly ignored. In the Northwest Provinces, acquired by the Company at a much later date, the thalookdars, zemindars, or whatever these landowners may have been called, were generally set aside; but the asserted rights of some of them became subjects of endless litigation in the courts of law; the landowners frequently obtained decrees against the Company, and many received a percentage in compromise of their rights or claims. In Oude, annexed in 1856, the thalookdaree system was particularly strong. Almost the whole country had by degrees become parcelled out among great thalookdars or zemindars. Though under a Mohammedan government, these men were almost universally Hindoos—native chiefs who had obtained great prescription, exercised great power and authority, and were in fact feudatories of the government. They were much more than mere middlemen or farmers of revenue. They had their own forts, troops, and guns; they obeyed their nawab or king so far as they chose or were compelled; they seized with the strong hand estates which had unquestionably belonged to village communities in earlier times; and they fought with each other as English barons or Scottish clan-chieftains were wont to do in past ages. Sir William Sleeman estimated the number of armed retainers, whose services these thalookdars could command, at scarcely less than one hundred thousand; while they had nearly five hundred pieces of cannon in their several forts or strongholds. Under this system the village proprietary rights, even if not actually thrown aside and disregarded, became more weak and undefined than when the villagers held directly from the government. Hence arose a very embarrassing question when the Company took possession of Oude. With whom was the settlement to be made? The thalookdars were strong and in possession; the village communities were dormant, broken, and ill defined. It would have taken some time to suppress the one and revive the other. The opinions of revenue officers in the Northwest Provinces

side of the British, and thereby lessen the difficulties of the position; but the wily Oudian, balancing the relative advantages of loyalty and rebellion, gave specious answers on which no dependence could be placed. It became necessary to prepare for a new defence against a new siege. All the old 'garrisons' were strengthened, and new ones formed; all the guns and mortars were placed in effective positions, and all the soldiers told off to regular duties. As Outram and Havelock had brought scarcely any provisions with them into the Residency; and as those found in the palaces were articles of luxury rather than of solid food, a very careful commissariat adjustment became necessary—it being now evident that the daily rations must of necessity be small in quantity and coarse in quality. The enemy renewed their old system of firing, day after day, into the British position; they broke down the bridges over canals and small streams between the Residency and the Alum Bagh; and they captured, or sought to capture, every one who attempted to leave the intrenchment. On the other hand, the British made frequent sorties, to capture guns, blow up buildings, and dislodge parties of the enemy. Six days after the entry of Outram and Havelock, a soldier was found under circumstances not a little strange. Some of the garrison having sallied forth to capture two guns on the Cawnpore road, a private of the Madras Europeans was discovered in a dry well, where the poor fellow had been hiding several days. He had fortunately some tea-leaves and biscuits in his pockets, on which he had managed to support life; he had heard the enemy all round him, but had not dared to utter a sound. The well contained the dead body of a native sepoy; and the atmosphere hence became so pestilential and frightful that the poor European was wont to creep out at night to breathe a little fresh air. Great was his joy when at length he heard friendly voices; he shouted loudly for help, in spite of his exhausted state, and was barely saved from being shot by his countrymen as a rebel, so black and filthy was his appearance.

Throughout the month of October did this state of affairs in Lucknow continue. Outram had brought his guns into the intrenchment by clearing a passage for them through the palaces; he had destroyed Phillips' or Philip's Battery, with which the enemy had been accustomed greatly to annoy the garrison; he had blown up and cleared away a mass of buildings on the Cawnpore road; he had strengthened all the points of the position held by himself and Havelock; but still he could neither send aid to the Alum Bagh, nor receive aid from it. He could do nothing but maintain his position, until Sir Colin Campbell should be able to advance from Cawnpore with a new army. A few messages, in spite of the enemy's vigilance, were sent and received. Outram was glad to learn that a convoy of provisions had reached the Alum Bagh from Cawnpore, and that Greathed was marching down the Doab with a column from Delhi. As for Lucknow itself, matters remained much as before—sorties, firing, blowing up, &c.; but it must at the same time be admitted that Outram was more favourably placed in this respect than Inglis had been; his fighting-men were three or four times as numerous, and were thus enabled to guard all the posts with an amount of labour less terribly exhausting. Danger was, of course, not over; cannon-balls and bullets still did their work. The authoress of the *Lady's Diary* on one day recorded: 'An 18-pounder came through our unfortunate room; it broke the panel of the door, and knocked the whole of the barricade down, upsetting everything. My dressing-table was sent flying through the door, and if the shot had come a little earlier, my head would have gone with it. The box where E. usually sits to nurse baby was smashed flat.' Breakfasts of chupatties and boiled peas were now seldom relieved by better fare; many a diner rose from his meal nearly as hungry as when he sat down. Personal attire was becoming more and more threadbare. Poor Captain Fulton's very old flannel-shirt, time-worn and soiled, sold by auction for forty-five rupees—four pounds ten shillings sterling.

Little news could be obtained from the city itself, beyond the limits of the British position; but that little tended to shew that the rebels had set up a natural son of the deposed king as 'Padishah' of Oude, as a sort of tributary prince to the King of Delhi. Being a child only eight or ten years old, the real power was vested in a minister and a council of state. The minister was one Shirreff-u-Dowlah; the commander-in-chief was Hissamut-u-Dowlah; the council of state was formed of the late king's principal servants, the chieftains and thalookdars of Oude, and the self-elected leaders of the rebel sepoys; while the army was officered in the orthodox manner by generals, brigadiers, colonels, majors, captains, subalterns, &c. There was a strange sort of democracy underlying the despotism; for the sepoys elected their officers, and the officers their commander; and as those who built up felt that they had the right to pull down, the tenure of office was very precarious. The mongrel government at Lucknow was thus formed

ran strongly in favour of village proprietaries; still stronger in the Punjaub; and Oude was treated somewhat in the same way. The result in many cases was to eject the thalookdars, and make direct settlements with the village communities. When the Revolt began, the thalookdars at first behaved well to the British personally; with the butchery by a rabble they had no sympathy; and many were the Europeans whose lives they saved. But, the Company's government being for a time upset; and the period since the annexation having been too short to destroy the strength of the thalookdars, or to enable the village proprietors to acquire a steady possession of their rights—the thalookdars almost universally resumed what they considered to be their own. There is evidence, too, that in this course of proceeding they met with a considerable amount of popular support. It was in this way they became committed against the British government. Till Havelock's retreat from his unsuccessful attempt to relieve Lucknow in August, the thalookdars adopted a temporising policy; but when they saw him and Outram retreat across the Ganges to Cawnpore, they thought their time had arrived. They began to act in concert—not because they had much sympathy with mutinous sepoys, with the decrepit king of Delhi, or with the deposed king of Oude—but in the hope that, amid the general anarchy, they might regain their old influence.

of three elements—regal, aristocratic, and military, each trusting the other two only so far as self-interest seemed to warrant. The worst news received was that a small body of Europeans, including Sir Mountstuart Jackson and his sister, fugitives from Seetapoor, were in the hands of the rebels, in one of the palaces in Lucknow, and that a terrible fate impended over them.

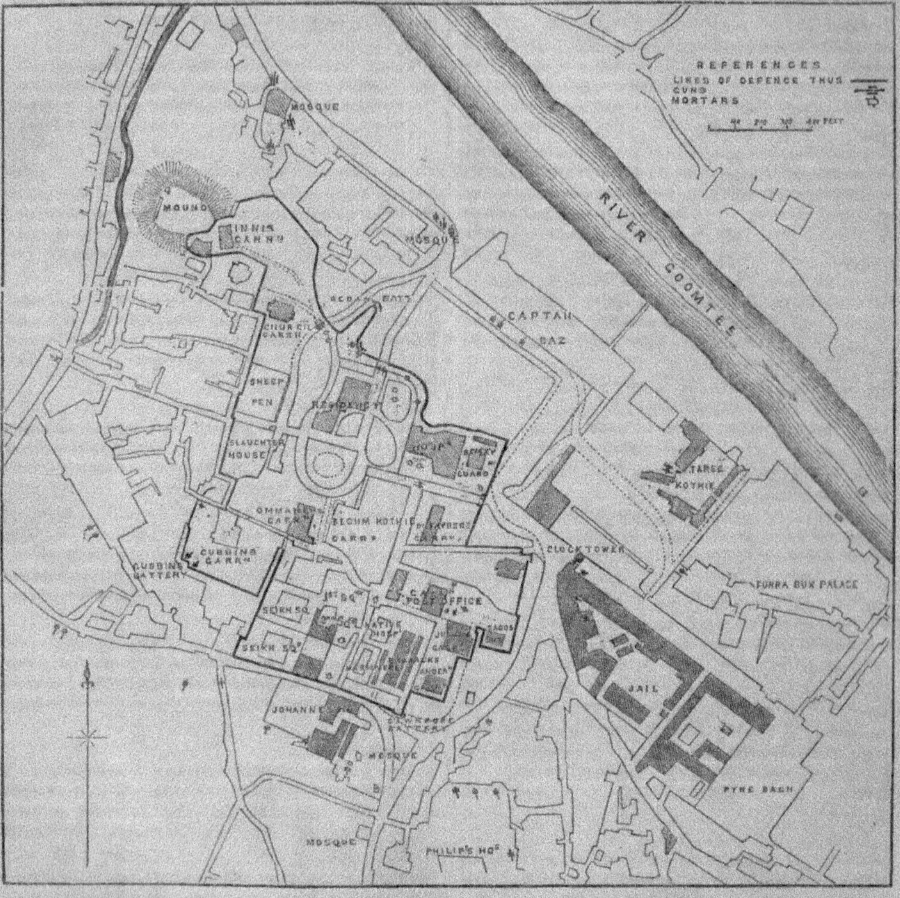

The Residency and its Defences, Lucknow.

November began with very low resources, but with raised hopes; for it was known that the commander-in-chief was busily making arrangements for a final relief of the garrison. Brigadier—or, as his well-earned initials of K.C.B. now entitled him to be called, Sir John—Inglis remained in command of the old or Residency intrenchment; Sir Henry Havelock took charge of the new or palatial position; while Sir James Outram commanded the whole. Labour being abundant, great improvements were made in all parts; sanitary plans were carried out, and hospitals made more comfortable; overcrowded buildings were eased by the occupancy of other places; cool weather brought increase of health; and improvements were visible in every particular except two—food and raiment. On the 9th of the month, Mr Cavanagh, who in more peaceful times had been an 'uncovenanted servant' of the Company, or clerk to a civil officer in Lucknow, made a journey on foot to a point far beyond the Alum Bagh under most adventurous circumstances,* to

* See NOTE, at the end of this chapter.

communicate in person full details of what was passing within the Residency, to concert plans in anticipation of the arrival of Sir Colin, and perhaps to act as a guide through the labyrinthine streets of the city. As an immediate consequence of this expedition, a system of semaphore telegraphy was established from the one post to the other, by which it was speedily known that Mr Cavanagh had succeeded in his bold attempt, and that Sir Colin arrived at the Alum Bagh on the 11th. Arrangements were now at once made to aid the advance of the commander-in-chief as effectively as possible. Day after day Havelock sent out strong parties to clear some of the streets and buildings in the southeastern half of the city—blowing up batteries and houses, and dislodging the enemy, in order to lessen the amount of resistance which Sir Colin would inevitably encounter.*

All this time, while the British in Lucknow were stoutly maintaining their ground against the enemy, some of their companions-in-arms—near at hand, but as inaccessible as if fifty miles distant—had their own troubles to bear. The position of the small detachment at the Alum Bagh was as trying as it was unexpected. When Havelock left a few hundred soldiers at that post, with four guns, vehicles, animals, baggage, ammunition stores, camp-followers, sick, and wounded, he never for an instant supposed that he would be cut off from them, and that the Residency and the Alum Bagh would be the objects of two separate and distinct sieges. Such, however, was the case. Not a soldier could go from the one place to the other; and it was with the utmost difficulty that a messenger could convey a small note rolled up in a quill. The place, however, was tolerably well armed and fortified; and as the enemy did not swarm in any great numbers between it and Cawnpore, reinforcements were gradually able to reach the Alum Bagh, although they could not push on through the remaining four miles to the Residency. On the 3d of October, a convoy of 300 men of the 64th regiment, with provisions, under Major Bingham, started from Cawnpore, and safely reached the Alum Bagh; he could not penetrate further, but the supplies thus obtained at the Alum Bagh itself were very valuable. On the 14th, a second convoy, under Major M'Intyre of the 78th Highlanders, was despatched; but he was attacked by the enemy in such force, that he could not reach the Alum Bagh; he returned, and had some difficulty in preventing the supplies from falling into the hands of the enemy. Another attempt afterwards succeeded. Colonel Wilson, commanding at Cawnpore, received the small detachments of British troops sent up from time to time from the lower provinces, as well as the supplies coming in from every quarter. His duty was, not to make conquests, but to send men and provisions to the Alum Bagh or the Residency as often as any opportunity occurred for so doing. He knew that the Alum Bagh batteries commanded all the approaches, and that the ground was cleared and exposed for five hundred yards on all sides; he did not therefore apprehend any serious calamity to the miscellaneous force shut up in that place, provided he could send provisions in good time. The three or four miles from the Alum Bagh to the Residency were, it is true, beset by difficulties of a most formidable character; bridges were broken, and lines of intrenchment formed, while mutineers and rebels occupied the district in great force; but they directed their attention rather to the Residency than to the Alum Bagh, thereby leaving the latter comparatively unmolested. Much sickness arose within the place, owing to the deficiency of space and of fresh air; and in the intervals between the arrivals of the convoys, provisions were scanty, and the distress was considerable. Nevertheless, the occupants of the Alum Bagh, with such men as Havelock and Inglis near them, never for an instant thought of succumbing; they would fight and endure till aid arrived.

Having thus watched the proceedings of the beleaguered garrisons at the Residency and the Alum Bagh, we may now trace the footsteps of Sir Colin Campbell, in his operations for their relief.

The commander-in-chief, as has already been stated, remained at Calcutta many weeks after his arrival in India. He was called upon to remodel the whole military machinery, and to arrange with the governor-general the system of strategy which would be most desirable under the actual state of affairs. He watched with intense interest the progress of events on the banks of the Jumna and the Ganges. He gave due praise to Wilson for the conquest of Delhi, and to Greathed for the conquering march through the Doab. He admired, as a soldier might well admire, the struggles of Havelock's gallant little army ere Outram had joined him; the combined operations of Havelock and Outram; and the wonderful defence made by Inglis against a host of opponents. He sent up from Calcutta, as soon as they arrived, reinforcements for the lamentably small British army; and he sent orders for brigading and marshalling, at Allahabad and at Cawnpore, such troops as could arrive from Calcutta on the one hand, and from Delhi on the other. At last, he himself departed

* One of the two hard-worked and sorely tried chaplains, in a letter to a relation when the dangers were past, employed a few simple words that really described the position of the Residency enclosure better than any long technical details. English friends had talked and written concerning the 'impregnable fort' in which the garrison were confined; to which he replied: 'We were in no fort at all; we occupied a few houses in a large garden, with a low wall on one side, and only an earthen parapet on the other, in the middle of a large city, the buildings of which completely commanded us, and swarming with thousands of our deadly foes, thirsting for our blood. God gave us protection and pluck, the former in a wonderful degree, or not one of us would be here to tell about it. . . . . The engineers calculated that all those months never one second elapsed without a shot being thrown in at us, and at times upwards of seventy per second, besides round shot and shell.' This probably means that the *average* was a shot per second for nearly five months—*twelve or fourteen million deadly missiles* thrown into this narrow and crowded space.

from Calcutta on the 28th of October, travelling like a courier, narrowly escaping capture by rebels on the way, and arriving at Cawnpore on the 3d of November—utterly heedless of the glitter and trappings that usually surround a commander-in-chief in India.

By what steps the various regiments reached Cawnpore, need not be traced in detail. As fast as they arrived, so did some degree of tranquillity succeed to anarchy. A portion of railway had for some weeks been finished from Allahabad to Lohunda, forty-two miles towards Futtehpoor, but had been stopped in its working by the mutiny; arrangements were now made, however, for bringing it into use, and for finishing the section between Lohunda and Futtehpoor. The English regiments, from China and elsewhere, went up from Calcutta by road or river, in the modes so often described; and were engaged in occasional skirmishes on the way, at times and places which have in like manner been mentioned. Benares was the converging point for the road and river routes; from thence the troops went up by Mirzapore to Allahabad; thence to Lohunda by rail; and, lastly, to Futtehpoor and Cawnpore by road-march or bullock-vehicles. A column under Colonel Berkeley was on its way; another under Colonel Hinde was in or near Rewah; another under Colonel Longden was near Jounpoor; while Colonel Wroughton, with the Goorkhas furnished by Jung Bahadoor, was on the Goruckpore frontier of Oude. True, some of these so-called columns were scarcely equal to one regiment in strength; but each formed a nucleus around which other troops might accumulate. Greathed's column, now better known as Hope Grant's, was the main element in Sir Colin's present force. It crossed the Ganges from Cawnpore into Oude on the 30th of October, about 3500 strong, with 18 guns, and advanced without opposition towards the Alum Bagh, near which it encamped, and awaited the arrival of the commander-in-chief.

A little may usefully be said here concerning the proceedings of the naval brigade, already noticed as having been placed under the command of Captain Peel, and as having arrived safely at Allahabad after a very wearisome voyage up the Ganges. On the 4th of October Sir Colin Campbell, then at Calcutta, telegraphed to Peel: 'In the course of about a week there will be a continuous stream of troops, at the rate of about ninety a day, passing into Allahabad, which I trust will not cease for the next three months.' Captain Peel was employed during October in facilitating the passage of troops and artillery up to Cawnpore. On the 20th Lieutenant Vaughan joined him, bringing 126 more naval officers and seamen, which raised the strength of the naval brigade to 516. Most of these new arrivals were sailors of the merchant service at Calcutta, who had agreed with much alacrity to join the brigade. On the 23d he sent off 100 seamen to Cawnpore, in charge of four siege train 24-pounders. On the 27th he despatched 170 more, in charge of four 24-pounders and two 8-inch howitzers; and on the same day a military escort was provided for a large amount of ammunition. Next, Captain Peel himself started for Cawnpore; and was soon afterwards joined on the road by Colonel Powell with the head-quarters of H.M. 53d regiment. Rather unexpectedly, a battle took place on the way. While at Thurea, on the 31st, news reached them that the Dinapoor mutineers, with three guns, had crossed the Jumna, and were about either to attack Futtehpoor, or to march towards Oude. Powell and Peel had with them troops and sailors numbering altogether about 700, in charge of a large and valuable convoy of siege and other stores. They marched that same evening to the camping-ground of Futtehpoor, where they were joined by some of the 93d Highlanders; and on the morning of the 1st of November a column of about 500 men marched twenty-four miles to Kudjna. The enemy were here found, with their guns commanding the road, their right occupying a high embankment, screened by a grove, and their left on the other side of the road. A part of the column advanced against the guns, while the rest rendered support on either side. A sharp battle of two hours' duration ensued, during which the enemy kept up so severe a fire of musketry that many of the English fell, including Colonel Powell, who received a musket-ball in the forehead. Captain Peel, although a sailor, then took the command; he carried a force round the upper end of the embankment, divided the enemy, and drove them from all their positions, capturing their camp and two of their tumbrils. His men were so worn out by 72 miles of marching in three days, that he could not organise a pursuit. Collecting his dead and wounded, which amounted in number to no less than 95, he marched back to Binkee; and after a little rest, the column, minus those who fell in this battle, continued the march towards Cawnpore. It was supposed the enemy numbered not fewer than 4000 men, of whom one half were mutinous sepoys from the Bengal army, and the other half rebels whom they had picked up on the way. After leaving some of his men at Cawnpore, to serve as artillerymen, Peel advanced with his heavy guns, and about 250 sailors, towards the Alum Bagh.

Understanding, then, that regiments and detachments of various kinds were working their way, at the close of October and early in November, towards Cawnpore, and across the Ganges into Oude, we may resume our notice of Sir Colin Campbell's movements.

Remaining at Cawnpore no longer than was necessary to organise his various military arrangements, the commander-in-chief crossed the Ganges on the 9th of November, and joined Hope Grant's column on the same day at camp Buntara, six miles short of the Alum Bagh. Wishing to have the aid of other detachments which were then on the road, he remained at Buntara till the morning of the 12th, when he started with the force which he had collected with so much trouble.* Advancing towards the Alum Bagh, he defeated a party of the enemy in a skirmish at a small fort called Jellalabad, a little way to the right of the main road, and five or six miles from the city. This fort being taken and blown up, Sir Colin pushed on and encamped for the night outside the Alum Bagh. Knowing that Havelock and Outram two months before had suffered severely in cutting their way through the city, Campbell now formed a plan of approach at the extreme eastern or rather southeastern suburb, and of battering down the enemy's defences step by step, and day after day, so as to form a passage for his infantry with comparatively small loss. This he had reason to hope; because there was a large open space at that end of the city, which—although containing many mosques, palaces, and other buildings—had few of those deep narrow lanes which had proved so dangerous to the former force. Hence the tactics of the next few days were to consist of a series of partial sieges, each directed against a particular stronghold, and each capture to form a base of operations for attacks on other posts nearer the heart of the city, until at length the Residency could be reached. The palaces, buildings, and gardens that would be encountered in this route were the Dil Koosha palace and park, the Martinière college, the Secunder Bagh, the Shah Nujeef, the palace Mess-house, the Observatory, the Motee Mehal, the Keisah or Kaiser Bagh, and various palatial buildings, of which the names are not clearly rendered; until at length those posts would be reached (the Chuttur Munzil, the Pyne Bagh, the Fureed Buksh palace, the Clock Tower, and the Taree Kothee) which were held by Havelock, and lastly those (the Residency and the other buildings within Inglis's original intrenchment) which were held by Outram.

After changing the garrison at the Alum Bagh, giving a little rest to troops who had recently had much heavy marching, and receiving an addition of about 630 men† from Cawnpore, Sir Colin commenced his arduous operations on the morning of the 14th, with a miscellaneous force of about 4000 men. As he approached the Dil Koosha park, the leading troops encountered a long line of musketry-fire; he quickly sent up reinforcements; and after a running-fight of about two hours, he drove the enemy down the hill to the Martinière college, across the garden and park of the Martinière, and far beyond the canal. This was effected without any great loss on either side. Campbell had now secured the Dil Koosha ('Heart's Delight') and the Martinière (Martine's college for half-caste children). Hope Grant's brigade, flanked by Bourchier's field-battery and Peel's heavy guns, was brought to the side of the canal (which enters the river Goomtee close to the Martinière), where they effectually kept the enemy in check. When night came, Sir Colin found he had made a good beginning; he had not only secured the easternmost buildings of Lucknow, but he had brought with him fourteen days' provisions for his own troops, and an equal proportion for those under Outram and Havelock; he had also brought all his heavy baggage (except tents, left at the Alum Bagh), and was therefore prepared to make a stand for several days at the Dil Koosha if necessary.

After further completing his arrangements on the 15th, and exchanging messages or signals with Havelock and Outram, the commander-in-chief resumed his operations on the 16th. Leaving every description of baggage at the Dil Koosha, and supplying every soldier's haversack with three days' food, he crossed the canal and advanced to the Secunder Bagh—a high-walled enclosure of strong masonry, about a hundred and twenty yards square, loopholed on all sides for musketry, and held in great force by the enemy. Opposite to it was a village at a distance of about a hundred yards, also loopholed and guarded by musketeers. After a determined struggle of two hours, during which artillery and infantry were brought to bear against them in considerable force, the enemy were driven out of the Secunder Bagh, the village, and a range of barracks hard by—all of which speedily became valuable strongholds to the conquerors. Sir Colin described this as a very desperate encounter, no less than 2000 of the enemy having fallen, chiefly after the storming of the Secunder Bagh itself by parties of the 53d and 93d regiments, aided by the 4th Punjaub infantry and a few miscellaneous troops. Indeed the enemy, well armed, crowded the Secunder Bagh in such numbers, that he said 'there never was a bolder feat of arms' than the storming. Captain Peel's naval siege-train then went to the front, and advanced towards the Shah Nujeef—a domed mosque with a garden, which had been converted into a strong post by the enemy; the wall of the enclosure had been loopholed with great care; the entrance had been covered by a regular work in masonry; and the top of the building had been crowned with a parapet. Peel was aided by a field-battery and some mortars; while the village to the left had been cleared of the enemy by Brigadier Hope and Colonel Gordon. A heavy cannonade was maintained against the Shah Nujeef for no less a space than three hours. The enemy defended the post very obstinately, keeping up an unceasing fire of musketry from the mosque and the defences in the garden. At last Sir Colin ordered the place to be stormed, which was effected in an intrepid manner by the 93d Highlanders, a battalion of detachments, and the naval brigade. In his

* H.M. 8th, 53d, 75th, and 93d foot.
2d and 4th Punjaub infantry.
H.M. 9th Lancers.
Detachments 1st, 2d, and 5th Punjaub cavalry.
Detachment Hodson's Horse.
Detachments Bengal and Punjaub Sappers and Miners.
Naval brigade, 8 guns; Bengal H.A., 10 guns.
Bengal horse field-battery, 6 guns; Heavy field-battery.
—About 700 cavalry and 2700 infantry, besides artillery.

† Detachments H.M. 23d and 82d foot.
Detachments Madras horse-artillery, royal artillery, royal engineers, and military train.

dispatch, the commander-in-chief said: 'Captain Peel led up his heavy guns with extraordinary gallantry to within a few yards of the building, to batter the massive stone-walls. The withering fire of the Highlanders effectually covered the naval brigade from great loss; but it was an action almost unexampled in war. Captain Peel behaved very much as if he had been laying the *Shannon* alongside an enemy's frigate.'

While Sir Colin and his troops were thus engaged, Havelock contributed towards the success of the general plan by the capture of a range of buildings in advance of the palace of Fureed Buksh. It had been agreed by signal and secret message, that as soon as Sir Colin should reach the Secunder Bagh, the outer wall of the advance garden of the Fureed Buksh (Havelock's most eastern post), in which the enemy had before made several breaches, should be blown in by mines previously prepared; that two powerful batteries erected in the enclosure should then open on the insurgents in front; and that after the desired effect had been produced, the troops should storm two buildings known as the Hern Khana or Deer-house and the Engine-house. This was successfully accomplished. At about eleven o'clock, the operations began. The mines were exploded; the wall was demolished; the works beyond were shelled by mortars; two of the mines at the Hern Khana were charged with destructive effect; and the infantry—eager for a little active work after being many weeks pent up within their intrenchment—dashed through the Chuttur Munzil and carried all before them, capturing the several buildings which had been marked out by previous arrangement.

Thus ended the important operations of the 16th, sanguinary in Sir Colin's force, but much less so in that of Havelock—operations during which the Secunder Bagh, the Shah Nujeef, the Hern Khana, the Engine-house, and many minor buildings, were captured. On the 17th, the commander-in-chief, after overcoming many obstacles, opened a communication between the canal and the left rear of a range of barracks, that facilitated his subsequent proceedings. Captain Peel meanwhile began to operate with his now famous naval brigade against a building called in the maps the Mess-house—a large structure, defended by a ditch twelve feet broad, and scarped with masonry, and by a loopholed mud-wall beyond the ditch. As a part of Sir Colin's general plan—that of employing artillery as much as possible, to save his infantry—a cannonading was continued for several hours against this Mess-house; and then it was stormed and taken without much difficulty by various detachments of the 53d, the 90th, the Punjaubees, and other regiments. This done, the troops pressed forward with great vigour, and lined a wall that separated the Mess-house from the Motee Mehal ('Pearl Palace'). This last-named place consisted of a wide enclosure containing many buildings. Here the enemy determined to make one last desperate stand; they fought with energy and determination for an hour, but then gave way. Sir Colin's troops broke an opening through the wall, aided by the sappers, and then they poured through, rushing onward until they reached the part of the city which for seven or eight weeks had been in the hands of Havelock. On the evening of this day the British found themselves in possession of nearly the whole river-side of Lucknow from the iron bridge to the Dil Koosha.

It may not be amiss here to mention that these operations during the second decade of November were conducted by the following officers: Sir Colin Campbell commanded the whole. General Mansfield officiated as chief of the staff. Brigadier Hope Grant was in immediate command of the column, formerly known as Greathed's, which constituted the chief part of Sir Colin's force. Colonel Greathed, now raised to brigadier-general as a mark of Sir Colin's estimate of his services, commanded one of the brigades of infantry. Brigadiers Russell and Adrian Hope took two other infantry brigades. Brigadier Little commanded the cavalry, Brigadier Crauford the artillery, Lieutenant Lennox the engineers, and Captain Peel the naval brigade. The operations brought the honorary distinction of K.C.B. to Grant and Peel, who became Sir James Hope Grant and Sir William Peel. Sir Colin's advance to the Residency, however, with the collateral struggles to which it gave rise, was severe in its results to his force, though less so than the operations of Outram and Havelock in September. He had to mourn the loss of 122 killed and 345 wounded. Out of this number there were 10 officers killed and 33 wounded. Sir Colin himself received a slight wound, but not such as to check his activity for an hour.* The loss of the enemy was frightfully severe; the exact amount was not known to the British, but it must have reached three or four thousand. They fought at the Secunder Bagh and the Shah Nujeef with a fierceness which rendered immense slaughter inevitable; for Peel's powerful artillery swept them down fearfully.

Whether the transports of joy that animated the British in Lucknow on the 17th of November were equal in intensity to those which had broken forth fifty-three days before, can never be exactly measured; men's emotions are not susceptible of such nice estimate. Suffice it to say, that as Inglis, on the 25th of September, had warmly grasped the hands of his deliverers Havelock and Outram; so did Outram, Havelock, and Inglis now

* The officers killed were Lieutenant-colonel Biddulph; Captains Hardy, Wheatcroft, Dalzell, and Lumsden; Lieutenants Mayne, Frankland, and Dobbs; Ensign Thompson; and Midshipman Daniel. The wounded were Sir Colin Campbell; Brigadier Russell; Lieutenant-colonels Ewart and Hale; Majors Alison and Barnston; Captains Alison, Anson, Grant, Hammond, Travers, Walton, and Burroughs; Lieutenants Salmond, Milman, Ford, Halkett, Munro, French, Wynne, Cooper, Welch, Goldsmith, Wood, Paul, M'Queen, Oldfield, and Henderson; Ensigns Watson, Powell, and M'Namara; Midshipman Lord A. P. Clinton; and Assistant-surgeon Veale.

welcome with all fervour Sir Colin Campbell and those who with him had just fought their way through the hostile streets of Lucknow. Then, when a few hours had enabled the new-comers to spread forth some of the supplies which their commissariat had provided, and the old inmates had done what little they could to render quiet eating and drinking possible—then were experienced once again the luxuries of wheaten bread, fresh butter, oranges, and other articles which are never luxuries save to those who have been long unable to obtain them. And then the feast of letters and newspapers from England was scarcely less delightful; for so close had been the investment of the Residency, that the inmates had been practically shut out from the world during the greater part of the summer and autumn.

The jubilation was, however, soon ended. Almost immediately on Sir Colin's arrival, an announcement was made that every European was to leave Lucknow and retire to Cawnpore. Many in the garrison had fondly hoped that the success of the commander-in-chief would have restored British control over the city; that comfort was about to succeed discomfort; that officers and civilians would resume their former duties under their former easy conditions; and that the ladies and children might rest a while in quiet, to recover health and strength before retiring to Calcutta or to the Hills. But such was not to be. Campbell had come to Lucknow almost solely to liberate them; and his plan of strategy—or, more probably, the number of available troops at his command—did not permit him to leave his small force in the Oudian capital; for there was hot work to look forward to. The enemy, notwithstanding their losses, still numbered fifty thousand fighting-men in and near Lucknow, shewing no symptoms of retreat, but rather a determination to defend the rest of the city street by street. To attack them further would have been to sacrifice a force already much reduced, and to risk the necessity for a third relief. Sir Colin issued an order, therefore, not only that all were to depart, but to depart quickly. The sick and wounded were to be removed directly from the Residency to the Dil Koosha—a distance of four miles in a straight line, but five or six if it were necessary to take a circuitous route to avoid the enemy; the women and children were to follow the same route on the next day; and the bulk of the soldiers were to depart when all else had been provided for. An encampment was prepared in the Dil Koosha park, with such necessaries and comforts as could be hastily brought together for sick, wounded, women, and children. The sojourn at the Dil Koosha was to be a brief one, sufficient only for the organisation of a convoy to Cawnpore. Only a small amount of personal baggage was allowed for each person; and thus those who possessed property were forced to leave most of it behind. The property, it is true, was very scanty; but the garrison felt vexed at leaving even a trifle as a booty to the rebels. As the ordnance stores and the Company's treasure (twenty-three lacs of rupees, safely preserved through all the trying scenes of half a year) were to be removed to the Dil Koosha about the same time as the non-combatants, and as all this was to be effected without exciting the suspicions of the rebels, the utmost vigilance and caution were needed.

The exodus from the Residency, and the escape to the Dil Koosha, through nearly the whole length of the city of Lucknow, will never be forgotten by those who took part therein. Many delicate ladies, unprovided with vehicles or horses, had to walk over five or six miles of very rough ground, exposed at one place to the fire of the enemy's musketry. The authoress of the *Lady's Diary*, with two other ladies, secured a carriage to convey them. 'We had a pair of starved horses of Mr Gubbins's to drag us; but the wretched animals had been on siege-fare so long that they had forgotten the use of their legs, and had no strength, so came to a stand-still every five minutes, invariably choosing the most dangerous parts of the road for their halt. At one place we were under so hot a fire that we got out and ran for our lives—leaving the vehicle to its fate; and two poor natives, who were helping to push it on behind, were shot. At the Fureed Buksh we had to wait a long time, as the carriage could not be got through a gateway till some stores were cleared away. Some of the officers of the 90th invited us inside, and gave us wine and water, which was very refreshing. We walked after that every step of the way to Secunderabad [Secunder Bagh], where we all had to wait several hours till doolies arrived to take on all the women; and we proceeded under a strong escort to Dil Koosha. The road to Secunderabad was frightfully dangerous in places. In one spot we were passing a 24-pounder manned by some sailors of the naval brigade; they all called out to us to bend low and run as fast as we could; we had hardly done so when a volley of grape whizzed over our heads and struck a wall beyond. At Secunderabad we found the place overflowing with women and children of the Lucknow garrison. . . . . At about nine o'clock P.M. we started again in doolies. The crowd and confusion were excessive, the enemy hovering round and firing occasional shots, and we were borne along in the most solemn silence; the only sounds were the tramp, tramp, tramp of the doolie-bearers and the screaming of the jackals. It was an awful time; one felt as if one's life hung in a balance, with the fate we had so long dreaded; but our merciful Father, who has protected us through so many and great dangers, brought us in safety to Dil Koosha, where we arrived about two o'clock in the morning.' They found shelter in the hastily prepared Dil Koosha encampment, already mentioned; and then, for the first time during five months, they snatched a little sleep beyond the Residency intrenchment. Mrs (now Lady) Inglis behaved on this occasion in a manner worthy of her name; a doolie or hospital-litter was prepared for her accommodation; but she refused it, in order that the sick and wounded might be better attended to. Mr Rees gives an extract from a letter of this lady, in which the incidents of the day are narrated nearly in the same terms as by the chaplain's wife; but the following few additional facts may be given: 'The road was quite safe except in three places, where it was overlooked by the enemy's position, and where we had to run. One poor woman was wounded at one of these places. We arrived at Secunder Bagh about six, and found every one assembled there, awaiting an escort and doolies to carry us on. When I tell you that upwards of two thousand men had been hastily buried there the day before, you can fancy what a place it was. . . . . We were regaled with tea and plenty of milk, and bread and butter—luxuries we had not enjoyed since the commencement of our troubles. At ten o'clock we recommenced our journey; most of the ladies were in palanquins, but we had a covered-cart drawn by two obstinate bullocks. We had a force of infantry and cavalry with us, but had not proceeded half a mile when the column was halted, and an order sent back for reinforcements; some noise was heard, and it was believed we might be attacked. However, it proved a false alarm; and after two disagreeable and rather anxious hours, we arrived safely at the Dil Koosha, and were quartered in tents pitched for our reception.' The charnel-house at the Secunder Bagh, mentioned in this extract, was the place where most of the slaughter of the enemy had occurred, and where the dead bodies had been hastily interred; the atmosphere around it was for many days in a frightful state.

The military movement in this evacuation of the Residency was spoken of by Sir Colin, in his official dispatch, as something masterly. He told how Outram so planned that each corps and regiment, each detachment and picket, should be able to march out silently in the dead of the night, without exciting suspicion among the myriads of enemies near; and yet that there should be guns and riflemen so posted as to repel the enemy if they should attempt any serious molestation of the retiring troops. It must be remembered that Outram and Havelock's gallant and much-enduring men had many things to effect after the non-combatants had departed from the Residency. They were called upon to bring away as many of the stores as could conveniently be conveyed, and to destroy those which, if left behind, would too much strengthen the enemy; they had to escort and protect their weaker companions, and to maintain a bombardment of the Kaiser Bagh and other posts, to deceive the enemy. The last of the men came out as quietly and cautiously as possible, in the dead of the night between the 22d and 23d of November, leaving lights burning, that the departure might not be suspected. They silently passed through the streets and roads, and safely reached the Dil Koosha. Captain Waterman, through some misconception, was left behind, and found himself, at two o'clock in the morning, the only living man in the intrenched position which had lately been so crowded. The situation was a terrible one, surrounded as he was by fifty thousand vindictive armed enemies. In an agony of mind, he ran past the Taree Kothee, the Fureed Buksh, the Chuttur Munzil, the Motee Mehal, the Secunder Bagh, and the Martinière, to the Dil Koosha, which he reached in a state of mental and bodily prostration. Sir Colin was among the last to leave the place. So cleverly was the evacuation managed (without the loss of one man), that the enemy continued to fire into the Residency enclosure long after the British had quitted it. What the scene was among the women and children, we have just been informed; what it was among the soldiers, is well described in a letter from one of the officers: 'An anxious night indeed that was! We left at twelve o'clock, having withdrawn all our guns from position, so that if the scoundrels had only come on, we should have had to fight every inch of our way while retiring; but the hand of Providence, which had watched the little garrison for so long a time, never left it to the last. The eye of the wicked was blinded while we marched breathlessly with beating hearts from our post, and, forming into line, walked through the narrow defiles and trenches leading from the ever-memorable Bailey guard. Out we went, while the enemy's guns still pounded the old wall, and while the bullets still whistled over the buildings; and, after a six miles' walk in ankle-deep sand, we were halted in a field and told to make ourselves comfortable for the night. Here we were in a pretty plight. Nothing to cover ourselves, while the cold was intense; so we lay down like so many sheep huddled together to keep ourselves warm, and so lay till the morning, when we rose stiff and cold, with a pretty prospect of the chance of finding our servants in a camp of 9000 men.'

The world-renowned 'Residency' at Lucknow being thus abandoned, it may be well to give in a note* Sir James Outram's comments on the eight

* 'I am aware of no parallel to our series of mines in modern war. Twenty-one shafts, aggregating 200 feet in depth, and 3291 feet of gallery, have been executed. The enemy advanced twenty mines against the palaces and outposts; of these they exploded three, which caused us loss of life, and two which did no injury; seven have been blown in; and out of seven others the enemy have been driven, and their galleries taken possession of by our miners—results of which the engineer department may well be proud. The reports and plans forwarded by Sir Henry Havelock, K.C.B., and now submitted to his excellency, will explain how a line of gardens, courts, and dwelling-houses, without fortified *enceinte*, without flanking defences, and closely connected with the buildings of a city, has been maintained for eight weeks in a certain degree of security; notwithstanding the close and constant musketry-fire from loopholed walls and windows, often within thirty yards, and from every lofty building within rifle-range, and notwithstanding a frequent though desultory fire of round-shot and grape from guns posted at various distances, from seventy to five hundred yards. This result has been obtained by the skill and courage of the engineer and quartermaster-general's departments, zealously aided by the brave officers and soldiers, who have displayed the same cool determination and cheerful alacrity in the toils of the trench and amid the concealed dangers of the mine that they had previously exhibited when forcing their way into Lucknow at the point of the bayonet, and amid a most murderous fire.'

weeks' defence of that place, as a sequel to Brigadier Inglis's account (p. 336) of the previous three months' defence before Outram arrived. To Outram was due the planning and execution of the strategical movement by which the evacuation of the Residency was accomplished. The commander-in-chief, in a general order issued on the 23d, thus spoke of it: 'The movement of retreat last night, by which the final rescue of the garrison was effected, was a model of discipline and exactness. The consequence was, that the enemy was completely deceived, and the force retired by a narrow, tortuous lane—the only line of retreat open—in the face of fifty thousand enemies, without molestation.'*

Great and universal was the grief throughout the camp when the rumour rapidly spread that Havelock, the gallant Christian soldier, was dead. He shared the duties of Outram at the Dil Koosha on the 23d and 24th, but died the next day, stricken down by dysentery, brought on by over-fatigue. All men talked of him as a religious as well as a brave man—as one, more than most men of his time, who resembled some of the Puritans of the sixteenth and seventeenth centuries. A few words may give the outline of his career. Henry Havelock was born near Sunderland in 1795. He was educated at the Charterhouse, and then studied for the bar for a short time; but afterwards adopted the military profession, following the example of his elder brother William. He entered the 95th regiment just after the battle of Waterloo, and during forty-two years saw a good deal of active service. After serving eight years in the United Kingdom, he exchanged into the 13th regiment, and went to India in 1823. He joined in the first Burmese war, of which he afterwards wrote and published a narrative. He served in various capacities twenty-three years before he became a captain, having no patronage in high places to facilitate his advancement. Then he served in the Afghan campaign, of which he wrote a memoir; and took a leading part in the memorable defence of Jelalabad. Rising gradually in office and in influence, he served in later periods at Gwalior, Moodkee, Ferozshah, Sobraon, the Sutlej, and other scenes of battle. When the Persian war broke out at the close of 1856, he was put in command of one division of the Anglo-Indian army; and when that war ended, he returned to India. What he achieved during 1857 the foregoing pages have shewn. All classes in England mourned his death. The Duke of Cambridge as commander-in-chief, Lords Palmerston and Panmure as ministers of the crown, the Earl of Derby as chief representative of the party at that time in opposition, the Court of Directors, the Court of Proprietors, the corporation of London, public functionaries and municipal bodies, religious and missionary societies—all sought to pay respect to the noble soldier who was at once pious, daring, and skilful. His widow, made Lady Havelock in virtue of his knighthood, received a pension of £1000 a year. His son received a baronetcy from the Queen, the rank of major from the commander-in-chief, and a pension of £1000 a year from the House of Commons. The public afterwards took up the subject of a monument to the hero, and a provision for his daughters, as matters not unworthy of support by voluntary efforts independent of the government. With or without a monument, the name of Henry Havelock will be held in grateful remembrance by the nation.

Sir Colin Campbell, like all around him, mourned the loss of his gallant coadjutor; but his thoughts had no time to dwell on that topic. He had to think of the living, to plan the march from the Dil Koosha to the Alum Bagh, and thence onward to Cawnpore. Certain state-prisoners had to be guarded, as well as the women and children, the sick and the wounded, the treasure and the stores. The whole army was thrown into two divisions: one under Brigadier Hope Grant, to form an escort from the Dil Koosha to the Alum Bagh; the other, under Outram, to keep the enemy at bay until the convoy was safely on its road. It was on the 24th that this novel and picturesque procession set out. The distance to the Alum Bagh was about four miles; and over the whole length of very rough road was a stream of bullock-carriages, palanquins, carts, camels, elephants, guns, ammunition and store wagons, soldiers, sailors (of the naval brigade), sick, wounded, women, children, and prisoners. The delays were great, the stoppages many, the fatigue distressing, the dust annoying; and all gladly rested their weary limbs at the Alum Bagh when night came.

It had been fully intended to afford the troops and their convoy several days' repose at the Alum Bagh; but on the 27th, Sir Colin was surprised to hear very heavy firing in the direction of Cawnpore. No news had reached him from that place for several days; therefore fearing some disaster, he felt it necessary to push forward as quickly as possible. Leaving Outram in command of part of the force at the Alum Bagh, and placing the rest under the immediate command of Hope Grant, he resumed his march at nine o'clock on the morning of the 28th. Messages now reached him, telling of a reverse which General Windham had suffered at Cawnpore, at the hands of the Gwalior mutineers. Sir Colin hastened forward, convoy and all; but he and a few officers took the start, and galloped on to Cawnpore that same night. The nature of Windham's disaster will come for notice in the next chapter; here we have only to speak of its

* The fate of the few English prisoners at Lucknow is not clearly traceable; but one account has stated that four Englishmen were put to death on the night when the Residency was finally evacuated. When the English troops, the women and children, the guns and baggage, and a quarter of a million sterling in silver, had safely reached the Dil Koosha, the leaders among the rebels became enraged beyond measure at a manœuvre which completely balked them. A few of them rushed to the Kaiser Bagh, where the unfortunate prisoners were confined, tied four of them—Sir Mountstuart Jackson, Mr Orr, Mr Barnes, and Sergeant Martin—to guns, and blew them away. The ladies were said to have been spared at the intercession of one of the begums or princesses of Oude.

immediate effect upon Sir Colin's plans. The enormous train of helpless women, children, sick, and wounded, could cross the Ganges and quit Oude only by a bridge of boats; if that were broken, the result might be tragical indeed. Orders were sent for the heavy guns to hurry on, and to take up such a position as would prevent the enemy from destroying or attacking the bridge; while a mixed force of infantry, cavalry, and horse-artillery was to cross quickly, and command the Cawnpore end of the bridge. Happily all this was effected just in time. When the passage was rendered safe, the artillery, the remaining troops, and the non-combatants, were ordered to file over the bridge; this they did, occupying the bridge in a continuous stream for *thirty hours*—unmolested, owing to Sir

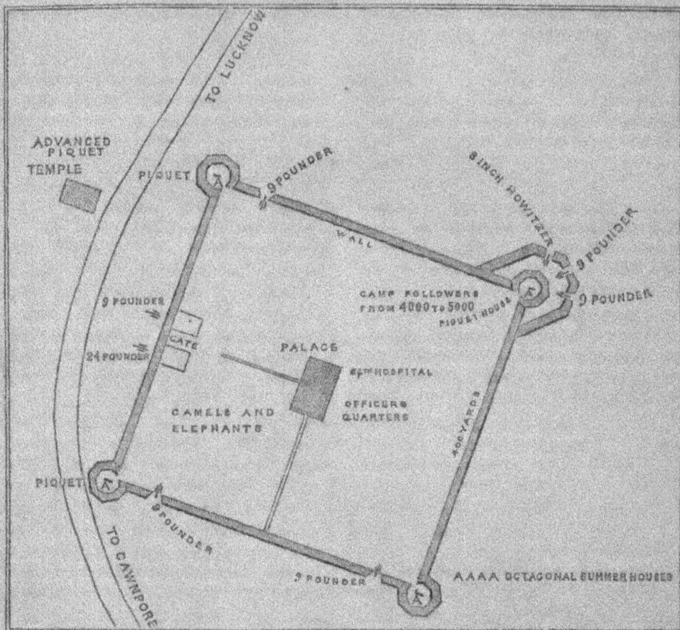

Fort of Alum Bagh, near Lucknow.

Colin's prompt plans, by the enemy's guns. All having safely crossed, the troops encamped around the ruinous old intrenchment rendered memorable by the gallant spirit and hapless fate of Sir Hugh Wheeler; while the women, children, sick, and wounded, were put temporarily into occupation of the old foot-artillery lines.

Although Sir Colin Campbell abandoned Lucknow for a while, he did not abandon the Alum Bagh. This post, a compact enclosure, capable of being defended on all sides, would afford an important base for future operations if maintained. Taking Hope Grant's division back with him to Cawnpore, he left Outram with three to four thousand men to hold the Alum Bagh against all odds, furnishing him with as large a supply as possible of provisions and stores. This force consisted of all the remaining or available companies of H.M. 5th, 78th, 84th, and 90th foot, the Madras Europeans, the Ferozpore Sikhs, three field-batteries, some heavy guns, two squadrons of the military train acting as dragoons, and a body of irregular cavalry. While the enemy were busily engaged in refortifying the city, so as to make it more formidable than ever, Sir James was making the Alum Bagh proof against all their attacks. The position thus occupied included not only the Alum Bagh itself, but a standing camp about three-quarters of a mile distant, and the bridge of Bunnee, which was separately held by 400 Madras sepoys and two guns.

Serious work and anxious thoughts occupied the mind of the commander-in-chief. He could do little in active military operations while so many helpless beings were depending on him for protection. Hence the sojourn of those who, from sex, age, or sickness, could render no active service at Cawnpore, was rendered as brief as possible. Vehicles, animals, provisions, and stores, were quickly collected; and on the 3d of December the march was resumed towards Allahabad—under an escort of H.M. 34th foot, two guns, and some cavalry. How the released Europeans fared on their journey; how they were cheered and greeted at Allahabad; how they felicitated themselves on once again sleeping in safety; and how they ultimately reached Calcutta by steamers on the Ganges—need not be told in detail. Let it suffice to say that when the ladies and children, with the invalided officers, who had passed through so wonderful a series of events, were approaching Calcutta, Lord Canning issued a notification, in which he said: 'No one will wish to obtrude upon those who are under bereavement or sickness any show of ceremony which shall impose fatigue or pain. The best welcome which can be tendered upon such an occasion is one which shall break in as little as possible upon privacy and rest. But the rescue of these sufferers is a victory beyond all price; and in testimony of the public joy with which it is hailed, and of the admiration with which their heroic endurance and courage are viewed,' it was ordered that a royal salute should be fired from the ramparts of Fort William as soon as the steamer arrived; that all ships-of-war in the river should be dressed in honour of the day; that officers would be appointed to conduct the passengers on shore; and that the state-barges of the governor-general should be in attendance.

Thus ended a great achievement. The women, children, sick, and wounded, who had to be brought away from the very heart of a city swarming with deadly enemies, and escorted through a country beset by mutinous sepoys and rebellious chieftains, were not fewer than *two thousand* in number. Let it be remembered, that while this helpless train of persons was on the way through Oude, behind them was the enormous hostile force of Lucknow, while in front of them were the Gwalior mutineers flushed by a recent victory. That all should have passed through this perilous ordeal with scarcely the loss of one life, reflects lasting credit on the generals who planned and executed the manœuvre. Of the five noble officers whose names are imperishably connected with the extraordinary sieges and defences of Lucknow—Inglis, Havelock, Neill, Outram, and Campbell—two fell before the grateful thanks of their countrymen at home could reach them; but the remaining three, when Christmas arrived, had the infinite satisfaction of knowing that their arduous labours had been rewarded by the safe arrival, at or near Calcutta, of the tender and weakened, the broken-down and invalided—those who had so long formed the European community in the Lucknow Residency.

Note.

Cavanagh's Adventure.—At p. 362 it is mentioned that Mr Cavanagh, an uncovenanted civil servant of the Company in the Residency at Lucknow, volunteered to make the perilous journey from that post to the commander-in-chief's camp many miles beyond the Alum Bagh, in order to establish more complete correspondence between Sir James Outram and Sir Colin Campbell than was possible by the simple medium of a small note enclosed in a quill. Mr Cavanagh's account of his hair-breadth run was afterwards published in the Blue-books; and as it affords a good idea of the state of Lucknow and its environs at the time, we will reprint it here:

'While passing through the intrenchment of Lucknow, about ten o'clock A.M. on the 9th inst., I learned that a spy had come in from Cawnpore, and that he was going back in the night as far as the Alum Bagh with dispatches to his excellency, Sir Colin Campbell, the commander-in-chief, who, it was said, was approaching Lucknow with 5000 or 6000 men.

'I sought out the spy, whose name is Kanoujee Lall, and who was in the court of the deputy-commissioner of Duriabad before the outbreak in Oude. He had taken letters from the intrenchment before, but I had never seen him till now. I found him intelligent, and imparted to him my desire to venture in disguise to the Alum Bagh in his company. He hesitated a great deal at acting as my guide, but made no attempt to exaggerate the dangers of the road. He merely urged that there was more chance of detection by our going together, and proposed that we should take different roads, and meet outside of the city, to which I objected. I left him to transact some business, my mind dwelling all the time on the means of accomplishing my object.

'I had, some days previously, witnessed the preparation of plans which were being made by direction of Sir James Outram to assist the commander-in-chief in his march into Lucknow for the relief of the besieged, and it then occurred to me that some one with the requisite local knowledge ought to attempt to reach his excellency's camp beyond or at the Alum Bagh. The news of Sir Colin Campbell's advance revived the idea, and I made up my mind to go myself at two o'clock, after finishing the business I was engaged upon. I mentioned to Colonel R. Napier, chief of Sir James Outram's staff, that I was willing to proceed through the enemy to the Alum Bagh, if the general thought my doing so would be of service to the commander-in-chief. He was surprised at the offer, and seemed to regard the enterprise as fraught with too much danger to be assented to; but he did me the favour of communicating the offer to Sir James Outram, because he considered that my zeal deserved to be brought to his notice.

'Sir James did not encourage me to undertake the journey, declaring that he thought it so dangerous that he would not himself have asked any officer to attempt it. I, however, spoke so confidently of success, and treated the dangers so lightly, that he at last yielded, and did me the honour of adding, that if I succeeded in reaching the commander-in-chief, my knowledge would be a great help to him.

'I secretly arranged for a disguise, so that my departure might not be known to my wife, as she was not well enough to bear the prospect of an eternal separation. When I left home, about seven o'clock in the evening, she thought I was gone on duty for the night to the mines; for I was working as an assistant field-engineer, by order of Sir James Outram.

'By half-past seven o'clock my disguise was completed, and when I entered the room of Colonel Napier, no one in it recognised me. I was dressed as a budmash, or as an irregular soldier of the city, with sword and shield, native-made shoes, tight trousers, a yellow silk koortah over a tight-fitting white muslin shirt, a yellow-coloured chintz sheet thrown round my shoulders, a cream-coloured turban, and a white waistband or kumurbund. My face, down to the shoulders, and my hands, to the wrists, were coloured with lampblack, the cork used being dipped in oil to cause the colour to adhere a little. I could get nothing better. I had little confidence in the disguise of my features, and I trusted more to the darkness of the night; but Sir James Outram and his staff seemed satisfied. After being provided with a small double-barrelled pistol, and a pair of broad pyjamahs over the tight drawers, I proceeded with Kanoujee Lall to the right bank of the river Goomtee, running north of our intrenchment, accompanied by Captain Hardinge, of the irregular cavalry.

'Here we undressed and quietly forded the river, which was only about four and a half feet deep, and about a hundred yards wide at this point. My courage failed me while in the water, and if my guide had been within reach, I should perhaps have pulled him back and abandoned the enterprise; but he waded quickly through the stream. Reaching the opposite bank, we went crouching up a ditch for three hundred yards, to a grove of low trees on the edge of a pond, where we stopped to dress. While we were here, a man came down to the pond to wash, and went away again without observing us.

'My confidence now returned to me, and with my tulwar resting on my shoulder we advanced into the huts in front, where I accosted a matchlockman, who answered to my remark that the night was cold: "It is very cold—in fact, it is a cold night." I passed him, adding that it would be colder by and by.

'After going six or seven hundred yards further, we reached the iron bridge over the Goomtee, where we were stopped and called over by a native officer who was seated in an upper-storied house, and seemed to be in command of a cavalry picket, whose horses were near the place saddled. My guide advanced to the light, and I stayed a little back in the shade. After being told that we had come from Mundeon—our old cantonment, and then in the possession of the enemy—and that we were going into the city to our homes, he let us proceed. We continued on along the left bank of the river to the stone bridge, which is about eight or nine hundred yards from the iron bridge, passing unnoticed through a number of sepoys and matchlockmen, some of whom were escorting persons of rank in palanquins preceded by torches.

'Recrossing the Goomtee by the stone bridge, we went by a sentry unobserved, who was closely questioning a dirtily dressed native, and into the chowk or principal street of the city of Lucknow, which was not illuminated as much as it used to be previous to the siege, nor was it so crowded. I jostled against several armed men in the street without being spoken to, and only met one guard of seven sepoys, who were amusing themselves with some women of pleasure.

'When issuing from the city into the country, we were challenged by a chowkeedar, or watchman, who, without stopping us, merely asked who we were. The part of the city traversed that night by me seemed to have been deserted by at least a third of its inhabitants.

'I was in great spirits when we reached the green fields, into which I had not been for five months. Everything around us smelt sweet, and a carrot I took from the road-side was the most delicious I had ever tasted. I gave vent to my feelings in a conversation with Kanoujee Lall, who joined in my admiration of the province of Oude, and lamentation that it was now in the hands of wretches whose misgovernment and rapacity were ruining it.

'A further walk of a few miles was accomplished in high spirits. But there was trouble before us. We had taken the wrong road, and were now quite out of our way in the Dil Koosha Park, which was occupied by the enemy. I went within twenty yards of two guns to see what strength they were, and returned to the guide, who was in great alarm, and begged I would not distrust him because of the mistake, as it was caused by his anxiety to take me away from the pickets of the enemy. I bade him not to be frightened of me, for I was not annoyed, as such accidents were not unfrequent even when there was no danger to be avoided. It was now about midnight. We endeavoured to persuade a cultivator, who was watching his crop, to shew us the way for a short distance, but he urged old age and lameness; and another, whom I peremptorily told to come with us, ran off screaming, and alarmed the whole village. We next walked quickly away into the canal, running under the Char Bagh, in which I fell several times, owing to my shoes being wet and slippery and my feet sore. The shoes were hard and tight, and had rubbed the skin off my toes, and cut into the flesh above the heels.

'In two hours more we were again in the right direction, two women in the village we passed having kindly helped us to find it. About two o'clock we reached an advanced picket of sepoys, who told us the way, after asking where we had come from, and whither we were going. I thought it safer to go up to the picket, than to try to pass them unobserved.

'Kanoujee Lall now begged I would not press him to take me into the Alum Bagh, as he did not know the way in, and the enemy were strongly posted around the place. I was tired, and in pain from the shoes, and would therefore have preferred going into the Alum Bagh; but, as the guide feared attempting it, I desired him to go on to the camp of the commander-in-chief, which he said was near Bunnee (a village eighteen miles from Lucknow) upon the Cawnpore road. The moon had risen by this time, and we could see well ahead.

'By three o'clock we arrived at a grove of mango-trees, situated on a plain, in which a man was singing at the top of his voice. I thought he was a villager, but he got alarmed on hearing us approach; and astonished us, too, by calling out a guard of twenty-five sepoys, all of whom asked questions. Kanoujee Lall here lost heart for the first time, and threw away the letter intrusted to him for Sir Colin Campbell. I kept mine safe in my turban. We satisfied the guard that we were poor men travelling to Umroula, a village two miles this side of the chief's camp, to inform a friend of the death of his brother by a shot from the British intrenchment at Lucknow, and they told us the road. They appeared to be greatly relieved on discovering that it was not their terrible foe, who was only a few miles in advance of them. We went in the direction indicated by them, and after walking for half an hour we got into a jheel or swamp, which are numerous and large in Oude. We had to wade through it for two hours up to our waists in water, and through weeds; for before we found out that we were in a jheel, we had gone too far to recede. I was nearly exhausted on getting out of the water, having made great exertions to force our way through the weeds, and to prevent the colour being washed off my face. It was nearly gone from my hands.

'I now rested for fifteen minutes, despite the remonstrances of the guide, and went forward, passing between two pickets of the enemy, who had no sentries thrown out. It was near four o'clock in the morning when I stopped at the corner of a tope or grove of trees to sleep for an hour, which Kanoujee Lall entreated I would not do; but I thought he overrated the danger, and, lying down, I told him to see if there was any one in the grove who would tell him where we then were.

'We had not gone far when I heard the English challenge "Who comes there?" with a native accent. We had reached a British cavalry outpost: my eyes filled with joyful tears, and I shook the Sikh officer in charge of the picket heartily by the hand. The old soldier was as pleased as myself when he heard whence I had come; and he was good enough to send two of his men to conduct me to the camp of the advance-guard. An officer of her Majesty's 9th Lancers, who was visiting his pickets, met me on the way, and took me to his tent, where I got dry stockings and trousers, and, what I much needed, a glass of brandy—a liquor I had not tasted for nearly two months.

'I thanked God for having safely conducted me through this dangerous enterprise, and Kanoujee Lall for the courage and intelligence with which he had conducted himself during this trying night. When we were questioned, he let me speak as little as possible. He always had a ready answer, and I feel that I am indebted to him in a great measure more than to myself for my escape. It will give me great satisfaction to hear that he has been suitably rewarded.

'In undertaking this enterprise, I was actuated by a sense of duty, believing that I could be of use to his excellency the commander-in-chief when approaching, for its relief, the besieged garrison, which had heroically resisted the attack of thirty times its own number for nearly five months, within a weak and irregular intrenchment; and, secondly, because I was anxious to perform some service which would insure to me the honour of wearing our Most Gracious Majesty's Cross.

'My reception by Sir Colin Campbell and his staff was cordial and kind to the utmost degree; and if I never have more than the remembrance of their condescension and of the heartfelt congratulation of Sir James Outram and of all the officers of his garrison on my safe return to them—I shall not repine, though to be sure having the Victoria Cross would make me a prouder and a happier man.

'JAMES CAVANAGH.

'*Camp, Alum Bagh, Nov. 24.*'

GROUP OF MAHRATTA ARMS.—From the Collection of Sir S. Meyrick: *a a*, Helmet; *b*, Sword; *c*, Musket; *d*, Knife and Sheath; *e*, Mace; *f*, Shield.

CHAPTER XXII.

CLOSING EVENTS OF THE YEAR.

THE expedition of Sir Colin Campbell to Lucknow in November, followed by the extraordinary rescue of the British residents at that city, formed an episode in the history of the Indian Revolt well worthy of being treated singly and separately from other matters. This having been done, the present chapter may conveniently be devoted to the closing events of the year in other places, touching only upon such occurrences as immediately affected the mutiny or the plans for its suppression. As in the former chapters *—relating, the one to July and August, and the other to September and October—the survey (applicable in this case to November and December) may usefully begin in the Calcutta provinces, and thence travel westward.

Calcutta itself, for reasons more than once stated, was not likely to be materially affected by mutinous proceedings. The interests of the native towns-people, concerned in supplying the wants of a larger number of Europeans than resided at any other city in India, led them to prefer scenes of quiet, even if the Bengalee character had been more warlike than is its wont; while the frequent landing of British troops from other shores kept in awe such of the sepoy soldiers as still remained in arms. A naval squadron anchored in the Hoogly, with sufficient power of metal to batter the city to ruins if danger arose. The natives, except a few of fanatical character, were more disposed to seek for holiday than for war; and holiday occasionally fell to their share, in the proceedings of the British themselves. On one day, towards the close of November, there were 4500 British troops temporarily garrisoned at Calcutta, and 11 ships-of-war anchored in the river. The troops comprised H.M. 19th, 20th, 42d, 54th, 79th, and 97th regiments of foot, or portions of them, together with one battalion of the 60th Rifles, and one of the Rifle brigade. A review of most of these fine troops was held on the Calcutta volunteers' parade-ground, before the journey to the upper provinces commenced. The Calcutta government commenced operations for reorganising the vast regions which had been thrown into confusion by the Revolt. A plan was sketched out for separating the divisions of Delhi and Meerut from the Northwest Provinces, and transferring them to the government of the Punjaub—in order that they might share in the peculiar system of executive rule which had been found to work well in the Punjaub, under the energetic control of Sir John Lawrence. The rest of the Northwest Provinces could not be permanently reorganised until the warlike operations had made further advance. Another proceeding on the part of the government was to send out a commission to the Andaman Islands, to examine how far they were suited as a penal settlement for rebels or traitors sentenced to transportation; the commission comprised naval and medical officers, who were empowered to select a spot healthy in situation and easily defended.

In the easternmost districts of India, mutiny shewed itself in small degree. It could hardly be other than slight, however; for the Hindustani troops were few in number, and the general population not ill affected. Three companies of the 34th Bengal native infantry, it will be remembered,* were stationed at Chittagong at the very beginning of the troubles in March and April; they not only remained faithful when the other companies of the same regiment became mutinous at Berhampore, but made a very high-flown declaration of their loyalty. After remaining 'true to their salt' throughout the whole of the summer and autumn, these three companies at length yielded to the general mania. They broke out into mutiny at Chittagong on the 18th of November, burnt their lines, blew up the magazine, looted the treasury, and commenced a search for Europeans. These latter escaped, chiefly in boats upon the river. The mutineers then released the convicts from the jail, and decamped. They moved northward, apparently tending toward Tipperah,

* Chap. xvii., pp. 277-291; chap. xx., pp. 338-358.

* See p. 103.

where a petty rajah held his court. Directly this was known, Major Byng, commanding a Silhet native regiment, marched down from the hills, and met the mutineers. A brief conflict ensued, in which the major unfortunately received a mortal wound; but the misguided men of the 34th, meeting with no kind of sympathy from the Silhetees, were almost wholly annihilated within a few days.

There were at that time two companies of the 73d native regiment at Dacca; and as soon as the authorities received from the magistrate of Chittagong news of what had occurred at the last-mentioned place, they resolved to disarm those two companies, as a precaution against mischief. The sepoys, however, hearing the news from Chittagong more speedily than the authorities, prepared for resistance. A party of volunteers disarmed a few scattered sepoys; but as the others had artillery to assist them, a hundred English sailors, with two or three howitzers, were told off to deal with them. A sharp contest ensued at the sepoy barracks, with balls, grape, and musketry; until at length the sailors, determined on a closer attack, rushed upon the sepoys, drove them out of the barracks, and killed many on the spot. The rest set off on a hasty march to Jelpigoree, the head-quarters of the regiment. So utterly was that part of India denuded of British troops, that there were none to repel even one or two hundred mutineers; and many villages were plundered on the road. The check came from a quarter where apparently the mutineers least expected it—from the men of their own regiment. The motives of the native troops were as inscrutable now as at any former time; for although the two companies thus rebelled, fought, and fled, the bulk of the regiment remained faithful. They had even quietly permitted two hundred Goorkhas to join the regiment—that step having been adopted by the authorities to infuse new blood into the corps. An officer of the 73d, writing from Jelpigoree on the 3d of December, said: 'Our men have sworn to their native officers (not to us) that they will do their duty; and our spies, who have hitherto proved so trustworthy, declare that we may fully depend on the regiment. Yesterday the test commenced by our ordering accoutrements and ammunition to be served out to our two hundred Goorkhas. This was done cheerfully, and is a very good indication of the prevailing feeling. A strange scene it was, watching the sepoys doling out ammunition to Goorkhas to fight against their own (the sepoys') comrades, and it did one's heart good to see it: we are all under arms, and very sanguine.' These men actually joined in routing the mutinous companies of their own regiment, and in driving them towards Bhotan, where they died miserably among an unsympathising population.—Such discrepancies in conduct between different regiments and different companies of the same regiment, threw great difficulties in the way of any logical tracing of the causes of the Revolt.

In a wide region of Bengal westward of Calcutta, the only incidents requiring notice were two or three in which the Shekhawuttie battalion shewed that it still remained faithful to the Company's raj—almost the last relic of the once magnificent Bengal army. With this regiment Colonel Forster put down the recusant Rajah of Pachete, whose domain touched the grand trunk-road above Raneegunge. After hovering some time on the verge of treason, this man at length refused to obey the British resident at Rugonauthpoor, Mr Lushington, who was obliged to intrench himself in self-defence. Colonel Forster hastened thither; and by his own boldness of bearing, and the faithfulness of his Shekhawutties, he captured the rajah, a fort of no inconsiderable strength, much wealth, and a mass of treasonable correspondence—without firing a shot. Shortly afterwards, Forster marched to Sumbhulpore, where a band of ruffians, headed by one of their own class, had commenced a course of violence that needed and obtained a prompt check.

Let us hasten on to the busier scenes of the northwest, viewing them in connection with Cawnpore as a central point of strategy, and with Sir Colin Campbell as leader of all the British operations. This may the more appropriately be done; because there were no events on the Lower Ganges, between Calcutta and Benares, requiring notice, so far as concerned the months of November and December.

Cawnpore was a centre in military matters for the following reasons. On one side of it was Lucknow, so important in relation to the occupancy of Oude; Allahabad, on another side, was on the great line of route for troops from Calcutta; Agra and Delhi, towards the northwest, lay on the path of approach from the Punjaub; while on the south and southwest were the roads along which armies or columns of armies might march from the two southern provinces of Madras and Bombay. Hence Sir Colin Campbell made earnest endeavours to maintain a good position at Cawnpore, as a convenient base of operations. Colonel Wilson, as commandant, was instructed to attend to the wants of Lucknow so far as he could, and to watch the movements of insurgent troops in the neighbourhood. This continued throughout October. In November, when Sir Colin went with his small army to relieve Lucknow, he left General Windham—well known in Crimean warfare as the 'hero of the Redan'—in command at Cawnpore, not to fight, but to keep communication safely open from Lucknow *viâ* Cawnpore to Allahabad. Sir Colin, it will be remembered,* hurried back to Cawnpore at the end of November on account of events that had occurred during his absence. What those events were, we have now to narrate.

The series of disasters that occurred to General Windham originated in part in the want of good communication between him and Sir Colin

* Chap. xxi., p. 362.

Campbell. Whether the messengers were stopped by the way, does not clearly appear; but Sir Colin remained in ignorance that the Gwalior mutineers were approaching Cawnpore; while Windham received no replies to letters sent by him, asking for instructions for his guidance. Sir Colin knew nothing of Windham's troubles until, on the 27th of November, he heard at the Alum Bagh the noise of artillery-firing at Cawnpore; while Windham received no aid or advice until Sir Colin himself appeared late on the following day. Whether or not there were defective tactics in the subsequent management of the affair, this uncertainty at the beginning was unquestionably disadvantageous. Windham knew, about the middle of the month, that the Gwalior and Indore mutineers, swelled to 20,000 strong by reinforcements of rebels from various quarters, had reached within about thirty miles of Cawnpore, on the Calpee road; and a week later he found that they were within twenty miles. As the troops at his command barely exceeded 2000 men, and as he received no news from Campbell, he considered how best to maintain his position. He was in an intrenchment or intrenched fort, far distant from the one formerly occupied by Sir Hugh Wheeler, and placed close to the Ganges, so as to command the bridge of boats; there being within the intrenchment the requisite buildings for the daily necessities of his force. As the city of Cawnpore lay between him and the Calpee road, he deemed it necessary to take up a new position. Leaving some of his troops, therefore, in the intrenchment, he formed with the remainder a new camp at Dhuboulee, close to the canal westward of the city, at a point where he believed he would be able to watch and frustrate the enemy.

On the 26th, finding that the mutineers were approaching, he went out to encounter them. He started at three in the morning with about 1200 infantry (chiefly of the 34th, 82d, 88th, and Rifles, 100 Sikh cavalry and eight guns), and marched eight or nine miles to Bhowsee, near the Pandoo Nuddee—leaving his camp-equipage and baggage near the city. Brigadier Carthew was second in command; and the chief officers under him were Colonels Walpole, Kelly, and Maxwell. The enemy were found strongly posted on the opposite side of the dry bed of the Pandoo Nuddee. The British advanced with a line of skirmishers along the whole front, with supports on each flank, and a reserve in the centre. The enemy opened a heavy fire of artillery from siege and field guns; but such was the eagerness of the British troops to engage, that they carried the position with a rush, cheering as they went; and a village, half a mile in the rear of the enemy, was rapidly cleared. The mutineers hastily took to flight, leaving behind them two howitzers and one gun. At this point, apparently for the first time, Windham became aware that he had been engaging the advanced column only of the enemy, and that the main force was near at hand. Rendered uneasy by his position, he resolved on retiring to protect the city, camp, cantonment, intrenchment, and bridge of boats. This he did.

So far, then, the operations of the 26th were to a certain extent successful. But disaster followed. He encamped for the night on the Jewee Plain, on the Calpee side of Cawnpore, having the city between him and the intrenchment. Whether Windham did not know that the enemy were so near in great force, whether his camping-ground was ill chosen, or whether he left his flanks unprotected, certain it is that, about noon on the 27th, when his men were preparing for a camp-dinner, they were surprised by an onslaught of the enemy in immense force, from behind a thick cover of trees and brushwood, beginning with an overwhelming artillery cannonade. For five hours did this attack continue, chiefly near the point of junction of the Delhi and Calpee roads. Distracted by an attack on three sides of him, Windham hastened to see what was doing on the fourth side, towards the city; and here he ascertained that the mutineers had turned his flanks, got into the city, and were beginning to attack the intrenchment near the bridge. Retreat was at once resolved on; and although the general's dispatch did not state the fact, the private letters shew that the retreat was *sauve qui peut*. For, in truth, it became a matter of speed, whether the British could rush back to the intrenchment in time to save it. They did so; but at the expense of a large store of tents, saddlery, harness, camp-equipage, and private property—all of which had to be abandoned in the hasty scamper from the camp to the intrenchment. This booty the enemy at once seized upon, and either appropriated or burned according to its degree of usefulness. No less than five hundred tents fed a bonfire that night—a loss quite irreparable at that time to the British.

Bitter was the mortification with which the troops contemplated this day's work. One of the officers said in a private letter: 'You will read the account of this day's fighting with astonishment; for it tells how English troops, with their trophies and their mottoes, and their far-famed bravery, were repulsed and lost their camp, their baggage, and their position, by [to?] the scouted and degraded natives of India.' The beaten 'Feringhees,' as the enemy had now a right to call them, did certainly retreat to their intrenchment amid overturned tents, pillaged baggage, men's kits, fleeing camels, elephants, horses, and servants. Another officer who had just come up from Allahabad, and who was within the intrenchment on the afternoon of this day, thus described the scene: 'Saw our troops retreating into the outer intrenchment. A regular panic followed. Trains of elephants, camels, horses, bullock-wagons, and coolies came in at the principal gate, laden with stuff. The principal buildings are the General Hospital, the Sailors' Hospital, the Post-office, and the Commissariat-cellars. Around these houses, which are scattered, crowds of camels, bullocks, and horses were collected, fastened by ropes to stakes in the ground, and among the animals, piles of trunks, beds, chairs, and miscellaneous furniture and baggage. There was scarcely room to move. Met one of the chaplains hastening into the intrenchment. He had left everything in his tent outside. The servants almost everywhere abandoned their masters when they heard the guns. Mounted officers were galloping across the rough ground between the inner and outer intrenchments, and doolie after doolie, with its red curtains down, concealing some poor victim, passed on to the hospitals. The poor fellows were brought in, shot, cut, shattered, and wounded in every imaginable way; and as they went by, raw stumps might be seen hanging over the sides of the doolies, literally like torn butcher-meat. The agonies which I saw some of them endure during the surgical operations were such as no tongue or pen can describe. The surgeons, who did their utmost, were so overworked, that many sufferers lay bleeding for hours before it was possible to attend to them.' During the hasty retreat, one of the guns had been overturned in a narrow street in Cawnpore. The British could not wait to bring it away; but at night General Windham ordered 100 men of the 64th to aid a few seamen of the naval brigade in an expedition to secure the gun. It was a delicate task, in a city crowded with the enemy; how it was done, one of the officers of the naval brigade has told.*

What was next to be done, became an important question. General Windham assembled his superior officers, and conferred with them. If he could have obtained reliable information concerning the position of the enemy's artillery, he would have proposed a night-attack; but, in ignorance on this important point, it was resolved to defer operations till the morrow. Early on the 28th, accordingly, the force was divided into four sections, thus distributed: One, under Walpole, was to defend the advanced portion of the town on the left side of the canal; a second, under Wilson, was to hold the intrenchment, and establish a strong picket on the extreme right; a third, under Carthew, was to hold the Bithoor road in advance of the intrenchment, receiving support from the picket there if needed; while the fourth section, under Windham himself, was to defend the portion of the town nearest the Ganges on the left of the canal, and support Walpole if needful. These several arrangements were especially intended to protect the intrenchment and the bridge of boats—so important in relation to Sir Colin Campbell's operations in Oude. The British position was to be wholly defensive. A severe struggle ensued. The Gwalior mutineers were now joined by another force under Nena Sahib, and a third under his brother Bhola Sahib; altogether the insurgents numbered 21,000. They marched unmolested towards the city and cantonment; and then were the few British sorely pressed indeed. Walpole was speedily engaged in very hard fighting; and it was on his side only that anything like a victory was achieved. Aided by Colonels Woodford and Watson, and Captain Greene, Walpole repulsed a vigorous attack made by the enemy, and captured two 18-pounder guns. Carthew, who struggled from morning till night against a most formidable body of the enemy, was at length obliged to retire from his position. Wilson, eager to render service at an exposed point, led his section of troops—chiefly consisting of H. M. 64th foot—against four guns planted by the enemy in front of Carthew's position. He and his gallant men advanced in the face of the enemy, and under a murderous fire, for more than half a mile, up a ravine commanded by high ground in front as well as on both sides. From the ridge in front, the four 9-pounders played upon them as they rushed forward. After reaching and almost capturing the guns, they were encountered by a very large force of the enemy who had hitherto been hidden; further progress was impossible; they retreated, and saw their officers falling around them in mournful number. Colonel Wilson himself was killed; as were also Major Stirling, Captain M'Crea, and Captain Morphey; while many other officers were wounded. It was a defeat and a loss, for which no counterbalancing advantage was gained.

Thus the 28th had increased the humiliation of the preceding day. Tents, baggage, officers, prestige—all had suffered. The mutineers revelled in the city as conquerors on the night of the 28th, seizing everything which had belonged to the British. More than 10,000 rounds of Enfield cartridges, the mess-plate of four Queen's regiments, paymasters' chests, and a large amount of miscellaneous property, fell into their hands. On the morning of the 29th the insurgents began to bombard the intrenchment and the bridge of boats. Had not Sir Colin Campbell arrived at that critical time, it is hard to say what might have been the amount of disaster; for the enemy were in immense strength; and if the bridge of boats had been broken, the fate of the refugees from Lucknow might have been sad indeed. All that day did the firing of the enemy continue. All that day did the living stream from Lucknow approach

* 'We marched off under the guidance of a native, who said he would take us to the spot where the gun lay. We told him he should be well rewarded if he brought us to the gun, but if he brought us into a trap, we had a soldier by him "at full cock" ready to blow his brains out. We passed our outside pickets, and entered the town through very narrow streets without a single nigger being seen, or a shot fired on either side. We crept along; not a soul spoke a word, all was still as death; and after marching in this way into the very heart of the town, our guide brought us to the very spot into which the gun was capsized. The soldiers were posted on each side, and then we went to work. Not a man spoke above his breath, and each stone was laid down quietly. When we thought we had cleared enough, I ordered the men to put their shoulders to the wheel and gun, and when all was ready, and every man had his pound before him, I said "Heave!" and up she righted. We then limbered up, called the soldiers to follow, and we marched into the intrenchments with our gun without a shot being fired. When we got in, the colonel returned us his best thanks, and gave us all an extra ration of grog; we then returned to our guns in the battery.'

the bridge. Sir Colin immediately assumed command at Cawnpore. Mortifying as it was to him to leave the enemy in possession of the city and everything west of it, he had no alternative. One holy duty pressed upon him—to protect the helpless Lucknow convoy until it could be sent on to Allahabad. He despatched Hope Grant with a column, to keep open the road from Cawnpore through Futtehpoor to Allahabad; while he employed all his other troops in keeping the enemy at bay. The officers in the intrenchment, looking over their earthworks, could see the six miles' train of women, children, sick, wounded, bearers, servants, camp-followers, horses, oxen, camels, elephants, wagons, carts, palanquins, doolies, advancing along the road to the bridge; and most narrowly were the movements of the enemy watched, to prevent any interruption to the passage of the cavalcade over the frail bridge.

This unfortunate series of events at Cawnpore greatly disconcerted Sir Colin Campbell. In his first dispatch to government relating to them, he referred almost without comment to Windham's own narrative. Three weeks afterwards a singularly worded dispatch was issued from his camp near Cawnpore, expressing a regret at an 'omission' in his former dispatch; and adding, 'I desire to make my acknowledgment of the great difficulties in which Major-general Windham, C.B., was placed during the operations he describes in his dispatch; and to recommend him and the officers whom he notices as having rendered him assistance to your lordship's protection and good offices.' Lord Canning shortly afterwards issued a general order, containing an echo of Sir Colin's dispatch. General Windham continued for a time with the commander-in-chief. If official dissatisfaction with his management at Cawnpore existed, it was either hushed up or smoothed away by subsequent explanations.

The month of December opened amid events that caused sufficient anxiety to Sir Colin Campbell. The convoy of Lucknow fugitives had not yet been sent away; the Gwalior mutineers had not yet been defeated. He was compelled to act on the defensive until his helpless non-combatants were provided for. During one week, from the 26th of November to the 2d of December, the loss in British officers had been very considerable in and near Cawnpore; for 10 were reported killed, 32 wounded, and 2 missing. The commander-in-chief, therefore, while repelling the still audacious insurgents, had to promote and establish numerous officers, as well as to reorganise his force.

It was a great relief to Sir Colin when the convoy left Cawnpore on its march towards Allahabad. He was then free to act as a military commander; and the enemy did not long delay in giving him an opportunity of proving his powers of command. On the 5th of December the enemy's artillery attacked his left pickets, while their infantry shewed on the same quarter; they also fired on the British pickets in the Generalgunje—an old bazaar extending along the canal in front of the line occupied by the camp. Brigadier Greathed had held this advanced position supported by Peel's and Bourchier's guns. Sir Colin resolved to take the offensive on the following day. The enemy occupied a strong position. Their centre was in the city of Cawnpore, and lined the houses and bazaars overhanging the canal and the barricaded streets; their right stretched away to a point beyond the crossing of the main trunk-road over the canal; while their left occupied the old cantonment, from which General Windham's post had been principally assailed. The canal, along which were placed the centre and the right, was thus the main feature of the enemy's position, and could only be passed by two bridges. The enemy's camp was two miles in rear of their right, on the Calpee road, which was intended to be their line of advance and retreat. Sir Colin well studied this position before he formed his plan. 'It appeared to me,' he said in his dispatch, 'that if the enemy's right were vigorously attacked, it would be driven from its position without assistance being able to come from other parts of the line: the wall of the town, which gave cover to our attacking columns on the right, being an effective obstacle to the movement of any portion of the enemy's troops from their left to their right.' In fact, his quick eye saw that the Gwalior mutineers had placed one-half their force in such a spot that it could not help the other half, provided the attack were made in a certain fashion. It was really a large and powerful army to which he was now confronted; so many other mutinous regiments had joined the Gwalior Contingent, that their force was now estimated at little short of 25,000 men, with about 40 pieces of artillery.

On the morning of the 6th, the commander-in-chief assigned to all his several corps and regiments their respective duties.* General Windham opened a heavy bombardment at nine o'clock, from the intrenchment in the old cantonment, to induce the enemy to believe that the attack would be in that quarter. For two hours, the rest of the force was quietly taking up its position—Greathed's column in front of the enemy's centre, and the other columns in rear of the old cavalry lines, effectually masked from observation. When it was judged that Windham's fire had drawn the enemy's attention away from the real point of attack, Sir Colin sent his cavalry and horse-artillery by a detour on the left, to cross the canal a mile and a half higher up, and assail the enemy's rear; while the infantry deployed in parallel lines

* The regiments or portions of regiments—made up into four brigades of infantry, one of cavalry, one of artillery, and one of engineers—were the following: H.M. 8th, 23d, 32d, 38th, 42d, 53d, 64th, 82d, and 93d foot; Rifle Brigade; 2d and 4th Punjaub infantry; H. M. 9th Lancers; 1st, 2d, and 5th Punjaub cavalry; Hodson's Horse; horse-artillery; light field-battery; heavy field-battery; Naval brigade; Queen's and Company's Engineers; Sappers and Miners.

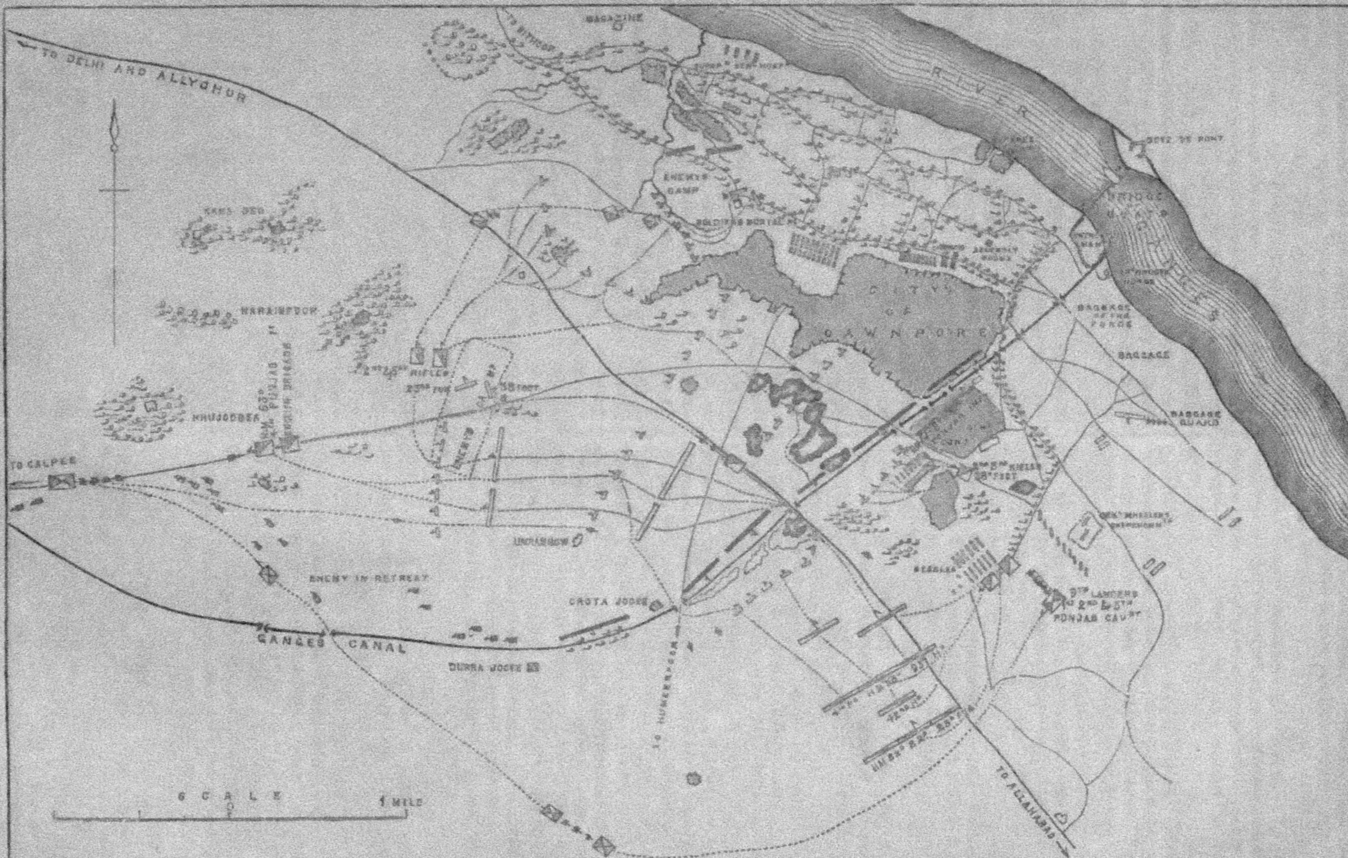

The Battle of Cawnpore, December 6, 1857.

fronting the canal. Captain Peel was the first man to cross the canal bridge for the attack on the enemy's camp; the heavy guns followed him; and in a few minutes the enemy were astonished at finding themselves in the heat of battle on a side not at all contemplated by them. Their defeat was equal to their surprise. Sir Colin's regiments crossed the canal by various bridges, reached the enemy's camp, cut their forces in two, and then completely routed them—pursuing them for fourteen miles on the Calpee road, and capturing guns and wagons as they went. In all this work the sailors of the naval brigade pushed forward with an energy which seems to have struck even the commander-in-chief, accustomed as he was to deeds of daring. In his official dispatch he said: 'I must here draw attention to the manner in which the heavy 24-pounder guns were impelled and managed by Captain Peel and his gallant sailors. Through the extraordinary energy and good-will with which the latter have worked, their guns have been constantly in advance throughout our late operations, from the relief of Lucknow till now—as if they were light field-pieces. The service rendered by them in clearing our front has been incalculable. On this occasion there was the sight beheld of 24-pounder guns advancing with the first line of skirmishers.' Before Sir Colin returned to camp in the evening, the enemy had been driven entirely and completely away from Cawnpore. The four infantry brigades engaged in this hot day's work were headed by Brigadiers Greathed, Adrian Hope, Walpole, and Inglis. Windham was only employed in masking the real nature of the attack. Sir Colin mentioned this matter in the following peculiar terms: 'Owing to his knowledge of the ground, I requested Major-general Windham to remain in command of the intrenchment, the fire of which was a very important feature in the operations of the 6th of December; although I felt and explained to General Windham that it was a command hardly worthy of his rank.'

There was a subsidiary operation in this battle of the 6th. After the capture of the enemy's camp, in the afternoon, General Mansfield was sent to occupy a position called the Subadar's Tank, in rear of the enemy's left, and about a mile and a half from the intrenchment. Having taken measures for the safeguard of the captured camp, and for maintaining a good post on the Calpee road, Mansfield advanced towards the Tank—struggling over broken ground and through enclosures, and driving parties of the enemy before him. After a good deal of manœuvring, in ground that greatly assisted the rebels, Mansfield succeeded in securing the position sought, and had the satisfaction of seeing large bodies of the enemy's infantry and cavalry move off westward in full retreat. As it was not practicable to communicate with Sir Colin after sunset, the position taken up being almost isolated; and as there were considerable numbers of the enemy still in occupation of the town and the old cantonment—Mansfield strengthened the pickets all round his position, and bivouacked his troops for the night, where they were left undisturbed by the enemy.

The mutineers were so thoroughly worsted in these operations on the 6th, that they retired from Cawnpore, irresolute touching their future plans—some marching in one direction, some in another. After securing and consolidating his position on the 7th, Sir Colin prepared further work for his lieutenants. On the 8th, he gave orders to Brigadier Hope Grant to march to Bithoor, and, if it should appear to him desirable, to advance further to Serai Ghat, a ferry over the Ganges about twenty-five miles above Cawnpore. This energetic officer set off with a strong column of 2800 men* and 11 guns, and marched through Bithoor to Soorajpore, three miles short of Serai Ghat. Here he bivouacked for the night. Early in the morning of the 9th, leaving a portion of his column to guard the baggage, he advanced with the main body, and found the enemy assembling on the bank of the river. The opposing forces soon got engaged in an artillery action, in which Grant's guns narrowly escaped being lost in a quicksand at the river-side. After a sharp firing for half an hour, the enemy's guns were silenced and then withdrawn. Then came up a force of the rebels' cavalry, to endeavour to capture Grant's guns; but he promptly sent forward his own cavalry, which advanced upon them, drove them away, pursued them, and cut up a considerable number. The nature of the ground, however, was such that most of the enemy reached the cover of trees and houses before the British could intercept them. Hope Grant's infantry was not engaged in this conflict; the retreat of the enemy taking place before their aid was needed. The enemy left behind them fourteen brass guns and howitzers, one iron 18-pounder, together with a large store of wagons and ammunition—all of which were speedily secured by the conquerors. These trophies were brought away by the exertions of the infantry, who had much difficulty to contend against along the quicksands. The troops had been marching and fighting for thirty hours, with few and short intervals, and had scarcely eaten for twenty-four hours; so that a supper, a night's rest, and a quiet day on the 10th, were very welcome to them. This affair at Serai Ghat completely succeeded; but the most extraordinary fact relating to it has yet to be mentioned. Hope Grant's casualty-list *was a blank!* In his dispatch he said: 'I am truly grateful to God, and happy to say, that though the fire of grape from the enemy was most

* 42d Highlanders,	403
53d foot,	413
93d Highlanders,	806
4th Punjaub rifles,	332
9th Lancers,	327
6th Punjaub cavalry,	85
Hodson's Horse,	109
Horse-artillery,	83
Foot-artillery,	139
Sappers,	100

severe and well placed, falling among the artillery like hail, I had not a single man even wounded, and only one horse of Captain Middleton's battery killed. It was truly marvellous and providential. Thirteen guns, most of them 9-pounders and 24-pounder howitzers, were playing with grape on the gallant artillery, and with round-shot upon the cavalry, the former within about five hundred yards—and his excellency is well aware with what precision these rebels fire their guns—yet not one single man was wounded.' It requires all one's faith in the honour of a truthful man to credit such a marvellous announcement.

In the various operations from the 3d to the 8th of December inclusive, Sir Colin suffered a loss of 13 killed and 86 wounded—a mere trifle compared with the strength of his force and the kind of enemy with whom he had to deal. Among the killed were Lieutenants Salmond and Vincent; and among the wounded, General Mansfield, Lieutenant-colonel Horsford, Captains Longden, Forbes, and Mansfield, Lieutenants Neill and Stirling, Ensigns Wrench, Graham, and Dyce. Lieutenant Stirling afterwards died from the effects of a wound which was at first reputed curable.

The occurrences narrated in the last few pages will have shewn by what steps Sir Colin Campbell obtained a firm footing at Cawnpore, as a centre from which he and his officers might operate in various directions. He had removed the British from Lucknow; he had furnished to Outram such a force as would enable that general to hold the Alum Bagh against all assailants; and he had dispersed the formidable rebel army which so endangered Windham and the British interests at Cawnpore. In the latter half of December he prepared to start off, with one portion of his force, towards Furruckabad; while Walpole was to proceed to Etawah, and Hope Grant to Futtehpoor; leaving Seaton to operate near Minpooree, Franks near Benares, and other brigadiers and colonels in various directions as rapidly as small columns could be brought together. The object appeared to be, to attack and disperse the enemy in various parts of the Northwest Provinces, and either permit or compel them to retreat into Oude—where a great effort, made early in the ensuing year, might possibly crush the rebellion altogether. So much of these operations as took place in December may briefly be noticed here, before proceeding to the affairs of Central India.

The whole region around Benares, Mirzapore, Allahabad, Goruckpore, and Jounpoor was thrown into occasional uneasiness—not so much by rebellious manifestations at those places, as by temptations thrown out by the Oudians. Mahomed Hussein was still powerful as a leader near the Oudian frontier; and he left no means untried to rally numerous insurgents around his standard. As the British could spare very few troops for service in this quarter, Mahomed Hussein remained throughout the most of the year master in and near Goruckpore. Even if the British were enabled to defeat him occasionally, they had no cavalry wherewith to organise a pursuit, and he speedily returned to his old quarters. Thus, towards the close of December, Colonel Rowcroft, with a mixed body of English sailors, Sikh police, and Goorkha irregulars, defeated this chieftain near Mujhowlee; but, unable to pursue him without cavalry, the victory was of little effect. Jung Bahadoor, as we have seen in a former chapter, sent a strong body of Goorkhas several weeks earlier to aid in the pacification of this part of India; and the gallant little Nepaulese warriors enabled the few English officers to effect that which would have been impracticable without such assistance. Jung Bahadoor himself, in conformity with an engagement made with Viscount Canning, prepared to join in the scene in person. He descended with 9000 picked men from his mountains in December, to attack the Oudian rebels near Goruckpore and Azimghur, and drive them back to their own country. It was just at the close of the year that he began to encounter the enemy, and to obtain successes which left Franks, Rowcroft, Longden, and other officers, free to engage in such operations as Sir Colin Campbell might plan for them at the opening of the new year.

Allahabad and Mirzapore, though often threatened, remained safely in British hands. In the Rewah district, southwest of those cities, the rajah still continued faithful, and Captain Osborne still carried on those energetic operations by which he had so long and so wonderfully maintained his post in a territory where he was almost the sole Englishman, and where many of the rajah's troops were burning with impatience to join the insurgents elsewhere. Osborne was incessantly on the watch, and almost incessantly in motion, to keep open the important line of route between Mirzapore through Rewah to Jubbulpoor—part of the available postal route between Calcutta and Bombay. There was a nest of rebels at Mylhere that gave him much trouble; but, aided by the faithful portion of the rajah's troops, he defeated them at Kunchynpore and Zorah; and finally, on the 28th of December, stormed and captured Mylhere itself.

In Oude, as the last chapter sufficiently shewed, British power was represented simply and solely by Sir James Outram and his companions in the Alum Bagh and at the Bridge of Bunnee. Lucknow was quite in the hands of the enemy, as were all the provincial districts of Oude. Sir James maintained his post steadily; not strong enough to make conquests, but holding the key to a position that might become all-important as soon as the commander-in-chief should resume operations in that quarter. So well did he keep watch and guard, that the movements of any insurgent troops in his vicinity became speedily known to him. On the 22d of December, the rebels made a clever attempt to obtain possession of the road to Cawnpore. They posted 1200 men inside a jungle, with a sandy plain in front and a road close at hand.

Sir James, detecting the intended plan, silently moved out two regiments in the dead of the night. The soft sand deadened all sound; and dawn found them within the enemy's pickets. A rattling volley and a cheer startled the enemy, who, after one discharge of their muskets, fled, leaving a hundred of their number dead on the field, besides four guns and several ammunition-wagons. One good result of this victory was, to induce some of the villagers to bring supplies for sale to the camp.

In Rohilcund, nothing could at present be effected to wrest the province from the enemy, until the Doab had been cleared from the host of rebels and marauders who infested it.

The proceedings of certain columns in the Doab, both before and after Sir Colin's victory at Cawnpore, must here be noticed.

Colonel Seaton, during the month of November, was placed in command of a column—consisting of one wing of the 1st Bengal Europeans, the 7th Punjaub infantry, a squadron of Carabiniers, Hodson's Horse, a troop of horse-artillery, and two companies of Sappers and Miners. Seaton started from Delhi, and worked his way southeastward, between the Jumna and the Ganges, clearing off small portions of the enemy as he went. After picking up at Allygurh a small force from the Agra garrison under Major Eld, he started again on the 13th of December, towards Etawah and Minpooree. The self-styled Rajah of Minpooree, who had fled at the approach of Greathed's column in October, afterwards returned to his old haunts, and expelled the officials established there by Greathed. His palace had been blown up, and his treasury and jewel-house looted; yet he possessed influence enough to collect a band of retainers in his service. To punish this rebel was one of the duties intrusted to Colonel Seaton. On the 14th, he fell in with a body of the insurgents, 4000 strong, at Gunjeree, on a small stream called the Neem Nuddee. His column suddenly surprised them, disordered them by a brilliant charge of Carabiniers, and drove them in confusion along the Futteghur road—capturing several guns on the way. Hodson's Horse cut down many of them during a brief pursuit. On the 15th, the column marched to Khasgunj, and on the 16th to Sahawur—in each case only to learn that the enemy had just fled. Seaton, determined not to give them up readily, marched on to Putialah, several miles further on the Furruckabad road, where he came up with them on the morning of the 17th. They were drawn up in a good position, with their centre and left posted behind ravines, and their right abutting on a tope of trees in front of the village. After having caused this position to be well reconnoitred by Captain Hodson and Lieutenant Greathed, Colonel Seaton began the contest with a sharp fire of light artillery, to which the enemy promptly responded. He then ordered the cavalry round to the right, to avoid the ravines, and to attack the enemy in flank. While this was being done, the infantry, deploying into line, advanced boldly on the enemy's right, charged with the bayonet, and speedily drove them out of the tope and village. The rout was complete, the cavalry having got round beyond the ravines, and reached a point whence they could pursue the fleeing enemy. Thirteen guns, camp-equipage, baggage, ammunition, and stores fell into the hands of the conquerors; while no less than 600 of the enemy were computed to have fallen in the field or during the pursuit. Leaving Furruckabad and its chieftain to be dealt with by Sir Colin Campbell, Colonel Seaton moved on towards Minpooree. He found the enemy awaiting him, posted a mile west of the city, with their front screened by large trees, under cover of which their guns opened upon the column as it came up. Seaton, by a flank-movement, disconcerted them, and they commenced a retreat, which resulted in the loss of six guns and a large number of men. The colonel at once took possession of Minpooree.

Brigadier Showers, another officer to whom the management of a column was intrusted, started, like Seaton, from Delhi, and, like him, sought to regain towns and districts which had long been a prey to misrule. This column began its operations in October, and during the following month returned to Delhi, after having retaken Nunoond, Dadree, and other places southwest of the city, together with many lacs of rupees which the rebels had looted from the several treasuries of the Company. Between Delhi and the Sutlej, General Van Cortlandt maintained tranquillity by the aid of a small force. Colonel Gerrard was the commander of another small column; consisting of one European regiment and a miscellaneous body of native troops. With this he marched to Rewaree, and thence to the town of Narnoul in Jhujjur, where a rebel chief, Sunnand Khan, had taken post with a number of armed retainers. Gerrard defeated them, and captured their stronghold, but his own gallant life was forfeited. Another small force, divided into detachments according to the services required, took charge of the triangular space of country included between Agra, Muttra, and Allygurh. Colonel Riddell and Major Eld moved about actively within this space —now watching the movements of rebellious chieftains, now cutting off the advance of mutineers from Rohilcund.

Colonel Walpole of the Rifle Brigade, in the higher capacity of brigadier, was intrusted by Sir Colin Campbell with the command of a column, consisting of H.M. 88th foot, two battalions of the Rifle Brigade, three squadrons of the 9th Lancers, the 1st Punjaub cavalry, Bourchier's battery, and Blunt's troop of horse-artillery. His duty was to sweep along the western half of the Doab, near the Jumna, and clear it of rebels. He started from Cawnpore on the 18th of December, and on the following day reached Akburpore, half-way to Calpee. Here he remained a few days, settling the surrounding country, which had long been disturbed by the Gwalior mutineers. From thence he proceeded towards Etawah, to clear the country in the direction of Agra and Dholpore.

It will thus be seen that, while Sir Colin was engaged in the larger operations at Lucknow and Cawnpore, and soon after the completion of those operations, small columns of troops were marching and fighting in various parts of the Northwest Provinces, clearing away bands of insurgents. The mutinied sepoy regiments still kept together in large bodies, mostly in Oude or on its borders; the insurgents here adverted to were rather marauders and plunderers, who were influenced very little either by creed or by nationality in taking up arms; they were retainers of ambitious petty chieftains, or they were reckless men, who hoped in the scramble to enrich themselves with plunder.

The commander-in-chief himself took the field just before the close of the year. Having made arrangements for the security of Cawnpore after the great victory over the Gwalior mutineers, and having marked out separate paths of duty to be followed by Seaton, Walpole, Hope Grant, Franks, Rowcroft, and other officers, he directed his attention towards Furruckabad, which had long been in hostile hands. This city, near the point of junction of Oude, Rohilcund, and the Doab, it was important to place again under British control. Colonel Seaton was ordered to direct his march towards that point, after other operations in the Doab; and Sir Colin now arranged to co-operate with him. Leaving Cawnpore in the last week of December, he marched up the great trunk-road, by way of Meerun-ke-Serai. It was not, however, until the year 1858 had arrived, that Campbell, Walpole, and Seaton, meeting from various points, effected a thorough capture of Furruckabad, and of the long deserted cantonment at Futteghur. Here, however, as in many other quarters, the commander-in-chief had to bear the vexation of losing his prey; the enemy, wonderfully alert in their movements, escaped from those places just before he reached them; he captured both the towns, but the enemy were still at large to fight elsewhere.

Let us on to Delhi.

Ever since the conquest in September, the imperial city had gradually assumed a state somewhat more orderly than was possible immediately after the siege. Many weeks after the conquest, when the *Delhi Gazette* had again got into working-order, it contained a graphic account of the city in its condition at that time. On the road from Kurnaul to Delhi was an almost continuous line of dead carcasses of camels, horses, and bullocks, with their skins dried into parchment over the mouldering bones. Here and there were remains of intrenchments, where battles had been fought on the road. From Badulla Serai to the Lahore Gate of the city every tree was either levelled with the ground, or the branches lopped off with round-shot. The garden-houses of the wealthy citizens were in almost every instance masses of ruins, with the bleaching remains of men and beasts around them. Here and there might be seen a perfectly white skeleton of a human being; while on all sides lay scattered fragments of red and blue clothing, cartouch-boxes, round-shot, fragments of shell, and grape-shot. Near the Subzee Mundee every tree was a mere bare trunk, with the branches and foliage gone, and shot-marks visible all around. The gaily ornamented residences near at hand were masses of blackened ruins, with sand-bags and loopholed screens which told of many a scene of fiery warfare. With the exception of the Moree Bastion and the Cashmere Gate, the northern wall of the city did not exhibit much evidence of devastation. The Cashmere Gate breach had been repaired. The main-guard was wholly destroyed. St James's Church was full of shot-holes, even up to the ball and cross. Most of the houses in this part of the city were utter ruins, some blackened as if by fire. The Bank, formerly the residence of the Begum Sumroo, had nothing but the walls and fragments of verandah remaining; and in a like state was the house of Sir T. Metcalfe. In the narrow street leading from Skinner's house to the Chandnee Chowk, every house bore visible proof of the showers of musket-balls that must have fallen; and every door was completely riddled. The roads were still cut up with shot and shell furrows. In many of the streets might be seen the *débris* of archways, which had been built up by the city people, but broken into by our troops. Shop-doors and huge gates lay about in all directions, many of which were well backed up by heavy stone-work, logs of wood, &c.; and remains of sand-bag defences were numerous. In short, the city showed that it had been obstinately defended, and that its conquest must have been terrible work for besiegers as well as besieged.

The aged king and his family still continued to be the subjects of newspaper gossip, mostly in a strain of fierce invective against the authorities for shewing lenity. It was stated in a former chapter,* that Mrs Hodson, wife to the gallant officer who had captured the king, made public the result of a visit to the royal captives, as shewing that no undue luxury marked their prison-life. But still the charges and insinuations continued. Newspaper paragraphs circulated the news that Jumma Bukht, son or grandson of the king, was allowed to ride about the streets of Delhi on an elephant, with an English colonel behind him; and that indulgence was granted to men whose only desert was speedy hanging. Captain (Major) Hodson himself made public a refutation of this charge, shewing the absurd way in which a very trifling incident had been magnified into a state proceeding. A military commission was appointed to try such leaders of the mutiny as were captured in or near Delhi. By sentence of

* P. 336.

this tribunal, twenty subordinate members of the royal family were executed on the 18th of November. Shortly afterwards, various chiefs of Goorgaon, Jhujjur, and Babulgurh were similarly put upon their trial, and sentenced according to the strength of the evidence brought against them.

The subject of prize-money remained for many weeks, or even months, involved in much controversy in Delhi. Notwithstanding the ruin and devastation, the amount of property recovered was very large, including forfeitures declared against those who were convicted of treason. This wealth reverted to the state, as a slight set-off for the vast expenses incurred. Some of the officers and soldiers, however, fondly hoped that it would be regarded as booty for the troops; and were thrown rather into discontent by an announcement that the reward of the conquerors of Delhi was to consist of six months' 'batta' or pay. It was just one of those questions on which much might be said on both sides. By a subsequent arrangement, much of the personal property lately belonging to the rebels was set apart, and treated as prize-money to be shared by the soldiers engaged in the capture.

St James's Church, Delhi.

The leniency question, the prize-money question, and the paucity of reward to the engineer officers engaged in the siege of Delhi, were among many subjects made matter for controversy during the later weeks of the year. But these we may pass over without further comment. Suffice it to say that the re-conquered city remained in British hands, and was gradually brought under the control of the British authorities. As to the aged king, preparations were made for subjecting him to a regular trial, to be commenced shortly after the arrival of the new year.

Of the Punjaub, little need be said. Happily for British interests in India, the same powerful mind continued to wield the destinies of the remote province. Sir John Lawrence, watchful over everything that occurred, not only maintained the Punjaub in quiet, but sent frequent reinforcements to other provinces. During the summer and autumn, the number of Sikh and Punjaubee regiments which he raised was something marvellous. Occasionally some of the wild tribes exhibited signs of insubordination; but they were met with such a determined front, and they received so little sympathy from the mass of the people, that their turbulence fell harmless. John Lawrence saved the Punjaub, and the Punjaub saved British India.

In all the portion of the empire included within the Saugor territories, Bundelcund, the Mahratta states, and Rajpootana, the months of November and December differed from the previous months principally in this circumstance—that the new mutinies were fewer, because the materials for mutiny were becoming exhausted; but that the battles were more numerous, because small armies were gradually being sent up from Madras and Bombay.

In October and November, many military operations in the Mahratta and Saugor countries were placed in doubt, so far as concerned the comprehension of them in England, by a difference of only one letter in the names of two commanders. The movements of Brigadier Steuart were often attributed to Brigadier Stuart, and *vice versâ*. Steuart commanded a column in the Deccan, which marched to Hosungabad, and then across the Nerbudda to Sehore. His duty was to protect Saugor on the right, Indore on the left, and Bhopal in the centre. By these movements, Saugor and Jubbulpoor were rendered tolerably safe. Holkar, at Indore, was sadly troubled by the mutinous feeling among his own troops. In order to maintain British influence in that important quarter, the Bombay government organised a new column, which, strengthened by other troops, would form a Malwah Field Force, to be placed under the command of Sir Hugh Rose; while Sir Robert Hamilton was ordered to resume his old appointment as British resident at Holkar's court.

Brigadier Stuart, portions of whose column were engaged in and near Neemuch, Mundisore, Dhar, Mehidpore, Rampoora, and Kotah in October, swept off many parties of rebels from the regions bordering on Malwah and Rajpootana. Nevertheless the state of affairs remained very unsettled. Many petty chieftains, incited by the numerical weakness of the British, and by the unexpected stand made by rebels elsewhere, appeared by tacit agreement to consider this the proper time to set up as little kings on their own account, each relying on the services of retainers who probably thought that something good might come to their share in the scramble.

At a somewhat later date, when Stuart was in command of the Malwah Field Force, before its name was changed to the 'First Brigade of the Nerbudda Field Force,' he had a contest with the Mundisore rebels. Being joined by a portion of the Hyderabad Contingent under Major Orr, Stuart approached within three or four miles of Mundisore on the 21st of November. This town is a few miles south of Neemuch, on the road to Indore. The brigadier encamped until a good reconnaissance could be effected. The rebel enemy at Mundisore, hearing of his approach, had posted pickets entirely covering the country over which he was advancing; they also mustered in some force outside the walls, and appeared inclined to attack. In the afternoon he found that the enemy were advancing in form, threatening his centre and both flanks at the same time. They advanced steadily, in great numbers and with banners flying: and he went forth to meet them. The struggle was a brief one. Major Orr easily repulsed the enemy's attack on the left flank; Captain Orr and Lieutenant Dew checked that on the right; a few rounds of artillery preserved the centre; and the enemy, giving way at all points, retreated into the town. Brigadier Stuart had now another matter to consider. He heard that a rebel army of 5000 men, employed in besieging Neemuch, intended to raise the siege, and to join their companions at Mundisore. This he resolved to prevent if possible by intercepting them. Accordingly, early on the 22d, he marched to such a position as would command the approaches to Mundisore; and later in the day his cavalry were engaged with a party of rebel horse under Heera Singh—one of many Rajpoot chieftains who took up arms at that disturbed period. Keeping a sharp watch during the night, Stuart prepared on the morning of the 23d to control the Neemuch and Mundisore road both from the north and the south. The enemy appeared, and took up a strong position with their right in and beyond the village of Goraria, their right centre covered by a date nullah and lines of date-trees, their battery of six guns on rising ground, with a large mud-hut protecting their gunners, and their left stretched along the ridge running east from the village. The battle that ensued was a very severe one. Stuart was obliged to recall a body of infantry, who charged a village that seemed full of the enemy; the rebels took possession of the houses, from which they kept up a very galling fire. The British could doubtless have taken the village; but the brigadier found his rear attacked by a second body of the enemy, requiring a new distribution of his troops. The engagements of this day resulted in a sort of drawn battle. On the 24th, the village was shelled for three hours; and was then captured by H.M. 86th and a native regiment, with considerable loss on both sides. During the ensuing night the enemy evacuated Mundisore and the whole vicinity, dispersing in flight throughout the country, after having lost at least fifteen hundred men during the four days. The brigadier then moved his camp to Mundisore, and made arrangements for dismantling the fort and destroying the guns before leaving the neighbourhood. By this series of operations, not only was Mundisore cleared of rebels, but Neemuch was relieved from a force which pressed very threateningly upon it.

The siege of Neemuch must now be noticed. The small English garrison at this station had for months been threatened by the Mundisore rebels; but it was not until the 8th of November that a formidable attack was actually made. A force of 5000 infantry, with three guns, advanced to within two miles of the town; and as it was impossible to meet such numbers in the open field, Captain Simpson prepared for the best defence he could make within the fort. Intrenchments had been formed some time before; but unfortunately they were too extensive to be effectively defended by the few hands in the garrison; and they thus speedily became occupied by the enemy. On the 9th, the enemy marched in full force into the bazaar and cantonment, plundering wherever they went. They then placed their guns at convenient distances, and began playing steadily against the fort. This cannonading was continued for several days. The rebels managed to build batteries for their guns in such positions that, from the foliage and other obstacles, they were unobservable from the walls of the fort. After about a fortnight of this battering, the rebels resolved to attempt an escalade. They brought forward huge ladders on wheels, affording room for four men abreast, and placed them against the walls of the fort; but here they were met by such steady and continuous volleys of musketry that not a man could enter. A Beloochee Mohammedan, belonging to the 12th Bombay native infantry, doing duty in Neemuch, performed an act of gallantry that won for him much and well-deserved applause. One of the besiegers, in retreating from the withering musketry-fire from the fort, dropped a splendid Mussulman green flag on the ground. The Beloochee at once offered to capture this flag. Under cover of a tremendous fire of musketry, he and a havildar were lowered by a rope from one of the enclosures; quick as lightning the flag was secured, and in a few minutes waved on the walls of Neemuch. The movements of Brigadier Stuart, recorded in the last paragraph, now disturbed the rebels; they departed, and Neemuch was for a time spared further molestation.

This narrative may pass over without particular mention the other regions of the vast empire of India. Disturbances there were in November and December, but not of such grave importance as to call for record. At Saugor and at Jubbulpore, the Europeans cried loudly for more troops, but they were still able to defend themselves against actual attacks. At Gwalior and at Bhopal, at Indore and at Mhow, although the vexations were many, the continued fidelity of Scindia and Holkar lessened the calamities that might otherwise have befallen the British. In Rajpootana and Gujerat, petty chieftains would from time to time unfurl the flag of rebellion, and collect a band of fighting retainers around them; but these territories were within practicable reach of Bombay, whence columns marched for the pacification of the upper country. Some portions of the Nizam's territory were occasionally troubled by insubordinate troops belonging to the contingent; as the Nizam and his prime-minister, however, remained firm in their alliance with the British, and as the distance was very great to the turbulent regions of the Jumna, serious danger was averted. In the South Mahratta country, around Kolapore, Sholapore, Satara, and Poonah, indications once now and then appeared that fanatic Mohammedans were ready to unfurl the green flag against the infidel Feringhees; but the near vicinity of the presidential city of Bombay, and the quiet demeanour of the natives further south, prevented the intended conspiracies from becoming serious in magnitude. In the Madras presidency, tranquillity was almost wholly undisturbed.

Thus ended the extraordinary year 1857—the most momentous that the English had ever experienced in India.

Notes.

Proposed Re-organisation of the Indian Army.—In closing the narrative for the year 1857, it may be useful to advert to two important subjects which occupied the attention of the East India Company—the state of the army, and the causes of the mutiny. Instead of rushing to conclusions on imperfect data, the Court of Directors instructed the governor-general to appoint two commissions of inquiry, empowered to collect information on those two subjects. The letters of instruction were both dated the 25th of November; the first ran as follows:

'1. We trust that when success, by the blessing of Divine Providence, shall have attended your efforts to put down the mutiny of the native army of your presidency, and to re-establish the authority of the government in the disturbed districts, you will be enabled to take advantage of the services of select officers of ability and experience, to assist you, by investigation and by practical counsel founded thereon, in forming wise conclusions on the most important subject which must soon press for decision—namely, the proper organisation of our army in India.

'2. To this end we authorise you to appoint, as soon as circumstances will permit, a commission, composed of military officers of the armies of the three presidencies (with whom should be associated officers of the Queen's army who have had experience of Indian service), on whose knowledge, experience, and judgment you can rely; together with one or more civil servants, whom you may consider to be specially qualified for such a duty by their knowledge of the native character and general administrative experience.

'3. In framing instructions for the guidance of this commission, we are desirous that the following heads of inquiry should be specified, in addition to any others which you may consider to deserve their attention:

'1st, Should corps be raised each in a prescribed district, and be recruited there, and there only?

'2d, Should corps be composed of troops or companies, each of which shall consist of separate tribes or castes; or should the tribes or castes be mixed up together in the whole regiment?

'3d, Should a company or companies of Europeans form a component part of a native regiment?

'4th, What alterations should be made in your recruiting regulations relating to tribes and castes, with a view to determine the future composition of the native army?

'5th, Will it be expedient to enlist natives of other tropical countries, equally qualified for service in India, with the natives of the country; and if so, should they be formed in separate regiments, or in companies, or otherwise?

'6th, Whether, in native infantry regiments, the discontinuance of the grades of native commissioned officers, and the substitution of a European sergeant and corporal to each company, is advisable; and if so, whether, in lieu of the prospect of distinction and emolument arising out of these grades, it would be advisable to establish graduated scales of good-service pay and retiring pensions, claimable after specified periods of service?

'7th, Whether the system of promotion generally, by seniority, to the grades of native commissioned officers (if these are retained), should not be altered and assimilated to the systems in force at Madras and Bombay?

'8th, If separate corps are to be maintained for military and police purposes, what will be the best organisation for each branch respectively?

'9th, Have the powers of commanding officers of native corps, and the powers of officers in charge of companies, been diminished? What consequences have been the result? Is it desirable that those powers should be increased, or what other measures should be adopted for the improvement of discipline?

'10th, Should cadets be trained and drilled in European regiments before they are posted to native regiments; or what would be the best mode of drilling and training cadets before they are posted to native regiments?

'11th, Should the special rules regulating punishment in the native army be retained; or should they be assimilated to the rules which obtain in the British army; or ought there to be any, and what, changes in those rules, or in the system of punishment?

'12th, How can the demands for European officers for staff and detached employments be best provided for, without injuring the efficiency of regiments?

'4. It is to be understood that the inquiries to be made by the commission, and the opinions to be offered by them, are to have reference to the several branches of the native army—infantry, regular and irregular; cavalry, regular and irregular; artillery, and Sappers and Miners; and, with respect to the artillery, and Sappers and Miners, whether they should be composed, as heretofore, of Europeans and natives, or be entirely European?

'5. To aid your government in forming an opinion as to the proportion which the European should bear to the native portion of the army in India generally, and at each presidency separately, we would recommend that your government should call upon the commission to give their opinions on this very important question; and we can entertain no doubt that the enlarged knowledge and experience of the members of the commission will enable them to furnish you with valuable information on this head.

'6. Having obtained opinions on all these heads of inquiry, and on such other heads as you may deem to be essential to the thorough development of the important questions at issue, you will refer the views of the commission for the consideration of the commander-in-chief, and will then furnish us with the results of your careful deliberation upon the whole of the measures which should, in your judgment, be taken for the organisation and maintenance, in the utmost practicable state of efficiency, of whatever military force you may think it desirable to form.

'7. The commission itself may be instructed to make to the governor-general in council any suggestions or recommendations which occur to them, although not on matters comprised in the specified heads of inquiry.'

Proposed Inquiry into the Causes of the Mutiny.—The second letter adverted to above was in the following terms:

'1. Although we are well aware that, from the period when the mutiny of the Bengal army assumed a formidable aspect, your time must necessarily have been too much engrossed by the pressing exigencies of the public service during each passing day, and in taking provident measures for the future, to admit of your directing much of your attention to past events, we have no doubt that you have not omitted to take advantage of all the means and opportunities at your command for the important purpose of investigating the causes of the extraordinary disaffection in the ranks of that army, which has, unhappily, given rise to so much bloodshed and misery.

'2. In this persuasion, and as a review of the voluminous records containing the details of the events which have occurred since the first display of disaffection at Barrackpore, has entirely failed to satisfy our minds in regard to the immediate causes of the mutiny, we desire that you will lose no time in reporting to us your opinions on the subject, embracing the following heads, together with any others which you may deem it necessary to add, in order to the full elucidation of the subject:

'1st, The state of feeling of the sepoy towards the government for some time preceding the outbreak.

'2d, Any causes which of late years may be thought likely to have affected their loyalty and devotion to the service.

'3d, Whether their loyalty had been affected by the instigations of emissaries of foreign powers, or native states, or by any general measures of our administration affecting themselves or any other classes of our subjects?

'4th, Whether the proposed use of the new cartridges was to any, and what, extent the cause of the outbreak?

'5th, Whether the objects which the mutineers are supposed to have had in view were directed to the subversion of the British power in India, or to the attainment of pecuniary or other advantages?

'6th, Whether the progress of the mutiny can be traced to general combination or concert, or was the result of separate impulses at the several stations of regiments; and, if the former, how the combination was carried on without any knowledge or suspicion of it on the part of the regimental officers?

'3. If, however, you should not feel yourselves to be in possession of information sufficient to form a well-grounded opinion upon the causes and objects of the mutiny, we authorise you to appoint a special mixed commission for a preliminary investigation into the same, to be composed of officers selected from all branches of the services of India, in whose personal experience and soundness of judgment you have entire confidence. In that case, you will lose no time in reporting to us your sentiments upon the conclusions arrived at by the commission.'

Colonel E. H. Greathed.

CHAPTER XXIII.

A SECOND YEAR OF REBELLION.

When, at the opening of 1858, the stirring events of the preceding year came to be passed in review, most men admitted that the progress of the Indian Revolt had outrun their expectations and falsified their hopes. Some had believed that the fall of Delhi would occur after a few days of besieging, bringing with it a pacification of the whole country. Some, allowing that this capture might very probably be retarded several weeks, did not the less look to a general pacification as a natural result. Others, relying on the heroic Havelock and the energetic Neill, prepared to date the termination of the rebellion from the expected capture of Lucknow. Others, recognising Sir Colin Campbell as 'the right man in the right place,' strengthened themselves in the belief that he would march at once from Calcutta to Cawnpore, and put down all the rebels before the summer was well over. Some believed that the sepoys, lamenting the ill success of their treachery to the British government, would return to their allegiance without inoculating other portions of the Indian community with the virus of lawlessness. Others had fondly hoped that, under the pressure of public opinion in England, such large numbers of fine troops would have been sent over in the summer and autumn, as would suffice to quell the mutiny even though the sepoys remained obstinate.

All these hopes were dashed. The gloomy prophets, on this occasion, were in the ascendant. The mutiny had spread to almost every native regiment in the Bengal army. It had been accompanied by an unexpected display of military organisation among the revolted sepoys. It had incited many ambitious chieftains to try their chance for an increase of power. It had been encouraged and extended by the long delay in the conquest of Delhi. It had further received a certain glow of triumph from the extraordinary events at Lucknow, which left the rebels perfect masters of the city at the end of the year. It had been permitted to grow to unwonted magnitude by the extreme slowness with which British troops arrived at Indian ports. Lastly, it had become surrounded by very un-English attributes, in the savage feeling of vengeance engendered in the minds of English officers and soldiers by the sepoy atrocities.

It is true that Englishmen had much to be proud of, in the achievements of their countrymen during the past year. They could point to the sagacity of Sir Henry Lawrence, in quietly fortifying and provisioning the Residency at Lucknow at a time when less acute observers saw no storm in the distance. They could admire, and wonder while they admired, the heroism with which Sir Hugh Wheeler and his companions had so long maintained a wretchedly weak position against a large army of mutineers headed by an arch-traitor. They could follow with delight the footsteps of Sir Henry Havelock, winning victory after victory over forces five or ten times as strong as his own. They could shew how, in a hot climate, Neill had advanced from the east and Nicholson from the west, fighting energetically against all obstacles, and dying like true soldiers at the head of their columns. They could ask the world whether a garrison was ever more nobly defended, under circumstances of trying difficulty, than the Residency under Inglis; and whether a garrison was ever brought away from the middle of a hostile city under more extraordinary conditions, and with more complete success, than was achieved in the 'Exodus from Lucknow' under Campbell, Outram, and Havelock. They could point to Sir John Lawrence for an example of what a civilian could do, maintaining a large and recently conquered country at peace by the energy of his own individual character, raising regiment after regiment of trustworthy native troops, and sending an army to reconquer Delhi before a single additional soldier could arrive from England. They could point to the exertions of numerous individuals, any one of whom would have been a hero if his heroism had not been eclipsed by that of men better known to fame.

These recollections afforded some consolation under the disappointment occasioned by the long continuance of the war waged by the mutineers. Yet were they far from being an adequate reward for the blood and treasure expended; the prevailing natural feeling was one of disappointment. Nor were theorists less at fault in their estimate of causes, than practical men in their expectation of results. Still was the question put, 'What was the cause of the mutiny?' And still were the answers as diverse as ever. From May to December the theories multiplied faster than the means of solving them. On the religious side, men banded themselves chiefly into two parties. One said that the native troops in India had revolted because we, as a nation, had tampered with their religion. We had nearly put down infanticide and suttee; we paid less respect than formerly to their idols and holy places; we had allowed pious officers to preach to the sepoys in their regiments, and missionaries to inveigh against brahmins and temples; and we so clumsily managed a new contrivance in the fabrication and use of cartridges, as to induce a suspicion in the native mind that a personal insult to their religious prejudices was intended. On the other hand, religious Christians contended that the revolt was a mark of God's anger against the English nation. They urged that a people possessing the Bible ought long ago, by government as well as by individual efforts, to have distributed it throughout the length and breadth of India; that we ought to have encouraged churches and chapels, ministers and missionaries, Bible-classes and Scripture-readers; that we ought to have disregarded caste prejudices, and boldly proclaimed that Hindooism and Moslemism were worse than mockeries, and that no expectations of happiness in this life or the next were sound but such as rested on Biblical grounds—in short, that England had had a magnificent opportunity, and a deep obligation, to teach with all her power the way of salvation to two hundred million benighted beings; and that, failing this, the Revolt had been a consequent and deserved calamity. Another class of reasoners attributed the outbreak to the want of sympathy between the Europeans and the natives in the general relations of life. A young man was sent out to India by the Company, either as a writer in the civil service or as a cadet in the army; he learned the immediate duties of his office, studied just so much of the vernacular languages and customs as were absolutely needed, rose in the middle years of his life to higher offices and emoluments, and returned to end his days in England. He held the natives in contempt; he neither knew nor cared what passed in their inmost hearts; he treated India as a conquered country, held especially for the benefit of the Company's servants. Hence, according to the view now under notice, the natives, having nothing for which to love and respect the British, were glad to avail themselves of any pretext to expel the foreign element from their land. Military men, acquainted with the Bombay and Madras armies, insisted that the mutiny had arisen from the organisation of that of Bengal; in which the Brahmin sepoys and Rajpoot sowars had been so pampered and petted, that they began to deem themselves masters instead of subjects, and to aim at a sort of military despotism on their own account. Other speculators, pointing to the fact that Mohammedans have in all ages been intensely fanatical, regarded the mutiny as only one among many indications of an attempt to revive the past glories of the Moguls, when the followers of Mahomet were the rulers in India. Others again, keeping clear of the larger questions of creed and race, attributed the troubles to the policy of annexation, which had been pursued to so extraordinary a degree in recent years. These reasoners urged that, whatever may have been the faults and follies of the King of Oude, five million natives unquestionably looked up to him as their sovereign, and felt their prejudices shocked and their alarm excited, when, in 1856, he was rudely hurled from his throne, and made a pensioner dependent on a company of merchants. Another class of theorists, impressed with a horror of taxation, pitied the poor Hindoos who had to pay so much to the Company for permission to live on the soil, so much for the salt monopoly, so much for other dues; and sought to find a reason for the mutiny in the desire to throw off these imposts. Commercial men, estimating nations and countries by a standard familiar to themselves, had long complained that the Company did not encourage independent commerce in India; and now they said: 'If you had acted with English good sense, the revolt would never have occurred. Afford facilities for the construction of railways, canals, and docks; build ships and steamers; develop your mineral wealth in coal and iron; sell or let plots of land to men who will bring English experience and English machinery to bear on its cultivation; grow tea and coffee, sugar and cocoa, timber and fruits, cotton and flax, corn and pulse, on the soils favourable to the respective produce—do all this, or afford facilities for others to do it, and the natives of India will then have something more profitable to think of than mutiny and bloodshed.'

We point to these various theories for the purpose of remarking, that the controversies relating to them were as warmly conducted at the end of the year as when the news of the cartridge troubles first reached England. The higher the position, the more extensive the experience, of public men, the more chary were they in committing themselves to any special modes of explanation; it was by those who knew little, that the boldest assertions were hazarded. An opinion was gradually growing up among cautious reasoners, that the revolt must have been the composite resultant of many co-ordinate or co-existent causes, each of which contributed towards it in a particular way; but such reasoners would necessarily perceive that a true solution could only be arrived at when all the separate items were known, and properly estimated. Hence the authorities, both in England and in India, recommended and followed a plan that may thus be enunciated—first suppress the mutiny; then collect gradually evidence of its various predisposing causes; and, finally, make use of that evidence in remodelling the institutions of British India on a firmer basis. The NOTES at the end of the last chapter shewed that the Company took the common-sense view, of inquiring into the probable causes of the mutiny before planning the re-organisation of Indian affairs. The candid acknowledgment by the Directors, that the voluminous documents hitherto produced had 'entirely failed to satisfy their minds in regard to the immediate causes of the mutiny,' was full of significance, and, it may be added, of caution to others.

So far as concerns the present Chronicle, the treatment will necessarily be affected by the character of the struggle. At the beginning of 1858, scarcely any symptoms of further mutiny were presented. The Bengal army was gone, scattered in anarchy; the armies of Bombay, Madras, and the Punjaub, were almost wholly sound; and the daily events consisted mainly of military operations against the revolted sepoy regiments of the Bengal army, and against such chieftains as had brought their retainers into the field for selfish purposes. Hence the narrative may march on more rapidly than before.

All the interest of the military operations in India, at the opening of the new year, grouped itself around the commander-in-chief. Slow as had been the arrival of British troops in India, during the months when Wheeler, Havelock, Neill, Outram, Inglis, Barnard, Wilson, and Nicholson were struggling against difficulties, the disembarkations were very numerous in November and December. When the old year gave place to the new, it was estimated that 23,000 British troops had landed at Calcutta since the troubles began, besides others put on shore at Bombay, Madras, and Kurachee.* They had advanced

* A return was prepared by order of parliament, of the odds and ends composing what was called the *sea-kit* of English soldiers going out to India, the cost at which they were estimated, and the mode of paying for them:

Articles.	Price.		
Two canvas frocks at 3*s*. 3*d*. (jackets substituted for frocks in the case of sergeants),	£0	6	6
One pair canvas trousers,	0	3	4
One neck handkerchief,	0	0	8
One pair of shoes,	0	6	0
Three pounds of marine soap, at 7*d*.,	0	1	9
Two pounds of yellow soap, at 7*d*.,	0	1	2
Nine balls of pipeclay,	0	0	9
One quart tin-pot, with hook,	0	1	0
One scrubbing-brush,	0	0	8
Three tins of blacking,	0	1	0
One clasp-knife,	0	1	0
One bag in lieu of haversack,	0	0	10
Needles and thread,	0	1	0
Three pounds of tobacco, at 2*s*. 8*d*.,	0	8	0
Two flannel-belts,	0	2	0
Two check-shirts, at 2*s*. 6*d*.,	0	5	0
	£2	0	8

'The prices,' as the return tells us, 'are unavoidably liable to variation, but those in the above list will serve as a general standard for guidance. These extra necessaries are paid for by the men to whom they are issued, out of pay advanced for the purpose. Tobacco is issued to such men only as are in the habit of using it; and if any man be provided already with any of the into the upper provinces, by those routes and modes which have so often been adverted to, and were placed under the brigadiers whom Sir Colin Campbell had appointed to conduct the various operations planned by him. We have first, therefore, to notice such of the proceedings of the commander-in-chief as took place during the month of January; turning attention afterwards to military proceedings in other quarters.

Sir Colin Campbell, as the last chapter shewed, rescued Cawnpore and General Windham from trouble at the close of November and the beginning of the following month. He did not move from the vicinity of that city till towards the end of December. Writing to Viscount Canning on this subject, on the 6th of January, he said: 'I am informed by the civil authorities that my protracted stay at Cawnpore was of much benefit; and I am convinced that, apart from any immediate military object, it is necessary, for the re-establishment of authority, that the march of the troops should be deliberate. Time is thus afforded to the magistrates and special commissioners to visit rebellious towns and villages, and again display to the people in unmistakable manner the resolution of your lordship's government to visit punishment on all those who during the last few months have set aside their allegiance.' He at the same time glanced rapidly at the chief military operations which had marked the month of December in the Gangetic and Jumna regions—such as Outram's defence at the Alum Bagh; Adrian Hope's clean sweep of Nena Sahib's property at Bithoor;* Walpole's expedition to Etawah and Minpooree; Seaton's energetic movements with a column from Delhi; and Windham's expedition to Futtiah.

When the vehicles had returned to Cawnpore, after conveying the Lucknow fugitives to Allahabad, the commander-in-chief prepared to move his head-quarters to Furruckabad and Fort Futteghur, near which places many insurgent chieftains required to be dealt with. He started on the 24th of December and marched to Chowrepore. After remaining there some time to organise his force into brigades, &c., he renewed his march on the 28th, and reached Meerun-ke-Serai. At the several halting-places of himself and his brigadiers, he made arrangements for destroying the country-boats on the Ganges, in order to prevent molestation of the Doab from the Oude side of the river when the troops should have moved on. On the 31st he arrived at Goorsaigunje; Greathed, Windham, and Hope Grant all being with him. On the first day of the new year, Sir Colin sent forth two regiments under Adrian Hope to secure the iron suspension-bridge over the Kallee Nuddee, a very important point on the road from Cawnpore to Futteghur. A party of sailors were quite delighted to assist in this work, replacing with ropes some of the ironwork which the rebels had begun to destroy. On the 2d the enemy, hovering in villages near the bridge, attacked Sir Colin's pickets and advanced columns; but they were speedily defeated and driven across the Ganges into Rohilcund.* Proof was here afforded that the insurgents had not forgotten the advantages of organisation. 'The rebels,' said the commander-in-chief in his dispatch, 'who were dispersed on this occasion, consisted of three or four battalions of the 41st and other corps of native infantry. In the 41st, the rebels had begun with much system to organise a second battalion, their recruits being dressed in a neat uniform.' On the 3d, Sir Colin reached Futteghur, the old British station near the city of Furruckabad. Fortunately, the enemy, who had held Futteghur for at least six months, now retreated so precipitately that they had not time to destroy the government property within the place. Sir Colin found a large amount of stores of the most valuable description, belonging to the gun and clothing agencies. Having secured these important items of military property, he sent a large stock of grain to Cawnpore, to lighten the labours of the commissariat for the supply of Sir James Outram at the Alum Bagh. The Nawab of Furruckabad had long been among the most ferocious leaders of the insurgents; and the commander-in-chief now proceeded to such measures as would punish him severely for his treachery. 'The destruction of the Nawab's palaces is in process. I think it right that not a stone should be left unturned in all the residences of the rebellious chiefs. They are far more guilty than their misguided followers.'

On the 6th of January, then, the commander-in-chief was on the banks of the Ganges at Futteghur. With him were the brigades and columns of Hope Grant, Adrian Hope, Walpole, Windham, Seaton, Greathed, and Little; Inglis, with a movable column, was restoring order in a part of the Doab

above articles, and such are in a serviceable condition, a duplicate supply is not given.'

It will at once be understood that the ordinary equipment of the soldier is not here mentioned; only the extras for the sea-voyage being included. The 'nine balls of pipeclay' constitute perhaps the worst item in the list.

* Before the final departure from the neighbourhood of Cawnpore, the British troops did their best to despoil one who received more execration than any other man in India. An officer writing at the close of the year, said: 'We have made very good use of our delay at Cawnpore. The Highland brigade was encamped at Bithoor, and employed in raising all Nena Sahib's valuables from a well. The operation was a most difficult one, as the well was deep and full of water. However, it was very successful; for not including their last day's work (a very good one) they raised 75½ pounds of gold in various shapes, and 252 pounds of silver. The last day they got an enormous quantity of gold and silver, so heavy that a man could just carry it. I hope they will come upon Bajee Rao's jewels. There are two more wells yet to open. The Nena is "beating his breast" at our well-successes.'

* One incident of this affair was afterwards thus described by an officer present: 'A brigade was sent to repair the suspension-bridge. They commenced work on the 1st, and by morning of the 2d had finished it all but one or two planks, which they were laying down, when the chief saw the villagers come out of the village opposite. He desired some one to go and tell them not to be afraid, as they would not be hurt; when all of a sudden bang came a round-shot from amongst them, which killed four men of the 53d. The enemy were then discovered to be in force; the naval brigade soon opened on them, pitching into the village for about two hours, they returning it with an 18-pounder and a 9-pounder. When the firing commenced, we were all sent for, the bridge was soon finished, and then the chief with his force crossed, turned them out of the village, and pursued them with cavalry and artillery for about eight miles.'

between Cawnpore and Etawah; while Outram was still at the Alum Bagh. Sir Colin scarcely moved from that spot during the remainder of the month. He was waiting for more troops from Calcutta, and for vast stores of warlike material from the upper provinces. It may here be remarked that the enormous weight of stores and ammunition required for an army, and the vast distances to be traversed in India, gave a stupendous character to some of the convoys occasionally prepared. Thus, on the 22d of January, about 3000 troops started from Agra for the Cawnpore regions, having in charge 19 guns of various calibre, and 1500 carts laden with stores and ammunition. There were 750 rounds of ammunition for each of 24 guns, and 500 for each of 44 howitzers and mortars—all required by the commander-in-chief. Several ladies, *en route* to Calcutta, took advantage of the protection of this force. The above numbers give a very imperfect idea of the convoy; for native servants and camp-followers, together with animals of draught and burden, always accompany such a train in swarms almost inconceivable.

When the English public found that the whole of the autumn months, and the winter so far as the end of January, had passed away without any great achievement except the relief of Lucknow, portions of them began to complain and to censure. They could not and would not find fault with Sir Colin, because he was a general favourite; and therefore they rushed to a conclusion inimical to Viscount Canning, who from the first had been made to bear the burden of a vast amount of anonymous abuse. A story arose that the governor-general and the commander-in-chief were at 'cross-purposes,' that Campbell was doing nothing because Canning thwarted him. The Duke of Cambridge and Lord Panmure took occasion, in the House of Lords, to give authoritative contradictions to these rumours; and among other evidence adduced was a letter written by Sir Colin to his royal highness—the one as commander-in-chief in India, the other as commander-in-chief of all the Queen's forces generally—just when he was about to set off to head the military operations at Cawnpore and Lucknow. 'Now that I am on the point of leaving Calcutta,' he said, 'I would beg, with the greatest respect to the governor-general, to record the deep sense of the obligation I entertain towards his lordship. Our intercourse has been most cordial, intimate, and unreserved. I cannot be sufficiently thankful for his lordship's confidence and support, and the kindly manner in which they have been afforded, to my great personal satisfaction. One at a distance, and unacquainted with the ordinary mode of transacting business in this country, could hardly estimate the gain to the public service which has thus been made. But I allude principally to my own feelings of gratification.' Whether or not the governor-general and the commander-in-chief were divided in opinion touching the best policy to pursue, it is certain that men in lower though influential positions differed widely in their views on this point. Some were anxious that Lucknow should be attacked at once. They urged that that city being the chief seat of rebellion, a crushing of the force there would dishearten the rebels elsewhere; whereas every day lost would add to the strength of Lucknow. Even our victories increased the number and desperation of its defenders; and, therefore, till this central point was captured, the revolt would always have a nucleus, a flag around which the discontented might rally. On the other hand, it was urged that Rohilcund should be cleared before Lucknow could be profitably seized. Large bands still roaming over that province might interrupt the commander-in-chief's communications, if he left them in his rear while engaged in Oude. Again, Sir Colin was waiting for more troops. It was asserted that, even if he could conquer sixty or eighty thousand fighting-men in the streets of Lucknow, he could not leave a force there while he was endeavouring to clear out Rohilcund. So far as can be judged from attainable evidence, it appears that Sir Colin himself held this second opinion—resolving to clear the outworks before attacking the central stronghold of rebellion.

Leaving the commander-in-chief for a while, we may suitably direct attention to the proceedings of other generals in other parts of the wide field of operations—beginning with those connected with Sir James Outram.

The Alum Bagh, never once out of English hands since the month of September, remained a very important stronghold. The reader will perhaps recall to mind the relation which that fort bore to the operations at Lucknow; but a short recapitulation may not be misplaced here. When Havelock and Outram, on the 25th of September, advanced to Lucknow, they left Colonel M'Intyre, of the 78th Highlanders, in command at the Alum Bagh, with orders to maintain that post until further instructions reached him. He had with him 280 English soldiers of various regiments, a few Sikhs, 4 guns, 128 sick and wounded, between 4000 and 5000 native camp-followers, large numbers of cattle, and a valuable store of baggage, ammunition, and other military appliances. His supply of food for the natives was very scanty, and those poor creatures soon suffered terribly from hunger. After a few days, they stealthily collected crops of rice and grain in fields near at hand, under protection of the guns; but this resource was soon exhausted. It is a familiar occurrence in the annals of Indian warfare, that the camp-followers and army-servants exceed by five or ten fold the number of actual combatants; and thus is to be explained the strange composition of the miscellaneous body collected within the walls of the Alum Bagh. Unable to receive aid or even instructions from the Residency, M'Intyre maintained his position as best he could. A convoy of provisions reached him from Cawnpore on the 7th of October, under Major Bingham, and another on the 25th under Major Barnston. Some of the troops remained with him on each occasion, raising his force altogether to 900 fighting-men and ten guns. Meanwhile he fortified his position with bastions and other defence-works, and contended successfully against the enemy, who constructed five batteries in various parts of the exterior, and brought artillery-fire to bear against him day after day. They also held the neighbouring fort of Jelalabad, which formed a sixth base of attack. So steadily and actively, however, did the colonel maintain his defence, that the enemy's fire occasioned him very little loss. Matters continued thus until the middle of November, when Sir Colin Campbell, conquering Jelalabad, and reaching Alum Bagh, made a few changes in the garrison. Then, in the last week of the month, Sir James Outram became master of the Alum Bagh, with a picked force of 3000 to 4000 men. He easily maintained his position throughout December, and gave the enemy a severe defeat on the 22d, at a place called Guilee, three miles from Alum Bagh on the Dil Koosha road. The opening of the year 1858 found Outram still at his post, and the enemy still endeavouring or hoping to cut off his communications and starve him out.* Some of his troops were away, conveying a supply of provisions from Cawnpore; and the enemy, knowing this, resolved to attack him on the 12th of January in his weakened state. Fathoming their intentions, he prepared for defence. At sunrise they appeared, to the immense number of at least 30,000, and formed a wide semicircle in front and flank of his position. Outram, massing his troops into two brigades, sent them out to confront the enemy. Then commenced a very fierce battle; for while the main body of the enemy attacked these two brigades, a second proceeded to assault the fort of Jelalabad, while a third by a detour reached the Alum Bagh itself, and endeavoured to cut off Outram's communications with it. From sunrise till four o'clock in the afternoon did the struggle continue, every British gun being incessantly engaged in repelling the advances of dense masses of the enemy. Foiled at every point, the insurgents at length withdrew to the city or to their original positions in the gardens and villages. It was a very serious struggle, for the enemy fought well and were in overwhelming numbers; nevertheless, their discomfiture was complete. Four days afterwards they made another attack, in smaller numbers, but with greater boldness: the result was the same as before—complete defeat and severe loss. Thus did this skilful and watchful commander frustrate every hostile attempt made by the swarms of insurgents who surrounded him.

We turn our attention next further eastward. The Nepaulese leader, Jung Bahadoor, with Brigadier MacGregor as representative of British interests, entered Goruckpore on the 6th of January, thus taking possession of a city which for many months had been almost entirely in the hands of rebels. The force was Goorkha, the officers were Nepaulese and English. Jung Bahadoor and Brigadier MacGregor being the two leaders, the brigades were thus commanded—the first by Run Singh and Captain Plowden, the second by Sunmuck Singh and Captain Edmonstone, the third by Junga Doge and Lieutenant Foote, and the artillery by Loll Singh and Major Fitzgerald. This singular combination was made because, although Jung Bahadoor was entitled to appoint his own native officers, it was nevertheless desirable that English officers should be at hand to advise or even control if necessary. The advancing force had first to effect a passage over a nullah, the bridge of which was broken, and the banks stoutly defended by the enemy; this was done after a short but sharp conflict. The enemy fled from the nullah through a jungle towards the city, pursued by the Goorkhas; but the latter could not equal the sepoys in running over loose sand, and therefore could not come up with them. All the baggage having crossed the nullah, Jung Bahadoor steadily advanced towards the city, attacked by new parties of the enemy in skirmishing form on both flanks. Many hundreds of the rebels rushed into the river Ribtee, to effect a safe crossing to the other side, adjacent to the Oude frontier; but they were shot down or drowned in considerable numbers in this attempt to escape. Goruckpore was entered, and taken possession of in the English name. It is curious to trace, in the military dispatch of Brigadier MacGregor to the Calcutta authorities, the same conventional 'mention' of Nepaulese officers as is customary in the British army. Colonel Loll Singh 'proved himself a good artillery officer;' Captain Suzan Singh's 'very effective fire was much admired;' Brigadier Junga Doge 'reaped, conjointly with the artillery, the principal honours of the day;' Brigadier Sunmuck Singh's brigade 'was well in advance;' Brigadier Run Singh's brigade 'was most skilfully led through the forest;' and Brigadier Jodh Adhikaree was only shut out from praise by the fact that his brigade was not brought into action. The names of the British officers were set forth in parallel order, each to receive praise by the side of his Nepaulese companion. The English commander of a military force, we may here remark, must often be embarrassed while writing his dispatches; for unless he mentions the name of almost every officer, he gives offence; while it taxes his powers of composition to vary the terms in which encomiums are expressed. When Goruckpore

* Sir James Outram's total force in and near the Alum Bagh, at the beginning of the year, was made up of the following elements:

H.M. 5th, 75th, 78th, 84th, and 90th foot.
1st Madras Europeans.
Brasyer's Ferozpore Sikhs.
12th irregular cavalry.
Hardinge's corps.
Military train.
Engineer park.
Artillery park.
Madras Sappers and Miners.
Royal artillery, under Eyre and Maude.
Bengal artillery, under Olphert.

was once again placed under British control, the authorities quickly put down the so-called government which had been introduced by Mahomed Hussein, the self-appointed nazim or chief. Such of his adherents as had clearly been rebellious were quickly tried, and many of them executed. All the convicted natives who were not sentenced to hanging were made to do sweeper's work, within the church, jail, and other buildings, without respect to their caste, creed, or former dignity. Mushurruff Khan, and other rebellious leaders in the district between Goruckpore and the Oude frontier, were one by one captured, to the manifest pacification of the country villages and planters' estates.

In the wide stretch of country between Patna and Allahabad, and between the Ganges on the south and Nepaul on the north, everything was awaiting the completion of the commander-in-chief's plans. In and near Arrah, Azimghur, Ghazeepore, Jounpoor, Benares, and Mirzapore, there were bodies of malcontents ready to break out into open rebellion as soon as any favourable opportunities should occur for so doing, but checked by the gradually increasing power of the British. On one occasion, towards the close of the month, Brigadier Franks marched out of Secundra, near Allahabad, against a body of 500 rebels, who were posted with several guns at Nussunpore. He totally defeated them, and captured two of their guns. About the same time, on the 22d of the month, Colonel Rowcroft, with detachments of H.M. 10th foot, sailors, Sikhs, and Goorkhas, proceeded from Azimghur towards the Oudian frontier, there to aid in hemming in the rebels. Indeed, Jung Bahadoor, Franks, and Rowcroft, at the end of the month, feeling that all was pretty secure on the east of the frontier, were gradually drawing a cordon round the Oudians, from Nepaul in the north to the Ganges on the south—ready to concur in any large scheme of operations which Sir Colin Campbell might be enabled to initiate.

The brigadiers who were more immediately under the eye of Sir Colin Campbell were employed during the month of January, as has already been implied, in clearing away bands of insurgents in the Doab and neighbouring districts. To detail the various minor contests will be unnecessary; one or two will suffice as samples of all. On the 27th of the month, Brigadier Adrian Hope had a smart contest with the enemy at Shumshabad. Taking with him a small column,* he started from Futteghur on the previous day, and proceeded through Kooshinabad to Shumshabad, where he found the enemy in considerable force. They occupied a commanding knoll on the edge of the plateau overlooking the plain stretching towards the river. On the knoll was a Mussulman tomb, surrounded by the remains of an old intrenchment, upon which they had raised a sand-bag battery; their front was defended by a ravine impassable for cavalry or guns. Hope, having formed his plan of attack, moved over some broken ground towards the enemy's camp. They at once opened with a well-directed fire of round-shot. Silencing these guns by a flank fire, Hope ordered his infantry to advance out of a hollow where they had been screened; they did so, rushed upon the camp, and captured it. Then began a pursuit of the fleeing enemy by Hope's cavalry, and the securing of several guns and much ammunition which they had left behind them. The brigadier believed the insurgents to consist of two of the mutinied Bareilly regiments, accompanied by a motley group of rebels anxious for plunder. About the same day, another district near Furruckabad became the scene of a fierce encounter. A body of rebels about 5000 strong, with four guns, being heard of at a distance of some miles from the city, a force was sent out—consisting of H.M. 42d and 53d foot, the 4th Punjaubees, two squadrons of H.M. 9th Lancers, two of Hodson's Horse, a horse-battery, and two troops of horse-artillery. The enemy's guns were planted on the site of an old mud-fort on rising ground, whence they opened fire as soon as the British came in sight. The morning being densely foggy, the column proceeded cautiously to prevent a surprise. The action that ensued was chiefly carried on by artillery and cavalry, and was marked by several deaths on the side of the British owing to the blowing up of tumbrils. Among the wounded was the gallant Hodson, whose name had become so well known in connection with an active and useful body of Punjaub or Sikh irregular cavalry. The result of this, as of almost all similar contests, was the defeat and dispersion of the enemy. A glance at a map will shew that at Furruckabad and Futteghur (the latter a military station near the former), the commander-in-chief was in an admirable position to send out detachments on special service. Bareilly, Allygurh, Agra, Muttra, Minpooree, Gwalior, Etawah, Calpee, Cawnpore, and Lucknow, formed an irregular circle of which Furruckabad was the centre.

On the first day of the year the little colony at Nynee Tal received one of the alarms to which it had been so often subjected for six months; but, as in all the other instances, the danger was promptly averted. The subsidiary station at Huldwanee, eighteen miles distant, was attacked early in the morning by a large number of the Bareilly rebels. Some time previously, a force of about 600 Goorkhas had been sent to that station; but owing to the absence of the commandant at Almora, and to the neglect in making any defensive arrangements, the place was not well prepared to resist a surprise. The enemy opened an artillery fire most unexpectedly, for their approach

* 9th Lancers, two squadrons.
Hodson's Horse, 200.
Bengal H.A. one troop.
Bengal F.A. 4 guns.
42d Highlanders.
53d foot.
4th Punjaub rifles.

was not in the least anticipated. The gallant little Goorkhas, however, speedily turned out, met the enemy hand to hand, defeated them, pursued them three or four miles from the station, and cut down a considerable number of them.

Of the two imperial or once imperial cities, Agra and Delhi, little need be said in connection with the events of January. Agra, it will be remembered, was never out of British hands during the turmoils of 1857, although severely pressed; and when Delhi on the one side, and Cawnpore on the other, were recovered, there was less chance than ever that Agra would fall into the hands of the enemy. The citizens resumed their ordinary employments, and the British authorities re-established their civil control.*

After four months of strict military occupancy, the city of Delhi was thrown open to natives who during that interval had been excluded. On the 18th of January an order to this intent came into operation. Each person availing himself of it had to pay one rupee four annas to the kotwallee or police authority; for this he was provided with a ticket, which insured him certain facilities for living and trading within the city. The Chandnee Chowk began to resume its former lively appearance; a military band resumed its evening music in the open space fronting the English church; and, 'but for the shot-holes all around,' as an eye-witness observed, 'the signs of many sanguinary months were passing away.' A formal charge was drawn up, and judicial proceedings commenced, against the imprisoned king; but as the trial chiefly took place in February, we may defer for a few pages any notice of the proceedings.

Everything westward of Delhi may happily be dismissed in the same language which has so often sufficed in former chapters. Sir John Lawrence, with his able coadjutors Montgomery, Cotton, and Edwardes, still held the whole length and breadth of the Punjaub at peace or nearly so. And the same may in like manner be said of Sinde, where Mr Frere and General Jacob held sway.

Of the state of the widely scattered and diversely governed regions of Central India and Rajpootana at the beginning of the year, it is difficult to give a correct picture. Unlike the Hindustani regions, they were inhabited by a very motley population —Bundelas, Rajpoots, Rohillas, Mahrattas, Bheels, Jâts, Ghonds, all mingled, and governed by chieftains who cared much more for their own petty authority than for the kings of Delhi and Lucknow, or for castes and creeds. Luckily the two principal Mahratta leaders, Scindia and Holkar, still remained faithful to the British, and thus rendered possible what would have been impossible without their assistance. If to Central India and Rajpootana, we add Bundelcund and the Saugor territories, we shall have a wide sweep of country approached nearest at one point by the Calcutta presidency, at another by the Madras presidency, and at a third by that of Bombay. As, however, Calcutta had no troops to spare for that part of India, Madras and Bombay sent up columns and 'field-forces' as fast as they could be provided; and thus it is that we read of small military bodies under Stuart, Steuart, Roberts, Whitlock, Rose, Raines, and other officers. According to the number of troops composing them, and the districts in which their services were required, these columns received various names—such as 'Rajpootana Field-force,' 'Nerbudda Field-force,' 'Malwah Field-force,' and 'Central India Field-force.' The mere naming might be of small consequence, were it not that confusion arose occasionally by different appellations being employed at different times for the very same force. At various periods during the month encounters took place, a few of which may briefly be noticed.

On the 6th of January, a small force of about 500 miscellaneous troops, with guns, set out from Camp Muddah in Rajpootana, under Major Raines, to rout a body of rebels at Rowah. They found the village strongly fortified by a hedge fronting a deep ditch and breastwork of earth, thick and loopholed. After a reconnaissance the major advanced; when the enemy opened fire, bringing down branches of trees with a crash among the British. When a hot artillery and infantry fire had been maintained for some time, about 200 men of the 10th Bombay N.I. received orders to storm the village; they advanced in admirable order, dashed forward, cleared the hedge, mounted to the opposite side, and compelled the insurgents to make a precipitate retreat. The village was burned to ashes, and the force returned to camp—having marched over deep sand in a thick jungle for twenty-two miles. One of the horrors of war was illustrated forcibly in a few brief words contained in an officer's narrative of this engagement: 'The villagers were mowed down in sections by the artillery, as they were entering a cave on the sides of the rock in rear of the village.' Nothing perplexed the English officers more than to determine how far to compassionate the native villagers; sometimes these poor creatures suffered terribly and undeservedly;

* The condition of the British quarters in Agra at the beginning of the year was briefly told by one of the writers in the *Mofussilite* newspaper, after the severe pressure on the garrison had ceased: 'The fort is being abandoned by every one who has a house which can be made in the least degree habitable; but many people will still be compelled to remain within its gloomy walls for an indefinite period; as in many instances the destruction of houses has been so complete, that it will be a work of time and a matter of considerable expense to place them in anything like decent repair. . . . . As we are fortunate enough to possess a good house with a pucka roof, which has been put into excellent repair, we intend publishing next Tuesday's paper in that building—the former printing-office of the *Mofussilite*. We shall all be put to great straits for furniture, crockery, and such like things; for although a charpoy (stump-bedstead), a teapoy, and a couple of broken chairs, were as much as we could find room for in one of our little cells of the fort, yet we shall soon require rather more when we dwell in roomier habitations. Our distant friends must know that it is a rare thing to see two plates of the same pattern on any table, and that none but those upon whom fortune has smiled indulge in glass tumblers. Tin pots are the height of our ambition. Port, sherry, brandy, Allsopp, and Bass, are beverages generally as unknown to this community as they were to Robinson Crusoe.'

but on other occasions they unquestionably assisted the rebels.'

Sir Hugh Rose had a short but decisive encounter with a body of rebels at Ratgurh or Rutgurh towards the close of the month. This was a town in Central India, between Saugor and Bhopal, in and near which many chieftains had unfurled the banner of rebellion, at the head of whom was Nawab Fazil Mahomed Khan. Ratgurh was a strong place, in good repair, and supplied with a year's provisions. The rebels intended to have made a bold stand; but they lost heart when they saw siege-artillery brought up to a position which they had deemed unattainable, and applied to the breaching of their fort. Many of the defenders abandoned the fort during the night, letting themselves down by ropes from the rocks, &c. On the next day some of their number, aided by many mutinous sepoys, emerged from the thick jungles in the neighbourhood, attacked the videttes guarding the rear of Sir Hugh's camp, and attempted to relieve the fort; but they were driven across the river Betwah, and the fort securely captured. It is worthy of note how many of the

Houses in the Chandnee Chowk, Delhi.

contests during the wars of the mutiny partook of the nature of sieges. Mud-forts have been famous in India for centuries, and the natives exhibit much tact in defending them. As long as guns attack from a safe distance, such strongholds may be long defended; but a storming by British bayonets utterly paralyses the garrisons. Sir Hugh bent his attention towards Saugor also, which had for many months been invested by a large body of the enemy. With the second brigade of the Central India Field-force, reinforced by the 3d Europeans and the 3d native cavalry from the Poonah division, he laid his plans for an effective relief of that place. General Whitlock, with a Madras column, was also bound for Saugor; but it was expected that Rose would reach that place before him.

In another region, much nearer Calcutta, a small military affair presented itself for notice. Just before the commencement of the new year, Sumbhulpore was relieved from a trouble that had pressed upon it, in the presence of a miscellaneous body of rebels. A small force of less than 300 troops, consisting of Madras native infantry, Ramgurh infantry, and Nagpoor irregular cavalry, made a forced march from Nagpoor to Sumbhulpore; and on the 30th of December Captain Wood marched out with this force to chastise a body of rebels encamped in a gorse-land near the city. The victory was speedy and decisive, and was rendered more valuable by the capture of three native chieftains who had been leaders in the rebellion. The rebels were not sepoys, but escaped convicts.

The large and important regions of Nagpoor and Hyderabad exhibited nearly the same features at the beginning of the year as they had done during the summer and autumn. Containing very few pure Hindustanis of the Brahmin and Rajpoot castes, and being within comparatively easy reach of the trusty and trusted native troops of the Madras presidency, they were seldom disturbed by symptoms of mutiny. The British commissioners or residents had, it is true, much to render them anxious; but the perils were not so great as those which weighed down their brother-officials in other regions. The Deccan, or Hyderabad, or the Nizam's Country—for it was known by all three names—had from the first been more troubled by marauders than by regular military mutineers. The villages of Mugrool, Janappul, Sind Kaid, Rungeenee, and Dawulgaum, mostly distant about twenty or thirty miles from Jaulnah, were infested during January by predatory bands of Rohillas and Bheels, who alarmed the villages by acts of plunder, dacoitee, and cruelty. They even went so far as to plunder the treasure-chest of a regiment of the Hyderabad Contingent, while on the way from Aurungabad to Jaulnah, and barely two miles from the last-named place. The officer commanding at Jaulnah sent a small force in pursuit; but the marauders, here as elsewhere, were swift of foot, and made clear off with their booty. These Bheels, a half-savage mountain tribe, gave annoyance in more districts than one. Captain Montgomery, superintendent of police at Ahmednuggur, a city between Jaulnah and Bombay, found it necessary to go out and attack a strong body of them, who held a position in a jungle twelve miles from Chandore. He had with him a miscellaneous force of Bombay native troops; but after three successive attempts he was beaten back from the enemy's position, and wounded, as well as three of his officers.

The Nagpoor force, though never very closely in league with the mutineers further north, contrived to rouse suspicion and bring down punishment early in the year. The Nagpoor irregulars had been disarmed by Brigadier Prior very early in the history of the Revolt; but Mr Plowden, commissioner of the Nagpoor territory, believing that they might be trusted, advised that their weapons should again be given to them. The conduct of the men throughout the rest of the year justified this reliance; but, with the strange inconsistency that so often marked the proceedings of the natives, they stained the first month of the year with a deed of violence. On the 18th of January, at Raepore, a place on the road between Nagpoor and Cuttack, a party of Mussulman gunners in the Nagpoor artillery suddenly rose, murdered Sergeant-major Sidwell, and called on the 3d Nagpoor irregular infantry to assist them in exterminating the Europeans. Either the 3d were innocent in the matter, or their hearts failed them; for they not only remained firm, but at once assisted in disarming the gunners. On the 22d, Lieutenant Elliott, deputy-commissioner, rode into Raepore, and immediately brought the gunners to trial; all but one were found guilty, and were hung that same evening, amid frantic appeals to their comrades to save them for the sake of their common faith—an appeal to which the infantry did not respond.

It may be observed, in relation to all the military operations in the month of January, that there were certain rebel leaders whose personal movements were seldom clearly known to the British officers. Nena Sahib of Bithoor, Koer Singh of Jugdispore, and Mohammed Khan of Bareilly, were unquestionably urging the sepoys and rebels to continue the struggle against the Company's 'raj;' but their own marchings and retreatings from place to place were veiled in much obscurity. There was, in truth, a very intelligible motive for this; for a price was placed upon the head of each, and he could not fully know whether any traitor were at his elbow. Some of the leaders, such as the Rajah of Minpooree and the Nawab of Furruckabad, were believed to have joined their fortunes with those of the defenders of Lucknow; while Mahomed Hussein, as we have seen, was hovering between Oude and Goruckpore, according to the strength of the Goorkhas sent against him. It was known that many of the Gwalior mutineers, after their severe defeat in December, had collected again in Bundelcund; but it was not clearly ascertained who among them assumed the post of leader.

SIR JAMES OUTRAM.

CHAPTER XXIV.

MILITARY OPERATIONS IN FEBRUARY.

IMPATIENT as the whole British nation was to hear of a brilliant and successful termination of the struggle in India, every telegram, every weekly mail, shewed that the time for this satisfaction was still far distant. The mutineers were beaten, but not crushed; the rebellious chieftains were checked, but not extinguished; their deluded followers were disappointed in the results obtained, but not deterred from making further efforts. England, with all her delays and waverings of opinion, had sent over a large, fine, and complete army; the Punjaub had supplied such a force of reliable troops as no one would have ventured beforehand to anticipate; generals had been brought into notice by the exigencies of public affairs who possessed those fine soldierly attributes which a nation is proud to recognise; the authorities, steady at their posts, never for a moment doubted that the British 'raj' would be established on a firmer basis than ever—and yet everything was in turmoil in India. Blood and treasure were being daily expended; but the time had not arrived when any adequate return was obtained for these losses. January having passed, men speculated whether Lucknow and Oude—to say nothing of other cities and provinces—would fall permanently into British hands during the month of February. What was the response to this much-mooted question, the present chapter will shew.

The gallant commander-in-chief, Sir Colin Campbell, being the chief actor in the busy military scenes of the period, it may be well to trace his movements during the month of February, before noticing the marchings and battles of other generals.

It will be remembered, from the details given in the last chapter, that Sir Colin, after the capture of Furruckabad and Futteghur early in January, remained during the greater part of that month encamped in that neighbourhood, organising the military arrangements necessary for an advance into Oude. These arrangements involved the arrival of siege-guns from Delhi and Agra, and the concentration at one point of different columns under his brigadiers. Among various subsidiary operations, Captain Taylor, of the Engineers, was sent to the Alum Bagh, to report as far as possible on the defensive works thrown up by the enemy in and near Lucknow, and to gather a strong engineer force to aid the commander-in-chief. Sir Colin remained nearly stationary during these preliminary proceedings, elaborating the details of his plan of strategy, in conjunction with his chief of the staff, General Mansfield. When his troops and his missiles, his *personnel* and *matériel*, were pretty well collected, he returned from Futteghur to Cawnpore on the 4th of February. Viscount Canning had shortly before gone up from Calcutta to Allahabad; and Sir Colin started off on the 8th to meet him. What these two representatives of British power agreed on during their interview, they of course kept to themselves; but every one felt the probability that some extensive scheme of policy, military and political, to be worked out by soldiers and civilians in unison, was discussed and mutually accepted. Returning again to Cawnpore, the commander-in-chief made the last arrangements for giving activity to the force which had been so slowly and with so much difficulty collected. Fain would many critics have censured the old general for delay; fain would they have urged that in two months he had only fought two battles—at Cawnpore and at Furruckabad—while the world was impatiently waiting to hear of the reconquest of Oude; but as he kept his own council with remarkable reticence, criticism gave way to a belief that there must have been good and sufficient cause for the caution which marked all his proceedings.

On or about the 11th of February, all the preparatory operations were completed, and an army, larger than any which had up to that time appeared against the rebels, began to cross the Ganges from Cawnpore into Oude. It had originally been intended to effect the crossing of a portion of the army at Futteghur; but Cawnpore was afterwards selected. The crossing was necessarily a slow and difficult one, on account of the vast *impedimenta* of an Indian army. To increase the facilities, a second bridge of boats was constructed. Even with this addition the passage across the Ganges lasted several days; for each bullock-cart carried but little. A small portion only of the ammunition, irrespective of all other equipage and baggage, required the services of fifteen hundred carts. The artillery was on an enormous scale; the siege-guns, the naval-brigade guns, the field-guns, and the horse-artillery guns, numbered not much less than two hundred in all. After crossing, the army distributed itself at certain places on the line of route from Cawnpore to Lucknow. For instance, on the 15th of the month, the head-quarters were still at Cawnpore; one portion of the army was encamped at Onao, one march from Cawnpore; another at Busherutgunje, a march and a half from Cawnpore; a third at Nawabgunge, two marches from Cawnpore; a fourth, under Outram, at the Alum Bagh; and a fifth at Sheorajpore, twenty miles from Cawnpore on the Allygurh road. Sir Colin himself still remained with head-quarters at Cawnpore—partly to provide for the safety of convoys of ladies and children passing down from Agra through Cawnpore to Allahabad; partly to await the entry into Oude, from the east, of the forces under Jung Bahadoor and Brigadier Franks; and partly to watch the proceedings of a large body of the enemy near Calpee, who were threatening again to overrun the Doab unless strongly held in check.

It may here usefully be stated that Sir Colin organised his Oudian army before any of the regiments began to cross into that province. As a permanent record of the component elements of that fine force, we give the details in a note at the end of the present chapter; but a summary may not be out of place here. The 'army of Oude,' as tabulated on the 10th of February, comprised such regiments and corps as were at that time under the more immediate command of Sir Colin Campbell; and took no account of the separate forces under Jung Bahadoor, Franks, Seaton, Macgregor, Windham, Inglis, Van Cortlandt, Rose, Stuart, Steuart, Orr, Whitlock, Greathed, Penny, M'Causland, Roberts, and other officers whose services were required elsewhere, or who had not reached the Oudian frontier at that date. The army of Oude, thus limited in its meaning, was systematically classified. There were three divisions of infantry, under Outram, Walpole, and a third general afterwards to be named. These were subdivided into six brigades, under Hamilton, Russell, Franklyn, Adrian Hope, Douglas, and Horsford—two brigades to each division. Each brigade was further divided into three regiments or battalions. The Queen's regiments of infantry in the six brigades were the 5th, 23d, 34th, 38th, 42d, 53d, 78th, 79th, 84th, 90th, and 93d, and two battalions of the Rifle Brigade. The other infantry regiments were Company's Europeans, Sikhs, and Punjaubees; the Goorkhas were in corps not yet incorporated in the army of Oude. A fourth division of infantry, under Franks, Wroughton, and Puhlwan Singh, was provided for, but did not at that time form a part of the army of Oude. The cavalry formed one division, under Hope Grant, and was separated into two brigades, under William Campbell and Little. The Queen's cavalry regiments in this division were the 2d Dragoon Guards, the 7th Hussars, and the 9th Lancers; the other cavalry were Sikhs, Punjaubees, and a few volunteers and irregulars of miscellaneous origin. The artillery division, under Archdale Wilson (the conqueror of Delhi), comprised a field-artillery brigade under Wood, a siege-artillery brigade under Barker, a naval brigade under Peel, and an engineer brigade under Napier.

Not until the last day of February did the commander-in-chief cross over the Ganges, and take command of the army destined to besiege and finally capture the great city of Lucknow. Meanwhile Sir James Outram, at the Alum Bagh, had been daily in communication with the other officers, and had prepared detailed plans of everything relating to Lucknow and its defences, so far as he was acquainted with them. The engineers, too, had been busily engaged in preparing that vast store of siege-materials which is necessary for the attack of strongly defended fortifications.

What the army of Oude effected during the month of March, the next chapter will shew. Before quitting this part of the February operations, however, it may be well to notice episodically the remarkable connection between the newspaper press and the battle-field in recent times. In the great wars of former days, correspondents residing at the chief cities in foreign countries were wont to send such items of information as they could pick up to the editors of English newspapers; and military officers, cautiously and anonymously, sent occasional criticisms on the details of the battles in which they were engaged. It was left for the period of the Crimean war, however, to commence, or at least to perfect, a system by which a non-military writer is sent out at enormous expense, to join an army in the field or at a siege, to bear some danger and much privation, to see with his own eyes everything that can be seen, and to write such descriptions of the scenes as shall be intelligible to ordinary newspaper readers. Mr W. H. Russell, of the *Times*, gave an importance to such communications never before equalled, by the brilliant style in which he described the military operations in Bulgaria and the Crimea during the Russian war of 1854-5; and the system was ably carried out by special correspondents connected with the staff of some of the other London newspapers. When the Indian mutiny was half a year old, Mr Russell started from England, to do that for India which he had before done for the Crimea—mix in the turmoil of war, and describe battles in a graphic and vivid way. What he saw and what he did in February initiated him into many of the peculiarities of Indian life, when scenes of slaughter had not yet come under his notice. Leaving Calcutta on the 4th of February, he went like other travellers to Raneegunge by railway, and thence to Benares by gharry dâk—a four-wheeled, venetian-blinded, oblong vehicle, driven by a native with 'mail post guard' inscribed on his brass belt-plate, and drawn at the rate of seven miles an hour by a single horse, the horse being changed at post-houses at every few miles' distance. On the way were troops going up with great regularity, travelling 35 miles per day in bullock-carts, and supplied with comfortable meals and sleeping-places at the dâk-bungalows. Travelling thus by way of Burdwan, Nimeaghat, Sheergotty, and Noubutpore, he arrived at Benares; this city, 'long, straggling, and Turkish looking,' was completely commanded by a new fort at Rajghat, built since the troubles of the preceding summer. Thence to Allahabad the fields were rich with corn, and the roads thronged by natives and trains of bullock-hackeries laden with cotton for the Benares and Mirzapore markets. Arrived at Allahabad, Mr Russell commenced his camp-life, messing generally with some of the officers, and sleeping under a tent. Viscount Canning and his suite were at that time living under canvas within the fort; while all around were evidences of military preparation for the English regiments sent up from Calcutta. Thence he travelled for fifty miles by the second portion of the great trunk-railway. The rebels in the preceding June had attacked the locomotives in an extraordinary way, if his account is to be taken as anything more than mere raillery: 'They fired musketry at the engines for some time at a distance, as if they were living bodies; then advanced cautiously, and finding that the engines did not stir, began to belabour them with sticks, all the time calling them names and abusing them.' By horse-dâk Mr Russell proceeded through Futtehpoor to Cawnpore, where he, like all others, was struck with astonishment that poor Sir Hugh Wheeler's 'intrenchment' could ever have held out so long as it did. Sir Colin Campbell was then at Cawnpore, living in a small subaltern's tent, working incessantly, and provided with an amount of personal 'baggage' so marvellously small as to shew how little the old soldier regarded luxuries. Mr Russell remained at Cawnpore till the 27th, when he joined the army in the march towards Lucknow. He had provided, in true Indian fashion, for the carriage of himself and baggage, a saddle-horse, a horse-gharry, and four camels. His account of the preparations for his march is not only amusing from the way in which it is told, but is instructive on matters relating to travelling in India.* The

* 'I have not as yet said one word of the two other camels which were appointed to carry my tent. Under the eaves of that tent had gathered a strange population—they came as sparrows come to a house, without the knowledge or consent of the owner; but the analogy fails in other respects except noise, because the natives require to be paid. There are two men who belong to the tent-post, as in England certain gentlemen belong to horses; then there is a man to carry water, who belongs to a large skin to contain that liquid; next there is a cleaner or sweeper; then there is a khitmutgar or servant, and there is his and my master, one Simon, "an assizes man" he says himself, but he only means that he is a follower of St Francisco d'Assisi; and then follow camel-keepers, and horse-keepers, and grass-cutters; so that I feel very much as Sancho did in his government of Barataria. On the morning of the 27th, soon after midnight, commenced a tumult in camp, the like of which I never heard before; first began a loud tapping of all the tent-pegs, as if an army of gigantic woodpeckers were attacking us. This was caused by the kélassies, or tent-men, loosening the tent-pegs, so that they might be drawn easily from the ground when the word to march was given. Then followed a most hideous grumbling, growling, roaring noise, as if many thousands of aldermen were choking all at once, only that it was kept up for hours; that was caused by the camels objecting to the placement of the smallest article on their backs, and continuing their opposition till they stalked off with their loads. Then came the trumpeting of elephants, the squeaking of bullock cart-wheels, the hum and buzz of thousands of voices, and at last the first bugle-call, which announced that the time for turning out had arrived. Daylight was still striving with the moonlight for mastery, and casting a sort of neutral tint over the camping-ground, on which blazed the flames of many watchfires, when the heads of our columns began to cross the bridge of boats at Cawnpore. There was but a waste of baked earth where, at sunset, had been a camp—only a few tents belonging to the commander-in-chief and the head-quarters' staff, were left behind; and for

end of February found Mr Russell, a civilian immersed in all the bustle of an army, ready to see and hear whatever the month of March should present to his attention.

Leaving for the present the commander-in-chief and his army, we shall briefly trace the operations, so far as they occurred in the month of February, of such of his generals as were employed in duties away from his immediate control and supervision.

Sir James Outram at once presents claims for notice; for though appointed general of one of the divisions of the army of Oude, he held an independent command until the month had expired. During more than three months this distinguished officer had never seen Sir Colin Campbell; during more than five months he had never once been away from the vicinity of Lucknow and the Alum Bagh. He marched with Havelock and Neill from Cawnpore to the capital of Oude in September, and relieved or rather reinforced Inglis; he commanded the British Residency at Lucknow during October, with Havelock and Inglis as his subordinates; he aided Sir Colin to effect the 'rescue' in November; and then he commanded at the Alum Bagh throughout the whole of December, January, and February. What he did in the first two of these months, we have seen in former chapters; what were his military proceedings in February, a few lines will suffice to shew.

Whether the enemy supposed that, by another attack on the Alum Bagh, they might disturb the extensive plans of the British; whether they were influenced by a sudden impulse to achieve a limited success; or whether another motive existed, presently to be mentioned—they fought another battle with Sir James Outram, and received their usual defeat. On the morning of the 21st of February, no less than 20,000 of the enemy attacked the Alum Bagh. Having filled all the trenches with as many men as they could hold, and placed large masses of infantry in the topes as a support, they commenced a simultaneous movement round both flanks of Outram's position—threatening at the same time the whole length of front, the north-east corner of the Alum Bagh, and the picket and fort at Jelalabad. Outram, perceiving at a glance the nature of the attack, strengthened the several endangered points. At the Alum Bagh and Jelalabad posts the enemy received a severe check, having come within range of the grape-shot which the British poured out upon them. He detached about 250 cavalry, and two field-pieces, under Captain Barrow, to the rear of Jelalabad; here Barrow came suddenly upon 2000 of the enemy's cavalry, and 5000 infantry, whom he kept at bay so effectually with his two field-guns, that they were quite frustrated in their intended scheme of attack. The enemy's attack on Outram's left flank was made by no fewer than 5000 cavalry and 8000 *infantry*. To oppose these he sent only four field-guns and 120 men of the military train, under Major Robertson; but this mere handful of men, with the guns, drove away the enemy. A large convoy was at the time on the road from Cawnpore; and the escort for this convoy had taken away most of Outram's cavalry. It is not surprising that the enemy should select such a time for attacking the Alum Bagh and endeavouring to intercept the convoy; but it is certainly a matter for wonder that such a large army should suffer itself to be beaten by a few hundred men. The casualty-list, too, was as surprising as anything else; for Outram had only 9 wounded and *none* killed; whereas the enemy's loss was adverted to in the following terms: 'The reports from the city state the enemy to have lost 60 killed and 200 wounded in their attack on the Alum Bagh, and about 80 or 90 killed in front of Jelalabad. This was exclusive of their loss on the left flank, and along our front, where our heavy artillery had constant opportunities of firing shell and shrapnel into the midst of their moving masses. I consider their loss to have been heavier than on any of their previous attacks.' At this very time the bulk of Sir Colin's army was approaching the Alum Bagh; the enemy well knew that fact, and had only been induced to hazard the attack on the 21st by the temporary absence of some of Outram's troops. The attack having failed, they hastened back to strengthen their defensive arrangements at Lucknow.

It may now be well to notice what was doing eastward of Oude. The strong Goorkha force under Jung Bahadoor, and the effective column of miscellaneous troops under Brigadier Franks, had greatly improved the condition of that portion of country which lay between Oude and Lower Bengal, around the cities and stations of Patna, Dinapoor, Arrah, Buxar, Ghazeepore, Azimghur, Goruckpore, Jounpoor, Benares, and Mirzapore. Mutineers there were, and marauders connected with rebel chieftains; but their audacity, except in the immediate vicinity of Oude, was checked by the increasing power of the forces brought to bear against them.

Brigadier Franks, one of the most energetic and admired of the officers whom the wars of the mutiny brought forth, had since the month of December commanded a column called the Jounpoor Field-force, which had been employed in chastising and expelling bodies of rebels from the Azimghur, Allahabad, and Jounpoor districts. During these operations, he had defeated the enemy at many places. The time was now approaching when Franks was to join Sir Colin

hours the bridges echoed to the tramp of men and horse, the rumble of artillery, and the tread of innumerable elephants, and camels, and oxen. The Ganges is at this season at its lowest, and the bridges are not, I should think, more than 300 yards long; one is used for the exit, the other for the entrance of Cawnpore. They lead to a level sandy plain, overflowed by the Ganges for several hundred yards in the rainy season, on which there were now moving, as far as the eye could reach, the strings of baggage animals and the commissariat carts of the army, with their fantastic followers.'

in the final operations against Lucknow; and when his Jounpoor field-force, losing its individuality, was to form the fourth division of infantry in the army of Oude, with Franks as its general of division. That change, however, was not likely to occur until the month of March had arrived. About the middle of February he was with his force at Budleepore, a town on the route from Jounpoor to Sultanpore in Oude. His force comprised H.M. 10th, 20th, and 97th regiments, six regiments of Goorkhas, and twenty guns. Colonel Puhlwan Singh commanded the Goorkhas, and Colonel Maberley the artillery. The force was a strong one, containing 2300 Europeans and 3200 Goorkhas, and an excellent park of guns. There was one month's provisions collected; and Franks was awaiting the orders of Sir Colin for an advance into Oude. Colonel Wroughton was with him, having no distinct military command, but acting as a medium of communication between Franks and Puhlwan Singh; being familiar with the Goorkhas, his services were valuable in giving such instructions to the Nepaulese auxiliaries as would enable them to understand and obey the orders of the brigadier.

Although placed in an expectant attitude, until he could receive instructions from Sir Colin, and until he heard of Jung Bahadoor's crossing of the frontier into Oude, Brigadier Franks was quite ripe for an encounter with the enemy whenever and wherever he could meet with them. They gave him an opportunity before the month was out, and he made ample use of it. He crossed the frontier into Oude near Singramow, on the 19th, and received speedy proof that a very large body of the enemy was before him—ordered, apparently, by the self-appointed authorities at Lucknow, to prevent him from approaching that city. Franks, however, cleverly deceiving the rebel leader, Nazim Mahomed Hossein, attacked his army in detail, first at Chandah and then at Humeerpoor. The section of the rebels at Chandah, under Bunda Hossein, comprised among other troops the mutinous sepoys of the 20th, 28th, 48th, and 71st Bengal native regiments. Franks attacked them in a strong position. They were in the fort and intrenchments, and crowning a long row of hillocks in front of the town; every neighbouring tope and village was full of them. Nevertheless he defeated them, and captured six of their guns. Giving his troops only a very brief rest, he marched on to Humeerpoor, two or three miles distant, on that same evening, and attacked a still larger force under the Nazim himself. The defeat was equally significant. 'Our Enfield rifles did it all,' wrote one of the English officers. The enemy retreated during the night, and Franks and his brave men bivouacked, after having, in the two engagements, inflicted a loss on their opponents of six guns and 800 men killed and wounded. The brigadier himself had been in the saddle fifteen hours on this severe day. After resting on the 20th, Franks and his opponent the Nazim, the one at Humeerpoor and the other at Warree, sought which should be the first to obtain possession of the pass, jungle, and fort of Badshaigunje. By a forced march, the English brigadier outmanœuvred the Nazim, gained the fort, and waited till reinforcements could reach him. The two forces came in sight of each other again on the 23d, by which time the Nazim and Bunda Hossein had swelled their motley army to no less than 25,000 men, comprising 5000 revolted sepoys, 1100 sowars, and the rest rabble; having with them 25 guns. The result of this encounter was a severe battle, fought near Sultanpore. The enemy had taken up a very wide position; their centre resting on the old cantonment and sepoy lines, thence extending through villages and topes, and screened in front by hillocks and nullahs. Franks turned the enemy's right by a detour, drew them into a hot struggle, and won a complete victory. No less than 1800 insurgents were killed and wounded, including two or three rebel chieftains. The victors captured twenty pieces of artillery, and the whole of the enemy's standing camp, baggage, ammunition, &c. The result of this battle was that the enemy were frustrated in the attempt to check the advance of Franks into Oude; he found the roads to Lucknow and Fyzabad entirely open to him. If he had had cavalry, he would have pursued and cut up the enemy in retreat; but 250 horse, long and anxiously expected from Allahabad, did not arrive at Sultanpore until the day after the battle. These three actions, two on the 19th and one on the 23d, were marked by that anomaly which the military operations in India so often exhibited—the disparity between the losses on the two sides. Nothing but a full trust in the truthfulness of a gallant officer would render credible the fact that, after conflicts in which 2600 of the enemy were killed and wounded, the conqueror could write as follows: 'I am proud to announce that, through the glorious conduct of the officers and men of this force, European and Nepaulese, I have been enabled by manœuvring to achieve these brilliant results with the loss on our side, in all three actions, of only 2 men killed and 16 wounded'—and this, be it remembered, in contesting against four times his own numbers.

While this Jounpoor field-force was thus actively engaged, a small body of English sailors were slowly advancing by another route into Oude. Ever active to be up and doing, a band of about 250 tars, belonging to the steam-frigate *Pearl*, were delighted at being formed into a naval brigade, and offered a chance of meeting and well belabouring the 'Pandies.' Under Captain Sotheby, they were sent up the river Gogra in the Company's steamer *Jumna*. They embarked near Dinapoor, and disembarked on the 20th at Nowraine, twenty miles short of Fyzabad. The enemy had two forts at that place, both of which were speedily taken, together with guns and ammunition, and the enemy driven away with great loss. Jung Bahadoor, with his Nepaulese contingent, was at the time not far distant; and Colonel Rowcroft, with 2000 Goorkhas, aided in the attack.

The proceedings of the Nepaulese leader must now be noticed. The English officers frequently, though cautiously, complained of the slowness of his movements; and Sir Colin Campbell was becoming impatient for his appearance near the great scene of conflict at Lucknow. He had been many weeks in the region around Goruckpore, with a fine army of 9000 Goorkhas; and though he had aided in putting down many bands of insurgents, it was now hoped that he would at once advance towards the centre of Oude. This he did, but not rapidly, during the month of February.

On the 26th, while Jung Bahadoor and Brigadier Macgregor were on the march from Mobarukhpoor to Ukberpoor, on the way to Fyzabad, they learned that a small body of rebels were in a fort at Berozepoor. A portion of the body-guard went to the place, and relied on a promise made by the rebels that they would evacuate the fort in forty minutes. Instead of departing, the enemy prepared for a defence; and a desperate fight ensued around a small fort distinguished by much novelty of construction. The fort was so completely surrounded by an impenetrable hedge of bamboos, that the besiegers were in much doubt concerning the nature of the defences within. At one place they were stopped by a ditch, at another by a high mud-wall and bastion, at another by a row of lofty bamboo-stakes. The place being very small, an attempt was made to storm it by assault; but so many were the obstacles, that a clearance by cannonade became necessary; and it was not until after much artillery firing, and much loss of life, that the fort was captured. So peculiar was the construction of the place, that Captain Holland was obliged to drag a 6-pounder gun through a bamboo-fence and an outer ditch, before he could breach a mud-wall which had until then been invisible. It was certainly no small achievement, in a military point of view, for the enemy to have constructed a fort entirely novel to the besiegers, and capable of being defended for several hours by less than forty men against many hundreds. When all was over, Brigadier Macgregor, wishing to know something more of the nature and construction of this little fort of Berozepoor, requested Lieutenant Sankey, of the Madras Engineers, to examine and report thereon—seeing that there might be like forts elsewhere, with which it would be well to be familiar. Near the village of Berozepoor, then, the fort was built. It was only sixty feet square, with circular bastions at the angles, and a banquette just within the parapet on which musketeers might stand. The mud-rampart was fifteen feet above the level of the ground, very thick at the bottom and loopholed for musketry at the top. It was surrounded by a ditch, this again by a belt of high bamboos, which was in turn encircled by another ditch ten or twelve feet deep. A row of newly planted bamboo slips, eight or ten feet high, was placed on the immediate lip of the counterscarp of the outer ditch. Lieutenant Sankey said in his report: 'Viewed from the outside, nothing very suspicious or formidable was discoverable about the place. It had all the appearance of an ordinary clump of bamboos at the corner of a village; which latter, like all inhabited places in this part of the country, was very well screened in foliage.' He found it, however, 'a very hedgehog of fortification. Nothing could be more difficult of approach; every portion bristling with thorns, and intercepted by ditches and banks.'

A little must now be said concerning a few isolated operations, belonging to the month of February, near the Jumna and the Ganges, in which Seaton, Maxwell, and Hope Grant were concerned. Colonel Seaton, at the close of the month, was at Mahomedabad, a few miles distant from Futteghur. He had with him a detachment of the 82d foot, 300 of De Kantzow's horse, 350 of De Kantzow's foot, and 40 Sikh troopers. After waiting for the arrival of the 4th Punjaub infantry, the 3d Europeans, Alexander's Horse, and nine guns, he was enabled to organise an efficient column for chastising the rebels in a number of villages around Futteghur. Those operations, however, scarcely commenced until the month of March.

Colonel Maxwell had the gratification of defeating a body of insurgents who had for a long time given much anxiety to the British officers—anxiety arising from a doubt concerning the plans and movements of the insurgents. The Gwalior mutineers are here alluded to. They did not allow the month to pass away wholly without giving signs of activity; though those signs were few and unimportant. Colonel Maxwell, commanding a detachment sent out from Cawnpore, suddenly found himself attacked on the 4th by the mutineers, who marched from Calpee to his camp at Bhogneepore. The broken nature of the ground, the cover of the crops, and the dimness of the light at five o'clock on a winter's morning, prevented Maxwell from forming a correct estimate of numbers; but he had every reason for believing them to be in great strength. He could only bring against them five companies of H.M. 88th foot, 50 troopers, and 2 guns; yet with this small force he maintained a running-fight for four hours. The enemy disputed every inch of the ground, making a stand at Chowra, a place three or four miles distant from the camp. He pursued them until they retreated across a small river, keeping up the fire of their skirmishers to the very last. It is difficult to understand what could have been the nature of the enemy's fire; for while, after the battle, the bodies of eighty rebels were found dead upon the field, Colonel Maxwell recorded only five wounded (none killed) in his own little force. Among the wounded was Lieutenant Thompson, one of the few who escaped alive from Cawnpore.

About the middle of February, it became known

that bodies of the enemy were in motion near the fords or ghats on the left bank of the Ganges, between Futteghur and Cawnpore, ready for any mischief that might present itself. To clear away these rebels, a movable column was organised, consisting of H.M. 34th, 38th, and 53d regiments, squadrons of the 7th Hussars and 9th Lancers, squadrons of Hodson's Horse and Watson's Horse, a company of Sappers and Miners, and a few guns. This column was to start from the main Lucknow road at a point near Bunnee, and to proceed on a line inclining towards the Ganges at such an angle as to sweep the rebels towards the west, where, at present, they would be less mischievous than if near the banks of the river. Sir Hope Grant took command of this column, which consisted of 3246 men (2240 infantry, 636 cavalry, 326 artillery, and 44 native Sappers). One of his achievements with this column consisted in the storming and capture of the town of Meeangunje or Meagunje, on the 23d of February. In the course of his various marchings, he learned that a body of the enemy had taken up a strong position at Meeangunje, a town between Lucknow and Futteghur. They had 2000 infantry in the town, 300 cavalry outside, and five or six guns. Hope Grant's force being stronger than theirs, a victory was naturally to be expected, although the position was a strong one. Meeangunje was surrounded by a stone wall fourteen feet high, and had three strong gates, opening into the Lucknow, Cawnpore, and Rohilcund roads respectively; there were also numerous bastions on all sides. At each of the gates the enemy placed guns behind strong breastworks, and the breastworks themselves were covered by trees. After a careful reconnoitring, Grant found a weak point on the fourth side of the town, where he could bring two heavy guns within three or four hundred yards of the wall, at a place where a postern-gate pierced it. Telling off part of his force to command the Lucknow road, another part to the Rohilcund road, and the rest to await behind a village the result of the cannonading, he opened fire. In less than an hour, the two heavy guns made a practicable breach in the wall. Grant at once ordered H.M. 53d to advance to the assault. The regiment separated into two wings, one of which, after entering the breach, proceeded under Colonel English through the left of the town; while the other, under Major Payne, penetrated to the right. This work was admirably done; the infantry advancing through a labyrinth of lanes, and driving the enemy before them at every yard. The town was captured, and with it six guns. The enemy, in endeavouring to escape by the several gates, were killed or captured to the number of nearly a thousand altogether. Here occurred another of those inexplicable anomalies already adverted to; Sir Hope Grant, in language too distinct to be misinterpreted, stated that his loss was only 2 killed and 19 wounded.

The Doab had undergone a wonderful improvement during the winter months. District after district was gradually falling out of the enemy's hands, and into the power of the British. Nevertheless, there was much need for caution. The insurgents were cunning, and often appeared where little expected. The commander-in-chief's operations, in February as in December, were influenced by the necessity of providing for the safety of non-combatants escaping from the scenes of strife. In the earlier month, as we have already seen, Sir Colin could not chastise the Gwalior mutineers until he had sent off the women, children, sick, and wounded from Lucknow to Cawnpore, Futtehpoor, and Allahabad; and now, in February, he had to secure the passage of a convoy from Agra, comprising a large number of ladies and 140 children. Protected by the 3d Bengal Europeans, some irregular horse, and two guns, these helpless persons left Agra on the 11th of February, and proceeded by way of Ferozabad and Minpooree to Cawnpore—thence to be forwarded to Allahabad. On the way, the convoy watched narrowly for any indications of the presence of Nena Sahib, who was reported to be in movement somewhere in that quarter.

Of Delhi, the chief matter here to be noticed, is the trial of the old imprisoned king, for complicity in the mutiny and its atrocities. Without formally limiting the account to the month of February, the general course of the investigation may briefly be traced.

The trial commenced on the 27th of January, in the celebrated imperial chamber of the Dewani Khas, the 'Elysium' where in former days Mogul power had been displayed in all its gorgeousness. The tribunal was a court-martial, all the members being military officers. The president was Colonel Dawes (in lieu of Brigadier Showers, who, though first appointed, had been obliged to leave for service elsewhere). The other members were Major Palmer, Major Redmond, Major Sawyers, and Captain Rothney. Major Harriott, deputy-judge-advocate-general, officiated as government prosecutor. The charges against the king were set forth under four headings.* It may be doubted

* 'COPY OF CHARGES PREFERRED AGAINST MAHOMED BAHADOOR SHAH, EX-KING OF DELHI.

'1. For that he, being a pensioner of the British government in India, did at Delhi, at various times between the 10th of May and 1st of October 1857, encourage, aid, and abet Mahomed Bukht Khan, Subadar of the regiment of artillery, and divers others, non-commissioned officers and soldiers, unknown, of the East India Company's army, in the crimes of mutiny and rebellion against the state.

'2. For having, at Delhi, at various times between the 10th of May and 1st of October 1857, encouraged, aided, and abetted Mirza Mogul, his own son, a subject of the British government in India, and divers other unknown inhabitants of Delhi and of the North-west Provinces of India, also subjects of the said British government, to rebel and wage war against the state.

'3. For that he, being a subject of the British government in India, and not regarding the duty of his allegiance, did at Delhi, on the 11th of May 1857, or thereabouts, as a false traitor against the state, proclaim and declare himself the reigning king and sovereign of India, and did then and there traitorously seize and take unlawful possession of the city of Delhi; and did, moreover, at various times between the 10th of May and 1st of October 1857, as such false traitor aforesaid, treasonably conspire, consult, and agree with Mirza Mogul, his son, and with Mahomed Bukht Khan, subadar of the regiment of artillery, and divers other false traitors unknown, to raise, levy, and make insurrection, rebellion, and war against the state; and, further to fulfil and perfect his treasonable design of overthrowing and destroying the British whether the wearisome legal phraseology ('to raise, levy, and make insurrection, rebellion, and war'—'treasonably conspire, consult, and agree with,' &c.) was well fitted for the purpose; but this may depend on the mode in which the English was translated into Hindustani.

It was impossible for the spectators to regard without emotion the appearance of the aged monarch, the last representative of a long line of Indian potentates, thus brought as a culprit before a tribunal of English officers. Even those who considered him simply as a hoary-headed villain were interested by the proceedings. After being in attendance some time, sitting in a palanquin outside the court, under a guard of Rifles, he was summoned within at about noon. He appeared very infirm, and tottered into court supported on one side by his favourite son, Jumma Bukht, and on the other by a confidential servant. He sat coiled up on a cushion at the left of the president; and 'presented such a picture of helpless imbecility as, under other circumstances, must have awakened pity.' His son stood a few yards to the left, and the guard of Rifles beyond all.

After the members of the court, the prosecutor, and the interpreter, had taken the usual oaths, the prosecutor proceeded to read the charges against the prisoner. He next addressed the court in a concise and explanatory manner; and announced that, though the king would be tried to ascertain whether he were guilty or not guilty, no capital sentence could be passed upon him, in consequence of his life having been guaranteed to him by Sir Archdale Wilson, through Captain Hodson. When the king was asked, through the interpreter, whether he was guilty or innocent, he professed to be ignorant of the nature of the charges against him. This, however, was affected ignorance, for the charges had long before been presented to him, translated into his own language. After considerable delay, he pleaded 'not guilty.'

During several sittings of the court, occupying many weeks, numerous witnesses were examined. Among them were Jutmull, Mukkhun Lall, Captain Forrest, Sir Theophilus Metcalfe, Hussun Uskeree, Bukhtawar, Kishen, Chunee, Golam, Essamoola Khan, and other persons, European, Eurasian or half-caste, and native. The evidence brought against the king was of very varied character, tending to shew that he both aided in inciting the mutiny, and in encouraging the atrocities of the mutineers. Some of the evidence proved that, so long ago as the summer of 1856, the King of Delhi had been in correspondence with the Shah of Persia, touching an overturning of the English 'raj' in India; in a manner and at a time corresponding with the advance of the Persians towards Herat. Other portions confirmed the fact that many of the massacres at Delhi, at the beginning of the Revolt, were sanctioned by the palace profligates, and even committed immediately under the king's own apartments. Sir T. Metcalfe, in his evidence, stated it as his opinion, derived from an intimate acquaintance with Delhi and its inhabitants, that the Revolt was the legitimate fruit of a Mussulman conspiracy; that the courts of Delhi and Lucknow were concerned in this conspiracy; that the war with Persia helped to strengthen it; that the Hindoos were used as tools in the matter by the Mohammedans; and that the affair of the greased cartridges was regarded as a lucky opportunity for enlisting Hindoo prejudices.

During the trial the king displayed a mingled silliness and cunning that revealed much of his character. Sometimes, while the evidence was being taken, he would coil himself up on his cushion, and appear lost in the land of dreams. Except when anything particular struck him, he paid, or appeared to pay, no attention whatever to the proceedings. On one of the days he was aroused from sleep, to reply to a question put by the court. Sometimes he would rouse up, as if by some sudden impulse, and make an exclamation in denial of a witness's statement. Once, when the intrigues of Persia were under notice, he asked whether the Persians and the Russians were the same people. On the twelfth day of the trial, the king was more animated than usual; he several times declared his innocence of everything; and amused himself by twisting and untwisting a scarf round his head.

Without tracing the incidents of the trial day by day, or quoting the evidence, it may suffice to say that the guilt of the aged sinner was sufficiently proved, on some if not all of the charges. The safety of his life being guaranteed, imprisonment became the only probable punishment. He was sentenced for the rest of his days to transportation—either to one of the Andaman Islands (a group in the eastern portion of the Bay of Bengal), or to some other place that might be selected. It may not be inappropriate to mention that some of the witnesses proved that Mr Colvin at Agra, and Sir Theophilus Metcalfe at Delhi, were told of a forthcoming Mohammedan conspiracy many weeks before the Meerut outbreak; so utterly, however, did these authorities disregard the rumour, that they did not even report it to the Calcutta government. There were only a few men in India, in the spring of 1857, who believed that the British 'raj' was 'on the edge of a volcano.'

government in India, did assemble armed forces at Delhi, and send them forth to fight and wage war against the said British government.

4. For that he, at Delhi, on the 16th of May 1857, or thereabouts, did, within the precincts of the palace at Delhi, feloniously cause and become accessory to the murder of 49 persons, chiefly women and children, of European and mixed European descent; and did, moreover, between the 10th of May and the 1st of October 1857, encourage and abet divers soldiers and others in murdering European officers and other English subjects, including women and children, both by giving and promising such murderers service, advancement, and distinction; and further, that he issued orders to different native rulers, having local authority in India, to slay and murder Christians and English people whenever and wherever found in their territories; the whole or any part of such conduct being a heinous offence under the provisions of Act 16, of 1857, of the Legislative Council of India.

'FREDERICK J. HARRIOTT, Major,
'*Deputy-judge-advocate-general, Government Prosecutor.*

'*Jan. 8, 1858.*'

In connection with the fate of the old king, much attention was necessarily bestowed on the past conduct of his favourite young wife, the intriguing Sultana Zeenat Mahal, the 'dark, fat, shrewd, but sensual-looking woman,' whom Mrs Hodson visited in the prison,* in relation to the Revolt. Ever since the year 1853, a feud had existed in the royal family, arising out of the polygamic troubles so frequent in oriental countries. The king, instigated by Zeenat Mahal, wished to name the child of his old age, Mirza Jumma Bukht, heir to the throne of Akbar; but the British government insisted on recognising the superior claims of an elder son, Mirza Fukhr-oo-deen. Strife and contest immediately commenced, and never ceased until one obstacle was removed from the path. Mirza Fukhr-oo-deen died in 1856, as alleged, of cholera, but not without suspicion of foul play. From that time till the beginning of the mutiny in the following year, the imperial palace was a focus of intriguing. The sultana bent her whole energies towards obtaining the heirship to the throne of the Moguls for her own son. She was known to have declared that this object would be persistently and steadily pursued, and to have opened many communications thereon with the authorities at Calcutta. When, however, it was announced that a grandson of the king should, after him, possess all that remained of imperial power, her plans were at once dashed. It thenceforward became a question with her whether, by an overturn of the English 'raj,' she could obtain that which was denied to her by the government; and when other sources of revolt and rebellion appeared, there was an intelligible reason why she should encourage the insurgents. Nothing came out at the trial so clear as to fix guilt unquestionably upon her; but there remained on men's minds a suspicion to which collateral circumstances afforded much probability.

Transferring attention from Delhi to Rohilcund and the Hills, it may at once be explained that little occurred during the month of February requiring detailed notice. The time had not yet arrived when Sir Colin Campbell could send strong columns to sweep away the rebels in that quarter. Bareilly was still the head-quarters of a rebel force, which ruled almost the whole of Rohilcund. Khan Bahadoor Khan, the self-appointed chief, had still around him a large body of revolted sepoys and insurgent retainers; and in the whole region between Oude on the one side, and Delhi and Meerut on the other, very little was under British control. The time, however, for making a demonstration in this quarter was approaching. Among other military arrangements planned about the middle of February, was the formation of a movable column at Meerut, to be held in readiness to march anywhere at a short notice. It was to consist of a squadron of Carabiniers, a wing of the 60th Rifles, a wing of the Belooch battalion, the 1st Punjaub infantry, the Moultanee horse, a field-battery, two 18-pounders, and one 8-inch howitzer. There was at the same time at Looksar, near Roorkee, a small force under Captain Brind, consisting of a squadron of Carabiniers, Hughes's irregular cavalry, detachments of Coke's Rifles, of the Nusseree battalion, and of the 3d Punjaub infantry, and a troop of horse-artillery. At Roorkee another corps was to be formed, under Major Coke, to consist of Punjaub regiments about to arrive. It was proposed that these three bodies—the movable column at Meerut, Brind's corps at Looksar, and Coke's corps at Roorkee—should ultimately form a Rohilcund field-force, under General Penny. What was effected by means of this force, will come for notice in a future page; little could be achieved until the commander-in-chief had broken the strength of the enemy in Oude, now the great centre of rebellion.

The hilly country in and around Kumaon, although too far removed from the Jumna regions to be frequently engaged in the horrors of war, was nevertheless occasionally made a battle-ground between hostile forces. Early in February, Colonel M'Causland, commanding in Kumaon, formed a camp at Huldwanee, to protect the Kumaon hills, and to clear the Barbur and Turale districts of rebels. He found two formidable bodies of the enemy threatening that region. One, under a leader named Fuzul Huq, consisting of 4000 men and 6 guns, was encamped at Sunda, in a strong position on the banks of the Sookhee river, about fifteen miles from Huldwanee, on the Peleebheet road. The other, under Khali Khan, consisting of 5000 men and 4 guns, was encamped at Churpurah, on the Paha Nuddee, sixteen miles from Huldwanee, on the Bareilly road. So far as could be judged, it appeared as if these 9000 men intended to make a combined attack on Huldwanee, and then to force the hill-passes. To encounter these enemies, M'Causland's force was but small, consisting of 700 Goorkha infantry, 200 horse, and 2 field-guns; nevertheless he resolved to confront them boldly. On the 9th of February he commenced a movement intended to prevent the junction of the two hostile forces. In the dead of the night, leaving his tents to be guarded by a few men in a barricaded square called the Mundee, he marched out as quietly as possible to the place occupied by Khali Khan's army. He came up to them at daybreak on the 10th, and found them encamped in a strong position; with their rear and left protected by the Paha Nuddee, a small village filled with infantry on their right flank, their front protected by rough ground intersected with nullahs and long jungle-grass, and the road commanded by four pieces of artillery. So completely did he surprise them, that when his cavalry first appeared, the rebels thought their allies under Fuzul Huq had arrived. Finding the enemy's right flank the best to attack, the colonel sent most of his men to that point, covered by the fire of his

* Chap. xx., p. 357.

two guns. The contest was sharp and severe. In about an hour the Goorkhas had captured the enemy's guns, cut down every artilleryman serving them, and dislodged the enemy from the village. Meanwhile the few horse made a gallant charge, repulsing a superior body of the enemy's cavalry, and taking a standard. The colonel's two guns worked immense execution among the enemy's cavalry, 'into which' (to use the professional language of the commander) 'they poured shrapnel with beautiful precision and tremendous effect.' The victory was complete. The enemy lost their guns, ammunition, standing-camp, baggage, 300 killed, and 600 wounded. The colonel, having thus defeated nearly six times his number, returned to Huldwanee—his gallant Goorkhas having marched thirty-four miles and fought a severe battle in thirteen hours. It was deemed necessary to return at once, lest their prolonged absence from Huldwanee should tempt Fuzul Huq, whose army was not far distant, to make a dash on the camp and station.

Nynee Tal was deeply interested in all these movements. During February it was hemmed in by the rebels on one side, and by the hill-snows on the other. The enemy, deterred by the gallant force at Huldwanee, hoped to penetrate to the little colony by a detour through the Kulleedougee Pass. This hope, however, was not worth much to them; for the pass was long and fatiguing; and near its top was a small body of Goorkhas, who, with a few guns, were determined to make a stout resistance if any attack were made.

The Punjaub and Sinde were nearly at peace. The few instances of turbulence, or of military operation, may pass without record here.

In that vast range of country which has in so many chapters required attention, comprising Rajpootana, Gujerat, Central India, the Mahratta States, Bundelcund, and the Saugor territories, the month of February exhibited the gradual strengthening of British columns sent up from Bombay and Madras, and the success of numerous small engagements in which the names of Rose, Roberts, Orr, Whitlock, Stuart, Steuart, and other officers are concerned. Being small in themselves, these engagements hardly need separate notice; but taken collectively, they tended to assist the commander-in-chief's plans towards the general pacification of India.

The month of February witnessed the conclusion of a series of services rendered by a small force under somewhat remarkable circumstances. Mention has frequently been made of Captain Osborne, political agent at Rewah, almost the only Englishman within a turbulent district. Fortunately, the Rajahs of Rewah and Nagode remained faithful to the British; they, with the aid of Osborne, formed a corps of such of their native troops as they felt could be trusted; and this corps was placed under Colonel Hinde for active service. It was November when the corps was first organised; but, the troops being undisciplined, badly equipped, and badly armed, and the arrangements for marching and camping being very defective, it was the middle of December before the corps started from the town of Rewah. The duty to be performed was to keep open and safe the road from Rewah to Jubbulpoor (one of the great highways of India), and to capture such forts by the way as were in hostile hands. Imperfect as were the materials at his command, Colonel Hinde nevertheless, between the middle of December and the middle of February, captured six forts, forty guns, two mortars, and two standards; rendered the great road to the Deccan secure; re-established dâk and police bungalows; restored order in the Myhere territory; annexed the small territory of the rebellious chieftains of Bijeeragooghar; appointed tehsildars and police therein; and captured a large number of turbulent rebels. The six forts taken were Kunchunpore, Goonah, Myhere, Jokai, Khunwara, and Bijeeragooghar. These services having been rendered, Captain Osborne recalled the corps to Rewah; and the governor-general thanked both him and Colonel Hinde for what they had effected in a troubled region, with very limited means. It is pleasant—amid the treachery of so many 'Pandies' and 'Singhs'—to read that Osborne and Hinde had a good word to say for Dinbund Pandy, Lullaic Singh, Sewgobind Pandy, Davy Singh, and Bisseshur Singh—Rewah and Nagode native officers, who were both faithful and brave in the hour of need.

Brigadier Whitlock, with a Madras column, was rendering service in the country between Nagpoor and Bundelcund. He had various skirmishes with bands of rebels at Jubbulpoor and Sleemanabad; and when he had restored something like order in that region, he moved off towards Cawnpore, there to take part if necessary in the operations of the army of Oude.

Few Europeans in India had better reason than those at Saugor to welcome the approach of some of their countrymen as deliverers. So far back as the month of June, the officers, their ladies, and the civilians, had been shut up in the fort by orders of Brigadier Sage, on account of the suspicious symptoms presented by the 31st, 42d, and other native regiments. There they remained throughout the whole of the autumn and part of the winter, too strong to be seriously molested, and too well supplied with food to suffer those privations which were so sadly experienced at Lucknow. Sir Hugh Rose arrived with his force at Saugor on the 3d of February, and liberated those who had so long been confined within the fort. No battle was needed to effect this; for though the garrison were almost entirely without reliable troops, they were not besieged by any considerable force of the enemy. Rose, who had collected a force with much difficulty from various quarters, prepared after the relief of Saugor to attack numerous bands of rebels in that part of India. He assaulted the strong fortress of Garra Kotah, at the confluence of the Sonah and the Guddarree; he captured it, pursued and cut up the enemy, and then marched towards Jhansi, where busy work awaited him in the following month.

General Roberts, towards the close of February, was collecting a force at and near Nusseerabad, for operations in that part of Rajpootana. He went with the head-quarters of H.M. 95th from Deesa to Beaur, and thence to Nusseerabad, where he arrived on the 22d. He was to be joined shortly afterwards by the 72d Highlanders from Deesa, and by 200 of the Sinde horse under Major Green; and when strengthened by other regiments, especially a good body of cavalry, he intended to march towards Kotah, a very strong fortress which had long been in the hands of a rebel chieftain.

The regions forming the central and southern

Moulvies, or Mohammedan Religious Teachers.

portions of the Bombay presidency were a little disturbed by fanatical Mohammedans, who, though unable to bring any very large number of conspirators into their plan of action, did nevertheless make many attempts to raise the green flag, the symbol of Moslem supremacy. There were no mutinies of whole regiments, however, or even companies of regiments. Indeed the instigators of mischief were rather rioters than soldiers; and the authorities only regarded these outbreaks seriously as sparks that might possibly kindle inflammable materials elsewhere.

The Nizam's country, generally peaceful on account of his fidelity to the English, became a field of temporary struggle owing to the insubordination of a minor chieftain, the Rajah of Shorapore. His small territory, bounded on one side by the river Kistnah, occupied an angle in the dominions of the Nizam. Wishing, perhaps, to rise from the rank of a petty chieftain to one of greater power, he had for some time displayed hostility towards the British. But his career now came to an end. A force left Belgaum at the end of January, to advance to Shorapore; another left Kulladghee for the same destination; while a third advanced from Madras. The Nizam, at the same time, acting in harmony with his prime minister and Colonel Davidson, issued a proclamation denouncing as rebels any of his subjects who should assist the chief of Shorapore. These various measures had the desired result; the insurgents were dispersed, Shorapore seized, and the chief made prisoner.

In reference to such occurrences as the one described in the last paragraph, it may be observed that many of the residents, or British representatives at the courts of native princes, exhibited a wisdom and intrepidity which claim for them a rank by the side of the military heroes whose names are much better known to the world. Such a one was Colonel Davidson, British resident at the Nizam's court at Hyderabad in the Deccan.

During many months, he, with a few hundred faithful troops, maintained English prestige amongst a fanatic Mussulman population of two or three hundred thousand men, who often threatened the handful of British in the city. 'Disaffected persons,' a well-informed authority has said, 'thronged to the Nizam's palace by day and by night, with imprecations upon their lips against Europeans. It was impossible to tell when mutiny might break out among the native soldiers; and it was certain that the rabble were only awaiting their opportunity to glut themselves with English blood. Yet amidst all this the British resident never faltered or wavered; and by mere force of character he preserved peace in the city and district, and succeeded in securing to our side the Nizam and his minister Salar Jung. This Salar Jung was a young and well-educated man, who for his friendship to the British was hated by the Mussulmans.' The position of this minister was almost as dangerous as that of the resident; for if the attack of the 17th of July * had succeeded, he would have shared the common fate of the British. Colonel Davidson not only secured Hyderabad, but was subsequently enabled to send a considerable cavalry force for service elsewhere.

Among other political arrangements of the month, was the termination of a short governorship in the regions around Allahabad. On the 4th of August, in the preceding year, after the Northwest Provinces had been thrown into anarchy by the mutiny, a 'lieutenant governorship of the Central Provinces' was established, and placed in the hands of Mr John Peter Grant, one of the members of the Supreme Council at Calcutta. A few weeks afterwards, on the 19th of September, some of the other provinces in the Jumna regions were placed under a 'chief-commissioner of the Northwest Provinces.' Both of these offices were abolished by the governor-general in council, on the 9th of February; and Viscount Canning, then at Allahabad, took under his immediate authority and control the whole of the provinces lately placed under those officers. He became in fact, though not in name, and for a temporary period, governor of a presidency of which Allahabad was the capital. At or about the same time, Meerut and Delhi were handed over to the chief-commissioner of the Punjaub. Thus, all the political power between Calcutta and the Afghan frontier being in the hands of Canning and Lawrence, and all the military power in Sir Colin Campbell, it was hoped that greater energy and precision would be thrown into the combined operations.

* See chap. xvii., p. 231.

Notes.

Sir Colin Campbell's Army of Oude.—On the 10th of February, as stated in the text of this chapter, the commander-in-chief made a formal announcement of the component elements of the army with which he was about to enter Oude. These particulars we give here in a note, as a permanent record of an interesting matter in the military history of the Revolt. It must be clearly borne in mind, however, that this army of Oude comprised only such troops as were at that date under the immediate command of Sir Colin. Columns, corps, and field-forces, under Franks, Seaton, Jung Bahadoor, Macgregor, Windham, Van Cortlandt, Penny, M'Causland, Greathed, Roberts, Rose, Steuart, Stuart, Whitlock, and other officers, were rendering active or defensive services in various parts of India; and it depended on the course of circumstances whether any and which of these could assist in the grand operations against Lucknow.

'*Head-quarters, Camp Cawnpore, Feb.* 10.

'The troops now in Oude, and those advancing into that province, are formed into divisions and brigades, and staff-officers are attached as follows; the whole being under the personal command of his Excellency the Commander-in-chief.

'Such appointments as now appear for the first time will take effect from this date.

Artillery Division.

'Staff.—Major-general Sir A. Wilson, K.C.B., Bengal Artillery, commanding; Major E. B. Johnson, Bengal Artillery, Assistant Adjutant-general; Lieutenant R. Biddulph, Royal Artillery, Deputy-assistant-quartermaster-general; Lieutenant-colonel C. Hogge, Bengal Artillery, Director of Artillery in the Ordnance Department; Captain C. H. Barchard, 20th Regiment Native Infantry, Aid-de-camp; Lieutenant H. G. Deedes, 60th Royal Rifles, Extra Aid-de-camp.

'Brigade of Field-artillery.—Brigadier D. E. Wood, C.B., Royal Horse-artillery; Lieutenant J. S. Frith, Bengal Horse-artillery, Major of Brigade.—E troop Royal Horse-artillery; F Troop Royal Horse-artillery; 1st Troop 1st Brigade Bengal Artillery; 2d Troop 1st Brigade Bengal Artillery; 2d Troop 3d Brigade Bengal Artillery; 3d Troop 3d Brigade Bengal Artillery; 3d Company 14th Battalion Royal Artillery, and No. 20, Light Field-battery; 2d Company 3d Battalion Bengal Artillery, and No. 12 Light Field-battery.

'Brigade of Siege-artillery.—Brigadier G. R. Barker, C.B., Royal Artillery; Lieutenant A. Bunny, Bengal Horse-artillery, Major of Brigade.—3d Company 8th Battalion Royal Artillery; 6th Company 11th Battalion Royal Artillery; 5th Company 12th Battalion Royal Artillery; 5th Company 13th Battalion Royal Artillery; 4th Company 1st Battalion Bengal Artillery; 1st Company 5th Battalion Bengal Artillery; 3d Company 5th Battalion Bengal Artillery; Detachment Bengal Artillery recruits.

'The Naval Brigade will form part of the division under Sir Archdale Wilson, but will be under the immediate command of Captain W. Peel, C.B., Royal Navy, and independent of the Brigade of Siege-artillery.

'Engineer Brigade.—Brigadier R. Napier, Bengal Engineers, Chief-engineer; Major of Brigade, Lieutenant H. Bingham, Veteran Establishment, Brigade Quartermaster; Lieutenant-colonel H. D. Harness, Royal Engineers, commanding Royal Engineers; Captain A. Taylor, Bengal Engineers, commanding Bengal Engineers.—4th Company Royal Engineers; 23d Company Royal Engineers; Head-quarters Bengal

Sappers and Miners; Punjaub Sappers and Miners; corps of Pioneers.

Cavalry Division.

'Brigadier-general J. H. Grant, C.B., commanding; Captain W. Hamilton, 9th Lancers, Deputy-assistant-adjutant-general; Lieutenant F. S. Roberts, Bengal Horse-artillery, Deputy-assistant-quartermaster-general; Captain the Hon. A. H. A. Anson, her Majesty's 84th Regiment, Aid-de-camp.

'1st Brigade.—Brigadier A. Little, her Majesty's 9th Lancers; Captain H. A. Sarel, her Majesty's 17th Lancers, Major of Brigade.—Her Majesty's 9th Lancers; 2d Battalion Military Train; 2d Punjaub Cavalry; Detachment 5th Punjaub Cavalry; Wale's Horse.

'2d Brigade.—Brigadier W. Campbell, her Majesty's 2d Dragoon Guards; Captain H. Forbes, 1st Light Cavalry, Major of Brigade.—Her Majesty's 2d Dragoon Guards; her Majesty's 7th (Queen's Own) Hussars; Volunteer Cavalry; Detachment 1st Punjaub Cavalry; Hodson's Horse.

1st Infantry Division.

'Major-general Sir J. Outram, G.C.B., Bombay Army, commanding; Captain D. S. Dodgson, 30th Native Infantry, Deputy-assistant-adjutant-general; Lieutenant W. R. Moorsom, her Majesty's 52d Light Infantry, Deputy-assistant-quartermaster-general; Lieutenant F. E. A. Chamier, 34th Native Infantry, Aid-de-camp; Lieutenant Hargood, 1st Madras Fusiliers, Extra Aid-de-camp.

'1st Brigade.—Brigadier D. Russell, her Majesty's 84th Regiment.—Her Majesty's 5th Fusiliers; her Majesty's 84th Regiment; 1st Madras Fusiliers.

'2d Brigade.—Brigadier C. Franklyn, her Majesty's 84th Regiment.—Her Majesty's 78th Highlanders; her Majesty's 90th Light Infantry; Regiment of Ferozpore.

2d Infantry Division.

'Captain R. C. Stewart, her Majesty's 35th Regiment, Deputy-assistant-adjutant-general; Captain D. C. Shute, Deputy-assistant-quartermaster-general.

'3d Brigade.—Brigadier W. Hamilton, her Majesty's 78th Highlanders, commanding; Captain G. N. Fendall, her Majesty's 53d Regiment, Major of Brigade.—Her Majesty's 34th Regiment; her Majesty's 38th Regiment; her Majesty's 53d Regiment.

'4th Brigade.—Brigadier the Hon. A. Hope, her Majesty's 93d Highlanders; Captain J. H. Cox, her Majesty's 75th Regiment, Major of Brigade.—Her Majesty's 42d Highlanders; her Majesty's 93d Highlanders; 4th Punjaub Rifles.

3d Infantry Division.

'Brigadier-general R. Walpole, Rifle Brigade, commanding; Captain C. A. Beerwell, 71st Regiment Native Infantry, Deputy-assistant-adjutant-general; Captain T. A. Carey, 17th Regiment Native Infantry, Deputy-assistant-quartermaster-general.

'5th Brigade.—Brigadier Douglas, her Majesty's 79th Highlanders.—Her Majesty's 23d Fusiliers; her Majesty's 79th Highlanders; 1st Bengal Fusiliers.

'6th Brigade.—Brigadier A. H. Horsford, Rifle Brigade.—2d Battalion Rifle Brigade; 3d Battalion Rifle Brigade; 2d Punjaub Infantry.

'Captain C. C. Johnson, Deputy-assistant-quartermaster-general, will be attached to army head-quarters. Deputy-judge Advocate-general to the Force.—Captain A. C. Robertson, Her Majesty's 8th (the King's) Regiment. Field Paymaster.—Captain F. C. Tombs, 18th Regiment Native Infantry. Baggage Master.—Lieutenant J. Morland, 1st Bengal Fusiliers. Provost Marshal.—Captain A. C. Warner, 7th Light Cavalry. Postmaster.—Major C. Apthorp, 41st Native Infantry. Superintending Surgeon.—J. C. Brown, M.B., Bengal Horse-artillery. Field Surgeon.—Surgeon Wilkie. Medical Storekeeper.—Assistant-surgeon Corbyn, M.D.

'All staff appointments connected with Major-general Sir J. Outram's force not specified above will hold good until the junction of that force with army head-quarters.

'All appointments not filled up in the above order are to be temporarily provided for under the orders of officers commanding divisions and brigades.

'The following is the General Staff of the army advancing into Oude:

'Commander-in-chief.—His Excellency General Sir Colin Campbell, G.C.B., Her Majesty's service.

'Military Secretary to Commander-in-chief.—Major A. Alison, her Majesty's service (wounded). Acting Secretary and Aid-de-camp.—Colonel A. C. Sterling, C.B., her Majesty's service. Aid-de-camp.—Captain Sir D. Baird, 98th foot. Aid-de-camp.—Lieutenant F. M. Alison, 72d Highlanders. Aid-de-camp.—Captain W. T. Forster, 18th foot. Commandant at head-quarters, and interpreter.—Captain J. Metcalfe, Bengal infantry. Surgeon.—Staff-surgeon J. J. Clifford, M.D., her Majesty's service. Chief of the Staff.—Major-general W. R. Mansfield, her Majesty's service. Deputy-assistant Adjutant-general to the Chief of the Staff.—Captain R. J. Hope Johnstone, Bombay infantry. Aid-de-camp to the Chief of the Staff.—Captain C. Mansfield, 33d foot (wounded). Acting Aid-de-camp.—Lieutenant D. Murray, 64th foot. Deputy-adjutant-general of the Army.—Major H. W. Norman, Bengal infantry. Assistant Adjutant-general of the Army.—Captain D. M. Stewart, Bengal infantry. Deputy-adjutant-general, her Majesty's troops.—Colonel the Hon. W. L. Pakenham, C.B. Assistant-quartermaster-general of the Army.—Captain G. Allgood, Bengal infantry. Deputy-assistant-quartermaster-general.—Captain C. C. Johnson, Bengal infantry. Acting quartermaster-general of her Majesty's Forces.—Captain C. F. Seymour, 84th foot. Judge Advocate-general.—Lieutenant-Colonel K. Young, Bengal infantry. Deputy Judge Advocate-general.—Captain A. C. Robertson, 8th foot. Principal Commissariat Officer.—Captain C. M. Fitzgerald Bengal infantry. Commissary of Ordnance.—Captain W. T. Brown, Bengal artillery. Field Paymaster.—Captain F. C. Tombs, Bengal infantry. Provost Marshal.—Captain A. C. Warner, Bengal cavalry. Baggage Master.—Lieutenant J. Morland, Bengal infantry. Principal Medical Officer, Queen's Troops.—Dr J. C. Tice. Superintending Surgeon.—Surgeon J. C. Brown, Bengal artillery.'

Mohammedan Rebel Leaders.—Whatever may have been the proximate causes of the Revolt, it is certain that the rebel leaders were found relatively more numerous among the Mohammedans than among the Hindoos. They talked more frequently and fiercely about fighting for the faith; and they dragged into the meshes of a net many Hindoos who would otherwise have remained free from treasonable entanglement. Several native proclamations have been noticed in earlier chapters of this work; and we now present another, illustrative of Mussulman intrigues. It purports to come from Prince Mirza Mahomed Feroze Shah, and was dated the 3d of Rajub 1274, corresponding to the 17th of February 1858:

'Be it known to all the Hindoo and Mohammedan inhabitants of India that to rule over a country is one of the greatest blessings from Heaven, and it is denied to a tyrant or an oppressor. Within the last few years the British commenced to oppress the people in India under different pleas, and contrived to eradicate Hindooism and Mohammedanism, and to make all the people embrace Christianity. The Almighty Power observing this, diverted the hearts of the people to a different course, and now every one has turned to annihilate the English, and they have nearly done so. Through avarice and ambition, the British have shewn some resistance, though in vain. Through Divine mercy, that will in a short time be reduced to nothing. Let this also be known to all the Hindoos and Mussulmans, that the English bear the bitterest enmity towards them. Should they again become predominant in this country—which, God forbid—they will destroy religion, property, and even the life of every one. A brief sketch of the views and intentions of the Supreme Court and Parliament is hereby given, in order to warn the people that they should get rid of habits of negligence, and strive in unity to destroy the infidels. When the Indian troops mutinied to save their religion, and killed all infidels in several places, the wise men of England were of opinion that had the British authorities in India kept the following things in view, the mutiny would never have broken out: 1. They should have destroyed the race of the former kings and nobles. 2. They should have burnt all books of every other religion. 3. They should not have left even a biswa of ground to any of the native rulers. 4. They should have intermarried among the natives, so that after a short time all would have become one race. 5. They should not have taught the use of artillery to the natives. 6. They should not have left arms among the natives. 7. They should not have employed any native until he consented to eat and drink with Europeans. 8. The mosques and Hindoo temples should not have been allowed to stand. 9. Neither Moulvies nor Brahmins should have been allowed to preach. 10. The several cases brought into the courts should have been decided according to English laws. 11. English priests should have performed all nuptial ceremonies of the natives according to their English customs. 12. All prescriptions of the Hindoo and Mussulman physicians should have been prohibited, and English medicines furnished instead. 13. Neither Hindoo nor Mussulman fakeers should have been allowed to convert people without the permission of English missionaries. 14. European doctors only should have been allowed to assist native women in childbed.—But the authorities did not take means to introduce these measures. On the contrary, they encouraged the people: so much so, that they at last broke out. Had the authorities kept in view the maxims above alluded to, the natives would have remained quiet for thousands of years. These are now the real intentions of the English; but all of us must conjointly exert ourselves for the protection of our lives, property, and religion, and to root out the English from this country. Thus we shall, indeed, through Divine mercy, gain a great victory over them. I (the prince) now draw a brief sketch of my travels, and I hope the people will pay attention to what I say. Before the destruction of the English, I went on a pilgrimage to Mecca, and on my return I observed that the English were in a bad and hazardous position. I therefore offered thanks to God, because it is in my nature to follow the principles of my religion and to promulgate justice. I persuaded many at Delhi to raise a religious war; I then hastened towards Gwalior, where the majority of the military officers promised to kill the English and take up my cause. A small portion of the Gwalior army accompanied me. I had not the least intention to announce war before I had everything in order; but the army became very enthusiastic, and commenced fighting with the enemy (the English). Though our army was then but a handful, and that of the enemy very large in numbers, still we fought manfully; and, though apparently we were defeated, in reality we were victorious over our enemy, for we killed 1000 of them. Since then I have been collecting as well as exhorting the people. I have exerted myself in procuring ammunition up to this day, now four months since the commencement. Thank God, an army of 150,000 old and new men are now bound by a solemn oath to embrace my cause. I have collected considerable treasury and munitions of war in many places, and in a short time I shall clear the country of all infidels. Since the real purpose of this war is to save religion, let every Hindoo and Mussulman render assistance to the utmost. Those that are old should offer their prayers. The rich, but old, should assist our sacred warriors with money. Those in perfect health, as well as young, should attend in person. But all those who are in the service of either Mirza Birjish Kadur Bahadoor in Lucknow and of Khan Bahadoor Khan at Bareilly should not venture out to join us, for these rulers are themselves using their best endeavours to clear the country of all infidels. All who join us should do so solely with a view of promulgating their religion, not with that of worldly avarice. Thus victory will certainly smile upon us; then distinguished posts will be conferred on the people at large. The delay in defeating the English has been caused by people killing innocent children and women without any permission whatever from the leaders, whose commands were not obeyed. Let us all avoid such practices, and then proclaim a sacred war. Lastly, the great and small in this campaign will be equal, for we are waging a religious war. I (the prince) do now proclaim a sacred war, and exhort all, according to the tenets of their religion, to exert themselves. The rest I leave to God. We shall certainly conquer the English, consequently I invite the people again to my assistance.—Printed at Bareilly, by Shaick Nisar Ally, under the supervision of Moulvie Mahomed Kootoob Shah.'

Goorkhas in their native country, Nepaul.

CHAPTER XXV.

FINAL CONQUEST OF LUCKNOW: MARCH.

THE month at length arrived which was to witness the great siege of Lucknow, the capture of that important city, and the commencement of a re-establishment of British influence in Oude. The city which, excepting a small portion near and around the Residency, had been wholly in the hands of the rebels since the beginning of July, was to revert to the Company's possession in March, by a series of military operations which it is the purpose of this chapter to trace.

The extraordinary events in that city have been too frequently dwelt on in past chapters to render any lengthened notice here necessary. The reader will only have to bear in mind that Lawrence maintained the Residency intact until his death early in July; that Inglis continued the defence until September; that Outram and Havelock held the same position until November; and that from thence to March the city was wholly in the hands of the enemy—the Alum Bagh alone being held by Outram. Concerning the buildings and general arrangement of Lucknow, it may be useful here to freshen the recollection by a few descriptive details. The city lies on the right bank of the river Goomtee, which there runs nearly from northwest to southeast. All the buildings on the opposite or left bank of the river are merely suburban. After winding round the buildings called the Martinière and the Dil Koosha, the river changes its course towards the south. The southeastern extremity of the city is bounded by a canal, which enters the Goomtee near the Martinière. There is no defined boundary on the southwest, west, or northwest, the urban giving way to the rural in the same gradual way as in most English towns. Between the crowded or commercial part of the city, and the river, extends—or extended at the time of the

Revolt (for it will be convenient to adopt the past tense in this description)—a long series of palaces and gardens, occupying collectively an immense area, and known by the several names of the Taree Kothee, Fureed Buksh, Pyne Bagh, Chuttur Munzil, Kaiser Bagh, Shah Munzil, Motee Mehal, Shah Nujeef, Secunder Bagh, &c. Still further in the same line, were the buildings once famous as the Residency, the Muchee Bhowan, the great Emanbarra, and the Moosa Bagh. In short, for a distance of at least five miles, there was a string of royal or governmental buildings along the right bank of the river, forming a belt between it and the poorer or denser streets of the city. There was a stone bridge beyond the Muchee Bhowan, an iron bridge near the Residency, and—in peaceful times—a bridge of boats near the Motee Mehal. As to the general aspect of the city, when seen from a distance, writers have been at a loss for similes applicable to it, owing chiefly to the vast space over which the buildings are dotted. 'If,' in the quaint words of one writer, 'Clapham were overrun by a Mohammedan conqueror, who stuck up domes, cupolas, and minarets on half the meeting-houses and mansions; and if that pleasant suburb, when all the trees are green, were spread for eighteen or twenty miles over a dead level surface—the aspect it would present might in some degree give one a notion of Lucknow.'

The city, in the interval between November and March, had been fortified by the rebels in great strength. Although not enclosed like Delhi by a fortified wall, its many square miles of area, full of narrow streets and high houses, and occupied by an enormous military force in addition to the ordinary population, constituted a formidable stronghold in itself. But the rebels did not neglect the usual precautions of defensive warfare. Rightly judging that the English commander would avoid a hand-to-hand contest in the streets, and would direct his attack towards the south-eastern suburb, they spared no labour in strengthening that side of the city. In considering their plan of fortification, they treated the courts and buildings of the Kaiser Bagh as a sort of citadel, and interposed a triple series of obstacles between it and the besiegers. First, exterior of the three, was a line of defence extending from the river to a building known as Banks's house, once occupied by Major Banks; the canal formed the wet ditch of this line, and within the canal was a rampart or elevated earthwork. The second defence consisted of an earthwork beginning at the river-side near the Motee Mehal, the Mess-house, and the Emanbarra. The third or interior defence was the principal rampart of the Kaiser Bagh itself. All these lines consisted of well-constructed earthen parapets or ridges, fronted by wide and deep ditches, and strengthened at intervals by bastions. Not relying wholly on these formidable lines, the enemy had loopholed and fortified almost every house and enclosure, constructed strong counter-guards in front of the gateways, and placed isolated bastions, stockades, and traverses across the principal streets. The three lines of defence all abutted at one end on the river Goomtee, and at the other on the great street or road called the Huzrutgunje; which street was among the principal of those loopholed and bastioned. It was estimated that the enemy defended their works with nearly 100 guns and mortars. The insurgent troops were variously computed at 40,000 to 80,000 in number; the estimate could not be a precise one, because it was impossible to determine how many peasants from the country or desperate characters from the city joined the regular sepoys. There is, however, reason to believe that, at the beginning of March, the city contained 30,000 revolted sepoys, 50,000 volunteers and armed retainers of chieftains, and an ordinary city population of no less than 300,000 souls. It was a terrible thought that a city should be bombarded containing so large a number of living beings; but, as one of the stern necessities of the war, it was imperative. The chieftains of Oude, and the revolted sepoys of the Company's army, were there in great number; and until they were subdued, nothing could be effected towards the pacification of this part of India.

It may not be out of place here to notice a few of the individuals who, during the interregnum in Oude, assumed sovereign or governing power. The newly set up king was a boy of eight or ten years old, a son of the deposed king living at that time under surveillance at Calcutta. As a boy, he was a puppet in the hands of others. The prime mover in all the intrigues was his mother, the Begum Huzrut Mehal, who professed to be regent during his minority, and to be assisted by a council of state. She was a woman of much energy of character, and conducted public affairs in an apartment of the Kaiser Bagh. Morally she was tainted in full measure with oriental vices. Like Catherine of Russia she raised one of her paramours, Mummoo Khan, to the office of chief judge, and did not scruple openly to acknowledge her relations towards him. While executing the Begum's commands in all that related to the management of the newly formed government, he enriched himself at the expense of the people generally. The chief minister was one Shirreff-u-Dowlah, and the generalissimo Hissamut-u-Dowlah; but Mummoo Khan, held up by courtly favour, had sources of power superior to both. Another notability was a Moulvie or Mussulman fanatic who, though professing allegiance to the boy-king of Oude, was suspected of aiming at the throne himself. Most of the officers of the government purchased their places by large gifts to the Begum or her favourite, knowing that they would obtain an ample return during the anarchy of the period. The eunuchs of the royal palaces held, nominally if not really, military commands. The whole city of Lucknow, it is quite evident, was a hideous mass of intrigue, in which the various members of the royal family sought how best they could obtain power and wealth at the expense of the bulk of the people; while their ministers and officers were parasitical just so far as might be subservient to their own interests. The trading classes generally had very little reason to rejoice at the temporary cessation of the British 'raj.' The Begum and the Moulvie leader were regarded as the chief instruments in the opposition to the British. Every measure was resorted to that could raise the fanaticism of the native population. The English, and especially their Sikh allies, were represented as systematically murdering all who fell into their hands. On one occasion, shortly before the arrival of Sir Colin, the Begum rode through the streets of the city on an elephant, as one might imagine our Elizabeth appearing before her troops at Tilbury; and she used all her arts to induce the several chieftains to make her cause theirs.

These preliminaries settled, the narrative may be proceeded with. How the troops under the commander-in-chief approached Lucknow in February, and what were the components of the army of Oude, in generals and soldiers, the last chapter shewed.

When, on the 1st of March, Sir Colin Campbell was within a few miles of Lucknow, in his camp at Buntara, he fully considered all the information obtainable up to that time concerning the defences of the city. One result of the inquiry, was to convince him that a necessity would arise for operating from both sides of the Goomtee river, whenever the actual assault should take place.* This would be necessary, or at least desirable, because such a course would enable him to enfilade (that is, attack laterally or at the extremities) many of the enemy's newly constructed works; and because he would thus be able to cut off the enemy from their external sources of supply. It is true that he could not hope wholly to surround a city which, with its fortified suburbs, had a circuit of little less than twenty miles; still he would make an important approach towards that condition by cannonading from both sides of the river. One of his earliest preparations, therefore, had relation to the means of crossing the river; and to this end his engineers were busily engaged in fitting casks so that they might be placed across the river as a floating-bridge. The former bridge of boats, opposite some of the palaces, had been removed by the insurgents; while the iron and stone bridges were well watched by them.

On the 2d, Sir Colin marched at daybreak from his camp at Buntara, diverged from the road to the Alum Bagh, and took that which went near the Jelalabad fort towards the eastern margin of the suburbs. With a portion only of his army, he advanced to the Dil Koosha, the palace and park at the easternmost extremity of the city. The chief officers with him at the time of this advance were Generals Lugard, Adrian Hope, Hope Grant, Little, and Archdale Wilson. His main object at first, with a force of five or six thousand men, was to march to such a spot, near the Dil Koosha, as would enable him to form a camp just beyond reach of the enemy's guns; and to protect his enormous siege-train as it gradually arrived, until the time was come for commencing active operations. Not only the siege-train, but the countless appendages of an Indian army, would equally require protection during its passage from Buntara to the Dil Koosha. Mr Russell, who accompanied this expedition in person, says that no language can correctly convey an idea of the vastness in the number of elephants, camels, oxen, horses, camp-followers, and vehicles that daily demanded the commander-in-chief's attention at this period. 'Who really can bring before his mind's eye a train of baggage-animals twenty-five miles long, a string of sixteen thousand camels, a siege-train park covering a space of four hundred by four hundred yards, with twelve thousand oxen attached to it, and a following of sixty thousand non-combatants?' Even the doolies or litter-carriages for wounded men constituted a formidable item. To each company of a regiment there were ten doolies, and to each dooly were six coolies or native porters: thus there were nearly five hundred dooly-carriers for each average regiment; and even with this large supply, if the sick and wounded in any one regiment exceeded eighty men, there would be more than the coolies could properly attend to.

The force with which Sir Colin started from Buntara brought a few guns only. These were dragged along the centre of the line of route; the infantry were on either side of them, the cavalry and horse-artillery outside all, and the baggage in the rear. Each soldier took a small quantity of food with him. The march was through a flat well-cultivated country, past the Jelalabad fort, but a mile or so distant from the Alum Bagh. The skirmishers at the head of the column, as they approached the Dil Koosha, found a body of insurgent troopers watching their progress. When the column began to close on the advance-guard, the enemy opened fire with several guns which were in position in strong bastions along the line of canal—the outermost of the three lines of defence before adverted to. This fire was heavy and well sustained. It was not difficult to capture the Dil Koosha itself; but Sir Colin's troops were much annoyed by the enemy's fire over the open country, until they could secure the Dil Koosha and the Mahomed Bagh as advanced pickets, with heavy guns placed in battery to oppose the enemy's artillery. This once effected, a secure base for further operations was obtained, with the right resting on the river. It was a good day's work, not in conquest, but in the preparations for conquest.

When Sir Colin came to reconnoitre the enemy's position, he found that the new lines of defence, constructed since November, were vast and well planned. He further saw that no immediate attack

* The plans of Lucknow at pp. 621 and 362 will convey an idea of the situation of the city relatively to the river.

could be successfully made upon them by infantry, without such a sacrifice of life as he had determined if possible to avoid. To fight with artillery, before sending in his foot-soldiers to fight, was his plan; and he now at once sent back a messenger to the camp at Buntara, for the rest of the troops and heavy siege-artillery to advance without delay. All during the following night was the road from Buntara to the Dil Koosha filled with an apparently endless train of soldiers, guns, commissariat-carts, beasts of burden and of draught, and camp-followers—ready to swell the large number already at the last-named place. This train was protected on either side by cavalry and horse-artillery, ready to dash out against any of the enemy that should threaten interruption.

During the whole day on the 3d, the operations consisted chiefly in this bringing forward of guns and bodies of troops to positions necessary to be occupied when the regular siege began. When the remainder of the siege-train had arrived, and also General Walpole's division, Sir Colin's position embraced all the open ground on the southeastern margin of the city, with his right flank resting on the Goomtee, and his left in the direction of the Alum Bagh. The Alum Bagh and the Jelalabad fort were both occupied by portions of his troops, and the country between them was controlled by Hodson's Irregular Horse; while a strong brigade of cavalry, under Brigadier W. Campbell, swept the suburbs northwest of the Alum Bagh. By this arrangement, almost the entire southern half of the city was invested by his forces. The Dil Koosha was head-quarters, surrounded by the tents in which the soldiers took their few brief hours of repose. The palace, built in an Italian style, still retained much of the splendour belonging to it in more peaceful days, when it was the 'Heart's Delight' of the sensual monarch; but now it was well guarded by 42d Highlanders, ready to grapple with princelings and sepoys at any moment. From the roof of this palace could be seen the chief buildings of the city, as well as the vast defensive preparations which the enemy had made. The sepoys in the Martinière maintained a rifle-fire against such of the British as made their appearance on the flat roof of the Dil Koosha; but the distance was too great to render the fire dangerous.

The operations of the 4th were a sequel to those of the 3d—not an actual commencement of the siege, but a furtherance of the arrangements necessary to render the siege successful. The camp was extended from the Dil Koosha to Bibiapore, a house and enclosure a little further down the right bank of the river. From the glimpses obtained by the skirmishers and pickets, and from the information brought in by spies, it was ascertained that many of the inhabitants, terrified at the formidable preparations for the siege, were fleeing from the city on the opposite side; and that the 'authorities' were endeavouring to check this flight, wishing the inhabitants to fight for their property and their lives within the city itself. There were intelligible reasons for this on both sides. The citizens, whether their love for their native royal family was great or small, had little inclination to sacrifice their own personal interests to that sentiment; while, on the other hand, the rebel leaders cared not how many townsmen were ruined, so long as the privileges and profits of government remained with themselves, rather than reverting to the British.

It was on the 5th that General Franks joined the commander-in-chief, with that corps which now became the fourth division of the army of Oude. He had fought his way half across the province, from the Jounpoor frontier, defeating many bodies of rebels on the way, and arriving at Lucknow precisely at the time which had been agreed on. Jung Bahadoor and his large Nepaulese army did *not* arrive at the time specified: a want of punctuality which disturbed both the plans and the equanimity of Sir Colin. The components of the army of Oude, as laid down by the commander-in-chief on the 10th of February, were enumerated in a note at the end of the last chapter. At present, on the 5th of March, when Franks had arrived, the army before Lucknow consisted approximately of the following numbers of troops—First division of infantry, under Outram, about 5000 strong; second, under Lugard, 5400; third, under Walpole, 4300; fourth, under Franks, 4800; cavalry, under Hope Grant and other commanders, distributed among the infantry divisions; artillery, including the naval brigade, 1100; and engineers, 1700. The army of Oude was often said to consist of 30,000 troops, of whom 18,000 were British and the rest native; but such an estimate was worth little unless the exact day be named to which it applied. The army varied both by arrivals and departures.

The portion of the siege-plan connected with the left bank of the river had never been lost sight of during the preparatory operations on the right. While the infantry, cavalry, artillery, and commissariat were busily engaged in camping near the Dil Koosha, the engineers were collecting the casks, fascines of fagots, ropes, and timbers, necessary for forming a bridge, or rather two bridges, across the Goomtee, at some point below where the enemy were in greatest force. The spot selected was near head-quarters at Bibiapore, where the river was about forty yards wide. The enemy, uneasy at the proceedings of the engineers, gradually assembled in considerable numbers on the opposite bank; but as the British brought up guns to oppose them, the engineering works proceeded without much molestation. These bridges exemplified some of the contrivances which military commanders are accustomed to adopt, in the course of their onerous duties. The groundwork of each was a collection of empty beer-casks, lashed by ropes to timber cross-pieces, and floated off one by one to their positions; a firm roadway of planking was afterwards fixed on the top of the whole range from end to end. Firm indeed must the construction necessarily have been; for troopers on their horses, heavy guns and mortars, ammunition-wagons, and commissariat carts, all would have to pass over these bridges, secure so far as possible from accident to man or beast.

To Sir James Outram was intrusted the command of that portion of the army which was to cross by these bridges of casks, and operate against the city from the left bank of the Goomtee. This gallant officer had been in and near the Alum Bagh for a period of just one hundred days, from November to March, defending himself successfully against numerous attacks made on him by the enemy, as narrated in former chapters. It was right that he should now have the most important command under Sir Colin. He took his departure from the Alum Bagh—leaving that important post, which he had so long and so well defended, to the care of Brigadier Franklyn and of the 5th and 78th Queen's regiments of foot. The force intrusted to him consisted of Walpole's division of infantry, together with regiments and detachments from other divisions.* Franks with his division took Walpole's place near the Dil Koosha. The plan of attack agreed upon was, that Outram, after crossing the Goomtee, should advance up the left bank; while the troops in position at the Dil Koosha were to remain at rest until it should have become apparent that the first line of the enemy's works, or the rampart running along the canal and abutting on the Goomtee, had been turned. Sir James, arriving at the Dil Koosha from the Alum Bagh, effected his crossing safely on the 6th, and pitched his camp for the night on the left bank of the river, near the race-course. It was a formidable burden for the bridges to bear, comprising, besides the infantry and cavalry, thirty guns, and a large train of baggage and ammunition animals; nevertheless the floating fabrics bore up well, and fully answered their intended purpose. English troops of the line, Highlanders, lancers, hussars, dragoons, artillery, engineers, commissariat, horses, oxen, camels, elephants—all passed safely over, and speedily fell into orderly array on the other side of the river. This was, of course, not done without a little fighting. The enemy could not be blind to the proceeding, nor to the consequences likely to result from it. There was skirmishing in front of the Chukkur Walla Kothee, or Yellow House, a circular building on the left bank of the river; and there was much prancing about of leading personages who hastily came out of the city; but nothing disturbed Sir James from securely encamping at night.

While Outram was thus crossing the river on the 6th, Sir Colin remained simply on the defensive near the Dil Koosha, deferring all active operations until the subsidiary force had got into fighting order on the left bank. The enemy maintained a continuous fire from the Martinière; but the gunnery was not good, and very little mischief was occasioned. One of the most striking circumstances connected with the position and proceedings of the commander-in-chief was that he *carried the electric telegraph with him* from camp to camp, from post to post. Chiefly through the energy of Lieutenant Patrick Stewart, poles were set up and wires extended wherever Sir Colin went. Calcutta, Allahabad, Cawnpore, Buntara, and the Alum Bagh, could all communicate instantly; and now a wire made its appearance through a drawing-room window at the Dil Koosha itself, being stretched over a row of poles along the line of route which the commander-in-chief and his troops had followed. Nay, the wires even followed Outram over the river, and made their appearance—for the first time in the history of Oude—on the left bank. No sooner did Sir Colin advance a few miles, than Stewart followed him with poles and wires, galvanic batteries and signalling apparatus—daring all dangers, conquering all difficulties, and setting up a talking-machine close to the very enemy themselves. It may almost literally be said that, wherever he lay down his head at night, Sir Colin could touch a handle, and converse with Lord Canning at Allahabad before he went to sleep. The value of the electric telegraph was quite beyond all estimate during these wars and movements: it was worth a large army in itself.

On the 7th, Sir James Outram, while making his arrangements on the opposite side of the river, was attacked in great force by the enemy. On the preceding day, he had baffled them in all their attempts, with a loss of only 2 killed and 10 wounded; and he was not now likely to be seriously affected even by four or five times his number. The enemy occupied the race-course stand with infantry, and bodies of cavalry galloped up to the same spot with the intention of disturbing Outram's camp. He resisted all the attacks, chased them to a distance with his cavalry, and maintained his advantageous camping-ground.* The road from Fyzabad and from the cantonment passed near his camp; and as all that region had for many months been entirely in the hands of

* 23d Fusiliers.
79th Highlanders.
Rifle Brigade, two battalions.
1st Bengal Europeans.
3d Punjaub infantry.
2d Dragoon Guards.
9th Lancers.
1st, 2d, and 5th Punjaub cavalry, detachment.
D'Aguilar's troop, horse-artillery.
Remington's troop, royal artillery.
M'Kinnon's troop, " " .
Gibbon's light field-battery.
Middleton's " " .
Head-quarters, field-artillery brigade.

* Mr Russell, all day on the 6th and 7th, was watching the proceedings from a position such as has seldom before been occupied by a newspaper writer. He was on the roof of the Dil Koosha, taking his chance of such shots as came from the Martiniere, and viewing Outram's marchings and fightings by means of a telescope. Sometimes his resolution was nearly baffled by heat and dust. 'The wind was all but intolerable—very hot and very high, and surcharged with dust. I had a little camp-table and chair placed on the top of the building, and tried to write; but the heat and the dust were intolerable. I tried to look out, but the glasses were filled with dust; a fog would be just as good a medium.'

the rebels, there was a liability at any moment of some sudden onslaught being made on him. The commander-in-chief had foreseen this, when he placed at the disposal of Outram a division strong enough to form a compact little army in itself.

The result of a careful reconnaissance made on the 8th, by Sir Colin, resulted in instructions to Outram to arrange his batteries during the night, and on the following day to attack the enemy's position, the key to which was the Chukkur Walla Kothee. On the morning of the 9th, accordingly, Sir James made the attack with excellent effect; the enemy being driven out at all points, and the Yellow House seized. He advanced his whole force for some distance through ground affording excellent cover for the enemy. He was by that means enabled to bring his right flank forward to occupy the Fyzabad road, which he crossed by a bridge over a nullah, and to plant his batteries for the purpose of enfilading the works upon the canal. During this day's operations, much skirmishing took place between his Sikhs and Rifles and the enemy; but the most obstinate contest was maintained within the Yellow House itself, where a few fanatics, shutting themselves up, resisted for several hours all attempts to dislodge them. They were at length expelled, fighting desperately to the last. Outram was then enabled to take the villages of Jeamoor and Jijowly, and to advance to the Padishah Bagh or King's Garden, opposite the Fureed Buksh palace, and to commence an enfilade fire on the lines of the Kaiser Bagh defences.

While Outram was engaged in these successful operations of the 9th on the left bank of the Goomtee, a very heavy fire was kept up against the Martinière, from mortars and guns placed in position on the Dil Koosha plateau. Sir Colin had purposely deferred this assault until Outram had captured the Yellow House, and commenced that flank attack which so embarrassed the enemy. The sailors of the naval brigade were joyously engaged on this day; for the thicker the fight, the better were they pleased. They commanded four great guns on the road near the Dil Koosha; and with these they battered away, not only against the Martinière, but also against a cluster of small houses near that building. Captain Sir William Peel managed to throw not only shot and shell, but also rockets, into enclosures which contained numerous insurgent musketeers—a visitation which necessarily prompted a hasty flight. It had well-nigh been a bad day for the British, however; for Peel received a musket-ball in the thigh while walking about fearlessly among his guns; the ball was extracted under the influence of chloroform; but the wound nearly proved fatal through the eagerness of the gallant man to return to the fray. He was, however, spared for the present. The enemy resisted this day's attack with a good deal of resolution; for they fired shot right over the Martinière towards the Dil Koosha, from guns in their bastions on the canal line of defence. When the cannonading had proceeded to the desired extent, a storming of the Martinière took place, by troops under the command of Sir Edward Lugard and other able officers. The instructions given by the commander-in-chief for this enterprise were minute and complete,* and were carried out to the letter. The infantry marched forward from their camp behind the Dil Koosha, their bayonets glittering in the sun; and it was remarked that the sight of these terrible bayonets appeared to throw the enemy into more trepidation than all the guns and howitzers, mortars and rockets. A bayonet-charge by the British was more than any of the 'Pandies' could bear. Silently and swiftly the Highlanders and Punjaubees marched on, the former towards the Martinière, and the latter towards the trenches that flanked that building; while the other regiments of Lugard's column followed closely in the rear. Distracted by Outram's enfilade fire from the other side of the river, and by Lugard's advance in front, the enemy made but a feeble resistance. The 42d Highlanders and the Punjaubee infantry climbed up the intrenchment abutting on the river, and rushed along the whole line of works, till they got to the neighbourhood of Banks's house. Meanwhile, another body of infantry advanced to the Martinière, and captured the building and the whole of the enclosure surrounding it. All this was done with very little bloodshed on either side; for Lugard's men, in obedience to orders, did not fire; while the enemy escaped from the walls and trenches without maintaining a hand-to-hand contest. This abandonment of the defence-works would not have taken place so speedily had not Outram's flanking fire enfiladed the whole line; but the insurgent artillerymen found it impossible to withstand the ordeal to which they

* 'He (Sir Edward Lugard) will employ for the purpose the 4th brigade, with the 38th and 53d regiments of the 3d brigade in support.

'The 42d Highlanders will lead the attack, and seize, as a first measure, the huts and ruined houses to the left of the Martinière, as viewed from the brigadier-general's front.

'While the movement is being made upon the huts in question, the wall below the right heavy battery will be lined very thickly, with at least the wing of a regiment, which will be flanked again by a troop of R.A. The huts having been seized, this extended wing behind the wall will advance right across the open on the building of the Martinière, its place being taken immediately by a regiment in support, which will also move rapidly forward on the building. But the attack on the huts is not to stop there. As soon as they are in, the Highlanders must turn sharp on the building of the Martinière, also following up the retreating enemy. The heavy guns of the right battery, as well as those belonging to the troop, will search the intrenchments of the tank and the brushwood to the right while this advance is going forward.

'The whole line of the ruined huts, Martinière, &c., having been seized, the engineers attached to the 2d division for the operation will be set to work immediately by the brigadier-general to give cover to the troops.

'The men employed in the attack will use nothing but the bayonet. They are absolutely forbidden to fire a shot till the position is won. This must be thoroughly explained to the men, and they will be told also that their advance is flanked on every side by heavy and light artillery, as well as by the infantry fire on the right.

'The brigadier-general will cause his whole division to dine at 12 o'clock. Inlying pickets will remain in camp. The 90th foot, now in the Mahomed Bagh, will be relieved by a regiment from Brigadier-general Franks's division. The troops will not be allowed to pass the lines of huts and the building without orders.'

were now exposed. Sir Colin's plan had been so carefully made, and so admirably carried out, that this capture of the enemy's exterior line of defence was effected almost without loss.

On the 10th, while Outram was engaged in strengthening the position which he had taken up, he sent Hope Grant with the cavalry of the division to patrol over the whole of the country between the left bank of the Goomtee and the old cantonment. This was done with the view of preventing any surprise by the approach of bodies of the rebels in that quarter. An extensive system of patrolling or reconnaissance had formed from the first a part of Sir Colin's plan for the tactics of the siege. Outram on this day brought his heavy guns into a position to rake the enemy's lines, to annoy the Kaiser Bagh with a vertical and direct fire, to attack the suburbs in the vicinity of the iron and stone bridges, and to command the iron bridge from the left bank; all of which operations he carried out with great success. The enemy, however, still held the right end of the iron bridge so pertinaciously, that it was not until after a very heavy cannonading that the conquest was effected.

On the city side of the river, on this day, the operations consisted mainly in securing the conquests effected on the 9th. At a very early hour in the morning, while yet dusk, the rebel sepoys advanced in great strength to reoccupy the defence-line of the canal, apparently not knowing that the Highlanders and Punjaubees had maintained that position during the night; they were speedily undeceived by a volley of musketry which put them to flight. At sunrise a disposition of troops and heavy guns was made by Lugard for an attack on Banks's house; and this house, captured about noon, was at once secured as a strong military post.

Thus did this remarkable siege go on day after day. Nothing was hurried, nothing unforeseen. All the movements were made as if the city and its environs formed a vast chess-board on which the commander-in-chief could see the position of all the pieces and pawns. Nay, so fully had he studied the matter, that he had some such command over the ground as is maintained by a chess-player who conducts and wins a game without seeing the board. Every force, every movement, was made conducive to one common end—the conquest of the city without the loss of much British blood, and without leaving any lurking-place in the hands of the enemy.

The conquest and fortifying of Banks's house enabled Sir Colin to commence the second part of his operations. Having captured the enemy's exterior line of defence, he had now to attack the second or middle line, which (as has been already shewn) began at the river-side near the Motee Mehal, the Mess-house, and the Emanbarra. The plan he formed was to use the great block of houses and palaces extending from Banks's house to the Kaiser Bagh as an approach, instead of sapping up towards the second line of works. 'The operation,' as he said in his dispatch, 'had now become one of an engineering character; and the most earnest endeavours were made to save the infantry from being hazarded before due preparation had been made.' The chief engineer, Brigadier Napier, placed his batteries in such positions as to shell and breach a large block of the palaces known as the Begum Kothee. This bombardment, on the 11th, was long and severe; for the front of the palaces was screened by outhouses, earthworks, and parapets, which required to be well battered before the infantry could make the assault. The 8-inch guns of the naval brigade were the chief instruments in this formidable cannonade. At length, about four o'clock in the afternoon, Napier announced that the breaches were practicable, and Lugard at once made arrangements for storming the Begum Kothee. He had with him the 93d Highlanders, the 4th Punjaub Rifles, and 1000 Goorkhas, and was aided in the assault by Adrian Hope. His troops speedily secured the whole block of buildings, and inflicted a very heavy loss on the enemy. The attack was one of a desperate character, and was characterised by Sir Colin as 'the sternest struggle which occurred during the siege.' From that point Napier pushed his engineering approaches with great judgment through the enclosures, by the aid of the sappers and the heavy guns; the troops immediately occupying the ground as he advanced, and the mortars being moved from one position to another as the ground was won on which they could be placed. Outram was not idle during these operations. He obtained possession of the iron bridge, leading over the river from the cantonment to the city, and swept away the enemy from every part of the left bank of the river between that bridge and the Padishah Bagh; thus leaving him in a position to enfilade the central and inner lines of defence established by the enemy among the palaces.

It was while these serious and important operations were in progress, on the 11th of March, that the commander-in-chief was called upon to attend to a ceremonial affair, from which he would doubtless have willingly been spared. The preceding chapters have shewn how Jung Bahadoor, descending from the Nepaulese mountains with an army of 9000 Goorkhas, rendered a little service in the Goruckpore and Jounpoor districts, and then advanced into Oude to assist in the operations against Lucknow. His movements had been dilatory; and Sir Colin was forced to arrange all the details of the siege as if no reliance could be placed in this ally. At length, however, on the afternoon of the 11th, Jung Bahadoor appeared at the Dil Koosha; he and Sir Colin met for the first time. The meeting was a curious one. The Nepaul chieftain, thoroughly Asiatic in everything, prepared for the interview as one on which he might lavish all his splendour of gold, satin, pearls, and diamonds; the old Highland officer, on the other hand, plain beyond the usual plainness of a soldier in all that concerned personal indulgences,* was somewhat tried even by the necessity for his full regimentals and decorative appendages. A continuous battle was going on, in which he thought of his soldiers' lives, and of the tactics necessary to insure a victory; at such a time, and in such a climate, he would gladly have dispensed with the scarlet and the feathers of his rank, and of the oriental compliments in which truth takes little part. A tasteful canopy was prepared in front of Sir Colin's mess-tent; and here were assembled the commander-in-chief, Archdale Wilson, Hope Grant, a glittering group of staff-officers and aids-de-camp, a Highland guard of honour, an escort of Lancers, bands, pipers, drums, flags, and all the paraphernalia for a military show. Sir Colin was punctual; Jung Bahadoor was not. Sir Colin, his thoughts all the while directed towards Lugard's operations at the Begum Kothee, felt the approaching ceremony, and the delay in beginning it, as a sore interruption. At length the Nepaulese chieftain appeared. Jung Bahadoor had, as Nepaulese ambassador, made himself famous in London a few years before, by his gorgeous dress and lavish expenditure; and he now appeared in fully as great splendour. The presentations, the greetings, the compliments, the speeches, were all of the wonted kind; but when Captain Hope Johnstone, as one of the officers of the chief of the staff, entered to announce that 'the Begum Kothee is taken,' Sir Colin broke through all ceremony, expressed a soldier's pleasure at the news, and brought the interview to a termination. Jung Bahadoor returned to his own camp; and the commander-in-chief instantly resumed his ordinary military duties. Sir Colin was evidently somewhat puzzled to know how best to employ his gorgeous colleague; although his courtesy would not allow him to shew it. The Goorkhas moved close to the canal on the 13th; and on the following day Sir Colin requested Jung Bahadoor to cross the canal, and attack the suburbs to the left of Banks's house. As he was obliged, just at that critical time, to mass all the available strength of his British troops in the double attack along the banks of the Goomtee, the commander-in-chief had few to spare for his left wing; and he speaks of the troops of the Nepaulese leader as being 'most advantageously employed for several days,' in thus covering his left.

We return to the siege operations. So great had been the progress made on the 11th, that the development of the commander-in-chief's strategy became every hour more and more clear. Outram's heavy fire with guns and mortars produced great effect on the Kaiser Bagh; while the Begum Kothee became a post from which an attack could be made on the Emanbarra, a large building situated between the Begum Kothee and the Kaiser Bagh.* The Begum Kothee palace, when visited by the officers of the staff on the morning of the 12th, astonished them by the strength which the enemy had given to it. The walls were so loopholed for musketry, the bastions and cannon were so numerous, the ditch around it was so deep, and the earthen rampart so high, that all marvelled how it came to be so easily captured on the preceding day. The enemy might have held it against double of Lugard's force, had they not been paralysed by the bayonet. It was a strange sight, on the following morning, to see Highlanders and Punjaubees roaming about gorgeous saloons and zenanas, still containing many articles of dress and personal ornaments which the ladies of the palace had not had time to carry away with them. Whither the inmates had fled, the conquerors at that time did not know, and in all probability did not care. It was a strange and unnatural sight; splendour and blood appeared to have struggled for mastery in the various courts and rooms of the palace, many contests having taken place with small numbers of the enemy.† From this building,

* When Sir Colin started from Buntara to the Dil Koosha on the 2d of March, Mr Russell says of his personal appearance: 'He wears a serviceable air which bespeaks confidence and resolution, and gives the notion of hard work and success. Everything about him is for service, even down to the keen-edged sabre in a coarse leather sheath, not dangling and clattering from his side and hitting the flanks of his horse from gaudy sling-belts, but tucked up compactly by a stout shoulder-belt just over his hip. . . . And so of his nether man; not clothed in regulation with gold stripes, but in stout brown corduroy, warranted to wear in any climate. The chief of the staff and the officers of the staff for the most part follow the example of the commander-in-chief.'

* It is well to bear in mind the distinction between two great Emanbarras at Lucknow; one, called the Emanbarra of Ghazee-u-deen Hyder, just mentioned; and the other, the Emanbarra of Azof-u-Dowlah, between the Muchee Bhowan and the Moosa Bagh.

† The graphic writer to whom we have more than once adverted was among those who hastened to the Begum Kothee as a spectator on this morning. Among the scenes that met his view he said: 'I saw one of the fanatics, a fine old sepoy with a grizzled moustache, lying dead in the court, a sword-cut across his temple, a bayonet-thrust through his neck, his thigh broken by a bullet, and his stomach slashed open, in a desperate attempt to escape. There had been five or six of these fellows altogether, and they had either been surprised and unable to escape, or had shut themselves up in desperation in a small room, one of many looking out on the court. At first, attempts were made to start them by throwing in live shell. A bag of gunpowder was more successful; and out they charged, and, with the exception of one man, were shot and bayoneted on the spot. The man who got away did so by a desperate leap through a window, amid a shower of bullets and many bayonet-thrusts. Such are the common incidents of this war. From court to court of the huge pile of buildings we wandered through the same scenes—dead sepoys—blood-splashed gardens—groups of eager Highlanders, looking out for the enemy's loopholes—more eager groups of plunderers searching the dead, many of whom lay heaped on the top of each other, amid the ruins of rooms brought down upon them by our cannon-shot. Two of these were veritable chambers of horrors. It must be remembered that the sepoys and matchlockmen wear cotton clothes, many at this time of year using thickly quilted tunics; and in each room there is a number of *resais*, or quilted cotton coverlets, which serve as beds and quilts to the natives. The explosion of powder sets fire to this cotton very readily, and it may be easily conceived how horrible are the consequences where a number of these sepoys and Nujeebs get into a place whence there is no escape, and where they fall in heaps by our shot. The matches of the men and the discharges of their guns set fire to their cotton clothing; it is fed by the very fat of the dead bodies; the smell is pungent and overpowering, and nauseous to a degree. I looked in at two such rooms, where, through the dense smoke, I could see piles of bodies; and I was obliged to own that the horrors of the hospital at Sebastopol were far exceeded by what I witnessed. Upwards of 300 dead were found in the courts of the palace, and, if we put the wounded carried off at 700, we may reckon that the capture of the place cost the enemy 1000 men at least. The rooms of the building round the numerous courts were for the most part small and dark, compared with the great size of the corridors and garden enclosures. The state-saloon, fitted up for darbars and entertainments, once possessed some claims to magnificence, which were, however, now lying under our feet in the shape of lustres, mirrors, pier-glasses, gilt tables, damask, silk and satin, embroidered fragments of furniture, and marble tables, over which

we have said, Sir Colin determined that progress should be made towards the Emanbarra, not by open assault, but by sapping through a mass of intermediate buildings.

The 12th was the day when the sapping commenced; but so many and so intricate were the buildings, that three days were occupied in this series of operations; seeing that it was necessary to destroy or at least to render innoxious such houses as might have concealed large bodies of the enemy. Lugard's troops having been hotly engaged on the 11th, they were now relieved by others under Franks. The work was of formidable character; for the flat roofs of many of the houses were covered with two or three feet of earth, baked in the sun, and loopholed for musketry. Every such house had to be well scrutinised, before a further advance was made. The sappers made passages, either actually underground, or through the lower portions of the walls and enclosures surrounding the buildings. On the 13th these approaches were so far completed that a large number of guns and mortars could be brought forward, and placed in position for bombarding

Gateway of the Emanbarra at Lucknow.

the Emanbarra. On this day, too, Jung Bahadoor's troops took possession of a mass of suburban houses southward of the city, between Sir Colin's camp and the Alum Bagh; after which the commander-in-chief paid a return visit to the Nepaulese chieftain, who strove to display still more magnificence than at the former interview.

The 14th of March was one of the busy days of the siege. The sap was carried on so successfully that the Emanbarra could be bombarded by heavy guns and mortars, and then taken. Directly this was done, Brasyer's Sikhs, pressing forward in pursuit of the fleeing enemy, entered the Kaiser Bagh—the third or inner line of defence having been turned without a single gun being fired from it. Supports were quickly thrown in, and the British troops found themselves speedily in a part of the city already well known to Campbell and Outram during their operations of November—surrounded by the Mess-house, the Taree Kothee, the Motee Mehal, and the Chuttur Munzil. All these buildings were near them, and all were occupied by them before night closed in. As fast as the infantry seized these several positions, so did the engineers proceed to secure the outposts towards the south and west. As in many other cases when it was the lot of the English in India to fight their greatest battles, or bear their greatest sufferings, on Sundays; so was it on a Sunday that these busy operations of the 14th took place. The front walls of the Kaiser Bagh and the Motee Mehal were extensively mined; insomuch that

one made his way from place to place with difficulty. The camp-followers were busily engaged in selecting and carrying away such articles as attracted their fancy—shawls, *resais*, cushions, umbrellas, swords, matchlocks, tom-toms or drums, pictures, looking-glasses, trumpets; but the more valuable plunder disappeared last night. It will be long before a Begum can live here in state again. Every room and wall and tower are battered and breached by our shot.'

when the artillery had effected its dread work, the infantry could approach much more safely than if exposed to the sight of sharp-shooters and matchlockmen. It is true that neither English nor Highlanders, neither Sikhs nor Goorkhas, would have hesitated to rush forward and storm these buildings without a sap; but as Sir Colin was well supplied with heavy guns, he acted steadily on the plan of employing them as much as possible before sending on his men—feeling that the loss of men would be more difficult to replace than that of guns and missiles, at such a time and in such a country. In his dispatch relating to the operations of the 14th of March, he said: 'The day was one of continued exertion; and every one felt that, although much remained to be done before the final expulsion of the rebels, the most difficult part of the undertaking had been overcome. This is not the place for a description of the various buildings sapped into or stormed. Suffice it to say that they formed a range of massive palaces and walled courts of vast extent, equalled perhaps, but not surpassed, in any capital of Europe. Every outlet had been covered by a work, and on every side were prepared barricades and loopholed parapets. The extraordinary industry evinced by the enemy in this respect has been really unexampled. Hence the absolute necessity for holding the troops in hand, till at each successive move forward the engineers reported to me that all which could be effected by artillery and the sappers had been done, before the troops were led to the assault.'

A little must here be said concerning the share which Sir James Outram had in the operations of the 12th and two following days. All his tactics, on the left bank of the river, were especially intended to support those of the commander-in-chief on the right bank. On the 12th his heavy guns, at and near the Padishah Bagh, poured forth a torrent of shot, to dislodge the enemy from certain positions near the city. His head-quarters were established under a small tope of trees near a ruined mosque; and he, as well as Lugard and Walpole, lived as simply as possible under tents. The Padishah Bagh itself—a suburban palace with beautiful saloons, halls, terraces, orange-groves and fountains—was held by H.M. 23d. The left bank of the river being occupied as far up as the iron suspension bridge, Outram planted two or three guns to guard that position from any hostile attack from the north; while two or three regiments of his own infantry, in convenient spots near the bridge, kept up a musketry-fire against such of the enemy as were visible and within reach on the opposite or city side of the river. This musketry-fire was continued all day on the 13th, while the batteries of heavy guns were being brought further and further into position. On the 14th, the same operations were continued; but the conquest of the Kaiser Bagh was so sudden and unexpected on this day, that the proceedings on the left bank of the river were relatively unimportant.

When the morning of the 15th arrived, Sir Colin Campbell felt that he might call Lucknow his own; for although much remained to be done, the conquests achieved were vast and important. The Mahomed Bagh, the Dil Koosha, the Martinière, the Secunder Bagh, the Emanbarra, the Mess-house, the Shah Munzil, the Motee Mehal, the Begum Kothee, and the Kaiser Bagh, were all in his hands—constituting by far the strongest and most important of the palatial buildings along the banks of the river. Moreover, the natives were evidently dismayed; vast numbers were leaving the city on the Rohilcund side; and spies brought information that the rebel leaders encountered much difficulty in keeping the sepoys steadily at the defence-works. The progress made by the British had surprised and alarmed the insurgents, and tended to paralyse their exertions. Some of the British officers had entertained a belief that the Kaiser Bagh was the key to the enemy's position, whereas others had looked rather to the Begum Kothee. The latter proved to be right. The enemy had greatly relied on the last-named building; insomuch that, when it was captured, they rushed in wild confusion to the Kaiser Bagh, intent rather upon flight than upon a stubborn resistance. The garrison of the Kaiser Bagh, disconcerted by this irruption of their brother insurgents, were rendered almost unable, even if willing, to make a manful resistance. The British were almost as much surprised by the speedy capture of the Kaiser Bagh, as the enemy were by the loss of the Begum Kothee. When the great palace changed hands, the smoke and blood and cries of war were strangely mingled with the magnificence of kiosks, mosques, corridors, courts, gardens, terraces, saloons, mirrors, gilding, chandeliers, tapestry, statues, pictures, and costly furniture, in this strange jumble of oriental and European splendour.

A soldier loses all his heroism when the hour for prize and plunder arrives. Those, whether officers or spectators, who have described the scene which was presented when these Lucknow palaces were conquered, tell plainly of a period of wild licence and absorbing greed. On the one hand there were palaces containing vast stores of oriental and European luxuries; on the other, there were bands of armed men, brave and faithful, but at the same time poor and unlettered, who suddenly found themselves masters of all these splendours, with very little check or supervision on the part of their officers. At first, in a spirit of triumphant revenge, costly articles were broken which were too large to be carried away; glass chandeliers were hurled to the ground, mirrors shattered into countless fragments, statues mutilated and overturned, pictures stabbed and torn, doors of costly wood torn from their hinges. But when this destruction had been wreaked, and when the troops had forced their way through courts and corridors strewn with sepoys' brass lotas or drinking-vessels, charpoys, clothing, belts, ammunition, muskets, matchlocks, swords, pistols, chupatties, and other evidences of precipitate flight —when this had all occurred, then did the love of plunder seize hold of the men. The Kaiser Bagh had been so quickly conquered, that the subaltern officers had not yet received instructions how to control the movements of the troops in this matter. Sikhs, Highlanders, English, were soon busily engaged. In one splendid saloon might be seen a party of Sikhs melting down gold and silver lace for the sake of the precious metals; in another, a quantity of shawls, lace, pearls, and embroidery of gold and silver, was being divided equally among a group of soldiers. In a sort of treasure-room, apparently belonging to some high personage, a few men of two British regiments found caskets and boxes containing diamonds, emeralds, rubies, pearls, opals, and other gems, made into necklaces, bracelets, ear-rings, girdles, &c.; together with gold-mounted pistols, jewel-hilted swords, saddle-cloths covered with gold and pearls, gold-handled riding-canes, jewelled cups of agate and jade, japanned boxes filled with crystal and jade vessels. And, as it appeared that every one felt himself permitted or at least enabled to retain whatever he could capture, the camp-followers rushed in and seized all that the soldiers had left. Coolies, syces, khitmutgars, dooly-bearers, and grass-cutters, were seen running hither and thither, laden with costly clothing, swords, firelocks, brass pots, and other articles larger in bulk than the actual soldiers could readily have disposed of. It was a saturnalia, during which it is believed that some of the troops appropriated enough treasure, if converted into its value in money, to render them independent of labour for the rest of their lives. But each man kept, in whole or in part, his own secret.

Let us on from this extraordinary scene. The 15th was chiefly employed in securing what had been captured, removing powder, destroying mines, and fixing mortars for the further bombardment of the positions still held by the enemy, on the right bank of the Goomtee, and in the heart of the city. As the infantry and artillery could fulfil this duty, without the aid of horse, two bodies of cavalry, under Walpole and Hope Grant, were sent out to prevent, if possible, the escape of the enemy on the sides of the city not subject to immediate attack. One of these generals proceeded towards the Sundeela road, and the other to that leading to Seetapoor. Whether this flight of the enemy disappointed or not the expectations of the commander-in-chief, was a question which he kept to himself. The city, for all practical military purposes, was twenty miles in circumference; and he could not have guarded all the outlets without a very much larger army than that which was at his disposal. Like as at Sebastopol, the siege was not aided by a complete investiture of the place besieged. It is possible that the capture of the Kaiser Bagh, and the consequent flight of the enemy, occurred too early for Sir Colin to be enabled to put in operation certain manœuvres on the other side of the city. Be this as it may, large numbers of rebel sepoys, and a still larger of the regular inhabitants of the city escaped during the 14th and 15th, mostly over the stone bridge—as if hopeful of safety in Rohilcund and Upper Oude.

On the 16th Sir James Outram, after ten days of active operation on the left bank of the Goomtee, crossed over by a bridge of casks opposite the Secunder Bagh; and he then advanced through the Chuttur Munzil towards the Residency. To lessen the chance of the enemy's retreat as much as possible, he marched right through the city, not only to the iron bridge near the Residency, but to the stone bridge near the Muchee Bhowan. All this was an enterprise of remarkable boldness, for the buildings to be successively conquered and entered were very numerous. Outram shifted his own head-quarters to Banks's house, on the city side of the river; and it was here that he received a letter from the Begum, or mother of the young boy-king, containing some sort of proposition for compromise or cessation of hostilities. Whatever it may have been, no successful result attended this missive: the progress and conquest went on as before. His troops, as they advanced to the Chuttur Munzil, the Pyne Bagh, the Fureed Buksh, and the Taree Kothee, found all these buildings abandoned by the enemy—who had been too much dismayed by the operations of the 16th to make a bold stand. At length he approached the Residency, the enclosed spot whose name will ever be imperishably associated with Inglis's defence of the British garrison, and in which Outram himself had passed many anxious weeks between September and November. Hardly a building remained standing within the enclosure; all had been riddled and shattered during the long period from July to November, and most of them subsequently destroyed by the enemy. Up to this time Outram's march of the 16th through the city had been almost unopposed; but he now ascertained that the houses and palaces between the iron and stone bridges were occupied by the enemy in considerable force. Hard fighting at once commenced here, in which the 20th, 23d, and 79th regiments were actively engaged. They advanced at a rapid pace from the Residency towards the iron bridge. A 9-pounder, planted to command a road by the way, fired grape into them; but it was speedily captured. By that time the large guns were brought into position, to play upon the stone bridge, the Emanbarra of Azof-u-Dowlah, and other structures northwest of the iron bridge. At that time Grant and his troopers were near the stone bridge on the left side of the river, while Outram's guns were firing on it from the right bank; as a consequence, no more escape was permitted by that channel; and the fugitives therefore ran along the right bank of the river, to a part of the open country northwest of Lucknow, not yet controlled by the English. Many of the rebel sepoys resolved to make a stand at the Moosa Bagh, a building at the extreme limits of the city in this direction; but the day was too far advanced to attack them at that spot; and the troops were glad to rest for the night in the splendid saloons and courts of the Emanbarra—one of the grandest among the many grand structures in Lucknow.

While Outram was engaged in these operations on the 16th, obtaining a mastery along almost the whole right bank of the river, the enemy very unexpectedly made an attack on the Alum Bagh, which was only held by a small English force under Brigadier Franklyn. Sir Colin Campbell immediately requested Jung Bahadoor to advance to his left up the canal, and take in reverse the post from which the enemy was making the attack. The Nepaulese chieftain performed this service successfully, capturing the post and the guns, and expelling the enemy.

When the morning of the 17th arrived, the commander-in-chief found himself so undoubtedly the master of Lucknow, that he was enabled to dispense with the services of some of his gallant artillery officers, whose aid was much wanted at Futteghur and elsewhere. Still, though the great conquest was mainly effected, the minor details had yet to be filled up. There were isolated buildings in which small knots of the enemy had fortified themselves; these it would be necessary to capture. It was also very desirable to check the camp-followers in their manifest tendency for plundering the shops and private houses of the city. Sir Colin did not wish the townsmen to regard him as an enemy; he encouraged them, so far as they had not been in complicity with the rebels, to return to their homes and occupations; and it was very essential that those homes should, in the meantime, be spared from reckless *looting*. In some of the streets, pickets of soldiers were placed, to compel the camp-followers to disgorge the plunder which they had appropriated; and thus was collected a strange medley of trinkets and utensils, which the temporary holders gave up with sore unwillingness. Here and there, where a soldier had a little leisure and opportunity, he would hold a kind of mock-auction, at which not only camp-followers but officers would buy treasures for a mere trifle; but these instances were few, for there was not much ready cash among the conquerors. Sir Colin found it necessary to issue an order concerning the plundering system.* Outram and Jung Bahadoor took part in a series of operations, on the 17th, intended to obtain control over the northwest section of the city. The one set forth from the river, the other from the vicinity of the Alum Bagh; and during the day they cleared out many nests of rebels. There was also an action on the margin of the city, in which the enemy managed to bring together a considerable force of horse, foot, and artillery; their guns were captured, however, and themselves put to flight.

Sir Colin, responsible for many places besides Lucknow, and for many troops besides those under his immediate command, now made daily changes in the duties of his officers. Major (now Lieutenant-colonel) Vincent Eyre and Major (now also Lieutenant-colonel) Turner, two of the most distinguished artillery officers, departed for Futteghur and Idrapore; and Franklyn went to Cawnpore. Inglis succeeded Franklyn at the Alum Bagh. Sir Archdale Wilson and Brigadier Russell took their departure on sick-leave.

A considerable force of the enemy still lingered around the Alum Bagh, irresolute as to any actual attacks, but loath to quit the neighbourhood until the last ray of hope was extinguished. With these rebels Jung Bahadoor had many smart contests. He had been instructed by Sir Colin to obtain secure possession of the suburbs of the city near the Char Bagh—the bridge that carried the Cawnpore road over the canal.

It was on this day, the 17th, and partly in consequence of the success attending the operations of the Goorkhas, that two English ladies, Mrs Orr and Miss Jackson, were delivered from the hands of enemies who had long held them in bondage. It will be remembered that on the night of the 22d of November,* the insurgents in Lucknow, enraged at the safe evacuation of the Residency by the British, put to death certain English prisoners who had long been in confinement in the Kaiser Bagh. Among them were Mr Orr and Sir Mountstuart Jackson. So far as any authentic news could be obtained, it appeared that Mrs Orr and Miss Jackson had been spared; partly, as some said, through the intervention of the Begum. During the subsequent period of nearly four months, the fate of those unhappy ladies remained unknown to their English friends. On the day in question, however (the 17th of March), Captain M'Neil and Lieutenant Bogle, both attached to the Goorkha force, while exploring some of the deserted streets in the suburb, were accosted by a native who asked their protection for his house and property. The man sought to purchase this protection by a revelation concerning certain English ladies, who, he declared,

* 'It having been understood that several small pieces of ordnance captured in the city have been appropriated by individuals, all persons having such in their possession are directed at once to make them over to the commissary of ordnance in charge of the park.

'It is reported to the commander-in-chief that the Sikhs and other native soldiers are plundering in a most outrageous manner, and refuse to give up their plunder to the guards told off for the express purpose of checking such proceedings. His excellency desires that strong parties, under the command of European officers, be immediately sent out from each native regiment to put a stop to these excesses.

'Commanding officers of native regiments are called upon to use their best endeavours to restore order, and are held responsible that all their men who are not on duty remain in camp, and that those who are on duty do not quit their posts.

'All native soldiers not on duty are to be confined to camp till further orders, and all who may now be on duty in the city are to be relieved and sent back to camp.

'All commanding officers are enjoined to use their best endeavours to prevent their followers quitting camp.'

* Chap. xxi. p. 369.

were in confinement in a place known to him. Almost immediately another native brought a note from Mrs Orr and Miss Jackson, begging earnestly for succour. M'Neil and Bogle instantly obtained a guard of fifty Goorkhas, and, guided by the natives, went on their errand of mercy. After walking through half a mile of narrow streets, doubtful of an ambush at every turning, they came to a house occupied by one Meer Wajeed Ali, who held, or had held, some office under the court. After a little parleying, M'Neil and Bogle were led to an obscure apartment, where were seated two ladies in oriental costume. These were the prisoners, who had so long been excluded from every one of their own country, and who were overwhelmed with tearful joy at this happy deliverance. It was not clearly known whether this Meer Wajeed Ali was endeavouring to buy off safety for himself by betraying a trust imposed in him; but the two English officers deemed it best to lose no time in securing their countrywomen's safety, whether he were a double-dealer or not; they procured a palanquin, put the ladies into it, and marched off with their living treasure—proud enough with their afternoon's work. When these poor ladies came to tell their sad tale of woe, with countenances on which marks of deep suffering were expressed, it became known that, though not exposed to any actual barbarities or atrocities, like so many of their countrywomen in other parts of India, their lives had been made very miserable by the unfeeling conduct of their jailers, who were permitted to use gross and insulting language in their presence, and to harrow them with recitals of what Europeans were and had been suffering. They had had food in moderate sufficiency, but of other sources of solace they were almost wholly bereft. It was fully believed that they would not have been restored alive, had the jailer obeyed the orders issued to him by the Moulvie.

After a day of comparative repose on the 18th, a combined movement against the Moosa Bagh was organised on the 19th. This was the last position held by the enemy on the line of the Goomtee, somewhat beyond the extreme northwest limit of the city. Outram moved forward directly against the place; Hope Grant cannonaded it from the left bank; while William Campbell, approaching on the remote side from the Alum Bagh, prevented retreat in that direction. Some said the Begum was there, some the Moulvie or fanatic chieftain; but on this point nothing was known. All that was certain was that several thousand insurgents, driven from other places, had congregated within the buildings and courts of the Moosa Bagh. Outram's troops started from the Emanbarra on this expedition early in the morning; he himself joined them from Banks's house, while Sir Colin rode over to see in person how the work was effected. Opposite the Moosa Bagh, which was a large structure surrounded by an enclosed court, was the residence of Ali Nuckee Khan, vizier or prime-minister to the deposed King of Oude; and in other parts of the vicinity were numerous mansions and mosques. If the rebels had held well together, they might have made a stout resistance here, for the buildings contained many elements of strength; but discord reigned; the Begum reproached the thalookdars, the thalookdars the sepoys; while the Moulvie was suspected of an intention to set up as King of Oude on his own account. Outram's column was to make the direct attack; Hope Grant's cavalry and horse-artillery were to command certain roads of approach and exit on the river-side; while William Campbell's cavalry, aided by two or three infantry regiments, were to command the opposite side. The contest can hardly be called a battle or a siege; for as soon as the rebels clearly ascertained that the British were approaching, they abandoned court after court, house after house, and escaped towards the northwest, by the only avenue available. Although they did not fight, they escaped more successfully than Sir Colin had wished or intended. Whether the three movements were not timed in unison, or whether collateral objects engaged the attention of Brigadier Campbell, certain it is that few of the enemy were killed, and that many thousands safely marched or ran out. The open country, covered with enclosures and corn-fields, enabled the sepoys better to escape than the British to pursue them. A regiment of Sikhs was sent to occupy the Moosa Bagh; and now was Lucknow still more fully than before in the hands of the commander-in-chief.

On the 20th, further measures were taken, by proclamation and otherwise, to induce the peaceful portion of the inhabitants to return to their homes. This was desirable in every sense. Until the ordinary relations of society were re-introduced, anything like civil government was simply impossible; while, so long as the houses, deserted by their proper inhabitants, served as hiding-places for fanatics and budmashes, the streets were never for an instant safe. Many officers and soldiers were shot by concealed antagonists, long after the great buildings of the city had been conquered. Moreover, the Sikhs and Goorkhas were becoming very unruly. The plunder had acted upon them as an intoxicating indulgence, shaking the steady obedience which they were wont to exhibit when actively engaged against the enemy. Even at a time when Sir Colin was planning which of his generals he could spare, for service elsewhere or for sick-leave, and which regiments should form new columns for active service in other districts—even at such a time it was discovered that bodies of the enemy were lurking in houses near Outram's head-quarters, bent upon mischief or revenge; and there was much musketry-fire necessary before they could be dislodged. The 'sick-leave,' just adverted to, was becoming largely applied for. Many officers, so gallant and untiring as to be untouched by any suspicion of their willingness to shirk danger and hard work, gave in; they had become weakened in body and mind by laborious duties, and needed repose.

The Moulvie, who had held great power within Lucknow, and whose influence was even now not extinguished, commanded a stronghold in the very heart of the city. Sir Edward Lugard was requested to dislodge him on the 21st. This he did after a sharp contest; and Brigadier W. Campbell, with his cavalry, placed himself in such a position, that he was enabled to attack the enemy who were put to flight by Lugard, and to inflict heavy loss on them during a pursuit of six miles. The conquest of the Moulvie's stronghold had this useful effect among others; that it enabled Sir Colin to expedite the arrangements for the return of such of the inhabitants as were not too deeply steeped in rebellion to render return expedient. Among those who fell on this occasion, on the side of the enemy, was Shirreff-u-Dowlah, the chief-minister of the rebel boy-king, or rather of his mother the Begum; this man had been in collision with the Moulvie, each envious of the other's authority; and there were those who thought it was by a treacherous blow that he now fell. Even in this, the last contest within the city, the sappers had to be employed; for the Moulvie had so intrenched himself, with many hundred followers, that he could not be dislodged by the force at first sent against him; the engineers were forced to sap under and through

Major Hodson, Commandant of Hodson's Horse.

some surrounding buildings, before the infantry could obtain command of that in which the Moulvie was lodged.

This was the last day of those complicated scenes of tactics and fighting which formed collectively the siege of Lucknow, and which had lasted from the 2d to the 21st of March. Concerning the cavalry expeditions, during the third week of this period, it is pretty evident that they had been fruitless in great results. Sir Hope Grant had cut up a few hundred fugitive rebels in one spot, and intercepted more in another; Brigadier William Campbell had rendered useful service both in and beyond the suburbs of the city; but the proofs were not to be doubted that the mutinied sepoys and rebel volunteers had safely escaped from the city, not merely by thousands, but by tens of thousands; and that they still retained a sufficiency of military organisation to render them annoying and even formidable. When this news reached England, it damped considerably the pleasure afforded by the conquest of Lucknow. The nation asked, but asked without the probability of receiving a reply, whether the enemy had in this particular foiled a part of the commander-in-chief's plan; and whether the governor-general shared the opinions of the commander concerning the plan of strategy, and the consequences resulting from it?

The losses suffered by the British army during the operations at Lucknow, though necessarily considerable, were small in comparison with those which would have been borne if artillery had not been so largely used. Sir Colin from the first determined that shells and balls should do as much of the dread work as possible, clearing away or breaching the enemy's defence-works before he sent in his infantry to close quarters. During the entire series of operations, from the 2d to the 21st of March, he had 19 officers killed and 48 wounded. The whole of the generals and brigadiers escaped untouched; and there were only two officers among the wounded so high in military rank as lieutenant-colonel. The killed and wounded among the troops generally were about 1100. The enemy's loss could hardly have been less than 4000. One of the deaths most regretted during these operations was that of Major Hodson; who, as the commander of 'Hodson's Horse,' and as the captor of the King of Delhi, had been prominently engaged in the Indian wars. It was on the day marked by the conquest of the Begum Kothee that he fell. Having no especial duty on that day, and hearing that Brigadier Napier was busily engaged in engineering operations connected with the attack on that palace, he rode over to him, and joined in that storming attack which Sir Colin characterised as 'the sternest struggle which occurred during the siege.' Hodson, while assisting in clearing the court-yards and buildings near the palace of parties of the enemy lurking there, was shot by a sepoy. His orderly, a large powerful Sikh, carried him in his arms to a spot beyond the reach of shot, whence he was carried in a dooly to Banks's house, where surgical aid could be obtained. Some of his own irregular troopers cried over him like children. The shot had passed through the liver, and he died after a night of great agony. A spot was chosen for his grave near a tope of bamboos behind the Martinière. Sir Colin and his staff attended the funeral, at which the old chief was much affected; he had highly valued Hodson, and did not allow many hours to elapse before he wrote a graceful and feeling letter to the widow of the deceased officer. As soon as possible a telegraphic message was sent to bring down Captain Daly, the commandant of the famous corps of Guides; he was every way fitted to command a similar body of irregular cavalry, 'Hodson's Horse.'

No sooner was the city of Lucknow clearly and unequivocally in the hands of Sir Colin Campbell, than he completely broke up the lately formidable 'army of Oude.' The troops had nothing more immediately to do at that spot; while their services were urgently needed elsewhere. With regret did the soldiers leave a place where such extraordinary gains had fallen to the lot of some among their number; or, more correctly, this regret endured only until the very stringent regulations put an effectual stop to all plundering. The regiments were re-organised into brigades and divisions; new brigadiers were appointed in lieu of those on 'sick-leave;' and a dispersion of the army commenced.

It is impossible to read Sir Colin Campbell's mention of Jung Bahadoor without feeling that he estimated at a small price the value of the services yielded by the Nepaulese leader. Whether it was that the arrival of the Goorkha army was delayed beyond the date when the greatest services might have been rendered, or that Sir Colin found it embarrassing to issue orders to one who was little less than a king, it is plain that not much was effected by Jung Bahadoor during the operations at Lucknow. He came when the siege was half over; he departed a fortnight afterwards; and although the commander-in-chief said in a courteous dispatch: 'I found the utmost willingness on his part to accede to any desire of mine during the progress of the siege; and from the first his Highness was pleased to justify his words that he was happy to be serving under my command'—although these were the words used, there was an absence of any reference to special deeds of conquest. It was a pretty general opinion among the officers that the nine thousand soldiers of the Nepaulese army were far inferior in military qualities to those Goorkhas who had for many years formed two or three regiments in the Bengal army. When the looting in the city began, Jung Bahadoor's Goorkhas could scarcely be held in any control; like the Sikhs, they were wild with oriental excitement, and Sir Colin was more anxious concerning them than his own European troops. Viscount Canning, who was in intimate correspondence with the commander-in-chief through the medium of the electric telegraph, exchanged opinions with him in terms known only to themselves; but the announcement made public was to the effect that the governor-general solicited the aid of the Goorkha troops in the neighbourhood of Allahabad, and invited Jung Bahadoor to a personal conference with him at that city. It was during the last week in March that the Nepaulese allies quitted Lucknow, and marched off towards the Oude frontier.

Of the troops which remained at Lucknow, after the departure of some of the brigades, it need only be said in this place that they began to experience the heat of an Indian equinox, which, though much less than that of summer, is nevertheless severely felt by Europeans. A letter from an assistant-surgeon in the division lately commanded by Brigadier Franks, conveyed a good impression of camp-troubles at such a time.*

When the governor-general wrote the usual thanks and compliments after the conquest of Lucknow, he adverted very properly to the

* 'Though we are all in the town, our camp and hospital are still in the old place. While I write this in my tent in camp, the thermometer is at 100 degrees; not a breath of wind, and the flies —I can pity the Egyptians now—the tent is filled with them, and everything edible covered with them. We drink and eat flies, and in our turn are eaten by them. They nestle in your hair, and commit the most determined suicides in your tea or soup. Old-fashioned looking crickets come out of holes and stare at you; lizards run wildly across the tent; and ants by the thousand ply their wonted avocations utterly unmindful of your presence. When night arrives, it becomes a little cooler, the candles are lit, all the flies (save the suicides) have gone to roost upon the tent-poles, and you fancy that your troubles are over. Vain hope! the tent-doors are open; in flies a locust, hops into some dish, kicks himself out again, hitting you in the face, and finally bolts out at the opposite door. Then comes a flock of moths, all sizes and shapes, which dart madly at the lights. At last you put out your candle, and get into bed, when a new sound commences. Hum, hum, something soft and light settles on your face and hands: a sensation of red-hot needles intimates that the mosquitoes are upon you. The domestic flea and bug also abound; their appetites quite unimpaired by the climate. Jackals and pariah dogs yell and howl all night. Day dawns, and you have your flies down upon you lively as ever. This will give you some idea of our tent comforts.'

previous operations, which, though not conquests in the ordinary sense of the term, had won so much fame for Inglis, Havelock, Neill, Outram, and Campbell; and then after mentioning some of the most obvious facts connected with the siege,* praised all those whom Sir Colin had pointed out as being worthy of praise. Concerning the proclamation which Lord Canning issued, or proposed to issue, to the natives of Oude, it will be convenient to defer notice of it to a future chapter; when attention will be called to the important debates in the imperial legislature relating to that subject.

Here this chapter may suitably end. It was designed as a medium for the remarkable episode of the final conquest of Lucknow in the month of March; and will be best kept free from all topics relating to other parts of India.

* 'From the 2d to the 16th of March a series of masterly operations took place, by which the commander-in-chief, nobly supported in his well-laid plans of attack by the ability and skill of the general officers, and by the indomitable bravery and resolution of the officers and men of all arms, drove the rebels successively from all their strongly fortified posts, till the whole fell into the possession of our troops. That this great success should have been accomplished at so little cost of valuable lives, enhances the honour due to the leader who has achieved it.' After mentioning the remarkable services rendered by Outram during more than five months in the Residency and the Alum Bagh, Viscount Canning could not do other than recognise the crowning service of that distinguished man, as the second in command under Campbell during the great operations of March.

Note.

Lucknow Proclamations.—When Sir Colin Campbell had effectually conquered Lucknow, and had gathered information concerning the proceedings of the rebels since the preceding month of November, it was found that no means had been left untried to madden the populace into a death-struggle with the British. Among other methods, printed proclamations were posted up in all the police stations, not only in Lucknow, but in many other parts of Oude.

One of these proclamations, addressed to the Mohammedans, ran thus:

'God says in the Koran: "Do not enter into the friendship of Jews and Christians; those who are their friends are of them—that is, the friends of Christians are Christians, and friends of Jews are Jews. God never shews his way to infidels."

'By this it is evident that to befriend Christians, is irreligious. Those who are their friends are not Mohammedans; therefore all the Mohammedan fraternity should with all their hearts be deadly enemies to the Christians, and never befriend them in any way; otherwise, all will lose their religion, and become infidels.

'Some people, weak in faith and worldly, think that if they offend the Christians, they will fall their victims when their rule is re-established. God says of these people: "Look in the hearts of these unbelievers, who are anxious to seek the friendship of Christians through fear of receiving injury," to remove their doubts and assure their wavering mind. It is also said that "God will shortly give us victory, or will do something by which our enemies will be ashamed of themselves." The Mussulmans should therefore always hope, and never believe that the Christians will be victorious and injure them; but, on the contrary, should hope to gain the victory and destroy all Christians.

'If all the Mohammedans join and remain firm to their faith, they would no doubt gain victory over the Christians, because God says that the victory is due to the faithful from Him; but if they become cowards and infirm to their religion, and do not sacrifice their private interest for the public good, the Europeans will be victorious, and, having subdued the Mohammedans, they will disarm, hang, shoot, or blow them away, seize upon their women and children, disgrace, dishonour, and christianise them, dig up their houses and carry off their property; they will also burn religious and sacred books, destroy the musjids, and efface the name of Islam from the world.

'If the Mohammedans have any shame, they should all join and prepare themselves to kill the Christians without minding any one who says to the contrary; they should also know that no one dies before his time, and when the time comes, nothing can save them. Thousands of men are carried off by cholera and other pestilence; but it is not known whether they die in their senses, and be faithful to their own religion.

'To be killed in a war against Christians is a proof of obtaining martyrdom. All good Mohammedans pray for such a death; therefore, every one should sacrifice his life for such a reward. Every one is to die assuredly, and those Mohammedans who would spare themselves now will be sorry on their death for their neglect.

'As it is the duty of all men and women to oppose, kill, and expel the Europeans for deeds committed by them at Delhi, Jhujur, Rewaree, and the Doab, all the Mohammedans should discharge their duty with a willing heart; if they neglect, and the Europeans overpower them, they will be disarmed, hung, and treated like the inhabitants of other unfortunate countries, and will have nothing but regret and sorrow for their lot. Wherefore this notice is given to warn the public.'

Another proclamation, addressed principally to zemindars and Hindoos in general, but to Mohammedans also, was couched in the following terms:

'All the Hindoos and Mohammedans know that man loves four things most: 1, his religion and caste; 2, his honour; 3, his own and his kinsmen's lives; 4, his property. All these four are well protected under native rulers; no one interferes with any one's religion; every one enjoys his respectability according to his caste and wealth. All the respectable people—Syad, Shaikh, Mogul, and Patan, among Mohammedans; and Brahmins, Chatrees, Bys, and Kaeths, among the Hindoos—are respected according to their castes. No low-caste people like chumars, dhanook, and passees, can be equal to and address them disrespectfully. No one's life or property is taken unless for some heinous crime.

'The British are quite against these four things—they want to spoil every one's caste, and wish both the Mohammedans and Hindoos to become Christians. Thousands have turned renegades, and many will become so yet; both the nobles and low caste are equal in their eyes; they disgrace the nobles in the presence of the ignoble; they arrest or summon to their courts the gentry, nawabs, and rajahs at the instance of a chumar, and disgrace them; wherever they go they hang the respectable people, kill their women and children; their troops dishonour the women, and dig up and carry off their buried property. They do not kill the mahajuns, but dishonour their women, and carry off their money. They disarm the people wherever they go, and when the people are disarmed, they hang, shoot, or blow them away.

'In some places, they deceive the landholders by

promising them remittance of revenue, or lessen the amount of their lease; their object is that when their government is settled, and every one becomes their subject, they can readily, according to their wish, hang, disgrace, or christianise them. Some of the foolish landholders have been deceived, but those who are wise and careful do not fall into their snares.

'Therefore, all the Hindoos and Mohammedans who wish to save their religion, honour, life, and property, are warned to join the government forces, and not to be deceived by the British.

'The passees (low-caste servants) should also know that the chowkeedaree (office of watchmen) is their hereditary right, but the British appoint burkundauzes in their posts, and deprive them of their rights; they should therefore kill and plunder the British and their followers, and annoy them by committing robbery and thefts in their camp.'

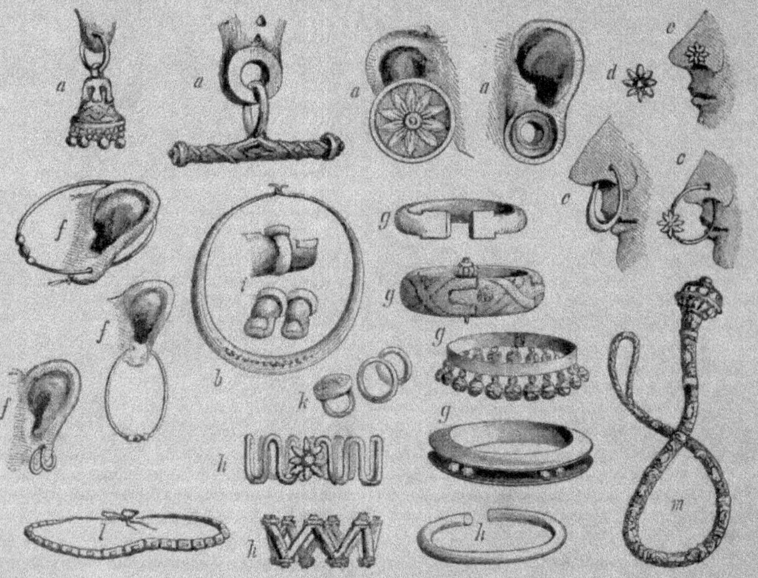

HINDOO METALLIC ORNAMENTS.

a Women's Earrings. *b* Parsee Women's Neck-ring. *c* Women's Nose-rings. *d* Women's Forehead Ornament. *f* Men's Earrings. *g* Women's Anklets. *h* Women's Armlets. *i* Women's Toe-rings. *k* Women's Finger-rings. *l* Women's Necklace. *m* Men's Necklace.

BARRACKPORE.

CHAPTER XXVI.

MINOR EVENTS IN MARCH.

HAVING briefly narrated in the last chapter the progress of Sir Colin Campbell's army in Oude, from the beginning towards the close of March; it now becomes expedient to watch the operations of those military officers who, during the same month, were engaged in services in other parts of India. The achievements were not so great in magnitude or notoriety, but they do not the less require to be noticed: seeing that they illustrate the state of feeling among the native population, the fluctuations of fortune among the rebels, and the struggles of British officers amid great difficulties.

As in former chapters, there will be a convenience in beginning with the Calcutta regions, and transferring attention successively to the west, northwest, and southwest.

The Anglo-Indian capital was shorn of somewhat of its splendour during the spring months, by the absence of the governor-general at Allahabad; but in truth this was a secondary matter; for it was not a time for levees, gaieties, or vice-regal presentations and splendour. Calcutta experienced a panic so late in the history of the mutiny as the 3d of March—one of many to which a somewhat excitable population had been exposed. A telegraphic message was received from Barrackpore, to the effect that the sepoys of two native regiments at that station—the 2d and the 23d B. N. I.—were deserting in bodies of ten or twelve; and that the deserters were supposed to be making their way to Calcutta. The officers of the volunteer guards were at once requested to send pickets to certain unprotected buildings in Calcutta. Very speedily these pickets were told off; cavalry patrolled the streets all night; the artillerymen remained watchful within the fort; and the English troops present were kept under arms. The rumour proved to have been greatly exaggerated, and the suspected danger passed away—but not without causing much trepidation among the unwarlike portion of the Calcutta community.

So numerous were the European troops that arrived at Calcutta during the winter, and so obvious the necessity for increasing the strength of that branch of the army in India, that preparations were made for accommodating them within easy reach of the capital. Barrackpore, although well supplied with sepoy lines, had never held European troops in large number. It was now resolved, instead of building new European barracks at that place, to increase those at Chinsura. This town, about twenty miles from Calcutta, on the banks of the Hoogly, had already a fine European barrack and military hospital, in a very healthy spot. About the month of March, many hundred men were set to work, to increase the barrack accommodation to a level with the wants of five thousand European troops, and to raze all the buildings within five hundred yards on all sides, to form parade-grounds, &c.

In the regions north and east of Calcutta, the materials for rebellion were pretty nearly exhausted. There had from the first been only a small amount of disturbance in those districts; and it became gradually evident that the town and village population were desirous of continuing their peaceful avocations, uninterrupted by mutinous sepoys or fanatical Mohammedans.

It was in many ways fortunate that the recently acquired province of Pegu had remained peaceful during the dangerous periods of the mutiny. Had revolt or treason been at work in that quarter, the embarrassment of the government would have been seriously aggravated. Disturbances, it is true, did take place; but they were not of such magnitude as to give occasion for alarm. This was mainly owing to the policy of the King of Burmah. We had taken from him a rich province, a slice out of his empire, by a mingled course of war and politics; and he was no more likely to be content with that result than any other defeated monarch. But he was a shrewd observant man; he measured the power of England, and saw reason to believe that he would weaken rather than strengthen himself by any hostility at this time. There were not wanting those near him who urged him to a different policy. Burmah, like other countries, had its war-party, who kept up a spirit of bitterness towards the British. This party was headed by the king's brother, and by many of the old dispossessed Burman officials of Pegu. There is reason to believe that, had the strength of the rebels in Oude remained much longer unbroken, the King of Burmah might have been drawn or driven into hostility in spite of himself. Whenever news came over from the opposite side of the Bay of Bengal, the Mohammedans resident in Burmah made the most of such parts of it as indicated a decline of the English 'raj,' and gave strength to a feeling among the Burmese which the king might not much longer have been able to resist. In the early part of 1857 there were four European regiments in Pegu; but the urgent demands from India had led to the withdrawal of all these, except a wing of the 2d Madras Europeans at Toungoo, and a few of H. M. 29th at Thayetmyo; and even of native Madras troops in Pegu, the number was but small. There was a time, in the autumn of that year, when the war-party might have wrought serious mischief to British interests; but when steam-frigates, corvettes, gun-boats, and regiments from various quarters began to shew themselves at Rangoon or in the Irrawaddy, or were known to be passing up the Bay towards Calcutta, the chances were altered. Instead of fighting, the king did a much wiser thing, whether from humane or from politic motives—he subscribed ten thousand rupees towards the Mutiny Relief Fund.

West and southwest of Calcutta, in a part of India very imperfectly known to Europeans, tranquillity was occasionally disturbed, not so much by mutinous sepoys, as by ambitious chieftains desirous of strengthening themselves in a time of anarchy and uncertain allegiance. In the region around Chyabassa, many petty occurrences from time to time kept the few Europeans in anxiety. There were not many rebel sepoys in that quarter, it is true; but, on the other hand, there were few troops of any kind to aid Captain Moncrieff, the senior assistant-commissioner. A semi-savage tribe, called Coles or Koles, infested the neighbourhood. On the 25th of March, three thousand of these Coles, with a medley of guns, muskets, and native weapons of all kinds, assembled at Chuckerderpore, where Moncrieff had a small camp of marines and two guns; they were, however, dispersed by a mere handful of men, and three of their guns taken. This district was kept in an agitated state mainly by the machinations of a turbulent chieftain, the Rajah of Porahat.

Let us advance, however, to those regions where the audacity of the insurgents was more seriously felt—the regions of the Middle Ganges and the Lower Jumna. The Lower Ganges, between Calcutta and Dinapoor, remained peacefully in the hands of cultivators and traders, who were glad enough to be free from the visitations of fighting-men; but from Dinapoor upwards the sources of discordance were numerous. A few mutineers lurked about, aided by a much larger proportion of desperate characters, who took service under chieftains (mostly Mohammedan) bent upon increasing their own power at the expense of the British.

The Azimghur district, nearly north of Benares, became in March the scene of a conflict which certainly gave a triumph for a time to the enemy, although it was favourable to the British in the first instance. This conflict took place on the 21st at Atrowlia, between a body of insurgents on the one side, and a small force under Colonel Millman of H.M. 37th, commandant of the Azimghur field-force. Being in camp at Koelsa, he received information from Mr Davies, magistrate of Azimghur, that a considerable body of mutineers was in the neighbourhood of Atrowlia, a place about twenty-five miles from that city. The colonel immediately set out, with about 260 infantry, cavalry, and gunners, and two pieces of ordnance—his troops being British and Madrasses. At daybreak on the 22d, he espied the enemy—chiefly sepoys of the Dinapoor brigade, who had followed the fortunes of Koer Singh—posted in several topes of mango-trees. His infantry of the 37th, his Madras cavalry under Colonel Cumberlege, and his two guns, speedily discomfited the enemy and put them to flight; but his day's work was not ended. While his men were halting in the neighbourhood of Atrowlia, and breakfast was being prepared among the topes of trees, news was suddenly brought that the rebels were advancing in great force. Millman, immediately proceeding with some skirmishers to ascertain their strength, found them strongly posted behind a mud-wall, in the midst of topes of trees and sugar-canes. He sent back orders for his troops to advance; but the enemy increased in number so rapidly, that he could not contend against them; he retired slowly from Atrowlia to his camp at Koelsa, followed by the enemy, who fired at a distance, and endeavoured to turn his flanks. He made one dash with his cavalry; but news, or at least a rumour, reaching the camp, that no fewer than 5000 rebels were approaching, such a panic was created among his camp-followers, that many of the hackery-drivers left their carts, and all the cooks ran away. The colonel, perplexed both by his foes and his camp-followers, and conscious that his camp was untenable in case of a night-attack, and that adequate supplies would be wanting for his men—deemed it expedient to retreat to Azimghur, which he did the same day. He was compelled to abandon a portion of his tents and baggage, which fell into the hands of the enemy.

This was a vexatious and serious discomfiture. It told unfavourably in two directions; for while it paralysed the exertions of the few British officers and troops in that region, it afforded to the rebels an excuse for vaunting abroad their prowess and success. The natives, inexplicable in character to Europeans, were often incredulous to rumours of defeat among their own countrymen; but rumours on the other side spread among them with astounding rapidity, encouraging them to schemes of resistance which they might possibly otherwise have avoided.

It was a natural consequence of the withdrawal from Atrowlia, and the retreat to Azimghur, that the last-named station should itself become imperiled; for a wide range of country was thus left wholly at the mercy of Koer Singh and his associates. The British in Azimghur proceeded to intrench themselves within the jail, which was surrounded by a deep ditch; and every man was set to work to strengthen the fortifications. The rebels gradually approached, to the number of four or five thousand; and then the small garrison was fairly besieged—all the rest of the city being in the hands of the insurgents. A messenger was despatched to Benares on the 26th, to announce the state of affairs; but all that the authorities at that place could do, on the spur of the moment, was to send fifty dragoons in carts, drawn by bullocks and pushed on by coolies. A telegraphic message was at the same time sent to Allahabad; consequent upon which a wing of H.M. 13th foot, and the depôt of the 2d, started off to Benares, for service at that place or at Azimghur. There was a rumour that Koer Singh intended to attack Ghazeepore or Benares, or both, on his way from Azimghur to Arrah; and this rumour led to much entreaty for aid to the threatened stations.

It will hereafter be seen that Azimghur needed the care of Sir Colin Campbell. Meanwhile we may notice the state of affairs in a district somewhat further north.

The neighbourhood of Goruckpore was the scene of a contest early in March. At that time there were assembled about 200 men of the naval brigade, under Captain Sotheby, 200 Bengal yeomanry cavalry, 900 Goorkhas, a few Sikhs and four guns—under Colonel Rowcroft. This motley but stanch garrison was attacked on the 5th in great force by several influential rebels, who had with them an army of 12,000 men, including 3500 sepoys of mutinied Bengal regiments. Between eight o'clock and noon, Rowcroft not only defeated this greatly superior force, but chased the enemy seven miles, nearly to their encampment at Bilwa or Belwar. The enemy lost 400 or 500 in killed and wounded, eight guns, and much ammunition. Among the leaders of the rebels were the Nazim Mahomed Hussein, Rajah Dabie Buksh of Gonda, the Rajah of Churdah, and Mehudee Ali Hussein, who were all mounted on elephants. This victory was a very fortunate one; for not only was Goruckpore saved from being a second time overrun by insurgents, but Colonel Rowcroft received news that many thousand villagers on the banks of the Gogra were ready to rise in rebellion if he had been defeated. This kind of peril was constantly impressed on the minds of the British officers; the consequences of a disaster were always more than they could safely calculate.

A defeat was experienced by a small force in the Allahabad district towards the close of March, owing to the want of due information concerning the position and strength of the enemy. Two companies of H.M. 54th, a hundred Sikhs, a few Madras cavalry, and two guns, went out to attack some rebels at a place called Suraon, between Allahabad and Gopeegunje. Insufficiently informed of the locality, the force came suddenly to a spot surrounded by a jungle, in which a large body of rebels were concealed. Much to the astonishment of the magistrate of the district, those rebels possessed six pieces of artillery; a fire was opened, which wrought much mischief to the British force, and eventually compelled it to retreat. This was a small affair, but it rendered the authorities uneasy; for it shewed that within a few hours of Allahabad, where the governor-general had temporarily taken up his quarters, there were not only insurgents ready for mischief, but that those insurgents, in some way and from some source not easily accounted for, had possessed themselves of artillery.

Jung Bahadoor's participation in the later stages of the siege of Lucknow was noticed in the last chapter. He had entered Oude from the east; and shortly before his junction with Sir Colin, his advanced division had a sharp engagement with a force of the enemy, which may briefly be noticed here. Captain Plowden was in charge of this division; and under him were a few English and many Nepaulese officers, commanding the Goorkha regiments of which the division consisted. Having received information that the Nazim Mahomed Hussein, with a force of 4000 men, intended to dispute the passage of Jung Bahadoor's army at the road to Lucknow over the Kandoo Nuddee, Captain Plowden prepared to contest the matter with him. His division consisted of seven Goorkha regiments, about 4000 strong, with thirteen guns. On the morning of the 5th of March, he found the enemy drawn up in detached parties near the bridge; he opened fire with his guns, and then charged with infantry in line. His progress was much disturbed by an intervening space of bush-jungle and deep ravines; nevertheless his Goorkhas charged resolutely, drove back the enemy at all points, pursued them for two or three miles, killed 600 of their number, and captured a gun—without losing more than 17 in killed and wounded. Captain Plowden, in his dispatch, told how he had been aided by the Nepaulese General Khurruk Bahadoor, the two brigadiers Junga Doje and Run Sing Bahadoor, Colonel Teela Bickrum Singh Tappah, and other officers whose names present a formidable appearance. The Nepaulese army pursued its way to Lucknow, and rendered a small amount of assistance. When their services had terminated at that city, Jung Bahadoor took a few of the best regiments with him to Allahabad, on his expedition to an interview with the governor-general; but the main body of his army marched off *viâ* Nawabgunge, on the Fyzabad route, towards the Nepaul and Goruckpore frontier. Whether Jung Bahadoor was negotiating with Lord Canning concerning the price at which the services of the Goorkhas were to be purchased; or whether any project was afoot for transferring some of the Goorkha regiments formally to the British service—was not made publicly known; but it was understood that the main Nepaulese force would remain near Nawabgunge until after the interview between the two great personages.

Of the wildly excited province of Oude, it is scarcely necessary to say much here. The great event of the month, the siege of Lucknow, has already been recorded; the other parts of the province were still almost wholly in the hands of the insurgents. It will, however, contribute towards an understanding of the state of the province in March, if we advert to a few facts concerning the temporary occupants of the city of Lucknow, and the arrangements made by Sir Colin affecting his army.

First, a word or two concerning the soldiery. It would be quite impossible to say which regiments of the Queen's army rendered most service or behaved most valiantly; but the defence of Lucknow had been so extraordinary in its character, that the government deemed it right to notice specially the courage and fortitude of the 32d infantry—Inglis's main prop during his defence of the Residency from the 1st of July till the arrival of Havelock and Outram near the end of September. There was put forth an announcement to the effect that 'her Majesty, in consideration of the enduring fortitude and persevering gallantry displayed in defence of the Residency at Lucknow, has been graciously pleased to command that the 32d be clothed, equipped, and trained as a light infantry regiment, from the 26th of February 1858. Her Majesty has also been pleased to command that the word "Lucknow" shall be borne on the regimental colour of the 32d light infantry, in commemoration of the enduring fortitude and persevering gallantry displayed in the defence of the Residency of Lucknow for eighty-seven days.' Many of the other royal regiments had borne more fighting in the open field; but none equalled the 32d in long enduring privation and heroism, owing to the extraordinary circumstances in which the regiment had been placed.

Next, concerning the city itself, the place which had undergone so strange a series of sieges and defences. In Lucknow, after the recapture, the shopkeepers gradually returned, opened their places of business, and resumed commercial dealings. Many parts of the city had been so battered by shot and shell that the buildings were scarcely habitable; but as this only occurred to a small extent in the trading streets, there was little interruption on that ground to the return of the inhabitants. The chief obstacles were—the complicity of many of the towns-people in the proceedings of the mutineers, and the impoverishment of others by several days of fighting, anarchy, and plunder. The troops destined for the defence of the city were quartered in some among the many palaces, not so much battered by cannonading as the others. A clear space was formed around the Kaiser Bagh, by the demolition of small buildings; and operations were made for opening a wide street or avenue entirely through the city, from the iron bridge to the canal—strategic precautions, intended to give the garrison control over the city in case of a turbulent rising. Precautions were in truth still necessary. Lucknow had contained more ruffians, more desperate characters ready for any lawless enterprises, than most other cities in India; and the British authorities felt by no means certain that the lurking-places in the narrow streets were yet cleared of them. The officers bore in mind, with regret and resentment, that two of their companions had been murdered in the city when the siege might have been deemed fairly over. These two were Lieutenants Cape and Thackwell. They rode from the camp into the city, but for what purpose was not clearly known to their companions. They got off their horses, tied them to a doorpost, and went into a house. It is supposed that budmashes, prowling about, shot them; but the only certainty is that, when some of the Madras fusiliers went out to search for them, the headless trunks of the two unfortunate officers were all that remained to reveal the secret of their fate.

The details given in the last chapter will have rendered evident the fact that the escape of the rebels from Lucknow after the siege was far more complete than the English public had expected or wished. How far it disappointed those immediately responsible, no one but themselves knew. A secrecy enveloped the plans of the commander-in-chief; he told just so much as he wished to be known, and kept the rest to himself, or shared it with the governor-general. Whether foreseen or not, however, the escape of the rebels was very marked and significant. Sir Hope Grant and other cavalry leaders endeavoured to check them, but the check was of small account; in truth, the cavalry were too few for a belt of country so wide. When the fact became indisputably clear that the main body of insurgents had got away, the question arose—whither? The camping-grounds of the fugitive rebels were very imperfectly known to the British authorities. It was supposed, but on uncertain information, that, at the end of the month of March, Nena Sahib was at Bareilly, with 2000 men, and many members of his family; that the Begum of Oude was at Khyrabad, with nearly 10,000 men; that 2000 more were near Shahjehanpoor; and that Khan Bahadoor Khan was concocting some scheme of operations with the Nena, having Rohilcund for its theatre. These were the suppositions, founded on vague data.

One thing Sir Colin speedily decided on. It was useless to keep a fine army at Lucknow, while so much serious work had to be done elsewhere. As already mentioned, he broke up his 'army of Oude' into separate portions. Jung Bahadoor having taken his departure with his nine thousand Nepaulese, the commander-in-chief proceeded to organise columns or divisions for special service in various directions. On the 29th of March Sir Colin issued a general order, pointing to the forthcoming duties of these portions of the army. The 5th and 78th regiments were to march from the Alum Bagh to Cawnpore. The artillery at the Alum Bagh was to be divided, some to return to the camp at Lucknow, the rest to join the 5th regiment. The troops to be left at Lucknow were to be formed into a division under Sir Hope Grant. This was to comprise H.M. 20th, 28th, 33d, 53d, 90th, and 93d infantry, the 2d Dragoon Guards, three Punjaub regiments of horse, and various detachments of artillery and engineers, with Brigadiers W. Campbell and Barker as subordinate commanders. Sir Edward Lugard was to form and command a division to be called the 'Azimghur Field-force,' to consist of H.M. 10th regiment, various detachments of cavalry, artillery, and engineers, and whatever troops might at that time be in the Azimghur district. The infantry of this force was to form a brigade under Brigadier Douglas; and the destination was the district from which the force was named—a district, as we have lately seen, greatly endangered by the presence of a large rebel force. Indeed, so urgent was the need for aid in that quarter, that Lugard started off at once. Another division, for service in Rohilcund, was placed under the command of General Walpole. It comprised H.M. 42d, 79th, and 93d infantry, two battalions of the Rifle Brigade, the 1st Bengal Europeans, two regiments of native infantry, H.M. 7th Hussars and 9th Lancers, three regiments of Punjaub cavalry, the Naval Brigade from H.M. steamer *Shannon*, and various detachments of artillery and engineers. Everything portended that this division would have hot work before it—hot both in the common and the figurative sense; for the powerful sun of the month of April would soon pour down on the heads of the troops; while it was quite certain that Rohilcund contained a large number of mutinied sepoys, rebel leaders, and desperate men ready for any deeds of violence and anarchy.

It may here suitably be mentioned, that Sir Colin Campbell's experience of Oudian warfare taught him the necessity of caution in all attacks on the forts with which that province was so fully provided. His officers would have dashed at them, as at other obstacles; but he forbade enterprises likely to be followed by losses which good guns might obviate. On the 24th of March, just when the army of Oude was about to be broken up, he issued a general order concerning the arrangements to be made for attacking such strongholds.*

Quitting Oude for a time, and transferring attention to the important and fertile Doab between the Ganges and the Jumna, we shall see that the month of March found that part of India still much distracted by fighting and lawless violence. True, Allahabad was in British hands at one end of it, Delhi at the other, Cawnpore and Agra

* 'The commander-in-chief prohibits columns from moving to the attack of forts, whether large or small, without at least two heavy guns, or a heavy gun and a heavy howitzer. If possible, such columns should always have mortars also; namely, two 8-inch and two 5½-inch. Arrangements are to be made by the inspector-general of ordnance to insure the presence of a proportion of heavy guns, howitzers, mortars, and cohorns, at all stations where British regiments are quartered. Wherever there is a possibility of movable columns being organised, the necessary elephant and bullock draught should be maintained. When an expedition against a fort is deemed absolutely necessary, and heavy ordnance cannot be obtained, a special reference is to be made to the chief of the staff by telegraph. If, however, the station be removed from the wire, the general officer commanding the division or station must, of course, exercise a discretionary power; but the commander-in-chief begs that it may be recollected, as a principle, that, except in cases of the most absolute necessity, forts are not to be attacked with light guns only.'

at intermediate points; but nevertheless there were numerous bands of rebels roaming about the open country. Whether two or three of these towns were on river-banks just beyond the Doab, does not affect the question, which is not one of mere geographical nomenclature.

The Lower Doab was brought more fully than before within the influence of military control, by the opening of a further portion of the great trunk-railway to Futtehpoor, placing that town within a few hours' distance of Allahabad. This opening took place on the 25th of March; when Viscount Canning, with nearly all the civil officers of the last-named city, made the inaugurating journey to Futtehpoor, amid the holiday accompaniments of flags, triumphal arches, bands of music, feasting, and speech-making. Further to the northwest, Cawnpore remained a kind of central point, whence troops could be sent to quarters where they were most needed. A few regiments only were kept there, sufficient to guard against sudden surprises. All the British who entered the place beheld with melancholy interest the cross erected near the terrible well by the men of the 32d, in memory of the women and children of that regiment, included among the victims of Nena Sahib.

There was an important town, southwest of Cawnpore, which seemed likely to be a scene of warfare. During the month of March, it became very apparent that Calpee was a spot which would speedily require attention on the part of the military authorities. When Sir Colin Campbell defeated the Gwalior mutineers at Cawnpore, many weeks earlier, they fled from that neighbourhood. Rumours spread around that a considerable portion of the defeated force had fled southwest to Calpee, fortified themselves there, and called upon the neighbouring zemindars for supplies of men and money—both of which were forthcoming. The truth of this rumour, doubtful for a time, became confirmed as the spring advanced. It was now certain that rebels in great force occupied Calpee, well supplied with artillery and other munitions of war, and eagerly watching for a chance of making an attack on Cawnpore—should that oft-besieged place be left at any time insufficiently guarded. To what extent Nena Sahib or his brothers were connected with this Calpee force, was not known. The struggles in and near that town belong to a month beyond that to which this chapter relates.

The great city of Agra remained peacefully in the hands of the British. Occasionally, small columns were sent out to attack and disperse bodies of mutineers who were working mischief in the country districts; but the formidable brigades of mutinied regiments were not in that quarter. As one instance; on the 11th of March, Brigadier Showers found it necessary to chastise some rebels at Bah, in the Agra district. He set forth with two companies of the 8th foot, 400 of the Sikh police, two guns, a howitzer, and a mortar; and encountered a motley force of 4000 rebels—comprising three troops of insurgent cavalry, three companies of infantry, and a body of escaped convicts. These ruffians had assaulted and captured the town of Bah, plundered all the houses, carried off the cattle, and murdered some of the wealthier inhabitants. This body of rebels appeared to have come from the direction of the Gwalior territories across the Chumbul. Many of their leaders had been in the civil service of the Company, but turned rebels when they thought rebellion would be more profitable. Against these men Brigadier Showers marched from Agra. A strange wild contest ensued. The enemy did not stand to fight a battle, but made use of ravines, rocks, temples, topes, and villages as places whence masked attacks might be effected. There were no roads thereabouts, and Showers experienced much difficulty in struggling through jungles and ravines.

It was often difficult for the officers in command to muster troops enough to put down these bands of insurgents. At one period during the month, Colonel Riddell marched out from Minpooree to aid in intercepting fugitives from Lucknow. While he was gone, information arrived that Etawah was threatened by a large body of rebels. No aid being available from Minpooree, a telegraphic message was sent on to Futteghur (Furruckabad); and Colonel Seaton immediately ordered a regiment of Bengal Europeans to march to the threatened spot. These minor operations were often very harassing to the troops, who had to march great distances, and wage contests which did not bring them so much glory as a regular siege or a great battle. Officers naturally preferred those battle-fields which would bring their names in honourable form into the official gazettes; and private soldiers those which might earn for some of them the Victoria Cross; but many weary months passed over some of the corps, during which the troops were engaged in harassing pursuit of marauders and ruffians whom they heartily despised, and to conquer whom brought them very little increase of military reputation.

Speaking generally, it may be said that, at the end of March, the efforts made by the British officers in the Doab were directed chiefly to prevent the escape of rebels across the Ganges from Oude. One small force was watching to this intent at and near Cawnpore; another was in the Minpooree district; a third was marching down the road from Meerut to Futteghur; while two others, under Chamberlain and Coke, were endeavouring to control the Gangetic valley between Futteghur and Roorkee.

Further to the northwest, the region around Delhi was nearly all in British hands, and the city itself wholly so—all the mutinous regiments being far away. The authorities, after Delhi had remained several months peacefully in their hands, resolved on the formation of a camel corps, under a peculiar system of organisation.

It was completed by the end of March, by a native named Lalla Jotee Pershaud, under the superintendence of Captain Chalmers, assistant commissary-general. The camels, 400 in number, were selected with great care, in the Bikaneer district. The drivers were armed each with a sword and fusil; and each camel was fitted to carry a European soldier if necessary. The drivers, equivalent to troopers or cavalry-men, were carefully selected from the natives of Rajpootana. The purpose in view was to form a corps of armed men capable of moving with great rapidity to any spot where their services might be urgently needed. Lalla Jotee Pershaud was a wealthy and influential man; and it was intended to make the officering of the corps such as would render it an acceptable compliment to friendly natives of good position.

As to the city itself, no semblance of fighting was presented. The conquest by Sir Archdale Wilson, half a year before, had been so complete, that no enemy remained to fight with. The British kept just sufficient reliable troops in the place to defend it from surprise; but the authority was mainly transferred to civil commissioners, who gradually re-established order and reorganised the revenue department. The old king still resided there, waiting for his time of punishment. A special tribunal tried and executed a large number of rebels.

A curious struggle of opinions arose on the question—What should be done with Delhi? Not only within that city itself, but all over India, the controversy was maintained with much earnestness. The opinions resolved themselves into three varieties—advocating destruction, decay, and conservation, respectively. When the city was captured, a very general desire was expressed, under the influence of fierce indignation, to destroy the place altogether, leaving not one stone upon another to tell where Delhi had been—or rather, leaving the stones to tell where Delhi had ceased to be. The destructives, if these persons may thus be called, argued that Delhi should be extinguished from the list of cities, because it was the centre of disaffection, the scene of the first and worst stroke levelled at British power; that the Mohammedans of India would ever think they had a national rallying-point, so long as Delhi remained; and that the destruction of this rallying-point would impress them with an idea of British power. The place has a charm for native ears; it is a sign, a symbol, a standard, a flag of nationality, the memory of which should be effaced, as something dangerous to the future security of the British 'raj.' Delhi, they urged, should be regarded rather as a dynastic than a commercial capital; everything in it recalls the past greatness of a race which had just been foremost in mutiny. For all these reasons—destroy Delhi. Gradually there arose a second party, who suggested decay rather than destruction. They said: 'Destroy Delhi, and it would be perpetually an object of regret to the followers of Islam; but Delhi decayed would excite only a feeling of contempt. No tradition of sovereignty could attach to a dirty little village in which a population of pauper Mussulmans, around the ruins of old palaces, scrambled for the charity of a contemptuous traveller.' They recommended that the European troops at Delhi should be removed to Hansi, where they might be easily accommodated; that the arsenal should be removed to Ferozpore; or that an entirely new European city should be built, lower down the Jumna; and that Delhi should then be left to be supported by natives alone, burdened by a special taxation as a punishment for treason—this, it was believed, would gradually rob the city of all its dignity and importance. But there arose a third party, to which, it was reputed, no less a personage than Sir John Lawrence belonged, urging the preservation of Delhi. The grounds for this advice were many and important. It was pointed out, among other things—that Delhi is admirably placed, geographically and politically; that its site was selected by men who looked primarily to the maintenance of power in the northwestern regions of India; that, as a commercial entrepôt, it is the point at which the two great streams of Central Asian trade diverge to Calcutta and Bombay; that, as a military cantonment, the city commands the Jumna at the best point for crossing the river; that it is the most central point from which the marauding Goojurs and Meewatties could be controlled; that the imperial palace would form an admirable fortress, to be garrisoned by British troops; and that the walls, brought at one point within a narrower sweep, would keep out plunderers and protect the magazine.

Whatever was to be the course pursued, Delhi remained, at the period to which this chapter relates, undestroyed. The city-wall was still standing, with the breaches hastily earthed up; all the gates had been closed, except the Cashmere, Lahore, and Calcutta Gates, but none destroyed; the fractured Cashmere Gate had been replaced by a temporary wooden barrier; the English church had been painted and repaired; the college, riddled by cannon and musket balls, had been converted into a barrack; the magazine remained as poor Willoughby had left it, half blown up; and the palace had not suffered very materially from the siege. Concerning the principal street of the city, an eye-witness wrote as follows: 'The Chandnee Chowk is the only street we have seen in India to which the terms of descriptive admiration bestowed on European cities justly apply. If the traveller does not examine details too minutely, the cheerful picturesque aspect of the Chandnee Chowk may remind him for a moment of the Parisian boulevards. In the centre of a spacious street is a double row of well-grown trees, on either side a broad roadway flanked by irregular picturesque buildings. But if we speak of this street as being in 1858 cheerful, we can allude only to its architectural structure. Neither its associations nor its own present accompaniments and accessories are other than gloomy. Every house has been plundered; and the little show of property, as it begins again under the protection of British bayonets slowly to accumulate, cannot disguise the ruin which 1857 has created. To a stranger, the population that flows up and down the shining street would seem large; but to one who saw Delhi and the Chandnee Chowk before the rebellion, it is but as the ghost of the former life of the place that moves to and fro. There is the mosque where Nadir Shah sat and witnessed his great massacre. There is the Kotwallee or police-station, whereat were exposed the bodies of murdered Europeans, and afterwards of their murderers the princes, whom Hodson slew. In front of this building stand now three large gibbets, whereon have been already justly executed between two and three hundred of those who joined in the murder and rapine of the 11th of

Kootub Minar, near Delhi.

May, and on which more culprits are destined yet to pay for their crimes. Everywhere the demeanour of the native population is more than respectful to the Europeans—it is cringing. Fear possesses every soul. Never was a conquest more thorough than is for the present that of Delhi and its neighbourhood by the British. The present disposition of the native mind in Delhi towards us, of terror and trembling obedience, is one which no wise man can wish permanently to continue. It is a disposition, however, which no wise man will deny that it was necessary temporarily to create, if the mild uniformity of British rule was ever again to be asserted in Delhi.' In connection with these observations, it may be stated that the cringing servility of the natives, so manifest at Delhi, was by no means so evident in Oude and the Doab. A sullen haughtiness, or perhaps a fierce vindictiveness, was visible on the countenances of a very large percentage of those natives with whom the British came into contact, telling of discontent or of hostile passion.

Of Rohilcund it is not necessary to say much in this chapter. The greater part of it still continued, as it had been for nine months, in the hands of the rebels; and in addition to this, many of the escaped mutineer regiments from Lucknow had unquestionably directed their steps to this province, to swell the numbers of those who were in arms against the British. General Walpole was sent out against them with a powerful column; what he achieved, we shall see in the proper place.

That part of Rohilcund which constitutes the 'Hills,' the group of healthy hill-stations at the base of the Himalaya, though nearly cut off from communication with the Jumna regions, maintained itself bravely, never once falling into the hands of the armed insurgents. Colonel M'Causland, military commandant in Kumaon, so steadily and watchfully maintained British interests in that remote hilly province, that he generally detected hostile machinations in time to frustrate them. He had chiefly Goorkhas for troops, Rohilcund rebels for opponents; and he seldom failed to baffle and defeat those rebels, whether his force were great or small. Early in March he heard that the insurgents had sent a detachment to collect revenue—that is, to plunder—at Sitargunje, a place twenty-five miles from his camp at Huldwanee. He determined to surprise them; and although the success was not so great as he could have wished, through the unexpected absence of the larger part of the enemy's force, still those who were met with were speedily vanquished. He intrusted the enterprise to Captain Baugh, who commanded the Nepaul Contingent in the Kumaon brigade. Baugh started off on the evening of the 3d, taking with him about 220 horse and foot, and two mountain howitzers. To expedite matters, he mounted his infantry and artillery on elephants; but during the night his progress was retarded 'by an elephant carrying one of the mountain howitzers falling sick.' Arriving at Sitargunje early in the morning of the 4th, he found that the main body of rebels had departed on the preceding day to a village about six miles distant. Most of those remaining were within the government tehseel, a high building forty or fifty yards square; and these did not fight; they fell or escaped as their individual luck determined. Captain Baugh brought away from the place whatever he thought might be most useful. Finding that the main body of the insurgents, under Fuzul Huq, numbered not less than 5000 men, with six guns, he did not deem it prudent to march after them with his little force to Butteree, the village where they were on that day encamped, about midway between Huldwanee and Bareilly.

The Punjaub and Sirhind continued to be nearly free from anarchy. Yet there were symptoms which, if left unattended to, might have led to evil. The 4th regiment Bengal native cavalry, one of the last remaining links in that fine army, was disarmed and unhorsed at Umballa during the month of March. After ten months of faithfulness, amid the treachery of so many of their compatriots, these troopers at length exhibited a tendency to insubordination, not safely to be overlooked. In the Punjaub generally the movements of troops were very frequent and rapid, shewing that the authorities were well on the alert. Wishing to obtain a healthy military station west of the Indus, the brigadier in command laid the foundation of Campbellpore—a station named in honour of the commander-in-chief. This custom was often adopted in India: witness Jacobabad and Sleemanabad.

One of the most instructive facts brought to light during the wars of the mutiny, was the ardour with which some of the natives of India joined in waging battle with others. During the first and second Sikh wars, the sepoys of the Bengal native army unquestionably fought heroically against the Sikhs, winning battles in a way that excited the admiration of their British officers. And now the Sikhs shewed themselves equally willing to aid the British against the sepoys, and equally able to vanquish them in the field. Two inferences may legitimately be drawn from this—that success depended rather on the British officers than on the kind of troops whom they commanded; and that the maintenance of an army formed of any one nation in India is not so safe as the admixture of nationalities, each to act as a check upon the other. The subject is adverted to in this place, because the month of March witnessed the return of the Guides to Peshawur, and the honours that marked that event. It will be remembered* that this celebrated corps, chosen among the Punjaubees for their activity and intelligence, consisted of two small regiments, one of infantry and one of cavalry; that they made an extraordinary march of 750 miles, from Peshawur to Delhi, in the hot weather of June 1857; and that they served most gallantly in the operations against that city during the autumnal months. They remained until February in and near Delhi, and then returned to their native country. Major-general Cotton, commanding in the Peshawur division, made a point of giving the gallant fellows an honorary reception. He caused all the troops in the Peshawur cantonment to be paraded on the 16th of March. On the approach of the Guides to the parade-ground, the assembled troops saluted and the guns fired; the major-general delivered an address; a *feu de joie* and an ordnance salute of twenty guns followed; and the Guides marched past him in full military array. Captain Battye, who had commanded the cavalry portion of the force, was killed almost immediately on the arrival of the Guides at Delhi; but Captain Daly lived to return. Cotton addressed Daly and his companions first, welcoming them back to Peshawur; and then he addressed the Peshawur force generally, telling them of the wonderful march which the Guides had made nine months before, and of their deeds at Delhi. 'Within three hours after reaching Delhi, the Guides engaged the enemy, and every one of their officers was wounded. For nearly four months, officers and men were almost constantly in action, sometimes twice a day. They took 600 men to Delhi, and received 200 recruits during the siege. Not one man deserted to the enemy or from the corps; but no less than 350 were killed and wounded, and 120 fell to rise no more. I need not dwell on their separate deeds of valour, their general actions, their skirmishes, or their single combats; but as a specimen of the spirit that animated the corps, I will mention that a mere boy, Singh by name,

* Chap. xiv., p. 234.

bore a wounded European soldier out of the battle.'

In connection with this subject, it may be remarked that the personal character of the British officers has always exercised a very notable influence over the native troops of India. In Brigadier Hodgson's *Opinions on the Indian Army*, an anecdote is related, illustrative of the power possessed over the sepoys by any commander whose prowess and genius they had learned to value. A native officer, speaking to him of events which he had himself witnessed, said: 'During the campaign against the Mahrattas, in the year 1804, we made a tremendous forced march of 54 miles in 30 hours, and surprised Holkar and his cavalry at Furruckabad, and routed them with great slaughter. We had marched 250 miles in 13 days. The troops had been upon very short commons for some time; and you, sir, know what a tyrant a hungry belly is. The sepahees (sepoys) began to be very loud in their grumblings, and expressed their discontent pretty freely. This was reported. A short time afterwards, Lick Sahib Bahadoor (Lord Lake) was observed riding past the column *eating dry pulse.* This fact spread rapidly through the ranks; and from that moment, not the whisper of a murmur was heard. I believe, sir, had a man grumbled after that, he would have run the risk of being put to death by his companions—such was the love and veneration the sepahees had for Lick Sahib Bahadoor.'

Some of the half-savage mountain tribes of Peshawur and the Afghan frontier gave occasional trouble; but neither there nor in Sinde were the authorities prevented from sending reinforcements to the more troubled provinces. In connection with Sinde, it may be mentioned that Mr Frere, commissioner of that province, communicated a singular document to Lord Elphinstone, governor of the Bombay presidency. It was not directly connected with the mutiny or its instigators; but was nevertheless deemed important by Mr Frere, as illustrating phases of Hindoo character concerning which Europeans know so little. The information was given by Mr Macdonald, deputy-collector of Larkhana, in his weekly digest under date 20th of March. We transcribe it in a footnote.*

We may now conveniently turn our attention to Central India—that region, south of the Jumna, in which Mahrattas and Bundelas were so strong. We have stated in former chapters that Sir Hugh Rose, a distinguished Bombay officer, was placed in command of various regiments and detachments known collectively as the 'Central India Field-force.' He was gradually working his way northward to the notorious city of Jhansi, defeating rebels everywhere on his road. On the 4th of March, Sir Hugh Rose was enabled to telegraph the following news, from his camp at Peeplia: 'Yesterday, the troops under my command forced the pass of Mudenpore, after a short but very vigorous resistance. The troops, British and native, behaved gallantly. The pass is extremely strong, and the enemy suffered severely. They numbered about 4000 or 5000 Pathans and Bundelas, and 600 or 700 sepoys of the 52d and other regiments. I sent Major Orr in pursuit; and he cut up 50 or 60 rebels, of whom a large proportion were sepoys. The enemy are scattered in every direction. They have abandoned the little fortress of Seraj, a fort or arsenal which is the property of the Rajah of Shagurh, in which I shall have a small force to keep up my communication with Saugor. I am now in communication with my first brigade (under Brigadier Stuart) at Chendaree, and this gives me command of the whole of the country up to Jhansi, with the exception of two or three forts, which I can take.' About a week later, he sent news to Bombay that the capture of the pass of Mudenpore—on the line of hills which separated the British district of Saugor from the little state of Shagurh—and the defeat of the rebels on the 3d, had produced advantages far exceeding those at first anticipated by him. The rebels had successively abandoned several strongholds which they had possessed—first the fort of Seraj, with four guns, a rude manufactory for powder, shot and shell, carriages and tents; then the town and fort of Murrowra, with a triple line of defences; then the town and fort of Multhone; next the pass

* 'A circumstance well worthy of note has taken place during the last week; it calls for remark, inasmuch as it exposes the peculiar superstitions of the Hindoo shopkeepers of this country. In the talooka of Nuseerabad, below the hills which form the western boundary of Sinde, and not far south of the jaghire of Ghybee Khan, the Sirdar of the Chandia tribe, there stands the ancient and still important town of Hamal. It is situated on a mound close to the great Western Trunk-road, which runs from the town of Dost Allee, in Kumbur, to that of Gool Mahomed Luggaree; this part of the country is annually flooded by the hill-torrents, and for this reason all the towns are built on eminences, and surrounded by strong bunds. About twelve months ago, a certain shopkeeper of the town went out to his field with his donkey to work. On returning in the evening he loaded the ass, and was proceeding homewards, when the animal fell down and died. The Hindoos of that town consider that if, through any man's carelessness, the death of a beast of burden is caused, that man must make a pilgrimage to the town of Narrainsir, a few miles south of Lucput, in the Runn of Kutch, and there, shaving his head and performing other numerous ceremonies, expiate his fault. Consequently, when this unfortunate man returned home and reported the death of the donkey, he was at once told that, unless he immediately made the requisite pilgrimage to Narrainsir, and there expiated his fault, they would neither eat nor drink with him, nor hold any intercourse whatever with him. As the poor man thought the ass's death was in no way brought about by any fault of his, he appealed to the punchayets (Hindoo juries of five persons each) of Larkhana, Guerrilla, and Kumbar, other large towns in the Larkhana district. They returned answer that the punchayet of Hamal was wrong in its decision, and that they acquitted the man of all blame as to the cause of the ass's death. A controversy was at once raised throughout this part of the country, and it ended in all the punchayets of the towns of the Katcha country siding with the punchayet of Hamal, and the punchayets of the towns on the plain near the river taking part with Larkhana. The dispute came to a climax during the past week, when the Larkhana punchayet, in the name and acting for the minor towns near the river, issued a notice that the Hindoos of these towns would no longer associate with, nor have any intercourse with those of Hamal, Ghybee Dherah, and other towns of the Katcha country. This challenge was at once accepted, and the punchayets of the Katcha country issued a counter-notice, forbidding all Hindoos of their towns to hold intercourse with those of the district towns above mentioned; marriages before agreed upon have been broken off, agencies broken up, partnerships dissolved, and even the ties of relationship are no longer binding. To such an extent do the superstitious feelings of these men act upon their social conduct.'

of Goonah; then the pass and town of Hurat; and lastly, the fort of Cornel Gurh. As all the passes had been fortified and barricaded, their precipitate abandonment by the rebels was fortunate for Sir Hugh. Another result was the occupation by him of the hitherto independent district of Shagurh; the rajah having joined the rebels, Sir Robert Hamilton and Sir Hugh Rose resolved to punish him by 'annexing' his small territory, or at least occupying it until instructions could be received from Calcutta. Accordingly, on the 10th of March, the British flag was hoisted at Murrowra, in Shagurh, in presence of Rose's second brigade, under a salute of twenty-one guns. The encampment of the brigade at this time was about twenty-five miles from Jhansi. Rose and Hamilton were well on the alert; for Balla Sahib, brother of the Nena, was at that time heading an army of rabble, and levying contributions in various parts of Bundelcund. What troops this rebel had with him, was not clearly known; but it was found that the Rajah of Chuanpore had been mulcted by him of seven lacs of rupees; and the Rajah of Churkaree, resisting a similar demand, had had his town destroyed by fire, and was compelled to take refuge in his fort. Mr Carne, British resident in Churkaree, narrowly escaped capture at the hands of the rebels.

While Rose was thus engaged, Brigadier Stuart, with the first brigade of the Central India Field-force, was clearing out various rebel haunts in districts lying southward of Jhansi. On the morning of the 6th of March, Stuart's column or brigade set out from his camp near the Chendaree fort, and marched six or eight miles to Khookwaas, a fort near which a large body of rebels were assembled. The route being through a thick jungle nearly the whole distance, the 25th and 86th regiments advanced cautiously, in skirmishing order. Arriving at a small pass near the fort, Stuart found that the enemy had barricaded the road, and lined the hills on either side with matchlock-men. The engineers soon cleared away the barricades; while a small party of the 86th rushed up the hills and dislodged the matchlock-men. Shortly afterwards, however, it was ascertained that the chief body of the enemy had taken up a position behind the wall of an enclosure about a mile from the fort. The 86th dashed forwards to gain this enclosure; two of the officers, Lieutenant Lewis and Captain Keating, climbed to its top before any of their men, and jumped down into the interior of the enclosure. The troops soon cleared out the enclosure, and then pursued their operations against the fort itself. Working his way steadily onwards, defeating and expelling bodies of insurgents from neighbouring villages, Stuart was at length enabled, on the 17th, to capture the fort of Chendaree itself. This place, situated in Malwah, about a hundred miles from Gwalior, is in a district which was assigned by Scindia in 1844, according to agreement with the British government, to assist in the maintenance of the Gwalior Contingent. The fort—consisting of a strong rampart of sandstone, flanked by circular towers, and crowning a high hill—was in the hands of insurgents at the date now under notice; and it was Brigadier Stuart's duty to capture it. After cannonading on the evening of the 16th, he formed a practicable breach in the walls, and resolved to take the place by assault on the following morning. This he did very effectually. The 25th and 86th regiments, by an impetuous rush, carried everything before them. Captain Keating was severely wounded whilst foremost with the storming-party. The enemy mostly escaped, on account of the simple failure of a letter. On the preceding evening, the brigadier received a message informing him that Captain Abbott was within available distance with a considerable body of irregular cavalry; and in return a letter was despatched to Abbott, requesting him to gallop forward and invest the north side of the fort. This letter did not reach Abbott in time; and as a consequence, there was no obstacle to the escape of the rebels northward. All the guns, eight of iron and two of brass, were taken. The fort was given up to the keeping of one of Scindia's lieutenants or soubahs, in friendly relation with the British; and the inhabitants of the town resumed their peaceful avocations, apparently glad to get rid of the presence of the rebels.

Stuart's operations at Chendaree greatly facilitated the advance of Sir Hugh Rose towards Jhansi. He marched on, with the second brigade of his Central India Field-force, and reached that blood-stained city on the 21st of March. He gave a sketch of his operations from the 20th to the 25th in the following brief telegraphic form: 'On the 20th my cavalry invested as much as possible the fort and town of Jhansi. The next day the rest of my force arrived. The rebels have fortified the walls of the town, and, shutting themselves up in the town and fort, have not defended the advanced position of Jhansi. The ranee has left her palace in the town, and has gone into the fort. The rebel garrison numbers about 1500 sepoys, of whom 500 are cavalry, and 10,000 Bundelas, with 30 or 40 cannon. Their position is strong; but I have occupied two good positions, one a breaching, the other a flanking one. I have been delayed by the want of a plan of Jhansi, and consequently have been obliged to make long and repeated reconnaissances. I opened a flanking fire, vertical and horizontal, yesterday (the 25th), and hope to open a breaching fire to-morrow, or at latest the next day.' We shall see in a later page that Sir Hugh completely succeeded in his assault, early in April.

The present may be a proper place in which to advert to a matter which greatly agitated the public mind from time to time, both in England and India—namely, the conduct of the insurgents towards those of the British who unfortunately fell into their power. Jhansi was one of the stations in respect to which horror was most distressingly expressed. The morbid taste for horrors engendered by the incidents of the Revolt gave rise to many exaggerations. The terrible news from Delhi, Cawnpore, Jhansi, and other places, during the early months of the struggle, produced mischief in two ways; it created a demand for indiscriminate sanguinary vengeance; and it produced a tendency, not only to believe, but to exaggerate, all rumours of atrocities as committed by the natives. In England as well as at Calcutta, controversies almost of a fierce character arose on these points; the advocates on one side treating it as a point of honour to believe the tragedies in their worst form; while those on the other, in bitter terms demanded proof that the rumours were true. It was extremely difficult to disprove any statements concerning atrocities committed; for in most cases there were no Europeans left behind to give trustworthy testimony. Circumstances became known, during the progress of the military operations, which led to an inference that, though inhuman slaughter of innocent persons unquestionably took place soon after Delhi fell into the hands of the insurgents, it was not preceded by so much of hideous barbarity towards the women and children as had at first been reported and believed. It also became more and more evident, as time advanced, that many of the inscriptions on the wall of the slaughter-room at Cawnpore must have been written *after* the departure or death of the hapless persons whose writing they professed to be, by some one who failed to see the cruelty of the hoax he was perpetrating. This subject is adverted to in the present place, because the month of March lightened a little the terrible severity of the story of Jhansi, one of those which made a distressing impression on the public mind. It will be remembered * that, early in June of the preceding year, the British at Jhansi, upwards of fifty in number, were all put to death by the insurgents, acting at the instigation of a woman, the ranee or chieftainess of Jhansi; the destruction was so complete, that no European was left to tell the true incidents. Nine months afterwards, in the month of March, some of the English newspapers in India gave a detail of revolting indignities said to have been inflicted on the females of the party at Jhansi—greatly adding to the distress already felt by the relatives of the murdered persons. Jhansi had by that time been restored to British rule; and Captain Pinkney, superintendent of Jhansi, Jaloun, and Chendaree, determined to ascertain how far the real facts could be got at. After a diligent inquiry in various quarters, he arrived at a belief that the massacre, however barbarous, had not been deepened in atrocity by the frightful circumstances put forth in the newspapers. The truth appeared to him to be as follows: When the British in the fort were unable longer to hold out through want of food, they surrendered to the rebels, who swore that they would spare all their lives. No sooner, however, were the fort-gates opened, than the rebels entered, bound the men, and took them as well as the women and children to a place outside the city-walls called the Jokun Bagh. Here the men were placed in one group, and the women and children in another. The rebels and the ranee's armed servants then murdered all the men, Major Skene being the first cut down by the jail darogah, one Bukshish Ali. After this the women and children were put to death with swords and spears. The dead bodies were stripped, and left two days in the Jokun Bagh, when they were all thrown into a neighbouring stream. Shortly after the writing of Captain Pinkney's report, a letter was sent to the supreme government by Sir Robert Hamilton, political agent in Central India, in which a few of the facts were somewhat differently stated. According to his account, when the unhappy Europeans reached the Jokun Bagh, 'they were stopped on the roadside under some trees. They were accompanied by a crowd of mutinous sepoys, irregular sowars, disaffected police, fanatic Mussulmans, men in the service of the ranee, inhabitants of the town, and rabble. Here Bukshish Ali, jail darogah, called out: "It is the ressaldar's order that all should be killed;" and immediately cut down Captain (Major) Skene, to whom he was indebted for his situation under government. An indiscriminate slaughter of the men, women, and children then commenced; all were mercilessly destroyed, and their bodies left strewn about the road, where they remained until the third day, when, by permission of the same ressaldar, they were all buried in two gravel-pits close by.' Execrable as this was, it was far less harrowing than the newspaper narratives which had given rise to the investigation. Captain Pinkney ascertained that the total number of Europeans thus barbarously murdered was sixty-seven, of whom just about one half were women and children. Sir Robert Hamilton caused the ground around the two gravel-pits to be cleared, and an enclosing wall to be built; he and all the other officials, on a selected day, attended a funeral-service at the spot, delivered by the Rev. Mr Schwabe, chaplain to the station; and he also planned the erection of an obelisk. Strange that India should become the ground for so many obelisks and crosses erected in memory of Europeans ruthlessly murdered by natives. One hundred and two years before, in 1756, Suraj-u-Dowlah, after conquering Calcutta from the Company's servants, drove a hundred and forty-six adult Europeans, on a sultry June evening, into a dungeon only twenty feet square; and of those miserable creatures, a hundred and twenty-three died during the night, of heat, thirst, pressure, suffocation, and madness. An obelisk was afterwards set up, to mark this terrible 'Black Hole of Calcutta.' And now, in the middle of the nineteenth century, the English again found themselves engaged in erecting these damning memorials of native brutality, at Cawnpore and at Jhansi.

* Chap. xl., p. 179.

Leaving Jhansi and its mournful recollections for a while, we pass over from the Mahratta territories into Rajpootana; where numerous petty chieftains kept the territory in a state of much agitation. There were scarcely any of the mutinied Bengal regiments in that part of India; but the Kotah Contingent, and other auxiliary corps which had revolted, sided with some of the chieftains in hostilities against the British. So far as concerns the operations of the month of March, those of the Kotah insurgents were the chief that call for attention. We have in former pages alluded to a 'Rajpootana Field-force,' formed of several regiments sent up from Bombay. The first division of this force set forth from Nuseerabad on the 10th of March, for service against Kotah. It

Obelisk built on the Site of the Black Hole, Calcutta, to commemorate the Murder of the One Hundred and Twenty-three Englishmen.—From a Drawing in the India House.

consisted of H.M. 95th foot, a wing of the 83d, the 10th Bombay infantry, the Sinde horse, and some horse and foot artillery. Siege-material of formidable character accompanied the column; comprising eighteen field-pieces, of which ten were 8-inch mortars and howitzers, and an immense supply of ammunition. The second division, that started on the following day, consisted of H.M. 72d foot, a wing of the 83d, the 1st Bombay Lancers, a mountain train, Brown's battery, and an engineering corps. The 8th Hussars, with detachments of horse and foot artillery, were afterwards to join the columns. Several of the guns in the siege-train were drawn by elephants. Brigadier-general Lawrence accompanied this field-force, but only in a political capacity; the military command was held by General Roberts. The conquest of Kotah was looked forward to as a difficult enterprise, not only from the force of the enemy in men and guns, but from the peculiar position of the town itself. Kotah is bounded by the deep river Chumbul on one side, and by a lake on the other; and there was a probability that batteries would have to be erected on the opposite side of the river. The approach to it by land from Nuseerabad was also beset by many obstacles. It would be necessary to traverse the Mokundurra Pass, a long and narrow valley between two parallel ranges of hills, easily rendered formidable by a small number of men. It was altogether a larger and more important operation than the conquest of the numerous petty forts with which Rajpootana abounded. Many persons in India thought that those forts might safely be left to themselves; since the hill-chieftains were more frequently incited by hostility towards each other than towards the British, and since it was very little better than a waste of power to pursue them into the wilds and jungles which intersect that part of India. One favourable circumstance in connection with Kotah was, that the rajah was faithful, and as much opposed as the British to the insurgents.

The middle of the month was occupied by the march of Roberts's force from Nuseerabad, over a difficult country. Surmounting all obstacles, the general arrived at Kotah on the 22d of March, and encamped a mile or two distant, on the north bank of the Chumbul. The rebels were in possession of the south bank, having with them a powerful array of guns, many of large calibre. The fort, the palace, and half the city, were held by the rajah, with Rajpoots and troops from Kerowlie. On the 25th, a portion of the British, about 300 in number, under Major Heatley, crossed the river, to aid the rajah at a critical moment. The rebels had that morning made a desperate attempt to escalade the walls, and drive the rajah's troops into their only remaining stronghold, the castle; but this attempt was frustrated; had it succeeded, the rebels would have commanded the ferry over the river. Portions of H.M. 83d, and of the Bombay troops, formed the small force which crossed the river on the 25th. Two days afterwards, 600 men of H.M. 95th, with two 9-pounders, crossed over. On the 30th General Roberts was able to announce by telegraph, 'I this day assaulted the town of Kotah with complete success, and comparatively trifling loss. No officer killed. The whole town is in my possession.' Upwards of fifty guns were captured. The victory was gained by a clever flank-movement, which turned the enemy's position, and rendered their defences useless. This was a point in tactics which the rebels seldom attended to sufficiently; they repeatedly lost battles by allowing their flanks to be turned.

Eastward of the Mahratta and Rajpoot territories, there were isolated bodies of insurgents in the Saugor regions, between the Jumna on the north and Nagpoor on the south. But General Whitlock, with a field-force gathered from the Madras presidency, kept these rebels under some control. His movements, however, scarcely need record here.

The South Mahratta country kept up just so much disturbance as to demand the vigilant attention of the authorities, without exciting any serious apprehension. In the month of March there was much of this disturbance, near the frontier between the two presidencies of Bombay and Madras, at Belgaum. On the one side, the Bombay government offered a large reward for the apprehension of three brothers, rebel leaders, Baba Desaee, Nena Desaee, and Hunmunt Desaee; while the governor of the Madras presidency put in force a disarming statute on his side of the frontier. One of the leaders, Hunmunt Desaee, after many contests, was driven, with the wives and families of others among the insurgents, into a tower on the summit of a peak in the Coonung range; it was a one-storied structure, with a ladder leading to an entrance trap-door. Such towers had been used by the military police in that range, and Hunmunt defended himself here as long as he could. There were other traitors in this part of the country. Towards the close of March, Mr Manson, one of the Company's civil servants, obtained a clue to a conspiracy in which several natives —Naga Ramchunder, Balla Bhoplay, Bhow Shrof Chowdry, and others—were concerned; having for its object the collecting of guns unknown to the British authorities, and the inciting of other natives to acts of rebellion. One of these men was the chief of Jamkhundie, one a money-lender, and two others were Brahmins. The money-lender was supposed to have assisted the mutineers of Kolapore with pecuniary means for carrying on their operations. By lodging these mischief-makers in safe keeping at Belgaum and Satara, preparatory to a trial, the authorities checked an incipient disturbance.

This little patch of country, inhabited to a considerable extent by the southern Mahrattas, was the only part of the Bombay presidency south of the city itself which was in any anxiety concerning the proceedings of the insurgents. And indeed, northward of the city, there were no manifestations of rebellion short of the regions around Gujerat and Rajpootana; where even those who were disposed to be peaceful found themselves embarrassed and imperiled by the turbulence of their neighbours. In Gujerat, Sir Richmond Shakespear commenced and steadily carried on a general disarming of the population; the Guicowar or native sovereign cordially assisted him, and the two together collected many guns and thousands of stands of arms. As to the Madras presidency, it was quite at peace. From Cuttack in the north to Travancore in the south, there were no rebellious regiments, and few chieftains who ventured to endanger their safety by disputing the British 'raj.' In the Nagpoor and Saugor territories, belonging rather to the Bengal than to the Madras presidency, the elements of convulsion surged occasionally, but not to a very alarming extent. The Nizam's country was troubled in a way which shews how desirable it is that orientals should not be tempted by anarchy or weakness in the governing power. The regular troops were moderately steady; but the news of mutiny elsewhere excited all the turbulent elements of the Deccan. Robber chieftains and city ruffians rose, not so much against the British, as against any who had property to lose. The town of Mulgate, held by a chieftain who commanded a motley band of Rohillas and Arabs, resisted the Nizam's authority for some time; but it fell, and the leaders were taken prisoner.

This chapter will have shewn that, when the last day of March arrived, the attention of the military authorities in India was chiefly directed to those districts which had Azimghur, Bareilly, Calpee, and Jhansi for their chief cities, and which swarmed with large bodies of rebels ready to make a desperate resistance. It was left for the months of April and May to develop the strategic operations against those places.

Notes.

So frequent is the mention, in all matters relating to the local government of India, of 'covenanted' and 'uncovenanted' service, and so peculiar the duties of those covenanted servants who bear or bore the title of 'collectors'—that it may be well to sketch briefly the Company's remarkable system, so far as it refers to those two subjects. The collectors and magistrates suffered much and braved much during the mutiny, owing to their peculiarly intimate relations with the natives; and their duties deserve on that account a little attention in the present work. For many reasons it will be desirable, as in the volume generally, to adopt the past tense in speaking of this system—bearing in mind, however, that the system was fully in operation during the mutiny, except when the officials were actually driven away from their districts.

'Covenanted' and 'Uncovenanted' Service.—The 'services' supported by the East India Company were of four kinds—civil, military, naval, and ecclesiastical. The military has already been frequently noticed; the Company supported a military force of something near three hundred thousand men, involving various engagements on the one hand with the British crown, and on the other with native princes. The naval service was limited to a force of about sixty vessels and five thousand men, employed chiefly in surveying, coast-guarding, mail-conveyance, and the prevention of piracy. The ecclesiastical service, maintained by the Company for their own servants only, consisted of three Church of England bishops, about a hundred and forty Protestant clergymen, three Roman Catholic bishops, and about eighty Roman Catholic priests. The Protestants were liberally supported; the Roman Catholics simply received a grant, in aid of larger funds to be derived by them from other quarters. But it was the civil service that constituted the most remarkable feature in the Company's organisation, embracing all the persons engaged in the collection of revenue or the administration of justice.

The civil service was of two kinds, covenanted and uncovenanted. The uncovenanted civil servants were very much like *employés* in other countries, paid reasonably for their services, but having no peculiar privileges—no declared provision for life, no claim to promotion by seniority, no stipulated furlough or leave of absence, no claimable pension. They comprised Europeans, Eurasians or half-castes, and natives. Subordinate duties, fiscal and judicial, were intrusted to them, according to their range of ability and supposed honesty, as judged by the local governments. The Europeans in this class were chiefly persons who had gone out to India in some other capacity, or were sons of officers already in service in India. The European and Eurasian uncovenanted servants barely reached three thousand in number. The class was mainly composed of natives—Mohammedans more generally than Hindoos. The employment of natives as uncovenanted servants of the Company was commenced by Lord William Bentinck (1828 to 1835), and steadily increased under other governors-general; insomuch that the judicial administration of the lower courts fell almost wholly into the hands of natives. The humbler offices in the revenue department were also filled by them. A few of the uncovenanted servants received salaries ranging from £500 to £800 per annum; but in the greater number of instances the amount was far lower.

The covenanted servants comprised nominated or favoured persons who, after receiving a special education in the Company's seminary at Haileybury, were subjected to examination in England, and then sent out to India at the Company's expense. They entered into a covenant, prescribed by ancient custom, 'That they shall obey all orders; that they shall discharge all debts; and that they shall treat the natives of India well.' Until 1853 (when a system of public competition was established by the charter granted to the Company in that year), the appointment of persons to this favoured service was wholly in the patronage of the directors. After a certain amount of tuition and examination, the young men ('writers,' as they were sometimes called) were conveyed to India, where they pursued further studies, chiefly in oriental languages, at Calcutta, Madras, or Bombay. While so studying, they received an 'out-of-employ allowance.' At length they commenced employment as 'assistants' to magistrates and collectors in country districts, as soon as they possessed a certain amount of knowledge of vernacular languages, criminal law, and revenue law. Their daily duties were partly magisterial, partly fiscal. After some years' practice, the assistant was competent for promotion. He became collector or magistrate of a district, under regulations differing in the different presidencies. In Bengal, the offices of judge, magistrate, and collector were held by three different persons, all 'covenanted;' in the other presidencies the offices of magistrate and collector were held by the same person; in the 'non-regulation provinces' (Punjaub, Nagpoor, Sinde, &c.), all three offices were held by one person. The local government had a voice in the selection of persons to fill these offices; but the principle of promotion by seniority was extensively acted on, and was almost claimed as a right by the 'covenanted.' The salaries paid were very munificent. The lowest assistant received £500 per annum, and the amount rose gradually to £10,000 per annum, the salary of a member of the Supreme Council at Calcutta.

Such were the chief points of difference between the covenanted and uncovenanted services of the East India Company. It was not so much a distinction of race, colour, or creed, as a means of favouring selected persons in England, and of giving those persons a special education to fit them for civil duties in India.

Collectors and Collectorates.—We shall next notice in a succinct way the remarkable duties of such of the covenanted civil servants as filled the office of collector—especially in those districts where the collector was also the magistrate. In the Northwest Provinces, to which the mutiny was mainly confined, the collector-magistrate of each district was in many matters controlled by the commissioner of the province in which the district was situated; but he had in a larger degree than the commissioner an intimate knowledge of the villages and villagers of India, their incomes, hopes, fears, wants, and peculiarities; and he became more deeply involved in anxieties and dangers consequent on the mutiny.

The term 'collector' very inadequately expresses the status and duties of the official so named. So far from being a mere tax-gatherer, he was a revenue judge, an executive district authority, with large powers and heavy responsibilities. As collector and magistrate, he was responsible to two different departments—to the higher judicial courts for his conduct as a magistrate, and to the revenue department in all that concerned his collectorship. He had two sets of assistants, with duties clearly defined and separated. The magisterial duties being dismissed without further description, as susceptible of easy comprehension, we shall dwell only on the collectorship.

The duties of the collector were fivefold. He was collector of government revenue; registrar of landed property in his district; revenue judge between landlord and tenant; ministerial officer of courts of justice; and treasurer and accountant of the district. None but a man of varied and extensive attainments, united to zeal and industry, could adequately fulfil so many duties; many of the great names in the recent years of Indian history are those of men who laid the foundations for their greatness as collectors. The districts over which the collectors presided varied greatly in size and wealth; but in all cases they comprised several thousand villages each, and yielded revenue varying from one to two hundred thousand pounds per annum—for the whole of which the collector was responsible. In the whole of India, the collectorates were somewhat under a hundred and seventy in number, for the most part identical with districts, but in a few cases comprising whole provinces newly annexed; and these collectorates yielded, in 1856, revenue to the amount of about thirty millions sterling.

The collector-magistrate had generally two assistants, like himself 'covenanted' servants of the Company. Besides these there were 'uncovenanted' servants, European and native, sufficient in number for the duties to be rendered. The district was marked out into sub-districts containing from one to two hundred villages each. The collector resided at the head-station of the district, with a staff of clerks, writers, and record-keepers. Each sub-district was under the revenue management of a responsible native officer, who had subordinates under him to keep his accounts and conduct the details of his office. Carrying down the classification still more minutely, every village in every sub-district had its headman and its native accountant, who were in intimate correspondence concerning the revenue of the village.

The chief official of the district, as collector of government revenue, obtained this revenue mainly from three sources—land-tax, spirit and drug duty, and stamps. The second and third items were so small in amount, that many well-wishers of the Company urged the abandonment of those imposts; and at anyrate only a small share of the collector's attention was devoted to them. The land-tax was the great source of revenue; and until the government of India undergoes an entire revolution both in spirit and in practice, such must continue to be the case. So decided was the importance of this tax compared with all others, that of the thirty millions sterling raised in 1856, no less than seventeen millions resulted from land-tax. The land-tax formed the great fund out of which the vast expenses for the executive government, military and civil, were mainly paid. Hence the importance of the revenue-collector and his land-tax duties. The assessment of the land, for the realisation of the tax, differed in different presidencies, according to the relations existing between the state, the landowners, the farmers, and the labourers. In Bengal the revenue was collected in gross from great and powerful zemindars, the state having little or nothing to do with the actual cultivators. In Madras no zemindars or great men were recognised; the state drew the tax from the ryots or cultivators, each on his own bit of land. In Bombay the Madras system existed in a modified form. In Oude nothing could be done till the annexation in 1856, when the peculiar *thalookdaree* system * laid a foundation for many troubles in the following year. In the Northwest Provinces the assessment depended on the peculiar village tenures, which had existed from time immemorial, and according to which the ownership of the soil could not be interfered with by the state so long as the village paid the revenue. Great as may have been, and great as were, the differences between the Hindoo, Mohammedan, and English governments, this village system maintained its ground century after century. The tenure of land in these provinces, recognised by the Company as among those institutions which they wished to respect, were mainly three in number:

Zemindaree—denoting those estates where the property was held collectively without any territorial division, whether the owners were one, few, or many.

Puttidaree—those estates where the property was partially or entirely divided, and held separately by the coparceners.

Bhyacharuh—estates held by coparcenary communities, where actual possession had overborne law; it was a kind of Puttidaree founded on actuality rather than right.

Whichever of these systems prevailed, the Company respected it in assessing the land-tax; and thus each piece of land was represented in the tax-books by the name of a particular tax-payer or community of tax-payers. The actual assessment, the percentage on produce, depended on circumstances specially ascertained in each district; but the two guiding principles laid down by the Company, when they established a revenue-system for the Northwest Provinces were—that the rate should be light enough to leave a wide margin of profit to the cultivators; and that it should be fixed without alteration for a considerable period of years. The collector, knowing how much was assessed upon every village or every piece of land, was armed with powers sufficient to enforce payment. Whether the assessment was 'light' or not, was a standing controversy between those who respectively supported the zemindaree, the ryotwaree, and the village systems. The Company's advocates generally urged that, though the ratio of tax to produce seemed heavy, any comparison with English land-tax would be fallacious; seeing that the villagers and cultivators in India were not called upon to pay, in addition to land-tax, any such imposts as excise, tithes, church-rates, county-rates, poor-rates, or income-tax. The excellences and defects of the system, however, are not discussed here; we simply describe the system itself.

The collector, having a definite amount to receive, from a definite number of villages, represented by a definite number of persons, could neither increase nor lessen, anticipate nor postpone, the tax, without special reasons. If a district suffered from drought, the government often deferred or wholly remitted the tax; but this only under well-defined circumstances. The collector's register recorded all changes in ownership or occupancy by death or private transfer; and as he knew each year who *ought* to pay, he was intrusted with certain powers to enforce payment by imprisonment, distraint of personal property, annulment of lease, sequestration of profits, transfer of defaulting share to a solvent shareholder of the same community, farming of the estate to a stranger, or sale by public auction.

In most districts, until the time of the Revolt, the collection of revenue was an easy task, occupying only a portion of the collector's thoughts in May and June, November and December. 'So complete the machinery,' said a writer in the *Calcutta Review*, 'so prosperous the provinces, so well adjusted the assessment, that the golden shower fell uninterruptedly; and the collector, who had without an effort of his own transmitted a royal ransom half-yearly to the public treasury, was scarcely aware of the financial feat which he and his subordinates had performed.' But when a drought, an inundation, or any great calamity interfered with the growth or harvesting of the crop, the collector's duties were most trying and laborious; seeing that he had to listen to petitions for relief or delay from hundreds or thousands of villages in his district.

His ordinary duties as a collector of revenue occupied only a small portion of his time and thoughts. As registrar of landed property, he kept maps and registers of land, drawn out with a degree of minuteness scarcely paralleled in any other country in the world; and these maps and registers were renewed or corrected annually, to shew the size, position, ownership, and crop of every cultivated field in the whole district. As revenue judge between landlord and tenant, he was often called upon to assist the responsible landowner to collect his rent from the cultivators, or to assist the cultivator in resisting oppression by the landlord; it was a duty requiring a knowledge both of law and of revenue matters. As a ministerial officer of the courts of justice, he had to put in force, somewhat in the manner of a sheriff, all decisions of the judge relating to land, transfers of property, or arrears of land-tax; and his local knowledge often enabled him to assist the judge in arriving at an equitable decision. As treasurer and accountant, he took care of the bags of silver coin in which the land-tax and the other taxes were chiefly paid, tested and weighed the

* Chap. xxi., p. 360.

coin before making up his accounts, paid monthly stipends to some of the military and civil officers of the district, kept a minute debtor and creditor account, and transmitted his accounts and his surplus silver to Calcutta. In addition to all these duties, the collector, considered as the European who possessed most knowledge on various subjects in his district, performed miscellaneous duties scarcely susceptible of enumeration. 'Everything that is to be done by the executive, must be done by him, in one of his capacities; and we find him, within his jurisdiction, publican [tax-gatherer], auctioneer, sheriff, road-maker, timber-dealer, enlisting sergeant, sutler, slayer of wild beasts, wool-seller, cattle-breeder, postmaster, vaccinator, discounter of bills, and registrar-general—in which last capacity he has also to tie the marriage-knot for those who object to the Thirty-nine Articles. Latterly, he has been made schoolmaster of his district also. Every new measure of government places an extra straw on the collector's back. Whatever happens to be the prevailing hobby, the collector suffers. One day specimens are called for, for the Exhibitions of London or Paris; the next day, the cry is for iron and timber for the railway, or poles for the telegraph.'

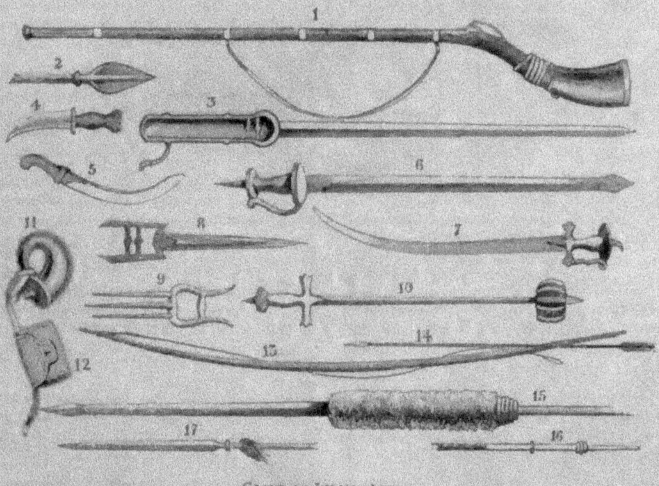

GROUP OF INDIAN ARMS.

1. Matchlock. 2. Head of a Hunting-spear. 3. Potta. 4. Creece. 5. Knife. 6. Hunting Tulwar. 7. Common Tulwar. 8. Kundeer. 9. Kundeer. 10. Ballagondacka. 11. Powder-horn. 12. Pouch for balls. 13. Bow. 14. Arrow. 15. Borsee Spear—carried before chiefs, &c. 16. Bottom end of a Spear. 17. Head of common Spear.

Zemindar, Hindoo landowner.

CHAPTER XXVII.

DISCUSSIONS ON REBEL PUNISHMENTS.

BEFORE entering on the military struggles that marked the month of April, it may be desirable to notice the phases of public feeling concerning the amount of punishment due to the mutineers and rebels in India. The discussions on this subject undoubtedly influenced the course of proceeding adopted both by the military and the civil authorities; although it may not be possible to measure the exact amount of that influence, or the exact date at which it was felt. Some of the proceedings of Viscount Canning at Calcutta, in reference to this matter, belonged to the month of March; some of the discussions in the imperial parliament, and at the India House, bearing on Canning's line of policy, belonged to later months; but it will be useful to give a rapid sketch, in this place, of the nature of the discussion generally, and of the remarkable tone given to it by party politics in England. All reference to the debates concerning the re-organisation of the Indian government, whether at home or in India itself, may more fittingly be postponed to a later chapter.

Almost from the first, a large portion of the Anglo-Indian population cried aloud for most summary and sanguinary vengeance on rebels and mutineers of all kinds, Mohammedan and Hindoo, towns-people and country peasants. General Neill was idolised for a time by this class—not so much because he was a gallant soldier and a skilful commander, as because he was supposed to be terribly severe in his treatment of insurgents. This matter has been adverted to in former pages, as well as the torrents of abuse that were poured upon the governor-general for 'clemency'—a word used in a mocking and bitter spirit. Many of the censors afterwards joined the ranks of those who abused the same governor-general for a policy supposed to be antagonistic to that of 'clemency.' The fact is again mentioned here, owing to its connection with a controversy that gave rise to formidable parliamentary struggles many months afterwards. The proceedings of four different bodies—the Calcutta government, the Board of Control, the Houses of Parliament, and the Court of Directors—must be briefly noticed to shew the course of this controversy.

At first, when the mutiny was still in its earlier stages, the friends and relations of those who had suffered barbarous treatment at the hands of the natives gave utterance to a wild demand for vengeance, springing not unnaturally from an excited state of feeling. The following, from one of the Calcutta journals, is a fair example of this kind of writing in its milder form: 'Not the least amongst the thousand evils which will follow in the track of the rebellion is the indurating effect it will have upon the feelings of our countrywomen when the struggle is over. There are many hundreds of English ladies who lie down nightly to dream of horrors too great for utterance; who scarcely converse except upon one dreadful subject; and who would be found almost as willing as their husbands and fathers to go out and do battle with the mutineers, *if they could only insure the infliction of deep and thorough vengeance.* It is a contest with murderers who are not satisfied with their life's blood, that they have to expect daily. Their very servants are perhaps in league to destroy them. They suffer almost hourly worse than the pains of death. Many have already died by homicidal hands; but more from the pangs of starvation and travel, from the agonies of terror, and the slow process of exhaustion. *And all this while friends and relatives sigh vainly for the coming of the day of retribution.*' The italicised passages shew only a very moderate use of the words 'vengeance' and 'retribution,' but may suffice to indicate the feeling here adverted to.

The Calcutta government, as has been duly recorded in the proper chapters, from time to time issued orders and proclamations relating to the treatment which the mutineers were to receive, or which was to be meted out to non-military natives who should shew signs of insubordination. There was, as one instance, the line of policy contested between Mr Colvin and Lord Canning. The former issued, or intended to issue, a proclamation to the mutineers of the Northwest Provinces, in which, among other things, he promised that 'soldiers engaged in the late disturbances, who are desirous of going to their own homes, and who give up their arms at the nearest government civil or military post, and retire quietly, shall be permitted to do so unmolested;' whereas Lord Canning insisted that this indulgence or leniency should not be extended to any regiments which had murdered or ill-used their officers, or committed cruel outrages on other persons. Then there were several orders and statutes proclaiming martial law in the disturbed districts; appointing commissioners to try mutineers by a very summary process; authorising military officers to deal with rebel towns-people as well as with revolted sepoys; enabling the police to arrest suspected persons without the formality of a warrant; making zemindars and landowners responsible for the surrendering of any ill-doers on their estates; and other measures of a similar kind. When, in the month of July, Viscount Canning found it needful to check the over-zeal of some of the tribunals at Allahabad, who were prone to hang accused persons without sufficient evidence of their guilt, he was accused of interference with the righteous demand for blood. It is true, that these were, in the first instance, merely newspaper accusations; but as the English public looked to newspapers for the chief part of their information concerning India, these controversies gave rise to a very unhealthy excitement; and weeks, or even months, often passed before the truth could be known—as was strikingly evidenced in the case of the lieutenant-governor of the Central Provinces, whose supposed 'clemency' (in a matter of which, as soon appeared, he knew absolutely nothing) was held over him as a reproach for nearly four months. In September appeared a proclamation at Agra, warning the natives of the possible consequences of any complicity on their parts in the proceedings of the mutineers. Part of the proclamation ran as follows: 'The government of these provinces calls on all landowners and farmers, with their tenantry, and on all well-disposed subjects, to give all possible assistance to the authorities in bringing those outcasts (mutineers and rebels) to justice. Landowners and farmers of land, especially, are reminded of the terms of their engagement not to harbour or countenance criminals and evil-disposed persons. The government requires proofs of the fidelity and loyalty of all classes of its subjects, in recovering the arms, elephants, horses, camels, and other government property, which have been feloniously taken by the offenders. All persons are warned against purchasing or bartering for any such property of the state under the severest penalties; and rewards will be paid to those who, immediately on obtaining possession of the same, bring them to the nearest civil or military station.'

So far as concerns the imperial parliament, little took place during the year 1857 touching on the subject of the present chapter. The opposition party sought to shew that her Majesty's ministers were responsible for the outbreak; some members of both Houses broached their views concerning the causes of the mutiny; others criticised the mode in which troops were sent to India; some condemned, others defended, Viscount Canning; many put forth suggestions concerning the future government of India; many more sought to overwhelm with guilt the East India Company; while missionaries, civil servants, Indian judges, aristocratic officers, favoured commanders, were made subjects of frequent and warm debate—but the members of the legislature generally held aloof from that excessive demand for a sanguinary policy towards the insurgents, so much dwelt on by many of the Anglo-Indians. After passing an act, containing among other provisions clauses relating to 'The Punishment of Mutiny and Desertion of Officers and Soldiers in the Service of the East India Company,' parliament was prorogued on the 28th of August. During the recess, the press was busy on those accusations and reclamations already adverted to—in turn correcting, and corrected by, the official documents which from time to time appeared. Commercial troubles having agitated the country during the autumn, parliament met again on the 3d of December, for a short session before Christmas. Although the purpose of meeting was prescribed and limited, the members of the legislature did not deem it necessary or desirable to remain silent on a subject so uppermost in men's thoughts as the mutiny in India. Speeches were made, motions brought forward, explanations given, and returns ordered, on the state of the army, the mode of sending over troops, the conduct of the government, and various other matters bearing on the struggle in the East. The speech from the throne contained many allusions to that struggle, but none that bore on the mode of punishing the rebels. The Earl of Derby, in a speech on the opening-night, sought to discourage the cry for vengeance raised in many quarters. After urging that England should deal with the mutineers in justice and not in revenge, he added: 'For every man taken with arms in his hands there ought to be a righteous punishment, and that punishment death. For those miscreants who have perpetrated unmentionable and unimaginable atrocities upon women, death is too mild a sentence. On them should be inflicted the heavier punishment—a life embittered by corporal punishment in the first instance, and afterwards doomed to the most degrading slavery. Be they Brahmins of the highest caste, they should be forced to undergo the lowest, most degrading, most hopeless slavery. But, while he would take this course, he earnestly deprecated the extension of a feeling of hostility to the whole native population. From letters which he had seen, he feared that every white man in India who had suffered in any way by the mutiny came to regard every man with a black face as his enemy. Now, that was a feeling which should be restrained, if not by Christianity, at least by motives of sound policy. Measures should be taken to convince the natives that the English are their masters; but they must also be convinced that the English are their benefactors. We should not try to govern India by the sword alone.' This sentiment was also well expressed by Mr Mangles, chairman of the East India Company, at the Haileybury examination on the 7th of December. Addressing the assembled professors, prizemen, students, and Company's officers present, he adverted to the sudden rupture of friendly relations in India, and added: 'For many years to come, there must exist strong mistrust and suspicion, if not more bitter feelings, between those who rule and those who are subject. It is impossible that it should be otherwise, after the scenes which have been passed through, the treacheries and murders—and worse than murders—that have been rife throughout the land. But, gentlemen, you are bound to struggle with those feelings and subdue them. It will be your duty to remember that only a small part, an infinitesimal part, of the population of India have been engaged in these frightful and scandalous outrages.' [Here many striking instances of fidelity were brought to notice.] 'It would therefore be most unjust to bring the charge of treachery against the whole people of India. It will be your duty, under these circumstances, to struggle against the suspicion and distrust which have been engendered by recent events, and to endeavour to win the affections of the people over whom you are called upon to exercise power. If we cannot govern India in that way, we ought to give up the country and come away.'

When parliament met for the usual session, in February, a question was put by the Earl of Ellenborough, concerning the policy intended to be pursued towards the rebels. Adverting to a rumour of some very wholesale series of military executions in Central India, he said: 'Without questioning the justice of the sentence in that particular case, he doubted if capital punishment was so efficacious as a severe flogging. The natives were not afraid of death, but shrank from corporal pain. Besides, it is quite impossible to hang all the mutineers, and the continued exhibition of unrelenting severity must inevitably create a blood-feud between the natives and their European masters.' Earl Granville, on the part of the government, replied that no particular instructions had been sent out to Viscount Canning on this matter, because the utmost reliance was placed on the justice and firmness of that nobleman: he added, that he agreed in the opinion that the frequent spectacle of capital punishment must have the worst possible effect; and he concluded by stating that the governor-general was directing his thoughts towards the possibility of transporting some of the evil-doers to the Andaman Islands.

Now occurred a change in political matters which threw Indian discussions into a new channel. Hitherto, the subject of the punishment of mutineers had been discussed in parliament with reference rather to persons than to property. The ministry, however, having been changed on grounds quite irrespective of Indian affairs, and the Earl of Derby having succeeded Viscount Palmerston as premier, India was dragged into the consequences of this change. The Earl of Ellenborough, admitted on all hands to be a well-informed statesman on Indian matters, however opinions might differ concerning his temper and prudence, was appointed president of the Board of Control. When governor-general of India, many years earlier, he had been in frequent collision with the East India Company, as represented both by the Court of Directors and by the Calcutta government; and it was thought probable that his new assumption of authority in Indian affairs would be marked by something notable and important. It was so. The singular termination of his ministerial career was closely and immediately connected with the subject to which this chapter relates, in a way that may now be briefly narrated.

At first this question of punishment had to be discussed by the new government in the same manner as before—that is, in relation to the sanguinary vengeance advocated by many writers of letters and newspaper articles, especially at Calcutta. On the 18th of March, Mr Rich moved in the House of Commons for the production of certain papers which he expected would throw light on this matter. He contended that the conduct of the army, in the punishment of the insurgents, was merciless and cruel. He intimated the necessity of requiring the authorities in India to act strictly up to the instructions of Lord Canning, who, he thought, deserved honour for his firmness and humanity. The Calcutta journals, he asserted, recommended that Oude should be made one wide slaughter-house, in which extermination should be the rule rather than the exception; and it was but right that the government should at once check this terrible feeling of sanguinary animosity. Most of the speakers in the debate that followed agreed in the view taken by Mr Rich; and more than one of them broached the doctrine that the insurgents in Oude ought not to be treated like rebel sepoys—seeing that, whether wisely or unwisely, they were fighting for what they deemed national independence.

During the first half of the month of April, nothing occurred in parliament involving any very great collision of opinions on this particular subject; but towards the close of the month a clashing of views on Oude affairs became manifest to the public. Throughout the first ten months of the mutiny, while Viscount Palmerston was at the head of affairs, the opposition party, in both Houses of Parliament, frequently appeared as advocates for the deposed royal family of Oude, dwelling on the injustice involved in the deposition. Much of this advocacy may have been sincere, but much also was mere special pleading; for the speakers well knew that, if in office, they would not and could not seek to undo what had been done. No sooner did a change of ministry take place, than the new occupants of office became much more cautious in denouncing the 'annexation of Oude;' seeing that, if an iniquity at all, it was one in which the Marquis of Dalhousie, the Calcutta government, the Court of Directors, the Crown, and both Houses of Parliament, were all implicated. Every one now saw that the practical question before the country was —not the rights or wrongs of the annexation— but the treatment of insurgents engaged in the warlike struggle. It became known that the Secret Committee of the Court of Directors had sent a letter to the governor-general in council, dated the 24th of March, relating to the treatment which it was desirable that rebels and mutineers should receive. So peculiar and anomalous were the functions of this Secret Committee, that although nominally belonging to the Court of Directors, it was little other than the mouthpiece of the president of the Board of Control. The letter was really from the Earl of Ellenborough, rather than from any one else.

Before pursuing this narrative, it may be well to say a few words concerning the organisation and functions of this Secret Committee—one of the many anomalies connected with our government of India. Mr Arthur Mills (*India in 1858*) described the relation between the Secret Committee, the Court of Directors, and the Board of Control, in the following terms: 'The Court of Directors meets weekly at the East India House for the transaction of business, the ordinary details of which are discharged by three committees—1. Finance and home; 2. Political and military; 3. Revenue, judicial, and legislative. There is also a "Secret Committee," with peculiar functions altogether different from those of the three ordinary committees. The office of the Secret Committee is purely ministerial. It receives from India all dispatches on matters with respect to which secrecy is deemed important—including those which relate to war, peace, or negotiations with native powers or states within the limits of the charter, or other states or princes; and forwards such dispatches to the Board of Control. The Secret Committee also transmits to India, after signature, dispatches prepared by that Board, which it is bound to do, under oath, "without disclosing the same." The Secret Committee is composed, as prescribed by act of parliament, of three directors. The court may elect whom they please; but the chairman, deputy-chairman, and senior member of the court, are almost invariably appointed. The papers of the Secret Committee are in charge of the examiner at the East India House, who is clerk to the committee. . . . There is also a secret department in the Board of Control, for the purpose of carrying on written and oral communications with the Secret Committee of the Court of Directors. The oral communications are for the most part carried on through the president personally; in the written communications he is assisted by a senior clerk, and occasionally by the secretaries of the Board. On the arrival of secret dispatches from India, the copy intended for the Board is sent to the senior clerk in the secret department, who prepares a *précis* of all the letters and enclosures, which he lays before the president; who thereupon gives him instructions, oral or written, for the preparation of an answer, or sometimes drafts one himself. It is then copied in official form, and transmitted to the Secret Committee of the East India House.'

The secret dispatch, produced by the authority

here described, began by expressing a hope * that, as soon as Lucknow should fall before the conquering arm of Sir Colin Campbell, the governor-general would feel himself sufficiently strong to act towards the natives with the generosity as well as the justice which is congenial to the British character. The subsequent paragraphs laid down the propositions that it would be better, except in aggravated instances, to award punishment such as is usual against enemies captured in regular war, than against rebels and mutineers—the exceptions being those in which the fighting by the insurgents 'exceeded the licence of legitimate hostilities;' that the insanity of ten months ought not to blot out the recollection of a hundred years of fidelity; that the punishment of death had been far too frequently awarded; and that the governor-general ought sternly to resist the entreaties of those who would urge him to the adoption of a sanguinary policy.

The 6th of May was the date on which the battle may be said to have begun in parliament, on the policy to be pursued towards Oude. Mr Bright, in the House of Commons, asked the ministers whether there was any authenticity in a certain proclamation concerning Oude, said to have been issued by Viscount Canning; whether, if authentic, it had been issued in accordance with any directions from the home government; and, if not so sanctioned, what steps the government intended to take in relation to it? These questions came upon the House generally by surprise, as indicating a revelation of things hitherto hidden; and it was then for the first time made public, by the minister who replied to these questions—that the government had, three weeks before, received a dispatch containing a copy of the proclamation adverted to; that the matter was immediately taken into consideration by the government; that a *secret* dispatch had been sent off, stating the views of the government on the matter; and that there would be no objection to produce both the proclamation and the dispatch. This announcement was the forerunner of a storm, in which the passion of party was strongly mixed up. On the 7th, in the House of Lords, the Earl of Ellenborough moved for the production of certain papers, analogous to those ordered by the other House on the preceding night; and then arose a debate whether Viscount Canning had really issued the proclamation he intended; whether it was a proper proclamation to issue; whether it was right that the Earl of Ellenborough should reprimand Viscount Canning in so imperious a way as he was accused of doing; whether the secret dispatch containing that reprimand should have been kept so entirely concealed from the Court of Directors; whether it should have been sent out to Calcutta at the time it was; and whether a so-called *secret* dispatch ought to make its appearance among parliamentary papers, unrelieved by any comments on it by Viscount Canning. There was unquestionably something strange in the mode of proceeding; for the dispatch, although not made known to the Court of Directors until the morning of the 7th, had been communicated to certain members of both Houses on the 6th. Earl Granville urged that, if the government wished to get rid of Viscount Canning, the usual course might have been adopted for so doing; but that it was neither just nor generous to keep him in office, and yet give publicity to such insulting censure on him. The Earls of Derby and Ellenborough replied that it was not intended to dismiss Viscount Canning, or even to censure him; but to induce him to make such modifications in his proposed proclamation as would render the policy adopted in Oude less severe.

It now becomes necessary to attend to this much-canvassed proclamation itself, before noticing the further debates concerning it.

The proclamation in question, and the explanations bearing on it, were dated at a period when, from the absence of an electric telegraph between England and India, they could not of course be known in the former country. On the 3d of March, while at Allahabad, paying anxious attention to the daily telegrams received from Oude, Viscount Canning sent a proclamation and an explanatory letter to that province, relating to the treatment to be meted out to rebels.* Although Sir Colin Campbell commanded the army of Oude, and conducted the military operations, Sir James Outram was chief-commissioner of the province; and on his shoulders rested, at that time, all that could be effected in the way of civil government. The proclamation was to be at once a sentence, a warning, and a threat, addressed to the inhabitants of Oude. It announced that Lucknow, after months of anarchy, was now again in British hands; it dwelt on the fact that many of the citizens, even those who had shared the bounty of the government, had joined the insurgents; and it declared, that the day of retribution for evil-doers had arrived. It proceeded to name six rajahs, thalookdars, and zemindars, who had remained faithful amid great temptation, and who were not only to retain their estates, but were to receive additional rewards. It promised a proportionate reward to all other chieftains who could prove that they had been loyal. With these exceptions, the whole proprietary right to the soil of Oude was declared to be forfeited to the British crown—subject only to such indulgences as might, as a matter of *favour*, be conceded to individuals, conditional on their immediate submission to the supreme authority, their surrendering of arms, and their steady assistance in the maintenance of order and discipline; and conditional, also, on their innocence of shedding the blood of Englishmen and Englishwomen in the cruel outrages which had taken place. The stringent and startling

* See Note G, at the end of the chapter.

* See notes A and B, at the end of the chapter; where many of the documents here referred to are printed in full.

clause in this proclamation was that which related to the confiscation: declaring that, with the few specified exceptions, 'the proprietary right in the soil of the province is confiscated to the British government, which will dispose of that right in such manner as it may seem fitting.' In the letter to Sir James Outram accompanying this draft of a proclamation, Viscount Canning stated that the proclamation was not to be issued until Lucknow had been fully conquered by Sir Colin Campbell; and that, when so issued, it was to be addressed only to the non-military inhabitants of Oude, without in the slightest degree offering pardon or lenity to rebel sepoys. The proclamation was spoken of as a very indulgent one; seeing that it promised an exemption, almost general, from the penalties of death and imprisonment, to Oudian chieftains and others who had gone against the government; the confiscation of estates was treated as a merciful diminution of punishment, rather than as a severe measure of justice. Sir James Outram was to exercise his judgment as to the mode and the time for issuing the proclamation, in the English, Hindee, and Persian languages. He was supplied with suggestions, rather than strict instructions, how to deal with those Oudians who had been inveterate opponents of the government, but without being concerned in actual murder; how to regard those who had fought in the insurgent ranks, but shewed a willingness to surrender their arms; and how to draw a line between the chieftains on the one hand and their less responsible retainers on the other.

Such being the general character of the proposed proclamation and its accompanying letter, we proceed with the debate.

After the discussions on Friday the 7th of May, the conduct of the government underwent much discussion out of parliament; the supporters of Viscount Canning contending that the publication of the secret dispatch was unfair to that nobleman, even if the dispatch itself were defensible. On the 10th, the Earl of Shaftesbury gave notice of a resolution condemnatory of the publication; and Mr Cardwell gave notice of a similar resolution in the House of Commons. In the course of an irregular discussion, it appeared that the government had not received a single official dispatch from Viscount Canning since that which contained the draft of his proposed proclamation, and they were quite in the dark whether the proclamation had been issued, altered or unaltered. It also became known that the *late* president of the Board of Control, Mr Vernon Smith, had received a letter from Viscount Canning, stating that the proclamation would require an explanatory dispatch, which he had not had time to prepare.

On the next day, March 11th, parliament was surprised by an announcement that the Earl of Ellenborough, without consulting his colleagues, had resigned into the Queen's hands his seals of office as president of the Board of Control. Amid the courteous expressions of regret on the part of the other ministers, at losing so important a coadjutor, it soon became evident that the publication of the secret dispatch had emanated from the Earl of Ellenborough, without the knowledge or consent of the Earl of Derby and the cabinet. He found that he had drawn them into trouble; and he resolved to take the whole blame on himself—resigning office to shield others from censure. There was a generosity in this which touched his colleagues. The Earl of Derby candidly admitted that there were parts of the secret dispatch which he could not quite approve, and that the publication of it was indefensible; but that he deeply regretted the resignation of the Earl of Ellenborough.

This will be the proper place in which to notice the celebrated dispatch fraught with such important consequences. On the 24th of March, after Viscount Canning's proclamation had been penned, but long before any news concerning it could reach England, the Secret Committee wrote to him on the subject of the treatment of the rebels generally. The letter was virtually from the Earl of Ellenborough; although, on account of the absurd system of double government, it professed to emanate from a committee sitting in Leadenhall Street. The general character of this letter was noticed in a recent paragraph, and the letter itself is given in Note G; it may therefore be passed without further notice here. When, on the 12th of April, a draft-copy of Viscount Canning's proposed proclamation reached England, the Earl of Ellenborough wrote the much-discussed 'secret dispatch,' purporting, as before, to come from the Secret Committee of the Court of Directors. A few days elapsed before the writing, and a few more before the forwarding, of this document. The earl* expressed his apprehension that the proposed proclamation would raise such a ferment in Oude as to render pacification almost impossible. He declared his belief that the mode of settling the land-tenure when the British took possession of Oude had been in many ways unjust, and had been the chief cause of the general and national character of the disaffection in that province. He asserted that the Oudians would view with dismay a proclamation which cut them off, as a nation, from the ownership of land so long cherished by them; and would deem it righteous to battle still more energetically than before against a government which could adopt such a course of policy. He went through a process of argument to shew that the Oudians regretted the dethronement of their native king; that their regret ought to be at least respected; that they had never, as a nation, acknowledged British suzerainty; that they ought not to be treated as rebels in the same sense as the inhabitants of those parts of India which had long been under British control; and that the conflict in which they had engaged should

* See Note H.

on this account be regarded rather as legitimate war than as rebellion. The haughty and stinging portions of the dispatch were contained in the fifteenth and two following clauses or paragraphs; in which the earl, addressing the greatest British functionary in India, said: 'Other conquerors, when they have succeeded in overcoming resistance, have excepted a few persons as still deserving of punishment; but have, with a generous policy, extended their clemency to the great body of the people. You have acted upon a different principle. You have reserved a few as deserving of special favour, and you have struck with what they will feel as the severest of punishment the mass of the inhabitants of the country. We cannot but think that the precedents from which you have departed

East India House.

will appear to have been conceived in a spirit of wisdom superior to that which appears in the precedent you have made.'

Such was the celebrated secret dispatch, the writing and promulgation of which led to the resignation of the Earl of Ellenborough. That resignation produced an exciting controversy in and out of parliament. As the offender, the president of the Board of Control, had sacrificed himself, was it necessary or desirable to make the ministry generally responsible for his supposed or alleged misdeeds? Party considerations speedily became mixed up with the discussion of this question. The Whigs had recently been displaced by the Conservatives, under circumstances that occasioned much irritation; and each party availed itself of the India controversy as a handle to be employed against the other. On the one side it was contended that Viscount Canning deserved praise rather than censure, for his untiring attention to the affairs of India during a troubled period; that, even if his proposed proclamation were injudicious, it was not right to publish the secret dispatch relating thereto, until he had explained the reasons for framing his proclamation; and that the ministers ought not to be shielded from blame simply on account of the resignation of their colleague. On the other hand, the ministers endeavoured to shew that this resignation ought to be taken into account; and when this failed, they took up the cause of the Oudians, contending that the inhabitants of that province were in a different category from the other natives of India.

When the great debates on this subject came on in both Houses, on the 14th of May, the ministers dwelt forcibly on the conduct of Mr Vernon Smith, who had received a letter or letters from Viscount Canning, which he ought, in the interests of the public, to have communicated to the government, but which he shewed only to members of his own party. It was urged—and the argument made a great impression both in and out of parliament—that if the Earl of Ellenborough had known of Viscount Canning's intention to send home an explanation concerning the intent and scope of the proclamation, it might possibly have led to a modification of the secret dispatch, or even to an abandonment of it. In the House of Lords, the case against the government was argued by Lords Shaftesbury, Argyll, Somerset, Cranworth, Grey, Newcastle, and Granville; while the arguments on the other side were maintained by Lords Ellenborough, Derby, Carnarvon, Chelmsford, and Donoughmore. The Earl of Shaftesbury had couched his resolution in such a form * as he thought was calculated to insure Viscount Canning fair-play whenever his intentions and proceedings should be really known. Without undertaking to defend the proclamation, in the absence of any proof whether that document had or had not undergone modification, he contended that the dispatch passed on the governor-general a cruel and unmerited censure; that this so-called 'secret' dispatch was evidently intended by its writer to be a public one, administering rebuke that should be known to all the world; that its publication was perilous, even seditious, inasmuch as it encouraged the people of Oude to persevere in rebellion, and virtually absolved them from all blame for their past conduct. The Earl of Ellenborough, in reply, defended every word of the dispatch; he insisted that it would be impossible to govern India peacefully even for a day, if the proclamation were acted on in its full spirit. He cared not for office; he resigned because he had unintentionally embarrassed his colleagues, not because he regretted any part of his conduct. The Earl of Derby, and other members of the cabinet, described the resolutions as a party manœuvre to overthrow the government; claimed an acquittal on the plea that their colleague had taken all the blame of the publication to himself; and complained that the governor-general had not sent one single letter to the new government, explanatory of his plans and motives. When the debate was ended, the result shewed a very close division—there being contents, 159, non-contents, 168; giving a majority of 9 for ministers.

Far more exciting and influential was the debate in the Commons on the same night. From the day when Mr Cardwell gave notice of his resolutions, the case was regarded as a serious one for the ministers; seeing that he was a distinguished member of an independent party in the House, and would be able to bring a large accession to the regular opposition votes. The very fact of the Earl of Ellenborough having resigned, seemed to afford proof that the publication of the dispatch, if not the writing of it, was disapproved by some of the ministers, and would weaken them in the approaching debate. Mr Cardwell's resolutions,† like those of the Earl of Shaftesbury, did not bind the House to any approval of the much-talked-of proclamation, whether issued or unissued; they related only to the unfairness of the dispatch in the absence of further news from India, and to the still greater unfairness of making the reproof contained in that dispatch patent to all the world. The members of the Whig opposition, and all who sided with them in the debate, adhered pretty closely to this line of argument; but the ministers and their supporters travelled much further. They felt that the only justification for the dispatch and its publication was to be found in the proclamation; and they therefore gave the proclamation as black a character as it could well receive. Viscount Canning was abused in round terms as a tyrant and spoliator; and those who supported him were accused of being influenced purely by factious motives in bringing forward the resolutions. The attack against the government was maintained by Mr Cardwell, Lord John Russell, Mr Vernon Smith, Mr Lowe, Colonel Sykes, and others, and resisted by the solicitor-general, Lord Stanley, Mr Baillie, &c. The debate was adjourned to the 17th, when it became evident that many of the independent members intended to support the government—partly because they disapproved of the Canning proclamation; partly because they suspected the Whigs of an intention to make this Indian question a stepping-stone to a return to office; and partly because they condemned the conduct of the late president of the Board of Control, in withholding Canning's letter. This last-named circumstance told very seriously against the Whig party; the Conservatives made the most of it, and won over many adherents from among the independent members. Again was the debate adjourned, to the 18th. It now became still more evident that the division-list would present an aspect far different from that at first expected; the prophesied majority for the resolutions gradually fell, and the ministers began to look confidently to a decision in their favour. A new element had entered into the case. If the Derby ministry would have resigned office when beaten, there was a sufficient number of independent members ready to carry the motion against them; but as there was a threat of a dissolution, and as many seats would be endangered by a general election, self-interest became mixed up with patriotism. Another adjournment took place, to the 20th, on which day the House was addressed by Sir James Graham, Mr Bright, Sir R. Bethell, Mr Labouchere, and other members of influence. The current of debate set in very much in favour of the govern-

* '1. That it appears, from papers laid upon the table of this House, that a dispatch has been addressed by the Secret Committee of the Court of Directors, to the governor-general of India, disapproving a proclamation which the governor-general had informed the court he intended to issue after the fall of Lucknow.

'2. That it is known only from intelligence that has reached this country, by correspondence published in newspapers, that the intended proclamation has been issued, and with an important modification, no official account of this proceeding having yet been received; that this House is still without full information as to the grounds upon which Lord Canning had acted, and his answer to the objections made to his intended proclamation in the dispatch of the Secret Committee cannot be received for several weeks.

'3. That, under these circumstances, this House is unable to form a judgment on the proclamation issued by Lord Canning, but thinks it right to express its disapprobation of the premature publication by her Majesty's ministers of the dispatch addressed to the governor-general; since this public condemnation of his conduct is calculated to weaken the authority of the governor-general of India, and to encourage those who are now in arms against this country.'

† 'That this House, whilst it abstains from expressing any opinion on the policy of any proclamation which may have been issued by the governor-general of India with relation to Oude, has seen with great and serious apprehension that her Majesty's government have addressed to the governor-general of India, through the Secret Committee of the East India directors, and have published, a dispatch condemning in strong terms the conduct of the governor-general. And this House is of opinion that such a course upon the part of her Majesty's government must tend, under the present circumstances of India, to produce a most prejudicial effect, by weakening the authority of the governor-general, and encouraging further resistance on the part of those who are still in arms against us.'

ment. It transpired that many eminent men in India—including Sir James Outram, Sir John Lawrence, General Mansfield, and General Franks—had all in various ways expressed an opinion that Lord Canning's proclamation, if issued in the form originally intended, would be productive of some mischief in Oude.

This, therefore, will be a convenient place in which to notice the officially recorded opinions of Outram on the subject—the only ones which were presented before the House in a formal and undoubted manner. The documents received from India shewed that Sir James entertained many misgivings concerning the proclamation and its probable tendency. The proclamation and its accompanying letter being sent to him from Allahabad, he replied on the 8th, in a communication * pointing out to Viscount Canning the paragraphs which appeared to him mischievous. He declared his belief that there were not a dozen landowners throughout the whole of Oude who had not in some way or other assisted the rebels during the past struggle; and that, therefore, there would be hardly any exceptions to the sweeping confiscation proposed by the governor-general. He asserted most distinctly his conviction that, as soon as the proclamation should be made public, nearly all the chiefs and thalookdars would retire to their domains, and prepare for a desperate resistance. He expressed an opinion that the landowners had been very unjustly treated in the land-settlement after the annexation; that, apart from this, their sympathy with the rebels was an exceedingly natural feeling, under the peculiar circumstances of Oude; that it was not until the mutiny was many weeks old that they turned against us; that they ought to be regarded rather as honourable enemies than as rebels; that they would be converted into relentless enemies if their lands were confiscated, maintaining a guerrilla war which would 'involve the loss of thousands of Europeans by battle, disease, and exposure;' but that if their lands were insured to them, they would probably be more attached to British rule than ever they had yet been. It is evident that Sir James Outram had already discussed this subject with the governor-general, for he apologises for 'once more' urging his views upon his lordship. A brief reply † was immediately sent to this letter, proposing a very slight increase of leniency in the treatment of the landowners, but leaving the general spirit of the proclamation untouched. Later in the month, the governor-general replied more at length to the arguments of Sir James. He admitted ‡ that the inhabitants of Oude were far differently placed from those of Bengal and the Northwest Provinces, in respect to allegiance to the British crown; both because the annexation had been recent, and because it had been no voluntary act on the part of the Oudians. But he would not admit that, on those grounds, the rebel thalookdars should be treated so indulgently as Outram proposed. He urged that exemption from death, transportation, and imprisonment, was a great boon, sufficiently marking the treatment of the Oudians from that of other natives. Without entering on the question whether the settlement of the land-claims had been unjust, he offered his reasons for thinking that that matter had not had much to do with the complicity of the thalookdars in the rebellion. He attributed this complicity mainly to 'the repugnance which they feel to suffer any restraint of their hitherto arbitrary powers over those about them; to a diminution of their importance by being brought under equal laws; and to the obligation of disbanding their armed followers, and of living a peaceful and orderly life.' He maintained that if Sir James's suggestion were acted on, the rebels would be treated, not merely as honourable enemies, but as enemies *who had won the day;* and that this would be accepted by the natives as a confession of fear and weakness, encouraging them to regard rebellion as likely to be a profitable game. In short, Viscount Canning insisted on his proclamation being maintained in its chief features.

It was impossible that such a letter as that of Sir James Outram could fail, when made known, to exert a considerable influence in the House of Commons. The resemblance between it and the Earl of Ellenborough's dispatch was very close, except in relation to discourteous and haughty language, which Outram neither did nor could use. On the 21st of May, after five nights' debate, marked by speeches from almost all the eminent men in the House, the contest ended in a kind of drawn battle. Influenced by a great variety of motives, the opponents of the government urged upon Mr Cardwell the withdrawal of his resolutions. They did not wish to be compelled to vote. Some had been impressed by the recorded opinion of Outram, and the rumoured opinions of Lawrence and other eminent men in India; some disliked party tactics, even against their opponents; some were afraid of a general election, if their votes should lead to a dissolution of parliament. All the leaders of the Whig party joined in a wish to withdraw the resolutions; and this was done. The affair had, however, been so managed throughout as to give a good deal of triumph to the Conservative government, and to strengthen that government for the rest of the session.

What was the ultimate fate of the much-condemned proclamation, will remain to be shewn in a later page. Two further documents relating to this matter are given in Notes I and K.

* See Note C. † See Note D. ‡ See Note E.

Notes.

The official documents referred to in this chapter are of so much importance, in reference to the political history of the Indian Revolt, and to the opinions entertained by public men concerning the feelings of the natives, that it may be well to present the chief of them in full. Owing to the length of time necessary for the transmission of letters between England and India, two or more of these documents were crossing the ocean at the same time, in opposite directions, and therefore could not exactly partake of the nature of question and answer. We shall attempt no other classification than that of placing in one group the documents written in India; and in another those written in London—observing, in each group, the order of dates.

A.

The first document here given is a letter dictated by Viscount Canning when at Allahabad, and signed by his secretary, Mr Edmonstone. It was addressed to Sir James Outram, in his capacity of chief-commissioner of Oude, and was written at a time when the fall of Lucknow was soon expected:

'ALLAHABAD, *March* 3, 1858.

'SIR—I am directed by the Right Honourable the Governor-general, to enclose to you a copy of a proclamation which is to be issued by the chief-commissioner at Lucknow, as soon as the British troops under His Excellency the Commander-in-chief shall have possession or command of the city.

'2. This proclamation is addressed to the chiefs and inhabitants of Oude only, and not to the sepoys.

'3. The governor-general has not considered it desirable that this proclamation should appear until the capital is either actually in our hands or lying at our mercy. He believes that any proclamation put forth in Oude in a liberal and forgiving spirit would be open to misconstruction, and capable of perversion, if not preceded by a manifestation of our power; and that this would be especially the case at Lucknow—which, although it has recently been the scene of unparalleled heroism and daring, and of one of the most brilliant and successful feats of arms which British India has ever witnessed—is still sedulously represented by the rebels as being beyond our power to take or to hold.

'4. If an exemption, almost general, from the penalties of death, transportation, and imprisonment, such as is now about to be offered to men who have been in rebellion, had been publicly proclaimed before a heavy blow had been struck, it is at least as likely that resistance would have been encouraged by the seeming exhibition of weakness, as that it would have been disarmed by a generous forbearance.

'5. Translations of the proclamation into Hindee and Persian accompany this dispatch.

'6. It will be for the chief-commissioner in communication with His Excellency the Commander-in-chief, to determine the moment at which the proclamation shall be published, and the manner of disseminating it through the province; as also the mode in which those who may surrender themselves under it shall be immediately and for the present dealt with.

'7. This last question, considering that we shall not be in firm possession of any large portion of the province when the proclamation begins to take effect, and that the bulk of our troops, native as well as European, will be needed for other purposes than to keep guard through its districts—is one of some difficulty. It is clear, too, that the same treatment will not be applicable to all who may present themselves.

'8. Amongst these there may be some who have been continuously in arms against the government, and who have shown inveterate opposition to the last, but who are free from the suspicion of having put to death or injured Europeans who fell in their way.

'9. To these men their lives are guaranteed and their honour; that is, in native acceptation—they will neither be transported across sea, nor placed in prison.

'10. Probably the most easy and effectual way of disposing of them, in the first instance, will be to require that they shall reside in Lucknow under surveillance and in charge of an officer appointed for that purpose.

'11. Their ultimate condition and place of residence may remain to be determined hereafter, when the chief-commissioner shall be able to report fully to the governor-general upon the individual character and past conduct of each.

'12. There will be others who, although they have taken up arms against the government, have done so less heartily, and upon whom, for other causes, the chief-commissioner may not see reason to put restraint. These, after surrendering their arms, might be allowed to go to their homes, with such security for their peaceable conduct as the chief-commissioner may think proper to require.

'13. One obvious security will be that of making it clearly understood by them, that the amount of favour which they shall hereafter receive, and the condition in which they shall be re-established, will be in part dependent upon their conduct after dismissal.

'14. The permission to return to their homes must not be considered as a reinstatement of them in the possession of their lands, for the deliberate disposal of which the government will preserve itself unfettered.

'15. There will probably be a third class, less compromised by acts of past hostility to the government, in whom the chief-commissioner may see reason to repose enough of confidence to justify their services being at once enlisted on the side of order, towards the maintenance of which in their respective districts they might be called upon to organise a temporary police.

'16. The foregoing remarks apply to the thalookdars and chiefs of the province. As regards their followers who may make submission with them, these, from their numbers, must of necessity be dismissed to their homes. But before this is done, their names and places of residence should be registered, and they should receive a warning that any disturbance of the peace or resistance of authority which may occur in their neighbourhood, will be visited, not upon the individual offenders alone, but by heavy fines upon the villages.

'17. I am to observe that the governor-general wishes the chief-commissioner to consider what has been above written as suggestions rather than instructions, and as indicating generally the spirit in which his lordship desires that the proclamation should be followed up, without tying down the action of the chief-commissioner in matters which may have to be judged under circumstances which cannot be foreseen.

'18. There remains one more point for notice.

'19. The proclamation is addressed to the chiefs and inhabitants of Oude, not to mutineers.

'20. To the latter, the governor-general does not intend that any overture should be made at present.

'21. But it is possible that some may surrender themselves, or seek terms, and it is necessary that the chief-commissioner should be prepared to meet any advances from them.

'22. The sole promise which can be given to any mutineer is, that his life shall be spared; and this promise must not be made if the man belongs to a regiment which has murdered its officers, or if there be other *primâ facie* reason to suppose that he has been implicated in any specially atrocious crime. Beyond the guarantee of life to those who, not coming within the above-stated exception, shall surrender themselves, the governor-general cannot sanction the giving of any specific pledge.

'23. Voluntary submission will be counted in mitigation of punishment, but nothing must be said to those who so submit themselves which shall bar the government from awarding to each such measure of secondary punishment as in its justice it may deem fitting.—I have, &c.,

(Signed) 'G. F. EDMONSTONE.

'*Allahabad, March* 3, 1858.'

B.

The proclamation referred to in the above letter ran as follows:

'PROCLAMATION.

'The army of His Excellency the Commander-in-chief is in possession of Lucknow, and the city lies at the mercy of the British government, whose authority it has for nine months rebelliously defied and resisted.

'This resistance, begun by a mutinous soldiery, has found support from the inhabitants of the city and of the province of Oude at large. Many who owed their prosperity to the British government, as well as those who believed themselves aggrieved by it, have joined in this bad cause, and have ranged themselves with the enemies of the state.

'They have been guilty of a great crime, and have subjected themselves to a just retribution.

'The capital of their country is now once more in the hands of the British troops.

'From this day it will be held by a force which nothing can withstand, and the authority of the government will be carried into every corner of the province.

'The time, then, has come at which the Right Honourable the Governor-general of India deems it right to make known the mode in which the British government will deal with the thalookdars, chiefs, and landholders of Oude, and their followers.

'The first care of the governor-general will be to reward those who have been steadfast in their allegiance at a time when the authority of the government was partially overborne, and who have proved this by the support and assistance which they have given to British officers.

'Therefore the Right Honourable the Governor-general hereby declares that

'Drigbejjie Singh, Rajah of Bulrampore;
'Koolwunt Singh, Rajah of Pudnaha;
'Rao Hurdeo Buksh Singh, of Kutiaree;
'Kasheepershand, Thalookdar of Sissaindee;
'Zuhr Singh, Zemindar of Gopaul Kheir; and
'Chundeeloll, Zemindar of Moraon (Baiswarah),

are henceforward the sole hereditary proprietors of the lands which they held when Oude came under British rule, subject only to such moderate assessment as may be imposed upon them, and that those loyal men will be further rewarded in such manner and to such extent as, upon consideration of their merits and their position, the governor-general shall determine.

'A proportionate measure of reward and honour, according to their deserts, will be conferred upon others in whose favour like claims may be established to the satisfaction of the government.

'The governor-general further proclaims to the people of Oude that, with the above-mentioned exceptions, the proprietary right in the soil of the province is confiscated to the British government, which will dispose of that right in such manner as it may seem fitting.

'To those thalookdars, chiefs, and landholders, with their followers, who shall make immediate submission to the chief-commissioner of Oude, surrendering their arms and obeying his orders, the Right Honourable the Governor-general promises that their lives and honour shall be safe, provided that their hands are unstained with English blood murderously shed.

'But, as regards any further indulgence which may be extended to them, and the condition in which they may hereafter be placed, they must throw themselves upon the justice and mercy of the British government.

'To those among them who shall promptly come forward and give to the chief-commissioner their support in the restoration of peace and order, this indulgence will be large, and the governor-general will be ready to view liberally the claims which they may thus acquire to the restitution of their former rights.

'As participation in the murder of Englishmen and Englishwomen will exclude those who are guilty of it from all mercy, so will those who have protected English lives be specially entitled to consideration and leniency.

'By order of the Right Honourable the Governor-general of India.

'G. F. EDMONSTONE,
'*Secretary to the Government of India.*'

C.

Sir James Outram, not fully satisfied with this proclamation, directed his secretary, Mr Couper, to write as follows to Mr Edmonstone:

'CAMP, CHIMLUT, *March* 8, 1858.

'SIR—I am directed to acknowledge the receipt of your letter, No. 191, dated 3d inst., enclosing a proclamation to be issued to the landholders, chiefs, and inhabitants of Oude, upon the fall of the capital.

'2. In this proclamation a hereditary title in their estates is promised to such landholders as have been steadfast in their allegiance, and, with these exceptions, the proprietary right in the soil of the province is confiscated.

'3. The chief-commissioner desires me to observe that, in his belief, there are not a dozen landowners in the province who have not themselves borne arms against us, or sent a representative to the durbar, or assisted the rebel government with men or money. The effect of the proclamation, therefore, will be to confiscate the entire proprietary right in the soil; and this being the case, it is, of course, hopeless to attempt to enlist the landowners on the side of order; on the contrary, it is the chief-commissioner's firm conviction that as soon as the chiefs and thalookdars become acquainted with the determination of the government to confiscate their rights, they will betake themselves at once to their domains, and prepare for a desperate and prolonged resistance.

'4. The chief-commissioner deems this matter of such vital importance, that, at the risk of being deemed importunate, he ventures to submit his views once more, in the hope that the Right Hon. the Governor-general may yet be induced to reconsider the subject.

'5. He is of opinion that the landholders were most unjustly treated under our settlement operations, and even had they not been so, that it would have required a degree of fidelity on their part quite foreign to the usual character of an Asiatic, to have remained faithful to our government under the shocks to which it was exposed in Oude. In fact, it was not until our rule was virtually at an end, the whole country overrun, and the capital in the hands of the rebel soldiery, that the thalookdars, smarting as they were under the loss of their lands, sided against us. The chief-commissioner thinks, therefore, that they ought hardly to be considered as rebels, but rather as honourable enemies, to whom terms, such as they could without loss of dignity accept, should be offered at the termination of the campaign.

'If these men be given back their lands, they will at once aid us in restoring order; and a police will soon be organised with their co-operation, which will render unnecessary the presence of our enormous army to re-establish tranquillity and confidence.

'But, if their life and freedom from imprisonment only be offered, they will resist; and the chief-commissioner foresees that we are only at the commencement of a guerrilla war for the extirpation, root and branch, of this class of men, which will involve the loss of thousands of Europeans by battle, disease, and exposure. It must be borne in mind that this species of warfare has always been peculiarly harassing to our Indian forces, and will be far more so at present, when we are without a native army.

'6. For the above reasons, the chief-commissioner earnestly requests that such landholders and chiefs as have not been accomplices in the cold-blooded murder of Europeans may be enlisted on our side by the restoration of their ancient possessions, subject to such restrictions as will protect their dependents from oppression. If his lordship agree to this proposition, it will not yet be too late to communicate his assent by electric telegraph before the fall of the city, which will probably not take place for some days. Should no such communication be received, the chief-commissioner will act upon his present instructions, satisfied that he has done all in his power to convince his lordship that they will be ineffectual to re-establish our rule on a firm basis in Oude.—I have, &c.,

(Signed) 'G. COUPER,

'*Secretary to Chief-commissioner.*

'*Chief-commissioner's Office, Camp, Chimlut, March* 8.'

D.

Mr Edmonstone, on the part of Viscount Canning, wrote the following brief reply, suggesting an additional clause to the proclamation, and promising a more detailed communication at a future time :

'ALLAHABAD, *March* 10, 1858.

'SIR—Your secretary's letter of the 8th instant was delivered to me at an early hour this morning, by Captain F. Birch, and it will receive a detailed reply in due course.

'Meanwhile, I am desired by the Right Honourable the Governor-general to subjoin a clause which may be inserted in the proclamation (forwarded with my letter, No. 191, of the 3d instant), after the paragraph which ends with the words, "justice and mercy of the British government."

'"To those amongst them who shall promptly come forward, and give to the chief-commissioner their support in the restoration of peace and order, this indulgence will be large, and the governor-general will be ready to view liberally the claims which they may thus acquire to a restitution of their former rights."

'2. This clause will add little or nothing to your discretionary power, but it may serve to indicate more clearly to the thalookdars the liberal spirit in which the governor-general is prepared to review and reciprocate any advances on their part.

'3. It is expected that you will find means to translate this additional clause into the vernacular languages, and that you will be able to have copies of the proclamation, so amended, prepared in sufficient numbers for immediate use. If more should be required, the magistrate of Cawnpore will lithograph them on your requisition.

'4. It is very important, as you will readily see, that every copy of the vernacular version of the proclamation sent to you, with my letter of the 3d instant, should be carefully destroyed.—I have, &c.,

(Signed) 'G. F. EDMONSTONE,

'*Secretary, Government of India, with the Governor-general.*

'*Allahabad, March* 10, 1858.'

E.

It was not until after a lapse of three weeks that the promised detailed reply was sent to Sir James Outram, in the following terms :

'ALLAHABAD, *March* 31, 1858.

'SIR—In replying at once on the 10th inst. to your secretary's letter of the 8th, in which you urged reasons against the issue of the proclamation to the thalookdars and landholders of Oude, which had been transmitted to you by the Right Hon. the Governor-general, my answer was confined to communicating to you the addition which his lordship was willing to make to that proclamation, without entering into the general questions raised in your letter. The governor-general desires me to express his hope that you will not have supposed that the arguments adduced by you were not fully weighed by him, or that your opinion upon a subject on which you are so well entitled to offer one, has not been received with sincere respect, although he was unable to concur in it.

'2. I am now directed by his lordship to explain the grounds upon which the course advocated in your letter—namely, that such landholders and chiefs as have not been accomplices in the cold-blooded murder of Europeans should be enlisted on our side by the restoration of their ancient possessions, subject to such restrictions as will protect their dependents from oppression—is, in the opinion of the governor-general, inadmissible.

'3. The governor-general entirely agrees with you in viewing the thalookdars and landholders of Oude in a very different light from that in which rebels in our old provinces are to be regarded. The people of Oude had been subjects of the British government for little more than one year when the mutinies broke out; they had become so by no act of their own. By the introduction of our rule many of the chiefs had suffered a loss of property, and all had experienced a diminution of the importance and arbitrary power which they had hitherto enjoyed; and it is no marvel that those amongst them who had thus been losers should, when they saw our authority dissolved, have hastened to shake off their new allegiance.

'4. The governor-general views these circumstances as a palliation of acts of rebellion, even where hostility has been most active and systematic. Accordingly, punishment by death or imprisonment is at once put aside by the proclamation in the case of all who shall submit themselves to the government, and who are not murderers; and whilst confiscation of proprietary rights in the land is declared to be the general penalty, the means of obtaining more or less of exemption from it, and of establishing a claim to restitution of rights, have been pointed out, and are within the reach of all without injury to their honour. Nothing more is required for this than that they should promptly tender their adhesion, and help to maintain peace and order.

'5. The governor-general considers that the course thus taken is one consistent with the dignity of the government, and abundantly lenient. To have followed that which is suggested in your secretary's letter would, in his lordship's opinion, have been to treat the rebels not only as honourable enemies, but as enemies who had won the day.

'In the course of the rebellion, most of the leaders in it, probably all, have retaken to themselves the lands and villages of which they were deprived, by the summary settlement which followed the establishment of our government in Oude. If upon the capture of Lucknow by the commander-in-chief, before our strength had been seen or felt in the distant districts, and before any submission had been received or invited from them, the rights of the rebel chiefs to all their ancient possessions had been recognised by the government, it is not possible that the act would not have been viewed as dictated by fear or weakness. It would have led the people of Oude, and all who are watching the course of events in that province, to the conclusion that rebellion against the British government cannot be a losing game; and although it might have purchased an immediate return to order, it would not assuredly have placed the future peace of the province upon a secure foundation.

'6. You observe, indeed, that the landholders were most unjustly treated under our settlement. The governor-general desires me to observe that if this were unreservedly the case, or if the proceedings of the commissioners by which many of the thalookdars were deprived of portions of their possessions had been generally unjust, he would gladly have concurred in your recommendation, and would have been ready, at the risk of any misinterpretation of the motives of the government, to reinstate the thalookdars at once in their old possessions. But it is not so. As a question of policy, indeed, the governor-general considers that it may well be doubted whether the attempt to introduce into Oude a system of village settlement in place of the old settlement under thalookdars was a wise one; but this is a point which need not be discussed here. As a question of justice, it is certain that the land and villages taken from the thalookdars had, for the most part, been usurped by them through fraud or violence.

'7. That unjust decisions were come to by some of our local officers in investigating and judging the titles of the landowners is, the governor-general fears, too true; but the proper way of rectifying such injustice is by a re-hearing where complaint is made. This, you are aware, is the course which the governor-general is prepared to adopt, and to carry out in a liberal and conciliatory spirit. It is a very different one from proclaiming that indiscriminate restitution of all their ancient possessions is at once to be yielded to the landowners.

'8. That the hostility of the thalookdars of Oude who have been most active against the British government has been provoked, or is excused, by the injustice with which they have been treated, would seem to be your opinion.

'But I am to observe, that there are some facts which deserve to be weighed before pronouncing that this is the case.

'9. No chiefs have been more open in their rebellion than the rajahs of Churda, Bhinga, and Gonda. The governor-general believes that the first of these did not lose a single village by the summary settlement, and certainly his assessment was materially reduced. The second was dealt with in a like liberal manner. The Rajah of Gonda lost about 30 villages out of 400; but his assessment was lowered by some 10,000 rupees.

'10. No one was more benefited by the change of government than the young Rajah of Naupara. His estates had been the object of a civil war with a rival claimant for three years, and of these he was at once recognised as sole proprietor by the British government, losing only six villages out of more than a thousand. His mother was appointed guardian, but her troops have been fighting against us at Lucknow from the beginning.

'11. The Rajah of Dhowrera, also a minor, was treated with equal liberality. Every village was settled with his family; yet these people turned upon Captain Hearsey and his party, refused them shelter, pursued them, captured the ladies, and sent them into Lucknow.

'12. Ushruf Bux Khan, a large thalookdar in Gonda, who had long been an object of persecution by the late government, was established in the possession of all his property by us; yet he has been strongly hostile.

'13. It is clear that injustice at the hands of the British government has not been the cause of the hostility which, in these instances at least, has been displayed towards our rule.

'14. The moving spirit of these men and of others amongst the chiefs of Oude must be looked for elsewhere; and, in the opinion of the governor-general, it is to be found mainly in the repugnance which they feel to suffer any restraint of their hitherto arbitrary powers over those about them, to a diminution of their importance by being brought under equal laws, and to the obligation of disbanding their armed followers, and of living a peaceful and orderly life.

'The penalty of confiscation of property is no more than a just one in such cases as have been above recited; and although considerations of policy and mercy, and the newness of our rule, prescribe a relaxation of the sentence more or less large according to the features of each case, this relaxation must be preceded by submission, and the governor-general cannot consent to offer all, without distinction, an entire exemption from penalty, and the restoration of all former possessions, even though they should not have been guilty of the murder of Europeans.—I have, &c.,

(Signed) 'G. F. Edmonstone,
'Secretary to the Government of India, with the Governor-general.

'Allahabad, March 31, 1858.'

F.

The following document, though not pertaining to the affairs of Oude, may usefully be given here, bearing as it does on the treatment proposed to be adopted towards mutineers and rebels. It was written, in the name of Viscount Canning, by the secretary to the government of the Northwest Provinces, and was addressed to the functionaries of the disturbed province of Rohilcund:

'Agra, *April* 28, 1858.

'Sir—I am directed to communicate to you the general principles which the Right Honourable the Governor-general desires to see followed by all civil and other officers who will exercise judicial or magisterial powers in Rohilcund, on the re-entry of British troops into that province.

'2. The condition of Rohilcund has been, in some respects, peculiar. The progress of the Revolt in the interior has until lately suffered little check. The people, left to themselves, have in many quarters engaged actively in hostilities against each other; but direct opposition to British authority has been mainly confined to the several Sudder towns, to the frontier on the Ganges, and to the expeditions against Nynee Tal.

'3. Under these circumstances, his lordship considers it just to distinguish, by a widely differing treatment, the simple bearing of arms, or even acts of social violence committed at a period when the check of lawful government was removed, from acts directly involving treason against the state, or a deliberate defiance of its authority. Excepting instances of much aggravation, it is not the wish of government that public prosecutions should be set on foot on account of offences of the former class.

'4. Further, in respect of treason and defiance of British authority, his lordship desires that criminal proceedings shall be taken only against leaders, and against such persons, whether high or low, as have distinguished themselves by activity and rancour against the government, or by persistence in opposition to its authority after the advance of troops and the re-occupation of stations. The governor-general will admit to amnesty all other classes, even though they have borne arms on the side of the rebels, provided that they tender an early and complete submission. But continuance in opposition will exclude from pardon.

'5. The governor-general has reason to believe that an impression exists in Rohilcund that the Mohammedan population, as such, is to be proscribed and crushed. It is likely that the rumour has been raised and fostered by the rebel leaders to excite apprehension and mistrust of the government. His lordship desires that every appropriate occasion may be taken to disabuse the people of this gross error. Such suspected rebels as may be brought to trial will be tried each by his own acts. Each will stand or fall by the line of conduct which he shall be proved to have followed. The government will maintain, as it has always maintained, a strict impartiality in its administration. Equal justice will be shared by all its subjects, whether Hindoos or Mohammedans. You will make public these views, and instruct the chief district officers to make them widely known, in such manner as may appear to be most effectual.

'6. It will be your care, in accordance with the injunctions of his lordship's orders, embodied in the circular order dated the 19th February, to bring forward, for early notice by the governor-general, the several examples of conspicuously faithful conduct exhibited by many of the inhabitants of Rohilcund, under circumstances of peculiar difficulty.—I have, &c.,

'W. Muir,
'Sec. to Govt. N.W. P.'

G.

We now transfer attention to four of the documents written in London. The first was nominally from the 'Secret Committee,' really from the Earl of Ellenborough, and was suggested by the state of affairs in India during the second half of the month of February:

'The Secret Committee of the Court of Directors of the East India Company, to the Governor-general of India in Council, March 24, 1858.

'The telegram from Calcutta, dated the 22d ult., which

arrived this morning, conveys intelligence of the concentration of the force under the commander-in-chief, and of that under Jung Bahadoor, upon Lucknow; and we trust we may indulge the expectation that, ere this, that city has been evacuated by the rebels, and that no considerable corps remains united against us in the field.

'2. If this happy result should have been attained, it will be very satisfactory to us to learn that you have deemed yourselves sufficiently strong to be enabled to act towards the people with the generosity, as well as the justice, which are congenial to the British character.

'3. Crimes have been committed against us which it would be a crime to forgive; and some large exceptions there must be, of the persons guilty of such crimes, from any act of amnesty which could be granted; but it must be as impossible, as it would be abhorrent from our feelings, to inflict the extreme penalty which the law might strictly award upon all who have swerved from their allegiance.

'4. To us it appears that, whenever open resistance shall have ceased, it would be prudent, in awarding punishment, rather to follow the practice which prevails after the conquest of a country which has defended itself to the last by desperate war, than that which may perhaps be lawfully adopted after the suppression of mutiny and rebellion, such acts always being excepted from forgiveness or mitigation of punishment as have exceeded the licence of legitimate hostilities.

'5. While we may be unable to forget the insanity which, during the last ten months, has pervaded the army and a large portion of the people, we should at the same time remember the previous fidelity of a hundred years, and so conduct ourselves towards those who have erred as to remove their delusions and their fears, and re-establish, if we can, that confidence which was so long the foundation of our power.

'6. It would be desirable that, in every case, the disarming of a district, either by the seizure of arms or by their surrender, should precede the application to it of any amnesty; but there may be circumstances which would render expedient a different course of proceeding. Upon these exceptional cases, you and the officers acting under your orders must decide.

'7. The disarming of a district having been effected, with exceptions, under your licence, in favour of native gentlemen, whose feelings of honour would be affected by being deprived of the privilege of wearing arms, and of any other persons in whom you may confide, we think the possession of arms should be punished in every case by a severe penalty; but unless the possession of arms should be combined with other acts, leading to the conclusion that they were retained for the perpetration of crimes, that penalty should not be death. Of course the possession of arms by Englishmen must always remain lawful.

'8. Death has of late been but too common a punishment. It loses whatever terror it might otherwise have when so indiscriminately applied; but, in fact, in India there is not commonly a fear of death, although there ever must be a fear of pain.

'9. In every amnestied district, the ordinary administration of the law should as soon as possible be restored.

'10. In carrying these views into execution, you may meet with obstruction from those who, maddened by the scenes they have witnessed, may desire to substitute their own policy for that of the government; but persevere firmly in doing what you may think right; make those who would counteract you feel that you are resolved to rule, and that you will be served by none who will not obey.

'11. Acting in this spirit, you may rely upon our unqualified support.'

II.

Three or four weeks afterwards, was written the 'secret dispatch' which gave rise to so vehement a debate in parliament:

'*April* 19, 1858.

'Our letter of the 24th of March 1858 will have put you in possession of our general views with respect to the treatment of the people in the event of the evacuation of Lucknow by the enemy.

'2. On the 12th inst., we received from you a copy of the letter, dated the 3d of March, addressed by your secretary to the secretary to the chief-commissioner in Oude, which letter enclosed a copy of the proclamation to be issued by the chief-commissioner as soon as the British troops should have command of the city of Lucknow, and conveyed instructions as to the manner in which he was to act with respect to different classes of persons, in execution of the views of the governor-general.

'3. The people of Oude will see only the proclamation.

'4. That authoritative expression of the will of the government informs the people that six persons, who are named as having been steadfast in their allegiance, are henceforward the sole hereditary proprietors of the lands they held when Oude came under British rule, subject only to such moderate assessment as may be imposed upon them; that others in whose favour like claims may be established will have conferred upon them a proportionate measure of reward and honour; and that, with these exceptions, the proprietary right in the soil of the province is confiscated to the British government.

'5. We cannot but express to you our apprehension that this decree, pronouncing the disinherison of a people, will throw difficulties almost insurmountable in the way of the re-establishment of peace.

'6. We are under the impression that the war in Oude has derived much of its popular character from the rigorous manner in which, without regard to what the chief landholders had become accustomed to consider as their rights, the summary settlement had, in a large portion of the province, been carried out by your officers.

'7. The landholders of India are as much attached to the soil occupied by their ancestors, and are as sensitive with respect to the rights in the soil they deem themselves to possess, as the occupiers of land in any country of which we have a knowledge.

'8. Whatever may be your ultimate and undisclosed intentions, your proclamation will appear to deprive the great body of the people of all hope upon the subject most dear to them as individuals, while the substitution of our rule for that of their native sovereign has naturally excited against us whatever they may have of national feeling.

'9. We cannot but in justice consider that those who resist our authority in Oude are under very different circumstances from those who have acted against us in provinces which have been long under our government.

'10. We dethroned the King of Oude, and took possession of his kingdom, by virtue of a treaty which had been subsequently modified by another treaty, under which, had it been held to be in force, the course we adopted could not have been lawfully pursued; but we held that it was not in force, although the fact of its not having been ratified in England, as regarded the provision on which we rely for our justification, had not been previously made known to the King of Oude.

'11. That sovereign and his ancestors had been uniformly faithful to their treaty engagements with us, however ill they may have governed their subjects.

'12. They had more than once assisted us in our difficulties, and not a suspicion had ever been entertained of any hostile disposition on their part towards our government.

'13. Suddenly the people saw their king taken from amongst them, and our administration substituted for his, which, however bad, was at least native; and this sudden change of government was immediately followed by a summary settlement of the revenue, which, in a very considerable portion of the province, deprived the most influential landholders of what they deemed to be their property—of what certainly had long given wealth, and distinction, and power to their families.

'14. We must admit that, under these circumstances, the hostilities which have been carried on in Oude have rather the character of legitimate war than that of rebellion, and that the people of Oude should rather be regarded with indulgent consideration, than made the objects of a penalty exceeding in extent and in severity almost any which has been recorded in history as inflicted upon a subdued nation.

'15. Other conquerors, when they have succeeded in overcoming resistance, have excepted a few persons as still deserving of punishment, but have, with a generous policy, extended their clemency to the great body of the people.

'16. You have acted upon a different principle. You have reserved a few as deserving of special favour, and you have struck with what they will feel as the severest of punishment the mass of the inhabitants of the country.

'17. We cannot but think that the precedents from whom you have departed will appear to have been conceived in a spirit of wisdom superior to that which appears in the precedent you have made.

'18. We desire that you will mitigate in practice the stringent severity of the decree of confiscation you have issued against the landholders of Oude.

'19. We desire to see British authority in India rest upon the willing obedience of a contented people; there cannot be contentment where there is general confiscation.

'20. Government cannot long be maintained by any force in a country where the whole people is rendered hostile by a sense of wrong; and if it were possible so to maintain it, it would not be a consummation to be desired.'

I.

The Court of Directors, before the secret dispatch became known to them, adopted courteous language in the following letter of instructions sent to Viscount Canning, referring to an earlier communication:

'*May* 5, 1858.

'1. You will have received, by the mail of the 25th of March, a letter from the secret committee, which has since been laid before us, respecting the policy which it becomes you to pursue towards those natives of India who have recently been in arms against the authority of the British government.

'2. That letter emphatically confirms the principles which you have already adopted, as set forth in your circular of the 31st of July 1857, by impressing upon you the propriety of pursuing, after the conquest of the revolted provinces, a course of policy distinguished by a wise and discriminating generosity. You are exhorted to temper justice with mercy, and, except in cases of extreme criminality, to grant an amnesty to the vanquished. In the sentiments expressed by the secret committee we entirely concur. While there are some crimes which humanity calls upon you to punish with the utmost severity, there are others of a less aggravated character, which it would be equally unjust and impolitic not to pardon and to forget.

'3. The offences with which you will be called upon to deal are of three different kinds. Firstly, high crimes, instigated by malice prepense, and aggravated by treachery and cruelty. Secondly, offences the results rather of weakness than of malice, into which it is believed that many have been drawn by the contamination of example, by the fear of opposing themselves to their more powerful countrymen, or by the belief that they have been compromised by the acts of their associates, rather than by any active desire to embarrass the existing government. And, thirdly, offences of a less positive character, amounting to little more than passive connivance at evil, or at most to the act of giving such assistance to the rebels as, if not given, would have been forcibly extorted, and which in many cases it would have been death to refuse to bodies of licentious and exasperated mutineers.

'4. It is the first only of these offences, the perpetrators of which, and their accomplices, it will be your duty to visit with the severest penalty which you can inflict; and it is, happily, in such cases of exceptional atrocity, that you will have the least difficulty in proving both the commission of the offence and the identity of the offender. In the other cases you might often be left in doubt, not only of the extent of the offence committed, but of its actual commission by the accused persons; and although we are aware that the retribution which might be righteously inflicted upon the guilty may be in some measure restricted by too much nicety of specification, and that, in dealing with so large a mass of crime, it is difficult to avoid the commission of some acts of individual injustice, we may still express our desire that the utmost exertion may be made to confine, within the smallest possible compass, these cases of uncertain proof and dubious identity, even though your retributary measures should thus fall short of what in strict justice might be inflicted.

'5. As soon as you have suppressed the active hostility of the enemy, your first care will be the restoration of public confidence. It will be your privilege when the disorganised provinces shall no longer be convulsed by intestine disorder, to set an example of toleration and forbearance towards the subject people, and to endeavour by every means consistent with the security of the British empire in the east, to allay the irritation and suspicion, which, if suffered to retain possession of the minds of the native and European inhabitants of the country, will eventually lead to nothing less calamitous than a war of races.

'6. In dealing with the people of Oude, you will doubtless be moved by special considerations of justice and of policy. Throughout the recent contest, we have ever regarded such of the inhabitants of that country as—not being sepoys or pensioners of our own army—have been in arms against us as an exceptional class. They cannot be considered as traitors or even rebels, for they had not pledged their fidelity to us, and they had scarcely become our subjects. Many, by the introduction of a new system of government, had necessarily been deprived of the maintenance they had latterly enjoyed; and others feared that the speedy loss of their means of subsistence must follow from the same course. It was natural that such persons should avail themselves of the opportunity presented by the distracted state of the country, to strike a blow for the restoration of the native rule, under which the permitted disorganisation of the country had so long been to them a source of unlawful profit. Neither the disbanded soldiers of the late native government, nor the great thalookdars and their retainers, were under any obligation of fidelity to our government for benefits conferred upon them. You would be justified, therefore, in dealing with them as you would with a foreign enemy, and in ceasing to consider them objects of punishment after they have once laid down their arms.

'7. Of these arms they must for ever be deprived. You will doubtless, in prosecution of this object, address yourself in the first instance to the case of the great thalookdars, who so successfully defied the late government, and many of whom, with large bodies of armed men, appear to have aided the efforts of the mutinous soldiery of the Bengal army. The destruction of the fortified strongholds of these powerful landholders, the forfeiture of their remaining guns, the disarming and disbanding of their followers, will be amongst your first works. But, whilst you are depriving this influential and once dangerous class of people of their power of openly resisting your authority, you will, we have no doubt, exert yourself by every possible means to reconcile them to British rule, and encourage them, by liberal arrangements made in accordance with ancient usages, to become industrious agriculturists, and to employ in the cultivation of the soil the men who, as armed retainers, have so long wasted the substance of their masters and desolated the land. We believe that these landholders may be taught that their holdings will be more profitable to them under a strong government, capable of maintaining the peace of the country, and severely punishing agrarian outrages, than under one which perpetually invites, by its weakness, the ruinous arbitration of the sword.

'8. Having thus endeavoured, on the re-establishment of the authority of the British government in Oude, to re-assure the great landholders, you will proceed to consider, in the same spirit of toleration and forbearance, the condition of the great body of the people. You will bear in mind that it is necessary, in a transition state from one government to another, to deal tenderly with existing usages, and sometimes even with existing abuses. All precipitate reforms are dangerous. It is often wiser even to tolerate evil for a time, than to alarm and to irritate the minds of the people by the sudden introduction of changes which time can alone teach them to appreciate, or even, perhaps, to understand. You will be especially careful, in the readjustment of the fiscal system of the province, to avoid the imposition of unaccustomed taxes, whether of a general or of a local character, pressing heavily upon the industrial resources and affecting the daily comforts of the people. We do not estimate the successful administration of a newly acquired province according to the financial results of the first few years. At such a time we should endeavour to conciliate the people by wise concessions, and to do nothing to encourage the belief that the British government is more covetous of revenue than the native ruler whom it has supplanted.'

K.

The last document here given is a letter of instructions from the Court of Directors, kind and courteous towards the governor-general, but evidently conveying an opinion that the proposed proclamation, unless modified and acted on with caution, would be too severe for the purpose in view:

'*Political Department, 18th of May* (No. 20) 1858.

'1. The secret committee has communicated to us the governor-general's secret letter, dated 5th March (No. 9) 1858, with its enclosures, consisting of a letter addressed to the chief-commissioner of Oude, dated 3d of March, and of the proclamation referred to therein, which was to be issued by Sir James Outram to the chiefs and inhabitants of Oude as soon as the British troops should have possession or command of the city of Lucknow.

'2. We have also received communication of the letter addressed to your government by the secret committee, under date the 19th of April last, on the subject of the draft of proclamation.

'3. Our political letter of the 5th of May has apprised you of our strong sense of the distinction which ought to be maintained between the revolted sepoys and the chiefs and people of Oude, and the comparative indulgence with which, equally from justice and policy, the insurgents of that country (other than sepoys) ought to be regarded. In accordance with these views, we entirely approve the guarantee of life and honour given by the proposed proclamation to all thalookdars, chiefs, and landholders, with their followers, who should make immediate submission, surrender their arms, and obey the orders of the British government, provided they have not participated in the murder "of Englishmen or Englishwomen."

'4. We are prepared to learn that in publicly declaring that, with the exception of the lands of six persons who had been steadfast in their allegiance, the proprietary right in the soil of the province was confiscated to the British government, the governor-general intended no more than to reserve to himself entire liberty of action, and to give the character of mercy to the confirmation of all rights not prejudicial to the public welfare, the owners of which might not, by their conduct, have excluded themselves from indulgent consideration.

'5. His lordship must have been well aware that the words of the proclamation, without the comment on it which we trust was speedily afforded by your actions, must have produced the expectation of much more general and indiscriminate dispossession than could have been consistent with justice or with policy. We shall doubtless be informed, in due course, of the reasons which induced the governor-general to employ those terms, and of the means which, we presume, have been taken of making known in Oude the merciful character which we assume must still belong to your views. In the meantime, it is due to the governor-general that we should express our entire reliance that on this, as on former occasions, it has been his firm resolution to shew to all whose crimes are not too great for any indulgence, the utmost degree of leniency consistent with the early restoration and firm maintenance of lawful authority.

'We accordingly have to inform you, that on receiving communication of the papers now acknowledged, the Court of Directors passed the following resolution:

'"Resolved—That in reference to the dispatch from the secret committee to the governor-general of India, dated the 19th ult., with the documents therein alluded to, and this day laid before the Court of Directors, this court desires to express its continued confidence in the governor-general, Lord Canning, and its conviction that his measure for the pacification of Oude, and the other disturbed districts in India, will be characterised by a generous policy, and by the utmost clemency that is found to be consistent with the satisfactory accomplishment of that important object."—We are, &c.

(Signed) 'F. CURRIE,
'W. J. EASTWICK,
&c. &c.'

'*London, May* 18, 1858.

Ganges Transport Boat.

JUNG BAHADOOR, of Nepaul.

CHAPTER XXVIII.

MILITARY OPERATIONS IN APRIL.

THE British officers and soldiers in India looked forward, not without anxiety, to a hot-weather campaign in the summer of 1858. Much disappointment was felt, too, in England, when the necessity for such a campaign became manifest. Persons in all ranks had fondly hoped that, when Sir Colin Campbell had spent two or three months in preparing for the siege of Lucknow, he would be enabled so to invest that city as to render the escape of the mutineers impossible; and that in conquering it, the heart of the rebellion would be crushed out. The result did not answer to this expectation. Lucknow was conquered; but the prisoners taken could be reckoned simply by dozens; nearly all the rebels who were not killed escaped into the provinces. It is true that they were now a dispersed body instead of a concentrated army; but it is also true that, in abandoning Lucknow, they would retire to many towns and forts where guns could be found, and where a formidable stand might be made against British troops. Let the summer approach, and the ratio of advantages on the two sides would be changed in character. Hot weather may affect the sepoy, but it affects him relatively less than the Englishman.

It is heart-breaking work to a gallant soldier to feel his bodily strength failing through heat, at a time when his spirit is as heroic as ever. The rebels were astute enough to know this. The lithe Hindoo, with supple limbs and no superfluous flesh, can make great marches—especially when he retreats. His goods and chattels are few in number; his household arrangements simple; and it costs him little time or thought to shift his quarters at a short notice, in a period of peace. During war or rebellion, when he becomes a soldier, his worldly position is even more simple than before. A man who can live upon rice, parched corn, and water, and to whom it is a matter of much indifference whether he is clothed or not, has a remarkable freedom of movement, requiring little intricacy of commissariat arrangements. The English, during the war of the mutiny, had ample means of observing this mobility of the native rebel troops, and ample reasons for lamenting its consequences. If this were so during the winter, it would be still more decidedly the case during a hot-weather campaign, when exhaustion and *coups de soleil* work so terribly on the European constitution. It was this consideration, as we have said, that gave rise to much disappointment, both in India and in England, when the real sequel of the siege of Lucknow became apparent. The disappointment resolved itself in some quarters into adverse criticism on Sir Colin Campbell's tactics; but even these who deemed it wise and just to postpone such criticism, could not postpone their anxiety when they found that the rebels, fleeing from Lucknow, assumed such an attitude elsewhere as would render a summer campaign necessary.

The long sojourn of the commander-in-chief in and near the Oudian capital, and the frequent communications between him and the governor-general, told of serious and weighty discussions concerning the policy to be pursued. Rumours circulated of an antagonism of plans; of one project for leaving the rebels unmolested until after the hot season should have passed, and of another for crushing them in detail before they could succeed in re-combining. But whatever might have been the rumours, the policy adopted followed the latter of these two courses. The army of Lucknow, broken up into divisions or columns, was set again to work, to pursue and defeat those insurgents who kept the field with a pertinacity little expected when the mutiny began. So much of those operations as took place during the month of April, it is the purpose of this chapter to narrate; but a few words may previously be said concerning the state of affairs in Bengal, more dependent on Calcutta than on the army of Oude or the commander-in-chief.

The fact has already been adverted to that the supreme government, amid all the anxiety of the rebellion in the northwest, began in the spring of the year to take measures for the better protection of Lower Bengal. That province, the most important in the whole of India, had been very little affected by the mutiny, chiefly because there were few Mohammedan leaders inclined to become rebels; but the authorities could not close their eyes to the facts that the province was very insufficiently defended, and that any successful revolt there would be more disastrous than in other regions. So long as the delta of the Ganges remained in British hands, there would always be a base of operations for reconquering Upper India, if necessary; but that delta once lost, the services of a Clive, backed by a large army from England, would be again needed to recover it. A plan was therefore formed for locating five or six thousand European troops in Bengal, quartered at Calcutta, Dumdum, Chinsura, Barrackpore, Dinapoor, Benares, and one or two other places. It became very seriously contested whether any native army whatever would be needed in the province. The Bengalees are peaceful, and have few ambitious chieftains among them; hence, it was argued, a few thousand British troops, and a few hundred seamen of the Naval Brigade, would suffice to protect the province. There were 'divisional battalions' of native troops still at certain stations, as a sort of military police; but the regular Bengal native army had been extinguished, or had extinguished itself. So useful had a few hundred seamen become, that their employment led to many such suggestions as the following—'Wherever these seamen are, there is a feeling of absolute security at once from external attack and internal treachery. Bengal has now been nearly twelve months without a native army, and within that twelve months they have never once been missed. Why not retain this security? Why not strike off Bengal from the provinces to be occupied by a native force, and render our improvised force a permanent institution? A company of European sailors would be a nucleus for the armed police in each division. Why not keep them up as such, give them permanent allowances, recruit them primarily from the same useful class? There can be no want of men when once such a permanent opening is known. They would not only protect the great cities, and double the physical force on which all authority must ultimately rest, but act as a permanent check on the divisional battalions. We want such a check. These men may be as faithful as the sepoys have been false, as attached to Europeans as the sepoys have proved themselves hostile; but there can never be any proof of the fact. Let us not again trust armed natives without the precautions we take in our ships against our own sailors—a check by a different body.' All such considerations necessarily resolved themselves into a much larger inquiry, to be conducted deliberately and cautiously—how ought the army of India to be re-constituted?

Semi-barbarous tribes in many instances took advantage of the disturbed state of British influence in India, to make inroads into districts not properly belonging to them; and it sometimes happened that the correction of these evil-doers was a very difficult matter. Such an instance occurred in the month now under notice. On the borders of Assam, at the extreme northeast corner of India, were a wild mountain tribe called Abors, who had for some time been engaged in a system of marauding on the Assam side of the frontier. Captain Bivar, at Debrooghur, set forth to punish them, taking with him a mixed force of sailors and Goorkhas. The Abors retreated to their fastnesses, and Bivar attempted to follow them; but this was an unsuccessful manœuvre. The Abors brought down many of his men by poisoned arrows, and maimed others by rolling down stones upon them from the rocks; a portion of their numbers, meanwhile, making a circuit, fell upon the baggage-boats, and captured the whole of the baggage. Captain Bivar and his companions suffered many privations before they safely got back to Debrooghur. These, however, were minor difficulties, involving no very serious consequences. Throughout the northeast region of India there were few 'Pandies,' few sepoys of Hindustani race; and thus the materials for rebellion were deprived of one very mischievous ingredient.

The Calcutta authorities found it necessary to make stringent rules concerning ladies and children; and hence some of the magistrates and collectors, the representatives of the Company in a civil capacity in the country districts, were occasionally placed in troublesome circumstances by family considerations during times of tumult. From the first, the Calcutta government had endeavoured, by every available means, to prevent women and children from going to the scenes of danger: knowing how seriously the movements of the officers, military and civil, would be interfered with by the presence of helpless relatives during scenes of fighting and tumult. One of the magistrates, in Western Bengal, was brought into difficulty by disobedience to this order. His wife entreated that she might come to him at his station. She did so. Shortly afterwards a rumour spread that a large force of the enemy was approaching. The lady grew frightened, and the husband anxious. He took her to another place, and was thereby absent from his post at a critical time. The government suspended him from office for disobeying orders in having his wife at the station, and for quitting his district without leave at a time when his presence was imperatively needed.

One other matter may be mentioned here, in connection with the local government, before proceeding to the affairs of Oude and the northwest. The Calcutta authorities shared with the Court of Directors, the English government, and the House of Commons, the power of rewarding or honouring their troops for good services; the modes adopted were many; but amid the controversies which occasionally arose concerning military honours, medals, promotions, and encomiums, it was made very manifest during the wars of the mutiny that the Victoria Cross, the recognition of individual valour, was one of the most highly valued by the soldiery, both officers and privates. The paltriness of the bits of metal and ribbon, or the tastelessness of the design, might be abundantly criticised; but when it became publicly known that the Cross would be given *only* to those who had shewn themselves to be brave among the brave, the value of the symbol was great, such as a soldier or sailor could alone appreciate. From time to time notices appeared in the *London Gazette*, emanating from the War-office, giving the utmost publicity to the instances in which the Victoria Cross was bestowed. The name of the officer or soldier, the regiment or corps to which he belonged, the commanding officer who had made the recommendation, the dispatch in which the deed of bravery was recorded, the date and place of that deed, the nature of the deed itself—all were briefly set forth; and there can be little doubt that the recipients of the Cross would cherish that memorial, and the *Gazette* notice, to the end of their lives. Incidental notices of this honorary testimonial have been frequently made in former chapters; and it is mentioned again here because of its importance in including officers and privates in the same category. Thus, on the 27th of April, to give one instance, the *London Gazette* announced the bestowal of the Victoria Cross on Lieutenant-colonel Henry Tombs, of the Bengal artillery; Lieutenant James Hills, of the same corps; Lieutenant William Alexander Kerr, of the 24th Bombay native infantry; Sergeant John Smith, of the Bengal Sappers and Miners; Bugler Robert Hawthorne, of the 52d foot; Lance-corporal Henry Smith, of the same regiment; Sergeant Bernard Diamond, of the Bengal horse-artillery; and Gunner Richard Fitzgerald, of the same corps. Sergeant Smith and Bugler Hawthorne, it will be remembered, assisted poor Home, Salkeld, and Burgess in blowing up the Cashmere Gate at Delhi; unlike their heroic but less fortunate companions, they lived to receive the Victoria Cross.*

Let us now pass to the stormy northwest regions. Beginning with Lucknow as a centre, it will be convenient to treat of Sir Colin's arrangements at that place, and then to notice in succession the operations of his brigadiers in their movements radially from that centre, so far as they were connected with the month of April.

That portion of the army which remained in Lucknow found the month of April to open with a degree of heat very distressing to bear. A temperature of 100° F., under the shade of

* The following will give an idea of the mode in which the *Gazette* announcements were made: '24th Bombay N. I.—Lieutenant William Alexander Kerr; date of act of bravery, July 10, 1857.—On the breaking out of a mutiny in the 27th Bombay N. I. in July 1857, a party of the mutineers took up a position in the stronghold or *paga* near the town of Kolapore, and defended themselves to extremity. "Lieutenant Kerr, of the Southern Mahratta Irregular Horse, took a prominent share in the attack on the position; and at the moment when its capture was of great public importance, he made a dash at one of the gateways, with some dismounted horsemen, and forced an entrance by breaking down the gate. The attack was completely successful, and the defenders were either killed, wounded, or captured—a result that may with perfect justice be attributed to Lieutenant Kerr's dashing and devoted bravery." (Letter from the Political Superintendent at Kolapore to the Adjutant-general of the Army, dated September 10, 1857.)'

a tent, was not at all unusual. When the wind was calm, the pressure of temperature was not much felt; but the blowing of a hot wind was truly terrible—not only from the heat itself, but from the clouds of dust laden with particles of matter of the most offensive kind. Every organ of sense, every nerve, every pore, was distressed. And it was at such a time that a commander was called upon to plan, and officers and soldiers to execute, military operations with as much care and exactitude as if under a cool and temperate sky. There were putrefying bodies yet unburied in the vicinity, pools of recently dried blood in the streets and gardens, and abominations of every kind in this city of palaces: how these affected the air, in a temperature higher than is ever known in England, may be imperfectly, and only imperfectly, conceived.*

The last chapter told in what way the treatment of the Oude rebels engaged the attention of the imperial legislature, and what were the violent discussions to which that subject gave rise. In this place it will only be necessary to state that, long before Viscount Canning came to hear the views of the two Houses of Parliament, he found it necessary to determine, if not the policy itself, at least the names of those who would have the onerous task of re-establishing civil government in the distracted province. Mr Montgomery, who, as judicial commissioner of the Punjaub, had rendered admirable service to Sir John Lawrence, was selected by the governor-general to fill the office of chief-commissioner of Oude—aided by a staff of judicial and financial commissioners, civil and military secretaries, deputy-commissioners, commissioners of divisions, deputy-commissioners of districts, and other officers. It was believed that he combined the valuable qualities of sagacity, experience, firmness, and conciliation. Oude was to be parcelled out into four divisions, and each division into three districts. The intention was, that as soon as any part of the province was brought into some degree of order by Sir Colin and his brigadiers, Montgomery should take it in hand, and bring it to order in relation to judicial and revenue affairs. Large powers were given to him, in relation to 'proclamations' and everything else; and it remained for time to shew the result.

While on this subject, it may be well to advert to the conduct and position of one particular native of Oude. During many months the line of policy pursued by the influential Oudian landowner, Rajah Maun Singh, was a subject of much anxiety among the British authorities. His power in Oude was very considerable, and it was fondly hoped or wished that he might prove faithful in mutinous times. This hope was founded on two kinds of evidence, positive and negative—proofs that he had often befriended the poor European fugitives in the hour of greatest need, and that on many occasions he had *not* injured the British when he might easily have done so. Nevertheless it was impossible to get rid of the impression that he was 'playing fast and loose;' reserving himself for whichever party should gain the ascendency in the Indian struggle. So much importance was attached in England to this rajah's conduct, that the House of Commons ordered the production of any documents that might throw light upon it. The papers produced ranged over a period of six months. So early as June 1857, when the mutiny was only six or seven weeks old, Mr Tucker, commissioner of Benares, wrote to Maun Singh concerning the relations between him and the British government—acknowledging the steadiness of the rajah in maintaining the district of Fyzabad in a peaceful condition, so far as he could, and assuring him that it would be good policy for him to continue in the same path. He told him that although England was engaged in a war with China, and had only just concluded one with Persia, and that moreover her Hindustani troops had proved faithless, she would undoubtedly triumph over all opposition from within and without, and would equally remember those who had been true and those who had been false to her—to reward the one and punish the other. It was a letter of thanks for the past, and of warning for the future. During the same month, Maun Singh was in correspondence with Mr Paterson, magistrate of Goruckpore, giving and receiving friendly assurances, and impressing the magistrate with a belief in his sincere desire to remain faithful to the British government during a time of trouble. In the middle of July he was in correspondence with Mr Wingfield, British political agent with the Goorkha force at that time in the Goruckpore district. Maun Singh, it may here be remarked, had suffered severely in his estate, by the land-settlement made when the Company took possession of Oude; he had suffered, whether rightly or wrongly; and the Calcutta authorities were naturally anxious to know whether his losses had converted him into a rebel. He wrote to Mr Wingfield, promising to adhere faithfully to a course of friendliness towards the English. Mr Wingfield recommended the government to trust Maun Singh, to supply him with a certain amount of funds, and to believe that he was able and willing to keep the districts of Fyzabad and Sultanpore tolerably free from anarchy. He added: 'All I see and hear of Maun Singh makes me think him stanch up to this moment. He has exerted himself in every way to protect the women and children that were left at Fyzabad,

* 'Of the dust it is quite beyond the powers of writing to give a description. It is so fine and subtle, that long after the causes which raised it have ceased to exert their influence, you may see it like a veil of gauze between your eyes and every object. The sun, while yet six or seven degrees above the horizon, is hid from sight by it as though the luminary were enveloped in a thick fog; and at early morning and evening, this vapour of dust suspended high in air seems like a rain-cloud clinging to a hillside. When this dust is set rapidly in motion by a hot wind, and when the grosser sand, composed of minute fragments of talc, scales of mica, and earth, is impelled in quick successive waves through the heated atmosphere, the effect is quite sufficient to make one detest India for ever. Every article in your tent, your hair, eyes, and nose, are filled and covered with this dust, which deposits a coating half an inch thick all over the tent.'—W. H. Russell.

and to place them in safety. He sent four sergeants' wives and seven children to this place; but we cannot expect him to sacrifice himself for us. He has doubtless already made himself obnoxious to the rebels by his open adhesion to our cause; and if fortune goes against us at Lucknow, instead of being able to render us any assistance, he will himself have to take shelter here.' The Calcutta government authorised Mr Wingfield to thank Maun Singh for his actions and his promises, and to assist him with money to a certain prescribed amount. In August a letter was sent to the rajah himself by the government, thanking him for what he had done, and urging him to a continuance in the same course. Many months afterwards, the Calcutta authorities had again to discuss this subject. During the autumn, Maun Singh's former promises had been a good deal belied. He had been in and near Lucknow during the period when Havelock, Outram, and Campbell were engaged in warfare at that city; and it was more than suspected that he had aided the insurgents. True, he was a man who, having something of the feelings of a gentleman, rather succoured than persecuted hapless fugitives who were powerless for aught save suffering; but his proceedings in other ways were not satisfactory. When Outram commanded in the Residency, shut up with Havelock and Inglis, he exchanged many communications with the rajah, but to no satisfactory end. During the winter, rumours reached Maun Singh that the governor-general, regarding him as a traitor in spite of his many promises, intended to deprive him of his estates, as a punishment. He wrote a reproachful letter to Mr Brereton, the magistrate at Goruckpore—complaining that this was a poor reward for his services; that he went with his family to Lucknow because he was threatened by insurgents at Fyzabad; but that throughout the various sieges at Lucknow he never joined the rebels in attacking the British. Among various letters from the officials, were two which showed that Mr Wingfield had greatly modified his former favourable opinion of the Fyzabad rajah. On the 2d of February he wrote: 'Maun Singh is not the man to be selected as an object of clemency. He has not the excuse of having been hurried into insurrection by the force of example, the impetuosity of his feelings, or even regard for his personal safety. He withstood all these trials; for it was on mature reflection, and after weighing all the chances on either side, that he chose that of rebellion. As long as he thought the success of the insurrection was but transient, and that our government would speedily recover its position, he professed loyalty, and even supported us; but when he heard that the Goorkhas were not to march through Fyzabad, and that Havelock had been obliged to abandon his design of relieving the Residency and to retire on Cawnpore, he thought our case hopeless, and joined what appeared the triumphant side. He has now found out his mistake, and wishes to turn again.' Again, on the 12th of February Mr Wingfield wrote: 'On Maun Singh's conduct I look with some distrust, which his letter does not tend to remove. Our Fyzabad news-writer, whose information has invariably proved correct, reports that the rajah has had an interview with some of the sepoy officers, and agreed to their proposal to invade this (Goruckpore) district, and moved three of his guns down to the Ghat. It would be quite consistent with his known character for duplicity to infer that, while aiding the insurgents, he is trying to keep well with us.' The double-dealer had, indeed, his hands full of employment; for he had been sounding Sir James Outram at the Alum Bagh, before he applied to the Goruckpore authorities, at the very time that he had on hand some sort of negotiation with the rebels. He succeeded so far as this—that no party liked absolutely to throw him off. Mr Wingfield, in writing to the government, candidly admitted that, inscrutable and unreliable as Maun Singh was, matters would have gone worse for the British in Oude if he had not been there. 'It must be admitted that his neutrality up to the present time has paralysed the plans of the insurgents, and has made him the object of their indignation. Had he declared himself openly against us, the district of Goruckpore would long ago have been invaded.' On the 16th of February the governor-general sent orders from Allahabad, as to the mode in which any overtures from Maun Singh should be received. He directed that the rajah should be thanked for the humanity he had shewn towards individuals; reminded that strong suspicions were entertained of his complicity with the rebels; threatened with a full and searching inquiry into his past conduct; and recommended to submit himself—without any other conditions than a promise of his life and honour—to the British authorities. But Maun Singh did not follow this advice—he remained throughout the spring months balancing and trimming between loyalty and disloyalty.

Reverting to the state of affairs at Lucknow, it may here be observed that the commander-in-chief remained in that city until the middle of April. There was nothing Napoleonic, nothing rapid, in his movements after the conquest; but those who knew him best knew that he was organising plans of operation for all his brigadiers, and on all sides of the Oudian capital. So thoroughly was he master of his own secrets, and of his correspondence with the governor-general, that very little concerning his plans were known until the very day of operation. Even the higher officers had little but conjecture to rest upon; while the mere retailers of gossip were sorely puzzled for materials. It may be that the excessive publicity of the details of the Crimean war had rendered military authorities uneasy, and tended to render them chary of giving information of their plans in any subsequent wars. During the second week in the month, Sir Colin Campbell took a rapid gallop to Allahabad—a long distance and a somewhat perilous ride in such a disturbed state of the country; but he was not a man to care for distance or for danger, as personally affecting himself. He had many weighty questions to settle with Viscount Canning; and as the governor-general could not or would not go to the commander, the commander went to the governor-general. The result of the interview was the departure of Sir Colin Campbell himself, as well as his generals, for active service in districts distant from Lucknow.

It will be desirable to trace the movements of the generals and brigadiers singly before noticing those of the commander-in-chief and his head-quarters.

And first, for Sir James Outram. This eminent man, the second in influence among the military commanders in India, quitted Lucknow nearly at the same time as many other officers; but on a different mission. When that city was conquered, Outram at once became supreme authority there, as chief-commissioner of Oude. He collected round him a civil staff, and proceeded to enrol a police, establish police-stations, and restore order in the city. From these duties, however, he was summoned away. His services were needed at Calcutta. The supreme council in that city generally contained one military officer among its members, to advise on matters pertaining to war. General Low, who had for some time filled that position, retired to England; and Outram was chosen to supply his place. Personally, it was well that Sir James should quit the camp for a while, after half a year's incessant military employment in Oude; and professionally, it was desirable that the council at Calcutta should have the benefit of his assistance, in any plans for the reorganisation of the Indian army—a most important matter, towards which the attention of the authorities was necessarily much directed. Sir James did not forget his old companions-in-arms. As soon as he reached Calcutta, he gave orders that copies of one of the newspapers should be regularly sent to the hospitals of six of the British regiments at Cawnpore, Meerut, Lucknow, and Benares; he knew how irksome are the hours in a sick-room, and how joyfully a few books or journals are hailed in such a place.

The lines of operation marked out for the other generals naturally bore relation to the real or supposed position of the insurgent forces. The rumours which reached head-quarters concerning the concentration of rebel leaders in Rohilcund, even making allowance for exaggerations, told of a somewhat formidable organisation. Among the best-known names included in the list were Khan Bahadoor Khan, Nena Sahib, Fuzul Huq, Waladid Khan, and the Nawab of Furruckabad. Khan Bahadoor Khan was chief ruler; and he appears to have organised something like a regular government, with dewans, moonshees, naibs, darogahs, kotwals, nazims, and military commanders. Nena Sahib was there as a sort of distinguished refugee; as were also two shahzadas or princes of the royal family of Delhi. Nena Sahib is supposed to have arrived at Bareilly in Rohilcund, after Sir Colin's great victory at Lucknow, with four hundred troopers, and to have taken up his abode in the fine large native school-room built by the British in that city. One among many bazaar reports was, that Khan Bahadoor Khan began to entertain misgivings concerning the ultimate success of his rebel policy; but that Nena Sahib, acting on his fears, insisted that a drawing back would be ruinous. Another rumour, having much probability to recommend it, was to the effect that Nena Sahib looked to Central India, the region of Gwalior, Kotah, and Indore, as the field in which his own personal success might ultimately be best insured, on account of his great influence among the Mahrattas of that region; and it was supposed that, failing of success in Oude and Rohilcund, he would endeavour to cross the Ganges and the Jumna into Bundelcund and Central India. Hence one of the points of policy on the side of the commander-in-chief, was to guard those great rivers at as many ghats or passing-places as possible—in the hope that, confined to Oude and Rohilcund, the rebels might be crushed; and in the fear that, scattered over Central India, they might again become powerful. Whether his forces were sufficiently numerous for this duty, was one of the many questions that pressed upon Sir Colin Campbell. The trite saying of an enemy 'not knowing when they were beaten,' was many times revived by the British officers in those days; the mutineers seldom gained a victory; but on the other hand, they were not much disheartened by defeat; they retreated, only to collect and fight again; and thus the British troops seldom felt that a victory would give an unquestionably permanent advantage.

Of the leaders who had taken part in the conquest of Lucknow, Jung Bahadoor, the Nepaulese chieftain—as has been shown in a former chapter—went to Allahabad with a body-guard, to hold an interview with the governor-general. The rest of the Goorkha contingent retraced their steps by slow degrees towards their Nepaulese home. So late as the 22d of April, the main body of Goorkhas were no further from Lucknow than Nawabgunge, a town on the banks of the Gogra, northeast of the capital of Oude. On that day, they marched to Sutturgunje, and on the 23d to Durriabad. This town had a fort which might have made a stout resistance, but there were no rebel troops at hand to put the matter to proof. After remaining at Durriabad two days, the Goorkhas marched on the 25th to Shugahgunje, on the 26th to Mobarrukgunje, and on the 27th to Durabgunje—all of them places on or near the banks of the Gogra, on the route towards Fyzabad. Resting two days at Durabgunje, they marched on the 29th to Ayodha or Oude, the ancient Hindoo capital, afterwards supplanted by the Mohammedan Fyzabad, just at hand—which Fyzabad was in its turn supplanted by Lucknow. On the last day of the month, the Goorkhas were on one side of the river Gogra at Fyzabad, and a body of rebels on the other—each intently watching the other, but without fighting. Maun Singh was at that time at

Goorkha Havildar or Sergeant.

Fyzabad, friendly to the British. Little satisfaction appears to have been derived by any party from this co-operation of the Goorkhas with the British. In the preceding July and August, when Havelock was straining every nerve to bring a small force up to Lucknow, and when Inglis was contending against stupendous difficulties in that city—in those months, there was an army of three or four thousand Goorkhas near the eastern frontier of Oude, badly commanded and insufficiently employed. Why they were not pushed on to Lucknow, as an auxiliary force, was known only to the authorities; but, in its effect, this inactivity of the Goorkhas called forth much adverse criticism. Again, during the six months from the beginning of September to the beginning of March, the assistance from Nepaul was not of such a character as had been hoped by those who knew that the Goorkhas enlisted in the Sirmoor and Kumaon battalions were really brave and efficient troops, and who expected that Jung Bahadoor's Goorkhas would prove to be men of the same stamp. Why the aid rendered was so small, was a politico-military question, on which very little information was afforded. When, at last, a really large Nepaulese army entered Oude, its movements were so slow that Sir Colin began the siege of Lucknow without its aid; and when the siege was over, the army began to march back again, without participating further in the war. This was a very impotent result; and the Nepaulese episode was by no means a brilliant one in the history of the wars of the mutiny. So far as concerns the march during the month of April, from Lucknow towards the Nepaul frontier, it may be remarked that the Goorkhas dreaded the approaching hot weather, that their number of sick was very large, and that the carts for their baggage were so enormous in number as greatly to impede their movements.

Another of the generals concerned in the siege of Lucknow, Sir Edward Lugard, was intrusted by the commander-in-chief with service in a region infested by Koer Singh—the chieftain whose name had been so closely associated with the Dinapoor mutiny and the 'disaster at Arrah,' in the preceding summer. This rebel had worked round nearly in a circle—not metaphorically, but topographically. He had marched at the head of insurgents south and southwest from Arrah, then west into Bundelcund, then north into the Doab and Oude; and now it was his fortune to be driven east and southeast back to his old quarters in the neighbourhood of Arrah.

Before Lugard could cross the frontier into the provinces eastward of Oude, it was found necessary to bring smaller forces to bear upon bodies of rebels infesting those provinces, and threatening to command the region between the rivers Goomtee and Gogra. The city of Azimghur was in this way greatly indebted to the gallant exertions of Lord Mark Kerr. This officer, immediately on the arrival of news that Azimghur was beset by the enemy, started off from Benares on the 2d of April, with 450 men of H.M. 13th regiment and Queen's Bays, and two 6-pounder guns. Though impeded by a train of three hundred bullock-carts laden with ammunition, Kerr pushed forward with such rapidity that he arrived in the neighbourhood of Azimghur on the third day after quitting Benares. Here he was opposed by three or four thousand rebels, comprising a large proportion of sepoys of the too celebrated Dinapoor brigade. The rebels were commanded with some skill by a subadar of one of the mutinied regiments. They occupied a position of considerable strength, on the right and left sides of the main road; their right resting on a strong village, and their left protected by a ditch and embankment. Lord Mark succeeded in dislodging those of the enemy who were immediately in his front; but while thus engaged, his convoy in the rear was attacked by eight hundred rebels, who were with great difficulty beaten off, at the expense of the life of Captain Jones, who was guarding the convoy. Overcoming all resistance, Lord Mark succeeded in reaching a point near Azimghur, and remained there until the arrival of Lugard's column from Lucknow. This portion of the rebels did not return to the city after the action, but retired in good order, taking their guns and baggage with them.

Azimghur, however, needed the assistance of a larger force than Kerr could bring against it; for Koer Singh, with a formidable band of rebels, had to be contended against, in a region containing many large towns. Sir Edward Lugard, placed by Sir Colin Campbell in command of a column destined for service in this region, started from Lucknow during the last week in March; but the destruction of a bridge over the Goomtee at Sultanpore greatly delayed his progress, and compelled him to take a circuitous route by Jounpoor, which city he did not reach till the 9th of April. His column was a strong one; comprising three regiments of infantry, three of Sikh horse, a military train, three batteries of horse-artillery, and seven hundred carts full of warlike stores. On the evening of the 10th, he marched out from Jounpoor, to encounter Gholab Hossein, one of the rebel chuckladars or leaders. The enemy did not stay to fight, but retreated precipitately. They required close watching, however; for while Sir Edward was on the march from Jounpoor to Azimghur, a large rebel force got into his rear, and attempted to re-enter Jounpoor. This caused him to modify his plan, and to disperse the rebels before proceeding to Azimghur. In this he succeeded, but lost the services of Lieutenant Charles Havelock, nephew of the distinguished general. The gallant young officer, at the commencement of the mutiny, had been adjutant of the 12th Bengal native irregular cavalry, and was thrown out of employment by the revolt of that regiment. He then went as a volunteer with his uncle, and was for nine months more or less engaged in the operations in and around Lucknow. When Lugard left the army of Oude, and took command of the column whose operations are here being recorded, young Havelock accompanied him, holding a command in a Goorkha battalion. It was while Lugard was dispersing the rebels near Jounpoor, that the lieutenant was killed by a shot from a hut in an obscure village.

Sir Edward, resuming his march towards Azimghur, reached that city at length on the 15th, somewhat vexed at the numerous delays that had occurred on his journey. On his arrival at the bridge of boats which crossed the small river Tons at that city, he encountered a portion of Koer Singh's main army. They fought well, and with some determination; and it was not without a struggle that he defeated and dispersed them. Mr Venables, the civilian who had gained so high a reputation for courage during the earlier mutinous proceedings in the district, was wounded on this occasion. The East India Company had reason to be proud of its civilians, for the most part, during the troubles; Mr Venables was only one among many who nobly distinguished themselves. After this battle at the bridge, it soon became evident, as in many other instances, that the rebels had been too quick for their pursuers. Koer Singh and the main body of his force were quitting Azimghur on the one side just when Lugard entered it on the other; the fighting was merely with the rear-guard, and all the rest of the insurgents marched off safely. As it was by no means desirable that they should escape to work mischief elsewhere, Sir Edward, on the 16th, sent off Brigadier Douglas in pursuit of them, with the 37th and 84th regiments, some cavalry and artillery. Lugard himself proposed to encamp for a while at Azimghur.

We have now for a time to leave Sir Edward Lugard, and to notice the unsatisfactory result of the operations which he initiated. The town of Arrah was destined to be the scene of another discomfiture of British troops, as mortifying if not as disastrous as that which occurred early in the mutiny, and inflicted by the same hand—Koer Singh. When this indefatigable rebel was driven out of Azimghur, he separated from some of the other chieftains, at a point which he believed would enable him to cross the Ganges into the district of Shahabad, where Arrah would be near at hand. He marched with two thousand sepoys and a host of rabble. Brigadier Douglas pursued him with great rapidity, marching a hundred miles in five days of great heat; he came up with the rebels at Bansdeh, defeated them, and drove them to Beyriah, Koer Singh himself being wounded. On the 21st, a portion of Douglas's force again came up with the enemy while in the act of crossing the Ganges at Seeporeghat in the Ghazeepore district. It appeared that Koer Singh had cleverly outwitted Colonel Cumberlege, who, with two regiments of Madras cavalry, was endeavouring to aid Douglas in crushing him at a particular spot. Koer Singh did not wait to be crushed, but swiftly and silently marched to the Ganges at a spot not guarded by Cumberlege. When Douglas's troops came up, they killed a few of the rebels, and captured two guns, six elephants, and much ammunition and treasure—but the interception had not been prompt enough; for Koer Singh and the greater part of his force had safely crossed to the right bank of the river. The remainder of Douglas's column came up on the evening of this day, quite worn out with their long march, and needing some days' rest. Koer Singh, although beaten first by Lugard and then by Douglas, had baffled them both in reference to a successful flight; and now it was his fortune (though wounded) to baffle a third British officer. The rebels reached Koer Singh's hereditary domain of Jugdispore. The town of Arrah was at that time occupied by 150 men of H.M. 35th foot, 150 of Rattray's Sikhs, and 50 seamen of the Naval Brigade—the whole under Captain Le Grand. This officer, hearing of the approach of the rebels, and knowing that small bodies had often defeated large armies during the course of the war, sallied forth to prevent the march of Koer Singh to Jugdispore, or else to disturb him at that place. He found them posted in a jungle. They were nearly two thousand in number, but dispirited, and without guns. Le Grand's small force, with the two 12-pounder howitzers, encountered the enemy about two miles from Jugdispore, at daylight on the 23d. After an ineffectual firing of the howitzers, a bugle-call threw everything into confusion. Whether Le Grand, fearing to be surrounded, sounded a retreat, or whether some other signal was misinterpreted, it appears certain that his force fell into inextricable confusion; they abandoned guns and elephants, and fled towards Arrah, followed by numbers of the enemy, who shot and cut down many of them. The 35th suffered terribly; two-thirds of their number were either killed or wounded, including Captain Le Grand himself, Lieutenant Massey, and Dr Clarke. This mortifying calamity, in which the unfortunate Le Grand is said to have disobeyed instructions given by the superior officer of the district, gave rise to much bitter controversy. The 35th was one of those regiments of which the colonel was an old man, shattered in health, and not well fitted to head his troops in active service. It was also, in the heat of controversy, brought as a charge against him that he was a martinet in matters of discipline, and kept his soldiers in red cloth and pipe-clayed belts under the tremendous heat of an Indian sun. The charges, in this as in many similar cases, may have been overwrought; but all felt that the 35th had not behaved in such a way as English troops are wont to behave when well commanded—and hence the inference that they were *not* well commanded.

A new series of operations became necessary as a consequence of this disaster near Jugdispore. The news hastened the movements of Brigadier Douglas, who on the 25th crossed the Ganges at Seenaghat, and pushed on the 84th foot and two guns towards Jugdispore. It was, however, not till the month of May that that jungle-haunt of rebels was effectually cleared out. Meanwhile a little had been doing at another spot in the same region. When, after the action at the bridge of Azimghur, Koer Singh's force divided into three, one of these divisions, with several horse-artillery guns, marched towards Ghazeepore. Brigadier Gordon, at Benares, at once ordered two companies of H.M. 54th to proceed to Ghazeepore by hasty marches, half the number being carried on elephants or in ekahs. It was hoped that these troops, coming in aid of small numbers of royal troops, European cavalry, Madras cavalry, and two 6-pounder guns, already at Ghazeepore, would suffice to protect that important city from the rebels; and this hope was realised. Considerably to the northwest, between Goruckpore and the Oude frontier, Colonel Rowcroft maintained a small force, with which from time to time he repelled attacks made by the enemy. On the 17th of April, when at Amorah, his camp was attacked by three thousand rebels; the attack was not effectually resisted without eight hours' hard fighting. The sepoys, almost for the first time in the war, endeavoured to resist a cavalry charge in British fashion, by kneeling in a line with upturned bayonets; but a corps of Bengal yeomanry cavalry made the charge with such impetuosity that the enemy were overthrown and a victory gained.

Such, in brief, was the general character of the operations eastward of Oude. We have next to touch upon those of Sir Hope Grant, in Oude itself.

This gallant general, as colonel of a cavalry regiment, had commenced his share in the war as a subordinate to one or more brigadiers; but he had since proved himself well worthy of the command of a column under his own responsibility. When Sir Colin Campbell parcelled out among his chief officers various duties consequent on the flight of the insurgents from Lucknow, a column or division was made up, to be commanded by Sir Hope Grant, to look after such of the rebels as had taken a northerly direction. His column consisted of H.M. 38th foot, one battalion of the Rifle Brigade, a regiment of Sikhs, H.M. 9th Lancers (Hope Grant's own regiment), a small body of reliable native cavalry, two troops of horse-artillery, and a small siege and mortar train. It was known or believed that the Moulvie of Fyzabad had collected a force near Baree, about thirty miles north of Lucknow; and that the Begum of Oude, with several cart-loads of treasure, had fled for concealment to Bitowlie, the domain of a rebel named Gorbuccus Singh. To what extent Sir Hope Grant would be able to capture, intercept, or defeat the rebels in the service of these leaders, was a problem yet to be solved. He set out from Lucknow on the 11th of April, with Brigadier Horsford as his second in command. In the first three days the troops marched to Baree, on the Khyrabad road; and then was experienced one of the perplexities of the campaign. Every brigadier or divisional general was painfully impressed with the danger of moving in a country where the mass of the population was unfriendly. In many provinces the towns-people and villagers were for the most part disposed, if not to aid the British, at least to hold aloof; but the fact could not be concealed that the Oudians generally were in a rebellious state of feeling, and would gladly have aided to cut off the resources of Sir Colin's lieutenants. It was merely one among many examples, when Sir Hope Grant set out towards the Gogra, in hopes to overtake the Begum and her fleeing forces; his column or field-force was accompanied by no less than 6000 hackeries or vehicles of various kinds, forming a line of nearly twenty miles; and it was essentially necessary, while assuming the offensive in front, that the flanks and rear of this immense train should be protected—a difficult duty in a hostile country. Scarcely had Grant approached near Baree, when the cavalry of the Moulvie's rebel force got into his rear, and attempted to cut off the enormous baggage-train. Sir Hope was too good a general to be taken by surprise; but his rear-guard found enough to do to repel the attack made upon them, and to protect the enormous baggage-train. This done, and some horse-artillery guns captured, Sir Hope Grant resumed his march. Turning eastward from Baree, he marched towards the Gogra, in the hope of intercepting the flight of the Begum of Oude, her paramour Mummoo Khan, and a large force of rebels. On the 15th he reached Mohamedabad, on this route; and on the 17th he halted at Rammuggur for a few days, while a strong reconnoitring party set forth to ascertain if possible the exact position and strength of the rebels. The news obtained was very indefinite, and amounted to little more than this—that the Begum and Mummoo Khan were retreating northward with one large force, and the Moulvie westward with another; but that it would not be very easy to catch either, as the sepoys were celebrated for celerity of movement during a retreat. Sir Hope Grant dispersed various bodies of rebels, and disturbed the plans of the Begum and the Moulvie; but he returned to Lucknow towards the close of the month without having caught either of those wily personages, and with many of his troops laid prostrate by the heat of the sun.

Ghazeepore.

We turn now towards the west or northwest, on the Rohilcund side of Oude. It has already been mentioned, that after the fall of Lucknow, many of the rebel leaders fled to Rohilcund, with the hope of making a bold stand at Bareilly, Shahjehanpoor, Moradabad, and other towns in that province. Khan Bahadoor Khan, the self-appointed chief of Bareilly, was nominally the head of the whole confederacy in this region; but it depended on the chapter of accidents how long this leadership would continue. At any rate, Sir Colin Campbell saw that he could not allow this nest of rebels to remain untouched; Bareilly must be conquered, as Delhi and Lucknow had been. The veteran commander probably mourned in secret the necessity for sending his gallant troops on a long march, into a new field of action, with a sun blazing on them like a ball of fire; but seeing the necessity, he commanded, and they obeyed. His plan of strategy comprised a twofold line of action—an advance of one column northwestward from Lucknow; and an advance of another southeastward from Roorkee; the two columns to assist in clearing the border districts of Rohilcund, and then to meet at Bareilly, the chief city of the province. We will notice first the operations of the force on the north-east border.

Brigadier Jones, with the Roorkee field-force, commenced operations in the eastern part of Rohilcund, about the middle of April. His force consisted of H.M. 60th Rifles, the 1st Sikh infantry, Coke's Rifles, the 17th Punjaub infantry, the Moultan Horse, with detachments of artillery and engineers. The force numbered three thousand good troops in all, and was strengthened by eight heavy and six light guns. Major (now Brigadier) Coke, whose Punjaub riflemen had gained for themselves so high a reputation, commanded the infantry portion of Jones's column. The column marched from Roorkee on the 15th, and made arrangements for crossing to the left bank of the Ganges as soon as possible. A large number of the enemy having intrenched themselves at Nagul, about sixteen miles below Hurdwar on the left bank, Jones made his dispositions accordingly. He determined to send his heavy guns and baggage to the ghat opposite Nagul; while his main body should cross at Hurdwar, march down the river on the other side, and take the intrenchment in flank. This plan was completely carried out by the evening of the 17th—Nagul being taken, the enemy driven away with great loss, and the whole column safely encamped on that side of the Ganges which would afford easier access to the hot-bed of the rebels at Bareilly. Four days afterwards, Brigadier Jones encountered the Daranuggur insurgent force near Nageena or Nuggeena, on the banks of a canal. The insurgents maintained a fire for a time from nine guns; but Jones speedily attacked them with his cavalry, outflanked them, charged, captured the guns and six elephants, and put the enemy speedily to flight, after very considerable loss. Jones's killed and wounded were few in number; but he had to regret the loss of Lieutenant Gostling, who was shot through the heart while heading some of the troops. The brigadier resumed his march. Luckily for British interests, Mooradabad was not so deeply steeped in rebellion as Bareilly; and the Rajah of Rampore, not far distant, was faithful so far as his small power would extend. The benefit of this state of affairs was felt at the time now under notice. Feroze Shah, one of the Shahzadas or princes of Delhi in league with the Bareilly mutineers, marched on the 21st of April towards Mooradabad, to demand money and supplies. He was refused; and much fighting and pillage resulted as consequences. Brigadier Jones's column came up opportunely; he entered Mooradabad on the 26th, checked the plundering, drove out the rebels, captured many insurgent chieftains, and re-established the confidence of the townspeople. At the end of the month, Jones was still in Mooradabad or its neighbourhood, ready for co-operation in May with another column which we must now notice.

While Jones had been thus occupied, Bareilly and the rebels were threatened on the other side by the Rohilcund field-force. During the first two or three weeks after the conquest of Lucknow, Sir Colin Campbell was engaged in various plans which did not permit of the immediate dispatch of troops to Rohilcund; but on the 7th of April several regiments began to assemble at the Moosa Bagh, to form a small special army for service in that province. Why they were not despatched earlier, was one of the many problems which the commander-in-chief kept to himself. On the 9th this minor army, the Rohilcund field-force, set out, with General Walpole as its commander, and Brigadier Adrian Hope at the head of the infantry. The distance from Lucknow to Bareilly, about fifteen marches, was through a region so ill provided with roads that few or no night-marches could be made; it was necessary to have the aid of daylight to avoid plunging into unforeseen difficulties and dangers. As a consequence, the troops would be exposed to the heat of an Indian sun during their journey, and had to look forward to many trials on that account. Not the least among the numerous perplexities that arose out of the defective state of the roads, was the difficulty of dragging the guns which necessarily accompanied such a force; cavalry and infantry were, in all such cases, inevitably delayed by the necessity of waiting until the ponderous pieces of ordnance could arrive.*

Walpole's field-force, resting at night under shady groves, it was hoped might reach Bareilly about the 24th of the month; and this was the more to be desired, seeing that Rohilcund, from its position in relation to numerous rivers, becomes almost impassable as soon as the rains set in—about the end of May or the beginning of June. Marching onward in accordance with the plan laid down, Walpole came on the 14th of April to one of the

* It may here be remarked that the difficulty of moving heavy ordnance over the bad roads and roadless tracts of India, painfully felt by the artillery officers engaged in the war, suggested to the East India Company an inquiry into the possibility of employing locomotives for such a purpose. A machine, called 'Boydell's Traction Engine,' patented some time before in England, was tested with a view to ascertain the degree of its availability for this purpose. The peculiarity of this engine was, that it was a locomotive *carrying its own railway*. Six flat boards were ranged round each of the great wheels in such a way that each board came in succession *under* the wheel, and formed, for a few feet, a flat plankroad or tramway for the wheel to roll upon. It was supposed that the vehicle would move much more easily by this contrivance, than if the narrow periphery of the wheel ran upon soft mud or irregular pebbles and gravel. The motion of the wheel placed each plank down at its proper time and place, and lifted it up again, in such a way that there was always one of the boards flat on the ground, beneath the wheel. Colonel Sir Frederick Abbott and Colonel Sir Proby Cautley, on the part of the directors, tested this machine at Woolwich—where it drew forty tons of ordnance along a common road, uphill as well as upon the level. Another road-locomotive, by Messrs Napier, was tested for a similar purpose. The results were of good augury for the future; but the machines were not perfected early enough to be made applicable for the wars of the mutiny.

many forts which have so often been mentioned in connection with the affairs of Oude. The name of the place, situated about fifty miles from Lucknow, and ten from the Ganges, was variously spelled Rhodamow, Roodhamow, Roer, and Roowah; but whatever the spelling, the fort became associated in the minds of the British troops with more angry complainings than any other connected with the war; since it was the scene of a mortifying repulse which better generalship might have avoided, and which was accompanied by the death of a very favourite officer. Rhodamow was a small fort or group of houses enclosed by a high mud-wall, loopholed for musketry, provided with irregular bastions at the angles, and having two gates. It was a petty place, in relation to the largeness of the force about to attack it—nearly six thousand men. While marching through the jungle towards Rohilcund, Walpole heard that fifteen hundred insurgents had thrown themselves into this fort of Rhodamow; but the number proved to be much smaller. He attacked it with infantry without previously using his artillery, and without (as it would appear) a sufficient reconnaissance. He sent on the 42d Highlanders and the 4th Punjaub infantry to take the fort; but no sooner did the troops approach it than they were received by so fierce and unexpected a fire of musketry, from a concealed enemy, that not only was the advance checked, but the gallant Brigadier Adrian Hope was killed at the head of his Highlanders. The troops could not immediately and effectually reply to this fire, for their opponents were hidden behind the loopholed wall. Everything seems to have been thrown into confusion by this first fatal mistake; the supports were sent up too late, or to the wrong place; and the exasperated troops were forced to retire, amid yells of triumph from the enemy. The heavy guns were then brought to do that which they ought to have done at first; they began to breach the wall, but the enemy quietly evacuated the fort during the night, with scarcely any loss. Besides Adrian Hope, several other officers were either killed or wounded, and nearly a hundred rank and file. During this mortifying disaster, in which the Highlanders were particularly unfortunate in the loss of officers, Quarter-master Sergeant Simpson, of the 42d, displayed that daring spirit of gallantry which so endears a soldier to his companions. When the infantry had been recalled from the attack, Simpson heard that two officers of his regiment had been left behind, dead or wounded in the ditch outside the wall. He rushed out, seized the body of Captain Bramley, and brought it back amid a torrent of musketry; setting forth again, he brought in the body of Captain Douglas in a similar way, and he did not cease until seven had been thus brought away—to be recovered if only wounded, to be decently interred if dead. It was a day, however, the memory of which could not be sweetened by any such displays of gallantry, or by many subsequent victories; the men of the two Highland regiments felt as if a deep personal injury had been inflicted on them by the commander of the column. Sir Colin Campbell, when the news of this untoward event reached him, paid a marked compliment to Adrian Hope in his dispatch. 'The death of this most distinguished and gallant officer causes the deepest grief to the commander-in-chief. Still young in years, he had risen to high command; and by his undaunted courage, combined as it was with extreme kindness and charm of manner, had secured the confidence of his brigade in no ordinary degree.' Viscount Canning, in a like spirit, officially notified that 'no more mournful duty has fallen upon the governor-general in the course of the present contest than that of recording the premature death of this distinguished young commander.'

General Walpole pursued his march, and had a successful encounter on the 22d with a large body of the enemy at Sirsa. His cavalry and artillery attacked them so vigorously as to capture their guns and camp, and to drive them over the Ramgunga in such haste as to leave them no time for destroying the bridge of boats at that place. This achievement was fortunate, for it enabled Walpole on the 23d to transport his heavy guns quickly and safely over the Ramgunga at Allygunje. A few days after this, he was joined by the commander-in-chief, whose movements we must next notice.

It was immediately after Sir Colin Campbell's return from his interview with the governor-general at Allahabad, that he withdrew from Lucknow all the remaining troops, except those destined for the defence of that important city, and for the re-establishment of British influence in Oude. He formed an expeditionary army, which he headed himself—or rather, the army set forth from Lucknow to Cawnpore, and the commander-in-chief joined it at the last-named place on the 17th of April. The result of the conference at Allahabad had been, a determination to march up the Doab to Furruckabad, and to attack the Rohilcund rebels on a side where neither Jones nor Walpole could well reach them. The heat was great, the rivers were rising, and the rains were coming in a few weeks; and it became now a question whether the movements from Lucknow as a centre had or had not been too long delayed. Sir Colin with his column—for, being a mere remnant, it was too small a force to designate an army—took their departure from Cawnpore on the 18th, leaving that city in the hands of a small but (at present) sufficient body of troops. On the 19th he advanced to Kiliaupore, on the 20th to Poorah, and on the 21st to Urrowl—marching during early morn, and encamping in the hotter hours of the day. The day's work commenced, indeed, so early as one o'clock in the morning; when the elephants and camels began to be loaded with their burdens, the equipage and tents packed up, and the marching arrangements completed. Between two or three o'clock, all being in readiness, away went infantry, cavalry, artillery, engineers, commissariat, and a countless host of natives, horses, camels, elephants, bullocks, and vehicles—covering an area of which the real soldiers occupied but a very small part. They marched or rode till about six o'clock; when all prepared for breakfast, and for a hot day during which little active exertion was possible without imminent danger of *coup de soleil*. Sir Colin's train of munition and supplies was enormous; for, in addition to the usual baggage of an army, he had to take large commissariat supplies with him. The villagers held aloof in a manner not usual in the earlier stages of the mutiny, and in other parts of India; they did not come forward to engage in a traffic which would certainly have been profitable to them, in selling provisions to the army. Whether this arose from inability or disinclination, was a matter for controversy; but the fact itself occasioned embarrassment and uneasiness to a commander who had to drag with his army a huge train of animals and vehicles filled with food. The enormous number of natives, too, that accompanied the force, with their wives and families, exerted its usual cumbrous effect on the movements of the troops; so that the fighting-men themselves bore but a minute fractional ratio to the living and dead accompaniments of the column. It is useless to complain of this. An army of five thousand, or any other number, of British troops *must* have a large train of native attendants, to contend against the peculiarities of Indian climate and Indian customs. Mr Russell, marching with this portion of the late 'Army of Oude,' said: 'If the people we see around us, who are ten or twelve to one as compared with us in this camp, were—not to arm and cut our throats, or poison us, or anything of that kind—but simply bid us a silent good-bye this night, and leave us, India would be lost to us in a day. It requires only that, and all the power of England could not hold the eastern empire. We could not even strike our tents without these men to-morrow. We are dependent on them—even the common soldier is—for the water we drink and the meals we eat, for our transport, for all but the air we breathe; and the latter, it must be admitted, is not improved by them sometimes. The moment that such a thing becomes possible as a popular desertion, through patriotic or any other motives, from the service of the state, it becomes impossible to hold India except upon sufferance. It is the rupee, self-interest, and the necessities of a population trained to follow camps, which afford guarantees against such a secession—unlikely enough indeed in any nation, and scarcely possible in any war. . . . We are, in fact, waging war against Hindoos and Mussulmans by the aid and with the consent of other Hindoos and Mussulmans, just as Alexander was able to beat Porus by the aid of his Indian allies; and no European or other state can ever rule in India without the co-operation and assistance of a large proportion of the races which inhabit the vast peninsula.'

Sir Colin marched on the 22d to Meerun-ke-serai, near the ruins of the ancient city of Canouje; on the 23d to Gosaigunje; and on the 24th to Kamalgunje—approaching each day nearer to Furruckabad. Every day's camping-ground was selected near the Ganges, both for the sake of salubrity, and to check if possible the passage of rebel bands over the river from Oude into the Doab. On the 25th the column reached Furruckabad, or rather the adjacent English station of Futteghur. General Penny came from a neighbouring district to confer with the commander-in-chief on matters connected with the Rohilcund campaign, and then returned to the column or brigade which he commanded. Futteghur had regained a part of its former importance, as the place where most of the artillery-carriages and sepoy-clothing were made, and where vast quantities of timber and cloth had fallen as spoil to the enemy.

The sojourn at Futteghur was very brief. The electric telegraph had been busy transmitting information to and from Allahabad; and as Sir Colin's plans were already made, he lost no time in putting them in execution. The main plan comprised four movements—Campbell from Futteghur, Walpole from Lucknow, Jones from Roorkee, and Penny from Puttealee; all intended to hem the rebels into the middle of Rohilcund, and there crush them. The marches of Walpole and Jones have already been noticed; Penny was to march his column towards Meerunpore Muttra, between Shahjehanpoor and Bareilly, after crossing the Ganges near Nudowlee; while the commander-in-chief was to enter Rohilcund directly from Futteghur. In the middle of the night between the 26th and 27th his column, elephants and guns and all, crossed the Ganges by the bridge of boats, and entered the province which was to be a scene of hostilities. After a few hours the column reached the river Ramgunga, which it crossed by the bridge of boats fortunately secured by Walpole as the fruit of his victory at Allygunje; and soon afterwards the commander-in-chief effected a junction with Walpole, at Tingree near the Ramgunga. No very long time for repose was allowed; stern work was to be done, and the sooner commenced, the less would it be checked by heat and prohibited by rains. A march of a few hours brought the now united columns to Jelalabad—one of many places of that name in India. It was a fort which had lately been occupied by a small body of matchlockmen, who had precipitately abandoned it when news of Sir Colin's approach reached them. A small village lay near, and was governed by the fort. The Moulvie of Fyzabad was believed to have intended to make a stand at this place, but to have abandoned it for a larger stronghold at Shahjehanpoor. On the 29th, a further approach was made to Kanth. Each day was pretty well like that which preceded it—the same early marching, camping, and resting, and the same struggle with the camp-followers, who, however closely watched, pertinaciously plundered the villages through or near which they passed—thereby terrifying and exasperating all villagers alike, whether friendly or unfriendly to the British. This system of plunder by the camp-followers was one of the greatest troubles to which the generals of the several columns were exposed; severe punishments were threatened, but all in vain.

It was on the last day of the month that Sir Colin Campbell and General Walpole arrived at Shahjehanpoor; and then it was to learn that the wily and active Moulvie had again outmanœuvred them. The plan had been to draw a cordon more and more closely round the rebels at Shahjehanpoor and Bareilly, and thus to catch them as in a trap. But the Moulvie would not enter the trap. He held Shahjehanpoor, with a considerable force of men and guns, as long as he deemed it safe, and then escaped just at the right moment. It was well to regain Shahjehanpoor, after that place had been eleven months in the hands of rebels; but it was vexing to learn that the Moulvie had retreated towards Oude—the very province where his presence was least desired by the British. Nena Sahib, it was also ascertained, had quitted Shahjehanpoor a few days earlier, and just before leaving, had ordered the government buildings to be destroyed, in order that the British troops might find no shelter when they arrived. This cowardly, ruthless, but active and inventive chieftain succeeded in his aim in this matter; there were few roofed buildings left, and the encampment had to be effected under a tope of trees, with earthen intrenchments thrown up around.

It is evident, from this summary of Rohilcund affairs, that the operations against the rebels in that province did not advance far during the month of April, as concerns any effective crushing of the rebellion. The insurgents were beaten wherever met with; but their ubiquity and vitality greatly puzzled Sir Colin and his brigadier; and it remained to be seen how far the month of May would witness the re-establishment of British authority in Rohilcund and Oude. Some of the columns and field-forces had penetrated from the east and south as far as Shahjehanpoor, others from the west and northwest as far as Mooradabad; but Bareilly, the chief city in Rohilcund, had not been reached by any of them at the end of April.

Few events caused more regret in the army at this period than the death of Captain Sir William Peel, the gallant seaman who had earned so high a reputation as commander of the Naval Brigade. After his wound, received at Lucknow, he was carried in a doolie or litter to Cawnpore; and when at that station he gradually became able to walk about slowly by the aid of a stick. He soon, however, exhibited symptoms of small-pox, which, acting on a system at once ardent and debilitated, proved fatal. He died at Cawnpore after Sir Colin Campbell's force had departed from that place towards Futteghur; and thus the Queen and the country lost the services of an eminent son of an eminent statesman. Every one felt the justice of the special compliment paid to this gallant naval officer by the governor-general, in the official order issued immediately on the receipt of the news of Peel's death.* Throughout the Crimean, Persian, and Indian wars, the British navy had been engaged in less fighting than many of its ardent members wished; and it was therefore all the more incumbent on the authorities to notice the exertions of naval brigades when on shore.

Throughout the extent of the Upper Doab, the British officers found much difficulty in maintaining a fair stand against the rebels. Not that there were large bodies of trained sepoys in the field, as in the regions just described, and in Central India; but there were numerous chieftains, each at the head of a small band of followers, ready to harass any spot not protected by English troops. Brigadier Penny, in command of a field-force organised at Delhi, was watching the district between that city and the Ganges—ready to put down insurgents wherever he could encounter them, and hoping to assist the commander-in-chief in Rohilcund. Another column, under Brigadier Seaton, controlled the region around Futteghur before Sir Colin reached that place; and he, like Penny, Jones, Walpole, Hope Grant, Lugard, and all the other commanders of sections of the army, found an active watchfulness of the enemy necessary. One among Seaton's engagements in the month of April may be briefly noticed. On the 6th, when evening had darkened into night, he marched from Futteghur to attack a body of rebels concerning whom he had received information. He took with him about 1400 men—comprising 600 of H.M. 82d under Colonel Hall, 400 Sikhs under Captain Stafford, 150 cavalry under Lieutenant St John, and 200 of the Futteghur mounted-police battalion under Lieutenant de Kantzow—together with five guns under Major Smith. After marching all night, Seaton came up with the enemy at seven in the morning, at a place called Kankur. The enemy's force was very large, though not well organised, and included nearly a thousand troopers well mounted and armed. After an artillery-fire on both sides, and a sharp fire from Enfield rifles,

* '*Allahabad, April 30.*—It is the melancholy duty of the Right Honourable the Governor-general to announce the death of that most distinguished officer, Captain Sir William Peel, K.C.B., late in command of her Majesty's ship *Shannon*, and of the Naval Brigade in the Northwest Provinces.

'Sir William Peel died at Cawnpore, on the 27th instant, of small-pox. He had been wounded at the commencement of the last advance upon Lucknow, but had nearly recovered from the wound, and was on his way to Calcutta, when struck by the disease which has brought his honourable career to an early close.

'Sir William Peel's services in the field during the last seven months are well known in India and in England. But it is not so well known how great the value of his presence and example has been wherever during this eventful period his duty has led him.

'The loss of his daring but thoughtful courage, joined with eminent abilities, is a very heavy one to his country; but it is not more to be deplored than the loss of that influence which his earnest character, admirable temper, and gentle kindly bearing exercised over all within his reach—an influence which was exerted unceasingly for the public good, and of which the governor-general believes that it may with truth be said that there is not a man of any rank or profession who, having been associated with Sir William Peel in these times of anxiety and danger, has not felt and acknowledged it.'

the 82d rushed forward, entered the village, and worked terrible execution. The rebels fled, abandoning their camp, ammunition, and stores; together with papers and correspondence which threw light on some of the hitherto obscure proceedings of the mutineers. The rebel Rajah of Minpooree was the chief leader of the insurgents, and with him were Ismael Khan and Mohson Ali Khan.

The Minpooree district was much troubled by this rebellious rajah; but as Futteghur on the one side, and Agra on the other, were now in English hands, the rebels were more readily kept in subjection. Agra itself was safe, and so was the main line of road thence through Muttra to Delhi.

One of the few pleasant scenes of the month, at Delhi, was the awarding of honour and profit to a native who had befriended Europeans in the hour of greatest need. Ten months before, when mutiny was still new and terrible, the native troops at Bhurtpore rose in revolt, and compelled the Europeans in the neighbourhood to flee for their lives. The poor fugitives, thirty-two in number—chiefly women and children—roamed from place to place, uncertain where they might sleep in peace. On one day they arrived at the village of Mahonah. Here they met with one Hidayut Ali, a ressaldar (troop-captain), of a regiment of irregular cavalry which had mutinied at Mozuffernugger; he was on furlough or leave of absence at his native village, and did not join his mutinous companions. He received the fugitives with kindness and courtesy, fed them liberally, gave them a comfortable house, renewed their toil-worn garments, posted village sentries to give notice of the approach of any mutineers, disregarded a rebuke sent to him by the insurgents at Delhi, formed the villagers into an escort, and finally placed the thirty-two fugitives in a position which enabled them safely to reach Agra. This noble conduct was not forgotten. In April the commissioner held a grand durbar at Delhi, made a complimentary speech to Hidayut Ali, presented him with a sword valued at a thousand rupees, and announced that the government intended to bestow upon him the jaghire or revenues of his native village.

Good-fortune continued to mark the wide and important region of the Punjaub, in the absence of any of those great assemblages of rebels which so distracted the provinces further to the southeast. Nevertheless Sir John Lawrence found a demand on him for unceasing watchfulness. The longer the struggle continued in Hindostan and Central India, the more danger was there that the Punjaubees, imbibing an idea that the British were weak, would encourage a hope of regaining national independence. There was also a grave question involved in the constitution of the native army. When the troubles began in the month of May, and when Canning was beset with so many difficulties in his attempt to send up troops from Calcutta, John Lawrence came to the rescue in a manner deserving the lasting gratitude of all concerned in the maintenance of British rule in India. He felt a trusty reliance that the inhabitants of the Punjaub, governed as he (aided by Montgomery, Cotton, Edwardes, and other energetic men) had governed them, would remain faithful, and would be willing to accept active service as soldiers in British pay. His trust was well founded. He sent to Delhi those troops, without which the conquest of the city could not have been effected; and he continued to raise regiment after regiment of Sikhs and Punjaubees—equipping, drilling, and paying a number so large as to constitute in itself a powerful army. But there would necessarily be a limit to this process. The Sikhs were faithful so far; but what if they should begin to feel their power, and turn to a national object the arms which had been given to them to fight in the British cause? Not many years had elapsed since they had fought fiercely at Moultan and Lahore, Sobraon and Chillianwalla, Moodkee and Ferozshah, against those very English whom they were now defending; and it was at least possible, if not probable, that dreams of re-conquest might occupy their thoughts. Sir John Lawrence brought to an end his further raising of regiments; and there can be little doubt that the governor-general and the commander-in-chief appreciated the motives by which he had been influenced. In political affairs the Punjaub was very active; for not only did Lawrence become chief authority over a larger region than before, but many of his assistants were taken away from him. When Sir James Outram went to Calcutta as a member of the supreme council, Mr Montgomery was appointed chief-commissioner of Oude, and took with him many of the most experienced civilians from Lahore to Lucknow. This necessitated great changes in the *personnel* of the Punjaub civil service, the commissionerships and sub-commissionerships of districts, &c.

Peshawur, the most remote portion of Northwest India, was throughout the period of the Revolt more troubled by marauding mountaineers than by revolted sepoys. Very few Hindoos inhabited that region; the population was mostly Mussulman, especially among the hills; and these followers of Islam had but little sympathy with those in Hindostan Proper. The disturbances, such as they were, were of local character. In April, it became necessary to visit with some severity certain tribes which throughout the winter had been engaged in rebellion and rapine. General Cotton and Colonel Edwardes, two of the most trusted officers in the Indian army, collected a column at Nowsherah for service against the hillmen; and at the close of the month there were nearly four thousand men in rendezvous, ready for service. It comprised detachments of H.M. 81st and 98th foot; of the 8th, 9th, and 18th Punjaub infantry; of other native infantry; of the 7th and 18th irregular cavalry; of the Guide cavalry; and of various artillery and engineer corps. On the 28th of the month, Cotton was at a place among the hills called Mungultana, a stronghold of some of the frontier fanatics. The place was easily taken, and the insurgents dispersed; as they were at Jelemkhana, Sitana, and other places, soon afterwards; but it was hard work for the troops, over very bad roadless tracks in hot weather.

It was a strange but hopeful sign that, amid all the sanguinary proceedings in India—the ruthless barbarities of some among the sepoys and rebels, and the military retributions wrought by the British—amid all this, the peaceful, civilising agency of railways was steadily though slowly advancing. A recent chapter shewed that the grand trunk-railway was extended into the Doab, the very hot-bed of insurrection, during the month of March: the engineers, mechanics, and labourers having been accustomed to resume their operations as soon as the insurgents were driven away from any spot where the works were in progress. In the Madras and Bombay presidencies, little affected by rebellion, various railways were gradually advancing; and now, in the month of

Fort of Peshawur.

April, the province of Sinde was to have its heyday of railway rejoicing. In an earlier portion of the volume,* a brief account was given of the schemes, present and prospective, for supplying India with railways. Among those was one for a line, 120 miles in length, from Kurachee to Hydrabad in Sinde: expected, if no difficulties intervened, to be finished towards the close of 1859. This was to be one link in a vast and extensive chain, if the hopes of its projectors were ever realised. Kurachee is not at the mouth of the Indus; but it has an excellent harbour, in which large merchantmen can cast anchor; and engineers were enabled to shew that a little over one hundred miles of railway would connect this port with the Indus at a point above the delta of that river, and just where Hydrabad, the chief city of Sinde, is situated. Such a railway would, in fact, bear a remarkably close analogy to that in Egypt, from Alexandria to Cairo—each connecting a seaport with a capital, and avoiding delta navigation much impeded by shallows and shifting sands. From Hydrabad there are 570 miles of Indus available for river-steaming up to Moultan, in the Punjaub. From that city a railway would be planned through Lahore to Umritsir, where a junction would be formed with the grand trunk-line, and thus Kurachee connected with Calcutta by rapid means of travel—a great scheme, worthy of the age and the country. It could, however, only have small beginnings. On the 29th of April, the first sod of the 'Sinde Railway' was turned at Kurachee. It would be well if all rejoicings were based on such rational grounds as those which marked that day in the young Alexandria of Western India. Mr Frere,

* Chap. vii., Notes, p. 119.

commissioner of Sinde, presided over the ceremonies. All was gaiety. The 51st regiment lent its aid in military pomp; and all the notabilities of the place—political, military, naval, clerical, commercial, and engineering—were gathered together. And not only so; but the lookers-on comprised many of those who well marvelled what a railway could be, and how a carriage could move without visible means of draught or propulsion—Parsees, Hindoos, Beloochees, Sindians, Afghans, Punjaubees—all were there, with their picturesque garments, and their little less picturesque native vehicles. How the officiating dignitary turned the sod and wheeled the barrow; how the band played and the people cheered; how the chief personages celebrated the event by a dinner; how, at that dinner, a triumphant specimen of confectionary was displayed, comprising sweetmeat Kurachees, Calcuttas, rivers, mosques, ghats, temples, wheelbarrows, pick-axes, rails, locomotives, bridges, tunnels—need not be told: they belong to one remarkable aspect of modern European and American society, which becomes doubly interesting when exhibited among the less active, more sensuous orientals.

We now turn to that stormy, unsettled region southwest of the Jumna, comprising Bundelcund, Central India, and Rajpootana.

Probably no commander had a series of more uninterrupted successes during the wars of the mutiny than Sir Hugh Rose. Looking neither to Calcutta nor to the Punjaub, for aid, but relying on the resources of the Bombay presidency, he gradually accumulated a force for service in Central India which defeated the rebels wherever they were met with. We have seen that, in January, Sir Hugh was busily engaged in defeating and dispersing rebels at Ratgurh, and in various parts of the district between Bhopal and Saugor. We find him in February relieving the British garrison which had for so many months been shut up within the fort of the last-named city, and then clearing a vast range of country in the direction of Jhansi. Lastly, we have seen how, after subduing a district in which rebellious Mahrattas were very numerous, he approached nearer and nearer to Jhansi during the early weeks of March; that he arrived within a short distance of that city on the 21st of that month, with the second brigade of the Central India field-force; that the rebels fortified the walls of the town, and shut themselves up within the town and fort; that the mutinied sepoys and rebel Bundelas in the place were computed at eleven or twelve thousand; that the Ranee of Jhansi had left her palace to seek greater safety in the fort; that Rose's first brigade joined him on the 25th; and that he then commenced the siege in a determined manner. From this point, the narrative of Sir Hugh's operations may be carried into the following month.

Before the first week in April had terminated, this distinguished general had gained very considerable advantages over the enemy. At daybreak on the first of the month, his force encountered an army of the enemy outside the walls of Jhansi, and completely defeated them. The rebels were commanded by a Mahratta chieftain, Tanteea Topee, a relative of Nena Sahib, who had marched thither in the hope of being able to relieve his brother rebels shut up within the beleaguered city. Sir Hugh divided his force into two parts—one to continue the siege, and the other to meet Tanteea Topee in the field. The rebels, including among their number two regiments of the traitorous Gwalior Contingent, fought desperately; but Rose succeeded in turning their left flank with artillery and cavalry, breaking up their array, and putting them to flight. It was a severe contest, for the rebels defended themselves individually to the last, even when their order of battle was broken. Rose pursued them to the river Betwah, and captured all their guns and ammunition. During the pursuit, they endeavoured to check him by setting the jungle on fire; but his cavalry and horse-artillery, nothing daunted, galloped through the flames, and kept close at the heels of the fugitives. The whole line of retreat became strewed with dead bodies; and it was estimated that the day's sanguinary work had cost the enemy not less than fifteen hundred men.

This battle was followed by a result more favourable than Sir Hugh had ventured to hope. The ranee, shut up within Jhansi, well knew that Tanteea Topee was hastening to her assistance; for there was everywhere an intercommunication between the insurgents too close for the British to baffle. She knew of his approach, and hoped that he would be able to defeat and drive away the besiegers; but the battle of the Betwah dismayed her, and the result was very favourable to the British. In arranging for the siege, Sir Hugh divided his infantry into four detachments, two on the right and two on the left. H.M. 86th, and the 25th Bombay infantry, soon gained the walls, some by breach and others by escalade. Lieutenant Dartnell of the 86th, who was foremost in the assault, narrowly escaped being cut to pieces directly he entered the place. These two regiments were on the left attack. The attack on the right was less successful, owing to the use of defective ladders; the troops were for some time exposed to a murderous fire; but at length they entered the place, and joined their companions near the ranee's palace. A discovery was now made. The ranee had evacuated the place during the night, with such of her troops as could break through the cordon which Rose endeavoured to draw round Jhansi. In the endeavour of the garrison to escape, the slaughter was terrible; insomuch that, during the storming of the fort and the pursuit of the garrison, more than three thousand of the rebels were laid low, besides the fifteen hundred during the battle. Much of this slaughter was within the city itself; for the towns-people were believed to have favoured the rebels, and the soldiers took severe vengeance before their officers could check the bloodshed. All this stern fighting could not be carried on without loss on the part of the British. Sir Hugh had to lament the fall of Lieutenant-colonel Turnbull, Captain Sinclair, Lieutenants Meicklejohn and Park, and Dr Stack, besides a number of non-commissioned officers and privates. The evacuation of the place in so sudden a way greatly lessened his chance of loss, for its defence might have been long continued. 'Jhansi,' he said in his telegraphic dispatch, 'is not a fort, but its strength makes it a fortress; it could not have been breached; it could only have been taken by mining and blowing up one bastion after another.'

After this signal defeat of the rebels at Jhansi, the victorious army of Sir Hugh gradually prepared to move towards Calpee, a town on the Jumna, on the line of road from Jhansi to Cawnpore. Symptoms appeared to shew that a struggle would take place at this spot. Two rebel leaders made renewed exertions to regain lost ground in that region. The chief of these was Tantcea Topee, lately defeated at Jhansi; he had with him two mutinied infantry regiments, seven hundred cavalry, a large following of Ghazees or fanatics, and twelve guns. The other was Ram Rao Gobind, who had the command of three thousand rabble and four guns. These two leaders resolved to act on some common plan; and Sir Hugh Rose equally resolved to defeat them. Nevertheless this gallant officer had much need for careful planning long after he was master of Jhansi. He had a large number of sick and wounded, whose safety it would be necessary to provide for; and the roads around that city were still infested with remnants of the Kotah rebels and the Chanderee garrison. He himself remained at Jhansi until such time as he could resume his march without danger to those left behind; but he gave active employment to portions of his force. About the middle of the month he sent Major Orr with a column from Jhansi across the Betwah to Mhow, to clear that part of the country of rebels, and afterwards to join Rose and the main body of the force on the road to Calpee; the major had many small encounters with the rajahs of Bampore and Shagurh, and with detached parties of rebels. Some days afterwards, on the 21st, Sir Hugh despatched Major Gall, with detachments of cavalry and artillery, to a point on the Calpee road, to watch the enemy and aid Major Orr if necessary. Gall, besides other minor engagements, captured a fort belonging to the Rajah of Sumpter; the rebels in it proved to be disguised mutineers of the 12th Bengal native infantry, who fought desperately until all were killed. Sir Hugh, with his first brigade and head-quarters, did not take his departure from Jhansi until the 25th. He marched ten miles that day to Boregaum, on the Calpee road, and resumed his progress on subsequent days. His second brigade was soon to follow him—with the exception of detachments of the 3d Bombay Europeans, the 24th Bombay native infantry, and artillery, left under the charge of Colonel Liddell to protect Jhansi and the sick and wounded. Rumours reached Sir Hugh that four of the rebel leaders—the Ranee of Jhansi, Tantcea Topee, the Rajah of Shagurh, and the Rajah of Bampore—with seven thousand men and four guns, intended if possible to intercept him, and prevent his march to Calpee. To what result all these manœuvres on both sides led, was left to the month of May to determine.

While these operations were going on in and near the Jhansi district, General Whitlock, with a column of Madras troops, was engaged a little further eastward, in a district of Bundelcund having Banda for its chief town. He was frequently in contact with large or small bodies of rebels. One of these struggles took place on the 19th of April, when he encountered a force of seven thousand insurgents headed by the Nawab of Banda. Whitlock defeated the Nawab, captured Banda, killed five hundred of the enemy, and took several guns. After this victory, he gradually worked his way towards Calpee, to aid in Rose's operations.

The city of Saugor remained in a somewhat peculiar condition during the spring months—secure itself, but surrounded by a disturbed district. The European residents were living in cantonments, sufficiently protected by troops left there by General Whitlock after he relieved the place early in February. These troops were neither stationary nor idle; the vicinity was swarming with rebels and malcontents, whom it was necessary to check by frequent pursuit and defeat. Those two exceptions to the generally mutinous condition of the Bengal native army, the 31st and 42d regiments, still remained in and near Saugor—or such portions of them as had not become tainted by insubordination. Divided into small detachments, they assisted the European and Madras troops in keeping open the line of communication between Saugor and the district marked by the victorious operations of Sir Hugh Rose.

Turning to the Mahratta and Rajpootana states, we find that, on the 2d of April, a large body of rebels, many thousands in number, with ten guns, crossed the Parbuttee river at Copoind into Scindia's Gwalior territory. They were fleeing from Kotah, where a British force had severely handled them. Scindia still remained true to his alliance. Many of his officers, each with a small force, opposed the rebels at different points, drove them back across the river, and overturned many of their guns and wagons in the stream. The rebels, accompanied by large numbers of women and children, made their way by other routes towards Bundelcund.

Kotah, just mentioned, was closely connected with the insurgent and military operations in Rajpootana. It will be remembered * that in the month of March General Roberts, commanding the Rajpootana field-force, marched from Nuseerabad

* Chap. xxvi., p. 441.

towards Kotah, accompanied by Richard Lawrence as political representative; that many difficulties had to be surmounted on the march; that Kotah was reached on the 22d; and that Roberts captured that place just before the end of the month, defeating a large body of rebels, and obtaining possession of an extensive store of ordnance and ammunition. After this victory, Roberts remained a long time at Kotah. Many other places would have welcomed his appearance; but there were doubts how far Kotah could safely be left, seeing that the neighbourhood was in a very disaffected state. The Kotah rebels, on the other hand, were greatly disconcerted at the news of the fall of Jhansi, which interfered with their plans and hopes. They had been camping for a while at Kularus, on the road from Gwalior to Bombay, but began now to move off towards the south. Captain Mayne, with some of Scindia's troops, was at that place on the 11th of April, and found that the Kotah rebels, about four thousand strong, with six guns, had joined the rebel Rajah of Nirwur, six miles distant. Captain Mayne was preparing to watch and follow them, but the troops at his command consisted of only a few hundred men, and he could do little more than reconnoitre. Later in the month, General Roberts organised a column to look after the rebels at Goonah, Chupra, and other places. The column consisted of H.M. 95th foot, the 10th Bombay native infantry, a wing of the 8th hussars, a wing of the 1st lancers, and a troop of horse-artillery; and it started from Kotah for active service on the 24th. Thus the month of April passed away; Roberts himself remaining at Kotah; while some of his officers, each with a detachment of the Rajpootana field-force, were engaged in chastising bodies of rebels in the turbulent region on the border of the Rajpoot and Mahratta territories. Like Sir Hugh Rose at Jhansi, he had to consider how his conquered city would fare if he quitted it.

The province of Gujerat, lying as it does between Rajpootana and Bombay, was narrowly watched by the government of that presidency; and as one precaution, all the inhabitants were disarmed. On the 8th of April, a field-force, comprising about a thousand men of all arms, left Ahmedabad to conduct the disarming. Another column of about the same strength was preparing to march from the same station about a week later. It was expected that the difficulties of the troops would arise, not so much from the opposition of the natives, as from the gradually increasing heat of the weather.

Southward of Bombay there was still, as in the earlier months of the year, just so much of insubordination as to need careful watching on the part of the government, but without presenting any very alarming symptoms. The small Mahratta state of Satara was a little troubled. Two officers of the recently deposed rajah, his commander-in-chief and his commandant of artillery, were detected in treasonable correspondence with Nena Sahib. One of them, having been found guilty, was sentenced to be hanged; the indignity struck with horror one imbued with high-caste notions, and he asked to be blown away from a gun as a more noble death; this was refused; and under the influence of dismay and grief, he made a confession which afforded a clue to a further conspiracy. There was much in these southern Mahrattas which puzzled the authorities. To what extent the natives were bound into a brotherhood by secret compact, the English never could and never did know. Much comment was excited by an occurrence at Kolapore, where two native officers were blown away from guns, on conviction of being concerned in the mutiny and rebellion. It was remembered that those very men had sat on courts-martial which condemned numbers of their fellow-mutineers to the same punishment which was their own ultimate doom. One of the principal witnesses against them was a colleague whom they had sentenced to death, but who escaped by making a confession which implicated them. Many others, however, condemned by the court of which these two men were members, died without making a similar confession, although it was believed that they also might have implicated their judges.

Note.

Native Police of India.—So peculiar was the position of the native police of India—as a medium between the military and the civilians, and between the government and the people—that it may be desirable to say a few words on the organisation of that body. All parties agreed that this organisation was defective in many points, and numerous reforms were suggested; but the Revolt found the police system still in force unreformed. The information here given is obtained chiefly from a dispatch sent from the India House about six months before the Revolt began, at a time when few or none saw the dark shadow that was hovering over our eastern empire.

In Bengal, each district was subdivided into smaller jurisdictions, each having its local police. The police were charged with duties both preventive and detective. They were prohibited from inquiring into cases of a petty nature; but complaints in cases of a more serious character were usually laid before the police *darogah*—whose duties were something more than those of an English police superintendent, something less than those of an English magistrate. The darogah was authorised to examine the complaints brought before him, to issue process of arrest, to summon witnesses, to examine the accused, and to forward the case to the magistrate or collector-magistrate, or submit a report of his proceedings, according as the evidence seemed to warrant the one or the other course.

In the Northwest Provinces the native revenue-officers called *tehsildars* were, at the discretion of the government, invested with the powers of police darogahs; whereas in Bengal the revenue service was kept wholly distinct from the police or magisterial.

In the Madras presidency, the duties ordinarily performed in Bengal by the police darogahs were, even more generally than in the Northwest Provinces, performed by the tehsildar; indeed it was a recognised part of the system that the tehsildar and the darogah were the same person. This double function carried with it an increase of power. The Madras tehsildar-darogah was authorised, not only to inquire into petty cases (which the Bengal darogah was prohibited from doing), but also to proceed in certain specified instances to judgment, sentence, and the infliction of punishment.

In the Bombay presidency, the revenue and police functions were, until a recent period, combined in the same way as in Madras. The tehsildars, besides their revenue duties, were authorised in their police capacity to investigate all complaints of a criminal nature, and to exercise a penal jurisdiction in respect of certain petty offences. Within a few months before the Revolt, however, a change was made in the organisation. A new officer, a superintendent of police, was placed under the magistrate. The magistrate, confining himself for the most part to judicial and administrative matters, left to his superintendent of police the control of the executive police and the command of the entire stipendiary body, with the initiative in the prevention and detection of crime. To aid this superintendent in the supervision of the district police, there was placed in each police division an officer called joint-police *amildar*; whose duties, in regard to the preservation of the public peace and the investigation of serious crimes, were nearly similar to those of the Bengal darogah, but without including any power of punishing even for the most trivial offences.

It thus appears that, apart from the penal powers exercised by the Madras district police, the Bengal *darogah*, the Madras *tehsildar*, and the Bombay *amildar*, all acted to a certain extent judicially when engaged in investigating crimes of a serious nature. They examined the parties and the evidence, and they formed a judgment on the case to the extent of deciding whether it was one for the immediate arrest of the accused and transmission to the magistrate, or otherwise.

No doubt the founders of this police system anticipated beneficial results from it; but those results were not obtained. It was very inefficient for the detection of crime, and almost useless for prevention. There were defects both in organisation and in procedure. The police force attached to each division was too much localised and isolated; and the notion of combination between any separate parts of it, with a view of accomplishing extensive police objects, was seldom entertained. Although unable to check crime to the extent intended and hoped for, the police were very unscrupulous in their mode of wielding their authority, and bore a very general character for oppression and corruption. The great source of mischief was found to be, the want of efficient control and overlooking. The native police had a proneness to oriental modes of administering justice, in which bribery and barbarity perform a great part: this tendency required to be constantly checked by Europeans; and if the magistrate or collector-magistrate found his time too fully occupied to exercise this supervision, the police wrought much mischief, and brought the English 'raj' into disfavour. Where the district was smaller than usual, or where the magistrate was more than commonly zealous and active, the police were found to be more efficient through more supervision. Whenever it was found necessary to grapple effectually with any particular crimes, such as *thuggee* or *dacoitee*, the ordinary police proved to be wholly useless; an entirely separate instrumentality was needed. Besides the want of effective supervision, the native police were underpaid, and had therefore an excuse for listening to the temptations of bribery.

In the dispatch already adverted to, written by the Court of Directors, a course of improvement was pointed out, without which the native police, it was affirmed, could not rise to the proper degree of efficiency. The suggestions were briefly as follows: To separate the police from the administration of the land-revenue, in those provinces where those duties had been customarily united; in order that the native officer should not be intrusted with double functions, each of which would interfere with the other. To subject all the police to frequent visit and inspection, that they might feel the influence of a vigilant eye over them. To relieve the collector-magistrate from this addition to his many duties, by appointing in each district a European officer with no other duty than that of managing the police of the district, subject to a general superintendent of police for each presidency. To increase the salaries of the police, in order that the office might have a higher dignity in the estimation of the natives, and in order that the official might be less tempted to extortion or bribery. To empower the authorities to punish and degrade, more readily than was before possible, those police who oppressed the people or otherwise displayed injustice; and to reward those who displayed more than ordinary intelligence and honesty, a further suggestion was made, arising out of the organisation of the Punjaub under the Lawrences and their coadjutors; in which there was a preventive police with a military organisation, and a wholly distinct detective police with a civil organisation. This system was found to work so well, that the Court of Directors submitted to the Calcutta government an inquiry whether the police generally might not with advantage be thus separated into two parts, preventive and detective, each exercised by a different set of men.

The Revolt broke out before the reform of the police system could commence; and then, like other reforms, it was left to be settled in more peaceful days.

Summer Costumes, Indian Army.

CHAPTER XXIX.

PROGRESS OF EVENTS IN MAY.

WHEN, on the 10th of May 1858, the course of twelve months had been completed since the commencement of the mutiny, the nation looked back at the events of that period as a terrible episode in the history of British dominion. Into how many thousands of families mourning had been introduced by it, no one correctly knew; the problem was a dismal one, which few had the heart to investigate. Those who, not affected by private grief, or hiding their grief in a sense of public duty, viewed the twelvemonth's conflict in a national sense, saw in it a mingled cause for humiliation and pride—humiliation that British rule should be so trampled on by those who had been long and peacefully under it; pride that so many public servants, so many private persons, should have proved worthy of their country in a time of severe and bitter trial. In military matters, the once great Bengal native army had almost ceased to exist. Twenty thousand disarmed sepoys were in and near the Punjaub, carefully watched lest they should join the ranks of the insurgents; disarmed regiments were similarly detained elsewhere; others had been almost annihilated by twelve months of fierce warfare; others were still engaged as the nuclei of rebel armies; while the number of Bengal sepoys was very small indeed, reckoned by hundreds rather than thousands, who still fought faithfully on the side of the British. The Madras and Bombay troops had, happily for India and England's interest therein, remained almost wholly 'true to their salt;' enabling the governors of those two presidencies to send gallant field-forces into the disturbed northern and central provinces.

Sikhs, Punjaubees, Moultanese, Scindians, Beloochees, and hill-men on the Afghan frontier, had rendered services of such lasting importance in Hindostan, that they may almost be regarded as the preservers of the English 'raj;' this they had been enabled to do from two causes—the want of sympathy between the mutineers and those north-western tribes; and the admirable system of Punjaub government organised by the Lawrences. In civil matters, India had witnessed the almost total breaking up of the ordinary revenue and magisterial arrangements, in provinces containing at least fifty millions of souls; Europeans driven into hiding-places, even if not murdered; and treasuries plundered by bands of ruffians, who gladly hailed the state of anarchy brought on by the mutiny of the sepoy regiments. Among the superior members of the government, Viscount Canning still maintained his position, battling against unnumbered difficulties; Sir Colin Campbell still remained at the head of the army, well aware that his utmost skill as a military commander would long be needed; and Sir John Lawrence still held the Punjaub in his wonderful grasp, displaying governing powers of the very highest order at an eminently critical time. On the other hand, the Anglo-Indians had to mourn over a sad death-list. Henry Lawrence, Havelock, Colvin, Neill, Venables, Nicholson, William Peel, Adrian Hope, Wheeler, Barnard, Banks, Battye—all, and a vast many more gallant spirits, had sunk under the terrible pressure of the past twelve months.

Appropriating the present chapter to a rapid glance at the progress of events in the month of May, and beginning (as usual) with the Bengal regions, we may conveniently notice two or three arrangements made by the Calcutta government, bearing relation either to the state of the army, or to the condition of civilians affected by the mutiny.

Among the earliest measures taken to re-construct the Bengal army, so shattered by the mutiny, was one announced in a government notification on the 7th of May. It was to the effect that four regiments of Bengal *European* cavalry should be formed, in lieu of eight regiments of Bengal *native* cavalry, erased from the list of the establishment for mutinous conduct. Each regiment was to consist of 1 colonel, 2 lieutenant-colonels, 2 majors, 14 captains, 18 lieutenants, 8 cornets, 1 adjutant, 1 interpreter and quartermaster, 4 surgeons and assistants, 119 non-commissioned and subordinate officers of various kinds, and 700 privates; making a total of 870—an unusually large number for a cavalry regiment. In addition to these, there were to be native syces, grass-cutters, and quarter-masters, attached to each regiment; and various persons employed at the depôt. The pay was to be the same as in the royal dragoon regiments. Each regiment was to be divided into ten troops. As the officers were to be about doubly as numerous as the English officers in the disbanded native regiments, it was calculated that the four new would absorb the officers of eight old regiments. The regiments thus extinguished by this first process, were the 1st, 2d, 3d, 4th, 6th, 7th, 9th, and 10th Bengal native cavalry; the 5th and the 8th were left to be dealt with at some subsequent period. As for any larger measures connected with the reconstruction of a *native* Bengal army, these were left for determination at a later period, after collating the opinions of the most experienced authorities in India.

The distress experienced by the British troops from the intense heat of the Indian sun, and the severe strictures passed by the press and by members of the legislature on those regimental officers who permitted or compelled their soldiers to swelter in red cloth, led to the issuing of orders concerning light summer clothing. It was found that a kind of gray or dust-coloured linen called *khakee* or *curkey* was better suited than anything else—even white—as a material for clothing in the hot season; and hence the issuing of an order by the adjutant-general, on the 21st of May, to the effect noted below.* This question concerning appropriate clothing had long been discussed by military men in India: the officers of greatest experience being those who most disapproved the wearing of closely fitting garments in such a climate. General Jacob had resolutely contended against the adoption of English uniforms by the sepoys of the Company's army. He said: 'A sepoy of the line, dressed in a tight coat; trousers in which he can scarcely walk, and cannot stoop at all; bound to an immense and totally useless knapsack, so that he can scarcely breathe; strapped, belted, and pipe-clayed within an inch of his life; with a rigid basket-shako on his head, which requires the skill of a juggler to balance, and which cuts deep into his brow if worn for an hour; and with a leather-stock round his neck, to complete his absurd costume—when compared with the same sepoy, clothed, armed, and accoutred solely with regard to his comfort and efficiency—forms the most perfect example of what is madly called the "regular" system with many European officers, contrasted with the system of common sense now recommended for adoption.' The graphic description by Mr Russell, of the officers and men in Sir Colin Campbell's army of Oude, shews how eager soldiers are to get rid of their irksome uniforms when permitted, under the influence of a heat

* 'With the concurrence of the government, the commander-in-chief is pleased to direct that white clothing shall be discontinued in the European regiments of the Honourable Company's army; and that for the future the summer-clothing of the European soldiers shall consist of two suits of "khakee," corresponding in pattern and material with the clothing recently sanctioned for the royal army of England. Corps are to be permitted to wear out serviceable summer-clothing of the old pattern now in use; but in regiments in which this clothing requires to be renewed, the new pattern now established is to be introduced without delay. Commanding officers will take steps to obtain patterns from regiments of her Majesty's service. A complete suit, including cap-cover, should not exceed in cost 4-12 rupees. The summer-clothing now authorised will be supplied from the clothing agency of the presidency to all recruits of the Company's service arriving at Calcutta between 1st February and 1st October, to be issued with the least possible delay after arrival of the recruits.'

denoted by the cabalistic mark 100° F. or 110° F.: 'Except the Highlanders—and when they left Lucknow they were panting for their summer clothes, and had sent officers to Cawnpore to hurry them—not a corps that I have seen sport a morsel of pink or shew a fragment of English scarlet. The Highlanders wear eccentric shades of gray linen over their bonnets—the kilt is discarded, or worn out in some regiments; and flies, mosquitoes, and the sun are fast rendering it impossible in the others. Already many officers who can get trews have discarded the ponderous folds of woollen stuff tucked into massive wads over the hips, and have provided some defence against the baking of their calves by day, and have sought to protect their persons against the assaults of innumerable entomological enemies by night. The artillery had been furnished with excellent head-covers and good frocks of light stuff. . . . The 7th Hussars, the Military Train, have vestiary idiosyncrasies of their own; but there is some sort of uniformity among the men. Among the officers, individual taste and fantasy have full play. The infantry regiments, for the most part, are dressed in linen frocks, dyed carkey or gray slate-colour—slate-blue trousers, and shakos protected by puggerees, or linen covers, from the sun. The peculiarity of carkey is that the dyer seems to be unable to match it in any two pieces, and that it exhibits endless varieties of shade, varying with every washing, so that the effect is rather various than pleasing on the march or on the parade-ground. But the officers, as I have said, do not confine themselves to carkey or anything else. It is really wonderful what fecundity of invention in dress there is, after all, in the British mind when its talents can be properly developed. To begin with the head-dress. The favourite wear is a helmet of varying shape, but of uniform ugliness. . . . Whatever it might be in polished steel or burnished metal, the helmet is a decided failure in felt, or wicker-work, or pith, so far as external effect is concerned. It is variously fabricated, with many varieties of interior ducts and passages leading to escape-holes for imaginary hot air in the front or top, and around it are twisted infinite colours and forms of turbans with fringed ends and laced fringes. When a peacock's feather, with the iris end displayed, is inserted in the hole in the top of the helmet, or is stuck in the puggeree around it, the effect of the covering is much enhanced; and this style is rather patronised by some of the staff. The coat may be of any cut or material, but shooting-jackets hold their own in the highest posts; and a carkey-coloured jerkin, with a few inches of iron curb-chain sewed on the shoulders to resist sabre-cuts, is a general favourite. . . . . As to the clothing of the nether man, nothing but a series of photographs could give the least notion of the numerous combinations which can be made out of a leg, leather, pantaloons, and small-clothes. Long stage-boots of buff-coloured leather—for the manufacture of which Cawnpore is famous—pulled up over knee-breeches of leather or regimental trousers, are common. There are officers who prefer wearing their Wellingtons outside their pantaloons, thus exhibiting tops of very bright colours; and the boot and baggy trousers of the Zouave officer are not unknown.'

The next point to be adverted to affected civilians and private traders more extensively than the military. The compensation to sufferers by the mutiny, a much-disputed question for nearly twelve months, was put into a train for settlement by a government order issued at Calcutta in May. This order applied to Bengal only, as being a region quite large enough to be brought within one set of official rules. The compensation was to be for loss of property and effects, leaving losses affecting life or health to be settled by a distinct machinery. A Mr E. Jackson was appointed at Calcutta as commissioner to inquire into claims for compensation. A limit was named, the 26th of August, after which no claims would be received from persons resident in India: an extension of time being allowed for those who were not in that country. In cases where the amount claimed did not exceed fifty thousand rupees, the application to the commissioner was to be accompanied by a detailed statement of the particulars of the claim, and of the evidence adducible in support of it; but where the property was of higher amount, the regulation required only a general estimate to accompany the application, a further period of three months being allowed for the preparation and submission of the detailed statement of losses. It was at the same time very pointedly mentioned that these preliminary operations did not constitute an actual *claim* on the Company for any compensation whatever. 'It is to be understood that the registry of applications above provided for does not imply any recognition of claims to compensation; the Honourable Court of Directors having expressly reserved their final decision upon the question, whether or not compensation for losses sustained by the mutiny shall be awarded.' The Company probably deemed it wise, in the uncertainty how large might be the total aggregate sum claimed, to avoid any formal pledge that these compensations could be rightfully demanded and would be really paid. The above, we have said, applied to Bengal; but about the same time a similar notification appeared at Allahabad, applicable to the Northwest Provinces. Mr C. Grant and Mr E. H. Longden were named commissioners to record and register claims. The conditions were generally the same as those in Bengal; and to them was added an announcement that 'Applications will be received, subject to the same rules, from natives of the country for compensation, on account of loss of property caused by their known loyalty and attachment to the British government.' A similar announcement was afterwards made, extending the boon to the province of Oude.

Superadded to the arrangements made for the

succour of those who had borne pecuniary loss by the mutiny, was one dated May 25th. This was to the effect that some provision would be made for the relief of the destitute families of persons who had died after the loss of their property, even though the death were not occasioned by the mutiny. It was thereupon determined that grants of money should be given to families rendered impoverished by this double calamity; the grants to be regulated on the same principle as those allowed to European and native officers of the government.

DACCA.

One of the resolutions arrived at by the authorities at Calcutta gave very general satisfaction—except to a few officers jealous of any encroachments on the privileges of the army. Whether suggested at home, or in India, the movement was in the right direction. The regulation was to the effect that civilians who had distinguished themselves in the field since the commencement of the mutiny, or who should so distinguish themselves before the mutiny ended, should be allowed to participate in the honours which had hitherto been considered peculiar to the military service. The civil servants of the Company, as a body, greatly raised themselves in the estimation of the nation by the gallantry which many of them displayed under circumstances of great peril—not only in defending their posts against large bodies of insurgents, but in sharing those field and siege operations which are more immediately sources of honour to military men. What those honours were to be, depended partly on the crown, partly on the Company; but the object of the order was to shew that the civil position of a gallant man should not necessarily be a bar to his occupancy of an honoured place among military men.

In entering now upon the military operations of the month, it is satisfactory to know that nothing important presents itself for record in connection with the eastern regions of Bengal. There were few or no actual mutinies, for reasons more than once assigned in former chapters. Notwithstanding this safety, however—partly through the superstitious character of the natives of India, and partly through the uneasy feeling prevailing in the minds of Europeans during the mutiny—the newspapers were frequently engaged in discussing mysteries, rumours, and prophecies of a strange character. One, connected more with Bengal than with the other provinces, related to 'something white,' which was to be ominous of British rule in India. Where it arose, or how, remained as undiscoverable as the chupatty mystery; but the rumour put on various forms at different times and places. At Tipperah, the native story told of a 'white thing' which would be unprocurable after some time. At Chittagong, a particular day was named, when, 'out of four things, three would be given and one withheld;' and at Jessore, the bazaar-people became so excited concerning a prophetic rumour of an equally enigmatical kind, that the magistrate endeavoured to elicit something from his police-darogah that might explain it; but the man either could not or would not tell how the story arose. In Dacca and other places the prediction assumed this form—that after a certain period, a certain 'white thing' would cease to exist in India; and in some instances the exact interval was named, 'three months and thirteen days.'

Occasionally, the authorities found it necessary to watch very closely the proceedings of Mohammedan fanatics; who, at Burdwan, Jessore, Rungpoor, and other places, were detected in attempts to rouse up the people to a religious war. Fortunately, the townsmen and villagers did not respond to these appeals. Southwest of Calcutta, the Sumbhulpore district, disturbed occasionally by rebel bands intent on plunder, was kept for the most part tranquil by the firm management of Colonel Forster. In the month of May he hit upon the plan of inviting the still faithful chieftains of the districts to furnish each a certain number of soldiers to defend British interests, on promise of a due recognition of their services afterwards. The chieftains raised two thousand matchlockmen among them, and took up such positions as Colonel Forster indicated—a measure which completely frustrated and cowed the rebels.

We may pass at once to a consideration of the state of affairs in Behar or Western Bengal, comprising the districts around what may be called the Middle Ganges. This region, as former chapters have sufficiently told, and as a glance at a map will at once shew, contains many important cities and towns, which were thrown into great commotion by the mutiny—such as Patna, Dinapoor, Arrah, Buxar, Azimghur, Goruckpore, Ghazeepore, Jounpoor, Sasseram, Benares, Chunargur, and Mirzapore. It is true that many of these were formerly included within the government of the 'Northwest Provinces,' and then in that of the 'Central Provinces;' but this is a matter of little consequence to our present purpose; if we consider them all to belong to the Mid-Ganges region, it will suffice for the present purpose.

The condition of the region just defined, during May, depended mainly on the relation between Sir Edward Lugard on the one hand, and the Jugdispore rebels on the other. How it fared with this active general and the troops under his command, when April closed, we have already seen. It will be remembered that about the middle of that month, Koer Singh took up a strong position at Azimutgurh, from which Lugard deemed it necessary to dislodge him; that Lugard himself remained encamped at Azimghur with the bulk of his Azimghur field-force, in order that he might watch the proceedings of numerous bands of rebels under the Rajahs of Nuhurpoor and Naweejer and Gholam Hossein, hovering about the districts of Sandah, Mundoree, and Koelser; but that he made up a strong column to pursue Koer Singh. This column, placed under the command of Brigadier Douglas, consisted of the following troops: H.M. 4th foot; a wing of the 37th foot; a detachment of Punjaub Sappers; two squadrons of Sikh cavalry; a squadron of the Military Train; and nine guns and mortars. Then followed the series of cross-purposes, in which Koer Singh was permitted or enabled to work much more mischief than Sir Edward had anticipated. The events may briefly be recapitulated thus: On the 17th and 18th, Douglas, after starting with his column from Azimghur, came up with the rebels, defeated them at Azimutgurh, and chased them to Ghosee, Nugra, and Secunderpore. On the 19th he found that they intended to cross the Gogra before he could come up to them in pursuit—an intention which he strove to render nugatory. On the 20th he encountered them again, at Muneer Khas, defeated them with great slaughter, captured most of their munitions of war, and dispersed the rebels, the main body of whom fled towards Bullah and Beyriah. On the 21st, Douglas had the mortification, on reaching Sheopore, of finding that Koer Singh had outwitted the officer who had been ordered to guard the passage of the Ganges in the vicinity of Ghazeepore with about nine hundred men; the wily chief of Jugdispore had got in the rear of the detachment by a flank-movement, and had crossed the Ganges at an undefended spot. Then followed Captain Le Grand's disastrous expedition to Jugdispore on the 23d; the crossing of the Ganges on the 25th by Douglas, with his column; and the advance towards Arrah and Jugdispore to retrieve the disaster. To what results these operations led in the month of May, we have now to see.

Brigadier Douglas arrived at Arrah with a part of his force on the 1st of May, the rest having arrived two days earlier; but Douglas not being in sufficient force to effectually encompass the enemy, and the importance of thoroughly routing Koer Singh being evident, Sir Edward Lugard, leaving a few troops to guard Azimghur, set out for the Ganges with his main column, crossed over into the Shahabad district on the 3d and following days, and prepared for operations in the direction of Arrah and Jugdispore. The rebels, estimated at seven or eight thousand, were supposed to be intrenching themselves, and getting in supplies. On the 8th, Sir Edward arrived in the vicinity of Jugdispore, and came in sight of some of the rebels. Two companies of the 84th foot, with detachments of Madras Rifles, and Sikh horse, aided by two horse-artillery guns, were sent back to Arrah, to protect that place while operations were being directed against Jugdispore. The commissioner of Patna at the same time sent the steamer *Patna* up the Ganges, to watch the ghâts or ferries. On the 9th, Sir Edward marched his force from Beheea to an open plain a little to the west of Jugdispore. Here he intended to encamp for a while, to allow Colonel Corfield to come up with some additional troops from Sasseram. Circumstances occurred, however, to change his plan. In the afternoon of this day a large body of rebels formed outside the jungle, and moved in the direction of Arrah; but these were quickly followed by cavalry and horse-artillery, and driven back into the jungle. Another body, much more numerous, began to fire into Sir Edward's camp before he could get his baggage well up and tents fixed. This determined him to attack them at once. Dividing his force into three columns, he planned an assault on Jugdispore on three points at once. The place was carried after a little skirmishing, the rebels making only a slight resistance; they retired to Lutwarpore, in the jungle district, taking with them two guns which they had captured from the British in the preceding month. The loss on both sides was trifling. Leaving a strong party to retain Jugdispore, Lugard returned to his camp in the evening. According to the rumours prevalent, Koer Singh, who had so long been a source of annoyance to the British, had died of his wounds; and the rebels, under his brother Ummer Singh, were ill supplied and in much confusion. A nephew of Koer Singh, named Ritbhunghur Singh, gave himself up to the British a short time afterwards—hopeful of insuring forgiveness by being able to shew that, in earlier months, he had befriended certain Europeans in a time of great peril. On the 10th, after ordering all the fortifications at Jugdispore, and all the buildings which had belonged to Koer Singh, to be destroyed, Lugard prepared to follow the rebels into the jungle. He arranged that Colonel Corfield, with the Sasseram force, should approach Lutwarpore in one direction, while he himself intended to advance upon it from Jugdispore. On the 11th and 12th much fighting took place. Sir Edward took the rebels by surprise; they expected to be attacked from Arrah or Beheea, but he marched westward through a belt of jungle to Hettumpore, and attacked them on a side which they believed to be quite safe. Lugard and Corfield were everywhere successful. It was, however, a harassing kind of warfare, bringing more fatigue than glory; the rebels, though chastised everywhere, avoided a regular engagement, and retreated into the jungle after every partial skirmish. At Arrah, Jugdispore, Lutwarpore, Hettumpore, Beheea, Peroo, and Chitowra, Lugard defeated and cut them up at various times in the course of the month; yet he could not prevent them from recombining, and collecting around them a rabble of budmashes and jail-felons. Sir Edward hoped, at anyrate, to be able so to employ a strong detachment of cavalry as to prevent the rebels from crossing the river Sone, and carrying anarchy into other districts. They nevertheless continued to harass the neighbourhood by freebooting expeditions, if not by formidable military projects. After Lugard's defeat of the main force, some of the insurgents broke up into bands of a few hundreds each, and were joined by budmashes from the towns and revolted villages. One party attacked an indigo factory near Dumoran, and burned it to the ground; another effected a murderous outbreak at the village of Rajpore, near Buxar; another threatened the railway-bridge works at Karminassa. These mischievous proceedings naturally threw the whole district into agitation. The threat against the railway-works was fully carried out about the end of the month; for the devastators destroyed the engineers' bungalows and the workmen's sheds, set fire to all the wood and coal collected for brick-burning, destroyed everything they could easily lay their hands on, and effectually stopped the works for a time. Nothing could be done to quell these disturbances, until a British force appeared.

Practically, therefore, the 'Azimghur field-force,' under Sir Edward Lugard, succeeded in breaking down the military organisation of the rebels in that part of India, without being able to prevent the formation of roaming bands bent on slaughter and devastation. And even the limited amount of advantage gained was purchased at a high price; for the tremendous heat of the sun struck down the poor soldiers with fatal certainty; numbers of them were carried from Jugdispore to Arrah, towards the close of the month—prostrated by sickness, wounds, fatigue from jungle-fighting, and sun-stroke.

Somewhat further to the north, in the Goruckpore district, another group of rebels continued to harass the country, disturbing the operations of peaceful planters and traders. About the end of May, the rebel leader Mahomed Hussein, with four thousand men, suddenly made an attack upon the Rajah of Bansee, one of those who had remained faithful to the British government. The rajah was obliged to flee to a stronghold in a neighbouring jungle; and then his palace, with the town of Bansee, were plundered by the rebels. Mr Wingfield, the commissioner of Goruckpore, immediately started forth with two hundred and fifty Europeans and some guns to the relief of the rajah, whom he found besieged in his stronghold. The enemy fled precipitately on hearing of Wingfield's approach, notwithstanding the immense disparity of force. The energetic commissioner then proceeded with the rajah to attack some rebel villages; while a simultaneous advance was made on Amood by Colonel Rowcroft. The object of these demonstrations was to keep the rebels in check until the rains set in, and the waters of the Gogra rose. Towards the end of the month, four Europeans came into Goruckpore from a neighbouring station, where they had been suddenly attacked by a body of rabble under one Baboo Surdoun Singh, and other leaders. This was one among many evidences of a still disturbed condition of the Goruckpore district. The district was in a slight degree protected by the passage of a body of troops who, though retiring rather than fighting, exerted some kind of influence on the evildoer of the country. We speak of the Goorkhas of Jung Bahadoor's Nepaulese contingent. These troops retreated slowly from Oude towards their own country, neither receiving nor giving satisfaction from their late share in the warlike operations. After a sojourn of some time at Goruckpore, they resumed their march on the 17th of May, proceeding by brigades, and consuming much time in arranging and dragging their enormous supply of vehicles. They crossed the river Gunduck at Bagaha, with much difficulty. A distance of about thirty miles then brought them to Bettiah, and fourteen more to Segowlie—very near the frontier of the British dominions. It was early in the following month when the Goorkhas finally reached their native country, Nepaul—their leader Jung Bahadoor being, though still faithful as an ally, somewhat dissatisfied by his failure in obtaining notable advantage from the governor-general in return for services rendered. Viscount Canning had, many months earlier, received fierce newspaper abuse for not having availed himself more promptly of aid offered by Jung Bahadoor; but there now appeared much probability that caution had been all along necessary in dealing with this ambitious chieftain.

Directing attention next to the region of the Jumna and the Upper Ganges, we have to notice the continuance of insubordination around the Allahabad region, almost in the very presence of the governor-general himself, who still remained, with his staff, in that station. One of the most vexing symptoms of mischief at this place was the occurrence of incendiarism—the burning of buildings by miscreants who could not be discovered. On the 24th of May a new range of barracks was found to be on fire, and six bungalows were completely destroyed. The prevalence of a fierce wind, and the scarcity of water, frustrated for some time all attempts to extinguish the flames. One poor invalid soldier was burned to death, and many others injured. Beyond the limits of the city itself, it was a state of things very unexpected by the supreme authorities, that the road from Allahabad through Futtehpoor to Cawnpore—a road more traversed than any other by British troops throughout twelve months of anarchy—should in the middle of May be scarcely passable without a strong escort. Yet such was the case. The opposition to the British raj, though it had assumed a guerrilla character, was very harassing to deal with. The British were strong in a few places; but the rebels were in numerous small bodies, scattered all over the surrounding country; and these bodies occasioned temporary panics at spots where there was no force to meet them. The thorough knowledge of the country, possessed by some of the leaders, enabled them to baffle the pursuers; and thus it arose that these petty bands occasioned alarms disproportionate to the number of men comprising them. Sometimes they would occupy the great trunk-road, between Allahabad and Cawnpore, and close up all means of transit unless attacked and driven away by force. On the other hand, this district exhibited a remarkable union of the new with the old, the European with the oriental, the practical with the primitive—arising out of the opening of a railway through a part of the route. After reading, as we so often have in this volume, of toilsome marches by sunburnt and exhausted troops over rough roads and through jungle-thickets, it is with a peculiar feeling of interest that we find an announcement to the effect, that 'on the 26th of May a special train left Allahabad with a party of Sikhs to reinforce Futtehpoor, which was said to be threatened by a large force of the enemy.' Had this railway been opened when or soon after the Revolt began, there is at least a fair probability that the Cawnpore massacre might have been prevented—provided always that the railway itself, with its locomotives and carriages, were *not in rebels' hands*.

Allahabad, about the period now under notice, was made the subject of a very important project, one of many arising out of the mutiny. The Indian government had long and fully considered the various advantages likely to be derived from the founding of a great Anglo-Indian capital at some spot far removed from the three older presidential cities of Calcutta, Madras, and Bombay. The spot selected was Allahabad. The peculiarities of this very important station, before and during the mutiny, have been frequently noticed in past chapters. Occupying the point of the peninsula formed by the junction of the two grand rivers Ganges and Jumna, Allahabad is scarcely paralleled for situation by any other city in India. The one river brings down to it a stream of traffic from Kumaon, Rohilcund, Furruckabad, Cawnpore, Futtehpoor, and the southwestern districts of Oude; while the other brings down that from Kurnaul, Roorkee, Meerut, Delhi, Muttra, Agra, Calpee, and a wide range of country in Rajpootana, Bundelcund, and the Doab. On the other sides, too, it has an extraordinary number of large military and commercial towns within easy reach (in peaceful times), such as Lucknow, Fyzabad, Sultanpore, Goruckpore, Azimghur, Jounpoor, Benares, Ghazeepore, Mirzapore, Dinapoor, and Patna. Agra was at one time intended to have been converted into a presidential city, the capital of an Agra presidency; but the intention was not fully carried out; the Northwest Provinces were formed into a lieutenant-governorship, with Agra as the seat of government; but the events of the mutiny shewed the necessity of holding with a strong hand the position of Allahabad, as a centre of great influence; and Agra began to fall in relative importance.

It has been remarked that England has seldom built cities as a nation, as a government; cities have *grown*, like the constitution, without those preconceived theories of centralised organisation which are so prevalent on the continent of Europe. It has been much the same in India as in England.

The three presidential capitals—Calcutta, Madras, and Bombay—became what they are, not from the development of a plan, but from a series of incidents having little relative connection. 'Our three capitals are congeries of houses, without order, or beauty, or healthiness other than nature may have supplied. Our cantonments, which sometimes grow into cities, are generally stuck down in a plain as a kind of petrified encampment. Even when founding, as in Rangoon, it is with

FYZABAD.

the utmost difficulty we can compel successive governors to care whether the original plan be not set aside.' A problem arose whether Allahabad might not be an exception to this rule. Standing at the extreme end of the Doab, and bounded by two fine rivers on the north, south, and east, it is susceptible of any degree of enlargement by including additional ground on the west; it might be made one of the strongest forts in India; and its rivers, aided by the railway when finished, might make it a great centre of trade. Most of the conditions, therefore, were favourable to the building of a fine Anglo-Indian city on that spot. The river frontages, it is easily seen, might easily be defended against any attacks which orientals could bring against them. On the west or land side, it was proposed to construct a line of intrenchment, or a sort of intrenched camp, four miles in length, from river to river. This fortification would consist mainly of two great redoubts on the river-banks, each capable of holding an entire regiment, but each defensible by a small force if necessary. With these two redoubts, and one midway between them, and earthern embankments to connect the three, it would be possible to render Allahabad impregnable to any hostile force likely to be brought against it. Within the space thus marked out by the embankment and the rivers would be included a cantonment, a European town, and a native town. The cantonment, a complete military establishment for four or five regiments, would be near the western boundary, on the Jumna side. Eastward of this would be the new English town, built in plots of ground let on lease to builders (native or European), who would be required, in building houses, shops, and hotels, to conform to some general plan, having reference to the railway station as a centre of trade. Nearer the Ganges would be the native town; while at the point of junction of the two rivers would be the existing fort, extended and enlarged so as to form if needed a last stronghold for all the Europeans in Allahabad. Many of the details in the plan were suggested during a period of panic fear, when the natives were looked upon as if they were permanently bitter enemies; and, during the long course of years necessary for working out the idea, great modification in these details might be expected; but the general character of the scheme, as developed about the period to which this chapter relates, may be understood from the above brief sketch.

It was on the 5th of May that a notification appeared at Allahabad, signed by Mr Thornhill, officiating commissioner under the governor-general, concerning the leasing of land in that city for building purposes. The terms were evidently framed with the intention of attracting the notice of commercial firms, at Calcutta and elsewhere, to Allahabad as a future emporium of commerce. The regulations may be summarily noticed as follow: A new civil European town to be formed near the railway station at Allahabad, distinct from the cantonment, the native town, and the fort. Land, in plots of three acres each, to be let on lease by the government, for the erection of shops, hotels, warehouses, and other buildings requisite for a European population. Each plot to have a frontage of three hundred feet on a public road, with a smaller road in the rear. Some of the plots to be let for dwelling-houses; and these, as well as the hotels and shops, to receive a certain systematic arrangement, laid down by the authorities for the general convenience of the whole community. Priority of choice to be given to those who intend to construct hotels, on account of the great necessity for that species of accommodation in a newly collected community. Plots, competed for by two or more persons, to be sold by auction to the highest bidder. The lease to be for fifty years, unless a shorter time be specified by agreement; and the lessee to have the privilege of renewal, under approval as to conditions, but not with any rise of rental. The rent to be thirty rupees (about £3) per acre per annum. Leases to be transferable, and sub-letting to be permitted, on payment of a registration fee; provided the transferree or sub-lessee enter into an engagement to fulfil the necessary conditions to the government. Every lessee to specify the kind of structures he intends to build on his plot; to commence building within one year after obtaining the lease; and to finish in three years—on forfeiture both of the lease and of a money penalty, if the building fail in kind, value, or time. Lessees to be subject to such rates and taxes as may be imposed for municipal purposes, and to all regulations of police and conservancy. Lessees to be placed under stringent rules, concerning the employment of thatch or other inflammable materials for the roofs of buildings. As a general rule, one plot to one lessee; but if a special application be made, and supported on sufficient grounds, two or more plots to be leased together.—Such were the general regulations. At the time of issuing the order, there were about forty plots set out as a commencement to the system.

The turbulent province of Oude next calls for attention; and as Sir Colin Campbell's operations bore almost equal reference to Oude and Rohilcund, we will treat both provinces together.

It will be remembered, from the details given in the last chapter, that after the great conquest of Lucknow in March, a considerable time elapsed before any effective attempts were made to overtake and defeat the rebels who had escaped from that city. A few troopers and a few guns were, it is true, sent in pursuit, but with no resources for a long series of marchings and encampings. We have seen that Brigadier John Jones, with the Roorkee field-force, about three thousand strong—H.M. 60th Rifles, 1st Sikh infantry, Coke's Rifles, 17th Punjaub infantry, the Moultan Horse, and detachments of artillery and engineers—advanced into the heart of Rohilcund from the northwest, while Sir Colin Campbell and General Walpole operated from the Oude or southeastern side: the object being to hem in such of the rebels as had assembled in any force in Rohilcund. Recapitulating the narrative in a few words, we may remind the reader that Jones started from Roorkee on the 15th of the month; crossed the Ganges on the 17th; defeated a body of rebels at Nagul on the same day; and advanced during the next four days steadily on the road to Mooradabad. On the 22d, he fought and won the battle of Nageena; on the 23d, at Noorpoor, he struck into the high road from Mozuffernugger to Mooradabad, with a view of protecting one of the ghâts or ferries of the Ganges; on the 24th, he reached Chujlite, where he learned that Feroze Shah, one of the numerous princes of the House of Delhi, had taken and entered Mooradabad two days before; and on the 25th he reached that town, which had been hastily evacuated by Feroze Shah on the news of Jones's approach. Encamping outside the town, Jones ordered Lieutenant-colonel (formerly Major) Coke, who commanded the infantry portion of his force, to march into Mooradabad, and make a diligent search for a number of rebel chieftains believed to be hidden there. This search was attended with unexpected success. Coke placed parties of the Moultan cavalry at all the outlets of the city, to prevent escapes, and then he attacked and searched all the houses in which rebel chieftains were believed to be concealed. The capture of one of them was marked by a daring act of intrepidity on the part of an English officer. Nawab Mujjoo Khan, the chief of the rebels hereabouts, had caused himself to be proclaimed Nawab of Mooradabad, and had instigated the people to murder and plunder the Europeans in the place, many months earlier. To capture this villain was a point of some importance. Coke proceeded to the Nawab's house with two guns, a party of Sappers, and the 1st Punjaub infantry. The soldiers of the Nawab's guard making a stout resistance, many of them were shot down, including the son and nephew of the Nawab. Lieutenant Angelo then burst open the door of the room in which the Nawab and another of his sons were concealed, and captured them. While so occupied, he was fired upon by some of the Nawab's guard, from an upper room; whereupon he rushed up stairs, burst open the door, entered the room single-handed, and shot three men in succession with his revolver; some of his troops then coming up, he captured the rest of the guard. In short, the search was thoroughly successful. The names and titles of twenty-one rebel chieftains captured, containing many repetitions of Khan, Sheik, Ali, Hossein, Beg, and Shah, showed that these evil-doers were mostly Mohammedans—the Hindoos of Rohilcund having been much less extensively involved in rebellion. While Jones was thus operating in the northwest, Walpole was engaged, though less successfully, in the southeast. He started on the 9th from Lucknow, with the 'Rohilcund Field-force,' five thousand strong; received a mortifying discomfiture on the 14th at Fort Rhodamow, rendered more distressing by the death of Brigadier Adrian Hope; defeated the rebels at Sirsa on the 22d; and crossed the Ramgunga at Allygunje on the 23d. The commander-in-chief himself left Lucknow about the middle of the month; started from Cawnpore at the head of a small column on the 18th; advanced to Kilianpore, Poorah, Urrowl, Meerun-ke-serai, Gosaigunje, and Kamalgunje between that date and the 24th; entered Furruckabad and Futteghur on the 25th; crossed the Ganges on the 26th and 27th; joined Walpole's field-force on the banks of the Ramgunga on the 28th; marched to Kanth on the 29th; and reached Shahjehanpoor on the 30th, in force sufficient to retake that city, but not in time to capture the rebel Moulvie of Fyzabad, who escaped to work mischief elsewhere.—We thus call to mind that, at the end of April, Campbell and Walpole had advanced from the southeast as far as Shahjehanpoor; while Jones had advanced from the northwest to Mooradabad—the two forces being separated by the city of Bareilly, and a wide expanse of intervening country. About the same time General Penny was planning a march with a third column towards a point between Bareilly and Shahjehanpoor, after crossing the Ganges at Nudowlee; he was to march through the Budayoon district, and to unite his column with Sir Colin's main force at Meeranpore Kutra, six marches distant from Futteghur. Bareilly, the chief city of Rohilcund Proper, became the point to which the attention of the commanders of all three forces were directed. We have now to see to what result these combinations led in the following month.

On the 2d of May the Rohilcund field-force, of which Sir Colin Campbell now assumed the command in person, started from Shahjehanpoor, to commence operations against Bareilly. A small force was left behind for the defence of Shahjehanpoor, comprising one wing of the 82d foot, De Kantzow's Irregular Horse, four guns, and a few artillerymen and sappers, under Colonel Hall. What befel this small force will presently appear. Sir Colin marched on the 2d to Tilmul, over a fertile flat country, diversified with topes of trees, but nearly overwhelmed with dust, and inhabited by villagers who were thrown into great doubt by the approach of what they feared might be a hostile force. On the 3d he advanced from Tilmul to Futtehgunje; where he was joined by the force which General Penny had undertaken to bring into Rohilcund from the west.

At this point it is desirable, before tracing the further operations of the commander-in-chief, to notice the course of events which led to the death of General Penny. Being at Nerowlee, on the 29th of April, and believing that the rebels were in some force at the town of Oosait, Penny set out with a column for service in that direction. This column consisted of something under 1500 men: namely, 200 Carabiniers, 350 H.M. 64th, 250 Moultan Horse, 360 Belooch 1st battalion, 300 Punjaub 2d infantry, a heavy field-battery, and a light field-battery with four guns. The column left Nerowlee about nine in the evening; but various delays prevented Penny from reaching Oosait, seven miles distant, until midnight. It then appeared that the enemy had retired from Oosait, and, as native rumour said, had retreated to Datagunje. The column advanced deliberately, under the impression that no enemy was near; but when arrived at Kukerowlee, it suddenly fell into an ambuscade. From the language used by Colonel Jones of the Carabiniers, whose lot it was to write the official account of this affair, it is evident that General Penny had been remiss in precautionary measures; he shared the belief of Mr Wilson, a political resident who accompanied him, that no enemy was near, and under the influence of this belief he relaxed the systematic order of march which had been maintained until Oosait was reached. 'From this point,' we are told, 'military precautions were somewhat neglected, the mounted portion of the column being allowed very considerably to outmarch the infantry; and eventually, though an advanced-guard was kept up, it was held back immediately in front of the artillery.' Penny with his staff, and Mr Wilson, were riding at the head of the advanced-guard; when at four o'clock, near Kukerowlee, they came into the midst of a wholly unexpected body of the enemy; who poured out grape and round shot at not more than forty yards' distance, charged down from the left with horsemen, and opened fire with musketry in front. One of the first who fell was General Penny, brought low by grape-shot. Colonel H. R. Jones, who now took the command, made the best arrangements he could to meet the emergency. The four guns of the light field-battery were quickly ordered up to the front, and the cavalry were brought forward ready for a charge. There were, however, many difficulties to contend against. The enemy's right occupied a mass of sand-hills; their left was protected by thick groves of trees; the town of Kukerowlee was in their rear to fall back upon; and the dimness of the light rendered it impossible rightly to judge the number and position of the rebels. Under these circumstances, Colonel Jones deemed it best merely to hold his ground until daylight should suggest the most fitting course of procedure, and until the infantry should have arrived. When the 64th came up with the cavalry and artillery which Penny had imprudently allowed to go so far ahead, Colonel Bingham at once charged the enemy in front, and drove them into the town. This done, Jones ordered the artillery to shell the town; this completely paralysed the rebels, who soon began to escape from the opposite side. Hereupon Jones sent his cavalry in pursuit; many of the enemy were cut up, and one gun taken; but it was not deemed prudent to continue this pursuit to any great distance, in a district imperfectly known. This battle of Kukerowlee was thus, like nearly all the battles, won by the British; and had it not been for the unfortunate want of foresight on the part of General Penny, he might have been spared to write the dispatch which described it. He was the only officer killed. Those wounded were Captains Forster and Betty, Lieutenants Eckford, Davies, and Graham. Eckford's escape from death was very extraordinary. The first fire opened by the rebels shot his horse from under him; he then mounted an artillery-horse; a party of Ghazees—fanatics who have sworn to die for their 'deen' or faith—attacked him, wounded him, and stabbed his horse; Eckford fell off, and a Ghazee gave him a tremendous cut over the back of the right shoulder, and left him for dead; Surgeon Jones came up, and helped the wounded lieutenant along; but the enemy pursuing, Eckford was made to lie down flat on his face as if dead; the enemy passed on without noticing him, and he was afterwards rescued by some of his companions. Three days after this encounter with the rebels, Colonel Jones succeeded in bringing poor Penny's column into safe junction with Sir Colin's force at Futtehgunje—the mutineers and ruffians from the district of Budayoon retiring before him, and swelling the mass of insurgents at Bareilly.

While this was doing, another Jones was marching through Rohilcund in a different direction. It is necessary to avoid confusion in this matter, by bearing in mind that Brigadier John Jones commanded the 'Roorkee field-force;' while Colonel H. R. Jones held the temporary command of the column lately headed by General Penny. The brigadier, in pursuance of a plan laid down by Sir Colin, directed his march so that both might reach Bareilly on the same day, the one from Mooradabad and the other from Shahjehanpoor. While on his march, Jones expected to come up with the rebels at Meergunje, a place within a few miles of Bareilly. He found, however, that after constructing two batteries at the first-named place, they had apparently misdoubted their safety, and retreated to Bareilly. Cavalry, sent on in pursuit, overtook the rear of the rebels, cut down great numbers of them, and captured two guns. At an early hour on the 6th, the brigadier with his force arrived within a mile and a half of a bridge contiguous to Bareilly, known as Bahadoor Singh's bridge. His reconnoitring party was fired upon. A skirmish at once ensued, which lasted three hours, and ended in the capture of the bridge; the rebels were driven back with great slaughter into Bareilly. Just as Jones reached the margin of the city, he heard a cannonading which denoted the arrival of the commander-in-chief from the opposite direction.

Having thus noticed the coalescence of the forces under the two Joneses, we shall be prepared to trace the march of Sir Colin Campbell towards the common centre to which the attention of all was now directed.

After being reinforced at Futtehgunje by the column recently under the command of Penny, Sir Colin resumed his march on the 3d of May. As he advanced, he received news that the rebels were in much disorder. Several of the chiefs had left them; and Nena Sahib, a coward throughout, had sought safety by fleeing towards the border-region between Oude and Nepaul. The main body had been some time at Fureedpore; but when they heard of Sir Colin being at Futtehgunje they retreated to Bareilly—thereby running into the power of another column. The villagers, mostly Hindoos, told distressing tales of the extortions and wrongs they had suffered at the hands of the Mohammedan chieftains, during the twelve months that Rohilcund had been in the power of the rebels; they made great profession of their joy at seeing the arrival of an English army; but past experience had shewn that such profession should be received with much qualification. Certain it was, that Sir Colin Campbell, during his marches through Oude, the Doab, and Rohilcund, received very little aid, and very little correct information, from the villagers of the districts through which he passed; they were either timid, or double-dealing, or both. In one of his dispatches he said: 'In spite of the assumed friendship of the Hindoo portion of the population, I have not found it easier to obtain information in Rohilcund, on which trust could be put, than has been the case in dealing with the insurrection in other parts of the empire.' On the 4th, the commander-in-chief advanced from Futtehgunje to Fureedpore, only one march from Bareilly. Rumours now arrived that not only Nena Sahib, but the Delhi prince Feroze Shah, had sought safety by flight from Bareilly; but that Khan Mahomed Khan still remained at the head of the rebels. On this point, however, and on the number of the enemy's forces, no information was obtained that could be relied upon. As for Bareilly itself, supposing no fortifications to have been thrown up by the rebels, it could not long maintain a siege; seeing that, with the exception of a stream with rather steep banks, there was no obstacle to the entrance of a force from without. The city itself consisted mainly of a street two miles long, with numerous narrow streets and lanes branching off to the right and left; outside these streets and lanes were large suburbs of detached houses, walled gardens, plantations, and enclosures; and outside the suburbs were wide plains intersected by nullahs. It was at present uncertain whether the two forces, from Shahjehanpoor and Mooradabad,

Hindoo Fruit-girl.

could prevent the escape of the enemy over these lateral suburbs and plains; but such was certainly the hope and wish of the commander-in-chief.

Early in the morning of the 5th, Sir Colin left his camping-ground at Fureedpore, and advanced towards Bareilly. After a brief halt, the videttes detected a body of rebel cavalry in the distance; and Sir Colin at once marshalled his forces for an attack. The whole force was brigaded into two brigades of cavalry, under Jones and Hagart; one of artillery, under Brind; and two of infantry, under Hay and Stisted.* Without reference to the brigades, however, the order of advance was thus arranged: the 2d Punjaub cavalry formed a line of skirmishers on the left of the main-road; the Lahore light horse formed a similar line on the right; while across the road, and in support of these skirmishers, was a line formed by troops of the 9th Lancers and the 1st Punjaub cavalry, a troop of horse-artillery, and several field-guns. Then came the 78th Highlanders, and a body of Sappers and Engineers, along the road; the 93d foot on the right of the road; and the 42d Highlanders on the left. Next, supporting and flanking these, were

* *Cavalry.—1st Brigade*, under Brigadier Jones (6th Dragoon Guards). Head-quarters and two squadrons 6th Dragoon Guards, under Captain Bickerstaff; Captain Lind's Moultanee horse. *2d Brigade*, under Brigadier Hagart (7th Hussars). Her Majesty's 9th Lancers, under Major Coles; 2d Punjaub cavalry, under Major S. Browne; detachments of Lahore light horse, 1st Punjaub cavalry, 5th Punjaub cavalry, and 17th irregular cavalry.

Artillery.—Under Lieutenant-colonel Brind, C.B., B.A.; Lieutenant-colonel Tombs's troop, B.H.A.; Lieutenant-colonel Remington's troop, B.H.A.; Major Hammond's light field-battery, B.A., four guns; two heavy field-batteries, Captain Francis, B.A.; siege-train with Major Le Mesurier's company, B.A., under Captain Cookworthy's detachment, B.A., detachment R.E. Bengal and Punjaub; Sappers and Miners, under Lieutenant-colonel Harness, R.E., chief-engineer to the force.

Infantry.—Highland Brigade, under Lieutenant-colonel Leith Hay, C.B. (her Majesty's 93d Highlanders). Her Majesty's 42d Highlanders, under Lieutenant-colonel Cameron; her Majesty's 79th Highlanders, under Lieutenant-colonel Taylor, C.B.; her Majesty's 93d Highlanders, under Lieutenant-colonel Ross; 4th Punjaub Rifles, Lieutenant M'Queen; Belooch Battalion, Captain Beville. *Brigadier Stisted's* (78th) *Brigade*. Seven companies her Majesty's 64th foot, Lieutenant-colonel Bingham, C.B.; her Majesty's 78th Highlanders, Colonel Hamilton; 4 companies her Majesty's 82 foot, Colonel the Hon. P. Herbert, C.B.; 2d Punjaub infantry, Lieutenant-colonel Greene; 22d Punjaub infantry, Captain Stafford.

the 79th foot, the Carabiniers, the Moultan Horse, the remainder of the 9th Lancers and of the Punjaub cavalry, and a wing of the Belooch battalion. Then came the siege-train and the enormous array of baggage; flanked by the 64th foot, a wing of the 82d, the 2d Punjaub infantry, and the 4th Punjaub rifles. Lastly came the rear-guard, comprising the 22d Punjaub infantry, the 17th irregular cavalry, a squadron of the 5th Punjaub cavalry, and a troop of horse-artillery. As this strong force advanced, the rebels fired a few shot from a battery set up at the entrance to Bareilly; but they made scarcely any attempt to fortify or defend either the stream that crossed the high road, or the bridge over the stream. The enemy's infantry appeared to be mostly congregated in the old cantonment or sepoy-lines, while the cavalry were hovering about in topes of trees. The infantry scarcely shewed; but the cavalry, aided by horse-artillery, made demonstrations as if about to attack, in numbers estimated at two or three thousand. This did not stay the progress of Sir Colin, who was too strong to be affected by such an attempt. Advancing through a suburb on one side of the city, he ordered the 42d, the 79th, and a Sikh or Punjaub regiment, to explore a ruined mass of one-storied houses. What followed may best be told in the language of Mr Russell, who was with the army at the time: 'As soon as the Sikhs got into the houses, they were exposed to a heavy fire from a large body of matchlock-men concealed around them. They either retired of their own accord, or were ordered to do so; at all events, they fell back with rapidity and disorder upon the advancing Highlanders. And now occurred a most extraordinary scene. Among the matchlockmen, who, to the number of seven or eight hundred, were lying behind the walls of the houses, was a body of Ghazees or Mussulman fanatics, who, like the Roman Decii, devote their lives with solemn oaths to their country or their faith. Uttering loud cries, "Bismillah, Allah, deen, deen!" one hundred and thirty of these fanatics, sword in hand, with small circular bucklers on the left arm, and green cummerbungs, rushed out after the Sikhs, and dashed at the left of the right wing of the Highlanders. With bodies bent and heads low, waving their tulwars with a circular motion in the air, they came on with astonishing rapidity. At first they were mistaken for Sikhs, whose passage had already somewhat disordered our ranks. Fortunately, Sir Colin Campbell was close up with the 42d; his keen, quick eye detected the case at once. "Steady, men, steady; close up the ranks. Bayonet them as they come on." It was just in time; for these madmen, furious with bang, were already among us, and a body of them sweeping around the left of the right wing got into the rear of the regiment. The struggle was sanguinary but short. Three of them dashed so suddenly at Colonel Cameron that they pulled him off his horse ere he could defend himself. His sword fell out of its sheath, and he would have been hacked to pieces in another moment but for the gallant promptitude of Colour-sergeant Gardiner, who, stepping out of the ranks, drove his bayonet through two of them in the twinkling of an eye. The third was shot by one of the 42d. Brigadier Walpole had a similar escape; he was seized by two or three of the Ghazees, who sought to put him off his horse, while others cut at him with their tulwars. He received two cuts on the hand, but he was delivered from the enemy by the quick bayonets of the 42d. In a few minutes the dead bodies of one hundred and thirty-three of these Ghazees, and some eighteen or twenty wounded men of ours, were all the tokens left of the struggle.'

Sir Colin had not yet reached Bareilly. The little skirmishing that had occurred was in one of the suburbs. The enemy's cavalry, though powerless for any serious attack, succeeded in creating, by a dash across the plain towards the baggage, an indescribable amount of alarm among the camp-followers, bazaar-traders, horses, camels, bullocks, and elephants. There was not much real fighting throughout the day; but the heat was so intense, the poor soldiers suffered so much from thirst, so many were brought low by sunstroke, and all were so fatigued, that Sir Colin resolved to bivouac on the plain for the night, postponing till the next day an advance into, and the capture of, the city of Bareilly.

Whether this delay on the road to victory was sound or not in a military sense, it afforded the enemy an opportunity to escape, which they did not fail to take advantage of. On the morning of the 6th, it was ascertained that many of the leaders, and a large body of rebel troops, had quietly left the place. Guns were brought to bear upon certain buildings in the city, known or suspected to be full of insurgents; and it was while this cannonade was in progress that Sir Colin became aware of the arrival of Brigadier Jones, already adverted to. On the 7th the two forces advanced into the city, and took complete possession of it, but without capturing any of the leaders, or preventing the escape of the main body of rebels. A large quantity of artillery, mostly of recent native manufacture, fell into the hands of the victors, together with a great store of shell, shot, and powder, for the manufacture of which, materials and machinery had been provided by the rebels.

Before proceeding with the narrative of Bareilly affairs, it will be necessary to notice a very remarkable episode at Shahjehanpoor. It will be remembered that when Sir Colin Campbell started from that place on the 2d of May, to advance on Bareilly, he left behind him a small defensive force. In his dispatch he said: 'When I passed through Shahjehanpoor, I was informed that the Fyzabad Moulvie, and the Nawab of the former place, were at Mohumdee, with a considerable body of men who had retired from Shahjehanpoor; and I thought it would be impolitic to leave the district without evidence of our presence.' He therefore told off a small defensive force; comprising a wing of the 82d foot, Lieutenant De Kantzow's irregular horse, a few artillerymen, and four guns. In obedience to orders left by Sir Colin, Colonel Hall, of the 82d, marched this small force from the camp at Azeezgunje, to occupy the jail in the cantonment of Shahjehanpoor as a military post. There being no shade within the cantonment, he pitched his camp for a time in a tope of trees near the jail. He next formed the jail into a small intrenched position, with four guns, and as large a supply of provisions as he could procure. All this was done in one day, the 2d of May; and, indeed, not an hour was to be lost; for a spy appeared on the following morning to announce that a large body of rebels had arrived within four miles of the place. This announcement proved to be correct. A strong band of insurgents from Mohumdee in Oude, taking advantage of Sir Colin's departure from Shahjehanpoor, were advancing to regain possession of that station. Colonel Hall immediately sent his baggage and provisions into the jail, and ordered four companies of the 82d to guard the camp during this transfer. Going out to reconnoitre, he saw the enemy's cavalry approaching. Lieutenant De Kantzow would willingly have charged the enemy with his small body of horse; but the colonel, knowing the overwhelming force of the rebels, and noting his instructions to act on the defensive, forbade this charge. Both went into the jail, with their handful of troops, and prepared for a resolute defence. The rebels arrived, seized the old fort, plundered the town, put many of the principal inhabitants to death, and established patrols on the river's bank. It was computed that they were little less than eight thousand strong, with twelve guns. Against this strong force, Hall held his position for eight days and nights, sustaining a continuous bombardment, without thinking for an instant of yielding. Not until the 7th of the month did the commander-in-chief hear of this disaster at Shahjehanpoor. He at once made up a brigade; consisting of the 60th Rifles, the 79th Highlanders, a wing of the 82d foot, the 22d Punjaub infantry, two squadrons of Carabiniers, Cureton's Horse, with some artillery and guns. Brigadier Jones, who commanded this brigade, received at the same time from Sir Colin discretionary power to attack the enemy at Mohumdee after the relief of Hall at Shahjehanpoor, if he should so deem it expedient. Jones, at the head of his brigade, started from Bareilly on the 8th, and reached Shahjehanpoor on the 11th. At daybreak, a body of the enemy having been seen, Jones sent out the Mooltan Horse to pursue them; but a heavy mass of troops being now visible, it became necessary to draw up in order of battle. The enemy's cavalry began the battle; these were driven off by Jones's howitzers. Then the Highlanders and Rifles were pushed on as skirmishers, supported by horse-artillery; and in a short time the rebels were put to flight—allowing the brigadier to select his own point of entrance into Shahjehanpoor. Fortunately he made himself acquainted with the fact that many buildings in the suburbs had been loopholed for musketry, and with the probability that many others in the heart of the town had been similarly treated; he thereupon avoided the main street, and made a detour through the eastern suburbs. No enemy was visible within the town, until a strong party of troopers were found drawn up near the school-house; these were quickly dispersed by a few shrapnell shells, and a pursuit by the Carabiniers, leaving a gun and some ammunition-wagons behind them. Jones continued his march by the church, and across the parade-ground to the jail, where the gallant little garrison under Colonel Hall had so long defended themselves against an overwhelming force. The bold stand made by this officer was an enterprise that excited little attention amid the various excitements of the period; but Sir Colin Campbell did not fail to see that the defence had been prompt, energetic, and skilful. The adjutant-general, writing to the governor-general, said: 'I am directed by the commander-in-chief to inform his lordship that the lieutenant-colonel hardly does justice to himself in his report of this defence, which was conducted by him with prudence and skill, and consequently with trifling loss. I am to add that Lieutenant-colonel Hall, although he makes no mention of the fact, was himself wounded by a musket-bullet in the leg, from the effect of which he has not yet (May 29th) recovered.'

To return to Bareilly. After the operations which have now been briefly described, the insurgents were so completely driven out of Mooradabad, Bareilly, and Shahjehanpoor, the principal towns in this province, that it was no longer deemed necessary to keep up the 'Rohilcund field-force' in its collected form; the various brigades, cavalry and infantry, were broken up, and Sir Colin gave separate duties to his various officers, according to the tenor of the information received from various parts of the country. Some corps and detachments remained at Bareilly; some went to Lucknow; one or two Punjaub regiments set off towards Meerut; and General Walpole was placed in command in Kumaon and Rohilcund. It was just at this time, the 11th of May, that Sir Colin Campbell received an official notification from the Queen to thank his troops in her name for their gallant services in earlier months. The address was, of course, merely of a customary kind under such circumstances; but it constituted one among the list of honours to which soldiers look as some reward for their hard life.* The 'last stronghold'

* 'The commander-in-chief has received the most gracious commands of her Majesty the Queen to communicate to the army an expression of the deep interest felt by the Queen in the exertions of the troops, and the successful progress of the campaign.

'Sir Colin Campbell has delayed giving execution to the royal command, until he was able to announce to the army that the last stronghold of rebellion had fallen before the persevering attempts of the troops of her Majesty and the Hon. East India Company.

'It is impossible for the commander-in-chief to express adequately adverted to by him was Bareilly; he could not then know that another stronghold, Gwalior, was destined to be the scene of a much more sanguinary struggle.

Among the arrangements more immediately affecting Rohilcund, was the formation of a column for special service in the country districts. This column, placed under the command of Lieutenant-colonel (now Brigadier) Coke, comprised a wing of the 42d Highlanders, the 1st Punjaub rifles, the 1st Sikh infantry, a detachment of the 24th Punjaub infantry, a squadron of Carabiniers, the Moultan Horse, a detachment of the 17th irregular cavalry, and a considerable force of artillery. With three weeks' supplies for the European troops, and four weeks' for the native, this column set forth from Bareilly on the 12th of May.

The commander-in-chief, leaving instructions for the formation of efficient defences at Bareilly, started off to some more central station, where he could be in easy communication with the various columns engaged in different parts of Northern India. General Walpole took command of the whole of the Rohilcund troops; having under him Coke's brigade just adverted to, and Major Lennox to superintend the engineering works at Bareilly. Mr Alexander established himself as civil commissioner, to reorganise a government for that long-distracted province. Being thus satisfied that affairs were in a good train, Sir Colin started on the 15th, taking with him his head-quarters staff, the 64th foot, a wing of the 9th Lancers, and detachments of other troops. The veteran commander bore heat and fatigue in a manner that astonished his subordinates; he got through an amount of work which knocked up his aids-de-camp; and was always ready to advise or command, as if rest and food were contingencies that he cared not about. The natives, when any of them sought for and obtained an interview with him, were often a good deal surprised to see the commander of the mighty British army in shirt-sleeves and a pith-hat; but the keen eye and the cool manner of the old soldier told that he had all his wits about him, and was none the worse from the absence of glitter and personal adornment. His advance in the first instance was to Fureedpore, as a first stage towards Futteghur; his second to Futtehgunje; but here he heard news that changed his plans. To understand what occurred, we must revert to the affairs at Shahjehanpoor.

When Brigadier Jones had relieved Colonel Hall from his difficulties on the 11th, he found that he had been engaged with a fragment only of the enemy's force; and he prepared for the contingency of a hostile encounter. On the 15th he was attacked with great fury and in great force by the rebels, who were headed by the Moulvie of Fyzabad, the Begum of Oude, the Shahzada of Delhi, and (as some thought) by Nena Sahib. The struggle continued throughout the day, and needed all the activity and resources of the brigadier. So large was the body of rebels, indeed, that he could do nothing more than act on the defensive until reinforcements could reach him. This was the information received by Sir Colin when at Futtehgunje. He immediately re-arranged his forces. Leaving the 47th and 93d foot, the 17th Punjaub infantry, the 2d Sikh cavalry, and some horse and foot artillery, to guard Bareilly; he hastened towards Shahjehanpoor with the 64th foot, the Belooch battalion, the 9th Lancers, and some horse and foot artillery. On the 17th he marched to Tilhur; moving cautiously, for the rebels were known to be in great force not far distant. He rested during the mid-day heat, in a tope of mango-trees beyond the village of Tilhur. In the evening, information arrived that the Moulvie, with a large force, was strongly posted on the Mohumdee road, a few miles northeast of Shahjehanpoor. Mohumdee, which had been made a stronghold by the rebels, comprised a brick-fort, mounted with twelve or fifteen guns, strengthened in various ways, and protected within and without by troops. The Moulvie, as the most skilful of the insurgent leaders, held the chief command in these parts; but the Begum of Oude, and the Shahzada of Delhi, were believed to be near at hand. Mohumdee itself was about twenty miles from Shahjehanpoor; but the whole road was more or less commanded by the rebels. In the early morn of the 18th Sir Colin started again. Arriving at Shahjehanpoor, he passed the old camping-ground, made a partial circuit of the city to the bridge of boats, crossed the bridge, and traversed the city to the other side. It was found that the city had suffered considerably by the cannonading which Brigadier Jones had been compelled to inflict upon it, in his operations for the relief of the little garrison under Colonel Hall; and that many of the respectable inhabitants had deserted the place until more peaceful times, more facilities for quiet trade, should arrive.

When Sir Colin's force joined that under Brigadier Jones, and the two commanders compared notes, it was found that the brigadier's troops had suffered intensely from the heat. Mr Russell, who at that time—sick and hurt by a kick from a horse—was carried in a doolie or litter among the 'baggage' of Sir Colin's army, was not sufficiently in front to witness much of the fighting; but his diary is full of vivid pictures of camp-life under a burning sun: 'In Rose's attack on the enemy at Koonch, eight men fell dead in the ranks, and upwards of twenty officers and men had to be carried from the field through the heat of the sun. Nineteen of our casualties at Bareilly, ten of which

his sense of the high honour done to him in having been chosen by the Queen to convey her Majesty's most gracious acknowledgments to the army, in the ranks of which he has passed his life.

'The commander-in-chief ventures to quote the very words of the Queen:

'"That so many gallant, brave, and distinguished men, beginning with one whose name will ever be remembered with pride, Brigadier-general Havelock, should have died and fallen, is a great grief to the Queen. To all Europeans and native troops who have fought so nobly and so gallantly—and amongst whom the Queen is rejoiced to see the 93d—the Queen wishes Sir Colin to convey the expression of her great admiration and gratitude."'

were fatal, were caused in the same way. In fact, every march henceforth after ten o'clock in the morning must be attended with loss of life.'—'A peep into most of the tents would discover many of the head-quarters' staff panting on their charpoys, in the nearest possible approach to Adamite costume, and gasping for breath like carp on the banks of a moat. It may readily be imagined—if officers, each of whom has a tent to himself, with kuskus tatties, punkahs, and similar appliances to reduce the temperature, suffer so much from heat—what the men endure, packed ten or twelve in a tent, and in some regiments eighteen or twenty, without such resources, and without change of light clothing; and how heavily picket-duty, outlying and inlying, presses upon them.' In encamping after a twilight morning march, 'it may be easily imagined how anxiously each man surveys the trees about his tent as the site is marked out, and calculates what shelter it will give him, and at what time the sun will find out his weak points during the day; for indeed the rays do strike through every interstice like red-hot shot. There is no indecision of shadow, no infirmity of outline; for wherever the sun falls on the side of a tent, it seems to punch out a fervid blazing pattern on the gray ground of the canvas.'—'The motion of a doolie is by no means unpleasant; but I confess my experience of its comforts has now lasted quite long enough. It is a long cot slung from a bamboo-pole, borne on the shoulders of four men, two in front and two behind, who at a shuffling pace carry you along the road at the rate of four miles an hour; and two spare men follow as a relief. As the bottom of the litter hangs close to the ground, the occupant has more than his share of all the dust that is going; but if the curtains or tilts are let down, the heat becomes insupportable.'—'The march of Jones's column to the relief of Shahjehanpoor had told heavily upon the men. Upwards of thirty rank and file of the 79th fell out in marching to and through the city; and the 60th Rifles, accustomed though they be to Indian warfare, were deprived of the services of upwards of forty men from sun-stroke. It was pitiable, I was told, to see the poor fellows lying in their doolies, gasping their last. The veins of the arm were opened, and leeches applied to the temples; but notwithstanding every care, the greater number of the cases were fatal almost immediately; and even among the cases of those who recovered, there are few who are fit for active service again, except after a long interval of rest.'—'I own I am distressed when I see the 60th Rifles dressed in dark-green tunics, which absorb the heat almost as much as if they were made of black cloth, and their cloth forage-caps poorly covered with a few folds of dark cotton. What shall we say of the 79th Highlanders, who still wear that picturesque and extraordinary head-dress, with the addition of a flap of gray cloth over the ears! If it were white, perhaps it would afford some protection against the sun; but, as it is, this mass of black feathers is surely not the head-dress that would be chosen by any one, except a foolish fantastic savage, for the plains of India.'

Having arrived at Shahjehanpoor on the 18th, the commander-in-chief wished to give his troops a little needful rest during the heat of the day. A cavalry detachment, however, having gone out to reconnoitre, came in sight of a small mud-fort containing four guns; the guns fired upon the cavalry; the report of this firing brought forward a body of the enemy's troopers; and the appearance of these drew out Sir Colin and nearly the whole of his force. Thus a battle-array was very unexpectedly formed. Among the rebels was a large body of Rohilla troopers—active, determined, well mounted, and well armed; and as these men fought better than was wont among the enemy, and were supported by many guns, there followed a good deal of cavalry and artillery skirmishing. During the firing, a round-shot passed so close to Sir Colin Campbell and General Mansfield as greatly to endanger both, and to increase the desire among the soldiers generally that the commander-in-chief, who was very careful of his men's lives, would attach a little more value to his own. Although the result of the encounter was to drive off the enemy to a greater distance, it was not wholly satisfactory or decisive; Sir Colin had not intended to resume active service until his troops had been refreshed by a few hours' rest; but the reconnaissance had been so managed as to precipitate an engagement with the enemy. It was only a small part of the rebel force that was thus encountered on the 18th; the main body, eight or ten thousand strong, was at Mohumdee.

The commander-in-chief, finding himself too weak in cavalry to pursue the enemy with any effect, suspended operations for a few days; remaining at Shahjehanpoor until Brigadier Coke's column could join him from the district of Pileebheet. Coke, in accordance with a plan already noticed, was preparing to sweep round the country by way of Boodayoun to Mooradabad; but he now joined Sir Colin, on the 22d; and preparations were made for an immediate advance upon the rebel position at Mohumdee. Again were the enemy beaten, and again did the Moulvie and the other leaders escape. When the British marched to that place on the 24th they found that the rebels had evacuated their strong fort, after destroying the defence-works. They had also destroyed Kujoorea, a very strong doubly intrenched position, surrounded by thick bamboo-hedges, and having a citadel. Several guns were dug up at the last-named place; and much property was discovered which had once belonged to the unfortunate Europeans murdered by the rebels nearly twelve months earlier.

Throughout the operations in Oude and Rohilcund, from May 1857 till May 1858, one of the master-spirits among the rebels was the Moulvie of Fyzabad—a man whose name has been so often mentioned: 'A tall, lean, and muscular man, with lantern jaws, long thin lips, high aquiline nose, deep-set large dark eyes, beetle brows, long beard, and coarse black hair falling in masses over his shoulders.' During the investigations which were subsequently made into the plans and intrigues of the rebels in Oude, the fact was ascertained that this Moulvie had been known many years before as Ahmed Shah, a sort of inspired fanatic or fakeer. He travelled through the Northwest Provinces on some sort of miraculous mission which was a mystery to the Europeans; his stay at Agra was of considerable duration, and was marked by the exercise of much influence over the Mohammedan natives. Mr Drummond, magistrate of that city, kept an eye on him as a suspicious character; and it was afterwards regarded as a probability that the Moulvie had been engaged in some plotting inimical to the English 'raj.' The commencement of the mutiny in May 1857 may have been determined by unforeseen circumstances; but abundant proofs were gradually obtained that some sort of conspiracy had been long before formed, and hence a reasonable inference that the Moulvie may have been one of the conspirators. When the troops mutinied at Fyzabad in June, they placed the Moulvie at their head. He had been in that city in April, attended by several fanatic followers; and here he circulated seditious papers, openly proclaiming a religious war. Although the police on this occasion were ordered to arrest him, he and his followers made an armed resistance which could not be suppressed without military aid. The Moulvie was captured, tried, and condemned for execution; but the Revolt broke out before he could thus be got rid of, and then he suddenly changed character from a felon to a leader of a formidable body of armed men. Though sometimes eclipsed in power by other leaders, he maintained great influence over the rebels throughout the turbulent proceedings of the period. There can be little doubt that he had much of the sincerity of a true religious fanatic; and as he was an able man, and free from the dastardly cruelty that so stained the names of Nena Sahib and other leaders of unenviable notoriety, a certain kind of respect was felt for him by the British whom he opposed.

When the month of May ended, and Sir Colin Campbell had proceeded to Futteghur as a central station whence he could conveniently watch the progress of events, the Rohilcund and Roorkee field-forces were broken up; and the regiments which had composed them were set apart for various detached duties. Brigadier Seaton remained at Shahjehanpoor, with the 60th Rifles, the 82d foot, the 22d Punjaub infantry, Cureton's cavalry, two squadrons of the 6th Dragoon Guards, and some artillery. The 79th Highlanders, and various detachments of artillery, took their departure for Futteghur. The 64th went to Meerut; the 9th Lancers to Umballa; and Coke's Sikh brigade to Boodayoun or Pileebheet. At the end of the month all was quiet at and near Shahjehanpoor, and the peaceful portion of the inhabitants were returning; but it was doubtful how soon a new irruption of rebels from Oude would throw everything again into confusion. Indeed there were at that time many rebel leaders at the head of small bodies of insurgents, ready for mischief; among whom were Baboo Ramnarain of Islamnuggur, and Nizam Ali of Shahee—but these men could safely be regarded rather as guerrilla chieftains than as military leaders.

It was on this fitting occasion, when there seemed to be a lull in the din of war, that Sir Colin Campbell issued a congratulatory address to the troops of the Anglo-Indian armies. Although the address was not made publicly known to the troops by the adjutant-general until the following month, it was dated the 28th of May, and ran as follows:

'In the month of October 1857 the garrison of Lucknow was still shut up, the road from Calcutta to Cawnpore was unsafe, the communications with the northwest were entirely closed, and the civil and military functionaries had disappeared altogether from wide and numerous provinces. Under instructions from the Right Honourable the Governor-general, a large plan was designed, by which the resources of the three presidencies, after the arrival of reinforcements from England, should be made available for combined action. Thus, while the army of Bengal, gathering strength from day to day, has recovered the Gangetic Doab, restored the communications with the northwest of the empire, relieved the old garrison of Lucknow, afterwards taking that city, reoccupying Rohilcund, and finally insuring in a great measure the tranquillity of the old provinces—the three columns put in movement from Bombay and Madras have rendered like great and efficient services in their long and difficult marches on the Jumna, through Central India, and in Rajpootana. These columns, under Major-generals Sir Hugh Rose, K.C.B., Whitlock, and Roberts, have admirably performed their share in the general combination arranged under the orders of his lordship the governor-general. This combination was spread over a surface ranging from the boundaries of Bombay and Madras to the extreme northwest of India. By their patient endurance of fatigue, their unfailing obedience, and their steadfast gallantry, the troops have enabled the generals to fulfil their instructions. In no war has it ever happened that troops have been more often engaged than during the campaigns which have now terminated. In no war has it ever happened that troops should always contend against immense numerical odds, as has been invariably the case in every encounter during the struggle of the last year; and in no war has constant success without a check been more conspicuously achieved. It has not occurred that one column here, another there, has won more honour than the other portions of the army; the various corps have done like hard work, have struggled through the difficulties of a hot-weather campaign, and have compensated for paucity of numbers in the vast area of operations by continuous and unexampled marching, notwithstanding the season. It is probable that much yet remains for the army to perform; but now that the commander-in-chief is able to give the greater part of it rest for a time, he chooses this moment to congratulate the generals and troops on the great results which have attended their labours. He can fairly say that they have accomplished in a few months what was believed by the ill-wishers of England to be either beyond her strength, or to be the work of many years.'

This address is not fully intelligible without taking into account certain brilliant proceedings in Central India, hereafter to be noticed; but it is transcribed here as a suitable termination to the Rohilcund operations in the month of May. The other important affairs bearing relation to it will find their due place of record.

Oude itself has been very little mentioned in this chapter. The reason is, that the most important section of the rebels escaped from that province into Rohilcund, after the great siege of Lucknow, thereby determining the main scene of struggle during May. There was not, however, a total cessation of fighting in Oude. Sir Hope Grant, who had been left at Lucknow by Sir Colin Campbell, had more than one encounter with the rebels in the course of the month. Some of these operations brought him, on the 10th, to a place called Doundea Khera, a fort belonging to the rebel Ram Buksh. This fort, though of mud, was of considerable strength; it was square, with earthen walls and bastions of considerable thickness; it had four guns, and was rendered difficult of approach by a ditch and belt of prickly jungle. The fort was, however, found deserted when Sir Hope arrived. His work then consisted in destroying the fort, and such of the buildings as could be shewn to have belonged to Ram Buksh. This done, he advanced on the 12th to Nuggur. Hearing that two thalookdars or chieftains, Beni Madhoo and Shewrutten Singh, had assembled an army of fifteen thousand infantry, sixteen hundred cavalry, and eleven guns, at Sirsee, a village and fort about five miles off, Grant determined to attack them at once. He left all his baggage, supplies, &c., with tents struck, in a safe position, with a force of cavalry, infantry, and artillery for their protection. From the extreme difficulty of obtaining correct information in that country, Sir Hope was in much doubt concerning the ground occupied by the enemy; and eventually he found it stronger than he had expected. The rebels were drawn up on the banks of a nullah, with an extensive thick jungle in their rear, rendered still stronger by the fortified village of Towrie. At five in the afternoon the enemy's first gun opened fire; but as soon as Grant had formed his column, with cavalry and horse-artillery covering his right flank, the rebels were attacked with such boldness and vigour that they gave way, and were driven into the jungle, leaving two iron guns behind them. Grant's column was at one time almost surrounded by the rebels; but a prompt movement of some of the regiments speedily removed this difficulty. The rebels suffered severe loss, including that of one of their leaders, Shewrutten. Sir Hope Grant, deeming it imprudent to allow his troops to enter the jungle, bivouacked for the night on the ground where the battle had been fought, and returned on the morning of the 13th to his camp at Nuggur. During these operations, he found himself within a short distance of the small Hindoo temple in which Lieutenants Delafosse and Thomson, and several other Europeans, sought refuge after their escape from the boat-massacre at Cawnpore, eleven months earlier.* Much blood having been spilled on that occasion, one of the objects of the present expedition was to bring certain of the native miscreants to justice. Mr Elliott, assistant-commissioner, who accompanied the column, went on to the temple with a squadron of cavalry, took a few prisoners, and then destroyed the temple—which still exhibited the shot-holes resulting from the dastardly attack of a large body of natives on a few unarmed Europeans.

Towards the close of the month, Hope Grant found that a body of the enemy was threatening Bunnee, and endeavouring to obtain command of the high road between Lucknow and Cawnpore; this necessitated an expedition on his part to frustrate the design. As a means of better controlling approach to the capital, he blew up the stone-bridge over the Goomtee, thus leaving the iron suspension-bridge as the only mode of crossing.

Of Lucknow, little need be said in this chapter. The engineers were employed in constructing such batteries and strongholds, and clearing away such native buildings, as might enable a small British force to defend the place; while Mr Montgomery, the newly appointed chief-commissioner, was cautiously feeling his way towards a re-establishment of civil government. Viscount Canning had given him plenary powers, in reference to the issue of any proclamation to the natives—powers which required much tact in their exercise; for there was still a large amount of fierce opposition and vindictive feeling to contend against.

In the Doab, and the district adjacent to it, several minor affairs took place during the month, sufficient to indicate a very turbulent condition of portions of the population, even if not of great military importance. At one period of the month five thousand rebels, in two bodies, crossed the Kallee Nuddee, and marched along the western boundary of the Futteghur district, burning and destroying villages. They then crossed the Ganges into Oude by the Shorapore Ghât, taking with them several guns. Here, however, they were watched and checked by a small force under Brigadier Carthew, and by Cureton's Horse. About the same time, a party of a thousand rebels, with

* See Chap. viii., p. 138.

four guns, marched from Humeerpore to Asung, on the great trunk-road between Lullutpore and Cawnpore; they commanded that road for several days, until a force could be sent out to dislodge them. Higher up the Doab, the fort and village of Ayana, in the Etawah district, were taken by a party of Alexander's Horse, and a rebel chief, named Roop Singh, expelled. Colonel Riddell, who commanded a column from Etawah, encountered and defeated small bodies of rebels near Ooriya and Sheregurh, and then descended the Ganges in boats to Calpee, to take part in an important series of operations in which the Central India field-force was mainly concerned. Brigadier Showers, during the greater part of this month, was employed in various ways around Agra as a centre. Among other measures, he organised a corps of Jât cavalry, to defend the ghâts of the Ganges, and prevent rebels from crossing the river. Agra itself, with the brigadier at hand to check rising disturbances, remained free from serious troubles; though from time to time rumours were circulated which threw the Europeans into some uneasiness. As the native inhabitants still possessed a number of old firelocks, swords, and other weapons; it was deemed prudent to issue an order for disarming. An immense collection of queer native weapons was the result—not very formidable to English troops, but mischievous as a possible element of strength to the disaffected. Many of the guns in the fort were kept pointed towards the city, as a menace to evil-doers.

In reference to many parts of the Doab, there was ample reason for British officers feeling great uneasiness at the danger which still surrounded them in the Northwest Provinces, wherever they were undefended by troops. The murder of Major Waterfield was a case in point. About the middle of May the major and Captain Fanshawe were travelling towards Allygurh *vià* Agra. In the middle of the night, near Ferozabad, a band of a hundred and fifty rebels surrounded the vehicle, shot the driver, and attacked the travellers. The two officers used their revolvers as quickly as they could; but the unfortunate Waterfield received two shots, one in the head and one through the chest, besides a sword-cut across the body; he fell dead on the spot. Fanshawe's escape was most extraordinary. The rebels got him out of the carriage, and surrounded him; but they pressed together so closely that each prevented his neighbour from striking. Fanshawe quickly drew his sword, and swung it right and left so vigorously that he forced a passage for himself through the cowardly crew; some pursued him, but a severe sword-cut to one of them deterred the rest. The captain ran on at great speed, climbed up a tree, and there remained till the danger was over. His courage and promptness saved him from any further injury than a slight wound in the hand. Poor Waterfield's remains, when sought for some time afterwards, were found lying among the embers of the burned vehicle; they were carried into Agra, and interred with military honours. The native driver was found dead, with the head nearly severed from the body.

Nynee Tal, Mussouree, and the other hill-stations towards which the sick and the weak looked with so much yearning, were almost wholly free from disturbance during May. One of the few events calling for notice was an expedition from Huldwanee by Captain Crossman. Receiving news that two rebel leaders, Nizam Ali Khan and Kali Khan, were preparing for mischief at a place called Bahonee, he started off on the 8th of May, with two or three companies of his own regiment, and a hundred Goorkhas mounted on elephants. He missed the two leaders, but captured many other rebels, included Kali Khan's brother—all in the service of the notorious Khan Bahadoor Khan, self-appointed chief of Bareilly. After burning five rebel villages, in which great atrocities had been perpetrated against Christians many months before, Crossman returned to Huldwanee—having been in incessant movement for twenty-six hours.

Fortunately, the other regions of India presented so few instances—with a notable exception, presently to be mentioned—of rebellious proceedings, that a few paragraphs will suffice for their treatment.

During the earlier half of the month of May, minor engagements took place in the Nagpoor territory, for the dispersion of bands of marauders and insurgents. The rebels were so little influential, the troops sent against them so few in number, and the towns and villages so little known, that it is unnecessary to trace these operations in detail. The localities concerned were Arpeillee, Ghote, Ashtee, Koonserra, Chamoorshee, and others equally obscure. The insurgents were a contemptible rabble, headed by refractory zemindars; but as their country was almost a complete jungle, it was very difficult work for Lieutenant Nuttall and Captain Crichton to put them down. The first of these two officers had under him five companies of the Nagpoor irregular infantry, with one gun; the other was deputy-commissioner of the district. A party of two thousand rebels, under the zemindar of Arpeillee—about a hundred miles south of Nagpoor—ravaged many villages; and at one spot they brutally murdered Mr Gartlan and Mr Hall, electric-telegraph inspectors, taking away all the public and private property from the station. The marauders and murderers were gradually put down; and this necessary work, though difficult from the cause above mentioned, was facilitated by the peaceful tendencies of the villagers generally, who rather dreaded than favoured Yenkut Rao, Bapoo Rao, and the other rebel zemindars. It also tended to lessen the duration of the contest, and insure its success, that Milloo Potail, and some other chieftains, sided with the British. Bapoo Rao, the head rebel of the district, was believed to be bending his steps towards the Nizam's country; but as he would there fall into the hands of an ally of the British, little doubt was entertained that his career would soon be cut short.

The Nizam and his prime-minister kept the large territory of Hyderabad free from any extensive military disturbances; but the country districts were so harassed by bands of marauding Rohilla freebooters, that the Nizam requested the Bombay government to furnish a small force for putting down this evil. Accordingly a corps of a few hundred men were sent to the region between Aurungabad and Jaulnah—with very evident and speedy effect.

It will be remembered that, in connection with the events of the month of April, the intended disarming of the province of Gujerat was adverted to. This critical and important operation was carried out during May. Sir Richmond Shakespear, who held a military as well as a political position in that province, managed the enterprise so firmly and skilfully that village after village was disarmed, and rendered so far powerless for mischief. Many unruly chieftains regarded this affair as very unpalatable. It was a work of great peril, for the turbulent natives were out of all proportion more numerous than any troops Sir Richmond could command; but he brought to bear that wonderful influence which many Englishmen possessed over the natives—influence shewing the predominance of moral over physical power. The native sovereign of Gujerat, the Guicowar, had all along been faithful and friendly to the British; he trusted Sir Richmond Shakespear as fully as Scindia trusted Sir Robert Hamilton, and gave an eager assent to the disarming of his somewhat turbulent subjects. The Nizam, the Guicowar, Scindia, and Holkar—all remained true to the British alliance during the hour of trouble; if they had failed us, the difficulties of reconquest would have been immensely increased, if not insuperable.

Of the Bombay presidency mention may be postponed to the chapter relating to the month of June, so far as concerns the appearance and suppression of slight rebellious symptoms. One of the minor events in Bombay city at this period was the conferring of a baronetcy on a native gentleman, the high-minded liberal Jamsetjee Jejeebhoy. He had long before been knighted; but his continued and valuable assistance to the government through all trials and difficulties now won for him further honour. The Parsee merchant became Sir Jamsetjee Jejeebhoy, Bart.—perhaps the most remarkable among baronets, race and creed considered. Whatever he did, was done in princely style. In order that his new hereditary dignity might not be shamed by any paucity of wealth on the part of his descendants, he at once invested twenty-five lacs of rupees in the Bombay four per cents., to entail an income of ten thousand pounds a year on the holder of the baronetcy. A large mansion at Mazagon was for a like purpose entailed; and the old merchant-prince felt a commendable pride in thinking that Bombay might possibly, for centuries to come, count among its inhabitants a Sir Jamsetjee Jejeebhoy.

The reader will have observed that this chapter is silent concerning the brilliant campaign of Sir Hugh Rose in Central India, and of the subsidiary operations under Generals Roberts and Whitlock. It has been considered advantageous, on account of the great importance of Sir Hugh's exploits, and of the intimate manner in which his proceedings in June were determined by those of May, to treat those transactions in a separate chapter, apart from those connected with the names of Campbell, Lugard, Douglas, Grant, Walpole, Jones, and Penny. The narrative will next, therefore, take up the affairs of Central India during the months of May and June.

Note.

Transport of Troops to India.—Early in the session of 1858, many members of the legislature, anxious to witness the adoption of the speediest mode of transporting troops to India, insisted not only that the overland route *viâ* Suez ought to have been adopted from the first, but also that the government and the East India Company ought to receive national censure for their real or supposed remissness on this point. In former chapters the fact has been rendered evident that, among the many important questions pressed upon the attention of the government, none was more prominent than that which related to the mode of strengthening the British army in India. England, not a military country in the continental estimate of that phrase, could ill spare troops to wage a great war in her Eastern possessions; and yet such a course was absolutely necessary. With ninety-nine regiments of line-infantry, and a proportionate number of troops of other kinds, she had to defend nearly thirty colonies besides the home country. Nay, at the very time when the mutiny began, she had barely finished a war with Persia, and had just commenced another with China—superadded to the defensive requirements just adverted to. Had the Persian expedition not been brought to a successful termination in the spring of 1857, and had the regiments destined for China become practically engaged in hostilities in that country at that time, it is difficult to imagine how the governor-general could have sent up any reinforcements from Calcutta, or Lord Elphinstone from Bombay, until summer had far advanced. Under the particular circumstances of time and place, however, Generals Outram and Havelock were released from their duties in Persia time enough to conduct the important operations at Lucknow and elsewhere—bringing with them the Queen's troops and Company's troops which had been engaged in the war in that country; while, on the other side, troops intended for service in China were rendered available for the needs of India. Still, this did not affect the strictures passed in the home country. Members of the legislature inquired, and journalists inquired: 'Why was not the overland route adopted for or by troops sent from England?' Hence the appointment of a committee of the House of Commons—'To inquire concerning the measures resorted to, or which were available, and as to the lines of communication adopted for reinforcing our army during the pending Revolt in India, and report thereon to the House: with a view to ascertaining the arrangements which should be made towards meeting any future important emergencies involving the security of our Eastern dominions.'

As the report given in by the committee was comprised within a few paragraphs, we will present it unaltered here, and then touch upon a few matters of detail connected with the subject.

The committee agreed to report:

'1. That the inquiry which this committee has been appointed to conduct may be divided into three branches: the first, relating to the overland route to India; the second, to the employment of steamers, as compared with sailing-vessels, for the transport of troops round the Cape of Good Hope; and the third, to the use made during the mutiny of the military resources of this country and of the colonies.

'2. That the Court of Directors appear, from the first intelligence of the mutiny at Meerut, to have been sensible of the advantages of the overland route, and to have lost no time in recommending its adoption; but that political and other considerations deterred her Majesty's ministers from at once assenting to that recommendation.

'3. That the committee cannot judge of the validity of those political objections, as they felt themselves precluded from inquiring into them; but that they ceased to prevail in the first week of September, when the more serious character of the war and the lateness of the season for ships departing for Calcutta, led to a formal requisition from the Court of Directors, and to a compliance with it on the part of the cabinet.

'4. That it would have been desirable, independently of political considerations, to have taken advantage of the overland route at the earliest possible period; and, apart from such considerations, it is much to be regretted that the steps that were taken in September to transmit small bodies of troops by this route were not resorted to at an earlier date. That the transport, however, of any large body of troops would have required previous arrangements, and that the evidence laid before the committee leaves great room to doubt whether any considerable reinforcements could have been sent in the months of July and August, with a prospect of their arrival in India so far in advance of those sent round the Cape as to give any great advantage in favour of this route.

'5. That although the overland route may be advantageously employed in times of emergency, it would not be advisable that it should be relied upon as the ordinary route for the transmission of troops to India.

'6. That if steamers had been used in greater numbers, the reinforcements would have reached India more quickly than they did by sailing-vessels; but that no evidence has been laid before the committee to shew that, at the time the emergency arose, a greater amount of steam-transport was attainable; whilst it has been shown that grave doubts existed whether the supply of coal on the route would have been sufficient for a larger number of steam-vessels than were actually employed.

'7. That steamers should for the future be always made use of, as far as possible, in urgent cases; but that, for the transmission of the ordinary reliefs, the committee would not recommend the adoption of so costly a mode of transport.

'8. That the governors of Ceylon and the Mauritius gave early and valuable assistance to the government of India, and deserve great praise for the zeal and promptitude with which they acted; that the governor of the Cape, without loss of time, forwarded treasure and horses, together with a portion of the troops at his disposal, but that he did not send the whole amount of the force which he was instructed by the home government to transmit to India; that the committee have not the means of judging whether the circumstances of the colony did or did not justify Sir George Grey in taking this course.

'9. That the committee observe with satisfaction that the people of Canada displayed great readiness to afford assistance to the mother-country, and that the committee are of opinion that it is highly desirable to give every encouragement to such demonstrations of loyalty on the part of the colonies.

'10. That on the whole, considering the suddenness of the danger, and the distance to which the troops were to be sent, the committee are of opinion that great credit is due to the Court of Directors of the East India Company for the promptitude and efficiency with which they discharged the difficult task of transmitting reinforcements to the army in India during the past year.'

From the tenor of this report, it is evident that the East India directors were ready to adopt the overland route before the government gave in their adhesion. The 'political reasons' for avoiding that route were connected with the relations between Egypt and various European countries: relations often involving jealousy and diplomatic intrigue, and likely to be thrown into some perplexity by the passage of troops belonging to another nation. The ministers were unwilling to speak out plainly on this point, possibly for fear of giving offence to France; and the committee, though sorely against the wish of some of its members, refrained from pressing them on this point; hence the cautious phraseology of the report, throwing a sort of shield over the government.

In reference to the proceedings connected with the transport of troops to India, it may be well to advert to a few dates. The home government received, on the 9th of April, the first intimation that a disaffected spirit had made its appearance among the native troops at Barrackpore. On the 19th of May, Lord Ellenborough inquired in the House of Lords whether reinforcements were being sent to India; a reply in the affirmative was given, accompanied by an expression of opinion that the disaffection was of very minor character. Shortly afterwards, in the House of Commons, a similar belief was expressed by members of the government that the occurrences at Barrackpore were trifling, not likely to lead to serious results. At that period, as we have already seen,* the Bengal presidency, including the vast range of territory from Pegu to Peshawur, contained about 23,000 European troops and 119,000 native; the Madras presidency, 10,000 European and 50,000 native; the Bombay presidency, 5000 European and 31,000 native—making a total of about 38,000 Company's and Queen's European troops, and 200,000 native. These, the actual numbers, were exclusive of the large brigades of the Bombay army at that time engaged in, or not yet returned from, the Persian expedition. During May, the government and the East India directors decided that more European troops ought to be in India, in consideration both of the condition of India itself, and of the incidence of war in Persia and China; and the early dispatch of four regiments was decided on. At length, on the 27th of June, arrived a telegram announcing the revolt at Meerut and the seizure of Delhi by the mutineers. While Lord Elgin on the way to China, Lord Harris at Madras, Lord Elphinstone at Bombay, Sir Henry Ward at Ceylon, Sir James Higginson at Mauritius, and Sir George Grey at the Cape of Good Hope, were using their best exertions to send troops to aid Viscount Canning, the home authorities considered what best could be done in furnishing reinforcements from England. There were no less than 13,000 troops at the Cape of Good Hope at that time, including ten regiments of Queen's infantry; it was fully believed in England that the governor might well have spared the greater portion of these troops; and the smallness of the number really contributed by him led to much disappointment in India, and much adverse criticism in England.

When the authorities at the War-office commenced their arrangements for despatching troops to India, they had to provide for a sea-voyage of about fourteen thousand miles.

* Chapter xii., p. 203.

A question arose whether, without changing the route or shortening the distance, the duration of the voyage might not be lessened by the employment of steam-vessels instead of sailing-ships. The Admiralty, and most members of the government, opposed this change on various grounds, principally in relation to difficulties in the supply of fuel, but partly in relation to monsoons and other winds. By the 10th of July, out of 31 vessels chartered by the government and the Company for conveying troops to India, nearly all were sailing-ships. A change of feeling took place about that date; the nation estimated time to be so valuable, that the authorities were almost coerced into the chartering of some of the noble merchant-steamers, the rapid voyages of which were already known. Between the 10th of July and the 1st of December, 59 ships were chartered, of which 29 were screw-steamers. The autumnal averages of passages to India were greatly in favour of steamers. Within a certain number of weeks there were 62 troop-laden ships despatched from England to one or other of the ports, Calcutta, Madras, Bombay, Kurachee; the average duration of all the voyages was 120 days by sailing-vessels, and only 83 days by steamers—a diminution of nearly one-third. Extending the list of ships to a later date, so as to include a greater number, it was found that 82 ships carried 30,378 troops from the United Kingdom to India—thus divided: 55 sailing-ships carried 16,234 men, averaging 299 each; 27 steamers carried 14,144, averaging 523 each. It was calculated that 14,000 of these British soldiers arrived in India *five weeks earlier*, by the adoption of steam instead of sailing-vessels. It is impossible to estimate what amount of change might have been produced in the aspect of Indian affairs, had these steam-voyages been made in the summer rather than in the autumn; it might not have been permitted to the mutineers to rule triumphant at Lucknow till the spring of the following year, or the fidelity of wavering chieftains to give way under the long continuance of the struggle.

Besides the two inquiries concerning the promptness with which troops were sent, and the kind of vessels employed to convey them, there was a third relating to the route adopted. From the earliest news of the revolt at Meerut, many persons in and out of parliament strenuously recommended the use of the overland route, as being much shorter than any possible ocean-route. The Court of Directors viewed this proposal more favourably than the government. Until the month of September, 'political difficulties' were dimly hinted at by ministers, but without any candid explanations; and as the objections gave way in the month just named, the nation arrived at a pretty general conclusion that these difficulties had never been of a very insurmountable character. It is only fair to state, however, that many experienced men viewed the overland route with distrust, independently of any political considerations. They adverted to the incompleteness of the railway arrangements between Alexandria and Cairo; to the difficulty of troops marching or riding over the sandy desert from Cairo to Suez; to the wretchedness of Suez as a place of re-embarkation; and to the unhealthiness of a voyage down the Red Sea in hot summer weather. Nevertheless, it was an important fact that the East India directors, most of whom possessed personal knowledge concerning the routes to India, urged the government from the first to send at least a portion of the troops by the Suez route. It was not until the 19th of September that assent was given; and the 13th of October witnessed the arrival of the first detachment of English troops into the Indian Ocean *viâ* Suez. These started from Malta on the 1st of the month. On the 2d of October, the first regiment started from England direct, to take the overland route to India. The Peninsular and Oriental Steam-navigation Company, having practically almost a monopoly of the Suez route, conveyed the greater portion of the troops sent in this way; and it may be useful to note the length of journey in the principal instances. The following are tabulated examples giving certain items—such as, the name of the steamer, the date of leaving England, the number of troops conveyed, and the time of reaching Alexandria, to commence the overland portion of the journey:

Steamer.	Left England.	No. of Troops.	Days to Alexandria.
Sultan,	1857. Oct. 2	248	13 days.
Dutchman,	Oct. 14	256	17 "
Sultan,	Nov. 17	264	14 "
Euxine,	Dec. 2	236	15 "
Indus,	Dec. 4	83	14 "
Abeona,	Dec. 8	861	13 "
Pera,	1858. Feb. 4	231	15 "
Ripon,	Feb. 11	248	15 "
Sultan,	Feb. 24	244	13 "
Malabar,	Mar. 11	264	14 "
Ripon,	Mar. 27	420	14 "
Benares,	Ap. 8	907	17 "

Thus the voyage was made on an average in about 14½ days, from the shores of England to those of Egypt. The landing at Alexandria, the railway journey to Cairo, the journey by vans and donkeys across the desert, the short detention at Suez, and the embarkation in another steamer at that port, occupied a number of days varying from 2 to 17—depending chiefly on the circumstance whether or not a steamer was ready at Suez to receive the troops when they arrived from Alexandria; the average was about 5½ days. From Suez the voyages were made to Kurachee, Bombay, Ceylon, Madras, or Calcutta. The steamers took forward all the troops mentioned in the above list, as well as others which reached Alexandria by other means. Most of these troops were landed at Bombay or Kurachee, as being nearer than Calcutta; and the average length of voyage was just 16 days. The result, then, presented was this:

England to Alexandria,	14½	days' average.
Alexandria to Suez,	5½	"
Suez to India,	16	"
	36	"

Those which went to Calcutta instead of Bombay or Kurachee, were about 3 days longer. Comparing these figures with those before given, we arrive at the following remarkable conclusion:

Sailing-ships round Cape,	120	days' average.
Steamers "	83	"
Suez route,	36	"

This, as a question of time, triumphantly justified all that had been said by the advocates of the shortest route; nor did it appear that there were any counterbalancing disadvantages experienced. Between the 6th of November 1857, and the 18th of May 1858, more than 5000 officers and soldiers landed in India, who had travelled by the Suez overland route from England.

SIR HUGH ROSE.

CHAPTER XXX.

ROSE'S VICTORIES AT CALPEE AND GWALIOR.

THE fame of Sir Hugh Rose came somewhat unexpectedly upon the British people. Although well known to persons connected with India as a gallant officer belonging to the Bombay army, Rose's military services were not 'household words' in the mother-country. Henry Havelock had made himself the hero of the wars of the mutiny by victories won at a time when the prospects were stern and gloomy; and it was not easy for others to become heroes of like kind, when compared in the popular mind with such a noble soldier. Hence it may possibly be that the relative merits of Campbell, Havelock, Neill, Wilson, Nicholson, Outram, Hope Grant, Inglis, Rose, Roberts, Napier, Eyre, Greathed, Jones, Smith, Lugard, and other officers, as military leaders, will remain undecided for a long period—until dispatches, memoirs, and journals have thrown light on the minuter details of the operations. Be this as it may, Sir Hugh Rose won for himself a high name by a series of military exploits skilfully conceived and brilliantly executed.

To understand the true scope of Rose's proceedings in the months of May and June, it may be well to recapitulate briefly the state of matters at the close of the preceding month.

After Sir Hugh—with the 1st brigade of his Central India Field-force under Brigadier Stuart, and the 2d brigade under Brigadier Steuart—had captured the important city of Jhansi, in the early part of April, his subsequent proceedings were determined according to the manœuvres of the rebels elsewhere. Jhansi, as the strongest and most important place in Bundelcund, was a valuable conquest; but as the Ranee and Tanteea Topee—the one chieftainess of Jhansi, and the other a representative of the Mahratta influence of Nena Sahib in these parts—had escaped, with the greater part of their rebel troops, it became necessary to continue the attack against them wherever they might be. The safety of Jhansi, the succour of the sick and wounded, and the reconstruction of his field-force, detained Rose in that city until the 25th of the month; but Majors Orr and Gall were in the interim actively employed in chasing and defeating various bodies of rebels in the surrounding country. Orr was sent from Jhansi across the river Betwah to Mhow, to clear that region from insurgents, and then to join Rose on the way to Calpee; he captured a small fort at Goorwai, near the Betwah, and kept a sharp watch on the proceedings of the rebel Rajahs of Banpore and Shagurh. Gall, with two squadrons of the 14th Dragoons and three 9-pounders, was commissioned to reconnoitre the position and proceedings of the rebels on the Calpee road; he captured the fort of Lohare, belonging to the insurgent Rajah of Sumpter. Hearing that Tanteea Topee, Ram Rao Gobind, and other leaders, had made Calpee a stronghold, and intended to dispute the passage of the road from Jhansi to that place, Rose laid his plans accordingly. Calpee, though not a large place, was important as being on the right bank of the Jumna, and on the main road from Jhansi to Cawnpore. During the later days of April, Sir Hugh was on the road to Calpee with the greater part of his two brigades; the rest of his troops, under Orr, Gall, and one or two other officers, being engaged in detached services. At that same time, General Whitlock, after defeating many bodies of rebels in and near the Banda district, was gradually tending towards a junction with Rose at Calpee; while General Roberts was at Kotah, keeping a vigilant eye on numerous turbulent bands in Rajpootana.

When May arrived, Sir Hugh, needing the services of Majors Orr and Gall with his main force, requested General Whitlock to watch the districts in which those two officers had been engaged. Being joined on the 8th by his second brigade (except the regiments and detachments left to guard Jhansi), he resumed his march on the 9th. News reached him that Tanteea Topee and the Ranee intended to dispute his passage towards Calpee at a place called Koonch, with a considerable force of cavalry and infantry. As soon as he arrived at Koonch, he engaged the enemy, drove them from their intrenchment, entered the town, cut them up severely, pursued them to a considerable distance, and captured several guns. The heat on this occasion was fearful. Rose himself was three times during the day disabled by the sun, but on each occasion rallied, and was able to remount; he caused buckets of cold water to be dashed on him, and then resumed the saddle, all wet as he was. Thirteen of his gallant but overwrought soldiers were killed by sun-stroke. Nothing daunted by this severe ordeal, he marched on to Hurdwee, Corai, Ottah, and other villages obscure to English readers, capturing a few more guns as he went. Guided by the information which reached him concerning the proceedings of the rebels, Sir Hugh, when about ten miles from Calpee, bent his line of march slightly to the west, in order to strike the Jumna near Jaloun, a little to the northwest of Calpee. He had also arranged that Colonel Riddell, with a column from Etawah, should move down upon Calpee from the north; that Colonel Maxwell, with a column from Cawnpore, should advance from the east; and that General Whitlock should watch the country at the south. The purpose of this combination evidently was, not only that Calpee should be taken, but that all outlets for the escape of the rebels should as far as possible be closed.

On the 15th, the two brigades of Rose's force joined at a point about six miles from Calpee. A large mass of the enemy here made a dash at the baggage and rear-guard, but were driven off without effecting much mischief. When he reached the Jumna, Rose determined to encamp for a while in a well-watered spot; and was enabled, by a personal visit from Colonel Maxwell, to concert further plans with him, to be put in force on the arrival of Maxwell's column. On the 16th, a strong reconnoitring column under Major Gall proceeded along the Calpee road; it consisted of various detachments of infantry, cavalry, and horse-artillery. On the same day, the second brigade was attacked by the enemy in great force, and was not relieved without a sharp skirmish. On the 17th, the enemy made another attack, which was, however, repulsed with less difficulty. Nena Sahib's nephew was believed to be the leader of the rebels on these two occasions. It was not until the 18th that Rose could begin shelling the earthworks which they had thrown up in front of the town. Greatly to their astonishment, the enemy found that Maxwell arrived at the opposite bank of the Jumna on the 19th, to assist in bombarding the place; they apparently had not expected this, and were not prepared with defences on that side. On the 20th, they came out in great force on the hills and nullahs around the town, attempted to turn the flank of Sir Hugh's position, and displayed a determination and perseverance which they had not hitherto exhibited; but they were, as usual, driven in again. On the 21st, a portion of Maxwell's column crossed the Jumna and joined Rose; while his heavy artillery and mortars were got into position. On the 22d, Maxwell's batteries opened fire across the river, and continued it throughout the night, while Sir Hugh was making arrangements for the assault. The rebels, uneasy at the prospect before them, and needing nothing but artillery to reply to Maxwell's fire, resolved to employ the rest of their force in a vigorous attack on Rose's camp at Gulowlie. Accordingly, on that same day, the 22d, they issued forth from Calpee in great force, and attacked him with determination. Rose's right being hard pressed by them, he brought up his reserve corps, charged with the bayonet, and repulsed the assailants at that point. Then moving his whole line forward, he put the enemy completely to rout. In these assaults, the rebels had the advantage of position; the country all round Calpee was very rugged and uneven, with steep ravines and numerous nullahs; insomuch that Rose had much difficulty in bringing his artillery into position. The assaults were made by numbers estimated at not far less than fifteen thousand men. The 71st and 86th foot wrought terrible destruction amongst the dense masses of the enemy. About noon on the 23d, the victorious Sir Hugh marched on from Gulowlie to Calpee. The enemy, who were reported to have chosen Calpee as a last stand-point, and to have sworn either to destroy Sir Hugh's army or to die in the attempt, now forgot their oath; they fled panic-stricken after firing a few shot, and left him master of the town and fort of Calpee. This evacuation was hastened by the effect of Maxwell's bombardment from the other side of the river.

Throughout the whole of the wars of the mutiny, the mutineers succeeded in escaping after defeat; they neither surrendered as prisoners of war, nor remained in the captured towns to be slaughtered. They were nimble and on the watch, knew the roads and jungles well, and had generally good intelligence of what was going on; while the British were seldom or never in such force as to be enabled completely to surround the places besieged: as a consequence, each siege ended in a flight. Thus it had been in Behar, Oude, the Doab, and Rohilcund; and thus Rose and his coadjutors found it in Bundelcund, Rajpootana, and Central India. Sir Hugh had given his troops a few hours' repose after the hot work of the 22d; and this respite seems to have encouraged the rebels to flee from the beleaguered town; but they would probably have succeeded in doing the same thing, though with greater loss, if he had advanced at once. The British had lost about forty commissariat carts, laden with tea, sugar, arrack, and medical comforts; but their loss in killed and wounded throughout these operations was very inconsiderable.

Sir Hugh Rose inferred, from the evidences presented to his notice, that the rebels had considered Calpee an arsenal and a point of great importance. Fifteen guns were kept in the fort, of which one was an 18-pounder of the Gwalior Contingent, and two others 9-pounder mortars made by the rebels. Twenty-four standards were found, one of which had belonged to the Kotah Contingent, while most of the rest were the colours of the several regiments of the Gwalior Contingent. A subterranean magazine was found to contain ten thousand pounds of English powder in barrels, nine thousand pounds of shot and empty shells, a quantity of eight-inch filled shrapnell-shells, siege and ball ammunition, intrenching tools of all kinds, tents new and old, boxes of new flint and percussion muskets, and ordnance stores of all kinds—worth several lacs of rupees. There were also three or four cannon foundries in the town, with all the requisites for a wheel and gun-carriage manufactory. In short, it was an arsenal, which the rebels hoped and intended to hold to the last; but Sir Hugh's victory at Gulowlie, and his appearance at Calpee, gave them a complete panic: they thought more of flight than of fighting.

The question speedily arose, however—Whither had the rebels gone? Their losses were very large, but the bulk of the force had unquestionably escaped. Some, it was found, had crossed the Jumna into the Doab, by a bridge of boats which had eluded the search of the British; but the rest, enough to form an army of no mean strength, finding that Rose had not fully guarded the side of Calpee leading to Gwalior, retreated by that road with amazing celerity. Sir Hugh thereupon organised a flying column to pursue them, under the command of Colonel Robertson. This column did not effect much, owing in part to the proverbial celerity of the rebels, and in part also to difficulties of other kinds. Heavy rains on the first two days rendered the roads almost impassable, greatly retarding the progress of the column. The enemy attempted to make a stand at Mahona and Indoorkee, two places on the road; but when they heard of the approach of Robertson, they continued their retreat in the direction of Gwalior. The column reached Irawan on the 29th; and there a brief halt was made until commissariat supplies could be sent up from Calpee. An officer belonging to the column adverted, in a private letter, to certain symptoms that the villagers were becoming tired of the anarchy into which their country had been thrown. 'The feeling of the country is strong against the rebels now, whatever it may have been; and the rural population has welcomed our advent in the most unmistakable manner. At the different villages as we go along, many of them come out and meet us with earthen vessels full of water, knowing it to be our greatest want in such weather; and at our camping-ground they furnish us voluntarily with supplies of grain, grass, &c., in the most liberal manner. They declare the rebels plundered them right and left, and that they are delighted to have the English raj once more. It is not only the inhabitants of the towns and villages where we encamp who are so anxious to evince their good feeling; but the people, for miles round, have been coming to make their salaam, bringing forage for our camp with them, and thanking us for having delivered them from their oppressors. They say that for a year they have had no peace; but they have now a hope that order will be once more restored.' Concerning this statement it may suffice to remark, that though the villagers were unquestionably in worse plight under the rebels than under the British, their obsequious protestations to that effect were not always to be depended on; their fears gave them duplicity, inducing them to curry favour with whichever side happened at the moment to be greatest in power.

Colonel Robertson, though he inflicted some loss on the fugitives, did not materially check them. His column—comprising the 25th Bombay native infantry, the 3d Bombay native cavalry, and 150 Hyderabad horse—pursued the rebels on the Gwalior road, but did not come up with the main body. On the 2d of June he was joined by two squadrons of the 14th dragoons, a wing of the 86th foot, and four 9-pounders. On the next day, when at Moharar, about midway between Calpee and Gwalior (fifty-five miles from each) he heard news of startling import from the last-named city—presently to be noticed. About the same time Brigadier Steuart marched to Attakona on the Gwalior road, with H.M. 71st, a wing of the 86th, a squadron of the 14th Dragoons, and some guns, to aid in the pursuit of the rebels.

While these events were in progress on the south of the Jumna, Colonel Riddell was advancing from the northwest on the north side of the same river. On the 16th of May, Riddell was at Graya, with the 3d Bengal Europeans, Alexander's Horse, and two guns; he had a smart skirmish with a party of rebels, who received a very severe defeat. Some of the Etawah troops floated down the Jumna in boats, under the charge of Mr Hume, a magistrate, and safely joined Sir Hugh at Calpee. On their way they were attacked by a body of insurgents much more numerous than themselves; whereupon Lieutenant Sheriff landed with a hundred and fifty men at Bhijulpore, brought the rebels to an engagement, defeated them, drove them off, and captured four guns with a large store of ammunition. On the 25th, when on the banks of the Jumna some distance above Calpee, Colonel Riddell saw a camp of rebels on the other side, evidently resting a while after their escape on the 23d; he sent the 2d Bengal Europeans across, and captured much of the camp-equipage—the enemy not waiting to contest the matter with him.

When Calpee had been securely taken, and flying columns had gone off in pursuit of the enemy, to disperse if not to capture, Sir Hugh Rose conceived that the arduous labours of his Central India Field-force were for a time ended, and that his exhausted troops might take rest. He issued to them a glowing address, adverting with commendable pride to the unswerving gallantry which they had so long exhibited: 'Soldiers! you have marched more than a thousand miles, and taken more than a hundred guns. You have forced your way through mountain-passes and intricate jungles, and over rivers. You have captured the strongest forts, and beaten the enemy, no matter what the odds, whenever you met him. You have restored extensive districts to the government, and peace and order now where before for a twelvemonth were tyranny and rebellion. You have done all this, and you never had a check. I thank you with all sincerity for your bravery, your devotion, and your discipline. When you first marched, I told you that you, as British soldiers, had more than enough of courage for the work which was before you, but that courage without discipline was of no avail; and I exhorted you to let discipline be your watchword. You have attended to my orders. In hardships, in temptations and danger, you have obeyed your general, and you have never left your ranks; you have fought against the strong, and you have protected the rights of the weak and defenceless, of foes as well as of friends. I have seen you in the ardour of the combat preserve and place children out of harm's way. This is the discipline of Christian soldiers, and it is what has brought you triumphant from the shores of Western India to the waters of the Jumna, and establishes without doubt that you will find no place to equal the glory of your arms.'

Little did the gallant Sir Hugh suspect that the very day on which he issued this hearty and well-merited address (the 1st of June) would be marked by the capture of Gwalior by the defeated Calpee rebels, the flight of Scindia to Agra, and the necessity for an immediate resumption of active operations by his unrested Central India Field-force.

The rebels, it afterwards appeared, having out-marched Colonel Robertson, arrived on the 30th of May at the Moorar cantonment, in the neighbourhood of Gwalior, the old quarters of the Gwalior Contingent. Tanteea Topee, a leader whose activity was worthy of a better cause, had preceded them, to tamper with Scindia's troops. The Maharajah, when he heard news of the rebels' approach, sent an urgent message to Agra for aid; but before aid could reach him, matters had arrived at a crisis.

The position of the Maharajah of Gwalior had all along been a remarkable and perilous one, calling for the exercise of an amount of sagacity and prudence rarely exhibited by so youthful a prince. Although only twenty-three years of age, he had been for five years Maharajah in his own right, after shaking off a regency that had inflicted much misery on his country; and during these five years his conduct had won the respect of the British authorities. The mutiny placed him in an embarrassing position. The Gwalior Contingent, kept up by him in accordance with a treaty with the Company, consisted mainly of Hindustanis and Oudians, strongly in sympathy with their compatriots in the Jumna and Ganges regions. His own independent army, it is true, consisted chiefly of Mahrattas, a Hindoo race having little in common with the Hindustanis; but he could not feel certain how long either of the two armies would remain faithful. After many doubtful symptoms, in July 1857, as we have seen in former chapters, the Gwalior Contingent went over in a body to the enemy—thus adding ten or twelve thousand disciplined and well-armed troops to the rebel cause. Scindia contrived for two or three months to remain on neutral terms with the Contingent—on the one hand, not sanctioning their proceedings: on the other, not bringing down their enmity upon himself. During the winter they were engaged in encounters at various places, which have been duly noticed in the proper chapters. When Sir Hugh Rose's name had become as much known and feared in Central India as Havelock's had been in the Northwest Provinces many months before, the rebels began to look to Gwalior, the strongest city in that part of India, as a possible place of permanent refuge; and many of the Mahratta and Rajpoot chieftains appear to have come to an agreement, that if Scindia would not join them against the British, they would attack him, dethrone him, and set up another Maharajah in his stead. Meanwhile the Gwalior prince, a brave and shrewd man, as well as a faithful ally, looked narrowly at the circumstances that surrounded him. He had some cause to suspect his own national or regular army, but deemed it best to conceal his suspicions. There was every cause for apprehension, therefore, on his part, when he found a large body of insurgent troops approaching his capital—especially as some of the regiments of the old Gwalior Contingent were among the number.

Although aid from Agra or Calpee had not arrived, Scindia had courage and skill enough to make a bold stand against them, if his own troops had proved faithful; but treachery effected that which fair fighting might not easily have done. Siendia's body-guard remained faithful. Such was not, however, the case with the bulk of his infantry, who had been tampered with by Tanteea Topee, and had agreed to desert their sovereign in his hour of greatest need. This was doubtless the motive of the rebel leader in preceding the march of the Calpee fugitives. When the struggle began, Scindia's force comprised two or three thousand cavalry, six thousand infantry, and eight guns; that of the enemy consisted of four thousand cavalry, seven thousand infantry, and twelve guns—no overwhelming disparity, if Scindia's own troops had been true. The rebels did not want for leaders; seeing that they had the Ranee of Jhansi, the Nawab of Banda, Tanteea Topee, Rao Sahib, Ram Rao Gobind, and Luchmun Nena. Rao Sahib, nephew of the Nena, was the nominal leader of the Mahrattas in this motley force; but Tanteea Topee was really the man of action and power. Certainly the most remarkable among the number was the Ranee of Jhansi, a woman who—but for her cruelty to the English at that station—would command something like respect. Whether she had been unjustly treated by the Company, in relation to the 'annexations' in former years, was one among many questions of a similar kind on which opinions were divided; but supposing her to be sincere in a belief that territory had been wrongly taken from her, then did her conduct (barring her cruelty and her unbounded licentiousness) bear something like the stamp of heroism. At anyrate, she proved herself a very Amazon in these warlike contests—riding like a man, bearing arms like a man, leading and fighting like a man, and exhorting her troops to contend to the last against the hated Feringhees.

The battle between the Maharajah and the insurgents was of brief duration. The enemy, at about seven o'clock on the morning of the 1st of June, made their appearance in battle-array. Scindia took up a position about two miles eastward of the Moorar cantonment; placing his troops in three divisions, of which the centre was commanded by him in person. The rebels pushed on a cloud of mounted skirmishers, with zumborucks or camel-guns; these were steadily confronted by Scindia's centre division. But now did the treachery appear. It is not quite clear whether the right and left divisions of his force remained idle during the fighting of the centre division, waited for the capture of guns as a signal for revolt, marched over to the opposite side, and began to fire on such of their astonished companions as still remained true to Scindia; or whether the left division went over at the commencement of the fighting, and was followed soon after by the right; but at anyrate the centre, comprising the body-guard with some other troops, could not long contend against such immense odds. The body-guard fought manfully until half their number had fallen, and the rest fled. Scindia himself, too, powerless against such numerous opponents, sought safety in flight, and fortunately found it. Attended by a few faithful troops, the Maharajah galloped off by way of the Saugor Tal, the Residency, and the Phool Bagh, avoiding the Lashkar or permanent camp of his (late) army; he then took to the open country, by the Dholpore road, and reached Agra two days afterwards. The rebels sent a troop of cavalry sixteen or eighteen miles in pursuit, but he happily kept ahead of them. Most of the members of his family fled to Seepree, while his courtiers were scattered in all directions.

Directly the Maharajah had thus been driven out of his capital, the rebels entered Gwalior, and endeavoured to form a regular government. They chose Nena Sahib as 'Peishwa,' or head of all the Mahratta princes. They next set up Rao Sahib, the Nena's nephew, as chief of Gwalior. These selections appear to have been assented to by Scindia's traitorous troops as well as by the other rebels. All the troops were to have a certain number of months' pay for their services in this achievement. The army was nevertheless the great difficulty to be contended against by the rebel leaders. The insurgents from Calpee, and the newly revolted troops of Scindia, had worked together for a common object in this instance; but there was jealousy between them; and nothing could make them continue together without the liberal distribution of money—partly as arrears of pay, partly as an advance. Ram Rao Gobind, who had long before been discharged from Scindia's service for dishonesty, became prime-minister. The main bulk of the army, under the masculine Ranee of Jhansi, remained encamped in a garden called the Phool Bagh, outside the city; while pickets and guns were sent to guard all the roads of approach. The property of the principal inhabitants was sequestered, in real or pretended punishment for friendliness towards the Maharajah and the British. Scindia possessed an immense treasure in his palace, which he could not take away in his flight; this the rebels seized, by the connivance of the truculent treasurer, Ameerchand Batya; and it was out of this treasure they were enabled to reward the troops. They also declared a formal confiscation of all the royal property. Four petty Mahratta chieftains in the district of Shakerwarree—named Kunughat, Gholab Singh, Dooghur Shah, and Bukhtawar Singh—had some time previously declared themselves independent, and had been captured and imprisoned by Scindia for so doing; these men were now set at liberty by the newly constituted authorities, and received insignia and dresses of honour, on condition of raising forces in their several localities to oppose any British troops who might attempt to cross the Chumbul and approach Gwalior. The leaders mustered and reviewed their troops, plundered and burnt the civil station, and liberated such prisoners as they thought might be useful to them. They also sent letters of invitation to the Rajahs of Banpore, Shagurh, &c., to join them.

Thus did a body of rebels, collected from different quarters, and actuated by different motives, expel the Maharajah Scindia from the throne of Gwalior, and install a government avowedly and bitterly hostile to him and to the British with whom he was in alliance. Throughout twelve months' events at Gwalior, the more experienced of the Company's officers frequently directed their attention to a certain member of Scindia's family, in doubt whether treachery might have been exhibited in that quarter. This was a princess, advanced in life, whose influence at Gwalior was known to be considerable, and whose experience of the checkered politics of Indian princedoms had extended over a very lengthened period. She was known as the Baeza Baee of Gwalior. Sixty years before the mutiny began, she was the beauty of the Deccan, the young bride of the victorious Dowlut Rao Scindia of 1797; and she lived through all the vicissitudes of those sixty years. During thirty years of married life she exercised great influence over her husband and the court of Gwalior, exhibiting more energy of purpose than is wont among eastern women. In 1827 Scindia died without a legitimate son; and the widow, in accordance with Indian custom, adopted a kinsman of the late Maharajah to be the new Scindia. The Baeza Baee as regent, and Moodkee Rao as expectant rajah, had many quarrels during the next seven years: these ended, in 1834, in the installation of the young man as rajah, and in the retirement of the widowed princess to Dholpore. Tumults continued; for the princess was considered the more skilful ruler of the two, and many of the Mahrattas of Gwalior wished her to continue as regent. Whether from justice, or from motives of cold policy, the British government sided with Scindia against the Baeza Baee; and she was ordered to take up her abode in some district beyond the limits of the Gwalior territory. In 1843, when Moodkee Rao Scindia died, this territory came more closely than before under British influence; a new Scindia was chosen, with the consent of the governor-general, from among the relations of the deceased Maharajah; and with this new Scindia the aged Baeza Baee appears to have resided until the time of the mutiny. Nothing unfavourable was known against this venerable lady; but when it was considered that she was a woman of great energy, and that many other native princesses of great energy—such as the Ranee of Jhansi and the Begum of Oude—had thrown their influence in the scale against the English, it was deemed proper to watch her movements. And this the more especially, as she had some cause to complain of the English policy in the Mahratta dominions in past years. Although watched, however, nothing appeared to justify suspicion of her complicity with the rebels.

Great was the anxiety at all the British stations when the news arrived that Gwalior, the strongest and most important city in Central India, and the capital of a native sovereign uniformly true to the British alliance, had fallen into the hands of the rebels. In many minds a desponding feeling was at once manifest; while those who did not despond freely acknowledged that the situation was a critical one, calling for the exercise of promptness, skill, and courage. All felt that the conqueror of Jhansi and Calpee was the fit man to undertake the reconquest of Gwalior, both from his military fame and from the circumstances of his position—having around him many columns and corps which he could bring to one centre. It was in the true spirit of heroism that Sir Hugh Rose laid aside all thoughts of self when the exigencies of the service called for his attention. He had won a complete victory at Calpee, and believed that in so doing he had crushed the rebels in Bundelcund and Scindia's territory. Then, and then only, did he think of himself—of his exhausted frame, his mind worn by six months of unremitting duty, his brain fevered by repeated attacks of sun-stroke in the fearful heat of that climate. He knew that he had honestly done his part, and that he might with the consent of every one claim an exemption for a time from active service. He intended to go down to Bombay on sick-certificate—after having sent off a column in pursuit of the fleeing rebels, and made arrangements for his successor. Such were Sir Hugh's thoughts when June opened. The startling news from Gwalior, however, overturned all his plans. When he found that Scindia's capital was in the hands of the insurgents whom he had so recently beaten at Calpee, all thoughts concerning fatigue and heat, anxiety and sickness, were promptly dismissed from his mind. He determined to finish the work he had begun, by reconquering the great Mahratta city. No time was to be lost. Every day that Gwalior remained in the hands of the rebels would weaken the British prestige, and add strength to the audacity of the rebels.

Sir Hugh's first measure was to request the presence of General Whitlock at Calpee, to hold that place safely during the operations further westward. Whitlock was at Moudha, between Banda and Humeerpoor, when he heard the news; he at once advanced towards Calpee by the ford of the Betwah at Humeerpoor. Rose's next step was to organise two brigades for rapid march to Gwalior. Of those brigades the infantry consisted of H.M. 86th foot, a wing of the 71st Highlanders, a wing of the 3d Bombay Europeans, the 24th and 25th Bombay native infantry, and the 5th Hyderabad infantry; the cavalry comprised wings of the 4th and 14th Dragoons, the 3d Hyderabad cavalry, and a portion of the 3d Bombay native cavalry; the artillery and engineers consisted of a company of the Royal Engineers, Bombay Sappers and Miners, Madras Sappers and Miners, two light field-batteries, Leslie's troop of Bombay horse-artillery, and a siege-train consisting of two 16-pounders, three 18-pounders, eight 8-inch mortars, two 10-inch mortars, and one 8-inch howitzer. The first of these two brigades was placed under the command of Brigadier C. S. Stuart, of the Bombay army; the second under Brigadier R. Napier, of the Bengal Engineers. Arrangements were made for the co-operation of a third brigade from Seepree, under Brigadier Smith. Orders were at the same time given for bringing up Major Orr's column from the south, and for joining it with Smith's brigade somewhere on the road to Gwalior; Colonel Maxwell, with the 5th Fusiliers and the 88th foot, was invited to advance from Cawnpore to Calpee; while Colonel Riddell was instructed to cross the Chumbul with his Etawah column. Rose did not know what might be the number of insurgents against whom he would have to contend when he reached Gwalior, and on that account he called in reinforcements from various quarters.

Pushing on his two main brigades as rapidly as possible, Sir Hugh appeared in the vicinity of Gwalior on the ninth day after leaving Calpee—allowing his troops no more rest by the way than was absolutely needed. On the evening of the 15th of June he was at Sepowlie, about ten miles from the Moorar cantonment; and by six o'clock on the following morning he reached the cantonment itself. Sir Hugh galloped forward with his staff to a point about midway between the cantonment and the city; and there began to reconnoitre the position taken up by the enemy. Gwalior is very remarkable as a military position, owing to the relation which the city bears to a strong and lofty hill-fort. 'The rock on which the hill-fort is situated,' says Mr Thornton, 'is completely isolated; though seven hundred yards to the north is a conical hill surmounted by a very remarkable building of stone; and on the southeast, south, and southwest, are similar hills, which form a sort of amphitheatre at the distance of from one to four miles. The sandstone of the hill-fort is arranged in horizontal strata, and its face presents so steep a fracture as to form a perpendicular precipice. Where the rock was naturally less precipitous, it has been so scarped as to be rendered perpendicular; and in some places the upper part considerably overhangs the lower. The greatest length of the rock, which is from northeast to southwest, is a mile and a half; the greatest breadth three hundred yards. The height at the south end, where it is greatest, is 342 feet. On the eastern face of the rock, several colossal figures are sculptured in bold relief. A rampart runs round the edge of the rock, conforming to the outline of its summit; and as its height is uniform above the verge, its top has an irregular appearance. The entrance within the enclosure of the rampart is towards the north end of the east side; first, by means of a steep road, and higher up by steps cut in the face of the rock, of such a size and of so moderate a degree of acclivity that elephants easily make their way up. This huge staircase is protected on the outer side by a high and massive stone-wall, and is swept by several traversing guns pointing down it: the passage up to the interior being through a succession of seven gates. The citadel is at the northeastern extremity of the enclosure, and has a very striking appearance. Adjoining is a series of six lofty round towers or bastions, connected by curtains of great height and thickness. There are within the enclosure of the rampart several spacious tanks, capable of supplying an adequate garrison; though fifteen thousand men would be required fully to man the defences.' The town of Gwalior, it may suffice to state, was situated along the eastern base of the rock. The Lashkar, or permanent camp of the Maharajah, stretch out from the southwest end of the rock; whereas the Moorar, or cantonment of the old Gwalior Contingent, was on the opposite side of the town.

Such was the place which Sir Hugh Rose found

it necessary to reconnoitre, preparatory to a siege. The hill-fort, the Lashkar, the Moorar, the city, and the semicircular belt of hills, all needed examination, sufficient at least to determine at what points the rebel army was distributed, and what defences had been thrown up. He found that only a few troops were in the city itself, the main body being placed in groups on and near the surrounding hills and cantonments. Rumour assigned to the rebels a force of seventeen thousand men in arms; but the means for testing the truth of this rumour were wanting.

The examination made by Rose led him to a determination to attack the Moorar cantonment suddenly, before the other portions of the rebels could arrive from the more distant stations—to adopt, in fact, the Napoleon tactics, possible only when rapid movements are made. Brigadier Smith was operating on the hills south of the town, as we shall presently see; but Rose carried out his own portion of the attack independently. Orders were at once given. The cavalry and guns were placed on each flank; while the infantry, in two divisions, prepared to advance. The 86th headed the attack, as part of the second brigade. No sooner did the enemy find themselves attacked, than they poured out a well-directed fire of musketry and field-guns; but this was speedily silenced, and the rebels forced to make a precipitate retreat. Many of them escaped into the city over a stone-bridge, the existence of which was not correctly known to Sir Hugh. Four pieces of ordnance were at the same time dragged over the bridge to the Lashkar camp—somewhat to the vexation of the British, who wished to seize them: the capture, however, was not long delayed. The main body of rebels, after being driven through the whole length of the cantonment, were chased over a wide expanse of country. Some terrible fighting occurred during this chase. At one spot a number of the enemy had been driven into a fortified trench around a village, and here they maintained a desperate hand-to-hand struggle, until the trench was nearly choked with dead and wounded bodies. It was while rushing on at the head of a company of the 71st Highlanders in this contest that Lieutenant Neave fell, mortally wounded. The rebels engaged in this struggle included several men of the Maharajah's 1st regiment. A strong body of the enemy's cavalry were drawn up about half a mile from the bridge; but they did not venture forth; and Sir Hugh encamped for the night in the Moorar cantonment.

This, then, was the first scene in the conquest. Sir Hugh had obtained safe possession of the cantonment of Moorar, and had conquered and expelled such of the insurgents as had taken up a position there. Nevertheless this was only a preliminary measure; for the city and the rock-fort were still in the hands of the enemy. Either through want of means or want of foresight, the rebels had done little to strengthen this fort; or, perchance, reposing on the Indian idea that that famous fortress was impregnable, they deemed such a precaution unnecessary. Instead of attending to that duty, they disposed their forces so as to guard the roads of approach from Indoorkee, Seepree, and other places; and it was in this field-service that the mail-clad Amazon, the Ranee of Jhansi, engaged.

We must now trace the progress of Brigadier Smith, who had taken charge of the operations from the south, and who would need to obtain command of the hills southward of the city before he could reach Gwalior itself. This active officer had to make a long march before he could reach the scene of conflict. His column—comprising a wing of the 8th Hussars, a wing of the Bombay Lancers, H.M. 95th foot, the 10th Native Bombay infantry, and a troop of Bombay horse-artillery—started from Seepree, and was joined, on the 15th of June, at Antree, by Major Orr with his men of the Hyderabad Contingent. Setting out from that place, the brigadier, thus reinforced, arrived on the 17th at Kotah-ke-serai, a place about eight miles from Gwalior, on the little river Oomrah. Here was a small square fort, and also a native travellers' bungalow (implied by the words *ke-serai*). As he approached this place, the brigadier could see masses of the enemy's cavalry and infantry in motion at the base of some neighbouring hills—some of those already adverted to as forming a semicircular belt around the southern half of Gwalior. These hills it was necessary for him to cross to get to the Lashkar camping-ground. Two companies of infantry, belonging to the 10th and 95th regiments, were thrown across the river as skirmishers, with a squadron of Hussars as videttes; while the rest of his column remained south of the river, to guard the ford and the fort. After a little skirmishing, some of his cavalry crossed the river, and came under the fire of a battery until then unperceived. Much sharp fighting ensued; the enemy having been permitted to retain their hold of the hills on one side of the river, in consequence of a movement made by Smith under false information. The road from Jhansi to Gwalior crosses the hills that lie southward of the Lashkar; and, before debouching from these hills, it runs for several hundred yards through a defile along which a canal had been excavated; the eastern embankment of this canal, twenty or twenty-five feet in height, supplied an excellent cover for Smith's troops during their advance. It was while his column was thus marching through the defile, defended by three or four guns on a neighbouring hill, that the principal part of the day's fighting took place. When night came, Smith had secured the defile, the road, and the adjoining hills; while the enemy occupied the hills on the other side of the canal. The most distinguished person who fell in this day's fighting was the Ranee of Jhansi—an Amazon to the last. The account given of her death is simply as follows: 'The Ranee, in trying to escape over the canal which separated the camp from the Phool Bagh parade, fell with her horse, and was cut down by a Hussar; she still endeavoured to get over, when a bullet struck her in the breast, and she fell to rise no more.' The natives are said to have hastily burned her dead body, to save it from apprehended desecration by the Feringhees. During the night between the 17th and 18th, the enemy constructed a battery on one of their hills, from which they poured forth a well-directed fire, lessened in serious results by the greatness of the distance. It was not without much difficulty and constant firing that the brigadier, during the 18th, became master of the hills, and drove away the enemy, who were led with much energy by Tanteea Topee.

While Brigadier Smith was thus closely engaged on the southern hills, Sir Hugh Rose contented himself with maintaining his won position at the Moorar cantonment; he could not safely advance into the city until Smith had achieved his portion of the work. On the 18th, when the brigadier had

GWALIOR.

surmounted some of the southern hills, Sir Hugh, seeing that the enemy's strong positions were on that side of the city, joined him by a flank-movement of twelve miles—leaving only a sufficient number of troops to guard his camp at the Moorar. Rose bivouacked for the night in rear of Smith's position, thus enabling both to act together on the morrow. The enemy still occupied some of the heights nearest to the city; and from these heights, as well as from the rock-fort, on the 19th, they poured out a fire of shot, shell, and shrapnell. Rose, after narrowly examining the chief of the heights occupied by the enemy, resolve to capture it by storm. Two of the choice infantry regiments sent on in advance, ascended this height—the 71st on the right, the 86th on the left; other regiments supported them; while the artillery was plied wherever the most effective result could be produced. The scheme required that some of the guns should be taken across the canal, in order to form a battery on one of the hills; and the sappers executed this difficult work under a hot fire. The struggle was not a long one; the infantry ran intrepidly up to the enemy's guns, and captured them. The height was now gained; and large masses of the enemy came full in view in the plain below. The rebels, losing heart at their failures, became panic-stricken when the height was taken; they began to flee in all directions. Then was the time for Rose's cavalry to render useful service;

the troopers scoured the plain in all directions, cutting off the wretched fugitives in large numbers. By four o'clock in the day, Rose was master of Gwalior, to the inexpressible astonishment of the enemy. There was scarcely any fighting in the city itself, or in the Lashkar camp; nor was there much firing from the rock-fort; when the heights were gained, the rebels gave way on all sides. While Brigadier Smith advanced with cavalry and artillery to occupy the plain of the

THE RANEE OF JHANSI.

Phool Bagh, Sir Hugh pushed on to the palace. Very little opposition was encountered; few of the enemy being met with either there or at the Lashkar. After providing for the safety of the palace, by posting Europeans and Bombay infantry at the entrances, Sir Hugh made arrangements for the security of the city. This he found comparatively easy; for the regular inhabitants of the place had good reason to wish for the suppression of the rebels, and gladly aided the conquerors in restoring order.

Thus, on the night of the 19th, Sir Hugh Rose was virtually conqueror, though not thoroughly. The seizure of palace, city, and cantonments did not necessarily imply the seizure of the rock-fort, the bold fortress which for ages has rendered Gwalior so famous in India. In point of fact, the conquest of this fort was deferred until the 20th; Sir Hugh looked upon it as an easy achievement, because it became known that only a few natives remained within the place. The conquest was not effected without causing the death of a gallant officer—Lieutenant Arthur Rose, of the 25th Bombay native infantry. As soon as the city had fallen into the hands of the besiegers, the lieutenant was sent by the commanding-officer of his regiment to guard the Kotwallee or police-station. A shot or two being unexpectedly fired from the fort, Rose proposed to a brother-officer, Lieutenant Waller, the daring project of capturing it with the handful of men at their joint disposal—urging that, though the risk would be great, the honour would be proportionally great if the attempt succeeded. Off they started, taking with them a blacksmith. This man, with his lusty arm and his heavy hammer, broke in the outermost or lowermost of the many gates that guarded the ascent of the rock on which the fort was situated; then another, and another, until all the six gates were broken into, and entered by the little band of assailants. It is hardly to be expected, that if the gates were really strong and securely fastened, they could have been burst open in this way; but the confusion resulting from the fighting had probably caused some of the defensive arrangements to be neglected. At various points on the ascent the assailants were fired at by the few rebels in the place; and near the top a desperate hand-to-hand conflict took place, during which the numbers were thinned on both sides. While Rose was encouraging his men in their hot work, a musket was fired at him from behind a wall; and the bullet, striking him on the right of the spine, passed through his body. The man who had fired the fatal shot, a Bareilly mutineer, then rushed out, and cut him across the knee and the wrist with a sword. Waller came up, and despatched this fellow, but too late to save the life of his poor friend Rose.*

Several days before the conquest of Gwalior was finally completed, arrangements were made for reinstating Scindia upon the throne from which he had been so suddenly and unexpectedly hurled. Irrespective of the justice of Scindia's cause, Sir Robert Hamilton and Sir Hugh Rose wished him to return at once from Agra to Gwalior for another reason—to enable the British to judge who among the townsmen deserved punishment, and who were worthy of forgiveness. It was also very important to shew that the government meant promptly and firmly to support so faithful a man, as an encouragement to other native princes to maintain faith with the British. Even before Rose had reached Gwalior, and when the result of the approaching battle could not in any degree be foreseen, Hamilton, as political resident at the court of Gwalior, sent a dispatch to Scindia at Agra, requesting him to move down at once to the Chumbul, that he might be in readiness to present himself at Gwalior whenever the proper time should arrive. Accordingly the temporarily dethroned Maharajah set out from Agra on the 13th of June with all his retinue, escorted by a party of Meade's Horse, and by some of his own troopers who still remained faithful. He reached Dholpore on the 15th, where he joined Colonel Riddell's column. On the next he faintly heard the roar of cannon at his capital, thirty-seven miles distant; and in the evening an express arrived from Sir Robert Hamilton, announcing the capture of the cantonment—the first stage towards the capture of Gwalior itself. Crossing the Chumbul, and mounting his horse, Scindia galloped off, and rode all night, reaching Gwalior on the 17th. During the next three days, the presence and advice of the Maharajah were very valuable to the British authorities, contributing much towards the final conquest. On the 20th, when all the fighting was well-nigh over, Scindia was restored to his throne with as much oriental pomp as could be commanded in the limited time: Rose, Hamilton, and all the chief military and civil officers, accompanying him in procession from the camp to the palace. It was a good augury that the townsmen, who lined all the streets, seemed right glad to have him back again amongst them.

When Gwalior was fairly cleared of rebels, and Scindia reinstated as Maharajah, two official congratulatory documents were issued, one by Sir Colin Campbell, and the other by Viscount Canning—somewhat differing in character, but tending to the same end. Sir Colin congratulated Sir Hugh Rose on the successful result of his rapid advance upon Gwalior, and the restoration of Scindia. He adverted to these as a happy termination of Rose's brilliant campaign in Central India—a campaign illustrated by many engagements in the open field; by the relief of Saugor; by the capture of Ratgurh, Shagurh, and Chendaree; by the memorable siege of Jhansi; by the fall of Calpee; and lastly, by the re-occupation of Gwalior. While thanking Rose and his troops heartily for their glorious deeds, Sir Colin did not fail to notice two other generals who had shared in the hot work of those regions. 'It must not be forgotten that the advance of the Central India Field-force formed part of a large combination, and was rendered possible by the movement of Major-general Roberts, of the Bombay army, into Rajpootana, on the one side; and of Major-general Whitlock, of the Madras army, on the other; and by the support they respectively gave to Major-general Sir Hugh Rose as he moved onwards in obedience to his instructions.' Viscount Canning's proclamation was more formal, and was intended to meet the eye of Scindia quite as much as those of the gallant troops who had just reinstated him; it had a political object, to encourage native princes in a course of fidelity, by shewing that the British government would aid in maintaining them on their thrones, just in proportion to their good faith.*

* Brigadier Stuart, when he heard of the fatal termination of this bold and daring achievement, issued the following general order: 'Brigadier Stuart has received with the deepest regret a report of the death of Lieutenant Rose, 25th Bombay N. I., who was mortally wounded yesterday, on entering the fort of Gwalior, on duty with his men. The brigadier feels assured that the whole brigade unite with him in deploring the early death of this gallant officer, whose many sterling qualities none who knew him could fail to appreciate.'

* '*Allahabad, June* 24, 1858.—The Right Honourable the Governor-general has the highest gratification in announcing that the town and fort of Gwalior were conquered by Major-general Sir Hugh Rose on the 19th instant, after a general action in which the rebels, who had usurped the authority of Maharajah Scindia, were totally defeated. On the 20th of June, the Maharajah Scindia, attended by the governor-general's agent for Central India, and Sir Hugh Rose, and escorted by British troops, was restored to the palace of his ancestors, and was welcomed by his subjects with

The British had re-conquered every part of the city and neighbourhood of Gwalior, reinstated Scindia on his throne, wrought terrible execution on the insurgents, and compelled the main body to seek safety in flight. But the questions then arose, in this as in all previous instances—to what quarter had the fugitives retreated, and what amount of mischief might they produce during and in consequence of their retreat? It was soon ascertained that, while others had chosen a different route, the main body had taken the road to Kurowlee. Hence it became an object with Sir Hugh to send off a force in pursuit, in the hope of so completely cutting up the fugitives as to prevent them from reassembling as an organised army at any other spot. He invited the co-operation of Brigadier Showers from another quarter, but depended chiefly on the exertions of a flying column hastily made up, and placed under the command of Brigadier Napier. On the 20th, within a few hours after the capture of Gwalior, Napier set forth; and the next few days were marked by deeds of gallantry worthy of the name he bore. The column consisted of a troop of horse-artillery, a troop of the 14th Dragoons, a wing of the Hyderabad Contingent cavalry, and three troops of Meade's Horse—altogether about six hundred men, with six guns. Starting from the Moorar cantonment, and passing from the Residency into the open country, Napier reached Sunnowlie, twenty-four miles from Gwalior, by three o'clock the next morning. On approaching Jowra Alipore, a few hours afterwards, he descried the enemy in great force, with nearly thirty guns. Not waiting to consider how small his numbers were compared with those opposed to him, Napier resolved to grapple with the enemy. He moved his column to the cover of a rising-ground which afforded partial concealment; and finding the rebels disposed to move off, he at once attacked them, with a chivalrous daring worthy of all praise. The column galloped off to the right, towards the enemy's guns, of which nine were grouped in and around a small tope of trees. Captain Lightfoot's horse-artillery galloped up to the front, poured in two rounds of shot at a distance of five hundred yards, limbered up, and dashed off to the enemy's guns, even outstripping the supporting cavalry; these guns, being found deserted by the enemy, were at once captured. Of fighting, there was really little in amount. The enemy, supposed to be at least ten times as numerous as Napier's troops, and supplied with formidable artillery, scarcely made a stand at any point; the necessity for flight from Gwalior had produced a sort of panic, and they made but little resistance to Napier. They ran off in various directions, but chiefly towards the south. Their haste was too great, and the pursuit too prompt, to enable them to save any of their guns; Napier seized them all, twenty-five in number, together with numerous stands of arms. Great as was this achievement, however, considering the relative forces of the belligerents, the result was hardly satisfactory in a political point of view. The hope was not merely to recover Gwalior, but to crush the rebel forces. Gwalior, it is true, was taken, and artillery in much strength was captured; still the main body of the rebels escaped from Rose at Gwalior on the 19th, and the same main body escaped from Napier at Jowra Alipore on the 21st. Although they had few or no guns, they fled as an army and not as a rabble; they retained that sort of military organisation which might enable them to work mischief elsewhere. Napier, wishing to prevent this as far as possible, pursued them some distance; but as the rebels were wonderfully quick in their movements, they gradually increased the distance between them and their pursuer, until at length Napier was thirty miles behind. He then gave up a pursuit which was likely to be fruitless, and returned to Gwalior with the guns he had captured. It was afterwards made a subject for question whether Rose should not have placed a greater force of light cavalry at Napier's disposal; but there appears much probability that, when once in flight, the rebels would have succeeded in escaping, in this as in all similar instances. They had attained great mastery in the art of fleeing.

Who was the leader of the body of rebels adverted to in the preceding paragraph was not clearly known; perhaps there was no recognised leader in the hasty flight. Another body, however, estimated at five or six thousand in number, followed the orders of the indefatigable Tanteea Topee; he led them across the Chumbul, past Shree Muttra and Hindoun, and made towards Jeypoor—the chief city of the principal among the Rajpoot states. So far as could be ascertained, he hoped to obtain the assistance of insurgent chieftains in that region. He carried with him the crown-jewels, and an immense amount of treasure, that had belonged to Scindia. There was a possibility that Tanteea Topee, by bending a little to the north, would advance to Bhurtpore instead of Jeypoor. The population of Bhurtpore was warlike, and Tanteea Topee could not enter within the earthen walls if opposed; but it was impossible at that time to rely on any body of Rajpoot troops; and hence the British authorities watched with some anxiety the progress of the rebel leader.

every mark of loyalty and attachment. It was on the 1st of June that the rebels, aided by the treachery of some of Maharajah Scindia's troops, seized the capital of his highness's kingdom, and hoped to establish a new government under a pretender in his highness's territory. Eighteen days had not elapsed before they were compelled to evacuate the town and fort of Gwalior, and to relinquish the authority which they had endeavoured to usurp. The promptitude and success with which the strength of the British government has been put forth to the restoration of its faithful ally to the capital of his territory, and the continued presence of British troops at Gwalior to support his highness in the re-establishment of his administration, offer to all a convincing proof that the British government has the will and the power to befriend those who, like Maharajah Scindia, do not shrink from their obligations or hesitate to avow their loyalty. The Right Honourable the Governor-general, in order to mark his appreciation of the Maharajah Scindia's friendship, and his gratification at the re-establishment of his highness's authority in his ancestral dominions, is pleased to direct that a royal salute shall be fired at every principal station in India.'

When, a few weeks earlier, Sir Hugh Rose had thanked his gallant troops after the capture of Calpee, he hoped to be able to retire to Bombay, to recruit his shattered health after so much active service in hot weather. This hope was founded on what appeared to be rational grounds. The last stronghold of the enemy had fallen into his hands, with its guns, ammunition, and stores. Detached posts, it is true, might require to be carefully guarded; isolated bodies of rebels might need pursuit and punishment; but there did not appear to be any enterprise of such magnitude and importance as to demand the combined services of the different regiments in the Central India Field-force. Therefore it was that, almost immediately after the fall of Calpee, Sir Hugh issued the glowing address to his troops, already adverted to. His hope of retirement, however, was for a time frustrated by the defeat of Scindia by the rebels; but when he had retaken Gwalior, and reinstated the Maharajah upon the throne, Sir Hugh found himself enabled to fulfil his wish. Towards the close of June he issued another address to his troops, in which he said: 'The major-general commanding being on the point of resigning the command of the Poonah division of the Bombay army,* on account of ill health, bids farewell to the Central India Field-force; and at the same time expresses the pleasure he feels that he commanded them when they gained one more laurel at Gwalior. The major-general witnessed with satisfaction how the troops and their gallant comrades in arms—the Rajpootana brigade, under General Smith—stormed height after height, and gun after gun, under the fire of a numerous field and siege artillery, taking finally by assault two 18-pounders at Gwalior. Not a man in these forces enjoyed his natural strength or health; and an Indian sun, and months of marching and broken rest, had told on the strongest; but the moment they were told to take Gwalior for their Queen and country, they thought of nothing but victory. They gained it, restoring England's true and brave ally to his throne; putting to complete rout the rebel army; killing numbers of them; and taking from them in the field, exclusive of those in the fort, fifty-two pieces of artillery, all their stores and ammunition, and capturing the city and fort of Gwalior, reckoned the strongest in India. The major-general thanks sincerely Brigadier-general Napier, C.B., Brigadier Stuart, C.B.,† and Brigadier Smith, commanding brigades in the field, for the very efficient and able assistance which they gave him, and to which he attributes the success of the day. He bids them and their brave soldiers once more a kind farewell. He cannot do so under better aspects than those of the victory of Gwalior.'

Every one admitted that Sir Hugh Rose had well earned a season of repose, after his five months of marching, fighting, besieging, and conquering. It was on the 12th of January 1858 that he took command of his Central India Field-force at Sehore. On the 23d he captured the town of Ratgurh; on the 28th, defeated the enemy in the field; and on the 30th, captured the fort of Ratgurh. February came, and with it, the relief of Saugor and the capture of the fort of Garra Kotah. In March he forced the pass of Mudenpore; captured a series of strongholds which gave him command of Bundelcund; took and burned Churkaree; and occupied Tal Behut. In April he defeated the rebel army of Tanteea Topee, near Jhansi; captured that city; and afterwards stormed and captured the fort belonging to it. In May he took the fort of Koonch; then fought a severe battle near Calpee; and eventually captured the fort at that place. Lastly, in June, as we have just seen, he thoroughly defeated the Gwalior mutineers, captured that important Mahratta city and fort, and replaced Scindia on the throne of his ancestors. Second to Havelock—and it may be doubted whether even this exception should be made—there was no general engaged in the wars arising out of the mutiny, whose operations were so numerous and so uniformly successful as those of Sir Hugh Rose. It must at the same time be admitted that Havelock, from first to last, had far smaller forces at his command.

The Central India Field-force underwent a total break up after the capture of Gwalior. The 95th regiment remained for a time within the rock-fort. Two of the Queen's regiments of infantry, and one of the Bombay regiments, with detachments of cavalry and artillery, occupied the Moorar cantonment, until further directions could be received. At Jhansi were stationed the 3d Bombay Europeans, the 24th Bombay native infantry, with cavalry and artillery. Brigadier Smith's Rajpootana brigade, which had rendered such good service at the siege of Gwalior, was distributed into three portions—one remaining at Gwalior, and the others going to Seepree and Goonah. All these troops absolutely needed rest. Whatever exertions were necessary to check the career of the fugitive rebels, were intrusted to troops from other quarters, especially to General Roberts, who held command of all the available troops in Rajpootana. Nothing but dire necessity kept British soldiers in the field under a midsummer sun in the plains of India. As to Sir Hugh Rose, a triumphant reception awaited him at Bombay; all ranks strove to render him honour, as one who had brought great renown to the Bombay army.

* The Central India Field-force was a kind of offshoot from the Poonah division of the Bombay army.

† Brigadier Steuart, who had been with Sir Hugh Rose in the earlier scenes of the campaign, retired through ill health before the operations at Gwalior began. His brigade passed to the command of Napier.

DARJEELING—Hill Sanatarium in Sikkim.

CHAPTER XXXI.

STATE OF AFFAIRS AT THE END OF JUNE.

ALTHOUGH the military operations conducted by Sir Hugh Rose and his heroic companions, bearing relation to the reconquest of Gwalior, and the re-establishment of Scindia on his Mahratta throne, were the most interesting events in India during the month of June, the other provinces also witnessed struggles and contests which equally need to be chronicled; seeing that they all contributed towards the one great and earnestly desired result—the pacification of the Anglo-Indian empire. Terrible, it is true, were the labours of the gallant men who fought and marched against the rebels under the scorching heat of an Indian sun—heat which was that year excessive, even for India itself; but such labours were necessary, and were borne with a degree of cheerfulness which commands our admiration for the sterling qualities of British troops. Sir Colin Campbell yearned to place his brave men under shade and at rest, until such time as the rains should have cooled down the summer's fiery temperature; he did so to such an extent as was practicable; but this extent was not great. June, as we shall see, was a month of much fighting in the regions adjacent to the Ganges, the Jumna, the Chumbul, and the Sone.

Calcutta saw nothing of the governor-general during many months. He took up his abode at Allahabad; filling the offices not only of governor-general of the whole of India, but special governor of some of those disturbed regions which had at one time been called the Northwest Provinces, and at another the Central Provinces. This he had done in order that he might be in more easy communication with the commander-in-chief, and in more prompt receipt of intelligence from the various stations and camps in Oude, Behar, Rohilcund, the Doab, Bundelcund, Central India, and Rajpootana. How the weight of responsibility pressed on one who had to govern at such a time and in such a climate, few were aware; he worked on, early and late, thinking only how best he could act as the Queen's viceroy for India. Calcutta had not much more to do with Lord Canning's proceedings at that period, than the other presidential cities; for he had his staff of government employés with him at Allahabad.

Bengal was nearly at peace in June; few troubles disturbed the equable flow of commerce and industry. One slight transaction of an opposite kind may, however, be briefly noticed. A body of sailors sent from Calcutta had an opportunity of bringing some rebels to an account, and defeating them in the wonted style. A naval brigade, under Captain Moore, was stationed in the district of Singbhoom, southwest of Calcutta, near the frontier between the Bengal and Madras presidencies. The district comprised the four petty states of Singbhoom, Colchan, Surakella, and Khursawa, each of which had its rajah or chieftain. The only town of any note in the district was Chyebassa; and here was the Company's civil station. The Rajah of Singbhoom, at the period now under notice, was endeavouring, like many other rajahs, to strengthen himself by throwing off British supremacy. It happened, on the 9th of the month, when the brigade was encamped at Chuckerderpore, but when some of the officers had gone to Chyebassa, that the camp was suddenly attacked by the rajah's motley retinue of Koles, a half-savage tribe armed with battle-axes, bows and arrows, spears, and matchlocks. They invested the camp on all sides, and made a very fierce attack. The seamen poured in a few shells among them, which threw them into much disorder. After this a party of thirty went out, and committed much havoc among them in a hand-to-hand contest. Captain Moncrieff then rode in from Chyebassa, with a cavalry escort, and at once engaged with the rebels. After five hours' skirmishing, the mid-day sun exhausted alike Europeans and Koles; and nothing further occurred till the morning of the 10th. The rebels were so numerous that the brigade could only attack them on one side at once; and thus it was not until the arrival of a hundred Ramgurh troops and fifty Sikhs, at noon on the 11th, that the rajah and his Koles gave way—retreating to the jungles of Porahaut.

In other parts of Bengal there were petty chieftains of like character, who were quite willing to set up as kings on their own account—regardless of treaties existing between them and the Company, and actuated solely by the temptations afforded during a period of disorder. But the conditions were not favourable to them. The meek and cowardly Bengalees did not imitate the Hindustanis of the Doab and Oude; the hill-tribes were too few in number to be formidable; and the steady arrival of British troops at Calcutta strengthened the hands of the authorities in all the surrounding regions. Arrangements were gradually made for increasing the number of European troops at Calcutta, Dacca, Barrackpore, Berhampore, Hazarebagh, Jessore, and one or two other stations—so as to place the whole of Bengal more immediately under the eye of the military authorities.

These defensive measures extended as far north as Darjeeling—one of those healthy and temperate hill-stations which have so often been adverted to in former chapters as important *sanitaria* for the English in India. Simla, Landour, Kussowlie, Subathoo, Mussouree, Dugshai, Almora, and Nynee Tal, are all of this character; and to these may be added Darjeeling. A patch of hill-country, containing about three hundred square miles, and formerly belonging to the Rajah of Sikim, was obtained by the Company a few years ago, and Darjeeling established near its centre. The Himalayas bound it on the north, Nepaul on the west, Bhotan on the east, and two of the Bengal districts on the south. The hills and valleys are beautiful, and the climate healthy. Darjeeling is more particularly mentioned in this place, because, about the date to which this chapter refers, public attention was called to a project for establishing a settlement called Hope Town, on the slopes of a hill near Darjeeling. This settlement was to be for independent emigrants, colonists, or settlers, from the plains, or even from Europe; who, it was hoped, might be tempted to that region by a fertile soil and a magnificent climate, and thus gradually introduce English farming at the base of the Himalayas. A company or society purchased or leased about fourteen thousand acres of hill-land, in Darjeeling district, but not in immediate contiguity to Darjeeling town. It was announced that the locality contained clay for bricks, rubble for masonry, lime for mortar, timber for carpentry and for fuel, and all the essential requisites for building; water was abundant, from the mountain streams and springs; while peaceful natives in the neighbouring plains would be eager to obtain employment as artisans and labourers. The elevation of the land, varying from three to six thousand feet, offered much facility of choice. As the government had commenced a road from Darjeeling and Hope Town to Caragola Ghât on the Ganges, there would be good markets for hill produce in many parts of Bengal—perhaps in Calcutta itself. When the project of this Hope Town settlement was first formed in 1856, it was intended that the projectors should grant leases of small plots for farms or dwellings, for a fixed number of years, and at a rental so small as to attract settlers; while at the same time this rental should so far exceed what the speculators paid to the government as to enable them to construct a road, and build a schoolroom, church, library, and other component elements for a town. This, it may be observed, was only one among several colonising projects brought before public notice in India. The land containing many magnificent tracts, and the climate presenting many varieties of temperature, it has often been urged that that noble country presents advantages for settlement which ought no longer to be overlooked. So long as the East India Company's power existed, any colonising schemes would necessarily prove almost abortive; but now that British India owns no other ruler than the sovereign of England, there may in future years be an opening offered for the thorough examination and testing of this important question, that its merits and demerits may be fairly compared. Some of the advocates of colonisation have painted imaginary pictures so glowing as to represent India as the true Dorado or Golden Land of the widely spreading British empire; some of the opponents of colonisation, on the other hand, have asserted that British farmers could not live in India if they would, and would not if they could:—the future will strike out a practicable mean between these two extremes.

The controversy concerning Indian heat, in reference to the wants and constitutions of English settlers, bore very closely on the subject of colonisation, and on the difference between the hilly districts and the plains. In military matters, however, and in reference to the struggle actually going on, all admitted that the summer of 1858 had been more than usually fierce in its heat. A correspondent of one of the journals said: 'As if to try the endurance of Englishmen to the utmost, the season has been such as has not been known since 1833. Those who know Bengal will understand it when I say that on the 15th inst. one clergyman in Calcutta buried forty-eight Englishmen, chiefly sailors. In one ship the captain, chief-mate, and twenty-six men, had all apoplexy at once. Nine men from Fort-William were buried one morning from the same cause. Her Majesty's 19th, at Barrackpore, who are nearly all under cover, and who are most carefully looked after, have 200 men unfit for duty from immense boils. All over the country paragraph after paragraph announces the deaths of so many men at such a place from apoplexy.' The same writer mentions the case of a colonel who, just arrived with his regiment at Calcutta, and, unfamiliar with an Indian climate, marched off his men *with their stocks on*: in an hour afterwards he and his instructor in rifle-practice were both dead from apoplexy.

Before quitting Calcutta, it may be well to mention that the month of June was marked by an honourable and energetic movement for recording the services and cherishing the memory of Mr Venables, one of those civil servants of the Company who displayed an undaunted spirit, and considerable military talent, in times of great trial. It will be remembered that, after many months of active service, both civil and military, Mr Venables was wounded at Azimghur on the 15th of April;* from the effects of this wound he soon afterwards sank—dying as he had lived, a frank and gallant man. A committee was formed in Calcutta to found, by individual subscriptions, some sort of memorial worthy of the man. Viscount Canning took an early opportunity of joining in this manifestation; and in a letter to the committee he spoke of Mr Venables in the following terms: 'It will be a satisfaction to me to join in this good work, not only on account of the admiration which I feel for the high qualities which Mr Venables devoted to the public service, his intrepidity in the field, his energy and calm temper in upholding the civil authority, and his thoroughly just appreciation of the people and circumstances with which he had to deal; but also, and especially, on account of circumstances attending the last service which Mr Venables rendered to his country. After the capture of Lucknow, where he was attached to Brigadier General Franks' column, Mr Venables came to Allahabad. He was broken in health and spirits, anxious for rest, and looking forward eagerly to his return to England, for which his preparations were made. At that time the appearance of affairs near Azimghur was threatening; and I asked Mr Venables to forego his departure from India, and return to that district, with which he was intimately acquainted—there to assist in preserving order until danger should have passed away. He at once consented cheerfully; and that consent cost him his life. I am certain that the Court of Directors, who are fully informed of all particulars of Mr Venables's great services and untimely death, will be eager to mark, in such manner as shall seem best to them, their appreciation of the character of this brave, self-denying English gentleman; and I am truly glad to have an opportunity of joining with his fellow-countrymen in India in testifying the sincere respect which I feel for his memory.'

Beyond the limits of Bengal, one of the many interesting questions that pressed upon public attention bore relation to Nepaul and Jung Bahadoor. That gay, gorgeous, shrewd, and unscrupulous chieftain had gone back to his own country somewhat dissatisfied with his share in the Oude campaign, or with the advantages accruing from it. Queen Victoria had made him a Grand Cross of the Bath—a gentle knight 'sans peur et sans reproche,' according to the original meaning of that honourable distinction; but there were those who believed he would have better welcomed some more substantial recognition of his services, such as a fair slice out of the territory of Oude. Some doubted his fidelity to the British cause, and among these were several of the leaders among the rebels. There came to light a most remarkable correspondence, showing in what way Jung Bahadoor was tempted to swerve from his allegiance, and in what way he resisted the temptation. Several letters were made public—by what agency does not clearly appear—addressed by the Begum of Oude and her adherents to the Nepaulese chieftain. About the period to which this chapter relates, the rebel party at Lucknow

* Chapter xxviii., p. 460.

disseminated rumours to the effect that Jung Bahadoor, after his return to Nepaul, had been written to by the Begum, and that he had undertaken to throw in his lot with the 'patriots' of Oude. That the attempt was made is clear enough; but the nature of the response, so far as the published correspondence revealed it, certainly does not seem to implicate him. One letter, apparently written about the end of May, was signed by Mahomed Surfraz Ali, who designated himself ambassador of the King of Oude. It began by expressing astonishment that Nepaul should have aided the infidel British, after having in former days been in friendly alliance with Oude. 'The chiefs of every tribe,' it said, 'should fight for their religion as long as they live.' Considering that the Oude royal family were Mohammedans, and the Nepaulese Hindoos, the ambassador had some difficulty in so framing his letter as to prove that Jung Bahadoor ought to aid them rather than the English; and indeed his logic was somewhat lame. The ambassador stated that he was then writing at Toolseepore, whither he had been sent by the powerful Moulvie Ahmedoolah Shah, on the part of the King of Oude, to act as accredited agent or ambassador with the Nepaul authorities. He proceeded to state that seven letters, in the Persian language, had been written by Mahomed Khan Bahadoor, viceroy of Oude, to as many of the chief personages in Oude—among others, to Jung Bahadoor himself; and that two letters, in the Hindee language, had been written under the seal of the King of Oude, one addressed to the King of Nepaul, and one to Jung Bahadoor. Mahomed Surfraz Ali added: 'Neither I nor the servants of our government are acquainted with your titles, or those of your authorities, so we cannot address you properly. I am in hopes that you will send me word how we should address you; and pray forgive any mistakes or omissions in this letter.' He begged the favour of a letter, with the chieftain's seal attached, for presentation to the court of Oude. The letters purporting to be written by or for 'Ramzan Ali Khan Mirza Birjiz Kudr Bahadoor,' King of Oude, assumed quite a regal style, and almost claimed the alliance of the Nepaul Maharajah as a right. The royal letter-writer made short work of the causes of the mutiny: 'The British some time ago attempted to interfere with the faith of both the Hindoos and the Mohammedans, by preparing cartridges with cows' grease for the Hindoos, and that of pigs' for the Mohammedans, and ordering them to bite them with their teeth. The sepoys refused, and were ordered by the British to be blown away from guns on the parade-ground. This is the cause of the war breaking out, and probably you are acquainted with it. But I am ignorant as to how they managed to get your troops, which they brought down here, and began to commit every sort of violence, and to pull down temples, mosques, imaumbarahs, and sacred places. You are well aware of the treachery of the British; and it is proper you should preserve the standard of religion, and make the tree of friendship between you and me fresh.' The real correspondents, in this exchange of letters, were the Begum of Oude and Jung Bahadoor. The astute chieftain wrote a reply, couched in such terms as to suggest a probability that the British resident at Khatmandoo was at his elbow. One of his high-flown paragraphs ran thus: 'Since the star of faith and integrity, sincerity in words as well as in acts, and wisdom and comprehension, of the British, are shining as bright as the sun in every quarter of the globe, be assured that my government will never disunite itself from the friendship of the exalted British government, or be instigated to join with any monarch against it, be he as high as heaven. What grounds can we have for connecting ourselves with the Hindoos and Mohammedans of Hindostan?' And he ended with this bit of advice: 'As you have sent me a friendly letter, let me persuade you, that if any person, Hindoo or Mohammedan, who has not murdered a British lady or child, goes immediately to Mr Montgomery, the chief-commissioner of Lucknow, and surrenders his arms, and makes submission, he will be permitted to retain his honour, and his crime will be pardoned. If you still be inclined to make war on the British, no rajah or king in the world will give you an asylum; and death will be the end of it.' This reply, supposing it to be a spontaneous expression of the real sentiments of Jung Bahadoor, would have possessed very high value; but a large deduction must probably be made both from the spontaneity and the sincerity.

It may perhaps be well to notice that the royal house of Oude was at discord with itself in those days, and that the king's name was used 'as a tower of strength' by intriguers who cared little for rightful ownership. The real king—that is, the ex-king—was at Calcutta, a prisoner and a half-idiot, with depravity enough to enjoy plots, but not brains to execute them. The legitimate son and heir, so to speak, was in Europe, where he had lately buried his grandmother the dowager-queen of Oude, and was spending his father's money at a very rapid rate. The regal personages at Lucknow were the Begum and her son. The Begum was one of the king's many ladies; and her son was a weak-headed youth of thirteen years old—'illegitimate,' according to the assertions of the 'legitimate' son at that time in Europe. The exiled king and his two sons were, in reference to these machinations at Lucknow, mere tools or pretences; the real mover was the clever and ambitious Begum. In Nepaul, likewise, the real power was possessed, not by the maharajah, or sovereign, but by his all-controlling, king-making subject, Jung Bahadoor.

The proceedings of the Oudian intriguers during the month of June will presently be noticed in other ways; but it will be convenient first to attend to the affairs of Behar.

In former chapters it has been narrated, in

sufficient fulness for the purpose in view, how the western provinces of Behar were troubled by the Jugdispore and Dinapoor rebels, and with how many difficulties Sir Edward Lugard had to contend in bringing his 'Azimghur Field-force' to bear against them. The month of June offered no exception to this state of things. Most harassing indeed were the labours which they brought upon him, testing his patience and perseverance more, perhaps, than his military skill. Notwithstanding the numerous defeats which they had suffered, these mutinied sepoys and armed budmashes were continually moving from place to place—giving evidence of their presence by murder, plunder, and burning. The jungles around Jugdispore afforded many facilities for hiding and secret flight. One of the many defeats inflicted by Sir Edward occurred on the 27th of May. Immediately afterwards a body of several hundreds of those insurgents issued from the eastern portion of the jungle, and shewed themselves in their true character as marauders bent on mischief, rather than as soldiers fighting for a definite cause. On the 30th they burned an indigo factory at Twining Gunge, a place near Dumoran; whilst on the same day another body advanced to the village of Rajpore, within eight miles of Buxar, and murdered two natives in government service. From thence they wandered, during the next four or five days, among the neighbouring villages, working mischief at every step. In anything like a military sense, these bands of marauders were contemptible; but so numerous were the unemployed and half-fed ruffians in the disturbed districts, that there were always materials at hand for swelling the numbers of these freebooting insurgents. Lugard was compelled to keep his troops moving about, between Arrah and Buxar; while the authorities at Ghazeepore and Benares were on the alert to check any advance of the rebels towards those cities. On the 2d of June he divided his force into two wings, and established camps at Keshwa and Dalleepore, with a line of posts across the jungle. On the next day he cut a broad road through the jungle to connect the two camps. Having thus completely hemmed a considerable body of the rebels within the southern end of the jungle, he attacked them with his whole force on the 4th, with a very successful result—so far as regarded the maintenance of military superiority. The rebels attempted for a time to make a stand; but the 10th and 84th foot, charging with the bayonet, defeated them with great slaughter. Here again, however, was the old story repeated; his hope of capturing the main body of rebels was frustrated; they broke up into small bands, and fled in various directions.

Instead of describing numerous petty contests that occurred during the month, it may be well to illustrate the peculiar characteristics of the struggle by one particular instance, to shew that the British troops in Behar had more certainty of hard work than chance of glory. During the first week in June, Sir Edward intrusted to Brigadier Douglas the duty of intercepting a body of rebels from the Jugdispore district towards Buxar—a difficult duty, on account of the ingenuity of the rebels in eluding pursuit. Douglas started on the 7th, taking with him H.M. 84th foot, a troop of the 4th Madras cavalry, three troops of the military train, and three guns of the royal horse-artillery. On that and the two following days he marched to Buxar, by way of Shahpoor and Saumgunje. Between the 10th and the 13th he was busily engaged in the almost hopeless task of catching the rebels who were known to be marching and marauding not far distant. Now he would descry a few hundred of them in a tope of trees, and send his horse-artillery to disperse them with grape-shot; now he would cross the little river Surronuddee, or the Kurrumnassa, or hasten to the Sheapoor Ghât, in the hope of cutting off fugitives; now he would march through or near the villages of Ghamur, Chawsa, or Barra, in search either of rebels or of intelligence. His success by no means repaid him for his harassing exertions; he could seldom rely on information obtained concerning the movements of the rebels, and still more seldom could he catch the rebels themselves. In his dispatch relating to these operations, the brigadier said: 'Three men of the royal horse-artillery died during the night from the effects of the sun, and one man of the 84th. . . . The heat during the operations was intense, and the troops suffered much, particularly the 84th regiment, who have now been thirteen months in the field. I consider this regiment at present to be quite unfit for active service; the men have no positive disease, but they are so exhausted that they can neither eat nor sleep.' If they could have encountered the enemy, and thoroughly vanquished them in a regular battle, the over-worked and heat-worn soldiers would have borne this and more than this cheerfully; but they had to deal with rebels who eluded their search in an extraordinary way. Sir Edward Lugard, in a dispatch written on the 14th, dated from his camp at Narainpoor, near Jugdispore, adverted to this subject in the following terms: 'To shew the rapidity and secrecy with which the rebels conduct their movements, I beg to state, that in order to guard against the return of any party from the west towards the jungles, without my getting timely intelligence, so that I might intercept them, I posted at Roop-Saugor—a village thirteen miles to my southwest, on the track taken by the rebels in their flight—Captain Rattray, with his Sikh battalion. He again threw forward scouts some miles in the same direction, and constantly had parties patrolling in the different villages. But in spite of every precaution, the rebel force were at Medneepore, within four miles of him, before he could communicate with me, and passed on towards the jungle the same night. Every endeavour to obtain information from the people of the district has proved vain; scarcely ever has any intelligence been given to us, until the time has passed when advantage could be taken of it.'

In reference to these Jugdispore rebels, it has been remarked that they were neither Sikhs from the west, nor Poorbeahs from the east; but chiefly Bhojpoories of the Shahabad district, most of them born on Koer Singh's own estates. Moreover, causes have been assigned for thinking that these, as well as other rebels, adhered most to those leaders who could treat them best, whether in pay or plunder, without much reference to their military abilities. 'The extraordinary variations in the numbers of the insurgents may be partly accounted for by variations in the readiness of pay. Koer Singh, when he left Oude, had barely five hundred men in his train. As he marched, every straggling sepoy, every embarrassed scoundrel with a sword, enlisted in his service. By the time he reached Azimghur he had two thousand five hundred followers; most, but not all, well armed. The flight across the river dispersed them once more; and it was not till the check sustained by H.M. 35th that they thronged to him again. Apparently the leaders are well aware of the advantage this peculiarity affords. Thus, after their defeat by Sir E. Lugard, the great bulk of the Behar insurgents vanished; the work was apparently complete, and the military ends of the campaign to all appearance accomplished. The leaders, however, remained in the jungle, and in five days their followers were round them again; they had glided back in twos and threes, by paths on which no European would be met.'

After many weeks of fatiguing duty in this region, Sir Edward Lugard, worn with heat and sickness, resigned the command about the end of June; handing over to Colonel Douglas the office of chasing the Jugdispore rebels from place to place. Nor was it in that particular locality alone that this duty had to be fulfilled. Ummer Singh, equalling his deceased brother in activity, was no sooner defeated in one place than he made his appearance in another, carrying discord into villages where his presence was as little desired by natives as by Europeans. While Colonel Douglas was on his way towards the scene of his new command, news reached him that the English at Gayah had been driven into intrenchments by a party of a hundred and fifty rebel prisoners, who had been set at liberty by the native police employed to watch them, and were speedily joined by the jail convicts; all—prisoners, police, and convicts—became suddenly 'patriots,' and shewed their patriotism by threatening all the officials at the station. This is believed to have been done by some connivance with Ummer Singh. The Europeans at Gayah were thrown into a great ferment by this visitation; the few troops present were withdrawn into the intrenchment, as were likewise the civilians, ladies, and children. No immediate attack followed; but the incident furnished one among many proofs that the native police were, in most of the Bengal and Hindostan provinces, a source of more danger than protection to the British—except the Sikh police, who almost uniformly behaved well.

The transactions in Oude, during the month of June, told of rebels defeated but not disbanded, weakened but not captured. There were many leaders, and these required to be narrowly watched.

One of the first cares of the authorities was to place the important city of Lucknow in such a state of defence as to render it safe from attacks within and without. Various military works were planned by Colonel Napier, and were executed by Major Crommelin after Napier's departure. From the vast extent of Lucknow, and the absence of any very prominent features of the ground, it was a difficult city to defend except by a large body of troops. The point which gave the nearest approach to a command over the city was the old fort or Muchee Bhowan, near which was the great Emanbarra, capable of sheltering a large number of troops. It was decided to select several spots as military posts, to clear the ground round those spots, and to open streets or roads of communication from post to post. The Muchee Bhowan was selected as the chief of these posts; a second was near the iron bridge leading over the Goomtee to the Fyzabad road; a third was on the site of the Residency, now a heap of ruins; a fourth was at the Moosa Bagh. All suburbs and buildings lying on the banks of the river, likely to intercept the free march of troops from the Muchee Bhowan to the Moosa Bagh, were ordered to be swept away. Large masses of houses were also removed, to form good military roads from the Muchee Bhowan to the Char Bagh, the Moosa Bagh, the stone bridge, the iron bridge, and the old cantonment. The vast range of palaces, such as the Fureed Buksh, the Chuttur Munzil, the Kaiser Bagh, &c., were converted temporarily into barracks, and all the streets and buildings near them either pulled down or thrown open. The Martinière, the Dil Koosha, and Banks's house, were formed into military posts on the eastern side of the city. The two extremes of these posts, from northwest to southeast, were not far short of seven miles asunder; they would require a considerable number of troops for their occupancy and defence; but under any circumstances such would be required in the great capital of Oude for a long period to come.

The Alum Bagh continued to be maintained, as an important and useful station on the road from Lucknow to Cawnpore. It was destined to live in history as a place which Sir James Outram had defended for nearly four months against armed forces estimated at little short of a hundred thousand men. It was not originally a fort, only a palace in the midst of a walled garden; but it presented facilities for being made into useful shelter for troops. Another place, the bridge of Bunnee, over the river Sye, was also carefully maintained as an important military post between Lucknow and Cawnpore.

During the latter part of May, the English troops employed with Sir Hope Grant in various expeditions against the enemy suffered severely from the heat; and it was found necessary to give the 38th regiment a temporary sojourn in the Emanbarra at Lucknow, supplying their place by the 53d. On the 3d of June the Bunnee force moved out, to disperse a body of rebels who had posted themselves near Pooroa. There was another duty of a singular kind intrusted to those troops. The Rajah of Kupoorthully, a Sikh chieftain, who had rendered valuable services to the government in time of need, received as a reward an extensive jaghire or domain in Oude. In order that he might defend both himself and British interests in that domain, he was assisted in intrenching himself, and was supplied with guns, mortars, and ammunition; this was irrespective of his own force of four thousand Sikh troops.

Shortly after the opening of the month, rumours reached the authorities at Lucknow that a body of rebels, estimated at seventeen or eighteen thousand, had crossed the Gogra, and taken up a position at Ramnuggur Dhumaree, under the orders of Gorhuccus Singh. The correctness of this report was not certain—nor of others that Madhoo Singh was at the head of five thousand rebels at Goosaengunje, Benee Madhoo with a small number in the Poorwah district, and Dunkha Shah with a larger force near Chinhut. Still, though these numbers were probably exaggerated by alarmists, it was not considered prudent to leave the northeast region of Oude unprotected. Accordingly, a movable column was organised, to proceed towards Fyzabad.

Sir Hope Grant, intrusted at that time with the conduct of military affairs in Oude, himself conducted an expedition towards the districts just adverted to. A little before midnight on the 12th of June, acting on information which had reached him, he marched from Lucknow to Chinhut, and thence towards Nawabgunge, on the Fyzabad road. His force consisted of the 2d and 3d battalions of the Rifle Brigade, the 5th Punjaub Rifles, a detachment of Engineers and Sappers, the 7th Hussars, two squadrons of the 2d Dragoon Guards, Hodson's Horse, a squadron of the first Sikh cavalry, a troop of mounted police, a troop of horse-artillery, and two light field-batteries. Leaving a garrison column at Chinhut, under Colonel Purnell, and intrusting the same officer with the temporary charge of the baggage and supplies belonging to the column, Sir Hope resumed his march during the night towards Nawabgunge, where sixteen thousand rebels had assembled, with several guns. By daylight on the following morning he crossed the Beti Nuddee at Quadrigunje, by means of a ford. He had purposely adopted this route instead of advancing to the bridge on the Fyzabad road; in order that, after crossing the nullah, he might get between the enemy and a large jungle. As a strong force of rebels defended the ford, a sharp artillery-fire, kept up by Mackinnon's horse-artillery and Johnson's battery, was necessary to effect this passage. Having surmounted this obstacle, Sir Hope, approaching nearer to Nawabgunge, got into the jungle district. Here the rebels made an attempt to surround him on all sides, and pick off his men by repeated volleys of musketry. The general speedily changed the aspect of affairs. He sent a troop of horse-artillery to the front; Johnson's battery and two squadrons of horse were sent to defend the left; while a larger body confronted the rebels on the right—where the enemy apparently expected to find and to capture Sir Hope's baggage. The struggle was very fierce, and the slaughter of the rebels considerable; the enemy, fanatical as well as numerous, gave exercise for all Grant's boldness and sagacity in contending with them. The victory was complete—and yet it was indefinite; for the rebels, as usual, escaped, to renew their mischief at some other time and place. Nearly six hundred of their number were slain; the wounded were much more numerous. Hope Grant's list of killed and wounded numbered about a hundred. Many of the rebels were Ghazees or Mohammedan fanatics, far more difficult to deal with than the mutinied sepoys. Adverting to some of the operations on the right flank, Grant said in his dispatch: 'On arriving at this point, I found that a large number of Ghazees, with two guns, had come out on the open plain, and attacked Hodson's Horse. I immediately ordered up the other four guns under the command of Lieutenant Percival, and two squadrons of the 7th Hussars under Major Sir W. Russell, and opened grape upon them within three or four hundred yards with terrible effect. But the fanatics made the most determined resistance; and two men in the midst of a shower of grape brought forward two green standards, which they planted in the ground beside their guns, and rallied their men. Captain Atherley's two companies of the 3d battalion Rifle Brigade at this moment advanced to the attack, which obliged the rebels to move off. The cavalry then got between them and the guns; and the 7th Hussars, led gallantly by Sir W. Russell, supported by Hodson's Horse under Major Daly, swept through them—killing every man.' Whatever may have been the causes, proximate or remote, of the mutiny, it is quite evident that such Mussulman fanatics as these, with their green flag of rebellion and their cries of 'Deen! deen!' had been worked up, or had worked themselves up, to something like a sincere belief that they were fighting for their religion.

The chief body of rebels, as has just been stated, succeeded in escaping from Nawabgunge after the battle. They fled chiefly to Ramnuggur and Mahadeo on the banks of the Gogra, and to Bhitowlie at the junction of that river with the Chowka—with the apparent and probable intention of throwing up earthworks for the defence of those positions.

Just about the time when Sir Hope Grant defeated these Nawabgunge rebels—supposed to have been headed by the Begum of Oude and her paramour Mummoo Khan—the career of the energetic Moulvie was suddenly cut short at another. This remarkable man, Moulvie Ahmedullah Shah, died as he had long lived, struggling against the Feringhees and all who supported them. On the 15th of June, after having been driven from place to place by the various British columns and detachments, he arrived from Mohumdee at Powayne, a town

Principal Street in Lucknow.

about sixteen miles northeast of Shahjehanpoor. He had with him a considerable body of horse, and some guns. The Rajah of Powayne, named Juggernath Singh, having incurred the displeasure of the Moulvie by sheltering two native servants of the Company, was attacked by him. Juggernath Singh, and his two brothers Buldeo Singh and Komul Singh, went out to confront the Moulvie as best they could. A skirmish ensued, which lasted three hours. The most notable result was the death of the Moulvie; he received a shot, and fell; his head was at once severed; and the Rajah sent the head and trunk to Shahjehanpoor, to be delivered to Mr Gilbert Money, the commissioner. Glad as the British may have been to get rid of a formidable enemy, it is doubtful whether Mr Money received the bleeding gift with much gratification. The Rajah of Powayne, however, had long been an object of suspicion, on account of his unfeeling conduct towards some of the poor fugitives in the early days of the Revolt; and as the British cause was now obviously the winning cause, he was anxious, by his alacrity in dealing with the dead body of the Moulvie, to win favour with the authorities. A very large reward had been offered by the government to whoever could capture the Moulvie; and although some doubt was expressed whether this was intended to apply as well to the bleeding corpse as to the living man, the reward was paid to the Powayne chieftain.

It was unquestionably a great gain to the British to know that the Moulvie was really removed from the field of strife. As to the Begum, she still remained unsubdued, moving from place to place according as she could gather a large body of adherents around her. It was about the second week in June, so far as is rendered apparent by the correspondence, that she received Jung Bahadoor's very decisive rejection of the appeal made by her for his alliance, lately adverted to; and as she lost nearly at the same time her able coadjutor the Moulvie, her prospects became more gloomy. Of Nena Sahib, little more could be said than that he was true to his character—a coward in all things. Where he was at any particular time, the British seldom certainly knew: he had not the courage of the Moulvie, or the Begum, or the Ranee.

In connection rather with the province of Goruckpore than with that of Oude, though nearly on the boundary-line between the two, must be mentioned two encounters in which the naval brigade honourably distinguished itself. The *Shannon's* seamen, it will be remembered, supplied a naval brigade under the lamented Captain Sir William Peel, for service in Oude; but there was also another brigade furnished by the *Pearl*, of which Captain Sotheby was commander. During May and June, this brigade was associated with certain troops and marines in the maintenance of order on the Goruckpore frontier of Oude. While on detached service, Major Cox and Lieutenant Turnour came in contact with the enemy on the 9th of June. The lieutenant had under him two 12-pounder howitzers, a 24-pounder rocket-tube, and about fifty seamen of the *Pearl's* crew; Lieutenant Pym had the control of about twenty marines from the same ship; while Major Cox, who commanded the whole detachment, had under him a small military force comprising two hundred men of the 13th light infantry, two troops of Madras cavalry, two troops of Bengal cavalry, and twenty Sikhs. It was altogether a singular medley of combatants. Having heard that Mahomed Hussein was occupying the neighbouring village of Amorha or Amorah in great force, Major Cox resolved to attack him. He divided his detachment into two parts, one headed by himself, and the other by Major Richardson. The seamen and marines were attached to Richardson's party. Starting at two o'clock in the morning, they marched along the road leading through the village. When within a mile of Amorah, they received a heavy fire from the rebel skirmishers; these were immediately attacked and driven in by Pym and the marines; while the guns threw shot and shell on the main body. Attempting to retreat on the other flank, Cox met and frustrated them; and the result of the skirmish was a decisive abandonment of the village by the rebels. Nine days afterwards another force, similar in constitution but larger in numbers, comprising in its naval element about a hundred and ten seamen, set out from Captangunje to make another attack on Mahomed Hussein, who was posted with four thousand rebels at Hurreah, about eight miles off. On approaching near Hurreah, the enemy's skirmishers were descried thrown across the river Gogra, screened in thick bamboo jungles, villages, topes of trees, and a dry nullah. British skirmishers were quickly sent on ahead, drove in the enemy, and waded the river after them up to their waists; the guns followed, and the enemy were driven from tope to tope, and from every place of concealment, and chased for four miles. The heat was tremendous; insomuch that seven hours' marching, fighting, and pursuing nearly knocked up officers and men. Mahomed Hussein, however, was severely defeated, and this was deemed a sufficient reward for all the fatigues and privations. The *Pearl's* naval brigade counted this as the tenth time in which it had been in action in nine months.

It may be here mentioned that an endeavour was made, towards the end of June, to estimate the number of thalookdars and other petty chieftains who were in arms against the British in the province of Oude; together with the amount of force at their disposal. The estimate was not wholly reliable, for the means of obtaining correct information were very deficient. The list published in some of the Bombay newspapers, professing to be the nearest attainable approach to the truth, included the names of about thirty-five 'thalookdars,' 'rajahs,' and 'chuckladars,' holding among them about twenty-five mud-forts, with nearly a hundred guns, and forty thousand armed retainers. The chief items in this curious list were—'The three chuckladars Mahomed Hussein, Mehndee Hussein, and Shaik Padil Imam, have twenty-three guns and ten thousand men massed about Sultanpore; some occupying Saloun, ten kos from Roy Bareilly'—'At Nain, within nine kos of Roy Bareilly, four thalookdars, named Juggernath Buksh, Bugwan Buksh, Bussunth Singh, and Juggernath (?), have collected eight guns and six thousand men'—'Banie Madhao, thalookdar; at Sukerpore, a strong fort surrounded by jungle, a few kos from Roy Bareilly; nineteen guns and eight thousand men'—'Rajah Ali Buksh Khan, at Moham, a small fort twenty-five kos east of Lucknow; five guns and fifteen hundred men.' Most of the rebel gatherings here adverted to were in the region around Roy Bareilly, southeast of Lucknow.

But notwithstanding these high-sounding names and formidable numbers, the cause of regular government in Oude was gradually advancing. The rebels could no longer endanger; they could only annoy. Mr Montgomery, at Lucknow, intrusted with large powers by the governor-general, was gradually feeling his way. While Cronmelin took charge of the immediate defence of that city, and Hope Grant was grappling with the rebels in the open field, Montgomery was employed in re-establishing the network of judicial and revenue organisation, as favourable opportunities arose. The Rajah of Kapoorthully, lately adverted to, undertook the defence of the region between the Bunnee and Cawnpore; while Hope Grant kept a vigilant eye on the centre of Oude. The astute and double-dealing Maun Singh was placed in a singular position. He was distrusted by both parties, because he would not openly side with one against the other. As the chieftain of Shahgunje, on the river Gogra, very near the eastern frontier of Oude, he would be formidable either as a friend or a foe. He had a fort, guns, and men at his command. There could be no question that for thirteen months he had been watching the progress of events, to determine in which balance to throw his sword; and it was equally evident that he was gradually recognising more and more the value of English friendship—as a consequence, he was bitterly disliked by the rebel leaders. Taking a view of the state of Oude generally during June, it is necessary to make a distinction between the earlier and the later days of the month. The former was much less favourable than the latter. It could not truthfully be said that the pacification proceeded rapidly. Injury was wrought by the party-tactics concerning the famous proclamation penned by Viscount Canning and condemned by the Earl of Ellenborough. The violent discussions arising out of that collision of opinion could not be wholly concealed from the natives of India. It cannot be doubted that many of the reckless and unscrupulous speeches made in the British parliament became known to, and cherished by, the insurgent chieftains. When a halo of suffering virtue was thrown around the Oudian royal family, and when the Queen of England's viceroy in India was spoken of almost as a murderer and robber, the power of the government became necessarily shaken, and the difficulties of pacification increased. The proclamation was modified; nay, Mr Montgomery received discretionary powers to determine whether, and when, and where there should be a proclamation at all—the governor-general wisely leaving it to his sagacity to be guided by the circumstance of time and place. At the beginning of June little had been effected towards winning the submission of the malcontent thalookdars and chuckladars; the hopes of successful rebellion had not been sufficiently damped. Nevertheless, as the month advanced, and when the Moulvie was dead and the Gwalior rebels beaten, the Oudian landowners, by ones and twos, began to look out for a compromise, which might enable them safely to abandon a losing cause. One of the most embarrassing difficulties perhaps was this—that the rebel leaders made instant war against any thalookdars or chuckladars who gave in their submission to the British government under the modified proclamation—thereby deterring the more timid landowners from the adoption of this course. Maun Singh himself was besieged by an insurgent force; but his means of resistance were considerable.

One of the evidences afforded that the pacification of Oude was considered to be gradually approaching, was the disbandment of the corps of Volunteer Cavalry, which was composed almost wholly of officers and gentlemen, and which had rendered such eminent services at a time when European troops were doubly precious from their extreme rarity. In a notification issued at Calcutta, Viscount Canning, after mentioning some of the arrangements connected with the disbanding, thus spoke of the services of the corps: 'The Volunteer Cavalry took a prominent part in all the successes which marked the advance of the late Major-general Sir Henry Havelock from Allahabad to Lucknow; and on every occasion of its employment against the rebels—whether on the advance to Lucknow, or as part of the force with which Major-general Sir James Outram held Alum Bagh—this corps has greatly distinguished itself by its gallantry in action, and by its fortitude and endurance under great exposure and fatigue. The governor-general offers to Major Barrow, who ably commanded the Volunteer Cavalry, and boldly led them in all the operations in which they were engaged, his most cordial acknowledgments for his very valuable services: and to Captain Lynch, and all the officers and men who composed this corps, his lordship tenders his best thanks for the eminent good conduct and exemplary courage which they displayed during the whole time that the corps was embodied.' The farewell of Sir James Outram was more hearty, because less official.*

Directing our attention next to the Doab and Rohilcund, it becomes at once apparent that organisation and systematic government made great advances during the month of June. The Doab no longer contained any large body of armed rebels. There were numerous smaller bands, but these bands chiefly made use of the Doab as a route of passage. The hopes of the rebel leaders were directed mainly towards two regions—Oude, on the north of the Ganges; and Central India, on the south of the Jumna. According as the fortunes of war (or rather depredation) tended in the one direction or the other, so did groups of armed insurgents cross, or attempt to cross, those rivers by means of the ghâts or ferries. If the chances for rebel success appeared stronger at Lucknow or Fyzabad, Bareilly or Shahjehanpoor, this current tended northward, or rather northeastward: if Calpee or Jhansi, Gwalior or Jeypoor, excited the hopes of the insurgents, the current took an opposite direction. The Doab, in either case, was regarded rather as a line of transit than as a field of contest. Sir Colin Campbell, well acquainted with this fact, devoted a portion of his attention to the ghâts on the two great rivers. It became very important to check if possible the marching and countermarching of the rebels across the Doab; and several columns and detachments of troops were engaged in this duty during the month now under notice. The success of the few actual encounters depended very much on the course of events in Scindia's dominions, narrated in the last chapter. When Gwalior fell into the hands of Tanteea Topee and his associates, all the turbulent chieftains in the surrounding districts displayed an audacity and hopefulness which they had not exhibited during the preceding month; but when Sir Hugh Rose reconquered that city, and replaced Scindia on his throne, timidity succeeded to audacity, misgiving to hopefulness.

* 'My dear Barrow—We are about to separate, perhaps for ever; but, believe me, I shall ever retain you in affectionate remembrance, and ever speak with that intense admiration which I feel for the glorious volunteers whom you have commanded with such distinction. It would afford me much pleasure to shake every one of them by the hand, and tell them how warmly I feel towards them. But this is impossible; my pressing duties will not allow me even to write a few farewell lines to each of your officers: but I trust to your communicating to them individually my affectionate adieu and sincerest wishes for their prosperity. May God bless you and them.' From one like Sir James, who had had such special means of observing and appreciating the exertions of the volunteer cavalry, this warm and genial letter must have been doubly gratifying.

The commander-in-chief, after his participation in the reconquest and pacification of Rohilcund, returned to his former quarters at Futteghur, where he remained until the second week in June. Throughout the month he was personally engaged in no hostilities; he was occupied either in studying how to give his heat-worn soldiers repose, or how best to employ those whose services in the field were still indispensable. The governor-general much desired his presence at Allahabad, to confer with him personally on the military arrangements necessary during the summer and autumn. It afforded a significant proof of the scattered position of the British forces, that during the first week in June there were no soldiers that could be spared to escort Sir Colin from Futteghur to Allahabad. Quiet as the Doab was, compared with its condition earlier in the year, there were still rebel bands occasionally crossing and recrossing it, and these bands would have hazarded much to capture a prize so important as the commander-in-chief of the Anglo-Indian army. He could not safely move without an escort, and he had to delay his journey until a few troops came in from Shahjehanpoor and other stations. While at Futteghur he caused a search to be made in the bazaars of that place and Furruckabad for sulphur, in order that any stores of that substance might be seized by and for the government. The rebels of the various provinces still possessed many guns; the chieftains and landowners still owned more weapons of various kinds than they chose to acknowledge to the government; there was iron for the making of cannon-balls; there were charcoal and saltpetre towards the making of gunpowder; but there was one ingredient, sulphur, without which all the firearms of the insurgents would be useless; and as sulphur was an imported article in India, the government made attempts to obtain possession of any stores of that substance that might be in doubtful hands. Percussion-caps, too, were becoming scarce among the rebels; and, the materials and machinery for making more being wanting, they were perforce superseded by the less effective matchlock.

The state of the Doab at that time is well told in connection with a journey made by Mr Russell. After the Rohilcund campaign was over, this active journalist looked about him to determine what was best worth seeing and describing, in reference to his special duties. If he went with or after Sir Colin to Allahabad, he would get to the head-quarters of politics, where very few stirring military operations were to be witnessed; if he went northeast into Oude, or southwest into Central India, he might, after much danger and difficulty, become involved in the movements of some flying column, ill assorting with the necessities of a lame man—for he still suffered from an injury by a kick from a horse. Mr Russell therefore resolved upon a journey through the Upper Doab from Futteghur to Delhi, and thence by Umballa to the healthy hill-station of Simla. He travelled by Bhowgong, Eytah, Gosaigunje, and Allygurh, meeting with ample evidence on the way of the ruin resulting from thirteen months of anarchy. Of the dâk bungalows or stations he says: 'Let no one understand by this a pleasant roadside hostelry with large out-offices, spacious courtyard, teams of horses, and hissing ostlers; rather let him see a mud-hovel by the way, standing out, the only elevation in the dead level of baked earth, a few trees under which are tethered some wretched horses, and a group of men'—whose dress consisted of little beyond a turban. From Bhowgong to Eytah the country looked like a desert; and by the roadside, at intervals of ten miles or less, were thannahs or police-stations—small one-storied houses, bearing traces of the destructiveness of the rebel leader which had so often swept the district. He crossed the Kallee Nuddee at a point where the Company had never yet introduced the civilised agency of a regular bridge. The gharry was pushed and dragged down a shelving bank of loose sand, and then over a rickety creaky bridge of boats—the native attendants making much use of the primitive distended bladders and earthen jars as floating supporters. Arrived at Eytah, he found the place little other than a heap of blackened ruins, with enclosures broken down and trees lopped off at the stem. Yet here were three Englishmen, civil servants of the Company, engaged in re-establishing the machinery of regular government. Mr Russell, like every one else, tried all the varieties of language to express adequately the tremendous heat of an Indian June. He left Eytah at two in the afternoon. 'The gharry was like an oven; the metal-work burning so that it could not be borne in contact with the hand for an instant. The wind reminded me of the deadly blast which swept over us on the march to Futteghur that dreadful morning when we left Rohilcund. Not a tree to shade the road; on each side a parched, dull, dun-coloured plain, with the waving heat-lines dancing up and down over its blighted surface; and whirling dust-storms or "devils," as they are called, careering to and fro as if in demoniac glee in their own infernal region. On such a day as this Lake's men (half a century earlier) fell file after file on their dreadful journey. Could I have found shelter, I would gladly have stopped, for even the natives suffered, and the horses were quite done up; but in India, in peace and war, one's motto must be "No backward step!"—so on we went.' After passing through many small towns and poor villages, in which half the houses were either ruined or shut up, he reached Allygurh, where, 'being late, there was nothing ready at the bungalow but mosquitoes.' Pursuing his journey, he at length reached Delhi.

The imperial city was now wholly and safely under British control. Sentries guarded the bridge of boats over the Jumna, allowing no native to pass without scrutiny; the fort of the Selimgurh was garrisoned by a small but trusty detachment. The plan, once contemplated, of destroying the defences, had not been adopted; the majestic wall, though shattered and ball-pierced in parts, remained in other respects entire. The defences were, altogether, calculated to strike a stranger with surprise, at the height and solidity of the wall, the formidable nature of the bastions, the depth and width of the dry ditch, the completeness of the glacis, and the security of such of the gates as had not been battered down or blown in. Some of the streets of the city had escaped the havoc of war; but others exhibited the effects of bombardment and assault in a terrible degree, although nine months of peaceful occupation had intervened; houses pitted with marks of shot and bullet, public buildings shattered and half in ruins, trees by the wayside split and rent, doors and windows splintered, gables torn out of houses, jagged holes completely through the walls. Half the houses in the city were shut; and the other

SURAT.—From a View in the Library of the East India Company.

half had not yet regained their regular steady inhabitants. The mighty palace of the Moguls was nearly as grand as ever on the outside; but all within displayed a wreck of oriental splendour. The exquisite Dewani Khas, when Mr Russell was there, instead of being filled with turbaned and bejewelled rajahs, Mogul guards, and oriental magnificence, as in the olden days, was occupied by British infantry—infantry, too, engaged in the humblest of barrack domestic duties. 'From pillar to pillar and column to column extended the graceful arches of the clothes-line, with shirts and socks and drawers flaunting in the air in lieu of silken banners. Long lines of charpoys or bedsteads stretched from one end of the hall to the other—arms were piled against the columns—pouches, belts, and bayonets depended from the walls; and in the place where once blazed the fabulous glories of the peacock's throne, reclined a private of her Majesty's 61st, of a very Milesian type of countenance.'

The old king still remained a prisoner at Delhi. The drivelling, sensual descendant of Tamerlane, shorn of everything that could impart dignity, occupied some of the smaller apartments of the palace, with a few of his wives, children, and grandchildren, near him. All were fretful and discontented, as they well might be: for they had nothing to see, nowhere to go, no honours to receive, no magnificence to luxuriate in. When interrogated by visitors concerning the early days of the Revolt, he was peevish, and wished to change the subject; and when his youngest begum, and his son Jumma Bukht, were induced to converse, the absence of family unity—if such a thing is possible in an oriental palace—was apparent enough.

Considered politically, Delhi had the great advantage, during the spring months, of being placed under Sir John Lawrence. The province which contained the once imperial city was detached from the 'northwestern' group, and made—with Sirhind, the Punjaub, and the Peshawur Valley—one compact and extensive government, under the control of one who, morally speaking, was perhaps the greatest man in India. It was necessary to reconstruct a government; but much careful consideration was needed before the principle of construction could be settled. If the peaceful industrious population would return to their homes and occupations, their presence would doubtless be welcome; but the neighbouring villages still swarmed with desperate characters, whose residence in Delhi would be productive of evil. Many of the better class of natives feared that the imperial city would never recover; that the injury which its buildings had received during the siege, the disturbance of trade by the hurried exit of the regular inhabitants, the enormous losses by plunder and forfeiture, and the break-up of the imperial establishment in the palace, had combined to inflict a blow which would be fatal to the once great Mogul capital. Delhi, nevertheless, had outlived many terrible storms; and these prognostications might be destined to fail.

One consequence of the steady occupation of Delhi during the winter and spring was the gradual departure of troops to other districts where they were more needed. Among these was one of the native regiments. The 'gallant little Goorkhas,' as the British troops were accustomed to designate the soldiers of the Sirmoor and Kumaon battalions, held their high reputation to the very last. The Sirmoor battalion had marched down to Delhi at the very beginning of the disturbances, and during more than twelve months had been on continuous duty in and near that region. The time had now come when a respite could be given to their labours. They took their departure to the healthy hill-station of Deyrah Dhoon. As they marched out of Delhi, headed by their commandant, Colonel Reid, they were escorted over the bridge by the 2d Bengal Europeans, who cheered them lustily, and inspirited them with a melody, the meaning of which they had perchance by this time learned—'*Should auld acquaintance be forgot.*' An officer, well familiar with these 'jolly little Goorkhas,' remarked on this occasion: 'There is not in military history a brighter or purer page than the record of the services and faithful conduct of the Sirmoor Goorkha battalion during the past year. First in the field, always in front, prominent, and incessantly fighting throughout the entire campaign and siege-operations before Delhi, the regiment has covered itself with honour and glory. In our darkest days, there was never a whisper, a suspicion, the shadow of a doubt of the honest loyalty and fidelity of these brave, simple-minded, and devoted soldiers. When others turned traitors, robbers, assassins, these rushed without a moment's hesitation to our side, fought the good fight, bled, and died, faithful to their salt, honourable and true to the last.'

LAHORE.

The Punjaub—at Lahore and all the other cities and stations—was so steadily and watchfully governed, that no disturbances took place except of a very slight character—personally distressing, it is true, but not nationally or politically of any moment. One such was the following: On a certain day a number of disbanded sepoys, who had long before taken refuge in Cashmere, recrossed the frontiers, and attacked the Christians stationed at a place called Madhopore; they murdered a few, including children, under circumstances of great barbarity. No other reason could be assigned for this brutality than a vengeful thirst for European blood. Hastily they crossed again into Cashmere, taking with them a quantity of plunder. A demand was at once made upon the chief of Cashmere, Rumbeer Singh, to capture and give them up; which demand was shortly afterwards attended to, although he had exhibited a little remissness in this matter in one or two former instances. The Rajah of Cashmere was not wholly unsuspected, indeed, of unfavourable views towards the British; and, with a less firm man than John Lawrence at his elbow, he might possibly have made his mountain territory a retreat for rebels.

Sinde, the land of the Indus, remained firmly in the hands of Mr Frere and General Jacob, the one as civil commissioner and the other as military commandant. At one period during the month, however, Frere was called upon to settle a question of religious zealotry, which might have kindled into a flame if not promptly dealt with. A Mohammedan of respectable character came to him, while at Hydrabad, and complained of an inscription on the inner wall of an open-fronted shop belonging to the Christian Mission. The inscription comprised one or two quotations from the Koran, and an argument to disprove the divine authority of the Prophet of Islam, from the evidence of the Koran itself. It was prepared and written, in the Sindhi and Arabic languages, by the Rev. Mr Matchett; and the Rev. Mr Gell caused it to be conspicuously exhibited in the open shop where Bibles were sold or distributed. The complainant was one Gholam Ali, a Mohammedan lately returned from a pilgrimage to Mecca. He stated to Mr Frere that the inscription, visible to all the passers-by in the main bazaar of the city, was irritating and offensive to the Mohammedans. Mr Frere read the inscription; and in afterwards explaining to Lord Elphinstone the reasons which determined his decision on the subject, he said: 'I am willing to be judged by any one who has any acquaintance with the ordinary feelings of a bigoted Mohammedan population as to the probable effects of such a placard on them. I feel confident that any such unprejudiced person would agree with me, that there was much danger of its causing an outbreak of fanatical violence; and holding that opinion, I cannot think that I should have been justified in allowing it to remain. It is quite possible it might never have caused any breach of the peace; but I did not think the present a time to try unnecessary experiments as to how much a fanatical native population will or will not bear in the way of provocation.' Mr Frere wrote to the Rev. Mr Gell, the mission-superintendent, requesting him to remove the inscription; on the ground that, however well meant, it might produce more harm than good. This proceeding led to a violent outcry on the part of the missionaries and their supporters, and to an erroneous narrative forwarded to the government of Bombay—accusing Mr Frere of encouraging Mohammedanism and insulting Christianity. It was one of those numerous occasions, presented during the course of the Revolt and its suppression, in which the governing authorities had much difficulty in steering clearly through the opposite dangers of two religious extremes.

Sir Hugh Rose's operations in Central India during the month of June were treated so fully in the last chapter, that little need be added here on the subject. The recapture of Gwalior was the great event; all the operations in Rajpootana, Bundelcund, Goojerat, and Holkar's territory, were subordinate to it. When the month closed, General Roberts, with the 'Rajpootana Field-force,' was on the march from Nuseerabad to Jeypoor, to check the progress of the Gwalior fugitives in that direction. Brigadier Showers was at or near Futtehpore Sikri, guarding the Agra route. Major Ramsey was advancing from Rohilcund with the Kumaon battalion. The English residents at Jeypoor and Bhurtpore were actively engaged in supporting, so far as was practicable, the loyal tendencies of the rajahs of those two states, so as to enable them to resist the rebels if the latter were to enter either of those cities. The doubt was, not so much of the rajahs, as of the soldiery in their pay, whose fidelity could not wholly be relied on. The main body of Gwalior fugitives were at that time somewhere near Hindoun, a town about equidistant from Gwalior, Agra, and Jeypoor; whether they were about to advance to Ummerpore on the Jeypoor road, to Mhow on the Ulwar road, or to any other point, was not well known. Indeed, the rebels themselves seemed to be divided in opinion as to their future movements; they were looking around, to find some rajah, nawab, or nazim who would join them in rebellion; but those chieftains were becoming more and more cautious how they committed themselves in this way. The spectacle of rajahs blown away from guns, and nawabs hung from gallows, was by no means encouraging.

General Whitlock's field-force, at the end of June, was distributed in various parts of Bundelcund, keeping in subjection the petty chieftains here and there in arms; for there was no longer anything like a formidable army of rebels opposed to him. Brigadier Carpenter, with three or four hundred men, and two guns, was at Kirkee. Major Dallas, with the 1st Madras N.I., was assisting the civil authorities in re-establishing the revenue and judicial departments. Colonel Reede, with two hundred men and two guns, was sent to look after the safety of Humeerpoor and its neighbourhood. Brigadier Macduff, with a portion of H.M. 43d foot, went to Calpee. Brigadier Munsey, with a small column of infantry, cavalry, and artillery, was sent to Nowgong, to protect a convoy of stores on their way from Saugor. The remainder of the force encamped for a while at Banda as head-quarters, having with them Narain Rao and Madhoo Rao as prisoners, a large number of guns, and a considerable amount of treasure and jewels captured from the rebels. Whitlock's long-continued exertions, although not attended by any great battles, had gradually restored something like tranquillity to this distracted region. Bundelcund and the Saugor territory, from the Jumna to the Nerbudda, had for nearly twelve months been in a miserable condition. The various bands of mutineers passing from Dinapoor and elsewhere wrought great mischief; powerful villages preyed upon their weaker neighbours; and the self-installed nawabs and rajahs extorted every farthing they could get from the peasantry and towns-people. Many villages were completely deserted; many more had been burned to the ground, and the people plundered of all the grain and other property which they possessed. The lesson which the peaceful natives had received from the rebels was a severe one, calculated to teach them the advantages of regular government under British influence.

Among the many 'field-forces' which about this time were broken up, to relieve the troops from some of their exhausting labours in fiercely hot weather, was a small one called the 'Satpoora Field-force.' Satpoora is a town in Holkar's Mahratta dominions, about seventy-five miles southeast of Indore, and very near the boundary of the Nagpoor territory. Satpoora also gives name to a range of mountains which, running east and west, separates the valley of the Taptee from that of the Nerbudda; and it was in this sense that the designation 'Satpoora Field-force' was given to a small body of troops collected for the defence of the region in question. Major Evans, commanding this force, took farewell of his men on the 22d of June. In an order or address, dated from his camp at Jalwana, he thanked Captain Sealey and the artillery, Captain Langston and the Rifles, Captain Baugh and the 9th Bombay N. I., Captain Briggs and the 10th, Lieutenant Latouche and the Poonah horse—being the components of his force. He made special mention of a certain encounter on the 11th of April; 'when the insurgents, posted in positions from which they supposed they could not be driven, were at once attacked at three different points; and despite a most obstinate and deadly resistance, were signally defeated and dispersed.' He proceeded in commendatory terms to state that 'the effect on the enemy has been so dispiriting that they have never again dared to collect in force; the disaffected chiefs themselves wandering about in concealment. The force has therefore been disappointed in not being able again to shew their prowess, which all were so eager to do, and would have done so well, had opportunity offered.'

Gujerat, the Guicowar's territory—situated south of Rajpootana, and west of Holkar's territory—had, it will be remembered, been most happily and effectively disarmed by Sir Richmond Shakespear, political resident at the court of the Guicowar; thereby lessening the probability of any hostile outbreak. Gujerat became subject, however, during this month, to one of those strange mysteries in which orientals so much delight. The lotus, and the chupatties, and the 'something white,' had had their day; and now arose the mystery of *twigs.* It was ascertained that twigs or small branches had been circulated from village to village in the province of Gujerat, as signals or watchwords; but nothing could be learned concerning their meaning. An ancient custom existed in many parts of India, of measuring the footprints with straws or twigs whenever a robbery had been committed, then forwarding them from village to village, until the measurement was found to implicate some one villager; after which the village was made responsible. This and many other ancient customs were referred to; but nothing appeared to throw light on the meaning of the twigs thus transmitted through Gujerat.

To assist in the maintenance of tranquillity in the Deccan, a small field-force, composed of troops selected from the Poonah division of the Bombay army, was made up, and placed under the command of Colonel Gall. Starting from Poonah, the colonel arrived at Aurungabad on the 8th of June, and resumed his march on the following day to Jaulnah, a military station in the northwest corner of the Nizam's dominions. Large bands of Rohilla marauders, expelled from the city of Hyderabad by the Nizam's troops, were known to be in various villages in the Jaulnah district; and it was deemed expedient to hold Colonel Gall's force in readiness to watch and disperse these men, lest their machinations should assume a military form. A new cavalry corps named Beatson's Horse assisted in this object. This corps, organised by and under the active officer of that name, consisted of recruits from various parts of the Deccan, for active service in any regions where their presence might be deemed most useful. At present, their quarters were at Jaulnah, where they were regularly picketed around the encampment at night. Arrangements were also made for strengthening the Jaulnah district with a wing of the 92d Highlanders, and with several guns.

Of the presidency of Bombay it may happily be said that—partly owing to the scarcity of the Poorbeah element in the native army, partly to the sagacious and energetic government of Lord Elphinstone—the curse of rebellion was rendered very little apparent. Sinde, placed temporarily under that presidency, was well looked after by

Mr Frere; Gujerat was safe under Sir Richmond Shakespear; Rajpootana was watched by the vigilant eye of General Roberts; while the northern Mahratta states, so far as they were subject to Bombay influence, were under the care of Sir Robert Hamilton.

Certain occurrences in the South Mahratta country, however, deserve to be noticed both in their political and their military phases.

Nothing is more certain than that many of the insurgent bodies in India rose in arms on account of personal or local matters, bearing little relation to the great military revolt, or to the so-called national rebellion. The derangement of regular government furnished opportunity for those who had real or assumed grievances. An example of this kind was furnished in the South Mahratta country. The natives of one of the least known districts south of Bombay had been in the habit of cutting down trees wherever they pleased, for the purpose of planting the cleared ground with various kinds of grain. The Bombay government at length put a stop to this wholesale destruction of timber. This stoppage was looked upon by the natives as an infringement of their 'vested rights.' A mischief-maker—one of the many usually at hand when the populace are excited—appeared in the person of the Rajah of Jumbote, a place south-west of Belgaum. He believed, or persuaded the people to believe, that Nena Sahib held Poonah with a large force; that the British troops were kept in check almost everywhere; and that it was a favourable time for a rise against the constituted authorities who held sway there. Another cause for disaffection arose out of the Hindoo custom of adoption; and this was felt in the South Mahratta country as in other parts of India. Many circumstances arose during the Revolt, shewing that the natives are familiar with and attached to this custom. When a prince, a chief, or a landowner, had no legitimate heir, it was customary for him to name a successor or heir, generally from among his kinsmen. So long as the East India Company had no territorial rights in a particular province or region, there was no motive for interfering with this custom; but self-interest afterwards stepped in, in a way that may be very easily explained. The Company, we will suppose, made a treaty with a native prince, to the effect that a certain state or a certain revenue should belong to him 'and his heirs for ever.' If he had no legitimate heir, the Company was tempted to seize the golden prize after his death, under the plea that the *adopted* son was not a true representative. A Hindoo custom was interpreted in an English sense, and, being found wanting, was disallowed; thereby enriching the Company. English lawyers found no difficulty in supporting this course of proceeding, because it was consistent with English law. It was not, however, until the governor-generalship of the Marquis of Dalhousie, that this kind of confiscation was extensively acted on; and hence the interval between 1848 and 1858 was marked by much more irritation among native princely families, than had been before exhibited in connection with this particular subject. Be it right or wrong, thus to interpret a Hindoo usage by an English test, the history of the Revolt plainly shewed that many of the bitterest enemies of the government were persons whose domains or revenues had been disturbed by a refusal of the Company to acknowledge the principle of adoption in heirship. The miscreant Nena Sahib, the spirited but unscrupulous Ranee of Jhansi, many of the princes of the house of Delhi, and others whose names and deeds have often been recorded in these pages, had—for some years preceding the outbreak—brooded over their real or fancied wrongs in some such matters as these. Is it matter for surprise that they welcomed a day of revenge—a day that might possibly restore to them that of which they deemed themselves unjustly deprived?

The Rajah of Nargoond was one of those to whom, in a minor degree, this principle applied. He was a South Mahratta prince, holding a small territory eastward of Dharwar—separated from Bombay by the once disturbed Kolapore district. Being one of the tributaries to the Bombay government, he petitioned for leave to adopt an heir to his raj or rajahship; and the result of this petition was such as to render him a bitter enemy. His enmity made itself apparent about the date to which this chapter relates, in intrigues with the malcontents around him. A ruthless murder brought matters to an issue. Mr Manson, political agent for the South Mahratta country, having cause to suspect the rajah, set out from Belgaum to seek a personal interview with him, in the hope of dissuading him from rebel movements. They had been on terms of intimacy, which seemed to justify this hope. On the evening of the 29th of May, Mr Manson reached Ramdroog—the chieftain of which advised him to be on his guard, as the Rajah of Nargoond could not be relied on. The unhappy gentleman, believing otherwise, pushed on towards Nargoond. That same night his palanquin was surrounded by a body of the rajah's troops at Soorbund, fifteen miles from Nargoond, and the political agent was foully murdered, together with most of his escort.

The Bombay government at once issued orders to attack the insurgents, and deal severely with the disaffected chieftains. It had been already ascertained that in the Dharwar collectorate, besides the Rajah of Nargoond, there were Bheem Rao of Moondurg, and the Desaee of Hembegee, to be confronted. The South Mahratta country, being near the boundary-line between the Bombay and Madras presidencies, had facilities for receiving small bodies of troops from two directions, to quell any disturbances that might arise. A Madras column, setting out from Bellary under Major Hughes, proceeded northward, and invested the stronghold of Bheem Rao at Kopal or Copal. A message was sent to this chief, giving him three hours to remove the women and children from the place. He returned no answer; whereupon a cannonade was opened. A breach was made practicable; a storming-party entered; the rebels gave way at every point; and very speedily the town and fort were in Major Hughes's possession. Bheem Rao himself, as well as Kenchengowda, the Desaee of Hembegee, were among the slain on this occasion. While Hughes was thus occupied at Kopal, a small column of Bombay troops was engaged in another part of the South Mahratta country. Three or four hundred men, with two guns, started from Belgaum under Captain Paget, and joined a party of Mahratta horse under Colonel Malcolm at Noolgoond. They advanced on the 1st of June to Nargoond, the stronghold of the rebel

Kolapore.

rajah. This stronghold consisted of a fortress on the summit of a rock eight hundred feet high, with the town at its base. A reconnaissance being made, it was found that nearly two thousand rebels were encamped about a mile out of the town; and the rajah could be seen, on an elephant, brandishing his sword. Malcolm sent on the Mahratta horse to commence the attack; with the two guns, two companies of the 74th Highlanders, and one of the 28th Bombay infantry, to support. Of fighting there was scarcely any; the rebels very soon fled from the plain and the town, and left them in the hands of Malcolm. The rock-fortress, however, still remained unconquered. Early in the morning of the 2d, a storming-party was sent to ascend the steep and rugged pathway which led up to the gate of the fortress, prepared to blow it open with powder. Only one rebel was visible; and after a couple of rifles had been fired at him, the gate was forced open and an entrance obtained. Four men, the only occupants of the fortress, threw themselves over a precipitous wall in a panic terror, and were dashed to pieces—either not understanding or not believing the promise of quarter offered to them.

Thus fell the fortress of Nargoond, which had been regarded as a formidable stronghold ever since the days of Tippoo Saib. The rajah fled early in the fight, with seven of his principal followers. Mr Souter, police-superintendent at Belgaum, knowing the rajah's complicity in the murder of Mr Manson,* set out in pursuit of him. At sunset on the 2d, the rajah and his followers

* The governor of Bombay, in a public notification, used many expressions of respect towards the memory of the political agent. Adverting to the advice given to Mr Manson not to trust himself to the mercies of the Rajah of Nargoond, Lord Elphinstone said: 'But with that noble devotion to duty, of which the recent history of India has presented so many instances, Mr Manson determined to make a final effort to save the chief, by his personal influence, from the ruin impending over him.' He added that the facts shewed 'that a gallant and accomplished gentleman, who had proved himself a most valuable servant of the state, has been basely murdered.' And he concluded by announcing that 'the body of Mr Manson has been recovered, and has been buried at Kulladgee. The Right Hon. the Governor in Council will regard it as a sacred duty to make a provision for the families of the brave men who lost their lives in defending one whose untimely fate is now so deeply deplored.'

were discovered skulking in a belt of jungle on the banks of the Malpurba, near Ramdroog; all but one were captured, just as they were about to start for Punderpore. They were sent to Belgaum, to be tried by a special commission. As to the rajah, the last hour of this wretched man was marked by very unseemly circumstances. On the 11th of June he was brought to trial, before Captain Schneider, political agent at Belgaum. He was found guilty of the crimes imputed to him, and was sentenced to be hanged on the next day. Early in the morning of the 12th, two companies of H.M. 56th, and two of the 20th Bombay native infantry, marched into Belgaum from Dharwar to afford a guard during the execution. When the last hour was approaching, the rajah begged hard to be blown from a gun, as a less degrading death than hanging; but the authorities on the spot were not empowered to accede to this application. The gallows was erected, and the hanging effected; but the rope broke, and the wretched man fell to the ground, where an undignified struggle took place between him and his executioners. The extreme sentence of the law was at length carried out, but not without evidences of mismanagement that added to the painfulness of the whole scene.

In connection with the affairs of the Bombay presidency generally, a few observations may be made on the state of the native army. One of the questions that pressed upon the authorities during many months bore relation to the treatment of the disarmed sepoy regiments—regiments which, though disarmed for suspicious conduct, had not so far committed themselves as to receive any more severe punishment. In the Punjaub Sir John Lawrence was troubled with the safe keeping of many thousands of these men; he dared not re-arm them, for their fidelity was more than doubtful; and he would not disband and dismiss them, lest they should swell the ranks of the rebels. Lord Elphinstone, governor of Bombay, was affected by this difficulty only in a small degree, because the mutineers in the Bombay army were few in number. A proceeding took place, however, in the month now under notice, which will illustrate one of the modes adopted of dealing with these dangerous incumbrances. It will be remembered* that in the early part of August 1857 many parts of the South Mahratta country were thrown into agitation by the appearance of mutiny among certain of the Bombay native troops. Kolapore, Poonah, Satara, Belgaum, Dharwar, Rutnagherry, and Sawunt Waree were the chief places affected; a plot was discovered, in which some of the troops were leagued with certain Mohammedan fanatics—discovered in time to prevent the massacre of numerous Europeans. The 21st and 27th regiments were two of those implicated; or rather some of the companies in those regiments; while other companies, not actually detected in the conspiracy, were simply disarmed. In this disarmed state the men remained more than ten months, watched, but not treated otherwise as culprits. At length a settlement of their treatment was effected. Lord Elphinstone and his council decided as follows: That the native commissioned officers, present when the disarming took place, should be dismissed from the army, unless they could bring forward special proofs of fidelity—that of the native non-commissioned officers, the elder should be expelled, and the younger reduced to the ranks—that the sepoys or privates should not be expelled unless special grounds were assignable in their disfavour—that the 21st and 27th regiments should be formally erased from the Bombay army list, to mark with some stigma the conduct of those regiments—that two new regiments, to be called the 30th and 31st infantry, should be formed, with a rank lower in dignity than that of the other native infantry regiments of the Bombay army—that all the privates of the (late) 21st and 27th, with excepted instances, and such native officers as could clear themselves from ill charges, should form the bulk of the two new regiments—finally, that the vacancies in the list of officers (subadars, jemadars, havildars, naiks) should be filled by chosen sepoys who had worthily distinguished themselves in the campaigns of Rajpootana and Central India. Lord Elphinstone, in his order in council relating to this matter, dwelt upon the disgrace which had been brought upon the Bombay army by the misdeeds of some of the men of the late 21st and 27th regiments; adverted to the terrible deaths which most of them had met with in the Kolapore region; exhorted the rest to beware how they listened to the solicitations and machinations of traitors; and added: 'The Governor in Council trusts that the 30th and 31st regiments will, by their future conduct, shew their determination to render themselves worthy of the leniency with which they have been treated, and to wipe out the stain which the crimes of the 21st and 27th have left upon the character of the Bombay army; so that the recollection of their past misdeeds may be as effectually effaced from the minds of men, as their former numbers will be erased from the roll of the army.'

Another instance, somewhat analogous to this, was presented in the Punjaub. During the early days of the Revolt, the 36th and 61st Bengal regiments at Jullundur, and the 3d at Phillour, were among those which mutinied. Some of the sepoys in each, however, remained free from the taint; they stood faithful under great temptation. At a later date even these men were disarmed, from motives of policy; and they had none but nominal duties intrusted to them. At length Sir John Lawrence, finding that these men had passed through the ordeal honourably, proposed that they should be re-armed, and noticed in a way consistent with their merits. This was agreed to. About three hundred and fifty officers and men, the faithful exceptions of three unfaithful regiments, were formed into a special corps to be called the Wufadar Pultun or 'faithful regiment.' This new

* See Chap. xvii., pp. 289, 290.

corps was to be in four companies, organised on the same footing as the Punjaub irregular infantry; and was to be stationed at some place where the men would not have their feelings wounded and irritated by the taunts of the Punjaubee soldiery—between whom and the Hindustani sepoys the relations were anything but amicable. Any of the selected number who preferred it, might receive an honourable discharge from the army instead of entering any new corps. The experiment was regarded as an important one; seeing that it might afford a clue to the best mode of dealing with the numerous disarmed sepoys in the Punjaub.

The Bombay presidency was not so closely engaged in political and military matters as to neglect the machinery of peaceful industry, the stay and support of a nation. Another of those paths to commerce and civilisation, railways, was opened for traffic in India in June. It was a portion of a great trunk-line which, when completed, would connect Bombay with Madras. The length opened was from Khandalla to Poonah; and this, with another portion opened in 1853, completed a route from Bombay to Poonah, excepting a long tunnel under the range of hills called the Bhore Ghauts, which was not expected to be completed until 1860. On the day of ceremonial opening, a journey was made from Bombay to Poonah and back in eighteen hours, including four hours of portage or porterage at the Bhore Ghauts. There were intermediate stations at Kirkee and Tulligaum. The Company organised a scheme including conveyance across the ghauts, by palkees and gharries, as part of their passenger contract. An instructive index to the advancing state of society in India was afforded by the fact, that one of the great Parsee merchants of Bombay, Cursetjee Jamsetjee, was the leading personage in the hospitalities connected with this railway-opening ceremonial.

A few remarks on the sister presidency, and this chapter may close.

If Madras, now as in former months, was wholly spared from fighting and treason, it at least furnished an instance of the difficulty attending any collision on religious matters with the natives. The Wesleyan missionaries had a chapel and school in the district of Madras city called Royapettah. Many native children attended the school, for the sake of the secular instruction there given, without becoming formal converts. One of them, a youth of fifteen or sixteen, mentioned to the Rev. Mr Jenkins, the Wesleyan minister, his wish to become a Christian; it was found on inquiry, however, that the parents were averse to this; and Mr Jenkins left it to the youth whether he would join the mission or return to his parents. He chose the former course. Hereupon a disturbance commenced among the friends of the family; this was put down by the police; but as the youth remained at the mission-house, the religious prejudices of the natives became excited, and the disturbance swelled into a riot. A mob collected in front of the mission-house, entered the compound, threw stones and bricks at the house, forced open the door, and broke all the furniture. Mr Jenkins and another missionary named Stephenson, retreated from room to room, until they got into the bath-room, and then managed to climb over a wall into another compound, where they found protection. It was a mere local and temporary riot, followed by the capture of some of the offenders and the escape of others; but it was just such a spark as, in other regions of India, might have set a whole province into a flame. The missionaries, estimating the youth's age at seventeen or eighteen years, claimed for him a right of determining whether he would return to his parents (who belonged to the Moodelly caste), or enter the mission; whereas some of the zealots on the other side, declaring that his age was only twelve or thirteen, advocated the rightful exercise of parental authority. The magistrates, without entering into this question of disputed figures, recommended to the missionaries the exercise of great caution, in any matters likely to arouse the religious animosity of the natives; and there can be little doubt that, in the prevailing state of native feeling, such caution was eminently necessary.

Note.

Queen's Regiments in India in June.—Sufficient has been said in former chapters to convey some notion of the European element in the Indian army in past years; the necessity for increasing the strength of that element; the relation between the Queen's troops and the Company's troops; the difficulty of sparing additional troops from England; the mode in which that difficulty was overcome; and the controversy concerning the best route for troop-ships. It seems desirable to add here a few particulars concerning the actual number of European troops in India at or about the time to which this chapter relates, and the localities in which they were stationed.

The following list, correct as to the regiments, is liable to modification in respect of localities. Many of the regiments were at the time in detachments, serving in different places; in such cases, the station of the main body only is named. Other regiments were at the time on the march; these are referred to the station towards which they were marching.

QUEEN'S TROOPS IN THE BENGAL ARMY.

It may here be remarked, that the distinctions between 'fusiliers,' 'foot,' 'light infantry,' 'Highlanders,' and 'rifles,' are more nominal than real; these are all infantry regiments of the line, with a special number attached to each—except the particular corps called the 'Rifle Brigade.'

Cavalry.

2d Dra. Gds.,	Lucknow.	7th Lt. Dra.,	Lucknow.
6th " "	Meerut.	9th Lancers,	Umballa.
7th " "	Sealkote.	Mil. Trn., 2d bat.,	Benares.

Horse-artillery.

E Troop, .	Allahabad.	F Troop, .	Lucknow.

Foot-artillery.

2d Bat. 8th Com.	Benares.	11th Bat. 6th Com.	Lucknow.
3d " 5th "	Calcutta.	12th " 5th "	Lucknow.
5th " 4th "	Lucknow.	13th " 5th "	Bunnee.
6th " 1st "	Moultan.	13th " 6th "	Lucknow.
7th " 6th "	Rawul Pindee.	14th " 3d "	Agra.
8th " 7d "	Lucknow.	14th " 4th "	Allahabad.
9th " 3d "	Dumdum.	14th " 7th "	Futteghur.

Engineers.

4th Company,	Lucknow,	23d Company,	Lucknow.

Infantry.

5th Fusiliers,	Calpee.	60th Rif., 1st bat.	Shahjehanpoor.
7th " .	Meean Meer.	" " 2d "	Dinapoor.
8th foot, .	Agra.	61st . .	Delhi.
10th " .	Dinapoor.	70th . .	Peshawur.
13th Lt. Infantry,	Goruckpore.	73d . . .	Sheergotty.
19th foot, .	Barrackpore.	75th . .	Meerut.
20th " . .	Lucknow.	77th . . .	Calcutta.
23d Fusiliers,	Lucknow.	79th . .	Futteghur.
24th foot, .	Ferozpore.	80th . . .	Cawnpore.
27th " .	Umballa.	81st . .	Nowsherah.
29th " . .	Rangoon.	82d . . .	Shahjehanpoor.
32d Lt. Infantry,	Allahabad.	84th . .	Buxar.
34th foot, .	Azimghur.	87th . .	Jullundur.
35th " .	Dinapoor.	88th . .	Cawnpore.
37th " . .	Ghazeepore.	90th . . .	Lucknow.
38th " .	Lucknow.	93d . .	Bareilly.
42d Highlanders,	Bareilly.	97th . . .	Lucknow.
52d foot, .	Sealkote.	98th . .	Campbellpoor.
53d " . .	Lucknow.	Rif. Brig., 2d bat.	Lucknow.
54th " .	Allahabad.	" " 3d "	Lucknow.

QUEEN'S TROOPS IN THE BOMBAY ARMY.

The preceding list, relating to the Bengal army, gives the names and localities of regiments for the later weeks of June; the following, having reference to the Bombay army, applies to the earlier part of the same month; but the difference in this respect cannot be considerable.

Cavalry.

3d Drag. Guards,	Kirkee.	14th Light Drag.,	Calpee.
8th Hussars, .	Nuseerabad.	17th Lancers, .	Kirkee.

Horse-artillery.

D Troop, ... Poonah.

Foot-artillery.

1st Bat. 8th Com.,	Baroda.	11th Bat. 2d Com.,	Rajpootana.
4th " 3d "	Rajpootana.	11th " 7th "	Bombay.
6th " 1st "	Sinde.	14th " 5th "	Cen. India.
		14th " 8th "	Dharwar.

Engineers.

11th Company, .	Rajpootana.	21st Company, .	Cen. India.

Infantry.

4th foot, . .	Gujerat.	72d Highlanders,	Neemuch.
18th Royal Irish,	Poonah.	78th " .	Alum Bagh.
33d foot, . .	Poonah.	83d foot, .	Rajpootana.
51st " .	Kurachee.	86th " . .	Calpee.
56th " . .	Belgaum.	89th " .	Ahmedabad.
57th " .	Aden.	92d Highlanders,	Bombay.
64th " . .	Allygurh.	95th foot, . .	Rajpootana.
71st Highlanders,	Calpee.		

QUEEN'S TROOPS IN THE MADRAS ARMY.

The following list applies to the state of affairs about the third week in June:

Cavalry.

1st Drag. Guards,	Bangalore.	12th Lancers, .	Kurnool.

Horse-artillery.

H Troop, ... Mount.

Foot-artillery.

3d Bat. 2d Com.,	Bangalore.	14th Bat. 6th Com.,	Bundelcund.

Infantry.

1st foot, 1st Battalion, ...	Secunderabad.
43d "	Bundelcund.
44th "	Madras.
60th Rifles, 3d Battalion, ...	Bangalore.
66th foot, ...	Cannanore.
68th "	Rangoon.
69th "	Vizagapatam.
74th "	Bellary.

Summing up these entries, it will be seen that out of the 99 regiments of the line in the British army (the 100th, a new Canadian regiment, had not at that time completed its organisation), no less than 59 were in India in June 1858; with a proportion of the other branches of the military service. Nothing can more strikingly illustrate the importance attached to the state of our Indian possessions.

On the 1st of January 1857, there were about 26,000 royal troops and 12,000 Company's European troops in India. During the ensuing fifteen months, to April 1858, there were sent over 42,000 royal troops and 5000 Company's Europeans. These would have given a total of 85,000 British troops in India; but it was estimated that war, sickness, and heat had lessened this number to 50,000 available effective men. At that time the arrangements of the English authorities were such as to insure the speedy increase of this European element to not less than 70,000 men; and during the summer, still further advances were made in the same direction.

Almorah, Hill-station in Kumaon.

CHAPTER XXXII.

GRADUAL PACIFICATION IN THE AUTUMN.

IF the events of the three months—July, August, and September, 1858—be estimated without due consideration, it might appear that the progress made in India was hardly such as could fairly be called 'pacification.' When it is found how frequently the Jugdispore rebels are mentioned in connection with the affairs of Behar; how numerous were the thalookdars of Oude still in arms; how large an insurgent force the Begum held under her command; how fruitless were all the attempts to capture the miscreant Nena Sahib; how severely the friendly thalookdars and zemindars of Oude were treated by those in the rebel ranks, as a means of deterring others from joining the English; how active was Tanteea Topee in escaping from Roberts and Napier, Smith and Michel, with his treasure plundered from the Maharajah Scindia; how many petty chieftains in the Bundelcund and Mahratta territories were endeavouring to raise themselves in power, during a period of disorder, by violence and plunder—there may be some justification for regarding the state of India as far from peaceful during those three months. But notwithstanding these appearances, the pacification of the empire was unquestionably in progress. The Bengal sepoys, the real mutineers, were becoming lessened in number every week, by the sword, the bullet, the gallows, and privation. The insurgent bands, though many and apparently strong, consisted more and more exclusively of rabble ruffians, whose chief motive for action was plunder, and who seldom ventured to stand a contest even with one-twentieth part their number of English troops. The regiments and drafts sent out from England, both to the Queen's and the Company's armies, were regularly continued, so as to render it possible to supply a few British troops to all the points attacked or troubled. There was a steady increase in the number of Jâts, Goorkhas, Bheels, Scindians, Beloochees, &c., enlisted in British service, having little or no sympathy with the high-caste Hindustani Oudians who had been the authors of so much mischief. There was a re-establishment of civil government in all the provinces, and (excepting Oude) in nearly all the districts of each province; attended by a renewal of the revenue arrangements, and by the maintenance of police bodies who aided in putting down rebels and marauders. There was an almost total absence of anything like nationality in the motions of the insurgents, or unity of purpose in their proceedings; the decrepit Emperor of Delhi, and the half-witted King of Oude, both of them prisoners, had almost gone out of the thoughts of the natives—who, so far as they rebelled at all, looked out for new leaders, new paymasters, new plunder. In short, the British government had gained the upper hand in every province throughout India; and preparations were everywhere made to maintain this hold so firmly, that the discomfiture of the rebels became a matter almost of moral certainty. Much remained to be done, and much time would be needed for doing it; but the 'beginning of the end' was come, and men could speak without impropriety of the gradual pacification of India.

The events of these three months will not require any lengthened treatment; of new mutinies there was only one; and the military and other operations will admit of rapid recital.

Calcutta saw nothing of Viscount Canning during the spring, summer, and autumn. His lordship, as governor-general, appreciated the importance of being near Sir Colin Campbell, to consult with him daily on various matters affecting the military operations in the disturbed districts. Both were at Allahabad throughout the period to which this chapter relates. The supreme council, however, remained at the presidential capital, giving effect to numerous legislative measures, and carrying on the regular government of the presidency. Calcutta was now almost entirely free from those panics which so frequently disturbed it during the early months of the mutiny; rapine and bloodshed did not approach the city, and the English residents gradually sobered down. Although the violent and often absurd opposition to the governor-general had not quite ceased, it had greatly lessened; the dignified firmness of Lord Canning made a gradual conquest. Some of the newspapers, here as at Bombay, invented proclamations and narratives, crimes and accusations, with a disregard of truth which would hardly have been shewn by any journals in the mother-country; and those effusions which were not actually invented, too often received a colour ill calculated to convey a correct idea of their nature. Many of the journalists never forgot or forgave the restrictions which the governor-general deemed it prudent to place on the press in the summer of 1857; the amount of anonymous slander heaped on him was immense. One circumstance which enabled his lordship to live down the calumnies, was the discovery, made by the journalists in the following summer, that Lord Derby's government was not more disposed than that of Lord Palmerston to expel Viscount Canning from office—a matter which will have to be noticed more fully in another chapter. The more moderate journalists of the Anglo-Indian press, it must in fairness be stated, did their part towards bringing about a more healthy state of feeling.

That the authorities at Calcutta were not insensible to the value of newspapers and journals, in a region so far away from England, was shewn by an arrangement made in the month of August—which afforded at the same time a quiet but significant proof of an improved attention towards the well-being of soldiers. An order was issued that a supply of newspapers and periodicals should be forwarded to the different military hospitals in Calcutta at the public expense. Those for the officers' hospital* comprised some magazines of a higher class than were included in the list for the men's hospitals; but such were to be sent afterwards to the men's hospitals, when the officers had perused them.

In connection with military matters, in and near the presidential city, it may be mentioned that the neighbourhood of Calcutta was the scene of a settlement or colonisation very novel, and as unsatisfactory as it was novel. It has been the custom to send over a small number of soldiers' wives with every British regiment sent to our colonies or foreign territories. During the course of twelve months so many regiments arrived at Calcutta, that these soldiers' wives accumulated to eighteen hundred in number. They were consigned to the station at Dumdum, a few miles north of Calcutta; and were attended by three or four surgeons and one Protestant chaplain. The accommodation provided for them was sufficient for the women themselves, but not for the children, who added greatly to their number. Many of these women, being of that ignorant and ill-regulated class from which soldiers too frequently choose their wives, brought with them dirty habits and drinking tendencies; and these, when the fierce heat of an Indian summer came, engendered dysentery and diarrhœa, from which diseases a large number of women and children died. Other irregularities of conduct appeared, among a mass of women so strangely separated from all home-ties; and arrangements were gradually made for breaking up this singular colony.

The details given in former chapters, especially in the 'notes,' will have shewn how large was the number of regiments conveyed from the United Kingdom and the colonies to India; and when it is remembered that far more of these landed at Calcutta than at Madras, Bombay, or Kurachee, it will easily be understood how military an aspect they gave to the first-named city. Still, numerous as they were, they were never equal to the demand. Without making any long stay at Calcutta, they

* To the officers' hospital—*Calcutta Englishman*, *Bengal Hurkaru*, *Phœnix*, *Illustrated London News*, *Punch*, *Blackwood's Magazine*, *Fraser's Magazine*, *New Monthly Magazine*, *Monthly Army List*, four copies *Chambers's Journal*, four copies *Family Herald*. To the men's hospitals—two copies *Calcutta Englishman*, two copies *Bengal Hurkaru*, two copies *Phœnix*, two copies *Illustrated London News*, two copies *Punch*, two copies *Household Words*, twelve copies *Chambers's Journal*, twelve copies *Family Herald*.

marched to the scenes of action in the northwest. In the scarcity of regular troops, the Bengal government derived much valuable services from naval and marine brigades—men occupying a middle position between soldiers and sailors. Captain Sir William Peel's naval brigade has been often mentioned, in connection with gallant achievements in Oude; and Captain Sotheby's naval brigade also won a good name, in the provinces eastward of Oude. But besides these, there were about a dozen different bodies in Bengal, each consisting of a commandant, two under-officers, a hundred men, and two light field-guns. Being well drilled, and accustomed to active movements, these parties were held in readiness to march off at short notice to any districts where a few resolute disciplined men could overawe turbulent towns-people; and thus they held the eastern districts in quietness without drawing on the regular military strength of the presidency. The *Shannon* naval brigade acquired great fame; the heroic Peel had made himself a universal favourite, and the brigade became a noted body, not only for their own services, but for their connection with their late gallant commander. When the brigade returned down the Ganges, the residents of Calcutta gave them a public reception and a grand dinner. Sir James Outram was present at the dinner, and, in a graceful and appropriate way, told of his own experience of the services of the brigade at Lucknow in the memorable days of the previous winter. 'Almost the first white faces I saw, when the lamented Havelock and I rushed out of our prison to greet Sir Colin at the head of our deliverers, were the hearty, jolly, smiling faces of some of you *Shannon* men, who were pounding away with two big guns at the palace; and I then, for the first time in my life, had the opportunity of seeing and admiring the coolness of British sailors under fire. There you were, working in the open plains, without cover, or screen, or rampart of any kind, your guns within musket-range of the enemy, as coolly as if you were practising at the Woolwich target. And that it was a hot fire you were exposed to, was proved by three of the small staff that accompanied us (Napier, young Havelock, and Sitwell) being knocked over by musket-balls in passing to the rear of those guns, consequently further from the enemy than yourselves.' Such a speech from such a man was about the most acceptable compliment that the brigade could receive, and was well calculated to produce a healthy emulation in other quarters.

The authorities at all the stations were on the watch for any symptoms which, though trivial in themselves, might indicate the state of feeling among the soldiery or the natives generally. Thus, on the 10th of July, at Barrackpore, a chuprassee happening to go down to a tank near the lines, saw a bayonet half in and half out of the water. A search was thereupon ordered; when about a hundred weapons—muskets, sabres, and bayonets—with balls and other ammunition—were discovered at the bottom of the tank. These warlike materials were rendered almost valueless by the action of the water; but their presence in the tank was not the less a mystery needing to be investigated. The authorities, in this as in many similar cases, thought it prudent not to divulge the results of their investigation.

The great jails of India were a source of much trouble and anxiety during the mutiny. All the large towns contained such places of incarceration, which were usually full of very desperate characters; and these men were rejoiced at any opportunity of revenging themselves on the authorities. Such opportunities were often afforded; for, as we have many times had occasion to narrate, the mutineers frequently broke open the jails as a means of strengthening their power by the aid of hundreds or thousands of budmashes ready for any atrocities. So late as the 31st of July, at Mymensing, in the eastern part of Bengal, the prisoners in the jail, six hundred in number, having overpowered the guard, escaped, seized many tulwars and muskets, and marched off towards Jumalpore. The Europeans at this place made hurried preparations for defence, and sent out such town-guards and police as they could muster, to attack the escaped prisoners outside the station. About half of the number were killed or recaptured, and the rest escaped to work mischief elsewhere. It is believed, however, that in this particular case, the prisoners had no immediate connection with rebels or mutinous sepoys; certain prison arrangements concerning food excited their anger, and under the influence of this anger they broke forth.

So far as concerns actual mutiny, the whole province of Bengal was nearly exempt from that infliction during the period now under consideration; regular government was maintained, and very few rebels troubled the course of peaceful industry.

Behar, however, was not so fortunate. Situated between Bengal and Oude, it was nearer to the scenes of anarchy, and shared in them more fully. Sir Edward Lugard, as we have seen, was employed there during the spring months; but having brought the Jugdispore rebels, as he believed, to the condition of mere bandits and marauders, he did not think it well to keep his force in active service during the rainy season, when they would probably suffer more from inclement weather than from the enemy. He resigned command, on account of his shattered health, and his Azimghur field-force was broken up. The 10th foot, and the Madras artillery, went to Dinapoor; the 84th foot and the military train, under Brigadier Douglas, departed for Benares; the royal artillery were summoned to Allahabad; the Sikh cavalry and the Madras rifles went to Sasseram; and the Madras cavalry to Ghazeepore. Captain Rattray, with his Sikhs, was left at Jugdispore, whence he made frequent excursions to dislodge small parties of rebels.

A series of minor occurrences took place in this part of Behar, during July, sufficient to require the notice of a few active officers at the head of small bodies of reliable troops, but tending on the other hand to shew that the military power of the rebels was nearly broken down—to be followed by the predatory excursions of ruffian bands whose chief or only motive was plunder. On the 8th a body of rebels entered Arrah, fired some shot, and burnt Mr Victor's bungalow; the troops at that station being too few to effectually dislodge them, a reinforcement was sent from Patna, which drove them away. Brigadier Douglas was placed in command of the whole of this disturbed portion of Behar, from Dinapoor to Ghazeepore, including the Arrah and Jugdispore districts; and he so marshalled and organised the troops placed at his disposal as to enable him to bring small bodies to act promptly upon any disturbed spots. He established strong posts at moderate distances in all directions. The rebels in this quarter having few or no guns left, Douglas felt that their virtual extinction, though slow, would be certain. He was constantly on the alert; insomuch that the miscreants could never remain long to work mischief in one place. Meghur Singh, Joodhur Singh, and many other 'Singhs,' headed small bands at this time. On the 17th, Captain Rattray had a smart encounter with some of these people at Dehree, or rather, it was a capture, with scarcely any encounter at all. His telegram to Allahabad described it very pithily: 'Sangram Singh having committed some murders in the neighbourhood of Rotas, and the road being completely closed by him, I sent out a party of eight picked men from my regiment, with orders to kill or bring in Sangram Singh. This party succeeded most signally. They disguised themselves as mutinous sepoys, brought in Sangram Singh last night, and killed his brother (the man who committed the late murders by Sangram Singh's orders), his sons, nephew, and grandsons, amounting in all to nine persons—bringing in their heads. At this capture, all the people of the south [of the district?] are much rejoiced. The hills for the present are clear from rebels. I shall try Sangram Singh to-morrow.' The trunk-road from Calcutta to the upper provinces, about Sasseram, Jehanabad, Karumnassa, and other places, was frequently blocked by small parties of rebels or marauders; and then it became necessary to send out detachments to disperse them. As it was of immense importance to maintain this road open for traffic, military and commercial, the authorities, at Patna, Benares, and elsewhere, were on the alert to hunt down any predatory bands that might make their appearance.

Although Douglas commanded the district in which Jugdispore is situated, he did not hold Jugdispore itself. That place had changed hands more than once, since the day when Koer Singh headed the Dinapoor mutineers; and it was at the beginning of August held by Ummer Singh, with the chief body of the Behar rebels. Brigadier Douglas gradually organised arrangements for another attack on this place. His object was, if possible, so to surround Ummer Singh that he should only have one outlet of escape, towards Benares and Mirzapore, where there were sufficient English troops to bring him to bay. The rebels, however, made so many separate attacks at various places in the Shahabad district, and moved about with such surprising celerity, that Douglas was forced to postpone his main attack for a time, seeing that Jugdispore could not be invested unless he had most of his troops near that spot. All through the month of August we hear of partial engagements between small parties of rebels and much smaller parties of the English—ending, in almost every case, in the flight of the former, but not the less harassing to the latter. At one time we read of an appearance of these ubiquitous insurgents at Rasserah; at another at Arrah; at others at Belowtee, Nowadda, Jugragunje, Masseegunje, Roopsauguty, Doomraon, Burrarpore, Chowpore, Pah, Nurreehurgunje, Kuseea, Nissreegunje, and other towns and villages—mostly south of the Ganges and west of the Sone.

It is unnecessary to trace the operations in this province during September. There was no rebel army, properly so called; but there were small bands in various directions—plundering villages, burning indigo-works, molesting opium-grounds, murdering unprotected persons known or supposed to be friendly to the British, and committing atrocities from motives either of personal vengeance or of plunder. Of patriotism there was nothing; for the peaceful villages suffered as much from these ruffians as the servants of the state. The state of matters was well described by an eye-witness, who said that Shahabad (the district which contains Arrah and Jugdispore) 'is one of the richest districts in Behar, and is pillaged from end to end; it is what an Irish county would be with the Rockites masters of the opportunity.' It was a riot rather than a rebellion; a series of disorders produced by ruffians, rather than a manifestation of patriotism or national independence. To restore tranquillity, required more troops than Brigadier Douglas could command at that time; but everything foretold a gradual suppression of this state of disorder, when October brought him more troops and cooler weather.

We now pass on to the turbulent province of Oude—that region which, from the very beginning of the mutiny, was the most difficult to deal with. It will be remembered, from the details given in the former chapters, that Lucknow was entirely reconquered by the British; that the line of communication between that city and Cawnpore was safely in their hands; that after Sir Colin Campbell, Sir James Outram, and other generals had taken their departure to other provinces, Sir Hope Grant remained in military command of Oude; and that Mr Montgomery, who had been Lawrence's coadjutor in the Punjaub, undertook, as chief-commissioner of Oude, the difficult task of re-establishing civil government in that distracted country.

It may be well here to take some notice of an important state document relating to Oude and its government, its thalookdars and its zemindars.

During the spring and summer,* the two Houses of Parliament were hotly engaged in a contest concerning Viscount Canning and the Earl of Ellenborough, which branched off into a contest between Whigs and Conservatives, marked by great bitterness on both sides. The immediate cause was a proclamation intended to have been issued (but never actually issued) by Viscount Canning in Oude, announcing the forfeiture of all estates belonging to thalookdars and zemindars who had been guilty of complicity with the rebels. The Earl of Ellenborough, during his brief tenure of office as president of the Board of Control, wrote the celebrated 'secret dispatch' (dated April 19th),† in which he condemned the proposed proclamation, and haughtily reproved the governor-general himself. It was a dispatch, of which the following words were disapproved even by the earl's own party: 'We must admit that, under these circumstances, the hostilities which have been carried on in Oude have rather the character of legitimate war than that of rebellion, and that the people of Oude should rather be regarded with indulgent consideration, than made the objects of a penalty exceeding in extent and in severity almost any which has been recorded in history as inflicted upon a subdued nation. Other conquerors, when they have succeeded in overcoming resistance, have excepted a few persons as still deserving of punishment, but have, with a generous policy, extended their clemency to the great body of the people. You have acted upon a different principle. You have reserved a few as deserving of special favour, and you have struck with what they will feel as the severest of punishment the mass of the inhabitants of the country. We cannot but think that the precedents from which you have departed will appear to have been conceived in a spirit of wisdom superior to that which appears in the precedent you have made.'

It was not until the month of October that the English public were made acquainted with Viscount Canning's reply to this dispatch. During the interval of five or six months, speculation was active as to the mode in which he would view it, and the course he would adopt in relation to it. His reply was dated 'Allahabad, June 17th,' and, when at length publicly known, attracted general attention for its dignified tone. Even those who continued to believe that the much-canvassed proclamation would not have been a just one to issue, admitted (in most instances) the cogency of the governor-general's arguments against the Ellenborough dispatch—especially in relation to the unfairness of making public a professedly 'secret' dispatch. The reply was not addressed to the earl, whose name was not mentioned in it throughout; its address was to 'the Secret Committee of the Court of Directors,' in accordance with official rule; but the earl was responsible, and alone responsible, for the dispatch and the severe language it contained. The personal part of Viscount Canning's reply, the calm but indignant allusion to the ungenerous treatment he had received, was comprised in the first six clauses, which we give in a foot-note.* He proceeded to notice the strange way in which the Ellenborough dispatch almost justified the Oudians, as if they were fighting for a righteous cause—quite legitimate in a member of the legislature, proposing a reconsideration of the annexation of Oude; but quite unjustifiable in a minister serving Queen Victoria, who was at that moment, rightly or wrongly, the real Queen of Oude. Viscount Canning declined to discuss the policy which, two years earlier, had dictated the annexation; it was not his performance, nor was he

* See Chap. xxvii., pp. 450-461. † *Ibid*, p. 459.

* '1. The dispatch condemns in the strongest terms the proclamation which, on the 3d of March, I directed the chief-commissioner of Oude to issue from Lucknow.

'2. Although written in the Secret Committee, the dispatch was made public in England three weeks before it reached my hands. It will in a few days be read in every station in Hindostan.

'3. Before the dispatch was published in England, it had been announced to parliament by a minister of the Crown as conveying disapproval in every sense of the policy indicated by the governor-general's proclamation. Whether this description was an accurate one or not I do not inquire. The telegraph has already carried it over the length and breadth of India.

'4. I need scarcely tell your honourable committee that the existence of such a dispatch, even had it never passed out of the records of the Secret Department, would be deeply mortifying to me, however confident I might feel that your honourable committee would, upon reconsideration, relieve me of the censure which it casts upon me. Still less necessary is it for me to point out that the publication of the document, preceded as it has been by an authoritative declaration of its meaning and spirit, is calculated greatly to increase the difficulties in which the government of India is placed, not only by weakening the authority of the governor-general, but by encouraging resistance and delusive hopes in many classes of the population of Oude.

'5. So far as the dispatch and the mode in which it has been dealt with affect myself personally, I will trouble your honourable committee with very few words. No taunts or sarcasms, come from what quarter they may, will turn me from the path which I believe to be that of my public duty. I believe that a change in the head of the government of India at this time, if it took place under the circumstances which indicated a repudiation on the part of the government in England of the policy which has hitherto been pursued towards the rebels of Oude, would seriously retard the pacification of the country. I believe that that policy has been from the beginning merciful without weakness, and indulgent without compromise of the dignity of the government. I believe that wherever the authority of the government has been established, it has become manifest to the people in Oude, as elsewhere, that the indulgence to those who make submission, and who are free from atrocious crime, will be large. I believe that the issue of the proclamation which has been so severely condemned was thoroughly consistent with that policy, and that it is so viewed by those to whom it is addressed. I believe that that policy, if steadily pursued, offers the best and earliest prospect of restoring peace to Oude upon a stable footing.

'6. Firm in these convictions, I will not, in a time of unexampled difficulty, danger, and toil, lay down of my own act the high trust which I have the honour to hold; but I will, with the permission of your honourable committee, state the grounds upon which those convictions rest, and describe the course of policy which I have pursued in dealing with the rebellion in Oude. If, when I have done so, it shall be deemed that that policy has been erroneous, or that, not being erroneous, it has been feebly and ineffectually carried out, or that for any reason the confidence of those who are responsible for the administration of Indian affairs in England should be withheld from me, I make it my respectful but urgent request, through your honourable committee, that I may be relieved of the office of governor-general of India with the least possible delay.'

empowered to undo it when once done. But he felt it incumbent on him to point out the disastrous effects which might follow, if the Oudians were encouraged by such reasonings as those contained in the Ellenborough dispatch. Speaking of the Begum, the Moulvie, the Nazim, and other rebel leaders in Oude, he stated that there was scarcely any unity of plan or sympathy of purpose among them; 'but,' he added, 'I cannot think this want of unity will long continue. If it shall once become manifest that the British government hesitates to declare its right to possess Oude, and that it regards itself as a wrongful intruder into the place of the dynasty which the Begum claims to represent, I believe that this would draw to the side of the Begum many who have hitherto shewn no sympathy with the late ruling family, and that it is just what is wanting to give a national character to her cause. An uncompromising assertion of our authority in Oude is perfectly compatible with a merciful exercise of it; and I respectfully submit that if the government of India is not supported in making this assertion, and in declaring that the recent acts of the people of Oude are acts of rebellion, and that they may in strict right be treated as such, a powerful temptation will be offered to them to maintain their present struggle or to renew it.'

The governor-general's defence of the proclamation itself we need not notice at any length; the proclamation was never issued in its original form—the subject being left generally to the discretion of Mr Montgomery. The tenor of his reply may be thus briefly indicated—That he went to Allahabad to reside, chiefly that he might be able personally to investigate the state of Oude; that he soon decided to make a difference between mutinied sepoys and Oudian rebels; that the latter should not be put to death for appearing in arms against the authorities, unless they had committed actual murder; that the general punishment for Oudian rebellion should be confiscation of estates, a punishment frequently enforced against rebels in past years, both by the British and by the native governments; that it is a punishment which in no way affects the honour of the most sensitive Rajpoot or Brahmin; that it admits of every gradation, according to the severity or lightness of the offence; that it would enable the government to reward friendly thalookdars and zemindars with estates taken from those who had rebelled; that most of the thalookdars had acquired their estates by spoliation of the village communities, at a time when they (the thalookdars) were acting under the native government as 'nazims' (governors) or 'chuckladars' (collectors of government rents); that, as a matter of abstract right, it would be just to give these estates back again to the village communities; but that, as there would be insuperable difficulties to this course, it would be better to take the forfeited estates of rebellious thalookdars as government property, out of which faithful villages and individuals might be rewarded.

Another reply, written by Viscount Canning on the 7th of July, was to the dispatch of the Court of Directors dated the 18th of May. In that dispatch the directors, while expressing full confidence in the governor-general, courteously requested him to furnish an explanation of the circumstances and motives which led him to frame the proclamation. This explanation he most readily gave, in terms equivalent to those above indicated. He expressed, too, his thankfulness for the tone in which the directors had written to him. 'Such an expression of the sentiments of your honourable court would be to me a source of gratification and just pride under any circumstances; but the generous and timely promptitude with which you have been pleased to issue it, and the fact that it contains approval of the past, as well as trust for the future, has greatly enhanced its value. Your honourable court have rightly judged, that in the midst of difficulties no support is so cheering to a public servant, or so strengthening, as that which is derived from a declared approval of the spirit by which his past acts have been guided.'

It may be here remarked that some of the European inhabitants of Calcutta, who had from the first placed themselves in antagonism with Viscount Canning, prepared an address to the Earl of Ellenborough, thanking him for the 'secret' dispatch, denouncing the principles and the policy acted on by the governor-general, lamenting the earl's retirement after so brief a tenure of office, denouncing the Whigs, and expressing a hope that the earl, whether in or out of office, would long live to 'uphold the honour and interests of British India.'

We now proceed to a brief narrative of the course of events in Oude during July, August, and September.

The province, in the first of these three months, was in a remarkable condition. Mr Montgomery, as chief-commissioner, intrusted with large powers, gradually felt his way towards a re-establishment of British influence. Most of the dependants and adherents of the deposed royal family belonged to Lucknow; and it was hence in that city that they required most carefully to be watched. In the provinces, the late king's power and the present British power were regarded with about equal indifference or dislike. A sort of feudalism prevailed, inimical to the recognition of any central authority, except in merely nominal matters. There were rebel forces under different leaders at different spots; but it is doubtful whether any of them were fighting for the deposed king; each leader had an eye to the assumption of power by or for himself. Even the Begum, one of the king's wives, was influenced by motives very far removed from affection to her lord. Great as Montgomery's difficulties were, therefore, they were less than would have been occasioned by a concentration of action, a unity of purpose, among the malcontents. He re-organised civil tribunals and offices in such districts as were within his power, and waited for favourable opportunities to do the like in other districts.

General Sir Hope Grant was Mr Montgomery's coadjutor in these labours, bringing military power to bear where civil power was insufficient. In the early part of the month he remained at Lucknow, keeping together a small but efficient army, and watching the course of events around him. Later in the month, however, he deemed it necessary to take the field, and endeavour to chastise a large body of rebels who were setting up the Begum in authority at Fyzabad. On the 21st he started off in that direction, taking with him a force comprising the 1st Madras Europeans, the 2d battalion of the Rifle Brigade, the 1st Punjaub infantry, the 7th Hussars, Hodson's Horse, twelve light guns, and a heavy train. It was considered probable that, on his way, Grant would relieve Maun Singh, the powerful thalookdar so often mentioned, who was besieged in his fort at Shahgunje by many thousand rebels. This cunning time-server had drawn suspicion upon his acts and motives on many former occasions; but as it was more desirable to have him as a friend than an enemy, and as he had unquestionably earned the enmity of the rebels by his refusal to act openly against the British, it was considered prudent to pay some attention to his present applications for aid. Grant and Montgomery, the one as general and the other as commissioner, held possession of the road from Cawnpore to Lucknow, and the road from Lucknow to Nawabgunge; it was hoped that Grant's expedition would obtain command likewise of the road from Nawabgunge to Fyzabad. These are the three components of one main road which nearly intersects Oude from west to east; the possession of it would render practicable the gradual crushing of the rebel bands in different forts north and south of the road. The rebel leaders, about the middle of the month, were believed to comprise the Begum of Oude, her paramour Mummoo Khan, Beni Madhoo, Baboo Rambuksh, Bihonath Singh, Chandabuksh, Gholab Singh, Nurput Singh, the Shahzada Feroze Shah, Bhopal Singh, and others of less note; they had under their command sixty or seventy thousand armed men of various grades, and forty or fifty guns. More than half of the whole number were supposed to be with the Begum and Mummoo Khan, at Chowka-Ghât, beyond the river Gogra; and to these Sir Hope Grant directed his chief attention. Where Nena Sahib was hiding, the British authorities could never definitely learn; although it was known that he was near the northern or Nepaul frontier of Oude. It was believed that he, as well as the Begum, was becoming straitened for want of funds—appliances without which they could never hope to keep their rebel forces together.

The general, with his force from Lucknow, experienced no obstruction in his march towards Fyzabad. He arrived at a point within fourteen miles of that city by the 28th of July, having passed on his way through Nawabgunge—leaving the Rajah of Kupoorthulla to keep open his communications. His advance alarmed the rebel army which was at that time engaged in besieging Maun Singh in Shahgunje (twelve miles south of Fyzabad); it broke up into three divisions—one of which fled towards Gonda; a second marched for Sultanpore on the Goomtee; while a third made for Tanda on the Gogra. This precipitate flight shewed in a striking way the dread felt by the insurgents of an encounter with Sir Hope Grant; for their numbers are supposed to have been at least ten times as great as his. On the 29th, Grant entered Fyzabad, and there heard that a large body of rebels were escaping across the Gogra a mile or two ahead; he pushed on with cavalry and horse-artillery, but was only in time to send a few round-shot into their rear. On the following day, Maun Singh, now delivered from beleaguerment, had an interview with him. On the 2d of August, two of the three divisions of the rebel army contrived to join in the vicinity of Sultanpore, where they again formed a compact army of eighteen thousand men, with eleven guns. Notwithstanding the escape of the rebels, Grant's undisputed occupation of Fyzabad made a great impression in the whole province. This place was a centre of Mohammedan influence; while near it was the very ancient though decayed city of Ayodha or Oude, one of the most sacred of Hindoo cities. Religious quarrels had often broken out between the two communities; and now the British shewed themselves masters alike over the Mohammedan and the Hindoo cities.

It was a great advantage at this time that Hurdeo Buksh, a powerful zemindar of Oude, was enabled to give practical efficiency to the friendly feeling with which he had regarded the English throughout the mutiny. At his estate of Dhurrenpore, not far from Nawabgunge, he organised a small force of retainers, which, with two guns, he employed in fighting against some of the neighbouring thalookdars and zemindars who were hostile to British interests. Such instances were few in number, but they were gradually increasing; and to such agency the ultimate pacification of Oude would necessarily be in considerable part due.

While Grant was encamped at Fyzabad, he made arrangements for routing some of the rebel bodies stationed in places to the east and south-east, whither they had fled on his approach. He made up a column—comprising the 1st Madras Europeans, the 5th Punjaub Rifles, a detachment of Madras Sappers, a detachment of the 7th Hussars, 300 of Hodson's Horse, and a troop of horse-artillery. With this force, Brigadier Horsford was directed to proceed to Sultanpore, whither an important section of the rebels had retreated. Heavy rains prevented the departure of the brigadier so soon as had been intended; but he set forth on the 9th of August, and was joined on the way by a small force from Lucknow, comprising Brasyer's Sikhs and two horse-artillery guns. On the 13th, Horsford took possession of Sultanpore, after a tough opposition from sixteen or eighteen thousand rebels; he not only drove the enemy across the river Goomtee, but shelled them out of the cantonments on the opposite banks. The most determined of the combatants among the rebels were believed to be those regiments of mutinied sepoys which had been known as the Nuseerabad brigade; they had established three posts to guard the ghâts or ferries across the river, and held these ghâts for a time with such obstinacy as to occasion them a severe loss.

Sultanpore occupied an important position in relation to the rest of Oude; being on the same river (the Goomtee) as Lucknow, and on the high road from Allahabad to Fyzabad. It was evident that this place, from the relative positions of the opposing forces, could not long remain at peace. The rebels endeavoured to regain possession of it after their defeat; while Sir Hope Grant resolved to prevent them. They returned to the Goomtee, and occupied many villages nearly opposite the city. On the 24th of August, Grant made preparations for crossing the river and attacking them. This plan he put in execution on the following day; when twelve hundred foot and two guns effected the passage, and seized three villages immediately in front. The rebels, however, maintained a position from which they could send over shot into the British camp; this lasted until the 29th, when they were driven from their position, and compelled to retire towards Sassenpore, where they reassembled about seven thousand of their number, with eight guns.

The first days of September found this body of rebels separating and recombining, lessening and augmenting, in a manner that renders it difficult to trace the actual movements. The real mutinous sepoys, the 'Pandies' of the once mighty Bengal army, were now few among them; and the fluctuating numbers were made up chiefly of the adherents of the rebellious thalookdars and zemindars of Oude—the vassals of those feudal barons—together with felons and scoundrels of various kinds. On one day they appeared likely to retire to Amethee, the stronghold of a rebel named Lall Madhoo Singh; on another, they shewed symptoms of marching to Mozuffernugger, a place about ten miles from Sultanpore; while on a third, some of them made their appearance at a town about twenty miles from Sultanpore on the Lucknow road.

At this time (September) the position of the British in Oude, so far as concerned the possession of actual governing power, was very singular. They held a belt of country right across the centre of the province from east to west; while the districts north and south of that belt were either in the possession of rebels, or were greatly troubled by them. The position was thus clearly described by the Lucknow correspondent of the *Bombay Gazette:* 'The districts in our possession lie in a large ellipse, of which Lucknow and Durriabad are foci, the ends of one diameter being Cawnpore and Fyzabad. These cities are situated almost due east and west. Our civil jurisdiction extends, on the average, twenty-five miles all round Lucknow, and not much less round Durriabad. Our line of communication is uninterrupted from Cawnpore to Fyzabad, which latter borders on the Goruckpore district.' North of this belt or ellipse were various bodies of rebels under the Begum, Mummoo Khan, Feroze Shah, Hurdut Singh, and other leaders; while south of the belt were other bodies under Beni Madhoo, Hunmunt Singh, the Rajah of Gonda, &c. Irrespective of these, were Nena Sahib and some of his relations who, though not to be encountered, were known to be still in the northeast of Oude, near the Nepaul frontier. Sir Hope Grant had immediate control over both banks of the Goomtee, near Sultanpore, and was preparing for a decisive advance against the rebels as soon as he was joined by Brigadier Berkeley, who was sent from Allahabad on an expedition presently to be noticed.

The portion of Oude nearest to Rohilcund, where the energetic Moulvie had lately lost his life, was kept for a long time in a state of anarchy by a combination of rebel chieftains, who declared hostility against the Rajah of Powayne for having betrayed and killed the Moulvie. They at first quarrelled a good deal concerning the possession of the effects of the deceased leader; but the Begum put in a claim, which seems to have been acceded to. Although the authorities at Lucknow could not at this time spare a force to rout out the insurgents on this side of Oude, the service was rendered from Rohilcund, as will be shewn shortly.

In a district of Oude between Lucknow and the Rohilcund frontier, a gallant affair was achieved by Mr Cavanagh, who had gained so much renown by carrying the message from Sir James Outram at Lucknow to Sir Colin Campbell's camp. Being appointed chief civil officer of the Muhiabad district, he arranged with Captain Dawson and Lieutenant French to defend the district from rebels as well as they could, by the aid of a few native police and sowars. On the 30th of July a body of 1500 insurgents, with one gun, made a sudden attack on a small out-station defended only by about 70 men. The place was gallantly held until Cavanagh and French reached it. One bold charge sent the rebels fleeing in all directions; and the district was soon pacified. Mr Cavanagh had the tact to win over several small zemindars to the British cause, by threatening to punish them if insubordinate, and by undertaking to aid them if they were attacked by rebel bands; they combined to maintain four hundred matchlockmen at their own expense in the British cause. Many of the petty rajahs and zemindars had themselves been more than suspected; but the civil authorities were empowered to win them over, by an indulgent forgetfulness of their past conduct.

On another side of Oude, near Allahabad and the apex of the Doab, there were many bold and reckless thalookdars, who held out threats to all of their class who dared to profess friendship to the English. A loyal thalookdar, Baboo Rampursand Singh, was attacked by a number of these confederated chieftains with their retainers at Soraon; they took him and his family prisoners, destroyed his house, and sacked the village. As this course of proceeding would have deterred friendly thalookdars from a persistence in their loyalty, and still more certainly deterred waverers from making a choice adverse to the rebel cause, means were taken to check it. Brigadier Berkeley was placed in command of a 'Soraon Field-force,' hastily collected, comprising 200 of H.M. 32d foot, the 7th Punjaub infantry, about 150 other infantry, two troops of Lahore light horse, a detachment of Madras cavalry, detachments of horse and foot artillery, and nine guns and mortars. The brigadier set out for Allahabad, where the force had been collected, crossed the Ganges, marched to the Oude frontier, and came in sight of a body of rebels on the 14th of July, at the fort and village of Dehaign—one of the small forts in which Oude abounded. The rebels retired into the fort on his

Interior of Hindoo Rajah's House.

approach, allowing his skirmishers to take easy possession of the village. He encircled the fort with cavalry, and placed horse-artillery to watch any outlets of escape. A firing by heavy guns was not satisfactory to him, owing to the fort being completely hidden by trees and thick scrubby jungle; and he therefore resolved on storming the place by his infantry. The assault was speedily and thoroughly successful. About 250 of the rebels were killed in the fort and ditch; and about as many more were chased through the jungle and cut down by the cavalry and horse-artillery. The place was not properly a fort; it was a large area of jungle surrounded by a dilapidated earthen wall and ditch, and fenced with a thorny abattis, having a brick house in the centre. The rebels being driven out, Brigadier Berkeley caused the jungle to be cut, the walls to be levelled, and the house destroyed. After resting on the 15th, Berkeley proceeded on the 16th to the fort of Tiroul, seven miles north of Soraon. He found this fort in the middle of an impenetrable thorny jungle, through which a few paths were cut in directions known only to the natives; it was surrounded by a very thick thorny abattis; and it had walls, bastions, ditches, escarps, like a miniature fortress, with a stronghold in the centre to which the garrison could retire when closely pressed. There were only three guns on the bastions, but the walls were loopholed for musketry. So thick was the belt of trees and jungle around, that the brigadier could scarcely obtain a sight of the fort; he therefore deemed it prudent to employ his mortars and a 24-pounder howitzer before sending in his infantry to assault. This succeeded; the enemy evacuated the place during the night, leaving behind them their three guns and gun-ammunition. The infantry were on the alert to assist, but the enemy left them nothing to do. Fort Tiroul was then destroyed, as fort Soraon had been. The former was rather a superior example of an Oudian fort; although the walls and bastions were only of earth, they were of such considerable thickness, and were aided so greatly by loopholed parapets, ditches, breastworks, rifle-pits, thorny abattis, zigzag intrenchments, and thick jungle—that the enemy might have made a tough resistance to an infantry attack, if they had not been frightened out by shells and balls. By a somewhat similar train of operations, Brigadier Berkeley captured and destroyed a fort at Bhyspoor; and having thus finished the work intrusted to him, he returned with his temporary 'Soraon Field-force' to Allahabad. After a brief interval, he was again sent forth, to demolish other Oudian forts at places accessible from Allahabad, of which one was at Pertabghur; and then to advance to Sultanpore, to aid Sir Hope Grant. The two generals would then command a semicircle of country, within which most of the rebels in the eastern half of Oude would be enclosed; and an advance of other columns from Lucknow would completely hem them in. There were many symptoms, at the end of the month, that numerous zemindars and thalookdars were only waiting for a decent pretext, a decisive success of the British, to give in their adhesion.

The banks of the Ganges nearest to the province of Oude, even so low down as Allahabad, where the governor-general and the commander-in-chief were residing, required close watching; they were infested by bands of rebels, some of whom devastated the villages, while others sought to cross the Ganges into the Doab, and carry mischief into new districts. Towards the close of July—to cite one among many instances—it became known that the rebels had collected many boats on the Oude side of the river, ready to cross over into the Doab if the fortune of war should render this desirable. The authorities at once sent up the *Jumna* steamer, with a party of 130 Sikhs and two guns. At Manickpore and Kunkur, some distance up the river, they found more than twenty boats, which they succeeded in destroying; but the two forts were well armed with guns and rebels, and could not be safely attacked at that time—another and stronger expeditionary force was required to effect this. In August, and again in September, small forces were sent up from Allahabad by river, which had the desired effect of checking these insurgents.

Viscount Canning and Sir Colin Campbell both remained at Allahabad throughout the period to which this chapter relates—where, indeed, they had long been located. It was convenient for each in his special capacity, owing to its central situation. Sir Colin needed to be informed daily of the proceedings of all the brigades, columns, forces, and detachments which were out on active service. Gladly would he have kept them all under cover until the rainy season had passed; but the exigencies of the service prevented this: some troops were necessarily in the field—in Behar, in Oude, in Rohilcund, in Bundelcund, in the Mahratta states, in Rajpootana; and these, whether their number were few or many, were all working to one common end. At no other city could Sir Colin receive news from all those regions more promptly than at Allahabad. Again, Viscount Canning found it necessary to be in intimate communication with the commander-in-chief, in relation to all projects and arrangements involving military operations, on which the ultimate pacification of India so much depended. It was desirable, also, that he should be near Oude, the affairs of which were far more delicate than those of any other Indian province. Many events were likely to arise, concerning which the electric telegraph, though instantaneous, might be too curt and enigmatical, and which would be much better settled by a personal conference with the chief to whom the government of the Anglo-Indian empire was consigned.

Orders and dispatches, military and political, were issued in great number from Allahabad, which was the substitute for Calcutta at that time. Much progress had been made towards the construction of a new English town, with houses, hotels, offices, and shops; and much also in the building of new barracks, for the English troops which must necessarily continue to be stationed at this important place. The governor-general and the commander-in-chief were each surrounded with his staff of officials, for the transaction of business; and both worked untiringly for the public benefit.

From time to time Viscount Canning gave effect to several recommendations made by the generals and brigadiers for an acknowledgment of the fidelity and bravery of native soldiers. At a period when the treachery of the 'Pandies' of the Bengal army had been productive of such bitter fruit, it was doubly desirable to praise and reward such native troops as bore up well against the temptations to which they were exposed. On one day he issued orders for the promotion of certain officers and men of the Hyderabad Contingent, for conspicuous gallantry in the action at Banda; and in orders of subsequent dates, other well-deserving native troops were singled out for reward. Ressaldars were promoted to be ressaldar-majors, duffadars to be ressaldars or jemadars, bargheers and silladars to be duffadars, naiks to be havildars, and so on—these being some of the many designations of native military officers in India. One of the higher grade of native officers in the Hyderabad Contingent, Ressaldar-major Meer Dilawar Hossein, was made a member of the First Class of 'the Order of British India,' with the title of 'Sirdar Bahadoor.' Sometimes towns themselves were complimented, as a mode of gratifying the inhabitants, when good service had been rendered. Thus Sasseram became the subject of the following order: 'As a special mark of the consideration of government for the loyal services rendered by Shah Koobeeroodeen Ahmed of Sasseram, and his fellow townspeople, in repelling the mutineers, the Right Hon. the

Governor-general is pleased to confer upon Sasseram the name of Nasirool Hook-Kusbah, "Sasseram the aider or supporter of the rulers."'

Sir Colin Campbell's* daily duties of course bore relation chiefly to military matters. On one occasion, while at Allahabad, he reviewed the camel-corps as one of the reinforcements which from time to time arrived at that place. This was towards the close of July. It was a curious sight to see four hundred camels going through their military evolutions on the *maidan* or plain outside the city. These ungainly beasts performed almost all the usual cavalry movements. Besides an armed native driver, each camel carried an English soldier, who occupied the back seat, and was in a position to use his rifle. The camels had been trained to the word of command. On a recognised touch of the guiding-string, they dropped on their knees, the riflemen descended quickly, went on for a distance in skirmishing order, remounted on the recall being signalled, and the camels then rose in their wonted clumsy manner. This corps was likely to render very valuable service, by rapidly conveying a few skilled riflemen to distances and over tracts which would be beyond the reach of infantry.

The commander-in-chief, a man indefatigable in the performance of his duties, acquired for himself the reputation of being a general who insisted on all the duties of regimental service being properly attended to by the officers; to the effect that all alike should *work* for the common cause, in camps and barracks, as well as in the field. The following order, issued about the close of August, will shew how numerous were the duties thus marked out: 'The commander-in-chief begs that general officers commanding divisions and brigades will urge commanding-officers of her Majesty's regiments, troops, and batteries, to give their most particular attention to all points of interior economy; to examine and correct regimental books; to re-enlist soldiers of limited service willing to renew their engagements; to complete soldiers' clothing and necessaries, examine soldiers' accounts, soldiers' claims, and small account-books; to close, and render to the proper departments, the accounts of deceased officers and soldiers; to examine arms, accoutrements, and ammunition, and repair deficiencies; to continue judging-distance drills and musketry-instruction, as far as the climate will permit; to provide occupation for soldiers without harassing them by mere routine drills; to consider their comforts, diet, and amusements; to re-establish the regimental school, and encourage by every means the study of the Hindustani language, both by officers and soldiers disposed to study it; to ascertain by inquiry what means exist in the neighbourhood of their quarters, both in materials and workmen, to furnish their regiments with boots and clothing, in the event of failure of the usual supply; finally, to maintain the most exact discipline, the strict performance of all duties, and proper marks of respect to officers; which will be much assisted by a proper example on the part of officers, in dress and deportment, regularity in their duties, and treatment of native servants and followers.'

This last clause, 'treatment of native servants and followers,' related to a serious matter. Many of the younger officers, chiefly those whose knowledge of India had extended only over a few months, had acquired the habit of speaking and writing of the natives as if they were all fiends alike, to sabre and hang whom was a pleasurable duty. The atrocities of some were visited on all. The 'Pandies' who had begun the mutiny were now mixed up with others in the common designations of 'niggers' and 'devils;' and the officers above alluded to were far too prone to use the stick or the whip on the shoulders of natives, simply because they were natives, even when inoffensively employed. The observant correspondents of some of the London journals were too much struck with this dangerous tendency to allow it to pass unnoticed; they commented on it with severity. The letters from officers, made public in the journals published in India, furnished abundant proof of the feelings and language adverted to, conveyed in their own terms. Unless the mutiny were to end with general enmity on both sides, it was essential that an improved tone should prevail in this matter; and to this end, many hints were given by the authorities, in England as well as in India.

A few words will suffice to say all that need be said concerning the Doab and Rohilcund, the regions in which the mutiny really commenced.

Rohilcund was troubled with nothing beyond trifling disturbances during the month of July; and these came chiefly from Oude. Rebel leaders, with small bands of depredators, crossed the frontier, and harried some of the neighbouring villages. So little, however, was there of an organised rebel army in the province, that the predatory irruptions were easily quelled by means of small detachments of troops. At one period in the month a body of Oudians crossed into the northern part of Rohilcund, and combined with a rabble under one Nizam Ali in the wild Roodurpore tract of country. As it was considered possible that an attack on Pileebheet might be contemplated, the authorities at Bareilly sent a small force—comprising the Rohilcund Horse, a troop or two of Punjaub cavalry, and three companies of the Kumaon levies—to Pileebheet; this movement caused the insurgents to retire quickly. In the neighbourhood of Mohumdee, where much fighting had taken place during Sir Colin Campbell's campaign in the spring, bands of rebels still hovered about, looking for

* It may here be mentioned that, about the date to which these events refer, the commander-in-chief began to be frequently designated by his peerage-title. He had been created Baron Clyde of Clydesdale, in recognition of his valuable military services. To prevent confusion, however, it may be well, in the remaining pages of this work, to retain the more familiar appellation, Sir Colin Campbell.

any chances of success, and requiring to be carefully watched. One, of about four thousand men, was under Khan Bahadoor Khan of Bareilly; a second, under Khan Ali Nazim of Oude, numbered five thousand; and a third, under Wilayut Shah, mustered three thousand. These, with twenty or thirty guns, might have wrought much mischief if combined with the Oude rebels; but they were so placed on the frontier of the two provinces as to be nearly isolated, and afraid of any bold movements. The authorities, however, were on their guard. A force, including De Kantzow's Horse, was sent for the protection of Powayne; and Rajah Juggernath Singh, of that place, had about two thousand men who could be depended upon to oppose the rebels. In August, the town and station of Pileebheet were frequently threatened by one Kala Khan, who had three thousand budmashes at his beck, with four guns. As it was deemed necessary to defend Noria, a station about ten miles distant, a small force was sent out from Pileebheet to effect this. Kala Khan attacked the force at Sersown, and brought on an engagement in which his three thousand were opposed to about five hundred. He received a severe defeat, and lost his guns, three elephants, and a number of bullocks. This occurred during the last week in August. In September, matters remained nearly in the same state; the authorities in Rohilcund could not at once spare troops in sufficient number to put down the insurgents thoroughly; but the successes of Sir Hope Grant, in the central parts of Oude, would gradually but necessarily weaken the isolated bands of rebels on the frontier of the two provinces.

Meerut and Delhi had long been at peace. No symptoms of rebel armies appeared near those cities. Sir John Lawrence, having had the province of Delhi attached to his government of the Punjaub, was ruling it with the same vigour as his other provinces. All the natives, Hindoo and Mohammedan, saw that he was a man not to be trifled with. Many of the antiquated usages of the East India Company, in force in other provinces, he abrogated, and introduced a system more suitable to the actual condition of the country and its inhabitants. The 'regulations,' as they are called, he abolished altogether; and established in their place a system of government in which summary trial by *vivâ voce* examination was adopted. A military police was organised; and every village compelled to pay compensation for any damage done within its boundaries.

The district around Etawah was occasionally disturbed by a dacoit leader named Roop Singh, who collected a band of adherents, comprising a few of the Gwalior Contingent, a few of the mutinied troops from Scindia's own army, and numerous matchlockmen from the ravines of the Jumna. With this motley force he levied contributions from such of the villages as were not strong enough to resist him. He made his appearance at Ajeetmul and other places early in July; but was speedily routed out by a small detachment sent in pursuit. During August, this part of India was infested by men of the same class as those who troubled so many other provinces—reckless adventurers and escaped felons, who took advantage of the state of public affairs to plunder villages, and make exactions on every side. Some of them were headed by chieftains who could boast of a few hundred retainers, and who, with retainers and rabble together, gave more organisation to the plunderers. The principal among them was Roop Singh, mentioned above, who kept armed possession of a fort at Burhee, Bhurree, or Burhay, at the junction of the Chumbul with the Jumna, and occasioned great annoyance by attacking boats and levying toll as they passed. To keep these several mischief-makers in subjection required much activity on the part of the troops belonging to the district. Towards the close of the month, a force was sent out from Etawah purposely to take this fort and disperse the rebels. This was effectually accomplished on the 28th. Suspecting what was intended, the rebels attempted to check the progress of the boats carrying the detachment, at a place called Gurha Koodor, a fortified village three miles higher up. So long as the troops were in the boats, the rebels made a show of determination on shore; but a landing soon scattered them in all directions. The troops then re-embarked, floated down to Burhee, landed, took possession of the fort, and compelled Roop Singh to make a hasty retreat. This done, they collected and secured all the boats in the neighbouring parts of the rivers Jumna, Chumbul, and Koorarce, as a measure of precaution, clearing all the rebels from the vicinity of Dholpore. They then proceeded against the chief of Chuckernuggur, another leader of rebel bands whom it was necessary to put down. In September, Etawah, like the other districts around it, was very little troubled by warlike or mutinous proceedings.

Agra found no difficulty in maintaining order in and near the city. When, in June, the temporary success of Tanteea Topee and the Gwalior mutineers gave some cause for alarm, the authorities of Agra sent out troops to escort Scindia back to the capital of his dominions; and when, at a later date, those mutineers were fleeing from Gwalior, and were believed to be on the way to Bhurtpore or Odeypore, a detachment was sent out to check their approach. This detachment consisted of the 3d Bengal Europeans and a battery of guns, and was placed in aid of Brigadier Showers's force. The demonstration took effect; for (as we shall see more in detail presently), Tanteea Topee bent his steps southward, away from the threatened assault; and Showers was enabled to send back the detachment through Futtehpore Sikri to Agra. From that time, during the summer and autumn months, Agra and its neighbourhood were at peace.

Directing attention next to the Punjaub, we may remark that those who had the keenest sense of the value of loyal integrity in times of trouble, were anxious to see the day when some recognition should be shown of the services of three native rajahs, without whose co-operation it would scarcely have been possible for Sir John Lawrence to have sent those troops from the Punjaub which enabled Sir Archdale Wilson to recapture Delhi. These were the Rajahs of Putialah, Jheend, and Nabah—three small states which were at one time included within Sirhind, then among the 'Sikh protected states,' and then among the 'Cis-Sutlej states.' The rajahs were semi-independent, having most of the privileges of independent rulers, but being at the same time under certain engagements to the British government. If they had swelled the ranks of the insurgents, it is difficult to see how Hindostan could have been recovered; for these

UMRITSIR.

states intervene between Lahore and Umritsir on the one side, and Delhi on the other. From first to last the rajahs not only fulfilled their engagements, but more; and the government had abundant reason to be glad that these three territories had not been 'annexed;' for annexation, if not the cause, was unquestionably one of the aggravations to mutiny. Viscount Canning, in July, rewarded these three Sikh chiefs (for they were Sikhs, though not exactly Punjaubees) with estates and honours. The Rajah—or rather Maharajah, for he was of higher grade than the other two—of Putialah received certain territories in Jhujjur and Bhudour, on a certain military tenure in return for the revenues. He also received the gift of a house at Delhi which, once belonging to one of the begums of the imperial family, had been confiscated on account of her complicity in the mutiny. Lastly, his honorary titles were increased by the following: 'Furzund Khas, Munsoor Zuman, Ameer-ool-Omrah, Maharajah Dhurraj Rajahshur Sree Maharajah Rajgan, Nirundur Singh Mahundur Bahadoor'—an accumulation, the weight of which would be oppressive to any but an oriental prince. The translation is said to be: 'Special Son, Conqueror of the World, Chief of the Chiefs, Maharajah of Rajahs'—and so on. The Rajah of Jheend received the Dadree territory, thirteen villages in the Koolran Pergunnah, and a confiscated royal house at Delhi. The additions were: That he be allowed a salute of eleven guns; that his presents be increased from eleven to fifteen trays; that his state visits to the governor-general be returned by the secretary; and that his honorary titles be thus increased: 'Most cherished Son of true Faith, Rajah Surroop Singh Walee Jheend.' The Rajah of Nabah received similar presents, and the honorary appellations of—'Noble Son of good Faith, Berar Bunsee Sirmoor Rajah Bhurpoor Singh Malindur Bahadoor.' The revenues made over to these rajahs amounted—to the first, about £20,000 per annum; to the second, £12,000; to the third, £11,000.

We may smile at these extravagances of

compliment, but the services rendered deserved a solid reward as well as an addition to honorary titles. For, it must be remembered, the Rajah of Putialah maintained a contingent of 5000 troops—protected the stations of Umballa and Kurnaul at the outbreak of the mutiny—guarded the grand trunk-road from Kurnaul to Phillour, keeping it open for the passage of British and Punjaub troops—co-operated with General Van Cortlandt in Hissar—lent money when Sir John Lawrence's coffers were running low—and encouraged others by his own unswerving loyalty. Again: the Rajah of Jheend, whose contingent was very small, did not hesitate to leave his own territory undefended, and march towards Delhi—assisting to defend most of the stations between that city and Kurnaul, and to keep open the communication across the Jumna. Again: the Rajah of Nabah, at the very outset of the disturbances, proceeded to aid Mr Commissioner Barnes in maintaining Loodianah—supplied an escort for the siege-train—gallantly opposed the Jullundur mutineers—provided carriage for stores—and made loans to the Punjaub government in a time of monetary need. The districts given to these rajahs, at the suggestion of Sir John Lawrence, were so chosen as to furnish a prudent barrier of Sikhs between turbulent Mohammedans on the one side and equally turbulent Rajpoots on the other.

Nor did the authorities neglect to recognise the services of humbler persons, although, principally from the proverbial slowness of official movements, the recognition was often delayed to an unreasonable extent. Occasion has more than once presented itself, in former chapters, for noticing the bestowal of the much-prized Victoria Cross on officers and soldiers who had distinguished themselves by acts of personal valour. Owing to the dilatory official routine just adverted to, it was not until the 27th of July that Sergeant Smith and Bugler Hawthorne received the Victoria Cross for their intrepid services at the siege of Delhi ten months before. Their regiment, the 52d foot, was at Sealkote in the Punjaub on that date; and Brigadier Stisted had the pleasure of giving the honouring insignia to them. He told them that the Victoria Cross is in reality more honourable than the Order of the Bath, seeing that no one can obtain it except by virtue of well-authenticated acts of heroism. He gracefully admitted that his own Order of the Bath was due more to the pluck and bravery of his men than to his own individual services; and in reference to the Victoria Cross he added: 'I only wish I had it myself.' Another bestowal of this honour we will briefly mention, to shew what kind of spirit is to be found within the breasts of British troops. The award of the Cross, in this instance, was delayed no less than fourteen months after the achievement for which it was given; and the soldier may well have doubted whether he would ever receive it. The instance was that of Gunner William Connolly, of the Bengal horse-artillery; and the conduct for which his officer, Lieutenant Cookes, recommended him for this distinction, was recorded in a dispatch from which an extract is here given in a foot-note.*

A very unexpected event, in July, was the revolt of a regiment, or a portion of a regiment, in that region of India which was believed to be more vigorously governed and in better hands than any other—the Punjaub. The facts, as they afterwards came out (mostly, however, on hearsay evidence), appear to have been nearly as follow: The 18th Punjaub infantry, stationed at Dera Ismael Khan, on the western side of the Indus, contained among its numbers about a hundred Malwaie Sikhs, a peculiar tribe different from the other Sikhs of the Punjaub. These Malwaies planned a mutiny. On a particular night, some of them were to murder the officers of the station; the fort was to be seized; and the 39th Bengal native infantry, which had been disarmed some time previously, was to be re-armed from the magazines and stores of the fort. The two regiments of mutineers, perhaps joined by the Sikhs of Renny's regiment at Bunnoo, were then to embark in boats on the Indus, taking with them the guns, ammunition, and treasure, and were to float down to Dera Ghazee Khan; here they expected to be joined by the native garrison, with whom they would cross the Indus to Moultan; and lastly, with two regiments from the last-named place, they hoped to march upon Lahore. Such was the account, probably magnified in some of its particulars, obtained of the plans of the mutineers. So far as concerned the actual facts, the plot was discovered in time to prevent its execution. On the evening of the 20th, Major Gardiner of the 10th Punjaub infantry, and Captain Smith of the artillery, having received from some quarter a hint of what was intended, went down to the lines at ten o'clock at night, and summoned two of the

* 'I advanced my half-troop at a gallop, and engaged the enemy within easy musket-range. The sponge-man of one of my guns having been shot during the advance, Gunner Connolly assumed the duties of second sponge-man; and he had barely assisted in two discharges of his gun, when a musket-ball through the left thigh felled him to the ground. Nothing daunted by pain and loss of blood, he was endeavouring to resume his post, when I ordered a movement in retirement. Though severely wounded, he was mounted on his horse in the gun-team, rode to the next position which the guns took up, and manfully declined going to the rear when the necessity of his so doing was represented to him. About 11 o'clock A.M., when the guns were still in action, the same gunner, while sponging, was again knocked down by a musket-ball striking him on the hip, thereby causing great faintness and partial unconsciousness; for the pain appeared excessive, and the blood flowed fast. On seeing this, I gave directions for his removal out of action; but this brave man, hearing me, staggered to his feet and said: "No, sir; I'll not go there while I can work here;" and shortly afterwards he again resumed his post as sponge-man. Late in the afternoon of the same day, my three guns were engaged at a hundred yards from the walls of a village with the defenders—namely, the 14th native infantry, mutineers—amid a storm of bullets, which did great execution. Gunner Connolly, though suffering severely from his two previous wounds, was wielding his sponge with an energy and courage which attracted the admiration of his comrades; and while cheerfully encouraging a wounded man to hasten in bringing up ammunition, a musket-ball tore through the muscles of his right leg. With the most undaunted bravery, he struggled on; and not till he had loaded six times, did this man give way, when, through loss of blood, he fell into my arms; I placed him upon a wagon, which shortly afterwards bore him in a state of unconsciousness from the fight.'

men to appear. One, a sepoy, came first; he was ordered at once to be confined; but no sooner did he hear the order, than he ran off. Just as the guard were about re-capturing this man, a jemadar rushed out, cut down one of them, and wounded another. The sepoy and the jemadar, who were the ringleaders in the plot, escaped for a time, but were captured a few days afterwards. As soon as Sir John Lawrence heard of this occurrence, he ordered the disarmed 39th to be sent to Sealkote, where their movements could be more carefully watched.

Still more serious, in its nature if not in its intention, was the outbreak of the 62d and 69th Bengal native infantry, with a native troop of horse-artillery, at Moultan. These disarmed regiments, like many others in similar plight, were a source of embarrassment to the authorities. They could not safely be re-armed, for their Hindustani sympathies caused them to be suspected; while it was a waste of power to employ English soldiers to watch these unarmed men in their lines. At length it was determined to disband the two regiments, and let the men depart, a few at a time, and under necessary precautions, to their own homes. When this order was read out to them, they appeared satisfied; but a rumour or suspicion spread that there was an intention of destroying them piecemeal on the way. Whether this or any other motive actuated them, is not fully known; but they broke out into rebellion on the 31st of August. There were at Moultan at the time about 170 of the royal artillery, a wing of the 1st Bengal Europeans, the 11th Punjaub infantry, and the 1st Bengal irregular cavalry. Just as the mid-day gun fired, the two disarmed mutinous regiments rose in mutiny, seized anything they could find as weapons, and made a desperate assault on the troops at the station not in their plot. The 62d made their attack on the artillery stables and the European barracks; the 69th went at the guns and the artillery barracks. As these mutineers had few weapons but sticks, their attack appeared so strange, and was so wholly unexpected, that the loyal troops at the station were at first hardly prepared to resist them, and a few Europeans lost their lives; but when once the real nature of the mad attempt was clearly seen, the result was fearful. The misguided men were shot or cut down by all parties and in all quarters. Of thirteen hundred mutineers, few lived to return to their own Hindostan; three or four hundred were laid low in and near Moultan, others were shot by villagers, others were captured and brought in for military execution. It was the nearest approach to the utter annihilation of two regiments, perhaps, that occurred throughout the wars of the mutiny. The sepoys sometimes behaved more like madmen, at others more like children, than rational beings. In the present case they had scarcely a chance of success; for the Sikhs and Punjaubees around them displayed no affection for Hindustanis; the soldiery shot and cut them down, while the peasantry captured them for the sake of the reward offered. They possibly reckoned on the support of the 1st Bengal irregular cavalry; but this regiment remained loyal, and assisted in cutting down the sepoys instead of befriending them.

This occurrence strongly attracted the attention of the government. The disarmed sepoys, as has been more than once mentioned, were a source of much perplexity; it was not decided in what way best to set them free; and on the other hand, such an outbreak as this shewed that it would not be safe to re-arm them. There was at the same time a necessity for watching the Sikh and Punjaubee troops—now nearly 70,000 in number. Hitherto they had behaved admirably, fighting manfully for the government at times and places where the Hindustanis had been treacherous. That they had done so, afforded a justification for the confidence which Sir John Lawrence had placed in them; but that sagacious man saw that recruiting had gone quite far enough in this direction. It was just possible that the Punjaub army might become too strong, and rejoice in its strength by means of insubordination.

One of the incidents in the Punjaub during the month of August related to a physical rather than a moral outbreak—the overwhelming of a military station by a river torrent. The Indus, when about to enter the Punjaub from the Himalaya, passes through a narrow ravine in the Irhagan Hills. The rocks on either side here, undermined by the action of the water through unknown centuries, broke away and fell into the river. Half the water of the stream still continued to find its way onward; but the other half became dammed up, and accumulated into a vast lake. When the pressure of this body of water had augmented to an irresistible degree (which it did in fifteen days), it burst its barrier and rushed down with indescribable force, sweeping away villages on its banks. At Attock the level of the river rose fifty feet in one hour, carrying away the bridge of boats which constituted the only roadway over the Indus, and destroying workshops and timber-stores on the banks. The Cabool river, coming from Afghanistan, and joining the Indus at Attock, had its stream driven backwards or upwards with fearful rapidity; it speedily overflowed its banks, and destroyed nearly all the houses at the military station of Nowsherah. 'The officers,' said an eye-witness, 'not knowing when it would stop, but hoping the flood would soon subside, put all their things on the tops of their houses; but the water still continued rising, and house after house went down before it. . . . . The barracks were flooded and vacated by the troops; and all, gentle and simple, had to pass the night on some sand-hills.' The barracks, being 'pucka-built' (burnt bricks and mortar), were not destroyed, although flooded; the other buildings, being 'cutcha-built' (unburnt bricks and mud), were destroyed. The troops were at once removed to Peshawur; but the destruction of the boat-bridge at Attock threatened a serious interruption to military movements.

Nothing occurred in the Punjaub during September to need record here; nor did Sinde depart from its usual peaceful condition. Both of these large provinces, filling up the western belt of India from the Himalaya to the ocean, were held well in hand by the civil and military authorities.

Attention must now be transferred to those regions which, during many months, had been disturbed by anarchy and rebellion—Bundelcund, the Mahratta States, and Rajpootana. These large territories contained many petty chieftains, among whom a considerable number were prone to seize this opportunity to strengthen themselves by plundering their neighbours. Of patriotism, there was little enough; men appeared in arms for their own interests, or what they deemed their own interests, rather than for any common cause involving nationality or affection to native princes.

Bundelcund and the Saugor provinces were chiefly under the military control of General Whitlock, who had advanced from Madras with a force consisting chiefly of Madras troops, and had gradually established regular government in districts long troubled by violence and confusion. At the end of June, as the last chapter shewed, Whitlock's force was divided into a great many detachments, which overawed the turbulent at as many different stations; and the same state of matters continued, with slight variations, during the next three months. It must, however, be mentioned here, in relation to military commands, that—as one mode of facilitating the thorough discomfiture of the rebels—Viscount Canning made a new arrangement affecting the Saugor and Gwalior territories. That portion of India having been much disturbed during a period of more than twelve months, it was determined to establish there two military divisions instead of one, and to place in command of those divisions two of the generals who by hard fighting had become accustomed to the district and the class of inhabitants. General Whitlock was appointed to the Saugor division, which was made to extend to the Jumna, and to include the districts of Saugor, Jubbulpoor, Banda, Humeerpoor, and Calpee, with Saugor as the military head-quarters. General Napier was appointed to the Gwalior division, which was made to include Gwalior, Sepree, Goonah, and Jhansi. This arrangement, organised about the end of July, was to hold good whether any rebels should make a sudden outbreak, or whether the troops were fortunate enough to have a period of repose during the rainy season. Whitlock's force, consisting of H.M. 43d foot, the 1st and 19th Madras native infantry, with a proportion of cavalry and artillery—was mainly in two brigades, under Brigadiers Macduff and Rice.

Brief mention was made in the last chapter of a large capture of treasure by General Whitlock. This matter must here be noticed a little more fully, on account of its connection with the intricacies of Mahratta dynastic changes. During the general's operations in Bundelcund, he marched from Banda towards Kirwee in two brigades, intending to attack Narain Rao at the last-named place. This chieftain, a descendant of the Peishwa of the Mahrattas, possessed a rabble army, with which for a time he attempted to block up the roads of approach to Kirwee. The resistance made, however, was very slight; and shortly before Whitlock entered the place, Radha Govind, an adherent of Narain Rao, escaped from the town in the opposite direction, taking with him most of the armed men, and a large quantity of money and jewels, but no guns. Narain Rao, and another Mahratta leader named Madhoo Rao, remained at Kirwee. Their fears having been roused, they now resolved to surrender as a means of obtaining forgiveness for their rebellious proceedings. They came out to meet Whitlock, at a camping-ground a few miles from Kirwee. Delivering up their swords, they were kept securely for a time. Whitlock took possession of the town and palace, and found that the rebels had been busily engaged in casting cannon, making gunpowder, and enlisting men. In the palace and its precincts were discovered forty pieces of cannon, an immense supply of shot and powder, two thousand stands of arms, numerous swords and matchlocks, accoutrements of many of the rebel sepoy regiments, elephants and horses, and a vast store of wealth in cash and jewels. It was conjectured that the jewels might possibly be those which, half a century earlier, had mysteriously disappeared from Poonah, and were supposed to be in possession either of Scindia or Holkar, the most powerful of the Mahratta chiefs in those days; but the discovery now led to an opinion that the jewels had been stolen or appropriated by Bajee Rao, father of Narain Rao, and hidden by that family for half a century. As to the quantity and value of cash and jewels captured, it will be prudent to venture on no estimate. Some of the Anglo-Indian journals spoke of 'a hundred and forty cart-loads of gold ingots and nuggets, and forty lacs of rupees,' besides the jewels; but to whatever degree this estimate may have been exaggerated, the largeness of the sum gave rise to many inquiries concerning the history of the family to which it had belonged, and of which Nena Sahib was an 'adopted' member. It then transpired, that the first Peishwa of the Mahrattas, who died in 1720, was succeeded by Balajee Rao Sahib; one of Balajee's sons, Ragoba Dada, died in 1784; and from him were descended Narain Rao and Madhoo Rao, by one branch, and Nena Sahib by another—or rather, all these three individuals were adopted sons of Ragoba's descendants. According to the loose principles of oriental heirship, therefore, it was not difficult for any one among several Mahratta princes to set up a claim to the enormous wealth which, at a time of discord at the Peishwa's court, somehow disappeared from the treasury at Poonah.

Throughout India, there was no province which more strikingly illustrated than Bundelcund the misery which some of the villages must have suffered during many months of anarchy, when predatory bands were passing to and fro, and rebel leaders were forcing contributions from all who had anything to lose. Writing early in July concerning the Banda district, a British officer said: 'This district has suffered very extensively in the long interval of disorder to which it was abandoned; the various bands of mutineers passing up from Dinapoor did great mischief; various powerful villages preyed considerably upon their weaker neighbours; and, lastly, the Nawab and Narain Rao's officials extracted by torture every farthing they could get. Many villages are completely deserted, and many more have been burned to the ground, and the people plundered of all the grain and cattle and other property which they possessed. They have gained a very fair idea of what they are to expect under a native government; and I firmly believe they generally hail our return with delight.'

The difficulty of supplying English troops, or reliable native troops, to the numerous points where insurgents were known to be lurking, led occasionally to rebel successes little looked for by the authorities. Thus, on the first of August, a party of mutinous sepoys, headed by a subadar, took possession of the town of Jaloun, near the frontier of Scindia's territory; this they were enabled to do by the connivance of some of the inhabitants, who opened the gates for them. They were, however, speedily driven out by a small force from Calpee, under Brigadier Macduff. A slight but brilliant cavalry affair occurred about the middle of August, in a district of the Saugor territory placed under General Whitlock's care. A body of a thousand rebels, under Indur Goshun and other chiefs, had for some time been committing great havoc in the district, plundering the villages, and ill-using all the inhabitants who would not yield to their demands. After having thus treated Shahpoor, they advanced to Garrakotah with similar intent. To prevent this, a small force was sent from Saugor under Captain Finch. He made a forced march; and when within a few miles of them, seeing his infantry were tired out, he rushed forward with only sixty-seven troopers. So impetuous was the charge made by these horsemen on the rebels, that they killed a hundred and fifty, took many wounded prisoners, and brought away three hundred matchlocks and swords. The leader of the rebels, Indur Goshun, was among the slain. In another part of Bundelcund, between Banda and Rewah, about the middle of August, were three groups of rebels—one under Baboo Radha Govind and Gulabraee, a second under Runmunt Singh, and a third under Punjah Singh and Dere Singh. They were supposed to amount, in all, to six thousand men; but only three hundred of these were regular sepoys, and two hundred horsemen, the rest being adventurers and rabble. After ravaging many villages, they approached the station of Kirwee on the 13th. Brigadier Carpenter at once went out to meet them with a small force from Kirwee; he found Runmunt Singh's band drawn up as if for battle, but a few shots sent them fleeing. About the same time Punjah Singh and Dere Singh were defeated by a small force under Captain Griffin. Early in August, Captain Ashburner set out from Jhansi with five hundred men, on the duty of dispersing a few Bundela chiefs who had been engaged in rebellious machinations. The weather being very heavy, and the rebels swift of foot, a long period elapsed before anything decisive could be effected; but on the 1st of September, he came up with a body of rebels, occupying Mahoni and Mow Mahoni, two villages on the opposite banks of the small river Pooj, both surrounded by deep and difficult ravines, which rendered them strong places. After a little skirmishing, the rebels were driven by shot and shell out of Mahoni, and Ashburner crossed to attack a fort at Mow Mahoni. Symptoms soon appeared that the rebels were making off. Ashburner despatched fifty cavalry, all he had to spare at the moment, under Lieutenant Moore, to gallop after and cut them up in retreat. Moore effected this in dashing style.

We now turn to a region further west, in which the operations were more important than those of Bundelcund.

Referring to former chapters for the details of Sir Hugh Rose's victory over the Gwalior mutineers, and of his retirement to Bombay after a long season of incessant activity; we proceed to notice the operations of the troops after he parted company from them. His small but famous army, the 'Central India Field-force,' was broken up into detachments about the middle of July. The hope entertained was, that the fatigued soldiers might be able to go into quarters during the rainy season, as a means of recruiting their strength for any operations that might be necessary when the cooler and more tranquil weather of the autumn arrived. To understand this, it may be well to bear in mind that the rains of Britain furnish no adequate test of those of India, which fall in enormous abundance at certain seasons, rendering field-operations, whether for industry or war, very difficult. The detachments above adverted to could only in part obtain cessation of duties during the rainy season of 1858. At Jhansi were General Napier and Colonel Liddell; with a squadron of the 14th Light Dragoons, a wing of the 3d Bombay cavalry, the 3d Bombay Europeans, the 24th Bombay native infantry, a company of Bombay Sappers, and three guns of the late Bhopal Contingent. At Gwalior, under Brigadier Stuart, were three squadrons of the 14th Light Dragoons, Meade's Horse, a wing of the 71st Highlanders, the 86th foot, the 95th foot, the 25th Bombay native infantry, a company of Bombay artillery, a company of royal engineers, and a light field-battery. At Seepree, under Brigadier Smith, were two squadrons of the 8th Hussars, two of the 1st Bombay Lancers, the 10th Bombay native infantry, and a troop of Bombay horse-artillery. Lastly, at Goonah, were Mayne's irregular horse. Sir Hugh Rose himself was at that time at Bombay receiving the well-won congratulations of all classes, and resting for a while from his exhausting labours.

At Gwalior, where the rainy season soon began to shew symptoms, General Napier made preparations for the comfortable housing of his troops. The Maharajah, now more firmly knit than ever in bonds of amity with the British, lent his aid in this matter. Sir Robert Hamilton again took up his permanent residence in the city, gradually re-establishing political relations with the various petty states around. During July there was scarcely any fighting in Scindia's territory; and the component elements of the now-dissolved Central India Field-force were allowed to remain pretty well at peace.

Before tracing the Central India operations of August, it may be well to see what was doing in Rajpootana during July.

After the siege and capture of Gwalior by Sir Hugh Rose, as we have already narrated, the rebels made a hasty flight northwestward, across the river Chumbul, into Rajpootana; where a victory was gained over them by General Napier, who had been despatched after them for that purpose by Sir Hugh Rose. They appear to have separated, after that, into three bodies. The most important section, under Tanteea Topee and Rao Sahib, received the especial watchfulness of General Roberts, as comprising some of the best of the mutinied troops, and possessing a large amount of Scindia's property. Roberts took up the work which Rose had laid down. His 'Rajpootana Field-force,' now that detachments had been separated from it for service in various quarters, was by no means a large one. It comprised H.M. 83d foot, a wing of the 72d Highlanders, wings of the 12th and 13th Bombay native infantry, a few squadrons of the 8th Hussars and 1st Bombay Lancers, 400 Belooch horse, a light field-battery, and a siege-train of six pieces. The chief body of rebels, under Tanteea Topee and Rao Sahib, made their appearance, a few days after their defeat at Gwalior, at a point more than a hundred miles to the northwest, threatening Jeypoor. Roberts at once marched from Nuseerabad, to check these fugitives. He reached Jeypoor without opposition on the 2d of July; and there he learned news of Tanteea's miscellaneous force of about ten thousand men. The rebel leader was reported to have with him Scindia's crown-jewels and treasure, the former estimated at one million sterling value, and the latter at two millions. The treasure, being mostly in silver, was of enormous weight; and Tanteea had been endeavouring to exchange it for gold, on terms that would have tempted any money-changer in more peaceful times: seeing that fifty shillings' worth of silver was offered for gold mohurs worth only thirty shillings each. On the 5th Tanteea and his troops were at Dowlutpore, thirty-four miles south of Jeypoor; and it thereupon became a problem whether Roberts could overtake them before they reached the more southern states of Rajpootana; for he was on that day at Sanganeer, near Jeypoor. During the next few days, large bodies of rebels were seen, or reported to have been seen, at places whose names are not familiar to English readers—such as Chatsoo, Lalsoont, Tongha, Gureasa, Karier, Madhopore, Jullanee, Tonk, Bursoonie, Bhoomgurh, &c.—all situated in the northeast part of Rajpootana, and separated from the Gwalior region by the river Chumbul. We also find that General Roberts marched through or halted at many places whose names are equally unfamiliar—Sherdoss, Gurbroassa, Gloolousse, Donghur, Kukkor, Rumpore, and Bhugree. In fact, the rebels marched wherever they thought they could capture a stronghold which might serve them as a citadel; while Roberts tried every means to intercept them in their progress. On the 9th, the rebels took possession of the town of Tonk—situated on the river Bunnas, nearly due east of Nuseerabad, and about one-third of the distance from that station to Gwalior; they plundered it, captured three brass guns and a little ammunition, and besieged the Nawab in the neighbouring fort of Bhoomgurh. Roberts immediately sent on a detachment under Major Holmes, in advance of his main force; and the enemy hastily departed as soon as they heard of this. To enable him to keep up the pursuit more effectually, the general sent to Seepree for Colonel Smith's brigade. There was strong reason to suspect that the rebels wished to penetrate into Mewar and Malwah, provinces far to the south of Gwalior and Jeypoor, and in which the Mahrattas and Rajpoots counted many leaders who were ripe for mischief. To prevent this southward progress was one of the objects which General Roberts held well in view; this was the more necessary, because the country here indicated affords many mountain fastnesses from which it would be difficult to expel insurgent bands. Roberts was disappointed in not being able to come up with the Gwalior rebels at Tonk; but a few days' sojourn at that town greatly relieved his troops, who had suffered severely during a fortnight's marching in sultry weather, losing many of their number by sunstroke.

By the 23d of the month, when Major Holmes was still in pursuit of the enemy, who were reported to be approaching the fortress of Mandulghur in Mewar, Roberts broke up his temporary camp at Tonk, and recrossed the river Bunnas—his movements being greatly retarded by the swollen state of the stream and the swampy condition of the fields and roads. After wading for a whole week through an almost continuous slimy swamp, he came within twenty-four miles of Nuseerabad on the 1st of August. Sending all his sick to that station, he prepared to continue a pursuit of Tanteea Topee towards the south, with as great a rapidity as the state of the country would permit.

We now turn again to the Gwalior territory, to trace such operations as took place in the month of August.

About the middle of the month, there were no fewer than five detachments of the late Central India Field-force marching about the country on and near the confines of Scindia's Gwalior territory. Sir Hugh Rose's wish and expectation, that his exhausted troops would be able to remain quietly at quarters during the rainy season, were not realised; the state of affairs rendered active service still necessary. One detachment, under General Napier, had set out from Gwalior, and was on the way to Paoree, on an expedition presently to be mentioned; a second was at Burwa Saugor, on the river Betwah; a third at Nota, sixty miles from Jhansi, on the Calpee road; a fourth at Fyzabad (one of many places of that name), fifty miles from Jhansi on the Saugor road; and a fifth, consisting of Sappers and Miners, were preparing a bridge over the Betwah, ten miles from Jhansi. Colonel Liddell, at that period commandant of the Jhansi district, was on the alert to supply small detachments of troops to such places in the vicinity as appeared to need protection; and he himself started off to Burwa Saugor, near which place a rebel chieftain was marching about with three thousand men and two or three guns.

A circumstance occurred, early in August, which led to an expedition in a new direction, and to an eventual co-operation of General Napier with General Roberts in a pursuit of the rebels. This occurrence was an outbreak which required immediate attention. A petty Mahratta chieftain, Man Singh (not Maun Singh of Oude), who had conceived himself aggrieved by Scindia, put himself at the head of 2000 men, and on the 3d of the month, attacked and captured the strong fort of Paoree, southwest of Gwalior, and about eighteen miles from Seepree. Brigadier Smith, on hearing of this, started off on the 5th from the last-named station, with a force consisting of four squadrons of the 8th Hussars, the 1st Bombay Lancers, a wing of H.M. 95th foot, and three field-guns. On nearing Paoree, Man Singh sent a messenger to inquire what was the purpose of the brigadier, seeing that the quarrel was with Scindia and not with the English; he obtained an interview, and stated that his grievance arose from the refusal of Scindia to recognise his (Man Singh's) right to succeed his father in the principality of Nerwar and the country adjacent; and he further declared that he had no connection with the mutineers and rebels who were fighting against the English. Brigadier Smith, responsible for a time for the peace of that district, could not admit such a plea in justification of the maintenance of an armed force against the sovereign of the country; it would have been dangerous. Man Singh, thereupon, increasing the number of his retainers within the fort of Paoree to three or four thousand, prepared to defend himself. Scindia had some time before stored the fort with six months' provisions, in case he should deem it at any time necessary to defend the place from the rebels; but this proved to be an unlucky precaution, for Man Singh captured the place in a single night, and then had the six months' supplies to count upon. Brigadier Smith, finding his eleven hundred men too few to capture the fort, sent to Gwalior for a reinforcement and for a few siege-guns. In accordance with this requisition, a force of about 600 horse and foot, with five guns and four mortars, set out from Gwalior on the 11th. General Napier, feeling the importance of settling this matter quickly, resolved to attend to it in person; he started from Gwalior, reached Mahona on the 14th, and Seepree on the 17th, and joined Smith on the 19th. On the 23d, this demonstration had its effect on Man Singh, who, with another chieftain, Ajheet Singh, had been holding Paoree. Napier poured a vertical fire into the fort for twenty-four hours, and then commenced using his breaching-batteries. But the enemy did not await the result; they evacuated the place, and fled through a jungle country towards the south. Napier entered Paoree, garrisoned it, and hastily made up a column, with which Colonel Robertson started off in pursuit of the rebels. Robertson, after many days' rapid march, came up nearly to the rear of Man Singh's fleeing force; but that active leader, scenting the danger, made his rebels separate into three parties, with instructions to recombine at an appointed place; and for the present pursuit was unavailable. When August closed, Man Singh was at Sirsee, north of Goonah, with (it was supposed) about sixteen hundred men, but no guns. General Napier, having destroyed the fortifications at Paoree, and burst the guns, retired to Seepree, where he was encamped at the end of the month, making arrangements for a further pursuit of Man Singh in September.

While the forces in the Gwalior territory were thus employed, General Roberts was engaged in a more important series of operations in Rajpootana. On the 1st of August, as we have seen, Roberts was sufficiently near Nuseerabad to send his sick to that station, where they could be better attended to than on the march; while he himself would be more free to make a rapid advance southward. Major Holmes, many days before, had been sent from Tonk by Roberts, with a force consisting of 120 Bombay Lancers, 220 of H.M. 72d foot, four companies of the 12th Bombay N.I., and four guns—to pursue the retreating rebels in a certain (or rather an uncertain) direction. The duty was a most harassing one. It was difficult to obtain reliable information of the route taken by the rebels; and even when the route was known, they never once allowed him to overtake them—so rapid were their movements. So important was it considered to catch these Gwalior mutineers, that the Bombay government (with whom the operations in Rajpootana rested) sent out small expeditionary forces from various places, according as probabilities offered for intercepting the mutineers. Thus, on the 1st of August, Major Taylor started from Neemuch with a force, consisting of 300 of H.M. 72d Highlanders, 400 of the 13th Bombay N.I., 180 of the 2d Light Cavalry, a few engineers, four guns, and a military train. It was believed that, on that day, about seven thousand of the Gwalior mutineers were somewhere between Chittore and Rampoora, a few miles distant from Neemuch; and Major Taylor entertained a hope that he might intercept and defeat them. We have already seen that General Roberts had had a most harassing duty, attended with very little success, seeing that he could seldom manage to reach a town or village in

JEYPOOR.

which the rebels had halted, until after they had taken their departure; and it was now Major Taylor's turn to share the same ill-luck. He returned to Neemuch on the 7th, disappointed. His advance-guard had seen the rebels near Rampoora in great force; yet the latter, though many times stronger than himself in troops, would not stand the chance of an engagement. The rebels escaped, and Taylor returned with his mission unfulfilled.

One advantage, at any rate, the British could count upon at this period—the fidelity of many native rajahs, who would have terribly complicated the state of affairs if they had joined the rebels. Tanteea Topee sounded the Rajah of Jeypoor, then the Rajah of Kotah, next the Rajah of Ulwar, all of them native princes of Rajpootana; and it was on account of the refusal of those rajahs to receive or countenance him, that the rebel made such strangely circuitous marches from one state to another. Whither he went, however, thither did Roberts follow him. The general, after sending his sick to Nusserabad, marched to Champaneer on the 4th, and to Deolia on the 5th. At that time, it was believed that the rebels, checked in some of their plans by the floods, had turned aside from Mandulghur to Deekodee, in the direction of Odeypore. On the 8th—after a forced march with 500 of H.M. 83d, 200 Bombay infantry, 60 Gujerat horse, and three guns—General Roberts came up with a body of rebels near Sanganeer (not Sanganeer near Jeypoor), where they occupied a line on the opposite side of the river Rotasery. He speedily routed them; but as usual, they fled too rapidly for him to overtake them; they made towards the Odeypore road. Roberts, again disappointed of his prey, was forced to rest his exhausted troops for a while.

The general, when Major Holmes had rejoined

him after a fruitless pursuit of the mutineers, again considered anxiously the conditions and possibilities of this extraordinary chase. He had, each day, to endeavour to discover the locality of the rebels, then to guess at their probable future movements, and, lastly, to lay plans for overtaking or intercepting them. On the 11th, they were supposed to be at Lawah; and on the 12th, they marched to the crest of the Chutterbhoog Ghaut, with a view of passing from Mewar into Marwar. Captain Hall, commanding at Erinpoora, held a post at the foot of this ghaut, with a small force sufficient to deter the rebels. They thereupon changed their plan, retraced their steps to some distance, and marched over a rocky country to Kattara or Katario, a village near the Nathdwara Hills; here they encamped on the 13th. Meanwhile General Roberts, with his force strengthened by that of Major Holmes, started from the vicinity of Sunganeer on the 11th, and by the evening of the 13th had marched sixty-seven miles. On that night he was at Kunkrowlee, within eight miles of the rebels; but his troops were too much exhausted to proceed further without a little rest. On the forenoon of the 14th he descried the enemy defiling through a very hilly country covered with rocks and loose stones; he had, in fact, reached Kattara, the village mentioned above. They took up an excellent position on a line of rocky hills, on the crest of which they planted four guns, which they began to work actively. Roberts thereupon sent Major Holmes by a detour into that region; for, even if the rebels were not overtaken, it would be desirable to give them no rest to consolidate their plans. At length the general had the gratification of overtaking and defeating these insurgents, in search of whom he had been so long engaged. He advanced his troops through the defile, his horse-artillery beating off the enemy until the infantry could form into line. After a brief period, the rebels shewed symptoms of retiring. On mounting the crest, the infantry saw them endeavouring to carry away two of their guns with a small escort; a volley soon set them to flight, and rendered the guns an easy capture. The flight soon became a rout; the rebels escaped in various directions, and the victors came upon a camp covered with arms and accoutrements. The cavalry and horse-artillery followed the fugitives for ten miles, cutting down great numbers. Roberts captured all the guns which the enemy had brought from Tonk, four elephants, a number of camels, and much ammunition—with surprisingly little loss to himself.

It was at this time regarded, by some of the authorities, as a hopeful symptom that the rebels were now descending to a part of India inhabited by Bheels and other half-civilised tribes, who would think much more of the wealth than of the so-called patriotism of the mutineers. Most of Tanteea Topee's men were laden with silver coin, their share of the booty from Gwalior; this cash they carried with them, although in food and clothing they were ill provided; and there was a probability that, if once they ceased to be a compact army, they would individually be robbed by the Bheel villagers. Nevertheless, whatever may have been the hope or expectation in this respect, Roberts and his officers could never intercept the treasure which Tanteea Topee was known to have with him. This treasure, consisting of jewels and money (except the share of plunder distributed among the men) was carried on elephants; and so well were those elephants guarded, whether during fighting or fleeing, that the British could never capture them.

Few of the troops in British service had had harder work with little brilliant result than those in General Roberts's Rajpootana Field-force. The country is wild and rugged, the weather was rainy and hot at the same time, and the duty intrusted to the troops was to chase an enemy who would not fight, and who were celebrated for their fleetness in escaping. Hence it was with more than usual pleasure that the hard-worked men regarded their victory at Kattara; they felt they had a fair claim to the compliment which their commander paid them, in a general order issued the day after the battle.*

After the victory at Kattara, Roberts left the further pursuit of the rebels for a time to Brigadier Parkes. This officer had started from Neemuch on the 11th with a miscellaneous force of about 1300 men, comprising 72d Highlanders, native infantry, Bombay cavalry, royal engineers, royal artillery, Bheels, and Mewar troopers. By a series of forced marches, Parkes headed the rebels in such a way as greatly to aid General Roberts at Kattara. A few days' sojourn having refreshed them, the troops were again brought into action. Tanteea Topee, by amazing quickness of movement, traversed a wide belt of country eastward to the river Chumbul, which he crossed near Sagoodar on the 20th. Continuing his route, he arrived at Julra Patteen, a town on the main road from Agra to Indore; it was on the confines of the Rajpoot and Mahratta territories, and was held by a petty chieftainess or Rana. After a brief conflict, in which he was assisted by a few of the troops of the Rana, who broke their allegiance, he captured the place, levied contributions on the inhabitants, and took possession of all the guns, treasure, and ammunition he could find. Here, then, this extraordinary conflict took a new turn; a new region had to be attended to, although against the same offender as before; and new columns had to be despatched in pursuit. The flooding of the river Chumbul cut

* The major-general commanding has sincere pleasure in congratulating the troops under his command on the great success achieved by them yesterday. All have shewn most conspicuous gallantry in action; and the patient unmurmuring endurance of fatigue during the recent forced marches has enabled them to close with an enemy proverbially active in movements. The horse-artillery and cavalry (the latter nineteen hours in the saddle) have by their spirit and alacrity completed the success, and inflicted a most signal punishment on the rebels. The major-general tenders his hearty thanks to all, and doubts not but their brave and earnest devotion will meet with the approval of his excellency the commander-in-chief.

off Roberts and Parkes for a time from a further pursuit of Tanteea Topee; and therefore two new columns were sent, one from Indore under Colonel Hope, and one from Mhow under Colonel Lockhart. The great point now was to prevent Tanteea from getting into Malwah, and thence crossing the Nerbudda into the Deccan.

Before treating of the operations against this leader in September, it may be well to see what progress was made in checking the rebel leader who had appeared in Scindia's territory—Man Singh. General Napier made up a new force, comprising certain regiments from his own and Brigadier Smith's brigades, and placed it under the command of Colonel Robertson, with baggage and vehicles so arranged as to facilitate rapid movement. Setting out from Paoree on the 27th of August, the colonel marched eighteen miles to Bhanore; on the 28th, nineteen miles to Gunneish; and so on for several days, until he reached Burrumpore, near the river Parbuttee. Here, on the 2d of September, he learned that a body of rebels, under Man Singh, were a few miles ahead, endeavouring to reach a fort which they might seize as a stronghold. Pushing on rapidly, Robertson came up with them on the 5th, near the village of Bujeepore. They had not kept a good look-out; they had no suspicion that an active British officer was at their heels; consequently, when Robertson came suddenly upon them with horse and foot, while they were preparing their morning meal, their panic was extreme. They fled through the village, over a hill, across a river, and into a jungle; but the pursuers were so close behind them that the slaughter was very considerable. These rebels were nearly all good troops, from Scindia's bodyguard and from the Gwalior Contingent; they were supposed to have been among the fugitives from Gwalior with Tanteea Topee, but at what time or in what locality they had separated from that leader, and joined Man Singh, was not clearly known. About the middle of the month, Colonel Robertson was at Goonah; Brigadier Smith was searching for Man Singh; while General Napier was watching for any symptoms of the approach of the last-named leader towards Gwalior or its vicinity.

While affairs were thus progressing in the Mahratta country during September, new efforts were made to meet the existing state of things a little further to the west. When Tanteea Topee crossed the Chumbul towards Julra Patteen, and when that river began to swell, General Roberts's Rajpootana Field-force was unable conveniently to continue the pursuit of the rebel; and, therefore, arrangements were made from the south. As a means of hemming in the rebels as much as possible, and preventing them from carrying their mischief into other regions, a 'Malwah Field-force' was sent up from Mhow, under General Michel. Tanteea Topee does not appear to have regarded Julra Patteen as a stronghold in which it was worth his while to remain; he plundered the place of some treasure and many guns, and then took his departure. He must, however, have wavered considerably in his plans; for he took a fortnight in reaching Rajghurh—a place only sixty miles distant. He was probably seeking for any rajah or chieftain who would join his standard. At Rajghurh, Tanteea Topee was joined by some of the beaten followers of Man Singh, probably by Man Singh himself, and seemed to be meditating an attack upon Bhopal. Tanteea and Michel were now both contending which should reach a particular station first, on the Bhopal and Seronj road, as the possession of that station (Beora) would give the holder a powerful command over the district—especially as it was one of the telegraph stations, by which Calcutta and Bombay held communication with each other. Michel came up with Tanteea Topee on the 15th of September, before he reached Beora. The rebels would not meet him openly in the field, but kept up a running-fight. When they saw defeat awaited them, they thought more of their elephant-loads of treasure than of their guns; they escaped with the former, and abandoned the latter, which they had brought from Julra Patteen. At the expense of one killed and three wounded, General Michel gained a victory which cost the enemy three hundred men, twenty-seven guns, a train of draught bullocks, and much ammunition.

Towards the close of September, Tanteea Topee was in this remarkable position. He was near Seronj, on the high road from Gwalior to Bhopal, looking for any outlet that might offer, or for any chieftain who would join his standard. Roberts was on the west of him; Napier, Smith, and Robertson were on his north; Michel, Hope, and Lockhart, on the south; and Whitlock on the east. Active he assuredly had been; for since the fall of Gwalior he and his mutineers and budmashes had traversed a vast area of the Rajpoot and Mahratta territories; but he was now within the limits of a cordon, from which there was little chance of his ultimate escape.

Of the other parts of India, it is scarcely necessary here to say anything. The course of peaceful industry had been little disturbed, and the civil government had been steadily in the ascendant. All round the west and south of Rajpootana did this state of things continue, and so downward into the long-established districts of Surat, Poonah, Bombay, &c. It is well to observe, however, that even in the Bombay presidency, slight occurrences shewed from time to time that the leaven of Hindustani 'pandyism' was working mischief. The safety of that army depended on an admixture of different creeds and castes in its ranks; there were in it Rajpoots and Brahmins, as in the (late) Bengal native army, and these elements were sometimes worked upon by fermenters of mischief. Generally speaking, however, these, as well as the other components of the Bombay army, behaved well. Their faithfulness was shewn in the month of August, in connection with a circumstance which might else have been productive of disaster. Among the troops quartered at Gwalior after its reconquest by Sir Hugh Rose was the 25th Bombay N. I., containing, like other regiments of the same army, a small proportion of Hindustani Oudians. A non-commissioned officer of this regiment, a havildar-major, went to the adjutant, and told him that a Brahmin pundit, one Wamun Bhut, was endeavouring to tamper with the Hindustanis of the regiment, and, through them, with the regiment generally; he also expressed an opinion that there were persons in the city of Gwalior concerned in this conspiracy. Captain Little, when informed by the adjutant of this communication, laid a plan for detecting the plotters. He found Havildar-major Koonjul Singh, Naik Doorga Tewarree, and private Sunnoo Ladh ready to aid him. These three native soldiers, pretending to bend to the Brahmin's solicitations, gradually learned many particulars of the conspiracy, which they faithfully revealed to the captain. A purwannah or written order was produced, from no less a personage than Nena Sahib, making

POONAH.

magnificent promises if the regiment, or any portion of it, would join his standard; they were to kill all their officers, and as many Europeans as possible, and then depart to a place appointed. At length, on the 29th, the naik made an appointment to meet the two chief conspirators, a Brahmin and a Mahratta chief, under a large tree near the camp; where the havildar-major would expect to have an opportunity of reading the purwannah. Captain Little, with the adjutant and the quartermaster, arranged to move suddenly to the spot at the appointed time: they did so; the conspirators were seized, and the document taken from them. Two other leaders in the plot were afterwards seized: all four were blown from guns on the 7th of September; and many others were placed in confinement on evidence furnished by the purwannah itself. It became evident that Nena Sahib, a Mahratta, had many emissaries at work in this Mahratta territory, although he himself was hiding in inglorious security far away.

Lord Elphinstone, governor of Bombay, with his commander-in-chief, Sir Henry Somerset, established several new corps, as means of gradually increasing the strength of the Bombay army. Two Belooch regiments, a 2d regiment of South Mahratta Horse, and a Bombay Naval Artillery Brigade, were among the new components of the army.

The South Mahratta country, lower down the peninsula than Bombay, had quite recovered from the disturbances which marked it in earlier months. Satara, Kolapore, Sawuntwaree, Belgaum—all were peaceful. On the eastern or Madras side of the peninsula, too, troubles were few. It is true, there was a repetition in September of a dispute which had occurred three months before, between natives who wished to bring up their children in their own faith, and missionaries who wished to convert those children to Christianity; but this was a source of discord which the governor, if firm, could readily allay. Lord Harris had not an Indian reputation like that of Lawrence or Elphinstone; but he had tact and decision enough for the duties of his office—the maintenance of peace in a presidency where there were few or no Hindustani sepoys.

Of the large country of the Deccan, Hyderabad, or the Nizam's dominions, nothing disastrous has to be told. A pleasant proof was afforded of the continuance of friendly relations between the British and the Nizam, by a grand banquet given at Hyderabad on the 2d of July by Salar Jung to Colonel Davidson. These two officers—the one prime-minister to the Nizam, the other British resident at the Nizam's court—had throughout the mutinies acted in perfect harmony and good faith. All the British officers and their families at Secunderabad, the cantonment of the Hyderabad Contingent, were invited. The guests came from Secunderabad to the Residency at Hyderabad, and thence on elephants and in palanquins to the minister's palace. The entertainment was in celebration of the birth of the Nizam's son, Meer Akbar Ally, heir to the throne of the Deccan; and everything was done, by an admixture of oriental magnificence with European courtesies, to render it worthy of the occasion. It was, however, not so much the grandeur of the banquet, as the sentiment it conveyed towards the British at a critical time, that rendered this proceeding on the part of the Nizam's prime-minister important. The Nizam's dominions were at that time the scene of party struggles between two sets of politicians—the adherents of Salar Jung, and those of Shumsul Oomrah; but both of the leaders were fortunately advocates of an English alliance.

The northwest portion of the Nizam's dominions, around Aurungabad and Jaulnah, in near neighbourhood to some of the Mahratta states, was troubled occasionally by bands of marauders, who hoped to establish a link of connection between the anarchists of Hindostan and those of the Deccan. They were, however, kept in check by Colonel Beatson, who brought his corps of irregulars, 'Beatson's Horse,' to Jaulnah, there to remain during the rainy season—maintaining order in the surrounding districts, and holding himself ready to march with his troopers to any disturbed region where their services might be needed.

HYDERABAD.

Government Buildings, Madras.—From a Drawing by Thomas Daniell.

CHAPTER XXXIII.

LAST DAYS OF THE EAST INDIA COMPANY'S RULE.

THE demise of the great East India Company has now to be recorded—the cessation of functions in the mightiest and most extraordinary commercial body the world ever saw. The natives of India never did and never could rightly understand the relations borne by the Company to the crown and nation of England. They were familiar with some such name as 'Koompanee;' but whether this Koompanee was a king, a queen, a viceroy, a minister, a council, a parliament, was a question left in a state of ludicrous doubt. And no wonder. It has at all times been difficult even for Englishmen, accustomed to the daily perusal of newspapers, to understand the relations between the Crown and the Company. Men asked whether the Punjaub was taken possession of by the Queen or by the Company; and if by the Queen, why the Company was made to bear the expense of the Punjaub war? So of the war in Persia, the annexation of Oude, the disastrous campaign in Afghanistan, the Burmese war—were these operations conducted by and for the Queen, or by and for the Company?—who was to blame if wrong?—who to bear the cost whether right or wrong?—who to reap the advantage? Even members of parliament gave contradictory answers to these and similar questions; nay, the cabinet ministers and the Court of Directors disputed on these very points. The Company was gradually shorn of its trading privileges by statutes passed in the years 1813, 1833, and 1853; and as its governing privileges had, in great part, gone over to the Board of Control, it seemed by no means clear for what purpose the Company continued to exist. There was a guarantee of $10\frac{1}{2}$ per cent. on £6,000,000 of India stock, secured out of the revenues of India—the stock to be redeemable by parliament at cent. per cent. premium after the year 1874; and it appeared as if the whole machinery of the Indian government was maintained merely to insure this dividend, and to obtain offices and emoluments for persons connected with the Company. The directors always disowned this narrow view of the Company's position; and there can be no doubt that many of them and of their servants had the welfare of the magnificent Indian empire deeply at heart. Still, the anomaly remained, of a governing body whose governing powers no one rightly understood.

When the Revolt began in 1857, the nation's cry was at once against the East India Company. The Company must have governed wrongly, it was argued, or this calamity would never have occurred. Throughout a period of six months did a storm of indignation continue, in speeches, addresses, lectures, sermons, pamphlets, books, reviews, magazines, and leading articles in newspapers. By degrees the inquiry arose, whether the directors were free agents in the mode of governing India; whether the Board of Control did not overrule them; and whether the disasters were not traceable fully as much to the Board as to the directors? Hence arose another question, whether the double government—by a Court sitting in Leadenhall Street, and a Board sitting in Cannon Row—was not an evil that ought to be abolished, even without reference to actual blame as concerning the Revolt? The virulent abuse of the Company was gradually felt to be unjust; but the unsatisfactory nature of the double government became more and more evident as the year advanced.

There was a preliminary or short session of parliament held in that year, during a few days before Christmas, for the consideration of special business arising out of the commercial disasters of the autumn; but as every one knew that India and its affairs must necessarily receive some notice, the speech from the throne was looked for with much eagerness. On the 3d of December, when parliament met, the ministers put into the Queen's mouth only this very brief allusion to projected changes in the Indian government: 'The affairs of my East Indian dominions will require your serious consideration, and I recommend them to your earnest attention.' These vague words were useless without a glossary; but the glossary was not forthcoming. Ministers, when questioned and sounded as to their plans, postponed all explanations to a later date.

The first public announcement of the intentions of the government was made shortly before Christmas. A General Court of Proprietors of the East India Company was held on the 23d of December, for the discussion of various matters relating to India; and, in the course of the proceedings, the chairman of the Company announced that, on the 19th, an official interview had been held, by appointment, with Lord Palmerston. On this occasion, the prime minister informed the Court of Directors that it was the intention of the ministry, early in the approaching year, to bring a bill into parliament for the purpose of placing the government of British India under the direct authority of the crown. In this interview, as in the royal speech, no matters of detail were entered upon. The members of parliament in the one assembly, the proprietors of East India stock in the other, were equally unable to obtain information concerning the provisions of the intended measure. All that could be elicited was, that the 'double government' of India would cease; and a written notice or letter to this effect was transmitted from the First Lord of the Treasury to the Court of Directors on the 23d.

During the period of six or seven weeks between the preliminary and the regular sessions, the journalists had full scope for their speculations. Those who, from the first, had attributed the Revolt in India to the Company's misgovernment, rejoiced in the hoped-for extinction of that body, and sketched delightful pictures of happy India under imperial sway. Those who supported the Company and vested interests, predicted the utter ruin of British influence in India if 'parliamentary government' were introduced—a mode of government, as they alleged, neither cared for nor understood by the natives of that region, and utterly unsuited to oriental ideas. Those, the moderate thinkers, who believed that on this as on other subjects the truth lies between two extremes, looked forward hopefully to such a change as might throw new vigour, and more advanced ideas, into the somewhat antiquated policy of the East India Company, without destroying those parts of the system which had been the useful growth of long experience. Many things had transpired during the year, tending to shew that the Court of Directors had been more prompt than the Board of Control, in matters requiring urgent attention; and that, therefore, whatever might be the evils of the double government, it would not be just to throw all the onus on the Company.

Early in January 1858, on a requisition to that effect, a special Court of Proprietors was summoned, to meet on the 15th, for considering 'the communication addressed to the Court of Directors from the government respecting the continuance of the powers of this Company.' At this meeting, it transpired that the directors had written to Lord Palmerston, just before the Christmas vacation; but as no cabinet council had been held in the interim, and as no reply to that letter had been received, it had been deemed most courteous towards the government to withhold the publication of the letter for a time. A long debate ensued. One of the proprietors brought forward a resolution to the effect, 'That the proposed transfer of the governing power of the East India Company to the crown is opposed to the rights and privileges of the East India Company, fraught with danger to the constitutional interests of England, perilous to the safety of the Indian empire, and calls for the resistance of this corporation by all constitutional means.' Many of the supporters of this resolution carried their arguments to the verge of extravagance—asserting that 'our Indian empire, already tottering and shaking, will fall to the ground without hope of recovery, if the East India Company should be abolished'—and that 'by means of the enormous patronage that would be placed in the hands of the government, ministers would possess the power of corrupting the people of this country beyond the hope of their ever recovering their virtue or their patriotism.' Most of the defenders of the Company, however, adopted a more moderate tone. Colonel Sykes, speaking for himself and some of his brother-directors, declared: 'If we believed for one moment that any change in the present administration of the government of India would be advantageous to the people of India, would advance their material interests, and promote their comforts, we should gladly submit to any personal suffering or loss contingent upon that change.' He added, however, 'By the indefeasible principles of justice, and the ordinary usages of our courts of law, it is always necessary that a bill of indictment with certain counts should be preferred before a man is condemned; and I am curious to know what will be the counts of the indictment in the case of this Company; for at present we have nothing but a vague outline before us.' Finally it was agreed to adjourn the discussion, on the ground that, until the views of the government had been further explained, it would be impossible to know whether the words of the resolution were true, that the proposed change would be 'fraught with danger to the constitutional interests of England, and perilous to the safety of the Indian empire.'

On the renewal of the debate at the India House, on January 20th, the directors presented a copy of a letter which they had addressed to the government on the last day of the old year. In this letter they said: 'The court were prepared to expect that a searching inquiry would be instituted into the causes, remote as well as immediate, of the mutiny in the Bengal native army. They have themselves issued instructions to the government of India to appoint a commission in view to such an inquiry; and it would have been satisfactory to them, if it had been proposed to parliament, not only to do the same, but to extend the scope of the inquiry to the conduct of the home government, for the purpose of ascertaining whether the mutiny could, wholly or partially, be ascribed to mismanagement on the part of the court acting under the control of the Board of Commissioners. But it has surprised the court to hear that her Majesty's government—not imputing, so far as the court are informed, any blame to the home authorities in connection with the mutiny, and without intending any inquiry by parliament, or awaiting the result of inquiry by the local government—should, even before the mutiny was quelled, and whilst considerable excitement prevailed throughout India, determine to propose the immediate supersession of the authority of the East India Company; who are entitled, at least, to the credit of having so administered the government of India, that the heads of all the native states, and the mass of the population, amid the excitements of a mutinous soldiery inflamed by unfounded apprehension of danger to their religion, have remained true to the Company's rule. The court would fail in their duty to your lordship and to the country if they did not express their serious apprehension that so important a change will be misunderstood by the people of India.' This letter failed to elicit any explanatory response from the government. Lord Palmerston, in a reply dated January 18th, after assuring the directors that their observations would be duly considered by the government, simply added: 'I forbear from entering at present into any examination of those observations and opinions; first, because any correspondence with you on such matters would be most conveniently carried on through the usual official channel of the president of the Board of Control; and, secondly, because the grounds on which the intentions of her Majesty's government have been formed, and the detailed arrangements of the measure which they mean to propose, will best be explained when that measure shall be submitted to the consideration of parliament.' The directors about the same time prepared a petition to both Houses of Parliament, explanatory of the reasons which induced them to deprecate any sudden transference of governing power from the Company to the Crown. As this petition was very carefully prepared, by two of the most eminent men in the Company's service; as it contains a considerable amount of useful information; and as it presents in its best aspects all that could be said in favour of the Company—it may fittingly be transcribed in the present work. To prevent interruption to the thread of the narrative, however, it will be given in the Appendix (A), as the first of a series of documents.*

When these various letters and petitions came under the notice of the Court of Proprietors, they gave rise to an animated discussion. Most of the proprietors admired the petition, as a masterly document; and many of the speakers dwelt at great length on the benefits which the Company had conferred upon India. One of the directors, Sir Lawrence Peel, feeling the awkwardness of dealing with a government measure not yet before them, said: 'I have not signed the petition which you have just heard read; and I will shortly state the reason why. I entirely concur in the praises which have been bestowed upon that document. It is a most ably reasoned and worded production; it does infinite credit to those whose work it is; and it is much to the honour of this establishment that it has talent capable of producing such a document. But I have not signed the petition, because I have not thought it a prudent course to petition against a measure, the particulars of which I am not acquainted with.' The debate was further adjourned from the 20th to the 27th, and then to the 28th, when the speeches ran to great length. On one or other of the four days of meeting, most of the directors of the Company expressed their opinions—on the 15th, Mr Ross D. Mangles (chairman), and Colonel Sykes; on the 20th, Sir Lawrence Peel and Captain Eastwick; on the 27th, Mr Charles Mills, Sir Henry Rawlinson, Captain Shepherd, Mr Macnaghten,

* Some of the documents here adverted to will be given *verbatim*; others in a condensed form.

and Sir F. Currie (deputy-chairman); on the 28th, Mr Prinsep and Mr Willoughby. As might have been expected, a general agreement marked the directors' speeches; they were the arguments of men who defended rights which they believed to be rudely assailed. Some of the directors complained that the government notice was not explicit enough. Some thought that, at any rate, it clearly foreshadowed the destruction of the Company's power. Some contended that, if the Company did not speak out at once, it would in a few weeks be too late. Some insisted that the government brought forward the proposed measure in order to shift the responsibility for the mutiny to other shoulders. Some accused the ministers of being influenced by a grasping for patronage, a desire to appropriate the nominations to appointments. One of the few who departed from the general tone of argument was Sir Henry Rawlinson, who assented neither to the resolution nor to the petition. He dwelt at some length on the two propositions mainly concerned—namely, 'that the transfer of the government of India to the Crown would be unjust to the East India Company;' and that such transfer 'would be fatal to British rule in India.' Most of the other speakers had contended or implied that the first clause of this statement involved the second; that the transfer would be equally unjust to the Company, and injurious to India. Sir Henry combated this. He contended that the connection was not a necessary one. After a very protracted debate, the original resolution was passed almost unanimously; and then the petition to both Houses of Parliament was sanctioned as that of the Company generally.

Just at this period, the directors caused to be prepared, and published at a cheap price, an elaborate '*Memorandum of the Improvements in the Administration of India during the last Thirty Years.*' It was evidently intended to fall into the hands of such members of parliament as might be disposed to take up the cause of the Company in the forthcoming debates, and to supply them with arguments in favour of the Company, derived from a recital of the marked improvements introduced in Indian government. To this extent, it was simply a brief placed in the hands of counsel; but the *Memorandum* deserves to be regarded also in a historical light; for nothing but a very narrow prejudice could blind an observer to the fact that vast changes had been introduced into the legislative and administrative rule of India, during the period indicated, and that these changes had for the most part been conceived in an enlightened spirit—corresponding in direction, if not in intensity, with the improved state of public opinion at home on political subjects.

Parliament reassembled for the regular session on the 4th of February, fully alive to the importance of attending to all matters bearing on the welfare of India. Earl Grey, on the 11th, presented to the House of Lords the elaborate petition from the East India Company, lately adverted to. Characterising this as a 'state paper deserving the highest commendation,' the earl earnestly deprecated the abolition of the Court of Directors, and the transfer of their authority to the ministry of the day; grounding his argument on the assumption that the interposition of an independent body, well informed on Indian affairs, between the government and the natives of that country, was essential to the general welfare. He admitted the need for reform, but not abolition. The Duke of Argyll, on the part of the government, admitted that the Company's petition was temperate and dignified, but denied that its reasoning was conclusive. The Earl of Ellenborough, agreeing that the Queen's name would be powerfully influential as the direct ruler of India, at the same time doubted whether any grand or sweeping reform ought to be attempted while India was still in revolt. The Earl of Derby joined in this opinion, and furthermore complained of discourtesy shewn by the ministers toward the directors, in so long withholding from them a candid exposition of the provisions of the intended measure.

On the following day, the 12th of the month, the long-expected bill was introduced to the House of Commons by Lord Palmerston—or rather, leave to bring in the bill was moved. The first minister of the Crown, in his speech on the occasion, disowned any hostility to the Company, in reference either to the Revolt or to matters of general government. He based the necessity for the measure on the anomaly of the Company's position. When the commercial privileges were withdrawn, chiefly in 1833, the Company (he urged) became a mere phantom of what it had been, and subsided into a sort of agency of the imperial government, without, however, responsibility to parliament. Admitting the advantages of checks as securities for honesty and efficiency in administrative affairs, he contended that check and counter-check had been so multiplied in the 'double government' of India, as to paralyse action. He considered that complete authority should vest where complete responsibility was expected, and not in an irresponsible body of merchants. His lordship concluded by giving an outline of the bill by which the proposed changes were to be effected.

As the Palmerston Bill, or 'India Bill, No. 1,' as it was afterwards called, was not passed into a law, it will not be necessary to reprint it in this work; nevertheless, to illustrate its bearing on the subsequent debates, the pith of its principal clauses may usefully be given here: The government of the territories under the control of the East India Company, and all powers in relation to government vested in or exercised by the Company, to become vested in and exercised by the sovereign—India to be henceforth governed in the Queen's name—The real and personal property of the Company to be vested in Her Majesty for the purposes of the government of India—The appointments of governor-general of India, with ordinary members of the Council of India, and governors of the three presidencies, now made by the directors of the Company with the approbation of her Majesty, and other appointments, to be made by the Queen under her royal sign-manual—A council to be established, under the title of 'The President and Council for the Affairs of India,' to be appointed by her Majesty—This council to consist of eight persons, exclusive of its president—In the first nomination of this council, two members to be named for four years, two for six, two for eight, and two for ten years—The members of council to be chosen from among persons who had been directors of the East India Company, or ten years at least in the service of the Crown or Company in India, or fifteen years simply resident in India—Members of council, like the judges, only to be removable by the Queen, on an address from both Houses of Parliament—The president of the council eligible to sit in the Commons House of Parliament—Four members of council to form a quorum—Each ordinary member to receive a yearly salary of £1000; and the president to receive the salary of a secretary of state—The council to exercise the power now vested in the Company and the Board of Control; but a specified number of cadetships to be given to sons of civil and military servants in India—Appointments hitherto made in India to continue to be made in that country—Military forces, paid out of the revenues of India, not to be employed beyond the limits of Asia—Servants of the Company to become servants of the crown—The Board of Control to be abolished.

Such was the spirit of the bill which Lord Palmerston asked leave to introduce. Mr T. Baring moved as an amendment, 'That it is not at present expedient to legislate for the government of India.' Thereupon a debate arose, which extended through three evenings. The government measure was supported by speeches from Lord Palmerston, Sir Erskine Perry, Mr Ayrton, Sir Cornwall Lewis, Mr Roebuck, Mr Lowe, Mr Slaney, Sir W. Rawlinson, Mr A. Mills, Sir Charles Wood, and Lord John Russell; while it was opposed on various grounds by Mr T. Baring, Mr Monckton Milnes, Sir J. Elphinstone, Mr Ross D. Mangles, Mr Whiteside, Mr Liddell, Mr Crawford, Colonel Sykes, Mr Willoughby, Sir E. B. Lytton, and Mr Disraeli. The reasonings in favour of the government measure were such as the following: That the proper time for legislation had come, when the attention of the country was strongly directed to Indian affairs; that all accounts from India shewed that some great measure was eagerly expected; that it was dangerous any longer to maintain an effete, useless, and cumbrous machine, which the Court of Directors had virtually become; that the Company's 'traditionary policy' unfitted it to march with the age in useful reforms; that as the Board of Control really possessed the ruling power, the double government was a sham as well as an obstruction; that the princes of India felt themselves degraded in being the vassals and tributaries of a mere mercantile body; that, such was the anomaly of the double government, it was possible that the Company might be at war with a power with which her Majesty was at peace, thus involving the nation in inextricable embarrassment; that, with the exception of a very small section of the covenanted civil servants, the European community and the officers of the Indian army would prefer the government of the crown to that of the Company; that the natives of India having been thrown into doubt concerning the intentions of the Company to interfere with their religion, some authoritative announcement of the Queen's respect for their views on that subject would be very satisfactory; and that as the native Bengal army had disappeared, as India must in future be garrisoned by a large force of royal troops, and as the military power would then belong to the crown, it was desirable that the political power should go with it. Among the pleas urged on the opposite side were such as follow: That the natives of India would anticipate an increased stringency of British power, under the proposed *régime;* that the ministerial influence and patronage, in Indian matters, would be dangerous to England herself; that as the Whig and Conservative parties had both supported the system of double government in the India Bill of 1853, there was no reason for making this sudden change in 1858; that before any change of government was effected, it was imperatively necessary that an inquiry should be made into the causes and circumstances of the Revolt; that the direct exercise of governing power by a queen, formally designated 'Defender of the Faith,' could not be agreeable either to the Hindoos or the Mohammedans of India, whose ideas of 'faith' were so widely different from those of Christians; that, as all previous organic changes in the administration of the government of India had been preceded by an inquiry into the character of that government, so ought it in fairness to be in the present case; that if the proposed change were effected, European theories and novelties, owing to the pressure of public opinion on the ministry, would be attempted to be grafted on Asiatic prejudices and immobility, without due regard to the inherent antagonism of the two systems; and that the enormous extent, population, revenue, and commerce of India ought not to be imperiled by a measure, the consequences of which could not at present be foreseen.

This debate ended on the 18th; the House of Commons, by a majority of 318 to 173, granting leave for the introduction of the bill—it being understood that a considerable time would elapse before the second reading, in order that the details of the measure might be duly considered by all who took an interest in the matter.

Before, however, any very great attention could be given to the subject, either in or out of parliament, a most unexpected change took place in the political relations of the government. The same minister who, on the 18th of February, obtained leave to bring in the India Bill, was placed on the 19th in a minority which led to the resignation of himself and his colleagues. Circumstances connected with an attempted assassination of the Emperor of the French induced the Palmerston government to bring in a measure which proved obnoxious to the House of Commons; the measure was rejected by 234 against 219, and the government accordingly resigned. So far as concerned the immediate effect, the most important fact connected with India was the offer by the Earl of Derby, the new premier, of the presidency of the India Board to the Earl of Ellenborough. This nobleman had long been in collision with the East India Company and its civil servants. Twice already had he been president of the Board of Control, and in 1842-3-4 he had filled the responsible office of governor-general of India. In both offices, and at all times, he had cherished as much as possible the royal influence in India against the Company's, the military against the civil. As a consequence, his enemies were bitter, his friends enthusiastic. The author of an anonymous 'red pamphlet,' which attracted much notice during the Revolt, spoke of the Earl of Ellenborough as the one great man who could alone be the saviour of India—as the chivalrous knight who would shiver to atoms the 'vested rights' and 'traditionary policy' of the Court of Directors. It was natural, therefore, that the accession of the earl to the new government should be regarded as an important matter, either for good or evil.

It speedily became apparent that the new president of the Board of Control would find difficulty in framing a line of proceeding on Indian affairs. His own predilections were quite as much against the Company, as those of his predecessor; but many of his colleagues in the Derby government had committed themselves, when out of office, to a defence of the Company, and to a condemnation of any immediate alteration in the Indian government. Either he must change his opinions, or they belie their own words. The Court of Directors would fain have expected indulgent treatment from the Derby administration, judging from the speeches of the two preceding months; but their past experience of the Earl of Ellenborough threw a damp over their hope.

Three weeks after the vote which occasioned the change of government, Lord Palmerston proposed the postponement of the second reading of his India Bill until the 22d of April—a further lapse of six weeks; and this was agreed to. He would not withdraw the bill, because he still adhered to its provisions; he would not at once proceed with it, because his opponents were now in office, and he preferred to see what course they would adopt. The fate of India was thus placed in suspense for several weeks, simply through a party struggle arising out of French affairs; the great question—'Who shall govern India?'—was made subservient to party politics.

Although Lord Palmerston had named the 22d of April as the day for reconsidering his India Bill, this did not tie down the Derby ministry to the adoption of any particular line of policy. After many discussions in the cabinet, it was resolved that the ministers should 'eat their words' by legislating for India, although it had before been declared a wrong time for so doing; and that, throwing Lord Palmerston's bill aside, a new India Bill should be introduced.

Accordingly, on the 26th of March, Mr Disraeli, the new Chancellor of the Exchequer, moved for leave to bring in that which was afterwards called the 'India Bill No. 2.' As in a former instance, this bill may be most usefully rendered intelligible by a condensed summary: A secretary of state for India, to be appointed by the Queen—This secretary to be president of a Council of India—The council to consist of eighteen persons, nine nominated and nine elected—The nominated councillors to be appointed under the royal sign-manual by the crown, and to represent nine distinct interests—Those nine interests to be represented as follow: the first councillor to have belonged for at least ten years to the Bengal civil service; the second to the Madras service; the third to the Bombay service; and the fourth to the Upper or Punjaub provinces, under similar conditions; the fifth to have been British resident at the court of some native prince; the sixth to have served at least five years with the Queen's troops in India; the seventh, to have served the Company ten years in the Bengal army; and the eighth and ninth, similarly in the Madras and Bombay armies—The nine nominated members to be named in the bill itself, so as to give them parliamentary as well as royal sanction—The remaining eight members of the council to be chosen by popular election—Four of such elected members to be chosen from among persons who had served the Crown or the Company at least ten years in any branch of the Indian service, or had resided fifteen years in India; and to be chosen by persons who had been ten years in the service of the Crown or the Company, or possessed £1000 of India stock, or possessed £2000 of capital in any Indian railway or joint-stock public works—The other five of such elected members to be chosen from among persons who, for at least ten years, had been engaged in the commerce of India, or in the export of manufactured articles thither; and to be chosen by the parliamentary constituencies of five large centres of commerce and manufactures in the United Kingdom, namely, London, Liverpool, Manchester, Glasgow, and Belfast—the Secretary of State for India to have the power of dividing the council, thus constituted, into committees, and to exercise a general supervision over these committees—The secretary alone, or six councillors in union, to have power to summon a meeting of the council—The councillors not to be eligible to sit in parliament, but to have each £1000 per annum for their services—The patronage heretofore exercised by the East India Company to be now exercised by the Council—The army of India not to be directly affected by the bill—The revenues of India to bear the expenses of the government of India—A royal commission to be sent to India, to investigate all the facts and conditions of Indian finance.

It will be seen that this remarkable scheme was based on the idea of conciliating as many different interests as possible, in England and in India. Mr Disraeli, in the course of his speech, mentioned the names of the nine gentlemen whom it was proposed to nominate to the council on the part of the crown; and in relation to the vast powers of the secretary and council, he said: 'To establish a British minister with unrestricted authority, subject to the moral control of a body of men who by their special knowledge, their independence, their experience, their distinction, and their public merit, are, nevertheless, invested with an authority which can control even a despotic minister, and which no mere act of parliament can confer upon them, is, I admit, no ordinary difficulty to encounter; and to devise the means by which it may be accomplished is a task which only with the indulgence of this House and with the assistance of parliament we can hope to perform.'

Criticisms were much more numerous and contradictory on this than on Lord Palmerston's bill. It was no longer a contest of Conservatives against Whigs. The new bill was examined on its merits. The friends of the East India Company, expecting something favourable from the change of government, were much disappointed; they analysed the clauses of the bill, but found not what they sought. True, the old Indian interests were to be represented in the new council; but just one-half of the members were to be nominees of the crown, and five others were to be elected by popular constituencies over which the Company possessed no control. Even those who cared little whether the Company lived or died, provided India were well governed, differed among themselves in opinion whether the popular element would be usefully introduced in the manner proposed. The objections were more extensively urged out of parliament than within; for after the first reading of the bill, on the 26th of March, the further consideration of it was postponed to the 19th of April.

The Conservatives had reproved the Whigs for discourtesy to the East India Company, in not giving due notice of the provisions of 'Bill No. 1;' but now equal discourtesy (if discourtesy it were) was shewn by the first-named party in reference to 'Bill No. 2.' On the 24th of March, at a quarterly meeting of the Company, and only two days before Mr Disraeli introduced his measure—or rather the Ellenborough measure—into the House of Commons, the chairman of the Court of Directors was asked whether he knew aught concerning the provisions of a bill so nearly touching the interests of the Company; to which he replied: 'I know no more about the forthcoming bill than I knew of the last before its introduction into parliament.' On the 7th of April, however, at a special Court of Proprietors, the directors presented copies of the bills, 'No. 1' and 'No. 2;' and at the same time presented a Report against both. In the debate, on the 7th and 13th, arising out of the presentation of the Report, there was a pretty general opinion among the proprietors, that if Lord Palmerston's India Bill was bad, Mr Disraeli's was not one whit better, in reference to the interests of the Company; and there was a final vote for the following resolution: 'That this court concur in the opinion of the Court of Directors, that neither of the bills now before parliament is calculated to secure good government to India; and they accordingly authorise and request the Court of Directors to take such measures as may appear to them desirable for resisting the passing of either bill through parliament, and for introducing into any bill for altering the constitution of the government of India such conditions as may promise a system of administration calculated to promote the interests of the people of India, and to prove conducive to the general welfare.' One of the proprietors having expressed an opinion that the directors ought to prepare a third bill, more just than either of the other two, the chairman very fairly pointed out that it was not the Company's duty so to do.

Under somewhat unfavourable circumstances did the Derby ministry renew the consideration of Indian affairs after the Easter recess. Parliament, it is true, had not yet had time or opportunity to criticise 'Bill No. 2;' but that measure had been very unfavourably received both by the East India Company and by the newspaper press; and it became generally known that the ministers would gladly accept any decent excuse for abandoning or at least modifying the bill. This excuse was furnished to them by Lord John Russell. On the 12th of April, when the Commons resumed their sittings after the Easter vacation, his lordship expressed an opinion that the bill was ill calculated to insure the desired end; that its discussion was likely to be disfigured by a party contest; and that it would be better to agree to a set of resolutions in committee, on which a new bill might be founded. Mr Disraeli accepted this suggestion with an eagerness which led many members to surmise that a private compact had been made in the matter. He suggested that Lord John Russell should draw up the resolutions; but as his lordship declined this task, Mr Disraeli undertook it on the part of the government. Hereupon a new phase was presented by the debate. One member expressed his astonishment that the Chancellor of the Exchequer should be so ready to hand over the functions of government to the care of a private member. Another declared he could not see what advantage was to be gained by a resolution in committee in lieu of a bill in the whole House. The members of the late Whig government all condemned the plan suggested by Lord John and accepted by Mr Disraeli; but, pending the introduction of the proposed resolutions, they would not frustrate the plan. Mr Mangles, on the part of the East India Company, expressed an earnest hope that all party feeling would be excluded from the debates on India. The East India Company, he remarked, could hardly be expected to acquiesce in a measure for their own extinction; nevertheless, if such should be proved to be inevitable, the directors would give their best assistance to the perfecting of any measure which the House might think proper to adopt. Mr Disraeli finally promised to prepare a set of resolutions, and to bring them in for discussion on the 26th.

The state, then, to which this intricate discussion had been brought was this—the 'Bill No. 1,' proposed by Lord Palmerston, stood over for a second reading on the 22d of April; the 'Bill No. 2,' proposed by Mr Disraeli, was placed in abeyance for a time; while the 'resolutions,' to be prepared by Mr Disraeli on the suggestion of Lord John Russell, and intended as a means of improving 'Bill No. 2,' or perhaps of leading to a 'Bill No. 3,' were to be introduced on the 26th of April. It was pretty generally felt, both within and without the walls of parliament, that the whole subject was in great confusion, and that the ministers themselves had no definite notion of the best course to pursue. At the meeting of the East India Company on the 13th, Mr Mangles, who was a member of parliament as well as chairman of the Company, said: 'After the extraordinary occurrences we have witnessed within the last six weeks, in which we have seen a minister ousted who was supposed to have the support of a most commanding majority, and another minister placed in power without having a majority, or even a considerable minority, he would be a very bold man who would prophesy what the fate of any new measure in the House of Commons would be.'

On the 23d of April, Mr Disraeli announced his intention of abandoning 'Bill No. 2' altogether, and of postponing the preparation of 'Bill No. 3' until the House should have agreed to any 'resolutions' bearing on the subject. Lord Palmerston would not withdraw his 'Bill No. 1;' he simply held it in abeyance for a time, to watch the course of pending events. On the 26th, Mr Disraeli craved four days more for the preparation of his resolutions. He made a speech, in which he praised his own 'Bill No. 2' at the expense of his antagonist's 'Bill No. 1;' but, as he had 'voluntarily stifled his own baby'—to use the illustration of another speaker—his arguments fell with little force. The illustration, in truth, was so tempting, that it was long made use of both in and out of parliament. Lord Palmerston said: 'The measure, upon which the right honourable gentleman has pronounced so unbounded a funeral panegyric, has been murdered by himself. If he thought so well of the merits of the bill, why did he kill it?' Mr Gregory, wishing, by getting rid of the proposed 'resolutions,' to postpone all legislation on the subject until another year, moved as an amendment—'That at this moment it is not expedient to pass any resolutions for the future government of India.' A general desire prevailed in the House, however, that some measure or other should be passed into a law, to strengthen and render more definite the governing authority in India; and the amendment was withdrawn.

At length, on the 30th of April, the resolutions were proposed. They departed very widely from 'Bill No. 2.' The members of the council, instead of being definitely eighteen in number, were to be 'not less than twelve and not more than eighteen.' The scheme for representing classes, services, presidencies, and commercial communities in the council was given up; as was likewise the election of a portion of the members by parliamentary constituencies. As the whole of the fourteen resolutions, if agreed to, would require a separate agreement for each, and as every member would be allowed to speak on every resolution if he so chose, there were the materials presented for a very lengthened debate. There was a preliminary discussion, moreover, on a motion intended to extinguish the resolutions altogether. Lord Harry Vane moved—'That the change of circumstances since the first proposal by her Majesty's late advisers, to transfer the government of India from the East India Company to the Crown, renders it inexpedient to proceed further with legislation on the subject during the present session.' This proposal, however, was negatived by 447 to 57.

It would scarcely be possible, and scarcely worth while if possible, to follow all the intricacies of the debate on the 'resolutions.' Every part of the India question was opened again and again; every speaker considered himself at liberty to wander from principles to details, and back again; and hence the amount of speaking was enormous. Should there be a secretary of state for India, or only a president of a council? Should there be a council at all, or only a secretary with his subordinates, as in the home, foreign, colonial, and war departments? If a council, should it be wholly nominated, wholly elective, or part of each? Who should nominate, and who elect, and under what conditions? Should the secretary or president possess any power without his council, and how much? Should the East India Company, or not, be represented in the new council? By whom should the enormous patronage of the Court of Directors be hereafter exercised? What would become of the 'vested rights' of the Company, such as the receipt of dividends on the East India stock? In what relation would the governor-general of India stand to the new council? Would the local governments of the three presidencies be interfered with? Who would organise and support the Indian army? What would be done in relation to missionaries, idolatrous practices, caste, education, public works, manufactures, commerce,

&c., in India ?—These were some of the questions which were discussed, not once merely, but over and over again. Owing to the strange ministerial changes, the independent members in the House had had but few opportunities of fully expressing their sentiments; they did so now, at ample length. Many long nights of debate were spent over the resolutions; many amendments proposed; many alterations assented to by the ministers. It occupied three evenings—April 30, May 3, and May 7—to settle the first three resolutions; or rather, to agree to the first, to modify the second, and to withdraw the third. At this period occurred the exciting episode concerning the Oude proclamation, the censure of Viscount Canning, and the resignation of the Earl of Ellenborough.* As there was now no president of the Board of Control, the India resolutions could not conveniently be proceeded with; and therefore everything remained for a time at a dead-lock. Soon afterwards Lord Stanley, son of the Earl of Derby, accepted the seals of the office vacated by the Earl of Ellenborough. He had every claim to the indulgence of the House, in the difficulty of his new position; and this indulgence was willingly shewn to him; he was permitted to choose his own time, after the ceremony of his re-election, to bring the great question of India once again before the Commons House, in the hope of arriving at some practicable solution. For a period of one full month did the further consideration of the resolutions remain in abeyance, while these party tactics and ministerial changes were engaging public attention.

At length, on the 7th of June, when the subject was resumed, and when Lord Stanley took the lead on Indian affairs in the House of Commons, it began to be apparent that the resolutions were less valued by the government than they had before been. The debate concerning them, however, continued. When the time came for deciding how many members should compose the new Council of India, Mr Gladstone reopened the whole question by moving as an amendment, 'That, regard being had to the position of affairs in India, it is expedient to constitute the Court of Directors of the East India Company, by an act of the present session, to be a council for administering the government of India in the name of her Majesty, under the superintendence of such responsible minister, until the end of the next session of parliament.' Mr Gladstone proposed this amendment under a belief that it was not practicable, during the existing session of parliament, to perfect a scheme of government for India that would be worthy of the nation. The problem to be solved was one of the most formidable ever presented to any nation or any legislature in the history of the world, and the evils of delay would be insignificant in comparison with those of crude and hasty legislation. His suggestion, he contended, would not be inconsistent with the appointment of a new council in the following year, if it should be deemed desirable to make such appointment. Lord Stanley opposed this amendment—on the grounds that it had all the evils of a temporary and provisional measure; that the directors, as a council merely for one year, would be placed in an inconvenient position; that having been told that they were doomed, and that nothing could save them as a permanent body, they would slacken their zeal and energy, and impair the confidence of the public; that the much-condemned delays would still continue; and that the public service would derive no advantage. The friends of the East India Company supported this amendment; but it was rejected by 265 against 116. Mr Roebuck then made an attempt to extinguish the council both in theory and in fact. He contended that a Secretary of State, alone responsible for all his acts, relying upon his own mind for guidance and counsel, and having a more direct interest in doing right, was morally and mentally the best governor for India; he feared that a council would render the governing body practically irresponsible to the nation. Lord Stanley, on the other hand, insisted that it was quite impossible for any minister to act efficiently in such a difficult office without the aid of advisers possessing special information on Indian affairs; and as the House generally concurred in this view, Mr Roebuck's amendment was negatived without a division. Two evenings, June 7th and 11th, were spent in discussing two resolutions. On the 14th the House was engaged many hours in considering whether the council should be elective, or nominated, or both; great diversity of opinion prevailed; and the speakers, tempted by the peculiarity of the subject, wandered very widely beyond the limits of the immediate question. Lord John Russell thought that the members of the council ought to be wholly appointed by the Crown, on the responsibility of the minister; Sir James Graham thought that the Court of Directors ought to be *ex officio* members of the council, to insure practical knowledge on Indian affairs; but Lord Stanley contended that the advantages of two systems would be combined if one half of the council were nominated by the Crown, and the other half elected by a constituency of seven or eight thousand persons interested in or connected with Indian affairs; and the House, agreeing with this view, voted a resolution accordingly.

Midsummer was approaching. The House of Lords had not yet had an opportunity of discussing the Indian question either in principle or in detail; and it began now to be strongly felt that, as the resolutions really did not bind the Commons to any particular clauses in the forthcoming bill, their value was doubtful. Accordingly, on the 17th of June, after a long discussion on desultory topics, Lord Stanley proposed, amid some laughter in the House, to withdraw all the remaining resolutions—a proposition that was assented to with great alacrity, shewing that the legislators were

* See Chap. xxvii., p. 461.

by no means satisfied with the wisdom of their past proceedings.

Thus was completed the third stage in this curious legislative achievement. Lord Palmerston's 'India Bill No. 1' was laid aside, because he was expelled from office; Mr Disraeli's 'India Bill No. 2' was abandoned, because it was ridiculed on all sides; and now the 'resolutions' were given up when half-finished, because they were found to be inoperative and non-binding. Some of the supporters of the East India Company claimed, and not illogically, a little more respect for the Company than had lately been given; the difficulty of framing a new government for India shewed, by implication, that the old *régime* was not so bad as had been customarily asserted.

The 'India Bill No. 3' was brought in by Lord Stanley on the evening (June 17th) which witnessed the withdrawal of the resolutions. The bill comprised sixty-six clauses—of the more important of which a brief outline may be given here, to furnish means of comparison with bills 'No. 1' and 'No. 2:' The government of India to revert from the Company to the Crown—A Secretary of State to exercise all the powers over Indian affairs hitherto exercised by the Court of Directors, the Secret Committee, and the Board of Control—The Crown to determine whether to give these powers to one of the four existing secretaries of state, or to appoint a fifth—The Secretary to be assisted by a 'Council of India,' to consist of fifteen persons—The Court of Directors to elect seven of those members from among its own body, or from among persons who had at any time been directors; the remaining eight to be nominated by the Queen—Vacancies in the council to be filled up alternately by the Crown and by the council assembled for that purpose—A majority of all the members to be chosen from among persons who had served or resided at least ten years in India—Every councillor to be irremovable during good behaviour, to be prohibited from sitting in the House of Commons, to receive twelve hundred pounds a year as salary, to be allowed to resign when he pleases, and to be entitled to a retiring pension varying in amount according to the length of service—Compensation to be given to such secretaries or clerks of the Company as do not become officers of the new department—The Secretary of State to be president of the 'Council of India,' to divide the council into committees for the dispatch of business, and to appoint any member as vice-president—Council meetings to be called by the Secretary, or by any five members; and five to be a quorum—Questions to be decided in the council by a majority, but the Secretary to have a *veto* even over the majority—The Secretary may send and receive 'secret' dispatches, without consulting his council at all—Most of the appointments in India to be made as heretofore—Patronage of cadetships to be exercised partly by the council, but principally by the Secretary of State, and to be given in a certain ratio to sons of persons who have filled military or civil offices in India—The property, credits, debits, and liabilities of the Company, except India stock and its dividends, to be transferred from the Company to the Crown; and the council to act as trustees in these matters—The council to present annual accounts to parliament of Indian finance and all matters relating thereto—The council to guarantee the legalised dividend on India stock, out of the revenues of India.

The 'Bill No. 3,' of which the above is a slight programme, came on for second reading on the 24th of June. Lord Stanley—who, as admitted by opponents as well as supporters, entered with great earnestness upon the duties of his office—stated that he had endeavoured to avail himself of all the opinions expressed during the various debates, to prepare a measure that should meet the views of a majority of the House. In the discussion that ensued, Mr Bright wandered into subjects that could not possibly be treated in the bill; he re-opened the whole topic of Indian misgovernment—disapproved of governor-generals—condemned annexations—suggested new presidencies and new tribunals—and told the Commons how he would govern India if he were minister. The speech was vigorous, but inapplicable to the subject-matter in hand. The bill was read a second time without a division.

The East India Company were not silent at this critical period in their history. A meeting of proprietors on the 23d was made special for the consideration of 'Bill No. 3,' which was to be read a second time in the Commons on the following day; and at this meeting there was a general expression of disappointment that the Company had been treated as such a nullity. The only source of consolation was in the fact that seven members of the new council were to be chosen by the Court of Directors, from persons who then belonged or had formerly belonged to that court. The opinions of the Company were embodied in a letter addressed to Lord Stanley by the chairman and deputy-chairman, and presented to the House of Commons.

On the 25th, the House went into committee on the bill. Lord Palmerston proposed two amendments—that the members should be twelve in number instead of fifteen, and that all should be appointed by the Crown; but both amendments were rejected by large majorities as being inconsistent with the recent expression of opinion. At a further sitting on the 1st of July, the ministers shewed they had obtained a considerable hold on the House; for they succeeded in obtaining the rejection of amendments proposed by Lord Palmerston, Mr Gladstone, Sir James Graham, and Mr Vernon Smith. Lord Stanley, however, proposed many amendments himself on the part of the government; and these amendments were accepted in so friendly a spirit, that a large number of clauses were got through by the end of a long sitting on the 2d of July. One of the most interesting of the questions discussed bore relation to the Secret Committee of the past, and the proposed exercise of similar powers by the Secretary of State. Lord John Russell and Mr Mangles advocated the abolition of those powers altogether; while Sir G. C. Lewis recommended great caution in their exercise, if used. Mr Mangles, the late chairman of the Court of Directors, stated that the powers of the Secret Committee had been much more extensive than was generally supposed. 'During many years after the conquest of Sinde, the whole government of that province was conducted by the Secret Committee, and the Court of Directors knew nothing about it. He believed that much mischief had arisen from the Secret Committee undertaking to transact business with which it had no right to interfere. The real fact was, that nine-tenths of that which came before the Secret Committee might with safety be communicated to the whole world. He wished, therefore, that there should be no Secret Committee in future. It was a mere delusion and snare. The Court of Directors had shewn themselves to be as competent to keep a secret, when there was one, as the cabinet of her Majesty; and he had no reason to think otherwise of the proposed Indian Council.' The ministers, however, received the support of Lord Palmerston in this matter; and the continuance of the secret powers was sanctioned, although by a small majority only. On the 5th and 6th, the remaining clauses and amendments were gone through. Mr Gladstone proposed a clause enacting, 'That, except for repelling actual invasion, or under sudden or urgent necessity, her Majesty's forces in India shall not be employed in any military operation beyond the external frontier of her Indian possessions, without the consent of parliament.' Lord Palmerston opposed this clause; but Lord Stanley assented to it as a wholesome declaration of parliamentary power; and it was agreed to.

At length, on the 8th of July—five months after 'Bill No. 1' had been introduced by Lord Palmerston, and three or four months after the introduction of 'Bill No. 2' by Mr Disraeli—'Bill No. 3' was passed by the House of Commons, after a vehement denunciation by Mr Roebuck, who predicted great disaster from the organisation of the 'Council of India.' Lord Palmerston's bill was withdrawn on the next day; it never came on for a second reading.

The House of Lords justly complained of the small amount of time left to them for the discussion of the bill; but there was now no help for it, short of abandoning the measure for the session; and therefore they entered at once on the discussion. On the 9th, the bill was brought in and read a first time. Between that time and the second reading, the East India Company made one more attempt to oppose the measure. They agreed to a petition for presentation to the House of Lords. It was in part a petition, in part a protest. The propriety of adopting the petition was urged by such considerations as these: 'If we do not protest, every wrong that may be done for years to come will be laid at our doors; but with this protest upon record, history will do us the justice of stating that we have been deprived of our power without inquiry.' The Court of Proprietors also discussed whether counsel should be employed to represent the Company before the House of Lords. Many of the directors assented to this—but only so far as concerned technical and legal points; for, they urged, it would be very undignified to employ any hired counsel to argue the moral and political question, or to defend the conduct of the Company and the rights of India. It remained yet, however, an unsettled point whether counsel would be permitted to appear at all.

On the 13th of July, after a feeble attempt to attach importance to the Company's petition and protest, the bill was read a second time in the Lords. The most remarkable speech made on this occasion was that of the Earl of Ellenborough, Lord Stanley's predecessor at the Board of Control. He declared that, whether in or out of office, he could not approve of the measure, the parentage of which he gave to the House of Commons rather than to the government. He disapproved of the abandonment of popular election in the proposed council; disapproved of the strong leaven of 'Leadenhall Street' in its composition; disapproved of competitive examinations for the Indian artillery and engineers; and expressed a general belief that the scheme would not work well. When the bill went into committee on the 16th, the earl proposed that the members of the council should be appointed for five years only, instead of for life; but this amendment was negatived without a division. Lord Broughton, who, as Sir John Cam Hobhouse, had once been president of the India Board, opposed the whole theory of a council in the strongest terms. He described in anticipation the inconveniences he believed would flow from it. 'The council would only embarrass the minister with useless suggestions and minutes on the most trifling questions; and, if they were rejected, the minority would always be able to furnish weapons of attack against the Secretary in the House of Commons. The minister would gain no advice or knowledge from the council he could not obtain from others without the embarrassment of having official councillors.' The Earl of Derby contested these assertions simply by denying their truth; and they had no effect on the decision of the House. All the clauses were examined during three sittings, on the 16th, 19th, and 20th of the month, and were adopted with a few amendments. During the discussions, the Earl of Derby appeared as the friend of the 'middle classes.' The Earl of Ellenborough having repeated his objection to competitive examination for the engineers and artillery of the Indian army, on the ground that it would lower the 'gentlemanly' standard of those services, the premier replied that, 'He was not insensible to the advantages of birth and station: but he could not join with his noble friend in saying that because a person happened to be the son of a tailor, a grocer, or a cheesemonger, provided his mental qualifications were equal to those of his competitors, he was to be excluded from honourable competition for an appointment in the public service.'

On the 23d of July the India Bill was read a third time and passed by the House of Lords, with only a few observations bearing collaterally on Indian affairs. The Archbishop of Canterbury and some of the bishops made an appeal for the more direct encouragement of Christianity in India; but the Earl of Derby made a very cautious response. 'Due protection ought to be given to the professors of all religions in India, and nothing should be done to discourage the efforts of Christian missionaries. On the other hand, he deemed it essential to the interests, the peace, the well-being of England, if not also to the very existence of her power in India, that the government should carefully abstain from doing anything except to give indiscriminate and impartial protection to all sects and all creeds; and that nothing could be more inconvenient or more dangerous on the part of the state than any open or active assistance to any attempt to convert the native population from their own religions, however false or superstitious.' The Earls of Shaftesbury and Ellenborough joined in deploring the vindictive feeling which had sprung up between the Europeans and natives in India, and which, if continued, would neutralise all attempts at improvement. The Anglo-Indian press was severely reproved for the share it had taken in originating or fostering this feeling.

The Lords having introduced a few amendments in the India Bill, these amendments required the sanction of the Commons before they could be adopted. One of these affected the secret service of the new council; another, the mode of appointing the higher officials in India; a third, the principle of competitive examinations; a fourth, the application of Indian revenues; and so on. The Commons rejected some of these amendments, and accepted the rest, on the 27th. On the 29th the Lords met to consider whether they would abandon the amendments objected to by the Commons. This they agreed to do except in one instance—relating to competitive examinations for the Indian artillery and engineers; they still thought that commissions in these two services should be given only to 'gentlemen,' in the conventional sense of the term. The government, rather than run into collision with the Lords, recommended the Commons to assent to the slight amendment which had been made; and this was agreed to—but not without many pungent remarks on the course which the Upper House had thought proper to pursue. Sir James Graham adverted to a supercilious allusion by the Earl of Ellenborough to the 'John Gilpin class,' and added—'Where is hereditary wisdom found? In what consists the justice of the tenet that India must henceforward be governed by gentlemen, to the exclusion of the middle classes—a gentleman being defined to be something between a peer and those who buy and sell. Is this, I would ask, the only argument that can be advanced against the system of competitive examinations? Who, let me ask, founded, who won our Indian empire?—Those who bought and sold. Who extended it?—Those who bought and sold. Who now transfer that empire to the Crown? —Those who bought and sold; a company of merchants—merchants, forsooth, whose sons are now not thought worthy to have even inferior offices in India committed to their hands. But are not the sons of those who buy and sell entitled to the appellation of gentlemen? Definitions are dangerous; but I should, nevertheless, like to know what it is that constitutes a gentleman. Why, sir, it appears to me that if a man be imbued with strong Christian principles, if he have received an enlightened and liberal education, if he be virtuous and honourable—it appears to me that such a man as that is entitled to the appellation. And who will tell me that among the sons of those who buy and sell may not be found men possessing literary attainments and a refinement of mind which place them in a position to bear comparison with the highest born gentlemen in India? Who, let me ask, were the conquerors of the country? From what class have they sprung? Who was Clive?—The son of a yeoman. Who was Munro?—The son of a Glasgow merchant. Who was Malcolm?—The son of a sheep-farmer upon the Scotch border. These, sir, are the men who have won for us our Indian empire; and I entertain no fear that the sons of those who buy and sell, and who enter the Indian service by means of this principle of open competition, will fail to maintain a high position in our army, or that they will do anything to dishonour the English name.'

When the India Bill finally passed the Lords, the Earl of Albemarle recorded a protest against it—on the grounds that the home government established by it would be inefficient and unconstitutional; that the council would be too numerous; that it would be nearly half composed of the very directors who were supposed to be under condemnation; that those directors, by self-election to the council, would establish a vicious principle; that the members of the council would be irresponsible for the use of the great amount of patronage held by them; that the change in the mode of government was too slight to insure those reforms which India so much needed; that it was pernicious, and contrary to parliamentary precedent, to allow the members of the council to hold other offices, or to engage in commercial pursuits; that the practical effect of the council would be merely to thwart the Secretary of State for India, or else to screen him from censure; and that efficient and experienced under-secretaries would be far better than any council.

The bill received the royal assent, and became an act of parliament, on the 2d of August, under the title of 'An Act for the Better Government of India;' 21st and 22d of Victoria, cap. 106. A brief and intelligible abstract of all the provisions of this important statute will be found in the Appendix.

One clause in the new act provided that the Court of Directors should elect seven members to the new council of India, either out of the existing court, or from persons who had formerly been directors of the Company. On the 7th of August they met, and chose the following seven of their own number—Sir James Weir Hogg, Mr Charles Mills, Captain John Shepherd, Mr Elliot Macnaghten, Mr Ross Donelly Mangles, Captain William Joseph Eastwick, and Mr Henry Thoby Prinsep. Many of the public journals severely condemned this selection, as having been dictated by the merest selfish retention of power in the directors' own hands; but on the other side, it was urged that these seven gentlemen possessed a large amount of practical knowledge on Indian affairs; and, moreover, that the Company, owing the legislature no thanks for recent proceedings, were not bound to be disinterested in the matter.

A remarkable meeting was held by the East India Company on the 11th of August, to consider the state of affairs produced by the new act. The directors and proprietors met as if no one clearly knew what to think on the matter. They asked—What *is* the East India Company now? What does it possess? What can it do, or what has it got to do? Has it any further interest in the affairs of India? Is there now any use in a Court of Directors, or a Court of Proprietors, further than to distribute the dividends on India stock handed over by the new Council of India out of Indian revenues? Is the regular payment of that dividend well secured? Are the *trading* powers of the Company abolished; and if not, is there any profitable trade that can be entered upon? Are they to lose their house in Leadenhall Street, their museum, their library, their archives; and if so, why? If the Company at any time become involved in law-proceedings, will the costs come out of the dividends, or out of what other fund? The answers to these various questions were so very conflicting, and the state of doubt among all the proprietors so evident, that it was agreed—'That a committee of proprietors be appointed to act in concert with the chairman and deputy-chairman of the Court of Directors, for the purpose of obtaining counsel's opinion as to the present legal position of the Company under previous acts of parliament, as well as the present act—more especially as to the parliamentary guarantee of the Company's stock, and the position of the Company's creditors, Indian as well as European.'

The 1st of September 1858 was a day to be recorded in English annals—it witnessed the death of the once mighty East India Company as a governing body. 'On this day,' said one of the able London journals, 'the Court of Directors of the East India Company holds its last solemn assembly. To-morrow, before the shops and the counting-houses of our great metropolis shall have received their accustomed inmates, the greatest corporate body the world has ever seen will have shrivelled into an association of receivers of dividends. The great house in Leadenhall Street will stand as it has stood for long years, and well-nigh the same business will be done by well-nigh the same persons; but the government of the East India Company will have passed into a tradition. Thousands and tens of thousands, including many of the greatest and wisest in the land, intent upon pleasure at this pleasure-seeking period of the year, will, in all human probability, not give the great change a thought. But the first and second days of September 1858, which witness the extinction of the old and the inauguration of the new systems of Indian government, constitute an epoch in our national history—nay, in the world's history, second in importance to few in the universal annals of mankind. On this day the East India Company, which hitherto, through varied changes and gradations, has directed the relations of Great Britain with the vast continent of India, issues its last instructions to its servants in the east. On this day the last dispatches written by the authoritative "we" to our governor-general, or governors in council, will be signed by their "affectionate friends." To-morrow the *egomet* of her Majesty's Secretary of State will be supreme in the official correspondence of the Indian bureau. It may or may not be for the good of India, it may or may not be for the good of England, that the government of the East India Company should on this day cease to exist; but we confess we do not envy the feelings of the man who can contemplate without emotion this great and pregnant political change.' There was a disposition, on this last day of the Company's power, to look at the bright rather than the dark side of its character. 'It has the great privilege of transferring to the service of her Majesty such a body of civil and military officers as the world has never seen before. A government cannot be base, cannot be feeble, cannot be wanting in wisdom, that has reared two such services as the civil and military services of the East India Company. To those services the Company has always been just, has always been generous. In those services lowly merit has never been neglected. The best men have risen to the highest place. They may have come from obscure farmhouses or dingy places of business; they may have been roughly nurtured and rudely schooled; they may have landed in the country without sixpence or a single letter of recommendation in their trunks; but if they have had the right stuff in them, they have made their way to eminence, and have distanced men of the highest connections and most flattering antecedents. . . . . . Let her Majesty appreciate the gift—let her take the vast country and the teeming millions of India under her direct control; but let her not forget the great corporation from which she has received them, nor the lessons to be learned from its success.'

The last special General Court of the Company was held, as we have said, on the 1st of September. The immediate purpose was a generous one: the granting of a pension to the distinguished ruler of the Punjaub, Sir John Lawrence; and this was followed by an act at once dignified and graceful. It was an earnest tender of thanks, on the part of the East India Company generally, to its servants of every rank and capacity, at home and in India, for their zealous and faithful performance of duties; an assurance to the natives of India that they would find in Queen Victoria 'a most gracious

Old East India House, Leadenhall Street.

mistress;' an expression of hearty belief that the home-establishment, if employed by the Crown, would serve the Crown well as it had served the Company; a declaration of just pride in the sterling civilians and noble soldiers at that moment serving unweariedly in India; and an earnest hope and prayer 'That it may please Almighty God to bless the Queen's Indian reign by the speedy restoration of peace, security, and order; and so to prosper her Majesty's efforts for the welfare of her East Indian subjects that the millions who will henceforth be placed under her Majesty's direct as well as sovereign dominion, constantly advancing in all that makes men and nations great, flourishing, and happy, may reward her Majesty's cares in their behalf by their faithful and firm attachment to her Majesty's person and government.'

The East India House in Leadenhall Street was chosen by Lord Stanley as the office of the new Council for India, on account of its internal resources for the management of public business. During more than two centuries and a half, the city of London had contained the head-quarters of those who managed Anglo-Indian affairs. The first meeting of London merchants in 1599, on the subject of East India trade, was held at Founders' Hall. The early business of the Company, when formed, was transacted partly at the residences of the directors, partly in the halls of various incorporated companies. In 1621 the Company occupied Crosby Hall for this purpose. In 1638 a removal was made to Leadenhall Street, to the house of Sir Christopher Clitheroe, at that time governor of the Company. In 1648 the Company took the house of Lord Craven, adjoining Clitheroe's, and on the site of the present India House. In 1726 the picturesque old front of this mansion was taken down, and replaced by the one represented in the above cut. Finally, in 1796, the present India House was built,* and remained the head-quarters of the Company. Acquiring skill by gradual experience, the Company had rendered this one of the most perfectly organised establishments that ever existed. Ranged in racks and shelves, in chambers, corridors, and cellars, were

* See Engraving, p. 452.

the records of the Company's administration; prepared by governor-generals, judges, magistrates, collectors, paymasters, directors, secretaries, and other officials abroad and at home. These documents, tabulated and indexed with the greatest nicety, related to the whole affairs of the Company, small as well as great, and extended back to the earliest period of the Company's history. Declarations of war, treaties of peace, depositions of native princes, dispatches of governor-generals, proceedings of trials, appeals of natives, revenue assessments, army disbursements—all were fully recorded in some mode or other. The written documents relating to a hundred and fifty-five years of the Company's history, from 1704 to 1858, filled no less than a hundred and sixty thousand huge folio volumes. These documents were so thoroughly indexed and registered that any one could be found by a very brief search. It was mentioned with pride by the staff of the India House, that when Lord Stanley, in his capacity as Secretary of State for India, made his first official visit to Leadenhall Street, he was invited to test the efficiency of this registration department, by calling for any particular dispatch, or for any document bearing upon any act or policy of the Court of Directors, throughout a period of a century and a half; a promise was given that any one of these documents should be forthcoming in five minutes. His lordship thereupon asked for a report on the subject of some occurrence which took place under his own observation while on a tour in India. The document was speedily produced, and was found to contain all the details of the transaction minutely described.

After the Court of Directors had elected seven members to the new council, the government nominated the other eight. The greatest name on the list was Sir John Laird Muir Lawrence, who was expected to return to England, and for whom a place at the council-board was kept vacant. The other seven nominated members were Sir Henry Conyngham Montgomery, Sir Frederick Currie, Major-general Sir Robert John Hussey Vivian, Colonel Sir Proby Thomas Cautley, Lieutenant-colonel Sir Henry Creswicke Rawlinson, Mr John Pollard Willoughby, and Mr William Arbuthnot. It was considered that the fifteen members, in reference to their past experience of Indian affairs, might fairly represent the following interests:

Bengal Civil Service,	Prinsep, Mangles.
Madras " "	Montgomery.
Bombay " "	Willoughby.
Bengal Army,	Cautley.
Madras "	Vivian.
Bombay "	Eastwick.
The Punjaub,	Lawrence.
Afghan Frontier,	Rawlinson.
Native States,	Currie.
Indian Law,	Hogg, Macnaghten.
Shipping Interests,	Shepherd.
Finance,	Mills.
Indian Commerce,	Arbuthnot.

This classification, however, was not official; it was only useful in denoting the kind of knowledge likely to be brought to the council by each member. When, in the early days of September, Lord Stanley presided at the first meetings of the new council, he grouped the members into certain committees, for the more convenient dispatch of business. This grouping was based in part on the previous practice of the East India Company, and in part on suggested improvements. The committees were three in number, of five members each—partly nominated, and partly elected. The functions and composition of the committees were as follow:

FINANCE, HOME, AND PUBLIC WORKS.

Sir Proby Cautley,	Nominated.
Mr Arbuthnot,	
Mr Mills,	Elected.
Mr Macnaghten,	
Captain Shepherd,	

POLITICAL AND MILITARY.

Sir John Lawrence,	Nominated.
Sir R. Vivian,	
Sir H. Rawlinson,	
Mr Willoughby,	
Captain Eastwick,	Elected.

REVENUE, JUDICIAL AND LEGISLATIVE.

Sir H. Montgomery,	Nominated.
Sir F. Currie,	
Sir J. W. Hogg,	Elected.
Mr Mangles,	
Mr Prinsep,	

Lord Stanley appointed Sir G. R. Clerk and Mr Henry Baillie to be under-secretaries of state for India; and Mr James Cosmo Melvill, late deputy-secretary to the East India Company, to be assistant under-secretary. Mr John Stuart Mill, one of the most distinguished of the Company's servants in England, was earnestly solicited by Lord Stanley to assist the new government with his services; but he declined on account of impaired health. With a few exceptions, the valued and experienced servants of the Company became servants of the new council, as secretaries, clerks, examiners, auditors, record-keepers, &c.; for the rest, arrangements were to be gradually made in the form of compensations, pensions, or retiring allowances.

One of the first proceedings under the new *régime* was the appointment of a commission to investigate the complicated relations of the Indian army. The heads of inquiry on which the commission was to enter included almost everything that could bear upon the organisation and efficiency of the military force in the east, under a system where the anomalous distinction between 'Company's' troops and 'Queen's' troops would no longer be in force. Such an inquiry would necessarily extend over a period of many months, and would need to be conducted partly in India and partly in England.

In closing this narrative of the demise of the powerful East India Company as a political or governing body, it may be remarked that all the well-wishers of India felt the change to be a great and signal one, whether for good or harm. There were not wanting prophets of disaster. The influence of parliament being so much more readily brought to bear upon a government department than upon the East India Company, many persons entertained misgivings concerning the effect of the change upon the well-being of India. Before any long period could elapse, submarine cables would probably have been sunk in so many seas, and land-cables stretched across so many countries, that a message would be flashed from London to Calcutta in a few hours. Lord Palmerston once jocularly made a prediction, ten years before the Indian mutiny broke out, to the effect that the day would come when, if a minister were asked in parliament whether war had broken out in India, he would reply: 'Wait a minute; I'll just telegraph to the governor-general, and let you know.' A war in India did indeed come, before the period for the fulfilment of this prediction; but the time was assuredly approaching when the 'lightning-post,' as the natives of India felicitously call it, would be in operation. What would be the results? Some of the foreboders of disaster said: 'In any great crisis, it is true, which demands prompt action on the part of the governing country, this rapid intercommunication will be a source of strength; the resources of England will be brought to bear upon any part of India four or five weeks sooner than under existing circumstances. But, on the other hand, the ordinary work of government, at either end of the wire, will be greatly complicated and embarrassed by this frequent intercommunication of ideas. The Council of India will probably not be over-anxious to fetter the movements of the governor-general; nor will the Secretary of State for India be necessarily prone to send curt sentences of advice or remonstrance to the distant viceroy; but it is doubtful whether parliament would suffer the council or the Secretary to exercise this wise forbearance. There would be a tendency to govern India by the House of Commons through the medium of the electric telegraph. A sensitive governor-general would be worried to death in a few months by the interference of the telegraph with his free action; and an irritable one might be stung into indignant resignation in a much shorter time.' All such fears are groundless. If a message from England were perilous in its tendency through its ease and quickness of transmission, a message from India pointing out this perilous tendency would be equally easy and quick. The electric messenger does its work as rapidly in one direction as the other. A governor-general, worthy of the name, would take care not instantly to obey an order which he believed to be dangerous to the welfare of the country under his charge; the wire would enable him to converse with the authorities at home in a few hours, or, at any rate, a few days, and to explain circumstances which would probably lead to a modification of the order issued. The electric telegraph being one of the greatest boons ever given by science to mankind, it will be strange indeed if England does not derive from it—in her government of India, as in other matters—an amount of benefit that will immeasurably outweigh any temporary inconveniences.

Calcutta.—Company's Troops early in the Nineteenth Century.

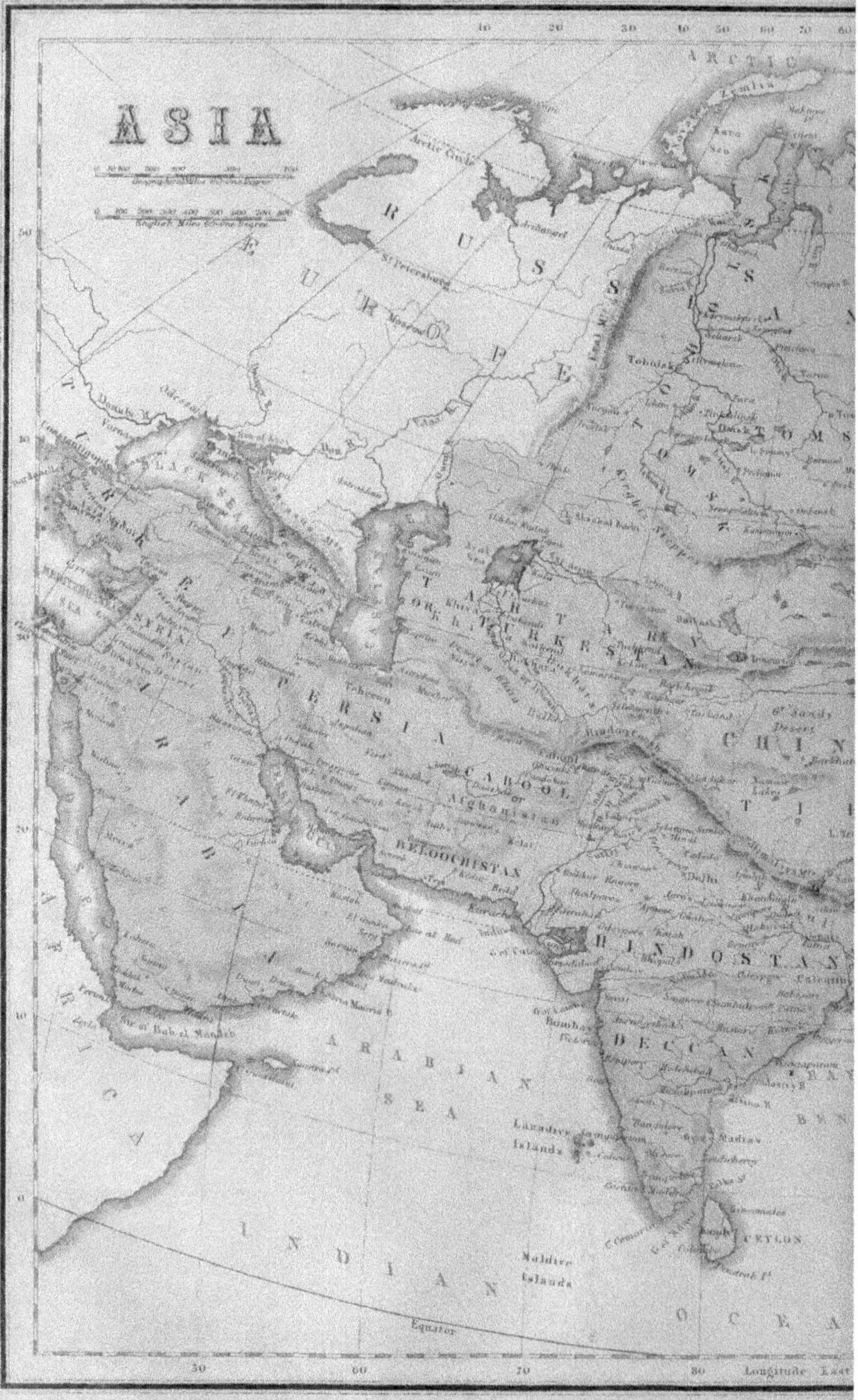
ASIA
RUSSIA
EUROPE
TARTARY
TURKESTAN
PERSIA
CABOOL or Afghanistan
BELOOCHISTAN
ARABIA
SYRIA
HINDOSTAN
DECCAN
CHINA
ARABIAN SEA
INDIAN OCEAN
AFRICA
CEYLON
Laccadive Islands
Maldive Islands
Equator
Arctic Circle
Bombay
Delhi
Calcutta
Madras
Tobolsk
Longitude East

W. & R. CHAMBERS.

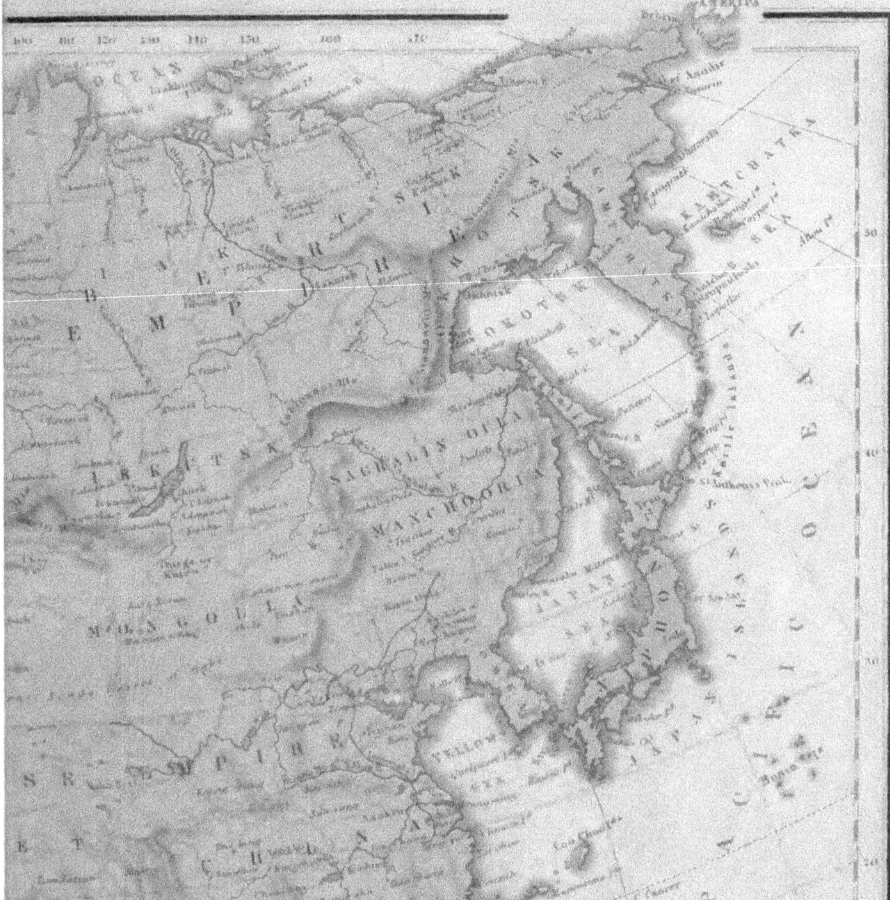

DON & EDINBURGH

ORMUZ—Entrance to the Persian Gulf.

SUPPLEMENTARY CHAPTER.

§ 1. THE PERSIAN EXPEDITION, 1856-7. § 2. THE CHINESE AND JAPANESE EXPEDITIONS, 1856-7-8.
§ 3. ENGLISH PROSPECTS IN THE EAST.

NOT the least among the many extraordinary circumstances connected with the Revolt in India was this—that England, at the very time when the Revolt began, had two Asiatic wars on her hands, one eastward and the other westward of her Indian empire. True, the Shah of Persia had consented to a treaty of peace before that date; true, the Emperor of China had not yet actually received a declaration of war; but it is equally true that British generals and soldiers were still holding conquered positions in the one country, and that hostilities had commenced in the other. We have seen in former chapters, and shall have occasion to refer to the fact again, that Viscount Canning was most earnestly desirous, when the troubles in India began, to obtain the aid of two bodies of British troops—those going to China, and those returning from Persia. It must ever remain an insoluble problem how the Revolt would have fared if there had been no Persian and Chinese expeditions. On the one hand, several additional regiments of the Company's army, native as well as European, would have been in India, instead of in or near Persia. On the other hand, there would not have been so many disciplined British troops at that time on the way from England to the east. Whether these two opposing circumstances would have neutralised each other, can only be vaguely guessed at.

There are other considerations, however, than that which concerns the presence or absence of British troops, tending to give these two expeditions a claim to some brief notice in the present work. The Persian war, if the short series of hostilities deserve that name, arose, mainly and in the first instance, out of apprehensions for the future safety of British India on the northwest. The Chinese war arose, mainly and in the first instance, out of that opium-traffic which had put so many millions sterling into the coffers of the East India Company. Other events, it is true, had tended to give a different colour and an intricate complication to the respective quarrels; but it can hardly be doubted that the India frontier-question in the one case, and the India opium-question in the other, were the most powerful predisposing causes in bringing about the two wars. Two sections of the present chapter are appropriated to such an outline of these two warlike expeditions as will show how far they were induced by India, and how far they affected India, before and during the Revolt. Any detailed treatment of the operations would be beyond the scope of the present volume. The expedition to Japan will claim a little notice as a peaceful episode in the Chinese narrative.

§ I. THE PERSIAN EXPEDITION, 1856-7.

Examining a map of Asia, we shall see that the country, called in its widest extent Afghanistan, is bounded on the east by India, on the west by Persia, and on the north by the territories of various Turcoman tribes. Whatever may be the fruitfulness or value of Afghanistan in other respects, it includes and possesses the only practicable route from Central Asia to the rich plains of India. So far as Persia, Bokhara, and Khiva are concerned, England would never for a moment think of doubting the safety of India; but when, in bygone years, it was known that Russia was increasing her power in Central Asia, acquiring a great influence over the Shah of Persia, and sending secret agents to Afghanistan, a suspicion arose that the eye of the Czar was directed towards the Indus as well as towards the Bosphorus, to India as well as to Turkey. Alarmists may have coloured this probability too highly, but the symptoms were not on that account to be wholly neglected. About midway between the Punjaub and the Caspian Sea is the city of Herat, near the meeting-point of Persia, Afghanistan, and Turkistan or Independent Tatary. It was this city, rather than any other, which caused the war with Persia. To what state does Herat belong, Persia or Afghanistan? The answer to this question is of great political importance; for as Russia has more influence in the first-named state than in the second, any aggressive schemes of the court of St Petersburg against India would be favoured by a declaration or admission that Herat belonged to Persia. In the course of twenty centuries Afghanistan has been in succession under Persian, Bactrian, Scythian, Hindoo, Persian, Saracenic, Turcoman, Khorasan, Mongol, Mogul, Persian, and Afghan rule; until at length, in 1824, three Afghan princes divided the country between them—one taking the Cabool province, another that of Candahar, and another that of Herat. There are therefore abundant excuses for Persians and Turcomans, Afghans and Hindoos, laying claim to this region, if they think themselves strong enough to enforce their claims. It is just such a complication as Russia would like to encourage, supposing her to have any designs against India—just such a complication, we must in justice add, as would lead England to seize Afghanistan, if she thought it necessary for the safety of her Indian empire. When Lord Auckland was governor-general of India, in 1837, he interfered in Afghan politics, in order to insure the throne of Cabool to a prince friendly to England and hostile to Russia and Persia; this interference led to the first Afghan war in 1838, the disastrous termination of which brought on the second Afghan war of 1842. Since the year last named, the Cabool and Candahar territories have remained in the hands of princes who were bound, by treaties of alliance, to friendly relations with England. Herat, however, further west and more inaccessible, became a prey to contentions which brought on the Persian war in 1856.

About the year 1833, disputes arose between Herat and Persia which have never since been wholly healed. The Shah claimed, if not the ownership of Herat, at least a tribute that would imply a sort of protective superiority. This tribute was suddenly withdrawn by Kamran Mirza, Khan of Herat, in or about the year just named; and certain clauses of a treaty were at the same time disregarded by him. Thence arose a warlike tendency in the court of Teheran—encouraged by Count Simonich, Russian ambassador; and discouraged by Mr Ellis, British ambassador. Negotiations failing, a Persian army began to march, and the Shah formally declared Herat to be a province of the Persian empire. The fortress of Ghorian fell, and after that the city of Herat was invested and besieged. Russia proposed a treaty in 1838, whereby Herat was to be given to the Khan of Candahar, on the condition that both of these Afghan states should acknowledge the suzerainty of Persia: the fulfilment of the conditions being guaranteed by Russia. This alarmed Sir John M'Neill, at that time British representative at Teheran; he suggested to Lord Palmerston that the British should send an army to support Herat, as a means of preventing the falling of the whole of Afghanistan into the clutches of Russia. Herat was defending itself bravely, and there might yet be time to save it. The Shah refusing to listen to M'Neill's representations, and various petty matters having given England an excuse to 'demand satisfaction,' an expedition was sent from India to the Persian Gulf in the summer of 1838. Nominally a dispute about Herat, it was really a struggle whether England or Russia should acquire most ascendency over the Shah of Persia. Three years of negotiation, on various minor grievances and differences, led to a treaty between England and Persia in 1841. There then followed many years of peace—not, however, unalloyed by troubles. Persia, urged on secretly by Russia, continually endeavoured to obtain power in the Herat territory; while the oriental vanity of the officials led them into many breaches of courtesy towards English envoys, consuls, and merchants. In 1851, it came to the knowledge of Colonel Sheil, at that time British minister at the court of Teheran, that Persia was quietly preparing for another attack on Herat. In spite of Sheil's remonstrances, the Shah sent an army against that city in 1852, captured the place, set up a dependent as subsidiary chief or khan, coined money with his own effigy, imprisoned and tortured many Afghan chiefs, and formally annexed the Herat territory as part of the great Persian empire. Colonel Sheil, failing in all his endeavours to counteract the policy of the Persian court, sent home to recommend that the British should despatch an expedition to the Persian Gulf. Under the influence of English pressure, the Shah signed another treaty in 1853—engaging to give up Herat; not to attack it again unless an attack came previously from the side of Cabool or Candahar; and to be content with the merely nominal suzerainty which existed in the time of the late Khan. The Persians, nevertheless, threw numberless obstacles in the way of carrying out this treaty; insomuch that Colonel Sheil was engaged in a perpetual angry correspondence with them. Faith in treaties is very little understood in Asia; and the court of Persia is thoroughly Asiatic in this matter. While this wrangle was going on, another embarrassment arose, out of the employment by the Hon. A. C. Murray, British representative, of a Persian named Mirza Hashem Khan, against the Shah's orders. A seizure of Hashem's wife by the authorities was converted by Mr Murray into a national insult, on the ground that Hashem was now in the service, and under the protection, of the British crown. Murray struck his flag from the embassy house, until the matter should be settled. A most undignified quarrel took place during the winter of 1855, and far into 1856—Mr Murray insisting on the supreme rights of the British protectorate; and the Persian authorities disseminating scandalous stories as to the motives which induced him to protect the lady in question.

The scene was next transferred to Constantinople; where, early in 1856, the Persian minister discussed the matter with Lord Stratford de Redcliffe, deploring the rupture, and laying all the blame on Mr Murray and the other British officials. In a memorandum drawn up at Teheran, for circulation in the different European courts, M'Neill, Sheil, Murray—all were stigmatised as mischief-makers, bent on humiliating Persia, and on disturbing the friendly relations between the Shah and Queen Victoria. In an autograph document from the Shah himself, Mr Murray was designated 'stupid, ignorant, and insane; one who has the audacity and impudence to insult even kings.'

Before this Murray quarrel was ended, hostilities broke out again at Herat. There were rival parties in that city; there was an attack threatened by Dost Mohammed of Cabool; an appeal was made to Persia for aid, by the Khan who at this time ruled Herat; and Persia marched an army of 9000 men in that direction. The British government, regarding this march as an infringement of the treaty of Herat, demanded the withdrawal of the troops, and threatened warlike proceedings if the demand were not attended to. The Persians, whether emboldened by secret encouragement from Russia, or actuated by any other motive, made a pretence of negotiating, but nevertheless proceeded with their expedition, captured Ghorian, and laid siege to Herat. Hereupon instructions were sent out to the governor-general of India, to prepare a warlike force for service in the Persian Gulf. Before those instructions could reach Bombay, Ferukh Khan arrived at Constantinople with full powers from the Shah to settle all points of difference between Persia and England. Lord Stratford de Redcliffe was empowered to treat with this plenipotentiary; they made great advances towards the settlement of the terms of a treaty; but while they were discussing (in November), news arrived that the Persians had captured the city of Herat after a long siege. This strange confusion between diplomacy at Constantinople and war at Herat, stringent orders from London and warlike alacrity at Bombay, totally disarranged the negotiations of Ferukh Khan and Lord Stratford de Redcliffe; those ministers could do nothing further. The governor-general declared war against Persia on the 1st of November, and the Persian plenipotentiary left Constantinople for Teheran in December.

Thus arose the Persian expedition—out of circumstances so complicated, that it is difficult to bear in mind the relations of one to another. The existence of intrigues among contending parties in the state of Herat; the frequent strife between the Afghans of Cabool and Candahar and those of Herat; the well-remembered and never-abandoned claims of Persia upon the last-named state; the open desire of Russia to obtain a hold over the Persian court; the concealed desire of the same astute power to approach nearer and nearer to the gates of India; the anxiety of England to see Afghanistan remain as a barrier between India and the centre of Asia; the tendency of Persia to disregard those courtesies to western nations which oriental potentates have never willingly conceded—all were concurrent causes in bringing about the British expedition to the Persian Gulf in 1856. The most powerful incentive, probably, although never acknowledged in diplomatic correspondence, was the wish to keep Russia as far as possible away from India.

But, it may be asked, what had the East India Company to do with this war? Why was India put to the expense of providing an armament for invading Persia? This, in truth, was one of the anomalies connected with the 'double government' of India. It was a war declared by Lord Palmerston's cabinet; but as it was founded on considerations relating to the safety of India, it was treated as an India war, to be conducted by the authorities in British India.

The providing of the army for the Persian Gulf devolved chiefly upon Lord Elphinstone, as governor of Bombay. The army was in two divisions, one of which left Bombay several weeks before the other. Numerous transport-vessels were chartered, besides many of the large mail-steamers, to carry troops, guns, and stores to the Persian Gulf. The commissariat and quartermasters' departments had to make great preparations—a thousand baggage-cattle; fodder for these, for draught-bullocks, and for cavalry and artillery horses; framework for fifteen hospitals; hutting for many thousand soldiers, &c. Means of transport had to be provided for most of these, as it would not be safe to rely on supplies obtained in an enemy's country.

Gradually, as the troops, guns, and stores reached the shores of Persia, the organisation of the force proceeded. It was thus constituted:

FIRST DIVISION.

1st Infantry Brigade, . .	H.M. 64th foot. 20th Bombay N.I.
2d " " .	2d Bombay Europeans. 4th Bombay Rifles.
Cavalry Brigade, . .	3d Bombay native cavalry. Poonah Horse.
Artillery " . .	Various detachments.

SECOND DIVISION

1st Infantry Brigade, . .	H.M. 78th Highlanders. 26th Bombay N.I.
2d " " .	23d Bombay N.I. Light Batt. B.N.I.
Cavalry Brigade, . .	H.M. 14th Dragoons. Jacob's Sinde Horse.
Artillery " . .	Troop horse-artillery. Two field-batteries.

The several divisions and brigades were thus commanded: The first division was placed under Major-general Stalker; and the four brigades of which it consisted were commanded by Brigadiers Wilson, Honner, Tapp, and Trevelyan. The second division was under Brigadier-general Havelock—who lived to become so famous in connection with the wars of the Indian mutiny; and the four brigades which it comprised were commanded by Brigadiers Hamilton, Hale, Steuart, and Hutt. Brigadier-general Jacob commanded in chief the cavalry of both divisions; while Major-general Sir James Outram held supreme command of the whole force.

The first division, as we have said, preceded the second by several weeks. General Stalker took his departure from Bombay on the 26th of November, with a fleet of nearly forty vessels under Admiral Sir Henry Leeke—a few of them war-steamers, but chiefly steam and sailing transports, carrying 10,000 soldiers, sailors, and men of all grades and employments. Stalker and Leeke, having brought all the troops and stores past Ormuz and up the Persian Gulf, captured the island of Karrack as a military depôt, and then effected a landing at Hallila Bay, about twelve miles south of Bushire. Although the opposition, from a few hundred Persian troops, was very insignificant, the landing was nevertheless a slow process, occupying three days and two nights—owing chiefly to the absence of any other boats than those belonging to the ships. There being no draught-cattle landed at that time, the troops were without tents or baggage of any kind; they therefore carried three days' rations in their haversacks. After being thus engaged on the 7th of December and two following days, Stalker and Leeke advanced towards Bushire—the one with the troops along the shore, the other with the fleet at easy distance. Bushire is an important commercial town on the northeast side of the gulf; whoever commands it, commands much of the trade of Persia. Stalker found the defences to be far stronger than he had anticipated. On the 9th he dislodged a body of Persian troops from a strong position they occupied in the old Dutch fort of Reshire. On the 10th, after a short bombardment, Bushire itself surrendered—with a promptness which shewed how few soldierly qualities were possessed by the garrison; for the place contained sixty-five guns, with a large store of warlike supplies. The governor of the city, and the commander of the troops, came out and delivered up their swords. The troops of the garrison, about two thousand in number, having marched out and delivered up their arms, were escorted by cavalry to a distance, and then set free. By the evening of the 11th the tents and cooking-utensils were landed; and an intrenched camp was formed outside Bushire as a temporary resting-place for the force—sufficient detachments being told off to hold the city and fort safely. So entirely had the expedition been kept secret from the Persians, that when, on the 29th of November, the first vessels of the fleet hove in sight, the governor of Bushire sent to Mr Consul Jones to ask what it meant; and he only then learned that our army and navy had come to capture the city. This plan was adopted, to obtain a 'material guarantee' sufficiently serious to influence the double-dealing Persian government.

Here the troops remained for several weeks. The second division, and the real head of the force, had not arrived; and General Stalker was not expected or authorised to undertake anything further at present. His camp, about a mile from Bushire, assumed every day a more orderly appearance; and steady trading transactions were carried on with the towns-people. The transport ships went to and fro between Bushire and Bombay, bringing guns and supplies of various kinds.

The political relations between the two countries, meanwhile, remained as indefinite as before. Mr Murray came from Bagdad to Bushire, to confer with the military and naval leaders on all necessary matters, and to negotiate with the Shah's government if favourable opportunity for so doing should offer. Herat remained in the hands of its conquerors, the Persians. Sir John Lawrence, in his capacity as chief authority in the Punjaub, held more than one interview with Dost Mohammed, Khan of Cabool, in order to keep that wily leader true to his alliance with England; and it was considered a fair probability that if Persia did not yield to England's demands, a second expedition would be sent from the Punjaub and Sinde through Afghanistan to Herat.

It was not until the last week in January, 1857, that Sir James Outram and his staff reached the Persian Gulf; nearly all the infantry had preceded him, but much of the artillery and cavalry had yet to come. Sir James sighted Bushire on the 30th; and General Stalker, long encamped outside the town, made prompt preparations for his reception. Outram was desirous of instant action. Stalker had been stationary, not because there was nothing to do, but because his resources were inadequate to any extensive operations. Shiraz, the most important city in that part of Persia, lying nearly due east of Bushire, is connected with it by two roads, one through Ferozabad, and the other through Kisht and Kazeroon; the Persians were rumoured to have 20,000 men guarding the first of these two roads, and a smaller number guarding the second. These reports were afterwards proved to be greatly exaggerated; but Sir James determined that, at any rate, there should be no longer sojourn at Bushire than was absolutely needed.

Information having arrived that a large body of Persians was at the foot of the nearest hills, Outram resolved to dislodge them. The troops were under Soojah-ool-Moolk, governor of Shiraz, and formed the nucleus of a larger force intended for the recapture of Bushire. Leaving the town to be guarded by seamen from the ships, and the camp by about 1500 soldiers under Colonel Shephard, with the *Euphrates* so moored that her guns could command the approaches—Outram started on the 3d of February, with about 4600 men and 18 guns. He took no tents or extra clothing; but gave to each soldier a greatcoat, a blanket, and two days' rations; while the commissariat provided three more days' rations. He marched round the head of Bushire creek to Char-kota, and on the 5th came suddenly upon the enemy's camp, which they had precipitately abandoned when they heard of his approach. This was near the town of Borasjoon, on the road to Shiraz. On the next two days he secured large stores of ammunition, carriages, camp-equipage, stores, grain, rice, horses, and cattle—everything but guns; these had been safely carried off by the enemy to the difficult pass of Mhak, in the mountains lying between Bushire and Shiraz; and as Sir James had not made any extensive commissariat arrangements, he did not deem it prudent to follow them at that time.

On the evening of the 7th, Outram began his march back to Bushire—after destroying nearly twenty tons of powder, and vast quantities of shot and shell; and after securing as booty such flour, grain, rice, and stores as belonged to the government rather than to the villagers. But now occurred a most unexpected event. The Persian cavalry, which retreated while Outram had been advancing, resolved to attack while he was retreating. They approached soon after midnight; and the British were soon enveloped in a skirmishing fire with an enemy whom they could not see. Outram fell from his horse, and Stalker had to take the command for a time. The enemy having brought four guns within accurate range, the position was for a time very serious. Stalker was enabled by degrees to get the regiments into array, so as to grapple with the enemy as soon as daylight should point out their position. When at length, on the morning of the 8th, the British saw the Persians, seven or eight thousand strong, drawn up in order near the walled village of Khoosh-aub, they dashed at them at once with cavalry and horse-artillery, so irresistibly that the plain was soon strewed with dead bodies; the enemy fled panic-stricken in all directions; and if Outram's cavalry had been more numerous (he had barely 500 sabres), he could almost have annihilated the Persian infantry. By ten o'clock all was over, the Persians leaving two guns and all their ammunition in the hands of the British. In the evening Outram resumed his march, and re-entered Bushire during the night of the 9th. His troops had marched ninety miles over ground converted into a swamp by heavy rains, and had seized a camp and won a battle, in a little more than six days. In a 'Field-force Order,' issued on February 10th, and signed by Colonel (afterwards Sir Edward) Lugard as chief of the staff, Outram warmly complimented his troops on this achievement.

After this dashing affair at Khoosh-aub, the patience of Sir James was sorely tried by a long period of comparative inactivity—occasioned in part by the rainy state of the weather, and in part by the non-arrival of some of the artillery and cavalry, without which his further operations would necessarily be much impeded. Brigadier-general Havelock arrived about this time, and took command of the second division, which had hitherto been under a substitute. The feeding of the army had become a difficult matter; for the Persian traders came in less readily after the battle of Khoosh-aub. Rumours gradually spread in the camp that an expedition was shortly to be sent out to Mohamrah, a town near the confluence of the Euphrates and the Karoon, about three days' sail up from Bushire; these rumours gave pleasurable excitement to the troops, who were becoming somewhat wearied of their Bushire encampment. Much had yet to be done, however, before the expedition could start; the northwest winds in the gulf delayed the arrival of the ships containing the cavalry and artillery. On the 4th of March, Sir James made public his plan. General Stalker was to remain at Bushire, with Brigadiers Wilson, Honner, and Tapp, in command of about 3000 men of all arms; while Outram and Havelock, with several of the brigadiers, at the head of 4000 troops, were to make an expedition to Mohamrah, where many fortifications were reported to have been recently thrown up, and where 10,000 or 12,000 Persian troops were assembled. During many days troop-ships were going up the Persian Gulf and the Euphrates—some conveying the troops already at Bushire; and others conveying cavalry and artillery as fast as they arrived from Bombay. The enemy eagerly watched these movements from the shore, but ventured on no molestation.

During the three weeks occupied by these

movements, events of an almost unprecedented character occurred at Bushire—the suicide of two British officers who dreaded the responsibility of the duties devolving upon them. These officers were —Major-general Stalker, commanding the first division of the army; and Commodore Ethersey, who had been placed in command of the Indian navy in the Persian Gulf when Sir Henry Leeke returned to Bombay. Stalker shot himself on the 14th of March. On that morning, Sir James Outram and Commander Jones had breakfasted with him in his tent. He displayed no especial despondency; but it had been before remarked how distressed he appeared on the subject of the want of barrack-accommodation for his troops—fearing lest he should be held responsible if the soldiers, during the heat of the approaching summer, suffered through want of shelter. On one or two other subjects he appeared unable to bear the burden of command; he dreaded lest Outram, by exposing himself to danger in any approaching conflict, might lose his life, and thereby leave the whole weight of the duty and responsibility on him (Stalker). Shortly after breakfast, a shot was heard in the tent, and the unfortunate general was found weltering in his blood. Commodore Ethersey followed this sad example three days afterwards. For three months he had been labouring under anxiety and despondency, haunted by a perpetual apprehension that neither his mental nor physical powers would bear up under the weight of responsibility incurred by the charge of the Indian navy during the forthcoming operations. Memoranda in his diary afforded full proof of this. An entry on the day after Stalker's suicide ran thus: 'Heard of poor Stalker's melancholy death. His case is similar to my own. He felt he was unequal to the responsibility imposed on him. . . . I have had a wretched night.' So deep had been his despondency for some time, and so frequently expressed to those around him, that the news of his suicide on the 17th excited less surprise than pain.

It had been Outram's intention to proceed against Mohamrah directly after his return from Borasjoon and Khoosh-aub; but the unexpected and vexing delays above adverted to prevented him from setting forth until the 18th of March. He was aware that the Persians had for three months been strengthening the fortifications of that place; he knew that the opposite bank of the river was on Turkish ground (Mesopotamia), on which he would not be permitted to erect batteries; and he therefore anticipated a tough struggle before he could master Mohamrah. His plan was, to attack the enemy's batteries with armed steamers and sloops-of-war; and then, when the fire had slackened, to tow up the troops in boats by small steamers, land them at a selected point, and at once proceed to attack the enemy's camp. The Persian army, 13,000 strong, was commanded by the Shahzada, Prince Mirza. Outram's force was rather under 5000, including only 400 cavalry: the rest having been left to guard Bushire and the encampment. Outram and Havelock arrived near Mohamrah on the 24th, and immediately began to place the war-ships in array, and to plant mortars on rafts in the river. On the 26th, the ships and mortars opened a furious fire; under cover of which the troops were towed up the river, and landed at a spot northward of the town and its batteries. The Persians, who had felt the utmost confidence that the landing of a British force, in the face of thirteen thousand men and a formidable array of batteries, would be an impossibility, were panic-stricken at this audacity. When, at about two o'clock, Outram advanced from the landing-place through date-groves and across a plain to the enemy's camp, the Persians fled precipitately, after exploding their largest magazine—leaving behind them all their tents, several magazines of ammunition, seventeen guns, baggage, and a vast amount of public and private stores. As Outram had, at that hour, been able to land not even one hundred cavalry, he could effect little in the way of pursuit; the Persians made off, strewing the ground with arms and accoutrements which they abandoned in their hurry. Commodore Young commanded the naval portion of this expedition, having succeeded the unfortunate Ethersey.

This action of Mohamrah scarcely deserved the name of a battle; for as soon as the ships and mortars had, by their firing, enabled the troops to land, the enemy ran away. Outram had scarcely any cavalry, and his infantry had no fighting—rather to their disappointment. The Persians having retreated up the river Karoon towards Ahwaz, Outram resolved to send three small armed steamers after them, each carrying a hundred infantry. Captain Rennie started on the 29th, in command of this flotilla: his instructions being, 'to steam up to Ahwaz, and act with discretion according to circumstances.' He proceeded thirty miles that day, anchored at night, landed, and found the remains of a bivouac. On the 30th he reached Ismailiyeh, and on the 31st Oomarra. Arriving near Ahwaz on the 1st of April, Rennie came up with the Persian army which had retreated from Mohamrah. Nothing daunted, he landed his little force of 300 men, advanced to the town, entered it, and allayed the fears of the inhabitants; while the Persians, thirty or forty times his number, retreated further northward towards Shuster, with scarcely any attempt to disturb him—such was the panic into which the affair at Mohamrah had thrown them. Captain Rennie, having had the satisfaction of putting to flight a large Persian army with a handful of 300 British, and having given to the inhabitants of Ahwaz such stores of government grain and flour as he could seize, embarked a quantity of arms, sheep, and mules, which he had captured, and steamed back to Mohamrah—earning and receiving the thanks of the general for his management of the expedition.

Just at this period a most sudden and unexpected event put an end to the operations. Captain Rennie's expedition returned to Mohamrah on the 4th of April; and on the 5th arrived news that peace had been signed between England and Persia. Outram's army, European and native, was rapidly approaching 14,000 men; such a force, under such a leader, might have marched from one end of Persia to the other; and both officers and soldiers had begun to have bright anticipations of honour, and perhaps of prize-money. It was with something like disappointment, therefore, that the news of the treaty was listened to; there had not been fighting enough to whet the appetites of the heroic; while soldiers generally would fain make a treaty at the sword's point, rather than see it done in the bureaux of diplomatists. Captain Hunt of the 78th Highlanders, who was concerned in the operations at Mohamrah and Ahwaz, and who wrote a volume descriptive of the whole campaign, told very frankly of the dissatisfaction in the camp: 'The news of peace with Persia having been signed at Paris on the 4th of March damped the elation of all, and considerable disgust was felt at this abrupt termination to what had promised to prove a brilliant campaign.'

How and where the treaty of peace was concluded, we must now shew, in connection with the proceedings of ministers, legislators, and ambassadors.

When the Persian expedition was determined on, parliament was not sitting, and no legislative sanction for the war could be obtained; but when the session opened in February 1857, the policy of the government was severely canvassed. Ministers were charged with involving the country in a war, without the nation itself being acquainted with the causes, or even consulted at all in the matter. The Earl of Clarendon explained the course of events at considerable length. He went into the case of Mr Murray, and the quarrel with the Persian government on matters of diplomatic etiquette—justifying that envoy in all that he had done. But the earl was particular in his assertions that the Murray dispute was not the cause of the war. The siege and capture of Herat furnished the *casus belli*. He dwelt on the immense value of that city as a military station. 'Herat is altogether a most important place for military operations; and an enemy once in possession of it is completely master of the position. Every government of this country has desired that Afghanistan should be protected; and it clearly cannot be protected if Herat remains in the power of Persia.' He expressed a conviction that 'the Russian government and the whole of the Russian people are under a belief that their destiny is to go forward, to conquer, and to hold new territory;' and that this disposition would be greatly tempted if Persia, backed up by Russia, were permitted to seize Herat. He stated finally that the Persian ambassador at Paris had recently expressed a wish to renew negotiations for peace, and that the British government would willingly listen to any overtures for that purpose. Lord Palmerston gave similar explanations in the House of Commons. The Earls of Derby and Malmesbury, Earl Grey, Lord John Russell, Mr Gladstone, and Mr Disraeli, all spoke disparagingly of the Persian expedition—either because it was not necessary; or because, if necessary, parliamentary permission for it ought to have been obtained. The latter was the strong point of opposition; many members asserted, not only that the nation was involved in a new war without its own consent, but that no one could understand whether war had been declared by the Crown or by the East India Company. Earl Grey moved an amendment condemnatory of the ministerial policy; but this was negatived. The ministers declined to produce the diplomatic correspondence at that time, because there was a hope of renewed negotiations with Furukh Khan at Paris.

At the close of February it became known to the public that the East India Company had, not unnaturally, demurred to the incidence of the expenses of the Persian war on their revenues. It appeared that, so early as the 22d of October the Court of Directors had written to the president of the Board of Control—adverting to 'the expedition for foreign service preparing at Bombay, under the orders (it is presumed) of her Majesty's government, communicated through the Secret Committee;' and suggesting for his consideration 'how far it may be just and proper to subject India to the whole of the charges consequent on those orders.' The directors, as a governing body, had no voice whatever in determining on the Persian war; and yet their soldiers and sailors were to take part in it, and the Indian revenues to bear all or part of the burden. It was ultimately decided that England should pay one-half of the expenses, the other half being borne by the Company out of the revenues of India.

Before the British public could learn one single fact connected with the landing of Sir James Outram or of the second division in Persia, they were surprised by the announcement that Lord Cowley and Furukh Khan had succeeded in coming to terms of pacification at Paris—the Persian ambassador having received from his sovereign large powers for this purpose. A provisional treaty was signed on the 4th of March, of which the following is a condensed summary: Peace to be restored between England and Persia—British troops to evacuate Persia as soon as certain conditions should be complied with—All prisoners of war to be released on both sides—The Shah to give an amnesty to any of his subjects who might have been compromised by and during the war—The Shah to withdraw all his troops from Herat and Afghanistan within three months after the ratification of the treaty—The Shah to renounce all claim upon Herat or any other Afghan state, whether for sovereignty or for tribute—In any future quarrel between Persia and the

Afghan khans, England to be appealed to as a friendly mediator—England to display equal justice to Persia and Afghanistan, in the event of any such appeal—Persia to have the power of declaring and maintaining war against any Afghan state in the event of positive insult or injury; but not to make such war a pretext for annexation or permanent occupation—Persia to liberate all Afghan prisoners, on condition of Persian prisoners being released by Afghans—All trading arrangements between England and Persia, in relation to consuls, ports, customs, &c., to be on an equal and friendly footing—The British mission, on its return to Teheran, to be received with due honours and ceremonials—Two commissioners to be named by the two courts, to adjudicate on British pecuniary claims against Persia—The British government to renounce all claim to any 'protection' over the Shah's subjects against the Shah's consent, provided no such power be given to [Russia or] any other court—England and Persia to aid each other in suppressing the slave-trade in the Persian Gulf—A portion of the English troops to remain on Persian soil until Herat should be evacuated by the Persians, but without any expense, and with as little annoyance as possible, to the Persian government—Ratifications to be exchanged at Bagdad within three months.

This treaty—which, if faithfully carried out, would certainly debar Persia from any undue interference with Afghan affairs—was signed at Paris on the very day (March 4th) when Sir James Outram announced to his troops at Bushire the intended attack on Mohamrah. Such was one of the anomalies springing from diplomacy at one place and war at another many thousand miles distant. Furukh Khan proceeded, on the 19th from Paris to London, where he was received by Queen Victoria as plenipotentiary extraordinary from the Shah of Persia, and where the arrangements for the fulfilment of the treaty were further carried out. The treaty having been forwarded to Teheran, was ratified by the Shah of Persia on the 14th of April, and the ratification arrived at Bagdad on the 17th. The English nation was still, as it had been from the beginning, without the means of judging whether the Persian war had been necessary or not; the government still withheld the state papers, on the ground that, as the ratification of the treaty would speedily be effected, it would be better to wait until then. When, later in the year, the Chancellor of the Exchequer asked the House of Commons for a vote of half a million sterling, 'on account of the expenses of the Persian war,' many members protested against the vote, on the ground that parliament had not been consulted in any way concerning the war. On the 16th of July Mr Roebuck moved a resolution—'That the war with Persia was declared, prosecuted, and concluded without information of such transactions being communicated to parliament; while expensive armaments were equipped without the sanction of a vote of this House; and that such conduct tends to weaken its just authority, and to dispense with its constitutional control over the finances of the country, and renders it requisite for this House to express its strong reprobation of such a course of proceeding.' The government policy was censured on many grounds by Mr Roebuck, Lord John Russell, Mr Gladstone, and Mr Disraeli; the first of these speakers even went so far as to attribute the mutiny in India to the withdrawal of troops for the Persian war. The House of Commons agreed, however, pretty generally in the opinion, that although the ministers might reasonably have been more communicative before they commenced hostilities with Persia, there was ground sufficient for the hostilities themselves; and the resolution was negatived by 352 to 38. The question was re-opened on the 17th, when the House granted the half-million asked by the Chancellor of the Exchequer towards defraying the expenses of this war; renewed attacks were made on the Asiatic policy of the Palmerston government, but the vote was agreed to; and nothing further occurred, during the remainder of the session, to disturb the terms of the pacification.

It is unnecessary to trace the course of events in Persia after the ratification of the treaty. The British officers, and the troops under their charge, had no further glory or honour to acquire; they would be called upon simply, either to remain quietly in Persia until Herat was evacuated, or to go through the troublesome ordeal of re-shipment back to Bombay. The troops all assembled in and near Bushire, where they resumed their former camp-life. The officers, having little to do, took occasional trips to Bassorah, Bagdad, and other places on the banks of the Euphrates and Tigris; while the soldiers were employed in destroying the fortifications of the encampment, now no longer needed. On the 9th of May Sir James Outram issued a 'Field-force Order'—thanking the troops for their services during this brief and rather uneventful war, and announcing the break-up of the force. Some of the regiments and corps were to return to India, as rapidly as means of transport could be obtained for them; while the rest, under Brigadier-general Jacob, were to form a small compact army, to remain at Bushire until all the terms of the treaty were fulfilled. Outram, Havelock, and a large number of officers, embarked within a few days for India; and by the time they reached Bombay and Madras, according to the place to which they were bound, the startling news reached their ears that a military mutiny had broken out at Meerut and Delhi. What followed, the pages of this volume have shewn. As to Persia, much delay occurred in carrying out the terms of the treaty, much travelling to and fro of envoys, and many months' detention of British troops at Bushire; but at length the Persians evacuated Herat, the British quitted the Gulf, and the singular 'Persian war,' marked by so few battles, came to an end.

[illegible]

§ 2. THE CHINESE AND JAPANESE EXPEDITIONS, 1856-7-8.

The occurrences westward of India having thus been briefly narrated, attention may now be directed to those on the east.

Viewed in relation to the circumstances which immediately preceded hostilities, it might almost be said that England declared war against China because a few persons went on board a small vessel to search for certain offenders, and because a Chinese official would not civilly receive visits from a British official. These trifling incidents, however, were regarded as symptoms of something greater: symptoms which required close diplomatic watching. To understand this matter, a brief summary of earlier events is needed.

During the first thirty years of the present century, in like manner as in earlier centuries, Europeans had no recognised right of residing in China, or even of visiting its ports. Merchants were allowed to reside at Canton, by official connivance rather than sanction; and even this was possible only at certain times of the year—they being required in other months to retire to Macao. They were liable to be expelled from Canton at any time, with or without assigned cause; their trade was liable to be stopped with equal suddenness; and, under the designation of 'barbarians,' all negotiation was denied to them except through the medium of a mercantile community called the Hong merchants. During many years, Indian opium was the chief commodity sold by the English to the Chinese, in exchange for tea and other produce. This opium-trade was always declared illegal by the Chinese government, though always covertly favoured by the Chinese officials. Quarrels frequently arose concerning this trade, and the quarrels sometimes ended in violence. The import of opium became so large that the exports were insufficient to pay for it; and when silver was thus found necessary to make up the balance, the imperial anger waxed stronger and stronger. The 'barbarians' were commanded not to bring any more opium; but, finding the trade too profitable to be abandoned, they continued their dealings in spite of the mandates of the celestial potentate.

The year 1831 may be said to have commenced the political or international stage of this difficulty. The governor-general of India wrote a letter to the governor of Canton, complaining of the conduct of the Chinese authorities, and demanding explanations, &c. Why his lordship, rather than any functionary in England, did this, was because the East India Company in those days sold opium on its own account, and made use of its political power to render that trade as profitable as possible—one of the pernicious anomalies arising out of the Company's double functions. In 1832, the governor of Canton vouchsafed a partial explanation, but only to the Hong merchants—refusing with superb scorn, to communicate either with the Company's merchants, or with the governor-general. In 1833 an imperial edict forbade the introduction of opium; but this, like many that preceded it, remained inoperative. In 1834 the Company's trading monopoly ceasing, private merchants thereupon engaged in the tea-trade with China. The English government sent three commissioners—Lord Napier, Mr (afterwards Sir) J. F. Davis, and Sir G. B. Robinson—as 'superintendents of British commerce in China.' The Chinese authorities refused to acknowledge these commissioners in any way, in spite of numerous invitations; while on the other hand the commissioners refused to retire from Canton to Macao. These disputes led to violence, and the violence brought a British ship-of-war up the Canton river. A compromise was the result—the commissioners retiring to Macao, and the Chinese authorities allowing the resumption of the opium-traffic. Lord Napier died towards the close of the year, and was succeeded as chief-superintendent by Mr Davis—Captain Elliot being appointed secretary, and afterwards third superintendent. During the next three years trade continued; but the Chinese officials were uniformly rude and insulting. The British government would not permit Captain Elliot to submit to these indignities; missives and counter-missives passed to and fro; and the year 1837 ended with threatening symptoms. In 1838 Admiral Maitland arrived in Canton river with a ship of war, to protect British interests—by cannon-balls, if not by friendly compact. The nearest approach to equality between the two nations was in an interview between Admiral Maitland and the Chinese Admiral Kwan; in which Maitland assured his brother-admiral that he would remain peaceful—until provoked. In 1839, as in previous years, the opium-trade was often violently interrupted by the Chinese authorities. The officers of the English government, political and naval, were placed in an embarrassing position in this matter; their duty was to protect Englishmen; but they could not compel the Chinese to trade in opium—for the Chinese government held the same power as all other despotic governments, of prohibiting or encouraging trade with other countries. In this year, when Maitland was absent, Elliot became powerless at Canton; he and all the English were made prisoners, and could not obtain release until they had destroyed all the opium in the English stores—more than twenty thousand chests. This was done: Elliot guaranteeing that the English government would repay the merchants. Commissioner Lin saw that the opium was wholly destroyed; and by the end of May almost every European had quitted Canton.

It was thus that commenced the first Chinese war—a war which had a bad moral basis on the English side; since it arose more out of the forced sale of an intoxicating drug, than out of any other circumstance. The British government, finding themselves bound by Captain Elliot's promise to pay an enormous sum for the opium destroyed, and feeling the importance of maintaining British supremacy in the east, resolved to settle the quarrel by warlike means. Fighting and negotiating alternated during 1840 and the two following years. At one time, Sir Gordon Bremer, at another, Sir Hugh Gough, commanded troops on the Chinese coast, acting in conjunction with ships-of-war; and according to the amount of naval or military success, so did the Chinese authorities manifest or not a disposition to treat. Commissioner Lin, then Commissioner Keshen, and afterwards Commissioner Key-ing, conducted negotiations—a perilous duty; for their imperial master did not scruple to punish, or even to put to death, those diplomatists who made a treaty distasteful to him; and nothing but the noise of cannon induced him to respect treaties when made. The chief military and naval events of the three years, in connection with this struggle, were the following: The British ship *Hellas* attacked by junks, and many of the crew killed; an attempt to burn the British fleet by fire-rafts; Chusan taken by the English; naval action near Macao; attack and capture of Chuen-pe and Tae-cok-tow; Hong-kong taken by the English; the Bogue forts, with 460 guns, taken by Sir Gordon Bremer; Canton attacked by the British, under Sir Hugh Gough, and only spared on the prompt payment of five million dollars; Amoy, with 300 guns, taken by the British; the cities of Ting-hae, Ching-hae, Ning-po, and several others on the coast, captured; several military engagements in the vicinity of the captured cities; an advance of a powerful squadron up the Yang-tsze-kiang; and a threatening of the great city of Nankin, which brought the emperor effectually to terms—all the previous offers of negotiation on the part of the Chinese having been mere expedients to save time.

The war ended thuswise. Sir Henry Pottinger arrived in the Chinese waters in April 1842, with full power as representative of the British Crown; and it was he who procured the important 'Treaty of Nankin,' signed by the respective plenipotentiaries in 1842, and the ratifications exchanged by the respective sovereigns in 1843. This treaty having had an important bearing on the later or second war with China, we will epitomise a few of its chief conditions: Lasting peace and friendship established between England and China—China to pay 21,000,000 dollars for the opium destroyed, and for the expenses of the war; the payments to be spread over four years—The ports of Canton, Amoy, Fuh-choo-foo, Ning-po, and Shang-hae, to be thrown open to British merchants, with consular facilities, and just and regular tariffs—The island of Hong-kong to become a permanent British possession—All British subjects, at that time confined in China, to be at once and unconditionally released—The Chinese emperor to give an amnesty to all his own subjects, in respect of any proceedings on their part friendly to the British—Correspondence in future to be conducted on terms of perfect equality between the officers of the two governments—The islands of Chusan and Kulangsoo to be held by the British until the fulfilment of all the conditions of the treaty, and then given up.

Under the influence of this Treaty of Nankin, trade rapidly extended between England and China. Instead of being confined to Canton, and conducted in a stealthy and undignified manner, it was openly carried on at five ports. The British government did not undertake to protect the opium-trade more than that in any other commodity; on the contrary, the representatives of the English government would gladly have seen that trade diminish; but in truth, the East India Company realised several millions sterling a year profit by it, and English merchants reaped many additional millions: insomuch that a very powerful influence was brought to back up this trade.

A 'Supplementary Treaty' was signed in October 1843, for regulating the terms of commercial intercourse at the five ports, and providing for the courteous reception of British representatives by the Chinese officials, in matters relating to mutual trade. During the thirteen years following the signature of the Treaty of Nankin, the trade between England and China gradually increased, though not at so rapid a rate as had been hoped by British manufacturers and merchants. The English had trading establishments, with consuls and other officials, at the five ports, and a colony or military settlement at Hong-kong; while there were always a few ships-of-war in the Chinese waters. The relations, however, were not wholly peaceful. The inhabitants of Canton had a general ill-will towards the English; so had the imperial viceroy; and violence arising out of this ill-will led to a brief period of hostilities. In April 1847, the English seized the Bogue Forts, in the Canton river, in order to obtain redress for various insults; this seizure was followed by a new convention.

Thus matters continued until October 1856. On the 8th of that month, an incident occurred, trivial in itself, which gave rise to the 'Second War with China.' Sir John Bowring was at that time chief representative of British interests in China, with Hong-kong as his head-quarters; Admiral Sir Michael Seymour commanded the royal ships in those seas; Commodore Elliot was under Seymour in the Canton and Hong-kong district; and Mr Parkes was consul at Canton. These were the English officials more immediately concerned in the matter. On the day here named, a Chinese officer and a party of soldiers boarded a *lorcha* or small vessel called the *Arrow*, anchored off Canton; and then seized twelve out of fourteen of the crew, bound them, and carried them away. The *Arrow* had a colonial register from the governor of Hong-kong, which placed it under British protection; the master, an Englishman, protested against the seizure, but was not listened to. The British flag, too, was hauled down from the lorcha. This was the statement on the part of the British. Most of the accusations, however, were stoutly denied by the officials of Canton, who asserted that the lorcha was Chinese, that the owner was Chinese, that the crew were Chinese, and that the boarding was effected simply to take into custody men who had committed some offence against Chinese laws.

When the seizure of the men from the *Arrow* became known, Mr Parkes remonstrated with the Chinese officer, on the ground that the crew were under British protection. No notice being taken of this remonstrance, Mr Parkes communicated with the highest dignitary in that part of China, whose name was Yeh Mingchin, and whose office was variously designated imperial commissioner, governor, and viceroy. The letter sent by Parkes to this functionary demanded that the twelve men should be brought back to the lorcha by the same officer who had taken them away, that an apology should be made, and an assurance given that the British flag should in future be respected. The men were sent back, after much negotiation; but Mr Parkes complained that the return 'was not made in the public manner which had marked the seizure, and that all appearance of an apology was pointedly avoided.' The facts were communicated to Sir John Bowring, and by him to Admiral Seymour. No real injury had been done, for the men had been reinstated; but there was an insult, which the English representatives conceived themselves bound to resent. They had often been piqued at the absence of respect shewn by the officers of the Celestial Empire, and were willing to avail themselves of any reasonable opportunity for bringing about a more diplomatic state of affairs.

The first act of war occurred on the part of the British. Sir John Bowring recommended to the admiral the seizure of a Chinese junk or war-boat, as a probable mode of bringing an apology. Sir Michael accordingly directed Commodore Elliot, of the *Sybille*, to carry out Bowring's instructions; and placed at his disposal the *Barracouta* steam-sloop and the *Coromandel* tender. A junk was seized; but this was a profitless adventure; for, being found to be private property, the junk was given up again. The admiral next sent the steam-frigates *Encounter* and *Sampson* up the Canton river; 'in the hope that the presence of such an imposing force would shew the high-commissioner the prudence of complying with our demands.' The Chinese viceroy remained, nevertheless, immovable; he made no apology. Mr Parkes thereupon went from Canton to Hong-kong, to consult with Bowring and Seymour as to the best course to be adopted. They all agreed that the seizure of the defences of the city of Canton would be the most judicious, both as a display of power without the sacrifice of life, and of the determination of the English to enforce redress—'experience of the Chinese character having proved that moderation is considered by the officials only as an evidence of weakness.'

Then commenced the second stage in the proceedings. On the 23d of October, Sir Michael Seymour went in person up to Canton, with the *Coromandel*, *Sampson*, and *Barracouta*, and accompanied by the marines and boat-crews of the *Calcutta*, *Winchester*, *Bittern*, and *Sybille*. He captured four forts a few miles below Canton, spiked the guns, destroyed the ammunition, and burned the buildings. Another, the Macao fort, in the middle of the river, mounting 86 guns, he retained and garrisoned for a time. Mr Parkes was then sent to announce to Yeh that the British admiral had come to enforce redress for insults received, and would remain in the river until redress was obtained. The high-commissioner sent a reply which was not deemed satisfactory. On the morning of the 24th, marines and sailors were sent to capture the 'Bird's Nest Fort,' the Shamin Fort, and others near Canton; this they did, spiking the guns and destroying the ammunition. On the afternoon of the same day, strong reinforcements were sent to the British factory, or trading-station of the merchants, to protect it from any sudden attack, and to guard against the floating of fire-rafts by the Chinese on the river.

'Apology' was the demand made by the British representatives; but no apology came; and thereupon the siege of Canton was proceeded with. On the 25th, a fort called the Dutch Folly, immediately opposite the city, was captured. The 26th being Sunday, nothing was done on that day. On the 27th, the admiral heightened his demands. He caused Consul Parkes to write to the Chinese commissioner, to the effect that as the required apology and reparation had not been given, the terms should be made more stringent. Henceforward, the field of contest was widened; it was no longer the lorcha and the flag alone that constituted the grievance. Sir John Bowring probably thought that the same amount of threat and of fighting, if fighting there must be, might be made to settle other annoyances, as well as those more immediately under notice. No reply being sent to Parkes's letter, the guns of the *Encounter* and *Barracouta* were brought to bear upon the Chinese commissioner's residence, and upon some troops posted on the hills behind a fort named by the English Gough's Fort. This enraged Yeh Mingchin, who issued a proclamation, offering a reward of thirty dollars for every Englishman's head.

Sir Michael, resolved to punish this obstinate viceroy, made preparations for a much more serious attack. He sent Captain Hall on shore, to warn the inhabitants of Canton to remove their persons and property from the vicinity of a certain portion of the city; this they did during the night of the 27th. On the 28th, a bombardment was kept up from the Dutch Folly, with a view of opening a clear passage to the wall of the city; and when this passage was opened by noon on the 29th, a storming-party was sent in under Commodore Elliot. Marines and sailors, with two field-pieces, advanced to the wall, and speedily obtained possession of the defences between two of the city-gates. One of the gates was then blown to pieces by gunpowder, and another body of seamen advanced to that spot under Captain Hall. Soon afterwards, Seymour, Parkes, and Elliot entered the city through this shattered gate, went to the high-commissioner's house, inspected it, remained there some time, and then returned to the ships. The motive for this visit was a singular one, unusual in European warlike politics, but having a significance in dealing with so peculiar a people as the Chinese; it was simply (in the words of the admiral's dispatch) 'to show his excellency that I had the power to enter the city.'

The month of November opened ominously. The British were determined to humble the pride of the Chinese officials; whereas, these officials showed no signs of yielding. Admiral Seymour now addressed a letter in his own name to the high-commissioner, adverting to the case of the *Arrow*; pointing threateningly to the fact that Canton was at the mercy of cannon-balls, and inviting him to terminate the unsatisfactory state of affairs by a personal interview. He claimed credit, rather than the reverse, for his conduct towards the city. 'It has been wholly with a view to the preservation of life, that my operations have hitherto been so deliberately conducted. Even when entering the city, no blood was shed, save where my men were assailed; and the property of the people was in every way respected.' Commissioner Yeh's reply to this letter was not deficient in courtesy or dignity; whether or not he believed his own assertions, he at least put them forth in temperate language. He maintained, as he had before asserted to Consul Parkes, that the seizure of the twelve men on board the *Arrow* was perfectly legal; that some of them had been released on their innocence of an imputed crime being proved; that the other three were given up when Parkes demanded them; that the *Arrow* was a Chinese vessel; that the authorities had no means of knowing that she had passed into the hands of an Englishman; that no flag was flying when the vessel was boarded, and, therefore, no flag could have been insultingly hauled down. The non-admission of English representatives into Canton was defended on the plea that, the less the two nations came in contact, the less were they likely to quarrel. Again was a letter written, and in more threatening terms than before. Sir Michael refused to discuss in writing the case of the *Arrow*, and insisted that nothing short of a personal interview between himself and Yeh, either on shipboard, or in Canton city, could settle the quarrel. Nothing daunted, Commissioner Yeh replied on the 3d, reiterating his assertions of the justice of his cause, and acceding to no propositions for a personal interview.

On the 6th a naval engagement took place on the river. The Chinese collected twenty-three war-junks in one spot, under the protection of the

French Folly fort, mounted with twenty six heavy guns. This fort was a little lower down the river than the Dutch Folly. Seymour resolved to disperse this junk-fleet at once. Commodore Elliot headed an attack by the guns, the crews, and the

Chinese War-junks.

boats of the *Barracouta* and *Coromandel*. A fierce exchange of firing took place; the Chinese having no less than a hundred and fifty guns in the junks and the fort. The fort was taken, the guns spiked, and the ammunition destroyed; the Chinese were driven out of the junks, and twenty-two of those vessels were burned. No fighting took place on the 7th. On the 8th the Chinese made a bold attempt to burn the British ships by fire-rafts; but the intended mischief was frustrated. The commissioner still being immovable, Bowring now suggested to Seymour that the next step ought to be the capture and destruction of the Bogue Forts—four powerfully armed defences on which the Chinese much relied. This was done after more fruitless negotiation.

Admiral Seymour had thus, by the middle of November, obtained full command of the Canton river; and he then stayed his operations for a while. The original cause of dispute, comparatively trifling, had now given place to a very grave state of affairs; and it remained to be seen whether the Palmerston ministry would lay all the blame on the obstinacy of Commissioner Yeh, or whether Bowring and Seymour would be considered to have exceeded their powers and their duties. So far as concerns the attitude of the Cantonese themselves, three deputations from the principal merchants and gentry waited on Mr Parkes between the 8th and 12th of November, to express their wishes that an amicable termination of the quarrel could be brought about; but at the same time to assert their conviction that, such was the inflexibility of the high-commissioner's character, he would never alter his expressed determination to refuse the English representatives admission into the city.

It may be well to remark in this place that the opium difficulty, which was unquestionably paramount above all others in the first war with China, had now lost much of its importance. The imperial government had in later years issued very few edicts against the traffic in this drug. Perhaps the quietness in this matter was mainly due to the fact that the export of silver to pay for the Indian opium was no longer needed—the increased sale of tea and silk being sufficient to make up an equivalent.

On the 26th of the month, other armed forts in the Canton river were taken by the English. The Chinese, in revenge for these proceedings, burned and destroyed almost all the European factories, mercantile buildings, and banks at Canton—leaving so little but ruins that Admiral Seymour could hardly find a roof to cover the seamen and marines when they afterwards landed. The commercial losses might be repaired; but an irreparable consequence of the incendiarism was the destruction of Dr Williams's printing establishment; including the large founts of Chinese type with which Morrison's Dictionary was printed; and comprising also more than 10,000 unsold volumes of books.

In this sort of piecemeal war, each successive attack irritated in its turn the opposite party; but the burning of the factories determined Bowring and Seymour to the adoption of a sterner policy than had hitherto been displayed. They resolved to bombard Canton itself, and to send an application to the governor-general of India for military aid—trusting that the home-government would hold them justified in adopting this course under difficulties and responsibilities of no light kind.

The year 1856 came to a close. The new year was ushered in with an attack by the Chinese on

Dutch Folly on the 1st of January. Six guns mounted on the Canton shore, and four on the opposite shore, fired into the Folly; but the small English force there stationed soon quelled this attack. On the 4th, a fleet of war-junks opened fire on the *Comus* and *Hornet* at the barrier in Macao Passage. No sooner did news of this attack reach Admiral Seymour, than he hastened forward in the *Coromandel*, towing all the available boats of the other ships. On nearing the junks, some of them undauntedly attacked the *Coromandel*, the boats, and a fort called the Teetotum Fort, which the English had before captured. The junks were heavily armed, and some of them had long snake-boats lashed to each side to row them along. A third fleet came down Sulphur Creek, and attacked the *Niger* and the *Encounter*. This was altogether a new aspect of the quarrel; the Chinese, not in the least humbled by the demands of Bowring and Seymour, became the assailants in the Canton river, and fought with a resolution hardly expected by their opponents. The attacks were not attended with very definite results. Not one junk was taken; they retired and collected into a somewhat formidable fleet of nearly four hundred.

The state of affairs was in every sense unsatisfactory to the English authorities. Commissioner Yeh was as firm as ever, and severely reproved the Canton gentry and merchants who had sent deputations to Sir Michael. He issued proclamations, denouncing the 'barbarians' in fiercer terms than before. Cruel massacres took place, whenever an isolated Englishman chanced to fall into the hands of the Chinese. Proclamations in the native language found their way to Hong-kong, inviting the seventy thousand Chinese residing in that island to rise against their English employers. Some of these Chinese were detected in attempts to introduce poison into the bread made for and sold to the English residents by the Chinese bakers. Against all this Bowring and Seymour could do little; and yet something, it was felt, must be attempted; for British trade at Canton was for a time ruined; and if matters were allowed to remain in their present state, the triumph of the Chinese would be most humiliating and pernicious to the English.

During the month of January (1857), while no progress was made in settling the differences at Canton, the spirit of the Chinese at Hong-kong became more and more hostile to the British; nor were those at Singapore unaffected by the taint. The warlike movements of the month—so far as that can be called war where no war had yet been declared—exasperated the Chinese, without making any impression on the obstinacy of Yeh. They consisted in the destruction of a portion of the city of Canton. Early on the morning of the 12th, bodies of marines and sailors set forth, armed with fireballs, torches, steeped oakum, &c.; they were conveyed in ships' boats, and landed on different parts of the suburbs of the city. The boats then retired a little way from the shore, while the *Barracouta*, *Encounter*, and *Niger*, kept watch in the middle of the river. The men advanced into the outer streets of the city, and commenced the work of destruction. The houses being mostly built of wood, they were easily ignited, and the breeze within an hour united all the fires into one vast sheet of flame. To increase the destruction, shot and shell were poured into the city from the ships and the fort. Throughout the whole of the day, did this miserable work continue—miserable in so far as it inflicted much suffering on the inhabitants, without hastening the capture of the city. On the 13th the attack ceased; Sir Michael Seymour made what arrangements he could to retain command of the passage of the Canton river; while the Cantonese provided for their houseless townspeople in hastily built structures. The British naval force under Sir Michael Seymour, comprising all the ships in the India and China seas, was by this time very formidable. It comprised the *Calcutta* (84), *Raleigh* (50), *Nanking* (50), *Sybille* (40), *Pique* (40), eight other sailing-vessels varying from 12 to 26 guns, twelve war-steamers, and seven steam gun-boats. These could have wrought great achievements in action at sea, with their 5000 seamen and marines; but there were scarcely any regular troops to conduct operations on land.

During February, the English consuls and traders could not but observe the increasing hostility of the Chinese. Dastardly assassinations occasionally took place; piracy was more rampant than ever; war-junks made their appearance wherever an English boat appeared to be insufficiently guarded; and proclamations were issued in the name of the emperor, applauding the firmness of Yeh. The merchants wished either that the affair of the *Arrow* had never been taken notice of by the British authorities, or else that the warlike operations had been carried on with more resolute effect. All the commercial relations had become disturbed, without any perceptible prospect of a return to peaceful trade. One of the worst features in the state of affairs was this —that as the English throughout the whole of the China seas were at all times few in number, they were obliged to employ Chinese servants and helpers; and these Chinamen were found now to be very little trustworthy. On the 23d of the month, the passenger-steamer *Queen* was on its way from Hong-kong to Macao; when suddenly the Chinese passengers joined with the Chinese crew in a murderous attack on the English passengers and officers, by which several lives were lost.

March arrived, but with it no solution of the Chinese difficulty. Even supposing Sir John Bowring, by this time, to have received instructions from home, warlike or otherwise, there had been no time to send him reinforcements of troops; and until such arrived, any extensive operations on land would be impracticable. Sir

John and his colleagues waited until their hands were strengthened.

In April, Seymour as well as Bowring remained quietly at Hong-kong, effecting nothing except the destruction of some junks. On the 6th, Commodore Elliot, with a fleet of armed boats from the *Sampson*, *Hornet*, *Sybille*, and *Nanking*, captured and destroyed eleven war-junks and two well-armed lorchas, after a chase and an engagement which lasted all day. Documents fell into the hands of the authorities at Hong-kong, tending to prove the complicity of the mandarins and many inhabitants of Canton in the various plots of incendiarism, kidnapping, and assassination, which had imperiled the persons and property of the English at that island. There were no present means of punishing these conspirators; but the discovery led to increased watchfulness.

The month of May witnessed no advance towards a settlement of Chinese difficulties. A great rebellion was distracting many inland provinces of the gigantic empire; but it did not appear that this could in any way help the English. Commissioner Yeh remained in his official residence at Canton, promising nothing, yielding nothing, and endeavouring to strengthen the city against the English. The Chinese, on the 3d, made an attempt to blow up the *Acorn* sloop-of-war in the Canton River, by means of a large iron tank filled with gunpowder, which was exploded close to the sloop; and a similar tank was afterwards found close to the *Hornet*—the first was exploded with little damage; the second was discovered before explosion.

Now occurred the sudden and startling outbreak in India, which wrought a most signal influence on the progress of affairs in China. Before this influence can usefully be traced, it will be necessary to glance briefly at the proceedings in England having reference to the Chinese quarrel.

It will be remembered that Sir John Bowring had incurred the heavy responsibility of commencing hostilities in October 1856, without special Foreign-office instructions; and that Sir Michael Seymour was equally without Admiralty instructions. These officers could not possibly receive an expression either of approval or condemnation, of advice or command, from England, until four or five months after the commencement of the troubles. It was near the close of the year when the British government received particulars of the first operations against Canton; and it was about the beginning of 1857 when the British newspapers and the nation took up the subject in earnest.

Immediately on the opening of the session of parliament in February 1857, ministers were eagerly pressed for information concerning the hostilities in China; because there was a general impression that an unduly severe punishment had been inflicted by Bowring and Seymour on the Chinese for a very small offence. On the 5th of February, the Earl of Ellenborough asked for the production of papers which might throw light on the affair of the lorcha *Arrow*, and prove whether it was an English or a Chinese vessel. The Earl of Clarendon, after promising the production of all the needful documents, stated that Sir John Bowring had not received any special instructions to demand admission into China; but that his general instructions authorised him 'to bear in mind the desirableness of obtaining that free access to Chinese ports which was mentioned in the treaty, and more particularly as regarded Canton.' Whether the means adopted by Bowring to obtain this free access were commendable, was a question on which the Houses of Parliament soon became fiercely engaged. Sir George Bonham, Bowring's predecessor, had not thought the admission into Canton a matter of great moment; and as Bowring was appointed by the Whigs, the Conservatives soon contrived to make a party question of it. Among the papers made public by the government about this time, was a dispatch written by the Earl of Clarendon to Sir John Bowring on the 10th of December 1856. The earl had just learned all that occurred at Canton between the 8th and the 15th of October; and he expressed an approval of the course pursued by Bowring and Parkes. Referring to voluminous documents which had been transmitted to him, he declared his opinions that the lorcha *Arrow* had a British master, British flag, and British papers, and was therefore a British vessel under the terms of the existing treaty; that if the Chinese authorities suspected there were pirates among the crew, they should have applied to the English consul, and not have taken the law into their own hands by boarding and violence—in short, he approved of what the British officials had done, so far as concerned the single week's proceedings which had alone come to his knowledge. Another mail brought over news of the seizure of the junks, and of the forcible entry of Sir Michael Seymour into Commissioner Yeh's house. This conduct met with the marked and clearly expressed commendation of the Earl of Clarendon, who, in a dispatch written on the 10th of January, complimented Seymour, Bowring, and Parkes on the moderation they had displayed under difficult circumstances.

On the 24th of February, the Earl of Derby moved a series of resolutions in the House of Lords: 'That this House has heard with deep regret of the interruption of amicable relations between her Majesty's subjects and the Chinese authorities at Canton; arising out of the measures adopted by her Majesty's chief-superintendent of trade to obtain reparation for alleged infractions of the Supplementary Treaty of the 8th of October 1843. That, in the opinion of this House, the occurrence of differences on this subject rendered the time peculiarly unfavourable for pressing on the Chinese authorities a claim for the admittance of British subjects into Canton, which had been left in abeyance since 1849; and for supporting the same by force of arms. That, in the opinion of this House, operations of actual hostilities ought not to have been undertaken without the express instructions, previously received, of her Majesty's government; and that neither of the subjects adverted to in the foregoing resolutions afforded sufficient justification for such operations.' These resolutions at once threw the whole blame on Sir John Bowring; his 'measures adopted' caused the 'interruption of amicable relations,' and the House 'heard with deep regret' this news. Of course, the ministers could not sanction the resolutions; they had already sent over approval of Bowring's conduct, and now they must manfully defend him. Hence arose a most exciting debate. The Treaty of 1842, the Supplementary Treaty of 1843, the Convention of 1847—all came into discussion, as well as the documents which had passed between the British and Chinese authorities. It became a party battle. All or nearly all the Whigs defended Sir John; all or nearly all the Conservatives attacked him. The judicial peers on the one side declared that the papers proved the *Arrow* to be a British vessel; those on the other asserted that the registry of that vessel at

CANTON.

Hong-kong had not been so conducted as to render this fact certain. The statesmen on the one side argued that Bowring was right to insist on being admitted into Canton by virtue of the treaty; those on the other contended that the right was not such as to justify him in bombarding the city. The general adherents of the one party believed the statement that the flag of the *Arrow* had been insultingly hauled down by the Chinese; those of the other credited the Chinese statement that the flag had not been hauled down. And so throughout the debate. It was quite as much a contest of Conservative against Whig, as of Bowring against Yeh. The Earl of Derby made a vehement appeal to the peers, for their condemnation of Sir John's conduct in going to war without express orders from home; and an earnest exhortation to the bishops 'to come forward on this occasion and vindicate the cause of religion, humanity, and civilisation from the outrage which had been inflicted upon it by the British representatives in Canton.' He declared that 'he should be disappointed indeed if the right reverend bench did not respond to this appeal.' The legal argument was very strongly contested against the government; Lords Lyndhurst, St Leonards, and Wensleydale all contending that, owing to some irregularities in the registry, the *Arrow* was virtually a Chinese vessel in October 1856, and that the Chinese authorities had a right to board it in search of pirates. On a division, the resolutions were negatived by 146 against 110—the bishops, notwithstanding the Earl of Derby's appeal, being as much divided as the other peers.

On the 26th the Commons took up the subject, in connection with a resolution proposed by Mr Cobden—'That this House has heard with concern of the conflicts which have occurred between the British and Chinese authorities in the Canton river; and, without expressing an opinion as to the extent to which the government of China may have afforded this country cause of complaint respecting the non-fulfilment of the treaty of 1842, this House considers that the papers which have been laid upon the table fail to establish satisfactory grounds for the violent measures resorted to at Canton in the late affair of the *Arrow*; and that a select committee be appointed to inquire into the state of our commercial relations with China.' This motion was more important than the one in the Lords, since it led to a dissolution of parliament. The debates extended through four evenings. Sir John Bowring was attacked by Mr Cobden, Sir E. Bulwer Lytton, Lord John Russell, Mr Warren, Mr Whiteside, Lord Goderich, Sir John Pakington, Sir F. Thesiger, Mr Sidney Herbert, Mr Roundell Palmer, Mr Milner Gibson, Mr Henley, Mr Roebuck, Mr Gladstone, and Mr Disraeli; while he was defended by Mr Labouchere, Mr Lowe, the Lord Advocate, Admiral Sir Charles Napier, Admiral Sir Maurice Berkeley, the Attorney-general, Sir George Grey, Sir Fenwick Williams 'of Kars,' Mr Serjeant Shee, Mr Bernal Osborne, and Lord Palmerston. It was not merely a contest between Liberals and Conservatives; for the Derby party were joined here by the small but influential Peel party; while the names of Russell, Cobden, Goderich, Milner Gibson, and Roebuck will shew to how large an extent the Liberals were dissatisfied with the proceedings in China. The arguments employed were such as have been more than once adverted to—that the *Arrow* was rather a Chinese than an English vessel; that the Chinese authorities had a right to board it, to search for pirates; that no British flag was hauled down, because none was flying on the lorcha at the time; that the return of the crew by the authorities ought to have satisfied Mr Parkes; that as Commissioner Yeh gave explanations, a demand ought not to have been made upon him for an apology also; that Sir John Bowring ought not to have extended the quarrel so as to include the question of his admission into Canton; that the seizure of the junks was illegal; and that the bombardment of Canton was not only illegal, but ferocious and unbefitting Christian men. Every one of these positions was disputed by the government; nevertheless the House of Commons sanctioned them, or the resolutions which implied them, by a majority of 263 over 247. This vote, arrived at on the 3d of March, determined Lord Palmerston to appeal to the country by dissolving the existing parliament and assembling a new one.

During the interregnum between the two parliaments, public opinion was much divided concerning Chinese affairs. Lord Palmerston was at that time in much favour, and his courage was admired in defending an absent subordinate when fiercely attacked; still it was not without a painful feeling that the nation heard of a great city being bombarded for trivial reasons. Those who most warmly defended Sir John Bowring were those who best knew the faithlessness of the Chinese authorities. By a combination of various causes, direct and indirect, a new House of Commons was elected more devoted to Lord Palmerston than the one which preceded it; and the Chinese war then became a settled question, so far as that branch of the legislature was concerned. During the interval of more than two months, between the adverse vote on the 3d of March and the assembling of the new parliament on the 7th of May, the government were making arrangements for bringing the Chinese difficulty to a satisfactory termination. They told off certain regiments to be sent to China; they appointed General Ashburnham to command them; they sent over the Earl of Elgin with large powers to control the whole of the proceedings; and they arranged with the French government a joint plan of action for obtaining, if possible, free commerce at all the Chinese ports. This scheme of policy was formed and partially put in execution; but the various portions of it were only by degrees made publicly known.

When parliament reassembled in May, numerous questions were put to the ministers in both Houses—concerning the appointment of General Ashburnham; the poisonings at Hong-kong; the treatment of Chinese prisoners; the relations between the East India Company and China in reference to the opium trade; the condition of Hong-kong as a British colony; the emigration of Chinese coolies—and other matters bearing upon the state of affairs in the Chinese seas. It speedily transpired that the French government had appointed Baron Gros, to act with the Earl of Elgin in the political negotiations with the Chinese; that the United States government would also send out a plenipotentiary; and that the Russian governor of the sterile provinces on the banks of the Amoor would be intrusted with similar powers by the court of St Petersburg. If peaceful efforts should fail to bring the Chinese government to amicable relations, war was to be carried on more energetically than before. In addition to the regiments of troops, the British government sent out the *Furious* steam-frigate, the *Surprise* and *Mohawk* dispatch-boats, thirteen steam gun-boats, and a steam transport. The Earl of Elgin left England on the 21st of April; General Ashburnham had started two or three weeks earlier; and the troops had gradually been shipped off as transport for them could be obtained. Certain regiments had been assigned to India, to relieve other regiments which had been long stationed there; but it was now proposed to send them first to China, whence, after settling the troubles, they might be transferred to India.

Little did the English government foresee how strangely their plans would be overturned by the formidable Revolt in India. In the earlier half of the month of June, the English nation directed no particular attention to the affairs of the east. The Persian war had come to a close; the Chinese difficulty was languidly waiting for a solution; and news of the Indian Revolt had not yet arrived.

But the close of the month witnessed a different state of things. The terrible tragedies at Meerut and Delhi were now known; and legislators and the press alike demanded that the comparatively unimportant Chinese expedition should not be allowed to absorb the services of Queen's troops so much needed in India. On the 29th, in the House of Lords, the Earl of Ellenborough said: 'We have sent to China that naval force which should, in my opinion, be left upon the shores of England, to give security to this country even under the auspices of the most profound peace. That naval force has been despatched to the Chinese waters—for what?—to carry on a contest between Sir John Bowring and Commissioner Yeh! Six battalions of troops have been sent out there for the same purpose; but I cannot help thinking that those six battalions will be found insufficient to bring under our control the numerous population of Canton. The consequence will be, that we shall find ourselves under the necessity of sending out further reinforcements. But are we, with India in danger, to fight the battle of the government? Are we, my lords, determined, happen what may, to persevere in that fatal policy which her Majesty's ministers have adopted?' Similar animadversions were made in the House of Commons by Mr Disraeli. The ministers, while announcing the immediate dispatch of more troops to India, did not promise that the Chinese expedition should be diverted from its purpose; for they underrated at that time the serious import of the sepoy revolt. Soon afterwards, however, when the news from India became more and more gloomy, orders were issued that some of the troops not yet embarked should be sent to India instead of China. As no such catastrophe as a mutiny in India could reasonably be anticipated when the Earl of Elgin was sent out, the ministers could not tell how far that plenipotentiary might accede to any application made to him by the governor-general of India for the use of the troops already approaching or in the Indian seas.

Such being the progress of opinion and of preparation in England in reference to the Chinese quarrel, we may resume the rapid sketch of operations in China itself.

When, at about the middle of May 1857, Viscount Canning received news at Calcutta of the disasters at Meerut and Delhi, he instantly, as we have seen in a former chapter,* transmitted telegraphic messages to Bombay, Ceylon, and Madras. He inquired whether the Earl of Elgin and General Ashburnham had arrived at either of those stations, on their way to China; and made earnest applications that the troops sent from England to China might be diverted from that route, and despatched to Calcutta instead. Canning and Elgin had both been intrusted by their sovereign with extensive powers; both, when they came to communicate, saw that the events in India were more critical than those in China; and both were of opinion that the Queen's troops were more wanted on the Jumna and Ganges than on the Canton or Pekin rivers. Hence arose an almost entire stoppage of the operations in the China seas till towards the close of the year. The slight events that marked the summer and autumn may be noticed in a few brief paragraphs.

Towards the close of May, before any considerable reinforcements could reach China, an attack was made by the British on a fleet of Chinese war-junks with very considerable effect. One of the many channels which the Canton river presents, called by the English Escape Creek, being known to contain a large fleet of junks, Commodore Elliot was ordered to make a vigorous demonstration in that quarter. On the 25th he entered the creek, with the *Hong-kong*, *Bustard*, *Staunch*, *Starling*, and *Forbes*, towing boats filled with men from the *Inflexible*, *Hornet*, and *Tribune*. He found forty-one mandarin junks, all heavily armed, moored across the creek; a brisk engagement ensued; and it was not until after the loss of many men, on the 25th and two following days, that the junks were destroyed.

The month of June opened with an engagement of more importance—the battle of Fatshan. This city is about seven miles distant in a straight line from Canton, but lying upon a different affluent of the Canton river. The expedition was not so much against Fatshan itself, as against a fleet of junks lying in the Fatshan branch or channel. Sir Michael Seymour himself accompanied this expedition. The channel was too narrow to admit any except small-craft; and therefore the work was to be done by gun-boats and row-boats. At three in the morning of the 1st of June the expedition started forth, the *Coromandel* towing three hundred marines in open boats. Many heavily armed forts line the Fatshan creek near the city, and these speedily opened fire as the boats advanced. When the *Coromandel* had nearly reached the town, the *Hong-kong*, *Haughty*, *Bustard*, *Forester*, *Plover*, *Opossum*, and other gun-boats, steamed up, each having its few but formidable guns, and each towing ships' boats full of 'blue-jackets.' The men landed at the foot of a hill which was crowned with a fort mounting twenty large guns, and which from that day was called Fort Seymour. The rush up the hill was exciting; commodores, captains, lieutenants, seamen, marines, all ran up, equally regardless of danger; and after a few rounds from the fort's guns, the Chinese, dismayed at the boldness of the English, took flight, and ran away from their guns. The assailants then hastened to attack the junks, which, mounting twelve guns each, were able to pour forth a tremendous fire of shot and shell. How the British escaped with so little loss in this encounter is a marvel. The seamen were in ecstasies at the boldness of the duty assigned to them. The boats' crews baffled the shots from so many hundred guns by rowing right up to the

* Chapter xiii., p. 211.

junks, *beneath* the line of fire of the guns; and when there, they did not cease till they had set fire to the junks, from which the crews escaped precipitately over the opposite sides. Out of the seventy-two junks, sixty-seven were destroyed.

Anxious were the speculations whether these renewed successes would or would not lead to any decisive termination of the struggle. Bowring and Parkes among the civilians, Seymour and Elliot among the naval commanders, knew well enough that without a military force this could not be done. They knew, moreover, that until the Earl of Elgin should arrive, they could not be placed fully in possession of the views of the home-government. They anxiously counted the days before the new arrivals would be announced. The Earl of Elgin and General Ashburnham were at Bombay on the day when the disastrous news from Meerut and Delhi reached that city. The general went on to Hong-kong, where he arrived on the 10th of June; but the earl, after reaching Singapore, gave orders that two of the approaching regiments should be diverted from the Chinese expedition to the service of Viscount Canning. This was ominous of the cessation of any effective operations on the China coast. Elgin, moreover, issued orders that, if Canning should make pressing application for more aid, other regiments should be similarly diverted to Calcutta. Meanwhile, at Canton, Yeh remained as impassable as ever; he did not yield an inch. The rich were flying from the city, the poor were half starved by the stoppage of all trade; nevertheless these miseries, bad enough to the Chinese themselves, did not improve the position of the English.

Early in July the Earl of Elgin arrived in the *Shannon* war-steamer. A large staff of military officers had now assembled at Hong-kong; but there was nothing for them to do, seeing that the regiments had not arrived, nor did it appear probable how soon Canning could spare them. A fleet and a staff of military officers were now in the Canton river almost in a state of idleness. The active correspondent of the *Times*, having no fighting to witness, made those rambling visits to Shang-hae and elsewhere which enabled him to give so graphic an account of the Chinese in their homes and shops and places of amusement. On the 13th the French admiral arrived at Hong-kong, to confer with Elgin on the policy to be pursued. At first there was an intention of steaming up to the Pei-ho river, on which the imperial city of Pekin stands, to bring the emperor to a conference. Within a few days, however, an urgent dispatch arrived from Viscount Canning, announcing that the revolt was spreading widely in India, and asking for further aid. The Earl of Elgin at once changed his plan. He set off to Calcutta, taking with him a force of fifteen hundred seamen and marines, mostly belonging to the *Shannon* and *Pearl* war-steamers. It was these hardy men who constituted the 'Naval Brigades' so often mentioned in past chapters of this work, and in service with which the gallant Captain Sir William Peel met his death. Elgin's determination was arrived at in part from this circumstance—that Baron Gros, the French high-commissioner or plenipotentiary, was not expected at Hong-kong until September; and that any negotiations at Pekin would be weakened in force unless the two countries acted in conjunction through their respective representatives.

August found the English officers and seamen very little satisfied with their position and duties in the Chinese waters. An occasional junk-hunt was all that occurred to break the monotony. Of fighting, such as men-of-war's men would dignify by the name, there was little or none. Yeh continued to govern Canton; the Cantonese continued to suffer by the suspension of their trade with the British. The four northern ports managed to retain a trade which was very lucrative to them—selling tea and silk to the English, and buying opium, which the Chinese dealers sold again at an enormous profit in the upper or inner provinces. As for the emperor at Pekin, the English authorities at Hong-kong had no means of determining to what extent he was cognizant of affairs in the south, nor how far he sanctioned the immovable line of policy followed by his viceroy at Canton.

In the early part of September, Yeh took advantage of the lull in warlike operations; he built more junks, cast more cannon, raised up several guns which had been sunk by the English, and collected a fleet of two hundred war-junks in the Canton and Fatshan waters, ready to encounter the 'barbarians' again in time of need. As a means of ascertaining what was in progress in this quarter, Commodore Elliot set forth from Hong-kong to make a reconnaissance. He started up the Canton river on the 9th, taking with him the gun-boats *Starling*, *Haughty*, and *Forester*, and the heavy boats of the *Sybille* and *Highflyer*. He steamed through some of the channels, which are so numerous as to convert the banks of the river into a veritable archipelago, difficult to explore on account of the shallowness of the water in the channels. He met with a vast array of trading-junks, which he did not molest because they were engaged in peaceful commerce; and a few war-junks, which he destroyed; but he did not reach any spot where war-junks in large numbers were congregated. One event of this month was the appearance of Russia on the scene. Admiral Count Putiatine, who had been appointed governor of the Russian province of Amoor, and who had made a rapid overland journey from St Petersburg to the mouth of the Amoor in seventy days, steamed from that river to the Pei-ho on a diplomatic mission. The purport of this mission was not revealed to the English; but there were many at Hong-kong who surmised that Russia, like the United States, was secretly planning that a goodly share of any contingent advantages arising from the struggle should fall to her—leaving all the odium of hostilities on the shoulders of England and France.

When October arrived, the stormy state of the China seas rendered it doubtful how soon the Earl of Elgin's diplomatic expedition to Pekin would take place. The British community at Hong-kong rather rejoiced at this; for they had all along advocated the simple formula—take Canton first, and negotiate with the emperor afterwards. The earl's intention to postpone his visit becoming clearly known, many of the staff-officers who had been in enforced idleness at Hong-kong took their departure—some to Calcutta, some to other places. When Baron Gros arrived in the *Audacieuse*, which was not until the middle of October, the talk of the fleet was that Canton would be really and effectually besieged, as a preliminary to any proceedings further north. The *Imperador* arrived towards the close of the month, bringing five hundred marines direct from England; and large accessions of warlike stores denoted a resolution on the part of the government to bring about some definite termination of this Chinese quarrel.

In November, General Ashburnham, apparently tired of doing nothing in China, gave up the military command and went to India, where a proffer of his services was courteously declined by Lord Canning and Sir Colin Campbell. His sudden return to England, without leave, gave rise to much comment in and out of parliament. General Straubenzee now became military commander in China, that is, commander of the British troops whenever they should arrive. Captain Sherard Osborne was collecting gun-boats from various quarters. Baron Gros undertook that France would operate in the capture of Canton, with three frigates, two corvettes, and four gun-boats, containing altogether about a thousand men. Mr Reed arrived in the *Minnesota*, as American commissioner to represent the interests of his country, but without any intention of taking part in the hostile demonstration. Throughout the whole affair, indeed, the United States 'fraternised' much more freely with Russia than with England and France.

At length the month arrived (December 1857) which was to witness the conquest of Canton. At the beginning of this month the European war-vessels in Chinese waters were really formidable in number. Besides the *Calcutta* (80), there were, including everything from steam-frigates down to gun-boats, a total of 70 European and American war-vessels, of which no less than 49 were British. On the 12th of the month, the Earl of Elgin sent a formal letter to Commissioner Yeh—announcing his arrival as ambassador extraordinary from Queen Victoria to the Emperor of China, and as plenipotentiary to settle all existing differences; expressing the pleasure which England would feel in being on friendly terms with China; enumerating the causes of complaint against the Chinese authorities; demanding 'the complete execution at Canton of all treaty engagements, including the free admission of British subjects into the city,' and 'compensation to British subjects and persons entitled to British protection for losses incurred in consequence of the late disturbances;' threatening a seizure of Canton if these terms were not acceded to; and hinting that the terms would in that case be rendered much more severe. On the 14th Yeh sent a reply, very tortuous and cunning, justifying the conduct of himself and his countrymen, but evading any direct notice of Elgin's demand and threat. On the 24th the British plenipotentiary wrote to announce that, as his desire for a peaceful termination of the dispute had not been properly met, he should at once prepare for war. The next day (Christmas-day) brought a second letter from Yeh, repeating his former arguments in a very discursive fashion, but evading everything in the way of concession.

When December had brought what few troops the home-government and Lord Canning thought they could spare for China, the available numbers appeared as follow—800 men of various services, principally of the 59th foot, from the garrison of Hong-kong; 2500 marines belonging to the various ships; 1500 naval brigade formed from the ships' crews for service on shore; and 900 French troops and seamen—making a total of 5700 men. These were aided by about 1000 Chinese and Malay coolies, as carriers and labourers—men who readily sold their patriotism for silver and copper. On the 16th, while the attempt at negotiation with Yeh was still going on, the English and French took possession of Honan, as a measure of precaution. This is an island just opposite Canton; its shore forms the Southwark of the great city. The merchants and traders were allowed all possible facilities for removing their families and goods from such buildings as the captors chose to appropriate—the wish being to inflict as small an amount of suffering as possible on the Chinese people, whom the Earl of Elgin carefully distinguished from the Chinese government. From the 16th to the 23d, steamers and gun-boats were daily arriving, and taking up positions mostly between Canton and the island. On the 22d a council was held, at which the Earl of Elgin and Baron Gros, having virtually declared war against China, gave up the command of the operations to the general and the two admirals—namely, General Straubenzee, Admiral Sir Michael Seymour, and Admiral R. de Genouilly. On the 23d, several military and naval officers steamed in gun-boats past the whole length of the city, landed at a point beyond its northwestern extremity, walked a mile and a half under the escort of a party of marines and sailors, mounted a hill, made accurate observations on a series of forts north of the city, and returned without the loss of a man. On the 24th there was a similar reconnaissance east and northeast of the city. These examinations satisfied the officers that the capture of the northern forts must be made from the east rather than the west. Christmas-day and the two following days were spent in making preparations for the bombardment; and in distributing papers along the shore, announcing to the Cantonese what calamity was in store for their city if Yeh did not yield before midnight on the 27th. The viceroy remained as immovable as ever, and so the terrible work began.

At daylight on the morning of the 28th of December the guns opened fire. Their number was enormous—some in war-steamers, some in gun-boats, some on Honan Island, some in the captured forts. The general orders were to fire at various parts of the city-wall, and over the city to the northern forts, but to work as little mischief as possible to the inhabited streets. Meanwhile the troops, marines, and naval brigade gradually effected a landing at about a mile from the eastern extremity of the city; they landed guns and vast quantities of stores and ammunition, and then proceeded by regular siege-operations to capture all the forts on the northern side of the city—the bombardment of the southern and western wall still continuing. These fearful operations continued throughout the last four days of the year, during which an immense number of fragile wooden buildings were burned—not purposely, but of necessity. The Chinese soldiers did not shew in any vast numbers, nor did they display much heroism; the assailants conquered one fort after another, until they held the whole of the eastern and northern margin of the city—having free communication with their ships by a line of route to their unmolested landing-place. Great as was the amount of burning of wooden tenements, the loss of life was very small; the allied killed and wounded were less than 150, and the Chinese loss was believed to be not more than double that number—so careful had the soldiers and sailors been to avoid bringing slaughter into a place containing a million of human beings.

Rarely has a city been held under a more singular tenure than Canton was held by the English and French on New-year's Day 1858. They were masters of all the defences, and naturally inferred that the city would formally yield. Nothing of the kind, however, took place. The Cantonese resumed trade in their streets and shops, but Yeh and his officers kept wholly out of sight. The ordinary usages of war were ignored by this singular people. Elgin, Gros, Straubenzee, Seymour, Genouilly—all came to the captured forts on the northern heights, and all were perplexed how to deal with these impassible Cantonese. On the 2d of January and two following days the captors lived in much discomfort on the heights; but on the 5th a very decided advance was made. Mr Parkes, and a few other Englishmen who were familiar with the Chinese language, had been busily engaged collecting information concerning the hiding-places of the dignitaries within the city; and, acting on the information thus obtained, Straubenzee sent several strongly armed parties into different districts of the city. The results were very important. The explorers captured Commissioner Yeh, the lieutenant-governor Peh-kwei, the Tatar general of the Chinese forces in and near Canton, fifty-two boxes of dollars in the treasury, and sixty-eight packages of silver ingots.

From the 5th of January to the 10th of February the city was placed under very anomalous government. In the first place, Yeh was sent as a sort of prisoner to Calcutta. In the next place, Yeh's palace became the head-quarters of the allied authorities; while other large buildings were appropriated as barracks. The Earl of Elgin decided that the Tatar general and the lieutenant-governor of Canton should be liberated. The general, Tseang-keun, was obliged to disarm and disband his troops, as a condition of his liberation. Elgin thought it prudent that Peh-kwei should be formally made governor of the city, to save it from pillage. On the 9th the installation of this functionary took place, in the presence of Elgin, Gros, Bowring, Parkes, Straubenzee, Seymour, Genouilly, and other officials. Colonel Holloway, Captain Martineau, and Mr Parkes were appointed commissioners, or a council of three, to assist Peh-kwei in his municipal duties. The city now became safely traversable by the English and French without much danger; the Chinese soldiers were disbanded; and the citizens were willing enough to go on with such trade as was left to them. The council of three insisted on organising an efficient street-police; on expediting the administration of justice; on visiting all the prisons; and on liberating such wretched captives as appeared to have been unjustly incarcerated. Although Peh-kwei protested loudly against this interference with his supreme authority, he was obliged to submit. This period was a saturnalia for pirates; the regular government being subverted, thousands of lawless men on the river carried on with impunity that system of piracy and plunder which the numerous creeks around Canton rendered so practicable. When this became fully known to the authorities now in the ascendant, Sir Michael Seymour put in force a severe measure of attack and reprisal against them.

How far the objects of the war had been attained, remained still a problem. Canton, it is true, was seized; but the imperial court at Pekin was invisible and inaccessible, and much evidently remained yet to be done. On the 10th of February the blockade was raised. The Canton river was speedily swarming with trading junks; the Honan warehouses were reopened and refilled; British merchants resumed their dealings with Chinese merchants; and within a few days many million pounds of tea were on their way to England. Shortly after the removal of the blockade, the Earl of Elgin and Baron Gros opened communications with Count Putiatine and Mr Reed; they proposed, in the names of England and France, that Russia and the United States should take part in the demands still necessary to be made upon the Emperor of China. These overtures were promptly met; but it must in justice be stated that, in the subsequent operations and negotiations for obtaining treaties, the Russian and American plenipotentiaries adopted a more secret and selfish policy than comported with the liberal offer made on the part of England and France. Elgin and Gros determined that Canton should remain in their power until full and satisfactory treaties had been obtained from the emperor. It affords a curious illustration of the indomitable perseverance of the English newspaper press, that the *Times* correspondent, Mr Wingrove Cooke, after seeing all the fighting in the Canton waters, and incurring as much hazard as his colleague Mr Russell had incurred in similar duties in the Crimea, contrived to obtain a passage in the ship (the *Inflexible*) which conveyed Yeh to Calcutta, and to draw forth many peculiarities in the character of that redoubtable Chinaman—a personage who, through the columns of that newspaper, soon became familiarly known in nearly every part of the globe; a man whose shipboard life was thus summed up, 'he eats a great deal, sleeps a great deal, and washes very little.'

Early in March, after the forwarding to Pekin of official dispatches under such circumstances as to render probable their receipt by the emperor, Elgin and Gros moved towards the north. This conveyance of letters was, as is usual in the Celestial Empire, a most complicated affair. Mr Lawrence Oliphant, the Earl of Elgin's private secretary, and Viscount de Contades, secretary of legation to Baron Gros, went from Canton to Shang-hae, bearing letters from the English and French plenipotentiaries, and also from those of America and Russia. After reaching Shang-hae, and being joined by the British, French, and American consuls, they pushed on in boats up the river, on whose banks stands the city of Soo-choo, the capital of that part of China. The governor endeavoured by every means to avoid an interview; but as the messengers would not be refused, he received them with an unwilling courtesy, and undertook to forward their letters to Pekin. The envoys then returned to Shang-hae. Certain arrangements were now made for the safety of Canton and Hong-kong, and vast stores were sent up to Shang-hae, in preparation for any contingencies. The Earl of Elgin and his suite, on their way to Shang-hae, sojourned for a while at Fuh-choo-foo. All the plenipotentiaries arrived at Shang-hae during the latter half of the month. They received answers from the court of Pekin to their several letters. The Chinese authorities endeavoured so to treat the subject as to keep the plenipotentiaries as far away from Pekin as possible. They alleged that, whether Yeh had or had not misused his authority at Canton, he was now dismissed, and was replaced by a viceroy who would be ready to listen to any reasonable representations; they recommended that the English and French plenipotentiaries had better return to the south, there to resume their superintendence of peaceful commerce; that the Russians should return to the north, and the Americans remain quietly at the trading ports. These replies did not purport to come from the emperor, who was too lofty a personage to recognise the plenipotentiaries; they came through the governor of the Shang-hae province, and were worded in the customary style of Chinese magniloquence.

The month of April found the Chinese quarrel apparently as far from solution as ever. The advice of the imperial authorities, that they should keep away from Pekin, and attend to their trading affairs, was not likely to be followed by the plenipotentiaries—one of whom, at any rate, had come from Europe for a far different purpose. Affairs did not progress very favourably at Canton. Pirates continued to infest the river; while an army of rebels—equally hostile to the imperialists and to the 'barbarians'—was marching towards the city from the interior. Many of the inhabitants, rendered uneasy by the strange confusion in the government and ownership of their city, fled from Canton. The English merchants found their trading arrangements sadly checked by these sources of disquietude; and they sighed for the return of those times when opium, and tea, and silk brought them large profits. Finding, as they had all along surmised, that nothing effectual could be done except in the immediate vicinity of Pekin, the plenipotentiaries took their departure from Shang-hae, and steamed northward. Count Putiatine, in the *America* steamer, anchored off the Pei-ho river on the 14th; a few hours afterwards arrived the *Furious* and the *Leven*, in the former of which was the Earl of Elgin; Mr Reed, in the *Mississippi*, made his appearance on the 16th; Baron Gros, in the *Audacieuse*, joined his brother-plenipotentiaries on the 23d; and Admirals Seymour and Genouilly arrived on the 24th. Letters were now sent off to Pekin, demanding the appointment of an official of high rank to meet the representatives of the four courts, to confer on the matters in dispute; and allowing six days for the return of an answer. This decisive step produced a more immediate effect than any course yet adopted; the emperor, unless wholly deceived by those around him, had now ample means of knowing that a formidable armament was at the mouth of the river on whose banks the imperial city is situated, and that Russia and America had joined England and France in this demonstration. Before the six days had expired, a messenger arrived to announce that Tao, or Tān, governor-general of the province, had been appointed as envoy to meet the plenipotentiaries. Meanwhile, the month of May was a troubled one in Canton. The new governor Hwang, and the lieutenant-governor Peh-kwei, were frequently detected in manœuvres not quite satisfactory to the English and French officers left in charge of the city. Many of the Cantonese themselves believed that Hwang had received secret orders from Pekin to retake Canton while the allies were engaged in the northern waters. There were machinations at

Pekin, rebel armies in the inner provinces, restless Tatars in the Canton province, pirates in the river, and unreliable Chinese authorities everywhere; insomuch that the continuance of quietude in the city was very problematical. During the month, about 1200 sepoys arrived from Calcutta; they had belonged to the 47th and 65th Bengal native infantry, disarmed in India as a matter of precaution, but not implicated in actual mutiny; the 70th had preceded them, and had behaved steadily in China.

The Earl of Elgin and Baron Gros experienced the customary difficulty in bringing the Chinese to anything like a candid agreement or understanding. The new envoy, Tao, was long in making his appearance; and when he did appear, his powers of treating were found to be so limited, and his attempts at evasion so many, that the aid of cannon-balls was again found to be necessary. Steamers were quickly sent down to Shang-hae, Hong-kong, and Canton, for reinforcements; and on the 20th of May hostile operations began. The banks of the Pei-ho being defended by forts, these forts were attacked one by one, and captured. The plenipotentiaries were by this means enabled to advance higher up the river, increasing their chance of a direct communication with the authorities at Pekin. The Chinese had not been idle; for throughout the month they had been seen drilling their troops in the forts, and sinking junks to bar the navigation of the river; but the gun-boats which the English and French had now brought up, and the boats of the war-ships, made light of these obstructions. The Russian and American ambassadors were pretty well satisfied with the trading concessions offered to them by the Chinese authorities; but the English and French were determined to be satisfied with nothing less than a definite settlement of all the points in dispute; and hence the attack on the forts, which evidently produced an immense excitement higher up the river.

June began with a battle, or at least, a skirmish, outside Canton—shewing that a peaceful occupation of that city was not readily to be looked for. A military force of 'braves' or Chinese soldiers having gradually been approaching from the north, General Straubenzee deemed it necessary to encounter and crush or disperse them at once. On the 2d, accompanied by Mr Parkes, he started off to the hills on the north of the city, having with him about a thousand men supplied with three days' rations. The braves, who were soon met with, kept up a skirmishing fight all day on the 3d, and then retired without much loss. Straubenzee returned to Canton on the 4th, also without much loss in actual fighting; but his soldiers had been stricken down in considerable number by the terrible heat of the sun. The expedition was scarcely to be considered satisfactory; for the braves were still hovering among the hills, very little disheartened by their defeat. As the month advanced, the state of affairs at Canton became worse and worse. Rockets were frequently fired at night into the posts held by the allies; the suburbs were full of armed ruffians ready for any mischief; the streets became unsafe to Europeans unless armed or guarded; occasional attacks were made on the police, and even on the sentries; headless bodies of Europeans were sometimes found in the river; two or three sailors were waylaid, cut down, and carried off; and placards were posted up about the city, couched in the most ferocious language against the 'foreign devils.' One of these placards designated the British consul as 'the red-haired barbarian Parkes.'

The state of affairs further north, during this month of June, was more favourable. The destruction of the forts on the banks of the Pei-ho had the effect of bringing the Chinese authorities again into a disposition for negotiation. The river was carefully examined from Ta-koo up to Tien-sing—a city of 300,000 inhabitants, situated on the high road to Pekin, at a point where the Great Canal of China enters the Pei-ho. The four plenipotentiaries steamed up to Tien-sing, where they were allowed to remain; seeing that the Chinese government, paralysed by the capture of the forts, no longer made an attempt to obstruct them. Governor Tao was dismissed, for having managed matters badly; and two mandarins of high rank, Kwei-liang and Hwa-sha-na, were appointed to negotiate with the barbarians. The plenipotentiaries took up their abode on shore, in a house provided by the mandarins; and a renewed series of negotiations commenced. Meanwhile, all hostilities were suspended; the war-junks and the gun-boats remained peacefully at anchor, and the trading-junks were allowed to pass up and down the river. About the middle of the month, some of the inhabitants of Tien-sing manifested a disposition to molest the plenipotentiaries and their suites; whereupon Sir Michael Seymour ordered up a few seamen and marines—who, perambulating the walls and streets of the city for a few hours, gave such a check to the citizens as to induce a more peaceful demeanour. One of the first definite results of the conferences which now ensued, was a treaty between China and the United States, signed on the 18th of June by Mr Reed and the two Chinese mandarins. America had from the first sought to obtain the best terms for herself, without much consideration for the other powers; and as her demeanour was more courteous than threatening, more submissive than dignified; as, moreover, her demands were not so extensive as those of England—she found less difficulty in settling the terms of a commercial treaty, which would open up a door for increased American trading with China; and with this Mr Reed was well satisfied. Count Putiatine about the same date signed a treaty as the representative of Russia. The policy of his court was to keep the other great powers as far from Pekin as possible, in order that nothing might check the gradual growth of Russian influence on the northern frontier of the Chinese empire. The terms of the Russian treaty were far more important than those of the American; they included the cession to Russia of a large area of country near the mouth of the great river Amoor, and of an amount of trading privileges such as had never before been conceded by China to any other country whatever.

The English and French treaties, especially the former, being more comprehensive in their character, could not be settled so readily as the American. Commissioner Key-ing, who had concluded the treaty of Nankin with Sir Henry Pottinger in 1842, was sent from Pekin to Tien-sing to assist Kwei-liang and Hwa-sha-na in the present instance; but the Earl of Elgin, seeing that Key-ing was disposed for a course of cunning and trickery, refused to treat with him; and the negotiations were left to the other two commissioners. All difficulties being gradually removed by three weeks of negotiation, treaties were at

HONG-KONG.

length signed on the 26th and 27th of June respectively by the Earl of Elgin and Baron Gros, with the two Chinese commissioners. The provisions were nearly the same for England and for France, except an indemnity to be given to the former nation for the expenses of the war and for certain losses incurred by the merchants. The more important clauses of the English treaty may be thus thrown into a summary: Confirmation of the former Treaty of Nankin—Agreement to appoint British ambassador at Pekin, and Chinese ambassador at London—Family and suite of British ambassador to have residence and security at Pekin, and facilities for travelling, transaction of business, and transmission of letters—British ambassador to correspond on terms of equality with the Chinese minister for foreign affairs—Christianity, whether Protestant or Catholic, to be tolerated, and Christian missionaries protected throughout the Chinese Empire—British subjects permitted to trade and to travel in the interior—Chin-kiang, on the great river Yang-tsze-kiang; Niuchwang, in Manchooria; Tang-choo, in the Gulf of Pe-che-lee; Tae-wan, in the island of Formosa; Swatow and Kiung-choo, in the island of Hainan, to be declared free ports; in addition to Canton, Amoy, Fuh-choo-foo, Ning-po, and Shang-hae, the five already opened; and in addition, also, to three other ports on the Yang-tsze-kiang, as soon as they should be freed from rebels—An Anglo-Chinese commission to prepare a commercial tariff, which is to be revised every ten years—Inland transit dues to be commuted for an *ad valorem* rate—Official correspondence to be conducted in English as the text or original, with a Chinese translation as an accompaniment—The Chinese character or symbol denoting 'barbarian' to be in future omitted in Chinese official documents relating to foreigners—British ships-of-war permitted to visit any ports in the empire, and their commanders to be treated on terms of equality by the Chinese officials—Both nations to assist in suppressing piracy in Chinese waters—Amount of indemnity to be settled by a separate article.

The Earl of Elgin would not quit Tien-sing until he had clearly ascertained that the emperor understood and accepted the terms of the treaty: this done, he returned on the 6th of July to Shang-hae.

It is impossible to avoid seeing that such a treaty, if faithfully carried out, would greatly revolutionise the commercial and social institutions of China. If British ships-of-war be permitted to visit any of the ports, and trading-ships have free entry to nearly a dozen of the number; if the great Yang-tsze-kiang be made a channel up which British manufactures may penetrate; if Christian missionaries may teach and preach, print and distribute, without opposition from the government; if a British official may reside at the imperial city, and the Chinese emperor condescend to appoint an ambassador to London; finally, if the vain assumption of superiority be discontinued in Chinese official documents relating to the English—an immense advance will have been made towards bringing China into the fraternity of nations. The great doubt was, whether so vast a change would not be too extensive to be made at once—too humiliating, in the Chinese view, for the imperial government to adopt in its integrity: especially as the British did not offer to assist the emperor against the rebels who ravaged his dominions. It was not expected that the formalities of ratification could all be completed before the summer of 1859. The Hon. Mr Bruce, brother to the Earl of Elgin, conveyed the treaty to England. No sooner was the tenor of the treaty known, than English merchants began to make inquiries and calculations concerning increased exports, of salt and other commodities, to the China seas. The indemnity question was felt to be one which could not be settled without long delay, in treating with so peculiar a people as the Chinese. Commissioners on both sides were to decide how much should be paid by China, for injury inflicted on British property at Canton, and for the expenses of the British expedition; they were also to decide on the revised tariff for imports and exports.

While the terms of this treaty were being settled at Tien-sing, the state of Canton became more and more disturbed. Street-murders were very frequent; bags of gunpowder were exploded in the streets, at moments when patrols were expected to pass; and missiles were hurled, from unseen quarters, into all parts of the city where Europeans resided. Many of the more peaceful citizens left Canton, and their houses were at once seized by ruffians, who posted up proclamations of most ultra-Chinese character. One of these proclamations was to the effect that, 'We have ascertained that there are only two or three thousand English and French dogs in the city; but our numbers are thousands on thousands; and if every one of us carry but a sword to kill every foreigner that we meet, we shall soon kill them all. If any one trade or supply provisions to the foreign dogs, we shall arrest and punish him according to the village regulations. All those who are in the employ of the foreign dogs must leave their employment in one month'—and terrible denunciations were hurled against all those who should disobey these behests. General Straubenzee and the other officials were much perplexed how to deal with this state of things; they began to fear that nothing less than a bombardment of the city would drive out the 'braves,' and restore peaceful trade; and yet it would be an anomaly to use cannon and muskets, beheading and imprisonment, against the subjects of an emperor with whom we had just made a treaty of peace. In this exigency, Sir John Bowring caused large posting-bills to be printed in Chinese—announcing that a treaty of peace had been signed between the two countries; that all animosity ought now to cease; that many Chinese, hitherto residing at Hong-kong as servants and traders, had been frightened away by threatening proclamations from some of the authorities on the mainland; that surreptitious attempts had been made to check the supply of provisions to Hong-kong; and that many inconveniences had thence arisen. The placard proceeded to warn all persons and communities against any interference with the peaceful resumption of commerce between the two nations. An attempt to distribute this placard or proclamation was clumsily made, and led to disaster. Two British officers, knowing the Chinese language, went with a few seamen in the gun-boat *Starling*, to the coast of the mainland nearly opposite the island of Hong-kong. Some difficulty being experienced in obtaining an interview with the official authorities, the sailors landed under a flag of truce, and attempted to post up the placards in the water-side suburbs of the town of Namtow; they were, however, attacked by Chinese soldiery, and driven back to the gun-boat, with the loss of one of their number and the wounding of another.

This untoward failure of course led to further fighting. As the attack made by the Chinese on the sailors was in defiance of a flag of truce, Sir John Bowring deemed himself justified in inflicting a punishment on the town. He made a requisition to General Straubenzee, who thereupon organised a small expeditionary force. He selected 700 men —59th foot, artillery, engineers, marines, and naval brigade—who were commanded by himself and Commodore Keith Stewart. They landed near Namtow on the 11th of August, and gave notice to the inhabitants that no injury would be done to them if they remained neutral; the attack being intended against the 'braves' or Chinese soldiers, who had originated the contest. Within a few hours a fort was attacked, the Chinese troops driven out, the fort destroyed, and two large brass guns brought away as trophies. The object in view was, not to injure the town or the inhabitants, but to prove to the authorities that any disregard of a flag of truce would subject them to a hostile demonstration.

Throughout these strange operations, in which war and peace were so oddly mingled—the one prevailing at Namtow, the other at Tien-sing—the city of Canton continued in a disturbed state. On the 21st of July, the 'braves' outside the city went so far as to plan an attack for the expulsion of the English and French altogether from the place. They were speedily beaten off. As before, however, it was a discomfiture, not a suppression; for the braves settled down in an encampment about four miles from Canton, ready for any exigencies. During a considerable time after the signing of the treaty at Tien-sing, Governor Whang either did not know of it, or else disregarded it; but in the course of the month of August, evidence gradually appeared that he had been officially informed of the treaty. He forbade the braves to make any further attacks. Many Chinese traders, who had been driven in disquietude from Canton, now returned; and Hong-kong began again to look out for Chinese servants and work-people. Governor Whang's proclamation, dated August 17th, contained a statement which bore an aspect of considerable probability: 'There are, both within and without the city, many villains and thieves who, pretending they are braves, take advantage of the state of affairs to create disturbances in order to plunder and rob, and from whose hands the citizens have suffered much. If such rascality be not speedily suppressed, how can the minds of the people be set at ease, or tranquillity restored? And unless the villains be apprehended, how can the districts be purged?' Wherefore he gave orders for the suppression of violence and hostile manifestations.

During the months of September and October—with the exception of a stroke of diplomacy at Japan, presently to be adverted to—Lord Elgin remained in the China seas, chiefly at Shang-hae, waiting for the Chinese commissioners who were to settle with him the minor details supplementary to the treaty. Former experience having shewn that the Chinese authorities viewed the obligations of a treaty somewhat lightly, it was not deemed prudent either to give up Canton, or to withdraw the powerful naval force from the China coast, until all the conditions of the treaty had been put in a fair train for fulfilment. Canton gradually recovered its trade and quietude; Hong-kong gradually got back its Chinese servants and artisans; and the English fleet vigorously put in operation that clause of the treaty which related to the suppression of piracy. Expeditions were fitted out from Hong-kong, which captured and destroyed hundreds of piratical junks.

One of the most remarkable episodes in this remarkable Chinese war bore relation to Japan—an empire consisting of many islands, lying north-eastward of China. Until a few years ago, the Japanese traded only with the Chinese and the Dutch. The Dutch were allowed to establish a trading station on the small island of Desima, which was connected with the larger island of Kiusiu or Kioosioo by a bridge. At the Kiusiu end of the bridge was the city of Nagasaki or Nangasaki, with the inhabitants of which only the Dutch were allowed to trade. One ship annually, and one only, was permitted to come to Desima from Java, bringing sugar, ivory, tin, lead, bar-iron, fine chintzes, and a few other commodities, and conveying away in exchange copper, camphor, lackered-wood ware, porcelain, rice, soy, &c. The Chinese, like the Dutch, were confined to the little island opposite Nagasaki, but their trading privileges were greater; at three different periods of the year they were wont to send laden junks from Amoy, Ning-po, and Shang-hae, and exchange Chinese commodities for Japanese. Such was the state of matters until a short time previous to the Russo-Turkish war; when the United States, taking advantage of an insult offered to American ships, induced or compelled the Japanese government to permit intercourse between the two countries, to be conducted at certain ports under certain regulations. Some time afterwards, similar privileges were accorded to Russia and England. The convention with England, signed at Nagasaki on the 9th of October 1855, provided for very little more than this—that British ships might resort to the three ports of Nagasaki, Simoda, and Hakodadi, for the purpose of effecting repairs, and obtaining fresh water, provisions, and such supplies as they might absolutely need. It was a denial of such aid to distressed ships that had led the United States to threaten the Japanese. France, not to be left behind by other nations, sent an expedition to obtain shipping privileges similar to those conceded to America, England, and Russia. On the 25th of May 1856, M. de Montravel presented himself before the governor of Nagasaki, accompanied by rather an imposing array of officers; he had no difficulty in procuring the desired concession. On the 11th of December in the same year, two British merchant-ships, about to enter the harbour at Nagasaki, to purchase certain supplies, were refused admission; whereupon the two captains sailed up close to the town, landed, and marched with a strong escort to the residence of the governor. He declined to receive them, but undertook that any letter from them should be conveyed to the emperor at Jedo or Yedo, the capital of Japan. This letter obtained the desired result; an imperial edict being issued on January 26, 1857, that ships from any of the four nations might enter Nagasaki as well as the other two ports—provided that none of the crews attempted to penetrate into the interior. This letter was, in fact, nothing more than the carrying out of an agreement, which the governor of Nagasaki had on a former occasion evaded. On the 17th of June 1857, Mr Townshend Harris, acting under the United States consul at Hong-kong, signed a treaty at Simoda with two Japanese commissioners. This treaty was a great advance, in commercial liberality, on anything previously known in that region.

Thus matters remained until the autumn of 1858; when, expeditions to China having been sent from England, France, Russia, and America, advantage was taken of the proximity of Japan to obtain by and for the first three countries the same trading privileges as had been granted to America. It was, throughout, a very singular race between four great nations, in which America obtained the first start. The Japanese had, during three or four years, seen much more of Europeans and Americans than at any former period, and had begun to acquire enlarged notions of international commerce; moreover, they had lately heard of the powerful armaments on the Canton and Pei-ho rivers, and of the treaties which those armaments had enforced; from whence the Earl of Elgin inferred that he might probably meet with success in an attempt to obtain an improved treaty of commerce. On the 3d of August he entered the port of Nagasaki, with the *Furious*, *Retribution*, and *Lee*—taking with him a steam-yacht as a present from Queen Victoria to the Emperor of Japan. On the following day he was joined by Sir Michael Seymour, with the *Calcutta* and *Inflexible*. It being deemed best that the yacht should be presented at Jedo if possible, the expedition set forth again, and proceeded to Simoda. Here it was ascertained that Mr Townshend Harris, United States consul, had just returned from Jedo with a new and very advantageous treaty of commerce between America and Japan; that Count Putiatine was at that very moment negotiating for a similar treaty between Russia and Japan; and that Mr Donker Curtius, Dutch consul, had been trying in a similar direction for Holland. The Earl at once saw that no time was to be lost, or he would be distanced by the other diplomatists. Procuring the aid of a Dutch interpreter, through the courtesy of Mr Harris, his lordship proceeded from Simoda towards Jedo on the 12th. Disregarding the rules laid down by the Japanese government concerning the anchoring-places of ships, the squadron, led by Captain Sherard Osborne, boldly pushed on to the vicinity of the city—to the utter astonishment of the natives, official and non-official. Boats approached, containing Japanese officers, who earnestly begged the British representative not to approach the great city, which had never yet been visited by a foreign ship; but as he was deaf to their entreaties, they prepared to give him a courteous reception on shore. Although the city was strongly protected by forts, there was no indication of a hostile repulsion of the strangers. During eight days did Elgin reside within the great city of Jedo, treated with every attention—possibly because there were British ships-of-war and a gun-boat just at hand. All the naval officers had opportunity of traversing the city during this interval, and met with signs of civilisation such as induced them to write home very glowing descriptions. The earl at first met with difficulties, arising from the circumstance that a conservative had just supplanted a liberal ministry (to use English terms) at Jedo, strengthening the prejudice against foreigners. Indeed, this change of ministry had arisen two or three days before, in consequence of the signing of the liberal treaty with America. Elgin, however, triumphed over this and all other difficulties; he arrived at Shang-hae again on the 3d of September, bringing with him a treaty of commerce between England and Japan, signed at Jedo on the 26th of August.

The treaty thus obtained was written in Dutch as the original, with English and Japanese translations. The chief clauses comprised the following provisions: England may appoint an ambassador to Jedo, and Japan an ambassador to London—The ambassadors to be free to travel in the respective empires—Each power may appoint consuls at the ports of the other—The ports of Hakodadi, Nanagawa, Nagasaki, Nee-e-gata, Hiogo, Jedo, and Osaca, to be opened to British traders at various times by the year 1863—British traders may lease ground and build dwellings and warehouses at those ports—The British may travel to distances within a certain radius of each port—In any dispute between British and Japanese, the British consuls to act as friendly arbitrators—If arbitration fail, British offenders to be tried by British laws, and Japanese by those of Japan—British residents may employ Japanese as servants or workmen—British may freely exercise their religion—Foreign and Japanese coin may be used indifferently for commercial purposes—Supplies for British vessels may be stored at certain ports free of duty—Japanese authorities to render aid to stranded British vessels—British captains may employ Japanese pilots—Goods may be imported at an *ad valorem* duty, without any transit or other dues, and may be re-exported duty free—British and Japanese to aid each other in preventing smuggling—Money, apparel, and household furniture of British subjects residing in Japan to be imported duty free—Munitions of war to be prohibited—All other articles to pay an *ad valorem* import-duty, varying from 5 to 35 per cent., according to a tariff to be specially prepared—Any trading privileges, granted hereafter to any other nation, to be granted equally to England.

This very important treaty—even more liberal in its provisions than that concluded with China—was to be ratified by the two courts, and the ratifications exchanged, within one year from the signature.

SIR EDWARD LUGARD.

§ 3. ENGLISH PROSPECTS IN THE EAST.

When, by the month of October 1858, it was known that the object of the Persian expedition had been fulfilled by the complete withdrawal of the Persians from Herat; that the purpose of the Chinese expedition had been even more than fulfilled, supposing the advantageous treaty made by the Earl of Elgin to be faithfully observed; and that a remarkable commercial treaty had been signed with Japan—the English nation felt, not unjustly, that their prospects of advancement in the east were greatly heightened. All depended, however, or would depend, on the result of the struggle in India; if that ended satisfactorily, the power of England in Asia would be greater than ever. That the Indian struggle *would* have a favourable termination, few doubted. There was much to be done; but as the whole empire cheerfully supported the government in the preparations for doing it, and as those preparations had been widely spread and deeply considered, success was very confidently looked forward to.

The arrangements for the final discomfiture (if not extinction) of the mutineers, and for bringing back a misguided peasantry to habits of order and of industry, will be noticed presently; but it may be desirable first to glance at two important subjects which much occupied the attention of thoughtful men—namely, the probable causes of the Revolt; and, consequent on those causes, the general character of the reforms proper to be introduced into the government of India, as an accompaniment to the change from the Company's *régime* to that of the Queen.

The complexity of Indian affairs was very remarkable; and in no instance more so than with reference to the first of the above two subjects of speculation. Down to the closing scene, men could not agree in their answers to the question—'What was the cause of the mutiny?' Military officers, cabinet ministers, commissioners, magistrates, missionaries, members of parliament, pamphleteers, writers in newspapers, as they had differed at first, so did they differ to the end. This discrepancy offers strong proof that the causes were many in number and varied in kind—that the Revolt was a resultant of several independent forces, all tending towards a common end. It may not be without value to shew in what directions public men sought for these causes. The following summaries present the views of a few among many who wrote on the subject:

Mr Gubbins,* who was financial commissioner of Oude (or Oudh) when the mutiny began, was requested by Mr Colvin, lieutenant-governor of the Northwest Provinces, to express his opinions concerning the causes of that catastrophe. He wrote out his opinions; and stated that Sir Henry Lawrence, shortly before his death, concurred mainly with them. In the first place, he did not attribute the mutiny to Russian intrigue—an explanation that had occurred to the minds of some persons. In the second place, he disbelieved that the mutiny was due to a Mohammedan conspiracy; the movement began among soldiers, of whom four-fifths or more were Hindoos; and certain Mohammedan sovereigns and leaders only joined it when they saw a probable chance of recovering dominion for their race and their religion. In the third place, Mr Gubbins equally denied that it was a national rebellion, a rising of a nation against its rulers; for, he urged, the villagers were throughout more disposed to remain neutral than to aid either side; we had no right to expect any great loyalty from them; and we received all that could fairly be looked for—the sympathy of some, the hostility of others, but the neutrality of the greater number. In the fourth place, he denied that the annexation of Oude caused the mutiny; there were certain persons—courtiers of the deposed king, shopkeepers at Lucknow, soldiers of the late king's army, and budmashes—who had suffered by the change; but the mass of the population, he contended, had been benefited by us, and had neither ground nor wish for insurrection. Having thus expressed his dissent from many modes of explanation, Mr Gubbins proceeded to give his own views, which traced the mutiny to three concurrent causes: 'I conceive that the native mind had been gradually alarmed on the vital subjects of caste and religion, when the spark was applied by the threatened introduction of the greased cartridge; that this spark fell upon a native army most dangerously organised, subject to no sufficient bonds of discipline, and discontented; and, above all, that this occurred at a time when Bengal and the Northwestern Provinces were so denuded of European troops as to leave the real power in the hands of the natives.'

Mr Rees,† confining his observations to the province with which he was best acquainted, attributed the mutiny to the mode of governing Oude by the English, superadded to the fierce hostility of the Mussulmans to Christians in general. Thousands of natives had been thrown out of employ by the change of government, and with them their retainers and servants; all alike were rendered impoverished and discontented. The shopkeepers of Lucknow, who had made large profits by supplying the palaces and harem of the king before his deposition, lost that advantage when an English commissioner took the king's place. New taxes and duties were imposed, as a means of substituting a regular for an irregular revenue; and these taxes irritated the payers. The Mohammedan teachers and fanatics, he urged, enraged at the substitution of a Christian for a Moslem government, were ready for any reactionary measures. Lastly, there were innumerable vagabonds, bravos, and beggars in the city, who had found bread in it under native rule, but who nearly starved under the more systematic English government. Hence, Mr Rees contended, the great city of Lucknow had for a year or more been ripe for rebellion, come from what quarter and in what way it might.

Colonel Bourchier,* like many military officers, sought for no other origin of the mutiny than that which was due to the state of the native army. The enormous increase in that army—by the contingents raised to guard the newly acquired territories in Central India, the Punjaub, and Oude—with no corresponding increase in the European force, encouraged a belief on the part of many of the natives that they had a fair chance of being able to drive the English altogether from the country. The colonel quoted an opinion expressed by the gallant and lamented Brigadier Nicholson, who possessed an intimate knowledge of the native character—'Neither greased cartridges, the annexation of Oude, nor the paucity of European officers, was the cause of the mutiny. For years I have watched the army, and felt sure they only wanted an opportunity to try their strength with us.'

Mr Ludlow † ridiculed the idea of the mutiny being sudden and unexpected. He pointed to the fact that Munro, Metcalfe, Napier, and other experienced men, had long ago predicted an eventual outbreak, arising mainly from the defective organisation of the military force. Mr Ludlow himself attributed the mutiny to many concurrent causes. The Brahmins were against us, because we were gradually sapping the foundations of their religion and power; the Mussulman leaders were against us, because we had reduced the Mogul rule to a shadow, and most of the nawabships likewise; the Mahrattas were against us, because we had gradually lessened the power of Scindia, Holkar, the Guicowar, the Peishwa, the Nena, and other leading men of their nation; the Oudians were against us, because, in addition to having

* *Account of the Mutinies in Oudh.*
† *Personal Narrative of the Siege of Lucknow.*

* *Eight Months' Campaign against the Bengal Sepoy Army.*
† *British India; its Races and its History.*

deposed their king, we had greatly lessened the privileges and emoluments of the soldiery who had heretofore served him; and lastly, the Hindoo sepoys were turned against us, because they believed the rumour that the British government intended to degrade their caste and religion by the medium of greased cartridges. Mr Ludlow treated the cartridge grievance as the spark that had directly kindled the flame; but he believed there were sufficient inflammable materials for the outbreak even if this particular panic had not arisen.

Mr Mead,* who, in connection with the press of India, had been one of the fiercest assailants of the Company in general, and of Viscount Canning in particular, insisted that the mutiny was a natural result of a system of government wrong in almost every particular—cruel to the natives, insulting to Europeans not connected with the Company, and blind even in its selfishness. More especially, however, he referred it to 'the want of discipline in the Bengal army; the general contempt entertained by the sepoys for authority; the absence of all power on the part of commanding officers to reward or punish; the greased cartridges; and the annexation of Oude.' The 'marvellous imbecility' of the Calcutta government—a sort of language very customary with this writer—he referred to, not as a cause of the mutiny, but as a circumstance or condition which permitted the easy spread of disaffection.

Mr Raikes,† who, as judge of the Sudder Court at Agra, had an intimate knowledge of the North-west Provinces, contended that, so far as concerned those provinces, there was one cause of the troubles, and one only—the mutiny of the sepoys. It was a revolt growing out of a military mutiny, not a mutiny growing out of a national discontent. Ever since the disasters at Cabool taught the natives that an English army *might* be annihilated, Mr Raikes had noticed a change in the demeanour of the Bengal sepoys. He believed that they indulged in dreams of ambition; and that they made use of the cartridge grievance merely as a pretext, in the beginning of 1857. The outbreak having once commenced, Mr Raikes traced all the rest as consequences, not as causes.—The villagers in many districts wavered, because they thought the power of England was really declining; the Goojurs, Mewatties, and other predatory tribes rose into activity, because the bonds of regular government were loosened; the Mussulman fanatics rose, because they deemed a revival of Moslem power just possible; but Mr Raikes denied that there was anything like general disaffection or national insurrection in the provinces with which he was best acquainted.

'Indophilus'‡—the *nom de plume* of a distinguished civilian, who had first served the Company in India, and then the imperial government in England—discountenanced the idea of any general conspiracy. He believed that the immediate exciting cause of the mutiny was the greased cartridges; but that the predisposing causes were two—the dangerous constitution of the Bengal sepoy army, and the Brahmin dread of reforms. On the latter point he said: 'In the progress of reform, we are all accomplices. From the abolition of suttee, to the exemption of native Christian converts from the forfeiture of their rights of inheritance; from the formation of the first metalled road, to covering India with a network of railways and electric telegraphs—there is not a single good measure which has not contributed something to impress the military priests with the conviction that, if they were to make a stand, they must do so soon, else the opportunity would pass away for ever.'

The Rev. Dr Duff,* director of the Free Church Scotch Missions in India, differed, on the one hand, from those who treated the outbreak merely as a military revolt, and, on the other, from those who regarded it as a great national rebellion. It was, he thought, something between the two—a political conspiracy. He traced it much more directly to the Mohammedan leaders than to the Hindoos. He believed in a long-existing conspiracy among those leaders, to renew, if possible, the splendour of the ancient Mogul times by the utter expulsion of the Christian English; the Brahmins and Rajpoots of the Bengal army were gradually drawn into the plot, by wily appeals to their discontent on various subjects connected with caste and religion; while the cartridge grievance was used simply as a pretext when the conspiracy was nearly ripe. The millions of India, he contended, had no strong bias one way or the other; there was no such nationality or patriotic feeling among them as to lead them to make common cause with the conspirators; but on the other hand they displayed very little general sympathy or loyalty towards their English masters. Viewing the subject as a missionary, Dr Duff strongly expressed his belief that we neither did obtain, nor had a right to obtain, the aid of the natives, seeing that we had done so little as a nation to Christianise them.

Without extending the list of authorities referred to, it will be seen that nearly all these writers regarded the 'cartridge grievance' as merely the spark which kindled inflammable materials, and the state of the Bengal army as one of the predisposing causes of the mutiny; but they differed greatly on the questions whether the revolt was rather Mohammedan or Hindoo, and whether it was a national rebellion or only a military mutiny. It is probable that the affirmative opinions were sounder than the negative—in other words, that every one of the causes assigned had really something to do with this momentous outbreak.

We now pass to the second of the two subjects

* *The Sepoy Revolt; its Causes and its Consequences.*
† *Notes on the Revolt in the Northwest Provinces.*
‡ *Letters of Indophilus to the 'Times.'*

* *The Indian Rebellion: its Causes and Results.*

indicated above—the views of distinguished men, founded in part on past calamities, on the reforms necessary in Indian government. And here it will suffice to indicate the chief items of proposed reforms, leaving the reader to form his own opinions thereon. During the progress of the Revolt, and in reference to the future of British India, a most valuable and interesting correspondence came to light—valuable on account of the eminence of the persons engaged in it. These persons were Sir John Lawrence and Colonel Herbert Edwardes—the one chief-commissioner of the Punjaub, the other commissioner of the Peshawur division of that province. Both had the welfare of India deeply at heart; and yet they differed widely in opinion concerning the means whereby that welfare could be best secured—especially in relation to religious matters. Early in the year 1858, Colonel Edwardes published a *Memorandum on the Elimination of all unchristian Principles from the Government of British India*. About the same time Mr MacLeod, financial commissioner, published a letter on the same subject; as did also, some time afterwards, Mr Arnold, director-general of public instruction in the Punjaub. Sir John Lawrence, on the 21st of April, addressed a dispatch to Viscount Canning, explanatory of his views on the matters treated by these three gentlemen, especially by Colonel Edwardes. The colonel had placed under ten distinct headings the 'unchristian elements' (as he termed them) in the Indian government; and it will suffice for the present purpose to give here brief abstracts of the statements and the rejoinders—by which, at any rate, the subject is rendered intelligible to those who choose to study it:

1. *Exclusion of the Bible and of Christian Teaching from the Government Schools and Colleges.*—Edwardes insisted that the Bible ought to be introduced in all government schools, and its study made a part of the regular instruction. Lawrence was favourable to Bible diffusion, but pointed out certain necessary limits. He would not teach native religions in government schools; he would teach Christianity only (in addition to secular instruction), but would not make it compulsory on native children to attend that portion of the daily routine. He would wish to see the Bible in every village-school throughout the empire—with these two provisoes: that there were persons able to teach it, and pupils willing to hear it. Who the teachers should be—whether clergymen, missionaries, lay Bible-readers, or Christianised natives—is a problem that can only very gradually receive its solution. Lawrence insisted that there must be no compulsion in the matter of studying Christianity; it must be an invitation to the natives, not a command. The four authorities named in the last paragraph all differed in opinion on this Bible question. Colonel Edwardes advocated a determined and compulsory teaching of the Bible. Mr MacLeod joined him to a considerable extent, but not wholly. Mr Arnold strongly resisted the project of teaching the Bible at all—on the grounds that it would infringe the principle of religious neutrality; that it would not be fair to the natives unless native religions were taught also; that it would seem to them a proselyting and even a persecuting measure; that it might be politically dangerous; and that we should involve ourselves in the sea of theological controversy, owing to the diversities of religious sects among Christians. Sir John Lawrence, as we have seen, adopted a medium between these extremes.

2. *Endowment of Idolatry and Mohammedanism by the Government.*—In British India, many small items of revenue are paid by the government for the support of temples, priests, idols, and ceremonies pertaining to the Hindoo and Mohammedan religions. Edwardes urged that these payments should cease, as a disgrace to a Christian government. Lawrence pointed out that this withdrawal could not be effected without a gross breach of faith. The revenues in question belonged to those religious bodies before England 'annexed' the states, and were recognised as such at the time of the annexation. They are a property, a claim on the land, like tithes in England, or like conventual lands in Roman Catholic countries. They are not, and never have been, regarded as religious offerings or gifts. We seized the lands; but if we were to withhold the revenues derived from those lands, on the ground that the religious services are heathen, it would be a virtual persecution of heathenism, and, as such, repugnant to the mild principles of Christianity. Lawrence believed that the payments might so be made as not to appear to encourage idolatry; but he would not listen to any such breach of faith as withholding them altogether.

3. *Recognition of Caste.*—Colonel Edwardes, in common with many other persons, believed that the British government had pandered too much to the prejudices of caste, and that this system ought to be changed. Lawrence pointed out that it was mainly in the Bengal army that this prevailed, and that the custom arose out of very natural circumstances. Brahmins and Rajpoots were preferred for military service, because they were generally finer men than those of lower castes, because they were (apparently) superior in moral qualifications, and because they were descended from the old soldiers who had fought under Clive and our early generals. Our officers became so accustomed to them, that at length they would enlist no others. Being more easily obtained from Oude than from any other province, it came to pass that the Bengal army gradually assumed the character of a vast aggregate of brotherhoods and cousinhoods—consisting chiefly of men belonging to the same castes, speaking the same dialects, coming from the same districts, and influenced by the same associations. It was the gradual growth of a custom, which the Revolt suddenly put an end to. Lawrence denied that the government had shewn any great encouragement to caste prejudices, except in the Bengal army. He believed that an equal error would be

committed by discouraging the higher and encouraging the lower castes. What is wanted is, a due admixture of all, from the haughty Brahmin and Rajpoot castes, down to the humble Trading and Sweeper castes. Whether all should be combined in one regiment, or different regiments be formed of different castes, would depend much on the part of India under notice. Christianised natives would probably constitute valuable regiments, as soon as their number becomes sufficiently great. On all these questions of caste, the two authorities differed chiefly thus—Edwardes would beat down and humble the higher castes; Lawrence would employ all, without especially encouraging any.

4. *Observance of Native Holidays in State Departments.*—Native servants of the government were usually allowed to absent themselves on days of festival or religious ceremony. Edwardes proposed to reform this, as being a pandering to heathen customs, unworthy of a Christian government. Lawrence contended that such a change would be a departure from the golden rule of 'doing unto others that which we would they should do unto us.' A Christian in a Mohammedan country would think

Fort St George, Madras; in 1780.

it cruel if compelled to work on Sunday, Good Friday, or Christmas-day; and so would the Hindoo and Mussulman of India, if compelled to work on their days of religious festival. Lawrence thought that the number might advantageously be lessened, by restricting the list to such as were especial religious days in the native faiths; but beyond this he would not curtail the privilege of holiday (holy day). He adverted to the fact that the Christian Sunday is made obvious to the natives by the suspension of all public works.

5. *Administration by the British of Hindoo and Mohammedan Laws.*—Edwardes deemed it objectionable that England should to so great an extent suffer native laws to be administered in India. Lawrence replied that it is the policy of conquerors to interfere as little as possible in those native laws which operate only between man and man, and do not affect imperial policy. He drew attention to the fact that Indian legislation had already made two important steps, by legalising the re-marriage of Hindoo widows, and by removing all possible civil disabilities or legal disadvantages from Christian converts; and he looked forward to the time when it might perhaps be practicable to abolish polygamy, and the making of contracts of betrothal by parents on behalf of infant children; but he strenuously insisted on the importance of not changing any such laws until the government can carry the good-will of the natives with them.

6. *Publicity of Hindoo and Mohammedan Processions.*—It was urged by Edwardes that religious processions ought not to be allowed in the public streets, under protection of the police. Lawrence joined in this opinion—not, however, on religious grounds, but because the processions led to quarrelling and fighting between rival communions, and because the Hindoo idols and pictures are often of a character quite unfitted for exhibition in public thoroughfares.

7. *Display of Prostitution in the Streets.*—This aspect of social immorality is far more glaring in many parts of India than in European cities, bad as the latter may be. Edwardes recommended,

and Lawrence concurred in the recommendation, that the police arrangements should be rendered more stringent in this matter.

8. *Restrictions on Marriage of European Soldiers.*—Great restrictions were, in bygone years, imposed by the Company on the marriage of European soldiers; and a shameful disregard shewn for the homes of those who were married. Edwardes condemned this state of things; and Lawrence shared his views to a great extent. He asserted that men are not better soldiers for being unmarried—rather the reverse; and that women and children, in moderate numbers, need not be any obstruction to military arrangements. Some change in this matter he recommended. He pointed out, however, that in reference to the comfort of married soldiers, great improvements had been introduced into the Punjaub, and improvements to a smaller extent in other parts of British India. He fully recognised the bounden duty of the government so to construct barracks as to provide for the proper domestic privacy of married soldiers and their families.

9. *Connection of the Government with the Opium-trade.*—Edwardes dwelt on the objectionable character of this connection. Lawrence replied that the English were not called upon to decide for the Chinese how far the use of opium is deleterious; and that, until we checked our own consumption of intoxicating liquors, we were scarcely in a position to take a high moral tone on this point. He nevertheless fully agreed that it was objectionable in any government to encourage the growth of this drug, actively supervising the storing and selling, and advancing money for this purpose to the cultivators. It was a revenue question, defensive wholly on financial grounds. How to provide a substitute for the £4,000,000 or £5,000,000 thus derived would be a difficult matter; but he thought the best course would be to sever the connection between the government and the opium-trade, and to lay a heavy customs duty on the export of opium from India.

10. *Indian Excise Laws.*—It was contended by Edwardes that the government encouraged intemperance by farming out to monopolists the right of manufacturing and selling intoxicating drugs and spirits. Lawrence contested this point. He asserted that there is less drunkenness in India, less spirit-drinking and drug-chewing, than under the former native rule, when the trade was open to all. As a question of morals, the Indian government does no more than that of the home country, in deriving a revenue from spirituous liquors; as a question of fact, the evils are lessened by the very monopoly complained of.

Sir John Lawrence, in a few concluding remarks, expressed a very strong belief that Christian civilisation may be introduced gradually into India if a temperate policy be pursued; but that rash zeal would produce great disaster. 'It is when unchristian things are done in the name of Christianity, or when Christian things are done in an unchristian way, that mischief and danger are occasioned.' He recommended that as soon as the supreme government had organised the details of a just and well-considered policy, 'it should be openly avowed and universally acted on throughout British India; so that there may be no diversities of practice, no isolated or conflicting efforts, which would be the surest means of exciting distrust; so that the people may see that we have no sudden or sinister designs; and so that we may exhibit that harmony and uniformity of conduct which befits a Christian nation striving to do its duty.' Finally, he expressed a singularly firm conviction that, so far as concerns the Punjaub, he could himself carry out 'all those measures which are really matters of Christian duty on the part of the government:' measures which 'would arouse no danger, would conciliate instead of provoking, and would subserve the ultimate diffusion of the truth among the people.'

It wants no other evidence than is furnished by the above very remarkable correspondence, to shew that the future government of India must, if it be effective, be based on some system which has been well weighed and scrutinised on all sides. The problem is nothing less than that of governing a hundred and eighty millions of human beings, whose characteristics are very imperfectly known to us. It is a matter of no great difficulty to write out a scheme or plan of government, plentifully bestrewed with personalities and accusations; there have been many such; but the calm judgment of men filling different ranks in life, and conversant with different aspects of Indian character, can alone insure the embodiment of a scheme calculated to benefit both India and England. Whether the abolition of the governing powers of the East India Company will facilitate the solution of this great problem, the future alone can shew; it will at any rate simplify the departmental operations.

The Queen's proclamation, announcing the great change in the mode of government, and offering an amnesty to evildoers under certain easily understood conditions, adverted cautiously to the future and its prospects. Before, however, touching on this important document, it may be well to say a few words concerning the military operations in the few weeks immediately preceding its issue.

These operations, large as they were, had resolved themselves into the hunting down of desperate bands, rather than the fighting of great battles with a military opponent. Throughout the whole of India, in the months of October and November, disturbances had been nearly quelled except in two regions—Oude, with portions of the neighbouring provinces of Rohilcund and Behar; and Malwah, with portions of Bundelcund and the Nerbudda provinces. Of the rest—Bengal, Assam and the Delta of the Ganges, Aracan and Pegu, the greater portion of Behar and the Northwest Provinces, the Doab, Sirhind and the hill regions, the Punjaub, Sinde, Cutch and Gujerat, Bombay and its vicinity, the Deccan under the Nizam, the Nagpoor territory, the Madras region, Mysore, the South Mahratta country, the south of the Indian peninsula—all were so nearly at peace as to excite little attention. Of the two excepted regions, a few details will shew that they were gradually falling more and more under British power.

In the Oude region the guiding spirit was still the Begum, one of the wives of the deposed king. She had the same kind of energy and ability as the Ranee of Jhansi, with less of cruelty; and was hence deserving of a meed of respect. Camp-gossip told that, under disappointment at the uniform defeat of the rebel troops whenever and wherever they encountered the English, she sent a pair of bangles (ankle-ornaments) to each of her generals or leaders—scoffingly telling him to wear those trinkets, and become a woman, unless he could vanquish and drive out the Feringhees. This had the effect of impelling some of her officers to make attacks on the British; but the attacks were utterly futile. There were many leaders in Oude who fought on their own account; a greater number, however, acknowledged a kind of suzerainty in the Begum. If she did not win battles, she at least headed armies, and carried on open warfare; whereas the despicable Nena Sahib, true to his cowardice from first to last, was hiding in jungles, and endeavouring to keep his very existence unknown to the English. The military operations in Oude during the month of October were not extensive in character. Sir Colin Campbell (Lord Clyde), waiting for the cessation of the autumnal rains, was collecting several columns, with a view of hemming in the rebels on all sides and crushing them. That they would ultimately be crushed, everything foretold; for in every encounter, large or small, they were so disgracefully beaten as to shew that the leaders commanded a mere predatory rabble rather than a brave disciplined soldiery. These encounters were mostly in Oude, but partly in Behar and Rohilcund. In the greater number of instances, however, the rebels ran instead of fighting, even though their number was tenfold that of their opponents. The skilled mutinied sepoys from the Bengal army were becoming daily fewer in number, so many having been struck down by war and by privation; their places were now taken by undisciplined ruffians, who, however strong for rapine and anarchy, were nearly powerless on the field of battle. Thousands of men in this part of India, who had become impoverished, almost houseless, during a year and a half of anarchy, had strong temptation to join the rebel leaders, from a hope of booty or plunder, irrespective of any national or patriotic motive. Sir Colin, when the month of November arrived, entered personally on his plan of operations; which was to bar the boundaries of Oude on three sides—the Ganges, Rohilcund, and Behar—and compel the various bodies of rebels either to fight or to flee; if they fought, their virtual annihilation would be almost certain; if they fled, it could only be to the jungle region on the Nepaul frontier of Oude, where, though they might carry on a hide-and-seek game for many months, their military importance as rebels would cease. In the dead of the night, between the 1st and 2d of November, the veteran commander-in-chief set forth from Allahabad with a well-selected force, crossed the Ganges, and advanced into Oude. His first work was to issue a proclamation,* sternly threatening all evildoers. A few days earlier, at Lucknow, Mr Montgomery, as chief-commissioner, had issued a proclamation for the disarming of Oude—requiring all thalookdars to surrender their guns, all persons whatever to surrender their arms, all leaders to refrain from building and arming forts; and threatening with fine and imprisonment those who should disobey. It was intended and believed that the three proclamations should all conduce towards a pacification—the Queen's (presently to be noticed) offering pardon to mutineers who yielded; the commander-in-chief's, threatening destruction to all towns and villages which aided rebels; and the commissioners's, lessening the powers for mischief by depriving the inhabitants generally of arms. With Sir Colin advancing towards the centre of Oude by Pertabghur, troops from Seetapoor, Hope Grant from Salone, and Rowcroft from the Gogra at Fyzabad, the Begum and her supporters were gradually so hemmed in that they began to avail themselves of the terms of the Queen's proclamation by surrender. It was to such a result that the authorities had from the first looked; but never until now had all the conditions for it been favourable. One of the first to surrender was Rajah Lall Madhoo Singh, a chieftain of great influence and energy, and one whose character had not been stained by deeds of cruelty.

In the Arrah or Jugdispore district, in like manner, the close of the scene was foreshadowed. Ummer Singh and his confederates had long baffled Brigadier Douglas; but now that troops were converging from all quarters upon the jungle-haunt, the rebels became more and more isolated from bands in other districts, their position more and more critical, and their final discomfiture more certain. Sir H. Havelock, son of the deceased general, and Colonel Turner, pressed them more and more with new columns, until their hopes were desperate. One excellent expedient was the cutting down of the Jugdispore

* 'The Commander-in-chief proclaims to the people of Oude that, under the order of the Right Hon. the Governor-general, he comes to enforce the law.

'In order to effect this without danger to life and property, resistance must cease on the part of the people.

'The most exact discipline will be preserved in the camps and on the march; and when there is no resistance, houses and crops will be spared, and no plundering allowed in the towns and villages. But wherever there is resistance, or even a single shot fired against the troops, the inhabitants must expect to incur the fate they have brought on themselves. Their houses will be plundered, and their villages burnt.

'This proclamation includes all ranks of the people, from the thalookdars to the poorest ryots.

'The Commander-in-chief invites all the well-disposed to remain in their towns and villages, where they will be sure of his protection against all violence.'

jungle, 23 miles in length by 4 in breadth; this useful work was begun in November by Messrs Burn, railway contractors.

In the other region of India above adverted to—comprising those districts of Malwah, Bundelcund, &c., which are watered by the Betwah, the Chumbul, the Nerbudda, and their tributaries—the leading rebel was Tanteea Topee, one of the most remarkable men brought forward by the Revolt. He had most of the qualities for a good general—except courage. He would not fight if he could help it; but in avoiding the British generals opposed to him, he displayed a cunning of plan, a fertility of resource, and a celerity of movement, quite noteworthy. The truth seems to have been, that he held power over an enormous treasure, in money and jewels, which he had obtained by plundering Scindia's palace at Gwalior; this treasure he carried with him wherever he went; and he shunned any encounters which might endanger it. He looked out for a strong city or fort, where he might settle down as a Mahratta prince, with a large store of available ready wealth at hand; but as the British did not choose to leave him in quietude, he marched from place to place. Between the beginning of June and the end of November he traversed with his army an enormous area of country, seizing guns from various towns and forts on the way, but usually escaping before the English could catch him. Former chapters have shewn by what strange circumvolutions he arrived at Julra Patteen; and a detail of operations would shew that his subsequent movements were equally erratic. He went to Seronj, then to Esagurh, then to Chunderee, then to Peshore, then arrived at the river Betwah, and wavered whether he should go southward to the Deccan or northward towards Jhansi. Everywhere he was either followed or headed, by columns and detachments under Michel, Mayne, Parkes, Smith, and other officers. Whenever they could bring him to an encounter, they invariably beat him most signally; but when, as generally happened, he escaped by forced marches, they tracked him. He picked up guns and men as he went; so that the amount of his force was never correctly known; it varied from three to fifteen thousand. One of the most severe defeats he received was at Sindwah, on the 19th of October, at the hands of General Michel; another, on the 25th, near Multhone, from the same active general. It was felt on all sides that this game could not be indefinitely continued. Tanteea Topee was like a hunted beast of prey, pursued by enemies who would not let him rest. When it had been clearly ascertained by General Roberts, in Rajpootana, that the fleet-footed and unencumbered rebel soldiery could escape faster than British troops could follow them, a new mode of strategy was adopted; columns from four different directions began to march towards a common centre, near which centre were Tanteea and his rebels; if one column could not catch him, another could head him and drive him back. Thus it was considered a military certainty that he must be run down at last. And if he fell, the great work of pacification in that part of India would be pretty well effected; for there was no rebel force of any account except that commanded by Tanteea Topee. After his defeat at Multhone, Tanteea was in great peril; Michel literally cut his army in two; and if he had pursued the larger instead of the smaller of these two sections, he might possibly have captured Tanteea himself. On the last day in October, the rebel leader crossed the Nerbudda river, thereby turning his back on the regions occupied by the columns of Roberts, Napier, Michel, Smith, and Whitlock. During November, he made some extraordinary marches in the country immediately southward of the Nerbudda—being heard of successively at Baitool, the Sindwara hills, and other little-known places in that region. He was no better off than before, however, for forces were immediately sent against him from Ahmednuggur, Kamptee, and other places; he had lost nearly all his guns and stores, his rebel followers, though laden with wealth, were footsore and desponding; and, for the first time, his companions began to look out for favourable terms of surrender. The Queen's proclamation was eminently calculated to withdraw his misguided followers from him; and the Nawab of Banda, the most influential among them, was the first to give himself up to General Michel.

Not only was a large measure of forgiveness held out to those who would return to their allegiance; but the British troops in India were becoming so formidably numerous as to render still more certain than ever the eventual triumph of order and good government. The Queen's troops in India at the beginning of November, those on the passage from England, and those told off for further shipment, amounted altogether to little short of one hundred thousand men. It affords a striking instance of triumph over difficulties, that between November 1857 and November 1858 the Peninsular and Oriental Steam-navigation Company conveyed no less than 8190 officers and soldiers to India by the overland route—in spite of the forebodings that that route would be unsuitable for whole regiments of soldiers; the burning Egyptian desert and the reef-bound Red Sea were traversed almost without disaster, under the watchful care of this company.

The 1st of November 1858 was a great day in India. On this day the transference of governing power from the East India Company to Queen Victoria was made known throughout the length and breadth of the empire. A royal proclamation* was issued, which many regarded as the Magna Charta of native liberty in India. At Calcutta, Bombay, Madras, Lahore, Kurachee, Delhi, Agra, Allahabad, Nagpoor, Mysore, Rangoon, and other great cities, this proclamation was read with every accompaniment of ceremonial splendour that could

* See Appendix.

give dignity to the occasion in the eyes of the natives; and at every British station, large or small, it was read amid such military honours as each place afforded. It was translated into most of the languages, and many of the dialects of India. It was printed in tens of thousands, and distributed wherever natives were wont most to congregate—in order that all might know that Queen Victoria was now virtually Empress of India; that the governor-general was now her viceroy; that the native princes might rely on the observance by her of all treaties made with them by the Company; that she desired no encroachment on, or annexation of, the territories of those princes; that she would not interfere with the religion of the natives, or countenance any favouritism in matters of faith; that creed or caste should not be a bar to employment in her service; that the ancient legal tenures and forms of India should, as far as possible, be adhered to; and that all mutineers and rebels, except those whose hands were blood-stained by actual murder, should receive a full and gracious pardon on abandoning their acts of insurgency. When these words were uttered aloud at Bombay (and the ceremony was more or less similar at the other cities named) the spectacle was such as the natives of India had never before seen. The governor and all the chief civilians; the military officers and the troops; the clergy of all the various Christian denominations; the merchants, ship-owners, and traders; the Mohammedans, Hindoos, Mahrattas, Parsees—all were represented among the throng around the spot from whence the proclamation was read, first in English, and then in Mahratta. And then the shouting, the music of military bands, the firing of guns, the waving of flags, the illuminations at night, the fireworks in the public squares, the blue-lights and manning of the ships, the banquets in the chief mansions—all rendered this a day to be borne in remembrance. Sir Jamsetjee Jejeebhoy, the Parsee baronet, vied with the Christians in the munificence of rejoicing; and indeed, so little did religious differences mar the harmony of the scene, that Catholic chapels, Mohammedan mosques, Hindoo pagodas, and Parsee temples were alike lighted up at night. It may not be that every one was enabled to assign good reasons for his rejoicing; but there was certainly a pretty general concurrence of opinion that the declared sovereignty of Queen Victoria, as a substitute for the ever-incomprehensible 'raj' of the East India Company, was a presage of good for British India. At Calcutta, the proclamation had the singular good-fortune of winning the approval of a community always very difficult to please. The Europeans consented to lay aside all minor considerations, in order to do honour to the great principles involved in the proclamation. The natives, too, took their share in the rejoicing. A public meeting was held early in the month, at which an influential Hindoo, Baboo Ramgopal Ghose, made an animated speech. He said, among other things: 'If I had power and influence, I would proclaim through the length and breadth of this land—from the Himalayas to Cape Comorin, from the Brahmaputra to the Bay of Cambay—that never were the natives more grievously mistaken than they have been in adopting the notion foisted on them by designing and ambitious men—that their religion was at stake; for that notion I believe to have been at the root of the late rebellion.' Some of the more intelligent natives rightly understood the nature of the great change made in the government of India; but among the ignorant, it remained a mystery—rendered, however, very palatable by the open avowal of a Queen regnant, and of a proclamation breathing sentiments of justice and kindness.

APPENDIX.

East India Company's Petition to Parliament, January 1858.—(See p. 563.)

TO the Right Honourable the Lords Spiritual and Temporal, and the Honourable the Commons of the United Kingdom of Great Britain and Ireland in Parliament assembled; The humble Petition of the East India Company, Sheweth:

That your petitioners, at their own expense, and by the agency of their own civil and military servants, originally acquired for this country its magnificent empire in the East.

That the foundations of this empire were laid by your petitioners, at that time neither aided nor controlled by parliament, at the same period at which a succession of administrations under the control of parliament were losing to the Crown of Great Britain another great empire on the opposite side of the Atlantic.

That during the period of about a century, which has since elapsed, the Indian possessions of this country have been governed and defended from the resources of those possessions, without the smallest cost to the British exchequer, which, to the best of your petitioners' knowledge and belief, cannot be said of any other of the numerous foreign dependencies of the Crown.

That it being manifestly improper that the administration of any British possession should be independent of the general government of the empire, parliament provided in 1783 that a department of the imperial government should have full cognizance of, and power of control over, the acts of your petitioners in the administration of India; since which time the home branch of the Indian government has been conducted by the joint counsels and on the joint responsibility of your petitioners and of a minister of the Crown.

That this arrangement has at subsequent periods undergone reconsideration from the legislature, and various comprehensive and careful parliamentary inquiries have been made into its practical operation; the result of which has been, on each occasion, a renewed grant to your petitioners of the powers exercised by them in the administration of India.

That the last of these occasions was so recent as 1853, in which year the arrangements which had existed for nearly three-quarters of a century were, with certain modifications, re-enacted, and still subsist.

That, notwithstanding, your petitioners have received an intimation from her Majesty's ministers of their intention to propose to parliament a bill for the purpose of placing the government of her Majesty's East Indian dominions under the direct authority of the Crown: a change necessarily involving the abolition of the East India Company as an instrument of government.

That your petitioners have not been informed of the reasons which have induced her Majesty's ministers, without any previous inquiry, to come to the resolution of putting an end to a system of administration which parliament, after inquiry, deliberately confirmed and sanctioned less than five years ago, and which, in its modified form, has not been in operation quite four years, and cannot be considered to have undergone a sufficient trial during that short period.

That your petitioners do not understand that her Majesty's ministers impute any failure to those arrangements, or bring any charge, either great or small, against your petitioners. But the time at which the proposal is made, compels your petitioners to regard it as arising from the calamitous events which have recently occurred in India.

That your petitioners challenge the most searching investigation into the mutiny of the Bengal army, and the causes, whether remote or immediate, which produced that mutiny. They have instructed the government of India to appoint a commission for conducting such an inquiry on the spot; and it is their most anxious wish that a similar inquiry may be instituted in this country by your [lordships'] honourable House, in order that it may be ascertained whether anything, either in the constitution of the home government of India, or in the conduct of those by whom it has been administered, has had any share in producing the mutiny, or has in any way impeded the measures for its suppression; and whether the mutiny itself, or any circumstance connected with it, affords any evidence of the failure of the arrangements under which India is at present administered.

That were it even true that these arrangements had failed, the failure could constitute no reason for divesting the East India Company of its functions, and transferring them to her Majesty's government. For, under the existing system, her Majesty's government have the deciding voice. The duty imposed upon the Court of Directors is, to originate measures and frame drafts of instructions. Even had they been remiss in this duty, their remissness, however discreditable to themselves, could in no way absolve the responsibility of her Majesty's government; since the minister for India possesses, and has frequently exercised, the power of requiring that the Court of Directors should take any subject into consideration, and prepare a draft-dispatch for his approval. Her Majesty's government are thus in the fullest sense accountable for all that has been done, and for all that has been forborne or omitted to be done. Your petitioners, on the other hand, are accountable only in so far as the act or omission has been promoted by themselves.

That under these circumstances, if the administration of India had been a failure, it would, your petitioners submit, have been somewhat unreasonable, to expect that a remedy would be found in annihilating the branch of the ruling authority which could not be the one principally in fault, and might be altogether blameless, in order to concentrate all powers in the branch which had necessarily the decisive share in every error, real or supposed. To believe that the administration of India would have been more free from error, had it been conducted by a minister of the Crown without the aid of the Court of Directors, would be to believe that the minister, with full power to govern India as he pleased, has governed ill because he has had the assistance of experienced and responsible advisers.

That your petitioners, however, do not seek to vindicate themselves at the expense of any other authority; they claim their full share of the responsibility of the manner in which India has practically been governed. That responsibility is to them not a subject of humiliation, but of pride. They are conscious that their advice and initiative have been, and have deserved to be, a great and potent element in the conduct of affairs in India. And they feel complete assurance, that the more attention is bestowed, and the more light thrown upon India and its administration, the more evident it will become, that the government in which they have borne a part, has been not only one of the purest in intention, but one of the most beneficent in act, ever known among mankind; that during the last and present generations in particular, it has been, in all departments, one of the most rapidly improving governments in the world; and that, at the time when this change is proposed, a greater number of important improvements are in a state of rapid progress than at any former period. And they are satisfied that whatever further improvements may be hereafter effected in India, can only consist in the development of germs already planted, and in building on foundations already laid, under their authority, and in a great measure by their express instructions.

That such, however, is not the impression likely to be made on the public mind, either in England or in India, by the ejection of your petitioners from the place they fill in the Indian administration. It is not usual with statesmen to propose the complete abolition of a system of government of which the practical operation is not condemned. It might therefore be generally inferred from the proposed measures, if carried into effect at the present time, that the East India Company having been intrusted with an important portion of the administration of India, have so abused their trust, as to have produced a sanguinary insurrection, and nearly lost India to the British empire; and that having thus crowned a long career of misgovernment, they have, in deference to public indignation, been deservedly cashiered for their misconduct.

That if the character of the East India Company were alone concerned, your petitioners might be willing to await the verdict of history. They are satisfied that posterity will do them justice. And they are confident that, even now, justice is done to them in the minds, not only of her Majesty's ministers, but of all who have any claim to be competent judges of the subject. But though your petitioners could afford to wait for the reversal of the verdict of condemnation which will be believed throughout the world to have been passed on them and their government by the British nation, your petitioners cannot look without the deepest uneasiness at the effect likely to be produced on the minds of the people of India. To them—however incorrectly the name may express the fact—the British government in India is the government of the East India Company. To their minds, the abolition of the Company will, for some time to come, mean the abolition of the whole system of administration with which the Company is identified. The measure, introduced simultaneously with the influx of an overwhelming British force, will be coincident with a general outcry, in itself most alarming to their fears, from most of the organs of opinion in this country, as well as of English opinion in India, denouncing the past policy of the government on the express ground that it has been too forbearing, and too considerate towards the natives. The people of India will at first feel no certainty that the new government, or the government under a new name, which it is proposed to introduce, will hold itself bound by the pledges of its predecessors. They will be slow to believe that a government has been destroyed, only to be followed by another which will act on the same principles, and adhere to the same measures. They cannot suppose that the existing organ of administration would be swept away without the intention of reversing any part of its policy. They will see the authorities, both at home and in India, surrounded by persons vehemently urging radical changes in many parts of that policy. Interpreting, as they must do, the change in the instrument of government as a concession to these opinions and feelings, they can hardly fail to believe that, whatever else may be intended, the government will no longer be permitted to observe that strict impartiality between those who profess its own creed and those who hold the creeds of its native subjects, which hitherto characterised it; that their strongest and most deeply rooted feelings will henceforth be treated with much less regard than heretofore; and that a directly aggressive policy towards everything in their habits, or in their usages and customs, which Englishmen deem objectionable, will be no longer confined to individuals and private associations, but will be backed by all the power of government.

And here your petitioners think it important to observe, that in abstaining as they have done from all interference with any of the religious practices of the people of India, except such as are abhorrent to humanity, they have acted not only from their own conviction of what is just and expedient, but in accordance with the avowed intentions and express enactments of the legislature, framed 'in order that regard should be had to the civil and religious usages of the natives,' and also 'that suits, civil or criminal, against the natives,' should be conducted according to such rules 'as may accommodate the same to the religion and manners of the natives.' That their policy in this respect has been successful, is evidenced by the fact that, during a military mutiny, said to have been caused by unfounded apprehensions of danger to religion, the heads of the native states and the masses of the population have remained faithful to the British government. Your petitioners need hardly observe, how very different would probably have been the issue of the late events if the native princes, instead of aiding in the suppression of the rebellion, had put themselves at its head, or if the general population had joined in the revolt; and how probable it is that both these contingencies would have occurred if any real ground had been given for the persuasion that the British government intended to identify itself with proselytism. It is the honest conviction of your petitioners, that any serious apprehension of a change of policy in this respect would be likely to be followed, at no distant period, by a general rising throughout India.

That your petitioners have seen with the greatest pain, the demonstrations of indiscriminate animosity towards the natives of India on the part of our countrymen in India and at home, which have grown up since the late unhappy events. They believe these sentiments to be fundamentally unjust; they know them to be fatal to the possibility of good government in India. They feel that if such demonstrations should continue, and especially if weight be added to them by legislating under their supposed influence, no amount of wisdom and forbearance on the part of the government will avail to restore that confidence of the governed in the intentions of their rulers, without which it is vain even to attempt the improvement of the people.

That your petitioners cannot contemplate without dismay the doctrine now widely promulgated, that India should be administered with an especial view to the benefit of the English who reside there—or that in its administration any advantages should be sought for her Majesty's subjects of European birth, except that which they will necessarily derive from their superiority of intelligence, and from the increased prosperity of the people, the improvement of the productive resources of the country, and the extension of commercial intercourse. Your petitioners regard it as the most honourable characteristic of the government of India by England, that it has acknowledged no such distinction as that of a dominant and a subject race; but has held that its first duty was to the people of India. Your petitioners feel that a great portion of the hostility with which they are assailed, is caused by the belief that they are peculiarly the guardians of this principle, and that, so long as they have any voice in the administration of India, it cannot easily be infringed; and your petitioners will not conceal their belief that their exclusion from any part in the government is likely, at the present time, to be regarded in India as a first successful attack on that principle.

That your petitioners, therefore, most earnestly represent to your [lordships'] honourable House that even if the contemplated change could be proved to be in itself advisable, the present is a most unsuitable time for entertaining it; and they most strongly and respectfully urge on your [lordships'] honourable House the expediency of at least deferring any such change until it can be effected at a period when it would not be, in the minds of the people of India, directly connected with the recent calamitous events, and with the feelings to which those events have either given rise, or have afforded an opportunity of manifestation. Such postponement, your petitioners submit, would allow time for a more mature consideration than has yet been given, or can be given in the present excited state of the public mind, to the various questions connected with the organisation of a government for India; and would enable the most competent minds in the nation calmly to examine whether any new arrangement can be devised for the home government of India uniting a greater number of the conditions of good administration than the present, and if so, which, among the numerous schemes which have been or may be proposed, possesses those requisites in the greatest degree.

That your petitioners have always willingly acquiesced in any changes which, after discussion by parliament, were deemed conducive to the general welfare, although such changes may have involved important sacrifices to themselves. They would refer to their partial relinquishment of trade in 1813; to its total abandonment, and the placing of their commercial charter in abeyance in 1833; to the transfer to India of their commercial assets, amounting to £15,858,000, a sum greatly exceeding that ultimately repayable to them in respect of their capital, independent of territorial rights and claims; and to their concurrence, in 1853, in the measure by which the Court of Directors was reconstructed, and reduced to its present number. In the same spirit, your petitioners would most gladly co-operate with her Majesty's government in correcting any defects which may be considered to exist in the details of the present system; and they would be prepared, without a murmur, to relinquish their trust altogether, if a better system for the control of the government of India can be devised. But as they believe that, in the construction of such a system, there are conditions which cannot, without the most dangerous consequences, be departed from, your petitioners respectfully and deferentially submit to the judgment of your [lordships'] honourable House their view of those conditions, in the hope that if your [lordships'] honourable House should see reason to agree in that view, you will withhold your legislative sanction from any arrangement for the government of India which does not fulfil the conditions in question in at least an equal degree with the present.

That your petitioners may venture to assume that it will not be proposed to vest the home portion of the administration of India in a minister of the Crown, without the adjunct of a council composed of statesmen experienced in Indian affairs. Her Majesty's ministers cannot but be aware that the knowledge necessary for governing a foreign country, and in particular a country like India, requires as much special study as any other profession, and cannot possibly be possessed by any one who has not devoted a considerable portion of his life to the acquisition of it.

That in constituting a body of experienced advisers, to be associated with the Indian minister, your petitioners consider it indispensable to bear in mind that this body should not only be qualified to advise the minister, but also, by its advice, to exercise, to a certain degree, a moral check. It cannot be expected that the minister, as a general rule, should himself know India; while he will be exposed to perpetual solicitations from individuals and bodies, either entirely ignorant of that country, or knowing only enough of it to impose on those who know still less than themselves, and having very frequently objects in view other than the interests or good government of India. The influences likely to be brought to bear on him through the organs of popular opinion will, in the majority of cases, be equally misleading. The public opinion of England, itself necessarily unacquainted with Indian affairs, can only follow the promptings of those who take most pains to influence it; and these will generally be such as have some private interest to serve. It is, therefore, your petitioners submit, of the utmost importance that any council which may form a part of the home government of India should derive sufficient weight from its constitution, and from the relation it occupies to the minister, to be a substantial barrier against those inroads of self-interest and ignorance in this country from which the government of India has hitherto been comparatively free, but against which it would be too much to expect that parliament should of itself afford a sufficient protection.

That your petitioners cannot well conceive a worse form of government for India, than a minister with a council whom he should be at liberty to consult or not at his pleasure, or whose advice he should be able to disregard without giving his reasons in writing, and in a manner likely to carry conviction. Such an arrangement, your petitioners submit, would be really liable to the objections in their opinion erroneously urged against the present system. Your petitioners respectfully represent that any body of persons associated with the minister, which is not a check, will be a screen. Unless the council is so constituted as to be personally independent of the minister; unless it feels itself responsible for recording an opinion on every Indian subject, and pressing that opinion on the minister, whether it is agreeable to him or not; and unless the minister, when he overrules their opinion, is bound to record his reasons—its existence will only serve to weaken his responsibility, and to give the colourable sanction of prudence and experience to measures in the framing of which those qualities have had no share.

That it would be vain to expect that a new council could have as much moral influence, and power of asserting its opinion with effect, as the Court of Directors. A new body can no more succeed to the feelings and authority which their antiquity and their historical antecedents give to the East India Company, than a legislature, under a new name, sitting in Westminster, would have the moral ascendency of the Houses of Lords and Commons. One of the most important elements of usefulness will thus be necessarily wanting in any newly constituted Indian Council, as compared with the present.

That your petitioners find it difficult to conceive that the same independence, in judgment and act, which characterises the Court of Directors will be found in any council all of whose members are nominated by the crown. Owing their nomination to the same authority, many of them probably to the same individual minister whom they are appointed to check, and looking to him alone for their re-appointment, their desire of recommending themselves to him, and their unwillingness to risk his displeasure by any serious resistance to his wishes, will be motives too strong not to be in danger of exercising a powerful and injurious influence over their conduct. Nor are your petitioners aware of any mode in which that injurious influence could be guarded against, except by conferring the appointments, like those of the judges, during good behaviour; which, by rendering it impossible to correct an error once committed, would be seriously objectionable.

That your petitioners are equally unable to perceive how, if the controlling body is entirely nominated by the minister, that happy independence of parliamentary and party influence which has hitherto distinguished the administration of India, and the appointment to situations of trust and importance in that country, can be expected to continue. Your petitioners believe that in no government known to history have appointments to offices, and especially to high offices, been so rarely bestowed on any other considerations than those of personal fitness. This characteristic, but for which, in all probability, India would long since have been lost to this country, is, your petitioners conceive, entirely owing to the circumstance that the dispensers of patronage have been persons unconnected with party, and under no necessity of conciliating parliamentary support; that consequently the appointments to offices in India have been, as a rule, left to the unbiassed judgment of the local authorities; while the nominations to the civil and military services have been generally bestowed on the middle classes, irrespective of political considerations, and in a large proportion on the relatives of persons who had distinguished themselves by their services in India.

That your petitioners therefore think it essential that at least a majority of the council which assists the minister for India with its advice, should hold their seats independently of his appointment.

That it is, in the opinion of your petitioners, no less necessary that the order of the transaction of business should be such as to make the participation of the council in the administration of India a substantial one. That to this end it is, in the opinion of your petitioners, indispensable that the dispatches to India should not be prepared by the minister, and laid before the council, but should be prepared by the council, and submitted to the minister. This would be in accordance with the natural and obvious principle, that persons, chosen for their knowledge of a subject, should suggest the mode of dealing with it, instead of merely giving their opinion on suggestions coming from elsewhere. This is also the only mode in which the members of the council can feel themselves sufficiently important, or sufficiently responsible, to secure their applying their minds to the subjects before them. It is almost unnecessary for your petitioners to observe, that the mind is called into far more vigorous action, by being required to propose, than by merely being called on to assent. The minister has necessarily the ultimate decision. If he has also the initiative, he has all the powers which are of any practical moment. A body whose only recognised function is to find fault, would speedily let that function fall into desuetude. They would feel that their co-operation in conducting the government of India was not really desired; that they were only felt as a clog on the wheels of business. Their criticism on what had been decided, without their being collectively consulted, would be felt as importunate as a mere delay and impediment; and their office would probably be seldom sought, but by those who were willing to allow its most important duties to become nominal.

That, with the duty of preparing the dispatches to India would naturally be combined the nomination and control of the home establishments. This your petitioners consider absolutely essential to the utility of the council. If the officers through whom they work are in direct dependence upon an authority higher than theirs, all matters of importance will in reality be settled between the minister and the subordinates, passing over the council altogether.

That a third consideration to which your petitioners attach great importance, is, that the number of the council should not be too restricted. India is so wide a field, that a practical acquaintance with every part of its affairs cannot be found combined in any small number of individuals. The council ought to contain men of general experience and knowledge of the world, also men specially qualified by financial and revenue experience, by judicial experience, diplomatic experience, military experience; it ought to contain persons conversant with the varied social relations, and varied institutions of Bengal, Madras, Bombay, the North-western Provinces, the Punjaub, and the native states. Even the present Court of Directors, reduced as it is in numbers by the act of 1853, does not contain all the varieties of knowledge and experience desirable in such a body; neither, your petitioners submit, would it be safe to limit the number to that which would be strictly sufficient, supposing all the appointments to be the best possible. A certain margin should be allowed for failures, which, even with the most conscientious selection, will sometimes occur. Your petitioners, moreover, cannot overlook the possibility, that if the nomination takes place by ministers at the head of a political party, it will not always be made with exclusive reference to personal qualifications; and it is indispensable to provide that such errors or faults in the nominating authority, so long as they are only occasional, shall not seriously impair the efficiency of the body.

That while these considerations plead strongly for a body not less numerous than the present, even if only regarded as advisers of the minister; their other office, as a check on the minister, forms, your petitioners submit, a no less forcible objection to any considerable reduction of the present number. A body of six or eight will not be equal to one of eighteen in that feeling of independent self-reliance which is necessary to induce a public body to press its opinion on a minister to whom that opinion is unacceptable. However unobjectionably in other respects so small a body may be constituted, reluctance to give offence will be likely, unless in extreme cases, to be a stronger habitual inducement in their minds than the desire to stand up for their convictions.

That if, in the opinion of your [lordships'] honourable House, a body can be constituted which unites the above enumerated requisites of good government, in a greater degree than the Court of Directors, your petitioners have only to express their humble hope that your endeavours for that purpose may be successful. But if, in enumerating the conditions of a good system of home government for India, your petitioners have, in fact, enumerated the qualities possessed by the present system, then your petitioners pray that your [lordships'] honourable House will continue the existing powers of the Court of Directors.

That your petitioners are aware that the present home government of India is reproached with being a double government; and that any arrangement by which an independent check is provided to the discretion of the minister, will be liable to a similar reproach. But they conceive that this accusation originates in an entire misconception of the functions devolving on the home government of India, and in the application to it of the principles applicable to purely executive departments. The executive government of India is, and must be, seated in India itself. The Court of Directors is not so much an executive as a deliberative body. Its principal function, and that of the home government generally, is not to direct the details of administration, but to scrutinise and revise the past acts of the Indian government—to lay down principles and issue general instructions for their future guidance—and to give or refuse sanction to great political measures, which are referred home for approval. These duties are more analogous to the functions of parliament than to those of an executive board; and it might almost as well be said that parliament, as that the government of India, should be constituted on the principles applicable to executive boards. It is considered an excellence, not a defect in the constitution of parliament, to be not merely a double but a triple government. An executive authority, your petitioners submit, may often with advantage be single, because promptitude is its first requisite. But the function of passing a deliberate opinion on past measures, and laying down principles of future policy, is a business which, in the estimation of your petitioners, admits of and requires the concurrence of more judgments than one. It is no defect in such a body to be double, and no excellence to be single, especially when it can only be made so by cutting off that branch of it which, by previous training, is always the best prepared—and often the only one which is prepared at all—for its peculiar duty.

That your petitioners have heard it asserted that, in consequence of what is called the double government, the Indian authorities are less responsible to parliament and the nation than other departments of the government of the empire, since it is impossible to know on which of the two branches of home government the responsibility ought to rest. Your petitioners fearlessly affirm that this impression is not only groundless, but the very reverse of the truth. The home government of India is not less, but more responsible than any other branch of the administration of the state; inasmuch as the president of the Board of Commissioners, who is the minister for India, is as completely responsible as any other of her Majesty's ministers; and, in addition, his advisers also are responsible. It is always certain, in the case of India, that the president of the Board of Commissioners must have either commanded or sanctioned all that has been done. No more than this, your petitioners would submit, can be known in the case of the head of any department of her Majesty's government. For it is not, nor can it rationally be supposed, that any minister of the Crown is without trusted advisers; and the minister for India must, for obvious reasons, be more dependent than any other of her Majesty's ministers, upon the advice of persons whose lives have been devoted to the subject on which their advice has been given. But in the case of India such advisers are assigned to him by the constitution of the government, and they are as much responsible for what they advise, as he for what he ordains; while, in other departments, the minister's only official advisers are the subordinates in his office, men often of great skill and experience, but not in the public eye, often unknown to the public even by name; official reserve precludes the possibility of ascertaining what advice they give, and they are responsible only to the minister himself. By what application of terms this can be called responsible government, and the joint government of your petitioners and the India Board an irresponsible government, your petitioners think it unnecessary to ask.

That, without knowing the plan on which her Majesty's ministers contemplate the transfer to the Crown of the servants of the Company, your petitioners find themselves unable to approach the delicate question of the Indian army, further than to point out that the high military qualities of the officers of that army have unquestionably sprung, in a great degree, from its being a principal and substantive army, holding her Majesty's commissions, and enjoying equal rank with her Majesty's officers; and your petitioners would earnestly deprecate any change in that position.

That your petitioners having regard to all these considerations, humbly pray your [lordships'] honourable House that you will not give your sanction to any change in the constitution of the Indian government during the continuance of the present unhappy disturbances, nor without a full previous inquiry into the operation of the present system. And your petitioners further pray, that this inquiry may extend to every department of Indian administration. Such an inquiry your petitioners respectfully claim, not only as a matter of justice to themselves, but because, when, for the first time in this century, the thoughts of every public man in the country are fixed on India, an inquiry would be more thorough, and its results would carry much more instruction to the mind of parliament and of the country, than at any preceding period.

E. I. Company's Objections to the First and Second India Bills: April 1858. (See p. 567.)

It is the duty of your Directors to lay before the Proprietors the two bills which have been introduced into parliament by the late and by the present ministry, for divesting the East India Company of all participation in the government of India, and for framing a new scheme of administrative agency.

On former occasions, when the ministers of the Crown have submitted measures to parliament for altering, in any manner, the constitution of the Indian government, the substance of the measures has been officially communicated to the Court of Directors, and an opportunity allowed to them of offering such remarks as their knowledge and experience in Indian affairs might suggest. The correspondence being afterwards laid before the Court of Proprietors, formed the most appropriate report which the Directors could make to their constituents on the measures under consideration by the legislature. In the present instance, this opportunity not having been afforded to them, it appears desirable that they should adopt the present mode of laying before the proprietary body the observations which it is entitled to expect from its executive organ, on the bills now before parliament, and on the present posture of the Company's affairs.

The Directors cannot but advert with feelings of satisfaction to the altered tone which public discussion has assumed in regard to the character of the East India Company, and the merits of the administration in which the Company has borne so important a part. The intention of proposing the abolition of the Company's government was announced in the midst of, and it may be surmised in deference to, a clamour, which represented the government of India by the Company as characterised by nearly every fault of which a civilised government can be accused, and the Company as the main cause of the recent disasters. But in the parliamentary discussions which have lately taken place, there has been an almost universal acknowledgment that the rule of the Company has been honourable to themselves and beneficial to India; while no political party, and few individuals of any consideration, have alleged anything seriously disparaging to the general character of the Company's administration. So far, therefore, the stand made by the Company against the calumnies with which they have been assailed, may be considered to have been successful.

But the admission generally made, and made explicitly by the proposers of both the bills, that the existing system works well, has not had the effect of inducing doubt of the wisdom of hastily abolishing it. Neither does it seem to have been remembered, that if the system has worked well, there must be some causes for its having done so, and that it would be worth while to consider what these are, in order that they might be retained in any new system. If the constitution which has made the Indian government what it is, must be abolished, because it is thought defective in theory, what is substituted should at least be theoretically unobjectionable. But the constitution of the East India Company, however anomalous, is far more in accordance with the acknowledged principles of good government than either of the proposed bills.

The nature of the case is, indeed, itself so anomalous, that something anomalous was to be expected in the means by which it could be successfully dealt with.

All English institutions and modes of political action are adapted to the case of a nation governing itself. In India, the case to be provided for is that of the government of one nation by another, separated from it by half the globe; unlike it in everything which characterises a people; as a whole, totally unacquainted with it; and without time or means for acquiring knowledge of it or its affairs.

History presents only two instances in which these or similar difficulties have been in any considerable degree surmounted. One is the Roman Empire; the other is the government of India by the East India Company.

The means which the bills provide for overcoming these difficulties consist of the unchecked power of a minister. There is no difference of moment in this respect between the two bills. The minister, it is true, is to have a council. But the most despotic rulers have councils. The difference between the council of a despot and a council which prevents the ruler from being a despot is, that the one is dependent on him, the other independent; that the one has some power of its own, the other has not. By the first bill, the whole council is nominated by the minister; by the second, one-half of it is nominated by him. The functions to be intrusted to it are left, in both, with some slight exceptions, to the minister's own discretion.

The minister is indeed subject to the control of parliament and of the British nation. But though parliament and the nation exercise a salutary control over their own affairs, it would be contrary to all experience to suppose that they will exercise it over the affairs of a hundred millions of Hindoos and Mohammedans. Habitually, they will doubtless be hereafter, as they have been heretofore, indifferent and inattentive to Indian affairs, and will leave them entirely to the minister. The consequence will be, that in the exceptional cases in which they do interfere, the interference will not be grounded on knowledge of the subject, and will probably be, for the most part, confined to cases where an Indian question is taken up from party motives, as the means of injuring a minister; or when some Indian malcontent, generally with objects opposed to good government, succeeds in interesting the sympathies of the public in his favour. For it is not the people of India, but rich individuals and societies representing class interests, who have the means of engaging the ear of the public through the press, and through agents in parliament. And it is important to remark, that by the provisions of either of the bills, the House of Commons will be rendered even less competent, in point of knowledge of Indian affairs, than at present, since by both bills all the members of the Council of India will be excluded from it.

The government of dependencies by a minister and his subordinates, under the sole control of parliament, is not a new experiment in England. That form of colonial government lost the United States, and had nearly lost all the colonies of any considerable population and importance. The colonial administration of this country has only ceased to be a subject of general condemnation since the principle has been adopted of leaving all the important colonies to manage their own affairs—a course which cannot be followed with the people of India. If the control of parliament has not prevented the habitual mismanagement of countries inhabited by Englishmen like ourselves, who had every facility for representing and urging their grievances, it is not likely to be any effectual protection to Mussulmans and Hindoos.

All governments require constitutional checks; but the constitutional checks applicable to a case of this peculiar kind must be found within the governing body itself.

Though England, as a whole, while desiring nothing but to govern India well, is necessarily ignorant of India, and feels, under ordinary circumstances, no particular interest in its concerns, there are in England a certain number of persons who possess knowledge of India, and feel an interest in its affairs. It seems, therefore, very desirable, for the sake of India, that England should govern it through, and by means of, these persons. This would be the case if the organ of government principally consisted of persons who have passed a considerable portion of their lives in India, or who feel that habitual interest in its affairs which is naturally acquired by having aided in administering them; and if this body, or a majority of it, were periodically elected by a constituency composed of persons in England who have served the government for a certain length of time in India, or whose interests are connected with that country by some permanent tie. It would be an additional advantage if this constituency had the power of requiring information, and compelling a public discussion of Indian questions. These are conditions which, to a considerable extent, the existing constitution of the East India Company fulfils.

The other great constitutional security for the good government of India lies in the forms of business. This is a point to which sufficient importance is not generally attached. The forms of business are the real constitution of India.

From the necessity of the case, recognised in both the proposed measures, the administration must be shared, in some proportion, between a minister and a council. The council may consist of persons possessing knowledge of India. The minister, except in very rare cases, can possess little or none. He is placed in office by the action of political party, which is governed by considerations totally unconnected with India; and, in the common course of politics, he is removed from office by the time he has been able to learn his duty. Even in the unusual case, of which present circumstances are an example, when the minister has made himself acquainted with India through the discharge of high functions in India itself, his knowledge is but the knowledge of one man; and one man's knowledge of a subject like India, until corrected and completed by that of other men, is, it may safely be affirmed, wholly insufficient, and if implicitly trusted, even dangerous. The good government, therefore, of India, by a minister and a council, depends upon the amount of influence possessed by the council; and their influence depends upon the forms of business.

However experienced may be the council, and however inexperienced the minister, he will have the deciding voice. The power will rest with one who may know less of the subject than any member of the council, and is sure to know less than the council collectively, if they are selected with ordinary judgment. The council will have no substantive power, but only moral influence. It is, therefore, all-important that this influence should be upheld. Unless the forms of business are such as to insure that the council shall exercise its judgment on all questions; that all matters requiring decision shall be considered by them, and their views recorded in the initiatory stage, before the minister has committed himself to an opinion—they will possess no more weight or influence than the same number of clerks in his office, whom also he can consult if he pleases; and the power of the minister will be practically uncontrolled.

In both the bills these considerations are entirely disregarded. The first bill does not establish any forms of business, but leaves them to be determined by the minister and his council; in other words, by the minister. Even, therefore, if the minister first appointed should be willing to establish forms which would be any restraint upon himself, a subsequent minister would have it in his power to alter the forms in any manner he pleased.

The second bill, unlike the first, does establish forms of business; but such alone as would effectually prevent the council from being a reality, and would render it a useless pageant.

To make the council a merely consultative body, without initiative, before whom subjects are only brought after the minister has made up his mind, is already a fatal inroad upon its usefulness. But by the second bill the council are not even a consultative body. The minister is under no obligation to consult them. They are not empowered to hold any regular meetings. They are to meet only when the minister convenes them, or on a special requisition by six members. He may send orders to India without their knowledge when the case is urgent, of which urgency he is the sole judge. When it is not urgent, his orders must be placed in the council-room for the perusal of the members for seven days, during which they are not required, but permitted, to give their opinion, not collectively, but individually. Their only power, therefore, is that of recording dissent from a resolution not only taken, but embodied in a dispatch. And as if this was not enough, provision is made that an office, always invidious, shall be incapable of being fulfilled in any but the most invidious manner. The members of council must come forward individually in declared opposition to the minister, by volunteering a protest against his announced intentions, or signing a requisition for a meeting of council to oppose them. Such a council is fitted to serve as a shield for the minister's responsibility when it may suit him to seek, and them to accord, their adhesion; rather than as a restraint on his power to administer India according to his individual pleasure.

The Directors are bound to admit, that the first of the bills contains several provisions indicative of a wish to assure to the council a certain, though small, amount of influence. The administration is to be carried on in the name of the president in council, and not, as by the second bill, in that of the Secretary of State alone. The council, as well as the president, has a voice in the appointment of the home establishment; while in the second bill all promotions and all appointments to the principal offices under the council, rest with the Secretary of State, exclusively; a provision which divests the council of all control or authority over their own establishment. Again, by Section XII. of the first bill, no grant involving increase of expenditure, and no appointment to office or admission to service, can be made without the concurrence of half the council. This, as far as it goes, is a real power; but its value is much diminished by the consideration that those by whom it is to be exercised are the nominees of the minister, dependent on him for their continuance in office after a few years.

In some other points the provisions of the second bill seem to have the advantage. Its council is more numerous; to which, however, little importance can be attached, if the council has no substantial power. It also recognises that the whole of the council ought not to be nominated by the minister, and that some part of it should be elected by a constituency specially qualified by a knowledge of India. But even in these, the best points of the bill, it is, in the opinion of the Directors, very far from unexceptionable. The nomination of even half the council by the minister, takes away all security for an independent majority. It may, indeed, be doubted whether there is any sufficient reason for the minister's nominating any portion, except the supposed reluctance of some eligible persons to encounter a canvass. The proportion of one-third, whom the minister now nominates to the Court of Directors, seems the largest which, consistently with full security for independence, can be so appointed.

The provision that each of the members nominated by the Crown shall be selected as the representative of some particular branch of the service in India, is still more objectionable. Not only would it preclude the nomination of the most distinguished man, if the seat in council appropriated to the department in which he had served were not at the time vacant, but it would introduce a principle which cannot be too strongly deprecated—that of class legislation. The council should comprise the greatest attainable variety of knowledge and experience; but its members should not consider themselves as severally the representatives of a certain number of class interests.

The clause which continues to the Proprietors the power of electing some portion of the council is, so far, deserving of support; and the principle of enlarging the constituency by the addition of persons of a certain length of Indian service and residence is, in itself, unexceptionable; but unless guarded by provisions, such as have never yet been introduced into any electoral system, so large and scattered a constituency as that proposed would greatly add to the inconvenience of canvass: especially as it is not certain that the new electoral body would adopt, from the old, the salutary custom of re-electing, as the general practice, whoever has been once chosen, and has not, by misconduct or incapacity, deserved to forfeit their confidence. The duties of a member of council would be entirely incompatible with a continually-recurring canvass of the constituency.

Respecting the proposition for giving the choice of five members of council to the parliamentary constituencies of five great towns, the Court of Directors can only express a feeling of amazement. It is not the mere fact of election by a multitude that constitutes the benefits of the popular element in government. To produce those benefits, the affairs of which the people are enabled to control the management must be their own affairs. Election by multitudinous bodies, the majority of them of a very low average of education, is not an advantage of popular government, but, on the contrary, one of its acknowledged drawbacks. To assign to such a constituency the control, not of their own affairs, but of the affairs of other people on the other side of the globe, is to incur the disadvantages of popular institutions without any of the benefits. The Court of Directors willingly admit the desirableness, if not necessity, of some provision for including an English element in the Council of India; but a more objectionable mode than the one proposed of attaining the object, could scarcely, in their opinion, be devised.

Besides the provisions which relate to the organ of government in England, the bills contain provisions relating to India itself, which are open to the strongest objection.

The appointments to the councils at Calcutta and at the subordinate presidencies, which are now made by the Court of Directors, with the approbation of the Crown, are transferred by both bills to the governor-general, and to the governors of Madras and Bombay. The Court of Directors are convinced that this change would greatly impair the chances of good government in India. One of the causes which has most contributed to the many excellences of Indian administration is, that the governor-general and governors have always been associated with councillors selected by the authorities at home from among the most experienced and able members of the Indian service, and who, not owing their appointments to the head of the government, have generally brought to the consideration of Indian affairs an independent judgment. In consequence of this, the measures of a government, necessarily absolute, have had the advantage, seldom possessed in absolute governments, of being always preceded by a free and conscientious discussion; while, as the head of the government has the power, on recording his reasons, to act contrary to the advice of his council, no public inconvenience can ever arise from any conflict of opinion. These important officers, who, by their participation in the government, form so salutary a restraint on the precipitancy of an inexperienced, or the wilfulness of a despotically tempered, governor-general or governor, are henceforth to be appointed by the great functionary whom they are intended to check. And this restraint is removed, when the necessity for an independent council will be greater than ever; since the power of appointing the governor-general, and of recalling him, is taken away from the Company, and from the body which is to be their substitute. It may be added that the authorities at home have had the opportunity of being acquainted with the conduct and services of candidates for council from the commencement of their career. The governor-general or governor would often have to nominate a councillor soon after their arrival in India, when necessarily ignorant of the character and merits of candidates, and would be entirely dependent on the recommendation of irresponsible advisers.

Another most objectionable provision demands notice, which is to be found only in the second bill. A commission, appointed in England, is to proceed to India, for the purpose of inquiring and reporting on the principles and details of Indian finance, including the whole revenue system, and, what is inseparably involved in it, the proprietary rights and social position of all the great classes of the community. The Court of Directors cannot believe that such a project will be persisted in. It would be a step towards the disorganisation of the fabric of government in India. A commission from England, independent of the local government of the country, deriving its authority directly from the higher power to which the local government is subordinate, and instructed to carry back to the higher power information on Indian affairs which the local government is not deemed sufficiently trustworthy to afford, would give a most serious shock to the influence of the local authorities, and would tend to impress all natives with the belief that the opinions and decisions of the local government are of small moment, and that the thing of real importance is the success with which they can contrive that their claims and objects shall be advocated in England. Up to the present time, it has been the practice of the home government to uphold in every way the authority of the governments on the spot; even when reversing their acts, to do so through the governments themselves, and to employ no agency except in subordination to them.

From this review of the chief provisions of the bills, which embody the attempts of two great divisions of English statesmen to frame an organ of government for India, it will probably appear to the proprietors, that neither of them is grounded on any sufficient consideration of past experience, or of the principles applicable to the subject; that the passing of either would be a calamity to India; and that the attempt to legislate while the minds of leading men are in so unprepared a state, is altogether premature.

The opinion of your Directors is, that by all constitutional means the passing of either bill should be opposed; but that if one or the other should be determined on for the purpose of transferring the administration, in name, from the East India Company to the Crown, every exertion should be used in its passage through committee to divest it of the mischievous features by which both bills are now deformed, and to maintain, as at present, a really independent council, having the initiative of all business, discharging all the duties, and possessing all the essential powers of the Court of Directors. And it is the Court's conviction, that measures might be so framed as to obviate whatever may be well founded in the complaints made against the present system—retaining the initiative of the council, and that independence of action on their part which should be regarded as paramount and indispensable.

E. I. Company's Objections to the Third India Bill: June 1858. (See p. 570.)

1. Although the bill which has been newly brought in by her Majesty's ministers 'for the better government of India,' has not yet been formally communicated to the Court of Directors, the Court, influenced by the desire which they have already expressed to give all aid in their power towards rendering the scheme of government, which it is the pleasure of parliament to substitute for the East India Company, as efficient for its purposes as possible, have requested us* to lay before your lordship,† and through you before her Majesty's government, a few observations on some portions of the bill.

2. Having in documents which have been presented to parliament expressed their sentiments fully on all the general features of the subject, the Court refrain from offering any further arguments on points upon which the government and the House of Commons seem to have pronounced a decided opinion. The joint government of a minister and a council, composed in majority of persons of Indian experience, deriving their appointments only partially from ministerial nomination, and all of them holding office on a tenure independent of the minister, is a combination which fulfils to a considerable extent the conditions of a good organ of government for India. The Court would have much preferred that in the constitution of the council more extensive recourse had been had to the elective principle. But if they cannot hope that this course will be adopted, they see many advantages in the provision by which one-half the number, instead of being named by the government, will be selected by a responsible body, intimately connected with India, to whom the qualification of candidates will in general be accurately known, and who will be under strong inducements to make such a choice as will tend to increase the credit and consideration of the body.

3. With regard to the qualifications prescribed for members of council, the Court desire to offer a suggestion. Her Majesty's present government have, on many occasions, expressed a desire to secure the Crown appointments against the evils of abuse of patronage. The security against such abuse has hitherto consisted in the strict limitation of the appointments to persons who have served a considerable number of years in India. While the Court fully agree with her Majesty's government in recognising the desirableness of an English element, it does not seem to them advisable that this element should extend to nearly half the council, only a bare majority being reserved for persons of Indian experience. Knowledge of India is, after all, the most important requisite for a seat in the Indian Council; while it is chiefly in the English nominations that there is any present danger lest appointments should be obtained through political or parliamentary influence—from which influence, unless introduced through that channel, the council, like the Court of Directors, may be expected to be altogether free. The Court, therefore, recommend that the qualification of ten years' Indian service or residence be made imperative on at least two-thirds instead of a mere majority of the fifteen members of council. They also think it questionable if the interests of India will be promoted by the exclusion of the whole of the members of the council from seats in parliament. These are the only modifications which we are requested to suggest in the provisions respecting the composition of the council.

[The remaining objections made by the Directors were little more than a repetition of those made against the first and second bills (given *in extenso* in a preceding page); and need not be reproduced here. The Directors expressed a dislike or apprehension of the subordinate position in which the Council would be placed; of the autocratic power to be possessed by the Secretary for India; of the transference of the powers of the Secret Committee wholly and solely to him; of the proposed mode of making appointments and exercising patronage; of any disturbance in the mode of auditing accounts; and of the appointment of any Commission of Inquiry in India which should appear derogatory to the dignity of the local governments. Many of these objections were listened to, and were productive of modifications during the discussion of the bill. The result will be seen in the next article of this Appendix.]

* The chairman and deputy-chairman.

† Lord Stanley, president of the Board of Control.

Abstract of Act for the Better Government of India—21 *and* 22 *Vict. cap.* 106.—*Received Royal Assent August* 2, 1858. (See p. 573.)

Transfer of Governing Powers.

I. Governing powers transferred from the East India Company to the Crown.

II. All rights, territories, revenues, and liabilities similarly transferred.

III. A Secretary of State to exercise all the governing powers heretofore exercised by Court of Directors, Court of Proprietors, and Board of Control.

IV. Provision concerning sitting of secretary and under-secretary in House of Commons.

V. Concerning re-election of secretaries to House of Commons.

VI. Secretary of State for India to receive salary equal to those of other secretaries of state.

Council of India.

VII. A Council of India, of 15 persons, to be formed.

VIII. Court of Directors to elect 7 members of this Council, from among persons possessing certain qualifications; and the Crown to appoint the other 8.

IX. Vacancies among the 8 to be filled up by the Crown; and among the other 7, by election by the Council.

X. Nine members of the Council, at least, must have had not less than ten years' experience in India.

XI. Members to hold office for life, or during good behaviour.

XII. Members not to sit in parliament.

XIII. Annual salary of £1200 to each member.

XIV. Members may resign; if after ten years' service, on a pension of £500, subject to certain conditions.

XV. Secretaries and other officers of Company to become officers of Council of India—subject to any changes afterwards made by Privy Council and sanctioned by parliament.

XVI. Secretary in Council to make all subsequent appointments in the home establishment.

XVII. Compensation to such officers of the Company as are not retained permanently by the Council.

XVIII. Any officer of the Company, transferred to the service of the Council, to have a claim to the same pension or superannuation allowance as if the change of government had not taken place.

Duties and Proceedings of the Council.

XIX. Council to conduct affairs of India in England; but all correspondence to be in the name of the Secretary of State.

XX. Secretary of State may divide the Council into committees.

XXI. Secretary of State to sit and vote as president, and appoint vice-president.

XXII. Five to be a quorum; meetings convened by Secretary of State not fewer than one each week.

XXIII. Secretary of State to decide questions on which members differ. Any dissentient member may require his opinion to be placed upon record.

XXIV. Secretary's proceedings to be open to all the Council, except in 'secret service' dispatches.

XXV. Secretary to give reasons for any exercise of his veto against the decision of the majority.

XXVI. Secretary allowed to overrule the two preceding clauses in urgent cases.

XXVII. Functions of the 'secret committee' transferred to Secretary of State.

XXVIII. Dispatches marked 'secret' not to be opened by members of Council.

Appointments and Patronage.

XXIX. Of the high appointments in India, some to be made by the Crown, some by the Council, and some by the Governor-general.

XXX. Inferior appointments to be made as heretofore, except transference of patronage from Court of Directors to Council.

XXXI. Special provision for civil service in India.

XXXII. Secretary in Council to make rules for examination of persons intended for junior situations in civil service of India.

XXXIII. Appointments to naval and military cadetships to vest in the Crown.

XXXIV. Competitive examinations for engineers and artillery of the Indian army.

XXXV. A certain ratio of cadetships to be given to the sons of persons who have served in India.

XXXVI. All the other cadetships to be in the gift of the members of the Council, subject to approval; the Secretary of State to have twice as many nominations as an ordinary member.

XXXVII. In all unchanged rules concerning appointments, power of Court of Directors to be vested in Council.

XXXVIII. The same in reference to any dismissal from service.

Transfer of Property.

XXXIX. Company's property, credits, and debits, to revert to the Crown—except the *East India Stock* and the dividends thereon.

XL. Secretary in Council may buy, sell, or borrow, in the name of the Crown, for the service of India.

Revenues.

XLI. Expenditure of revenues in India wholly under Secretary in Council.

XLII. Liabilities of Company, and dividends on India stock, to be borne by Secretary in Council out of revenues of India.

XLIII. Secretary in Council to keep a cash account with the Bank of England, and to be responsible for all payments in relation to India revenue.

XLIV. Transfer of cash balance from the Company to the Council.

XLV. A stock account to be opened at Bank of England.

XLVI. Transfer of stock accounts.

XLVII. Mode of managing Council's finances at the Bank.

XLVIII. Transfer of Exchequer bills, &c., from Company to Council.

XLIX. Power of issuing bonds, debentures, &c.

L. Provisions concerning forgery.

LI. Regulations of audit department.

LII. The Crown to appoint auditor of Indian accounts, to whom all needful papers are to be sent by Secretary in Council.

LIII. Annual accounts to be furnished to parliament of the revenue and expenditure of India; accompanied by reports on the moral and material progress of the several presidencies.

LIV. War in India to be made known to parliament within a specified period.

LV. India revenues not to pay for wars unconnected with India.

Existing Establishments.

LVI. Company's army and navy transferred to the Crown, but with all existing contracts and engagements holding good.

LVII. Future powers as to conditions of service.

LVIII. All commissions held under the Company to be valid as under the Crown.

LIX. Regulations of service to be subject to future change, if deemed necessary.

LX. Court of Directors and Court of Proprietors cease to hold power in reference to government of India.

LXI. Board of Control abolished.

LXII. Records and archives of Company to be given up to Council—except stock and dividend books.

LXIII. Powers of Governor-general, on assuming duties of that office.

LXIV. Existing enactments and provisions to remain in force, unless specially repealed.

Actions and Contracts.

LXV. Secretary in Council may sue and be sued as a body corporate.

LXVI. And may take the place of the Company in any still-pending actions.

LXVII. Treaties and covenants made by the Company to remain binding.

LXVIII. Members not *personally* liable for such treaties or covenants.

LXIX. A Court of Directors still to exist, but in smaller number than before, and having powers relating only to the management of the Company's dividend and a few minor subjects.

LXX. Quarterly courts not in future obligatory.

LXXI. Company's liability ceases, on all matters now taken under the care of the Council.

Saving of Certain Rights of the Company.

LXXII. Secretary in Council to pay dividends on India stock out of India revenue.

LXXIII. Dividends to constitute a preferential charge.

Commencement of the Act.

LXXIV. Commences thirty days after day of receiving royal assent.

LXXV. Company's orders to be obeyed in India until the change of government shall have been proclaimed in the several presidencies.

The Indian Mutiny Relief Fund. (See p. 226.)

This noble manifestation of kind feeling towards the sufferers in India, which originated in a public meeting held in London on the 25th of August 1857, assumed munificent proportions during the next following year, when the colonists and Englishmen residing abroad had had time to respond to the appeal made to them. In a report prepared by the Committee, on the 1st of November 1858, it was announced that the sum placed in their charge amounted, up to that time, to £431,729. They had remitted £127,287 to India, there to be distributed by auxiliary local committees; they had assisted sufferers after their return to, or during their residence in, the home country, to the extent of £35,757; and their management expenses had amounted to £6224. There remained, invested at interest, the sum of £265,461, applicable to further cases of need. It is interesting to notice the kind of persons to whom relief was afforded, on account of the varied privations to which the mutiny had subjected them. The sum of £35,757 expended in England, was mostly in donations to the following numbers and classes of persons:

32 Military officers.	423 Children of soldiers.
86 Widows and children of officers.	82 Other relatives of soldiers.
25 Wives of officers.	10 Clergymen and missionaries.
25 Orphans of officers.	6 Widows of Clergymen.
51 Other relatives of officers.	1 Wife of missionary.
13 Disabled soldiers.	23 Widows and orphans of civilians.
298 Widows of soldiers.	73 Planters, railway officials, &c.

Queen Victoria's Proclamation to the Princes, Chiefs, and People of India.—Read in the principal Cities of India, November 1, 1858. (See p. 612.)

VICTORIA, by the Grace of God, of the United Kingdom of Great Britain and Ireland, and of the Colonies and Dependencies thereof in Europe, Asia, Africa, America, and Australasia, Queen, Defender of the Faith.

Whereas, for divers weighty reasons, we have resolved, by and with the advice and consent of the Lords Spiritual and Temporal, and Commons in Parliament assembled, to take upon ourselves the government of the territories in India, heretofore administered in trust for us by the Honourable East India Company:

Now, therefore, we do by these presents notify and declare that, by the advice and consent aforesaid, we have taken upon ourselves the said government; and we hereby call upon all our subjects within the said territories to be faithful and to bear true allegiance to us, our heirs and successors, and to submit themselves to the authority of those whom we may hereafter from time to time see fit to appoint to administer the government of our said territories, in our name and on our behalf.

And we, reposing especial trust and confidence in the loyalty, ability, and judgment of our right trusty and well-beloved cousin and councillor, Charles John Viscount Canning, do hereby constitute and appoint him, the said Viscount Canning, to be our first Viceroy and Governor-general in and over our said territories, and to administer the government thereof in our name, and generally to act in our name and on our behalf: subject to such orders and regulations as he shall, from time to time, receive from us through one of our principal Secretaries of State.

And we do hereby confirm in their several offices, civil and military, all persons now employed in the service of the Honourable East India Company, subject to our future pleasure, and to such laws and regulations as may hereafter be enacted.

We hereby announce to the native Princes of India that all treaties and engagements made with them by or under the authority of the Honourable East India Company, are by us accepted, and will be scrupulously maintained; and we look for the like observance on their part.

We desire no extension of our present territorial possessions; and while we will permit no aggression upon our dominions or our rights to be attempted with impunity, we shall sanction no encroachment on those of others. We shall respect the rights, dignity, and honour of native princes as our own; and we desire that they, as well as our own subjects, should enjoy that prosperity and that social advancement which can only be secured by internal peace and good government.

We hold ourselves bound to the natives of our Indian territories by the same obligations of duty which bind us to all our other subjects; and those obligations, by the blessing of Almighty God, we shall faithfully and conscientiously fulfil.

Firmly relying ourselves on the truth of Christianity, and acknowledging with gratitude the solace of religion, we disclaim alike the right and the desire to impose our convictions on any of our subjects. We declare it to be our Royal will and pleasure that none be in anywise favoured, none molested or disquieted, by reason of their religious faith or observances, but that all shall alike enjoy the equal and impartial protection of the law; and we do strictly charge and enjoin all those who may be in authority under us that they abstain from all interference with the religious belief or worship of any of our subjects, on pain of our highest displeasure.

And it is our further will that, so far as may be, our subjects, of whatever race or creed, be freely and impartially admitted to offices in our service, the duties of which they may be qualified, by their education, ability, and integrity, duly to discharge.

We know and respect the feelings of attachment with which the natives of India regard the lands inherited by them from their ancestors, and we desire to protect them in all rights connected therewith, subject to the equitable demands of the State; and we will that, generally, in framing and administering the law, due regard be paid to the ancient rights, usages, and customs of India.

We deeply lament the evils and misery which have been brought upon India by the acts of ambitious men, who have deceived their countrymen by false reports, and led them into open rebellion. Our power has been shewn by the suppression of that rebellion in the field; we desire to shew our mercy by pardoning the offences of those who have been thus misled, but who desire to return to the path of duty.

Already in one province, with a view to stop the further effusion of blood, and to hasten the pacification of our Indian dominions, our Viceroy and Governor-general has held out the expectation of pardon, on certain terms, to the great majority of those who in the late unhappy disturbances have been guilty of offences against our government; and has declared the punishment which will be inflicted on those whose crimes place them beyond the reach of forgiveness. We approve and confirm the said act of our Viceroy and Governor-general, and do further announce and proclaim as follows:

Our clemency will be extended to all offenders, save and except those who have been or shall be convicted of having directly taken part in the murder of British subjects.

With regard to such, the demands of justice forbid the exercise of mercy.

To those who have willingly given asylum to murderers, knowing them to be such, or who may have acted as leaders or instigators in revolt, their lives alone can be guaranteed; but in appointing the penalty due to such persons, full consideration will be given to the circumstances under which they have been induced to throw off their allegiance; and large indulgence will be shewn to those whose crimes may appear to have originated in a too credulous acceptance of the false reports circulated by designing men.

To all others in arms against the government, we hereby promise unconditional pardon, amnesty, and oblivion of all offences against ourselves, our crown and dignity, on their return to their homes and peaceful pursuits.

It is our Royal pleasure that these terms of grace and amnesty should be extended to all those who comply with their conditions before the first day of January next.

When, by the blessing of Providence, internal tranquillity shall be restored, it is our earnest desire to stimulate the peaceful industry of India, to promote works of public utility and improvement, and to administer its government for the benefit of all our subjects resident therein. In their prosperity will be our strength, in their contentment our security, and in their gratitude our best reward. And may the God of all power grant unto us, and to those in authority under us, strength to carry out these our wishes for the good of our people.

Viscount Canning's Proclamation.—Issued at Allahabad, November 1, 1858. (See p. 612.)

Her Majesty the Queen having declared that it is her gracious pleasure to take upon herself the government of the British territories in India, the Viceroy and Governor-general hereby notifies that from this day all acts of the government of India will be done in the name of the Queen alone.

From this day, all men of every race and class who, under the administration of the Honourable East India Company, have joined to uphold the honour and power of England, will be the servants of the Queen alone.

The Governor-general summons them, one and all, each in his degree, and according to his opportunity, and with his whole heart and strength, to aid in fulfilling the gracious will and pleasure of the Queen, as set forth in her royal proclamation.

From the many millions of her Majesty's native subjects in India, the Governor-general will now, and at all times, exact a loyal obedience to the call which, in words full of benevolence and mercy, their Sovereign has made upon their allegiance and faithfulness.

CHRONOLOGICAL TABLE.

Events in India.

1857.

Jan. 22. Cartridge disturbances began at Dumdum.
Feb. 6. „ grievances inquired into at Barrackpore.
„ 11. General Hearsey warned government of disaffection.
„ 26. 19th Bengal N. I. riotous at Berhampore.
Mar. 26. Cartridge disturbances at Umballa.
„ 27. Proclamation explaining Cartridge question.
„ 29. 34th B. N. I. riotous at Barrackpore.
„ 31. 19th B. N. I. disbanded and dismissed.
Apr. 24. Cartridge disturbances at Meerut.
May 1. „ „ Lucknow.
„ 3. 7th Oude Infantry mutinied at Lucknow.
„ 5. 34th B. N. I. disbanded and dismissed.
„ 9. 3d B. N. C. punished at Meerut.
„ 10. COMMENCEMENT OF THE GREAT REVOLT AT MEERUT.
„ „ Troops in Company's pay on this day—38,000 Europeans, 200,000 Natives.
„ 11. Meerut mutineers (11th and 20th B. N. I., and 3d B. N. C.) marched to Delhi.
„ „ 38th, 54th, and 74th B. N. I., mutinied at Delhi.
„ 13. 16th, 26th, and 49th B. N. I., and 8th B. N. C., disarmed at Meean Meer near Lahore.
„ 14. General Anson departed from Simla, to head troops.
„ 16. B. N. Sappers and Miners mutinied at Meerut.
„ 17. 25th B. N. I. riotous at Calcutta.
„ 19. Anson's Proclamation concerning cartridges.
„ 20. 55th B. N. I. mutinied at Murdan.
„ „ 9th B. N. I. „ „ Allygurh and vicinity.
„ 21. First siege-column left Umballa for Delhi.
„ „ Europeans at Cawnpore began their intrenchment.
„ 22. 24th, 27th, and 51st B. N. I., with 5th B. N. C., disarmed at Peshawur.
„ 24. Colvin's proclamation—disapproved by Viscount Canning.
„ „ Portion of Gwalior Horse mutinied at Hattrass.
„ „ General Anson left Umballa for Delhi.
„ 27. „ „ died at Kurnaul.
„ „ Wilson's Field-force left Meerut for Delhi.
„ 28. Reed succeeded Anson provisionally.
„ „ 15th and 30th B. N. I. mutinied at Nusseerabad.
„ 30. Portions of 13th, 48th, and 71st B. N. I., with 7th N. C., mutinied at Lucknow.
„ „ Wilson defeated Delhi rebels at Ghazeeoodeen Nuggur.
„ 31. Wilson defeated Delhi rebels, near the Hindeun.
„ „ Barnard left Kurnaul to command army against Delhi.
„ „ 28th B. N. I. mutinied at Shahjehanpoor.
June 1. 44th and 67th B. N. I. disarmed at Agra.
June 3. 17th B. N. I. mutinied at Azimghur.
„ „ 41st B. N. I., 9th and 10th Oude Irreg. I., and 2d Oude Mil. Police, mutinied at Seetapoor.
„ „ 29th B. N. I. mutinied at Mooradabad.
„ „ 72d B. N. I., and a wing of 1st B. N. C., mutinied at Neemuch.
„ 4. 37th B. N. I., 13th Irreg. C., and Loodianah Sikhs, mutinied at Benares.
„ „ 12th B. N. I., and 14th Irreg. C., mutinied at Jhansi.
„ 5. 1st, 53d, and 56th B. N. I., and 2d B. N. C., mutinied at Cawnpore.
„ „ Wing of Loodianah Sikhs mutinied at Jounpoor.
„ 6. Barnard and Wilson joined forces at Bhagput.
„ „ 6th B. N. I. mutinied at Allahabad.
„ „ ? Hurrianah Battalion mutinied at Hansi.
„ „ ? Bhurtpore Levies mutinied at Bhurtpore.
„ 7. 36th and 61st B. N. I., and 6th B. C., mutinied at Jullundur.
„ 8. 22d B. N. I., and 6th Oude I., mutinied at Fyzabad.
„ „ ? Massacre of Europeans at Jhansi.
„ „ Barnard defeated Delhi rebels at Badulla Serai.
„ „ „ arrived with siege-army before Delhi.
„ 9. 15th Irreg. C. mutinied at Sultanpore.
„ „ Europeans driven from Futtehpoor by rebels.
„ 10. 1st Oude Irreg. I. mutinied at Pershadeepore.
„ „ Wing of 12th B. N. I., and 14th Irreg. C., mutinied at Nowgong.
„ „ ? Europeans driven from Neemuch by rebels.
„ 11. Neill relieved Allahabad from the rebels.
„ „ 60th B. N. I. mutinied at Rohtuk.
„ 12. First boat-party from Futteghur massacred by Nena Sahib.
„ 13. Press 'Gagging' Act passed at Calcutta.
„ „ 45th and 57th B. N. I. mutinied at Ferozpore.
„ 14. 43d and 70th B. N. I. and 2d N. C. disarmed at Barrackpore.
„ „ Gwalior Contingent mutinied at Gwalior.
„ 15. King of Oude under surveillance at Calcutta.
„ 18. 10th B. N. I. mutinied at Futteghur.
„ 19. Defeat of Nusseerabad rebels outside Delhi.
„ 23. Nagpoor Irreg. C. disarmed at Nagpoor.
„ „ Severe Battle outside Delhi.
„ 26. 33d and 35th B. N. I. disarmed at Phillour.
„ 27. First news of the Revolt reached England.
„ „ Boat-massacre at Cawnpore, by Nena Sahib.
„ 30. Disastrous Battle of Chinhut, near Lucknow.
„ „ 4th Irreg. C. mutinied at Mozuffernugger.
„ „ Europeans at Saugor intrench themselves in fort.
July 1. „ driven out of Indore.
„ „ 23d B. N. I. mutinied at Mhow.
„ „ Siege of Europeans in Lucknow began.
„ 2. Severe Battle outside Delhi.

July 2. Rohilcund mutineers entered Delhi.
" 3. Mussulman Conspiracy discovered at Patna.
" 4. Death of Sir H. Lawrence at Lucknow.
" " Kotah Contingent mutinied at Agra.
" 5. Death of Sir H. Barnard outside Delhi.
" " Reed took command of siege-army.
" " Disastrous Battle of Shahgunje, near Agra.
" 7. 14th B. N. I. mutinied at Jelum.
" " 58th B. N. I. disarmed at Rawul Pindee.
" " Havelock's column left Allahabad for Cawnpore.
" " 42d B. N. I., and 3d Irreg. C., mutinied at Saugor.
" 9. 46th B. N. I., and 9th C., mutinied at Sealkote.
" 11. Second boat-party from Futteghur arrived at Bithoor.
" 12. Nicholson defeated Sealkote mutineers.
" " Havelock defeated rebels at Futtehpoor.
" " Sir Colin Campbell left England for India.
" 14. Severe Battle outside Delhi.
" 15. Havelock defeated rebels at Aong.
" " " " " Pandoo Nuddee.
" " Massacre at Cawnpore, by Nena Sahib.
" 16. Havelock defeated Nena Sahib at Aherwa.
" 17. " entered Cawnpore victoriously.
" " " defeated Nena Sahib near Bithoor.
" " Reed resigned command before Delhi—Wilson succeeded.
" 20. Fierce Attack by rebels on Lucknow Garrison.
" 24. 12th Irreg. C. mutinied at Segowlie.
" 25. Havelock crossed Ganges into Oude.
" " 7th, 8th, and 40th B. N. I. mutinied at Dinapoor.
" 26. Nearly 6000 persons sheltered in Agra Fort, of whom 2000 children.
" 27. Mr Wake's defence of Arrah commenced.
" 29. 26th B. N. I. mutinied at Lahore.
" " Havelock defeated rebels at Onao.
" " " " " Busherutgunje.
" 30. Captain Dunbar's disaster at Arrah.
" 31. Ramgurh Infantry mutinied at Ramgurh.
" " Siege-army before Delhi = 6918 effectives, and 1116 sick and wounded.
Aug. 1. 63d B.N.I. and 11th Irreg. C. disarmed at Berhampore.
" " Severe Battle outside Delhi.
" " 27th Bombay N. I. mutinied at Kolapore.
" 2. Vincent Eyre defeated Koer Singh near Arrah.
" 8. 59th B. N. I. disarmed at Umritsir.
" " Nicholson arrived with his Column at Delhi.
" 10. Severe Battle outside Delhi.
" 12. Havelock's second victory at Busherutgunje.
" " Vincent Eyre defeated Koer Singh at Jugdispore.
" 13. Havelock retreated across Ganges to Cawnpore.
" 14. 5th Irreg. C. mutinied at Berhampore.
" 15–18. Hodson defeated rebels outside Delhi.
" 16. Havelock defeated Nena Sahib at Bithoor.
" 20. Fierce attack by the rebels on Lucknow Residency.
" 22. Jhodpore Legion mutinied at Erinpoora.
" 24. Montgomery defeated rebels at Allygurh.
" 25. Nicholson won Battle of Nujuffghur near Delhi.
" " Meeting in London at the Mansion-house, to establish Indian Mutiny Relief Fund.
" 28. 51st B. N. I. mutinied at Peshawur.
Sep. 5. Outram's Column left Allahabad for Cawnpore.
" " Fierce attack by rebels on Lucknow Residency.
" 7. Indore mutineers captured Dholpore.
" " Siege-army before Delhi = 13,000 men.
" 9. Mr Colvin died at Agra.
" 11. Cannonading of Delhi commenced.
" " Viscount Eyre defeated rebels at Koondun Puttee.
" 14. Delhi entered by storm—death of Nicholson.
" 15–20. Gradual Conquest of Delhi city and fortifications.
" " Outram joined Havelock and Neill at Cawnpore.
" 16. 50th B. N. I. mutinied at Nagode.
" 18. 52d B. N. I. mutinied at Jubbulpoor.
" 19. Outram and Havelock crossed Ganges into Oude.
" 20. Goorkhas defeated rebels at Mundoree.
" 21. Hodson captured King and Princes of Delhi.
Sep. 23. Outram and Havelock captured the Alum Bagh.
" 25. " " entered Lucknow Residency.
" " Death of Neill at Lucknow.
" 27. Outram and Havelock besieged in Residency.
" 28. Greathed defeated Delhi rebels at Bolundshuhur.
Oct. 3. Peel's Naval Brigade arrived at Allahabad.
" 5. Greathed defeated Delhi rebels at Allygurh.
" 9. 32d B. N. I. mutinied at Deoghur.
" 10. Greathed defeated Indore rebels near Agra.
" 15. Gwalior Contingent took the field, as a rebel army.
" " Rajah of Kotah's troops mutinied.
" 19. Greathed and Hope Grant retook Minpooree.
" 26. " " " arrived at Cawnpore.
" 28. Sir Colin Campbell started from Calcutta, for scene of hostilities.
Nov. 1. Peel's Naval Brigade defeated rebels at Kudjna.
" 9. Mr Cavanagh's adventure at Lucknow.
" " Europeans besieged in Fort of Neemuch.
" " Sir Colin Campbell crossed Ganges into Oude.
" 12. " " captured Jelalabad Fort.
" 14–17. " " fought his way into Lucknow.
" 18. Wing of 34th B. N. I. mutinied at Chittagong.
" 20. ? 73d B. N. I. mutinied at Dacca.
" 23. British evacuated Lucknow.
" 24. Stuart defeated Bundela rebels near Mundesoor.
" 25. Death of Havelock, outside Lucknow.
" 27, 28. Windham beaten by Gwalior rebels near Cawnpore.
" 29. Lucknow Garrison recross Ganges to Cawnpore.
Dec. 6. Sir Colin defeated 25,000 rebels at Cawnpore.
" 9. Hope Grant defeated rebels at Serai Ghât.
" 14–17. Seaton defeated rebels in Minpooree district.
" 19. Government announced to East India Company an approaching change in Company's powers.
" 28. Osborne reconquered Myhere from Bundela rebels.
" 30. Wood defeated rebels near Sumbhulpore.
" 31. East India Company protested against the proposed legislation for India.

1858.

Jan. 1. Bareilly mutineers defeated at Huldwanee.
" 3. Sir Colin Campbell arrived at Futteghur.
" 6. Jung Bahadoor and his Goorkha army entered Goruckpore.
" " Raines defeated a body of rebels at Rowah.
" 12. Outram defeated 30,000 rebels outside Alum Bagh.
" 27. Adrian Hope defeated rebels at Shumshabad.
" " Trial of the King of Delhi commenced.
" 28. East India Company petitioned Parliament against government proceedings.
Feb. 3. Rose liberated the Europeans at Saugor.
" 4. Sir Colin returned to Cawnpore from Futteghur.
" " Maxwell repulsed Gwalior rebels at Chowra.
" 9. Sir Colin and Canning met at Allahabad.
" " Delhi and Meerut divisions placed under Punjaub government.
" 10. M'Causland repulsed Bareilly rebels at Sunda.
" 11. Great convoy of women and children left Agra.
" 12. Lord Palmerston brought in India Bill No. 1.
" 12–18. Debates thereon—government majority, 318 to 173.
" 19. Franks defeated Bunda Hossein at Chundah.
" " " " Mahomed Hossein at Humeerpoor.
" 20. Palmerston Ministry resigned.
" 21. Derby Ministry formed—Lord Ellenborough at the India Board.
" " Outram repulsed 20,000 rebels at Alum Bagh.
" 23. Hope Grant took Meeangunje from Oude rebels.
" 26. Goorkhas captured fort of Mobarukhpoor in Oude.
" 28. Sir Colin crossed Ganges, to head his army.
Mar. 2. Sir Colin advanced to the Alum Bagh.
" 2–21. Gradual conquest of Lucknow from rebels.
" 3. Viscount Canning's Proclamation to the Oudians.
" 4. Rose defeated Bundelas at Mudenpore Pass.
" 5. Rowcroft repulsed 12,000 rebels at Goruckpore.

Mar. 5. Goorkhas defeated Oude rebels at Kandoo Nuddee.
„ 10. Rose defeated rebel Rajah of Shagurh.
„ „ Roberts headed the Rajpootana Field-force.
„ 11. Jung Bahadoor joined Sir Colin outside Lucknow.
„ „ Showers defeated a body of rebels at Bah.
„ 16. Return of the Guide Corps to Peshawur.
„ 17. Stuart captured Chendaree from rebels.
„ 21. Rose with Siege-army arrived before Jhansi.
„ „ Lucknow finally conquered by British.
„ 22. Millman repulsed by Azimghur rebels at Atrowlia.
„ „ Roberts with Siege-army arrived before Kotah.
„ 25. Moncrieff routed a body of Coles at Chuckerderpore.
„ 26. Mr Disraeli brought in India Bill No. 2.
„ 29. Army of Oude broken up into separate columns.
„ 30. Roberts captured Kotah.
Apr. 1. Rose defeated Tanteea Topee outside Jhansi.
„ 2. „ captured Jhansi—Ranee escaped.
„ „ Kerr defeated Dinapoor rebels near Azimghur.
„ „ Death of Captain Sir William Peel at Cawnpore.
„ 6. Seaton defeated Minpooree Rajah at Kankur.
„ 7. East India Company protested against both India Bills.
„ 12. House of Commons determined to proceed by Resolutions on India Bill.
„ 14. Disaster at Rhodamow under Walpole.
„ „ Death of Adrian Hope at Rhodamow.
„ 17. Rowcroft defeated rebels at Amorah.
„ „ Jones defeated Rohilcund rebels at Nagul.
„ 18. Sir Colin resumed operations from Cawnpore.
„ „ Douglas defeated Koer Singh at Azimutgurh.
„ „ „ „ „ Muneer Khas.
„ 19. Ellenborough's 'Secret Dispatch' written.
„ „ Whitlock took Banda, and defeated Nawab.
„ 21. Le Grand's disaster at Jugdispore.
„ „ Jones defeated Rohilcund rebels at Nageena.
„ „ Koer Singh eluded Douglas, and crossed Ganges.
„ 22. Walpole defeated rebels at Sirsa.
„ 25. Jones recovered Mooradabad from Oude rebels.
„ „ Sir Colin reached Futteghur.
„ 27. „ „ entered Rohilcund.
„ 28. „ „ joined Walpole at Ramgunga.
„ 30. „ „ entered Shahjehanpoor.
„ „ Penny's Column won Battle of Kukerowlee.
„ „ Death of Penny at Kukerowlee.
„ „ Mr Disraeli brought in 'Resolutions' in House of Commons.
May 3. Lugard crossed Ganges in pursuit of Koer Singh.
„ 3-11. Hall held fort of Shahjehanpoor against 8000 rebels.
„ 5. Sir Colin defeated rebels outside Bareilly.
„ 7. „ „ captured Bareilly—rebel leaders escaped.
„ „ Corps of Bengal European Cavalry determined on.
„ 9. Lugard defeated Koer Singh at Jugdispore—Koer Singh killed.
„ „ Rose marched in pursuit of Tanteea Topee and the Ranee.
„ 11. Rose defeated them at Koonch.
„ „ Jones relieved Hall at Shahjehanpoor.
„ „ Ellenborough resigned—Lord Stanley appointed to Board of Control.
„ 12. Lugard defeated Ummer Singh near Jugdispore.
„ „ Hope Grant defeated 16,000 Oude rebels at Sirsee.
„ 14-21. Great debates in parliament, on Canning's Proclamation and Ellenborough's Dispatch.
„ 15. Jones attacked in great force at Shahjehanpoor.
„ 15-23. Rose in fierce conflict with Tanteea Topee in and near Calpee.
„ 17. Jung Bahadoor returned to Nepaul.
„ 18. Sir Colin repulsed rebels at Shahjehanpoor.
„ 21. Light summer clothing ordered for troops.
„ 22. Coke joined Sir Colin from Pileebheet.
„ 23. Rose captured Calpee—Tanteea Topee, Ranee of Jhansi, and Nawab of Banda, fled towards Gwalior.
„ 24. Incendiarism at Allahabad.
„ „ Sir Colin captured fort of Mohumdee.
May 26. Railway opened from Allahabad to Futtehpoor.
„ 28. Sir Colin returned to Futteghur from Rohilcund and Oude.
„ „ Sir Colin thanked his army for past services.
„ 30. Rebel leaders from Calpee arrived at Gwalior.
June 1. Scindia defeated by Tanteea Topee and Calpee rebels.
„ 2. Rebels captured Gwalior—Scindia fled to Agra.
„ 4. Lugard defeated rebels in Jugdispore jungle.
„ 7. Lord Stanley resumed India debates in House of Commons.
„ 9. Mahomed Hossein defeated at Amorah.
„ 9-11. Moncrieff defeated rebels at Chuckerderpore.
„ 13. Hope Grant defeated 16,000 rebels at Nawabgunge.
„ 15. The Moulvie killed in action at Powayne.
„ 16. Rose arrived near Gwalior.
„ 16-19. Great Battle in and near Gwalior.
„ 17. Death of the Ranee of Jhansi at Gwalior.
„ „ Lord Stanley brought in India Bill No. 3.
„ „ Canning's reply to Ellenborough's Secret Dispatch.
„ 18. Mahomed Hossein defeated at Hurreah.
„ 20. Rose recaptured Gwalior, and reinstated Scindia.
„ 21. Napier left Gwalior in pursuit of Tanteea Topee.
„ 23. East India Company's objections to Bill No. 3.
„ 24. India Bill read second time in Commons.
„ 29. Mr Manson murdered by Rajah of Nargoond.
End of month. 30th and 31st Bombay N.I. formed, to contain faithful men from mutinous 21st and 27th.
„ „ Faithful men of mutinous 3d, 36th, and 61st Bengal N.I., formed into a new regiment in Punjaub.
July 2. Roberts with Rajpootana Field-force reach Jeypoor.
„ 8. India Bill passed the Commons.
„ 9. „ „ read a first time in Lords.
„ „ Tanteea Topee plundered Tonk—soon afterwards driven out by Holmes.
„ 12. Rajah of Nargoond hanged at Belgaum.
„ 13. India Bill read second time in the Lords.
„ 14-20. Berkeley captured several small forts in Oude.
„ 17. Rattray captured rebel chiefs at Dehree.
„ 21. Hope Grant set out from Lucknow to confront rebels.
„ 23. Roberts left Tonk in pursuit of Tanteea Topee.
„ 28. Hope Grant relieved Maun Singh from siege at Shahgunje.
„ 29. Hope Grant entered Fyzabad, and drove out rebels.
„ 30. Cavanagh defeated a body of rebels in Muhiabad.
„ 31. India Bill passed the Lords.
„ „ Outbreak of prisoners at Mymensing.
Aug. 1. Bundela rebels seized Jaloun—expelled by Macduff.
„ 2. India Bill (Act) received royal assent.
„ 3. Man Singh captured Paoree.
„ 7. Court of Directors elected seven members for new Council of India.
„ 8. Roberts defeated Tanteea Topee at Sunganeer.
„ 11. Parkes headed a column from Neemuch, to check Tanteea Topee.
„ 12. Tanteea Topee checked at Marwar frontier, by Erinpoora force.
„ 13. Horsford retook Sultanpore from Oude rebels.
„ „ Carpenter defeated rebels near Kirwee.
„ 14. Roberts defeated Tanteea Topee at Kattara.
„ 20. Tanteea Topee crossed Chumbul to Julra Patteen.
„ 23. Napier drove Man Singh out of Paoree.
„ 25-29. Hope Grant fighting with Oude rebels outside Sultanpoor.
„ 29. Brahmin plot discovered at Gwalior.
„ 31. Disarmed 62d and 69th B.N.I. mutinied at Moultan.
„ „ Man Singh encamped at Sirsee, north of Goonah.
Sept. 1. Ashburner defeated rebels near Mahoni.
„ „ Last day of E. I. Company's governing power.
„ 2. New Council of India commenced its sittings.
„ 5. Napier defeated Man Singh at Bujeepore.
„ 15. Michel defeated Tanteea Topee at Beora.

Sept. 16–30. Continuous chase after Tanteea Topee, by various British columns.
Oct. 3–8. Dawson besieged by Oude rebels at Sundeela.
„ 5. Eveleigh defeated rebels at Meeangunje.
„ 8. Barker and Dawson defeated rebels at Puuao.
„ 19. Tanteea Topee defeated by Michel at Sindwah.
„ 25. „ „ „ at Multhone.
„ 29. Beni Madhoo defeated at Poorwa.
„ 30. Mehndee Hossein defeated at Sufdergunje.
„ 31. Tanteea Topee crossed the Nerbudda.
Nov. 1. Queen's Proclamation issued.
„ „ Sir Colin's final plans laid.
November. Gradual defeat and surrender of rebels in Oude and Behar.
„ Gradual defeat and surrender of rebels in Central India.

Events in Persia.

1856.

(Summer). Persia sent an army against Herat.
Aug. 22. Orders received at Bombay to prepare fleet and army against Persia.
Oct. 22. East India Company protested against expense of Persian Expedition.
„ „ Orders received at Bombay for force to embark.
„ 26. Persians captured Herat.
Nov. 1. Governor-general declared war against Persia.
„ 20. Outram departed from England to command Persian Expedition.
„ 26. Stalker left Bombay for Persian Gulf.
Dec. 7. Stalker and 1st Division landed near Bushire.
„ 10. „ „ „ captured Bushire.

1857.

Jan. 30. Outram arrived at Bushire, with 2d Column.
Feb. 3. Debates in Parliament concerning Persia.
„ „ Outram marched from Bushire to Borasjoon.
„ 9. Night-attack by Persians at Khoosh-aub.
„ 12. ? Havelock arrived at Bushire.
Mar. 4. Treaty of Peace between England and Persia signed at Paris.
„ 14. Suicide of Stalker at Bushire.
„ 17. „ „ Ethersey at Bushire.
„ 19. Treaty of Peace ratified at London.
„ 26. Outram defeated Persians at Mohamrah.
Apr. 1. Rennie defeated Persians at Ahwaz.
„ 5. News of the Treaty reached Bushire.
„ 14. Treaty ratified at Teheran.
May 9. Outram's army in Persia broken up.
„ 12. ? Outram and Havelock left Persia for India.
(Autumn). Evacuation of Herat by the Persians, and consequent evacuation of Persia by the British.

Events in China and Japan.

1856.

Oct. 8. Affair of the Lorcha *Arrow* near Canton.
„ 23–25. Seymour captured Forts in Canton river.
„ 28, 29. Partial Bombardment of Canton.
Nov. 3. Yeh refused a personal conference.
„ 6. Naval action with junks in Canton river.
„ 8. Chinese employed fire-rafts against British ships.
„ 26. British captured other Forts below Canton.
Dec. 10. Bowring's proceedings approved by home government.
„ 11. Dispute at Nagasaki with Japanese authorities.

1857.

Jan. 1–4. Attacks and counter-attacks in Canton river.
„ 10. Bowring's further proceedings approved.
„ 26. Japanese edict favourable to English ships.
Feb. 3. Debates in parliament on Chinese affairs.
„ 12. Partial destruction of Canton by the British.
„ 24. Great debate in House of Lords on China.
Mar. 3. House of Commons condemned Chinese War—Ministers therefore dissolved parliament.
Apr. 6. War-junks destroyed in Canton river.
„ 7. ? Ashburnham left England for China.
„ 21. Elgin left England for China.
May 25. Attack on junks in Escape Creek.
June 1. Attack on junks in Fatshan Creek.
July (early). Elgin arrived at Hong-kong.
„ (end). Elgin proceeded to confer with Canning at Calcutta.
Sept. 9. Elliot made reconnaissance of Chinese junk-fleet.
Dec. 12. Elgin sent formal demands on Yeh.
„ 24. On Yeh's refusal, Elgin resolved on storm measures.
„ 28–31. Cannonading and fighting around Canton.
„ 31. British captured all the defences of Canton.

1858.

Jan. 5. Parkes captured Commissioner Yeh.
„ 9. Provisional government established at Canton.
Feb. 10. Blockade of Canton river ended.
Mar. (end). Elgin proceeded to Shang-hae.
Apr. 24. Elgin sent his demands to the emperor at Pekin.
„ 30. Emperor appointed a plenipotentiary.
May 20. Negotiations failing, Elgin resumed hostilities.
„ „ Forts on the Pei-ho destroyed by English.
June 3. Straubenzee encountered Chinese outside Canton.
„ 26. Elgin signed Treaty with China at Tien-sing.
July 6. „ returned to Shang-hae.
Aug. 3. „ went to Nagasaki in Japan.
„ 11. Namtow punished for breach of flag of truce.
„ 16. Elgin arrived at Jedo.
„ 26. „ signed Treaty with Japan at Jedo.
Sept. & Oct. Gradual settlement of details of Chinese tariff.

INDEX.

THE END.

Edinburgh:
Printed by W. and R. Chambers.

CPSIA information can be obtained
at www.ICGtesting.com
Printed in the USA
LVHW041946130323
741532LV00001B/281